LAWRENCE SANDERS

Three Complete Novels

ALSO BY LAWRENCE SANDERS

McNally's Risk
McNally's Luck
McNally's Secret
The Seventh Commandment
Sullivan's Sting
Capital Crimes
Timothy's Game
The Timothy Files
The Eighth Commandment
The Fourth Deadly Sin
The Passion of Molly T.
The Seduction of Peter S.
The Case of Lucy Bending
The Third Deadly Sin
The Tenth Commandment
The Sixth Commandment
The Tangent Factor
The Second Deadly Sin
The Marlow Chronicles
The Tangent Objective
The Tomorrow File
The First Deadly Sin
Love Songs
The Pleasures of Helen
The Anderson Tapes

LAWRENCE SANDERS

Three Complete Novels

THE FIRST DEADLY SIN

◎

THE SECOND DEADLY SIN

◎

THE THIRD DEADLY SIN

G. P. PUTNAM'S SONS NEW YORK

G. P. Putnam's Sons
Publishers Since 1838
200 Madison Avenue
New York, NY 10016

Published simultaneously in Canada

Library of Congress Cataloging-in-Publication Data

Sanders, Lawrence, date.
[Novels. Selections]
Lawrence Sanders : three complete novels.
p. cm.
Contents: The first deadly sin — The second deadly sin — The third deadly sin.
ISBN 0-399-13877-3
1. Delaney, Edward X. (Fictitious character)—Fiction.
2. Detective and mystery stories, American. 3. Detectives—United States—Fiction. I. Title. II. Title: Three complete novels.
PS3569.A5125A6 1993 93-18769 CIP
813'.54—dc20

Printed in the United States of America
1 2 3 4 5 6 7 8 9 10

Contents

THE FIRST DEADLY SIN

Part I

1

There was quiet. He lay on his back atop a shaft of stone called Devil's Needle, and felt he was lost, floating in air. Above him, all about him stretched a thin blue sac. Through it he could see scribbles of clouds, a lemon sun.

He heard nothing but his own strong heart, the slowly quieting of his breath as he recovered from his climb. He could believe he was alone in the universe.

Finally he stood and looked around him. Waves of foliage lapped at the base of his stone; it was a dark green ocean with a froth of autumn's russet. He could see the highway, the tarred roofs of Chilton, a steel ribbon of river uncoiling southward to the sea.

The air had the bite of Fall; it moved on a breeze that knifed lungs and tingled bare skin. He gulped this stern air like a drink; there was nothing he might not do.

He moved over to the cleft in the edge of the stone and began hauling up the nylon line clipped to his belt. At the end of the rope was his rucksack. In it were sandwiches, a thermos of black coffee, a first aid kit, spiked clamps for his climbing boots, pitons, an extra sweater and, buckled to the outside, his ice ax.

He had made the sandwiches himself, of stone-ground whole wheat said to be organically grown. The filling of one was sliced onions, of the other white radishes and plum tomatoes.

He sat on the smooth granite and ate slowly. The coffee was still warm, the sandwich bread fresh with a crunchy crust. Out of nowhere a blue jay appeared and greeted him with its two-note whistle. It landed on the stone, stared at him fearlessly. He laughed, tossed a crust. The bird took it up, then dropped it immediately and was gone in an azure flash.

Finished, he replaced sandwich wrappings and thermos in his rucksack. He lay back, using it as a pillow. He turned onto his side, bowing his spine, drawing up his knees. He determined to awake in half an hour. He was asleep almost instantly and dreamed of a woman hairless as a man's palm.

He awoke in half an hour and lighted a cigarette. The day was drawing on; he must be down and out of the park before dark. But there was time to smoke, time for silence, a final coffee, cold now and gritty with dregs.

He had been recently divorced. That was of no concern; it had happened to a stranger. But he was perplexed by what was happening to *him* since he and Gilda had parted. He was assembling a jigsaw puzzle. But he didn't have all the pieces, had no conception of what the completed picture might be.

He pulled off his knitted watch cap, exposing his shaven skull to watery sunlight. He pressed fingers to the smooth; soft skin slid on hard bone.

The divorce had just been obtained (in Mexico) but he had been separated from his wife for almost two years. Shortly after they agreed to live apart, he had shaved his head completely and purchased two wigs. One ("Ivy League") he wore to the office and on formal occasions. The other ("Via Veneto") was crisp curls and ringlets. He wore it to parties or when entertaining at home. Both wigs were in the dark brown shade of his own hair.

It was true his hair had been thinning since he was 24. At the time of his separation from Gilda, when he was 33, the front hairline had receded into a "widow's peak" and there was a small tonsure at the back of his head. But he was far from bald. His remaining hair had gloss and weight.

Nevertheless, he had shaved his entire skull when he purchased the wigs, though the coiffeur assured him it was not necessary; the artificial hair could be blended ("Absolutely undetectable, sir") with his natural hair.

When climbing, or swimming, or simply alone in his apartment, he preferred the shaven pate. He had developed a habit—almost a nervous tic—of caressing it with his fingertips, probing the frail cranium and that perilous stuff that lay beneath.

He pulled on his cap, tugging it down over his ears. He prepared for the descent by donning horsehide gloves, rough side out. He then lowered his rucksack to the boulders below. The end of the line was still clipped to his belt, a wide canvas band similar to that used by professional window washers.

The cleft, by which ascents to and descents from the flat top of Devil's Needle were made, was a chimney. It was a vertical crack in the granite shaft, four feet across at the base. It narrowed as it rose until, at the top, it was barely wide enough for a climber to scrape through to the summit.

The climber braced shoulders and back against one wall of the chimney. He bent his knees, placing the soles of his boots against the opposite wall. He then, literally, walked up the cleft, depending upon the strength of buttocks, thighs and calves to maintain sufficient pressure to keep from falling.

As he took small steps, not relaxing one foot to scrape it upward until the other was firmly planted, he "walked his shoulders" slowly higher—right, left, right, left. He continued tension in his bent legs to keep himself jammed between opposing walls of the chimney.

As the cleft narrowed toward the top of the 65-foot shaft, the climber's legs became increasingly bent until his knees were almost touching his chin and gains upward were measured in inches. At the top, it was necessary to apply pressure with knees instead of feet. The climber then reached up and grabbed two heavy pitons a previous conqueror of Devil's Needle had thoughtfully left embedded in the stone. With their aid, the man ascending could pull himself out of the narrow chimney, over the lip, onto the flat top. It was a bedsheet of stone.

The descent, though more difficult, was not excessively dangerous for an experienced climber. Gripping the pitons, he allowed his body to slide down into the cleft. He started by bracing his knees against one granite wall, his back against the other. Releasing the pitons, he then slowly "walked" downward, until the crack widened sufficiently so he could put the rubber-ridged soles of his boots against the opposing wall.

At this time of day, in September, as he began the descent, the top of Devil's Needle was washed with pale sunshine. But the slit into which he lowered himself was shaded and smelled rankly.

He braced his knees, took a deep breath, released the pitons. He was suspended in gloom, emptiness below. He hung a moment in blemished light, then placed flat hands against the facing wall to take some of the tension off his knees. He started the slow wiggle downward and out.

The cleft spread until it was wide enough to press his feet against the wall. Moving faster now, he twisted, struggled, writhed, his entire body in a steady left-right rhythm, shifting from foot to foot, shoulder to shoulder, until the stretched stone thighs popped him out and he was in murk.

He rested five minutes while his breathing eased. He coiled his nylon line, slung his rucksack. He hiked across boulders, through a meadow, along a dirt road to the ranger's cabin.

The park guardian was an older man, made surly by this visitor's refusal to heed his warning about climbing alone. He shoved the register angrily across the wooden counter. The climber signed in the Out column and noted the time.

His name was Daniel Blank.

2

Under the terms of the separation agreement, Gilda Blank had retained possession of their car: a four-door Buick sedan. Daniel thereupon purchased for himself a Chevrolet Corvette, a powerful machine of racy design. Since buying the sports car he had twice been arrested for speeding. He paid a fine in each case. One more similar violation would result in suspension of his license.

Now, standing beside his car to strip off canvas jacket, wool sweater and cotton T-shirt, he admired the car's clean feminine lines. He toweled off bare skull, face, neck, shoulders, arms, upper torso. The evening air was astringent as alcohol. He had a sense of healthy well-being. The hard climb, sculpted day, simple food all had left him with the exhilaration of a new start. He was beginning.

Daniel Blank was a tall man, slightly over six feet, and was now slender. In high school and college he had competed in swimming, track (220 high hurdles), and tennis, individual sports that required no teamwork. These physical activities had given his body a firm sheath of long muscle. His shoulders, pectorals and thighs were well-developed. Hands and feet were narrow fingernails and toenails long. He kept them shaped and buffed.

Shortly after his separation, he had taken a "physical inventory," inspecting his naked body minutely in the full-length mirror on the inside of his bathroom door. He saw at once that deterioration had begun, the flesh beneath his jaw had started to sag, his shoulders slumped, the lower abdomen protruded, it was soft and without tone.

He had at once begun a strict regimen of diet and exercise. In his methodical way he bought several books on nutrition and systems of physical training. He read them all carefully, making notes and devised for himself a program that appealed to him and that he felt would show almost immediate improvement in his physical appearance.

He was not a fanatic, he did not swear off drinking and smoking. But he cut his alcohol intake by half and switched to non-nicotine cigarettes made of dried lettuce leaves. He tried to avoid starches, carbohydrates, dairy products, eggs, blood meats. He ate fresh fruits, vegetables, broiled fish, salads with a dressing of fresh lemon juice. Within three months he had lost 20 pounds, his ribs and hip bones showed.

Meanwhile he had started a program of daily exercise, 30 minutes in the morning upon rising, 30 minutes in the evening before retiring.

The exercises Daniel Blank selected for himself came from a manual based on the training of Finnish gymnasts. All the movements were illustrated with photographs of young blonde women in white leotards. But Blank felt this was of no import; only the exercises counted, and these promised increased agility, pliancy, and grace.

The exercises had proved efficacious. His waist was now down to almost 32 inches. Since his hips were wide (though his buttocks were flat) and his chest enlarged from his youthful interest in running and swimming, he had developed a feminine "hourglass" figure. All his muscles regained their youthful firmness. His skin was smooth and blood-flushed. Age seemed stayed.

But the diet and exercise had also resulted in several curious side effects. His nipples had become permanently engorged and, since he ordinarily wore no undershirt, were obvious beneath the stuff of thin dress shirts or lisle pullovers. He did not find this displeasing. A heavier garment, such as a wool turtleneck sweater worn next to the skin, sometimes resulted in a not unpleasant irritation.

Another unexpected development was the change in appearance of his genitals. The testicles had become somewhat flaccid and hung lower than previously. The penis, while not growing in size (which he knew to be impossible at his age), had altered in color and elasticity. It now seemed to be slightly empurpled in a constant state of mild excitation. This also was not disagreeable. It might be caused by agitation against the cloth of the tighter trousers he had purchased.

Finally he found himself free of the diarrhea that had frequently plagued him during his marriage. He ascribed this to his new diet, exercise, or both. Whatever the reason, his bowel movements were now regular, without pain, and satisfying. His stool was firm.

He drove toward Manhattan. He had pulled on a fresh velour shirt. The radio was no more than a lulling hum. He followed an unlighted two-laner that led into the Thruway.

The speedometer climbed slowly: 50, 60, 70, 80. The car roared to catch the headlight glare. Trees flung backward; billboards and ghost houses grew out of darkness, blazed, flicked back into dark.

He loved speed, not so much for the sensual satisfaction of power as for the sense of lonely dislocation.

It was Saturday night; the Thruway was heavy with traffic pouring into the city. Now he drove with brutal hostility, switching lanes, cutting in and out. He hunched over the wheel, searching for openings to plunge through, for sudden breaks in the pattern enabling him to skin by more cautious drivers.

He came over the bridge; there were the hard edges, sharp corners, cheap lights of Manhattan. Slowed by signals, by trucks and buses, he was forced to move southward at moderate speed. He turned eastward on 96th Street; his city closed in.

It was a city sprung and lurching. It throbbed to a crippled rhythm, celebrated death with insensate glee. Filth pimpled its nightmare streets. The air smelled of ashes. In the schools young children craftily slid heroin into their veins.

A luncheonette owner was shot dead when he could not supply apple pie to a demanding customer. A French tourist was robbed in daylight, then shot and paralyzed. A pregnant woman was raped by three men in a subway station at 10:30 in the morning. Bombs were set. Acid was thrown. Explosions destroyed embassies, banks, and churches. Infants were beaten to death. Glass was shattered, leather slashed, plants uprooted, obscene slogans sprayed on marble monuments. Zoos were invaded and small animals torn apart.

His poisoned city staggered in a mad plague dance. A tarnished sun glared down on an unmeaning world. Each man, at night, locked himself within bars, hoping for survival in his iron cage. He huddled in upon himself, hoarding his sanity, and moved through crowded streets glancing over his shoulder, alert to parry the first blow with his own oiled blade.

The apartment house in which Daniel Blank lived was a raw building of glass and enameled steel. It was 34 stories high and occupied an entire city block on East 83rd Street. It was built in a U-shape; a black-topped driveway curved in front of the entrance. A stainless steel portico protruded so that tenants alighting from cars were protected from rain. The entrance step was covered with green outdoor carpeting.

Inside, a desk faced plate glass doors. Doormen were on duty 24 hours a day. They were able to inspect the underground garage, service entrances, hallways and elevators by closed-circuit TV. Behind them was a wide lobby with chairs and sofas of chrome and black plastic. There were abstract paintings on the walls and, in the center, a heavy bronze sculpture, nonrepresentational, entitled *Birth*.

Daniel Blank pulled into an alley alongside the curved driveway. It led down to the garage where tenants, for an additional rental, could park their cars, have them washed, serviced, and delivered to the main entrance when required.

He turned the Corvette over to the attendant on duty. He took his rucksack and outdoor clothes from the car, and rode the escalator to the main lobby. He went to the desk where tenants' mail was distributed, deliveries accepted, messages held.

It was almost 10:00 P.M.; no one was on duty at the mail desk. But one of the doormen went behind the counter. There was no mail in Blank's cubbyhole, but there was a small sheet of paper folded once. It said: "Brunch Sunday (tomorrow) at 11:30. Don't miss. Come early. Thousands of fantastic pipple. Love and kisses. Flo and Sam." He read the note, then tucked it into his shirt pocket.

The doorman, who had not spoken to him nor raised his eyes to Daniel's, went back behind his desk. His name was Charles Lipsky, and he had been involved with Blank in an incident that had occurred about a year previously.

Daniel had been waiting under the portico for a taxi to take him to work. He rarely drove his own car to the office since parking space near Ninth Avenue and 46th Street was almost non-existent. Doorman Lipsky had gone down to the street to whistle up a cab. He halted one and rode it up the driveway. He opened the door for Blank and held out his hand for the usual 25-cent tip.

As Daniel was about to pay him, a man he recognized as a tenant of the building came up the entrance step hauling a German shepherd pup on a long leather leash.

"Heel!" the man was shouting. "Heel!"

But the young dog hung back. Then he lay on the driveway, muzzle down between his paws, and refused to budge.

"Heel, you bastard!" the man screamed. He then struck the dog twice on the head with a folded newspaper he had been carrying under his arm. The dog cringed away. Whereupon the man kicked him heavily in the ribs.

Daniel Blank and Charles Lipsky saw all this clearly. Blank leaped forward. He could not endure the sight of an animal being mistreated; he couldn't even *think* of a horse pulling a load.

"Stop that!" he cried furiously.

The tenant turned on him in outrage. "Mind your own goddamned business!"

He then struck Daniel on the head with his folded newspaper. Blank pushed him angrily. The man staggered back, became entangled in the leather leash, stumbled off the step onto the driveway, fell awkwardly, and broke his left arm. Police were called, and the tenant insisted on charging Daniel Blank with assault.

In time, Blank and Lipsky were summoned to the 251st Precinct house to give sworn statements. Daniel said the tenant had abused his dog, and when he, Daniel, objected, the man had struck him with a folded newspaper. He had not pushed the man until after that first blow. Charles Lipsky corroborated this testimony.

The charge was eventually withdrawn, the case dropped. The dog owner moved from the building. Blank gave Lipsky five dollars for his trouble and thought no more of the matter.

But about six months after this incident, something of a more serious nature happened.

On a Saturday night, lonely and jangling, Daniel Blank put on his "Via Veneto" wig and strolled out into midnight Manhattan. He wore a Swedish blazer of black wool and a French body shirt in a lacy polyester weave, cut to cling to the torso. It was a style called *chemise de gigolo* and had a front that opened halfway to the waist. An ornate Maltese cross hung from a silver chain about his neck.

On impulse, nothing else, he stopped at a Third Avenue tavern he had seen before but never entered. It was called "The Parrot." There were two couples at the bar and two single men. No one sat at the tiny tables. The lone waiter was reading a religious tract.

Blank ordered a brandy and lighted a lettuce cigarette. He looked up and, unexpectedly, caught the eye of one of the single men in the mirror behind the bar. Blank shifted his gaze immediately. The man was three seats away. He was about 45, short, soft, with the meaty nose and ruddy face of a bourbon drinker.

The bartender had his radio tuned to WQXR. They were playing Smetana's *The Moldau.* The bartender was reading a scratch sheet, marking his choices. The couples had their heads together and were murmuring.

"You have beautiful hair."

Daniel Blank looked up from his drink. "What?"

The porky man had moved onto the barstool next to his.

"Your hair. It's beautiful. Is it a rug?"

His first instinct was to drain his drink, pay, and leave. But why should he? The dim loneliness of The Parrot was a comfort. People together and yet apart: that was the secret.

He ordered another brandy. He turned a shoulder to the man who was hunching closer. The bartender poured the drink, then went back to his handicapping.

"Well?" the man asked.

Blank turned to look at him. "Well what?"

"How about it?"

"How about what?"

Up to now they had been speaking in conversational tones: not loud, but understandable if anyone was interested in listening. No one was.

But suddenly the man leaned forward. He thrust his flabby face close: watery eyes, trembling lips: hopeful and doomed.

"I love you," he whispered with an anxious smile.

Blank hit him in the mouth and toppled him off the stool onto the floor. When the man got up, Blank hit him again, breaking his jaw. He fell again. Blank was frantically kicking him in the groin when the bartender finally came alive and rushed around the bar to pinion his arms and drag him away.

Once again the police were summoned. This time Blank thought it best to call his lawyer, Russell Tamblyn. He came to the 251st Precinct house and, shortly before dawn, the incident was closed.

The injured man who, it was learned, had a sad record of offenses including attempts to molest a child and to proposition a plain-clothed patrolman in a subway toilet—refused to sign a complaint. He said he had been drunk, knew nothing of what had happened, and accepted responsibility for the "unfortunate accident."

The detective who took Daniel Blank's statement was the same man who had taken his testimony in the incident involving the tenant who kicked his dog.

"You again?" the detective asked curiously.

The attorney brought the signed waiver to Daniel Blank, saying, "It's all squared away. He's not making a charge. You're free to go."

"Russ, I told you it wasn't my fault."

"Oh sure. But the man has a broken jaw and possible internal injuries. Dan, you've got to learn to control yourself."

But that wasn't the end of it. Because the doorman, Charles Lipsky, found out, even though nothing had been published in the newspapers. The bartender at The Parrot was Lipsky's brother-in-law.

A week later the doorman rang the bell of Blank's apartment. After inspection through the peephole, he was admitted. Lipsky immediately launched into a long, jumbled chronicle of his troubles. His wife needed a hernia operation; his daughter needed expensive treatment for an occluded bite; he himself was heavily in debt to loansharks who threatened to break his legs, and he needed five hundred dollars at once.

Blank was bewildered by this recital. He asked what it had to do with him. Lipsky then stammered that he knew what had happened at The Parrot. It wasn't Mr. Blank's fault, certainly, but if other tenants . . . If it became known . . . If people started talking . . .

And then he winked at Daniel Blank.

That knowing wink, that smirky wink, was worse than the victim's whispered, "I love you." Daniel Blank felt attacked by a beast whose bite excited and inflamed. Violence bubbled.

Lipsky must have seen something in his eyes, for he turned suddenly, ran out, slammed the door behind him. Since then they had hardly spoken. When necessary, Blank ordered and the doorman obeyed, never raising his eyes. At Christmas, Daniel distributed the usual amounts: ten dollars to each doorman. He received the usual thank-you card from Charles Lipsky.

Blank pushed the button; the door of the automatic elevator slid silently open. He stepped inside, pushed button C (for Close door), button 21 (for his floor), and button M (for Music desired). He rode upward to the muted strains of "I Got Rhythm."

He lived at the front end of one leg of the building's U. It was an exceptionally large four-room apartment with living room windows facing north, bedroom windows east, and kitchen and bathroom windows west, or really down into the apartment house courtyard. The walk to his door from the elevator was along a carpeted tunnel. The corridor was softly lighted, the many doors blind, air refrigerated and dead.

He unlocked his door, reached in and switched on the foyer light. Then he stepped inside, looked about. He closed the door, double-locked it, put on the chain, adjusted the Police Bar, a burglar-proof device consisting of a heavy steel rod that fitted into a slot in the floor and was propped into a recess bolted to the door.

Mildly hungry, Blank dropped clothing and gear on a foyer chair and went directly to the kitchen. He switched on the blued fluorescent light. He inspected the contents of his refrigerator, selected a small cantaloupe and sliced it in half, at right angles to the stem line. He wrapped half in wax paper and returned it to the refrigerator. He scooped seeds and soft pulp from the other half, then filled the cavity with Familia, a Swiss organic cereal. He squeezed a slice of fresh lemon over all. He ate it steadily, standing, staring at his reflection in the mirror over the kitchen sink.

Finished, he dumped melon rind into the garbage can and rinsed his fingers. Then he moved from room to room, turning the light on in the next before turning it off in the last. Undressing in nis bedroom he found the note in his shirt pocket: ". . . Thousands of fantastic pipple . . ." He placed it on his bedside table where he'd seen it upon awakening.

He closed the bathroom door tightly before taking a shower so hot it filled the air with heavy steam, clouding the mirrors and sweating the tiles. He lathered with an emollient soap of cocoa butter that slicked his skin. After rinsing in cool water and turning off the shower, he rubbed his wet body with a cosmetically treated tissue claiming to "restore natural oils to dry skin" and "smooth, soften, and lubricate the epidermis."

His twice-a-week maid had been in during the afternoon. His bed was made with fresh sheets and pillowcases. The top sheet and sateen comforter were turned down. It was hardly 11:00 P.M., but he was pleasantly weary and wanted sleep.

Naked, allowing water and tiny oil globules to dry on his exposed body, he moved about the apartment, drawing drapes, checking window latches and door locks. He stepped into the bathroom again to swallow a mild sleeping pill. He felt sure he would not need it, but he didn't want to think in bed.

The long living room was dimly lit by light from the bedroom. The end of the living room faced north, with drapes over wide plate glass windows that could not be opened. The east wall, abutting the bedroom, was almost 25 feet long and nine feet high.

This expanse, painted a flat white, Daniel Blank had decorated with mirrors. He had allowed a space four feet from the floor to accommodate a couch, chairs, end tables, lamps, a bookcase, a wheeled cart of hi-fi equipment. But above that four-foot level, the wall was covered with mirrors.

Not one mirror or fitted tiles of mirrors, but more than fifty individual mirrors adorned that wall; tiny mirrors and large mirrors, flat and beveled, true and exaggerative, round and square, oval and rectangular. The wall quivered with silver reflections.

Each mirror was framed and hung separately: frames of wood and metal, painted and bare, plain and ornate, modern and rococo, carved wood and bland plastic. Some were fogged antiques; one was a 3-by-4-inch sheet of polished metal: the mirror issued to Marines in World War II.

The mirrors were not arranged in a planned pattern on this nervous wall; they had been hung as they were purchased. But somehow, haphazardly, as the wall filled, frames and reflections had grown an asymmetrical composition. His city was there, sprung and lurching.

Padding back to the bedroom, naked, scented, oiled, Daniel Blank looked to his mirrored wall. He was chopped and fragmented. As he moved, his image jumped, glass to glass. A nose there. Ear. Knee. Chest. Navel. Foot. Elbow. All leaped, were held, disappeared to be born again in something new.

He stopped, fascinated. But even motionless he was minced and snapped, all of him divided by silvered glass that tilted this way and that. He felt himself and saw twenty hands moving, a hundred fingers probing: wonder and delight.

He went into the bedroom, adjusted the air-conditioner thermostat, slid into bed. He fell asleep seeing in the dim glow of the nightlight those myriad eyes reflecting him in framed detail. Waist in steel. Shoulder in carved oak. Neck in plastic. Knee in copper. Penis in worm-eaten walnut.

Art.

3

She had been one of the first women in Manhattan to leave off her brassiere. He had been one of the first men in Manhattan to use a necktie as a belt. She had been one of the first to adopt a workman's lunch pail as a purse. He had been one of the first to wear loafers without socks. The first! A zeal for the new bedeviled them, drove them.

No notice of Florence and Samuel Morton was made in the long, detailed separation agreement signed by the Blanks. Gilda took the Buick sedan, the Waterford crystal, the Picasso print. Daniel took the apartment lease, 100 shares of U.S. Steel, and the Waring blender. No one mentioned the Mortons. It was tacitly assumed they were Daniel's "best friends," and he was to have them. So he did.

They contradicted the folk saying, "Opposites attract." Husband and wife, they were obverse and reverse of the same coin. Where did Samuel leave off and Florence begin? No one could determine. They were a bifocal image. No. They were a double image, both in focus simultaneously.

Physically they were so alike that strangers took them for brother and sister. Short, bony-thin, with helmets of black, oily hair, both had ferrety features, the quick, sharp movements of creatures assailed.

He, married, had been a converter of synthetic textiles. She, married, had been a fabric designer. They met on a picket line protesting a performance of *The Merchant of Venice,* and discovered they had the same psychoanalyst. A year later they were divorced, married to each other, and had agreed to have no children because of the population explosion. Both gladly, cheerfully, joyfully, submitted to operations.

Their marriage was two magnets clicking together. They had identical loves, fears, hopes, prejudices, ambitions, tastes, moods, dislikes, despairs. They were one person multiplied by two. They slept together in a king-sized bed, entwined.

They changed their life styles as often as their underwear. They were ahead of everyone. Before it was fashionable, they bought pop art, op-art, and then switched back to realism sooner than art critics. They went through marijuana, amphetamines, barbiturates, speed, and a single, shaking trial of heroin, before returning to dry vermouth on the rocks. They were first to try new restaurants, first to wear Mickey Mouse watches, first to discover new tenors, first to see new movies, plays, ballets, first to wear their sunglasses pushed atop their heads. They explored all New York and spread the word: "This incredible little restaurant in Chinatown . . . The best belly-dancer on the West Side . . . That crazy junk shop on Canal Street . . ."

Born Jews, they found their way to Catholicism via Unitarianism, Methodism, and Episcopalianism (with a brief dabble in Marxism). After converting and confessing once, they found this groovy Evangelical church in Harlem where everyone clapped hands and shouted. Nothing lasted. Everything started. They plunged into Yoga, Zen, and Hare Krishna. They turned to astrology, took high colonics, and had a whiskered guru to dinner.

They threw themselves in the anti-Vietnam War movement and went to Washington to carry placards, parade and shout slogans. Once Sam was hit on the head by a construction worker. Once Flo was spat upon by a Wall Street executive. Then they spent three weeks in a New Hampshire commune where 21 people slept in one room.

"They did nothing but verbalize!" said Sam.

"No depth, no significance!" said Flo.

"A bad scene!" they said together.

What drove them, what sparked their search for "relevance," their hunger to "communicate," to have a "meaningful dialogue," to find the "cosmic flash," to uncover "universal contact," to, in fact, refashion the universe, was guilt.

Their great talent, the gift they denied because it was so vulgar, was simply this: both had a marvelous ability to make money. The psychedelic designs of Florence sold like mad. Samuel was one of the first men on Seventh Avenue to foresee the potential of the "youth market." They started their own factory. Money poured in.

Both, now in their middle 30s, had been the first with the new. They leeched onto the social chaos of the 1960s: the hippies, flower children, the crazy demand for denim jeans and fringed leather jackets and pioneer skirts and necklaces for men and Indian beads and granny glasses and all the other paraphernalia of the young, taken up so soon by their elders.

The Mortons profited mightily from their perspicacity, but it seemed to them a cheesy kind of talent. Without acknowledging it both knew they were growing wealthy from what had begun as a sincere and touching crusade. Hence their frantic rushing about from picket line to demonstration, from parade to confrontation. They wanted to pay their dues.

In further expiation, they sold the factory (at an enormous profit) and opened a boutique on Madison Avenue, an investment they were happily convinced would be a disaster. It was called Erotica, based on a unique concept for a store. The idea had come to them while attending religious services of a small Scandinavian sect in Brooklyn which worshipped Thor.

"I'm bored with idleness," he murmured.

"So am I," she murmured.

"A store?" he suggested. "Just to keep busy."

"A shop?" she suggested. "A fun thing."

"A boutique," he said.

"Elegant and expensive," she said. "We'll lose a mint."

"Something different," he mused. "Not hotpants and paper dresses, miniskirts and skinny sweaters, army jackets and newsboy caps. Something really *different*. What do people want?"

"Love?" she mused.

"Oh yes," he nodded. "That's it."

Their boutique, Erotica, sold only items related, however distantly, to love and sex. It sold satin sheets in 14 colors (including black), and a "buttock pillow" advertised merely "for added comfort and convenience." It carried Valentines and books of love poetry; perfumes and incense; phonograph records that established a mood; scented creams and lotions; phallic candles; amorous prints, paintings, etchings and posters; unisex lingerie; lace pajamas for men, leather nightgowns for women; and whips for both. An armed guard had to be hired to eject certain obviously disturbed customers.

Erotica was an instant success. Florence and Samuel Morton became wealthier. Depressed, they turned to blackstrap molasses and acupuncture. Making money was their tragic talent. Their blessing was that they were without malice.

And the first thing Daniel Blank saw upon awaking Sunday morning was the note on his bedside table, the invitation to brunch from Flo and Sam. They would, he remembered fondly, serve things like hot Syrian bread, iced lumpfish, smoked carp, six kinds of herring. Champagne, even.

He padded naked to the front door, unlocked chains and bars, took in his New York *Times*. He went through the ritual of relocking, carried the newspaper to the kitchen, returned to the bedroom, began his 30 minutes of exercise in front of the mirror on the closet door.

It was the quiet Sunday routine he had grown to cherish since living alone. The day and its lazy possibilities stretched ahead in a golden glow. His extensions and sit-ups and bends brought him warm and tingling into a new world; anything was possible.

He showered quickly, gloating to see his dried skin had softened and smoothed. He stood before the medicine cabinet mirror to shave, and wondered once again if he should grow a mustache. Once again he decided against it. It would, he felt, make him look older, although a drooping Fu Manchu mustache with his glabrous skull might be interesting. Exciting?

His face was coffin-shaped and elegant, small ears set close to the bone. The jaw was slightly aggressive, lips sculpted, freshly colored. The nose was long, somewhat pinched, with elliptic nostrils. His eyes were his best feature: large, widely spaced, with a brown iris. Brows were thick, sharply delineated.

Curiously, he appeared older full-face than in profile. From the front he seemed brooding. Lines were discernible from nose creases to the corners of his mouth. The halves of his face were identical; the effect was that of a religious mask. He rarely blinked and smiled infrequently.

But in profile he looked more alert. His face came alive. There was young expectation there: noble brow, clear eye, straight nose, carved and mildly pouting lips, strong chin. You could see the good bones of cheek and jaw.

He completed shaving, applied "Faun" after-shave lotion, powdered his jaw lightly, sprayed his armpits with a scented antiperspirant. He went back into the bedroom and considered how to dress.

The Mortons with their ". . . Thousands of fantastic pipple . . ." were sure to have a motley selection of the bizarre friends and acquaintances they collected: artists and designers; actors and writers; dancers and directors; with a spicy sprinkling of addicts, whores and arsonists. All, on a Sunday morning, would be informally and wildly costumed.

To be different—aloof from the mob, above the throng—he pulled on his conservative "Ivy League" wig, grey flannel slacks, Gucci loafers, a white cashmere turtleneck sweater, a jacket of suede in a reddish brown. He stuffed a yellow-patterned foulard kerchief in his breast pocket.

He went into the kitchen and brewed a small pot of coffee. He drank two cups black, sitting at the kitchen table and leafing through the magazine section of the Sunday *Times*. The ads proved that current male fashions had become more creative, colorful, and exciting than female.

At precisely 11:30, he locked his front door and took the elevator up to the Mortons' penthouse apartment on the 34th floor.

He was alone in the elevator, there was no one waiting for entrance at the Mortons' door and, when he listened, he could hear no sounds of revelry inside. Perplexed, he rang the bell, expecting the door to be answered by Blanche, the Mortons' live-in maid, or perhaps by a butler hired for the occasion.

But Samuel Morton himself opened the door, stepped quickly out into the corridor, closed but did not latch the door behind him.

He was a vigorous, elfin man, clad in black leather shirt and jeans studded with steel nailheads. He twinkled when he moved. His eyes, shining with glee, were two more nailheads. He put a hand on Daniel Blank's arm.

"Dan," he pleaded, "don't be sore."

Blank groaned theatrically, "Sam, not again? You promised not to. What's *with* you and Flo? Are you professional matchmakers? I told you I can find my own women."

"Look, Dan, is it so terrible? We want you to be happy! Is that so terrible? Your happiness—that's all! All right, blame us. But we're so happy together we want everyone to be happy like us!"

"You promised," Blank accused. "Sam, your cuffs are about a half-inch too long. After that disaster with the jewelry designer, you *promised*. Who's this one?"

Morton stepped closer, whispering . . .

"You won't believe. An original! I swear to God . . ." Here he held up his right hand. ". . . an *original!* She comes into the store last week. She's wearing a sable coat down to her ankles! It's a warm day, but she's wearing an ankle-length fur. And sable! Not mink. Dan—*sable!* And she's beautiful in an offbeat, kinky way. Marilyn Monroe she's not, but she's got this thing. She scares you! Yes. Maybe not beautiful. But something else. Something better! So in she comes wearing this long sable coat. Fifty thousand that coat—at least! And with her is this kid, a boy, maybe eleven, twelve, around there. And he *is* beautiful! The most beautiful boy I've ever seen—and you know I don't swing that way! But she's not married. The kid's her brother. Anyhow, we get to talking, and Flo admires her coat, and it turns out she bought it in Russia. Russia! And she lives in a townhouse on East End Avenue. Can you imagine? East End Avenue! A townhouse! She's got to be loaded. So one thing leads to another, and we invited her up for brunch. So what's so terrible?"

"Did you also tell her you were inviting a friend—male and divorced—who is living in lonely anguish and seeking the companionship of a good woman?"

"No. I swear!"

"Sam, I don't believe you."

"Dan, would I lie to you?"

"Of course. Like your 'thousands of fantastic pipple'."

"Well . . . Flo may have casually mentioned a few neighbors might stop by."

Daniel laughed. Sam grabbed his arm, pulled him close.

"Just take a look, a quick look. Like no woman you've ever met! I swear to you, Dan—an *original*. You have simply got to meet this woman! Even if nothing comes of it—naturally Flo and I are hoping—but even if nothing happens, believe me it will be an experience for you. Here is a new human being! You'll see. You'll see. Her name is Celia Montfort. My name is Sam and her name is Celia. Right away that tells a lot—no?"

The Mortons' apartment was a shambles, thrift shop, rats' nest, charity bazaar, gypsy camp: as incoherent as their lives. They redecorated at least twice a year, and these upheavals had left a squabble of detritus: chairs in Swedish modern, a Victorian love seat, a Sheraton lowboy, a wooden Indian, Chinese vases, chromium lamps, Persian rugs, a barber pole, a Plexiglas table, ormolu ashtrays, Tiffany glass, and paintings in a dozen trendy styles, framed and unframed, hung and propped against the wall.

And everywhere, books, magazines, prints, photographs, newspapers, posters, swatches of cloth, smoking incense, boxes of chocolates, fresh flowers, fashion sketches, broken cigarettes, a bronze screw propeller and a blue bedpan: all mixed, helter-skelter, as if giant salad forks had dug into the furnishings of the apartment, tossed them to the ceiling, allowed them to flutter down as they would, pile up, tilt, overlap, and create a setting of frenzied disorder that stunned visitors but proved marvelously comfortable and relaxing.

Sam Morton led Daniel to the entrance of the living room, tugging him along by the arm, fearful of his escaping. Blank waved a hand at Blanche, working in the kitchen, as he passed.

In the living room, Flo Morton smiled and blew a kiss to Dan. He turned from her to look at the woman who had been speaking when they entered, and who would not stop to acknowledge their presence.

"It is bad logic and worse semantics," she was saying in a voice curiously devoid of tone and inflection. " 'Black is beautiful'? It's like saying, 'Down is up.' I know they mean to affirm their existence and assert their pride. But they have chosen a battlecry no one, not even themselves, can believe. Because words have more than meaning, you see. The meaning of words is merely the skeleton, almost as basic as the spelling. But words also have emotional weight. The simplest, most innocent words—as far as definition is concerned—can be an absolute horror emotionally. A word that looks plain and unassuming when written or printed can stir us to murder or delight. 'Black is beautiful'? To the human race, to whites, blacks, yellows, reds, black can *never* be beautiful. Black is evil and will always seem so. For black is darkness, and that is where fears lie and nightmares are born. Blackhearted. Black sheep of the family. Black art: the magic practised by witches. Black mass. These are not racial slurs. They spring from man's primitive fear of the dark. Black is the time or place without light, where dangers lurk, and death. Children are naturally afraid of the dark. It is not taught them; they are born with it. And even some adults sleep with a nightlight. 'Behave yourself or the boogie man will get you.' I imagine even Negro children are told that. The 'boogie'—a black monster who comes out of the dark, the perilous dark. Black is the unknowable. Black is danger. Black is evil. Black is death. But 'Black is beautiful'? Never. They'll never get anyone to believe that. We are all animals. I don't believe we've been introduced."

She raised her eyes to look directly at Daniel Blank. He was startled. He had been so engrossed with her lecture, so intent on following her thought, that he had no clear idea of what she looked like. Now, as Florence Morton hastily introduced them, as he crossed the room to take Celia Montfort's proffered hand, he inspected her closely.

She sat curled up in the softness of a big armchair that was all foam, red velvet and cigarette burns. Strangely, for a Sunday morning, she was wearing an elegant evening shift of black satin. The neckline was straight across, the dress suspended from bare shoulders by spaghetti straps. She wore a thin choker of diamonds, and on the wrist of the hand she held out to Blank was a matching bracelet. He wondered if perhaps she had been to an all-night party and had been unable to go home to change. He thought so when he saw the silk evening slippers.

Her hair was so black it was almost purple, parted in the middle, and fell loosely below her shoulders without wave or curl. It gave her thin face a witch-like appearance, enhanced by long, slender hands, tapering fingers with stiletto nails.

Her bare arms, shoulders, the tops of her small breasts revealed by the low-cut gown: all gleamed against the red velvet. There was a peculiar, limpid *nakedness* to her flesh. The arms were particularly sensual: smooth, hairless, as seemingly boneless as tentacles: arms squeezed from tubes.

It was difficult to estimate her height or appreciate her figure while she was coiled into the armchair. Blank judged her a tall woman, perhaps five foot six or more, with a good waist, flat hips, hard thighs. But at the moment all that was of little importance to him; her face bewitched him, her eyes locked with his.

They were grey eyes, or were they a light blue? Her thin brows were arched, or were they straight? Her nose was—what? An Egyptian nose? A nose from a sarcophagus or bas-relief? And those parted lips: were they full and dry, or flat and moist? The long chin, like the toe of her silk slipper—was that enchanting or perhaps too masculine? As Sam Morton had said, not beautiful. But something there. Something better? It needed study.

He had the impression that at this time, noon on a bright Sunday, wearing Saturday night's stale finery, her face and body were smudged with weariness. There was a languor in her posture, her skin was pallid, and faint violet shadows were beneath her eyes. She had the scent of debauchery, and her toneless voice came from senses punished beyond feeling and passions spent.

Florence and Samuel immediately launched into a violent denunciation of her "Black is beautiful" comments. Daniel watched to see how she reacted to this assault. He saw at once she had the gift of repose: no twistings there, no squirmings, no fiddling with bracelet, fluffing hair, touching ears. She sat quietly, composed, and Daniel suddenly realized she was not listening to her critics. She was withdrawn from all of them.

She was gone but not, he guessed, daydreaming. She was not floating; she had pulled back within herself, sinking deeper into her own thoughts, hungers, hopes. Those eyes, indecipherable as water, attended them, but he had a sense of her estrangement. He wanted to be in her country, if only for a visit, to look around and see what the place was like.

Flo paused for an answer to a question. But there was no answer. Celia Montfort merely regarded her with a somewhat glassy stare, her face expressionless. The moment was saved by the entrance of Blanche, pushing a big-three-shelved cart laden with hot and cold dishes, a pitcher of Bloody Marys, an iced bottle of sparkling rosé.

The food was less unconventional than Blank had hoped, but still the poached eggs were sherried, the ham was in burgundy sauce, the mushroom omelette brandied, the walnut waffles swimming in rum-flavored maple syrup.

"Eat!" commanded Flo.

"Enjoy!" commanded Sam.

Daniel had a single poached egg, a strip of bacon, a glass of wine. Then he settled back with a bunch of chilled Concord grapes, listening to the Mortons' chatter, watching Celia Montfort silently and intently devour an immense amount of food.

Afterward they had small, warmed Portuguese brandies. Daniel and the Mortons carried on a desultory conversation about Art Deco, a current fad. Celia's opinion was asked, but she shook her head. "I know nothing about it." After that she sat quietly, brandy glass clasped in both hands, eyes brooding. She had no talent for small talk. Complain of bad weather and she might, he thought, deliver you a sermon on humility. Strange woman. What was it Sam had said—"She scares you." Why on earth should he have said that—unless he was referring to her disturbing silences, her alienation: which might be nothing more than egoism and bad manners.

She rose suddenly to her feet and, for the first time, Blank saw her body clearly. As he had guessed, she was tall, but thinner and harder than he had suspected. She carried herself well, moved with a sinuous grace, and her infrequent gestures were small and controlled.

She said she must go, giving Flo and Sam a bleak smile. She thanked them politely for their hospitality. Flo brought her coat: a cape of weighted silk brocade, as dazzling as a matador's jacket. Blank was now convinced she had not been home to that East End Avenue townhouse since Saturday evening, nor slept at all the previous night.

She moved to the door. Flo and Sam looked at him expectantly.

"May I see you home?" he asked.

She looked at him thoughtfully.

"Yes," she said finally. "You may."

The Mortons exchanged a rapid glance of triumph. They waited in the hallway, in their studded jumpsuits, grinning like idiots, until the elevator door shut them away.

In the elevator, unexpectedly, she asked: "You live in this building, don't you?"

"Yes. The twenty-first floor."

"Let's go there."

Ten minutes later she was in his bedroom, brocaded cape dropped to the floor, and fast asleep atop the covers of his bed, fully clothed. He picked up her cape, hung it away, slipped off her shoes and placed them neatly alongside the bed. Then he closed the door softly, went back into the living room to read the Sunday New York *Times,* and tried not to think of the strange woman sleeping in his bed.

At 4:30, finished with his paper, he looked in upon her. She was lying face up on the pillows, her great mass of black hair fanned out. He was stirred. From the shoulders down she had turned onto her side and slept holding her bare arms. He took a light wool blanket from the linen closet and covered her gently. Then he went into the kitchen to eat a peeled apple and swallow a yeast tablet.

An hour later he was seated in the dim living room, trying to recall her features and understand why he was so intrigued by her sufficiency. The look of the sorceress, the mysterious wizard, could be due, he decided, to the way she wore her long, straight hair and the fact, as he suddenly realized, that she wore no make-up at all: no powder, no lipstick, no eye shadow. Her face was naked.

He heard her moving about. The bathroom door closed; the toilet was flushed. He switched on lamps. When she came into the living room he noted that she had put on her shoes and combed her hair smooth.

"Don't you ever wear any make-up?" he asked her.

She stared at him a long moment.

"Occasionally I rouge my nipples."

He gave her a sardonic smile. "Isn't that in poor taste?"

She caught his lewd meaning at once. "Witty man," she said in her toneless voice. "Might I have a vodka? Straight. Lots of ice, please. And a wedge of lime, if you have it."

When he came back with identical drinks for both, she was curled up on his Tobia Scarpa sofa, her face softly illuminated by a Marc Lepage inflatable lamp. He saw at once her weariness had vanished with sleep; she was serene. But with a shock he saw something he had not noticed before: a fist-sized bruise on the bicep of her left arm: purple and angry.

She took the drink from his hand. Her fingers were cool, bloodless as plastic.

"I like your apartment," she said.

Under the terms of the separation agreement, Gilda Blank had taken most of the antiques, the overstuffed furniture, the velvet drapes, the shag rugs. Daniel was happy to see it all go. The apartment had come to stiffle him. He felt muffled by all that carved wood and heavy cloth: soft things that burdened, then swaddled him.

He had redecorated the almost empty apartment in severe modern, most of the things from Knoll. There was chrome and glass, black leather and plastic, stainless steel and white enamel. The apartment was now open, airy, almost spidery in its delicacy. He kept furniture to a minimum, leaving the good proportions of the living room to make their own statement. The mirrored wall was cluttered wit, but otherwise the room was clean, precise, and exalting as a museum gallery.

"A room like this proves you don't require roots," she told him. "You have destroyed the past by ignoring it. Most people have a need for history, to live in a setting that constantly reminds of past generations. They take comfort and meaning from feeling themselves part of the flow, what was, is, will be. I think that is a weak, shameful emotion. It takes strength to break free, forget the past and deny the future. That's what this room does. Here you can exist by yourself in yourself, with no crutches. The room is without sentiment. Are you without sentiment?"

"Oh," he said, "I don't think so. Without emotion perhaps. Is your apartment in modern? As austere as this?"

"It is not an apartment. It's a townhouse. It belongs to my parents."

"Ah. They are still living then?"

"Yes," she said. "They are still living."

"I understand you live with your brother."

"His name is Anthony. Tony. He's twenty years younger than I. Mother had him late in life. It was an embarrassment to her. She and my father prefer him to live with me."

"And where do they live?"

"Oh, here and there," she said vaguely. "There is one thing I don't like about this room."

"What is that?"

She pointed to a black cast iron candelabrum with twelve contorted arms. Fitted to each was a white taper.

"I don't like unburned candles," she said tonelessly. "They seem to me as dishonest as plastic flowers and wallpaper printed to look like brick."

"Easily remedied," he said, rose and slowly lighted the candles.

"Yes," she said. "That's better."

"Are you ready for another drink?"

"Bring the vodka and a bucket of ice out here. Then you won't have to run back and forth."

"Yes," he said, "I will."

When he returned, she had snuffed three of the tapers. She added ice and vodka to her glass.

"We'll snuff them at intervals. So they will be in various lengths. I'm glad you have the dripless kind. I like candles, but I don't like leavings of dead wax."

"Memories of past pleasures?"

"Something like that. But also too reminiscent of bad Italian restaurants with candles in empty Chianti bottles and too much powdered garlic in the sauce. I hate fakery. Rhinestones and padded brassieres."

"My wife—" he started. "My ex-wife," he amended, "wore a padded bra. The strange thing was that she didn't need it. She was very well endowed. Is."

"Tell me about her."

"Gilda? A very pleasant woman. We're both from Indiana. We met at the University. A blind date. I was a year ahead of her. We went together occasionally. Nothing serious. I came to New York. Then she came here, a year later, and we started seeing each other again. Serious, this time."

"What was she like? Physically, I mean."

"A large woman, with a tendency to put on weight. She loved rich food. Her mother is enormous. Gilda is blonde. What you'd call a 'handsome woman.' A good athlete. Swimming, tennis, golf, skiing—all that. Very active in charities, social organizations. Took lessons in bridge. Chinese cooking, and music appreciation. Things like that."

"No children?"

"No."

"How long were you married?"

"Ahh . . ." He stared at her. "My God, I can't remember. Of course. Seven years. Almost eight. Yes, that's right. Almost eight years."

"You didn't want children?"

"I didn't—no."

"She?"

"Yes."

"Is that why you divorced?"

"Oh no. No, that had nothing to do with it. We divorced because—well, why did we divorce? Incompatibility, I guess. We just grew apart. She went her way and I went mine."

"What was her way?"

"You're very personal."

"Yes. You can always refuse to answer."

"Well, Gilda is a very healthy, well-adjusted, outgoing woman. She likes people, likes children, parties, picnics, the theatre, church. Whenever we went to the theatre or a movie where the audience was asked to sing along with the entertainer or music, she would sing along. That's the kind of woman she was."

"A sing-alonger with a padded brassiere."

"And plastic flowers," he added. "Well, not plastic. But she did buy a dozen roses made of silk. I couldn't convince her they were wrong."

He rose to blow out another three candles. He came back to sit in his Eames chair. Suddenly she came over to sit on the hassock in front of him. She put a light hand on his knee.

"What happened?" she whispered.

"You guessed?" he said, not surprised. "A strange story. I don't understand it myself."

"Have you told the Mortons?"

"My God, no. I've told no one."

"But you want to tell me."

"Yes I want to tell you. And I want you to explain it to me. Well, Gilda is a normal, healthy woman who enjoys sex. I do too. Our sex was very good. It really was. At the start anyway. But you know, you get older and it doesn't seem so important. To her, anyway. But I don't mean to put her down. She was good and enthusiastic in bed. Perhaps unimaginative. Sometimes she'd laugh at me. But a normal, healthy woman."

"You keep saying healthy, healthy, healthy."

"Well, she was. Is. A big, healthy woman. Big legs. Big breasts. A glow to her skin. Rubens would have loved her. Well . . . about three years ago we took a summer place for the season on Barnegat Bay. You know where that is?"

"No."

"The Jersey shore. South of Bay Head. It was beautiful. Fine beach, white sand, not too crowded. One afternoon we had some neighbors over for a cook-out. We all had a lot to drink. It was fun. We were all in bathing suits, and we'd drink, get a little buzz on, and then go into the ocean to swim and sober up, and then eat and drink some more. It was a wonderful afternoon. Eventually everyone went home. Gilda and I were alone. Maybe a little drunk, hot from the sun and food and laughing. We went back into our cottage and decided to have sex. So we took off our bathing suits. But we kept our sunglasses on."

"Oh."

"I don't know why we did it, but we did. Maybe we thought it was funny. Anyway, we made love wearing those dark, blank glasses so we couldn't see each other's eyes."

"Did you like it?"

"The sex? For me it was a revelation, a door opening. I guess Gilda thought it was funny and forgot it. I can never forget it. It was the most sexually exciting thing I've ever done in my life. There was something primitive and frightening about it. It's hard to explain. But it shook me. I wanted to do it again."

"But she didn't?"

"That's right. Even after we came back to New York and it was winter, I suggested we wear sunglasses in bed, but she wouldn't. I suppose you think I'm crazy?"

"Is that the end of the story?"

"No. There's more. Wait until I blow out more candles."

"I'll get them."

She snuffed out three more tapers. Only three were left burning, getting down close to the iron sockets. She came back to sit on the ottoman again.

"Go on."

"Well, I was browsing around Brentano's—this was the winter right after Barnegat Bay—and Brentano's, you know, carries a lot of museum-type antique jewelry and semi-precious stones, coral and native handicrafts. Stuff like that. Well, they had a collection of African masks they were selling. Very primitive. Strong and somehow frightening. You know the effect primitive African art has. It touches something very deep, very mysterious. Well, I wanted to have sex with Gilda while we both wore those masks. An irrational feeling, I know. I knew it at the time, but I couldn't resist. So I bought two masks—they weren't cheap—and brought them home. Gilda didn't like them and didn't dislike them. But she let me hang them in the hallway out there. A few weeks later we had a lot to drink—"

"You got her drunk."

"I guess. But she wouldn't do it. She wouldn't wear one of those masks in bed. She said I was crazy. Anyway, the next day she threw the masks away. Or burned them, or gave them away, or something. They were gone when I got home."

"And then you were divorced?"

"Well, not just because of the sunglasses and the African masks. There were other things. We had been growing apart for some time. But the business with the masks was certainly a contributing factor. Strange story—no?"

She got up to extinguish the three remaining candles. They smoked a bit, and she licked her fingers, then damped the wicks. She poured both of them a little more vodka, then regarded the candelabrum, head cocked to one side.

"That's better."

"Yes," he agreed. "It is."

"Do you have a cigarette?"

"I smoke a kind made from dried lettuce leaves. Non-nicotine. But I have the regular kind too. Which would you like?"

"The poisonous variety."

He lighted it for her, and she strolled up and down before the mirrored wall, holding her elbows. Her head was bent forward; long hair hid her face.

"No," she said, "I don't believe it was irrational. And I don't believe you're crazy. I'm talking now about the sunglasses and the masks. You see, there was a time when sex itself, by itself, had a power, a mystery, an awe it no longer has. Today it's 'Shall we have another martini or shall we fuck?' The act itself has no more meaning than a second dessert. In an effort to restore the meaning, people try to increase the pleasure. They use all kinds of gadgets, but all they do is add to the mechanization of sex. It's the wrong remedy. Sex is not solely, or even mainly, physical pleasure. Sex is a rite. And the only way to restore its meaning is to bring to it the trappings of a ceremony. That's why I was so delighted to discover the Mortons' shop. Probably without realizing it, they sensed that today the psychic satisfactions of sex have become more important than physical gratifications. Sex has become, or should become, a dramatic art. It was once, in several cultures. And the Mortons have made a start in providing the make-up, costumes, and scenery for the play. It is only a start, but it is a good one. Now about you . . . I think you became, if not bored then at least dissatisfied with sex with your 'healthy, normal' wife. 'Is this all there is?' you asked. 'Is there nothing more?' Of course there is more. Much, much more. And you were on the right track when you spoke about "a revelation . . . a door opening' when you made love wearing sunglasses. And when you said the African masks were 'primitive' and 'somehow frightening.' You have, in effect, discovered the unknown or disregarded side of sex: its psychic fulfillment. Having become aware of it, you suspect—rightly so—that its spiritual satisfactions can far surpass physical pleasure. After all, there are a limited number of orifices and mucous membranes in the human body. In other words, you are beginning to see sex as a religious rite and a dramatic ceremony. The masks were merely the first step in this direction. Too bad your wife couldn't see it that way."

"Yes," he said. "Too bad."

"I must be going," she said abruptly, and marched into the bedroom to retrieve her cape.

"I'll see you home," he said eagerly.

"No. That won't be necessary. I'll take a cab."

"At least let me come down to call a cab for you."

"Please don't."

"I want to see you again. May I call you?"

"Yes."

She was out the door and gone almost before he was aware of it. The smell of snuffed candles and old smoke lingered in the room.

He turned out the lights and sat a long time in darkness, pondering what she had said. Something in him responded to it. He began to glimpse the final picture that might be assembled from the bits and pieces of his thought and behavior that had, until now, puzzled him so. That final picture shocked him, but he was neither frightened nor dismayed.

Once, late in the previous summer, he had been admiring his naked, newly slender and tanned body in the bedroom mirror. Only the nightlight was on. His flesh was sheened with its dim, rosy glow.

He noted how strange and somehow exciting the gold chain of his wrist watch looked against his skin. There was something there . . . A week later he purchased a women's belt, made of heavy, gold-plated links. He specified a chain adjustable to all sizes, and then had it gift-wrapped for reasons he could not comprehend.

Now, only hours after he had first met Celia Montfort, after she had slept in his bed, after she had listened to him and spoken to him, he stood naked again before the bedroom mirror, the room illuminated only by the caressing nightlight. About his wrist was the gold chain of his watch, and around his slim waist was the linked belt.

He stared, fascinated. Chained, he touched himself.

4

Javis-Bircham Publications, Inc. owned the office building, and occupied the top fifteen floors, on 46th Street west of Ninth Avenue. The building had been erected in the late 1930s, and was designed in the massive, pyramidal style of the period, with trim and decoration modeled after that of Rockefeller Center.

Javis-Bircham published trade magazines, textbooks, and technical journals. When Daniel Blank was hired six years previously, the company was publishing 129 different periodicals relating to the chemical industry, oil and petroleum, engineering, business management, automotive, machine tools, and aviation. In recent years magazines had been added on automation, computer technology, industrial pollution, oceanography, space exploration, and a consumer monthly on research and development. Also, a technical book club had been started, and the corporation was currently exploring the possibilities of short, weekly newsletters in fields covered by its monthly and bi-monthly trade magazines. Javis-Bircham had been listed as number 216 in Fortune Magazine's most recent list of America's 500 largest corporations. It had gone public in 1951 and its stock, after a 3-1 split in 1962, showed a 20-fold increase in its Big Board price.

Daniel Blank had been hired as Assistant Circulation Manager. His previous jobs had been as Subscription Fulfillment Manager and Circulation Manager on consumer periodicals. The three magazines on which he had worked prior to his employment at Javis-Bircham had since died. Blank, who saw what was happening, had survived, in a better job, at a salary he would have considered a hopeless dream ten years ago.

His first reaction to the circulation set-up at Javis-Bircham was unequivocal. "It's a fucked-up mess," he told his wife.

Blank's immediate superior was the Circulation Manager, a beefy, genial man named Robert White, called "Bob" by everyone, including secretaries and mail-room boys. This was, Blank thought, a measure of the man.

White had been at Javis-Bircham for 25 years and had surrounded himself with a staff of more than 50 males and females who seemed, to Blank, all "old women" who smelled of lavender and whiskey sours, arrived late for work, and were continually taking up office collections for birthdays, deaths, marriages, and retirements.

The main duty of the Circulation Department was to supply to the Production Department "print-run estimates": the number of copies of each magazine that should be printed to insure maximum profit for Javis-Bircham. The magazines might be weeklies, semi-monthlies, monthlies, quarterlies, semi-annuals or annuals. They might be given away to a managerial-level readership or sold by subscription. Some were even available to the general public on newsstands. Most of the magazines earned their way by advertising revenue. Some carried no advertising at all, but were of such a specialized nature that they sold solely on the value of their editorial content.

Estimating the "press run" of each magazine for maximum profitablity was an incredibly complex task. Past and potential circulation of each periodical had to be considered, current and projected advertising revenue, share of general overhead, costs of actual printing—quality of paper, desired process, four-color plates, etc.—costs of mailing and distributing, editorial budget (including personnel), publicity and public relations campaigns, etc., etc.

At the time Daniel Blank joined the organization, this bewildering job of "print-run estimation" seemed to be done "by guess and by God." Happy Bob White's staff of "old women" fed him information, laughing a great deal during their conversations with him. Then, when a recommendation was due, White would sit at his desk, humming, with an ancient slide rule in his hands, and within an hour or so would send his estimate to the Production Department.

Daniel Blank saw immediately that there were so mnay variables involved that the system screamed for computerization. His experience with computers was minimal; on previous jobs he had been involved mostly with relatively simple data-processing machines.

He therefore enrolled for a six months' night course in "The Triumph of the Computer." Two years after starting work at Javis-Bircham, he presented to Bob White a 30-page carefully organized and cogently reasoned prospectus on the advantages of a computerized Circulation Department.

White took it home over the weekend to read. He returned it to Blank on Monday morning. Pages were marked with brown rings from coffee cups, and one page had been crinkled and almost obliterated by a spilled drink.

White took Daniel to lunch and, smiling, explained why Blank's plan wouldn't do. It wouldn't do at all.

"You obviously put a lot of work and thought into it," White said, "but you're forgetting the personalities involved. The people. My God, Dan, I have lunch with the editors and advertising managers of those magazines almost every day. They're my friends. They all have plans for their books: an article that might get a lot of publicity and boost circulation, a new hot-shot advertising salesman who might boost revenue way over the same month last year. I've got to consider all those personal things. The human factors involved. You can't feed that into a computer."

Daniel Blank nodded understandingly. An hour after they returned from lunch he had a clean copy of his prospectus on the desk of the Executive Vice President.

A month later the Circulation Department was shocked to learn that laughing Bob White had retired. Daniel Blank was appointed Circulation *Director*, a title he chose himself, and given a free hand.

Within a year all the "old women" were gone, Blank had surrounded himself with a young staff of pale technicians, and the cabinets of AMROK II occupied half the 30th floor of the Javis-Bircham Building. As Blank had predicted, not only did the computer and auxiliary data-processing machines handle all the problems of circulation—subscription fulfillment and print-run estimation—but they performed these tasks so swiftly that they could also be used for salary checks, personnel records, and pension programs. As a result, Javis-Bircham was able to dismiss more than 500 employees and, as Blank had carefully pointed out in his original prospectus, the annual leasing of the extremely expensive AMROK II resulted in an appreciable tax deduction.

Daniel Blank was currently earning $55,000 a year and had an unlimited expense account, a very advantageous pension and stock option plan. He was 36.

About a month after he took over, he received a very strange postcard from Bob White. It said merely: "What are you feeding the computer? Ha-ha."

Blank puzzled over this. What had been fed the computer, of course, were the past circulation and advertising revenue figures and profit or loss totals of all the magazines Javis-Bircham published. Admittedly, White had been working his worn slide rule during most of the years from which those figures were taken, and it was possible to say that, in a sense, White had programmed the computer. But still, the postcard made little sense, and Daniel Blank wondered why his former boss had bothered to send it.

It was gratifying to hear the uniformed starter say, "Good morning, Mr. Blank," and it was gratifying to ride the Executive Elevator in solitary comfort to the 30th floor. His personal office was a corner suite with wall-to-wall carpeting, a private lavatory and, not a desk, but a table: a tremendous slab of distressed walnut on a wrought-iron base. These things counted.

He had deliberately chosen for his personal secretary a bony, 28-year-old widow, Mrs. Cleek, who needed the job badly and would be grateful. She had proved as efficient and colorless as he had hoped. She had a few odd habits: she insisted on latching all doors and cabinets that were slightly ajar, and she was continually lining up the edges of the ashtrays and papers with the edges of tables and desks, putting everything parallel or at precise right angles. A picture hanging askew drove her mad. But these were minor tics.

When he entered his office, she was ready to hang away his coat and hat in the small closet. His black coffee was waiting for him, steaming, on a small plastic tray on the table, having been delivered by the commissary on the 20th floor.

"Good morning, Mr. Blank," she said in her watery voice, consulting a stenographer's pad she held. "You have a meeting at ten-thirty with the Pension Board. Lunch at twelve-thirty at the Plaza with Acme, regarding the servicing contract. I tried to confirm, but no one's in yet. I'll try again."

"Thank you," he said. "I like your dress. Is it new?"

"No," she said.

"I'll be in the Computer Room until the Pension Board meeting, in case you need me."

"Yes, Mr. Blank."

The embarrassing truth was that, as Mrs. Cleek was probably aware, he had nothing to do. It was true he was overseer of an extremely important department—perhaps *the* most important department of a large corporation. But, literally, he found it difficult to fill his working day.

He could have given the impression of working. Many executives in similar circumstances did that. He could accept invitations to luncheons easily avoided. He could stalk corridors carrying papers over which he could frown and shake his head. He could request technical literature on supplies and computer systems utterly inadequate or too sophisticated for Javis-Bircham's needs, with a heavy increase of unnecessary correspondence. He could take senseless business trips to inspect the operations of magazine wholesalers and printing plants. He could attend dozens of conventions and trade meetings, give speeches and buy the bodies of hat-check girls.

But none of that was his style. He needed work; he could not endure inaction for long. And so he turned to "empire building," plotting how he might enlarge the size of the Circulation Department and increase his own influence and power.

And in his personal life he felt the same need for action after the brief hibernation following his divorce (during which period he vowed, inexplicably, to remain continent). This desire to "do" dated from his meeting with Celia Montfort. He punched his phone for an outside line, then dialed her number. Again.

He had not seen her nor had he spoken to her since that Sunday he was introduced at the Mortons' and she had napped on his bed. He had looked her up in the Manhattan directory. There it was: "Montfort, C." at an East End address. But each time he called, a male voice answered, lisping: "Mith Montforth rethidenth."

Blank assumed it was a butler or houseman. The voice, in spite of its flutiness, was too mature to be that of the 12-year-old brother. Each time he was informed that Mith Montfort was out of town and, no, the speaker did not know when she might return.

But this time the reply was different. It was "Mith Montforth rethidenth" again, but additional information was offered: Miss Montfort had arrived, had called from the airport, and if Mr. Blank cared to phone later in the day, Mith Montforth would undoubtedly be at home.

He hung up, feeling a steaming hope. He trusted his instincts, though he could not always say *why* he acted as he did. He was convinced there was something there for him with that strange, disturbing woman: something significant. If he had energy and the courage to act . . .

Daniel Blank stepped into the open lobby of the Computer Room and nodded to the receptionist. He went directly to the large white enameled cabinet to the right of the inner doors and drew out a sterile duster and skull cap hermetically sealed in a clear plastic bag.

He donned white cap and duster, went through the first pair of swinging glass doors. Six feet away was the second pair, and the space between was called the "air lock," although it was not sealed. It was illuminated by cold blue fluorescent lights said to have a germicidal effect. He paused a moment to watch the ordered activity in the Computer Room.

AMROK II worked 24 hours a day and was cared for by three shifts of acolytes, 20 in each shift. Blank was gratified to note that all on the morning shift were wearing the required disposable paper caps and dusters. Four men sat at a stainless steel table; the others, young men and women, sexless in their white paper costumes, attended the computer and auxiliary data-processing machines, one of which was presently chattering softly and spewing out an endless record that folded up neatly into partly serrated sheets in a wire basket. It was, Blank knew, a compilation of state unemployment insurance taxes.

The mutter of this machine and the soft start-stop whir of tape reels on another were the only sounds heard when Blank pushed through the second pair of swinging glass doors. The prohibition against unnecessary noise was rigidly enforced. And this glaring, open room was not only silent, it was dustproof, with temperature and humidity rigidly controlled and monitored. An automatic alarm would be triggered by any unusual source of magnetic radiation. Fire was unthinkable. Not only was smoking prohibited but even the mere possession of matches or cigarette lighters was grounds for instant dismissal. The walls were unpainted stainless steel, the lamps fluorescent. The Computer Room was an unadorned vault, an operating theatre, floating on rubber mountings within the supporting body of the Javis-Bircham Building.

And 90 percent of this was sheer nonsense, humbuggery. This was not an atomic research facility, nor a laboratory dealing with deadly viruses. The business activities of AMROK II did not demand these absurd precautions—the sterile caps and gowns, the "air lock," the prohibition against normal conversation.

Daniel Blank had decreed all this, deliberately. Even before it was installed and operating, he realized the functioning of AMROK II would be an awesome mystery to most of the employees of Javis-Bircham, including Blank's superiors: vice presidents, the president, the board of directors. Blank intended to keep the activities of the Computer Room an enigma. Not only did it insure his importance to the firm, but it made his task much easier when the annual "budget day" rolled around and he requested consistently rising amounts for his department's operating expenses.

Blank went immediately to the stainless steel table where the four young men were deep in whispered conversation. This was his Task Force X-1, the best technicians of the morning shift. Blank had set them a problem that was still "Top Secret" within this room.

From his boredom, in his desire to extend the importance of the Circulation Department and increase his personal power and influence, Blank had decided he should have the responsibility of deciding for each magazine the proportion between editorial pages and advertising pages. Years ago this ratio was dictated in a rough fashion by the limitations of printing presses, which could produce a magazine only in multiples of eight or 16 pages.

But improvements in printing techniques now permitted production of magazines of any number of pages—15, 47, 76, 103, 241: whatever might be desired, with a varied mix of paper quality. Magazine editors constantly fought for more editorial pages, arguing (sometimes correctly, sometimes not) that sheer quantity attracted readers.

But there was obviously a limit to this: paper cost money, and so did press time. Editors were continually wrangling with the Production Department about the thickness of their magazines. Daniel Blank saw a juicy opportunity to step into the fray and supersede both sides by suggesting AMROK II be given the assignment of determining the most profitable proportion between editorial and advertising pages.

He would, he knew, face strong and vociferous opposition. Editors would claim an infringement of their creative responsibilities; production men would see a curtailment of their power. But if Blank could present a feasible program, he was certain he could win over the shrewd men who floated through the paneled suites on the 31st floor. Then he—and AMROK II, of course—would determine the extent of the editorial content of each magazine. It seemed to him but a short step from that to allowing AMROK II to dictate the most profitable subject matter of the editorial content. It was possible.

But all that was in the future. Right now Task Force X-1 was discussing the programming that would be necessary before the computer could make wise decisions on the most profitable ratio between editorial and advertising pages in every issue of every Javis-Bircham magazine. Blank listened closely to their whispered conversation, turning his eyes from speaker to speaker, and wondering if it was true, as she had said, that she occasionally rouged her nipples.

He waited, with conscious control, until 3:00 P.M. before calling. The lisping houseman asked him to hang on a moment, then came back on the phone to tell him, "Mith Montfort requeth you call again in a half hour." Puzzled, Blank hung up, paced his office for precisely 30 minutes, ate a chilled pear from his small refrigerator, and called again. This time he was put through to her.

"Hello," he said. "How are you?" (Should he call her "Celia" or "Miss Montfort"?)

"Well. And you?"

"Fine. You said I could call."

"Yes."

"You've been out of town?"

"Out of the country. To Samarra."

"Oh?" he said, hoping she might think him clever, "you had an appointment?"

"Something like that."

"Where exactly is Samarra?"

"Iraq. I was there for only a day. Actually I went over to see my parents. They're currently in Marrakech."

"How are they?" he asked politely.

"The same," she said in her toneless voice. "They haven't changed in thirty years. Ever since . . ." Her voice trailed off.

"Ever since what?" he asked.

"Ever since World War Two. It upset their plans."

She spoke in riddles, and he didn't want to pry.

"Marrakech isn't near Samarra, is it?"

"Oh no. Marrakech is in Morocco."

"Geography isn't my strong point. I get lost every time I go south of 23rd Street."

He thought she might laugh, but she didn't.

"Tomorrow night," he said desperately, "tomorrow night the Mortons are having a cocktail party. We're invited. I'd like to take you to dinner before the party. It starts about ten."

"Yes," she said immediately. "Be here at eight. We'll have a drink, then go to dinner. Then we'll go to the Mortons' party."

He started to say "Thank you" or "Fine" or "I'm looking forward to it" or "See you then," but she had already hung up. He stared at the dead receiver in his hand.

The next day, Friday, he left work early to go home to prepare for the evening. He debated with himself whether or not to send flowers. He decided against it. He had a feeling she loved flowers but never wore them. His best course, he felt, was to circle about her softly, slowly, until he could determine her tastes and prejudices.

He groomed himself carefully, shaving although he had shaved that morning. He used a women's cologne, Je Reviens, a scent that stirred him. He wore French underwear—white nylon bikini briefs—and a silk shirt in a geometric pattern of white and blue squares. His wide necktie was a subtly patterned maroon. The suit was navy knit, single breasted. In addition to wrist watch, cufflinks, and a heavy gold ring on his right forefinger, he wore a gold-link identification bracelet loose about his right wrist. And the "Via Veneto" wig.

He left early to walk over to her apartment. It wasn't far, and it was a pleasant evening.

His loose topcoat was a black lightweight British gabardine, styled with raglan sleeves, a fly front, and slash pockets. The pockets, in the British fashion, had an additional opening through the coat fabric so that the wearer did not have to unbutton his coat to reach his trouser or jacket pockets but could shove his hand inside the concealed coat openings for tickets, wallet, keys, change, or whatever.

Now, strolling toward Celia Montfort's apartment through the sulfur-laden night, Daniel Blank reached inside his coat pocket to feel himself. To the passer-by, he was an elegant gentleman, hand thrust casually into coat pocket. But beneath the coat . . .

Once, shortly after he was separated from Gilda, he had worn the same coat and walked through Times Square on a Saturday night. He had slipped his hand into the pocket opening, unzipped his fly, and held himself exposed beneath the loose coat as he moved through the throng, looking into the faces of passersby.

Celia Montfort lived in a five-story greystone townhouse. The door bell was of a type he had read about but never encountered before. It was a bell-pull, a brass knob that is drawn out, then released. The bell is sounded as the knob is pulled and as it is released to return to its socket. Daniel Blank admired its polish and the teak door it ornamented . . .

. . . A teak door that was opened by a surprisingly tall man, pale, thin, wearing striped trousers and a shiny black alpaca jacket. A pink sweetheart rose was in his lapel. Daniel was conscious of a scent: not his own, but something heavier and fruitier.

"My name is Daniel Blank," he said. "I believe Miss Montfort is expecting me."

"Yeth, thir," the man said, holding wide the door. "I am Valenter. Do come in."

It was an impressive entrance: marble-floored with a handsome staircase curving away. On a slender pedestal was a crystal vase of cherry-colored mums. He had been right: she did like long-stemmed flowers.

"Pleath wait in the thudy. Mith Montfort will be down thoon."

His coat and hat were taken and put away somewhere. The tall, skinny man came back to usher him into a room paneled with oak and leather-bound books.

"Would you care for a drink, thir?"

Soft flames flickering in a tiled fireplace. Reflections on the polished leather of a tufted couch. On the mantel, unexpectedly, a beautifully detailed model of a Yankee whaler. Andirons and fireplace tools of black iron with brass handles.

"Please. A vodka martini on the rocks."

Drapes of heavy brocade. Rugs of—what? Not Oriental. Greek perhaps? Or Turkish? Chinese vases filled with blooms. An Indian paneled screen, all scrolled with odd, disturbing figures. A silvered cocktail shaker of the Prohibition Era. The room had frozen in 1927 or 1931.

"Olive, thir, or a twitht of lemon?"

Hint of incense in the air. High ceiling and, between the darkened beams, painted cherubs with dimpled asses. Oak doors and window mouldings. A bronze statuette of a naked nymph pulling a bow. The "string" was a twisted wire.

"Lemon, please."

An art nouveau mirror on the papered wall. A small oil nude of a middle-aged brunette holding her chin and glancing downward at sagging breasts with bleared nipples. A tin container of dusty rhododendron leaves. A small table inlaid as a chessboard with pieces swept and toppled. And in a black leather armchair, with high, embracing wings, the most beautiful boy Daniel Blank had ever seen.

"Hello," the boy said.

"Hello," he smiled stiffly. "My name is Daniel Blank. You must be Anthony."

"Tony."

"Tony."

"May I call you Dan?"

"Sure."

"Can you lend me ten dollars, Dan?"

Blank, startled, looked at him more closely. The lad had his knees drawn up, was hugging them, his head tilted to one side.

His beauty was so unearthly it was frightening. Clear, guileless blue eyes, carved lips, a bloom of youth and wanting, sculpted ears, a smile that tugged, those crisp golden curls long enough to frame face and chiselled neck. And an aura as rosy as the cherubs that floated overhead.

"It's awful, isn't it," the boy said, "to ask ten dollars from a complete stranger, but to tell you the truth—"

Blank was instantly alert, listening now and not just looking. It was his experience that when someone said "To tell the truth—" or "Would I lie to you?" the man was either a liar, a cheat, or both.

"You see," Tony said with an audacious smile. "I saw this absolutely marvelous jade pin. I know Celia would love it."

"Of course," Blank said. He took a ten dollar bill from his wallet. The boy made no move toward him. Daniel was forced to walk across the room to hand it to him.

"Thanks so much," the youth said languidly. "I get my allowance the first of the month. I'll pay you back."

He paid then, Blank knew, all he was ever going to pay: a dazzling smile of such beauty and young promise that Daniel was fuddled by longing. The moment was saved of souring by the entrance of Valenter, carrying the martini not on a tray but in his hand. When Blank took it, his fingers touched Valenter's. The evening began to spin out of control.

She came in a few moments later, wearing an evening shift styled exactly like the black satin she had been wearing when he first met her. But this one was in a dark bottle green, glimmering. About her neck was a heavy silver chain, tarnished, supporting a pendant: the image of a beast-god. Mexican, Blank guessed.

"I went to Samarra to meet a poet," she said, speaking as she came through the door and walked steadily toward him. "I once wrote poetry. Did I tell you? No. But I don't anymore. I have talent, but not enough. The blind poet in Samarra is a genius. A poem is a condensed novel. I imagine a novelist must increase the significance of what he writes by one-third to one-half to communicate all of his meaning. You understand? But the poet, so condensed, must double or triple what he wants to convey, hoping the reader will extract from this his full meaning."

Suddenly she leaned forward and kissed him on the lips while Valenter and the boy looked on gravely.

"How are you?" she asked.

Valenter brought her a glass of red wine. She was seated next to Blank on the leather sofa. Valenter stirred up the fire, added another small log, went to stand behind the armchair where Anthony coiled in flickering shadow.

"I think the Mortons' party will be amusing," he offered. "A lot of people. Noisy and crowded. But we don't have to stay long."

"Have you ever smoked hashish?" she asked.

He looked nervously toward the young boy.

"I tried it once," he said in a low voice. "It didn't do anything for me. I prefer alcohol."

"Do you drink a lot?"

"No."

The boy was wearing white flannel bags, white leather loafers, a white knitted singlet that left his slim arms bare. He moved slowly, crossing his legs, stretching, pouting. Celia Montfort turned her head to look at him. Did a signal pass?

"Tony," she said.

Immediately Valenter put a hand tenderly on the boy's shoulder.

"Time for your lethon, Mathter Montfort," he said.

"Oh, pooh," Tony said.

They walked from the room side by side. The lad stopped at the door, turned back, made a solemn bow in Blank's direction.

"I am very happy to have met you, sir," he said formally.

Then he was gone. Valenter closed the door softly behind them.

"A handsome boy," Daniel said. "What school does he go to?"

She didn't answer. He turned to look at her. She was peering into her wine glass, twirling the stem slowly in her long fingers. The straight black hair fell about her face: the long face, broody and purposeful.

She put her wine glass aside and rose suddenly. She moved casually about the room, and he swiveled his head to keep her in view. She touched things, picked them up and put them down. He was certain she was naked beneath the satin shift. Cloth touched her and flew away. It clung, and whispered off.

As she moved about, she began to intone another of what was apparently an inexhaustible repertoire of monologues. He was conscious of planned performance. But it was not a play; it was a ballet, as formalized and obscure. Above all, he felt *intent*: motive and plan.

"My parents are such sad creatures," she was saying. "Living in history. But that's not living at all, is it? It's an entombing. Mother's silk chiffon and father's plus-fours. They could be breathing mannequins at the Costume Institute. I look for dignity and all I find is . . . What is it I want? Grandeur, I suppose. Yes. I've thought of it. But is it impossible to be grand in life? What we consider grandeur is always connected with defeat and death. The Greek plays. Napoleon's return from Moscow. Lincoln. Superhuman dignity there. Nobility, if you like. But always rounded with death. The living, no matter how noble they may be, never quite make it, do they? But death rounds them out. What if John Kennedy had lived? No one has ever written of his life as a work of art, but it was. Beginning, middle, and end. Grandeur. And death made it. Are you ready? Shall we go?"

"I hope you like French cooking," he muttered. "I called for a reservation."

"It doesn't matter," she said.

The dance continued during dinner. She requested a banquette: they sat side by side. They ate and drank with little conversation. Once she picked up a thin sliver of tender veal and fed it into his mouth. But her free hand was on his arm, or in his lap, or pushing her long hair back so that the bottle green satin was brought tight across button nipples. Once, while they were having coffee and brandy, she crossed her knees. Her dress hiked up; the flesh of her thighs was perfectly white, smooth, glistening. He thought of good sea scallops and Dover sole.

"Do you like opera?" she asked in her abrupt way.

"No," he said truthfully. "Not much. It's so—so made up."

"Yes," she agreed, "it is. Artificial. But it's just a device: a flimsy wire coat hanger, and they hang the voices on that."

He was not a stupid man, and while they were seated at the banquette he became aware that her subtle movements—the touchings, the leanings, the sudden, unexpected caress of her hair against his cheek—these things were directorial suggestions, parts of her balletic performance. She was rehearsed. He wasn't certain of his role, but wanted to play it well.

"The voices," she went on, "the mighty voices that give me the feeling of suppressed power. With some singers I get the impression that there is art and strength there that hasn't been tapped. I get the feeling that, if they really let themselves go, they could crush eardrums and shatter stained glass windows. Perhaps the best of them, throwing off all restraint, could crush the world. Break it up into brittle pieces and send all the chunks whirling off into space."

He was made inferior by her soliloquies and made brave by wine and brandy.

"Why the hell are you telling me all this?" he demanded.

She leaned closer, pressed a satin-slicked breast against his arm.

"It's the same feeling I get from you," she whispered. "That you have a strength and resolve that could shatter the world."

He looked at her, beginning to glimpse her intent and his future. He wanted to ask, "Why me?" but found, to his surprise, it wasn't important.

The Mortons' party leavened their heavy evening. Florence and Samuel, wearing identical red velvet jumpsuits, met them at the door with the knowing smirks of successful matchmakers.

"Come in!" Flo cried.

"It's a marvelous party!" Sam cried.

"Two fights already!" Flo laughed.

"And one crying jag!" Sam laughed.

The party had a determined frenzy. He lost Celia in the swirl, and in the next few hours met and listened to a dozen disoriented men and women who floated, bumped against him, drifted away. He had a horrible vision of harbor trash, bobbing and nuzzling, coming in and going out.

Suddenly she was behind him, hand up under his jacket, nails digging into his shirted back.

"Do you know what happens at midnight?" she whispered.

"What?"

"They take off their faces—just like masks. And do you know what's underneath?"

"What?"

"Their faces. Again. And again."

She slipped away; he was too confused to hold her. He wanted to be naked in front of a mirror, making sure.

Finally, finally, she reappeared and drew him away. They flapped hands at host and hostess and stepped into the quiet corridor, panting. In the elevator she came into his arms and bit the lobe of his left ear as he said, "Oh," and the music from wherever was playing "My Old Kentucky Home." He was sick with lust and conscious that his life was dangerous and absurd. He was teetering, and pitons were not driven nor ice ax in.

There was Valenter to open the door for them, the sweetheart rose wilted. His face had the sheen of a scoured iron pot, and his lips seemed bruised. He served black coffee in front of the tiled fireplace. They sat on the leather couch and stared at blue embers.

"Will that be all, Mith Montfort?"

She nodded; he drifted away. Daniel Blank wouldn't look at him. What if the man should wink?

Celia went out of the room, came back with two pony glasses and a half-full bottle of marc.

"What is that?" he asked.

"A kind of brandy," she said. "Burgundian, I think. From the dregs. Very strong."

She filled a glass, and before handing it to him ran a long, red tongue around the rim, looking at him. He took it, sipped gratefully.

"Yes," he nodded. "Strong."

"Those people tonight," she said. "So inconsequential. Most of them are intelligent, alert, talented. But they don't have the opportunity. To surrender, I mean. To something important and shaking. They desire it more than they know. To give themselves. To what? Ecology or day-care centers or racial equality? They sense the need for something more, and God is dead. So . . . the noise and hysteria. If they could find . . ."

Her voice trailed off. He looked up.

"Find what?" he asked.

"Oh," she said, her eyes vague, "you know."

She rose from the couch. When he rose to stand alongside her, she unexpectedly stepped close, reached out, gently drew down the lower lid of his right eye. She stared intently at the exposed eyeball.

"What?" he said, confused.

"You're not inconsequential," she said, took him by the hand and led him upward. "Not at all."

Dazed by drink and wonder, he followed docilely. They climbed the handsome marble staircase to the third floor. There they passed through a tawdry wooden door and climbed two more flights up a splintered wooden stairway flecked with cobwebs that kissed his mouth.

"What *is* this?" he asked once.

"I *live* up here," she answered, turned suddenly and, being above him, reached down, pulled his head forward and pressed his face into the cool satin between belly and thighs.

It was a gesture that transcended obscenity and brought him trembling to his knees there on the dusty stairs.

"Rest a moment," she said.

"I'm a mountain climber," he said, and their whispered exchange seemed to him so inane that he gave a short bark of laughter that banged off dull walls and echoed.

"What?" he said again, and all the time he knew.

It was a small room of unpainted plank walls, rough-finished and scarred with white streaks as if some frantic beast had clawed to escape. There was a single metal cot with a flat spring of woven tin straps. On this was thrown a thin mattress, uncovered, the striped grey ticking soiled and burned.

There was one kitchen chair that had been painted fifty times and was now so dented and nicked that a dozen colors showed in bruised blotches. A bare light bulb, orange and dim, hung from a dusty cord.

The floor was patched with linoleum so worn the pattern had disappeared and brown backing showed through. The unframed mirror on the inside of the closed door was tarnished and cracked. The iron ashtray on the floor near the cot overflowed with cold cigarette butts. The room smelled of must, mildew, and old love.

"Beautiful," Daniel Blank said wonderingly, staring about. "It's a stage set. Any moment now a wall swings away, and there will be the audience applauding politely. What are my lines?"

"Take off your wig," she said.

He did, standing by the cot with the hair held foolishly in his two hands, offering her a small, dead animal.

She came close and caressed his shaven skull with both hands.

"Do you like this room?" she asked.

"Well . . . it's not exactly my idea of a love nest."

"Oh it's more than that. Much more. Lie down."

Gingerly, with some distaste, he sat on the stained mattress. She softly pressed him back. He stared up at the naked bulb, and there seemed to be a nimbus about it, a glow composed of a million shining particles that pulsed, contracted, expanded until they filled the room.

And then, almost before he knew it had started, she was doing things to him. He could not believe this intelligent, somber, reserved woman was doing those things. He felt a shock of fear, made a few muttered protests. But her voice was soft, soothing. After awhile he just lay there, his eyes closed now, and let her do what she would.

"Scream if you like," she said. "No one can hear."

But he clenched his jaws and thought he might die of pleasure.

He opened his eyes and saw her lying naked beside him, her long, white body as limp as a filleted fish. She began undressing him with practiced fingers . . . opening buttons . . . sliding down zippers . . . tugging things away gently, so gently he hardly had to move at all . . .

Then she was using him, *using* him, and he began to understand what his fate might be. Fear dissolved in a kind of sexual faint he had never experienced before as her strong hands pulled, her dry tongue rasped over his fevered skin.

"Soon," she promised. "Soon."

Once he felt a pain so sharp and sweet he thought she had murdered him. Once he heard her laughing: a thick, burbling sound. Once she wound him about with her smooth, black hair, fashioned a small noose and pulled it tight.

It went on and on, his will dissolving, a great weight lifting, and he would pay any price. It was climbing: mission, danger, sublimity. Finally, the summit.

Later, he was exploring her body and saw, for the first time, her armpits were unshaved. He discovered, hidden in the damp, scented hairs under her left arm, a small tattoo in a curious design.

Still later they were drowsing in each other's sweated arms, the light turned off, when he half-awoke and became conscious of a prescence in the room. The door to the corridor was partly open. Through sticky eyes he saw someone standing silently at the foot of the cot, staring down at their linked bodies.

In the dim light Daniel Blank had a smeary impression of a naked figure or someone dressed in white. Blank raised his head and made a hissing sound. The wraith withdrew. The door closed softly. He was left alone with her in that dreadful room.

5 One night, lying naked and alone between his sateen sheets, Daniel Blank wondered if this world might not be another world's dream. It was conceivable: somewhere another planet populated by a sentient people of superior intelligence who shared a communal dream as a method of play. And Earth was their dream, filled with fantasies, grotesqueries, evil—all the irrationalities they themselves rejected in their daily lives but turned to in sleep for relaxation. For fun.

Then we are all smoke and drifting. We are creatures of another world's midnight visions, moving through a life as illogical as any dream, and as realistic. We exist only in a stranger's slumber, and our death is his awaking, smiling at the mad, tangled plot his sleep conceived.

It seemed to Blank that since meeting Celia Montfort his existence had taken on the quality of a dream, the vaporous quality of a dream shot through with wild, bright flashes. His life had become all variables and, just before falling asleep to his own disordered dream, he wondered if AMROK II, properly programmed, might print out the meaning in a microsecond, as something of enormous consequence.

"No, no," Celia Montfort said intently, leaning forward into the candlelight. "Evil isn't just an absence of good. It's not just omission; it's commission, an action. You can't call that man evil just because he lets people starve to put his country's meager resources into heavy industry. That was a political and economic decision. Perhaps he is right, perhaps not. Those things don't interest me. But I think you're wrong to call him evil. Evil is really a kind of religion. I think he's just a well-meaning fool. But evil he's not. Evil implies intelligence and a deliberate intent. Don't you agree, Daniel?"

She turned suddenly to him. His hand shook, and he spilled a few drops of red wine. They dripped onto the unpressed linen tablecloth, spreading out like clots of thick blood.

"Well . . ." he said slowly.

She was having a dinner party: Blank, the Mortons, and Anthony Montfort seated around an enormous, candle-lighted dining table that could easily have accommodated twice their number in a chilly and cavernous dining hall. The meal, bland and without surprises, had been served by Valenter and a heavy, middle-aged woman with a perceptible black mustache.

The dishes were being removed, they were finishing a dusty beaujolais, and their conversation had turned to the current visit to Washington of the dictator of a new African nation, a man who wore white-piped vests and a shoulder holster.

"No, Samuel," Celia shook her head, "he is not an evil man. You use that word loosely. He's just a bungler. Greedy perhaps. Or out for revenge on his enemies. But greed and revenge are grubby motives. True evil has a kind of nobility, as all faiths do. Faith implies total surrender, a giving up of reason."

"Who was evil?" Florence Morton asked.

"Hitler?" Samuel Morton asked.

Celia Montfort looked slowly around the table. "You don't understand," she said softly. "I'm not talking about evil for the sake of ambition. I'm talking about evil for the sake of evil. Not Hitler—no. I mean saints of evil—men and women who see a vision and follow it. Just as Christian saints perceived a vision of good and followed that. I don't believe there have been any modern saints, of good *or* evil. But the possibility exists. In all of us."

"I understand," Anthony Montfort said loudly, and they all turned in surprise to look at him.

"To do evil because it's fun," the boy said.

"Yes, Tony," his sister said gently, smiling at him. "Because it's fun. Let's have coffee in the study. There's a fire there."

In the upstairs room the naked bulb burned in the air: a dusty moon. There was a smell of low tide and crawling things. Once he heard a faint shout of laughter, and Daniel Blank wondered if it was Tony laughing, and why he laughed.

They lay unclothed and stared at each other through the dark sunglasses she had provided. He stared—but did she? He could not tell. But blind eyes faced his blind eyes, discs of black against white skin. He felt the shivery bliss again. It was the mystery.

Her mouth opened slowly. Her long tongue slid out, lay flaccid between dry lips. Were her eyes closed? Was she looking at the wall? He peered closer, and behind the dark glass saw a far-off gleam. One of her hands wormed between her thighs, and a tiny bubble of spittle appeared in the corner of her mouth. He heard her breathing.

He pressed to her. She moved away and began to murmur. He understood some of what she said, but much was riddled. "What is it? What is it?" he wanted to cry, but did not because he feared it might be less than he hoped. So he was silent, listened to her murmur, felt her fingertips pluck at his quick skin.

The black covers over her eyes became holes, pits that went through flesh, bone, cot, floor, building, earth, and finally out into the far, dark reaches. He floated down those empty corridors, her naked hands pulling him along.

Her murmur never ceased. She circled and circled, spiraling in, but never named what she wanted. He wondered if there was a word for it, for then he could believe it existed. If it had no name, no word to label it, then it was an absolute reality beyond his apprehension, as infinite as the darkness through which he sped, tugged along by her hungry hands.

"We've found out all about her!" Florence Morton laughed.

"Well . . . not all, but some!" Samuel Morton laughed.

They had appeared at Daniel's door, late at night, wearing matching costumes of blue suede jeans and fringed jackets. It was difficult to believe them husband and wife; they were sexless twins, with their bony bodies, bird features, helmets of oiled hair.

He invited them in for a drink. The Mortons sat on the couch close together and held hands.

"How did you find out?" he asked curiously.

"We know everything!" Florence said.

"Our spies were everywhere!" Samuel said.

Daniel Blank smiled. It was almost true.

"Lots of money there," Flo said. "Her grandfather on her mother's side. Oil and steel. Plenty of loot. But her father had the family. He didn't inherit much but good looks. They said he was the handsomest man of his generation in America. They called him 'Beau Montfort' at Princeton. But he never did graduate. Kicked out for knocking up—someone. Who was it, Samovel?"

"A dean's wife or a scullery maid—someone like that. Anyway, this was in the late Twenties. Then he married all that oil and steel. He made a big contribution to Roosevelt's campaign fund and thought he might be ambassador to London, Paris or Rome. But FDR had more sense than that. He named Montfort a 'roving representative' and got him away from Washington. That was smart. The Montforts loved it. They drank and fucked up a storm. The talk of Europe. Celia was born in Lausanne. But then things went sour. Her parents got in with the Nazis, and daddy sent home glowing reports about what a splendid, kindly gentleman

Hitler was. Naturally, Roosevelt dumped him. Then, from what we can learn, they just bummed around in high style."

"What about Celia?" Daniel asked. "Is Tony really her brother?"

They looked at him in astonishment.

"You wondered?" Flo asked.

"You guessed?" Sam asked.

"We didn't get it straight," she acknowledged. "No one really knows."

"Everyone guesses," Sam offered. "But it's just gossip. No one *knows.*"

"But Tony could be her son," Flo nodded.

"The ages are right," Sam nodded. "But she's never been married. That anyone knows about."

"There are rumors."

"She's a strange woman."

"And who is Valenter?"

"What's his relationship to her?"

"And to Tony?"

"And where does she go when she goes away?"

"And comes back bruised? What is she *doing?*"

"Why don't her parents want her in Europe?"

"What's *with* her?"

"Who *is* she?"

"I don't care," Daniel Blank whispered. "I love her."

He worked late in his office on Halloween night. He had a salad and black coffee sent up from the commissary. As he ate, he went over the final draft of the prospectus he was scheduled to present to the Production Board on the following day: his plan to have AMROK II determine the ratio between advertising and editorial pages in every Javis-Bircham magazine.

The prospectus seemed to him temperate, logical, and convincing. But he recognized that it lacked enthusiasm. It was as stirring as an insurance policy, as inspirational as a corporate law brief; he poked it across the table and sat staring at it.

The fault, he knew, was his; he had lost interest. Oh the plan was valid, it made sense, but it no longer seemed to him of much import.

And he knew the reason for his indifference: Celia Montfort. Compared to her, to his relations with her, his job at Javis-Bircham was a game played by a grown boy, no worse and no better than Chinese Checkers or Monopoly. He went through the motions, he followed the rules, but he was not touched.

He sat brooding, wondering where she might lead him. Finally he rose, took his trench coat and hat. He left the prospectus draft on the table, with the garbage of his dinner and the dregs of cold coffee in the plastic cup. On his way to the executive elevator he glanced through the window of the Computer Room. The night shift, white-clad, floated slowly on their crepe soles over the cork floor, drifting through a sterile dream.

The rain came in spits and gusts, driven by a hacking wind. There were no cabs in sight. Blank turned up his coat collar, pulled down the brim of his hat. He dug toward Eighth Avenue. If he didn't find a cab, he'd take a crosstown bus on 42nd Street to First Avenue, and then change to an uptown bus.

Neon signs glimmered. Porno shops offered rubdowns and body painting. From a record shop, hustling the season, came a novelty recording of a dog barking "Adeste, Fideles." An acned prostitute, booted and spurred, murmured, "Fun?" as he passed. He knew this scruffy section well and paid no heed. It had nothing to do with him.

As he approached the subway kiosk at 42nd Street, a band of young girls came giggling up, flashing in red yellow green blue party dresses, coats swinging open, long hair ripped back by the wind. Blank stared, wondering why such beauties were on such a horrid street.

He saw then. They were all boys and young men, transvestites, on their way to a Halloween drag. In their satins and laces. In evening slippers and swirling wigs. Carmined lips and shadowed eyes. Shaved legs in nylon pantyhose. Padded chests. Hands flying and throaty laughs.

Soft fingers were on his arm. A mocking voice: "Dan!"

It was Anthony Montfort, looking back to flirt a wave, golden hair gleaming in the rain like flame. And then, following, a few paces back, the tall, skinny Valenter, wrapped in a black raincoat.

Daniel Blank stood and watched that mad procession dwindle up the avenue. He heard shouts, raucous cries. Then they were all gone, and he was staring after.

She went away for a day, two days, a week. Or, if she really didn't go away, he could not talk to her. He heard only Valenter's "Mith Montforth rethidenth," and then the news that she was not at home.

He became aware that these unexplained absences invariably followed their erotic ceremonies in the upstairs room. The following day, shattered with love and the memory of pleasure, he would call and discover she was gone, or would not talk to him.

He thought she was manipulating him, dancing out her meaningful ballet. She approached, touched, withdrew. He followed, she laughed, he touched, she caressed, he reached, she pulled back, fingers beckoning. The dance inflamed him.

Once, after four days' absence, he found her weary, drained, with yellow bruises on arms and legs, and purple loops beneath her eyes. She would not say where she had been or what she had done. She lay limp, without resistance, and insisted he abuse her. Infuriated, he did, and she thanked him. Was that, too, part of her plan?

She was a tangle of oddities. Usually she was well-groomed, bathed and scented, long hair brushed gleaming, nails trimmed and painted. But one night she came to his apartment a harridan. She had not bathed, as he discovered, and played the frumpish wanton, looking at him with derisive eyes and using foul language. He could not resist her.

She played strange games. One night she donned a child's jumper, sat on his lap and called him "Daddy." Another time—and how had she guessed *that?*—she bought him a gold chain and insisted he link it about his slim waist. She bit him. He thought her mad with love for him, but when he reached for her, she was not there.

He knew what was happening and did not care. Only she had meaning. She recited a poem to him in a language he could not identify, then licked his eyes. One night he tried to kiss her—an innocent kiss on the cheek, a kiss of greeting—and she struck his jaw with her clenched fist. The next instant she was on her knees, fumbling for him.

And her monologues never ended. She could be silent for hours, then suddenly speak to him of sin and love and evil and gods and why sex should transcend the sexual. Was she training him? He thought so, and studied.

She was gone for almost a week. He took her to dinner when she returned, but it was not a comfortable evening. She was silent and withdrawn. Only once did she look directly at him. Then she looked down, and with the middle finger of her right hand lightly touched, stroked, caressed the white tablecloth.

She took him immediately home, and he followed obediently up that cobwebbed staircase. In the upstairs room, standing naked beneath the blaring orange light, she showed him the African masks.

And she told him what she wanted him to do.

6

Daniel Blank inched his way up the chimney of Devil's Needle. He could feel the cold of the stone against his shoulders, against his gloved palms and heavy boots. It was dark inside the cleft; the cold was damp and smelled of death.

He wormed his way carefully onto the flat top. There had been light snow flurries the day before, and he expected ice. It was there, in thin patches, and after he hauled up the rucksack he used his ice ax to chip it away, shoving splinters over the side. Then he could stand on cleated soles and search around.

It was a lowery sky, with a look of more snow to the west. Dirty clouds scummed the sun; the wind knifed steadily. This would, he knew, be his last climb until spring. The park closed on Thanksgiving; there were no ski trails, and the rocks were too dangerous in winter.

He sat on the stone, ate an onion sandwich, drank a cup of coffee that seemed to chill as it was poured. He had brought a little flask of brandy and took small sips. Warmth went through him like new blood, and he thought of Celia.

She went through him like new blood, too; a thaw he knew in heart, gut, loins. She melted him, and not only his flesh. He felt her heat in every waking thought, in his clotted dreams. His love for her had brought him aware, had made him sensible of a world that existed for others but which he had never glimpsed.

He had been an only child, raised in a large house filled with the odors of disinfectant and his mother's gin. His father was moderately wealthy, having inherited from an aunt. He worked in a bank. His mother drank and collected Lalique glass. This was in Indiana.

It was a silent house and in later years, when Daniel tried to recall it, he had an absurd memory of the entire place being tiled: walls, floors, ceilings plated with white tile, enamel on steel, exactly like a gleaming subway tunnel that went on forever to nowhere. Perhaps it was just a remembered dream.

He had always been a loner; his mother and father never kissed him on the lips, but offered their cheeks. White tiles. The happiest memory of his boyhood was when their colored maid gave him a birthday present; it was a display box for his rock collection. Her husband had made it from an old orange crate, carefully sanding the rough wood and lining it with sleazy black cloth. It was beautiful, just what he wanted. That year his mother gave him handkerchiefs and underwear, and his father gave him a savings bond.

He was a loner in college, too. But in his sophomore year he lost his virginity at the one whore house in the college town. In his last two years he had a comforting affair with a Jewish girl from Boston. She was ugly but had mad eyes and a body that didn't end. All she wanted to do was screw. That was all right with him.

He found a piece of chalcedony and polished it in his rock tumbler and on the buffing wheel. It wasn't a priceless stone, but he thought it pretty. The Jewish girl laughed when he gave it to her on graduation day. "Fucking *goy,*" she said.

His graduation present from his parents was a summer in Europe, a grand tour of a dozen countries with enough time for climbing in Switzerland and visiting archeological digs in the south of France. He was waiting for his plane in New York, in a hotel bed with the Jewish girl who had flown down from Boston for a last bang, when a lawyer called to tell him his mother and father, driving home from his graduation, had gone off the highway, had been trapped in their car, and burned to death.

Daniel Blank thought less than a minute. Then he told the lawyer to sell the house, settle the estate, and bury his parents. Daniel himself would be home after his trip to Europe. The Boston girl heard him say all this on the phone. By the time he hung up, she was dressed and marching out of there, carrying her Louis Vuitton bag. He never saw her again. But it was a wonderful summer.

When he returned to his hometown late in August, no one would talk to him but the lawyer—and he as little as possible. Daniel Blank couldn't care less. He flew to New York, opened a bank account with his inheritance, then flew back to Bloomington and was finally accepted at the University of Indiana, going for an M.S. with emphasis on geology and archeology. During his second year he met Gilda, the woman he later married.

Two months before he was to get his degree, he decided it was all a lot of shit; he didn't want to spend the rest of his life shoveling dirt. He gave the best stone in his collection (a nice piece of jade) to Gilda, donated the remaining rocks to the University, and flew to New York. He played the part of a modestly moneyed bachelor in Manhattan for about six months. Then most of the cash was gone, but he hadn't sold off any of the stocks or bonds. He got a silly job in the circulation department of a national magazine. He found, to his amusement, that he was good at it. And he discovered he had an ambition unhampered by conscience. Gilda came to New York, and they were married.

He was not a stupid man; he knew the tiled emotions of his boyhood and youth had deadened him. And that house that smelled of CN and gin . . . those cheek-kisses . . . the Lalique glass. Other people fell in love and wept; he collected stones and scorned his parents' funeral.

What Celia Montfort had done for him, he decided, was to peel clean what had always been in him but had never been revealed. Now he could feel, deeply, and react to her. He could love her. He could sacrifice for her. It was *passion,* as warming as brandy on a bleak November afternoon. It was a fire in the veins, a heightened awareness, a need compounded of wild hope and fearful dread. He sought it, following the same instinct that had led him to discard his rock collection, those mementoes of dead history.

He started the climb down, still thinking of his love for Celia, of her naked and masked in the upstairs room, and of how quickly she had learned to slide her hand into his slitted pocket and fondle him as they walked in public.

Descending, he moved one boot too quickly. The heel hit the toe of the other boot, pressed against the opposite chimney wall. Then both legs dangled. For a long, stomach-turning moment he was suspended only by the pressure of his arms, clamped by shoulders and palms shoving against opposing walls. He forced himself to take a deep breath, eyes closed in the cold darkness. He would not think of the fast fall to the boulders below.

Slowly, smiling, he drew up one knee and planted a sole carefully against the opposite wall. His elbows were trembling with strain. He lifted the other boot into position and pressed. Now he could take the load off shoulders, arms, wrists, hands.

He looked up at the little patch of murky sky above the black hole he was in, and laughed with delight. He would descend safely. He could do anything. He had the strength to resist common sense.

Part II

1 Captain Edward X. Delaney, Commanding Officer of the 251st Precinct, New York Police Department, wearing civilian clothes, pushed open the door of the doctor's office, removed his Homburg (stiff as wood), and gave his name to the receptionist.

He planted himself solidly into an armchair, glanced swiftly around the room, then stared down at the hat balanced precisely on his knees. It was the "Observation Game": originally a self-imposed duty but now a diversion he had enjoyed for almost thirty years, since he had been a patrolman. If, for any reason, he was called upon to describe the patients in the waiting room . . .

"Left: male, Negro, dark brown, about 35, approximately 5 feet 10 inches, 160 pounds. Kinky black hair cut short; no part. Wearing plaid sports jacket, fawn-colored slacks, cordovan loafers. Necktie looped but not knotted. Heavy ring on right hand. Slight white scar on neck. Smoking cork-tip cigarette held between thumb and forefinger of left hand.

"Center: female, white, about 60–65; short, plump, motherly type. Uncontrollable tremor of right hand. Wearing black coat, soiled; elastic stockings, hole in left knee; old-fashioned hat with single cloth flower. Dark reddish hair may be wig. Approximately 5 feet 1 inch, 140 pounds. Fiddles with wen on chin.

"Right: male, white, about 50, 6 feet 2 inches. Extremely thin and emaciated. Loose collar and suit jacket show recent weight loss. Sallow complexion. Fidgety. Right eye may be glass. Nicotine-stained fingers indicate heavy smoker. Gnaws on lower lip. Blinks frequently."

He raised his eyes, inspected them again. He was close. The Negro's ring was on the left hand. The old woman's hair (or wig) was more brown than reddish. The thin man wasn't quite as tall as he had estimated. But Captain Delaney could provide a reasonably accurate description and/or identify these strangers in a line-up or courtroom if needed.

He was not, he acknowledged, as exact as some men in his judgment of physical characteristics. There was, for instance, a detective second grade attached to the 251st Precinct who could glance at a man for a few seconds and estimate his height within an inch and his weight within five pounds. That was a special gift.

But Captain Delaney also had an eye. That was for the Negro's necktie that was looped but not knotted, the old woman's wen, the thin man's continual blinking. Small things. Significant things.

He saw and remembered habits, tastes, the way a man dressed, moved, grimaced, walked, spoke, lighted a cigarette or spat into the gutter. Most important, Captain Delaney—the cop—was interested in what a man did when he was alone, or thought he was alone. Did he masturbate, pick his nose, listen to recordings of Gilbert & Sullivan, shuffle pornographic photos, work out chess problems? Or did he read Nietzsche?

There was a case—Delaney remembered it well; he had been a detective in the Chelsea precinct where it happened—three young girls raped and murdered within a period of 18 months, all on the roofs of tenements. The police thought they had their man. They carefully charted his daily movements. They brought him in for questioning and got nowhere. Then they established very close surveillance. Detective Delaney watched the suspect through binoculars from an apartment across the courtyard. Delaney saw this man, who had never been known to go to church, this man who thought he was alone and unobserved, this man went each night onto his knees and prayed before a reproduction of the face of Jesus Christ—one of those monstrous prints in which the eyes seem to open, close, or wink, depending upon the angle of view.

So they took the suspect in again, but this time, on Delaney's urging, they brought in a priest to talk to him. Within an hour they had a complete confession. Well . . . that was what one man did when he thought he was alone and unobserved.

It was the spastic twitch, the uncontrollable tic that Captain Delaney had an eye for. He wanted to know what tunes the suspect whistled, the foods he ate, how his home was decorated. Was he married, unmarried, thrice-married? Did he beat his dog or beat his wife? All these things told. And, of course, what he did when he thought he was alone.

The "big things" Captain Delaney told his men—things like a man's job, religion, politics, and the way he talked at cocktail parties—these were a facade he created to hold back a hostile world. Hidden were the vital things. The duty of the cop, when necessary, was to peek around the front at the secret urges and driven acts.

"Doctor will see you now," the receptionist smiled at him.

Delaney nodded, gripped his hat, marched into the doctor's office. He ignored the hostile stares of the patients who had, obviously, been waiting longer than he.

Dr. Louis Bernardi rose from behind his desk, holding out a plump, ringed hand.

"Captain," he said. "Always a pleasure."

"Doctor," Delaney said. "Good to see you again. You're looking well."

Bernardi caressed the bulged grey flannel waistcoat, straining at its tarnished silver buttons which, Barbara Delaney had told her husband, the doctor had revealed to her were antique Roman coins.

"It's my wife's cooking," Bernardi shrugged, smiling. "What can I do? He-he! Sit down, sit down. Mrs. Delaney is dressing. She will be ready to leave soon. But we shall have time for a little chat."

A chat? Delaney assumed men had a talk or a discussion. That "chat" was Bernardi. The Captain consulted a police surgeon; Bernardi was his wife's physician, had been for thirty years. He had seen her through two successful pregnancies, nursed her through a bad bout of hepatitis, and had recommended and seen to her recovery from a hysterectomy only two months previously.

He was a round man, beautifully shaved. He was soft and, if not unctuous, he was at least a smooth article. The black silk suit put forth a sheen; the shoes bore a dulled gleam. He was not perfumed, but he exuded an odor of self-satisfaction.

Contradicting all this were the man's eyes: hard, bright. They were shrewd little chips of quartz. His glance never wavered; his toneless stare could bring a nurse to tears.

Delaney did not like the man. He did not, for a moment, doubt Bernardi's professional competence. But he mistrusted the tailored plumpness, the secret smile, the long strands of oily hair slicked across a balding pate. He was particularly incensed by the doctor's mustache: a thin, carefully clipped line of black imprinted on the upper lip as if marked by a felt-tipped pen.

The Captain knew he amused Bernardi. That did not bother him. He knew he amused many people: superiors in the Department, peers, the uniformed men of his command. Newspapermen. Investigators. Doctors of sociology and criminal pathology. He amused them all. His wife and children. He knew. But on occasion Dr. Bernardi had made no effort to conceal his amusement. Delaney could not forgive him that.

"I hope you have good news for me, doctor."

Bernardi spread his hands in a bland gesture: the dealer who has just been detected selling a ruptured camel.

"Regrettably, I do not. Captain, your wife has not responded to the antibiotics. As I told her, my first instinctive impression was of a low-grade infection. Persistent and of some duration. It accounts for the temperature."

"What kind of infection?"

Again the gesture: hands spread wide and lifted, palms outward.

"That I do not know. Tests show nothing. Nothing on X-rays. No tumor, so far as I am able to determine. But still, apparently, an infection. What do you think of that?"

"I don't like it," Delaney said stonily.

"Nor do I," Bernardi nodded. "First of all, your wife is ill. That is of most importance. Second, it is a defeat for me. What is this infection? I do not know. It is an embarrassment."

An "embarrassment," Delaney thought angrily. What kind of a thing was that to say? The man didn't know how to use the king's English. Was he an Italian, a Lebanese, a Greek, a Syrian, an Arabian? What the hell *was* he?

"Finally," Dr. Bernardi said, consulting the file open on his desk, "let us consider the fever. It has been approximately six weeks since your wife's first visit complaining of, quote, 'Fever and sudden chills.' Unquote. On that first visit, a temperature a bit above normal. Nothing unusual. Pills for a cold, the flu, a virus—whatever you want to call it. No effect. Another visit. Temperature up. Not a great increase, but appreciable. Then antibiotics. Now, third visit and temperature is up again. The sudden chills continue. It worries me."

"Well, it worries her and it worries me," Delaney said stoutly.

"Of course," Bernardi soothed. "And now she finds many loose hairs in her comb. This is undoubtedly the result of the fever. Nothing serious, but still. . . . And you are aware of the rash on the insides of her thighs and forearms?"

"Yes."

"Again, undoubtedly the result of the fever stemming from the infection. I have prescribed an ointment. Not a cure, but it will take the itch away."

"She looks so healthy."

"You are seeing the fever, Captain! Don't believe the blush of health. Those bright eyes and rosy cheeks. He! It is the infection."

"What infection?" Delaney cried furiously. "What the hell *is* it? Is it cancer?"

Bernardi's eyes glittered.

"At this stage, I would guess no. Have you ever heard of a Proteus infection, Captain?"

"No. I never have. What is it?"

"I will not speak of it now. I must do some reading on it. You think we doctors know everything? But there is too much. There are young physicians today who cannot recognize (because they have never treated) typhus, smallpox or poliomyelitis. But that is by the by."

"Doctor," Delaney said, wearied by all this lubricious talk, "let's get down to it. What do we do now. What are our options?"

Dr. Bernardi leaned back in his swivel chair, placed his two forefingers together, pressed them against his plump lips. He regarded Delaney for a long moment.

"You know, Captain," he said with some malevolence, "I admire you. Your wife is obviously ill, and yet you say 'What do *we* do' and 'What are *our* options.' That is admirable."

"Doctor . . ."

"Very well." Bernardi sat forward sharply and slapped the file on his desk. "You have three options. One: I can attempt to reduce the fever, to overcome this mysterious infection, by heavier doses of antibiotics or with drugs I have not yet tried. I do not recommend this out of the hospital; the side effects can be alarming. Two: Your wife can enter a hospital for five days to a week for a series of tests much more thorough than I can possibly administer in this office. I would call in other men. Specialists. Neurologists. Gynecologists. Even dermatologists. This would be expensive."

He paused, looking at the Captain expectantly.

"All right, doctor," Delaney said patiently. "What's the third choice?"

Bernardi looked at him tenderly.

"Perhaps you would prefer another physician," he said softly. "Since I have failed."

Delaney sighed, knowing his wife's faith in this oleaginous man.

"We'll go for the tests. In the hospital. You'll arrange it?"

"Of course."

"A private room."

"That will not be necessary, Captain. It is only for tests."

"My wife would prefer a private room. She's a very modest woman. Very shy."

"I know, Captain," the doctor murmured, "I know. Shall you tell her or shall I?"

"I'll tell her."

"Yes," Dr. Bernardi said. "I believe that would be best."

The Captain went back to the reception room to wait for her, and practiced smiling.

It was a doxy of a day, merry and flirting. There was a hug of sun, a kiss of breeze. Walking north on Fifth Avenue, they heard the snap of flags, saw the glister of an early September sky. Captain Delaney, who knew his city in all its moods and tempers, was conscious of a hastened rhythm. Summer over, vacation done, Manhattan rushed to Christmas and the New Year.

His wife's hand was in his arm. When he glanced sideways at her, she had never seemed to him so beautiful. The blonde hair, now silvered and fined, was drawn up from her brow and pinned in a loose chignon. The features, once precise, had been softened by time. The lips were limpid, the line of chin and throat something. Oh she was something! And the glow (that damned fever!) gave her skin a grapy youthfulness.

She was almost as tall as he, walked erect and alert, her hand lightly on his arm. Men looked at her with longing, and Delaney was proud. How she strode, laughing at things! Her head turned this way and that, as if she was seeing everything for the first time. The last time? A cold finger touched.

She caught his stare and winked solemnly. He could not smile, but pressed her arm close to his body. The important thing, he thought—the most important thing—was that . . . was that she should out-live him. Because if not . . . if not . . . he thought of other things.

She was almost five years older than he, but she was the warmth, humor, and heart of their marriage. He was born old, with hope, a secret love of beauty, and a taste for melancholy. But she had brought to their home a recipe for lentil soup, thin nightgowns with pink ribbons, and laughter. He was bad enough; without her he would have been a grotesque.

They strolled north on Fifth Avenue, on the west side. As they approached the curb at 56th Street, the traffic light was about to change. They could have made it across safely, but he halted her.

"Wait a minute," he said. "I want to catch this."

His quick eye had seen a car—a station wagon with Illinois license plates—coming southward on Fifth Avenue. It attempted to turn westward onto 56th Street, going the wrong way on a one-way street. Immediately there was a great blaring of horns. A dozen pedestrians shouted, "One-way!" The car came to a shuddering halt, nosing into approaching traffic. The driver bent over the wheel, shaken. The woman beside him, apparently his wife, grabbed his arm. In the seat behind them two little boys jumped about excitedly, going from window to window.

A young uniformed patrolman had been standing on the northwest corner of the intersection, his back against a plate glass window. Now, smiling, he sauntered slowly toward the stalled car.

"Midtown Squad," Captain Delaney muttered to his wife. "They pick the big, handsome ones."

The officer wandered around to the driver's side, leaned down, and there was a brief conversation. The couple in the out-of-state car laughed with relief. The policeman cocked thumb and forefinger at the two kids in the back and clicked his tongue. They giggled delightedly.

"He's not going to ticket them?" Delaney said indignantly. "He's going to let them go?"

The patrolman moved back onto Fifth Avenue and halted traffic. He waved the Illinois car to back up. He got it straightened out and heading safely downtown again.

"I'm going to—" Captain Delaney started.

"Edward," his wife said. "Please."

He hesitated. The car moved away, the boys in the back waving frantically at the policeman who waved back.

Delaney looked sternly at his wife. "I'm going to get his name and tin number," he said. "Those one-way signs are plain. He should have—"

"Edward," she repeated patiently, "they're obviously on vacation. Did you see the luggage in the back? They don't know our system of one-way streets. Why spoil their holiday? With two little boys? I think the patrolman handled it beautifully. Perhaps that will be the nicest thing that happens to them in New York, and they'll want to come back again. Edward?"

He looked at her. ("Your wife is obviously ill . . . the fever . . . hair in her comb . . . you have three options . . . infection that . . .") He took her arm, led her carefully across the street. They walked the next block in silence.

"Well, anyway," he grumbled, "his sideburns were too long. You won't find sideburns like that in *my* precinct."

"I wonder why?" she said innocently, then laughed and leaned sideways to touch her head against his shoulder.

He had plans for lunch at the Plaza, window-shopping, visiting the antique shops on Third Avenue—things she enjoyed doing together on his day off. It was important that she should be happy for a time before he told her. But when she suggested a walk through the Park and lunch on the terrace at the zoo, he agreed instantly. It would be better; he would find a bench where they could be alone.

As they crossed 59th Street into the Park, he looked about with wonder. Now what had been there before the General Motors Building?

"The Savoy-Plaza," she said.

"Mindreader," he said.

So she was—where he was concerned.

The city changed overnight. Tenements became parking lots became excavations became stabbing office buildings while your head was turned. Neighborhoods disappeared, new restaurants opened, brick changed to glass, three stories sprouted to thirty, streets bloomed with thin trees, a little park grew where you remembered an old Irish bar had been forever.

It was his city, where he was born and grew up. It was home. Who could know its cankers better than he? But he refused to despair. His city would endure and grow more beautiful.

Part of his faith was based on knowledge of its past sins: all history now. He knew the time when the Five Points Gang bit off enemies' ears and noses in tavern brawls, when farm lads were drugged and shanghaied from the Swamp, when children's bordellos flourished in the Tenderloin, when Chinese hatchetmen blasted away with heavy pistols (and closed eyes) in the Bloody Triangle.

All this was gone now and romanticized, for old crime, war, and evil enter books and are leached of blood and pain. Now his city was undergoing new agonies. These too, he was convinced would pass if men of good will would not deny the future.

His city was an affirmation of life: its beauty, harshness, sorrow, humor, horror, and ecstasy. In the pushing and shoving, in the brutality and violence, he saw striving, the never-ending flux of life, and would not trade it for any place on earth. It could grind a man to litter, or raise him to the highest coppered roof, glinting in benignant sunlight.

They entered the Park at 60th Street, walking between the facing rows of benches toward the zoo. They stopped before the yak's cage and looked at the great, brooding beast, his head lowered, eyes staring at a foreign world with dull wonder.

"You," Barbara Delaney said to her husband.

He laughed, turned her around by the elbow, pointed to the cage across the way where a graceful Sika deer stood poised and alert, head proud on slim neck, eyes gleaming.

"You," Edward Delaney said to his wife.

They lunched lightly. He fretted with his emptied coffee cup: peering into it, turning it over, revolving it in his blunt fingers.

"All right," she sighed in mock weariness, "go make your phone call."

He glanced at her gratefully. "It'll just take a minute."

"I know. Just to make sure the precinct is still there."

The thick voice said, "Two hundred and fifty-first Precinct. Officer Curdy. May I help you?"

"This is Captain Edward X. Delaney," he said in his leaden voice. "Connect me with Lieutenant Dorfman, please."

"Oh. Yes, Captain. I think he's upstairs. Just a minute; I'll find him."

Dorfman came on almost immediately. " 'Lo, Captain. Enjoying your day off? Beautiful day."

"Yes. What's happening?"

"Nothing unusual, sir. The usual. A small demonstration at the Embassy again, but we moved them along. No charges. No injuries."

"Damage?"

"One broken window, sir."

"All right. Have Donaldson type up the usual letter of apology, and I'll sign it tomorrow."

"It's done, Captain. It's on your desk."

"Oh. Well . . . fine. Nothing else?"

"No, sir. Everything under control."

"All right. Switch me back to the man on the board, will you?"

"Yes, sir. I'll buzz him."

The uniformed operator came back on.

"Captain?"

"Is this Officer Curdy?"

"Yes, sir."

"Curdy, you answered my original call with: 'Two hundred and fifty-first Precinct.' In my memo number six three one, dated fourteen July of this year, I gave very explicit orders governing the procedure of uniformed telephone operators on duty. I stated in that memorandum that incoming calls were to be answered: 'Precinct two five one.' It is shorter and much more understandable than 'Two hundred and fifty-first Precinct.' Did you read that memo?"

"Yes, sir. Yes, Captain, I did read it. It just slipped my mind, sir. I'm so used to doing it the old way . . ."

"Curdy, there is no 'old way.' There is a right way and a wrong way of doing things. And 'Two five one' is the right way in my precinct. Is that clear?"

"Yes, sir."

He hung up and went back to his wife. In the New York Police Department he was known as "Iron Balls" Delaney. He knew it and didn't mind. There were worse names.

"Everything all right?" she asked.

He nodded.

"Who has the duty?"

"Dorfman."

"Oh? How is his father?"

He stared at her, eyes widening. Then he lowered his head and groaned. "Oh God. Barbara, I forgot to tell you. Dorfman's father died last week. On Friday."

"Oh Edward." She looked at him reproachfully. "Why on earth didn't you tell me?"

"Well, I meant to but—but it slipped my mind."

"Slipped your mind? How could a thing like that slip your mind? Well, I'll write a letter of condolence as soon as we get home."

"Yes, do that. They took up a collection for flowers. I gave twenty dollars."

"Poor Dorfman."

"Yes."

"You don't like him, do you?"

"Of course I like him. As a man, a person. But he's really not a good cop."

"He's not? I thought you told me he does his job very well."

"He does. He's a good administrator, keeps up on his paperwork. He's one of the best lawyers in the Department. But he's not a good cop. He's a reasonable facsimile. He goes through all the motions, but he lacks the instinct."

"And tell me, oh wise one," she said, "what is this great cop's instinct?"

He was glad to have someone to talk to about such things.

"Well," he said, "laugh if you like, but it does exist. What drove me to become a cop? My father wasn't. No one in my family was. I could have gone on to law school; my marks were good enough. But all I ever wanted was to be a cop. As long as I can remember. And I'll tell you why: because when the laundry comes back from the Chinaman—as you well know, my dear, after thirty years—I insist on—"

"Thirty-one years, brute."

"All right, thirty-one years. But the first year we lived in sin."

"You *are* a brute," she laughed.

"Well, we did: the most marvelous year of my life."

She put a hand over his. "And everything since then has been anti-climax?"

"You know better than that. All right, now let me get back to the instinct of a true cop."

"And the Chinaman's laundry."

"Yes. Well, as you know, I insist on putting my own clean clothes away in the bureau and dresser. Socks are folded once and piled with the fold forward. Handkerchiefs are stacked with the open edges to the right. Shirts are stacked alternately, collar to the rear, collar to the front—so the stack won't topple, you understand. And a similar system for underwear, pajamas, and so forth. And always, of course, the freshly laundered clothes go on the bottom of each pile so everything is worn evenly and in order. That's the word: 'order.' That's the way I am. You know it. I want everything in order."

"And that's why you became a cop? To make the world neat and tidy?"

"Yes."

She moved her head back slowly and laughed. How he loved to see her laugh. If only he could laugh like that! It was such a whole-hearted expression of pure joy: her eyes squinched shut, her mouth open, shoulders shaking, and a surprisingly full, deep guffaw that was neither feminine nor masculine but sexless and primitive as all genuine laughter.

"Edward, Edward," she said, spluttering a little, taking a lace-edged hanky from her purse to wipe her eyes. "You have a marvelous capacity for deluding yourself. I guess that's why I love you so."

"All right," he said, miffed. "You tell me. Why did I become a cop?"

Again she covered his hand with hers. She looked into his eyes, suddenly serious.

"Don't you know?" she asked gently. "Don't you *really* know? Because you love beauty. Oh, I know law and order and justice are important to you. But what you really want is a beautiful world where everything is true and nothing is false. You dreamer!"

He thought about that a long time. Then they rose, and hand in hand they strolled into the park.

In Central Park, there is an inclosed carrousel that has been a delight to generations of youngsters. Some days, when the wind is right, you can hear its musical tinkle from a distance; the air seems to dance.

The animals—marvelously carved and painted horses—chase each other in a gay whirl that excites children and hypnotizes their parents. On a bench near this merry-go-round, Barbara and Edward Delaney sat to rest, shoulders touching. They could hear the music, see the giddy gyrations through trees still wearing summer's green.

They sat awhile in silence. Then she said, not looking at him, "Can you tell me now?"

He nodded miserably. As rapidly as he could, he delivered a concise report of what Dr. Bernardi had told him. He omitted only the physician's fleeting reference to a "Proteus infection."

"I see no choice," he said, and gripped her hand harder. "Do you? We've got to get this cleared up. I'll feel better if Bernardi brings in other men. I think you will, too. It only means five days to a week in the hospital. Then they'll decide what must be done. I told Bernardi to go ahead, get the room. A private room. Barbara? Is that all right?"

He wondered if she heard him. Or if she understood. Her eyes were far away, and he did not know the smile on her soft lips.

"Barbara?" he asked again.

"During the war," she said, "when you were in France, I brought the children here when the weather was nice. Eddie could walk then but Elizabeth was still in the carriage. Sometimes Eddie would get tired on the way home, and I'd put him in the carriage with Liza. How he hated it!"

"I know. You wrote me."

"Did I? Sometimes we'd sit on this very bench where we're sitting now. Eddie would ride the merry-go-round all day if I let him."

"He always rode a white horse."

"You do remember," she smiled. "Yes, he always rode a white horse, and every time he came around he'd wave at us, sitting up straight. He was so proud."

"Yes."

"They're good children, aren't they, Edward?"

"Yes."

"Happy children."

"Well, I wish Eddie would get married, but there's no use nagging him."

"No. He's stubborn. Like his father."

"Am I stubborn?"

"Sometimes. About some things. When you've made up your mind. Like my going into the hospital for tests."

"You will go, won't you?"

She gave him a dazzling smile, then unexpectedly leaned forward to kiss him on the lips. It was a soft, youthful, lingering kiss that shocked him with its longing.

And late that night she still burned with that longing, her body kindled with lust and fever. She came naked into his arms and seemed intent on draining him, exhausting him, taking all for herself and leaving nothing.

He tried to contain her fury—so unlike her; she was usually languorous and teasing—but her rage defeated him. Once, thrashing about in a sweated paroxysm, she called him "Ted," which she had not done since their life together was born.

He did what he could to satisfy and soothe, wretchedly conscious that his words were not heard nor his caresses felt; the most he could do was be. Her storm passed, leaving him riven. He gnawed a knuckle and fell asleep.

He awoke a few hours later, and she was gone from the bed. He was instantly alert, pulled on his old patterned robe with its frazzled cord. Barefoot, he went padding downstairs, searching all the empty rooms.

He found her in what they still called the "parlor" of their converted brownstone, next door to the 251st Precinct house. She was on the window seat, clad in a white cotton nightgown. Her knees were drawn up, clasped. In the light from the hallway he could see her head bent forward. Her hair was down, hiding her face, drifting shoulders and knees.

"Barbara," he called.

Her head came up. Hair fell back. She gave him a smile that twisted his heart.

"I'm dying," she said.

2 Barbara Delaney's stay in the hospital for tests was longer than the five days predicted by Dr. Louis Bernardi. It became a weekend and five days, then two weekends and five days, and finally a total of fifteen days. To every inquiry by Captain Edward X. Delaney, the doctor answered only, "More tests."

From his daily—sometimes twice-daily—visits to his wife's private room, Delaney came away with the frightening impression that things were not going well at all. The fever persisted, up one day, down slightly the next. But the course was steadily upward. Once it hit almost 103; the woman was burning up.

He himself had been witness to the sudden chills that racked her body, set teeth chattering and limbs trembling. Nurses came hurrying with extra blankets and hot water bottles. Five minutes later she was burning again; blankets were tossed aside, her face rosy, she gasped for breath.

New symptoms developed during those fifteen days: headaches, urination so difficult she had to be catheterized, severe pain in the lumbar region, sudden attacks of nausea that left her limp. Once she vomited into a basin he held for her. She looked up at him meekly; he turned away to stare out the window, his eyes bleary.

On the morning he finally decided, against his wife's wishes, to dismiss Bernardi and bring in a new man, he was called at his Precinct office and summoned to an early afternoon meeting with Bernardi in his wife's hospital room. Lieutenant Dorfman saw him off with anguished eyes.

"Please, Captain," he said, "try not to worry. She's going to be all right."

Marty Dorfman was an extraordinarily tall (six-four) Jew with light blue eyes and red hair that spiked up from a squeezed skull. He wore size 14 shoes and couldn't find gloves to fit. He seemed constantly to be dribbled with crumbs, and had never been known to swear.

Nothing fitted; his oversize uniform squirmed on thin shoulders, trousers bagged like a Dutch boy's bloomers. Cigarette ashes smudged his cuffs. Occasionally his socks didn't match, and he had lost the clasp on the choker collar of his jacket. His shoes were unshined, and he reported for duty with a dried froth of shaving cream beneath his ears.

Once, when a patrolman, he had been forced to kill a knife-wielding burglar. Since then he carried an unloaded gun. He thought no one knew, but everyone did. As Captain Delaney had told his wife, Dorfman's paperwork was impeccable and he had one of the finest legal minds in the Department. He was a sloven, but when men of the 251st Precinct had personal problems, they went to him. He had never been known to miss the funeral of a policeman killed in line of duty. Then he wore a clean uniform and wept.

"Thank you, lieutenant," Delaney said stiffly. "I will call as soon as possible. I fully expect to return before you go off. If not, don't wait for me. Is that clear?"

"Yes, Captain."

Dr. Louis Bernardi, Delaney decided, was perfectly capable of holding the hand of a dying man and saying, "There there." Now he was displaying the X-rays proudly, as if they were his own Rembrandt prints.

"The shadows!" he cried. "See the shadows!"

He had drawn a chair up close to the bedside of Barbara Delaney. The Captain stood stolidly on the other side, hands clasped behind him so their tremble might not reveal him.

"What are they?" he asked in his iron voice.

"What is it?" his wife murmured.

"Kidney stones!" Bernardi cried happily. "Yes, dear lady," he continued, addressing the woman on the bed who stared at him sleepily, her head wavering slightly, "the possibility was there: a stubborn fever and chills. And more recently the headaches, nausea, difficulty in passing water, pain in the lower back. This morning, after more than ten days of exhaustive tests—which I am certain, he-he, you found exhausting as well as exhaustive—we held a conference—all the professional men who have been concerned with your condition—and the consensus is that you are, unhappily, suffering from a kidney calculus."

His tone was so triumphant that Delaney couldn't trust himself to speak. His wife turned her head on the pillow to look warningly at him. When he nodded, she turned back to Bernardi to ask weakly:

"How did I get kidney stones?"

The doctor leaned back in his chair, made his usual gesture of placing his two index fingers together and pressing them against his pouting lips.

"Who can say?" he asked softly. "Diet, stress, perhaps a predisposition, heredity. There is so much we don't know. If we knew everything, life would be a bore, would it not? He!"

Delaney grunted disgustedly. Bernardi paid no heed.

"In any event, that is our diagnosis. Kidney stones. A concretion frequently found in the bladder or kidneys. A hard, inorganic stone. Some no larger than a pinhead. Some quite large. They are foreign matter lodged in living tissue. The body, the living tissue, cannot endure this invasion. Hence, the fever, the chills, the pain. And, of course, the difficulty in urinating. Oh yes, that above all."

Once again Delaney was infuriated by the man's self-satisfaction. To Bernardi, it was all a crossword puzzle from the *Times*.

"How serious is it?" Barbara asked faintly.

A glaze seemed to come down over Bernardi's swimming eyes, a milky, translucent film. He could see out but no one could see in.

"We needed the blood tests and these sensitive plates. And then, since you have been here, the symptoms that developed gave us added indications. Now we know what we are facing."

"How serious is it?" Barbara asked again, more determinedly.

"We feel," Bernardi went on, not listening, "we feel that in your case, dear lady, surgery is indicated. Oh yes. Definitely. I am sorry to say. Surgery."

"Wait," Delaney held up his hand. "Wait just a minute. Before we start talking about surgery. I know a man who had kidney stones. They gave him a liquid, something, and he passed them and was all right. Can't my wife do the same?"

"Quite impossible," Bernardi said shortly. "When the stones are tiny, that procedure is sometimes effective. These X-rays show a large area of inflammation. Surgery is indicated."

"Who decided that?" Delaney demanded.

"We did."

" 'We'?" Delaney asked. "Who is 'we'?"

Bernardi looked at him coldly. He sat back, pulled up one trouser leg, carefully crossed his knees. "Myself and the specialists I called in," he said. "I have their professional opinions here, Captain—their written and signed opinions—and I have prepared a duplicate set for your use."

Captain Edward X. Delaney had interrogated enough witnesses and suspects in his long career to know when a man or woman was lying. The tip-off could come in a variety of ways. With the stupid or inexperienced it came with a physical gesture: a shifting away of the eyes, a nervous movement, blinking, perhaps a slight skim of sweat or a sudden deep breath. The intelligent and experienced revealed their falsehood in different ways: a too deliberate nonchalance, or an "honest" stare, eyeball to eyeball, or by a serious, intent fretting of the brows. Sometimes they leaned forward and smiled candidly.

But this man was not lying; the Captain was convinced of that. He was also convinced Bernardi was not telling the whole truth. He was holding something back, something distasteful to him.

"All right," Delaney grated, "we have their signed opinions. I assume they all agree?"

Bernardi's eyes glittered with malice. He leaned forward to pat Barbara's hand, lying limply atop the thin blue blanket. "There there," he said.

"It is not a very serious operation," he continued. "It is performed frequently in every hospital in the country. But all surgery entails risk. Even lancing a boil. I am certain you understand this. No surgery should ever be taken lightly."

"We don't take it lightly," Delaney said angrily, thinking this man—this "foreigner"—just didn't know how to talk.

During this exchange Barbara Delaney's head moved side to side, back and forth between husband and doctor.

"Very well," Delaney went on, holding himself in control, "you recommend surgery. You remove those kidney stones, and my wife regains her health. Is that it? There's nothing more you're not telling us?"

"Edward," she said. "Please."

"I want to know," he said stubbornly. "I want you to know."

Bernardi sighed. He seemed about to mediate between them, then thought better of it.

"That is our opinion," he nodded. "I cannot give you an iron-clad one hundred percent guarantee. No physician or surgeon can. You must know that. This, admittedly, will be an ordeal for Mrs. Delaney. Normal recuperation from this type of surgery demands a week to ten days in the hospital, and several weeks in bed at home. I don't wish to imply that this is of little importance. It is a serious situation, and I take it seriously, as I am certain you do also. But you are essentially a healthy woman, dear lady, and I see nothing in your medical record that would indicate anything but a normal recovery."

"And there's no choice but surgery?" Delaney demanded again.

"No. You have no choice."

A small cry came from Barbara Delaney, no louder than a kitten's mew. She reached out a pale hand to her husband; he grasped it firmly in his big paw.

"But we have no assurance?" he asked, realizing he was again repeating himself, and that his voice was desperate.

The translucent film over Bernardi's eyes seemed to become more opaque. Now it was the pearly cover on the eyes of a blind dog.

"No assurance," he said shortly. "None whatsoever."

Silence fell into the pastel room like a gentle rain. They looked at each other, all three, heads going back and forth, eyes flickering. They could hear the noises of the hospital: loudspeakers squawking, carts creaking by, murmured voices, and somewhere a radio playing dance music. But in this room the three looked into each others' eyes and were alone, swaddled in silence.

"Thank you, doctor," Delaney said harshly. "We will discuss it."

Bernardi nodded, rose swiftly. "I will leave you these documents," he said, placing a file on the bedside table. "I suggest you read them carefully. Please do not delay your decision more than twenty-four hours. We must not let this go on, and plans must be made."

He bounced from the room, light on his feet for such a stout man.

Edward X. Delaney had been born a Catholic and raised a Catholic. Communion and confession were as much a part of his life as love and work. He was married in the Church, and his children attended parochial schools. His faith was monolithic. Until 1945 . . .

On a late afternoon in 1945, the sun hidden behind a sky black with oily smoke, Captain Delaney led his company of Military Police to the liberation of a concentration camp in north Germany. The barbed wire gate was swinging wide. There was no sign of activity. The Captain deployed his armed men. He himself, pistol drawn, strode up to an unpainted barracks and threw open the door.

The things stared at him.

A moan came up from his bowels. This single moan, passing his lips, took with it Church and faith, prayer and confidence, ceremony, panoply, habit and trust. He never thought of such things again. He was a cop and had his own reasons.

Now, sensing what lay ahead, he yearned for the Church as a voluntary exile might yearn for his own native land. But to return in time of need was a baseness his pride could not endure. They would see it through together, the two of them, her strength added to his. The aggregate—by the peculiar alchemy of their love—was greater than the sum of the parts.

He sat on the edge of her bed, smiled, smoothed her hair with his heavy hand. A nurses' aide had brushed her hair smooth and tied it back with a length of thick blue knitting wool.

"I know you don't like him," she said.

"That's not important," he shook his great head. "What is important is that you trust him. Do you?"

"Yes."

"Good. But I still want to talk to Ferguson."

"You don't want to decide now?"

"No. Let me take the papers and try to understand them. Then I'll show them to Ferguson and get his opinion. Tonight, if possible. Then I'll come back tomorrow and we'll discuss it. Will that be all right?"

"Yes," she said. "Did Mary do the curtains?" She was referring to their Monday-to-Friday, 8-to-4 maid.

"Yes, she did. And she brushed and aired the living room drapes in the backyard. Tomorrow she'll do the parlor drapes if the weather holds. She wants so much to visit you but I said you weren't up to it. I've told all your friends that. Are you sure it's what you want?"

"Yes. I don't want anyone to see me like this. Maybe later I'll feel up to it. What did you have for breakfast?"

"Let's see . . ." he said, trying to remember. "A small orange juice. Cereal, no sugar. Dry toast and black coffee."

"Very good," she nodded approvingly. "You're sticking to your diet. What did you have for lunch?"

"Well, things piled up, and we had to send out for sandwiches. I had roast beef on whole wheat and a large tomato juice."

"Oh Edward," she said, "that's not enough. You must promise that tonight you'll—" Suddenly she stopped; tears flooded up to her eyes and out, down her cheeks. "Oh Jesus," she cried. "Why me?"

She lurched up to embrace him. He held her close, her wet face against his. His blunt fingers stroked her back, and he kept repeating, "I love you, I love you, I love you," over and over. It didn't seem enough.

He went back to the Precinct carrying her medical file. The moment he was at his desk he called Dr. Sanford Ferguson, but couldn't reach him. He tried the Medical Examiner's office, the morgue, and Ferguson's private office. No one knew where he was. Delaney left messages everywhere.

Then he put the medical file aside and went to work. Dorfman and two Precinct detectives were waiting to see him, on separate cases. There was a deputation of local businessmen to demand more foot patrolmen. There was a group of black militants to protest "police brutality" in breaking up a recent march. There was a committee of Jewish leaders to discuss police action against demonstrations held almost daily in front of an Egyptian embassy located in the precinct. There was an influential old woman with an "amazing new idea" for combatting drug addiction (put sneezing powder in cocaine). And there was a wealthy old man charged (for the second time) with exhibiting himself to toddlers.

Captain Delaney listened to all of them, nodding gravely. Occasionally he spoke in a voice so deliberately low his listeners had to crane forward to hear. He had learned from experience that nothing worked so well as quiet, measured tones to calm anger and bring people, if not to reason then to what was possible and practical.

It was 8:00 P.M. before his outer office had emptied. He rose and forced back his massive shoulders, stretching wide. This kind of work, he had discovered, was a hundred times more wearying than walking a beat or riding a squad. It was the constant, controlled exercise of judgment and will, of convincing, persuading, soothing, dictating and, when necessary, surrendering for a time, to take up the fight another day.

He cleaned up his desk, taking a regretful look at the paperwork that had piled up in one day and must wait for tomorrow. Before leaving, he looked in at lockups and squad rooms, at interrogation rooms and the detectives' cubbyholes. The 251st Precinct house was almost 90 years old. It was cramped, it creaked, and it smelled like all antique precinct houses in the city. A new building had been promised by three different city administrations. Captain Delaney made do. He took a final look at the Duty Sergeant's blotter before he walked next door to his home.

Even older than the Precinct house, it had been built originally as a merchant's townhouse. It had deteriorated over the years until, when Delaney bought it with the inheritance from his father's estate ($28,000), it had become a rooming house, chopped up into rat-and-roach-infested one-person apartments. But Delaney had satisfied himself that the building was structurally sound, and Barbara's quick eye had seen the original marble fireplaces and walnut paneling (painted over but capable of being restored), the rooms for the children, the little paved areaway and overgrown garden. So they had bought it, never dreaming he would one day be commanding officer of the Precinct house next door.

Mary had left the hall light burning. There was a note Scotch-taped to the handsome pier glass. She had left slices of cold lamb and potato salad in the refrigerator. There was lentil soup he could heat up if he wanted it, and an apple tart for dessert. It all seemed good to him, but he had to watch his weight. He decided to skip the soup.

First he called the hospital. Barbara sounded sleepy and didn't make much sense; he wondered if they had given her a sedative. He spoke to her for only a few moments and thought she was relieved when he said good-night.

He went into the kitchen, took off his uniform jacket and gun belt and hung them on the back of a chair. First he mixed a rye highball, his first drink of the day. He sipped it slowly, smoked a cigarette (his third of the day), and wondered why Dr. Ferguson hadn't returned his calls. Suddenly he realized it might be Ferguson's day off, in which case he had probably been out playing golf.

Carrying the drink, he went into the study and rummaged through the desk for his address book. He found Ferguson's home number and dialed. Almost immediately a jaunty voice answered:

"Doctor Ferguson."

"Captain Edward X. Delaney here."

"Hello, Captain Edward X. Delaney there," the voice laughed. "What the hell's wrong with you—got a dose of clap from a fifteen-year-old bimbo?"

"No. It's about my wife. Barbara."

The tone changed immediately.

"Oh. What's the problem, Edward?"

"Doctor, would it be possible to see you tonight?"

"Both of you or just you?"

"Just me. She's in the hospital."

"I'm sorry to hear that. Edward, you caught me on the way out. They've dragged me into an emergency cut-'em-up"—the doctor's slang for an autopsy. "I won't be home much before midnight. Too late?"

"No. I can be at your home at midnight. Will that be all right?"

"Sure. What's this all about?"

"I'd rather tell you in person. And there are papers. Documents. Some X-rays."

"I see. All right, Edward. Be here at twelve."

"Thank you, doctor."

He went back into the kitchen to eat his cold lamb and potato salad. It all tasted like straw. He put on his heavy, black-rimmed glasses, and as he ate slowly, he methodically read every paper in Barbara's medical file, and even held the X-rays up to the overhead light, although they meant nothing to him. There she was, in shadows: the woman who meant everything to him.

He finished eating and reading at the same time. All the doctors seemed to agree. He decided to skip the apple tart and black coffee. But he mixed another rye highball and, in his skivvie shirt, went wandering through the empty house.

It was the first time since World War II he and his wife slept under separate roofs. He was bereft, and in all those darkened rooms he felt her presence and wanted her: sight, voice, smell, laugh, slap of slippered feet, touch . . . *her*.

The children were there, too, in the echoing rooms. Cries and shouts, quarrels and stumblings. Eager questions. Wailing tears. Their life had soaked into the old walls. Holiday meals. Triumphs and defeats. The fabric of a family. All silent now, and dark as the shadows on an X-ray film.

He climbed stairs slowly to vacant bedrooms and attic. The house was too big for the two of them: no doubt about it. But still. . . . There was the door jamb where Liza's growth had been marked with pencil ticks. There was the flight of stairs Eddie had tumbled down and cut his chin and never cried. There was the very spot where one of their many dogs had coughed up his life in bright blood, and Barbara had become hysterical.

It wasn't much, he supposed. It was neither high tragedy nor low comedy. No great heights or depths. But a steady wearing away of the years. Time evened whatever drama there may have been. Time dimmed the colors; the shouting died. But the golden monochrome, the soft tarnish that was left had meaning for him. He wandered through the dim corridors of his life, thinking deep thoughts and making foolish wishes.

Dr. Sanford Ferguson, a bachelor, was a big man, made bigger by creaseless tweed suits worn with chain-looped vests. He was broad through the shoulders and broad through the chest. He was not corpulent but his thighs were as big around as another man's waist, and his arms were meaty and strong.

No one doubted his cleverness. At parties he could relate endless jokes that had the company helpless with laughter. He knew many dialects perfectly and, in his cups, could do an admirable soft-shoe clog. He was much in demand as an after-dinner speaker at meetings of professional associations. He was an ineffectual but enthusiastic golfer. He sang a sweet baritone. He could make a soufflé. And, unknown to everyone (including his older spinster sister), he kept a mistress: a middle-aged colored lady he loved and by whom he had fathered three sons.

He was also, Delaney knew, an experienced and cynical police surgeon. Violent death did not dismay him, and he was not often fooled by the obvious. In "natural deaths" he sniffed out arsenic. In "accidental deaths" he would pry out the fatal wound in a corpus of splinters.

"Here's your rye," he said, handing the highball to Delaney. "Now sit there and keep your mouth shut, and let me read and digest."

It was after midnight. They were in the living room of Ferguson's apartment on Murray Hill. The spinster sister had greeted Delaney and then disappeared, presumably to bed. The doctor had mixed a rye highball for his guest and poured a hefty brandy for himself in a water tumbler.

Delaney sat quietly in an armchair pinned with an antimacassar. Dr. Ferguson sat on a spindly chair at a fine Queen Anne lowboy. His bulk threatened to crush chair and table. His wool tie was pulled wide, shirt collar open: wiry hair sprang free.

"That was a nice cut-'em-up tonight," he remarked, peering at the documents in the file Delaney had handed over. "A truck driver comes home from work. Greenwich Village. He finds his wife, he says, on the kitchen floor. Her head's in the oven. The room's full of gas. He opens the window. She's dead. I can attest to that. She was depressed, the truck driver says. She often threatened suicide, he says. Well . . . maybe. We'll see. We'll see."

"Who's handling it?" Delaney asked.

"Sam Rosoff. Assault and Homicide South. You know him?"

"Yes. An old-timer. Good man."

"He surely is, Edward. He spotted the cigar stub in the ashtray on the kitchen table. A cold butt, but the saliva still wet. What would you have done?"

"Ask you to search for a skull contusion beneath the dead woman's hair and start looking for the truck driver's girlfriend."

Dr. Ferguson laughed. "Edward, you're wonderful. That's exactly what Rosoff suggested. I found the contusion. Right now he's out looking for the girlfriend. Do you miss detective work?"

"Yes."

"You were the best," Ferguson said, "until you decided to become Commissioner. Now shut up, lad, and let me read."

Silence.

"Oh-ho," Ferguson said. "My old friend Bernardi."

"You know him?" Delaney asked, surprised.

"I do indeed.

"What do you think of him?"

"As a physician? Excellent. As a man? A prick. No more talk."

Silence.

"Do you know any of the others?" Delaney asked finally. "The specialists he brought in?"

"I know two of the five—the neurologist and the radiologist. They're among the best in the city. This must be costing you a fortune. If the other three are as talented, your wife is in good hands. I can check. Now be quiet."

Silence.

"Oh well," Ferguson shrugged, still reading, "kidney stones. That's not so bad."

"You've had cases?"

"All the time. Mostly men, of course. You know who get 'em? Cab drivers. They're bouncing around on their ass all day."

"What about my wife?"

"Well, listen, Edward, it could be diet, it could be stress. There's so much we don't know."

"My wife eats sensibly, rarely takes a drink, and she's the most—most serene woman I've ever met."

"Is she? Let me finish reading."

He went through all the reports intently, going back occasionally to check reports he had already finished. He didn't even glance at the X-rays. Finally he shoved back from the table, poured himself another huge brandy, freshed the Captain's highball.

"Well?" Delaney asked.

"Edward," Ferguson said, frowning, "don't bring me in. Or anyone else. Bernardi is a bombastic, opinionated, egotistical shit. But as I said, he's a good sawbones. On your wife's case he's done everything exactly right. He's tried everything except surgery—correct?"

"Well, he tried antibiotics. They didn't work."

"No, they wouldn't on kidney stones. But they didn't locate *that* until they got her in the hospital for sensitive plates, and then the trouble passing urine started. That's recent, isn't it?"

"Yes. Only in the last four or five days."

"Well, then . . ."

"You recommend surgery?" Delaney asked in a dead voice.

Ferguson whirled on him. "I recommend nothing," he said sharply. "It's not my case. But you've got no choice."

"That's what he said."

"He was right. Bite the bullet, m'lad."

"What are her chances?"

"You want betting odds, do you? With surgery, very good indeed."

"And without?"

"Forget it."

"It's not fair," Delaney cried furiously.

Ferguson looked at him strangely. "What the fuck is?" he asked.

They stared at each other a long moment. Then Ferguson went back to the table, flipped through the X-rays, selected one and held it up to the light of a tilted desk lamp. "Kidney," he muttered. "Yes, yes."

"What is it, doctor?"

"He told you and I told you: calculus in the kidneys, commonly known as stones."

"That's not what I meant. Something's bothering you."

Ferguson looked at him. "You son of a bitch," he said softly. "You should never have left the detective division. I've never met anyone as—as *attuned* to people as you are."

"What is it?" Delaney repeated.

"It's nothing. Nothing I can explain. A hunch. You have them, don't you?"

"All the time."

"It's little things that don't quite add up. Maybe there's a rational explanation. The recent hysterectomy. The fever and chills that have been going on since then. But only recently the headaches, nausea, lumbar pain, and now the difficulty passing urine. It all adds up to kidney stones, but the *sequence* of symptoms is wrong. With kidney stones, pain at pissing usually comes from the start. And sometimes it's bad enough to drive you right up a wall. No record of that here. Yet the plates show. . . . You tell me she's not under stress?"

"She is not."

"Every case I've had is driven, trying to do too much, bedeviled by time, rushing around, biting fingernails and screaming at the waitress when the coffee is cold. Is that Barbara?"

"No. She's totally opposite. Calm."

"You can't tell. We never know. Still . . ." He sighed. "Edward, have you ever heard of Proteus infection?"

"Bernardi mentioned it to me."

Ferguson actually staggered back a step, as if he had been struck a blow on the chest. "He *mentioned* it to you?" he demanded. "When was this?"

"About three weeks ago, when he first told me Barbara should go into the hospital for tests. He just mentioned it and said he wanted to do some reading on it. But he didn't say anything about it today. Should I have asked him?"

"Jesus Christ," Ferguson said bitterly. "No, you shouldn't have asked him. If he wanted to tell you, he would have."

"You've treated cases?"

"Proteus? Oh yes, I have indeed. Three in twenty years. Mr. Proteus is a devil."

"What happened to them?"

"The three? Two responded to antibiotics and were smoking and drinking themselves to death within forty-eight hours."

"And the third?"

Ferguson came over, gripped Delaney by the right arm, and almost lifted him to his feet. The Captain had forgotten how strong he was.

"Go have your wife's kidney stones cut out," the doctor said brutally. "She'll either live or die. Which is true for all of us. No way out, m'lad."

Delaney took a deep breath.

"All right, doctor," he said. "Thank you for your time and your—your patience. I'm sorry to have bothered you."

"Bother?" Ferguson said gruffly. "Idiot."

He walked Delaney to the door. "I might just stop by to see Barbara," he said casually. "Just as a friend of the family."

"Yes," Delaney nodded dumbly. "Please do that. She doesn't want any visitors, but I know she'll be glad to see you."

In the foyer Ferguson took Delaney by the shoulders and turned him to the light.

"Have you been sleeping okay, Edward?" he demanded.

"Not too well."

"Don't take pills. Take a stiff shot. Brandy is best. Or a glass of port. Or a bottle of stout just before you get into bed."

"Yes. All right. Thank you. I will."

They shook hands.

"Oh wait," Ferguson said. "You forgot your papers. I'll get the file for you."

But when he returned, Delaney had gone.

He stopped at his home to put on a heavy wool sweater under his uniform jacket. Then he walked next door to the Precinct house. There was a civilian car parked directly in front of the entrance. Inside the windshield, on the passenger's side, a large card was displayed: PRESS.

Delaney stalked inside. There was a civilian talking to the Desk Sergeant. Both men broke off their conversation and turned when he tramped in.

"Is that your car?" he asked the man. "In front of the station?"

"Yes, that's mine. I was—"

"You a reporter?"

"Yes. I was just—"

"Move it. You're parked in a zone reserved for official cars only. It's clearly marked."

"I just wanted—"

"Sergeant," Delaney said, "if that car isn't moved within two minutes, issue this man a summons. If it's still there after five minutes, call a truck and have it towed away. Is that clear?"

"Yes, sir."

"Now look here—" the man started.

Delaney walked by him and went up to his office. He took a black-painted three-cell flashlight from the top drawer of his file cabinet. He also slipped a short, hard rubber truncheon into his jacket pocket and hung a steel "come-along" on his gun belt.

When he came out into the chilly night again, the Press car had been reparked across the street. But the reporter was standing on the sidewalk in front of the Precinct house.

"What's your name?" he asked angrily.

"Captain Edward X. Delaney. You want my shield number?"

"Oh . . . Delaney. I've heard about you."

"Have you?"

" 'Iron Balls.' Isn't that what they call you?"

"Yes."

The reporter stared, then suddenly laughed and held out his hand.

"The name's Handry, Captain. Thomas Handry. Sorry about the car. You were entirely right and I was entirely wrong."

Delaney shook his hand.

"Where you going with the flashlight, Captain?"

"Just taking a look around."

"Mind if I tag along?"

Delaney shrugged. "If you like."

They walked over to First Avenue, then turned north. The street was lined with stores, supermarkets, banks. Most of them had locked gates across doors and windows. All had a light burning within.

"See that?" Delaney gestured. "I sent a letter to every commercial establishment in my precinct requesting they keep at least a hundred-watt bulb burning all night. I kept after them. Now I have ninety-eight-point-two percent compliance. A simple thing, but it reduced breaking-and-entering of commercial establishments in this precinct by fourteen-point-seven percent."

He stopped in front of a shoe repair shop that had no iron gates. Delaney tried the door. It was securely locked.

"A little unusual, isn't it?" Handry asked, amused. "A captain making the rounds? Don't you have foot patrolmen for that?"

"Of course. When I first took over the 251st, discipline was extremely lax. So I started unscheduled inspections, on foot, mostly at night. It worked. The men never know when or where I may turn up. They stay alert."

"You do it every night?"

"Yes. Of course, I can't cover the entire precinct, but I do a different five or six blocks every night. I don't *have* to do it anymore, you understand; my men are on their toes. But it's become a habit. I think I enjoy it. As a matter of fact, I can't get to sleep until I've made my rounds. My wife says I'm like a householder who has to go around trying all the windows and doors before he goes to bed."

A two-man squad car came purring by. The passenger officer inspected them, recognized the Captain and threw him a salute, which he returned.

Delaney tried a few more un-gated doors and then, flashlight burning, went prowling up an alleyway, the beam flickering over garbage cans and refuse heaps. Handry stayed close behind him.

They walked a few more blocks, then turned eastward toward York Avenue.

"What were you doing in my Precinct house, Handry?" the Captain asked suddenly.

"Nosing around," the reporter said. "I'm working on an article. Or rather a series of articles."

"On what?"

"Why a man wants to become a policeman, and what happens to him after he does."

"Again?" Delaney sighed. "It's been done a dozen times."

"I know. And it's going to be done again, by me. The first piece is on requirements, screening, examination, and all that. The second will be on the Academy and probationary training. Now I'm trying to find out what happens to a man after he's assigned, and all the different directions he can go. You were originally in the detective division, weren't you?"

"That's right."

"Homicide, wasn't it?"

"For a while."

"They still talk about you, about some of your cases."

"Do they?"

"Why did you switch to patrol, Captain?"

"I wanted administrative experience," Delaney said shortly.

This time Handry sighed. He was a slender, dapper young man who looked more like an insurance salesman than a reporter. His suit was carefully pressed, shoes shined, narrow-brim hat exactly squared on his head. He wore a vest. He moved with a light-footed eagerness.

His face betrayed a certain tension, a secret passion held rigidly under control. Lips were pressed, forehead bland, eyes deliberately expressionless. Delaney had noted the bitten fingernails and a habit of stroking the upper lip downward with the second joint of his index finger.

"When did you shave your mustache?" he asked.

"You should have stayed in the detective division," Handry said. "I know I can't stop stroking my lip. Tell me, Captain—why won't policemen talk to me? Oh, they'll talk, but they won't really open up. I can't get into them. If I'm going to be a writer, that's what I've got to learn to do—how to get into people. Is it me, or are they afraid to talk for publication, or what the hell is it?"

"It isn't you—not you personally. It's just that you're not a cop. You don't belong. There's a gulf."

"But I'm trying to understand—really I am. This series is going to be very sympathetic to the police. I want it to be. I'm not out to do a hatchet job."

"I'm glad you're not. We get enough of that."

"All right, then you tell me: why *does* a man become a policeman? Who the hell in his right mind would want a job like that in this city? The pay is miserable, the hours are miserable, everyone thinks you're on the take, snot-nosed kids call you 'pig' and throw sacks of shit at you. So what the hell is the *point?*"

They were passing a private driveway alongside a luxury apartment house. Delaney heard something.

"Stay here," he whispered to Handry.

He went moving quietly up the driveway, the flashlight dark. His right hand was beneath his jacket flap, fingers on the butt of his gun.

He was back in a minute, smiling.

"A cat," he said, "in the garbage cans."

"It could have been a drug addict with a knife," Handry said.

"Yes," Delaney agreed, "it could have been."

"Well then, *why?*" Handry asked angrily.

They were strolling slowly southward on York Avenue heading back toward the Precinct house. Traffic was light at that hour, and the few pedestrians scurried along, glancing nervously over their shoulders.

"My wife and I were talking about that a few weeks ago," Delaney mused, remembering that bright afternoon in the Park. "I said I had become a cop because, essentially, I am a very orderly man. I like everything neat and tidy, and crime offends my sense of order. My wife laughed. She said I became a policeman because at heart I am an artist and want a world of beauty where everything is true and nothing is false. Since that conversation—partly because of what has happened since then—I have been thinking of what I said and what she said. And I have decided we are not so far apart—two sides of the same coin actually. You see, I became a policeman, I think, because there is, or should be, a logic to life. And this logic is both orderly and beautiful, as all good logic is. So I was right and my wife was right. I want this logic to endure. It is a simple logic of natural birth, natural living, and natural death. It is the mortality of one of us and the immortality of all of us. It is the on-going. This logic is the life of the individual, the family, the nation, and finally all people everywhere, and all things animate and inanimate. And anything that interrupts the rhythm of this logic—for all good logic does have a beautiful rhythm, you know—well, anything that interrupts that rhythm is evil. That includes cruelty, crime, and war. I can't do much about cruelty in other people; much of it is immoral but not illegal. I can guard against cruelty in myself, of course. And I can't do a great deal about war. I *can* do something about crime. Not a lot, I admit, but *something.* Because crime, *all* crime, is irrational. It is opposed to the logic of life, and so it is evil. And that is why *I* became a cop. I think."

"My God!" Handry cried. "That's great! I've got to use that. But I promise I won't mention your name."

"Please don't," Delaney said ruefully. "I'd never live it down."

Handry left him at the Precinct house. Delaney climbed slowly to his office to put away his "beat" equipment. Then he slumped in the worn swivel chair behind his desk. He wondered if he would ever sleep again.

He was ashamed of himself, as he always was when he talked too much. And what nonsense he had talked! "Logic . . . immortality . . . evil." Just to tickle his vanity, of course, and give him the glow of voicing "deep thoughts" to a young reporter. But what did all that blathering have to do with the price of beans?

It was all pretty poetry, but reality was a frightened woman who had never done an unkind thing in her life now lying in a hospital bed nerving herself for what might come. There were animals you couldn't see gnawing away deep inside her, and her world would soon be blood, vomit, pus, and feces. Don't you ever forget it, m'lad. And tears.

"Rather her than me" suddenly popped into his brain, and he was so disgusted with himself, so furious at having this indecent thought of the woman he loved, that he groaned aloud and struck a clenched fist on the desk. Oh, life wasn't all that much of a joy; it was a job you worked at, and didn't often succeed.

He sat there in the gloom, hunched, thinking of all the things he must now do and the order in which he must do them. Brooding, he glowered, frowned, occasionally drew lips back to show large, yellowed teeth. He looked like some great beast brought to bay.

3

In the Metropolitan Museum of Art there is a gallery of Roman heads. Stone faces are chipped and worn. But they have a quality. Staring into those socket eyes, at those broken noses, crushed ears, splintered lips, still one feels the power of men long dead. Kill the slave who betrayed you or, if your dreams have perished, a short sword in your own gut. Edward Delaney had that kind of face; crumbling majesty.

He was seated now in his wife's hospital room, the hard sunlight profiling him. Barbara Delaney stared through a drugged dimness and saw for the first time how his features had been harshened by violence and the responsibilities of command. She remembered the young, nervy patrolman who had courted her with violets and once, a dreadful poem.

The years and duty had not destroyed him, but they had pressed him in upon himself, condensing him. Each year he spoke less and less, laughed infrequently, and withdrew to some iron core that was his alone; she was not allowed there.

He was still a handsome man, she thought approvingly, and carried himself well and watched his weight and didn't smoke or drink too much. But now there was a somber solidity to him, and too often he sat brooding. "What is it?" she would ask. And slowly his eyes would come up from that inward stare, focus on her and life, and he would say, "Nothing." Did he think himself Nemesis for the entire world?

He had not aged so much as weathered. Seeing him now, seated heavily in sharp sunlight, she could not understand why she had never called him "Father." It was incredible that he should be younger than she. With a prescience of doom, she wondered if he could exist without her. She decided he would. He would grieve, certainly. He would be numb and rocked. But he would survive. He was complete.

In his methodical way, he had made notes of the things he felt they should discuss. He took his little leather-bound notebook from his inside pocket and flipped the pages, then put on his heavy glasses.

"I called the children last night," he said, not looking up.

"I know, dear. I wish you hadn't. Liza called this morning. She wanted to come, but I told her absolutely not. She's almost in her eighth month now, and I don't want her traveling. Do you want a boy or girl?"

"Boy."

"Beast. Well, I told her you'd call as soon as it's over; there was no need for her to come."

"Very good," he nodded. "Eddie was planning to come up in two weeks anyway, and I told him that would be fine, not to change his plans. He's thinking of getting into politics down there. They want him to run for district attorney. I think they call it 'public prosecutor' in that state. What do you think?"

"What does Eddie want to do?"

"He's not sure. That's why he wants to come up, to discuss it with us."

"How do you feel about it, Edward?"

"I want to know more about it. Who'll be putting up the campaign funds. What he'll owe. I don't want him getting into a mess."

"Eddie wouldn't do that."

"Not deliberately. Maybe from inexperience. He's still a young man, Barbara. Politics is new to him. He must be careful. Those men who want him to run have their own ambitions. Well . . . we'll talk about it when he comes up. He promised not to make any decision until he talks to us. Now then . . ." He consulted his notes. ". . . How do you feel about Spencer?"

He was referring to the surgeon introduced by Dr. Bernardi. He was a brusque, no-nonsense man without warmth, but he had impressed Delaney with his direct questions, quick decisions, his sharp interruptions of Bernardi's effusions. The operation was scheduled for late in the afternoon of the following day. Delaney had followed the surgeon out into the hall.

"Do you anticipate any trouble, doctor?" he asked.

The surgeon, Dr. K. B. Spencer, looked at him coldly.

"No," he said.

"Oh, I suppose he's all right," Barbara Delaney said vaguely. "What do you think of him, dear?"

"I trust him," Delaney said promptly. "He's a professional. I asked Ferguson to check him out, and he says Spencer is a fine surgeon and a wealthy man."

"Good," Barbara smiled faintly. "I wouldn't want a *poor* surgeon."

She seemed to be tiring, and there was a hectic flush in her cheeks. Delaney put his notebook aside for a moment to wring out a cloth in a basin of cold water and lay it tenderly across her brow. She was already on intravenous feeding and had been instructed to move as little as possible.

"Thank you, dear," she said in a voice so low he could hardly hear her. He hurried through the remainder of his notes.

"Now then," he said, "what shall I bring tomorrow? You wanted the blue quilted robe?"

"Yes," she whispered. "And the fluffy mules. The pink ones. They're in the righthand corner of my closet. My feet are swollen so badly I can't get into my slippers."

"All right," he said briskly, making a note. "Anything else? Clothes, makeup, books, fruit . . . anything?"

"No."

"Should I rent a TV set?"

She didn't answer, and when he raised his head to look at her, she seemed asleep. He took off his glasses, replaced his notebook in his pocket, began to tiptoe from the room.

"Please," she said in a weak voice, "don't go yet. Sit with me for a few minutes."

"As long as you want me," he said. He pulled a chair up to the bedside and sat hunched over, holding her hand. They sat in silence for almost five minutes.

"Edward," she breathed, her eyes closed.

"Yes. I'm here."

"Edward."

"Yes," he repeated. "I'm here."

"I want you to promise me something."

"Anything," he vowed.

"If anything should happen to me—"

"Barbara."

"If anything should—"

"Dear."

"I want you to marry again. If you meet a woman . . . Someone . . . I want you to. Will you promise?"

He couldn't breathe. Something was caught in his chest. He bowed his head, made a small noise, gripped her fingers tighter.

"Promise?" she demanded.

"Yes."

She smiled, nodded, slept.

4

Captain Delaney was detained by another demonstration at the embassy. By the time he got it squared away and the chanting marchers shunted off into side streets, it was late afternoon and almost time for Barbara's operation. He had one of the precinct squad cars rush him over to the hospital. He knew it was a breach of regulations, but he determined to make a full report on it, explaining the circumstances, and if they wanted to discipline him, they could.

He hurried up to her room, sweating under his longjohns and uniform jacket. They were wheeling her out as he arrived; he could only kiss her pale cheek and smile at her. She was on a cart, bundled up in blankets, the tube still attached to her arm, the jar of feeding fluid high on a rod clamped to the cart.

He left her on the second floor where the operating rooms were located. There was also a recovery ward, offices of physicians and surgeons, a small dispensary, and a large waiting room painted a bilious green and furnished with orange plastic couches and chairs. This brutal chamber was presided over by a handsome nurse, a woman of about 40, buxom, a blonde who kept poking tendrils of hair back under her starched cap.

Delaney gave his name, and she checked a frighteningly long list on her desk.

"Mrs. Barbara Delaney?"

"Yes."

"Captain, it will be another half-hour until the operation. Then Mrs. Delaney will go to the recovery ward. You won't be allowed to see her until she's returned to her room, and then only if her doctor approves."

"That's all right. I'll wait. I want to talk to the surgeon after the operation is finished."

"Well . . ." she said doubtfully, consulting her list. "I'm not sure you'll be able to. Dr. Spencer has two more scheduled after your wife. Captain, if you're hungry or want a cup of coffee, why don't you go downstairs to the cafeteria? Our paging system is connected there, and I can always call if you're needed."

"A good idea," he nodded approvingly. "Thank you. I'll do that. Do you happen to know if Dr. Bernardi is in the hospital?"

"I don't know, sir, but I'll try to find out."

"Thank you," he said again.

The food in the hospital cafeteria was, as he expected, wretched. He wondered how long they had to steam it to achieve that spongy texture and uniform color; the string beans were almost the same shiny hue as the mashed potatoes. And it all tasted as bad as it looked. Even liberal sprinklings of salt and pepper couldn't make the meat loaf taste like anything but wet wallboard. He thought of his wife's Italian stew, scented and spiced with rosemary, and he groaned.

He finally shoved the dishes away, hardly touched, and had a cup of black coffee and half a dish of chocolate pudding. Then he had another cup of coffee and smoked a cigarette. He was sweltering in the overheated cafeteria, but he never considered unhooking his choker collar. It wouldn't look right in public. He reflected on how you could always spot old cops, even in a roomful of naked men. The cops had a ring of blue dye around their necks: a lifetime of wearing that damned choker collar.

He returned to the waiting room on the second floor. The nurse told him she had located Dr. Bernardi; he was gowned and observing the kidney operation on Mrs. Delaney. The Captain thanked her and went out to the public telephone in the hall. He called the precinct. Lieutenant Rizzo had the duty and reported nothing unusual, nothing that required the Captain's attention. Delaney left the extension number of the waiting room in case he was needed.

He went back in, sat down, and looked around. There was an elderly Italian couple sitting on a couch in a corner, holding hands and looking scared. There was a young man standing propped against a wall, his face vacant. He was smoking a cigarette that threatened to burn his fingers. Seated on a plastic chair was a mink-clad matron, face raddled, showing good legs and a wattled neck. She seemed to be making an inventory of the contents of her alligator handbag.

Delaney was next to an end table scattered with magazines. He picked up a six-months-old copy of "Medical Progress," flipped through it, saw he could never understand it, put it aside. Then he sat solidly, silently, and waited. It was the detectives' art. Once, on a stake-out, he had sat in a parked car for 14 hours, relieving himself in an empty milk carton. You learned to wait. You never got to like it, but you learned how to do it.

A few things happened. The big, buxom nurse went off duty and was replaced by a woman half her size: a tough, dark, surprisingly young Puerto Rican girl with glowing eyes, a brisk way of moving, a sharp way of talking. She took all their names and why they were there. She straightened magazines on the tables. She emptied ashtrays. Then, unexpectedly, she sprayed the room with a can of deodorant and opened a window. The room began to cool; Delaney could have kissed her.

The vacant-faced young man was called and slouched out, staring at the ceiling. The mink-clad matron suddenly stood, wrapped her coat tightly about her, and pushed through the door without speaking to the nurse. The elderly Italian couple still sat patiently in the corner, weeping quietly.

New arrivals included a stiff, white-haired gentleman leaning on a cane. He gave his name to the nurse, lowered himself into a chair, and immediately fell asleep. Then there was a pair of hippie types in faded jeans, fringed jackets, beaded headbands. They sat cross-legged on the floor and began to play some game with oversize cards whose design Delaney could not fathom.

Finally he let himself glance at the wall clock. He was shocked to see it so late. He hurried to the desk and asked the nurse about his wife. She dialed, asked, listened, hung up.

"Your wife is in the recovery ward."

"Thank you. Can you tell me where Dr. Spencer is, so I can talk to him?"

"You should have asked before. Now I have to call again."

He let her bully him. "I'm sorry," he said.

She called, asked, hung up.

"Dr. Spencer is operating and not available."

"What about Dr. Bernardi?" he said doggedly, not at all fazed by her furious glare.

Again she called, asked, spoke sharply to the person on the other end, then punched the phone down.

"Dr. Bernardi has left the hospital."

"What? What?"

"Dr. Bernardi has left the hospital."

"But he—"

At that moment the door to the waiting room slammed back. It hit the wall with the sound of a pistol shot. Thinking of it later, Delaney decided that from that moment on, the night simply exploded and went whirling away.

It was the mink-clad matron, her wrinkled face crimson.

"They're killing him!" she screamed. "They're killing him!"

The little nurse came from behind her desk. She reached for the distraught woman. The matron raised one fur-covered arm and clubbed her down.

The others in the room looked up. Dazed. Bewildered. Frightened. Delaney rose lightly to his feet.

"They're killing him!" the woman screamed.

The nurse scrambled up, rushed out the door.

Delaney moved very slowly toward the hysterical woman.

"Oh yes," he said in a voice deliberately dulled, slowed. "They're killing him. Oh yes," he nodded.

The woman turned to him. "They're killing him," she repeated, not yelling now but pulling at the loose skin beneath her chin.

"Oh yes," Delaney kept nodding. "Oh yes."

He, to whom touching a stranger was anathema, knew from experience how important physical contact was in dealing with irrational or maddened people.

"Oh yes," he kept repeating, nodding his head but never smiling. "I understand. Oh yes."

He put a hand lightly, tentatively, on her furred arm.

"Oh yes," he kept nodding. "Oh yes."

She looked down at the hand on her arm, but she didn't throw him off.

"Oh yes," he nodded. "Tell me about it. I want to know all about it. Oh yes. Tell me from the beginning. I want to hear all about it."

Now he had his arm about her shoulders; she was leaning into him. Then an intern and attendant, white-clad, came flinging in, followed by the furious nurse. Delaney, leading the matron slowly toward a couch, waved them away with his free hand. The intern had enough sense to stop in his tracks and halt the others.

The old Italian couple, open-mouthed, and the hippie couple watched in silence. The white-haired gentleman slept on.

"They're killing him!" she screamed once more.

"Oh yes," he nodded, hugging her closer. "Tell me all about it. I want to know all about it."

He got her seated on a plastic couch, his arm still about her shoulders. The intern and his aides watched nervously but didn't approach.

"Tell me," Delaney soothed. "Tell me everything. Start from the beginning. I want to know."

"Shit," the woman said suddenly, and fumbled in her alligator bag for a handkerchief. She blew her nose with a tremendous fluttering blast that startled everyone in the room. "You're a beautiful man, you know that? You're not like those other mother-fuckers in this butcher shop."

"Tell me," he droned on, "tell me about it."

"Well," she said, dabbing at her nose, "it began about six months ago. Irving came home early from the office and complained about—"

Delaney heard a scuffling of feet and looked up. The room seemed filled with police uniforms. Oh God, he thought despairingly, don't tell me that stupid nurse called the cops because of one poor, sad, frightened, hysterical woman.

But it couldn't be. There was Captain Richard Boznanski of the 188th Precinct, just north of his. And he recognized a detective lieutenant and a man from the public relations section. A sergeant had his arm around Boznanski's waist and was half-supporting him.

Delaney pulled apart from the matron.

"Don't go away," she pleaded. "Please don't go away."

"Just for a minute," he whispered. "I'll be back. I promise I'll be back."

The loudspeaker was shouting: "Dr. Spencer, report to 201, please. Dr. Ingram, report to 201, please. Dr. Gomez, report to 201, please. Drs. Spencer, Ingram and Gomez, report to 201, please."

Delaney stalked over to Boznanski. He didn't like the way the man looked. His face was waxy white and covered with a sheen of sweat. His eyes seemed to move uncontrollably, and there was a tremor to his chin: his lips met and drew apart every second.

"Dick," Delaney urged, "what is it? What *is* it?"

Boznanski stared at him with dazed eyes. "Edward?" he said. "What are you doing here? Edward? How did you hear so soon?"

Delaney felt a hand on his arm and turned. It was Ivar Thorsen, Deputy Inspector, in charge of personnel in the patrol division. He drew Delaney to one side. He began to speak in a low voice, his light blue eyes never moving from Delaney's.

"It was an ambush, Edward. A call came in about a prowler. A two-man car checked it out. Jameson was black, Richmond white. It was a false alarm. At a housing project on 110th Street. They were returning to their car. Shotguns from the bushes. Jameson got his head blown off. Richmond took it in the chest and belly."

"Any chance?" Delaney asked, stone-faced.

"Well . . . no, I'd guess. I saw him. I'd guess no. But they're rounding up this team of surgeons to work on him. Listen, Edward, if Richmond dies, it'll be the fourth man Boznanski's lost this year. He's shook."

"I saw."

"Will you stay with him? The corridor's full of reporters, and they're moving in TV cameras. The Mayor and Commissioner are on their way. I've got a lot of crap to do—you know?"

"Yes."

"Just sit by him—you know."

"Sure."

Thorsen looked at him curiously, his ice eyes narrowing.

"What are you doing here, Edward?"

"My wife was operated on tonight. For kidney stones. I'm waiting to hear how she made out."

"Jesus," Thorsen breathed. "I'm sorry, Edward. I didn't know. How is she?"

"I'm trying to find out."

"Forget about Boznanski. The sergeant will stand by."

"No," Delaney said. "That's all right. I'll be here."

"They're killing him!" the matron cried, grabbing his arm. "They told me it was just a simple operation, and now they say there are complications. They're killing him!"

"Oh yes," Delaney murmured, leading her back to the couch. "I want to hear. I want to know all about it."

He lighted a cigarette for her, then started out into the hall. He fumbled in his pocket and found he had only a quarter. He was about to ask someone for change, then realized how stupid that was. He called Dr. Bernardi's office. He got an answering service. They told him they'd give the doctor his message.

He came back into the waiting room. The shaken nurse was behind her desk. He asked if Dr. Spencer was still in surgery. She said she'd check and also check on his wife in the recovery ward. He thanked her. She thanked him, softened and human.

He went back to Captain Richard Boznanski, seated now, his head thrown back, gasping for breath. He didn't look good. The sergeant was standing by, worried.

"Captain," he said, "is there any booze . . . ?"

Delaney looked at the man in the chair. "I'll try," he said.

"He came home early from work about six months ago," the mink-clad matron said at his elbow, "and he complained of this pain in his chest. He's always been a heavy smoker, and I thought—"

"Oh yes," Delaney said, holding her by the arm. "And what did they say it was?"

"Well, they weren't sure, and they wanted to do this exploratory."

"Oh yes," Delaney nodded. "Just a minute now, and I'll be right back."

He asked the nurse if she had any or could find any whiskey. She explained that regulations prohibited her from giving anything like that to patients or visitors. Delaney nodded and asked if she could find Dr. Bernardi's home phone number. She said she'd try. He asked if she could change a dollar. She couldn't, but she gave him what change she had and refused to accept the dollar he offered. He gave her a grateful smile.

He called Ferguson, who wasn't home. Delaney realized he had awakened the spinster sister. He explained the situation and asked, if Ferguson returned, if he would try to reach Bernardi and find out about Mrs. Delaney's condition. Then Ferguson could call Delaney in the waiting room.

The Captain stalked to the end of the second floor corridor. The swinging doors to the elevators were guarded by two patrolmen. They drew back to let him through.

The moment he stepped out he was surrounded by reporters, all shouting at once. Delaney held up a hand until the newsmen quieted.

"Any statements will have to come from Deputy Inspector Thorsen or others. Not from me."

"Is Richmond still alive?"

"As far as I know. A team of surgeons is working. That's all I know. Now if you'll . . ."

He pushed through the crush. They were setting up small TV cameras on tripods near the elevators. Then Delaney saw Thomas Handry leaning against a wall. He was the reporter who had accompanied Delaney on his midnight rounds. He pulled Handry aside. The man's eyes seemed huge and feverish.

"I told you, I told you," he said to Delaney.

"Do you have any whiskey?" the Captain asked.

Handry looked at him, bewildered.

"Take off your hat," Delaney commanded.

Handry snatched his hat away.

"Do you have any whiskey?" Delaney repeated.

"No, I don't, Captain."

"All I need is a shot. Ask around, will you? See if any of your boys is carrying a flask. Maybe one of the TV men has a pint. I'll pay for it."

"I'll ask, Captain."

"Thank you. Tell one of the men on the door to call me. I'll be in the waiting room."

"If no one's got anything, I'll go out for it."

"Thank you."

"Is Richmond dead?"

"I don't know."

He went back into the waiting room.

"Dr. Spencer is still in surgery," the nurse told him.

"Thank you. Did Dr. Ferguson call?"

"No. But I checked recovery. Your wife is sleeping peacefully."

"Thank you."

"An exploratory," the matron said, holding onto his elbow. "They said it would just be an exploratory. Now they won't tell me anything."

"What's his name?" Delaney asked. "Maybe I can find out what's going on."

"Modell," she said. "Irving Modell. And my name is Rhoda Modell. We have four children and six grandchildren."

"I'll try to find out," Delaney nodded.

He went back to the nurse. But she had heard his conversation with the woman.

"Not a chance," she said softly. "A few hours. Before morning. They took one look and sewed him up."

He nodded and glanced at the clock. Had time speeded up? It was past midnight.

"What I'd like—" he started, but then there was a patrolman next to him.

"Captain Delaney?"

"Yes."

"There's a reporter at the door. Guy named Handry. Says you—"

"Yes, yes."

Delaney walked back with him. The door was opened wide enough for Handry to give him a wrinkled brown paper bag.

"Thank you," Delaney said, and reached for his wallet. But Handry shook his head angrily and turned away.

He peeked into the bag. It was an almost full pint bottle of bourbon. He took several paper cups from the water cooler in the hallway and went back into the waiting room. Boznanski was still lolling in the chair, his head thrown back. Delaney filled a cup with bourbon.

"Dick," he said.

Boznanski opened his eyes.

"A sip," Delaney said. "Dick, just take a little sip."

He held the cup to the policeman's lips. Boznanski tasted, coughed, bent forward in dry heaves, then leaned back. Delaney fed him slowly, sip by sip. Color began to come back into the Captain's face. He straightened in his chair. Delaney poured a cup for the sergeant who drained it gratefully, in one gulp.

"Oh my," he said.

"May I sir?" a voice asked. And there was the white-haired gentleman, finally awake and holding out a quivering hand that seemed skinned with tissue paper. And the two hippies. And the old Italian couple. Just a taste for all: the sacramental cup.

"He's not going to make it, is he?" the matron asked suddenly, looking at Delaney. "I knew you wouldn't lie to me."

"I wouldn't lie to you." Delaney nodded, pouring her the few drops remaining in the bottle. "He's not going to make it."

"Ah Jesus," she sighed, rolling a pale tongue around the inside of the waxed paper cup. "What a miserable marriage that was. But aren't they all?"

There was noise outside in the corridor. Deputy Inspector Thorsen came in, composed as ever. He stalked directly to the seated Captain Boznanski and stared at him. Then he turned to Delaney.

"Thanks, Edward."

"What about Richmond?"

"Richmond? Oh. He's gone. They tried, but it was hopeless. Everyone knew it. Five surgeons working four hours."

Delaney looked up at the clock. It couldn't be two in the morning, it *couldn't* be. What had happened to time?

"The Mayor and Commissioner are out there now," Thorsen said in a toneless voice, "giving statements about the need for gun control laws and a new moral climate."

"Yes," Delaney said. He strode over to the nurse's desk. "Where can I find Dr. Spencer?" he asked harshly.

She looked at him with tired eyes. "Try the lounge. Turn right as you go out. Then, after you go through the swinging doors, there's a narrow door on the left that says 'No Admittance.' That's the surgeons' lounge."

"Thank you," Captain Delaney said precisely.

He followed her directions. When he pushed back the narrow door without knocking, he saw a small room, one couch and two armchairs, a TV set, a card table and four folding chairs. There were five men in the room wearing surgical gowns, skull caps, and masks pulled down onto their chests. Three were dressed in light green, two in white.

One man was standing, staring out a window. One was fiddling with the knobs on the TV set, trying to bring in a clear picture. One was trimming his fingernails with a small pocket knife. One was seated at the card table, carefully building an improbable house of leaned cards. One was stretched out on the floor, raising and lowering his legs, doing some kind of exercise.

"Dr. Spencer?" Delaney said sharply.

The man at the window turned slowly, glanced at the uniform, turned back to the window.

"He's dead," he said tonelessly. "I told them that."

"I know he's dead," the Captain said. "My name is Delaney. You operated on my wife earlier this evening. Kidney stones. I want to know how she is."

Spencer turned again to look at him. The other men didn't pause in their activities.

"Delaney," Spencer repeated. "Kidney stones. Well. I had to remove the kidney."

"What?"

"I had to take out one of your wife's kidneys."

"Why?"

"It was infected, diseased, rotted."

"Infected with what?"

"It's down in the lab. We'll know tomorrow."

The man building a house of cards looked up. "You can live with one kidney," he said mildly to Delaney.

"Listen," Delaney said, choking, "listen, you said there'd be no trouble."

"So?" Spencer asked. "What do you want from me? I'm not God."

"Well, if you're not," Delaney cried furiously, "who the hell is?"

There was a knock on the door. The man on the floor, the one lifting and lowering his legs, gasped, "Come in, come in, whoever you are."

A colored nurses' aide stuck her capped head through the opened door and looked about boldly.

"Any of you gentlemen a certain Captain Delaney?" she asked saucily.

"I'm Delaney."

"You have a call, Captain. In the waiting room. They say it's very, very, very important."

Delaney took a last look around. Spencer was staring out the window again, and the others were trying to stay busy. He stalked down the hall, pushed angrily through the swinging doors, slammed back into the waiting room. The little nurse handed him the phone, not looking up.

"Captain Edward X. Delaney here."

"Captain, this is Dorfman."

"Yes, lieutenant. What is it?"

"Sorry to bother you, Captain. At this hour."

"What is it?"

"Captain, there's been a murder."

Part III

1

The street was blocked off with sawhorses: raw yellow wood with "New York Police Department" stencilled on the sides. Below the barricades were oil lanterns, black globes with smoking wicks. They looked like 19th century anarchists' bombs.

The patrolman on duty saluted and pulled one sawhorse aside to let Delaney through. The Captain walked slowly down the center of the street, toward the river. He knew this block well; three years previously he had led a team of officers and Technical Patrol Force specialists in the liberation of a big townhouse that had been taken over by a gang of thugs and was being systematically looted. The house was near the middle of the block. A few lights were on; in one apartment the tenants were standing at the window, staring down into the street.

Delaney paused to survey the silent scene ahead of him. Understanding what was happening, he removed his cap, made the sign of the cross, bowed his head.

There were a dozen vehicles drawn up in a rough semicircle: squad cars, ambulance, searchlight truck, laboratory van, three unmarked sedans, a black limousine. Thirty men were standing motionless, uncovered heads down.

This city block had been equipped with the new street lights that cast an orange, shadowless glow. It filled doorways, alleys, corners like a thin liquid, and if there were no shadows, there was no brightness either, but a kind of strident light without warmth.

Into this brassy haze a morning mist seeped gently and collected in tears on hoods and roofs of cars and on black asphalt. It damped the hair and faces of the silent watchers. It fell as a shroud on the bundle crumpled on the sidewalk. The kneeling priest completed extreme unction and rose from his knees. The waiting men replaced their hats; there was a subdued murmur of voices.

Delaney stared at this night lithograph, then walked forward slowly. He came into a hard white beam from the searchlight truck; men turned to look at him. Lieutenant Dorfman came hurrying up, face twisted.

"It's Lombard, Captain," he gasped. "Frank Lombard, the Brooklyn councilman. You know—the one who's always talking about 'crime on the streets' and writing the newspapers what a lousy job the police are doing."

Delaney nodded. He looked around at the assembled men: patrolmen, precinct and Homicide North detectives, laboratory specialists, an inspector from the Detective Division. And a deputy commissioner with one of the Mayor's personal aides.

Now there was another figure kneeling alongside the corpse. Captain Delaney recognized the massive bulk of Dr. Sanford Ferguson. Despite the harsh glare of the searchlights, the Police Surgeon was using a penlight to examine the skull of the dead man. He stood away a moment while photographers placed a ruler near the corpse and took more flash photos. Then he kneeled again on the wet sidewalk. Delaney walked over to stand next to him. Ferguson looked up.

"Hullo, Edward," he smiled. "Wondering where you were. Take a look at this."

Before kneeling, Delaney stared down a moment at the victim. It was not difficult to visualize what had happened. The man had been struck down from behind. The back of his skull appeared crushed; thick black hair was bloodied and matted. He had fallen forward, sprawling heavily. As he fell, the left femur had snapped; the leg was now flung out at an awkward angle. He had fallen with such force that the splintered end of the bone had thrust out through his trouser leg.

As he fell, presumably his face smacked the sidewalk, for blood had flowed from a mashed nose, perhaps from a crushed mouth and facial abrasions. The pool of blood, not yet congealed, bloomed from his head in a small puddle, down into a plot of cracked earth about a scrawny plane tree at the curb.

Delaney kneeled carefully, avoiding a leather wallet lying alongside the body. The Captain turned to squint into the searchlight glare.

"The wallet dusted?" he called to men he couldn't see.

"No sir," someone called back. "Not yet."

Delaney looked down at the wallet.

"Alligator," he said. "They won't get much from that." He took a ballpoint pen from the inside pocket of his uniform jacket and gently prized open the wallet, touching only one edge. Dr. Ferguson put the beam of his penlight on it. They both saw the thick sheaf of green bills.

Delaney let the wallet fall closed, then turned back to the body. Ferguson put his light on the skull. Three men in civilian clothes came up to kneel around the corpse. The five bent over closely, heads almost touching.

"Club?" one of the detectives asked. "A pipe maybe?"

"I don't think so," Ferguson said, without looking up. "There's no crushing or depression. That's blood and matting you see. But there's a penetration. Like a puncture. A hole about an inch in diameter. It looks round. I could put my finger in it."

"Hammer?" Delaney asked.

Ferguson sat back on his heels. "A hammer? Yes, it could be. Depends on how deep the penetration goes."

"What about time, doc?" one of the other detectives asked.

"Looks to be within three hours tops. No, call it two hours. Around midnight. Just a guess."

"Who found him?"

"A cabby spotted him first but thought he was a drunk and didn't stop. The cabby caught up with one of your precinct squads on York Avenue, Captain, and they came back."

"Who were they?"

"McCabe and Mowery."

"Did they move the body or the wallet?"

"McCabe says they didn't touch the body. He says the wallet was lying open, face up, with ID card and credit cards showing in plastic pockets. That's how they knew it was Lombard."

"Who closed the wallet?"

"Mowery did that."

"Why?"

"He says it was beginning to drizzle, and they were afraid it might rain harder and ruin any latent prints on the plastic windows in the wallet. He says they could see it was a rough leather wallet and chances are there'd be a better chance of prints on the plastic than on the leather. So they closed the wallet, using a pencil. He says they didn't touch it. McCabe backs him up. McCabe says the wallet is within a quarter-inch at most from where they found it."

"When did the cabby stop them on York Avenue and tell them there was someone lying here?"

"About an hour ago. Closer to fifty minutes maybe."

"Doctor," Delaney asked, "can we roll him over now?"

"You got your pictures?" a detective roared into the darkness.

"We need the front," the reply came back.

"Careful of that leg," Ferguson said. "One of you hold it together while we roll him over."

Five pairs of hands took hold of the corpse gently and turned it face up. The five kneeling men drew back as two photographers came up for long shots and closeups of the victim. Then the circle closed again.

"No front wounds that I can see," Ferguson reported, his little flashlight beam zigzagging down the dead body. "The broken leg and facial injuries are from the fall. At least the abraded skin indicates that. I'll know better when I get him downtown. It was the skull penetration that did it."

"Dead before he hit the ground?"

"Could be if that puncture is deep enough. He's a—he was a heavy man. Maybe two twenty-five. He fell heavily." He felt the dead man's arms, shoulders, legs. "Solid. Not too much fat. Good muscle layer. He could have put up a fight. If he had a chance."

They were silent, staring down at the body. He had not been a handsome man, but his features were rugged and not unpleasant: strong jaw, full lips, a meaty nose (now crushed), thick black brows and walrus mustache. The teeth still unbroken were big, white, square—little tombstones. Blank eyes stared at the weeping sky.

Delaney leaned forward suddenly and pressed his face close to the dead man's. Dr. Ferguson grabbed him by the shoulder and pulled him back.

"What the hell are you doing, Edward?" he cried. "Kissing the poor bastard?"

"Smell him," Delaney said. "Smell the mustache. Garlic, wine, and something else."

Ferguson leaned forward cautiously, and sniffed at the thick mustache.

"Anise," he said. "Wine, garlic, and anise."

"That's an Italian dinner," one of the detectives said. "Maybe he stiffed the waiter and the guy followed him down here and offed him."

No one laughed.

"He is Italian," someone said. "His name isn't Lombard, it's Lombardo. He dropped the 'o' when he went into politics. His district in Brooklyn is mostly Jewish."

They looked up. It was Lieutenant Rizzo from the 251st.

"How do you know, lieutenant?"

"He's—was my wife's cousin. He was at our wedding. His mother lives around here somewhere. I called my wife. She's calling relatives, trying to find out the mother's address. My wife says Lombard came over from Brooklyn occasionally to have dinner with his mother. She's supposed to be a good cook."

The five men climbed shakily to their feet and brushed their damp knees. Dr. Ferguson signaled toward the ambulance, and two men came forward lugging a canvas body bag. A man came from the laboratory van with a plastic bag and a small pair of tongs to retrieve the wallet.

"Edward," Ferguson said, "I forgot to ask. How is your wife getting along?"

"She was operated on tonight. Or rather yesterday afternoon."

"And . . . ?"

"They had to take out one of her kidneys."

Ferguson was silent a moment, then . . . "Infected?"

"That's what Spencer told me. Bernardi observed the operation but I can't get hold of him."

"The prick. As soon as I get to a phone I'll try to find out what the hell is going on. Where can I reach you."

"The precinct house probably. We'll have to reshuffle schedules and figure out how many uniformed men we can spare for door-to-door questioning. They're taking our detectives away."

"I heard. Edward, I'll call if I learn anything. If I don't call, it means I haven't been able to reach Spencer or Bernardi."

Delaney nodded. Dr. Ferguson climbed into the back of the ambulance, and it went whining away. Lieutenant Dorfman was moving toward him, but the deputy commissioner came out of the darkness and clamped a hand on Delaney's elbow. The Captain didn't like to be touched; he tugged his arm gently away.

"Delaney?"

"Yes sir."

"My name's Broughton. B-r-o-u-g-h-t-o-n. I guess we never met."

They had, but Delaney didn't mention it. The two officers shook hands. Broughton, a thick, shapeless man, motioned Delaney toward the black limousine. He opened the back door, waved Delaney in, climbed in beside him.

"Go get a coffee, Jack," he commanded the uniformed driver.

Then they were alone. Broughton offered a cigar but Delaney shook his head. The deputy lighted up furiously, the end of the cigar flaring, the car filling with harsh smoke.

"It's a piece of shit," he said angrily. "Why the hell can't we get Havana cigars? We're defeating Communism by smoking horse shit? What kind of insanity is that?"

He sat back, staring out the window at the sidewalk where someone had chalked an outline around the corpse before it was removed.

"A lot of flak on this one, Captain," Broughton said loudly. "A *lot* of flak. The Commissioner cancelled a speech in Kansas City—Kansas *City,* for Chrissakes—and is flying back. You probably saw the Mayor's aide. His Honor is on our ass already. And don't think the fucking governor won't get in the act. You know this Lombard—the guy who got hisself killed?"

"I read his statements in the newspapers and I saw him on television."

"Yeah, he got the publicity. So you know what we're up against. 'Crime in the streets . . . no law and order . . . hoodlums and muggers running wild . . . shake up the police department . . . the Commissioner should resign . . . ' You know. The shithead was running for Mayor. Now he's knocked off, and if we don't pull someone in, it proves he was right. You understand how serious this is, Captain."

"I consider every homicide serious."

"Well . . . yeah . . . sure. But the politics involved. You understand that?"

"Yes sir."

"All right. That's one thing. Now the other thing. . . . This killing couldn't have happened at a worst time. You get the Commissioner's memo about precinct detectives?"

"Memorandum four six seven dash B dated eight October; subject: Detective division, reorganization of? Yes sir, I received it."

Broughton laughed shortly. "I heard about you, Delaney. Yeah, that's the memo." He belched suddenly, a ripe, liquid sound. He didn't excuse himself, but scratched in his crotch. "All right, we're pulling all the detectives out of the precinct houses. You're next on the list. You got the notification?"

"Yes."

"Starts on Monday. All detectives will be organized in special units—homicide, burglary and larceny, truck thefts, hotel thefts, and so on. Uniformed officers will make the first investigation of a crime. You're going to give your cops a crash course on what to look for. It's all spelled out in a manual you'll be getting. The investigating officers file a report. If it's a major theft, say, involving more than $1,500 in money or goods, the detective unit takes over. If it's a minor crime, say b-and-e or a mugging, the patrolman does what he can or reports it unsolvable. We tried it out in two test precincts, and we think it's going to work. What do you think?"

"I don't like it," Delaney said promptly. "It takes detectives out of the precincts and out of the neighborhoods. Sometimes they make their best busts just by knowing the neighborhood—who's missing, new hoods who have shown up, who's been flashing a roll. And of course they all have their neighborhood informers. Now, as I understand it, one specialized detective unit might be covering as many as four or five precincts. I like the idea of uniformed men getting experience in investigation work. They'll like that. They'll be functioning like detectives—which is what most of them thought police work was all about, instead of taking old people to hospitals and settling family squabbles. But while they're investigating and making out that preliminary report, they're off the beat, and I'll have less men on patrol and visible. I don't like that."

Broughton pried a fingertip roughly into one nostril, dug out some matter, rolled it into a ball between thumb and forefinger. He opened the car window and flicked it outside.

"Well, you're going to have to live with it," he said coldly. "At least for a year until we get some numbers and see what's happening to our solution rates. But now this son of a bitch Lombard gets hit right in the middle of the change-over. So we have Homicide North still in existence, the new homicide unit covering your precinct, and you still got your precinct detectives. Jesus Christ, all those guys will be walking up each other's heels, covering the same ground—and whose responsibility is it? It's going to be as fucked up as a Chinese fire drill. It is already. You got any ideas how to straighten it out?"

Delaney looked up in surprise. The final question had come so suddenly, so unexpectedly, that even though he had wondered about the reason for this private talk, he wasn't prepared for the demand.

"Can you give me twenty-four hours to think it over? Maybe I can come up with something."

"No good," Broughton said impatiently. "Right now I got to go out to the airport to pick up the Commissioner, and I got to have some suggestions on how to straighten out this mess. He'll want action. The Mayor and every councilman will be leaning on him. And if he don't produce, it's probably his ass. And if it's his ass, it's my ass too. You understand?"

"Yes."

"You agree that right now it's screwed up as far as organization goes?"

"Yes."

"Christ, you're a regular chatterbox, ain't you?" Broughton farted audibly and squirmed his buttocks on the car seat. "I been hearing how smart you are, Captain. Okay, here's your chance; give me a for-instance right now."

Delaney looked at him with distaste, recognizing the man's crude energy but angered by his bullying, disgusted by his personal habits, sensing a personality that reeked of the jungle.

"Try a temporary horizontal organization," he said tonelessly. "The Department, just like the army and most business corporations, is organized vertically. Responsibility and authority are vested in the man at the top. Orders come down the chain of command. Each division, precinct, unit, or whatever, has a definite assignment. But sometimes problems come up that can't be solved by this type of organization. It's usually a problem of limited duration that might never occur again. The Lombard homicide comes right in the middle of the reorganization of the detective division. All right, do what the army and most corporations do when they're faced with a unique situation that doesn't require a permanent organization. Set up a temporary task force. Call it 'Operation Lombard,' if you like. Appoint an overall commander. Give him full responsibility and authority to draw on any unit for personnel and equipment he needs. Detectives, patrolmen, specialists—anyone who'll help him do the job. The men are detached on a temporary basis. The whole operation is temporary. When and if Lombard's killer is found, the task force is disbanded, and the men go back to their regular units."

A light came into Broughton's muddy eyes. He laughed with glee and rubbed his palms together between his knees.

"They weren't kidding; you're a smart son of a bitch, Delaney. I like it. And I think the Commissioner will like it. A special task force: 'Operation Lombard.' It'll show we're doing something—right? That should satisfy the Mayor and the newspapers. How long do you think it'll take to break the Lombard thing?"

Delaney looked at him in astonishment.

"How would I know? How would anyone know? Maybe someone's confessing right now. Maybe it'll never be solved."

"Jesus, don't say that."

"Did you ever read solution statistics on homicides? If they're not solved within the first forty-eight hours, the solution probability drops off steeply and continues to plunge as time passes. After a month or two, solution probability is practically nil."

Broughton nodded glumly, got out of the car, spat his cold cigar into the gutter. Delaney got out too and stood there as the uniformed driver came running up. Broughton got in the front seat alongside the driver. As the limousine pulled away, the Captain saluted gravely, but it was not returned.

Delaney stood a moment, inspecting the street. The first contingent of uniformed patrolmen from his precinct came straggling up in twos and threes, to gather about the chalked outline on the sidewalk. The Captain moved over to listen to a sergeant giving them orders.

"Everyone got a flashlight?" he asked. "Okay, we spread out from here. We move slowly. Got that? slowly. We check every garbage can—" There was a groan from the massed men. "There was a pickup on this street yesterday afternoon so most of the cans should be empty. But even if they're full, spill them out. Every can has got to be searched. After you're through, try to kick most of the shit back in. We're calling for another sanitation pickup today, and the cans will be clawed through again when they're spilled into the garbage truck. Also, every area and alley, and put your light in every sewer and catch basin. This is a preliminary search. By tomorrow we'll have some sewer and street men here to take off the manhole covers and gratings and probe the sludge. Now, what we're looking for is anything that looks like a weapon. It could be a gun or a knife. But especially look for a club, a piece of pipe, an iron rod, a hammer, or maybe a rock with blood and matted hair on it. Anything with blood on it. And that includes a hat, clothing, a handkerchief, maybe a rag. If you're not sure, call me. Don't pass up anything. We do this block first. Then we cross York to the next block. Then we come back and do one block south and one block north. Got it? All right, get moving."

Delaney watched the searchlights spread out from where the dark blood still glistened in the morning mist. He knew it had to be done, but he didn't envy the men their task. It was possible they might find something. Possible. They would, he knew, also find gut-wrenching garbage, vomit, a dead cat, and perhaps the bloody body of an aborted baby.

By morning there would be more men doing the same thing, and more, and more. The search would spread farther and farther until it covered all his precinct and, finally, most of Manhattan.

Now he watched carefully as the men started their search. Then, suddenly, he realized his weariness had dropped away, or perhaps he was so exhausted he was numb. He clasped his hands behind his back and strolled down to the river fence. There he turned, faced toward York Avenue, and began to consider how the murder might have happened.

Lombard's body had been found on the sidewalk almost half-way between the river and York Avenue. If indeed he had dinner with his mother, it was reasonable to assume she lived between the river and the point where the victim was found. Lombard had fallen forward toward York. Had he, about midnight, been walking toward a bus line, a subway station, or perhaps his parked car for the trip home to Brooklyn?

Pacing slowly, Delaney inspected the buildings between the river and the spot where the body was found. They were all converted brownstones and townhouses. Fronts of the townhouses were flush; there were no areas where a killer might lurk, although it was conceivable he might have been in a lobby, ostensibly inspecting bells, his back turned to passersby. Delaney doubted that. Too much chance of being spotted by a tenant.

But the entrances to the converted brownstones were three or four steps down from the sidewalk. There were high bushes and boxes of ivy, still green, that offered some concealment for a crouching assassin. Delaney could not believe it. No killer, even if trained and wearing crepe-soled shoes, could leap from concealment, charge up three or four steps, and rush his victim from behind without making *some* noise. And Lombard would have turned to face his attacker, perhaps throw up an arm to protect himself, or make some movement to escape. Yet apparently he was struck down suddenly and without warning.

Barely moving, Delaney stared at the building fronts across the street. It was possible, he acknowledged, that the killer had waited in an outside lobby until Lombard passed on his way to York Avenue, had then come out on the sidewalk and followed him. But again, Lombard would surely have heard him or sensed his presence. And on this block at midnight, would a man as aware of street crime as Lombard allow a man to stalk him? The councilman could have run toward the traffic on York Avenue, or even dashed across the street to seek refuge in the big townhouse lobby with the doorman.

All this theorizing, of course, assumed that Lombard was a marked target, that the killer had followed him or at least been aware that he would be on this particular street at this particular time. But the suddenness and complete success of the attack were the points that interested Delaney at the moment. He retraced his steps to the river fence, turned around, and began again a slow walk toward York.

"What's Iron Balls up to, sarge?" a uniformed patrolman asked. He was stationed at the chalked outline on the sidewalk to shoo away the curious.

The sergeant stared across the street at the slowly pacing Captain.

"Why, he's looking for clues," he explained blandly. "He's sure to find a cancelled French postage stamp, or a lefthand glove with the little finger missing, or maybe a single turkey feather. Then he'll solve the murder and make deputy inspector. What the fuck do you think he's doing?"

The patrolman didn't know, and the sergeant didn't either.

Another possibility, Delaney was thinking, was that the killer was walking along with Lombard, the two were friends. But could the killer pull out a weapon, get behind his victim, and strike him directly from the rear without Lombard turning in alarm, dodging, or trying to ward off the blow?

The sticking point was still the suddenness of the attack and the fact that Lombard, a big, muscular man, had apparently offered no resistance, had allowed the killer to come up on him from behind.

Delaney stopped a moment and reflected; he was racing ahead too fast. Perhaps the killer didn't approach from the rear. Perhaps he came directly toward Lombard from York Avenue. If he was well-dressed, walking swiftly like a resident of the block anxious to get home at midnight, chances are Lombard would have inspected him as he approached. And if the man looked all right, Lombard might have moved aside slightly to let him pass.

The weapon, of course, would have to be concealed. But if it was a pipe or a hammer, there were a number of ways that could be done—in a folded newspaper, under a coat carried on the arm, even in a trick package. Then, the instant after passing Lombard, the victim's attention now on the area in front of him, the killer could bare his weapon, whirl, crush Lombard's skull. All in an instant, Lombard would have no warning. He would topple forward, already dead. The assassin would return his weapon to its cover, and retrace his steps to York Avenue or even continue on to his own apartment, if he was a resident of the block, or to the apartment of a friend, or to a car parked for a convenient getaway.

Delaney ran through it again. The more he inspected it, the stronger it looked. It *felt* right. It assumed the killer approaching Lombard was a stranger to him. But if he was well-dressed, "legitimate" looking, and apparently hurrying home, it was doubtful if Lombard or anyone else would cross the street to escape attack. The Captain discarded the notion that after the murder the killer went on to his own apartment or that of a friend; he would surely guess that every resident of the block would be questioned and his whereabouts checked at the time of the slaying. No, the killer either went back toward York or escaped in a car parked nearby.

Delaney returned to the fence blocking off East River Drive, crossed the street, and started down the sidewalk where the body had been found, heading in the direction the victim had been walking.

Now I am Frank Lombard, soon to be dead. I have just had dinner with my mother, I have come out of her apartment house at midnight, I am in a hurry to get home to Brooklyn. I walk quickly, and I look about constantly. I even look down into the bush-surrounded entrances to the brownstones. I am acutely aware of the incidence of street assaults, and I make certain no one is lurking, waiting to bash me on the head or mug me.

I look up ahead. There is a man coming toward me from York Avenue. In the shadowless glare of the new street lights I can see that the man is well-dressed, carrying a coat over his arm. He too is hurrying, anxious to get home. I can understand that. As he approaches, our eyes lock. We both nod and smile reassuringly. "It's all right," the smile says. "We're both well-dressed. We look okay. We're not muggers." I draw aside a little to give the man room to pass. The next instant I am dead.

Delaney stopped at the chalked outline on the sidewalk. It began to seem real to him. It explained why Lombard apparently made no move to defend himself, didn't have time to make a move. The Captain walked slowly down to York Avenue. He turned, started back toward the river.

Now I am the killer, carrying a coat across my arm. Under the coat, hidden, I am grasping the handle of a hammer. I am walking quickly, with purposeful strides. Ahead of me, in the orange glare, I see the man I am to kill. I walk toward him briskly. As I come up, I nod, smile, and move to pass him. Now he is looking straight ahead. I pass, lift the hammer free, whirl, raise it high and strike. He goes down, sprawling forward. I cover the hammer again, walk quickly back to York Avenue again and escape.

Captain Delaney paused again at the chalked diagram. Yes, it could have happened that way. If the killer had nerve and resolution—and luck, of course. Always luck. No one looking out a window. No one else on the street at that hour. No cab suddenly coming down from York, its headlights picking him up the instant he struck. But assuming the killer's luck, it all—ah, Jesus! The wallet! He had forgotten that damned wallet completely!

The wallet was the folding type, the kind a man customarily carries in a hip pocket. Indeed, Delaney had noted it had acquired a slight curve, taking its shape from the buttock. He carried the same type of wallet himself, and it began to curve after several months of use.

Lombard had been wearing a three-quarter car coat fastened in front with wooden toggles. In back, the coat and suit jacket beneath it had been pulled up high enough to expose his hip pockets. Now why had the killer paused long enough to frisk his victim for his wallet and then leave it open beside the body, even though it was stuffed with money? Every moment he tarried, every second, the killer was in deadly peril. Yet he took the time to search the corpse and remove the wallet. And then he left it open beside the body.

Why didn't he take the money—or the entire wallet? Not because he was frightened away by someone's appearance at a window or on the street. A man with nerve enough to approach his victim from the front would have nerve enough to take his loot, even if emperiled. A man can run just as fast with a wallet as without it. No, he just didn't want the money. What did he want? To check the identification of his victim—or did he take something from the wallet, something they didn't know about yet?

Delaney went back to York Avenue, turned, started back, and ran through it again.

Now I am the killer, carrying a coat across my arm. Under the coat . . .

Delaney knew as well as any man in the Department what the chances were of solving this particular homicide. He knew that in 1971 New York City had more murders than American combat deaths in Vietnam during the same period. In New York, almost five victims a day were shot, knifed, strangled, bludgeoned, set on fire or thrown from roofs. In such a horrific bloodbath, what was one more?

But if that became the general attitude, the *accepted* attitude, society's attitude—"What's one more?"—then the murder of Frank Lombard was an incident of no significance. When plague strikes, who cares enough to mourn a single soul?

When Captain Edward X. Delaney explained to the newspaperman why he had become a cop, he said what he thought: that he believed there was an eternal harmony in the universe, in all things animate and inanimate, and that crime was a dissonance in the chiming of the spheres. That is what Delaney thought.

But now, playing his victim-killer game in the first raw attempt to understand what had happened and to begin a possible solution of this crime, he was sadly aware that he had a deeper motive, more felt than thought. He had never spoken of it to anyone, not even Barbara, although he suspected she guessed.

It was perhaps due to his Catholic nurture that he sought to set the world aright. He wanted to be God's surrogate on earth. It was, he knew, a shameful want. He recognized the sin. It was pride.

---

2 What was it? He could not decipher its form or meaning. A frail thing there under white sheet and blue blanket, thin arms arranged outside. Heavy eyelids more stuck than shut, cheek bones poking, pale lips drawn back in a death's head grin, a body so frail it seemed even the blanket pressed it flat. And tubes, bandages, steel and plastic—new organs these—jars and drainage bags. He looked frantically for signs of life, stared, stared, saw finally a slow wearied rise and fall of breast no plumper than a boy's. He thought of the body of Frank Lombard and wondered. Where is the connection? Then realized he saw both through mist, his eyes damped and heavy.

"She's under heavy sedation," the nurse whispered, "but she's coming along just fine. Dr. Bernardi is waiting for you in the Surgeons' Lounge."

He searched for something he could kiss, a naked patch of skin free of tubes, needles, straps, bandages. All he wanted was to make a signal, just a signal. He bent to kiss her hair, but it was wire beneath his lips.

"I mentioned it," Bernardi said, inspecting his fingernails. Then he looked up at Delaney accusingly, daring him to deny it. "You'll remember I mentioned Proteus infection."

The Captain sat stolidly, craving sleep like an addict. They were at opposite sides of the card table in the Surgeons' Lounge. Cards were scattered across the surface, most of them face down but a queen of hearts showing, and a nine of spades.

"Proteus infection," Delaney repeated heavily. "How do you know?"

"That's what the lab tells us."

"And you think your lab is more knowledgeable than you and your associates who diagnosed my wife's illness as kidney stones?"

Again the opaque film coated the doctor's glistening eyes. His body stiffened, and he made a gesture Delaney had never seen him use before: he put the tip of his right forefinger in his right ear with the thumb stuck up in the air, exactly like a man blowing his brains out.

"Captain," he purred in his unctuous voice, "I assure you—"

"All right, all right," Delaney waved the apology away. "Let's not waste time. What is Proteus infection?"

Bernardi brightened, as he always did at an opportunity to display his erudition. Now he made his usual gesture of placing his index fingers together and pressing them against pouting lips.

"Proteus," he sang happily. "A Greek sea-god who could change his appearance at will. You should be interested in that, Captain. A million different shapes and disguises at will. That would complicate a policeman's task, would it not? He!"

Delaney grunted disgustedly. Bernardi paid no heed.

"And so the name was given to this particular infection. An infection is not an illness—but we needn't go into that. Suffice to say that Proteus infection frequently takes on the shape, appearance, form, and symptoms of a dozen other infections and illnesses. Very difficult to diagnose."

"Rare?" Delaney asked.

"Proteus rare?" the doctor said, eyebrows rising. "I would say no. But not too common. The literature is not extensive. That is what I was researching this morning, and why I did not return your calls. I was reading everything I could find on Proteus."

"What causes it?" Delaney asked, trying to keep the hatred out of his voice, to be as clinical and unemotional as this macaroni.

"I told you. Bacillus Proteus. B. Proteus. It exists in all of us. Usually in the intestinal tract. We have all kinds of good and bad little animalcules squiggling around inside us, you know. Sometimes, usually following an abdominal operation, B. Proteus goes on a rampage. Breaks loose. Sometimes in the urinary tract or in a specific organ. Rarely in the blood stream itself. The usual symptoms are high fever, chills, headaches, sometimes nausea. Which are—as I am certain you are aware—the symptoms of a dozen other infections. Proteus also causes certain changes in the blood, difficult to determine definitely. The recommended treatment for this infection is the employment of antibiotics."

"You tried that."

"True. But I assure you, Captain, I did not go through the entire spectrum. These so-called 'wonder drugs' are not all that wonderful. One of them may stifle a particular bacillus. At the same time it encourages the growth of another, more virulent bacillus. The antibiotics are not to be used lightly. In your wife's case, I believe the Proteus infection was triggered by her hysterectomy. But all the symptoms pointed to kidney stones, and there was nothing in the tests or plates to discourage that diagnosis. When Dr. Spencer got in there, we realized one kidney had to be removed. *Had* to. You understand?"

Delaney didn't answer.

"We saw there were still pockets of infection, small and scattered, that could not be removed by surgery. Now we must start again, hoping the main source of infection has been eliminated and we can clear up the remaining pockets with antibiotics."

"Hoping, doctor?"

"Yes. Hoping, Captain."

The two men stared at each other.

"She's dying, isn't she, doctor?"

"I wouldn't say that."

"No. You wouldn't."

He dragged to his feet, stumbled from the room.

Now I am the killer, Bacillus Proteus. I am in my wife's kidneys. I am . . .

He went back to the precinct house in hard afternoon sunlight. He thought he would be with her. He did not think he ought or should be with her, but that he would. He knew he could not attend her, for as long as it took, and still function efficiently as Captain Edward X. Delaney, New York Police Department. On his old portable he typed out a letter to Deputy Inspector Ivar Thorsen, Patrol Division, asking immediate retirement. He filled out the "Request for Retirement" form and told Thorsen, in a personal note, that the request was due to his wife's illness. He asked his old friend to expedite the retirement papers. He sealed, stamped the envelope, walked down to the corner postbox and mailed it. Then he returned to his home and rolled onto his bed without undressing.

He slept for perhaps three minutes or eight hours. The brilliant ringing of the bedside phone brought him instantly awake.

"Captain Edward X. Delaney here."

"Edward, this is Ferguson. Did you talk to Bernardi?"

"Yes."

"I'm sorry, Edward."

"Thank you."

"The antibiotics might work. The main source of the infection is gone."

"I know."

"Edward, I woke you up."

"That's all right."

"I thought you might want to know."

"Know what?"

"The Lombard homicide. It wasn't a hammer."

"What was it?"

"I don't know. The skull penetration was about three to four inches deep. It was like a tapered cone. The outside hole, the entrance, was about an inch in diameter. Then it tapered down to a sharp point. Like a spike. Do you want a copy of my report?"

"No. I've retired."

"What?"

"It's not my concern. I filed my retirement papers."

"Oh, Jesus. Edward, you can't. It's your life."

"I know."

Delaney hung up. Then he lay awake.

3

Three days later Captain Delaney received the telephone call he had been expecting: the assistant to Deputy Inspector Thorsen asked if he could meet with Thorsen that afternoon at four o'clock. Delaney went downtown via subway, wearing his uniform.

"Go right in, Captain," Thorsen's pretty secretary said when he gave his name. "They're expecting you."

Wondering who "they" might be, Delaney knocked once and pushed open the heavy oak door to Thorsen's office. The two men seated in leather club chairs rose to their feet, and the Deputy Inspector came forward smiling.

Ivar Thorsen was Delaney's "rabbi" in the Department. The term was current police slang for a superior officer or high official in city government who liked an officer personally, took an interest in his career, and generally guided and eased his advancement in rank. When a "rabbi" moved upward in the hierarchy, sooner or later his protege moved upward also.

Deputy Inspector Ivar Thorsen, a man in his late 50s, was called "The Admiral" by his subordinates, and it was easy to see why. Of relatively short stature, his body was slender and stringy, but all muscle and tendon; he bounced as he walked. His skin was fair and unblemished, features classically Nordic but without softness. His pale blue eyes could be distressingly piercing. The white hair seemed never combed but rigorously brushed until it hugged tightly the shape of his head from a leftside part that showed pink scalp.

He shook Delaney's hand, then turned to the other man in the room.

"Edward, I think you know Inspector Johnson."

"I surely do. Good to see you, inspector."

"Likewise, Edward," the grinning black Buddha said. He extended a huge hand. "How you been?"

"Can't complain. Well . . . I can, but no one will listen."

"I know, I know," the big man chuckled, and his heavy belly moved up and down. "Wish we could get together more often, but they keep me chained to those damned computers, and I don't get uptown as often as I'd like."

"I read your analysis of arrest and conviction percentages."

"You did?" Johnson exclaimed with genuine pleasure. "You must be the only cop in town who did."

"Wait a minute, Ben," Thorsen protested. "I read it."

"The hell," the black scoffed. "You started it maybe, and read the last paragraph."

"I swear I read every word."

"I give you five-to-one you didn't—and I can ask questions to prove it."

"I'll take that bet."

"Misdemeanor," Delaney said promptly. "I can place you both under arrest. Gambling laws."

"Not so," Johnson shook his great head. "The courts have held a private wager between two gentlemen cannot be prosecuted under anti-gambling statutes. See *Harbiner v. the City of New York.*"

"See *Plessy v. Novick,*" Delaney retorted. "The court held a private unpaid wager between two persons cannot be a matter for judicial decision only because the wager itself was illegal."

"Come on," Thorsen groaned. "I didn't ask you here to argue law. Sit down." He waved them to the club chairs, then took the upholstered swivel chair behind his glass-topped desk. He flicked on his intercom. "Alice, please hold all incoming calls except emergency."

Inspector Johnson turned toward Delaney and regarded him curiously.

"What did you think of my report, Edward?"

"The numbers were a shock, inspector. And the—"

"You know, Edward, if you called me Ben I really don't think I'd have you up for insolence and insubordination."

"All right, Ben. Well . . . the numbers were a shock, your analysis was brilliant, but I can't agree with your conclusion."

"What can't you agree with?"

"Suppose only five percent of felony arrests eventually produce convictions. From that you argue that we—the men on the beat—should make fewer arrests but better ones—arrests that will stand up in court. But aren't you disregarding the deterrent effect of mass arrests, even if we know the evidence will never stand up? The suspect may never be convicted, but after he goes through booking, a time in jail until he can raise bail—if he can—and the expense of a lawyer for his day in court, maybe he'll think twice before he strays again."

"Maybe, maybe not," Johnson rumbled. "I was aware of the deterrent angle when I wrote the report. As a matter of fact, I agree with it. But if I had come out recommending more arrests—whether or not they stood up in court—if I had recommended dragnet operations on prostitutes, drifters, homosexuals, gamblers—you know what would have happened? Some radical in the Department would have leaked that report to the press, and every civil liberties group would be down on our necks, and we'd be 'fascist pigs' all over again."

"You mean you tailored your convictions for the sake of public relations?"

"That's right," Johnson agreed blandly.

"Are public relations that important?"

"Got to be. For the Department. Your world is your own Precinct. My world is the Commissioner's office and, by extension, the Mayor's."

Delaney stared at the big black. Inspector Benjamin Johnson was on the Commissioner's staff, in charge of statistics and production analysis. He was an enormous man, a former All-American guard from Rutgers. He had gone to fat, but the result wasn't unpleasant; he still carried himself well, and his bulk gave him added dignity. His smile was appealing, almost childlike—a perfect disguise for what Delaney knew was a hard, complex, perceptive intelligence. A black didn't attain Johnson's rank and reputation by virtue of a hearty laugh and a mouthful of splendid teeth.

"Please," Thorsen raised a palm. "The two of you get together some night and fight it out over a beefsteak or soul food."

"Steak for me," Johnson said.

"I'll take the soul food," Delaney smiled.

"Let's get on with it," Thorsen said in his no-nonsense way. "First of all, Edward, how is Barbara feeling?"

Delaney came back to realities. He enjoyed "police talk" and could sit up all night arguing crime and punishment. But only with other cops. Civilians simply didn't *know*. Or perhaps it was like atheists arguing with priests. They were talking about different things, or in different languages. The atheist argued reason; the priest argued faith. In this case, the policeman was the atheist, the civilian the priest. Both were right and both were wrong.

"Barbara is not so good," he said steadily. "She hasn't snapped back from the operation the way she should—or at least the way I hoped she would. They've started her on antibiotics. The first didn't do a thing. They're trying another. They'll go on trying."

"I was sorry to hear your wife was ill, Edward," Johnson said quietly. "What exactly is it?"

"It's called Proteus infection. In her case it's an infection of the urinary tract. But the doctors wouldn't tell me a damned thing about how really ill she is and what her chances are."

"I know," Johnson nodded sympathetically. "The thing I hate most about doctors is when I go to one with a pain in my gut and explain exactly what the symptoms are, and the doctor says, 'That doesn't worry me.' Then I say, 'I know, goddamn it, it's *my* pain; why should it worry you?' "

Delaney smiled wanly, knowing Johnson was trying to cheer him up.

"I hate to hear about illnesses I never heard of before," Thorsen said. "There are so many things that can go wrong with the human body, it's a wonder any of us get through this life alive." Then, realizing what he had said and seeing the others' sad smiles, he added. "That's right—we don't, do we? Well, Edward, I have your application for retirement here. First of all let me confess, I haven't done a thing with it yet. It's perfectly in order. You have every right to retire if you wish. But we wanted to talk to you first. Ben, you want to take it from here?"

"No." Johnson shook his massive head. "You carry the ball."

"Edward, this concerns the Lombard homicide in your precinct. I know you know the man's reputation and the publicity he got and how important it is to the Department to come up with a quick solution and arrest. And, of course, it came in the middle of the reorganization of the Detective Division. Did you get the memo on the special task force Operation Lombard headed by Deputy Commissioner Broughton?"

Delaney paused before answering, wondering how much he should say. But Broughton was a slob—and what could the man do to him since he was retiring?

"Yes, I know," he nodded. "As a matter of fact, I suggested Operation Lombard to Broughton the morning of the murder. We had a private talk in his car."

Thorsen turned his head swiftly to look at Johnson. The two men stared at one another a moment. Then the inspector slammed a heavy palm down onto the arm of his leather chair.

"I told you," he said angrily. "I told you that stupid, racist son of a bitch didn't have the brains to come up with that idea himself. So it was you, Edward?"

"Yes."

"Well, don't expect a thank-you from brother Broughton. That bastard is strictly 'Hurray for me, fuck you.' He's flying mighty high right now."

"That's why we asked you here today, Edward," Thorsen said softly. "Broughton is flying high, and we'd like to bring him down."

Delaney looked from man to man, realizing he was getting involved in something he had vowed to avoid: the cliques and cabals that flourished in the upper echelons of the Department—and in all levels of government, and in the military, and in corporations, and in every human organization that had more than two members.

"Who is 'we'?" he asked cautiously.

"Inspector Johnson and myself, of course. And about ten or a dozen others, all of superior rank to us, who don't, for obvious reasons, want their names used at this time."

"What ranks?"

"Up to Commissioner."

"What are you trying to do?"

"First of all, we don't like Broughton. We believe he's a disgrace—hell, he's a catastrophe!—to the Department. He's amassing power, building a machine. This Operation Lombard is just another step up for him. If he can solve the murder."

"What motivates Broughton?" Delaney asked. "Ambition? What does he want? Commissioner? Mayor?"

Delaney looked at him, ready to laugh if Johnson was smiling. But he was not.

"Ben's not kidding, Edward. It's not impossible. Broughton is a relatively young man. He has an ego and hunger for power you wouldn't believe. Theodore Roosevelt went from the Commissioner's office to the White House. Why not Broughton? But even if he never gets to be President, or governor, or mayor, or even commissioner, we still want him out."

"Facist bastard," Johnson grumbled.

"So . . . ?" Delaney said.

"We have a plan. Will you listen to it?"

"I'll listen."

"I'm not even going to talk about discretion and all this being in strict confidence, etcetera. I know you too well for that. Edward, even if you retired today, you couldn't spend every waking hour with your wife. She's going to be in the hospital for the foreseeable future, isn't she?"

"Yes."

"If you retired today, you'd still have plenty of time on your hands. And I know you; after almost thirty years in the Department, you'd go nuts. All right . . . Now it's been three—no, almost four days since the Lombard homicide. It's been almost three days since the formation of Operation Lombard. Since then, Broughton has been drawing men and equipment from all over the city. He's built up a big organization, and it's still growing. I told you, the man's power-hungry. And I can also tell you that Broughton and Operation Lombard haven't come up with a thing. Not a lead, not a clue, not a single idea of how it was done, why it was done, and who did it. Believe me, Edward, they're no farther ahead at this moment than when you saw Lombard on the sidewalk."

"That doesn't mean they might not solve it tomorrow, tonight, or right now, while we're talking."

"True. And if Broughton brings it off, he'll crucify us. I mean Ben here and me and our friends. Broughton may be stupid, but he's shrewd. He knows who his enemies are. I tell you this man is capable of farming you out just because you suggested Operation Lombard from which he profited. He's the kind of man who can't stand to feel gratitude. He'll cut you down . . . somehow."

"He can't touch me. I'm retiring."

"Edward," Inspector Johnson said in a deep, throbbing voice, "suppose you didn't retire. Suppose you requested an indefinite leave of absence. We could swing it."

"Why should I do that?"

"It would relieve you of the responsibility of the Two-five-one. We'd put in an Acting Captain. An *Acting* Captain. You wouldn't be replaced. You agree it's possible your wife may recover faster than anyone expects, and then you'd want back to active duty? That's possible, isn't it?"

"Yes. It's possible."

"All right," Johnson said, seeming to look for words, to feel his way. "Now, say you're on leave of absence. You're relieved of responsibility. Now what we want you to do—" Then it all came out in rush: "Whatwewantyoutodoisfind-Lombard'skiller."

"What?"

"You heard me. We want you to solve the Lombard homicide before Broughton and his Operation Lombard do it."

Delaney looked from man to man, astonished.

"Are you insane?" he finally demanded. "You want me, a single cop not even on active duty, working outside the Department like some kind of—some kind of private detective, you expect me to bring in Lombard's killer before five hundred or a thousand detectives and uniformed men and specialists with all the resources of the Department behind them? Impossible."

"Edward," Thorsen said patiently. "We think there's a chance. A small chance, true, but it's worth taking. Yes, you'd have to work in civilian clothes. Yes, you'd be by yourself; you couldn't request personnel from the Department, or equipment. But we'll set up a contact, and through the contact we'll make certain you got anything you'd need: print identification, evidence analysis, lab work, criminal records. Whatever you need, you'll get. We'll cover it somehow so Broughton doesn't get wind of it. If he does, we're all down the drain."

"Listen," Delaney said desperately, "is it only you two out to get Broughton or are there really a dozen others all the way up to the Commissioner?"

"There are others," Thorsen said gravely, and Johnson nodded just as solemnly.

"It won't work," Delaney said definitely. He stood and began to pace back and forth, hands clasped behind him. "You know how many men you need for a homicide investigation like this? Men to search sewers. Men to dig in garbage cans. Men to ring doorbells and ask questions. Men to investigate Lombard's private life, his business life, his political life. Men to trace him back to the day he was born, trying to find an enemy. How in God's name could I—or any one man—do all that?"

"Edward," Johnson said softly, "you wouldn't have to do all that. That's what Operation Lombard is doing right now, and I swear to you, you'd get a Xerox copy of every report filed. Anytime a patrolman or detective or specialist puts anything down on paper about the Lombard off, you'll see a copy within twenty-four hours."

"That's a promise," Thorsen nodded. "Just don't ask how we'll do it."

"I won't, I won't," Delaney said hastily. "But just what more do you think I could do than Operation Lombard is doing right now?"

"Edward," Thorsen sighed, "don't put yourself down. I remember once I had dinner at your house, and we were talking about something you had done and let your division commander take the credit for—you were a lieutenant then—and Barbara got angry and told you that you should assert yourself more. She was right. Edward, you have a talent, a drive, a genius—call it whatever the hell you like—for investigative work. You know it but won't admit it. I know it and shout it every chance I get. It was my idea to bring you in on this, this way. If you say yes, fine. Then we'll go to work. If you say no, and want to go through with your retirement, okay and no hard feelings."

Delaney walked over to one of the windows and stared down into the crowded street. People were scurrying between honking cars in a traffic jam. There was bright movement, surge and thrust. He heard the horns, a siren, the far-off hoot of a liner putting to sea, the drone overhead of a plane slanting down to Kennedy Airport.

"No leads at all?" he asked, without turning around.

"None whatsoever," Thorsen said. "Not a thing. Not even a theory that makes sense. A blank. A compete blank. Broughton is beginning to show the strain."

Delaney turned around with a bleak smile. He looked at Inspector Johnson and spoke to him.

"Ben, I gave him the solution probability figures on homicide. You know how they drop off after forty-eight hours?"

"Yes," Johnson nodded. "It's been almost four days now, with probability dropping every minute for Broughton."

"For me too," Delaney said ruefully. "If I took this on," he added hastily.

He turned back to the window, his hands jammed into his pockets now. He wished with all his heart he could discuss this with Barbara, as he had discussed every important decision in his career. He needed her sharp, practical, aggressive, *female* intelligence to probe motives, choices, possibilities, safeguards. He tried, he strained to put himself in her place, to think as she might think and decide as she might decide.

"I'd be in civilian clothes," he said, his back to them. "Could I use my tin?"

"Yes," Johnson said immediately. "But as little as possible."

Delaney began to realize how completely they had thought this out, planned it, worried it for flaws, before they approached him.

"How often would I report?"

"As often as possible. Once a day or, if not, whenever you have something or a request for something."

"Who would I report to?"

"Me," Thorsen said promptly. "I'll give you a clean number."

"Don't tell me you think your home phone is tapped?"

"I'll give you a clean number," Thorsen repeated.

Delaney made up his mind and said what he thought Barbara would want him to say.

"If I'm on leave of absence but not retired, I can still be racked up on Departmental charges. If Broughton finds out about this, he'll fix me good. I met the man. I know what he is. I'll do what you want if I get a signed letter from either of you, or both of you, authorizing this investigation."

He turned to face them. They looked at him, then at each other.

"Edward . . ." Thorsen started, then stopped.

"Yes?"

"It's our ass."

"I know it. Without the letter, it's my ass. Mine alone. If Broughton discovers what's going on."

"Don't you trust—" Thorsen began.

"Now wait just one fat minute," Johnson held up his hamhand. "Let's not get all riled here and start talking about trust and friendship and saying things we might be sorry for later. Just let me think a minute. Edward has a very good point, Ivar. It's something we didn't consider. Now just let me think and see if I can come up with something that will satisfy all the parties concerned."

He stared off into the middle distance, while the other two watched him expectantly. Finally Johnson grunted and heaved himself to his feet. He scrubbed his curly grey hair with knuckles, then motioned toward Thorsen. The two men went over to one corner and began to speak in low voices, Johnson doing most of the talking and gesturing frequently. Delaney took his seat again in the club chair and wished he was with his wife.

Finally the whispering ceased. The two men came over to stand before his chair.

"Edward," Johnson rumbled, "if we got a letter addressed to you personally, authorizing your unofficial or semi-official investigation into the death of Frank Lombard, and if this letter was signed by the Commissioner, would that satisfy you?"

Delaney looked up in amazement.

"The Commissioner? Why on earth would he sign a letter like that? He just appointed Broughton commander of Operation Lombard."

Inspector Johnson sighed heavily. "Edward, the Commish is a man of some ability. About a middleweight, I'd guess. And he's well-meaning and kind. All to the good. But this is the first time he's operated in New York. He's never had to keep afloat in a school of barracudas. Not the kind we got. He's learning—but the question is, will they give him time to learn? He's just beginning to realize a good executive has got to spend as much time protecting his ass as he does coping with the problems in front of him. Nine times out of ten, it's those strong, efficient executive assistants with the long knives who do a top man in. I think the Commissioner may just be starting to realize what Broughton is doing between those farts and belches. Broughton has some palsy-walsys on the Mayor's staff, you know. There's also another factor. This is something never talked about in business management manuals, but it exists in the Department, in federal, state and local government, in business, and in the military. I think the Commissioner is physically frightened of Broughton. I can't give you any evidence, but that's what I feel. It was the source of a lot of Joe McCarthy's power. Plenty of those old, frail Senators were physically afraid of Joe. Well, we've got a man, a friend—real Machiavelli type—a Deputy the Commissioner trusts who could maybe put a bug in his ear. 'Look Commissioner, Broughton is a fine fellow—a little crude for my taste but he gets things done—and maybe he'll bring off this Operation Lombard thing and find the killer. But look, Commissioner, wouldn't it be wise to have an ace in the hole? I mean if Broughton falls on his face, you really should have a back-up plan in the works. Now it just so happens I've got this smart-ass Captain who right now is on leave of absence, and this smart-ass Captain is the best detective this town ever saw, and if you ask him nice, Commissioner, and write him a po-lite letter, this smart-ass Captain just might be willing to smell around and find Frank Lombard's killer for you. Without Broughton knowing a thing about it, of course.' "

Delaney laughed. "Do you think he'll go for that? Do you really think he'll give me a letter of authorization?"

"If we git it, will you do it?"

"Yes."

4

The following evening, as he was preparing to leave for the hospital, an envelope was delivered to his home by commercial messenger. The envelope contained a letter signed by the Commissioner, authorizing Captain Edward X. Delaney to undertake a "discreet inquiry" into the homicide of Frank Lombard. There was also a letter signed by the Chief of Patrol granting Captain Delaney an indefinite leave of absence "for personal reasons." Delaney began to appreciate the clout swung by Thorsen, Johnson, and their friends.

He was about to call Ivar Thorsen from his home, but after dialing two digits he hung up and sat a moment, staring at the phone. He remembered the Deputy Inspector had stressed that the number he had been given was "clean." He pulled on his overcoat, walked two blocks to a public phone booth and called from there? The "clean" number proved to be an answering service. He gave only his last name and the number of the phone he was calling from. Then he hung up and waited patiently. Thorsen was back to him within three minutes.

"I got the papers," Delaney said. "Quick work."

"Yes. Where are you calling from."

"A public phone booth two blocks from my house."

"Good. Keep doing that. Use different booths."

"All right. Have you made any decision on an Acting Captain?"

"Not yet. Any suggestions?"

"I have a lieutenant. Dorfman. Know him?"

"No. But a *lieutenant?* I'm not sure we can swing it. That's a boss precinct,

Edward. It should have a captain or deputy inspector. I don't believe there's any precedent for a lieutenant commanding a precinct."

"Consider it, will you? Look up Dorfman's file. Four commendations. A good administrator. A fine lawyer."

"Can he hack it?"

"We'll never know until he gets the chance, will we? There's another thing."

"What's that?"

"He trusts me. More than that, he likes me. He'd make a perfect contact. The man to handle the requests I'll have for records, print identification, research, lab analysis, things like that. It could be shuffled in with the usual precinct paper. No one could spot it."

"How much would you tell him?"

"As little as possible."

There was a silence.

"There's another factor," Delaney said quickly. "I gave Broughton the idea for Operation Lombard and the homicide was in my precinct. It would be natural for him to think I was pissed-off and jealous. He'll be suspicious of any possible interference from me. I'm guessing how his mind works from what you and Johnson told me about him."

"You guess right."

"Well, he'll hear I've gone on leave of absence, and he'll relax. He'll relax even more if he hears Dorfman has been appointed Acting Captain. A *lieutenant?* And a man with no detective experience? Broughton will cross off my old Precinct as a potential trouble spot, and I'll be able to use Dorfman as a contact with little possibility of discovery."

"It's a thought," Thorsen said. "And a good one. Let me discuss it with—with others. Maybe we can swing it. I'll get back to you. Anything else?"

"Yes. I know Broughton came out of patrol. Who's straw boss of his detectives on Operation Lombard?"

"Chief Purley."

"Oh God. He's good."

"You're better."

"Keep telling me that. I need all the reassurance I can get."

"When are you starting?"

"As of now."

"Good. You'll have the Xerox tomorrow. You understand?"

"Yes."

"Keep me informed."

The two men hung up without saying goodby.

Delaney took a cab to the hospital, pressed back into a corner of the rear seat, biting at his thumbnail. He was beginning to feel the old, familiar excitement. Forget his reasoning and emotions about police work. His gut reaction was obvious: the chase was on and he was the hunter.

He came into her room smiling determinedly, taking from his pocket a silly little thing he had bought her: a cheap, brilliant brooch, a rhinestoned penguin she could pin to her hospital gown. She held her arms out to him; he bent to embrace her.

"I was hoping you'd come."

"I told you I would. Better?"

She smiled brightly and nodded.

"Here." He handed her the penguin. "From Tiffany's. A little over a hundred thousand."

"Beautiful," she laughed. "What I've always wanted."

He helped her pin it to the shoulder of her gown. Then he took off his overcoat, pulled a chair over to the bed, sat down and took one of her hands in his.

"Truly better?"

"Truly. I think I should start seeing people. Some close friends."

"Good," he said, being careful to avoid false heartiness. "Eddie will be up next week. What about Liza?"

"No, Edward. Not in her condition. Not yet."

"All right. Shall I call your friends?"

"I'll do it. Most of them I want to see call me every day. I'll tell them I'd like to see them. You know—two or three a day. Not everyone at once."

He nodded approvingly and looked down at her smiling. But her appearance shocked him. She was so thin! The tubes and jars were gone, her face was flushed with the familiar fever, but the frailty was what tore his heart. She who had always been so active, strong, vibrant . . . Now she lay flaccid and seemed to strain for breath. The hand he was not holding picked weakly at blanket fluff.

"Edward, are you eating all right?"

"Fine."

"Sticking to your diet?"

"I swear."

"What about sleep?"

He held out a hand, palm down, then turned it over, then flipped it back and forth a few times.

"So-so. Listen, Barbara, there's something I must tell you. I want to—"

"Has something happened? Are the children all right?"

"The children are fine. This doesn't concern them. But I want to talk to you for about an hour. Maybe more. It won't tire you, will it?"

"Of course not, silly. I've been sleeping all day. I can tell you're excited. What is it?"

"Well . . . four days ago—actually early in the morning following your operation—there was a homicide in my precinct."

He described to her, as concisely and completely as he could, the discovery and appearance of Frank Lombard's body. Then he went on to tell her how important it was to solve Lombard's murder in view of the man's public criticism of the Department, and how the current reorganization of the Detective Division hampered efficient handling of the case. Then he described his private talk with Deputy Commissioner Broughton.

"He sounds like a horrible man!" she interrupted.

"Yes . . . Anyway, the next day I filed for retirement."

She came up from the bed in shock, then fell back, her eyes filling with tears.

"Edward! You didn't?"

"Yes. I wanted to spend more time with you. I thought it was the right decision at the time. But it didn't go through. This is what happened . . ."

He recounted his meeting with Deputy Inspector Thorsen and Inspector Johnson. He detailed their plan for Delaney to make an independent investigation of the Lombard homicide, in an effort to humiliate Broughton. As he spoke, he could see Barbara come alive. She propped herself on one elbow and leaned forward, eyes shining. She was the politician of the family and dearly loved hearing accounts and gossip of intradepartmental feuding, the intrigues and squabbles of ambitious men and factions.

Delaney told her how he had demanded a letter of authorization from a superior officer before he would agree to the Lombard investigation.

"Barbara, do you think I did the wise thing?"

"You did exactly right," she said promptly. "I'm proud of you. In that jungle, the first law is 'Save yourself.' "

Then he told her about receiving the Commissioner's letter, the authorization of indefinite leave of absence, and his most recent conversation with Thorsen.

"I'm glad you recommended Dorfman," she nodded happily. "I like him. And I think he deserves a chance."

"Yes. The problem is making a lieutenant even an *acting* commander of a precinct. And of course they can't suddenly promote him without possibly alerting Broughton. Well . . . we'll see what happens. Meanwhile, I'll be getting copies of all the Operation Lombard reports tomorrow."

"Edward, it doesn't sound like you have much to go on."

"No, not much. Thorsen says that so far Operation Lombard has drawn a blank. They don't have any description of a possible suspect, how he killed, or why he killed."

"You say 'he.' Couldn't it have been a woman?"

"Possibly, but the probability percentages are against it. Women murder with gun, knife, and pistol. They rarely bludgeon. And when they do, it's usually when the victim is asleep."

"Then you're really starting from scratch?"

"Well . . . I have two things. They don't amount to much and I expect Chief Pauley has them too. Lombard was a tall man. I'd guess about six feet. Now look . . ." Delaney rose to his feet and looked around the hospital room. He found a magazine, rolled it up tightly, and gripped one end. "Now I'm the killer with a hammer, a pipe, or maybe a long spike. I'm striking down at the victim's skull." He raised the magazine above his head and brought it down viciously. "See that? I'll do it again. Watch the position of my right arm." Again he raised the magazine and brought it down in a feigned crushing blow. "What did you see?"

"Your arm wasn't extended. Your right arm was bent. The top of the magazine was only about six inches above your head."

"Correct. That's the way a man would normally strike. When you're hammering in a nail, you don't raise your arm to its full length above your head; you keep your elbow bent the better to control the accuracy of the blow. You raise your arm just high enough to provide what you estimate to be sufficient force. It's an unconscious skill, based on experience. To drive a carpet tack, you might raise a hammer only an inch or two. To drive a spike, you'd raise the hammer to your head level or higher."

"Was Lombard killed with a hammer?"

"Ferguson says no. But it was obviously something swung with sufficient force to penetrate his brain to a depth of three to four inches. I haven't seen Ferguson's report yet."

"Could the killer be lefthanded?"

"Could be. But probability is against it, unless the nature and position of the wound indicate otherwise, and then it might be due to the position of the victim at the moment of impact."

"There are so many possibilities."

"There surely are. Barbara, are you getting tired?"

"Oh no. You can't stop now. Edward, I don't understand the significance of what you just showed me—how a man strikes with his elbow bent."

"Just that Lombard was about six feet tall. If the killer raised the weapon about six inches above his own head—which is about the limit any man would raise a tool or weapon before striking downward—and the puncture was low on Lombard's skull (not so far down as to be in that hollow where the spine joins the skull, but up from that toward the crown of the skull), then I'd guess the killer to be approximately of Lombard's height or maybe a few inches taller. Yes, it's a guess. But based, it seems to me, on what little physical evidence is available. And I've got to start guessing *somewhere.*"

"You said you had two things, Edward. What's the other?"

"Well . . . I worked this out the morning of the murder. While I was on the scene. Just to satisfy my own curiosity, I guess. What bothered me most about the murder was why a man of Lombard's size and strength, with his awareness of street crime, alone on a deserted street at midnight, why he would let an assailant come up behind him and chop him down without making any apparent effort to defend himself. Here's how I think it was done . . ."

He acted it out for her. First he was Lombard, in his overcoat, walking briskly around the hospital room, head turning side to side as he inspected entrances and outside lobbies. "Then I see a man coming toward me from York Avenue. Coming *toward* me." Delaney-Lombard, explaining as he performed, peeked ahead, watching the approaching figure. He slowed his steps, ready to defend himself or run to safety if danger threatened. But then he smiled, reassured by the stranger's appearance. He moved aside to let the smiling stranger pass, and then . . .

"Now I'm the killer," Delaney told a wide-eyed Barbara. He took off his overcoat and folded it over his left arm. Beneath the coat, hidden, the rolled up magazine was grasped in his left hand. His right arm swung free as he marched briskly around the hospital room. "I see the man I want to kill. I smile and continue to walk quickly like a resident of the block anxious to get home."

Delaney-killer turned his head as he passed Lombard. Then his right hand swooped under the coat. The rolled-up magazine was transferred. At the same time Delaney-killer whirled and went up on his toes. Now he was behind the victim. The magazine whistled down. The entire action took a few seconds, no longer.

"Then I bend over—"

"Get him!" Barbara cried. "Edward, get him! Get him!"

He straightened in astonishment, riven by the hatred and venom in her voice. He rushed to the bed, tried to take her in his arms, but she would not be comforted.

"Get him!" she repeated, and it was a curse. "You can do it, Edward. You're the only one who can do it. Get him! Promise me? It's not right. Life is too precious. Get him! Get him!"

And even after he calmed her, a nurse had been summoned, a sedative had been administered, Barbara was sleeping, and he left the hospital, still he heard that virulent "Get him! Get him!" and vowed he would.

5

Xerox Copies of the Operation Lombard reports constituted a bundle of almost 500 sheets of typed papers, official forms, photostats, transcriptions of tape recordings, signed statements, etc. In addition, there was a separate envelope of more than 30 photo copies: Lombard in death and in life, his wife, mother, two brothers, political and business associates, and close friends. The dead man and his wife had been childless.

Captain Delaney, impressed with this mass of material spread out on the desk in his study, and realizing the urgency with which Operation Lombard was working, set out to organize the documents into manila folders marked Physical Evidence, Personal History, Family, Business (Lombard had been an active partner in a Brooklyn law firm), Politics, and Miscellaneous.

It took him almost two hours to get the material filed in some kind of rough order. Then he mixed a rye highball, put his feet up on the desk, and began reading. By two in the morning he had read every report and stared at every photo in every file. He was doubly impressed with the thoroughness of Broughton's investigation, but as far as first impressions went, Ivar Thorsen was right: there was nothing—no leads, no hints, no mysteries at all—except who killed Frank Lombard.

He started his second reading, going slower this time and making notes on a pad of long yellow legal notepaper. He also set aside a few documents for a third reading and study. Dawn was lightening the study windows when he closed the final folder. He rose to his feet, stretched and yawned, put his hands on his hips and bent his torso backward until his spine cracked.

Then he went into the kitchen and drank a large glass of tomato juice with a lemon wedge squeezed into it. He made a carafe of three cups of instant coffee, black, and carried that into the study along with a dry and stale bagel.

He consulted his notes and, sipping coffee, read for the third time Dr. Sanford Ferguson's medical report. It was one of Ferguson's usual meticulous autopsies; the eight-page statement included two sketches showing the outside wound in actual size and a profile outline of the human skull showing the location and shape of the penetration. It looked like an elongated isosceles triangle. The outside wound was roughly circular in shape, slightly larger than a quarter.

The essential paragraph of the report was as follows:

"The blow caused a penetrating wound, fracturing the right occipital bone, lacerating the dura, piercing the right occipital lobe. Laceration of the cerebellum caused hemorrhaging with resultant rupture into the posterior fossa and 4th ventrical causing acute compression of the brain stem with subsequent death."

Delaney made several additional notes on the autopsy report. He had questions he knew could only be answered in a personal interview with Ferguson. How he would explain to the doctor his interest in the Lombard homicide was a problem he'd face when he came to it.

His other notes concerned the interviews with the widow, Mrs. Clara Lombard. She had been interviewed five times by three different detectives. Delaney nodded approvingly at Chief Pauley's professionalism. It was standard detective procedure: you send three different detectives for the first three interviews. Then the three get together with their chief, discuss the subject's personality, and select the detective who has established the closest rapport with her, the one she feels most *simpatia* with. He returns for the two final interviews.

Delaney began to get a picture of the widow from the typed reports. (The first three were transcriptions made from tape recordings.) Mrs. Clara Lombard seemed to be a flighty, feather-brained women, trying hard to appear devastated by the tragedy of her husband's violent death, but still capable of infantile laughter, jokes of a dubious nature, sudden inquiries about insurance money, questions about probating the will, illogical threats of legal action against New York City, and statements that could only be construed as outright flirtation.

Delaney wasn't interested in all that; careful investigation showed that although Clara was a very social woman—a happy party-goer with or without her husband—she had no boyfriend, and no one, not even her women friends, even hinted she might have been unfaithful.

The portion of her testimony that interested Delaney most was concerned with Frank Lombard's wallet. That damned wallet irritated the Captain . . . its position near the body . . . the fact that it had been deliberately removed from the hip pocket . . . it was lying open . . . it was still full of money . . .

To Delaney's surprise, in only one interview had Mrs. Lombard been handed a detailed inventory of the wallet. This document was included in the Physical Evidence file. Clara had been asked if, to her knowledge, anything was missing. She had replied no, she thought all her late husband's identification and credit cards were there, and the sum of money—over two hundred dollars—was what he customarily carried. Even two keys, one to his home, one to his office—in a "secret pocket" in the wallet—were there.

Delaney didn't accept her statement. How many wives could tell you exactly what their husbands carried in their wallets? How many husbands could list exactly what their wife's purse contained? As a matter of fact, how many men knew exactly how much money they had in their own wallets? To test this,

Delaney thought a moment and guessed he had fifty-six dollars in the wallet in his hip. Then he took it out and counted. He had forty-two—and wondered where his money was going.

The only other Operation Lombard report that interested him was an interview with the victim's grieving mother. Delaney read this transcription again. As he had suspected, Mrs. Sophia Lombard lived in a converted brownstone between the East River and the point where her son's body had been found.

Mrs. Lombard had been questioned—and very adroitly, Delaney acknowledged; that was Chief Pauley's doing—on the circumstances of her son's visits to her. Did he come every week? The same night every week? The same time every night? In other words, was it a regular, established routine? Did he call beforehand? How did he travel over from Brooklyn?

The answers were disappointing and perplexing. Frank Lombard had no regular schedule for dining with his mother. He came to see her when he could. Sometimes two weeks, sometimes a month would elapse before he could make it. But he was a good boy, Mrs. Sophia Lombard assured her interrogator; he called every day. On the day he could come to dinner, he would call before noon so Mrs. Lombard could go out and shop in the markets along First Avenue for the things he liked.

Lombard didn't drive his car over from Brooklyn because parking space was hard to find near his mother's apartment. He would take the subway, and a bus or taxi from the subway station. He didn't like to walk on the streets at nights. He always left for his Brooklyn home before midnight.

Did Mrs. Clara Lombard ever accompany her husband to his mother's home for dinner?

"No," Mrs. Sophia Lombard said shortly. And reading that reply, Delaney smiled, understanding the discord that must have existed in *that* family.

Delaney replaced the reports in their folders, and put all the Operation Lombard file in a small safe in the corner of the study. As he well knew, an experienced "can man" could be into that in one minute flat. And two inexperienced thieves could carry it out between them to sledge it open later.

His eyes were sandy and his bones ached. It was almost seven a.m. He dumped the cold coffee, went upstairs, undressed and rolled into bed. Something was nagging at his mind, something he had read in the Operation Lombard reports. But that had happened to him frequently: a lead sensed but not recognized. It didn't worry him; he tried not to think about it. He knew from experience that it would come to him eventually, sliding into his mind like a remembered name or a tune recalled. He set the alarm for eight-thirty, closed his eyes and was instantly asleep.

He arrived at the precinct house a little after nine a.m. The Desk Sergeant was a policewoman, the second of her rank in New York to be assigned to such duty. He went over to the log with her, and asked questions. She was a tall, powerfully built woman with what he termed to himself, without knowing why, a *thunderous* body. In truth, he was intimidated by her, but could not deny her efficiency. The book was in order; nothing had been neglected that could have been done—a sad, sad list of drunks, missing persons, beaten wives, stolen welfare checks, mistreated children, burglaries, Peeping Toms, prostitutes, dying oldsters, homosexuals, breaking-and-entering, exhibitionists . . . People. But the moon was full, and Delaney knew what that meant.

He climbed the creaking wooden steps to his office and, on the landing, met Detective Lieutenant Jeri Fernandez who was, or had been, in command of detectives assigned to the 251st.

"Morning, Captain," Fernandez said glumly.

"Good morning, lieutenant," Delaney said. He looked at the man sympathetically. "Having a rough time, aren't you?"

"Oh shit!" Fernandez burst out. "Half my men are gone already. The others will be gone within a week. Okay, that's one thing. But the paper work! All our open cases have to be transferred to the proper unit covering this precinct. Jesus, it's a mess."

"What did you get?"

"I drew a Safe, Loft and Truck Division in midtown," Fernandez said disgustedly. "It covers four precincts including the Garment Center. How does that grab you? I'm second in command, and we'll be getting dicks from all over Manhattan. It'll take us at least a year to set up our snitches. What great brain dreamed up this idea?"

Delaney knew how Fernandez felt. The man was a conscientious, efficient, but unimaginative detective. He had done a good job in the 251st, training his men, being hard when he had to be hard and soft when he had to be soft. Now they were breaking up his crew and farming them out to specialized divisions. And Fernandez himself would now be number two man under a detective captain. He had a right to his anger.

"I would have guessed Broughton would have grabbed you for Operation Lombard," Delaney said.

"Not me," Fernandez said with a sour grin. "I ain't white enough."

They nodded and separated. Delaney went on to his office, marveling how quickly a man's prejudices and record spread throughout the Department. More fool Broughton, he thought; Fernandez could have been a big help. Unimaginative he might have been, but when it came to dull, foot-flattening routine, he was excellent. The important thing was to know how to use men, to take advantage of their particular talents and the best in them.

The moment he was at his desk he called the hospital. The head floor nurse told him his wife was down in the lab, having more X-ray plates taken, but she was doing "as well as can be expected." Trying to conceal his distaste for that particular phrase, Delaney thanked her and said he'd call later.

Then he called Dr. Sanford Ferguson and, unexpectedly, was put through to him immediately at his office.

"That you, Edward?"

"Yes. Can we get together?"

"How's Barbara?"

"Doing as well as can be expected."

"I seem to recognize the words. Is it about Barbara you want to see me?"

"No. The Lombard homicide."

"Oh? I was glad to hear you hadn't retired. Now it's an indefinite leave of absence."

"News travels fast."

"It was on the Telex about ten minutes ago. Edward, what's this about Lombard? I thought Broughton was handling it."

"He is. But I want to see you, to talk to you. Can you make it?"

"Well . . ." Ferguson was cautious, and Delaney didn't blame him. "Look, I've got to go up to 34th Street today. It's my sister's birthday, and I want to get her something. At Macy's. Any suggestions?"

"When in doubt, a gift certificate."

"Won't work. I know her. She wants something personal."

"A silk scarf. That's what I always buy for Barbara. She's got enough silk scarves to make a parachute."

"Good idea. Well then, how about lunch?"

"Fine."

"I know a good chop house near Macy's. Do you like mutton chops?"

"Hate them."

"Idiot. That heavy, gamy taste . . . nothing like it."

"Can I get a broiled kidney?"

"Of course."

"Then let's have lunch at your chop house."

"Good. You get there at twelve-thirty. I'll be finished shopping by then and will be there before you. Ask the head waiter for my table. He knows me. It will be in the bar, not the main dining room. All right?"

"Of course. Thank you."

"For what? I haven't done anything for you yet."

"You will."

"Will I? In that case you're paying for the lunch."

"Done," Captain Edward X. Delaney said.

Ferguson gave him the address of the chop house and they hung up.

"Oysters!" Ferguson boomed happily. "I definitely recommend the oysters. The horseradish is freshly ground. Then I'll have the mutton chop."

"Very good, sir," the waiter said.

"Oysters for me also," Delaney nodded. "Then I'll have the broiled kidney. What comes with that?"

"Home-fries and salad, sir."

"Skip the potatoes, please. Just the salad. Oil and vinegar."

"I'll have everything," Ferguson cried, and drained half his martini.

"What did you buy your sister?" Delaney asked.

"A silk scarf. What else? Come on, Edward, what's this all about? You're on leave of absence."

"Do you really want to know?"

Dr. Sanford Ferguson was suddenly sober and quiet. He stared at Delaney a long moment. "No," he said finally. "I really don't want to know. Except . . . will my name be brought into it?"

"I swear to you—no."

"That's good enough for me."

Their oysters were brought, and they looked down at them, beaming. They went through the business with the horseradish sauce and the hot stuff. They swallowed, looked at each other, groaned with pleasure.

"All right," Ferguson said. "What do you want?"

"About your report on the Lombard—"

"How did you get my report?"

Delaney looked at him steadily. "You said you didn't want to know."

"That's right; I don't. All right, what about the report?"

"I have a few questions." Delaney took a short list out of his side pocket, put it on the cloth before him, donned his heavy glasses, consulted it, then leaned toward Ferguson.

"Doctor," he said earnestly, "your official reports are most complete. I don't deny it. But they're couched in medical language. As they should be, of course," he added hastily.

"So?"

"I have some questions about what your medical terms mean."

"Edward, you're jiving me."

"Well . . . really what the significance is."

"That's better," Ferguson smiled. "You can read a PM as well as a third-year medical student."

"Yes. Also, I happen to know, doctor, that you include in your official reports only that which you objectively observe and which could be substantiated by any other capable surgeon doing the identical post-mortem. I also know that in an autopsy—in *any* investigation—there are impressions, feelings, hunches—call them what you like—that can never be part of an official report because the physical evidence doesn't exist. And its those impressions, feelings and hunches that I want from you."

Ferguson slipped a dipped oyster into his mouth, swallowed, rolled his eyes.

"You're a bastard, Edward," he said amiably. "You really are a bastard. You'll use anyone, won't you?"

"Yes," Delaney nodded. "I'll use anyone. Any time."

"Let's start from word one," Ferguson said, busily stirring his oyster sauce. "Let's start with head wounds. Much experience?"

"No. Not much."

"Edward, the human skull and the human brain are tougher beyond your comprehension. Ever read a detective novel or see a movie where a man has a single bullet fired into his head and dies instantly? Practically impossible. I've had cases of victims with five bullets in their heads who lived. They were vegetables, true, but they lived. Three years ago I had a would-be suicide who fired a bullet at his head with a low-calibre revolver. Twenty-two, I think. The slug bounced off his skull and hit the ceiling. Literally. Commit suicide by firing a bullet into your temple? Forget it. The slug could pass completely through, come out the other side, and you still wouldn't be dead. You might live hours, weeks, or years. Maybe you couldn't talk, or move, or control your bowels, but you'd be alive. How are your oysters, Edward?"

"Very good. Yours?"

"Marvelous. There's only one way of committing sure suicide—instantaneous suicide—by a gunshot to the head. That's by using a pistol or revolver of reasonably heavy calibre, say a thirty-eight at least—a rifle or shotgun would do as well, of course—put the muzzle deep into your mouth aimed at the back of your head, close your lips and teeth firmly about the barrel, pull the trigger, and splatter your brains onto the opposing wall. Some of these little oysterettes, Edward?"

"Yes, thank you."

"Now about the Lombard homicide. The entry was made from the back, low on the crown. About halfway to where the spine joins the skull. The only other spot where death might be instantaneous."

"You think the killer had a surgeon's knowledge?"

"Oh God, no," Ferguson said, signaling the waiter to remove their emptied oyster plates. "Yes, to hit that spot deliberately would require a surgeon's experience. But the victim would have to be on an operating table. No killer swinging a weapon violently could hope to hit it. It was luck. The killer's luck, not Lombard's luck."

"Was death instantaneous?" Delaney asked.

"Close to it. If not instant, then within a few seconds. A half-inch to the right or left and the man might have lived for hours or weeks."

"It was that close?"

"I told you the human skull and brain are much tougher than most people realize. Do you know how many ex-soldiers are walking around today with hunks of shrapnel in their brains? They live normally, except for occasional crushing headaches, but we can't operate. And they'll live out their normal lives and die from smoking too many cigarettes or eating too much cheese."

The mutton chop, broiled kidney, and salads were served. Ferguson got his home fries, a big plate with plenty of onions. After consultation with the head waiter, who was 343 years old, they ordered a bottle of heavy burgundy.

"To get back to Lombard," Delaney said, digging into his broiled kidney, "was it really a circular wound?"

"Oh you're so smart," Ferguson said without rancor. "You're so fucking smart. My report stated it *appeared* to be a circular penetration. But I had the impression it could have been triangular. Or even square. Look, Edward, you've never probed a brain penetration. You think it's like pounding a spike into modeling clay, and then you pull out the spike and you've got a nice, clean perfect cavity? It's nothing like that. The wound fills up. Brain matter presses in. There is blood. Bits of bone. Hair. All kinds of crap. And you expect me to—How's the kidney?"

"Delicious," Delaney said. "I've been here before, but I forgot how much bacon they give you."

"The mutton chop is fine," Ferguson said, dipping into his little dish of applesauce. "I'm really enjoying this. But about that Lombard wound . . . In addition to the impression I had that the opening was not necessarily circular in shape, I also had the feeling that the penetration curved downward."

"Curved?"

"Yes. Like a limp cone. The tip of the weapon lower than the shaft. A curve. Like a hard-on just beginning to go soft. You understand?"

"Yes. But why are you so uncertain about the shape of the wound and the shape of the penetration? I know what you wrote, but what do you guess?"

"I think, I *guess* that Lombard fell forward with such force that it wrenched the weapon out of the killer's hand. And that the killer then bent forward and twisted his tool or weapon to remove it from Lombard's skull. If the spike was triangular or square, the twisting would result in a roughly circular shape."

"And it would mean the weapon was valuable to the killer," Delaney said. "He took the time to recover it. It was valuable intrinsically, or valuable because it might be traced to the killer. Murderers who use a hammer or pipe or rock usually wear gloves and leave the weapon behind."

"Beautiful," Dr. Ferguson said, draining his wine. "I love to listen to you think."

"I'm glad it wasn't a hammer," Delaney said. "I never really believed it was."

"Why not?"

"I've handled three hammer cases. In two of them the handle broke. In the third, the head snapped off."

"So you knew how tough the human skull is? But you let me talk."

"That's the name of the game. Anything else?"

"What else? Nothing else. It's all smoke. On the evidence, the penetration was circular, but it might have been triangular. It might have been square. It hit the one spot that killed the man instantly. Do I think the killer has surgical knowledge? No. It was a lucky hit."

"Dessert?" Delaney asked.

"Just coffee for me, thanks."

"Two coffees, please," Delaney ordered. "Any ideas, any guesses, any wild suggestions at all as to what the weapon might have been?"

"None whatsoever."

"Was there anything inside the wound you didn't expect to find? Anything that wasn't in your report?"

Ferguson looked at him sternly a moment, then relaxed and laughed. "You never give up, do you? There were traces of oil."

"Oil? What kind of oil?"

"Not enough for analysis. But undoubtedly hair oil. The rest of his hair was heavily oiled, so I assume the oil in the wound came from the hair driven into it."

"Anything else?"

"Yes. Since you're paying, I'll have a brandy."

After Ferguson took a cab back to his office, Delaney walked slowly toward Sixth Avenue. He realized he was only a few blocks from the flower market and sauntered down there. He was in no hurry. He knew from experience that each investigation had a pace of its own. Some shouted of a quick solution and were wrapped up in hours. Others had the feel of slow growth and the need for time. The Lombard homicide was one of those. He consoled himself that Broughton, who *was* in a hurry, was getting nowhere. But was he doing any better? As Dr. Ferguson had said, it was all smoke.

He found what he was looking for in the third flower shop he visited: violets, out of season. They were the flowers with which he had courted Barbara. They were sold by street vendors in those days, old ladies with baskets next to old men selling chestnuts. He would buy a bunch for Barbara and ask, "Fresh roasted violets, lady?" She was always kind enough to laugh. Now he bought the last two bunches the store had and took a cab to the hospital.

But when he tiptoed into her room she was sleeping peacefully and he didn't have the heart to awaken her. He unwrapped the violets and looked around the room for something to put them in, but there was nothing. Finally he sat in the straight chair, his uniformed bulk overflowing it. He grasped the tender violets in his big fist and waited quietly, watching his wife sleep. He glanced once at the dusty windows. The sharp November sunlight was diluted and softened.

Perhaps, the sad, hunkering man wondered, a marriage was like one of those stained glass windows he had seen in a modest village church in France. From the outside, the windows were almost opaque with the dirt and grime of centuries. But when you went inside, and saw the sunlight leaping through, diffused by the dust, the colors struck into your eye and heart with their boldness and purity, their youth and liveliness.

His marriage to Barbara, he supposed, must seem dull and dusty to an outsider. But seen from within, as father of a family, it was all bright and beguiling, touching and, finally, holy and mysterious. He watched his wife sleep and *willed* his strength to her, making her whole and laughing again. Then, unable to endure his thoughts, he stood and placed the violets on her bedside table with a scribbled note: "Fresh roasted violets, lady?"

When he got back to his office, Dorfman was waiting for him with a sheet of paper torn from the telex.

"Captain," he said in a choked voice, and Delaney was afraid he might weep, "is this—"

"Yes, lieutenant, it's correct. As of now, I'm on leave of absence. Come on in and let's talk about it."

Dorfman followed him inside and took the scarred chair next to Delaney's desk.

"Captain, I had no idea your wife was so ill."

"Well, as far as I can guess, it's going to be a long haul, and I wanted to spend as much time with her as possible."

"Is there anything I can do?"

"Thank you, no. Well, perhaps there is something. You might call her. I have a feeling she'd like to see you. Whenever you can spare the time."

"I'll call her right away," Dofrman cried.

"Wait a few hours. I've just come from there, and she's sleeping."

"I'll call just before my watch ends. Then if she wants to see me, I can go right over. What can I bring—flowers, candy, what?"

"Oh nothing, thanks. She has everything she needs."

"Maybe a cake?" Dorfman said. "A nice cake. She can share it with the nurses. Nurses love cake."

"Fine," Delaney smiled. "I think she'd like a cake from you."

"Captain," Dorfman mourned, his long horse-face sagging again, "I suppose this means we'll be getting an Acting Captain?"

"Yes."

"Do you have any idea who it will be, sir?"

Delaney debated a moment, briefly ashamed of manipulating a man so honest and sincere. But it was the sensible thing to do, to cement Dorfman's trust and affection.

"I recommended you for the job, lieutenant," he said quietly.

Dorfman's pale blue eyes widened in shock.

"Me?" he gasped. Then, "Me?" he repeated with real pleasure

"Wait a minute," Delaney held up his hand. "I recommended you, but I don't think you'll get it. Not because your file isn't good enough or you couldn't handle the job, but your rank is against you. This precinct calls for a captain or deputy inspector. You understand that?"

"Oh sure, Captain. But I certainly do appreciate your recommending me."

"Well, as I said, I don't think you're going to get it. So if I were you, I wouldn't mention it to a soul. Particularly your wife. Then, if they turn you down, it'll just be your disappointment, and no one will think they considered you and passed you over, for one reason or another."

"I won't mention it, sir."

Delaney considered whether or not to hint to Dorfman the services as a contact he might be asked to provide in the Captain's investigation of the Lombard homicide. Then he decided against it. This wasn't the right time, and he had given the man enough to think about.

"In any event," Delaney said, "if you get the job or don't get it, remember I'm still living next door and if there is ever anything I can help you with, don't hesitate to give me a call or ring my bell. I mean that. Don't get the idea you'll be bothering me or annoying me. You won't. As a matter of fact, I'd appreciate knowing what's going on over here. This is my precinct and, with luck, I hope to be back in command some day."

"I hope so too, Captain," Dorfman said fervently. "I really do hope so." He rose and stuck out a hand. "Best of luck, sir, and I hope Mrs. Delaney is feeling better real soon."

"Thank you, lieutenant."

After Dorfman left, Delaney sat swinging back and forth slowly in his swivel chair. Was a man as gentle and sensitive as the lieutenant capable of administering a busy precinct in the New York Police Department? It was a job that occasionally demanded ruthlessness, a certain amount of Broughton-type insensibility. But then, Delaney reflected, ruthlessness could be an acquired trait. Even an assumed trait. He certainly hoped *he* had not been born with it. Dorfman could learn to be ruthless when necessary, just as he, Delaney, had learned. He did it, but he didn't enjoy it. Perhaps that was the essential difference between Broughton and him: he didn't enjoy it.

Then he slammed his swivel chair level and reached into his bottom desk drawer to haul out a long card file. The grey metal box was dented and battered. Delaney opened it and began searching for what he wanted. The cards were filed by subject matter.

Soon after Patrolman Edward X. Delaney was promoted to detective third grade—more years ago than he cared to remember—he became aware that despite the enormous resources of the New York Police Department, he frequently came up against problems that could only be solved, or moved toward solution, by civilian experts.

There was, for instance, a retired detective, delighted to cooperate with his former colleagues, who had established and maintained what was probably the world's largest collection of laundry marks. There was an 84-year-old spinster who still operated a shop on Madison Avenue. She could glance at an unusual button you showed her, and name the material, age, and source. There was a Columbia University professor whose specialty was crickets and grasshoppers. There was an amateur archeologist, all of whose "digs" had been made within city limits. He could examine rocks and soil and place them within a few blocks of their origin. A Bronx recluse was one of the world's foremost authorities on ancient writing, and could read hieroglyphics as quickly as Delaney read English.

All these experts were willing—nay, *eager* to cooperate with police investigations. It was a welcome interruption of their routine, gave them a chance to exhibit their expertise in a good cause. The only problem was shutting them up; they all did seem to talk excessively, like anyone whose hobby is his vocation. But eventually they divulged the information required.

Delaney had them all in his card file, carefully added to and maintained for almost twenty years. Now he flipped through the cards until he found the one he was looking for. It was headed: "Weapons, antique and unusual." The man's name was Christopher Langley, an assistant curator of the Arms and Armor Collection of the Metropolitan Museum of Art. (The card following his was "Weapons, modern," and that man was a retired colonel of Marines.)

Delaney called the Metropolitan (the number on the card), asked for the Arms and Armor Section, and then asked for Christopher Langley.

"I'm sorry, sir," a young, feminine voice replied. "Mr. Langley is no longer with us. He retired about three years ago."

"Oh. I'm sorry to hear that. Do you happen to know if he's living in New York?"

"Yes sir, I believe he is."

"Then he'll be in the phone book?"

There was a moment's silence.

"Well . . . no sir. I believe Mr. Langley has an unlisted number."

"Could you tell me what it is? I'm a personal friend."

"I'm sorry, sir. We cannot reveal that information."

He was tempted to say, "This is Captain Edward X. Delaney, New York Police Department, and this is official business." Or, he could easily get the number from the phone company, as an official police inquiry. But then he thought better of it. The fewer people who knew of his activities, the better.

"My name is Edward Delaney," he said. "I wonder if you'd be kind enough to call Mr. Langley at the number you have, tell him I called, and if he wishes to contact me, he can reach me at this number." He then gave her the phone number of the 251st Precinct.

"Yes sir," she said. "I can do that."

"Thank you."

He hung up, wondering what percentage of his waking hours was spent on the telephone, trying to complete a call, or waiting for a call. He sat patiently, hoping Langley was in. He was: Delaney's desk phone rang within five minutes.

"Delaney!" Christopher Langley cried in his remarkably boyish voice (the man was pushing 70). "Gosh, I asked for *Lieutenant* Delaney and your operator said it was *Captain* Delaney now. Congratulations! When did that happen?"

"Oh, a few years ago. How are you, sir?"

"Physically I'm fine but, gee, I'm bored."

"I heard you had retired."

"Had to do it, you know. Give the young men a chance—eh? The first year I dabbled around with silly things. I've become a marvelous gourmet cook. But my gosh, how many *canetons à l'orange* can you make? Now I'm bored, bored, bored. That's why I was so delighted to hear from you."

"Well, I need your help, sir, and was wondering if you could spare me a few hours?"

"As long as you like, dear boy, as long as you like. Is it a big caper?"

Delaney laughed, knowing Langley's fondness for detective fiction.

"Yes sir. A very big caper. The biggest. Murder most foul."

"Oh gosh," Langley gasped. "That's marvelous! Captain, can you join me for dinner tonight? Then afterwards we can have brandy and talk and you can tell me all about it and how I can help."

"Oh I couldn't put you to that—"

"No trouble at all!" Langley cried. "Gee, it'll be wonderful seeing you again, and I can demonstrate my culinary skills for you."

"Well . . ." Delaney said, thinking of his evening visit to Barbara, "it will have to be a little later. Is nine o'clock too late?"

"Not at all, not at all! I much prefer dining at a late hour. As soon as I hang up, I'll dash out and do some shopping." He gave Delaney his home address.

"Fine," the Captain said. "See you at nine, sir."

"Gosh, this is keen!" Langley said. "We'll have frogs' legs sautéed in butter and garlic, *petits pois* with just a hint of bacon and onion, and *gratin de pommes de terre aux anchois*. And for dessert, perhaps a *crème pralinée*. How does that sound to you?"

"Fine," Delaney repeated faintly. "Just fine."

He hung up. Oh God, he thought, there goes my diet, and wondered what happened when sautéed frogs' legs met broiled kidney.

A young woman was walking toward Central Park, between Madison and Fifth Avenues, pushing a baby carriage. Suddenly a wooden rod, about nine inches long, was projecting from her breast. She slumped to her knees, falling forward, and only the fast scramble of a passerby prevented the baby carriage from bouncing into Fifth Avenue traffic.

Delaney, who was then a detective lieutenant working out of Homicide East (as it was then called) arrived on the scene shortly after the woman died. He joined the circle of patrolmen and ambulance attendants staring down incredulously at the woman with the wooden spike driven through her breast, like some modern vampire.

Within an hour they had the missile identified as a quarrel from a crossbow. Delaney went up to the Arms and Armor Department of the Metropolitan Museum of Art, seeking to learn more about crossbows, their operation, range, and velocity of the bolts. That was how he met Christopher Langley.

From the information supplied by the assistant curator, Delaney was able to solve the case, to his satisfaction at least, but it was never prosecuted. The boy responsible, who had shot the bolt at a stranger from a townhouse window across the street, was the son of a wealthy family. They got him out of the country and into a school in Switzerland. He had never returned to the United States. The District Attorney did not feel Delaney's circumstantial evidence was sufficiently strong to warrant extradition proceedings. The case was still carried as open.

But Delaney had never forgotten Christopher Langley's enthusiastic cooperation, and his name was added to the detective's "expert file." Delaney frequently recalled a special memory of the skinny little man. Langley was showing him through a Museum gallery, deserted except for a grinning guard who evidently knew what to expect.

Suddenly the assistant curator plucked a two-handed sword from the wall, a sixteenth-century German sword as long as he was tall, and fell into a fighting stance. The blade whirled about his head in circles of flashing steel. He chopped, slashed, parried, thrust.

"That's how they did it," he said calmly, and handed the long sword to Delaney.

The detective took it, and it almost clattered to the floor. Delaney estimated its weight as thirty pounds. The wiry Christopher Langley had spun it like a feather.

When he opened the door to his apartment on the fifth floor of a converted brownstone on East 89th Street, he was exactly as Delaney remembered him. In another age he would have been called a fop or dandy. Now he was a well-preserved, alert, exquisitely dressed 70-year-old bachelor with the complexion of a maiden and a small yellow daisy in the lapel of his grey flannel Norfolk jacket.

"Captain!" he said with pleasure, holding out both hands. "Gosh, this *is* nice!"

It was a small, comfortable apartment the ex-curator had retired to. He occupied the entire top floor: living room, bedroom, bath, and a remarkably large kitchen. There was a glass skylight over the living room which, Delaney was glad to see, had been fitted with a guard of iron bars.

Langley took his hat and overcoat and hung them away.

"Not in uniform tonight, Captain?"

"No. As a matter of fact, I am not on active duty. I'm on leave of absence."

"Oh?" Langley asked curiously. "For long?"

"I don't know."

"Well . . . do sit down. There—that's a comfortable chair. Now what can I bring you? Cocktail? Highball?"

"Oh, I don't—"

"I have a new Italian aperitif I'm trying for the first time. It's quite dry. Very good on the rocks with a twist of lemon."

"Sounds fine. Are you having one?"

"Of course. Just take me a minute."

Langley bustled into the kitchen, and the Captain looked around. The walls of the living room were almost solid bookcases with deep, high shelves to accommodate volumes on antique weaponry, most of them out-size "art books" illustrated with color plates.

Only two actual weapons were on display: an Italian arquebus of the 17th century with exquisitely detailed silver chasing, and an African warclub. The head was intricately carved stone. Delaney rose to his feet and went over to inspect it. He was turning it in his hands when Langley came back with their drinks.

"Mongo tribe," he said. "The Congo. A ceremonial ax never used in combat. The balance is bad but I like the carving."

"It's beautiful."

"Isn't it? Dinner in about ten minutes. Meanwhile, let's relax. Would you like a cigarette?"

"No, thank you."

"Good. Smoking dulls the palate. Do you know what the secret of good French cooking is?"

"What?"

"A clear palate and butter. Not oil, but butter. The richest, creamiest butter you can find."

Delaney's heart sank. The old man caught his look of dismay and laughed.

"Don't worry, Captain. I've never believed you had to eat a lot of one dish to enjoy it. Small portions and several dishes—that's best."

He was as good as his word; the portions were small. But Delaney decided it was one of the best dinners he had ever eaten and told the host so. Langley beamed with pleasure.

"A little more dessert? There is more, you know."

"Not for me. But I'll have another cup of coffee, if you have it."

"Of course."

They had dined at a plain oak table covered with a black burlap cloth, a table, Delaney was sure, doubled as Langley's desk. Now they both pushed back far enough to cross their legs, have a cigarette, drink coffee, sip the strong Portuguese brandy Langley had served.

"About this—" Delaney had started, but just then the apartment doorbell rang, in the familiar "shave and a haircut, two bits" rhythm, and the Captain was surprised to see Langley's face go white.

"Oh gracious," the old man whispered. "It's her again. The Widow Zimmerman! She lives right below me."

He bounced to his feet, trotted across the room, looked through the peephole, then unlocked and opened the door.

"Ahh," he said. "Good evening, Mrs. Zimmerman."

Delaney had a clear view of her from where he sat. She was perhaps 60, taller than Langley by about six inches, certainly heavier than he by fifty pounds. She balanced a beehive of teased brassy hair above her plump face, and her bare arms looked like something you might see on a butcher's block. She was so heavily girdled that her body seemed hewn from a single chunk of wood; when she walked, her legs appeared to move only from the knees down.

"Oh, I do hope I'm not disturbing you," she simpered, looking at the Captain boldly over Langley's shoulder. "I know you've got company. I heard you go out to shop and then come back. I heard your bell ring and your guest arrive. One of your fantastic foreign dinners, I'm sure. Now I just happened to bake a fresh prune strudel today, and I thought you and your guest might enjoy a nice piece for dessert, and here it is."

She held out the napkin-covered dish to Langley; he took it with the tips of his fingers.

"That's very kind of you, Mrs. Zimmerman. Won't you come—"

"Oh, I won't interrupt. I wouldn't think of it."

She waited expectantly, but Langley did not repeat his invitation.

"I'll just run along," the Widow Zimmerman said, pouting at Delaney.

"Thank you for the strudel."

"My pleasure. Enjoy."

She gave him a little-girl smile. He closed the door firmly behind her, bolted and chained it, then put his ear to the panel and listened as her steps receded down the stairs. He came back to the table and whispered to Delaney . . .

"A dreadful woman! Continually bringing me food. I've asked her not to, but she does. I'm perfectly capable of cooking for myself. Been doing it for fifty years. And the food she brings! Strudel and chopped liver and stuffed derma and pickled herring. Gracious! I can't throw it away because she might see it in the garbage cans and be insulted. So I have to wrap it like a gift package and carry it three or four blocks away and dump it into a litter basket. She's such a problem."

"I think she's after you," Delaney said solemnly.

"Oh my!" Christopher Langley said, blushing. "Her husband—her late husband—was such a nice, quiet man. A retired furrier. Well, let me put this in the kitchen, and then please go on with what you were saying."

"Did you read in the papers about the murder of Frank Lombard?" the Captain asked when Langley had rejoined him.

"Goodness, I certainly did. Everything I could find. A fascinating case. You know, whenever I read about a real-life murder or assault, I always look for a description of the weapon. After all, that was my life for so many years, and I'm still interested. But in all the accounts of the Lombard killing, the description of the weapon was very vague. Hasn't it been identified yet?"

"No. It hasn't. That's why I'm here. To ask your help."

"And as you know, I'll be delighted to give you every assistance I can, dear boy."

Delaney held up his hand like a traffic cop.

"Just a minute, sir. I want to be honest with you. As I told you, I am not on active duty. I am on leave of absence. I am not part of the official investigation into the death of Frank Lombard."

Christopher Langley looked at him narrowly a moment, then sat back and began to drum his dainty fingers against the table top.

"Then what is your interest in the Lombard case?"

"I am conducting a—a private investigation into the homicide."

"I see. Can you tell me more?"

"I would prefer not to."

"May I ask the purpose of this—ah—private investigation?"

"The main purpose is to find the killer of Frank Lombard as quickly as possible."

Langley stared at him a long, additional moment, then let off his finger drumming and slapped the table top with an open palm.

"All right," he said briskly. "Was it a striking weapon or a swinging weapon? That is: do you visualize it as a knife, a dagger, a dirk, a poniard—something of that sort—or was it a sword, pole, battleax, club, mace—something of that sort?"

"I'd say the percentages would be in favor of the swinging weapon."

"The percentages!" Langley laughed. "I had forgotten you and your percentages. This is a business to you, isn't it?"

"Yes. It's a business. And sometimes the only things you have to work with are the percentages. But what you said about a striking weapon—a knife or dagger—surely a blade couldn't penetrate a man's skull?"

"It could. And has. If blade and handle are heavy enough. The Marines' combat knife in World War Two could split a man's skull. But most blades would glance off, causing only superficial wounds. Besides, Lombard was struck on the head from behind, was he not?"

"That's correct."

"Then that would probably rule out a striking weapon. An assailant using a blade and coming from behind would almost certainly go in between the shoulder blades, into the ribs, sever the spine, or try for the kidneys."

Delaney nodded, marveling at the gusto with which this impish man ticked off these points on his fingers, an enthusiasm made all the more incredible by his age, diminutive physique, elegant appearance.

"All right," Langley went on, "let's assume a swinging weapon. One-hand or two-hand?"

"I'd guess one-hand. I think the killer approached Lombard from the front. Then, as he passed, he turned and struck him down. During the approach the weapon could have been concealed beneath a coat on the killer's arm or in a newspaper folded under his arm."

"Yes, that certainly rules out a halberd! You're talking about something about the size of a hatchet?"

"About that."

"Captain, do you believe it was an antique weapon?"

"I doubt that very much. Once again, the percentages are against it. In my lifetime I've investigated only two homicides in which antique weapons were used. One was the crossbow case in which you were involved. The other was a death caused by a ball fired from an antique duelling pistol."

"Then we'll assume a modern weapon?"

"Yes."

"Or a modern tool. You must realize that many modern tools have evolved from antique weapons. The reverse is also true, of course. During hand-to-hand combat in Korea and Vietnam, there were several cases of American soldiers using their Entrenching tool, shovel, or Entrenching tool, pickmattock, as a weapon both for offense and defense. Now let's get to the wound itself. Was it a crushing, cutting, or piercing blow?"

"Piercing. It was a penetration, about three to four inches long."

"Oh my, that *is* interesting! And what was the shape of the penetration?"

"Here I'm going to get a little vague," Delaney warned. "The official autopsy of the examining surgeon states that the outside wound was roughly circular in shape, about one inch in diameter. The penetration dwindled rapidly to a sharp point, the entire penetration being round and, as I said, about three or four inches deep."

"Round?" Langley cried, and the Captain was surprised at the little man's expression.

"Yes, round," he repeated. "Why—is anything wrong?"

"Is the surgeon certain of this? The roundness, I mean?"

"No, he is not. But the wound was of such a nature that precise measurements and analysis were impossible. The surgeon had a feeling—just a guess on his part—that the spike that penetrated was triangular or square, and that the weapon became stuck in the wound, or the victim in falling forward, wrenched the weapon out of the killer's hand, and that the killer then had to twist the weapon back and forth to free it. And this twisting motion, with a square or triangular spike, would result in—"

"Ah-ha!" Langley shouted, slapping his thigh. "That's exactly what happened! And the surgeon believes the spike could have been triangular or square?"

"Believes it *could* have been—yes."

"*Was,*" Langley said definitely. "It was. Believe me, Captain. Do you know how many weapons there are with tapering round spikes that could cause the kind of wound you describe? I could name them on the fingers of one hand. You will find round spikes on the warclubs of certain Northwest Coast Indian tribes. There is a Tlingit warclub with a jade head that tapers to a point. It is not perfectly round, however. Thompson Indians used a warclub with a head of wood that was round and tapered: a perfect cone. The Tsimshian Indians used horn and bone, again round and tapered. Esquimo tribes used clubs with spikes of bone or narwhale or walrus tusks. Do you understand the significance of what I am saying, Captain?"

"I'm afraid not."

"The materials used in weapons that had a cone spike were almost always *natural* materials that tapered naturally—such as teeth or tusks—or were soft materials, such as wood, that could be tapered to a cone shape easily. But now let's move on to iron and steel. Early metal weapons were made by armorers and blacksmiths working with a hammer on a hot slug held on an anvil. It was infinitely easier and faster to fashion a flat spike, a triangular spike, or a square spike, than a perfect cone that tapered to a sharp point. I can't recall a single halberd, partison or *couteaux de brèche* in the Metropolitan that has a round spike. Or any war hammer or war hatchet. I seem to remember a mace in the Rotterdam museum that had a round spike, but I'd have to look it up. In any event, early weapons almost invariably were fashioned with flat sides, usually triangular or square, or even hexagonal. A perfectly proportioned round spike was simply too difficult to make. And even after dies and stamping of iron and steel came into existence, the same held true. It is cheaper, faster, and easier to make blades and spikes with flat sides than round ones that taper to a point. I think your surgeon's 'guesses' are correct. Using your famous 'percentages.' "

"Interesting," Delaney nodded, "and exactly what I came to you for. But there's another thing I should tell you. I don't know what it means, if anything, but perhaps you will. The surgeon has a feeling that the sharp tip of the penetration was lower than the opening wound. You understand? It was not a straight, tapered penetration, but it curved gently downward. Maybe I should make a little drawing."

"Oh gosh," Langley chortled, "that's not necessary. I know exactly what you mean." He leaped to his feet, rushed to a bookcase, ran his fingers over the bindings, grabbed out a big book, and hustled it back to the table. He turned to the List of Illustrations, ran his finger down, found what he was looking for, and flipped pages. "There," he said. "Take a look at that, Captain."

Delaney stared. It was a one-handed club. The head had a hatchet blade on one side, a spike on the other. The spike was about an inch across at the head, tapered to a sharp point and, as it tapered, curved downward.

"What is it?" he asked.

"Iroquois tomahawk. Handle of ash. Those are feathers tied to the butt. The head is iron, probably cut out of a sheet of hot metal with shears or hammered out with a chisel and then filed sharp. White traders carried them and sold them for pelts."

"Are you suggesting . . . ?"

"Heavens, no. But note how that flat spike curves downward? I could show you that same curve in warclubs and war-axes and halberds of practically every nation, tribe, and race on earth. Very effective; very efficient. When you hack down on a man, you don't want to hit his skull with a horizontal spike that might glance off. You want a spike that curves downward, pierces, penetrates, and kills."

"Yes," Delaney said. "I suppose you do."

The two men sat in silence a few moments, staring at the color photo of the Iroquois tomahawk. How many had *that* killed, Delaney wondered, and then, leafing slowly through the book, was suddenly saddened by the effort, art, and genius that the human race had expended on killing tools, on powder and shot, sword and stiletto, bayonet and bludgeons, crossbow and Centurion tank, blowpipe and cannon, spear and hydrogen bomb. There was, he supposed, no end to it.

But what was the need, or lust, behind all this interest, ingenuity, and vitality in the design and manufacture of killing tools? The lad with his slingshot and the man with his gun: both showing a dark atavism. Was killing then a passion, from the primeval slime, as valid an expression of the human soul as love and sacrifice?

Suddenly depressed, Delaney rose to his feet and tried to smile at his host.

"Mr. Langley," he said brightly, "I thank you for a pleasant evening, a wonderful dinner, and for your kind cooperation. You've given me a lot to think about."

Christopher Langley seemed as depressed as his guest. He looked up listlessly.

"I haven't helped, Captain, and you know it. You're no closer to identifying the weapon that killed Frank Lombard than you were three hours ago."

"You *have* helped, sir," Delaney insisted. "You've substantiated the surgeon's impressions. You've given me a clearer idea of what to look for. In a case like this, every little bit helps."

"Captain . . . "

"Yes, Mr. Langley?"

"In this 'private investigation' of yours, the weapon isn't the only thing. I know that. You're going to interview people and check into past records and things like that. Isn't that true?"

"Yes."

"Well, gosh, then you can only spend so much time trying to identify the weapon. Isn't that so?"

"Yes."

"Captain, let me do it. Please. Let me *try.*"

"Mr. Langley, I can't—"

"I know you're not on active duty. I know it's a private investigation. You told me. But still . . . you're trying. Let me help. Please. Look at me. I'm seventy. I'm retired. To tell you the truth, Captain, I'm sick of gourmet cooking. My whole life was. . . . Oh God, what am I supposed to do—sit up here and wait to die? Captain, please, let me *do* something, something important. This man Lombard was murdered. That's not right. Life is too precious."

"That's what my wife said," Delaney said wonderingly.

"She knew," Langley nodded, his eyes glistening now. "Let me do some work, some *important* work. I know weapons. You know that. I might be a help to you. Truly. Let me try."

"I don't have any funds," Delaney started. "I can't—"

"Forget it," the old man waved him away. "This will cost nothing. I can pay for cabs and books, or whatever. But let me work. At an important job. You understand, Captain? I don't want to just drift away."

The Captain stared, wondering if the ex-curator was prey to his own gloomy thoughts. Langley was far from being stupid, and how did an intelligent man justify a lifetime devoted to killing tools? Perhaps it was true, as he had said, that he was simply bored with retirement and wanted to work again. But his insistence on something "important," "important" work, an "important" job led Delaney to wonder if the old man, his life drawing to a close, was not, in a sense, seeking a kind of expiation, or at least hungering to make a sunny, affirmative gesture after a career celebrating shadows and the bog.

"Yes," Captain Delaney said, clearing his throat. "I understand. All right. Fine. I appreciate that, sir. If I find out anything more relating to the weapon, I'll make sure you know of it. Meanwhile, see what you can come up with."

"Oh!" Langley cried, effervescent again. "I'll get on it right away. There are some things I want to check in my books tonight, and tomorrow I'll go to the museums. Maybe I'll get some ideas there. And to hardware stores. To look at tools. Captain, am I a detective now?"

"Yes," Delaney smiled. "You're a detective."

He moved toward the door, and Langley scampered to get his coat and hat from the closet. He gave his unlisted phone number to the Captain, and Delaney carefully copied it into his pocket notebook. Langley unlocked the door, then leaned close.

"Captain," he whispered, "one final favor . . . When you go down the stairs, please try to tiptoe past the Widow Zimmerman's door. I don't want her to know I'm alone."

6

The home of the late Frank Lombard was on a surprisingly pastoral street in the Flatbush section of Brooklyn. There were trees, lawns, barking dogs, shrieking children. The house itself was red brick, two stories high, its ugliness hidden in a tight cloak of ivy that was still green and creeped to the eaves.

There was an asphalt driveway leading to a two-car garage. There were four cars, bumper to bumper, on the driveway, and more in front of the house, two double-parked. Captain Delaney observed all this from across the street. He also observed that one of the double-parked cars was a three-year-old, four-door Plymouth, and had the slightly rusted, slightly dusty, nondescript appearance of an unmarked police car. Two men in civilian clothes were in the front seat.

Delaney approved of a guard being stationed for the protection of the widow, Mrs. Clara Lombard. It was very possible, he thought, there was also a personal guard inside the house; Chief Pauley would see to that. Now the problem was, if Delaney went through with his intention to interview the widow, would one of the cops recognize him and report to Broughton that Captain Delaney had been a visitor.

The Captain pondered this problem a few minutes on the next corner, still watching the Lombard home. While he stood, hands shoved deep in his civilian overcoat pockets, he saw two couples leave the house, laughing, and another car double-park to disgorge two women and a man, also laughing.

Delaney devised a cover story. If the guards made him, and he was eventually braced by Broughton, he would explain that because the homicide occurred in his precinct, he felt duty-bound to express his condolences to the widow. Broughton wouldn't buy it completely; he'd be suspicious and have the widow checked. But that would be all right; Delaney did feel duty-bound to express his condolences, and would.

As he headed up the brick-paved walk to the door, he heard loud rock music, screams of laughter, the sound of shattering glass. It was a party, and a wild one.

A man answered his ring, a flush-faced, too-handsome man wearing not one, but two pinkie rings.

"Come in come in come in," he burbled, flourishing his highball glass and slopping half of it down the front of his hand-tailored, sky-blue silk suit. "Always room for one more."

"Thank you," Delaney said. "I'm not a guest. I just wanted to speak to Mrs. Lombard for a moment."

"Hey, Clara!" the man screamed over his shoulder. "Get your gorgeous ass out here. Your lover is waiting."

The man leered at Delaney, then plunged back into the dancing, drinking, laughing, yelling mob. The Captain stood patiently. Eventually she came weaving toward him.

A zaftig blonde who reminded him of Oscar Wilde's comment about the widow "whose hair turned quite gold from grief." She overflowed an off-the-shoulder cocktail dress that seemed capable of standing by itself, so heavily encrusted was it with sequins, rhinestones, braid, a jeweled peacock brooch and, unaccountably, a cheap tin badge, star-shaped, that said "Garter Inspector." She looked down at him from bleary eyes.

"Yeah?"

"Mrs. Clara Lombard?"

"Yeah."

"My name is Delaney, Captain Edward X. Delaney. I am the former commanding officer of the—"

"Jesus," she breathed. "Another cop. Haven't I had enough cops?"

"I would like to express my condolences on the death—"

"Five," she said. "Or six times. I lost count. What the hell is it now? Can't you see I've got a houseful of people? Will you stop bugging me?"

"I just wanted to tell you how sorry I—"

"Thanks a whole hell of a lot," she said disgustedly. "Well, screw all of you. This is a going-away party. I'm shaking New York, and the whole lot of you can go screw."

"You're leaving New York?" he asked, amazed that Broughton would let her go.

"That's right, buster. I've sold the house, the cars, the furniture-everything. By Saturday I'll be in sunny, funny Miami and starting a new life. A brand new life. And then you can all go screw yourselves."

She turned away and went rushing back to her party. Delaney replaced his hat, walked slowly down to the corner. He watched the traffic, waiting for the light to change. Cars went rushing by, and the odd thing that had nagged him since his reading of the Operation Lombard reports whisked into his mind, as he knew it would. Eventually.

In the interview with the victim's mother, Mrs. Sophia Lombard, she had stated he never drove over from Brooklyn because he couldn't find parking space near her apartment; he took the subway.

Delaney retraced his steps, and this time the outside guards stared at him. He rang the bell of the Lombard home again. The widow herself threw open the door, a welcoming smile on her puffy face—a smile that oozed away as she recognized Delaney.

"Jesus Christ, you again?"

"Yes. You said you're selling your car?"

"Not car—cars. We had two of them. And forget about getting a bargain; they're both sold."

"Your husband—your late husband drove a car?"

"Of course he drove a car. What do you think?"

"Where did he usually carry his driver's license, Mrs. Lombard?"

"Oh God," she shouted, and immediately the pinkie-ringed man was at her shoulder.

"Wassamatta, honey?" he inquired. "Having trouble?"

"No trouble, Manny. Just some more police shit. In his wallet," she said to Delaney. "He carried his driver's license in his wallet. Okay?"

"Thank you," Delaney said humbly. "I'm sorry to bother you. It's just that the license wasn't in his wallet when we found him." He refrained from mentioning that she had stated nothing was missing from the wallet. "It's probably around the house somewhere."

"Yeah, yeah," she said impatiently.

"If you come across it while you're packing, will you let us know? We've got to cancel it with the State."

"Sure, sure. I'll look, I'll look."

He knew she wouldn't. But it didn't make any difference; she'd never find it.

"Anything else?" she demanded.

"No, nothing. Thank you very much, Mrs. Lombard, for your kind cooperation."

"Go screw yourself," she said, and slammed the door in his face.

He went back to his home and methodically checked the inventory of personal effects taken from the body of Frank Lombard, and Mrs. Sophia Lombard's statement about her son's visiting habits. Then he sat a long time in the growing darkness. Once he rose to mix a weak rye highball and sat nursing that, sipping slowly and still thinking.

Finally he pulled on his overcoat and hat again and went out to find a different phone booth. He had to wait almost fifteen minutes before Deputy Inspector Ivar Thorsen got back to him, a period during which three would-be phone users turned away in disgust. One of them kicked the phone booth in anger before he left.

"Edward?" Thorsen asked.

"Yes. I've got something. Something I don't think Broughton has."

He heard Thorsen's swift intake of breath.

"What?"

"Lombard was a licensed driver. He owned two cars. His wife has sold them, incidentally. She's leaving town."

"So?"

"She says he carried his driver's license in his wallet. That makes sense. The percentages are for it. The license wasn't in the wallet when it was found. I checked the inventory."

There was a moment's silence.

"No one would kill for a driver's license," Thorsen said finally. "You can buy a good counterfeit for fifty bucks."

"I know."

"Identification?" Thorsen suggested. "A hired killer. He takes the license to prove to his employer he really did hit Lombard."

"What for? It was in all the papers the next day. The employer would know the job had been done."

"Jesus, that's right. What do you think? Why the driver's license?"

"Identification maybe."

"But you just said—"

"Not a hired killer. I have two ideas. One, the killer took the license as a souvenir, a trophy."

"That's nuts, Edward."

"Maybe. The other idea is that he took the license to prove to a third party that he had killed. Not killed *Lombard*, but killed someone, *anyone*. If the stories were in the papers, and the killer could present the victim's driver's license, that would prove *he* was the killer."

The silence was longer this time.

"Jesus, Edward," Thorsen said finally. "That's wild."

"Yes. Wild." (And suddenly he remembered a sex killing he had investigated. The victim's eyelids had been stitched together with her own hairpins.)

Thorsen came on again: "Edward, are you trying to tell me we're dealing with a crazy?"

"Yes. I think so. Someone like Whitman, Speck, Unruh, the Boston Strangler, Panzram, Manson. Someone like that."

"Oh God."

"If I'm right, we'll know soon enough."

"How will we know?"

"He'll do it again."

Part IV

1

He thought she was wearing a loose-fitting dress of black crepe with white cuffs. Then he saw the cuffs were actually bandages about both wrists. But he was so inflamed with what he wanted to tell her that he didn't question the bandages, knowing. Instead, he merely held up before her eyes Frank Lombard's driver's license. She would not look at it, but took him by the arm and drew him slowly, step by step, to the upstairs room. Where he was impotent.

"It's all right," she soothed. "I understand. Believe me, I understand and love you for it. I told you sex should be a ritual, a ceremony. But a rite has no consummation. It's a celebration of a consummation. Do you understand? The ritual celebrates the climax but does not encompass it. It's all right, my darling. Don't think you've failed. This is best. That you and I worship the fulfillment—a continuing celebration of an unknowable finality. Isn't that what prayer is all about?"

But he was not listening to her, so livid was he with the need to talk. He snapped on that cruel overhead light and showed her the driver's license and newspaper headlines, proving himself.

"For you," he said. "I did it for you." Then they both laughed, knowing it was a lie."

"Tell me everything," she said. "Every detail. I want to know everything that happened."

His soft scrotum huddled in her hand, a dead bird.

He told her, with pride, of the careful planning, the long hours of slow thought. His first concern, he said, had been the weapon.

"Did I want a weapon that could be discarded?" he asked rhetorically. "I decided not, not to leave a weapon that might be traced to me. So I chose a weapon I would take with me when I left."

"To be used again," she murmured.

"Yes. Perhaps. Well . . . I told you I'm a climber. I'm not an expert; just an amateur. But I have this ice ax. It's a tool of course, but also a very wicked weapon. All tempered steel. A hammer on one side of the head for pitons, and a tapered steel pick on the other. There are hundreds just like it. Also, it has a leather-wrapped handle and a rawhide thong hanging from the butt. Heavy enough to kill, but small and light enough to carry concealed. You know that coat I have with slits in the pockets, so that I can reach inside?''

''Do I not!'' she smiled.

''Yes,'' he smiled in reply. ''I figured I could wear that coat, the front unbuttoned and hanging loose. My left hand would be through the slit, and I could carry the ice ax by the leather throng, dangling from my fingers but completely concealed. When the time came to use it, I could reach inside the unbuttoned coat with my right hand and take the ax by the handle.''

''Brilliant,'' she said.

''A problem,'' he shrugged. ''I tried it. I practised. It worked perfectly. If I was calm and cool, unhurried, I could transfer the ax to my right hand in seconds. *Seconds!* One or two. No more. Then, after, the ax would disappear beneath my coat again. Held by my left hand through the pocket slit.''

''Did you see his eyes?'' she asked.

''His eyes?'' he said vaguely. ''No. I must tell you this in my own way.''

She leaned forward to put her lips on his left nipple; his eyes closed with pleasure.

''I didn't want to travel too far,'' he said. ''The farther I went, carrying the concealed ice ax, the greater the danger. It had to be in my own neighborhood. Near. Why not? The murder of a stranger. A crime without motive. What difference if it was next door or a hundred miles away? Who could connect me?''

''Yes,'' she breathed. ''Oh yes.''

He told her how he had walked the streets for three nights, seeking the lonely blocks, noting the lighting, remembering bus stops and subway stations, lobbies with doormen, deserted stretches of unattended stores and garages.

''I couldn't plan it. I decided it would have to be chance. Pure chance. 'Pure.' That's a funny word, Celia. But it was pure. I swear to you. I mean, there was no sex connected with it. I mean, I didn't walk around with an erection. I didn't have an orgasm when I did it. Nothing like that. Do you believe me?''

''Yes.''

''It really was pure. I swear it. It was religious. I was God's will. I know that sounds insane. But that's how I felt. Maybe it is mad. A sweet madness. I was God on earth. When I looked at people on shadowed streets . . . Is *he* the one? Is *he* the one? My God, the *power!*''

''Oh yes. Darling, oh yes.''

He was so tender with her in that awful room . . . so tender. And then, the memory of the two times he had been unfaithful to his wife . . . He had enjoyed both adventures; both women had been his wife's superior in bed. But he had not loved her the less for that. Instead, unaccountably, his infidelity had increased his affection for and kindness toward his wife. He touched her, kissed her, listened to her.

And now, telling this woman of murder, he felt the same thaw: not increased sexuality but heightened sweetness because he had a new mistress. He touched Celia's cheek, kissed her fingertips, murmured, saw to her comfort, and in all things acted the gentle and *parfait* lover, loving her the more because he loved another most.

''It was not someone else doing it,'' he assured her. ''You've read these stories where the killer blames it on someone else. Another *him.* Someone who took over, controlled his mind and guided his hand. It was nothing like that. Celia, I have never had such a feeling of being myself. You know? It was a sense of *oneness,* of *me.* Do you understand?''

''Oh yes. And then?''

''I hit him. We smiled. We nodded. We passed, and I transferred the ax to my right hand. Just as I had rehearsed. And I hit him. It made a sound. I can't describe it. A sound. And he fell forward so heavily that it pulled the ax out of my hand. I didn't know that might happen. But I didn't panic. Jesus, I was cool.

Cold! I bent down and twisted the ax to pull it free. Tough. I had to put my foot on the back of his neck and pull up on the ax with both hands to free it. I did that. I did it! And then I found his wallet and took his driver's license. To prove to you."

"You didn't have to do that."

"Didn't I?"

"Yes. You did."

They both laughed then, and rolled on the soiled bed, holding.

He tried, again, to enter into her and did not succeed, not caring, for he had already surpassed her. But he would not tell her that since she knew. She took his penis into her mouth, not licking or biting, but just in her mouth: a warm communion. He was hardly conscious of it; it did not excite him. He was a god; she was worshipping.

"One other thing," he said dreamily. "When, finally, on the night, I looked down the street and saw him walking toward me through that orange glow, and I thought yes, now, he is the one, I loved him so much then, *loved* him."

"Loved him? Why?"

"I don't know. But I did. And respected him. Oh yes. And had such a sense of gratitude toward him. That he was giving. So much. To me. Then I killed him."

2

"Good morning, Charles," Daniel called, and the doorman whirled around, shocked by the friendly voice and pleasant smile. "Looks like a sunny day today."

"Oh. Yes sir," Lipsky said, confused. "Sunny day. That's what the paper said. Cab, Mr. Blank?"

"Please."

The doorman went down to the street, whistled up a taxi, rode it back to the apartment house entrance. He got out and held the door open for Daniel.

"Have a good day, Mr. Blank."

"You too, Charles," and handed him the usual quarter. He gave the driver the address of the Javis-Bircham Building.

"Go through the park, please. I know it's longer but I've got time."

"Sure."

"Looks like a nice sunny day today."

"That's what the radio just said," the driver nodded. "You sound like you feel good today."

"Yes," Blank smiled. "I do."

"Morning, Harry," he said to the elevator starter. "A nice sunny morning."

"Sure is, Mr. Blank. Hope it stays like this."

"Good morning, Mrs. Cleek," Blank said to his secretary as he hung away his hat and coat. "Looks like it's going to be a beautiful day."

"Yes sir. I hope it lasts."

"It will." He looked at her closely a moment. "Mrs. Cleek, you seem a bit pale. Are you feeling all right?"

She blushed with pleasure at his concern. "Oh yes, Mr. Blank, I feel fine."

"How's that boy of yours?"

"I got a letter from him yesterday. He's doing very well. He's in a military academy, you know."

Blank didn't, but nodded. "Well, you do look a bit weary. Why don't you plan on taking a few Fridays off? It's going to be a long winter. We all need relaxation."

"Why . . . thank you very much, Mr. Blank. That's very kind of you."

"Just let me know in advance and arrange for someone from the pool to fill in. That's a pretty dress."

"Thank you very much, Mr. Blank," she repeated, dazed. "Your coffee is on your desk, and a report came down from upstairs. I put it next to your coffee."

"What's it about?"

"Oh, I didn't read it, sir. It's sealed and confidential."

"Thank you, Mrs. Cleek. I'll buzz when I want to do letters."

"Thank you again, Mr. Blank. For the days off, I mean."

He smiled and made a gesture. He sat down at his bare table and sipped coffee, staring at the heavy manila envelope from the president's office, stamped CONFIDENTIAL. He didn't open it, but taking his plastic container of coffee walked to the plate glass windows facing west.

It was an extraordinarily clear day, the smog mercifully lifted. He could see tugboats on the Hudson, a cruise liner putting out to sea, traffic on the Jersey shore, and blue hills far away. Everything was bright and glittering, a new world. He could almost peer into a distant future.

He drained his coffee and looked into the plastic cup. It was white foam, stained now, and of the consistency of cottage cheese. It bulged in his grip and felt of soap. He flicked on his intercom.

"Sir?" Mrs. Cleek asked.

"Would you do me a favor?"

"Of course, sir."

"On your lunch hour—well, take your usual hour, of course, but then take some more time—grab a cab over to Tiffany's or Jensen's—someplace like that—and buy me a coffee cup and saucer. Something good in bone China, thin and white. You can buy singles from open stock. If it's patterned, pick out something attractive, something you like. Don't be afraid to spend money."

"A coffee cup and saucer, sir?"

"Yes, and see if you can find a spoon, one of those small silver French spoons. Sometimes they're enameled in blue patterns, flowered patterns. That would be fine."

"One coffee cup, one saucer, and one spoon. Will that be all, sir?"

"Yes—no. Get the same thing for yourself. Get two sets."

"Oh, Mr. Blank, I couldn't—"

"Two sets," he said firmly. "And Mrs. Cleek, from now on when the commissary delivers my coffee, will you pour it into my new cup and leave it on my desk that way?"

"Yes, Mr. Blank."

"Keep track of what you spend, including cab fares there and back. I'll pay you personally. This is not petty cash."

"Yes, Mr. Blank."

He clicked off and picked up the president's envelope, having no great curiosity to open it. He searched the outside. Finally, sighing, he tore open the flap and scanned the two-sheet memo swiftly. It was about what he had expected, considering the lack of zeal in his prospectus. His suggestion of having AMROK II compute the ratio between editorial and advertising in all Javis-Bircham magazines was approved to this extent: it would be tried on an experimental basis on the ten magazines listed on the attached page, and would be limited to a period of six months, after which time a production management consultant would be called in to make an independent evaluation of the results.

Blank tossed the memo aside, stretched, yawned. He couldn't, he realized, care less. It was a crock of shit. Then he picked up the memo again and wandered out of the office.

"I'll be in the Computer Room," he said as he passed Mrs. Cleek's desk. She gave him a bright, hopeful smile.

He went through the nonsense of donning the sterile white skull cap and duster, then assembled Task Force X-1 about the stainless steel table. He passed around the second sheet of the president's memo, deeming it wise, at this time, not to tell them of the experimental nature and limited duration of the project.

"We've got the go-ahead," he said, with what he hoped they would think was enthusiasm. "These are the magazines we start with. I want to draw up a schedule of priorities for programming. Any ideas?"

The discussion started at his left and went around the table. He listened to all of them, watching their pale, sexless faces, not hearing a word that was said.

"Excellent," he said occasionally. Or, "Very good." Or, "I'll take a raincheck on that." Or, "Well . . . I don't want to say no, but . . ." It didn't make any difference: what they said or what he said. It had no significance.

Significance began, I suppose, when my wife and I separated. Or when she wouldn't wear the sunglasses to bed. Oh, it probably began much sooner, but I wasn't aware of it. I was aware of the glasses, the masks. And then, later, the wigs, the exercises, the clothes, the apartment . . . the mirrors. And standing naked in chains. I was aware of all that. I mean, I was conscious of it.

What was happening to me—*is* happening to me—is that I am feeling my way—*feeling:* that's a good word—feeling in the sense of emotion rather than the tactile sense—*feeling* my way to a new perception of reality. Before that, before the sunglasses, I perceived and reasoned in a masculine, in-line way, vertical, just like AMROK II. And now . . . and now I am discovering and exploring a feminine, horizontal perception of reality.

And what that requires is to deny cold order—logical, intellectual order, that is—and perceive a deeper order, glimpsing it dimly now, somewhere, an order much deeper and broader because . . . The order I have known up to now has been narrow and restricted, tight and disciplined. But it cannot account for . . . for all.

This feminine, horizontal perception applies to breadth, explaining the apparent illogic and seeming madness of the universe—well, this perception does not deny science and logic but offers something more—an emotional consciousness of people and of life.

But is it only emotional? Or is it spiritual? At least it demands a need to accept chaos—a chaos outside the tight, disciplined logic of men and AMROK II, and seeks a deeper, more fundamental order and logic and significance within that chaos. It means a new way of life: the truth of lies and the reality of myths. It demands a whole new way to perceive a—

No, that's not right. Perception implies a standing aside and observing. But this new world I am now in requires participation and sharing. I must strip myself naked and plunge—if I hope to know the final logic. If I have the courage . . .

Courage . . . When I told Celia of the power I felt when selecting my victim, and the love I had for him when he was selected—all that was true. But I didn't mention the fear—fear so intense it was all I could do to control my bladder. But isn't that part of it? I mean emotion—*feeling.* And from emotion to a spiritual exaltation, just as Celia is always speaking of ceremony and ritual and the beauty of evil. That is *her* final logic. But is it mine? We shall see. We shall see.

I must open myself, to everything. I grew in a tiled house of Lalique glass and rock collections. Now I must become warm and tender and accept everything in the universe, good and evil, the spread and the cramped. But not just accepting. Because then I'd be a victim. I must plunge to the heart of life and let its heat sear me. I must be moved.

To *experience* reality, not merely to perceive it: that is the way. And the final answer may be dreadful to divine. But if I can conquer fear, and kill, and feel, and learn, I will bring a meaning out of the chaos of my new world, give it a logic few have ever glimpsed before, and then I'll know.

Is there God?

---

3 He pulled that brass plunger, standing at her teak door, grasping the bundle of long-stemmed roses, blood-colored, and feeling as idiotic and ineffectual as any wooer come to call upon his lady-love with posies, vague hope, a vapid smile.

"Good-afternoon, Valenter."

"Good-afternoon, thir. Do come in."

He was inside, the door closed behind him, when the tall, pale houseman spoke in tones Daniel was certain were a burlesque, a spoof of sadness. That long face fell, the muddy eyes seemed about to leak, the voice was suited for a funeral chapel.

"Mither Blank, I am thorry to report Mith Montfort hath gone."

"Gone? Gone where?"

"Called away unexthpectedly. She athked me to prethent her regreth."

"Oh shit."

"Yeth thir."

"When will she be back? Today?"

"I do not know, thir. But I thuthpect it may be a few dayth."

"Shit," Blank repeated. He thrust the flowers at Valenter. "Put these in some water, will you? Maybe they'll last long enough for her to see them."

"Of courth, thir. Mather Tony ith in the thtudy and would like you to join him, thir."

"What? Oh. All right."

It was a Saturday noon. He had imagined a leisurely lunch, perhaps some shopping, a visit to the Mortons' Erotica, which was always crowded and entertaining on a Saturday afternoon. And then, perhaps, a movie, a dinner, and then . . . Well, anything. Things went best, he decided, when they weren't too rigidly programmed.

The boy languished on the tufted couch—a beauty!

"Dan!" he cried, holding out a hand.

But Blank would not cross the room to touch that languid palm. He sat in the winged armchair and regarded the youth with what he believed was amused irony. The roses had cost twenty dollars.

"About Celia," Tony said, looking down at his fingernails. "She wanted me to make her apologies."

"Valenter already has."

"Valenter? Oh pooh! Have a drink."

And suddenly, Valenter was there, leaning forward slightly from the waist.

"No, thank you," Blank said. "It's a little early for me."

"Oh come," Tony said. "Vodka martini on the rocks with a twist of lemon. Right?"

Daniel considered a moment. "Right," he smiled.

"What will your son have?" the waiter asked, and they both laughed.

"My son?" Blank said. He looked to Tony. "What will my son have?"

They were in a French restaurant, not bad and not good. They didn't care.

Tony ordered oysters and frogs' legs, a salad doused with a cheese dressing. Blank had a small steak and endive with oil and vinegar. They smiled at each other. Tony reached forward to touch his hand. "Thank you," he said humbly.

Daniel had two glasses of a thick burgundy, and Tony had something called a "Shirley Temple." The boy's knee was against his. He didn't object, wanting to follow this plot to its denouement.

"Do you drink coffee?" he asked. They flirted.

"How is school?" he asked, and Tony made a gesture, infinitely weary.

They were strolling then, hands brushing occasionally, up Madison Avenue, and stopped to smile at a display of men's clothing in a boutique.

"Oh," Tony said.

Daniel Blank glanced at him. The lad was in sunlight, brazen. He gleamed, a gorgeous being.

"Let's look," Blank said. They went inside.

"Ooh, thank you," Tony said later, giving him a dazzling smile. "You spent so much money on me."

"Didn't I though?"

"Are you rich, Dan?"

"No, I'm not rich. But not hurting."

"Do you think the pink pullover was right for me?"

"Oh yes. Your coloring."

"I would have loved those fishnet briefs, but I knew even the small size would be too large for me. Celia buys all my underwear in a women's lingerie shop."

"Does she?"

They sat on a park bench unaccountably planted in the middle of a small meadow. Tony fingered the lobe of Dan's left ear; they watched an old black man stolidly fly a kite.

"Do you like me?" Tony asked.

Daniel Blank would not give himself time to fear, but twisted around and kissed the boy's soft lips.

"Of course I like you."

Tony held his hand and made quiet circles on the palm with a forefinger.

"You've changed, Dan."

"Have I?"

"Oh yes. When you first started seeing Celia, you were so tight, so locked up inside yourself. Now I feel you're breaking out. You smile more. Sometimes you laugh. You never did that before. You wouldn't have kissed me three months ago, would you?"

"No, I wouldn't have, Tony, perhaps we should get back. Valenter is probably—"

"Valenter," Tony said in a tone of great disgust. "Pooh! Just because he—" Then he stopped.

But Valenter was nowhere about, and Tony used his own key to let them in. Daniel's roses were arranged in a Chinese vase on the foyer table. And in addition to the roses' sweet musk, he caught another odor: Celia's perfume, a thin, smoky scent, Oriental. He thought it odd he had not smelled it in this hallway at noon.

And the scent was there in the upstairs room to which Tony led him by the hand, resolute and humming.

He had vowed not only to perceive but to experience, to strip himself bare and plunge to the hot heart of life. The killing of Frank Lombard had been a cataclysm that left him riven, just as an earthquake leaves the tight, solid earth split, stretched open to the blue sky.

Now, alone and naked with this beautiful, rosy lad, the emotions he sought came more quickly, easily, and fear of his own feelings was already turning to curiosity and hunger. He sought new corners of himself, great sweetness and great tenderness, a need to sacrifice and a want to love. Whatever his life had lacked to now, he resolved to find, supply, to fill himself up with things hot and scented, all the emotions and sentiments which might illume life and show its mystery and purpose.

The boy's body was all warm fabric: velvet eyelids, silken buttocks, the insides of his thighs a sheeny satin. Slowly, with a deliberate thoughtfulness, Daniel Blank put mouth and tongue to those cloths, all with the fragrance of youth, sweet and moving. To use youth, to pleasure it and take pleasure from it, seemed to him now as important as murder, another act of conscious will to spread himself wide to sentient life.

The infant moved moaning beneath his caresses, and that incandescent flesh heated him and brought him erect. When he entered into Tony, penetrating his rectum, the boy cried out with pain and delight. Dimly, far off, Blank thought he heard a single tinkle of feminine laughter, and smelled again her scent clinging to the soiled mattress.

Later, when he held the lad in his arms and kissed his tears away—new wine, those tears—he thought it possible, probably even, that they were manipulating him, for what reason he could not imagine. But it was of no importance. Because whatever the reason, it must certainly be a selfish one.

Suddenly he *knew;* her slick words, her lectures on ritual, her love of ceremony and apotheosis of evil—all had the stench of egotism; there was no other explanation. She sought, somehow, to set herself apart. Apart and above. She wanted to conquer the world and, perhaps, had enlisted him in her mandarin scheme.

But, enlisted or not, she had unlocked him, and would find he was moving beyond her. Whatever her selfish motive, he would complete his own task: not to conquer life, but to become one with it, to hug it close, to feel it and love it and, finally, to know its beautiful enigma. Not as AMROK II might know it, but in his heart and gut and gonads, to become a secret sharer, one with the universe.

4

After wrenching his ice ax from the skull of Frank Lombard, he had walked steadily homeward, looking neither to the right nor to the left, his mind resolutely thoughtless. He had nodded in a friendly fashion to the doorman on duty, then ascended to his apartment. Only after he was inside, the battery of chains and locks in place, did he lean against the wall, still coated, close his eyes, drew a deep breath.

But there was still work to be done. He put the ax aside for the moment. Then he stripped naked. He examined coat and suit for stains, of any kind. He could see none. But he placed coat and suit in a bundle for the drycleaner, and shirt, socks and underclothing in the laundry hamper.

Then he went into the bathroom and held the ice ax so that the head was under water in the toilet bowl. He flushed the toilet three times. Practically all the solid matter—caked blood and some grey stuff caught in the saw-tooth serrations on the bottom point of the pick—was washed away.

Then, still naked, he went into the kitchen and put a large pot of water on to boil. It was the pot he customarily used for spaghetti and stew. He waited patiently until the water boiled, still not reflecting on what he had done. He wanted to finish the job, then sit down, relax, and savor his reactions.

When the water came to a rolling boil he immersed the ice ax head and shaft up to the leather around the handle. The tempered steel boiled clean. He dunked it three times, swirling it about, then turned the flame off under the pot, and held the ax head under the cold water tap to cool it.

When he could handle it, he inspected the ax carefully. He even took a small paring knife and gently pried up the top edge of the blue leather-covered handle. He could see no stains that might have leaked beneath. The ax smelled of steel and leather. It shone.

He took the little can of sewing machine oil from his kitchen closet and, with his bare hands, rubbed oil into the exposed steel surfaces of the ax. He applied a lot of oil, rubbing strongly, then wiped off the excess with a paper towel. He started to discard the towel in his garbage can, then thought better of it and flushed it down the toilet. The ice ax was left with a thin film of oil. He hung it away in the hall closet with his rucksack and crampons.

Then he showered thoroughly under very hot water, using a small brush on hands and fingernails. After he dried, he used cologne and powder, then donned a short cotton kimono. It was patterned with light blue cranes stalking across a dark blue background. Then he poured himself a small brandy, went into the living room, sat on the couch before the mirrored wall, and laughed.

Now he allowed himself to remember, and it was a beloved dream. He saw himself walking down that oranged street toward his victim. He was smiling, coat rakishly open, left hand inside the slit pocket, right arm swinging free. Was he snapping the fingers of his right hand? He might have been.

The smile. The nod. The hot surge of furious blood when he whirled and struck. The sound. He remembered the sound. Then the victim's incredible plunge forward that pulled the ice ax from his grasp, toppled him forward. Then, quickly pulling the ax free, search, wallet, and the steady walk homeward.

Well then . . . what did he feel? He felt, he decided, first of all an enormous sense of pride. That was basic. It was, after all, an extremely difficult and dangerous job of work, and he had brought it off. It was not too unlike a difficult and dangerous rock climb, a technical assignment that demanded skill, muscular strength and, of course, absolute resolve.

But what amazed him, what completely amazed him, was the *intimacy!* When he spoke to Celia about his love for the victim, he only hinted. For how could she understand? How could anyone understand that with one stroke of an ice ax he had *plundered* another human being, knowing him in one crushing blow, his loves, hates, fears, hopes—his *soul.*

Oh! It was something. To come so close to another. No, not close, but *in* another. Merged. Two made one. Once, he had suggested in a very vague, laughing, roundabout fashion to his wife that it might be fun if they sought out another woman, and the three might be naked together. In his own mind he had visualized the other woman as thin and dark, with enough sense to keep her mouth shut. But his wife didn't understand, didn't pick up on what he was suggesting. And if she had, she would have attributed it to his depraved appetites—a man naked in bed with two women.

But sex had nothing to do with it. That was the whole point! He wanted another woman both he and his wife could love because that would be a new, infinitely sweet intimacy between them. If he and his wife had gone to bed with a second woman, simultaneously sucked her hard nipples, caressed her, and their lips—his and his wife's—perhaps meeting on foreign flesh, well then . . . well then that would be an intimacy so sharp, so affecting, that he could hardly dream of it without tears coming to his eyes.

But now. Now! Recalling what he had done, he felt that sense of heightened intimacy, of entering into another, merging, so far beyond love that there was no comparison. When he killed Frank Lombard, he had become Frank Lombard, and the victim had become Daniel Blank. Linked, swooning, they swam through the endless corridors of the universe like two coupling astronauts cast adrift. Slowly tumbling. Turning. Drifting. Throughout all eternity. Never decaying. Never stopping. But caught in passion. Forever.

5 Whenever Daniel Blank saw Florence and Samuel together, he remembered a film he had once seen on the life of sea otters. The pups! They nuzzled each other, touched, frolicked and frisked. And the Mortons' close-fitting helmets of black oily hair were exactly like pelts. He could not watch them without amused indulgence.

Now, seated in the couch in his apartment, they insisted on sharing one Scotch-on-the-rocks—which he had replenished four times. They were clad in their black leather jumpsuits, sleek as hides, and their bright eyes and ferrety features were alive and curious.

Since they were so ready—ready? eager!—to reveal intimate details of their private lives, they assumed all their friends felt the same. They wanted to know how his affair with Celia Montfort was coming along. Had they been physically intimate? Was it a satisfying sex relationship? Had he discovered anything more about her they should know? What was Anthony's role in her household? And Valenter's?

He answered in generalities and tried to smile mysteriously. After awhile, balked by his reticence, they turned to each other and began to discuss him as if they were alone in their own apartment. He had endured this treatment before (as had all their silent friends), and sometimes he found it entertaining. But now he felt uncomfortable and, he thought, perhaps fearful. What might they not stumble on?

"Usually," Sam said, speaking directly to Flo, "when a man like Dan is asked point-blank if his sex relations with a particular woman are satisfactory, he will say something like, 'How on earth would I know? I haven't been to bed with her.' That means, A, he is telling the truth and has not been to bed with her. Or B, he has been to bed with her and is lying to protect the lady's reputation."

"True," Flo nodded solemnly. "Or C, it was so bad he doesn't want to mention it because he has failed or the lady has failed. Or D, it was absolutely marvelous, so incredible he doesn't want to talk about it; he wants to keep this wonderful memory for himself."

"Hey, come on," Dan laughed. "I'm not—"

"Ah yes," Sam interrupted. "But when a man like Dan replies to the question, 'How was sex with this particular woman?' by answering, 'It was all right,' what are we to understand from that? That he has been to bed with the lady but the experience was so-so?"

"I think that is what Dan would like us to believe," Flo said thoughtfully. "I think he is concealing something from us, Samovel."

"I agree," he nodded. "What could it be? That he has not yet made the attempt?"

"Yes," Flo said. "That makes psychological sense. Dan is a man who was married several years to a woman his physical and mental inferior. Correct?"

"Correct. And during that time sex became a routine, a habit. Suddenly separated and divorced, he looks around for a new woman. But he feels uncertain. He has forgotten how to operate."

"Exactly," Flo approved. "He is unsure of himself. He fears he may be rejected. After all, the boy isn't a mad rapist. And if he is rejected, then he will think the failure of his marriage was his fault. And his ego can't accept that. So in Dan's approach to this new woman, he is careful. He is wary. Did you ever know a wary lover to succeed?"

"Never," Sam said definitely. "Successful sex always demands aggression, either attack on the man or surrender on the part of the woman."

"And surrender on the part of the woman is as valid a method of aggression as attack on the part of the man."

"Of course. You remember reading—"

But at this point, tiring of their game, Daniel Blank went into the kitchen to pour himself a fresh vodka. When he returned to the living room, they were still at it, their voices louder now, when the bell of the hall door rang so stridently they were shocked to silence. Daniel Blank, to whom an unexpected knock or ring now came as a heart flutter or spasm of the bowels, behaved, he assured himself later, with nonchalant coolness.

"Now who on earth can that be?" he inquired of no one.

He rose and moved to the hallway door. Through the peephole he caught a glimpse of a woman's hair—long, blonde hair—and a padded coat shoulder. Oh my God, he thought, it's Gilda. What's she doing here?

But when he unhooked the chain and opened the door, it wasn't Gilda. It was and it wasn't. He stared, trying to understand. She stared back just as steadily. It wasn't until his mouth opened in astonishment that she broke into a laugh, and then he saw it was Celia Montfort.

But what a Celia! Wearing a blonde wig down to her shoulders, with the tips curled upward. Thick makeup including scarlet lip rouge. A tacky tweed suit with a ruffled blouse. A necklace of oversize pearls. Crimson nail polish. And, obviously, a padded brassiere.

She had never seen his ex-wife, never seen a photo of her, but the resemblance was startling. The physical bulk was there, the gross good health, high color, muscular swagger, a tossing about of elbows and shoulders.

"My God," Daniel said admiringly, "you're marvelous."

"Am I like her?"

"You wouldn't believe. But why?"

"Oh . . . just for fun, as Tony would say. I thought you'd like it."

"I do. I really do, My God, you're so like her. You really should have been an actress."

"I am," she said. "All the time. Aren't you going to ask me in?"

"Oh, of course. Listen, the Mortons are here. I'll announce you as Gilda. I want to see their reactions."

He preceded her to the doorway of the living room.

"It's Gilda," he called brightly, then stepped aside.

Celia came to the doorway and stood posed, sweeping the Mortons with a beaming smile.

"Gilda!" Sam cried, bouncing to his feet. "This is—" He stopped.

"Gilda!" Florence cried, waving. "How nice that—" She stopped.

Then Celia and Daniel burst out laughing, and within a moment the Mortons were laughing too.

Flo came over to embrace Celia, then patted the padded shoulders of her suit and the tweed behind.

"A padded ass," she reported to the men. "And sponge rubber tits. My God, sweetie, you thought of everything."

"Do you think I'm like?"

"Like?" Sam said. "A dead ringer. Even the makeup."

"Perfect," Flo nodded. "Even to the fingernails. How did you do it?"

"Guessed," Celia said.

"You guessed right," Daniel said. "Now would you like to take off your jacket and get comfortable?"

"Oh no. I'm enjoying this."

"All right. Vodka?"

"Please."

He went into the kitchen to prepare new drinks for all of them. When he came back, Celia had turned off all the lights except for one standing lamp, and in the gloom she looked even more like his ex-wife. The resemblance was shattering, even to the way she sat upright in the Eames chair, her back straight, feet firmly planted on the floor, knees slightly spread as if the thickness of her thighs prevented a more modest pose. He felt . . . something.

"Why the disguise?" Flo asked.

"What's the point?" Sam asked.

Celia Montfort fluffed her blonde wig, smiled her secret smile.

"Haven't you ever wanted to?" she asked them all. "Everyone wants to. Walk away from yourself. Quit your job, desert wife or husband and family, leave your home and all your possessions, strip naked if that is possible, and move to another street, city, country, world, and become someone else. New name, new personality, new needs and tastes and dreams. Become someone entirely different, entirely new. It might be better or it might be worse, but it would be *different.* And you might have a chance, just a chance, in your new skin. Like being born again. Don't you agree, Daniel?"

"Oh yes," he nodded eagerly. "I do agree."

"I don't," Sam said. "I like who I am."

"And I like who I am," Flo said. "Besides, you can never change, really."

"Can't you?" Celia asked lazily. "What a drag."

They argued the possibility of personal change, *essential* change. Blank listened to the Mortons' hooted denials and sensed the presence of an obscene danger: he was tempted to refute them, calmly, a cool, sardonic smile on his lips, by saying, "I have changed. I killed Frank Lombard." He resisted the tempation, but toyed with the risk a moment, enjoying it. Then he contented himself with an unspoken, "I know something you don't know," and this childish thought, for reasons he could not comprehend, made them immeasurably dear to him.

Eventually, of course, they were all talked out. Daniel served coffee, which they drank mostly in silence. At an unseen signal, Flo and Sam Morton rose to their feet, thanked Daniel for a pleasant evening, congratulated Celia Montfort on her impersonation, and departed. Blank locked and chained his door behind them.

When he returned to the living room, Celia was standing. They embraced and kissed, his mouth sticking to the thick rouge on her lips. He felt her padded ass.

"Shall I take it off?" she asked.

"Oh no. I like it."

They emptied ashtrays, carried glasses to the kitchen sink.

"Can you stay?" he asked.

"Of course."

"Good."

She went into the bathroom. He moved around the apartment, checking windows, turning off lights, putting the iron bar on the hallway door. When he walked across the living room he saw his ghostly reflection jump from mirror to mirror, bits and pieces.

When he came back into the bedroom she was sitting quietly on the bed, staring.

"What do you want?" she asked, looking up at him.

"Oh, leave the wig on," he said quickly. "And the brassiere and girdle. Or whatever it is. You'll want to take off the suit and blouse."

"And slip? And stockings?"

"Yes."

"The pearls?"

"No, leave them on. Would you like a robe? I have a silk robe."

"All right."

"Is it too warm in here?"

"A little."

"I'll turn down the heat. Are you sleepy?"

"More tired than sleepy. The Mortons tire me. They never stop moving."

"I know. I showered this morning. Shall I shower now?"

"No. Let me hold you."

"Naked?"

"Yes."

Later, under a single light blanket, she held him, and through her silk robe he felt padded brassiere and girdle.

"Mommy," he said.

"I know," she murmured. "I know."

He curled up in her arms, began weeping quietly.

"I'm trying," he gasped. "I really am trying."

"I know," she repeated. "I know."

The thought of fucking her, or attempting it, offended him, but he could not sleep.

"Mommy," he said again.

"Turn over," she commanded, and so he did.

"Ahh," she said. "There."

"Oh. Oh."

"Am I hurting you?"

"Oh yes! Yes."

"Am I Gilda now?"

"Yes. But she never would."

"More?"

"Slowly. Please."

"What is my name?"

"Celia."

"What?"

"Gilda."

"What?"

"Mommy."

"That's better. Isn't that better?"

He slept, finally. It seemed to him he was awake a moment later.

"What?" he said. "What is it?"

"You were having a nightmare. You screamed. What was it?"

"A dream," he said, snuggling into her. "I had a bad dream."

"What did you dream?"

"All confused."

He moved closer to her, his hands on cotton batting and sponge rubber.

"Do you want me to do it again?" she asked.

"Oh yes," he said thankfully. "Please."

In the morning when he awoke, she was lying beside him, sleeping naked, having sometime during the night taken off her wig, robe, costume. But she still wore the pearls. He touched them. Then he moved stealthily down beneath the blanket until he was crouched, completely covered, and smelled her sweet warmth. He spread her gently. Then he drank from her, gulping from the fountain, greedy he, until he felt her come awake. Still he persisted, and she moved, reaching down under the blanket to press the back of his head. He groaned, almost swooning, fevered with the covered heat. He could not stop. Afterwards she licked his mouth.

And still later, when they were dressed and at the kitchen table, she said, "You'll do it again?"—more of a statement than a question.

He nodded wordlessly, knowing what she meant, and beginning to comprehend the danger she represented.

"From the front?" she asked. "Will you? And look into his eyes, and tell me?"

"Difficult," he said.

"You can do it," she said. "I know you can."

"Well . . ." He glowed. "It needs planning. And luck, of course."

"You make your own luck."

"Do I? Well. I'll think about it. It's an interesting problem."

"Will you do something for me?"

"Of course. What?"

"Come to me immediately afterwards."

He thought a moment.

"Perhaps not immediately afterwards. But soon. That night. Will that do?"

"I may not be home."

He was instantly suspicious. "Do you want to know the night? I don't know that myself. And won't."

"No, I don't want to know the night, or the place. Just the week. Then I'll stay home every night, waiting for you. Can you tell me the week?"

"Yes. I'll tell you that. When I'm ready."

"My love," she said. "The eyes," she said.

---

6 Bernard Gilbert took life seriously—and he had a right to be mournful. Orphaned at an early age he had been schlepped around from uncle to aunt, cousin to cousin, six months at each, and always assured that the food he was eating, his bed, his clothes—all this came from the labor of his benefactors, at their expense.

At the age of eight he was shining shoes on the street, then delivering for a delly, then waiting on table, then selling little pieces of cloth, then bookkeeper in a third-rate novelty store. And all the time going to school, studying, reading books. All joylessly. Sometimes, when he had saved enough money, he went to a woman. That, too, was joyless. What could he do?

Through high school, two miserable years in the army, City College, always working, sleeping four or five hours a night, studying, reading, making loans and paying them back, not really thinking of *why?* but obeying an instinct he could not deny. And suddenly, there he was, Bernard Gilbert, C.P.A., in a new black suit, a hard worker who was good with numbers. This was a life?

There was a spine in him. Hard work didn't daunt him, and when he had to, he grovelled and shrugged it away. Much man. Not a swaggering, hairy-chested conqueror, but a survivor. A special kind of bravery; hope never died.

It came in his 32nd year when a distant cousin unexpectedly invited him for dinner. And there was Monica. "Monica, I'd like you to make the acquaintance of Bernard Gilbert. He's a C.P.A."

And so they were married, and his life began. Happy? You wouldn't believe! God said, "Bernie, I've been shitting on you for 32 years. You can take it, and it's time you deserve a break. Enjoy, kid, enjoy!"

First of all, there was Monica. Not beautiful, but handsome and strong. Another hard worker. They laughed in bed. Then came the two children, Mary and Sylvia. Beautiful girls! And healthy, thank God. The apartment wasn't much, but it was home. *Home!* His home, with wife and children. They all laughed.

The bad memories faded. It all went away: the cruelties, the hand-me-down clothes, the insults and crawling. He began, just began, to understand joy. It was a gift, and he cherished it. Bernard Gilbert: a melancholy man with sunken cheeks always in need of a shave, stooped shoulders, puzzled eyes, thinning hair, a scrawny frame: a man who, if he had his life to live over again, would have been a violinist. Well . . .

He had a good job with a large firm of accountants where his worth was recognized. In the last few years he had started to moonlight, doing the tax returns of self-employed people like doctors, dentists, architects, artists, writers. He made certain his employers knew about it; they didn't object, since he was doing it on his own time and it didn't conflict with their own commercial accounts.

His private business grew. It was hard, putting in an eight-hour day and then coming home for another two to four hours' work. But he talked it over with Monica—he talked *everything* over with Monica—and they agreed that if he stuck to it, maybe within five to ten years he might be able to cut loose and start his own business. It was possible. So Monica took a course in accounting, studied at home, and after awhile she could help him at night, in addition to cooking and cleaning and taking care of Mary and Sylvia. They were both hard workers, but they never thought of it, would have been surprised if someone had told them they worked hard. What else?

So there they were in a third-floor walk-up on East 84th Street. It wasn't a fancy apartment, but Monica had painted it nice, and there were two bedrooms and a big kitchen where Monica made matzoh brie like he couldn't believe, it was so good, and a record player with all of Isaac Stern's recordings, and a card table where he could work. It wasn't luxury, he acknowledged, but he wasn't ashamed of it, and sometimes they had friends or neighbors in and laughed. Sometimes they even went out to eat, with the children, at an expensive restaurant, and were very solemn, giggling inside.

But the best times were when he and Monica would finish their night's work, and would sit on the couch, after midnight, the children asleep, and they just were there, listening to Vivaldi turned down low, just together. He would have worked his ass off for the rest of his life for moments like that. And when Monica brushed her lips across his sunken cheek. . . . Oh!

He was thinking of moments like that when he got off the First Avenue bus. It wasn't even midnight. Well, maybe a little later. He had been downtown, working on the books of a medical clinic. It was a possible new account, a good one and a big one. The meeting with the doctors had taken longer than he had expected. Patiently he explained to them what the tax laws said they could do and what they could not do. He felt he had impressed them. They said they'd discuss it and let him know within a week. He felt good about it, but resolved not to be too optimistic when he discussed it with Monica. In case . . .

He turned into his own block. It had not yet been equipped with the new street lights, and far ahead, in the gloom, he saw a man walking toward him. Naturally, he was alerted—at that hour, in this city. But as they drew closer he saw the other man was about his age, well-dressed, coat flapping wide. He was striding along jauntily, left hand in his pocket, right arm swinging free.

They came close. Bernard Gilbert saw the other man was staring at him. But he was smiling. Gilbert smiled in return. Obviously the man lived in the neighborhood and wanted to be friendly. Gilbert decided he would say, "Good evening."

They were two steps apart, and he had said, "Good—" when the man's right hand darted beneath the open flap of his coat and came out with something with a handle, something with a point, something that gleamed even in the dull street light.

Bernard Gilbert never did say, "—evening." He knew he halted and drew back. But the thing was in the air, swinging down. He tried to lift a defending arm, but it was too heavy. He saw the man's face, handsome and tender, and there was no hate there, nor madness, but a kind of ardor. Something struck high on Bernard Gilbert's forehead, slamming him down, and he knew he was falling, felt the crash of sidewalk against his back, wondered what had happened to his newfound joy, and heard God say, "Okay, Bernie, enough's enough."

Part V

1 Three times a week a commercial messenger arrived at Captain Delaney's home with copies of the most recent Operation Lombard reports. Delaney noted they were becoming fewer and shorter, and Chief Pauley was sending his detectives back to recheck matters already covered: Lombard's private life and political career; possible links with organized crime; any similar assaults or homicides in the 251st Precinct, neighboring precincts, and eventually all of Manhattan, then all of New York; and then queries to the FBI and the police departments of large cities asking for reports of homicides of a similar nature.

Delaney admired Chief Pauley's professional competence. The Chief had assembled a force of almost 500 detectives brought in from all over the city. Many of these men Delaney knew personally or by reputation, and they included assault specialists, weapons technicians, men familiar with the political jungle, and detectives whose success was based on their interrogative techniques.

The result was nil: no angle, no handle, no apparent motive. Chief Pauley, in a confidential memo to Deputy Commissioner Broughton, had even suggested a possibility that Delaney himself had considered: the snuff had been committed by a policeman angered by Lombard's public attacks on the efficiency of the Department. Pauley didn't believe it.

Captain Delaney didn't either. A policeman would probably kill with a gun. But most career cops, who had seen mayors, commissioners, and politicians of all ranks come and go, would shrug off Lombard's criticism as just some more publicity bullshit, and go about their jobs.

The more Delaney pondered the killing, the more Operation Lombard reports he studied, the more firmly he became convinced that it was a motiveless crime. Not motiveless to the killer, of course, but motiveless to any rational man. Lombard had been a chance victim.

Delaney tried to fill up his hours. He visited his wife in the hospital twice a day, at noon and in the early evening. He did some brief interrogations of his own, visiting Frank Lombard's partner, his mother, and a few of his political associates. For these interviews Delaney wore his uniform and badge, risking Broughton's wrath if he should somehow discover what Delaney was up to. But it was all a waste of time; he learned nothing of value.

One evening, despairing of his failure to make any meaningful progress, he took a long pad of legal notepaper, yellow and ruled, and headed it "The Suspect." He then drew a line down the center of the page. The lefthand column he headed "Physical," the righthand column "Psychological." He resolved to write down everything he knew or suspected about the killer.

Under "Physical" he listed:

"Probably male, white."

"Tall, probably over six feet."

"Strong and young. Under 35?"

"Of average or good appearance. Possibly well-dressed."

"Very quick with good muscular coordination. An athlete?" Under "Psychological" he listed:

"Cool, determined."

"Driven by unknown motive."

"Psychopath? Unruh type?"

At the bottom of the page he made a general heading he called "Additional Notes." Under this he listed:

"Third person involved? Because of stolen license as 'proof of homicide.' "

"Resident of 251st Precinct?"

Then he reread his list. It was, he admitted, distressingly skimpy. But just the act of writing down what he knew—or guessed, rather; he *knew* nothing—made him feel better. It was all smoke and shadows. But he began to feel someone was there. Someone dimly glimpsed . . .

He read the list again, and again, and again. He kept coming back to the notation "Driven by unknown motive."

In all his personal experiences with and research on psychopathic killers he had never come across or read of a killer totally without motive. Certainly the motive might be irrational, senseless, but in every case, particularly those involving multiple murders, the killer had a "motive." It might be as obvious as financial gain; it might be an incredible philosophical structure as creepy and cheap as an Eiffel Tower built of glued toothpicks.

But however mad the assassin, he had his reasons: the slights of society, the whispers of God, the evil of man, the demands of political faith, the fire of ego, the scorn of women, the terrors of loneliness . . . whatever. *But he had his reasons.* Nowhere, in Delaney's experience or in his readings, existed the truly motiveless killer, the quintessentially evil man who slew as naturally and casually as another man lighted a cigarette or picked his nose.

There was no completely good man alive upon this earth and, Delaney believed—hoped!—there was no completely evil man. It was not a moral problem; it was just that no man was complete, in any way. So the killer of Frank Lombard had crushed his skull for a reason, a reason beyond logic and sense, but for a purpose that had meaning to him, twisted and contorted though it might be.

Sitting there in the gloom of his study, reading and rereading his sad little "Portrait of a Killer," Edward Delaney thought of this man existing, quite possibly not too far from where he now sat. He wondered what this man might be thinking and dreaming, might be hoping and planning.

In the morning he made his own breakfast, since it had been arranged that their day-only maid, Mary, would go directly from her home to the hospital, bringing Barbara fresh nightgowns and an address book she had requested. Delaney drank a glass of tomato juice, doggedly ate his way through two slices of unbuttered whole wheat toast, and drank two cups of black coffee. He scanned the morning paper as he ate. The Lombard story had fallen back to page 14. It said, in essence, there was nothing to say.

Wearing his winter overcoat, for the November day was chill, and the air smelled of snow, Delaney left the house before ten a.m. and walked over to

Second Avenue, to a phone booth in a candy store. He dialed Deputy Inspector Thorsen's answering service, left his phone booth number, hung up, waited patiently. Thorsen was back to him within five minutes.

"I have nothing to report," Delaney said flatly. "Nothing."

Thorsen must have caught something in his tone, for he attempted to soothe. "Take it easy, Edward. Broughton doesn't have anything either."

"I know."

"But I have some good news for you."

"What's that?"

"We were able to get your Lieutenant Dorfman a temporary appointment as Acting Commander of the Two-five-one Precinct."

"That's fine. Thank you."

"But it's only for six months. After that, either you'll be back on the job or we'll have to put in a captain or deputy inspector."

"I understand. Good enough. It'll help with the problem of Lombard's driver's license."

"What's the problem?"

"I'm on leave of absence, but I'm still on the Department list. I've got to report the license is missing."

"Edward, you worry too much."

"Yes. I do. But I've got to report it."

"That means Broughton will learn about it."

"Possibly. But if there is another killing, and I think there will be, and Chief Pauley's boys find the victim's license is missing—or anything like it—they'll check back with Lombard's widow down in Florida. She'll tell them I asked about the license and she couldn't find it. Then my ass will be in a sling. Broughton will have me up for withholding evidence."

"How do you want to handle it?"

"I've got to check the book, but as I recall, precinct reports of lost or stolen drivers' licenses are sent to Traffic Department personnel who then forward the report to the New York State Department of Motor Vehicles. I'll tell Dorfman about it and ask him to file the usual form. But Broughton might learn about it from Traffic. If they get a report that Frank Lombard's license is missing, someone will start screaming."

"Not to worry. We have a friend in Traffic."

"I thought you might have."

"Tell Dorfman to make out the usual form, but to call me before he sends it in. I'll tell him the man to send it to in Traffic. It will get to the State, but no one will tip Broughton. Does that satisfy you?"

"Yes."

"You're playing this very cautiously, Edward."

"Aren't you?"

"Yes, I guess we are. Edward, tell me . . ."

"What?"

"Are you making any progress at all? Even if it's something you don't want to talk about yet?"

"Yes," Delaney lied, "I'm making progress."

He walked back to his home, head bent, hands deep in overcoat pockets, trundling through the damp, gloomy day. His lie to Thorsen depressed him. It always depressed him when it was necessary to manipulate people. He would do it, but he would not enjoy it.

Why was it necessary to keep Thorsen's morale high? Because . . . because, Delaney decided, the Lombard homicide was more than just an intramural feud between the Broughton forces and the Thorsen-Johnson forces. In fact, he acknowledged, he had accepted their offer, not because he instinctively disliked

Broughton and wanted him put down, or had any interest in Departmental politics, but because . . . because . . . because . . .

He groaned aloud, knowing he was once again at the bone, gnawing. Was it the intellectual challenge? The atavistic excitement of the chase? The belief he was God's surrogate on earth? Why did he do it! For that universe of harmony and rhythm he had described so glowingly to Thomas Handry? Oh shit! He only knew, mournfully, that the time, mental effort and creative energy spent exploring his own labyrinthine motives might better be spent finding the man who sent a spike smashing into the skull of Frank Lombard.

He came up to his own stoop, and there was Lieutenant Dorfman ringing his bell. The lieutenant turned as he approached, saw Delaney, grinned, came bouncing down the steps. He caught up Delaney's hand, shook it enthusiastically.

"I got it, Captain!" he cried. "Acting Commander for six months. I thank you!"

"Good, good," Delaney smiled, gripping Dorfman's shoulder. "Come in and have a coffee and tell me about it."

They sat in the kitchen, and Delaney was amused to note that Dorfman was already assuming the prerogatives of his new rank; he unbuttoned his uniform blouse and sat sprawled, his long, skinny legs thrust out. He would never have sat in such a position in the Captain's office, but Delaney could understand, and even approve.

He read the teletype Dorfman had brought over and smiled again.

"All I can tell you is what I said before: I'm here and I'll be happy to help you any way I can. Don't be shy of asking. There's a lot to learn."

"I know that, Captain, and I appreciate anything you can do. You've already done plenty recommending me."

Delaney looked at him closely. Here it was again: using people. He forced ahead.

"I was glad to do it," he said. "In return, there is something you can do for me."

"Anything, Captain."

"Right now, I am going to ask you for two favors. In the future, I will probably ask for more. I swear to you I will not ask you to do anything that will jeopardize your record or your career. If you decide my word is not sufficient—and believe me, I wouldn't blame you if you thought that—then I won't insist. All right?"

Dorfman straightened in his chair, his expression puzzled at first, then serious. He stared at Delaney a long moment, their eyes locked.

"Captain, we've worked together a long time."

"Yes. We have."

"I can't believe you'd ask me to do anything I shouldn't do."

"Thank you."

"What is it you want?"

"First, I want you to file a report with the Traffic Department of a missing driver's license. I want it clearly stated on the report that I was the one who brought this matter to your attention. Before the report is sent in, I ask you to call Deputy Inspector Thorsen. He will give you the name of the man in the Traffic Department to send the report to. Thorsen has assured me the report will be forwarded to the New York State Department of Motor Vehicles in the usual manner."

Dorfman was bewildered.

"That's not much of a favor, Captain. That's just routine. Is it your license?"

"No. It's Frank Lombard's."

Dorfman stared at him again, then slowly began to button up his uniform jacket.

"Lombard's?"

"Yes. Lieutenant, if you want to ask questions, I'll try to answer them. But please don't be insulted if I say that in this matter, the less you know, the better."

The tall, red-headed man stood, began to pace about the kitchen, hands thrust into his trouser pockets. He counted the walls, didn't look at Delaney.

"I've been hearing things," he said. "Rumors."

"I imagine you have," Delaney nodded, knowing there was scarcely a man in the Department, down to the lowliest probationary patrolman, who wasn't dimly aware of the feuds and schisms amongst high-level commanders. "You don't want to get involved in it, do you?"

Dorfman stopped and gripped the top rail of a kitchen chair with reddish hands, knuckles bulging. Now he looked directly at Delaney.

"No, Captain, I don't want to get involved at all."

"What I've asked so far is pure routine, is it not? I'm asking you to report a missing driver's license. That's all."

"All right. I'll call Thorsen, get the name of the man at the Traffic Department, and file a report. Do you know the license number?"

"No."

"What is the second favor you want, Captain?"

There was something in his voice, something sad. The Captain knew Dorfman would do as he, Delaney, requested. But somehow, subtly, their relationship had changed. Dorfman would pay his debt as long as he was not compromised. But once he paid what he felt was enough, they would no longer be mentor and student, captain and lieutenant. They would no longer be friends. They would be professional associates, cautious, pleasant but reserved, watchful. They would be rivals.

Delaney had, he acknowledged, already destroyed a cordial relationship. In some small way he had corrupted faith and trust. Now, to Dorfman, he was just another guy who wanted a favor. But there was no help for it, no turning back.

"The second favor," Delaney said, accenting the word "favor" somewhat ironically, "is that I would appreciate it, lieutenant—" and again he deliberately accented the word "lieutenant"—"if you would keep me personally informed of any assaults or homicides in the Two-five-one Precinct in which the circumstances and particularly the wound are similar to the Lombard homicide."

"That's all?" Dorfman asked, and now the irony was his.

"Yes."

"All right, Captain," Dorfman nodded. He hooked his collar, tugged his jacket straight. The stains and crumbs were missing now. He was Acting Commander of the 251st Precinct.

He strode to the door without another word. Then, hand on the knob, he paused, turned to face Delaney, and seemed to soften.

"Captain," he said, "in case you're interested, I already have orders to report any assault or homicide like that to Chief Pauley."

"Of course," Delaney nodded. "He couldn't do anything else. Report to him first."

"Then to you?"

"Then to me. Please."

Dorfman nodded, and was gone.

Delaney sat without moving. Then he held out his right hand. It was trembling, a bit. It had not gone as well as he had hoped or as badly as he had feared. But, he assured himself again, it had to be done—and perhaps it would have happened in the ordinary course of events. Dorfman was a natural worshipper, almost a hanger-on, and if he was to make anything of himself, eventually he would have to be cast adrift, sink or swim. And Delaney laughed ruefully at his own rationalizing. There was, he admitted disgustedly, too goddamn much Hamlet in him.

It was almost time to leave for the hospital. He consulted his little pocket notebook and checked off the items Mary had taken care of. He had already donned his overcoat and hard Homburg, his hand reaching for the outside doorknob, when the phone rang. He picked up the extension in the hall and said, "Captain Edward X. Delaney here."

"Captain, this is Christopher Langley."

"Mr. Langley. Good to hear from you. How are you, sir?"

"Very well, and you?"

"Fine. I've been intending to call, but I didn't want you to feel I was pressuring you. So I thought it best to say *nothing*. You understand?"

There was silence for a moment, then Langley said, "I think I do understand. Gee, this is great! But it's been over a week since we met. Could we have lunch today, Captain? There's something I'd like your advice on."

"Oh?" Delaney said. "I'm afraid I can't make lunch. My wife is in the hospital, and I'm just leaving to visit her."

"I'm sorry to hear that, Captain. Nothing serious, I hope?"

"Well . . . we don't know. But it will take time. Listen, Mr. Langley, what you wanted to talk to me about—is it important?"

"It might be, Captain," the thin, flutey voice came back, excited now. "It's not anything final, but it's a beginning. That's why—"

"Yes, yes," Delaney interrupted. "Mr. Langley, would it be possible for you to meet me at the hospital? I do want to see you. Unfortunately, I can't have lunch with you, but we'll have a chance to talk and discuss your problem."

"Excellent!" Christopher Langley chortled, and Delaney knew he was enjoying this cloak-and-dagger conversation. "I'll be glad to meet you there. I hope you may be able to help me. At least it will give me an opportunity to meet your wife."

Delaney gave him the address and room number, and then rang off. The Captain stood a moment, his hand still on the dead phone, and hoped, not for the first time, that he had acted correctly in entrusting the important job of weapon identification to this elderly dandy. He started to analyze his motives for enlisting Langley's aid: the man's expertise; the need to recruit a staff, however amateur; Langley's plea for "important" work; Delaney's need—

He snorted with disgust at his own maunderings. He wanted to *move* on the Lombard homicide, and it seemed to him he had spent an unconscionable amount of time interrogating himself, probing his own motives, as if he might be guilty of—of what? Dereliction of duty? He resolved to be done, for this day at least, with such futile searchings. What was necessary was to *do*.

Barbara was seated in a wheelchair at the window, and she turned her head to give him a dazzling smile when he entered. But he had come to dread that appearance of roseate good health—the bright eyes and flushed cheeks—knowing what it masked. He crossed the room swiftly, smiling, kissed her cheek, and presented her with what might have been the biggest, reddest Delicious apple ever grown.

"An apple for the teacher," he said.

"What did I ever teach you?" she laughed, touching his lips.

"I'd tell you, but I don't want to get you unnecessarily excited."

She laughed again and turned the enormous apple in her slim fingers, stroking it. "It's beautiful."

"But probably mealy as hell. The big ones usually are."

"Maybe I won't eat it," she said faintly. "Maybe I'll just keep it next to my bed and look at it."

He was concerned. "Well . . . yes," he said finally. "Why not? Listen, how *are* you? I know you must be bored with me asking that, but you know I *must* ask it."

"Of course." She reached out to put a hand on his. "They started the new injections this morning. Two days before they know." *She* was comforting *him*.

He nodded miserably. "Is everything all right?" he asked anxiously. "I mean the food? The nurses?"

"Everything is fine."

"I asked for Temples at that stand on First Avenue. They expect them next week. I'll bring them over then."

"It's not important."

"It *is* important," he said fiercely. "You like Temples, you'll get Temples."

"All right, Edward," she smiled, patting his hand. "It's important, and I'll get Temples."

Then she was gone. It had happened several times recently, and it frightened him. Her body seemed to stiffen, her eyes took on an unfocused stare. She ceased speaking but her lips moved, pouting and drawing apart, kissing, over and over, like a babe suckling, and with the same soft, smacking sound.

"Listen," he said hurriedly, "when Eddie was here last week, I thought he looked thin. Didn't you think he looked thin?"

"Honey Bunch," she said.

"What?" he asked, not understanding and wanting to weep.

"My Honey Bunch books," she repeated patiently, still looking somewhere. "What happened to them?"

"Oh," he said. "Your Honey Bunch books. Don't you remember? When Liza told us she was pregnant, we packed up all the children's books and sent them off to her."

"Maybe she'll send them back," she murmured, turning her head to look at him with blind eyes. "My Honey Bunch books."

"I'll get some for you."

"I don't want new ones. I want the old ones."

"I know, I know," he said desperately. "The old ones with the red covers and the drawings. I'll get them for you, Barbara. Barbara? Barbara?"

Slowly the focus of her eyes shortened. She came back. He saw it happen. Then she was looking at him.

"Edward?"

"Yes," he said, "I'm here."

She smiled, gripped his hand. "Edward," she repeated.

"Listen, Barbara, there is someone coming here to meet me. Christopher Langley. He's an ex-curator of the Metropolitan. I told you about him."

"Oh, yes," she nodded. "You told me. He's trying to identify the weapon in the Lombard case."

"Exactly!" he cried delightedly, and leaned forward to kiss her cheek.

"What was that for?" she laughed.

"For being you."

"Edward, when Eddie was here last week, didn't you think he looked a little thin?"

"Yes," he nodded. "I thought he looked a little thin."

He lurched his chair closer, clasping her hands, and they talked of little things: the drapes in the study, whether or not to draw out accumulated dividends on his insurance policy to help pay hospital costs, what he had for breakfast, a rude attendant in the X-ray lab, a nurse who had unaccountably broken into tears while taking Barbara's temperature. He told her about Dorfman's promotion. She told him about a pigeon that came to her windowsill every morning at the same time. They spoke in low, droning voices, not really hearing each other, but gripping hands and singing a lovely duet.

They came out of it, interrupted by a timid but persistent rapping on the hospital room door. Delaney turned from the waist. "Come in," he called.

And into the room came dashing the dapper Christopher Langley, beaming.

And behind him, like a battle-ship plowing into the wake of a saucy corvette, came the massive Widow Zimmerman, also beaming. Both visitors carried parcels: brown paper bags of curious shape.

Delaney sprang to his feet. He shook Langley's little hand and bowed to the Widow. He introduced his wife to both. Barbara brightened immediately. She liked people, and she particularly liked people who knew what they were and could live with it.

There was talk, laughter, confusion. Barbara insisted on being moved back to the bed, knowing Edward would want to talk to Langley privately. The Widow Zimmerman planted her monumental butt in a chair alongside the bed and opened her brown paper bag. Gefilte fish! And homemade at that. The two men stood by, nodding and smiling, as the Widow expounded on the nutritive and therapeutic qualities of gefilte fish.

Within moments the good Widow had leaned forward over the bed, grasped one of Barbara's hands in her own meaty fists, and the two women were deep in a whispered discussion of such physical intimacy that the men hastily withdrew to a corner of the hospital room, pulled up chairs, leaned to each other.

"First of all, Captain," the little man said, "let me tell you immediately that I have not identified the weapon that killed Frank Lombard. I went through my books, I visited museums, and I saw several weapons—antique weapons—that could have made that skull puncture. But I agree with you: it was a modern weapon or tool. Gosh, I *thought* about it! Then, last week, I was walking down my street, and a Con Edison crew was tearing up the pavement. To lay a new cable, I suppose. They do it all the time. Anyway, they had a trench dug. There was a man in the trench, a huge black, and even in this weather he was stripped to the waist. A magnificent torso. Heroic. But Captain. An ordinary pick. A wooden handle as long as a woodsman's ax, and then a steel head with a pick on each side, tapering to a point. Much too large to be the Lombard weapon, of course. And I remembered you felt the killer carried it concealed. Extremely difficult to carry a concealed pick."

"Yes," Delaney nodded, "it would be. But the pick idea is interesting."

"The shape!" Langley said, hunching forward. "That's what caught my eye. A square spike tapering to a sharp point. More than that, each spike of the pick curved downward, just as your surgeon described the wound. So I began wondering if that pick, customarily used in excavation and construction work, might have a smaller counterpart—a one-handed pick with a handle no longer than that of a hatchet."

Delaney brooded a moment. "I can't recall ever seeing a tool like that."

"I don't think there is one," Langley agreed. "At least, I visited six hardware stores and none of them had anything like what I described. But at the seventh hardware store I found this. It was displayed in their window."

He opened his brown paper bag and withdrew a tool: magician and rabbit. He handed it to Delaney. The Captain took it in his blunt fingers, stared, turned it over and over, hefted it, gripped it, swung it by the handle, peered at the head. He sniffed at the wood handle.

"What the hell *is* it?" he asked finally.

"It's a bricklayer's hammer," Langley said rapidly. "Handle of seasoned hickory. Head of forged steel. Notice the squared hammer on one side of the head? That's for tapping bricks into place in the mortar. Now look at the spike. The top surface curves downward, but the bottom side is horizontal. The spike itself doesn't curve downward. In addition, the spike ends in a sharp, chisel point, used to split bricks. I knew at once it wasn't the weapon we seek. But it's a start, don't you think?"

"Of course it is," Delaney said promptly. He swung the hammer in short, violent strokes. "My God, I never knew such a tool existed. You could easily split a man's skull with this."

"But it isn't what we want, is it?"

"No," Delaney acknowledged, "it isn't. The spike doesn't curve downward, and the end comes to a chisel edge about—oh, I'd guess an inch across. Mr. Langley, there's something else I should have mentioned to you. This has a wooden handle. I admit Lombard might well have been killed with a wood-handled weapon, but my experience has been that with wood-handled implements, particularly old ones, the handle breaks. Usually at the point where it's been compressed into the steel head. I'd feel a lot better if we could find a tool or weapon that was made totally of steel. This is just a feeling I have, and I don't want to inhibit your investigation, sir."

"Oh, it won't, it won't!" the little man cried, bouncing up and down on his chair in his excitement. "I agree, I agree! Steel would be better. But I haven't told you everything that happened. In the store where I found this bricklayer's hammer, I asked the proprietor why he stocked them and how many he sold. After all, Captain, how many bricklayers are there in this world? And how many hammers would they need? Look at that tool. Wouldn't you judge that an apprentice bricklayer, buying a tool as sturdy as that, would use it for the rest of his professional career?"

Delaney hefted the hammer again, swinging it experimentally.

"Yes," he nodded, "I think you're right. The handle might possibly break, but this thing could last fifty, a hundred years."

"Exactly. Well, the hardware store owner said—and it's amazing how willing and eager men are to talk about their jobs and specialties—"

"I know," Delaney smiled.

"Well, he said he stocked those hammers because he sold twenty or thirty a year. And not only to bricklayers! He sold them, he said, to 'rock hounds'—a term, as he explained it, that applies to the people who search for precious and semiprecious stones—gemmologists and others of their ilk. In addition, he sold a few hammers to amateur archeologists. I then asked if he knew of a similar hammer on which the spike, instead of ending in a wide chisel edge, came to a sharp, tapered point. He said he had heard of such a hammer but had never seen it—a hammer made especially for rock hounds, prospectors, and archeologists. And this hammer had a spike, a pick, that tapered to a sharp point. I asked him where it might be available, but he couldn't say, except that I might try hobby and outdoor stores. What do you think, Captain?"

Delaney looked at him. "First of all," he said, "I think you have done remarkably well. Much better than I could have done." He was rewarded by Langley's beam of pleasure. "And I hope you will be willing to track this thing down, to try to find the rock hound's hammer with a spike that curves downward and tapers to a point."

"Willing?" Christopher Langley shouted delightedly. "Willing?" And the two women at the bed, still speaking softly, broke off their conversation and looked over inquiringly.

"Willing?" Langley asked in a quieter voice. "Captain, I cannot stop now. I never knew detective work could be so fascinating."

"Oh yes," Delaney nodded solemnly, "fascinating."

"Well, I haven't had so much fun in my life. After we leave here, Myra and I—"

"Myra?" Delaney interrupted.

"The Widow Zimmerman," the old dandy said, casting his eyes downward and blushing. "She has several admirable qualities."

"I'm sure."

"Well, I made a list of hobby shops from the Yellow Pages. We're going to have lunch in the Times Square area, and then we're going around to all the addresses I have and try to locate a rock hound's hammer. Is that the right way, Captain?"

"Exactly the right way," Delaney assured him. "It's just what I'd do. Don't be discouraged if you don't find it in the first four or five or dozen or fifty places you visit. Stick to it."

"Oh, I intend to," Langley said stoutly, straightening up. "This is important, isn't it, Captain?"

Delaney looked at him strangely. "Yes," he nodded, "it *is* important. Mr. Langley, I have a feeling about you and what you're doing. I think it's *very* important."

"Well," Christopher Langley said, "then I better get to it."

"May I keep this hammer?"

"Of course, of course. I have no use for it. I'll keep you informed as to our progress."

"Our?"

"Well . . . you know. I must take the Widow Zimmerman to lunch. She has been very kind to me."

"Of course."

"But I've told her nothing, Captain. *Nothing.* I swear. She thinks I'm looking for a rock hammer for my nephew."

"Good. Keep it that way. And I must apologize for my phone conversation this morning. I'm probably being overcautious. I doubt very much if my phone is being tapped, but there's no point in taking chances. When you want to reach me from now on, just dial my home phone and say something innocuous. I'll get back to you within ten or fifteen minutes from an outside phone. Will that be satisfactory?"

Then the ex-curator did something exceedingly curious. He made an antique gesture Delaney had read about in Dickens' novels but had never seen. Langley laid a forefinger alongside his nose and nodded wisely. Captain Delaney was delighted.

"Exactly," he nodded.

Then they were gone, waving goodby to Barbara and promising to visit her again. When the door closed behind them, Barbara and Edward looked at each other, then simultaneously broke into laughter.

"I like her," Barbara told him. "She asked very personal questions on short acquaintance, but I think it was from genuine interest, not just idle curiosity. A very warm, out-going, goodhearted woman."

"I think she's after Langley."

"So?" she challenged. "What's wrong with that? She told me she's been very lonely since her husband died, and he's all alone, too. It's not good to be alone when you get old."

"Look at this," he said, changing the subject hastily. "It's a bricklayer's hammer. This is what Langley's come up with so far."

"Is that what killed Lombard?"

"Oh no. But it's close. It's an ugly thing, isn't it?"

"Yes. Evil-looking. Put it away, please, dear."

He put it back in the brown paper sack and placed it atop his folded overcoat, so he wouldn't forget it when he left. Then he drew up a chair alongside her bed.

"What are you going to do with the gefilte fish?" he smiled.

"I may try a little. Unless you'd like it, Edward?"

"No, thank you!"

"Well, it was nice of her to bring it. She's one of those women who think food solves all problems and you can't be miserable on a full stomach. Sometimes they're right."

"Yes."

"You're discouraged, aren't you, Edward?"

He rose and began to stalk up and down at the foot of her bed, hands shoved into his hip pockets.

"Nothing is happening!" he said disgustedly. "I'm not *doing* anything."

"You're convinced the killer is crazy?"

"It's just an idea," he sighed, "but the only theory that makes any sense at all. But if I'm right, it means we have to wait for another killing before we learn anything more. That's what's so infuriating."

"Isn't that hammer Langley brought a lead?"

"Maybe. Maybe not. But even if Lombard had been murdered with a hammer exactly like that, I'd be no closer to finding the killer. There must be hundreds—thousands!—of hammers exactly like that in existence, and more sold every day. So where does that leave me?"

"Come over here and sit down." She motioned toward the chair at the bedside. He slumped into it, took her proffered hand. She lifted his knuckles to her face, rubbed them softly on her cheek, kissed them. "Edward," she said. "Poor Edward."

"I'm a lousy cop," he grumbled.

"No," she soothed. "You're a good cop. I can't think of anything you could have done that you haven't done."

"Operation Lombard did it all," he said dispiritedly.

"You discovered his driver's license was missing."

"Oh sure. Whatever the hell that means."

After 30 years of living with this man, she was almost as familiar with police procedure as he. "Did they check license numbers of parked cars?" she asked.

"Of course. Chief Pauley saw to that. The license number of every parked car in a five-block area was taken down on three successive nights. Then the owners were looked up and asked if they saw anything on the night of the murder. What a job that must have been! But Broughton has the manpower to do it, and it had to be done. They got nothing. Just like the questioning of residents in the neighborhood. Zero."

"Occam's Razor," she said, and he smiled, knowing what she meant.

Several years ago he had come across the unfamiliar phrase "Occam's Razor" in a criminologist's report dealing with percentages and probabilities in homicide cases in the Boston area. Delaney trusted the findings since the percentages quoted were very close to those then current in New York: the great majority of homicides were committed by relatives or "friends" of the victim—mothers, fathers, children, husbands, wives, uncles, aunts, neighbors . . . In other words, most killings involved people who knew each other.

In light of these findings, the Boston criminologist had stated, it was always wise for investigating officers to be guided by the principle of "Occam's Razor."

Intrigued by the phrase, Delaney had spent an afternoon in the reading room of the 42nd Street library, tracking down Occam and his "Razor." Later he told Barbara what he had discovered.

"Occam was a fourteenth century philosopher," he reported. "His philosophy was 'nominalism,' which I don't understand except that I think he meant there are no universal truths. Anyway, he was famous for his hard-headed approach to problem solving. He believed in shaving away all extraneous details. That's why they call his axiom 'Occam's Razor.' He said that when there are several possible solutions, the right one is probably the most obvious. In other words, you should eliminate all the unnecessary facts."

"But you've been doing that all your life, Edward."

"I guess so," he laughed, "but I call it 'Cut out the crap.' Anyway, it's nice to know a fourteenth century philosopher agrees with me. I wish I knew more about philosophy and could understand it."

"Does it really bother you that you can't?"

"Nooo . . . it doesn't bother me, but it makes me realize the limitations of my intelligence. I just can't think in abstractions. You know I tried to learn to play chess three times and finally gave up."

"Edward, you're more interested in people than things, or ideas. You have a very good intelligence for people."

Now, in the hospital room, when Barbara mentioned Occam's Razor, he knew what she meant and smiled ruefully.

"Well," he said, rubbing his forehead, "I wonder if old Occam ever tried solving an irrational problem by rational means. I wonder if he wouldn't begin to doubt the value of logic and deductive reasoning when you're dealing with—"

But then the door to the hospital room swung open, and Dr. Louis Bernardi glided in, olive skin gleaming, his little eyes glittering. A stethoscope was draped about his neck.

He offered Delaney a limp hand, and with the forefinger of his left hand lovingly caressed his ridiculous stripe of a mustache.

"Captain," he murmured. "And you, dear lady," he inquired in a louder voice, "how are we feeling today?"

Barbara began to explain that her feet continued to be swollen uncomfortably, how the rash had reappeared on the insides of her thighs, that the attack of nausea had seemed to worsen with the first injection of the antibiotic.

To each complaint Bernardi smiled, said, "Yes, yes," or "That doesn't bother me."

Why should it bother you, Delaney thought angrily. It's not happening to you, you little prick.

Meanwhile the doctor was taking her pulse, listening to her heart, gently pushing up eyelids to peer into her staring eyes.

"You're making a fine recovery from surgery," he assured her. "And they tell me your appetite is improving. I am so very happy, dear lady."

"When do you think—" Delaney began, but the doctor held up a soft hand.

"Patience," he said. "You must have patience. And I must have patients. He!"

Delaney turned away in disgust, not understanding how Barbara could trust this simpering popinjay.

Bernardi murmured a few more words, patted Barbara's hand, smiling his oleaginous smile, then turned to go. He was almost at the door when Delaney saw he was leaving.

"Doctor," he called, "I want to talk to you a minute." He said to Barbara, "Be right back, dear."

In the hall, the door of the room closed, he faced Bernardi and looked at him stonily. "Well?" he demanded.

The doctor spread his hands in that familiar bland gesture that said nothing. "What can I tell you? You can see for yourself. The infection still persists. That damned Proteus. We are working our way through the full spectrum of antibiotics. It takes time."

"There's something else."

"Oh? What is that?"

"Recently my wife has been exhibiting signs of—well, signs of irrationality. She gets a curious stare, she seems suddenly withdrawn, and she says things that don't make too much sense."

"What kind of things?"

"Well, a little while ago she wanted some children's books. I mean books she owned and read when she was a child. She's not under sedation, is she?"

"Not now, no."

"Pain-killers? Sleeping pills?"

"No. We are trying to avoid any possibility of masking or affecting the strength of the antibiotics. Captain, this does not worry me. Your wife has undergone major surgery. She is under medication. The fever is, admittedly, weakening her.

It is understandable that she might have brief periods of—oh, call it wool-gathering. He! I suggest you humor her insofar as that is possible. Her pulse is steady and her heart is strong."

"As strong as it was?"

Bernardi looked at him without expression. "Captain," he said softly—and Delaney knew exactly what was coming—"your wife is doing as well as can be expected."

He nodded, turned, glided away, graceful as a ballet dancer. Delaney was left standing alone, impotent fury hot in his throat, convinced the man knew something, or suspected something, and would not put it into words. He seemed blocked and thwarted on all sides: in his work, in his personal life. What was it he had said to Thomas Handry about a divine order in the universe? Now order seemed slipping away, slyly, and he was defeated by a maniacal killer and unseen beasts feeding on his wife's flesh.

From the man on the beat to the police commissioner—all cops knew what to expect when the moon was full: sleepwalkers, women who heard voices, men claiming they were being bombarded by electronic beams from a neighbor's apartment, end-of-the-world nuts, people stumbling naked down the midnight streets, urinating as they ran.

Now Delaney, brooding on war, crime, senseless violence, cruel sickness, brutality, terror, and the slick, honeyed words of a self-satisfied physician, wondered if this was not The Age of the Full Moon, with order gone from the world and irrationality triumphant.

He straightened, set his features into a smile, reentered his wife's hospital room.

"I suddenly realized why solving the Lombard killing is so important to me," he told her. "It happened in the Two-five-one Precinct. That's my world."

"Occam's Razor," she nodded.

Later, he returned home and Mary fixed him a baked ham sandwich and brought that and a bottle of cold beer into his study. He propped the telephone book open on his desk, and as he ate he called second-hand bookstores, asking for original editions of the Honey Bunch books, the illustrated ones.

Everyone he called seemed to know immediately what he wanted: the Grosset & Dunlap editions published in the early 1920s. The author was Helen Louise Thorndyke. But no one had any copies. One bookseller took his name and address and promised to try to locate them. Another suggested he try the chic "antique boutiques" on upper Second and Third Avenues, shops that specialized in nostalgic Americana.

Curiously, this ridiculous task seemed to calm him, and by the time he had finished his calls and his lunch, he was determined to get back to work, to work steadily and unquestioningly, just doing.

He went to his book shelves and took down every volume he owned dealing, even in peripheral fashion, with the histories, analyses and detection of mass murderers. The stack he put on the table alongside his club chair was not high; literature on the subject was not extensive. He sat down heavily, put on his thick, horn-rimmed reading glasses, and began to plow through the books, skipping and skimming as much as he could of material that had no application to the Lombard case.

He read about Gilles de Rais, Verdoux, Jack the Ripper and in more recent times, Whitman, Speck, Unruh, the Boston strangler, Panzram, Manson, the boy in Chicago who wrote with the victim s lipstick on her bathroom mirror, "Stop me before I kill more." It was a sad, sad chronicle of human aberration, and the saddest thing of all was the feeling he got of killer as victim, dupe of his own agonizing lust or chaotic dreams.

But there was no pattern—at least none he could discern. Each mass killer, of tens, hundreds, reputedly thousands, was an individual and had apparently acted from unique motives. If there was any pattern it existed solely in each man: the modus operandi remained identical, the weapon the same. And in almost every case, the period between killings became progressively shorter. The killer was caught up in a crescendo: more! more! faster! faster!

One other odd fact: the mass killer was invariably male. There were a few isolated cases of women who had killed several times; the Ohio Pig Woman was one, the Beck-Fernandez case involved another. But the few female mass murderers seemed motivated by desire for financial gain. The males were driven by wild longings, insane furies, mad passions.

The light faded; he switched on the reading lamp. Mary stopped by to say good-night, and he followed her into the hall to double-lock and chain the front door behind her. He returned to his reading, still trying to find a pattern, a repeated cause-effect, searching for the percentages.

It was almost five in the evening when the front doorbell chimed. He put aside the article he was reading—a fascinating analysis of Hitler as a criminal rather than a political leader—and went out into the hallway again. He switched on the stoop light, peered out the etched glass panel alongside the door. Christopher Langley was standing there, a neat white shopping bag in one hand. Delaney unlocked the door.

"Captain!" Langley cried anxiously. "I hope I'm not disturbing you? But I didn't want to call, and since it was on my way home, I thought I'd take the chance and—"

"You're not disturbing me. Come in, come in."

"Gee, what a marvelous house!"

"Old, but comfortable."

They went into the lighted study.

"Captain, I've got—"

"Wait, just a minute. Please, let me get you a drink. Anything?"

"Sherry?"

"At the moment, I'm sorry to say, no. But I have some dry vermouth. Will that do?"

"Oh, that's jim-dandy. No ice. Just a small glass, please."

Delaney went over to his modest liquor cabinet, poured Langley a glass of vermouth, took a rye for himself. He handed Langley his wine, got him settled in the leather club chair. He retreated a few steps out of the circle of light cast by the reading lamp and stood in the gloom.

"Your health, sir."

"And yours. And your wife's."

"Thank you."

They both sipped.

"Well," Delaney said, "how did you make out?"

"Oh, Captain, I was a fool, *such* a fool! I didn't do the obvious thing, the thing I should have done in the first place."

"I know," Delaney smiled, thinking of Occam's Razor again. "I've done that many times. What happened?"

"Well, as I told you at the hospital, I had gone through the Yellow Pages and made a list of hobby shops in the midtown area, places that might sell a rock hound's hammer with a tapered pick. The Widow Zimmerman and I had lunch—I had stuffed sole: marvelous—and then we started walking around. We covered six different stores, and none of them carried rock hammers. Some of them didn't even know what I was talking about. I could tell Myra was getting tired, so I put her in a cab and sent her home. She is preparing dinner for me tonight. By the by, she's an awful cook. I thought I'd try a few more stores before calling it a day. The next one on my list was Abercrombie & Fitch. And of course they carried a rock hound's hammer. It was so obvious! It's the largest store of its kind in the city, and I should have tried them first. That's why I say I was a fool. Anyway, here it is."

He leaned over, pulled the tool from his white shopping bag, handed it to Captain Delaney.

The hammer was still in its vacuum-packed plastic coating, and the cardboard backing stated it was a "prospector's ax recommended for rock collectors and archeologists." Like the bricklayers' hammer, it had a wood handle and steel head. One side of the head was a square hammer. The other side was a pick, about four inches long. It started out as a square, then tapered to a sharp point. The tool came complete with a leather holster, enabling it to be worn on a belt. The whole thing was about as long as a hatchet: a one-handed implement.

"Notice the taper of the pick," Langley pointed out. "It comes to a sharp point, but still the pick itself does not curve downward. The upper surface curves, but the lower surface is almost horizontal, at right angles to the handle. And, of course, it has a wooden handle. But still, it's closer to what we're looking for—don't you think?"

"No doubt about it," Delaney said definitely. "If that pick had a downward curve, I'd say this is it. May I take off the plastic covering?"

"Of course."

"You're spending a lot of money."

"Nonsense."

Delaney stripped off the clear plastic covering and hefted the ax in his hand.

"This is almost it," he nodded. "A tapered spike coming to a sharp point. About an inch across at the base of the pick. And with enough weight to crush a man's skull. Easily. Maybe this really is it. I'd like to show it to the police surgeon who did the Lombard autopsy."

"No, no," Christopher Langley protested. "I haven't told you the whole story. That's why I stopped by tonight. I bought this in the camping department, and I was on my way out to the elevators. I passed through a section where they sell skiing and mountain climbing gear. You know, rucksacks and crampons and pitons and things like that. And there, hanging on the wall, was something very interesting. It was an implement I've never seen before. It was about three feet long, a two-handed tool. I ruled it out immediately as our weapon: too cumbersome to conceal. And the handle was wood. At the butt end was a sharp steel spike, about three inches long, fitted into the handle. But it was the head that interested me. It was apparently chrome-plated steel. On one side was a kind of miniature mattock coming to a sharp cutting edge, a chisel edge. And the other side was exactly what we're looking for! It was a spike, a pick, about four or five inches long. It started out from the head as a square, about an inch on each side. Then it was formed into a triangle with a sharp edge on top and the base an inch across. Then the whole thing tapered, and as it thinned, it curved downward. Captain, *the whole pick curved downward,* top and bottom! It came to a sharp point, so sharp in fact that the tip was covered with a little rubber sleeve to prevent damage when the implement wasn't being used. I removed the rubber protector, and the underside of the tip had four little saw teeth. It's serrated, for cutting. I finally got a clerk and asked him what this amazing tool was called. He said it's an ice ax. I asked him what it was used for, and he—"

"What?" Delaney cried. "What did you say?"

"I asked the clerk what it was used—"

"No, no," the Captain said impatiently. "What did the clerk say it was called?"

"It's an ice ax."

"Jesus Christ," Delaney breathed. "Leon Trotsky. Mexico City. Nineteen-forty."

"What? Captain, I don't understand."

"Leon Trotsky. He was a refuge from Stalin's Russia—or perhaps he escaped or was deported; I don't remember exactly; I'll have to look it up. Trotsky and Lenin and Stalin were equals at one time. Then Lenin died. Then Stalin wanted to be Numero Uno. So Trotsky got out of Russia, somehow, and made his way to Mexico City. They caught up with him in nineteen-forty. At least it was said the assassin was an agent of the Russian Secret Police. I don't recall the details. But he killed Trotsky with an ice ax."

"Surely you don't think there's any connection between that and Frank Lombard's death?"

"Oh no. I doubt that very much. I'll look into it, of course, but I don't think there's anything there."

"But you think Lombard may have been killed with an ice ax?"

"Let me freshen your drink," Delaney said. He went over to the liquor cabinet, came back with new drinks for both of them. "Mr. Langley, I don't know whether being a detective is a job, a career, a profession, a talent or an art. There are some things I do know. One, you can't teach a man to be a *good* detective, anymore than you can teach him to be an Olympic miler or a great artist. And two, no matter how much talent and drive a man starts out with, he can never become a *good* detective without experience. The more years, the better. After you've been at it awhile, you begin to see the patterns. People repeat, in motives, weapons, methods of entrance and escape, alibis. You keep finding the same things happening over and over again; forced windows, kitchen knives, slashed screens, tire irons, jammed locks, rat poison—the lot. It all becomes familiar. Well, what bugged me about the Lombard killing, nothing *familiar* in it. Nothing! The first reaction, of course, going by percentages, was that it had been committed by a relative or acquaintance, someone known to Lombard. Negative. The next possibility was that it was an attempted robbery, a felony-homicide. Negative. His money hadn't even been touched. And worst of all, we couldn't even identify the weapon. But now you walk in here and say, 'Ice ax.' Magic words! Click! Trotsky was killed with an ice ax. Suddenly I've got something *familiar*. A murder weapon that's been used before. It's hard to explain, I know, Mr. Langley, but I feel better about this than I've felt since it started. I think we're moving now. Thanks to you."

The man glowed.

"But I'm sorry," Delaney said. "I interrupted you. You were telling me what the clerk at Abercrombie & Fitch said when you asked him what the ice ax was used for. What did he say?"

"What?" Langley asked again, somewhat dazed. "Oh. Well, he said it was used in mountain climbing. You could use it like a cane, leaning on the head. The spike on the butt of the handle bites into crusty snow or ice, if you're hiking across a glacier, for instance. He said you could get this ice ax with different ends on the butt—a spike, the way I saw it, or with a little wheel, like a ski pole, for soft snow, and so forth. So then I asked him if there was a shorter ice ax available, a one-handed tool, but with the head shaped the same way. He was very vague; he wasn't sure. But he thought there was such an implement, and he thought the whole thing might be made of steel. Think of that, Captain! A one-handed tool, all steel, with a spike that curves downward and tapers to a sharp point as it curves. How does that strike you?"

"Excellent!" Captain Delaney crowed. "Just excellent! It's now a familiar weapon, used in a previous homicide, and I feel very good about it. Mr. Langley, you've done wonders."

"Oh," the old man smiled, "it was mostly luck. Really."

"You make your own luck," Delaney assured him. "And my luck. Our luck. You followed through. Did the clerk tell you where you can buy a one-handed ice ax?"

"Well . . . no. But he did say there were several stores in New York that specialized in camping and mountain climbing equipment—axes, hatchets, crampons, special rucksacks, nylon rope and things of that sort. The stores must be listed somewhere. Probably in the Yellow Pages. Captain, can I stick with this?"

Delaney took two quick steps forward, clapped the little man on both arms.

"Can you?" he declaimed. "*Can* you? I should think you can! You're doing just fine. You try to pin down that one-handed, all-steel ice ax, who sells them, who buys them. Meanwhile, I want to dig into the Trotsky murder, maybe get a photo of the weapon. And I want to get more information on mountain climbers. Mr. Langley, we're moving. We're really *doing* now! I'll call you or you call me. The hell with security. I just feel—I *know*—we're heading in the right direction. Instinct? Maybe. Logic has nothing to do with it. It just *feels* right."

He got Langley out of there, finally, bubbling with enthusiasm and plans of how he intended to trace the ice ax. Delaney nodded, smiled, agreeing to everything Langley said until he could, with decency, usher him out, lock the front door, and come back into the study. He paced up and down in front of his desk, hands shoved into hip pockets, chin on chest.

Then he grabbed up the telephone directory, looked up the number, and dialed Thomas Handry's newspaper. The switchboard operator gave him the City Room where they told him Handry had left for the day. He asked for Handry's home phone number, but they wouldn't give it to him.

"Is it an unlisted number?" he asked.

"Yes, it is."

"This is Captain Edward X. Delaney, New York Police Department," the Captain said in his most pontifical tones. "I'm calling on official business. I can get Handry's phone number from the telephone company, if you insist. It would save time if you gave it to me. If you want to check on me, call your man at Centre Street. Who is he—Slawson?"

"Slawson died last year."

"I'm sorry to hear that. He was a good reporter."

"Yes. Just a minute, Captain."

The man came back and read off Handry's home phone number. Delaney thanked him, hung up, waited a few seconds, then lifted the receiver again and dialed. No answer. He waited ten minutes and called again. Still no answer.

There wasn't much in the refrigerator: half of that same baked ham he had had for lunch and some salad stuff. He sliced two thick slices of ham, then sliced a tomato and cucumber. He smeared mustard on the ham, and salad dressing on the rest. He ate it quickly, crunching on a hard roll. He glanced several times at his watch as he ate, anxious to get back to the hospital.

He slid plate and cutlery into the sink, rinsed his hands, and went back into his study to call Handry again. This time he got through.

"Hello?"

"Thomas Handry?"

"Yes."

"Captain Edward X. Delaney here."

"Oh. Hello, Captain. How are you?"

"Well, thank you. And you?"

"Fine. I heard you're on leave of absence."

"Yes, that's true."

"I understand your wife is ill. Sorry to hear that. I hope she's feeling better."

"Yes. Thank you. Handry, I want a favor from you."

"What is it, Captain?"

"First of all, I want some information on the murder of Leon Trotsky in Mexico City in nineteen-forty. I thought you might be able to get it from your morgue."

"Trotsky in Mexico City in nineteen-forty? Jesus, Captain, that was before I was born."

"I know."

"What do you want?"

"Nothing heavy. Just what the newspapers of the time reported. How he was killed, who killed him, the weapon used. If there was a photograph of the weapon published, and you could get a photostat, that would help."

"What's this all about?"

"The second thing," Delaney went on, ignoring the question, "is that I'd like the name and address of the best mountain climber in New York—the top man, or most experienced, or most skillful. I thought you might be able to get it from your Sports Desk."

"Probably. Will you please tell me what the hell this is all about?"

"Can you have a drink with me tomorrow? Say about five o'clock?"

"Well . . . sure. I guess so."

"Can you have the information by then?"

"I'll try."

"Fine. I'll tell you about it then." Delaney gave him the address of the chop house where he had lunched with Dr. Ferguson. "Is that all right, Handry?"

"Sure. I'll see what I can do. Trotsky and the mountain climber. Right?"

"Right. See you tomorrow."

Delaney hurried out and got a cab on Second Avenue. He was at the hospital within fifteen minutes. When he gently opened the door of his wife's room, he saw at once she was sleeping. He tiptoed over to the plastic armchair, switched off the floor lamp, then took off his overcoat. He sat down as quietly as he could.

He sat there for two hours, hardly moving. He may have dozed off a few minutes, but mostly he stared at his wife. She was sleeping calmly and deeply. No one came into the room. He heard the corridor sounds dimly. Still he sat, his mind not so much blank as whirring, leaping, jumping about without order or connection: their children, Handry, Langley, Broughton, the Widow Zimmerman, the ice ax, Thorsen and Johnson, a driver's license—a smear of thoughts, quick frames of a short movie, almost blending, looming, fading . . .

At the end of the two hours he scrawled a message in his notebook, tore the page out, propped it on her bedside table. "I was here. Where were you? Love and violets. Ted." He tiptoed from the room.

He walked back to their home, certain he would be mugged, but he wasn't. He went back into his study and resumed his readings of the histories, motives and methods of mass murderers. There was no one pattern.

He put the books aside, turned off the study lights shortly after midnight. He toured the basement and street floor, checking windows and locks. Then he trudged upstairs to undress, take a warm shower, and shave. He pulled on fresh pajamas. The image of his naked body in the bathroom mirror was not encouraging. Everything—face, neck, breasts, abdomen, ass, thighs—seemed to be sinking.

He got into bed, switched off the bedside lamp, and lay awake for almost an hour, turning from side to side, his mind churning. Finally he turned on the lamp, shoved his feet into wool slippers, went padding down to the study again. He dug out his list, the one headed "The Suspect." Under the "Physical" column he had jotted "An athlete?" He crossed this out and inserted "A mountain climber?" At the bottom, under "Additional Notes," he wrote "Possesses an ice ax?"

It wasn't much, he admitted. In fact, it was ridiculous. But when he turned out the study lights, climbed once more to the empty bedroom, and slid into bed, he fell asleep almost instantly.

2 "You didn't give me much time," Thomas Handry said, unlocking his attache case. "I guessed you'd be more interested in the assassination itself rather than the political background, so most of the stuff I've got is on the killing."

"You guessed right," Captain Delaney nodded. "By the way, I read all your articles on the Department. Pretty good, for an outsider."

"Thanks a whole hell of a lot!"

"You want to write poetry, don't you?"

Handry was astonished, physically. He jerked back in the booth, jaw dropping, took off his Benjamin Franklin reading glasses.

"How did you know that?"

"Words and phrases you used. The rhythm. And you were trying to get inside cops. It was a good try."

"Well . . . you can't make a living writing poetry."

"Yes. That's true."

Handry was embarrassed. So he looked around at the paneled walls, leather-covered chairs, old etchings and playbills, yellowed and filmed with dust.

"I like this place," he said. "I've never been here before. I suppose it was created last year, and they sprayed dirt on everything. But they did a good job. It really does look old."

"It is," Delaney assured him. "Over a hundred years. It's not a hype. How's your ale?"

"Real good. All right, let's get started." He took handwritten notes from his attache case and began reading rapidly.

"Leon Trotsky. Da-dah da-dah da-dah. One of the leaders of the Russian Revolution, and after. A theorist. Stalin drives him out of Russia, but still doesn't trust him. Trotsky, even overseas, could be plotting. Trotsky gets to Mexico City. He's suspicious, naturally. Very wary. But he can't live in a closet. A guy named Jacson makes his acquaintance. It's spelled two ways in newspaper reports: J-a-c-s-o-n and J-a-c-k-s-o-n. A white male. He visits Trotsky for at least six months. Friends. But Trotsky never sees *anyone* unless his secretaries and bodyguards are present. August twentieth, nineteen-forty, Jacson comes to visit Trotsky, bringing an article he's written that he wants Trotsky to read. I couldn't find what it was about. Probably political. Jacson is invited into the study. For the first time the secretaries aren't notified. Jacson said later that Trotsky started reading the article. He sat behind his desk. Jacson stood at his left. He had a raincoat, and in the pockets were an ice ax, a revolver, and a dagger. He said—"

"Wait a minute, wait a minute," Delaney protested. "Jacson had an ice ax in his raincoat pocket? Impossible. It would never fit."

"Well, one report said it was in the raincoat pocket. Another said it was concealed by Jacson's raincoat."

" 'Concealed.' That's better."

"All right, so Trotsky is reading Jacson's article. Jacson takes the ice ax from under his raincoat, or out of the pocket, and smashes it down on Trotsky's skull. Trotsky shrieks and throws himself on Jacson, biting his left hand. Beautiful. Then he staggers backward. The secretaries come running in and grab Jacson."

"Why the revolver and dagger?"

"Jacson said they were to be used to kill himself after he killed Trotsky."

"It smells. Did Trotsky die then, in his study?"

"No. He lived for about twenty-six hours. Then he died."

"Any mention of the direction of the blow?"

"On top of Trotsky's head, as far as I can gather. Trotsky was seated, Jacson was standing."

"What happened to him?"

"Jacson? Imprisoned. One escape try failed, apparently planned by the GPU. That's what the Russian Secret Police was called then. I don't know where Jacson is today, or even if he's alive. There was a book published on Trotsky last year. Want me to look into it?"

"No. It's not important. Another ale?"

"Please. I'm getting thirsty with all this talking."

They sat silently until another round of drinks was brought. Delaney was drinking rye and water.

"Let's get back to the weapon," he said, and Handry consulted his notes.

"I couldn't locate a photo, but the wonderful old lady who runs our morgue, and who remembers *everything,* told me that a magazine ran an article on the killing in the 1950s and published a photo of the ice ax used, so apparently a photo does exist, somewhere."

"Anything else?"

"It was the kind of ice ax used in mountain climbing. First, Jacson said he bought it in Switzerland. Now the testimony gets confused. Jacson's mistress said she had never seen it in Paris or New York, prior to their trip to Mexico. Then Jacson said he like mountaineering and had bought the ax in Mexico and used it when climbing—wait a minute; I've got it here somewhere—when climbing the Orizaba and Popo in Mexico. But then later it turned out that Jacson had lived in a camp in Mexico for awhile, and the owner's son was an enthusiastic mountaineer. He and Jacson talked about mountain climbing several times. This son owned an ice ax, purchased four years previously. The day following the attack on Trotsky, and Jacson's arrest, the camp owner went looking for his son's ice ax, but it had disappeared. Confusing, isn't it?"

"It always is," Delaney nodded. "But Jacson could have purchased the ax in Switzerland, Paris, New York, or stolen it in Mexico. Right?"

"Right."

"Great," Delaney sighed. "I didn't know you could buy the damned thing like a candy bar. Was Jacson really a GPU agent?"

"Apparently no one knows for sure. But the ex-chief of the Secret Service of Mexican Police says he was. Says it in a book he wrote about the case anyway."

"You're sure Jacson hit Trotsky only once with the ice ax?"

"That's one thing everyone seems to agree on. One blow. You need anything else on this?"

"Nooo. Not right now. Handry, you've done excellently in such a short time."

"Sure. I'm good. I admit it. Now let's get to New York's best mountain climber. Two years ago—about eighteen months, to be exact—that would have been an easy question to answer. Calvin Case, thirty-one, married, internationally recognized as one of the most expert, bravest, most daring mountaineers in the world. Then, early last year, he was the last man on the rope of a four-man team climbing the north wall of the Eiger. That's supposed to be the most difficult climb in the world. The guy I spoke to on our Sports Desk said Everest is pure technology, but the north wall of the Eiger is pure guts. It's in Switzerland, in case you're wondering, and apparently it's practically sheer. Anyway, this guy Calvin Case was tail-end Charlie on the rope. He either slipped or an outcrop crumbled or a piton pulled free; my informant didn't remember the details. But he did remember that Case dangled, and finally had to cut himself loose from the others, and fell."

"Jesus."

"Yes. Incredibly, he wasn't killed, but he crushed his spine. Now he's paralyzed from the waist down. Bed-ridden. Can't control his bladder or bowels. My man tells me he's on the sauce. Won't give any interviews. And he's had some good offers for books."

"How does he live?"

"His wife works. No children. I guess they get along. But anyway, I got another guy, active, who's now the number one New York climber. But right now he's in Nepal, preparing for some climb. Who do you want?"

"Do I have a choice? I'll take this Calvin Case. Do you have his address?"

"Sure. I figured you'd want him. I wrote it down. Here." He handed Delaney a small slip of paper. The Captain glanced at it briefly.

"Greenwich Village," he nodded. "I know that street well. A guy took a shot at me on a rooftop on that street, years ago. It was the first time I had ever been shot at."

"He didn't hit?" Handry asked.

"No," Delaney smiled. "He didn't hit."

"Did you?"

"Yes."

"Kill him?"

"Yes. Another ale?"

"Well . . . all right. One more. You having another drink?"

"Sure."

"But I've got to go to the john first. My back teeth are floating."

"That door over there, in the corner."

When Handry came back, he slid into the booth and asked, "How did you know I want to write poetry?"

Delaney shrugged. "I told you. Just a guess. Don't be so goddamned embarrassed about it. It's not shameful."

"I know," Handry said, looking down at the table, moving his glass around. "But still . . . All right, Captain, now you talk. What the hell is this all about?"

"What do you think it's about?"

"You ask me for a rundown on Trotsky, killed with an ice ax. A mountaineer's tool. Then you ask me for the name of the top mountain climber in New York. It's something to do with mountain climbing, obviously. The ice ax is the main thing. What's it all about?"

Delaney, knowing he would be asked, had carefully considered his answers. He had prepared three possible replies, of increasing frankness, still not certain how far he could trust the reporter. But now that Handry had made the Trotsky-ice ax-mountain climbing connection, he went directly to his second reply.

"I am not on active duty," he acknowledged. "But Frank Lombard was killed in my precinct. You may think it's silly, but I consider that my responsibility. The Two-five-one Precinct is my home. So I'm conducting what you might call an unofficial investigation. Operation Lombard is handling the official investigation. I'm sure you know that. Whatever I do, whatever I ask you to do, is outside the Department. As of the date of my leave of absence, I have no official standing. Whatever you do for me is a personal favor—you to me."

Thomas Handry stared at him a long moment. Then he poured himself a full glass of ale and drained off half of it. He set the glass down, a white foam mustache on his upper lip.

"You're full of shit," he informed Captain Edward X. Delaney.

"Yes," Delaney nodded miserably. "That's true. I think Lombard was killed with an ice ax. That's why I asked you for background on Trotsky and mountain climbers. That's all I've got. I asked you to look into it because I trust you. All I can promise you is first whack at the story—if there is a story."

"Do you have a staff?"

"A staff? No, I don't have a staff. I have some people helping me, but they're not in the Department. They're civilians."

"I'll get the story? Exclusively?"

"You'll get it. If there is a story."

"I could get a story published right now. Leave-of-absence police captain personally investigating a murder in his old precinct. Harmonicas and violins. 'I want revenge,' states Captain Edward X. Delaney. Is that what you want?"

"No. What do you want?"

"To be in on it. Okay, Captain? Just to know what's going on. You can use me as much as you want. I'm willing. But I want to know what you're up to."

"It may be nothing."

"Okay, it's nothing. I'll take the gamble. A deal?"

"You won't publish anything without my go-ahead?"

"I won't."

"I trust you, Handry."

"The hell you do. But you've got no choice."

---

3 It was a faint dream. He followed a man down a misted street. Not a man, really, but something there, a bulk, in the gilded gloom. Like the night when Frank Lombard was killed: orange light and soft rain.

The figure stayed ahead of him, indecipherable, no matter how fast he moved to see what it was he chased. He never closed. He felt no fear nor panic; just a need, a want for the shadow moving through shadows.

Then there was a ringing; not the siren of a squad car or the buffalo whistle of a fire engine, but the ringing of an ambulance, coming closer, louder; he drifted up from sleep and fumbled for the telephone.

Before he could identify himself he recognized Dorfman's voice.

"Captain?"

"Yes."

"Dorfman. There's been an assault on East Eighty-fourth. About halfway between First and Second. Sounds like the Lombard thing. A man tentatively identified as Bernard Gilbert. He's not dead. They're waiting for the ambulance now. I'm on my way."

"Did you call Chief Pauley?"

"Yes."

"Good."

"You want to meet me there?"

"No. You can handle it. Go by the book. Where they taking him?"

"Mother of Mercy."

"Thank you for calling, lieutenant."

"You're welcome."

Then he switched on the light, stepped into slippers, pulled on a robe. He went down to the study, flipping wall switches as he went, and finally lighted the lamp on his desk. The house was cold and damp; he pulled his overcoat on over his bathrobe. Then he consulted his desk calendar: 22 days since the Frank Lombard homicide. He made careful note of this on a fresh sheet of paper, then called Deputy Inspector Thorsen's answering service. He left his name and number.

Thorsen called him in minutes, sounding sleepy but not angry.

"What is it, Edward?"

"I'm calling from my home, but it's important. There's been a Lombard-type assault in the Two-five-one. Eighty-fourth Street. A man tentatively identified as Bernard Gilbert. He's still alive. They're taking him to Mother of Mercy. That's all I've got."

"Jesus," Thorsen breathed. "Sounds like you were right."

"No comfort in that. I can't go over there."

"No. That wouldn't be wise. Is it certain it's a Lombard-type thing?"

"I told you all I know."

"All right, assuming it is, what will Broughton do now?"

"If the wound is similar to the one that killed Lombard, Chief Pauley will try to establish a link between Lombard and this Bernard Gilbert. If he can't, and I don't believe he will, unless it's pure coincidence, he'll realize they were both chance victims, and he's faced with a crazy. Then he'll check every mental institution in a five-state area. He'll have men checking private doctors and psychiatrists and recently released inmates. He'll pull in every known nut in the city for questioning. He'll do what he has to do."

"Do you think it'll work?"

"No. Broughton has had about five hundred dicks working for him. Figure each detective has a minimum of three or four snitches on his wire. That means about two thousand informers, all over the city, and they've come up with zilch. If there was a crazy running wild—a crazy with a record—*someone* would know about it, or notice something weird, or hear some talk. Our man is new. Probably no record. Probably normal-appearing. I've already got him on my list as a good appearance, possibly well-dressed."

"What list?"

Delaney was silent a moment, cursing his lapse. That list was *his*.

"A stupid list I made out of things I suspect about the guy. It's all smoke. I don't *know* anything."

Now Thorsen was silent a moment. Then . . .

"I think maybe you and Johnson and I better have a meeting."

"All right," Delaney said glumly.

"And bring your list."

"Can it wait until I see the reports on this Bernard Gilbert assault?"

"Sure. Anything I can do?"

"Will you have a man at the scene—or involved in the investigation?"

"Well . . ." Thorsen said cautiously, "maybe."

"If you do, a couple of things . . . Is anything missing from the victim's wallet? Particularly identification of any kind? And second, does he—or did he—use hair oil of any kind?"

"Hair oil? What the hell is that all about?"

Delaney frowned at the telephone. "I don't know. I honestly don't know. Probably not important. But can you check?"

"I'll try. Anything else?"

"One more thing. If this Bernard Gilbert dies, and it's proved similar to the Lombard snuff, the papers are going to get hold of it, so you better be prepared for 'Maniacal Killer on Loose' type of thing. It's going to get hairy."

"Oh God. I suppose so."

"Most of the pressure will be on Broughton."

"And the Commish."

"Him, too, of course. But it will affect Chief Pauley most. He's sure to get hundreds of phony leads and false confessions. They'll all have to be checked out, of course. And there's a good possibility there may be imitative assaults and homicides in other parts of the city. It usually happens. But don't be spooked by them. Eventually they'll be weeded out . . ."

He had more conversation with Deputy Inspector Thorsen. They agreed that since Dorfman was recently appointed Acting Commander of the 251st Precinct, and since Thorsen was head of personnel of the patrol division, it would be entirely logical and understandable if Thorsen went to the scene of the Gilbert assault, ostensibly to check up on how Dorfman was handling things. Thorsen promised to call Delaney back as soon as possible, and he would, personally, try to check out the question of missing identification from Bernard Gilbert's wallet and whether or not the victim used hair oil.

The moment he hung up, Delaney dialed the home number of Dr. Sanford Ferguson. It was getting on to 2:00 a.m., but the doctor was awake and cheerful.

"Edward!" he said. "How's by you? I just came in from an on-the-spot inspection of a luscious young piece. Couldn't have been over twenty-six or seven. Oh so lovely."

"Dead?"

"Oh so dead. Apparently cardiac arrest. But doesn't that strike you as odd, Edward? A luscious young piece with a shattered heart?"

"Married?"

"Not legally."

"Is the boy friend a doctor or medical student?"

There was silence a moment.

"You bastard," Ferguson said finally, "you scare me, you know that? In case you're interested, the boy friend is a pharmacist."

"Beautiful," Delaney said. "Well, he probably found a younger, more luscious piece. But doctor, why I called . . . There's been an assault in the Two-five-one Precinct. Tonight. Preliminary reports are that the wound and weapon used are similar to the Lombard homicide. The victim in this case, still alive, a man named Bernard Gilbert, will be taken or has been taken to Mother of Mercy."

"Dear old Mother."

"I wondered if you've been assigned to this?"

"No, I have not."

"I wondered if you could call the attending doctors and surgeons at Mother of Mercy and find out if it really is a Lombard-type penetration, and whether he'll live or not, and—you know—whatever they'll tell you."

Again there was silence. Then . . .

"You know, Edward, you want a lot for one lousy lunch."

"I'll buy you another lousy lunch."

Ferguson laughed. "You treat everyone differently, don't you?"

"Don't we all?"

"I guess so. And you want me to call you back with whatever I can get?"

"If you would. Please. Also, doctor, if this man should die, will there be an autopsy?"

"Of course. On every homicide victim. Or suspected victim."

"With or without next-of-kin's consent?"

"That's correct."

"If this man dies—this Bernard Gilbert—could you do the autopsy?"

"I'm not the Chief Medical Examiner, Edward. I'm just one of the slaves."

"But could you wangle it?"

"I might be able to wangle it."

"I wish you would. If he dies."

"All right, Edward. I'll try."

"One more thing . . ."

Ferguson's laughter almost broke his eardrum; Delaney held the phone up in the air until the doctor stopped spluttering.

"Edward," Ferguson said, "I love you. I really do. With you it's always 'I want two things' or 'I'd like three favors.' But then you always say, 'Oh, just one more thing.' You're great. Okay, what's your 'one more thing'?"

"If you should happen to talk to a doctor or surgeon up at Mother of Mercy, or if you should happen to do the postmortem, find out if the victim used hair oil, will you?"

"Hair oil?" Ferguson asked. "Hair oil," Ferguson said. "Hair oil!" Ferguson cried. "Jesus Christ, Edward, you never forget a thing, do you?"

"Sometimes," Captain Delaney acknowledged.

"Nothing important, I'll bet. All right, I'll keep the hair oil in mind if I do the cut-'em-up. I'm certainly not going to bother the men in emergency at Mother of Mercy with a thing like that right now."

"Good enough. You'll get back to me?"

"If I learn anything. If you don't hear from me, it means I've drawn a blank."

Delaney rejected the idea of sleep, and went into the kitchen to put water on for instant coffee. While it was heating, he returned to the study and from a corner closet he dragged out a three-by-four ft. bulletin board to which he had pinned a black-and-white street map of the 251st Precinct. The map was covered with a clear plastic flap that could be wiped clean. In the past, while on active duty, Delaney had used the map to chart location and incidence of street crimes, breaking-and-entering, felonious assaults, etc. The map was a miniature of the big one on the wall of the commander's office in the precinct house.

Now he wiped the plastic overlay clean with a paper tissue, returned to the kitchen to mix his cup of black coffee, brought it back with him and sat at the desk, the map before him. He sharpened a red grease pencil and carefully marked two fat dots: on East 73rd Street where Lombard had been killed and on East 84th Street where Gilbert had been assaulted. Alongside each dot he wrote the last name of the victim and the date of the attack.

Two red dots, he acknowledged, hardly constituted a pattern, or even a crime wave. But from his experience and reading of the histories of mass murders, he was convinced additional assaults would be confined to a limited area, probably the 251st Precinct, and the assailant was probably a resident of the area. (Probably! Probably! Everything was probably.) The assassin's success in the Lombard killing would certainly make him feel safe in his home territory.

Delaney sat back and stared at the red dots. He gave Chief Pauley about three days to acknowledge there was no connection between the victims. Then Pauley would opt for a psychopathic killer and would do all those things Delaney had mentioned to Deputy Inspector Thorsen.

In addition, Delaney guessed, Chief Pauley, with no announcement and no publicity, would put on 10 or 20 decoys on the streets of the 251st Precinct, from about ten p.m. till dawn. In civilian clothes, newspapers clutched under one arm, the detectives would scurry up one street and down the next, apparently residents hurrying home in the darkness, but actually inviting attack. That's what Delaney would do. He was certain, knowing Pauley's thoroughness, that the Chief would do it, too. It might work. And it might only serve to drive the killer farther afield if he recognized the decoys for what they were. But you took your chances and hoped. You had to do *something*.

He was still staring at the red dots on the map overlay, sipping cooled black coffee and trying to compute percentages and probabilities, when the desk phone rang. He snatched it up after one ring.

"Captain Edward X. Delaney here."

"Thorsen. I'm calling from a tavern on Second Avenue. They had taken Gilbert to the hospital by the time I arrived. Broughton and Pauley are with him, hoping he'll regain consciousness and say something."

"Sure."

"Gilbert's wallet was on the sidewalk next to him, just like in the Lombard case. Someone's at his home now, trying to find out what, if anything, is missing."

"Was there money in it?"

"Dorfman tells me yes. He thinks it was about fifty dollars."

"Untouched?"

"Apparently."

"How is Dorfman managing?"

"Very well."

"Good."

"He's a little nervous."

"Naturally. Any prediction on whether Gilbert will live?"

"Nothing on that. He is a short man, about five-six or five-seven. He was hit from the front. The penetration went in high up on the skull, about an inch or so above where the hairline would have been."

" 'Would have been'?"

"Gilbert is almost completely bald. Dorfman says just a fringe of thin, grey hair around the scalp, above the ears. But not in front. He was wearing a hat, so I assume some of the hat material was driven into the wound. Jesus, Edward, I don't like this kind of work. I saw the blood and stuff where he lay. I want to get back to my personnel records."

"I know. So you have nothing on whether or not he used hair oil?"

"No, nothing. I'm a lousy detective, I admit."

"You did all you could. Why don't you go home and try to get some sleep?"

"Yes. I'll try. Anything else you need?"

"Copies of the Operation Lombard reports as soon as you can."

"I'll put the pressure on. Edward . . ."

"Yes?"

"When I saw the pool of blood there, on the sidewalk, I got the feeling . . ."

"What?"

"That this business with Broughton is pretty small potatoes. You understand?"

"Yes," Delaney said gently. "I know what you mean."

"You've got to get this guy, Edward."

"I'll get him."

"You sure?"

"I'm sure."

"Good. I think I'll go home now and try to get some sleep."

"Yes, you do that."

After he hung up, Delaney drew his list, "The Suspect," from his top drawer and went through it, item by item. None of his notations had been negated by what Thorsen had told him. If anything, his supposition had been strengthened. Certainly a swinging blow high on the skull of a short man would indicate a tall assailant. But why the attack from the front when the rear attack on Lombard had been so successful? And couldn't Gilbert see the blow coming and dodge or throw up an arm to ward it off? A puzzle.

He was almost ready to give it up for the night, to try to grab a few hours of sleep before dawn, when the phone rang. He reached for it, wondering again how much of his life was spent with that damned black thing pressing his ear flat and sticky.

"Captain Edward X. Delaney here."

"Ferguson. I'm tired, I'm sleepy, I'm irritable. So I'll go through this fast. And don't interrupt."

"I won't."

"You just did. Bernard Gilbert. White male. About forty years old. Five feet six or seven. About one-fifty. Around there. I'll skip the medical lingo. Definitely a Lombard-type wound. Struck from the front. The penetration went in about two inches above the normal hair line. But the man is almost totally bald. That answers your hair oil question."

"The hell it does. Just makes the cheese more binding."

"I'll ignore that. Foreign matter in the wound from the felt hat he was wearing. Penetration to a depth of four or five inches. Curving downward. He's in a deep coma. Paralyzed. Prognosis: negative. Any questions?"

"How long do they figure?"

"From this instant to a week or so. His heart isn't all that strong."

"Will he recover consciousness?"

"Doubtful."

Delaney could tell Ferguson's patience was wearing thin.

"Thank you, doctor. You've been a great help."

"Any time," Ferguson assured him. "Any two o'clock in the morning you want to call."

"Oh, wait a minute," Delaney said.

"I know," Ferguson sighed. " 'One more thing.' "

"You won't forget about the autopsy."

Ferguson began to swear—ripe, sweaty curses—and Delaney hung up softly, smiling. Then he went to bed, but didn't sleep.

It was something he hated and loved: hated because it kept his mind in a flux and robbed him of sleep; loved because it was a challenge: how many oranges could he juggle in the air at one time?

All difficult cases came eventually to this point of complexity; weapon, method, motives, suspects, alibis, timing. And he had to juggle them all, catching, tossing, watching them all every second, relaxed and laughing.

It had been his experience that when this point came in a difficult, involved investigation, when the time arrived when he wondered if he could hold onto all the threads, keep the writhings in his mind, at that point, at that time of almost total confusion, if he could just endure, and absorb more and more, then somehow the log jam loosened, he could see things beginning to run free.

Right now it was a jam, everything caught up and canted. But he began to see key logs, things to be loosened. Then it would all run out. Now the complexity didn't worry him. He could accept it, and more. Pile it on! There wasn't anything one man could do that a better man couldn't undo. That was a stupid, arrogant belief, he admitted. But if he didn't hold it, he really should be in another line of business.

4

Four days later Bernard Gilbert died without regaining consciousness. By that time Chief Pauley had established, to his satisfaction, that there was no link between Lombard and Gilbert, except the nature of the attack, and he had set in motion all those things Captain Delaney had predicted: the check-up of recent escapes from mental institutions, investigation of recently released inmates, questioning of known criminals with a record of mental instability, the posting of decoys in the 251st Precinct.

Delaney learned all this from copies of Operation Lombard reports supplied by Deputy Inspector Thorsen. Once again there were many of them, and they were long. He studied them all carefully, reading them several times. He learned details of Bernard Gilbert's life. He learned that the victim's wife, Monica Gilbert, had stated she believed the only thing missing from her husband's wallet was an identification card.

The accountants for whom Bernard Gilbert worked audited the books of a Long Island manufacturer doing secret work for the U. S. government. To gain access to the premises of the manufacturer, it was necessary for Bernard Gilbert to show a special identification card with his photo attached. It was this special identification card that was missing. The FBI had been alerted by Chief Pauley but, as far as Delaney could determine, the federal agency was not taking any active role in the investigation at this time.

There was a long memo from Chief Pauley to Deputy Commissioner Broughton speculating on the type of weapon used in the Lombard and Gilbert assaults. The phrase "a kind of ax or pick" was used, and Delaney knew Pauley was not far behind him.

At this point the news media had not yet made the Lombard–Gilbert connection. In fact, Gilbert's attack earned only a few short paragraphs on inside pages. Just another street crime. Delaney considered a few moments whether to tip off Thomas Handry, then thought better of it. He'd learn soon enough, and meanwhile Chief Pauley would be free of the pressures of screaming headlines, crank calls, false confessions, and imitative crimes.

It was the timing of his own activities that concerned Captain Delaney most. He wanted to keep up with the flood of Operation Lombard reports. He wanted desperately to interrogate Monica Gilbert himself. He needed to visit Calvin Case, the crippled mountain climber, and learn what he could about ice axes. He wanted to check the progress of Christopher Langley without giving the sweet old man the feeling that he, Delaney, was leaning on him. And, of course, the two visits a day to Barbara in the hospital—that came first.

Two days after the Gilbert attack, while the victim floated off somewhere, living and not living, but still breathing. Delaney thought long and hard on how to approach Monica Gilbert. She was sure to be spending many hours at her husband's bedside. And it was certain she would be guarded by Operation Lombard detectives, probably a two-man team outside her house, although there might be an interior man, too.

The Captain considered and rejected several involved plans for a clandestine meeting with her, unobserved by Operation Lombard. They all seemed too devious. He decided the best solution would be the obvious: he would call for an appointment, give his name, and then walk right up to her door. If he was braced or recognized by Broughton's dicks he would use the same cover story he had prepared when he had gone to question the widow of Frank Lombard: as ex-commander of the 251st Precinct he had come to express his sympathy.

It worked—up to a point. He phoned, identified himself, made an appointment to see her at her home at 4:00 p.m., when she returned from Mother of Mercy. He thought it likely she would repeat the conversation to her guard, as she had been instructed. Or perhaps her phone was tapped. Anything was possible. So, when he walked over a few minutes before four, and one of the dicks in the unmarked police car parked outside her brownstone cranked down his window, waved, and called, "Hi, Captain," he wasn't surprised. He waved back, although he didn't recognize the man.

Monica Gilbert was a strong, handsome woman, hairy, wearing a shapeless black dress that didn't quite conceal heavy breasts, wide hips, pillar thighs. She had been brewing a pot of tea, and he accepted a cup gratefully. There were two little girls in the room, peeking out from behind their mother's skirts. They were introduced to him as Mary and Sylvia, and he rose to bow gravely. They ran giggling from the room. He saw no sign of an interior guard.

"Milk?" she asked. "Sugar?"

"Thank you, no. I take it straight. How is your husband?"

"No change. Still in a coma. They don't hold out much hope."

She said all that in a flat monotone, not blinking, looking at him directly. He admired her control, knowing what it cost.

Her thick black hair, somewhat oily, was combed back from a wide, smooth brow and fell almost to her shoulders. Her large eyes appeared blue-grey, and were her best feature. The nose was long but proportionate. All of her was big. Not so much big as assertive. She wore no makeup, had made no effort to pluck heavy eyebrows. She was, he decided, a complete woman, but he knew instinctively she would respond to soft speech and a gentle manner.

"Mrs. Gilbert," he said in a low voice, leaning forward to her, "I know you must have spent many hours with the police since the attack on your husband. This is an unofficial visit. I am not on active duty; I'm on leave of absence. But I was commander of this precinct for many years, and I wanted to express my regrets and sympathy personally."

"Thank you," she said. "That's very kind of you. I'm sure everything is being done . . ."

"I assure you it is," he said earnestly. "A great number of men are working on this case."

"Will they get the man who did it?"

"Yes," he nodded. "They will. I promise you that."

She looked at him strangely a moment.

"You're not involved in the investigation?"

"Not directly, no. But it did happen in my precinct. What was my precinct."

"Why are you on leave of absence?"

"My wife is ill."

"I'm sorry to hear that. You live in the neighborhood?"

"Yes. Right next door to the precinct house."

"Well, then you know what it's like around here—robberies and muggings, and you can't go out at night."

"I know," he nodded sympathetically. "Believe me, I know, and hate it more than you do."

"He never hurt anyone," she burst out, and he was afraid she might weep, but she did not.

"Mrs. Gilbert, will it upset you to talk about your husband?"

"Of course not. What do you want to know?"

"What kind of a man is he? Not his job, or his background—I've got all that. Just the man himself."

"Bernie? The dearest, sweetest man who ever lived. He wouldn't hurt a fly. He worked so hard, for me and the girls. I know that's all he thinks about."

"Yes, yes."

"Look around. Does it look like we're rich?"

Obediently he looked around. In truth it was a modest apartment: linoleum on the floor, inexpensive furniture, paper drapes. But it was clean, and there were some touches: a good hi-fi set, on one wall an original abstraction that had color and flash, a small wooden piece of primitive sculpture that had meaning.

"Comfortable," he murmured.

"Paradise," she said definitely. "Compared to what Bernie had and what I had. It's not right, Captain. It's just not right."

He nodded miserably, wondering what he could say to comfort her. There was nothing. So he got on with it, still speaking in a quiet, gentle voice, hoping to soothe her.

"Mrs. Gilbert," he asked, remembering Ferguson's comment about the victim's heart, "was your husband an active man?" Realizing he had used the past tense, he switched immediately to the present, hoping she hadn't caught it. But the focus of her eyes changed; he realized she had, and he cursed himself. "I mean, is he active physically? Does he exercise? Play games?"

She stared at him without answering. Then she leaned forward to pour him another cup of tea. The black dress left her arms bare; he admired the play of muscle, the texture of her skin.

"Captain," she said finally, "for a man not involved in the investigation, you're asking a lot of unusual questions."

He realized then how shrewd she was. He could try lying to her, but was convinced she'd know.

"Mrs. Gilbert," he said, "do you really care how many men are working on this, or who they are, or what their motives are? The main thing is to catch the man who did it. Isn't that true? Well, I swear to you, I want to find the man who struck down your husband more than you do."

"No!" she cried. "Not more than I do." Her eyes were glittering now, her whole body taut. "I want the one who did it caught and punished."

He was astonished by her fury. He had thought her controlled, perhaps even phlegmatic. But now she was twanging, alive and fiery.

"What do you want?" he asked her. "Vengeance?"

Her eyes burned into his.

"Yes. That's exactly what I want. Vengeance. If I answer your questions, will it help me get it?"

"I think so."

"Not good enough, Captain."

"Yes, if you answer my questions it will help find the man who did this thing to your husband."

"Your husband" were the key words, as he had hoped they would be. She started talking.

Her husband was physically weak. He had a heart murmur, arthritis of the left wrist, intermittent kidney pains, although examinations and X-rays showed nothing. His eyes were weak, he suffered from periodic conjunctivitis. He did not exercise, he played no games. He was a sedentary man.

But he worked hard, she added in fierce tones; he worked so hard.

Delaney nodded. Now he had some kind of answer to what had been bothering him: why hadn't Bernard Gilbert made a response to a frontal attack, dodged or warded off the blow? It seemed obvious now: poor musculature, slow physical reactions, the bone-deep weariness of a man working up to and beyond his body's capacity. What chance did he have against a "strong, young, cool, determined psychopath with good muscular coordination"?

"Thank you, Mrs. Gilbert," Captain Delaney said softly. He finished his tea, rose to his feet. "I appreciate your giving me this time, and I hope your husband makes a quick recovery."

"Do you know anything about his condition?"

This time he did lie. "I'm sure you know more than I do. All I know is that he's seriously injured."

She nodded, not looking at him, and he realized she already knew.

She walked him to the door. The two delightful little girls came scampering out, stared at him, giggled, and pulled at their mother's skirt. Delaney smiled at them, remembering Liza at that age. The darlings!

"I want to do something," she said.

"What?" he asked, distracted. "I don't understand."

"I want to *do* something. To help."

"You have helped."

"Isn't there anything else I can do? You're doing something. I don't know what you're up to, but I trust you. I really feel you're trying to find who did it."

"Thank you," he said, so moved. "Yes, I'm trying to find who did it."

"Then let me help. Anything! I can type, take shorthand. I'm very good with figures. I'll do anything. Make coffee. Run errands. Anything!"

He couldn't trust himself to speak. He tried to nod brightly and smile. He left, closing the door firmly behind him.

Out on the street the unmarked police car was still parked in the same position. He expected a wave. But one of the detectives was sleeping, his head thrown back, his mouth open. The other was marking a racing sheet. They didn't even notice him. If they had been under his command he'd have reamed their ass out.

5 The next day started well, with a call from a book dealer informing Captain Delaney that he had located two volumes of the original Honey Bunch series. The Captain was delighted, and it was arranged that the books would be mailed to him, along with the invoice.

He took this unexpected find as a good omen, for like most policemen he was superstitious. He would tell others, "You make your own luck," knowing this wasn't exactly true; there was a good fortune that came unexpectedly, sometimes unasked, and the important thing was to recognize it when it came, for luck wore a thousand disguises, including calamity.

He sat at his study desk and reviewed a list of "Things to Do" he had prepared. It read:

"Interrogate Monica Gilbert.

"Calvin Case re ice ax.

"Ferguson re autopsy.

"Call Langley.

"Honey Bunch."

He drew a line through the final item. He was about to draw a line through the first and then, for a reason he could not understand, left it open. He searched, and finally found the slip of paper Thomas Handry had given him, bearing the name, address and telephone number of Calvin Case. He realized more and more people were being drawn into his investigation, and he resolved to set up some kind of a card file or simple directory that would list names, addresses, and phone numbers of all the people involved.

He considered what might be the best way to handle the Calvin Case interview. He decided against phoning; an unexpected personal visit would be better. Sometimes it was useful to surprise people, catch them off guard with no opportunity to plan their reaction.

He walked over to Lexington Avenue, shoulders hunched against the raw cold, and took the IRT downtown. It seemed to him each time he rode the subway—and his trips were rare—the graffiti covered more and more of interior and exterior surfaces of cars and platforms. Sexual and racist inscriptions were, thankfully, relatively rare, but spray cans and felt-tipped markers had been used by the hundreds for such records as: "Tony 168. Vic 134. Angie 127. Bella 78. Iron Wolves 127." He knew these to be the first names of individuals and the titles of street gangs, followed by their street number—evidence: "I was here."

He got off at 14th Street and walked west and south, looking about him constantly, noting how this section had changed and was changing since he had been a dick two in this precinct and thought he might leave the world a better place than he found it. Now if he left it no worse, he'd be satisfied.

The address was on West 11th Street, just off Fifth Avenue. The rents here, Delaney knew, were enormous, unless Case was fortunate enough to have a rent-controlled apartment. The house itself was a handsome old structure in the Federal style. All the front windows had white-painted boxes of geraniums or ivy on the sills. The outside knob and number plate were polished brass. The garbage cans had their lids on; the entryway had been swept. There was a little sign that read "Please curb your dog." Under it someone had written, "No shit?"

Calvin Case lived in apartment 3-B. Delaney pushed the bell and leaned down to the intercom. He waited, but there was no answer. He pushed the bell again, three long rings. This time a harsh masculine voice said, "What the hell. Yes?"

"Mr. Calvin Case?"

"Yes. What do you want?"

"My name is Captain Edward X. Delaney. Of the New York Police Department. I'd like to talk to you for a few minutes."

"What about?" The voice was loud, slurred, and the mechanics of the intercom made it raucous.

"It's about an investigation I'm conducting."

There was silence. It lasted so long that Delaney was about to ring again when the door lock buzzed, and he grabbed the knob hastily, opened the door, and climbed carpeted steps to 3-B. There was another bell. He rang, and again he waited for what he thought was an unusually long time. Then another buzzer sounded. He was startled and did nothing. When you rang the bell of an apartment door, you expected someone to inquire from within or open the door. But now a buzzer sounded.

Then, remembering the man was an invalid, and cursing his own stupidity, Delaney rang again. The answering buzz seemed long and angry. He pushed the door open, stepped into the dark hallway of a small, cluttered apartment. Delaney shut the door firmly behind him, heard the electric lock click.

"Mr. Case?" he called.

"In here." The voice was harsh, almost cracked.

The captain walked through a littered living room. Someone slept in here, on a sofa bed that was still unmade. There were signs of a woman's presence: a tossed nightgown, a powder box and makeup kit on an end table, lipsticked cigarette butts, tossed copies of "Vogue" and "Bride." But there were a few plants at the windows, a tall tin vase of fresh rhododendron leaves. Someone was making an effort.

Delaney stepped through the disorder to an open door leading to the rear of the apartment. Curiously, the door frame between the cluttered living room and the bedroom beyond had been fitted with a window shade with a cord pull. The shade, Delaney guessed, could be pulled down almost to the floor, shutting off light, affording some kind of privacy, but not as sound-proof as a door. And, of course, it couldn't be locked.

He ducked under the hanging shade and looked about the bedroom. Dusty windows, frayed curtains, plaster curls from the ceiling, a stained rag rug, two good oak dressers with drawers partly open, newspapers and magazines scattered on the floor. And then the bed, and on the opposite wall a shocking big stain as if someone had thrown a full bottle, watched it splinter and the contents drip down.

The smell was . . . something. Stale whiskey, stale bedclothes, stale flesh. Urine and excrement. There was a tiny log of incense smoking in a cast iron pot; it made things worse. The room was rotting. Delaney had smelled odors more ferocious than this—was there a cop who had not?—but it never got easier. He breathed through his mouth and turned to the man in the bed.

It was a big bed, occupied at some time in the past, Delaney imagined, by Calvin Case and his wife. Now she slept on the convertible in the living room. The bed was surrounded, by tables, chairs, magazine racks, a telephone stand, a wheeled cart with bottles and an ice bucket, on the floor an open bedpan and plastic "duck." Tissues, a half-eaten sandwich, a sodden towel, cigarette and cigar butts, a paperback book with pages torn out in a frenzy, and even a hard-cover bent and partly ripped, a broken glass, and . . . and everything.

"What the fuck do you want?"

Then he looked directly at the man in the bed.

The soiled sheet, a surprising blue, was drawn up to the chin. All Delaney saw was a square face, a square head. Uncombed hair was spread almost to the man's shoulders. The reddish mustache and beard were squarish. And untrimmed. Dark eyes burned. The full lips were stained and crusted.

"Calvin Case?"

"Yeah."

"Captain Edward X. Delaney, New York Police Department. I'm investigating the death—the murder—of a man we believe—"

"Let's see your badge."

Delaney stepped closer to the bed. The stench was sickening. He held his identification in front of Case's face. The man hardly glanced at it. Delaney stepped back.

"We believe the man was murdered with an ice ax. A mountain climber's ax. So I came—"

"You think I did it?" The cracked lips opened to reveal yellowed teeth: a death's head grin.

Delaney was shocked. "Of course not. But I need more information on ice axes. And as the best mountain climber—you've been recommended to me—I thought you might be—"

"Fuck off," Calvin Case said wearily, moving his heavy head to one side.

"You mean you won't cooperate in finding a man who—"

"Be gone," Case whispered. "Just be gone."

Delaney turned, moved away two steps, stopped. There was Barbara, and Christopher Langley, and Monica Gilbert, and all the peripheral people: Handry and Thorsen and Ferguson and Dorfman, and here was this . . . He took a deep breath, hating himself because even his furies were calculated. He turned back to the cripple on the soiled bed. He had nothing to lose.

"You goddamned cock-sucking mother-fucking son-of-a-bitch," he said steadily and tonelessly. "You shit-gutted ass-licking bastard. I'm a detective, and I detect *you*, you punky no-ball frigger. Go ahead, lie in your bed of crap. Who buys the food? Your wife—right? Who tries to keep a home for you? Your wife—right? Who empties your shit and pours your piss in the toilet? Your wife—right? And you lie there and soak up whiskey. I could smell you the minute I walked in, you piece of rot. It's great to lie in bed and feel sorry for yourself, isn't it? You corn-holing filth. Go piss and shit in your bed and drink your whiskey and work your wife to death and scream at her, you crud. A man? Oh! You're some man, you lousy ass-kissing turd. I spit on you, and I forget the day I heard your name, you dirt-eating nobody. You don't exist. You understand? You're no one."

He turned away, almost out of control, and a woman was standing in the bedroom doorway, a slight, frail blonde, her hair brushing the window shade. Her face was blanched; she was biting on a knuckle.

He took a deep breath, tried to square his shoulders, to feel bigger. He felt very small.

"Mrs. Case?"

She nodded.

"My name is Edward X. Delaney, Captain, New York Police Department. I came to ask your husband's help on an investigation. If you heard what I said, I apologize for my language. I'm very sorry. Please forgive me. I didn't know you were there."

She nodded dumbly again, still gnawing her knuckle and staring at him with wide blue eyes.

"Good-day," he said and moved to pass her in the doorway.

"Captain," the man in the bed croaked.

Delaney turned back. "Yes?"

"You're some bastard, aren't you?"

"When I have to be," Delaney nodded.

"You'll use anyone, won't you? Cripples, drunks, the helpless and the hopeless. You'll use them all."

"That's right. I'm looking for a killer. I'll use anyone who can help."

Calvin Case used the edge of his soiled blue sheet to wipe his clotted eyes clear.

"And you got a big mouth," he added. "A *biiig* mouth." He reached to the wheeled cart for a half-full bottle of whiskey and a stained glass. "Honey," he called to his wife, "we got a clean glass for Mister Captain Edward X. Delaney, New York Police Department?"

She nodded, still silent. She ran out, then came back with two glasses. Calvin Case poured a round, then set the bottle back on the cart. The three raised glasses in a silent toast, although what they were drinking to they could not have said.

"Cal, are you hungry?" his wife asked anxiously. "I've got to get back to work soon."

"No, not me. Captain, you want a sandwich?"

"Thank you, no."

"Just leave us alone, hon."

"Maybe I should just clean up a—"

"Just leave us alone. Okay, hon?"

She turned to go.

"Mrs. Case," Delaney said.

She turned back.

"Please stay. Whatever your husband and I have to discuss, there is no reason why you can't hear it."

She was startled. She looked back and forth, man to man, not knowing.

Calvin Case sighed. "You're something," he said to Captain Delaney. "You're really something."

"That's right," Delaney nodded. "I'm something."

"You barge in here and you take over."

"You want to talk now?" Delaney asked impatiently. "Do you want to answer my questions?"

"First tell me what it's all about."

"A man was killed with a strange weapon. We think it was an ice ax and—"

"Who's 'we'?"

"*I* think it was an ice ax. I want to know more about it, and your name was given to me as the most experienced mountaineer in New York."

"Was," Case said softly. "*Was.*"

They sipped their drinks, looked at each other stonily. For once, there were no sirens, no buffalo whistles, no trembles of blasting or street sounds, no city noises. It was on this very block, Delaney recalled, that a fine old town house was accidentally demolished by a group of bumbling revolutionaries, proving their love of the human race by preparing bombs in the basement. Now, in the Case apartment, they existed in a bubble of silence, and unconsciously they lowered their voices.

"A captain comes to investigate a crime?" Case asked quietly. "Even a murder? No, no. A uniformed cop or a detective, yes. A captain, no. What's it all about, Delaney?"

The Captain took a deep breath. "I'm on leave of absence. I'm not on active duty. You're under no obligation to answer my questions. I was commander of the Two-five-one Precinct. Uptown. A man was killed there about a month ago. On the street. Maybe you read about it. Frank Lombard, a city councilman. A lot of men are working on the case, but they're getting nowhere. They haven't even identified the weapon used. I started looking into it on my own time. It's not official; as I told you, I'm on leave of absence. Then, three days ago, another man was attacked not too far from where Lombard was killed. This man is still alive but will probably die. His wound is like Lombard's: a skull puncture. I think it was done with an ice ax."

"What makes you think so?"

"The nature of the wound, the size and shape. And an ice ax has been used as a murder weapon before. It was used to assassinate Leon Trotsky in Mexico City in nineteen-forty."

"What do you want from me?"

"Whatever you can tell me about ice axes, who makes them, where you buy them, what they're used for."

Calvin Case looked at his wife. "Will you get my axes, hon? They're in the hall closet."

While she was gone the men didn't speak. Case motioned toward a chair, but Delaney shook his head. Finally Mrs. Case came back, awkwardly clutching five axes. Two were under an arm; she held the handles of the other three in a clump.

"Dump 'em on the bed," Case ordered, and she obediently let them slide onto the soiled sheet.

Delaney stood over them, inspected them swiftly, then grabbed. It was an all-steel implement, hatchet-length, the handle bound in leather. From the butt of the handle hung a thong loop. The head had a hammer on one side, a pick on the other. The pick was exactly like that described by Christopher Langley; about five inches long, it was square-shaped at the shaft, then tapered to a thinning triangle. As it tapered, the spike curved downward and ended in a sharp point. On the underside were four little saw teeth. The entire head was a bright red, the leather-covered handle a bright blue. Between was a naked shaft of polished steel. There was a stamping on the side of the head: a small inscription. Delaney put on his glasses to read it: "Made in West Germany."

"This—" he began.

"That's not an ice ax," Calvin Case interrupted. "Technically, it's an ice hammer. But most people call it an ice ax. They lump all these things together."

"You bought it in West Germany?"

"No. Right here in New York. The best mountain gear is made in West Germany, Austria and Switzerland. But they export all over the world."

"Where in New York did you buy it?"

"A place I used to work. I got an employees' discount on it. It's down on Spring Street, a place called 'Outside Life.' They sell gear for hunting, fishing, camping, safaris, mountaineering, backpacking—stuff like that."

"May I use your phone?"

"Help yourself."

He was so encouraged, so excited, that he couldn't remember Christopher Langley's phone number and had to look it up in his pocket notebook. But he would not put the short ice ax down; he held it along with the phone in one hand while he dialed. He finally got through.

"Mr. Langley? Delaney here."

"Oh, Captain! I should have called, but I really have nothing to report. I've made a list of possible sources, and I've been visiting six or seven shops a day. But so far I—"

"Mr. Langley, do you have your list handy?"

"Why yes, Captain. Right here. I was just about to start out when you called."

"Do you have a store named Outside Life on your list?"

"Outside Life? Just a minute . . . Yes, here it is. It's on Spring Street."

"That's the one."

"Yes, I have it. I've divided my list into neighborhoods, and I have that in the downtown section. I haven't been there yet."

"Mr. Langley. I have a lead they may have what we want. Could you get there today?"

"Of course. I'll go directly."

"Thank you. Please call me at once, whether you find it or not. I'll either be home or at the hospital."

He hung up, turned back to Calvin Case, still holding the ice ax. He didn't want to let it go. He swung the tool in a chopping stroke. Then he raised it high and slashed down.

"Nice balance," he nodded.

"Sure," Case agreed. "And plenty of weight. You could kill a man easily."

"Tell me about ice axes."

Calvin Case told him what he could. It wasn't much. He thought the modern ice ax had evolved from the ancient alpenstock, a staff as long as a shepherd's crook. In fact, Case had seen several still in use in Switzerland. They were tipped with hand-hammered iron spikes, and used to probe the depth of snow, try the consistency of ice, test stone ledges and overhangs, probe crevasses.

"Then," Case said, "the two-handed ice ax was developed." He leaned forward from the waist to pick up samples from the foot of his bed. Apparently he was naked under the sheet. His upper torso had once been thick and muscular. Now it had gone to flab: pale flesh matted with reddish hair, smelling rankly.

He showed the long ice axes to Delaney, explaining how the implement could be used as a cane, driven into ice as a rope support, the mattock side of the head used to chop foot and hand holds in ice as capable of load-bearing as granite. The butt end of the handle varied. It could be a plain spike for hiking on glaciers, or fitted with a small thonged wheel for walking on crusted snow, or simply supplied with a small knurled cap.

"Where did you get all these?" Delaney asked.

"These two in Austria. This one in West Germany. This one in Geneva."

"You can buy them anywhere?"

"Anywhere in Europe, sure. Climbing is very big over there."

"And here?"

"There must be a dozen stores in New York. Maybe more. And other places too, of course. The West Coast, for instance."

"And this one?" Delaney had slipped the thong loop of the short ice ax over his wrist. "What's this used for?"

"Like I told you, technically it's an ice hammer. If you're on stone, you can start a hole with the pick end. Then you try to hammer in a piton with the other side of the head. A piton is a steel peg. It has a loop on top, and you can attach a line to it or thread it through."

Delaney drew two fingers across the head of the ax he held. Then he rubbed the tips of the two fingers with his thumb and grinned.

"You look happy," Case said, pouring himself another whiskey.

"I am. Oiled."

"What?"

"The ax head is oiled."

"Oh . . . sure. Evelyn keeps all my stuff cleaned and oiled. She thinks I'm going to climb again some day. Don't you, hon?"

Delaney turned to look at her. She nodded mutely, tried to smile. He smiled in return.

"What kind of oil do you use, Mrs. Case?"

"Oh . . . I don't know. It's regular oil. I buy it in a hardware store on Sixth Avenue."

"A thin oil," Calvin Case said. "Like sewing machine oil. Nothing special about it."

"Do all climbers keep their tools cleaned and oiled?"

"The good ones do. And sharp."

Delaney nodded. Regretfully he relinquished the short-handled ice ax, putting it back with the others on the foot of Case's bed.

"You said you worked for Outside Life, where you bought this?"

"That's right. For almost ten years. I was in charge of the mountaineering department. They gave me all the time off I wanted for climbs. It was good publicity for them."

"Suppose I wanted to buy an ice ax like that. I just walk in and put down my money. Right?"

"Sure. That one cost about fifteen dollars. But that was five years ago."

"Do I get a cash register receipt, or do they write out an itemized sales check?"

Case looked at him narrowly. Then his bearded face opened into a smile; he showed his stained teeth again.

"Mr. Detective," he grinned. "Thinking every minute, aren't you? Well, as far as Outside Life goes, you're in luck. A sales slip is written out—or was, when I worked there. You got the customer's name and address. This was because Sol Appel, who owns the place, does a big mail order business. He gets out a Summer and Winter catalogue, and he's always anxious to add to his list. Then, on the slip, you wrote out the items purchased."

"After the customer's name and address were added to the mailing list, how long were the sales slips kept? Do you know?"

"Oh Jesus, years and years. The basement was full of them. But don't get your balls in an uproar, Captain. Outside Life isn't the only place in New York where you can buy an ice ax. And most of the other places just ring up the total purchase. There's no record of the customer's name, address, or what was bought. And, like I told you, most of these things are imported. You can buy an ice ax in London, Paris, Berlin, Vienna, Rome, Geneva, and points in between. And in Los Angeles, San Francisco, Boston, Portland, Seattle, Montreal, and a hundred other places. So where does that leave you?"

"Thank you very much," Captain Delaney said, without irony. "You have really been a big help, and I appreciate your cooperation. I apologize for the way I spoke."

Calvin Case made a gesture, a wave Delaney couldn't interpret.

"What are you going to do now, Captain?"

"Do now? Oh, you mean my next step. Well, you heard my telephone call. A man who is helping me is on his way to Outside Life. If he is able to purchase an ice ax like yours, then I'll go down there, ask if they'll let me go through their sales slips and make a list of people who have bought ice axes."

"But I just told you, there'll be thousands of sales checks. *Thousands!*"

"I know."

"And there are other stores in New York that sell ice axes with no record of the buyer. And stores all over the world that sell them."

"I know."

"You're a fool," Calvin Case said dully, turning his face away. "I thought for awhile you weren't, but now I think you are."

"Cal," his wife said softly, but he didn't look at her.

"I don't know what you think detective work is like," Delaney said, staring at the man in the bed. "Most people have been conditioned by novels, the movies and TV. They think it's either exotic clues and devilishly clever deductive reasoning, or else they figure it's all rooftop chases, breaking down doors, and shootouts on the subway tracks. All that is maybe five percent of what a detective does. Now I'll tell you how he mostly spends his time. About fifteen years ago a little girl was snatched on a street out on Long Island. She was walking home from school. A car pulled up alongside her and the driver said something. She came over to the car. A little girl. The driver opened the door, grabbed her, pulled her inside, and took off. There was an eyewitness to this, an old woman who 'thought' it was a dark car, black or dark blue or dark green or maroon. And she 'thought' it had a New York license plate. She wasn't sure of anything. Anyway, the parents got a ransom note. They followed instructions exactly: they didn't call the cops and they paid off. The little girl was found dead three days later. *Then* the FBI was called in. They had two things to work on: it *might* have been a New York license plate on the car, and the ransom note was handwritten. So the FBI called in about sixty agents from all over, and they were given a crash course in handwriting identification. Big blowups of parts of the ransom note were pasted on the walls. Three shifts of twenty men each started going through every application for an automobile license that originated on Long Island. They worked around the clock. How many signatures? Thousands? Millions, more likely. The agents set aside the possibles, and then handwriting experts took over to narrow it down."

"Did they get the man?" Evelyn Case burst out.

"Oh, sure," Delaney nodded. "They got him. Eventually. And if they hadn't found it in the Long Island applications, they'd have inspected every license in New York State. Millions and millions and millions. I'm telling you all this so you'll know what detective work usually is: common sense; a realization that you've got to start somewhere; hard, grinding, routine labor; and percentages. That's about it. Again, I thank you for your help."

He was almost at the shaded doorway to the living room when Calvin Case spoke in a faint, almost wispy voice.

"Captain."

Delaney turned. "Yes?"

"If you find the ax at Outside Life, who'll go through the sales slips?"

Delaney shrugged. "I will. Someone will. They'll be checked."

"Sometimes the items listed on the sales slips are just by stock number. You won't know what they are."

"I'll get identification from the owner. I'll learn what the stock numbers mean."

"Captain, I've got all the time in the world. I'm not going any place. I could go through those sales checks. I know what to look for. I could pull out every slip that shows an ice ax purchase faster than you could."

Delaney looked at him a long moment, expressionless. "I'll let you know," he nodded.

Evelyn Case saw him to the outside door.

"Thank you," she said softly.

When he left the Case home he walked directly over to Sixth Avenue and turned south, looking for a hardware store. Nothing. He returned to 11th Street and walked north. Still nothing. Then, across Sixth Avenue, on the west side, he saw one.

"A little can of oil," he told the clerk. "Like sewing machine oil."

He was offered a small, square can with a long neck sealed with a little red cap.

"Can I oil tools with this?" he asked.

"Of course," the clerk assured him. "Tools, sewing machines, electric fans, locks . . . anything. It's the biggest selling all-purpose oil in the country."

Thanks a lot, Delaney thought ruefully. He bought the can of oil.

He shouldn't have taken a cab. They still had sizable balances in their savings and checking accounts, they owned securities (mostly tax-exempt municipal bonds) and, of course, they owned their brownstone. But Delaney was no longer on salary, and Barbara's medical and hospital bills were frightening. So he really should have taken the subway and changed at 59th Street for a bus. But he felt so encouraged, so optimistic, that he decided to buy a cab to the hospital. On the way uptown he took the little red cap off the oil can and squeezed a few drops of oil onto his fingertips. He rubbed it against his thumb. Thin oil. It felt good, and he smiled.

But Barbara wasn't in her room. The floor nurse explained she had been taken down to the lab for more X-rays and tests. Delaney left a short note on her bedside table: "Hello. I was here. See you this evening. I love you. Edward."

He hurried home, stripped off overcoat and jacket, loosened his tie, rolled up his cuffs, put on his carpet slippers. Mary was there and had a beef stew cooking in a Dutch oven. But he asked her to let it cool after it was done; he had too much to do to think about eating.

He had cleaned out the two upper drawers of a metal business file cabinet in the study. In the top drawer he had filed the copies of the Operation Lombard reports. Methodically, he had divided this file in two: Frank Lombard and Bernard Gilbert. Under each heading he had broken the reports down into categories: Weapon, Motive, Wound, Personal History, etc.

In the second drawer he had started his own file, a thin folder that consisted mostly, at this time, of jotted notes.

Now he began to expand these notes into reports, to whom or for what purpose he could not say. But he had worked this way on all his investigations for many years, and frequently found it valuable to put his own instinctive reactions and questions into words. In happier times Barbara had typed out his notes on her electric portable, and that was a big help. But he had never solved the mysteries of the electric, and now would have to be content with handwritten reports.

He started with the long-delayed directory of all the people involved, their addresses and telephone numbers, if he had them or could find them in the book. Then he wrote out reports of his meeting with Thorsen and Johnson, of his interviews with Lombard's widow, mother, and associates, his talks with Dorfman, with Ferguson. He wrote as rapidly as he could, transcribing scribbles he had made in his pocket notebook, on envelopes of letters, on scraps of paper torn from magazines and newspaper margins.

He wrote of his meeting with Thomas Handry, with Christopher Langley, with Calvin Case. He described the bricklayers' hammer, the rock hounds' hammer, and Case's ice ax—where they had been purchased, when, what they cost, and what they were used for. He wrote a report of his interrogation of Monica Gilbert, his purchase of the can of light machine oil, his filing of a missing driver's license report.

He should have done all this weeks ago, and he was anxious to catch up and then to keep his file current with daily additions. It might mean nothing, it probably meant nothing, but it seemed important to him to have a written record of what he had done, and the growing mass of paper was, somehow, reassuring. At the rear of the second file drawer he placed the bricklayers' hammer, the rock hounds' hammer, and the can of oil: physical evidence.

He worked steadily, stopping twice just long enough to get bottles of cold beer from the kitchen. Mary was upstairs, cleaning, but she had turned the light out under the stew. He lifted the lid and sniffed experimentally. The steam smelled great.

He wrote as clearly and as swiftly as he could, but he admitted his handwriting was miserable. Barbara could read it, but who else could? Still, his neat manila file folders grew: "The Suspect," Weapon, Motive, Interrogations, Timing, Autopsies, etc. It all looked very official and impressive.

Late in the afternoon, still writing as fast as he could, Mary departed, with a firm command to eat the stew before he collapsed from malnutrition. He locked the door behind her, went back to his reports and then, a few minutes later, the front door bell chimed. He threw his pen down in anger, thought, then said aloud, "Please, God, let it be Langley. With the ax."

He peered through the narrow glass side panels, and it was Langley. Bearing a paper-wrapped parcel. And beaming. Delaney threw open the door.

"Got it!" Langley cried.

The Captain could not tell him he had held the same thing in his hands a few hours previously; he would not rob this wonderful little man of his moment of triumph.

In the study they inspected the ice ax together. It was a duplicate of the one Calvin Case owned. They went over it, pointing out to each other the required features: the tapering pick, the downward curve, the sharp point, the all-steel construction.

"Oh yes," Delaney nodded. "Mr. Langley, I think this is it. Congratulations."

"Oh . . ." Langley said, waving in the air. "You gave me the lead. Who told you about Outside Life?"

"A man I happened to meet," Delaney said vaguely. "He was interested in mountain climbing and happened to mention that store. Pure luck. But you'd have gotten there eventually."

"Excellent balance," Langley said, hefting the tool. "Very well made indeed. Well . . ."

"Yes?" Delaney said.

"Well, I suppose my job is finished," the old man said. "I mean, we've found the weapon, haven't we?"

"What we think is the weapon."

"Yes. Of course. But here it is, isn't it? I mean, I don't suppose you have anything more for me to do. So I'll . . ."

His voice died away, and he turned the ice ax over and over in his hands, staring at it.

"Nothing more for you to do?" Delaney said incredulously. "Mr. Langley, I have a great deal more I'd like you to do. But you've done so much already, I hesitate to ask."

"What?" Langley interrupted eagerly. "What? Tell me what. I don't want to stop now. Really I don't. What's to be done? Please tell me."

"Well . . ." Delaney said, "we don't know that Outside Life is the only store in New York that sells this type of ice ax. You have other stores on your list you haven't visited yet, don't you?"

"Oh my yes."

"Well, we must investigate and make a hard list of every place in New York that sells this ice ax. This one or one like it. That involves finding out how many American companies manufacture this type of ax and who they wholesale to and who the wholesalers retail to in the New York area. Then—you see here? On the side of the head? It says 'Made in West Germany.' Imported. And maybe from Austria and Switzerland as well. So we must find out who the exporters are and who, over here, they sell to. Mr. Langley, that's a hell of a lot of work, and I hesitate to ask—"

"I'll do it!" Christopher Langley cried. "My goodness, I had no idea detective work was so—so involved. But I can understand why it's necessary. You want the source of every ice ax like this sold in the New York area. Am I correct?"

"Exactly," Delaney nodded. "We'll start with the New York area, and then we'll branch out. But it's so much work. I can't—"

Christopher Langley held up a little hand.

"Please," he said. "Captain, I *want* to do it. I've never felt so *alive* in my life. Now what I'll do is this: first I'll check out all the other stores on my list to see if they carry ice axes. I'll keep a record of the ones that do. Then I'll go to the library and consult a directory of domestic tool manufacturers. I'll query every one of them, or write for their catalogues to determine if they manufacture a tool like this. At the same time I'll check with European embassies, consulates and trade commissions and find out who's importing these implements to the U.S. How does that sound?"

Delaney looked at him admiringly. "Mr. Langley, I wish I had had you working with me on some of my cases in the past. You're a wonder, you are."

"Oh . . ." Langley said, blushing with pleasure, "you know . . ."

"I think your plan is excellent, and if you're willing to work at it—and it's going to be a lot of hard, grinding work—all I can say is 'Thank you' because what you'll be doing is important."

Key word.

"Important," Langley repeated. "Yes. Thank you."

They agreed Delaney could retain possession of the Outside Life ice ax. He placed it carefully in the rear of the second file cabinet drawer. His "exhibits" were growing. Then he walked Langley to the door.

"And how is the Widow Zimmerman?" he asked.

"What? Oh. Very well, thank you. She's been very kind to me. You know . . ."

"Of course. My wife thought very well of her."

"Did she!"

"Oh yes. Liked her very much. Thought she was a very warm hearted, sincere, out-going woman."

"Oh yes. Oh yes. She is all that. Did you eat any of the gefilte fish, Captain?"

"No, I didn't."

"It grows on you. An acquired taste, I suspect. Well . . ."

The little man started out. But the Captain called, "Oh, Mr. Langley, just one more thing," and he turned back.

"Did you get a sales check when you bought the ice ax at Outside Life?"

"A sales check? Oh, yes. Here it is."

He pulled it from his overcoat pocket and handed it to Delaney. The Captain inspected it eagerly. It bore Langley's name and address, the time ("Mountain ax–4B54C") and the price, $18.95, with the city sales tax added, and the total.

"The clerk asked for my name and address because they send out free catalogues twice a year and want to add to their mailing list. I gave my right name. That was all right, wasn't it, Captain?"

"Of course."

"And I thought their catalogue might be interesting. They do carry some fascinating items."

"May I keep this sales check?"

"Naturally."

"You're spending a lot of money on this case, Mr. Langley."

He smiled, tossed a hand in the air, and strutted out, the debonair boulevardier.

After the door was locked behind him, the Captain returned to his study, determined to take up his task of writing out the complete reports of his investigation. But he faltered. Finally he gave it up; something was bothering him. He went into the kitchen. The pot of stew was on the cold range. Using a long-handled fork, he stood there and ate three pieces of lukewarm beef, a potato, a small onion, and two slices of carrot. It all tasted like sawdust but, knowing Mary's cooking, he supposed it was good and the fault was his.

Later, at the hospital, he told Barbara what the problem was. She was quiet, almost apathetic, lying in her bed, and he wasn't certain she was listening or, if she was, if she understood. She stared at him with what he thought were fevered eyes, wide and brilliant.

He told her everything that had happened during the day, omitting only the call from the bookseller about the Honey Bunch books. He wanted to surprise her with that. But he told her of Langley buying the ice ax and how he, Delaney, was convinced that a similar tool had been used in the Lombard and Gilbert attacks.

"I know what should be done now," he said. "I already have Langley working on other places where an ice ax can be bought. He'll be checking retailers, wholesalers, manufacturers and importers. It's a big job for one man. Then I must try to get a copy of Outside Life's mailing list. I don't know how big it is, but it's bound to be extensive. Someone's got to go through it and pull the names and addresses of every resident of the Two-five-one Precinct. I'm almost certain the killer lives in the neighborhood. Then I want to get all the sales slips of Outside Life, for as many years as they've kept them, again to look for buyers of ice axes who live in the Precinct. And that checking and cross-checking will have to be done at every store where Langley discovers ice axes are sold. And I'm sure some of them won't have mailing lists or itemized sales checks, so the whole thing may be a monumental waste of time. But I think it has to be done, don't you?"

"Yes," she said firmly. "No doubt of it. Besides, it's your only lead, isn't it?"

"The only one," he nodded grimly. "But it's going to take a lot of time."

She looked at him a few moments, then smiled softly.

"I know what's bothering you, Edward. You think that even with Mr. Langley and Calvin Case helping you, checking all the lists and sales slips will take too much time. You're afraid someone else may be wounded or killed while you're messing around with mailing lists. You're wondering if perhaps you shouldn't turn over what you have right now to Operation Lombard, and let Broughton and his five hundred detectives get on it. They could do it so much faster."

"Yes," he said, grateful that she was thinking clearly now, her mind attuned to his. "That's exactly what's worrying me. How do you feel about it?"

"Would Broughton follow up on what you gave him?"

"Chief Pauley sure as hell would. I'd go to him. He's getting desperate now. And for good reason. He's got *nothing*. He'd grab at this and really do a job."

They were silent then. He came over to sit by her bedside and hold her hand. Neither spoke for several minutes.

"It's really a moral problem, isn't it?" she said finally.

He nodded miserably. "It's my own pride and ambition and ego . . . And my commitment to Thorsen and Johnson, of course. But if I don't do it, and someone else gets killed, I'll have a lot to answer for."

She didn't ask to whom.

"I could help you with the lists," she said faintly. "Most of the time I just lie here and read or sleep. But I have my good days, and I could help."

He squeezed her hand, smiled sadly. "You can help most by telling me what to do."

"When did you ever do what I told you to do?" she scoffed. "You go your own way, and you know it."

He grinned. "But you help," he assured her. "You sort things out for me."

"Edward, I don't think you should do anything immediately. Ivar Thorsen is deeply involved in this, and so is Inspector Johnson. If you go to Broughton, or even Chief Pauley, and tell them what you've discovered and what you suspect, they're sure to ask who authorized you to investigate."

"I could keep Thorsen and Johnson out of it. Don't forget, I have that letter from the Commissioner."

"But it would still be a mess, wouldn't it? And Broughton would probably know Thorsen is involved; the two of you have been so close for so long. Edward, why don't you have a talk with Ivar and Inspector Johnson? Tell them what you want to do. Discuss it. They're reasonable men; maybe they can suggest something. I know how much this case means to you."

"Yes," he said, looking down, "it does. More every day. And when Thorsen went to the scene of the Gilbert attack, he was really spooked. He as much as said that this business of cutting Broughton down was small stuff compared to finding the killer. Yes, that's the best thing to do. I'll talk to Thorsen and Johnson, and tell them I want to go to Broughton with what I've got. I hate the thought of it—that shit! But maybe it has to be done. Well, I'll think about it some more. I'll try to see them tomorrow, so I may not be over at noon. But I'll come in the evening and tell you how it all came out."

"Remember, don't lose your temper, Edward."

"When did I ever lose my temper?" he demanded. "I'm always in complete control."

They both laughed.

---

6 He shaved with an old-fashioned straight razor, one of a matched pair his father had used. They were handsome implements of Swedish steel with bone handles. Each morning, alternating, he took a razor from the worn, velvet-lined case and honed it lightly on a leather strop that hung from the inside knob of the bathroom door.

Barbara could never conceal her dislike of the naked steel. She had bought him an electric shaver one Christmas and, to please her, he had used it a few times at home. Then he had taken it to his office in the precinct house where, he assured her, he frequently used it for a "touch-up" when he had a meeting late in the afternoon or evening. She nodded, accepting his lie. Perhaps she sensed that the reason he used the straight razors was because they had belonged to his father, a man he worshipped.

Now, this morning, drawing the fine steel slowly and carefully down his lathered jaw, he listened to a news broadcast from the little transistor radio in the bedroom and learned, from a brief announcement, that Bernard Gilbert, victim of a midnight street attack, had died without regaining consciousness. Delaney's hand did not falter, and he finished his shave steadily, wiped off excess lather, splashed lotion, powdered lightly, dressed in his usual dark suit, white shirt, striped tie, and went down to the kitchen for breakfast, bolstered and carried along by habit. He stopped in the study just long enough to jot a little note to himself to write a letter of condolence to Monica Gilbert.

He greeted Mary, accepted orange juice, one poached egg on unbuttered toast, and black coffee. They chatted about the weather, about Mrs. Delaney's condition, and he approved of Mary's plan to strip the furniture in Barbara's sewing room of chintz slipcovers and send them all to the dry cleaner.

Later, in the study, he wrote a pencilled rough of his letter of condolence to Mrs. Gilbert. When he had it the way he wanted—admitting it was stilted, but there was no way of getting around *that*—he copied it in ink, addressed and stamped the envelope and put it aside, intending to mail it when he left the house.

It was then almost 9:30, and he called the Medical Examiner's office. Ferguson wasn't in yet but was expected momentarily. Delaney waited patiently for fifteen minutes, making circular doodles on a scratch pad, a thin line that went around and around in a narrowing spiral. Then he called again and was put through to Ferguson.

"I know," the doctor said, "he's dead. I heard when I got in."

"Did you get it?"

"Yes. The lump is on the way down now. The big problem in my life, Edward, is whether to do a cut-'em-up before lunch or after. I finally decided before is better. So I'll probably get to him about eleven or eleven-thirty."

"I'd like to see you before you start."

"I can't get out, Edward. No way. I'm tied up here with other things."

"I'll come down. Could you give me about fifteen minutes at eleven o'clock?"

"Important?"

"I think so."

"You can't tell me on the phone?"

"No. It's something I've got to show you, to give you."

"All right, Edward. Fifteen minutes at eleven."

"Thank you, doctor."

First he went into the kitchen. He tore a square of paper towel off the roller, then a square of wax paper from the package, then a square of aluminum foil.

Back in the study he took from the file drawer the can of light machine oil and the ice ax Christopher Langley had purchased at Outside Life.

He removed the cap from the oil can and impregnated the paper towel with oil. He folded it carefully into wax paper, then wrapped the whole thing in aluminum foil, pressing down hard on the folds so the oil wouldn't seep out. He put the package in a heavy manila envelope.

Then he sharpened a pencil, using his penknife to scrape the graphite to a long point. He placed the ice ax head on a sheet of good rag stationery and carefully traced a profile with his sharpened pencil, going very slowly, taking particular care to include the four little saw teeth on the underside of the point.

Then he took out his desk ruler and measured the size of the spike where it left the head, as a square. Each of the four sides, as closely as he could determine, was fifteen-sixteenths of an inch. He then drew a square to those dimensions on the same sheet of paper with the silhouette of the pick. He folded the sheet, tucked it into his breast pocket. He took the envelope with the oil-impregnated paper towel and started out. He pulled on his overcoat and hat, shouted upstairs to Mary to tell her he was leaving, and heard her answering shout. At the last minute, halfway out the door, he remembered his letter of condolence to Monica Gilbert and went back into the study to pick it up. He dropped it in the first mailbox he passed.

"Better make this quick, Edward," Dr. Ferguson said. "Broughton is sending one of his boys down to witness the autopsy. He wants a preliminary verbal report before he gets the official form."

"I'll make it fast. Did the doctors at Mother of Mercy tell you anything?"

"Not much. As I told you, Gilbert was struck from the front, the wound about two inches above the normal hair line. The blow apparently knocked him backward, and the weapon was pulled free before he fell. As a result, the penetration is reasonably clean and neat, so I should be able to get a better profile of the wound than on the Lombard snuff."

"Good." Delaney unfolded his paper. "Doctor, this is what I think the penetration profile will look like. It's hard to tell from this, but the spike starts out as a square. Here, in this little drawing, are the dimensions, about an inch on each side. If I'm right, that should be the size of the outside wound, at scalp and skull. Then the square changes to a triangular pick, and tapers, and curves downward, coming to a sharp point."

"Is this your imagination, or was it traced from an actual weapon?"

"It was traced."

"All right. I don't want to know anything more. What are these?"

"Four little saw teeth on the underside of the point. You may find some rough abrasions on the lower surface of the wound."

"I may, eh? The brain isn't hard cheddar, you know. You want me to work with this paper open on the table alongside the corpse?"

"Not if Broughton's man is there."

"I didn't think so."

"Couldn't you just take a look at it, doctor? Just in case?"

"Sure," Ferguson said, folding up the paper and sliding it into his hip pocket. "What else have you got?"

"In this envelope is a folded packet of aluminum foil, and inside that is an envelope of wax paper, and inside that is a paper towel soaked in oil. Light machine oil."

"So?"

"You mentioned there were traces of oil in the Lombard wound. You thought it was probably Lombard's hair oil, but it was too slight for analysis."

"But Gilbert was bald—at least where he was hit he was bald."

"That's the point. It couldn't be hair oil. But I'm hoping there will be oil in the Gilbert wound. Light machine oil."

Ferguson pushed back in his swivel chair and stared at him. Then the doctor pulled his wool tie open, unbuttoned the neck of his flannel shirt.

"You're a lovely man, Edward," he said, "and the best detective in town, but Gilbert's wound was X-rayed, probed and flushed at Mother of Mercy."

"If there was any oil in it, there couldn't be any now?"

"I didn't say that. But it sure as hell cuts down on your chances."

"What about the Olfactory Analysis Indicator?"

"The OAI? What about it?"

"How much do you know about it, doctor?"

"About as much as you do. You read the last bulletin, didn't you?"

"Yes. Sort of inconclusive, wasn't it?"

"It surely was. The idea is to develop a sniffer not much larger than a vacuum cleaner. Portable. It could be taken to the scene of a crime, inhale an air sample, and either identify the odors immediately or store the air sample so it could be taken back to the lab and analyzed by a master machine. Well, they're a long way from that right now. It's a monstrous big thing at this point, very crude, but I saw an impressive demonstration the other day. It correctly identified nine smokes from fifteen different brands of cigarettes. That's not bad."

"In other words, it's got to have a comparison to go by? Like the memory bank in a computer?"

"That's right. Oh-ho. I see what you're getting at. All right, Edward. Leave me your machine oil sample. I'll try to get a reading on tissue from Gilbert's wound. But don't count on it. The OAI is years away. It's just an experiment now."

"I realize that. But I don't want to neglect any possibility."

"You never did," Dr. Ferguson said.

"Should I wait around?"

"No point in it. The OAI analysis will take three days at least. Probably a week. As far as your drawing goes, I'll call you this afternoon or this evening. Will you be at home?"

"Probably. But I may be at the hospital. You could reach me there."

"How's Barbara?"

"Getting along."

Ferguson nodded, stood, took off his tweed jacket, hung it on a coat tree, began to shrug into a stained white coat.

"Getting anywhere, Edward?" he asked.

"Who the hell knows?" Captain Delaney grumbled. "I just keep going."

"Don't we all?" the big man smiled.

Delaney called Ivar Thorsen from a lobby phone. The answering service got back to him a few minutes later and said Mr. Thorsen was not available and would he please call again at three in the afternoon.

It was the first time Thorsen had not returned his call, and it bothered Delaney. It might be, of course, that the deputy inspector was in a meeting or on his way to a precinct house, but the Captain couldn't shake a vague feeling of unease.

He consulted his pocket notebook in which he had copied the address of Outside Life. He took a taxi to Spring Street, and when he got out of the cab, he spent a few minutes walking up and down the block, looking around. It was a section of grimy loft buildings, apparently mostly occupied by small manufacturers, printers, and wholesalers of leather findings. It seemed a strange neighborhood for Outside Life.

That occupied the second and third floors of a ten-story building. Delaney walked up the stairs to the second floor, but the sign on the solid door said "Offices and Mailing. Store on third floor." So he climbed another flight, wanting to look about before he talked to—to— He consulted his notebook again: Sol Appel, the owner.

The "store" was actually one enormous, high-ceilinged loft with pipe racks, a few glass showcases, and with no attempts made at fashionable merchandizing. Most of the stock was piled on the floor, on unpainted wooden shelves, or hung from hooks driven into the whitewashed walls.

As Langley had said, it was a fascinating conglomeration: rucksacks, rubber dinghies, hiking boots, crampons, dehydrated food, kerosene lanterns, battery-heated socks, machetes, net hammocks, sleeping bags, outdoor cookware, hunting knives, fishing rods, reels, creels, pitons, nylon rope, boating gear—an endless profusion of items ranging from five-cent fishhooks to a magnificent red, three-room tent with a mosquito-netted picture window, at $1,495.

Outside Life seemed to have its devotees, despite its out-of-the-way location; Delaney counted at least forty customers wandering about, and the clerks were busy writing up purchases. The Captain found his way to the mountaineering department and inspected pitons, crampons, web belts and harnesses, nylon line, aluminum-framed backpacks, and a wide variety of ice axes. There were two styles of short-handled axes: the one purchased by Langley and another, somewhat similar, but with a wooden handle and no saw-tooth serrations under the spike. Delaney inspected it, and finally found "Made in U.S.A." stamped on the handle butt.

He halted a scurrying clerk just long enough to ask for the whereabouts of Mr. Appel. "Sol's in the office," the departing clerk called over his shoulder. "Downstairs."

Delaney pushed open the heavy door on the second floor and found himself in a tiny reception room, walled with unfinished plywood panels. There was a door of clear glass leading to the open space beyond, apparently a combination warehouse and mailing room. In one corner of the reception room was a telephone operator wearing a wired headset and sitting before a push-pull switchboard that Delaney knew had been phased out of production years and years ago. Outside Life seemed to be a busy, thriving enterprise, but it was also obvious the profits weren't going into fancy offices and smart decoration.

He waited patiently until the operator had plugged and unplugged half a dozen calls. Finally, desperately, he said, "Mr. Appel, please. My name is—"

She stuck her head through the opening into the big room beyond and screamed, "Sol! Guy to see you!"

Delaney sat on the single couch, a rickety thing covered with slashed plastic. He was amused to note an overflowing ashtray on the floor. The single decoration in the room was a plaque on the plywood wall attesting to Mr. Solomon Appel's efforts on behalf of the United Jewish Appeal.

The glass door crashed back, and a heavy, sweating man rushed in. Delaney caught a confused impression of a round, plump face (the man in the moon), a well-chewed, unlit cigar, a raveled, sleeveless sweater of hellish hue, unexpectedly "mod" jeans of dark blue with white stitching and a darker satin down one leg, and Indian moccasins decorated with beads.

"You from Benson & Hurst?" the man demanded, talking rapidly around his cigar. "I'm Sol Appel. Where the hell are those tents? You promised—"

"Wait, wait," Delaney said hastily. "I'm not from Benson & Hurst. I'm—"

"Gatters," the man said positively. "The fiberglass rods. You guys are sure giving me the rod—you know where. You said—"

"Will you wait a minute," Delaney said again, sighing. "I'm not from Gatters either. My name is Captain Edward X. Delaney. New York Police Department. Here's my identification."

Sol Appel didn't even glance at it. He raised his hands above his head, palms outward, in mock surrender.

"I give up," he said. "Whatever it was, I did it. Take me away. Now. Please get me out of this nuthouse. Do me a favor. Jail will be a pleasure."

"No, no," Delaney laughed. "Nothing like that. Mr. Appel, I wanted—"

"You're putting on a dance? A dinner? You want a few bucks? Of course. Why not? Always. Any time. So tell me—how much?"

He was already reaching for his wallet when Delaney held out a restraining hand and sighed again.

"Please, Mr. Appel, it's nothing like that. I'm not collecting for anything. All I want is a few minutes of your time."

"A few minutes? Now you're really asking for something valuable. A few minutes!" He turned back to the opened glass door. "Sam!" he screamed. "You, Sam! Get the cash. No check. The cash! You understand?"

"Is there any place we can talk?" the Captain asked.

"We're talking, aren't we?"

"All right," Delaney said doubtfully, glancing at the switchboard operator. But she was busy with her cords and plugs. "Mr. Appel, your name was given to me by Calvin Case, and I—"

"Cal!" Appel cried. He stepped close and grabbed Delaney's overcoat by the lapels. "That dear, sweet boy. How is he? Will you tell me?"

"Well . . . he's—"

"Don't tell me. He's on the booze. I know. I heard. I wanted him back. 'So you can't walk,' I told him. 'Big deal. You can think. No? You can work. No?' That's the big thing—right, Captain—uh, Captain—"

"Delaney."

"Captain Delaney. That's Irish, no?"

"Yes."

"Sure. I knew. The important thing is to work. Am I right?"

"You're right."

"Of course I'm right," Sol Appel said angrily. "So any time he wants a job, he's got it. Right here. We can use him. Tell him that. Will you tell him that?" Suddenly Appel struck his forehead with the heel of his hand. "I should have been to see him," he groaned. "What kind of schmuck am I? I'm really ashamed. I'll go to see him. Tell him that, Chief Delaney."

"Captain."

"Captain. Will you tell him that?"

"Yes, certainly, if I speak to him again. But that isn't the—"

"You're taking up a collection for him? You're making a benefit, Captain? It will be my pleasure to take a table for eight, and I'll—"

Delaney finally got him calmed down, a little, and seated on the plastic couch. He explained he was involved in an investigation, and the cigar-chomping Sol Appel asked no questions. Within five minutes Delaney had discovered that Outside Life had a mailing list of approxmiately 30,000 customers who were sent Summer and Winter catalogues. The mailings were done with metal addressing plates and printed labels. There was also a typed master list, and Sol Appel would be happy to provide a copy for Captain Delaney whenever he asked.

"I assure you, it'll be held in complete confidence," the Captain said earnestly.

"Who cares?" Appel shouted. "My competitors can meet my prices? Hah!"

Delaney also learned that Outside Life kept sales checks for seven years. They were stored in cardboard cartons in the basement of the loft building, filed by month and year.

"Why seven years?" he asked.

"Who the hell knows?" Appel shrugged. "My father—God rest his soul—he only died last year—I should live so long—Mike Appel—a mensch. You know what a mensch is, Captain?"

"Yes. I know. My father was an Irish mensch."

"Good. So he told me, 'Sol,' he said a hundred times, 'always keep the copies of the sales checks for seven years.' Who the hell knows why? That's the way he did it, that's the way I do it. Taxes or something; I don't know. Anyway, I keep them seven years. I add this year's, I throw the oldest year's away."

"Would you let me go through them?"

"Go through them? Captain, there's got to be like a hundred thousand checks there."

"If I have to, can I go through them?"

"Be my guest. Sarah!" Sol Appel suddenly screamed. "You, Sarah!"

An elderly Jewish lady thrust her head through the switchboard operator's window.

"You called, Sol?" she asked.

"Tell him 'No'!" Appel screamed, and the lady nodded and withdrew.

Now that Delaney wanted to leave, Appel wouldn't let him depart. He shook his hand endlessly and talked a blue streak . . .

"Go up to the store. Pick out anything you like. Have them call me before you pay. You'll get a nice discount, believe me. You know, you Irish and us Jews are much alike. We're both poets—am I right? And who can talk these days? The Irish and the Jews only. You need a cop, you find an Irishman. You need a lawyer, you find a Jew. This stuff I sell, you think I understand it? Hah! For me, I go camping on Miami Beach or Nassau. You float on the pool there in this plastic couch with a nice, tall drink and all around these girlies in their little bitty bikinis. That, to me, is outside life. Captain, I like you. Delaney—right? You in the book? Sure, you're in the book. Next month, a Bar-Mitzvah for my nephew. I'll call you. Bring nothing, you understand? Nothing! I'll go see Calvin Case. I swear I'll go. You've got to work. Sarah! Sarah!"

Delaney finally got out of there, laughing aloud and shaking his head, so that people he passed on the stairway looked at him strangely. He didn't think Appel would remember to invite him to the Bar-Mitzvah. But if he did, Delaney decided he would go. How often do you meet a *live* man?

Well, he had found out what he wanted to know—and, as usual, it wasn't as bad as he had feared or as good as he had hoped. He walked west on Spring Street and, suddenly, pierced by the odor of frying sausage and peppers, he joined a throng of Puerto Ricans and blacks at an open luncheonette counter and had a slice of sausage pizza and a glass of sweet cola, resolutely forgetting about his diet. Sometimes . . .

He took two subways and a bus back to his home. Mary was having coffee in the kitchen, and he joined her for a cup, telling her he had already eaten lunch, but not saying what it was.

"Whatever it was, it had garlic in it," she sniffed, and he laughed.

He worked in his study until 3:00 P.M., bringing his reports up to date. The file of his own investigation was becoming pleasingly plump. It was nowhere near as extensive as the Operation Lombard reports, of course, but still, it had width to it now, it had width.

At 3:00 P.M., he called Deputy Inspector Thorsen. This time the answering service operator asked him to hold while she checked. She was back on again in a few minutes and told him Thorsen asked him to call again at seven in the evening. Delaney hung up, now convinced that something was happening, something was awry.

He put the worry away from him and went back to his notes and reports. If "The Suspect" was indeed a mountain climber—and Delaney believed he was—weren't there other possible leads to his identity other than the mailing list of Outside Life? For instance, was there a local or national club or association of mountain climbers whose membership list could be culled for residents of the 251st Precinct? Was there a newsletter or magazine devoted to mountaineering with a subscription list that could be used for the same purpose? What about books on mountain climbing? Should Delaney inquire at the library that served the 251st Precinct and try to determine who had withdrawn books on the subject?

He jotted down notes on these questions as fast as they occurred to him. Mountain climbing was, after all, a minor sport. But could you call it a *sport?* It really didn't seem to be a pastime or diversion. It seemed more of a—of a—well, the only word that came to his mind was "challenge." He also thought, for some reason, of "crusade," but that didn't make too much sense, and he resolved to talk to Calvin Case about it, and carefully made a note to himself to that effect.

Finally, almost as a casual afterthought, he came back to the problem that had been nagging him for the past few days, and he resolved to turn over everything he had to Broughton and Chief Pauley. They could follow through much faster than he could, and their investigation might, just might, prevent another death. He would have liked to stick to it on his own, but that was egotism, just egotism.

He was writing out a detailed report of his meeting with Sol Appel when the desk phone rang. He lifted the receiver and said absently, "Hello."

" 'Hello'?" Dr. Sanford Ferguson laughed. "What the hell kind of a greeting is that—'Hello?' Whatever happened to 'Captain Edward X. Delaney here'?"

"All right. Captain Edward X. Delaney here. Are you bombed?"

"On my way, m'lad. Congratulations."

"You mean the drawing was accurate?"

"Right on. The outside wound—I'm talking about the skull now—was a rough square, about an inch on each side. For the probe I used glass fiber. You know what that is?"

"A slender bundle of glass threads, flexible and transmitting light from a battery-powered source."

"You know everything, don't you, Edward? Yes, that's what I used. Tapering, curving downward to a sharp point, and I even found some evidence of heavier abrasions on the lower surface, a tearing. That could be accounted for by those little saw teeth. Not definite enough to put in my official report, but a possible, Captain, a possible."

"Thank you, doctor. And the oil?"

"No obvious sign of it. But I sent your rag and a specimen of tissue to the lab. I told you, it'll take time."

"They won't talk?"

"The lab boys? Only to me. It's just a job. They know from nothing. Happy, Edward?"

"Yes. Very. Why are you getting drunk?"

"He was so small. So small, so frail, so wasted and his heart wasn't worth a damn and he had a prick about the size of a thimble. So I'm getting drunk. Any objections?"

"No. None."

"Get the bastard, Edward."

"I will."

"Promise?"

"I promise," Captain Edward X. Delaney said.

He got to the hospital shortly after 5:30, but the visit was a disaster. Barbara immediately started talking of a cousin of hers who had died twenty years ago, and then began speaking of "this terrible war." He thought she was talking about Vietnam, but then she spoke of Tom Hendricks, a lieutenant of Marines, and he realized she was talking about the Korean War, in which Tom Hendricks had been killed. Then she sang a verse of "Black is the color of my true love's hair," and he didn't know what to do.

He sat beside her, tried to soothe her. But she would not be still. She gabbled of Mary, of the drapes in the third-floor bedrooms, Thorsen, violets, a dead dog—and who had taken her children away? He was frightened and close to weeping. He pushed the bell for the nurse, but when no one came, he rushed into the corridor and almost dragged in the first nurse he saw.

Barbara was still babbling, eyes closed, an almost-smile on her lips, and he waited anxiously, alone, while the nurse left for a moment to consult her medication chart. He listened to a never-ending stream of meaningless chatter: Lombard and Honey Bunch and suddenly, "I need a hundred dollars," and Eddie and Liza, and then she was at the carrousel in the park, describing it and laughing, and the painted horses went round and round, and then the nurse came back with a covered tray, removed a hypodermic, gave Barbara a shot in the arm, near the wrist. In a few moments she was calm, then sleeping.

"Jesus Christ," Delaney breathed, "what happened to her? What was that?"

"Just upset," the nurse smiled mechanically. "She's all right now. She's sleeping peaceably."

"Peacefully," the Captain said.

"Peacefully," the nurse repeated obediently. "If you have any questions, please contact your doctor in the morning."

She marched out. Delaney stared after her, wondering if there was any end to the madness in the world. He turned back to the bed. Barbara was, apparently, sleeping peacefully. He felt so goddamned frightened, helpless, furious.

It wasn't 7:00 P.M., so he couldn't call Thorsen. He walked home, hoping, just hoping, he might be attacked. He was not armed, but he didn't care. He would kick them in the balls, bite their throats—he was in that mood. He looked around at the shadowed streets. "Try me," he wanted to shout. "Come on! I'm here."

He got inside, took off his hat and coat, treated himself to two straight whiskies. He calmed down, gradually. What a thing that had been. He was home now, unhurt, thinking clearly. But Barbara . . .

He sat stolidly sipping his whiskey until 7:00 P.M. Then he called Thorsen's number, not really caring. Thorsen called him back almost immediately.

"Edward?"

"Yes."

"Something important?"

"I think so. Can you get Johnson?"

"He's here now."

Then Delaney became aware of the tone of the man's voice, the tightness, urgency.

"I've got to see you," the Captain said. "The sooner the better."

"Yes," Thorsen agreed. "Can you come over now?"

"Your office or home?"

"Home."

"I'll take a cab," Captain Delaney told him. "About twenty minutes, at the most."

He hung up, then said, "Fuck 'em all," in a loud voice. But he went into the kitchen, found a paper shopping bag in the cabinet under the sink, brought it back to the study. In it he placed the three hammers and the can of machine oil—all his "physical evidence." Then he set out.

Mrs. Thorsen met him at the door, took his coat and hat and hung them away. She was a tall silver-blonde, almost gaunt, but with good bones and the most beautiful violet eyes Delaney had ever seen. They chatted a few moments, and she asked about Barbara. He mumbled something.

"Have you eaten tonight, Edward?" she asked suddenly.

He tried to think, not remembering, then shook his head.

"I'm making some sandwiches. Ham-and-cheese all right? Or roast beef?"

"Either or both will be fine, Karen."

"And I have some salad things. In about an hour or so. The others are in the living room—you know where."

There were three men in the room, all seated. Thorsen and Inspector Johnson rose and came forward to shake his hand. The third man remained seated; no one offered to introduce him.

This man was short, chunky, swarthy, with a tremendous mustache. His hands lay flat on his knees, and his composure was monumental. Only his dark eyes moved, darting, filled with curiosity and a lively intelligence.

It was only after he was seated that Delaney made him: Deputy Mayor Herman Alinski. He was a secretive, publicity-shy politico, reputed to be the mayor's trouble-shooter and one of his closest confidants. In a short biographical sketch in the *Times,* the writer, speculating on Alinski's duties, had come to the conclusion that, "Apparently, what he does most frequently is listen, and everyone who knows him agrees that he does that very well indeed."

"Drink, Edward?" Thorsen asked. "Rye highball?"

Delaney looked around. Thorsen and Johnson had glasses. Alinski did not.

"Not right now, thank you. Maybe later."

"All right. Karen is making up some sandwiches for us. Edward, you said you had something important for us. You can talk freely."

Again Delaney became conscious of the tension in Thorsen's voice, and when he looked at Inspector Johnson, the big black seemed stiff and grim.

"All right," Delaney said. "I'll take it from the top."

He started speaking, still seated, and then, in a few moments, rose to pace around the room, or pause with his elbow on the mantel. He thought and spoke better, he knew, on his feet, and could gesture freely. None of the three men interrupted, but their heads or eyes followed him wherever he strode.

He began with Lombard's death. The position of the body. His reasons for thinking the killer had approached from the front, then whirled to strike Lombard down from behind. The shape and nature of the wound. Oil in the wound. The missing driver's license. His belief that it was taken as evidence of the kill. Then Langley, his expertise, and the discovery of the bricklayers' hammer which led to the rock hounds' hammer which led to the ice ax.

At this point he unpacked his shopping bag and handed around the tools. The three men examined them closely, their faces expressionless as they tested edges with thumbs, hefted the weight and balance of the tools.

Delaney went on: the Bernard Gilbert attack. The missing ID card. His belief that the assailant was psychopathic. A resident of the 251st Precinct. And would kill again. The information supplied by Handry: the Trotsky assassination and the name of Calvin Case. Then the interview with Case. The oil on the ice ax heads. He handed around the can of oil.

He had them now, and the three were leaning forward intently, Thorsen and Johnson neglecting their drinks, the Deputy Mayor's sharp eyes darting and glittering. There wasn't a sound from them.

Delaney told them about the interview with Sol Appel at Outside Life. The mailing list and itemized sales checks. Then he related how he had traced a profile of the ice ax head. How he had given that and a sample of machine oil to the surgeon who did the autopsy on Gilbert. How the profile on the wound checked out. How the oil would be analyzed on the OAI.

"Who did the post?" Inspector Johnson asked.

Alinski's head swivelled sharply, and he spoke for the first time. "Post?" he asked. "What's post?"

"Post-mortem," Delaney explained. "I promised to keep the surgeon's name out of it."

"We could find out," Alinski said mildly.

"Of course," the Captain said, just as mildly. "But not from me."

That seemed to satisfy Alinski. Thorsen asked how much Delaney had told the surgeon, had told Langley, Handry, Case, Mrs. Gilbert, Sol Appel.

Only as much as they needed to know, Delaney assured him. They knew only that he was engaged in a private investigation of the deaths of Lombard and Gilbert, and they were willing to help.

"Why?" Alinski asked.

Delaney shrugged. "For reasons of their own." There was silence for a few minutes, then Alinski spoke softly:

"You have no proof, do you, Captain?"

Delaney looked at him in astonishment.

"Of course not. It's all smoke, all theory. I haven't told you or shown you a single thing that could be taken into court at this time."

"But you believe in it?"

"I believe in it. For one reason only—there's nothing else to believe in. Does Operation Lombard have anything better?"

The three men turned heads to stare wordlessly at each other. Delaney could tell nothing from their expressions.

"That's really why I'm here," he said, addressing Thorsen. "I want to turn—"

But at that moment there was a kicking at the door; not a knocking, but three sharp kicks. Thorsen sprang up, stalked over, opened the door and relieved his wife of a big tray of food.

"Thank you dear," he smiled.

"There's plenty more of everything," she called to the other men. "So don't be polite if you're hungry; just ask."

Thorsen put the loaded tray on a low cocktail table, and they clustered around. There were ham-and-cheese sandwiches, roast beef sandwiches, chunks of tomato, radishes, dill pickles, slices of Spanish onions, a jar of hot mustard, olives, potato chips, scallions.

They helped themselves, all standing, and Thorsen mixed fresh drinks. This time Delaney had a rye and water, and Deputy Mayor Alinski took a double Scotch.

Unwilling to sacrifice the momentum of what he had been saying, and the impression he had obviously made on them, Delaney began talking again, speaking between bites of his sandwich and pieces of scallion. This time he looked at Alinski as he spoke.

"I want to turn over everything I've got to Chief Pauley. I admit it's smoke, but it's a lead. I've got three or four inexperienced people who can check sources of the ax and the Outside Life mailing list and sales checks. But Pauley's got five hundred dicks and God knows how many deskmen if he needs them. It's a question of time. I think Pauley should take this over; he can do it a lot faster than I can. It might prevent another kill, and I'm convinced there will be another, and another, and another, until we catch up with this nut."

The other three continued eating steadily, sipping their drinks and looking at him. Once Thorsen started to speak, but Alinski held up a hand, silencing him. Finally the Deputy Mayor finished his sandwich, wiped his fingers on a paper napkin, took his drink back to his chair. He sat down, sighed, stared at Delaney.

"A moral problem for you, isn't it, Captain?" he asked softly.

"Call it what you like," Delaney shrugged. "I just feel what I have is strong enough to follow up on, and Chief Pauley is—"

"Impossible," Thorsen said.

"Why impossible?" Delaney cried angrily. "If you—"

"Calm down, Edward," Inspector Johnson said quietly. He was on his third sandwich. "That's why we wanted to talk to you tonight. You obviously haven't been listening to radio or TV in the last few hours. You can't turn over what you have to Chief Pauley. Broughton canned him a few hours ago."

"Canned him?"

"Whatever you want to call it. Relieved him of command. Kicked him off Operation Lombard."

"Jesus Christ!" Delaney said furiously. "He can't do that."

"He did it," Thorsen nodded. "And in a particularly—in a particularly brutal way. Didn't even tell the Chief. Just called a press conference and announced he was relieving Pauley of all command responsibilities relating to Operation Lombard. He said Pauley was inefficient and getting nowhere."

"But who the hell is—"

"And Broughton is going to take over personal supervision of all the detectives assigned to Operation Lombard."

"Oh God," Delaney groaned. "That tears it."

"You haven't heard the worst," Thorsen went on, staring at him without expression. "About an hour ago Pauley filed for retirement. After what Broughton said, Pauley knows his career is finished, and he wants out."

Delaney sat down heavily in an armchair, looked down at his drink, swirling the ice cubes.

"Son of a bitch," he said bitterly. "Pauley was a good man. You have no idea how good. He was right behind me. Only because I had the breaks, and he didn't. But he would have been on to this ice ax thing in another week or so. I know he would; I could tell it by the reports. God damn it! The Department can't afford to lose men like Pauley. Jesus! A good brain and thirty years' experience down the drain. It just makes me sick!"

None of them said anything, giving him time to calm down. Alinski rose from his chair to go over to the food tray again, take a few radishes and olives. Then he came over to stand before Delaney's chair, popping food.

"You know, Captain," he said gently, "this development really doesn't affect your moral problem, does it? I mean, you can still take what you have to Broughton."

"I suppose so," Delaney said morosely. "Canning Pauley, for God's sake. Broughton's out of his mind. He just wanted a goat to protect his own reputation."

"That's what we think," Inspector Johnson said.

Delaney looked up at Deputy Mayor Alinski, still standing over him.

"What's it all about?" he demanded. "Will you please tell me what the hell this is all about?"

"Do you really want to know, Captain?"

"Yeah, I want to know," Delaney grunted. "But I don't want you to tell me. I'll find out for myself."

"I think you will," Alinski nodded. "I think you are a very smart man."

"Smart? Shit! I can't even find one kill-crazy psychopath in my own precinct."

"It's important to you, isn't it, Captain, to find the killer? It's the most important thing."

"Of course it's the most important thing. This nut is going to keep killing, over and over and over. There will be shorter intervals between murders. Maybe he'll hit in the daytime. Who the hell knows? But I can guarantee one thing: he won't stop now. It's a fever in his blood. He can't stop. Wait'll the newspapers get hold of this. And they will. Then the shit will hit the fan."

"Going to take what you have to Broughton?" Thorsen asked, almost idly.

"I don't know. I don't know what I'll do. I have to think about it."

"That's wise," Alinski said unexpectedly. "Think about it. There's nothing like thought—long, deep thought."

"I just want all of you to know one thing," Delaney said angrily, not understanding why he was angry. "The decision is mine. Only mine. What I decide to do, I'll do."

They would have offered him something, but they knew better.

Johnson came over to put a heavy hand on Delaney's shoulder. The big black was grinning. "We know that, Edward. We knew you were a hard-nose from the start. We're not going to lean on you."

Delaney drained his drink, rose, put the empty glass on the cocktail table. He repacked his paper shopping bag with hammers and the can of oil.

"Thank you," he said to Thorsen. "Thank Karen for me for the food. I can find my own way out."

"Will you call and tell me what you've decided, Edward?"

"Sure. If I decide to go to Broughton, I'll call you first."

"Thank you."

"Gentlemen," Delaney nodded around, and marched out. They watched him go, all of them standing.

He had to walk five blocks and lost two dimes before he found a public phone that worked. He finally got through to Thomas Handry.

"Yes?"

"Captain Edward X. Delaney here. Am I interrupting you?"

"Yes."

"Working?"

"Trying to."

"How's it coming?"

"It's never as good as you want it to be."

"That's true," Delaney said, without irony and without malice. "True for poets and true for cops. I was hoping you could give me some help."

"That photo of the ice ax that killed Trotsky? I haven't been able to find it."

"No, this is something else."

"You're something else too, Captain—you know that? All for you and none for me. When are you going to open up?"

"In a day or so."

"Promise?"

"I promise."

"All right. What do you want?"

"What do you know about Broughton?"

"Who?"

"Broughton, Timothy A., Deputy Commissioner."

"That prick? Did you see him on TV tonight?"

"No, I didn't."

"He fired Chief Pauley. For inefficiency and, he hinted, dereliction of duty. A sweet man."

"What does he want?"

"Broughton? He wants to be commissioner, then mayor, then governor, then President of these here You-nited States. He's got ambition and drive you wouldn't believe."

"I gather you don't approve of him."

"You gather right. I've had one personal interview with him. You know how most men carry pictures of their wives and children in their wallets? Broughton carries pictures of himself."

"Nice. Does he have any clout? Political clout?"

"Very heavy indeed. Queens and Staten Island for starters. The talk is that he's aiming for the primary next year. On a 'law and order' platform. You know, 'We must clamp down on crime in the streets, no matter what it costs.' "

"You think he'll make it?"

"He might. If he can bring off his Operation Lombard thing, it's bound to help. And if Lombard's killer turns out to be a black heroin addict on welfare who's living with a white fifteen-year-old hippie with long blonde hair, there'll be no stopping Broughton."

"You think the mayor's worried?"

"Wouldn't you be?"

"I guess. Thank you, Handry. You've made a lot of things a lot clearer."

"Not for me. What the hell is going on?"

"Will you give me a day—or two?"

"No more. Gilbert died, didn't he?"

"Yes. He did."

"There's a connection, isn't there?"

"Yes."

"Two days," Handry said. "No more. If I don't hear from you by then, I'll have to start guessing. In print."

"Good enough."

He walked home, the shopping bag bumping against his knee. Now he could understand something of what was going on—the tension of Thorsen, Johnson's grimness, Alinski's presence. He really didn't want to get involved in all that political shit. He was a cop, a professional. Right now, all he wanted to do was catch a killer, but he seemed bound and strangled by this maze of other men's ambitions, feuds, obligations.

What had happened, he realized, was that his search for the killer of Lombard and Gilbert had become a very personal thing to him, a private thing, and he resented the intrusion of other men, other circumstances, other motives. He needed help, of course—he couldn't do everything himself—but essentially it was a duel, a two-man combat, and outside advice, pressures, influence were to be shunned. You knew what you could do, and you respected your opponent's ability and didn't take him lightly. Whether it was a fencing exhibition or a duel to the death, you put your cock on the line.

But all that was egotism he admitted, groaning aloud. Stupid male *machismo*, believing that nothing mattered unless you risked your balls. It should not, it *could* not affect his decision which, as Barbara and Deputy Mayor Alinski had recognized, was essentially a moral choice.

Thinking this way, brooding, his brain in a whirl, he turned into his own block, head down, *schlepping* along with his heavy shopping bag, when a harsh voice called, "Delaney!"

He stopped slowly. Like most detectives in New York—in the world!—he had helped send men up. To execution, or to long or short prison terms, or to mental institutions. Most of them vowed revenge—in the courtroom, in threats phoned by their friends, in letters. Very few of them, thankfully, ever carried out their threats. But there were a few . . .

Now, hearing his name called from a dark sedan parked on a poorly lighted street, realizing he was unarmed, he turned slowly toward the car. He let the shopping bag drop to the sidewalk. He raised his arms slightly, palms turned forward.

But then he saw the uniformed driver in the front seat. And in the back, leaning toward the cranked-down window, the bulk and angry face of Deputy Commissioner Broughton. The cigar, clenched in his teeth, was burning furiously.

"Delaney!" Broughton said again, more of a command than a greeting. The Captain stepped closer to the car. Broughton made no effort to open the door, so Delaney was forced to bow forward from the waist to speak to him. He was certain this was deliberate on Broughton's part, to keep him in a suppplicant's position.

"Sir?" he asked.

"Just what the fuck do you think you're doing?"

"I don't understand, sir."

"We sent a man to Florida. It turns out that Lombard's driver's license is missing. The widow says you spoke to her about it. You were seen entering her house. You knew the license was missing. I could rack you up for withholding evidence."

"But I reported it, sir."

"You reported it? To Pauley?"

"No, I didn't think it was that important. I reported it to Dorfman, Acting Commander of the Two-five-one Precinct. I'm sure he sent a report to the Traffic Department. Check the New York State Department of Motor Vehicles, sir. I'm certain you'll find a missing license report was filed with them."

There was silence for a moment. A cloud of rank cigar smoke came billowing out the window, into Delaney's face. Still he stooped.

"Why did you go see Gilbert's wife?" Broughton demanded.

"For the same reason I went to see Mrs. Lombard," Delaney said promptly. "To present my condolences. As commander and ex-commander of the precinct in which the crimes occurred. Good public relations for the Department."

Again there was a moment's silence.

"You got an answer for everything, you wise bastard," Broughton said angrily. He was in semi-darkness. Delaney, bending down, could barely make out his features. "You been seeing Thorsen? And Inspector Johnson?"

"Of course I've been seeing Deputy Inspector Thorsen, sir. He's been a friend of mine for many years."

"He's your 'rabbi'—right?"

"Yes. And he introduced me to Johnson. Just because I'm on leave of absence doesn't mean I have to stop seeing old friends in the Department."

"Delaney, I don't trust you. I got a nose for snots like you, and I got a feeling you're up to something. Just listen to this: you're still on the list, and I can stomp on you any time I want to. You know that?"

"Yes, sir."

"Don't fuck me, Delaney. I can do more to you than you can do to me. You *coppish?*"

"Yes. I understand."

So far he had held his temper under control and now, in a split-second, he made his decision. His anger wasn't important, and neither was Broughton's obnoxious personality. He brought the shopping bag closer to the car window.

"Sir," he said, "I have something here I'd like to show you. I think it may possibly help—"

"Go fuck yourself," Broughton interrupted roughly, and Delaney heard the belch. "I don't need your help. I don't want your help. The only way you can help me is to crawl in a hole and pull it in over your head. Is that clear?"

"Sir, I've been—"

"Jesus Christ, how can I get through to you? Fuck off, Delaney. That's all I want from you. Just fuck off, you shithead."

"Yes, sir," Captain Edward X. Delaney said, almost delirious with pleasure. "I heard. I understand."

He stood and watched the black sedan pull away. See? You worry, brood, wrestle with "moral problems" and such crap and then suddenly a foul-mouthed moron solves the whole thing for you. He went into his own home happily, called Deputy Inspector Thorsen and, after reporting his meeting with Broughton, told Thorsen he wanted to continue the investigation on his own.

"Hang on a minute, Edward," Thorsen said. Delaney guessed Inspector Johnson and Deputy Mayor Alinski were still there, and Ivar was repeating the conversation to them. Thorsen was back again in about two minutes.

"Fine," he said. "Go ahead. Good luck."

7

He seemed to be spending a lot of time doodling, staring off into space, jotting down almost incomprehensible notes, outlining programs he tore up and discarded as soon as they were completed. But he was, he knew, gradually evolving a sensible campaign in the two weeks following the meeting in Thorsen's home.

He sat down with Christopher Langley in the Widow Zimmerman's apartment and, while she fussed about, urging them to more tea and crumbcake, they went over Langley's firm schedule for his investigation. The little man had already discovered two more stores in Manhattan that sold ice axes, neither of which had mailing lists or kept a record of customers' purchases.

"That's all right," Delaney said grimly. "We can't be lucky all the time. We'll do what we can with what we have."

Langley would continue to look for stores in Manhattan where the ice ax was sold, then broadening his search to the other boroughs. Then he would check tool and outdoor equipment jobbers and wholesalers. Then he would try to assemble a list of American manufacturers of ice axes. Then he would assemble a list of names and addresses of foreign manufacturers of mountaineering gear who exported their products to the U.S., starting with West Germany, then Austria, then Switzerland.

"It's a tremendous job," Delaney told him.

Langley smiled, seemingly not at all daunted by the dimensions of his task.

"More crumbcake?" the Widow Zimmerman asked brightly. "It's homemade."

Langley had told the truth; she was a lousy cook.

Delaney had another meeting with Calvin Case, who announced proudly that he was now refraining from taking his first drink of the day until his bedside radio began the noon news broadcast.

"I have it prepared," Case said, "but I don't touch it until I hear that chime. Then . . ."

Delaney congratulated him, and when Case repeated his offer of help, they began to figure out how to handle the Outside Life sales checks.

"We got a problem," Case told him. "It'll be easy enough to pull every sales slip that shows a purchase of an ice ax during the past seven years. But what if your man bought it ten years ago?"

"Then his name should show up on the mailing list. I'll have someone working on that."

"Okay, but what if he bought the ice ax some place else but maybe bought some other mountain gear at Outside Life?"

"Well, couldn't you pull every slip that shows a purchase of mountain climbing gear of any type?"

"That's the problem," Case said. "A lot of stuff used in mountaineering is used by campers, back-packers, and a lot of people who never go near a mountain. I mean stuff like rucksacks, lanterns, freeze-dried foods, gloves, web belts and harnesses. Hell, ice fishermen buy crampons, and yachtsmen buy the same kind of line mountaineers use. So where does that leave us?"

Delaney thought a few minutes. Case took another drink.

"Look," Delaney said, "I'm not going to ask you to go through a hundred thousand sales checks more than once. Why don't you do this: why don't you pull every check that has anything at all to do with mountain climbing? I mean *anything*. Rope, rucksacks, food—whatever. That will be a big stack of sales checks—right? And it will include a lot of non-mountain climbers. That's okay. At the same time you make a separate file of every sales check that definitely lists the purchase of an ice ax. After you've finished with all the checks, we'll go through your ice ax file first and pull every one purchased by a resident of the Two-five-one Precinct, and look 'em up. If that doesn't work, we'll pull every resident of the Precinct from your general file of mountaineering equipment purchases. And if that doesn't work, we'll branch out and take in everyone in that file."

"Jesus Christ. And if that doesn't work, I suppose you'll investigate every one of those hundred thousand customers in the big file?"

"There won't be that many. There have got to be people who bought things at Outside Life several times over the past seven years. Notice that Sol Appel estimates a hundred thousand sales checks in storage, but only thirty thousand on his mailing list. I'll check with him, or you can, but I'd guess he's got someone winnowing out repeat buyers, and only *new* customers are added to the mailing list."

"That makes sense. All right, suppose there are thirty thousand individual customers. If you don't get anywhere with the sales checks I pull, you'll investigate all thirty thousand?"

"If I have to," Delaney nodded. "But I'll cross that bridge when I come to it. Meanwhile, how does the plan sound to you—I mean your making two files: one of ice ax purchases, one of general mountaineering equipment purchases?"

"It sounds okay."

"Then can I make arrangements with Sol Appel to have the sales checks sent up here?"

"Sure. You're a nut—you know that, Captain?"

"I know."

The meeting with Monica Gilbert called for more caution and deliberation. He walked past her house twice, on the other side of the street, and could see no signs of surveillance, no uniformed patrolmen, no unmarked police cars. But even if the guards had been called off, it was probably that her phone was still tapped. Remembering Broughton's threat to "stomp" him, he had no desire to risk a contact that the Deputy Commissioner would learn about.

Then he remembered her two little girls. One of them, the older, was surely of school age—perhaps both of them. Monica Gilbert, if she was sending her children to a public school, and from what Delaney had learned of her circumstances she probably was, would surely walk the children to the nearest elementary school, three blocks away, and call for them in the afternoon.

So, the next morning, he stationed himself down the block, across the street, and waited, stamping his feet against the cold and wishing he had worn his earmuffs. But, within half an hour, he was rewarded by the sight of Mrs. Gilbert and her two little girls, bundled up in snowsuits, exiting from the brownstone. He followed them, across the street and at a distance, until she left her daughters at the door of the school. She started back, apparently heading home, and he crossed the street, approached her, raised his hat.

"Mrs. Gilbert."

"Why, it's Captain . . . Delaney?"

"Yes. How are you?"

"Well, thank you. And thank you for your letter of condolence. It was very kind of you."

"Yes, well . . . Mrs. Gilbert, I was wondering if I could talk to you for a few minutes. Would you like a cup of coffee? We could go to a luncheonette."

She looked at him a moment, debating. "Well . . . I'm on my way home. Why don't you come back with me? I always have my second cup after the girls are in school."

"Thank you. I'd like that."

He had carefully brought along the Xerox copy of the Outside Life mailing list, three packs of 3x5 filing cards, and a small, hand-drawn map of the 251st Precinct, showing only its boundaries.

"Good coffee," he said.

"Thank you."

"Mrs. Gilbert, you told me you wanted to help. Do you still feel that way?"

"Yes. More than ever. Now . . ."

"It's just routine work. Boring."

"I don't care."

"All right."

He told her what he wanted. She was to go through the 30,000 names and addresses on the mailing list, and when she found one within the 251st Precinct, she was to make out a typed file card for each person. When she had finished the list, she was then to type out her own list, with two carbons, of her cards of the Precinct residents.

"Do you have any questions?" he asked her.

"Do they have to live strictly within the boundaries of this Precinct?"

"Well . . . use your own judgment on that. If it's only a few blocks outside, include them."

"Will this help find my husband's killer?"

"I think it will, Mrs. Gilbert."

She nodded. "All right. I'll get started on it right away. Besides, I think it's best if I have something to keep me busy right now."

He looked at her admiringly.

Later, he wondered why he felt so pleased with himself after his meetings with Calvin Case and Mrs. Gilbert. He realized it was because he had been discussing names and addresses. Names! Up to now it had all been steel tools and cans of oil. But now he had names—a reservoir, a Niagara of names! And addresses! Perhaps nothing would become of it. He was prepared for that. But meanwhile he was investigating *people,* not things, and so he was pleased.

The interview with Thomas Handry was ticklish. Delaney told him only as much as he felt Handry should know, believing the reporter was intelligent enough to fill in the gaps. For instance, he told Handry that both Lombard and Gilbert had been killed with the same weapon—had *apparently* been killed with the same weapon. He didn't specify an ice ax, and Handry, writing notes furiously, nodded without asking more questions on the type of weapon used. As a newspaperman he knew the value of such qualifiers as "apparently," "allegedly," and "reportedly."

Delaney took complete responsibility for his own investigation, made no mention of Thorsen, Johnson, Alinski or Broughton. He said he was concerned because the crimes had occurred in his precinct, and he felt a personal responsibility. Handry looked up from his notebook to stare at Delaney a long time, but made no comment. Delaney told him he was convinced the killer was a psychopath, that Lombard and Gilbert were chance victims, and that the murderer would slay again. Handry wrote it all down and, thankfully, didn't inquire why Delaney didn't take what he had to Operation Lombard.

Their big argument involved when Handry could publish. The reporter wanted to go at once with what he had been told; the Captain wanted him to hold off until he got the go-ahead from him, Delaney. It developed into a shouting match, louder and louder, about who had done more for whom, and who owed whom what. Finally, realizing simultaneously how ridiculous they sounded, they dissolved into laughter, and the Captain mixed fresh drinks. They came to a compromise; Handry would hold off for two weeks. If he hadn't received the Captain's go-ahead by then, he could publish anything he liked, guess at anything he liked, but with no direct attribution to Delaney.

His biggest disappointment during this period came when he happily, proudly brought Barbara the two Honey Bunch books he had received in the mail. She was completely rational, apparently in flaming good health. She inspected the books, and gave a mirthful shout, looking at him and shaking her head.

"Edward," she said, "what on *earth?*"

He was about to remind her she had requested them, then suddenly realized she obviously didn't remember. He hid his chagrin.

"I thought you'd like them," he smiled. "Just like the ones you sent to Liza."

"Oh, you're such an old dear," she said, holding up her face to be kissed.

He leaned over the hospital bed eagerly, hoping her cheerfulness was a presage of recovery. When he left, the two books were alongside her bed, on the floor. When he returned the next day, one was opened, spread, pages down, on her bedside table. He knew she had been reading it, but he didn't know if this was a good sign or a bad sign. She made no reference to the book, and he didn't either.

So his days were spent mostly on plans, programs, meetings, interviews, and there was absolutely no progress to report when he called Thorsen twice a week. Having assigned his amateur "staff" their tasks, he called each of them every other day or so, not to lean on them, but to talk, assure them of the importance of what they were doing, answer their questions, and just let them know that he was there, he knew it would take time, and not to become discouraged. He was very good at this, because he liked these people, and he knew or sensed their motives for helping him.

But when all his plans and programs were in progress, when all his amateurs were busy at their tasks, he found himself with nothing to do. He went back through his own notes and reports, and found the suggestions about a mountain climbers' magazine, an association or club of mountain climbers, a mention to check the local library on withdrawals of books on mountaineering.

Then he came across his list. "The Suspect." He had not made an addition to it in almost six weeks. He looked at his watch. He had returned from his evening visit to the hospital; it was almost 8:00 P.M. Had he eaten? Yes, he had. Mary had left a casserole of shrimp, chicken, rice, and little pieces of ham. And walnuts. He didn't like the walnuts, but he picked them out, and the rest was good.

He called Calvin Case.

"Captain Edward X. Delaney here. How are you?"

"Okay."

"And your wife?"

"Fine. What's on your mind?"

"I'd like to talk to you. Now. It's not about the sales checks. I know you're working away at them. It's something else. If I can find a cab, I could be at your place in half an hour."

"Sure. Come ahead. I've got something great to show you."

"Oh? I'll be right down."

Evelyn Case met him at the door. She was flushed, happy, and looked about 15 years old, in faded jeans, torn sneakers, one of her husband's shirts tied about her waist. Unexpectedly, she went up on her toes to kiss his cheek.

"Well!" he said. "I thank you."

"We're working on the sales checks, Captain," she said breathlessly. "Both of us. Every night. And Cal taught me what the stock numbers mean. And sometimes I come home during my lunch hour and help him."

"Good," he smiled, patting her shoulder. "That's fine. And you look just great."

"Wait till you see Cal!"

The apartment was brighter now, and smelled reasonably clean. The windows of Case's bedroom were washed, there were fresh paper drapes, a pot of ivy on his cart, a new rag rug on the floor.

But the cartons of Outside Life sales checks were everywhere, stacked high against walls in the hallway, living room, bedroom. Delaney had to thread his way through, walking sideways in a few places, sidling through the open bedroom doorway from which, he noted, the window shade had been removed.

"Hi," Calvin Case called, gesturing around. "How do you like this?"

He was waving at an incredible contraption, a framework of two-inch iron pipe that surrounded his bed and hung over it, like the bare bones of a canopy. And there were steel cables, weights, handles, pulleys, gadgets.

Delaney stared in astonishment. "What the hell *is* it?" he asked.

Case laughed pleased at his wonderment.

"Sol Appel gave it to me. He came up to see me. The next day a guy showed up to take measurements. A few days later three guys showed up with the whole thing and just bolted it together. It's a gym. So I can exercise from the waist up. Look at this . . ."

He reached up with both hands, grabbed a trapeze that hung from wire cables. He pulled his body off the bed. The clean sheet dropped away to his waist. His naked torso was still flaccid, soft muscles trembling with his effort. He let go, let himself fall back onto the bed.

"That's all," he gasped. "So far. But strength is coming back. Muscle tone. I can feel it. Now look at this . . ."

Two handles hung above his head. They were attached to steel cables that ran over pulleys on the crossbar above him. The cables ran down over the length of the bed, across pulleys on the lower crossbar, and then down. They were attached to stainless steel weights.

"See?" Case said, and demonstrated by pulling the handles down to his chest alternately: right, left, right, left. "I'm only raising the one-pound weights now," he admitted. "But you can add up to five pounds on each cable."

"And when he started he couldn't even raise the one-pound weights," Evelyn Case said eagerly to Captain Delaney. "Next week we're going to two-pound weights."

"And look at this," Case said, showing what appeared to be a giant steel hairpin hanging from his pipe cage. "It's for your grip. For biceps and pectorals."

He grasped the hairpin in both hands and tried to squeeze the two arms together, his face reddening. He barely moved them.

"That's fine," Delaney said. "Just fine."

"The best thing is this," Case said, and showed how a steel arm was hinged to swing out sideways from the gym. "I talked to the guys who put this thing together. They're from some physical therapy outfit that specializes in stuff like this. Well, they sell a wheelchair with a commode built into it. I mean, you sit on a kind of a potty seat. You wheel yourself around, and when you've got to shit, you shit. But Jesus Christ, you're mobile. I'm too heavy for Ev to lift me into a chair like that, but when I get my strength back, I'll be able to move this bar out and swing onto that potty chair by myself, and swing back into bed whenever I want to. I know I'll be able to do it. My arms and shoulders were always good. I've hung from my hands lots of times, and then pulled myself up."

"That sounds great," Delaney said admiringly. "But don't overdo it. I mean, take it easy at first. Build your strength up gradually."

"Oh sure. I know how to do it. We ordered one of those chairs, but it won't be delivered for a couple of weeks. By that time I hope I'll be able to flip myself in and out of bed with no sweat. The chair's got a brake you can set so it won't roll away from you while you're getting into it. You realize what that means, Delaney? I'll be able to sit up at that desk while I'm going through the sales checks. That'll help."

"It surely will," the Captain smiled. "How you doing with the booze?"

"Okay. I haven't stopped, but I've cut down—haven't I, hon?"

"Oh yes," his wife nodded happily. "I know because I'm only buying about half the bottles I did before."

The two men laughed, and then she laughed.

"Incidentally," Case said, "the sales checks are going a lot faster than I expected."

"Oh? Why is that?"

"I hadn't realized how much of Outdoor Life's business was in fishing and hunting gear, tennis, golf, even croquet and badminton and stuff like that. About seventy-five percent, I'd guess. So I can just take a quick glance at the sales slip and toss it aside if it has nothing to do with mountaineering."

"Good. I'm glad to hear that. Can I talk to you a few minutes? Not about the sales checks. Something else. Do you feel up to it?"

"Oh sure. I feel great. Hon, pull up a chair for the Captain."

"I'll get it," Delaney told her, and brought the straight-backed desk chair over to the bedside and sat where he could watch Case's face.

"A drink, Captain?"

"All right. Thank you. With water."

"Hon?"

She went out into the kitchen. The two men sat in silence a few moments.

"What's it all about?" Case asked finally.

"Mountain climbers."

Later, in his own study, Captain Delaney took out his list, "The Suspect," and began to add what Calvin Case had told him about mountain climbers while it was still fresh in his mind. He extrapolated on what Case had said, based on his own instinct, experience, and knowledge of why men acted the way they did.

Under "Physical" he added items about ranginess, reach, strength of arms and shoulders, size of chest, resistance to panic. It was true Case had said mountain climbers come "in all shapes and sizes," but he had qualified that later, and Delaney was willing to go with the percentages.

Under "Psychological" he had a lot to write: love of the outdoors, risk as an addiction, a disciplined mind, no obvious suicide compulsion, total egotism, pushing to—what was it Case had said?—the "edge of life," with nothing between you and death but your own strength and wit. Then, finally, a deeply religious feeling, becoming one with the universe—"one with everything." And compared to that, everything else was "just mush."

Under "Additional Notes" he listed "Probably moderate drinker" and "No drugs" and "Sex relations probably after murder but not before."

He read and reread the list, looking for something he might have forgotten. He couldn't find anything. "The Suspect" was coming out of the gloom, looming. Delaney was beginning to get a handle on the man, grabbing what he was, what he wanted, why he had to do what he did. He was still a shadow, smoke, but there was an outline to him now. He began to exist, on paper and in Delaney's mind. The Captain had a rough mental image of the man's physical appearance, and he was just beginning to guess what was going on in the fool's mind. "The poor, sad shit," Delaney said aloud, then shook his head angrily, wondering why he should feel any sympathy at all for this villain.

He was still at it, close to 1:00 A.M., when the desk phone rang. He let it ring three times, knowing—*knowing*—what the call was, and dreading it. Finally he picked up the receiver.

"Yes?" he asked cautiously.

"Captain Delaney?"

"Yes."

"Dorfman. Another one."

Delaney took a deep breath, then opened his mouth wide, tilted his head back, stared at the ceiling, took another deep breath.

"Captain? Are you there?"

"Yes. Where was it?"

"On Seventy-fifth Street. Between Second and Third."

"Dead?"

"Yes."

"Identified?"

"Yes. His shield was missing but he still had his service revolver."

"What?"

"He was one of Broughton's decoys."

Part VI

1 "I didn't want him to suffer," he said earnestly, showing her Bernard Gilbert's ID card. "Really I didn't."

"He didn't suffer, dear," she murmured, stroking his cheek. "He was unconscious, in a coma."

"But I wanted him to be happy!" Daniel Blank cried.

"Of course," she soothed. "I understand."

He had waited for Gilbert's death before he had run to Celia, just as he had run to her after Lombard's death. But this time was different. He felt a sense of estrangement, withdrawal. It seemed to him that he no longer needed her, her advice, her lectures. He wanted to savor in solitude what he had done. She said she understood, but of course she didn't. How could she?

They were naked in the dreadful room, dust everywhere, the silent house hovering about them. He thought he might be potent with her, wasn't sure, didn't care. It was of no importance.

"The mistake was in coming from in front," he said thoughtfully. "Perhaps the skull is stronger there, or the brain not as frail, but he fell back, and he lived for four days. I won't do that again. I don't want anyone to suffer."

"But you saw his eyes?" she asked softly.

"Oh yes."

"What did you see?"

"Surprise. Shock. Recognition. Realization. And then, at the final moment, something else . . ."

"What?"

"I don't know. I'm not sure. Acceptance, I think. And a kind of knowing calm. It's hard to explain."

"Oh!" she said. "Oh *yes!* Finitude. That's what we're all looking for, isn't it? The last word. Completion. Catholicism or Zen or Communism or Meaninglessness. Whatever. But Dan, isn't it true we need it? We all need it, and will abase ourselves or enslave others to find it. But is it one for all of us, or one for each of us? Isn't that the question? I think it's one absolute for all, but I think the paths differ, and each must find his own way. Did I ever tell you what a beautiful body you have, darling?"

As she spoke she had been touching him softly, arousing him slowly.

"Have you shaved a little here? And here?"

"What?" he asked vaguely, drugged by her caresses. "I don't remember. I may have."

"Here you're silk, oiled silk. I love the way your ribs and hip bones press through your skin, the deep curve from chest to waist, and then the flare of your hips. You're so strong and hard, so soft and yielding. Look how long your arms are, and how wide your shoulders. And still, nipples like buds and your sweet, smooth ass. How dear your flesh is to me. Oh!"

She murmured, still touching him, and almost against his will he responded and moved against her. Then he lay on his back, pulled her over atop him, spread his legs, raised his knees.

"How lovely if you could come into me," he whispered and, knowing, she made the movements he desired. "If you had a penis, too . . . Or better yet, if we both had both penis and vagina. What an improvement on God's design! So that we both might be inside each other, simultaneously, penetrating. Wouldn't that be wonderful?"

"Oh yes," she breathed. "Wonderful."

He held her weight down onto him, calling her "Darling" and "Honey" and saying, "Oh love, you feel so good," and it seemed to him the fabric of his life, like a linen handkerchief laundered too often, was simply shredding apart. Not rotting, but pulling into individual threads; light was coming through.

In her exertions, sweat dripped from her unshaven armpits onto his shoulders; he turned his head to lick it up, tasting salty life.

"Will you kill someone for me?" she gasped.

He pulled her down tighter, elevating his hips, linking his ankles around her slender back.

"Of course not," he told her. "That would spoil everything."

2

He grew up in that silent, loveless, white-tiled house and, an only child, had no sun to turn to and so turned inward, becoming contemplative, secretive even. Almost all he thought and all he felt concerned himself, his wants, fears, hates, hopes, despairs. Strangely, for a young boy, he was aware of this intense egoism and wondered if everyone else was as self-centered. It didn't seem possible; there were boys his age who were jolly and out-going, who made friends quickly and easily, who could tease girls and laugh. But still . . .

"Sometimes it seemed I might be two persons: the one I presented to my parents and the world, and the one I *was,* whirling in my own orbit. The outward me was the orderly, organized boy who was a good student, who collected rocks and stowed them away in compartmented trays, each specimen neatly labeled: 'Blank, Daniel: Good boy.'

"But from my earliest boyhood—from my infancy, even—I have dreamed in my sleep, almost every night: wild, disjointed dreams of no particular meaning: silly things, happenings, people all mixed up, costumes, crazy faces, my parents and kids in school and historical and literary characters—all in a churn.

"Then—oh, perhaps at the age of eight, but it may have been later—I began to lose myself in daytime fantasies, as turbulent and incredible as my nighttime dreams. This daydreaming had no effect on my outward life, on the image I presented to the world. I could do homework efficiently, answer up in class, label the stones I collected, kiss my parents' cold cheeks dutifully . . . and be a million miles away. No, not away, but down inside myself, dreaming.

"Gradually, almost without my being aware of it, daytime fantasies merged with nighttime dreams. How this developed, or exactly when, I cannot say. But daytime fantasies became extensions of nighttime dreams, and it happened that I would imagine a 'plot' that continued, day and night, for perhaps a week. And then, having been rejected in favor of a new 'plot,' I might come back to the old one for a day or two, simply recalling it or perhaps embellishing it with fanciful details.

"For instance, I might imagine that I was actually not the child of my mother and father, but was a foster child placed with them for romantic reasons. My true father was, perhaps, a well-known statesman, my mother a great beauty who had sinned for love. For various reasons, whatever, they were unable to acknowledge me, and had placed me with this dull, putty-faced, childless Indian couple. But the day would come . . .

"There was something else I became aware of during my early boyhood, and this may serve to illustrate my awareness of myself. Like most young boys of the same age—I was about twelve at the time—I was capable of certain acts of nastiness, even of minor crimes: wanton vandalism, meaningless violence, 'youthful high spirits,' etc. Where I differed from other boys of that age, I believe, was that even when caught and punished, I felt no guilt. No one could make me feel guilty. My only regret was in being caught.

"Is it so strange that someone can live two lives? No, I honestly believe most people do. Most, of course, play the public role expected of them: they marry, work, have children, establish a home, vote, try to keep clean and reasonably law-abiding. But each—man, woman, and child—has a secret life of which they rarely speak and hardly ever display. And this secret life, for each of us, is filled with ferocious fantasies and incredible wants and suffocating lusts. Not shameful in themselves, except as we have been taught so.

"I remember reading something a man wrote—he was a famous author—and he said if it was definitely announced that the world would end in one hour, there would be long lines before each phone booth, with people waiting to call other people to tell them how much they loved them. I do not believe that, I believe most of us would spend the last hour mourning, 'Why didn't I do what I *wanted* to do?'

"Because I believe each of us is a secret island ('No man is an island'? What shit!) and even the deepest, most intense love cannot bridge the gap between individuals. Much of what we feel and dream, that we cannot speak of to others, is shameful, judged by what society says we are allowed to feel and dream. But if humans are capable of it, how can it be shameful? Rather do as our natures dictate. It may lead to heaven or it may lead to hell—what does 'heaven' mean or 'hell'?—but the most terrible sin is to deny. *That* is inhuman.

"When I fucked that girl in college, and later with my wife, and all those in between, I found it exciting and pleasurable, naturally. Satisfying enough to ignore the grunts, coughs, farts, belches, bad breath, blood and . . . and other things. But a moment later my mind would be on my collection of semi-precious stones or the programming of AMROK II. I had enjoyed masturbation as much, and began to wonder how much so-called 'normal sex' is really masturbation *à deux*. All the groans and protestations of love and ecstasy are the public face; the secret reactions are hidden from the partner. I once fucked a woman, and all the time I was thinking of—well, someone I had seen at a health club I belonged to. God knows what *she* was thinking of. Island lives.

"Celia Montfort was the most intelligent woman I had ever met. Much more intelligent than I was, as a matter of fact, although I think she lacked my sensitivity and understanding. But she was complex, and I had never met a complex woman before. Or perhaps I had, but could not endure the complexity. But in Celia's case, it attracted me, fascinated me, puzzled me—for a time.

"I wasn't certain what she wanted from me, if she wanted anything at all. I enjoyed her lectures, the play of her mind, but I could never quite pin down who she was. Once, when I called for a dinner date, she said, 'There is something I want to ask you.'

" 'Yes?' I said.

"There was a pause.

" 'I'll ask you tonight,' she said finally. 'At dinner.'

"So at dinner I said, 'What did you want to ask me?'

"She looked at me and said, 'I think I better put it in a letter. I'll write you a letter, asking it.'

" 'All right." I nodded, not wanting to push.

"But, of course, she never wrote me a letter asking anything. She was like that. It was maddening, in a way, until I began to understand . . .

"Understand that she was as deep and moiling as I, and subject, as I was, to sudden whims, crazy passions, incoherent longings, foolish dreams . . . the whole bit. Irrational, I suppose you might say. If I didn't lie to myself—and it's extremely difficult not to lie to yourself—I had to recognize that some of my hostility toward her—and I recognized I was beginning to feel a certain hostility, because she *knew*—well, some of this was because I was a man and she was a woman. I am not a great admirer of the women's liberation movement, but I agree men are victims of a conditioning difficult to recognize and analyze.

"But once I stopped lying to myself, I could acknowledge that she upset me because she had a secret life of her own, an intelligence greater than mine and, when it pleased her, a sexuality more intense than mine.

"I could realize that and admit it to myself: she was the first woman I had been intimate with who existed as an individual, not just as a body. The Jewish girl from Boston had been a body. My wife had been a body. Now I knew a person—call it a 'soul' if it amuses you—as unfathomable as myself. And it was no more logical for me to expect to understand her than to expect her to understand me.

"Item: We have come from a sweated bed where we have been as intimate as man and woman can be physically intimate. I have tasted her. Then, dressed, composed, on our way to dinner, I grab her arm to pull her out of the way of a careening cab. She looks at me with loathing. 'You touched me!' she gasps.

"Item: She has been tender, sympathetic, but somewhat withdrawn all evening. We returned to her home and, only because I need to use the john, does she allow me inside the door. I know there will be no sex that night. That's all right with me. It is her prerogative; I am not a mad rapist. But, from the bathroom, I return to the study. She is seated in the leather armchair and, standing behind her, Valenter is softly massaging her neck and bare shoulders with loving movements. Curled in a corner, Tony is watching them curiously. What am I to make of all this?

"Item: She disappears, frequently and without notice, for hours, days, a week at a time. She returns without explanation or excuse, usually weary and bruised, sometimes wounded and bandaged. I ask no questions; she volunteers no information. We have an unspoken pact: I will not pry; she will not ask. Except about the killing. She can't get enough of *that!*

"Item: She buys an imported English riding crop, but I refuse. Either way.

"In fact, there is no end to her.

"Item: She treats a cab driver shamefully for taking us a block out of our way, and tells me loudly not to tip him. Three hours later she insists I give money to a filthy, drunken panhandler who smells of urine. Well . . .

"I think what was happening was this: we had started on one level, trying to find a satisfactory relationship. Then, sated or bored, the wild sex had calmed and we began to explore the psychic part of sex in which she, and I, believed so strongly. After that—it proving not completely satisfactory—we went on digging deeper, inserting ourselves into each other, yet remaining essentially strangers. I tried to tell her: to achieve the final relationship, you must penetrate. Is that not so?

"I must not see her again. I would resolve that, unable to cope with her *humanity,* and, at the last moment, when I was certain our affair was over, she would call and say things to me on the phone. Oh! So we would once again have lunch or dinner, and under the table cloth, beneath our joined napkins, she would touch me, looking into my eyes. And it would start again.

"I do owe her one thing: the killings. You see, I can acknowledge them openly. The murders. Daniel, I love you! I know what I have done, and will do, and I feel no guilt. It is not someone else doing them. It is I, Daniel Blank, and I do not deny them, apologize or regret. Any more than when I stand naked before a dim mirror and once again touch myself. To deny your secret, island life and die unfulfilled—that is the worst.

"I need, most of all, to go deeper and deeper into myself, peeling layers away—the human onion. I am in full possession of my faculties. I know most people would think me vicious or deranged. But is that of any importance? I don't think so. I think the important thing is to fulfill yourself. If you can do that, you come to some kind of completion where both of you, the two you's, become one, and that one merges and becomes part of and adds to the Cosmic One. What *that* might be, I do not know—yet. But I am beginning to glimpse its outlines, the glory it is, and I think, if I continue on my course, I will know it finally.

"With all this introspection, all this intent searching for the eternal verity, which may make you laugh—do *you* have the courage to try it?—the incredible thing, the amazing thing is that I have been able to keep intact the image I present to the world. That is, I function: I awake each morning, bathe and dress, in a fashion of careless elegance, take a cab to my place of work, and there, I believe, I do my job in an efficient and useful manner. It is a charade, of course, but I perform well. In all honesty, perhaps not as I did before . . . Am I going through the movements, marching out the drill? It's probably my imagination but, a few times, I thought memebers of my X-1 computer team looked at me a bit queerly.

"And one day my secretary, Mrs. Cleek, was wearing a pants suit—it's allowed at Javis-Bircham—and I complimented her on how well it looked. Actually, it was much too snug for her. But later in the day, while she was standing by me, waiting while I signed some letters, I suddenly reached to stroke her pudendum, obvious beneath the crotch of her pants. I didn't grab or squeeze; I just stroked. She drew away, making a small cry. I went back to signing letters; neither of us spoke of what had happened.

"There was one other thing, but since nothing came of it, it hardly seems worth mentioning. I had a dream, a nighttime dream that merged into a daytime fantasy, of doing something to the computer, AMROK II. That is, I wanted to—well, I suppose in some way I wanted to destroy it. How, I didn't know. It was just a vagrant thought. I didn't even consider it. But the thought did come to me. I think I was searching for more humanity, not less. For more *human*-ness, with all its terrible mystery.

"Now we must consider why I killed those men and why (Sigh! Sob! Groan!) I suppose I will kill again. Well . . . again, it's *human*-ness, isn't it? To come close, as close as you can possibly come. Because love—I mean physical love (sex) or romantic love—isn't the answer, is it? It's a poor, cheap substitute, and never quite satisfactory. Because, no matter how good physical love or romantic love may seem, the partners still have, each, their secret, island life.

"But when you kill, the gap disappears, the division is gone, you are one with the victim. I don't suppose you will believe me, but it is so. I assure you it is. The act of killing is an act of love, ultimate love, and though there is no orgasm, no sexual feeling at all—at least in my case—you do, you really do, enter into another human being, and through that violent conjunction—painful perhaps, but just for a split-second—you enter into all humans, all animals, all vegetables, all minerals. In fact, you become one with everything: stars, planets, galaxies, the great darkness beyond, and . . .

"Oh. Well. What this is, the final mystery, is what I'm searching for, isn't it? I'm convinced it is not in books or beds or conversation or churches or sudden flashes of inspiration or revelation. It must be worked for, and it will be, in me.

"What I'm saying is that I want to go into myself, penetrate myself, as deeply as I possibly can. I know it will be a long and painful process. It may prove, eventually, to be impossible-but I don't believe that. I think that I can go deep within myself—I mean *deep!*—and there I'll find it.

"Sometimes I wonder if it's a kind of masturbation, as when I stand naked before my full-length mirror, golden chains about wrist and waist, and look at my own body and touch myself. The wonder! But then I come back, always come back, to what I seek. And it has nothing to do with Celia or Tony or the Mortons or my job or anything else but me. Me! That's where the answer lies. And who can uncover it but me? So I keep trying, and it is not too difficult, too painful or exhausting. Except, in all truth, I must tell you this: If I had my life to live over again, I would want to lie naked in the sun and watch women oil their bodies. That's all I've ever wanted."

He should have stopped there; it was a logical end to his musings. But he would not, could not. He thought of Tony Montfort, what they had done, what they might do. But the dream was fleeting, flicking away a mosquito or something else that might bite. He thought of Valenter, and of a professor in his college who had smelled of earth, and of going into a women's lingerie shop to buy white bikini panties for himself. Because they fit better? Once a man on a Fifth Avenue bus had smiled at him.

He still had the nighttime dreams, the daytime fantasies, but he was aware that the images were becoming shorter. That is, they no longer overlapped from night to day, the "plots" were abbreviated, visions flickered by sharply. His mind was so charged, so jumping, that he became vaguely alarmed, went to a doctor, received a prescription for a mild tranquilizer. They worked on him as a weak sleeping pill. But his mind still jumped.

He could not penetrate deeply enough into himself. He lied to himself; he admitted it; he caught himself at it. It was difficult not to lie to himself. He had to be on guard, not every day or every hour but every minute. He had to question every action, every motive. Probing. Penetrating. If he wanted to discover . . . what?

He soothed an engorged penis in a Vaselined hand, probed his own rectum with a stiff forefinger pointing toward Heaven, opened his empty mouth to a white ceiling and waited for bliss. Throbbing warmth engulfed him, eventually, but not what he sought.

There was more. He knew there was more. He had experienced it, and he set out to find it again, bathing, dusting, perfuming, dressing, preparing for an assignation. We all—all of us—must fulfill our island life. Oh yes, he thought, we must. Taking up the ice ax . . .

"Blood is thicker than water," he said aloud, "and semen is thicker than blood."

He laughed, having no idea what that meant, or if, indeed, it meant anything at all.

3

A week or so after the death of Bernard Gilbert, Daniel Blank went on the stalk. It was not too unlike learning to climb. You had to master the techniques, you had to test your strength and, of course, you had to try your nerve, pushing it to its limit, but not beyond. You did not learn how to murder by reading a book, anymore than you could learn how to swim or ride a bicycle by looking at diagrams.

He had already acquired several valuable techniques. The business of concealing the ice ax under his top coat, holding it through the pocket slit by his left hand, then transferring it swiftly to his right hand shoved through the opened fly of his coat—that worked perfectly, with no fumbling. The death of Lombard had been, he thought, instantaneous, while Gilbert lingered four days. He deduced from this that a blow from the back apparently penetrated a more sensitive area of the skull, and he resolved to make no more frontal attacks.

He was convinced his basic method of approach was sound: the quick, brisk step; the eye-to-eye smile; the whole appearance of ease and neighborliness. Then the fast turn, the blow.

He had, of course, made several errors. For instance, during the attack on Frank Lombard, he had worn his usual black calfskin shoes with leather soles. At the moment of assault his right foot had slipped on the pavement, leather sliding on cement. It was not, fortunately, a serious error, but he had been off-balance, and when Lombard fell backward the ice ax was pulled from Blank's grasp.

So, before the murder of Bernard Gilbert, Blank had purchased a pair of light-weight crepe-soled shoes. It was getting on to December, with cold rain, sleet, snow flurries, and the rubber-soled shoes gave much better traction and stability.

Similarly, in the attack on Lombard, the leather handle of the ice ax had twisted in his sweated hand. Reflecting on this, he had, before the Gilbert assault, roughed the leather handle by rubbing it gently with fine sandpaper. This worked well enough, but he still was not satisfied. He purchased a pair of black suede gloves, certainly a common enough article of apparel in early winter weather. The grip between suede glove and the roughened leather of the ice ax handle was all that could be desired.

These were details, of course, and those who had never climbed mountains would shrug them off as of no consequence. But a good climb depended on just such details. You could have all the balls in the world, but if your equipment was faulty, or your technique wasn't right, you were dead.

There were other things to consider; you just didn't go out and murder the first man you met. He cancelled out rainy and sleety nights; he needed a reasonably dry pavement for that quick whirl after he had passed his victim. A cloudy or moonless night was best, with no strong wind to tug at his unbuttoned coat. And he carried as few objects and as little identification as possible; less to drop accidentally at the scene.

He went to his health club twice a week and worked out, and he did his stretch exercises at home every night, so strength was no problem. He was, he knew, in excellent physical condition. He could lift, turn, bend, probably better than most boys half his age. He watched his diet; his reactions were still fast. He meant to keep them that way, and looked forward to climbing Devil's Needle again in the spring, or perhaps taking a trip to the Bavarian Alps for more technical climbs. That would be a joy.

So there was the passion—just as in mountain climbing—and there was also the careful planning, the mundane details—weapon, shoes, gloves, smile—just as any great art is really, essentially, a lot of little jobs. Picasso mixed paints, did he not?

He took the same careful and thoughtful preparation in his stalk after Gilbert's death. A stupid assassin might come home from his job and eat, or dine out and then come home, and return to his apartment house at the same time. Sooner or later, the apartment house doorman on duty would become aware of his routine.

So Daniel Blank varied his arrivals and departures, carefully avoiding a regular schedule, knowing one doorman went off duty at 8:00 P.M., when his relief arrived. Blank came and he went, casually, and usually these departures and arrivals went unobserved by a doorman busy with cabs or packages or other tasks. He didn't prowl every night. Two nights in a row. One night in. Three out. No pattern. No formal program. Whatever occurred to him; irregularity was best. He thought of everything.

There was, he admitted, something strange that to this enterprise that meant so much to him emotionally, privately, he should bring all his talents for finicky analysis, careful classifying, all the cold, bloodless skills of his public life. It proved he supposed, he was still two, but in this case it served him well; he never made a move without thinking out its consequences.

For instance, he debated a long time whether or not, during an actual murder, he should wear a hat. At this time of year, in this weather, most men wore hats.

But it might be lost by his exertions. And, supposing he made a murder attempt and was not successful—the possibility had to be faced—and the intended victim lived to testify. Surely he would remember the presence of a hat more strongly than he would recall the absence of a hat.

"Sir, did he wear a hat?"

"Yes, he wore a black hat. A soft hat. The brim was turned down in front."

That would be more likely than if Blank wore no hat at all.

"Sir, did he wear a hat?"

"What? Well . . . I don't remember. A hat? I don't know. Maybe. I really didn't notice."

So Daniel Blank wore no hat on his forays. He was that careful.

But his cool caution almost crumbled when he began his nighttime reconnaissance following the death of Bernard Gilbert. It was on the third night of his aimless meanderings that he became aware of what seemed to be an unusual number of single men, most of them tall and well proportioned, strolling through the shadowed streets of his neighborhood. The pavements were alive with potential victims!

He might have been mistaken, of course; Christmas wasn't so far away, and people were out shopping. Still . . . So he followed a few of these single males, far back and across the street. They turned a corner. He turned a corner. They turned another corner. He turned another corner. But none of them, none of the three he followed cautiously from a distance, ever entered a house. They kept walking steadily, not fast and not slow, up one street and down another.

He stopped suddenly, half-laughing but sick with fear. Decoys! Policemen. Who else could they be? He went home immediately, to think.

He analyzed the problem accurately: (1) He could cease his activities at once. (2) He could continue his activities in another neighborhood, even another borough. (3) He could continue his activities in his own neighborhood, welcoming the challenge.

Possibility 1 he rejected immediately. Could he stop now, having already come so far, with the final prize within recognizable reach? Possibility 2 required a more reasoned dissection. Could he carry a concealed weapon—the ice ax—by taxi, bus, subway, his own car, for any distance without eventual detection: Or—possibility 3—might he risk it?

He thought of his options for two whole days, and the solution, when it came, made him smack his thigh, smile, shake his head at his own stupidity. Because, he realized, he had been analyzing, thinking along in a vertical, in-line, masculine fashion—as if such a problem could be solved so!

He had come so far from this, so far from AMROK II, that he was ashamed he had fallen into the same trap once again. The important thing here was to trust his instincts, follow his passions, do as he was compelled, divorced from cold logic and bloodless reason. If he was finally to know truth, it would come from heart and gut.

And besides, there was risk—the sweet attraction of risk.

There was a dichotomy here that puzzled him. In the planning of the crime he was willing to use cool and formal reason: the shoes, the gloves, the weapon, the technique—all designed with logic and precision. And yet when it came to the *reason* for the act, he deliberately shunned the same method of thought and sought the answer in "heart and gut."

He finally came to the realization that logic might do for method but not for motive. Again, to use the analogy of creative art, the artist thought out the techniques of his art, or learned them from others and, with patience, became a skilled craftsman. But where craft ended and art began was at the point where the artist had to draw on his own emotions, dreams, fervors and fears, penetrating deep into himself to uncover what he needed to express by his skill.

The same could be said of mountain climbing. A man might be an enormously talented and knowledgeable mountaineer. But it was just a specialized skill if, within him, there was no drive to push himself to the edge of life and know worlds that the people of the valley could not imagine.

He spent several evenings attempting to observe the operations of the decoys. So far as he could determine, the detectives were not being followed by "back-up men" or trailed by unmarked police cars. It appeared that each decoy was assigned a four-block area, to walk up one street and down the next, going east to west, then west to east, then circling to cover the north-south streets. And unexpectedly, hurrying past a decoy who had stepped into a shadowed store doorway, he saw they were equipped with small walkie-talkies and were apparently in communication with some central command post.

It was, he decided, of little significance.

Sixteen days after the attack on Bernard Gilbert, Daniel Blank returned home directly from work. It was a cold, dry evening with a quarter moon barely visible through a clouded sky. There was some wind, a hint of rain or snow in a day or so. But generally it was a still night, cold enough to tingle nose, ears, ungloved hands. There was one other factor: the neighborhood theatre was showing a movie Daniel Blank had seen a month ago when it opened on Times Square.

He mixed himself a single drink, watched the evening news on TV. Americans were killing Vietnamese. Vietnamese were killing Americans. Jews were killing Arabs. Arabs were killing Jews. Catholics were killing Protestants. Protestants were killing Catholics. Pakistanis were killing Indians. Indians were killing Pakistanis. There was nothing new. He fixed a small dinner of broiled calves' liver and an endive salad. He brought his coffee into the living room and had that and a cognac while he listened to a tape of the Brandenburg Concerto No. 3. Then he undressed, got into bed, took a nap.

It was a little after nine when he awoke. He splashed cold water on his face, dressed in a black suit, white shirt, modestly patterned tie. He put on his crepe-soled shoes. He donned his topcoat, pulled on the black suede gloves, held the ice ax under the coat by his left hand, through the pocket slit. The leather thong attached to the handle butt of the ax went around his left wrist.

In the lobby, doorman Charles Lipsky was at the desk, but he rose to unlock and hold the outer door open for Blank. The door was kept locked from 8:00 P.M., when the shift of doormen changed, to 8:00 A.M. the following morning.

"Charles," Blank asked casually, "do you happen to know what movie's playing at the Filmways over on Second Avenue?"

"Afraid I don't, Mr. Blank."

"Well, maybe I'll take a walk over. Nothing much on TV tonight."

He strolled out. It was that natural and easy.

He actually did walk over to the theatre, to take a look at the movie schedule taped to the ticket seller's window. The feature film would begin again in 30 minutes. He had the money ready in his righthand trouser pocket. He bought a ticket with the exact sum, receiving no change. He went into the half-empty theatre, sat in the back row without removing his coat or gloves. When the movie ended and at least fifty people left, he left with them. No one glanced at him, certainly not the usher, ticket taker, or ticket seller. They would never remember his arrival or departure. But, of course, he had the ticket stub in his pocket and had already seen the film.

He walked eastward, toward the river, both hands now thrust through the coat's pocket slits. On a deserted stretch of street he carefully slipped the leather loop off his left wrist. He held the ax by the handle with his left wrist. He held the ax by the handle with his left hand. He unbuttoned his coat, but he didn't allow the flaps to swing wide, holding them close to his body with hands in his pockets.

Now began the time he liked best. Easy walk, a good posture, head held high. Not a scurrying walk, but not dawdling either. When he saw someone approaching, someone who might or might not have been a police decoy, he crossed casually to the other side of the street, walked to the corner and turned, never looking back. It was too early; he wanted this feeling to last.

He *knew* it was going to be this night, just as you know almost from the start of a climb that it will be successful, you will not turn back. He was confident, alert, anxious to feel once again that moment of exalted happiness when the eternal was in him and he was one with the universe.

He was experienced now, and knew what he would feel before that final moment. First, the power: should it be you or shall it be you? The strength and glory of the godhead fizzing through his veins. And second, the pleasure that came from the intimacy and the love, soon to be consummated. Not a physical love, but something much finer, so fine indeed that he could not put it into words but only felt it, knew it, floated with the exaltation.

And now, for the first time, there was something else. He had been frightened and wary before, but this night, with the police decoys on the streets, held a sense of peril that was almost tangible. It was all around him, in the air, in the light, on the mild wind. He could almost *smell* the risk; it excited him as much as the odor of new-fallen snow or his own scented body.

He let these things—power, pleasure, peril—grow in him as he walked. He opened himself to them, cast off all restraint, let them flood and engulf him. Once he had "shot the rapids" in a rubber dinghy, on a western river, and then and now he had the not unpleasant sensation of helplessness, surrender, in the hands of luck or an unknown god, swept along, this way, that, the world whirling, and, having started, no way to stop, no way, until passion ran its course, the river finally flowed placid between broad banks, and risk was a happy memory.

He turned west on 76th Street. Halfway down the block a man was also walking west, at about the same speed, not hurrying but not dallying either. Daniel Blank immediately stopped, turned around, and retraced his steps to Second Avenue. The man he had seen ahead of him had the physical appearance, the *feel,* of a police decoy. If Blank's investigations and guesses were accurate, the man would circle the block to head eastward on 75th Street. So Blank walked south on Second Avenue and paused on the corner, looking westward toward Third Avenue. Sure enough, his quarry turned the corner a block away and headed toward him.

"I love you," Daniel blank said softly.

He looked about. No one else on the block. No other pedestrians. All parked cars dark. Weak moon behind clouds. Pavement dry. Oh yes. Walk toward the approaching man. Pacing himself so they might meet about halfway between Second and Third Avenues.

Ice ax gripped lightly in fingertips of left hand, beneath his unbuttoned coat. Right arm and gloved hand swinging free. Then the hearty tramp down the street. The neighborly smile. That smile! And the friendly nod.

"Good evening!"

He was of medium height, broad through the chest and shoulders. Not handsome, but a kind of battered good looks. Surprisingly young. A physical awareness, a tension, in the way he walked. Arms out a little from his sides, fingers bent. He stared at Blank. Saw the smile. His whole body seemed to relax. He nodded, not smiling.

They came abreast. Right hand darting into the open coat. The smooth, practised transfer of the ax to the free right hand. Weight on left foot. Whirl as smooth as a ballet step. An original art form. Murder as a fine art: all sensual kinetics. Weight onto the right foot now. Right arm rising. Lover sensing, hearing, pausing, beginning his own turn in his dear *pas de deux*.

And then. Oh. Up onto his toes. His body arching into the blow. Everything: flesh, bone, sinew, muscle, blood, penis, kneecaps, elbows and biceps, whatever he was . . . giving freely, complctely, all of him. The crunch and sweet thud that quivered his hand, wrist, arm, torso, down into his bowels and nuts. The penetration! And the ecstasy! Into the grey wonder and mystery of the man. Oh!

Plucking the ax free even as the body fell, the soul soaring up to the cloudy sky. Oh no. The soul entering into Daniel Blank, becoming one with his soul, the two coupling even as he had imagined lost astronauts embracing and drifting through all immeasurable time.

He stooped swiftly, not looking at the crushed skull. He was not morbid. He found the shield and ID card in a leather folder. He no longer had to prove his deeds to Celia, but this was for him. It was not a trophy, it was a gift from the victim. I love you, too.

So simple! It was incredible, his luck. No witnesses. No shouts, cries, alarms. The moon peeped from behind clouds and withdrew again. The mild wind was there. The night. Somewhere, unseen, stars whirled their keening courses. And tomorrow the sun might shine. Nothing could stop the tides.

"Good movie, Mr. Blank?" Charles Lipsky asked.

"I liked it," Daniel Blank nodded brightly. "Very enjoyable. You really should see it."

He went through the now familiar drill: washing and sterilizing the ice ax, then oiling the exposed steel. He put it away with his other climbing gear in the front hall closet. The policeman's badge represented a problem. He had tucked Lombard's driver's license and Gilbert's ID card under a stack of handkerchiefs in his top dresser drawer. It was extremely unlikely the cleaning woman, or anyone else, would uncover them. But still . . .

He wandered through the apartment, looking for a better hiding place. His first idea was to tape the identification to the backs of three of the larger mirrors on the living room wall. But the tape might dry, the gifts fall free, and then . . .

He finally came back to his bedroom dresser. He pulled the top drawer out and placed it on his bed. There was a shallow recess under the drawer, between the bottom and the runners. All the identification fitted easily into a large white envelope, and this he taped to the bottom of the drawer. If the tape dried, and the envelope dropped, it could only drop into the second drawer. And, while taped, it was in a position where he could easily check its security every day, if he wanted to. Or open the envelope flap and look at his gifts.

Then he was home free—weapon cleansed, evidence hidden, all done that reason told him should be done. He even saved the ticket stub for the neighborhood movie. Now was the time for reflection and dreaming, for pondering significance and meaning.

He bathed slowly, scrubbing, then rubbing scented oil onto his wet skin. He stood on the bathroom mat, staring at himself in the full-length mirror, unaccountably, he began to make the gyrations of a strip-tease dancer: hands clasped behind his head, knees slightly bent, pelvis pumping in and out, hips grinding. He became excited by his own mirror image. He became erect, not fully but sufficiently to add to his pleasure. So there he stood, pumping his turgid shaft at the mirror.

Was he mad? he wondered. And, laughing, thought he might very well be.

4

The following morning he was having breakfast—a small glass of apple juice, a bowl of organic cereal with skim milk, a cup of black coffee—when the nine o'clock news came on the kitchen radio and a toneless voice announced the murder of Detective third grade Roger Kope on East 75th Street the previous midnight. Kope had been promoted from uniformed patrolman only two weeks previously. He left a widow and three small children. Deputy Commissioner Broughton, in charge of the investigation, stated several important leads were being followed up, and he hoped to make an important statement on the case shortly.

Daniel Blank put his emptied dishes into the sink, ran hot water into them, went off to work.

When he left his office in the evening, he purchased the afternoon *Post*, but hardly glanced at the headline: "Killer Loose on East Side." He carried the paper home with him and collected his mail at the lobby desk. He opened envelopes in the elevator: two bills, a magazine subscription offer, and the winter catalogue from Outside Life.

He fixed himself a vodka on the rocks with a squeeze of lime, turned on the television set and sat in the living room, sipping his drink, leafing through the catalogue, waiting for the evening news.

The coverage of Kope's murder was disappointingly brief. There was a shot of the scene of the crime, a shot of the ambulance moving away, and then the TV reporter said the details of the death of Detective Kope were very similar to those in the murder of Frank Lombard and Bernard Gilbert, and police believed all three killings were the work of one man. "The investigation is continuing."

Later that evening Blank walked over to Second Avenue to buy the early morning editions of the *News* and the *Times*. "Mad Killer Strikes Again," the *News'* headline screamed. The *Times* had a one-column story low on the front page: "Detective Slain on East Side." He brought the papers home, added them to the afternoon *Post* and settled down with a kind of bored dread to read everything that had been printed on Kope's death.

The most detailed, the most accurate report, Blank acknowledged, appeared under the byline "Thomas Handry." Handry, quoting "a high police official who asked that his name not be used," stated unequivocally that the three murders were committed by the same man, and that the weapon used was "an ax-like tool with an elongated spike." The other papers identified the weapon as "a small pick or something similar."

Handry also quoted his anonymous informant in explaining how a police decoy, an experienced officer, could be struck down from behind without apparently being aware of the approach of his attacker or making any effort to defend himself. "It is suggested," Handry wrote, "the assailant approached from the front, presenting an innocent, smiling appearance to his victim, then, at the moment of passing, turned and struck him down. It is believed by the usually reliable source that the killer carried his weapon concealed under a folded newspaper or under his coat. Although Gilbert died from a frontal attack, the method used in Kope's murder closely parallels that in the Lombard killing."

Handry's report ended by stating that his informant feared there would be additional attacks unless the killer was caught. Another paper spoke of an unprecedented assignment of detectives to the case, and the third paper stated that a curfew in the 251st Precinct was under consideration.

Blank tossed the papers aside. It was disquieting, he admitted, that the term "ax-like tool" had been used in Handry's report. He had to assume the police knew exactly what the weapon was, but were not releasing the information. He did not believe they could trace the purchase of an ice ax to him; his ax was five years old, and hundreds were sold annually all over the world. But it did indicate he would be wise not to underestimate the challenge he faced, and he wondered what kind of a man this Deputy Commissioner Broughton was, trying so hard to take him by the neck. Or, if not Broughton, whoever Handry's anonymous "high police official" was. That business of approaching from the front, then whirling to strike—who had guessed *that?* There were probably other things known or guessed, and not released to the newspapers—but *what?*"

Blank went over his procedures carefully and could find only two obvious weak links. One was his continued possession of the victims' identification. But, after pondering, he realized that if it ever came to a police search of his apartment, they would already have sufficient evidence to tie him to the murders, and the identification would merely be the final confirmation.

The other problem was more serious: Celia Montfort's knowledge of what he had done.

5

Erotica, the sex boutique owned by Florence and Samuel Morton was located on upper Madison Avenue, between a gourmet food shop and a 100-year-old store that sold saddles and polo mallets. Erotica's storefront had been designed by a pop-art enthusiast and consisted of hundreds of polished automobile hubcaps which served as distorting mirrors of the street scene and passing pedestrians.

"It boggles the mind," Flo nodded.

"It blows the brain," Sam nodded.

Between them, they had come up with this absolutely marvy idea for decorating their one window for the Christmas shopping season. They had, at great expense, commissioned a display house to create a naked Santa Claus. He had the requisite tasseled red cap and white beard, but otherwise his plump and roseate body was nude except for a small, black patent leather bikini equipped with a plastic codpiece, an item of masculine attire Erotica was attempting to revive in New York, with limited success.

The naked Santa was displayed in the Madison Avenue window for one day. Then Lieutenant Marty Dorfman, Acting Commander of the 251st Precinct, paid a personal visit to Erotica and politely asked the owners to remove the display, citing a number of complaints he had received from local churches, merchants, and outraged citizens. So the bikini-clad Saint Nicholas was moved to the back of the store, the window filled with miscellaneous erotic Christmas gifts, and Flo and Sam decided to inaugurate the extended-hours shopping season with an open house; free Swedish glug for old and new customers and a dazzling buffet that included such exotic items as fried grasshoppers and chocolate-covered ants.

Daniel Blank and Celia Montfort were specifically invited to this feast and asked to return to the Mortons' apartment later for food and drink of a more substantial nature. They accepted.

The air was overheated—and scented. Two antique Byzantine censers hung suspended in corners; from their pierced shells drifted fumes of musky incense called "Orgasm," one of Erotica's best sellers. Customers checked their coats and hats with a dark, exquisite, sullen Japanese girl clad in diaphanous Arabian Nights pajamas beneath which she wore no brassiere—only sheer panties imprinted with small reproductions of Mickey Mouse. Incredibly, her pubic hair was blond.

Celia and Daniel stood to one side, observing the hectic scene, sipping small cups of spiced, steaming glug. The store was crowded with loud-voiced, flush-faced customers, most of them young, all wearing the kinky, trendy fashions of the day. They weren't clothed; they were costumed. Their laughter was shrill, their movements jerky as they pushed through the store, examining phallic candles, volumes of Aubrey Beardsley prints, leather brassieres, jockstraps fashioned in the shape of a clutching hand.

"They're so excited," Daniel Blank said. "The whole world's excited."

Celia looked up at him and smiled faintly. Her long black hair, parted in the middle, framed her witch's face. As usual, she was wearing no makeup, though her eyes seemed shadowed with a bone-deep weariness.

"What are you thinking?" she asked him, and he realized once again how ideas, abstract ideas, aroused her.

"About the world," he said, looking around the frantic room. "The ruttish world. About people today. How stimulated they all are."

"Sexually stimulated?"

"That, of course. But in other ways. Politically. Spiritually, I guess. Violence. The new. The terrible hunger for the new, the different, the 'in thing.' And what's in is out in weeks, days. In sex, art, politics, everything. It all seems to be going faster and faster. It wasn't always like this, was it?"

"No," she said, "it wasn't."

"The in thing," he repeated. "Why do they call it 'in'? Penetration?"

Now she looked at him curiously. "Are you drunk?" she asked.

He was surprised. "On two paper cups of Swedish glug? No"—he laughed—"I am not drunk."

He touched her cheek with warm fingers. She grabbed his hand, turned her head to kiss his fingertips, then slid his thumb into her wet mouth, tongued it, drew it softly out. He looked swiftly about the room; no one was staring.

"I wish you were my sister," he said in a low voice.

She was silent a moment, then asked, "Why did you say that?"

"I don't know. I didn't think about it. I just said it."

"Are you tired of sex?" she asked shrewdly.

"What? Oh no. No. Not exactly. It's just . . ." He waved at the crowded room. "It's just that they're not going to find it this way."

"Find what?"

"Oh . . . you know. The answer."

The evening had that chopped, chaotic tempo that now infected all his hours: life speeding in disconnected scenes, a sharply cut film, images and distortions in an accelerating frenzy: faces, places, bodies, speech and ideas swimming up to the lens, enlarging, then dwindling away, fading. It was difficult to concentrate on any one experience; it was best simply to open himself to sensation, to let it all engulf him.

"Something's happening to me," he told her. "I see these people here, and on the street, and at work, and I can't believe I belong with them. The same race, I mean. They seem to me dogs, or animals in a zoo. Or perhaps I am. But I can't relate. But if they are human, I am not. And if I am, they are not. I just don't recognize them. I'm apart from them."

"You *are* apart from them," she said softly. "You've done something so meaningful that it sets you apart."

"Oh yes," he said, laughing happily. "I have, haven't I? If they only knew . . ."

"How does it feel?" she asked him. "I mean . . . knowing? Satisfaction? Pleasure?"

"That, of course," he nodded, feeling an itch of joy at talking of these things in a crowded, noisy room (he was naked but no one could see). "But mostly a feeling of—of gratification that I've been able to accomplish so much."

"Oh yes, Dan," she breathed, putting a hand on his arm.

"Am I mad?" he asked. "I've been wondering."

"Is it important?"

"No. Not really."

"Look at these people," she gestured. "Are they sane?"

"No," he said. "Well . . . maybe. But whether they're sane or mad, I'm different from them."

"Of course you are."

"And different from you," he added, smiling.

She shivered, a bit, and moved closer to him.

"Do we have to go to the Mortons?" she murmured.

"We don't have to. I think we should."

"We could go to your place. Or my place. Our place."

"Let's go to the Mortons," he said, smiling again and feeling it on his face.

They waited until Flo and Sam were ready to leave. Then they all shared a big cab back to the Mortons' apartment. Flo and Sam gabbled away in loud voices. Daniel Blank sat on the monkey seat, smiled and smiled.

Blanche had prepared a roast duckling garnished with peach halves. And there were small roasted potatoes and a tossed salad of romaine and Italian watercress. She brought the duckling in on a carving board to show it around for their approval before returning it to the kitchen to quarter it.

It looked delicious, they agreed, with its black, crusty skin and gleaming peach juice. And yet, when Daniel Blank's full plate was put before him, he sat a moment and stared; the food offended him.

He could not say why, but it happened frequently of late. He would go into a familiar restaurant, alone or with Celia, order a dish that he had had before, that he knew he liked, and then, when the food was put before him, he had no appetite and could scarcely toy with it.

It was just so—so *physical.* That steaming mixture to be cut into manageable forkfuls and shoved through the small hole that was his mouth, to emerge, changed and compounded, a day later via another small hole. Perhaps it was the vulgarity of the process that offended him. Or its animality. Whatever, the sight of food, however well prepared, now made him queasy. It was all he could do, for politeness' sake, to eat a bit of his duckling quarter, two small potatoes, dabble in the salad. He wasn't comfortable until, finally, they were seated on sofas and in soft chairs, having black coffee and vodka stingers.

"Hey, Dan," Samuel Morton said abruptly, "you got any money to invest?"

"Sure," Blank said amiably. "Not a lot, but some. In what?"

"First of all, this health club you belong to—what does it cost you?"

"Five hundred a year. That doesn't include massage or food, if you want it. They have sandwiches and salads. Nothing fancy."

"Liquor?"

"You can keep a bottle in your locker if you like. They sell set-ups."

"A swimming pool?"

"A small one. And a small sundeck. Gymnasium, of course. A sauna. What's this all about?"

"Can you swim naked in the pool?"

"Naked? I don't know. I suppose you could if you wanted to. It's for men only. I've never seen anyone do it. Why do you ask?"

"Sam and I had this marvy idea," Florence Morton said.

"A natural," Sam said. "Can't miss."

"There's this health club on East Fifty-seventh Street," Flo said. "It started as a reducing salon, but it's not making it. It's up for grabs now."

"Good asking price." Sam nodded. "And they'll shave."

"It's got a big pool," Flo nodded. "A gym with all the machines, two saunas, locker room, showers. The works."

"And a completely equipped kitchen," Sam added. "A nice indoor-outdoor lounge with tables and chairs."

"The decor is hideous," Flo added. "Hideous. But all the basic stuff is there."

"You're thinking of opening a health club?" Celia Montfort asked.

"But different," Flo laughed.

"Totally different," Sam laughed.

"For men *and* women," Flo grinned.

"Using the same locker room and showers," Sam grinned.

"With nude sunbathing on the roof," Sam noted.

Blank looked from one to the other. "You're kidding?"

They shook their heads.

"You'd take only married couples and families for members?"

"Oh no," Flo said. "Swinging singles only."

"That's just the point," Sam said. "That's where the money comes from. Lonely singles. And it won't be cheap. We figure five hundred members at a thousand a year each. We'll try to keep the membership about sixty-forty."

"Sixty percent men and forty percent women," Flo explained.

Blank stared at them, shook his head. "You'll go to jail," he told them. "And so will your members."

"Not necessarily," Flo said. "We've had our lawyers looking into it."

"There are some encouraging precedents," Sam said. "There are beaches out in California set aside for swimming in the nude. All four sexes. The courts have upheld the legality. The law is very hazy in New York. No one's ever challenged the right to have mixed nude bathing in a private club. We think we can get away with it."

"It all hinges on whether or not you're 'maintaining a public nuisance,' " Flo explained.

"If it's private and well-run and no nudity in public, we think we can do it," Sam explained.

"No nudity in public?" Daniel Blank asked. "You mean fornication in the sauna or in a mop closet or underwater groping is okay?"

"It's all private," Flo shrugged.

"Who's hurting whom?" Sam shrugged. "Consenting adults."

Daniel looked at Celia Montfort. She sat still, her face expressionless. She seemed waiting for his reaction.

"We're forming a corporation," Flo said.

"We figure we'll need a hundred thousand tops," Sam said, "for lease, mortgage, conversion, insurance, etcetera."

"We're selling shares," Flo said.

"Interested?" Sam asked.

Daniel Blank patted his Via Veneto wig gently.

"Oh," he said. "No," he said. "I don't think so. Not my cup of tea. But I think, if you can get around the legal angle, it's a good idea."

"You think it'll catch on?" Sam asked.

"Profitable?" Flo asked.

"No doubt about it," Blank assured them. "If the law doesn't close you down, you'll make a mint. Just walk down Eighth Avenue, which I do almost every day. Places where you can get a woman to give you a rub-down, or you can paint her body, or watch films, or get tickled with feathers. And ordinary prostitution too, of course. Mixed nude bathing in a private pool? Why not? Yes, I think it's a profitable idea."

"Then why don't you want to invest?" Celia asked him.

"What? Oh . . . I don't know. I told you—not my style. I'm tired of it all. Maybe just bored. Anyway, it puts me off. I don't like it."

They stared at him, the three of them, and waited. But when he said nothing more, Celia spurred him on.

"What don't you like?" she asked quietly. "The idea of men and women swimming naked together? You think it's immoral?"

"Oh God no!" he laughed loudly. "I'm no deacon. It's just that . . ."

"It's just what?"

"Well," he said, showing his teeth, "sex is so—so inconsequential, isn't it? I mean, compared to death and—well, virginity. I mean, they're so absolute, aren't they? And sex never is. Always something more. But with death and virginity you're dealing with absolutes. Celia, that word you used? Finitudes. Was that it? Or finalities. Something like that. It's so nice to—its so warm to—I know life is trouble, but still . . . What you're planning is wrong. Not in the moral sense. Oh no. But you're skirting the issue. You know? You're wandering around and around, and you don't see the goal, don't even glimpse it. Oh yes. Profitable? It will surely be profitable. For a year or two. Different. New. The in-thing. But then it will fall away. Just die. Because you're not giving them the answer, don't you see? Fucking underwater or in a sauna. And then. No, no! It's all so—so superficial. I told you. Those people tonight. Well, there you are. What have they learned or won? Maybe masturbation is the answer. Have you ever considered that? I know it's ridiculous. I apologize for mentioning it. But still . . . Because, you see, in your permissive world they say porn, perv and S-M. That's how much it means, that you can abbreviate it. So there you are. And it offends me. The vulgarity. Because it might have been a way, a path, but is no longer. Sex? Oh no. Shall we have another martini or shall we fuck? That important. I knew a girl once . . . Well. So you've got to go beyond. I tell you, it's just not enough. So, putting aside sex, you decide what comes next. What number bus to the absolute. And so you—"

Celia Montfort interrupted swiftly.

"What Daniel is trying to say," she told the astounded Mortons, "is that in a totally permissive society, virginity becomes the ultimate perversion. Isn't that what you wanted to say, dear?"

He nodded dumbly. Finally, they got out of there. She was trembling but he was not.

6

He propped himself on his left elbow, let his right palm slide lightly down that silky back.

"Are you awake?"

"Yes."

"Tell me about this woman, Celia Montfort."

Soft laughter.

"What do you want to know about 'this woman, Celia Montfort'?"

"Who is she? What is she?"

"I thought you knew all about her."

"I know she is beautiful and passionate. But so mysterious and withdrawn. She's so locked up within herself."

"Yes, she is, luv. Very deep, is our Celia."

"When she goes away, unexpectedly, where does she go?"

"Oh . . . places."

"To other men?"

"Sometimes. Sometimes to other women."

"Oh."

"Are you shocked, darling?"

"Not really. I guess I suspected it. But she comes back so weary. Sometimes she's been hurt. Does she want to be? I mean, does she deliberately seek it?"

"I thought you knew. You saw those bandages on her wrists. I saw you staring at them. She tried to slash her veins."

"My God."

"She tried it before and will probably try it again. Pills or driving too fast or a razor."

"Oh sweetheart, why does she do it?"

"Why? She really doesn't know. Except life has no value for her. No real value. She said that once."

He kissed those soft lips and with his fingertips touched the closed eyes gently. The limpid body moved to him, pressed sweetly; he smelled again that precious flesh, skin as thin, as smooth as watered silk.

"I thought I made her happy."

"Oh you did, Dan. As much as any man can. But it's not enough for her. She's seen everything, done everything, and still nothing has meaning for her. She's run through a dozen religions and faiths, tried alcohol and all kinds of drugs, done things with men and women and children you wouldn't believe. She's burned out now. Isn't it obvious? Celia Montfort. Poor twit."

"I love her."

"Do you? I think it's too late for her, Dan. She's—she's beyond love. All she wants now is release."

"Release from what?"

"From living, I suppose. Since she's trying so hard to kill herself. Perhaps her problem is that she's too intelligent. She's painted and written poetry. She was very good but couldn't endure the thought of being just 'very good.' If she didn't have the talent of a genius, she couldn't settle for second-best. Always, she wants the best, the most, the final. I think her problem is that she wants to be *sure*. Of something, anything. She wants final answers. I think that's why she was attracted to you, darling. She felt you were searching for the same thing."

"You're so old for your age."

"Am I? I'm ancient. I was born ancient."

They laughed gently, together, and moved together, holding each other. Then kissing, kissing, with love but without passion, wet lips clinging. Blank stroked webbed hair and with a fingertip traced convolution of delicate ear, slender throat, thrust of rib beneath satin skin.

Finally they drew apart, lay on their backs, side by side, inside hands clasped loosely.

"What about Valenter?"

"What about him?"

"What is his role in your home?"

"His *role?* He's a servant, a houseman."

"He seems so—so sinister."

Mocking: "Do you think he's sleeping with brother or sister? Or both?"

"I don't know. It's a strange house."

"It may be a strange house, but I assure you Valenter is only a servant. It's your imagination, Dan."

"I suppose so. That room upstairs. Are there peepholes where other people can watch? Or is the place wired to pick up conversation?"

"Now you're being ridiculous."

"I suppose so. Perhaps I was believing what I wanted to believe. But why that room?"

"Why did I take you there? Because it's at the top of the house. No one ever goes there. It's private, and I knew we wouldn't be interrupted. It's shabby, I know, but it was fun, wasn't it? Didn't you think it was fun? Why are you laughing?"

"I don't know. Because I read so much into it that doesn't exist. Perhaps."

"Like what?"

"Well, this woman—"

"I know, 'this Celia Montfort.' "

"Yes. Well, I thought this Celia Montfort might be manipulating me, using me."

"For what?"

"I don't know. But I feel she wants something from me. She's waiting for something. From me. Is she?"

"I don't know, Dan. I just don't know. She is a very complex woman. I don't know too much about women; most of my experience has been with men, as you very well know. But I don't think Celia Montfort knows exactly what she wants. I think she senses it and is fumbling toward it, making all kinds of false starts and wrong turnings. She's always having accidents. Slipping, upsetting things. Knocking things over, falling and breaking this or that. But she's moving toward something. Do you have that feeling?"

"Yes. Oh yes. Are you rested now?"

"Yes, darling, I'm rested."

"Can we make love again?"

"Please. Slowly."

"Tony, Tony, I love you."

"Oh pooh," Tony Montfort said.

7

The strange thing, the strange thing, Daniel Blank decided, was that the world, his world, was expanding at the same time he, himself, was contracting. That is, Tony and Mrs. Cleek and Valenter and the Mortons—everyone he knew and everyone he saw on the streets—well, he loved them all. So sad. They were all so sad. But then, just as he had told Celia that night at the Erotica, he felt apart from them. But still he could love them. That was curious and insolvable.

At the same time his love and understanding were going out to encompass all living things—people, animals, rocks, the whirling skies—he pulled in within himself, chuckling, to nibble on his own heart and hug his secret life. He was condensing, coiling in upon himself, penetrating deeper and deeper. It was a closed life of shadow, scent, and gasps. And yet, and yet there were stars keening their courses, a music in the treacherous world.

Well, it came to this: should he or should he not be a hermit? He could twirl naked before a mirrored wall and embrace himself in golden chains. That was one answer. Or he could go out into the clotted life of the streets, and mingle. Join. Penetrate, and know them all. Loving.

He opted for the streets, the evil streets, and openness. The answer, he decided, was there. It was not in AMROK II; it was in Charles Lipsky, and all the other striving, defeated clods. He hated them for their weaknesses and vices, and loved them for their weaknesses and vices. Was he a Christ? It was a vagrant thought. Still, he acknowledged, he could be. He had Christ's love. But, of course, he was not a religious man.

So. Daniel Blank on the prowl. Grinning at the dull winter sky, determined to solve the mystery of life.

This night he had bathed, oiled and scented his slender body, dressed slowly and carefully in black suit, black turtleneck sweater, crepe-soled shoes, the slit-pocket topcoat with the ice ax looped over his left wrist within. He sauntered out to search for his demon lover, a Mongol of a man, so happy, so happy. It was eleven days after the murder of Detective third grade Roger Kope.

It had become increasingly difficult, he acknowledged. Since the death of the detective, the neighborhood streets at night were not only patrolled by plainclothes decoys, but two-man teams of uniformed officers appeared on almost every block and corner, wary and not at all relaxed after what happened to Kope. In addition, the assignment of more squad cars to the area was evident, and Daniel Blank supposed that unmarked police cars were also being used.

Under the circumstances he would have been justified in seeking another hunting ground, perhaps another borough. But he considered it more challenge than risk. Did you reject a difficult climb because of the danger? If you did, why climb at all? The point, the whole point, was to stretch yourself, probe new limits of your talent and courage. Resolution was like a muscle: exercised it grew larger and firmer; unused it became pale and flabby.

The key, he reasoned, might be the time factor. His three killings had all taken place between 11:30 P.M. and 12:30 A.M. The police would be aware of this, of course, and all officers warned to be especially alert during the midnight hour. They might be less vigilant before and after. He needed every advantage he could find.

He decided on an earlier time. It was the Christmas shopping season. It was dark by seven P.M., but the stores were open until nine, and even at ten o'clock people were scurrying home, laden with parcels and bundles. After 12:30 the streets were almost deserted except for the decoys and uniformed patrols. Neighborhood residents had read the newspaper reports folowing Kope's death; few ventured out after midnight. Yes, earlier would be best: any time from nine to ten-thirty. Mountain climbers judged carefully the odds and percentages; they were not deliberate suicides.

He needed camouflage, he decided, and after long consideration determined what he must do. The previous evening, on his way home from work, he stopped in a store on 42nd Street that sold Christmas cards, artificial trees, ornaments, wrapping paper, and decorations. The store had opened six weeks before Christmas and would go out of business on Christmas Eve. He had seen it happen frequently, all over the city.

He purchased two boxes, one about the size of a shoe box, the other flat and long, designed for a man's necktie or a pair of gloves. He bought a roll of Christmas wrapping paper, the most conventional he could find: red background with reindeer pulling Santa's sled imprinted on it. The roll itself was wrapped in cellophane. He bought a small package of stickers and a ball of cord that was actually a length of knitting yarn wound about a cardboard square.

He wore his thin, black suede gloves while making the purchase. The store was mobbed; the clerk hardly glanced at him. At home, still wearing the gloves, he prepared the two empty boxes as Christmas packages, wrapping them neatly in the reindeer paper, sticking down the end flaps with the gummed Santa Claus heads, then tying them up with red yarn, making very attractive bows on top. Finished, he had what were apparently two Christmas gifts, handsomely wrapped. He intended to leave them at the scene; the chances of their being traced to him, he believed, were absolutely minimal. He then shoved excess wrapping, stickers, cord and paper bag into his garbage can, took it to the incinerator room down the hall, and dumped it all down. Then he came back to his apartment and took off his gloves.

As he had expected, the doorman on duty when he left the following evening—it was not Charles Lipsky—hardly looked up when Daniel Blank passed, carrying his two empty Christmas boxes; he was too busy signing for packages and helping tenants out of cabs with shopping bags stuffed with bundles. And if he had noted him, what of that? Daniel Blank on his way to an evening with friends, bringing them two gaily wrapped presents. Beautiful.

He was so elated with his own cleverness, so surprised by the number of shoppers still on the streets, that he decided to walk over to The Parrot on Third Avenue, have a leisurely drink, kill a little time. "Kill time." He giggled, the ax clasped beneath his coat, the Christmas packages in his right arm.

The Parrot was almost empty. There was one customer at the bar, a middle-aged man talking to himself, making wide gestures. The lone waiter sat at a back table, reading a religious tract. The bartender was marking a racing form. They were the two who had been on duty when he had had the fight with the homosexual the previous year. They both looked up when he came in, but he saw no recognition in their faces.

He ordered a brandy, and when it was brought he asked the bartender if he'd have something, too.

"Thanks," the man said with a cold smile. "Not while I'm working."

"Quiet tonight. Everyone Christmas shopping, I suppose."

"It ain't that," the man said, leaning toward him. "Other Christmases we used to get a crowd when the stores closed. This year, no one. Know why?"

"Why?"

"This nutty killer on the loose," the man said angrily, his reddish wattles wagging. "Who the hell wants to be out on the streets after dark? I hope they catch him soon and cut his balls off. The son-of-a-bitch, he's ruining our business."

Blank nodded sympathetically and paid for his drink. The ax was still under his coat. He sat at the bar, coated, gloved, although the room was warm, and sipped his brandy with pleasure. The Christmas boxes were placed on the bar next to him. It was quiet and restful. And amusing, in a way, to learn that what he was doing had affected so many people. A stone dropped in a pool, the ripples going out, spreading . . .

He had the one drink, left a modest tip, walked out with his packages. He turned at the door to see if he should make a half-wave to the bartender or waiter, but no one was looking at him. He laughed inwardly; it was all so easy. No one cared.

The shoppers were thinning out; those still on the streets were hurrying homeward, packages under their arms or shopping bags swinging. Blank imitated their appearance: his two Christmas presents under one arm, his head and shoulders slightly bent against the cruel wind. But his eyes flicked everywhere. If he couldn't finish his business before 11:00, he would give it up for another night; he was determined on that.

He lost one good prospect when the man suddenly darted up the stairway of a brownstone and was gone while Daniel Blank was still practicing his smile. He lost another who stopped to talk to the doorman of an apartment house. A third looked promising, but too much like a detective decoy; a civilian wouldn't be walking *that* slowly. Another was lost because a uniformed patrol turned the corner after him unexpectedly and came sauntering toward Blank.

He would not be frustrated and tried to keep his rage under control. But still . . . what were they doing to him? He pulled his left wrist far enough from his coat pocket to read the time under a street lamp. It was almost 10:30. Not much left. Then he'd have to let it go for another night. But he couldn't. *Couldn't.* The fever was in his blood, blazing. The hell with . . . Damn the . . . Fix bayonets, lads, and over . . . now or . . . It had to be. His luck was so good. A winning streak. Always ride a winning streak.

And so it was. For there—incredibly, delightfully, free of prowling cars and uniformed patrols—the block was empty and dim, and toward him came striding a single man, walking swiftly, under one arm a package in Christmas wrapping. And in the buttonhole of his tweed overcoat, a small sweetheart rose. Would a police decoy carry a Christmas package? Wear a rose? Not likely, Daniel Blank decided. He began his smile.

The lover passed under a street lamp. Blank saw he was young, slender, mustached, erect, confident and, really, rather beautiful. Another Daniel Blank.

"Good evening!" Daniel called out, a pace away, smiling.

"Good evening!" the man said in return, smiling.

At the moment of passing, Blank transferred the ax and started his turn. And even as he did he was aware that the victim had suddenly stopped and started *his* turn. He had a dim feeling of admiration for a man whose instincts, whose physical reactions were so right and so swift, but after that it was all uncertain.

The ax was raised. The Christmas packages dropped to the sidewalk. Then there were two hands clamped on his lifted wrist. The man's package fell also. But his grip didn't loosen. Blank was pulled tight. Three arms were high in the air. They stood a second, carved in sweet embrace, breathing wintry steam into each other's open lips, close. The physical contact was so delicious that Daniel was fuddled, and pressed closer. Warmth. Lovely warmth and strength.

Sense came flooding back. He hooked a heel behind the man's left knee, pulled back and pushed. It wasn't enough. The man staggered but would not go down. But his grip on Blank's wrist loosened. He hooked again and shoved again, his entire body against the other body. Oh. He thought he heard a distant whistle but wasn't sure. They fell then, and Daniel Blank, rolling, heard and felt his bent left elbow crack against the pavement and wondered, idly, if it was broken, and thought perhaps it was.

Then they were flat, Blank lying on top of the man whose eyes were dull with a kind of weariness. His hands fell free from Blank's wrist. So he brought the ice ax up and down, up and down, up and down, hacking furiously, in an ecstasy, pressing close, for this was the best yet, and hardly aware of weak fingers and nails clawing at his face. Something warm there.

Until the young man was still, black eyes glaring now. Blank laid the ax aside a moment to snatch at the lapel rose, picked up the ax again, staggered to a snarling crouch, looked about wildly. There were whistles now, definitely. A uniformed cop came pounding down from the far corner, hand fumbling at his hip, and his partner across the avenue, blowing and blowing at that silly whistle. Blank watched a few seconds, looping the ax about his dead left wrist under his coat.

He was suddenly conscious of the pain, in his left elbow, in his bleeding face. Then he was running, holding his injured left elbow close to his body, calculating possibilities and probabilities, but never once considered casting aside the sweetheart rose.

The body on the sidewalk should stop them for a moment, one of them at least, and as he turned onto First Avenue he stopped running, shoved the rose into his righthand coat pocket, fished out a handkerchief from the breast pocket of his jacket and held it across his bleeding face, coughing and coughing. He went into a luncheonette, two doors down from the corner. Still coughing, his bleeding face concealed by his handkerchief, he walked steadily to the phone booth in the rear. He actually clamped the handkerchief with his shoulder and took a coin from his righthand pocket to put in and dial the weather service. He was listening to a disembodied voice say, "Small craft warnings are in effect from Charleston to Block Island," when, watching, he saw a uniformed cop run by the luncheonette with drawn gun. Blank left the phone booth immediately, still coughing, handkerchief to face. There was an empty cab stopped for a light at 81st Street. Luck. Wasn't it all luck?

He asked the driver, politely, to take him to the West Side bus terminal. His voice—to his own ears, at least—was steady. When the light changed and the cab started off, he pushed to the far left corner where the driver couldn't see him in his rear view mirror without obvious craning. Then Blank held out his right hand, fingers spread. They didn't seem to be trembling.

It was almost a twenty-minute trip to the bus terminal and he used every one of them, looking up frequently to make certain the driver wasn't watching. First he swung open his topcoat, unbuttoned his jacket, unhooked his belt. Then he gently slid the loop of the ice ax off his nerveless left wrist, put his belt through the loop, and buckled it again. Now the ax would bump against his thigh as he walked, but it was safe. He buttoned his jacket.

Then he spit onto his handkerchief and softly rubbed his face. There was blood, but much less than he had feared. He put the handkerchief beside him on the seat and, gripping his left hand in his right, slowly bent his left arm. It hurt, it ached, but the pain was endurable, the elbow seemed to be functioning, and he hoped it was a bad bruise, not a break or a chip. He bent his left elbow and put the forearm inside his jacket, resting on the buttons, like a sling. It felt better that way.

He spit more into his handkerchief, wiped his face again, and there was hardly any fresh blood. The shallow wounds were already clotting. Blank pushed his reddened handkerchief into his breast pocket. He dragged out his wallet with one hand, glanced at the taxi meter, then extracted three one-dollar bills, replaced his wallet, sat back in the seat, drew a deep breath and smiled.

The bus station was mobbed. No one stared at him, and he didn't even bother covering his face with his handkerchief. He went directly to the men's room. It, too, was crowded, but he was able to get a look at himself in the mirror. His wig was awry, his left cheek scratched deeply—they'd surely scab—his right cheek roughened but not cut. Only one scratch on his left cheek was still welling blood, but slowly.

There was a man washing his hands in the basin alongside. He caught Blank's eye in the mirror.

"Hope the other guy looks as bad," he said.

"Never laid a hand on him," Blank said ruefully, and the man laughed.

Daniel moistened two paper towels under the tap and went into one of the pay toilets. When he had locked the door, he used one wet towel to wipe his face again, then plastered toilet paper onto his scratched, wet cheek. He used the other dampened towel to sponge his coat and suit. He discovered an abrasion on the left knee of his trousers; the cloth had been scraped through and skin showed. He would have to throw away the entire suit, wrap it in brown paper and dump it in a trash basket on his way to work. Chances were a derelict would fish it out before the sanitation men got to the basket. In any event, Blank could tear out the labels and burn them. It wasn't important.

He tried his left arm again. The elbow joint worked but painfully—no doubt about that. He took off his jacket and rolled up his sleeve. A lovely swelling there, already discolored. But the elbow worked. He adjusted all his clothes and managed his topcoat so that it hung from his shoulders, continental style, both his arms inside, the ax swinging from his belt. He peeled the toilet paper carefully from his face and looked at it. Faintly pinkish. He flushed paper and towels down the drain, tugged his clothing smooth, and opened the toilet door, smiling faintly.

In the mirror over the basin he adjusted his wig and combed it slowly with his right hand.

Another man, a hatless bald-headed man, was drying his hands nearby. He stared at Blank. Daniel turned to stare back.

''Looking at something?'' he asked.

The man gestured apologetically. ''Your hair,'' he said, ''it's a rug. Right?''

''Oh yes.''

''I've been thinking,'' the man said. ''You recommend?''

''Absolutely. No doubt about it. But get the best you can afford. I mean, don't skimp.''

''It don't blow off?''

''Not a chance. I never wear a hat. You can swim in it. Even shower in it if you like.''

''You really think so?''

''Definitely,'' Blank nodded. ''Change your whole life.''

''No kidding?'' the man breathed, enthused.

He took a cab back to his apartment house, his coat hanging loosely from his shoulders.

''Hey, Mr. Blank,'' the doorman said. ''Another guy got killed tonight. Not two blocks from here.''

''Is that right?'' Daniel said, and shook his head despairingly. ''From now on I'm taking cabs *everywhere.*''

''That's the best way, Mr. Blank.''

He drew a hot tub, poured in enough scented bath oil to froth the water and spice the bathroom. He undressed and slid in carefully, leaving the cleaning of the ice ax until later. But, atop the sudsy water, he floated the sweetheart rose. He watched it, immersed to his chin in the steaming tub, soaking his sore elbow. After awhile his erection came up until the flushed head of his penis was above the surface, and the small rose bobbed about it. He had never been so happy in his life. He dreamed.

Part VII

1 "They had stopped at a wharf painted white, and now Honey Bunch followed her daddy and her mother up this and found herself at the steps of the cunningest bungalow she had ever seen. It was painted white and it had green window boxes and green shutters with little white acorns painted on them. Honey Bunch had never seen a white acorn, but she thought they looked very pretty on the shutters. There was a little sign over the porch of his bungalow and on it were the words 'Acorn House.' "

Captain Edward X. Delaney stopped. At his wife's request he had been reading aloud from "Honey Bunch: Her First Days in Camp," but when he glanced up at the hospital bed Barbara seemed asleep, breathing heavily, thin arms and white hands lying limply atop the single blanket. She never got out of bed any more, not even to sit in a wheelchair.

He had arrived in time to help her with the evening meal. She nibbled a muffin, ate a little mashed potatoes, a few string beans, but wouldn't taste the small steak.

"You've got to eat, dear," he said, as firmly as he could, and she smiled wanly as he took the spoon and held some custard to her lips. She ate almost all the custard, then pushed his hand away, averted her face; he didn't have the heart to insist.

"What have you been doing, Edward?" she asked weakly.

"Oh . . . you know; trying to keep myself busy."

"Is there anything new on the case?"

"What case?" he asked, and then was ashamed and dropped his eyes. He did not want to dissemble but it seemed cruel, in her condition, to speak of violent death.

"What is it, Edward?" she asked, guessing.

"There's been another one," he said in a low voice. "A detective. One of Broughton's decoys."

"Married?"

"Yes. Three small children."

Her eyes closed slowly, her face took on a waxen hue. It was then she asked him to read aloud to her from one of the "Honey Bunch" books he had brought her. He took it up gladly, eager to change the subject, opened the book at random and began reading aloud in a resolute, expressive voice.

But now, after only two pages, she seemed to be sleeping. He put the book aside, pulled on his overcoat, took his hat, started to step quietly from the room. But she called, "Edward," and when he turned, her eyes were open, she was holding a hand out to him. He returned immediately to her bedside, pulled up a chair, sat holding her hot, dry fingers.

"That makes three," she said.

"Yes," he nodded miserably. "Three."

"All men," she said vaguely. "Why all men? It would be so much easier to kill women. Or children. Wouldn't it, Edward? Not as dangerous for the killer."

He stared at her, the import of what she was saying growing in his mind. It could be nothing, of course. But it could be something. He leaned forward to kiss her cheek softly.

"You're a wonder, you are," he whispered. "What would I ever do without you?"

Back in his study, a rye highball in his big fist, he forgot about the chicken pie Mary had left on the kitchen table, and thought only of the significance of what his wife had suggested.

It certainly wasn't unusual for a psychopathic killer to be uninterested in or fearful of sex before killing (or even impotent) and then, during or after the murder, to become an uncontrollable satyr. There had been many such cases, but all, to his knowledge, involved women or children as victims.

But now the three victims were men, and Lombard and Kope had been big, muscular men, well able to defend themselves, given half a chance. Still, so far the killer had selected only men, slaying with an ice ax. As Barbara had said, it was a dangerous way to kill—dangerous for the assassin. How much easier to strike down a woman or use a gun against a man. But he had not. Only men. With an ax. Did that mean anything?

It might, Delaney nodded, it just might. Of course, if the next victim was a woman, the theory would be shot to hell, but just consider it a moment. The killer, a male, had killed three other men, risking. Playing amateur psychologist, Delaney considered the sexual symbolism of the weapon used: a pointed ice ax, an ax with a rigid spike. Was that so far-fetched? An ice ax with a drooping spike! Even more far-fetched?

He took his "Expert File" from the bottom drawer of his desk and found the card he wanted: "PSYCHIATRIST/CRIMINOLOGIST. Dr. Otto Morgenthau." There were short additional notes in Delaney's handwriting on the card, recalling the two cases in which Dr. Morgenthau had assisted the Department. One involved a rapist, the other a bomber. Delaney called the number listed: The doctor's office on Fifth Avenue in the 60s, not in the 251st Precinct.

A feminine voice: "Dr. Morgenthau's office."

"Could I speak to Dr. Morgenthau, please? This is Captain Edward X. Delaney, New York Police Department."

"I'm sorry, Captain, the doctor is unavailable at the moment."

That meant Morgenthau had a patient.

"Could he call me back?" Delaney asked.

"I'll try, sir. May I have your number?"

He gave it to her, hung up, then went into the kitchen. He tried some of the chicken pie; it was good but he really wasn't hungry. He covered the remainder carefully with plastic wrap and put it into the refrigerator. He mixed another rye highball and sat hunched in the swivel chair behind his study desk, sipping his drink, staring blankly at the telephone. When it rang, half an hour later, he let it ring three times before he picked it up.

"Captain Edward X. Delaney here."

"And here is Dr. Otto Morgenthau. How are you, Captain?"

"Well, thank you, doctor. And you?"

"Weary. What is it, Captain?"

"I'd like to see you, sir."

"*You*, Captain? Personally? Or Department business?"

"Department."

"Well, what is it?"

"It's difficult to explain over the phone, doctor. I was wondering—"

"Impossible," Morgenthau interrupted sharply. "I have patients until ten o'-clock tonight. And then I must—"

"The three men who were axed to death on the East Side," Delaney interrupted in his turn. "You must have read about it."

There was a moment of silence.

"Yes," Dr. Morgenthau said slowly, "I have read about it. Interesting. The work of one man?"

"Yes, sir. Everything points to it."

"What do you have?"

"Bits and pieces. I hoped you could fill in some of the gaps."

Dr. Morgenthau sighed. "I suppose it must be immediately?"

"If possible, sir."

"Be here promptly at ten o'clock. Then I will give you fifteen minutes. No more."

"Yes, sir. I'll be there. Thank you, doctor."

Delaney arrived five minutes early. The morose, matronly nurse was pulling on an ugly cloth coat, fastened in front with wooden toggles.

"Captain Delaney?"

"Yes."

"Please do doublelock the door after I leave," she said. "Doctor will call you when he is ready."

Delaney nodded, and after she marched out, he obediently turned the latch, then sat down in a straight chair, his hat hooked over one knee, and waited patiently, staring at nothing.

When the doctor finally appeared from his consulting room, Delaney rose to his feet, shocked at the man's appearance. The last time the Captain had seen him, Morgenthau was somewhat corpulent but robust, alert, with erect posture, healthy skin tone, clear and active eyes. But now Delaney was confronted by a wheyfaced man shrunken within clothing that seemed three sizes too large in all dimensions. The eyes were dull and hooded, the hair thinning and uncombed. There was a tremor to the hands and, Delaney noted, fingernails were dirty and untrimmed.

They sat in the consulting room, Morgenthau slumped behind his desk, Delaney in an armchair at one side.

"I'll be as brief as possible, doctor," he began. "I know how busy—"

"Just a moment," Morgenthau muttered, gripping the edge of the desk to pull himself upright. "Sorry to interrupt you, Captain, but I have just remembered a phone call I must make at once. A disturbed patient. I shall only be a few minutes. You wait here."

He hurried out, not to the reception room but to an inner office. Delaney caught a quick glimpse of white medical cabinets, a stainless steel sink. Morgenthau was gone almost ten minutes. When he returned, his walk was swift and steady, his eyes wide and shiny. He was rubbing his palms together, smiling.

"Well now," he said genially, "what have we got, Captain?"

Not pills, Delaney thought; the reaction was too swift for pills. Probably an amphetamine injection. Whatever it was, it had worked wonders for Dr. Otto Morgenthau; he was relaxed, assured, listened closely, and when he lighted a cigar his hands were unhurried and steady.

Delaney went through it all: the deaths of the three victims, the ice ax, what he had learned about mountaineers, the way he believed the crimes were committed, the missing identification—everything he felt Morgenthau needed to know, omitting the fact, naturally, that he, Delaney, was not on active duty and was not in charge of the official investigation.

"And that's about all we've got, doctor."

"No possible link between the three men?"

"No, sir. Nothing we've been able to discover."

"And what do you want from me?"

"What you were able to provide us before—a psychiatric profile of the criminal. They were of great help, doctor."

"Oh yes," Morgenthau nodded. "Rape and bombing. But they are sufficiently popular pastimes so that there is a large history available, many similar cases. So it is possible to analyze and detect a pattern. You understand? Make a fairly reasonable guess as to motivation, modus operandi, perhaps even physical appearance and habits. But in this case—impossible. Now we are dealing with multiple murder. It is, fortunately for all of us, a relatively rare activity. I am now eliminating political assassination which, I would guess, does not apply here."

"No, sir. I don't believe it does."

"So . . . the literature on the subject is not extensive. I tried my hand at a short monograph but I do not believe you read it."

"No, doctor, I didn't."

"No wonder," Morgenthau giggled. "It was published in an obscure German psychiatric journal. So then, I cannot, regretably, provide you with a psychiatric profile of the mass murderer."

"Well, listen," Delaney said desperately, "can you give me *anything?* About motivation, I mean. Even general stuff might help. For instance, do you think this killer is insane?"

Dr. Morgenthau shook his head angrily. "Sane. Insane. Those are legal terms. They have absolutely no meaning in the world of mental health. Well, I will try . . . My limited research leads me to believe mass murderers are generally one of three very broad, indefinite types. But I warn you, motivations frequently overlap. With multiple killers, we are dealing with individuals; as I told you, there are no definitive patterns I can discern. Well, then . . . the three main types . . . One: biological. Those cases in which mass murder is triggered by a physical defect, although the killer may have been psychologically predisposed. As an example, that rifleman up in the Texas tower who killed—how many people? I understand he had a brain tumor and had been trained as a skilled marksman and killer in the military service. Two: psychological. Here the environment in general is not at fault, but the specific pressures—usually familial or sexual—on the individual are of such an extreme nature that killing, over and over again, is the only release. Bluebeard might be such a case, or Jack the Ripper, or that young man in New Jersey—what was his name?"

"Unruh."

"Yes, Unruh. And then the third cause: sociological. This might be when the killer, in a different environment, might live out his days without violence. But his surroundings are so oppressive that his only recourse is fighting back, by killing, against a world he never made, a world that grinds him down to something less than human. This sociological motivation involves not only the residents of ghettoes, the brutalized minorities. There was a case a few years ago—again in New Jersey, I believe—where a 'solid citizen,' a middle-aged, middle-class gentleman who worked for a bank or insurance company—something like that—and passed the collection—"

The fifteen minutes Dr. Morgenthau had allotted Delaney had long since passed. But the doctor kept talking, as Delaney knew he would. It was hard to stop a man riding his hobby.

"—and passed the collection plate at his church every Sunday," Morgenthau was saying. "And then one day this fine, mild, upstanding citizen kills his wife, children, and his mother. Mark that—his mother! And then he takes off."

"I remember that case," Delaney nodded.

"Have they caught him yet?"

"No, I don't think so."

"Well, anyway, Captain, in the investigation, according to newspaper reports, it was discovered this pillar of the community was living in a much larger house than he could afford; it was heavily mortgaged and he was deeply in debt: insurance, cars, clothes, furniture, his children's education—all the social pressures to consider. A sociological motivation here, obviously, but as I told you, mass killers do not fit into neat classifications. What of the man's personality, background, childhood, his crimes considered as a part of the nation's or the world's social history? Charles Manson, for instance. What I am trying to prove to you is that despite these three quite loose classifications; each case of mass murder is specific and different from the others. Men who kill children and the man who killed all those nurses in Chicago and Panzram all seem to have had a similar childhood: physical abuse and body contact at an early age. Sexual pleasure at an infantile level. And yet, of the three I just mentioned, one kills children, one kills young women, and one kills young boys—or buggers them. So where is the pattern? Well, there is a superficial one perhaps. Most mass murders tend to be quiet, conservative, neat. They attract no attention until their rampage. Often they wear the same suit or the same cut and color suit for days on end."

Delaney had been taking notes furiously in his pocket notebook. Now he looked up, eyes gleaming.

"That's interesting, doctor. But Manson wasn't like that."

"Exactly!" Morgenthau cried triumphantly. "That's just what I've been telling you: in this field it is dangerous to generalize. Here is something else interesting . . . Wertham says mass murderers are not passionless; they only appear to be so. But—and this is what is significant—he says that when their orgy of killing is finished, they once again become apparently passionless and are able to describe their most blood-curdling acts in chilling detail, without regret and without remorse. You know, Captain, my field has its own jargon, just as yours does. And the—the—what do you call it?—the lingo changes frequently, just like slang. Five or ten years ago we spoke of 'CPI's.' These were 'Constitutional Psychopathic Inferiors.' Apparently normal, functioning effectively in society, the CPI's feel no guilt, apparently are born without conscience, have no remorse, and cannot understand what the fuss is all about when the law objects to them holding a child's hand over a gas flame, throwing a puppy out of a ten-story window, or giving apples studded with razor blades and broken glass to a Halloween trick-or-treat visitor. Most mass murders are CPI's, I would guess. Was that lecture of any help to you, Captain?"

"A very great help," Delaney said gravely. "You've made a number of things clear. But doctor . . . well, the fault is mine, I suppose, in asking you about 'motives.' You spoke mostly about causes. But what about *motives?* I mean, how does the killer justify to himself what he has done or is doing?"

Dr. Morgenthau stared at him a moment, then laughed shortly. His exhilaration was wearing off, his body seemed to be shrinking as he slumped down into his swivel chair. "Now I know why they call you 'Iron Balls,' " he said. "Oh yes, I know your nickname. During our first—ah—cooperation—I believe it was that Chelsea rapist—I made certain inquiries about you. You interested me."

"Did I?"

"You still do. The nickname is a good one for you, Captain."

"Is it?"

"Oh yes. You are surprisingly intelligent and perceptive for a man in your position. You are remarkably well-read, and you ask the right questions. But do you know what you are, Captain Edward X. Delaney? I mean beneath the intelligence, perception, patience, understanding. Do you know what you are, really?"

"What am I?"

"You are a cop."

"Yes," Delaney agreed readily. "That's what I am all right: a cop." The doctor was drifting away from him; he better finish it up fast.

"Iron balls," Dr. Morgenthau muttered. "Iron soul."

"Yes," Delaney nodded. "Let's get back to this problem of motives. How does the killer justify to himself what he is doing?"

"Highly irrational," Morgenthau said in a slurred voice. "Highly. Most fascinating. They all have elaborate rationalizations. It allows them to do what they do. It absolves them. It makes no sense to so-called 'normal' men, but it relieves the killer of guilt. What they are doing is *necessary.*"

"Such as?"

"What? Well, now we are getting into metaphysics, are we not? Have some ideas. Do a monograph some day. Captain, will you excuse . . ."

He started to lift himself from his chair, but Delaney held out an arm, the palm of his hand turned downward.

"Just a few more minutes," he said firmly, "and then I'll be out of your hair."

Morgenthau fell back into his chair, looked at the Captain with dull, weary eyes.

" 'Iron Balls,' " he said. "The mass killer seeks to impose order on chaos. Not the kind of order you and I want and welcome, but *his* kind of order. World in a ferment. He organizes it. He can't cope. He wants the security of prison. That dear, familiar prison. 'Catch me before I kill again.' You understand? He wants the institution. And if not that, order in the universe. Humanity is disorderly. Unpredictable. So he must work for order. Even if he must kill to attain it. Then he will find peace, because in an ordered world there will be no responsibility."

Delaney wasn't making notes now, but leaning forward listening intently. Dr. Morgenthau looked at him and suddenly yawned, a wide, jaw-cracking yawn. Delaney, unable to help himself, yawned in return.

"Or," Dr. Morgenthau went on, and yawned again (and Delaney yawned in reply), "we have the graffiti artist. Pico 137. Marv 145. Slinky 179. Goddamn it, world, I exist. I am Pico, Marv, Slinky. I have made my mark. You are required to acknowledge my existence. You mother-fuckers, *I am!* So he kills fifteen people or assassinates a President so the world says, 'Yes, Pico, Marv, Slinky, you do exist!' "

Delaney wondered if the man would last. Puffed lids were coming down over dulled eyes, the flesh was slack, swollen fingers plucked at folds of loose skin under the chin. Even the voice had lost its timbre and resolve.

"Or," Morgenthau droned, "or . . ."

Eyes rolled up into his skull until all Delaney could see were clotted whites. But suddenly, pulling himself partly upright, the doctor shook his head wildly, side to side, tiny drops of spittle splattering the glass top of his desk.

"Or alienation," he said thickly. "You cannot relate. Worse. You cannot feel. You want to come close. You want to understand. Truly you do. Come close. To another human being and through him to all humanity and the secret of existence. Captain? Iron Balls? You want to enter into life. Because emotion, feeling, love, ecstasy—all that has been denied you. I said metaphysical. But. That's what you seek. And you cannot find, except by killing. To find your way. And now, Captain Iron Balls, I must . . ."

"I'm going," Delaney said hastily, rising to his feet. "Thank you very much, doctor. You've been a big help."

"Have I?" Morgenthau said vaguely. He staggered upward, made it on the second try, headed toward his inner office.

Delaney paused with his hand on the knob of the reception room door. Then he turned.

"Doctor," he said sharply.

Morgenthau turned slowly, staggered, looked at him through unseeing eyes.

"Who?" he asked.

"Captain Delaney. One more thing . . . This killer we've been discussing has snuffed three men. No women or children. He kills with an ice ax, with a pointed pick. A phallus. I know I'm talking like an amateur now. But could he be a homosexual? Latent maybe? Fighting it. Is it possible?"

Morgenthau stared at him, and before Delaney's eyes he melted farther into his oversize clothes, his face decayed and fell, the light vanished from his eyes.

"Possible?" he whispered. "Anything is possible."

2

Delaney watched, with anger and dismay, as Operation Lombard fell apart. It had been a viable concept—a temporary horizontal organization cutting across precinct lines and the chain of command—and under Chief Pauley, with his talent for organization and administrative genius, it had had a good chance of succeeding. But Pauley had been fired, and under the direction of Deputy Commissioner Broughton, Operation Lombard was foundering.

It was not for lack of energy; Broughton had plenty of that—too much. But he simply didn't have the experience to oversee a manhunt of this size and complexity. And he didn't know the men working for him. He sent weapons specialists halfway across the country to interrogate a recaptured escapee from a mental institution, and he used interrogation experts to check birth and marriage records in musty libraries. He dispatched four men in a car with screaming siren to question a suspect, where one man on foot would have obtained better results. And his paper work was atrocious; from reading the Operation Lombard reports, Delaney could tell it was getting out of hand; Broughton was detailing men to tasks that had been checked out weeks ago by Chief Pauley; reports were in the file, if Broughton knew where to look.

It was Thomas Handry, now calling Delaney at least twice a week, who described another of Broughton's failures: his ineptitude at handling the news media. Broughton made the fatal error of continually promising more than he could deliver, and newsmen became disillusioned with his "An arrest is expected momentarily" or "I'll have a *very* important announcement tomorrow" or "We have a suspect in custody who looks very hot." According to Handry, few reporters now bothered to attend Broughton's daily news briefings; he had earned the sobriquet of "Deputy Commissioner Bullshit."

Medical Examiner Sanford Ferguson also called. He wanted to tell Delaney that the Olfactory Analysis Indicator report on tissue taken from Bernard Gilbert's wound had been inconclusive. There could have been trace elements of a light machine oil; it could also have been half a dozen similar substances. Ferguson was trying again with scrapings from the fatal wound of Detective Roger Kope.

"Did you tell Broughton anything about this?"

"That son of a bitch? Don't be silly. He's caused us more trouble—I can't begin to tell you. It's not the work we mind, it's the bastard's *manner.*"

Then Ferguson detailed some Departmental gossip:

Broughton was in real trouble. Demands from wealthy east side residents of the 251st Precinct for a quick solution to the three street murders were growing.

A citizens' group had been formed. The Mayor was leaning on the Commissioner, and there were even rumors of the Governor appointing a board of inquiry. The murder of Frank Lombard was bad enough—he had wielded a lot of political clout—but the killing of a police officer had intensified editorial demands for a more productive investigation. Broughton, said Ferguson, had a lighted dynamite stick up his ass.

"It couldn't happen to a nicer guy," he added cheerfully.

Delaney wasted no time savoring the comeuppance of Deputy Commissioner Broughton. Nor did he dwell too long on his own personal guilt in the death of Detective third grade Roger Kope. He had done all he could to alert Broughton to the weapon used and the method of attack. And besides, if the truth be known, he blamed Kope; no officer on decoy should have allowed himself to be taken that way. Kope knew what he was up against and what the stakes were. You could feel horror and sympathy for a man shot down from ambush. But Kope had failed—and paid for it.

Delaney had enough on his plate without guilt feelings about Detective Kope. His amateurs needed constant mothering: telephone calls, personal visits and steady, low-key assurance that what they were doing was of value. So when Christopher Langley called to invite him to dinner with the Widow Zimmerman, and to discuss Langley's progress and future activities later, Delaney accepted promptly. He knew Langley's business could be decided in that phone conversation, but he also knew his physical presence was important to Langley, and he gave up the time gladly.

The dinner, thankfully, was prepared by the dapper little gourmet and served in his apartment, although the Widow Zimmerman had provided an incredibly renitent cheese cake. Delaney brought two bottles of wine, white and red, and they drank them both with Langley's *poulet en cocotte du midi,* since he assured them the business of red for meat and white for fish was pure poppycock.

After the meal, the Widow Zimmerman cleaned up, moving about Christopher Langley's apartment as if she was already mistress—as indeed she probably was, Delaney decided, having intercepted their affectionate glances, sly touchings, and sudden giggles at comments the humor of which he could not detect.

Langley and Delaney sat at the cleared table, sipped brandy, and the ex-curator brought out his lists, records, and notes, all beautifully neat, written out in a scholar's fine hand.

"Now then," he said, handing a paper over to Delaney, "here is a list of all stores and shops in the New York area selling the ice ax. Some call it 'ice ax' and some call it 'ice hammer.' I don't think that's important, do you?"

"No. Not at all."

"Of the five, the three I had checked in red itemize their sales checks, so that the purchase of an ice ax would be on record. Of these three, one does no mail order business and hence has no mailing list. The other two do have mailing lists and send out catalogues."

"Good," Delaney nodded. "I'll try to get copies of the mailing lists and their sales checks."

"I should warn you," Langley said, "not all these stores carry the same ax I found at Outside Life. The axes are similar in design, but they are not identical. I found one from Austria, one from Switzerland, and one made in America. The other two were identical to the Outside Life ax made in West Germany. I've marked all this on the list."

"Fine. Thank you. Well . . . where do we go from here?"

"I think," Christopher Langley said thoughtfully, "I should first concentrate on the West German ax, the one Outside Life sells. They're by far the largest outlet for mountaineering equipment in this area—and the least expensive, incidentally. I'll try to identify the manufacturer, the importer, and all retail outlets in this country that handle that particular ax. How does that sound?"

"Excellent. Just right. You're doing a marvelous job on this, Mr. Langley."

"Oh well, you know . . ."

When he left them, the Widow Zimmerman was washing dishes, and Christopher Langley was drying.

Delaney spent the next two days checking on Langley's list of stores in the New York area that sold ice axes and kept itemized sales checks. The one that did no mail order business and had no mailing list was willing to cooperate and lend Delaney the sales slips. He made arrangements to have them delivered to Calvin Case. The Captain wasn't optimistic about results; this particular store kept the checks for only six months.

Of the other two stores, Delaney was able to obtain checks and mailing lists from only one. The owner of the other simply refused to cooperate, claiming his mailing list was a carefully guarded business secret, of value to competitors, and Delaney couldn't have it without a court order. The Captain didn't push it; he could always come back to it later.

So he now had two more shipments of itemized sales checks for Calvin Case and another mailing list for Monica Gilbert. He decided to tackle Case first. He called, then subwayed down about noon.

The change in Calvin Case was a delight. He was clean, his hair cut and combed, his beard trimmed. He sat in pajamas in his aluminum and plastic wheelchair at his desk, flipping through Outside Life sales checks. Delaney had brought him a bottle, the same brand of whiskey Case had been drinking when Delaney first met him. The crippled mountaineer looked at the bottle and laughed.

"Thanks a lot," he said, "but I never touch the stuff now until the sun goes down. You?"

"No. Thanks. It's a bribe. I've got bad news for you."

"Oh?"

"We've found two more stores that sell ice axes. Ice hammers, I guess you'd say. Anyway, these stores have itemized sales checks."

Unexpectedly, Calvin Case smiled. "So?" he asked.

"Will you be willing to go through them?"

"Is it going to help?"

"Damned right," Delaney said fervently.

"Pile it on," Case grinned. "I ain't going no place. The more the merrier."

"Very few receipts," Delaney assured him. "I mean," he added hastily, "compared to Outside Life. One store keeps them for six months, and the other store for a year. How you coming?"

"Okay. Another three days, I figure. Then what happens?"

"Then you'll have a file of all ice ax purchases made at Outside Life in the past seven years. Right? Then I'll give you a map of the Two-five-one Precinct, and you'll go through your file and pull every sales check for an ice ax in the Precinct."

Case stared at him a long moment, then shook his head.

"Delaney," he said, "you're not a detective; you're a fucking bookkeeper. You know that?"

"That's right," the Captain agreed readily. "No doubt about it."

He was going down the stairs when he met Evelyn Case coming up. He took off his hat, nodded, and smiled. She put down her shopping bag to grab him in her arms, hug him, kiss his cheek.

"He's wonderful," she said breathlessly. "Just the way he used to be. And it's all your doing."

"Is it?" Delaney asked wonderingly.

His next meet had to be with Monica Gilbert, for he now had another mailing list for her to check. But she called him first and told him she had completed the Outside Life mailing list, had made out a file card for every resident of the 251st

Precinct on the list, and had a typed record of those residents, a master and two carbon copies, just as he had instructed.

He was amazed and delighted she had completed her job so quickly . . . and a little worried that she had not been as meticulous as he wanted her to be. But he had to work with what he had, and he arranged to meet her at her home the following evening. She asked him if he would care to come for dinner but he declined, with thanks; he would dine early (he lied) before he visited his wife at the hospital, and then be over later. Though why he had accepted Christopher Langley's dinner invitation and not Monica Gilbert's, he could not have said.

He bought two stuffed toys for the young daughters: a black and a white poodle. When you pressed their stomachs, they made a funny barking, squeaking sound. When he arrived, Mary and Sylvia were already in their little nightgowns, but Mrs. Gilbert allowed them out of their bedroom to say hello to the visitor. They were delighted with their presents and finally retired (pushed) to their bedroom, arguing about which poodle had the more ferocious expression. For a half-hour afterwards the adults heard the squeal of pressed toys. But the sounds gradually grew more infrequent, then ceased, and then Monica Gilbert and Edward Delaney were alone, in silence.

Finally: "Thank you for thinking of the girls," she said warmly.

"My pleasure. They're lovely kids."

"It was very kind of you. You like children?"

"Oh yes. Very much. I have a son and a daughter."

"Married?"

"My daughter is. She's expecting. Any day now."

"Her first?"

"Yes."

"How wonderful. You'll be a grandfather."

"Yes," he laughed with delight. "So I will."

She served coffee and almond-flavored cookies, so buttery he knew immediately they were homemade. His mother had made cookies like that. He put on his heavy glasses to inspect what she had done, while he sipped black coffee and nibbled cookies.

He saw immediately he needn't have doubted her swift efficiency. There had been 116 residents of the 251st Precinct on the Outside Life mailing list. She had made out a file card for each one: last name first in capital letters, followed by the given name and middle initial. Beneath the name was typed the address, in two lines. Then she had made a master list and two carbons from the cards, now neatly filed alphabetically in a wooden box.

"Very good," he nodded approvingly. "Excellent. Now I have some bad news for you; I have another mailing list from another store." He smiled at her. "Willing?"

She smiled in return. "Yes. How many names?"

"I estimate about a third of the number of the Outside Life list; maybe less. And you'll probably find duplications. If you do, don't make out a separate card, just note on the Outside Life card that the individual is also on this list. Okay?"

"Yes. What happens now?"

"To your typed list, you mean? You keep one carbon. Just stick it away somewhere as insurance. I'll keep the other carbon. The original will go to friends in the Department. They'll check the names with city, state, and federal files to see if anyone listed has a criminal record."

"A record?"

"Sure. Been charged, been convicted of any crime. Been sentenced. Fined, on probation, or time in jail."

She was disturbed; he could see it.

"Will this help find the man who killed my husband?"

"Yes," he said decisively, paused a moment, staring at her, then asked, "What's bothering you?"

"It seems so—so unfair," she said faintly.

He became suddenly aware of her as a woman: the solid, warm body beneath the black dress, the strong arms and legs, the steady look of purpose. She was not a beautiful woman, not as delicate as Barbara nor as fine. But there was a peasant sensuality to her; her smell was deep and disturbing.

"What's unfair?" he asked quietly.

"Hounding men who have made one mistake. You do it all the time I suppose."

"Yes," he nodded, "we do it all the time. You know what the recidivist rate is, Mrs. Gilbert? Of all the men present in prison, about eighty percent have been behind bars at least once before."

"It still seems—"

"Percentages, Mrs. Gilbert: We've got to use them. We know that if a man rapes, robs, or kills once, the chances are he'll rape, rob, or kill again. We can't deny that. We didn't create that situation, but we'd be fools to overlook it."

"But doesn't police surveillance, the constant hounding of men with records, contribute to—"

"No," he shook his great head angrily. "If an ex-con wants to go straight, really wants to, he will. I'm not going to tell you there have never been frames of ex-cons. Of course there have. But generally, when a man repeats, he wants to go back behind bars. Did you know that? There's never been a study of it, to my knowledge, but my guess is that most two-and-three-time losers are asking for it. They need the bars. They can't cope on the outside. I'm hoping a check on your list will turn up a man or men like that. If not, it may turn up *something.* A similar case, a pattern of violence, *something* that may give me a lead."

"Does that mean if you get a report that some poor man on this list forged a check or deserted his wife, you'll swoop down on him and demand to know where he was on the night my husband and those other men were killed?"

"Of course not. Nothing like that. First of all, criminals can be classified. They have their specialties, and rarely vary. Some deal strictly in white-collar crime: embezzlement, bribery, patent infringement—things like that. Crimes against property, mostly. Then there's a grey area: forgery, swindling, fraud, and so forth. Still crimes against property, but now the victim tends to be an individual rather than the government or the public. And then there's the big area of conventional crime: homicide, kidnapping, robbery, and so forth. These are usually crimes of violence during which the criminal actually sees and has physical contact with his victim; and infliction of injury or death usually results. Or, at least, the potential is there. I'm looking for a man with a record in this last classification, a man with a record of violence, physical violence."

"But—but how will you *know?* What if one of the men on that list was arrested for beating his wife? That's certainly violent, isn't it? Does that make him the killer?"

"Not necessarily, though I'd certainly check him out. But I'm looking for a man who fits a profile?"

She stared at him, not understanding. "A profile?"

He debated if he should tell her, but felt a need to impress her, couldn't resist it, and wondered why that was.

"Mrs. Gilbert, I have a pretty good idea—a pretty good *visualization* of the man who's doing these killings. He's young—between thirty-five and forty—tall and slender. He's in good health and strong. His physical reactions are very fast. He's probably a bachelor. He may be a latent homosexual. He dresses very well, but conservatively. Dark suits. If you passed him on the street at night, you'd feel perfectly safe. He probably has a good job and handles it well. There's nothing about him that would make people suspect him. But he's addicted to danger, to taking risks. He's a mountain climber. He's cool, determined, and I'm positive he's a resident of this neighborhood. Certainly of this precinct. And tall. Did I say he was tall? Yes, I did. Well, he's probably six feet or over."

Her astonishment was all he could have asked, and he cursed his own ego for showing off in this fashion.

"But how do you know all this?" she said finally.

He rose to his feet and began to gather his papers together. He was so disgusted with himself.

"Sherlock Holmes," he said sourly. "It's all guesswork, Mrs. Gilbert. Forget it. I was just shooting off my mouth."

She followed him to the door.

"I'm sorry about what I said," she told him, putting a strong hand on his arm. "I mean about how cruel it is to check men with records. I know you've got to do it."

"Yes," he nodded. "I've got to do it. Percentages."

"Captain, please do everything you think should be done. I don't know anything about it. This is all new to me."

He smiled at her without speaking.

"I'll get on the new list tonight. And thank you, Captain."

"For what?"

"For doing what you're doing."

"I haven't done anything yet except give you work to do."

"You're going to get him, aren't you?"

"Listen," Delaney said, "could we—"

He stopped suddenly and was silent. She was puzzled. "Could we what?" she asked finally.

"Nothing," he said. "Good-night, Mrs. Gilbert. Thank you for the coffee and cookies."

He walked home, resolutely turning his mind from the thought of what a fool he had made of himself—in his own eyes if not in hers. He stopped at a phone booth to call Deputy Inspector Thorsen, and waited five minutes until Thorsen called him back.

"Edward?"

"Yes."

"Anything new?"

"I have a list of a hundred and sixteen names and addresses. I need them checked out against city, state, and federal records."

"My God."

"It's important."

"I know, Edward. Well . . . at least we've got some names. That's more than Broughton has."

"I hear he's in trouble."

"You hear right."

"Heavy?"

"Not yet. But it's growing. Everyone's leaning on him."

"About this list of mine—I'll get it to your office tomorrow by messenger. All right?"

"Better send it to my home."

"All right, and listen, please include the State Department of Motor Vehicles and the NYPD's Special Services Branch. Can you do that?"

"We'll have to do it."

"Yes."

"Getting close, Edward?"

"Well . . . closer."

"You think he's on the list?"

"He better be," Delaney said. Everyone was leaning on him, too.

He was weary now, wanting nothing but a hot shower, a rye highball, perhaps a sleeping pill, and bed. But he had his paper work to do, and drove himself to it. What was it Case called him—a fucking bookkeeper.

He finished his writing, his brain frazzled, and filed his neat folders away. He drained his highball, watery now, and considered the best way to handle results from the search of records of those 116 individuals, when they began to come in on printouts from city, state, and federal computers.

What he would do, he decided, was this: he would ask Monica Gilbert to make notations of any criminal history on the individual cards. He would buy five or six packages of little colored plastic tabs, the kind that could be clipped on the upper edge of file cards. He would devise a color code: a red tab attached to a card would indicate a motor vehicle violation, a blue tab would indicate a New York City criminal record . . . and so forth. When reports were in from all computers, he could then look at Monica Gilbert's file box and, without wasting time flipping through 116 cards, see at a glance which had one, two, three or more plastic tabs attached to their upper edges. He thought it over, and it seemed an efficient plan.

His mind was working so sluggishly that it was some time before he wondered why he hadn't brought Monica Gilbert's card file home with him, to keep in his own study. The computer printouts Thorsen would obtain would be delivered to him, Delaney. He could make handwritten notations on individual cards himself and attach the color-coded plastic tabs. It wasn't necessary for him to run over to Mrs. Gilbert's apartment to consult the file every time he needed to. So why . . . Still . . . She *was* efficient and he couldn't do everything . . . Still . . . Had he angered her? If she . . . Barbara . . .

He dragged himself up to bed, took no shower and no sleeping pill, but lay awake for at least an hour, trying to understand himself. Not succeeding, he finally slid into a thin sleep.

3

It began to come together. Slowly. What he had set in motion. The first report on the 116 names came from the New York State Department of Motor Vehicles: a neatly folded computer printout, an original and six copies. Delaney took a quick look, noted there were 11 individuals listed, tore off a carbon for his own file, and took the report over to Monica Gilbert. He explained what he wanted:

"It's easy to read once you get the hang of it. It's computer printing—all capitals and no punctuation—but don't let that throw you. Now the first one listed is Avery, John H., on East Seventy-ninth Street. You have Avery's card?"

Obediently she flipped through her file and handed him the card.

"Good. Now Avery was charged with going through an unattended toll booth without tossing fifty cents in the hopper. Pleaded guilty, paid a fine. It's printed here in a kind of official lingo, but I'm sure you can make it out. Now I'd like you to make a very brief notation on his card. If you write, 'Toll booth—guilty—fine,' it will be sufficient. I'd also like you to note his license number and make of car, in this case a blue Mercury. All clear?"

"I think so," she nodded. "Let me try the next one myself. 'Blank, Daniel G., on East Eighty-third Street; two arrests for speeding, guilty, fined. Black Corvette and then his license number.' Is that what you want on this card?"

"Right. In case you're wondering, I'm not going to lean on these particular people. This report is just possible background stuff. The important returns will come from city and federal files. One more thing . . ."

He showed her the multicolored plastic tabs he had purchased in a stationery store, and explained the color code he had written out for her. She consulted it and clipped red tabs onto the top edges of the AVERY and BLANK cards. It looked very efficient, and he was satisfied.

Calvin Case called to report he had finished going through the Outside Life sales checks and had a file of 234 purchases of ice axes made in the past seven years. Delaney brought him a hand-drawn map of the 251st Precinct, and by the next day Case had separated those purchases made by residents of the Precinct. There were six of them. Delaney took the six sales checks, went home, and made two lists. One was for his file, one he delivered to Monica Gilbert so she could make notations on the appropriate cards and attach green plastic tabs. He had hardly returned home when she called. She was troubled because one of the six ice ax purchasers was not included in her master file of Outside Life customers. She gave him the name and address.

Delaney laughed. "Look," he said, "don't let it worry you. We can't expect perfection. It was probably human error; it usually is. For some reason this particular customer wasn't included on the mailing list. Who knows—maybe he said he didn't want their catalogue; he doesn't like junk mail. Just make out a card for him."

"Yes, Edward."

He was silent. It was the first time she had used his given name. She must have realized what she had done for suddenly she said, in a rush, "Yes, Captain."

"Edward is better," he told her, and they said goodby.

Now he could call her Monica.

Back to his records, remembering to start a new list for Thorsen headed by the single ax purchaser not included on the original list. Two days later Monica Gilbert had finished going through the new mailing list he had given her, and 34 more names were added to her master file and to the new list for Thorsen. And two days after that, Calvin Case had finished flipping through sales checks of the two additional New York stores that sold ice axes, and the names of three more purchasers in the 251st Precinct were added to Monica's file, green plastic tabs attached, and the names also added to the new Thorsen list. Delaney had it delivered to the Deputy Inspector.

Meanwhile computer printouts were coming in on the original 116, and Monica Gilbert was making notations on her cards, and attaching colored tabs to indicate the source of the information. Meanwhile Calvin Case was breaking down his big file of Outside Life receipts of sales of any type of mountaineering equipment, to extract those of residents of the 251st Precinct. Meanwhile Christopher Langley was visiting official German agencies in New York to determine the manufacturer, importer, jobbers and retail outlets that handled the ice ax in the U.S. Meanwhile, Captain Edward X. Delaney was personally checking out the six people who had purchased ice axes at the other two stores. And reading "Honey Bunch" to his wife.

Ever since he had been promoted from uniformed patrolman to detective third grade, Delaney, following the advice of his first partner—an old, experienced, and alcoholic detective who called him "Buddy Boy"—had collected business cards. If he was given a card by a banker, shoe salesman, mortician, insurance agent, private investigator—whatever—he hung onto it, and it went into a little rubber-banded pack. Just as his mentor had promised, the business cards proved valuable. They provided temporary "cover." People were impressed by them; often they were all the identification he needed to be banker, shoe salesman, mortician, insurance agent, private investigtor—whatever. That little bit of pasteboard was a passport; few people investigated his identity further. When he passed printing shops advertising "100 Business Cards for $5.00" he could understand how easily conmen and swindlers operated.

Now he made a selection of his collected cards and set out to investigate personally the nine residents of the 251st Precinct who had purchased ice axes in the past seven years. He had arranged the nine names and addresses according to location, so he wouldn't have to retrace his steps or end the day at the other end of the Precinct. This was strictly a walking job, and he dug out an old pair of shoes he had worn on similar jobs in the past. They were soft, comfortable kangaroo leather with high laced cuffs that came up over his ankles.

He waited until 9:00 A.M., then began his rounds, speaking only to doormen, supers, landlords, neighbors . . .

"Good morning. My name's Barrett, of Acme Insurance. Here's my card. But I don't want to sell you anything. I'm looking for a man named David Sharpe. He was listed as beneficiary on one of our policies and has some money coming to him. He live here?"

"Who?"

"David Sharpe."

"I don't know him."

"This is the address we have for him."

"Nah, I never—wait . . . What's his name?"

"David Sharpe."

"Oh yeah. Chris', he move away almost two years ago."

"Oh. I don't suppose you have any forwarding address?"

"Nah. Try the post office."

"That's a good idea. I'll try them."

And plucking his business card back, Delaney trudged on.

"Good morning. My name's Barrett, of Acme Insurance. Here's my card. But I don't want to sell you anything. I'm looking for a man named Arnold K. Abel. He was listed as beneficiary on one of our policies and has some money coming to him. He—"

"Tough shit. He's dead."

"Dead?"

"Yeah. Remember that plane crash last year? It landed short and went into Jamaica Bay."

"Yes, I remember that."

"Well, Abel was on it."

"I'm sorry to hear that."

"Yeah, he was a nice guy. A lush but a nice guy. He always give me a tenner at Christmas."

And then something happened he should have expected.

"Good morning," he started his spiel, "I'm—"

"Hell, I know you, Captain Delaney. I was on that owners' protective committee you started. Don't you remember me? The name's Goldenberg."

"Of course, Mr. Goldenberg. How are you?"

"Healthy, thank God. And you, Captain?"

"Can't complain."

"I was sorry to hear you retired."

"Well . . . not retired exactly. Just temporary leave of absence. But things piled up and I'm spending a few hours a day helping out the new commander. You know?"

"Oh sure. Breaking him in—right?"

"Right. Now we're looking for a man named Simmons. Walter J. Simmons. He's not wanted or anything like that, but he was a witness to a robbery about a year ago, and now we got the guy we think pulled the job, and we hoped this Simmons could identify him."

"Roosevelt Hospital, Captain. He's been in there almost six months now. He's one of these mountain climbers, and he fell and got all cracked up. From what I hear, he'll never be the same again."

"I'm sorry to hear that. But he still may be able to testify. I better get over there. Thank you for your trouble."

"My pleasure, Captain. Tell me the truth, what do you think about this new man, this Dorfman?"

"Good man," Delaney said promptly.

"With these three murders we've had in the last few months and the dingaling still running around free? What's this Dorfman doing about that?"

"Well, it's out of his hands, Mr. Goldenberg. The investigation is being handled personally by Deputy Commissioner Broughton."

"I read, I read. But it's Dorfman's precinct—right?"

"Right," Delaney said sadly.

So the day went. It was a disaster. Of the nine ice ax purchasers, three had moved out of the precinct, one had died, one was hospitalized, and one had been on a climbing tour in Europe for the past six months.

That left three possibles. Delaney made a hurried visit to Barbara, then spent the evening checking out the three, this time questioning them personally, giving his name and showing his shield and identification. He didn't tell them the reason for his questions, and they didn't ask. The efforts of Delaney, New York Police Department, were no more productive than those of Barrett, Acme Insurance.

One purchaser was an octogenarian who had bought the ax as a birthday present for a 12-year-old great-grandson.

One was a sprightly, almost maniacal young man who assured Delaney he had given up mountain climbing for skydiving. "Much more machismo, man!" At Delaney's urging, he dug his ax out of a back closet. It was dusty, stained, pitted with rust, and the Captain wondered if it had ever been used, for anything.

The third was a young man who, when he answered Delaney's ring, seemed at first sight to fit the profile: tall, slender, quick, strong. But behind him, eyeing the unexpected visitor nervously and curiously, was his obviously pregnant wife. Their apartment was a shambles of barrels and cartons; Delaney had interrupted their packing; they were moving in two days since, with the expected new arrival, they would need more room. When the Captain brought up the subject of the ice ax, they both laughed. Apparently, one of the conditions she had insisted on, before marrying him, was that he give up mountain climbing. So he had, and quite voluntarily he showed Delaney his ice ax. They had been using it as a general purpose hammer; the head was scarred and nicked. Also, they had tried to use the spike to pry open a painted-shut window and suddenly, without warning, the pick of the ice ax had just snapped off. And it was supposed to be steel. Wasn't that the damndest thing? they asked. Delaney agreed despondently it was the damndest thing he ever heard.

He walked home slowly, thinking he had been a fool to believe it would be easy. Still, it was the obvious thing to trace weapon to source to buyer. It had to be done, and he had done it. Nothing. He knew how many other paths he could now take, but it was a disappointment; he admitted it. He had hoped—just hoped—that one of those cards with the green plastic tab would be the one.

His big worry was time. All this checking of sales receipts and list making and setting up of card files and questioning innocents—time! It all took days and weeks, and meanwhile this nut was wandering the streets and, as past histories of similar crimes indicated, the intervals between murders became shorter and shorter.

When he got home he found a package Mary had signed for. He recognized it as coming from Thorsen by commercial messenger. He tore it open and when he saw what it was, he didn't look any further. It was a report from the Records

Division, New York Police Department, including the Special Services Branch. That completed the check on criminal records of the original 116 names.

He had been doing a curious thing. As reports came in from federal, state, and local authorities, he had been tearing off a carbon for his files, then delivering the other copies to Monica Gilbert for notation and tabbing in her master file. He didn't read the reports himself; he didn't even glance at them. He told himself the reason for this was that he couldn't move on individuals with criminal records until *all* the reports were in and recorded on Monica's file cards. Then he'd be able to see at a glance how many men had committed how many offenses. That's what he told himself.

He also told himself he was lying—to himself.

The real reason he was following this procedure was very involved, and he wasn't quite sure he understood it. First of all, being a superstitious cop, he had the feeling that Monica Gilbert had brought him and would bring him luck. Somehow, through her efforts, solely or in part, he'd find the lead he needed. The second thing was that he hoped these computer printouts of criminal records would lead to the killer and thus prove to Monica he had merely been logical and professional when he had requested them. He had seen it in her eyes when he told her what he was about to do; she had thought him a brutal, callous—well, a *cop*, who had no feeling or sympathy for human frailty. That was, he assured himself, simply not true.

Unlacing his high shoes, peeling off his sweated socks, he paused a moment, sock in hand, and wondered why her good opinion of him was so important to him. He thought of her, of her heavy muscular haunches moving slowly under the thin black dress, and he realized to his shame that he was beginning to get an erection. He had had no sex since Barbara became ill, and his "sacrifice" seemed so much less than her pain that he couldn't believe what he was dreaming: the recent widow of a murder victim . . . while Barbara . . . and he . . . He snorted with disgust at himself, took a tepid shower, donned fresh pajamas, and got out of bed an hour later, wide-eyed and frantic, to gulp two sleeping pills.

He delivered the new report to her the next morning and refused her offer to stay for coffee and Danish. Did she seem hurt? He thought so. Then, sighing, he spent a whole day—time! time!—doing what he had to do and what he knew would be of no value whatsoever: he checked those purchasers of ice axes who had moved, died, were abroad, or hospitalized. The results, as he knew they would, added up to zero. They really had moved, died, were abroad, or hospitalized.

Mary had left a note that Mrs. Gilbert had called, and would the Captain please call her back. So he did, immediately, and there was no coolness in her voice he could detect. She told him she had completed noting all the reported criminal records in her master file, and had attached appropriately colored plastic tabs. He asked her if she'd care to have lunch with him at 1:00 P.M. the following day, and she accepted promptly.

They ate at a local seafood restaurant and had identical luncheons: crabmeat salads with a glass of white wine. They spent a pleasant hour and half together, talking of the pains and pleasures of life in the city. She told him of her frustrated efforts to grow geraniums in window boxes; he told her of how, for years, Barbara and he had tried to grow flowers and flowering shrubs in their shaded backyard, had finally surrendered to the soot and sour soil, and let the ivy take over. Now it was a jungle of ivy and, surprisingly, rather pretty.

He told her about Barbara while they sipped coffee. She listened intently and finally asked:

"Do you think you should change doctors?"

"I don't know what to do," he confessed. "He's always been her physician, and she has great faith in him. I couldn't bring someone else in without her permission. He's trying everything he can, I'm sure. And there are consultants in on this. But she shows no improvement. In fact, it seems to me she's just wasting away, just fading. My son was up to visit a few weeks ago and was shocked at how she looked. So thin and flushed and drawn. And occasionally now she's irrational. Just for short periods of time."

"That could be the fever, or even the antibiotics she's getting."

"I suppose so," he nodded miserably. "But it frightens me. She was always so—so sharp and perceptive. Still is, when she isn't floating off in never-never land. Well . . . I didn't invite you to lunch to cry on your shoulder. Tell me about your girls. How are they getting along in school?"

She brightened, and told him about their goodness and deviltry, things they had said and how different their personalities were, one from the other. He listened with interest, smiling, remembering the days when Eddie and Liza were growing up, and wondering if he was now paying for that happiness.

"Well," he said, after she finished her coffee, "can we go back to your place? I'd like to take a look at that card file. All the reports finished?"

"Yes," she nodded, "everything's entered. I'm afraid you're going to be disappointed."

"I usually am," he said wryly.

"Oh well," she smiled, "these are only the unsuccessful criminals."

"Pardon?" he asked, not realizing at first that she was teasing him.

"Well, when a man has a record, it proves he was an inefficient criminal, doesn't it? He got caught. If he was good at his job, he wouldn't have a record."

"Yes," he laughed. "You're right."

They stood and moved to the cashier's desk, Delaney had his wallet out, but the manager, who had apparently been waiting for this moment, moved in close, smiling, and said to the cashier, "No check for Captain Delaney."

He looked up in surprise. "Oh . . . hello, Mr. Varro. How are you?"

"Bless God, okay, Captain. And you?"

"Fine. Thanks for the offer, but I'm afraid I can't accept it, I'm not on active duty, you know. Leave of absence. And besides"—he gestured toward Monica Gilbert who was watching this scene closely—"this young lady is a witness, and I wouldn't want her to think I was accepting a bribe."

They all laughed—an easy laugh.

"Tell you what," Delaney said, paying his bill, "next time I'll come in alone, order the biggest lobster in the house, and let you pick up the tab. Okay?"

"Sure, okay," Varro smiled. "You know me. Anytime, Captain."

They walked toward Monica's apartment, and she looked up at him curiously. "Will you?" she asked. "Stop in for a free meal, I mean?"

"Sure," he said cheerfully. "He'd be hurt if I didn't. Varro is all right. The best men stop in for coffee almost every day. The squad car men do, too. Not all of them take, but I'd guess most of them do. It doesn't mean a thing. Happens in a hundred restaurants and bars and hotdog stands and pizza parlors in the Precinct. Are you going to say, 'Petty graft'? You're right, but most cops are struggling to get their kids to college on a cop's pay, and a free lunch now and then is more important than you think. When I said it doesn't mean a thing, I meant that if any of these generous owners and managers get out of line, they'll be leaned on like anyone else. A free cup of coffee doesn't entitle them to anything but a friendly hello. Besides, Varro owes me a favor. About two years ago he discovered he was losing stuff from his storeroom. It wasn't the usual pilferage—a can or package now and then. This stuff was disappearing in *cases*. So he came to me, and I called in Jeri Fernandez who was lieutenant of our precinct detective squad at that time. Jeri put a two-man stakeout watching the back alley. The first night they were there—the *first* night!—this guy pulls up to the back door in a station wagon, unlocks the door cool as you please, and starts bringing up cases and cartons and bags from the basement and loading his wagon. They waited until he had the wagon full and was locking the back door. Then they moved in."

"What did they do?" she asked breathlessly.

Delaney laughed. "They made him unload his station wagon and carry all that stuff back down to the basement again and store it neatly away. They said he was puffing like a whale by the time he got through. He was one of the assistant chefs there and had keys to the back door and storeroom. It really wasn't important enough to bring charges. It would have meant impounding evidence, a lot of paperwork for everyone, time lost in court, and the guy probably would have been fined and put on probation if it was his first offense. So after he finished putting everything back the way it was, Jeri's boys worked him over. Nothing serious. I mean he didn't have to go to the hospital or anything like that, but I suppose they marked him up some—a few aches and pains. And of course he was fired. The word got around, and Varro hasn't lost a can of salad oil since. That's why he wanted to buy our lunch."

He looked at her, smiling, and saw her shiver suddenly.

"It's a whole different world," she said in a low voice.

"What is?"

But she didn't answer.

She was right; the criminal records were a disappointment. What he had been hoping was that when the computer printouts were collated and entered on the file cards, there would be a few or several cards with a perfect forest of multicolored plastic tabs clipped to their upper edges, indicating significant criminal records that might show a pattern of psychopathic and uncontrollable violence.

Instead, the card file was distressingly bare. There was one card with three tabs, two with two tabs, and 43 with one tab. None of the nine purchasers of ice axes, who Delaney had already checked out, had a criminal record.

While he went through the tabbed cards, slowly, working at Monica's kitchen table, she had brought in mending, donned a pair of rimless spectacles, and began making a hem on one of the girl's dresses, working swiftly, making small stitches, a thimble and scissors handy. When he had finished the cards, he pushed the file box away from him, and the sound made her look up. He gave her a bleak smile.

"You're right," he said. "A disappointment. One rape, one robbery, one assault with a deadly weapon. And my God, have you ever seen so many income tax frauds in your life!"

She smiled slightly and went back to her sewing. He sat brooding, tapping his pencil eraser lightly on the table top.

"Of course, this is a good precinct," he said, thinking aloud as much as he was talking to her. "I mean 'good' in the sense of better than East Harlem and Bedford-Stuyvesant. The per capita income is second highest of all the precincts in the city, and the rates of crimes of violence are in the lower third. I'm speaking of Manhattan, Bronx, and Brooklyn now. Not Queens and Staten Island. So I should have expected a high preponderance of white-collar crime. Did you notice the tax evasions, unscrupulous repair estimates, stock swindles—things like that? But still . . . What I didn't really consider is that all these cards, all these individuals—by the way, did you see that there are only four women in the whole file?—these individuals are all presumably mountain climbers or have bought gifts for mountain climbers or are outdoorsmen of one type or another: hunters, fishermen, boat owners, hikers, campers, and so forth. That means people with enough money for a leisure hobby. And lack of money is usually the cause of violent crime. So what we've got is a well-to-do precinct and a file of people who can afford to spend money, heavy money, on their leisuretime activities. I guess I was foolish to expect mountain climbers and deep-sea fishermen to have the same percentage of records as people in the ghettos. Still . . . it is a disappointment."

"Discouraged?" she asked quietly, not looking up.

"Monica," he said, and at this tone of voice she did look up to find him smiling at her. "I'm never discouraged," he said. "Well . . . hardly ever. I'll check out the rape, the robbery, and the assault. If nothing comes of that, there's a lot more I can do. I'm just getting started."

She nodded, and went back to her mending. He took notes on the three records of violent crimes included on the file cards. For good measure, although he thought the chances were nil, he added the names and addresses of men convicted of vandalism, extortion, and safe-breaking. He glanced at his watch, a thick hunter his grandfather had owned, and saw he had time to check out three or four of the men with records.

He rose, she put aside her sewing and stood up, and they took off their glasses simultaneously, and laughed together, it seemed like such an odd thing.

"I hope your wife is feeling better soon," she said, walking him to the door.

"Thank you."

"I'd—I'd like to meet her," she said faintly. "That is, if you think it's all right. I mean, I have time on my hands now that the file is finished, and I could go over and sit with—"

He turned to her eagerly. "Would you? My God, that would be wonderful! I know you two will get along. She'll like you, and you'll like her. I try to get there twice a day, but sometimes I don't. We have friends who come to see her. At least at first they did. But—you know—they don't come too often anymore. I'll go over with you and introduce you, and then if you could just stop by occasionally . . ."

"Of course. I'll be happy to."

"Thank you. You're very kind. And thank you for having lunch with me. I really enjoyed it."

She held out her hand. He was surprised, a second, then grasped it, and they shook. Her grip was dry, her flesh firm, the hand unexpectedly strong.

He went out into the dull winter afternoon, the sky tarnished pewter, and glanced at his list to see who he should hit first. But curiously he was not thinking of the list, nor of Monica Gilbert, nor of Barbara. Something was nibbling at the edge of his mind, something that had to do with the murders. It was something he had heard recently; someone had said something. But what it was he could not identify. It hovered there, tantalizing, teasing, until finally he shook his head, put it away from him, and started tramping the streets.

He got home a little after ten that evening, his feet aching (he had not worn his "cop shoes"), and so soured with frustration that he whistled and thought of daffodils—anything to keep from brooding on false leads and time wasted. He soaked under a hot shower and washed his hair. That made him feel a little better. He pulled on pajamas, robe, slippers, and went down to the study.

During the afternoon and evening he had checked out five of the six on his list. The rapist and the robber were still in prison. The man convicted of assault with a deadly weapon had been released a year ago, but was not living at the address given. It would have to be checked with his parole officer in the morning. Of the other three, the safe-breaker was still in prison, the vandal had moved to Florida two months ago and considerately left a forwarding address, and Delaney was just too damned tired to look for the extortionist, but would the next day.

He stolidly wrote out reports on all his activities and added them to his files. Then he made his nightly tour of inspection, trying locks on all windows and outside doors. Lights out and up to bed. It wasn't midnight, but he was weary. He was really getting too old for this kind of nonsense. No pill tonight. Blessed sleep would come easily.

While he waited for it, he wondered if it was wise to introduce Monica Gilbert to his wife. He had said they would hit it off, and they probably would. Barbara would certainly feel sympathy for a murder victim's widow. But would she think . . . would she imagine . . . But she had asked him to . . . Oh, he didn't know, couldn't judge. He'd bring them together, once at least, and see what happened.

Then he turned his thoughts to what had been nagging his brain since he left Monica's apartment that afternoon. He was a firm believer in the theory that if you fell asleep with a problem on your mind—a word you were trying to remember, an address, a name, a professional or personal dilemma—you would awake refreshed and the magic solution would be there, the problem solved in your subconscious while you slept.

He awoke the next morning, and the problem still existed, gnawing at his memory. But now it was closer; it was something Monica had said at their luncheon. He tried to remember their conversation in every detail: she had talked about her geraniums, he had talked about his ivy; she had talked about her children, he had talked about Barbara. Then Varro tried to pick up the check, and he, Delaney, told her about the breakin at the restaurant. But what the hell did all that have to do with the price of eggs in China? He shook his head disgustedly and went in to shave.

He spent the morning tracking down the extortionist, the last man of the six in Monica Gilbert's file with a record of even mildly violent crime. Delaney finally found him pressing pants in a little tailor shop on Second Avenue. The extortionist was barely five feet tall, at least 55 and 175 pounds, pasty-faced, with trembling hands and watery eyes. What in Gods name did he ever extort? Delaney muttered something about "mistaken identity" and departed as fast as he could, leaving the fat little man in a paroxysm of trembling and watering.

He went directly to the hospital, helped feed Barbara her noon meal, and then read to her for almost an hour from "Honey Bunch: Her First Little Garden." Strangely, the reading soothed him as much as it did her, and when he returned home he was in a somber but not depressed mood—a mood to work steadily without questioning the why's or wherefore's.

He spent an hour on his personal affairs: checks, investments, bank balances, tax estimates, charitable contributions. He cleaned up the month's accumulated shit, paid what he had to pay, wrote a letter to his accountant, made out a deposit for his savings account and a withdrawal against his checking account for current expenses.

Envelopes were sealed, stamped, and put on the hall table where he'd be sure to see them and pick them up for mailing the next time he went out. Then he returned to the study, drew the long legal pad toward him, and began listing his options.

1. He could begin personally investigating *every* name in Monica's card file. He estimated there were about 155.

2. He could wait for Christopher Langley's report, and then contact, by mail or phone, every retail outlet for the West German ice ax in the U.S.

3. He could wait for Calvin Case's file of everyone in the 251st Precinct who had bought any kind of mountaineering equipment whatsoever from Outside Life and that other store that had supplied a mailing list, and then he could ask Monica to double-check her file to make certain she had a card for every customer.

4. He could go back to the store that refused to volunteer sales checks and mailing list, and he could lean on them. If that didn't work, he could ask Thorsen what the chances were for a search warrant.

5. He could recheck his own investigations of the nine ice ax purchases and the six men in the file with a record of violent crime.

6. He could finally get to his early idea of determining if there was a magazine

for mountain climbers and he could borrow their subscription list; if there was a club or society of mountain climbers and he could borrow their membership list; and if it was possible to check the local library on residents of the 251st Precinct who had withdrawn books on mountaineering.

7. If it came to it, he would personally check out every goddamn name of every goddamn New Yorker on the goddamn Outside Life mailing list. There were probably about 10,000 goddamn New Yorkers included, and he'd hunt down every goddamn one of them.

But he was just blathering, and he knew it. If he was commanding the 500 detectives in Operation Lombard he could do it, but not by himself in much less than five years. How many murder victims would there be by then? Oh? . . . probably not more than a thousand or so.

But all this was cheesy thinking. One thing was bothering him, and he knew what it was. When Monica called him to report that one of the ice ax purchasers in Calvin Case's file hadn't been included on her Outside Life mailing list, he had laughed it off as "human error." No one is perfect. People do make mistakes, errors of commission or omission. Quite innocently, of course.

What if Calvin Case, late at night and weary, flipped by the sales check of an ice ax purchaser?

What if Christopher Langley had missed a store in the New York area that sold axes?

What if Monica Gilbert had somehow skipped a record of violent crime on one of the computer reports she noted on her file cards?

And what if he, Captain Edward X. Delaney, had the solution to the whole fucking mess right under his big, beaky nose and couldn't see it because he was stupid, stupid, stupid?

Human errors. And professionals were just as prone to them as Delaney's amateurs. That was why Chief Pauley sent different men back to check the same facts, why he repeated interrogations twice, sometimes three times. My God, even computers weren't perfect. But was there anything he could do about it? No.

So the Captain read over his list of options again and tossed it aside. A lot of shit. He called Monica Gilbert.

"Monica? Edward. Am I disturbing you?"

"Oh no."

"Do you have a few minutes?"

"Do you want to come over?"

"Oh no. I just want to talk to you. About our lunch yesterday. You said something, and I can't remember what it was. I have a feeling it's important, and it's been nagging at me, and I can't for the life of me remember it."

"What was it?"

He broke up: a great blast of raucous laughter. Finally he spluttered, "If I knew, I wouldn't be calling, would I? What did we talk about?"

She wasn't offended by his laughter. "Talk about?" she said. "Let's see . . . I told you about my window boxes, and you told me about your backyard. And then you spoke about your wife's illness, and then we talked about my girls. Going out, the manager tried to pick up the check, and you wouldn't let him. On the way home you told me about the assistant chef who was robbing him."

"No, no," he said impatiently. "It must have been something to do with the case. Did we discuss the case while we were eating?"

"Nooo . . ." she said doubtfully. "After we finished coffee you said we'd come back to my place and you'd go over the cards. Oh yes. You asked if I had finished entering all the reports on the cards, and I said I had."

"And that's all?"

"Yes. Edward, what is this— No, wait a minute. I was teasing you. I said something about the records from the computers just showing unsuccessful criminals, because if they were good at their jobs, they wouldn't have any record, and you laughed and said that was so."

He was silent a moment.

"Monica," he said finally.

"Yes, Edward?"

"I love you," he said, laughing and keeping it light.

"You mean *that's* what you wanted?"

"That's *exactly* what I wanted."

His erratic memory flashed back now, and he recalled talking to Detective Lieutenant Jeri Fernandez on the steps leading up to the second floor of the precinct house. That was when they were breaking up the precinct detective squads.

"What did you get?" Delaney had asked.

"I drew a Safe, Loft, and Truck Division in midtown," Fernandez had said disgustedly.

Now Delaney called Police Information, identified himself, told the operator what he wanted: the telephone number of the new Safe, Loft and Truck Division in midtown Manhattan. He was shunted twice more—it took almost five minutes—but eventually he got the number and, carefully crossing his fingers, dialed and asked for Lieutenant Fernandez. His luck was in; the detective picked up the phone after eight rings.

"Lieutenant Fernandez."

"Captain Edward X. Delaney here."

There was a second of silence, then a jubilant, "Captain! Jesus Christ! This is great! How the hell are you, Captain?"

"Just fine, lieutenant. And you?"

"Up to my ears in shit. Captain, this new system just ain't working. I can tell you. It's a lot of crap. You think I know what's going on? I don't know what's going on. No one knows what's going on. We got guys in here from every precinct in town. They set us all down here, and we're supposed to know all about the garment business. Pilferage, hijacking, fraud, arson, safecracking, the mob—the whole bit. Captain, it's wicked. I tell you, it's *wicked!*"

"Take it easy," Delaney soothed. "Give it a little time. Maybe it'll work out."

"Work out my ass," Fernandez shouted. "Yesterday two of my boys caught a spade taking packages out of the back of a U.S. Mail parcel post truck. Can you imagine that? In broad daylight. It's parked at Thirty-fourth and Madison, and this nut is calmly dragging out two heavy packages and strolling off with them. The U.S. Mail!"

"Lieutenant," Delaney said patiently, "the reason I called, I need some help from you."

"Help?" Fernandez cried. "Jesus Christ, Captain, you name it you got it. You know that. What is it?"

"I remember your telling me, just before the precinct squad was broken up, that you had been working on your open files and sending them to the new detective districts, depending on the nature of the crime."

"That's right, Captain. Took us weeks to get cleaned out."

"Well, what about the garbage? You know—the beef sheets, reports on squeals, tips, diaries, and so forth?"

"All the shit? Most of it was thrung out. What could we do with it? We was sent all over the city, and maybe only one or two guys would be working in the Two-five-one. It was all past history anyway—right? So I told the boys to trash the whole lot and—"

"Well, thanks very much," Delaney said heavily. "I guess that—"

"—except for the last year," Fernandez kept talking, ignoring the Captain's interruption. "I figured the new stuff might mean something to somebody, so we kept the paper that came in the last year, but everything else was thrung out."

"Oh?" Delaney said, still alive. "What did you do with it?"

"It's down in the basement of the precinct house. You know when you go down the stairs and the locker room is off to your right and the detention cells on your left? Well, you go past the cells and past the drunk tank, then turn right. There's this hallway that leads to a flight of stairs and the back door."

"Yes, I remember that. We always closed off that hallway during inspections."

"Right. Well, along that hallway is the broom closet where they keep mops and pails and all that shit, and then farther on toward the back door there's this little storage room with a lot of crap in it. I think it used to be a torture chamber in the old days."

"Yes," Delaney laughed. "Probably was."

"Sure, Captain. The walls are thick and that room's got no windows, so who could hear the screams? Who knows how many crimes got solved in there—right? Anyways, that's where we dumped all the garbage files. But just for the last year. That any help?"

"A lot of help. Thank you very much, lieutenant."

"My pleasure, Captain. Listen, can I ask you a favor now?"

"Of course."

"It's a one-word favor: *Help!* Captain, you got influence and a good rep. Get me out of here, will you? I'm dying here. I don't like the spot and I don't like the guys I'm with. I shuffle papers around all day like some kind of Manchurian idiot, and you think I know what I'm doing? I don' know my ass from my elbow. I want to get out on the street again. The street I know. Can you work it, Captain?"

"What do you want?"

"Assault-Homicide or Burglary," Fernandez said promptly. "I'll even take Narcotics. I know I can't hope for Vice; I ain't pretty enough."

"Well . . ." Delaney said slowly, "I can't promise you anything, but let me see what I can do. Maybe I can work something."

"That's good enough for me," Fernandez said cheerfully. "Many thanks, Captain."

"Thank *you,* lieutenant."

He hung up and stared at the telephone, thinking of what Fernandez had told him. It was a long shot, of course, but it shouldn't take more than a day, and it was better than resigning himself to one of those seven options on his list, most of which offered nothing but hard, grinding labor with no guarantees of success.

When Monica Gilbert had repeated her teasing remark about successful criminals having no record, he had to recognize its truth. But Monica wasn't aware that between a criminal's complete freedom and formal charges against him existed a half-world of documentation: of charges dismissed, of arrests never made because of lack of adequate evidence, of suits settled out of court, of complaints dropped because of dollar bribery or physical threats, of trials delayed or rejected simply because of the horrific backlog of court cases and the shortage of personnel.

But most of these judicial abortions had a history, a written record that existed *somewhere.* And part of it was in detectives' paperwork: the squeals and beef sheets and diaries and records of "Charge dropped," "Refused to press charges," "Agreed to make restitution," "Let off with warning,"—all the circumlocutions to indicate that the over-worked detective, using patient persuasion in most cases, with or without the approval of his superior officer, had kept a case off the court calendar.

Most judicial adjustments were of a minor nature, and a product of the investigating officer's experience and common sense. Two men in a bar, both liquored up, begin beating on each others' faces with their fists. The police are called. Each antagonist wants the other arrested on charges of assault. What is the cop to do? If he's smart, he gives both a tongue-lashing, threatens to arrest both for disturbing the peace, and sends them off in opposite directions. No pain, no strain, no paperwork with formal charges, warrants, time lost in court—an ache in the ass to everyone. And the judge would probably listen incredulously for all of five minutes and then throw both plaintiff and defendant out of his court.

But if the matter is a little more serious than a barroom squabble, if damage has been done to property or someone has suffered obvious injury, then the investigating officer might move more circumspectly. It can still be settled out of court, with the cop acting as judge and jury. It can be settled by voluntary withdrawal of charges, by immediate payment of money to the aggrieved party by the man who has wronged him, by mutual consent of both parties when threatened with more substantial charges by the investigating officer, or by a bribe to the cop.

This is "street justice," and for every case that comes to trial in a walnut-paneled courtroom, a hundred street trials are held every hour of every day in every city in the country, and the presiding magistrate is a cop—plainclothes detective or uniformed patrolman. And honest or venal, he is the kingpin of the whole ramshackle, tottering, ridiculous, working system of "street justice," and without him the already overclogged formal courts of the nation would be inundated, drowned in a sea of pettifoggery, and unable to function.

The conscientious investigating officer will or will not make a written report of the case, depending on his judgment of its importance. But if the investigating officer is a plainclothes detective, and if the case involves people of an obviously higher social status than sidewalk brawlers, and if formal charges have been made by *anyone,* and one or more visits to the precinct house have been made, then the detective will almost certainly make a written report of what happened, who did what, who said what, how much injury or damage resulted. Even if the confrontation simply dissolves—charges withdrawn, no warrants issued, no trial—the detective, sighing, fills out the forms, writes his report, and stuffs all the paper in the slush heap, to be thrown out when the file is overflowing.

Knowing all this, knowing how slim his chances were of finding anything meaningful in the detritus left behind by the Precinct's detective squad when it was disbanded, Delaney followed his cop's instinct and phoned Lieutenant Marty Dorfman at the 251st Precinct, next door.

Their preliminary conversation was friendly but cool. Delaney asked after the well-being of Dorfman's family, and the lieutenant inquired as to Mrs. Delaney's health. It was only when the Captain inquired about conditions in the Precinct that Dorfman's voice took on a tone of anguish and anger.

It developed that Operation Lombard was using the 251st Precinct house as command headquarters. Deputy Commissioner Broughton had taken over Lieutenant Dorfman's office, and his men were filling the second floor offices and bull pen formerly occupied by the Precinct detective squad. Dorfman himself was stuck at a desk in a corner of the sergeants' room.

He could have endured this ignominy, he suggested to Delaney, and even endured Broughton's slights that included ignoring him completely when they met in the hallway and commandeering the Precinct's vehicles without prior consultation with Dorfman. But what really rankled was that apparently residents of the Precinct were blaming him, Dorfman, personally for not finding the killer. In spite of what they read in the papers and saw on television about Operation Lombard, headed by Deputy Commissioner Broughton, they knew Dorfman was commander of their precinct, and they blamed him for failing to make their streets safe.

"I know," Delaney said sympathetically. "They feel it's your neighborhood and your responsibility."

"Oh yes," Dorfman sighed. "Well, I'm learning. Learning what you had to put up with. I guess it's good experience."

"It is," Delaney said definitely. "The best experience of all—being on the firing line. Are you going to take the exam for captain?"

"I don't know what to do. My wife says no. She wants me to get out, get into something else."

"Don't do that," Delaney said quickly. "Hang in there. A little while longer anyway. Things might change before you know it."

"Oh?" Dorfman asked, interested now, curious, but not wanting to pin Delaney down. "You think there may be changes?"

"Yes. Maybe sooner than you think. Don't make any decisions now. Wait. Just wait."

"All right, Captain. If you say so."

"Lieutenant, the reason I called—I want to come into the Precinct house around eight or nine tomorrow morning. I want to go down to that storage room in the basement. It's off the hallway to the back door. You know, when you pass the pens and drunk tank and turn right. I want to go through some old files stored in there. It's slush left by the detective squad. It'll probably take me all day, and I may remove some of the files. I want your permission."

There was silence, and Delaney thought the connection might have been cut.

"Hello? Hello?" he said.

"I'm still here," Dorfman said finally in a soft voice. "Yes, you have my permission. Thank you for calling first, Captain. You didn't have to do that."

"It's your precinct."

"So I've been learning. Captain . . ."

"What?"

"I think I know what you've been doing. Are you getting anywhere?"

"Nothing definite. Yet. Coming along."

"Will the files help?"

"Maybe."

"Take whatever you need."

"Thank you. If I meet you, just nod and pass by. Don't stop to talk. Broughton's men don't have to—"

"I understand."

"Dorfman . . ."

"Yes, Captain?"

"Don't stop studying for the captain's exam."

"All right. I won't."

"I know you'll do fine on the written, but on the oral they ask some tricky questions. One they ask every year, but it takes different forms. It goes something like this: You're a captain with a lieutenant, three sergeants, and maybe twenty or thirty men. There's this riot. Hippies or drunks off a Hudson River cruise or some kind of nutty mob. Maybe a hundred people hollering and breaking windows and raising hell. How do you handle it?"

There was silence. Then Dorfman said, not sure of himself, "I'd have the men form a wedge. Then, if I had a bullhorn, I'd tell the mob to disperse. If that didn't work, I'd tell the men to—"

"No," Delaney said. "That isn't the answer they want. The right answer is this: you turn to your lieutenant and say. 'Break 'em up.' Then you turn your back on the mob and walk away. It might not be the *right* way. You understand? But it's the right answer to the question. They want to make sure you know how to use command. Watch out for a question like that."

"Thank you, Captain," Dorfman said, and Delaney hoped they might be easing back into their earlier, closer relationship.

He thought it out carefully in his methodical way. He would wear his oldest suit, since that basement storeroom was sure to be dusty. It was probably adequately lighted with an overhead bulb, but just in case he would take along his flashlight.

Now, the room itself might be locked, and then he'd be forced to make a fuss until he found someone with the proper key. But he had never turned in his ring of master keys which, his predecessor had assured him, opened every door, cell and locker in the Precinct house. So he'd take his ring of keys along.

He didn't know how long it would take to go through the detectives' old files, but he judged it might be all day. He wouldn't want to go out to eat; the less chance of being seen by Broughton's men, or by Broughton himself, moving around the stairs and corridors, the better for everyone. So he would need sandwiches, two sandwiches, that he would ask Mary to make up for him in the morning, plus a thermos of black coffee. He would carry all this, plus the flashlight and keys, in his briefcase, which would also hold the typed lists of the cards included in Monica Gilbert's file.

Anything else? Well, he should have some kind of cover story just in case, by bad luck, Broughton saw him, braced him, and wanted to know what the fuck he was up to. He would say, he decided, that he had just stopped by to reclaim some personal files from the basement storeroom. He would keep it as vague as possible; it might be enough to get by.

He awoke the next morning, resolutely trying not to hope, but attempting to treat this search as just another logical step that had to be taken, whether it yielded results or not. He ate an unusually large breakfast for him: tomato juice, two poached eggs on whole wheat toast, a side order of pork sausages, and two cups of black coffee.

While Mary was preparing his luncheon sandwiches and his thermos, he went into the study to call Barbara, to explain why he would be unable to see her that day. Thankfully, she was in an alert, cheery mood, and when he told her exactly what he planned to do, she approved immediately and made him promise to call her as soon as his search was completed, to report results.

His entry into the 251st Precinct house went easily, without incident. That intimidating woman, the blonde sergeant, was on the blotter when he walked in. She was leaning across the desk, talking to a black woman who was weeping. The sergeant looked up, recognized the Captain, and flapped him a half-salute. He waved in return and marched steadily ahead, carrying his briefcase like a salesman. He went down the worn wooden staircase and turned into the detention area.

The officer on duty—on limited duty since his right arm had been knifed open by an eleven-year-old on the shit—was tilted back against the wall in an ancient armchair. He was reading a late edition of the *Daily News;* Delaney could see the headline: "Maniac Killer Still on Loose." The officer glanced up, recognized the Captain, and started to scramble to his feet. Delaney waved him down, ashamed of himself for not remembering the man's name.

"How you coming along?" he asked.

"Fine, Captain. It's healing real good. The doc said I should be mustering in a week or so."

"Glad to hear it. But don't hurry it; take all the time you need. I'm going to that storeroom in the back hallway. I've got some personal files there I want to get."

The officer nodded. He couldn't care less.

"I don't know how long it'll take, so if I'm not out by the time you leave, please tell your relief I'm back here."

"Okay, Captain."

He walked past the detention cells: six cells, four occupied. He didn't look to the right or to the left. Someone whispered to him; someone screamed. There were three men in the drunk tank lying in each others' filth and moaning. It wasn't the noise that bothered him, it was the smell; he had almost forgotten how bad it was: old urine, old shit, old blood, old vomit, old puss—90 years of human pain soaked into floors and walls. And coming through the miasma, like a knife thrust, the sharp, piercing carbolic odor that stung his nostrils and brought tears to his eyes.

The storeroom was locked, and it took him almost five minutes to find the right key on the big ring. And when the latch snapped open, he paused a few seconds and wondered why he hadn't turned that ring of keys over to Dorfman. Officially, they should be in the lieutenant's possession; it was his precinct.

He shoved the door open, found the wall switch, flipped on the overhead light, closed the door behind him and looked around. It was as bad as he had expected.

The precinct house had opened for business in 1882 and, inspecting the storeroom, Delaney guessed that every desk blotter for every one of those 90 years was carefully retained and never looked at again. They were stacked to the ceiling. An historian might do wonders with them. The Captain was amused by the thought: "A Criminal History of Our Times"—reconstructing the way our great-grandparents, grandparents, and parents lived by analyzing the evidence in those yellowing police blotters. It could be done, he thought, and it might prove revealing. Not the usual history, not the theories of philosophers, discoveries of scientists, programs of statesmen; not wars, explorations, revolutions, and new religions.

Just the petty crimes, misdemeanors, and felonies of a weak and sinning humanity. It was all there: the mayhem, frauds, child-beating, theft, drug abuse, alcoholism, kidnapping, rape, murder. It would make a fascinating record, and he wished an historian would attempt it. Something might be learned from it.

He took off his coat, hat and jacket and laid them on the least dusty crate he could find. The windowless room had a single radiator that clanked and hissed constantly, spitting out steam and water. Delaney opened the door a few inches. The air that came in was carbolic-laden, but a little cooler.

He put on his glasses and looked at what else the room held.

Mostly cardboard cartons, overflowing with files and papers.

The cartons bore on their sides the names of whiskies, rums, gins, etc., and he knew most of them came from the liquor store on First Avenue, around the corner. There were also rough wooden cases filled with what appeared to be physical evidence of long forgotten crimes: a knitted woolen glove, moth-eaten; a rusted cleaver with a broken handle; a stained upper denture; a child's Raggedy-Ann doll; a woman's patent leather purse, yawning empty; a broken crutch; a window weight with black stains; a man's fedora with one bullet hole through the crown; sealed and bulging envelopes with information jotted on their sides; a bloodied wig; a corset ripped down with a knife thrust.

Delaney turned away and found himself facing a carton of theatrical costumes. He fumbled through them and thought they might have been left from some remote Christmas pageant performed in the Precinct house by neighborhood children, the costumes provided by the cops. But beneath the cheap cotton—sleazy to begin with and now rotting away—he found an ancient Colt revolver, at least twelve inches long, rusted past all usefulness, and to the trigger guard was attached a wrinkled tag with the faded inscription: "Malone's gun. July 16, 1902." Malone. Who had he been—cop or killer? It made no difference now.

He finally found what he was looking for: two stacks of relatively fresh cardboard cartons containing the last year's garbage from the detective squad's files. Each carton held folders in alphabetical order, but the cartons themselves were stacked helter-skelter, and Delaney spent almost an hour organizing them. It was then past noon, and he sat down on a nailed wooden crate (painted on the top: "Hold for Capt. Kelly") and ate one of his sandwiches, spiced salami and thickly sliced Spanish onion on rye bread thinly spread with mayonnaise—which he dearly loved—and drank half his thermos of coffee.

Then he got out his list of names from Monica's cards and went to work. He had to compare list to files, and had to work standing up or kneeling or crouching. Occasionally he would spread his arms wide and bend back his spine. Twice he stepped out into the hallway and walked up and down a few minutes, trying to shake the kinks out of his legs.

He felt no elation whatsoever when he found the first file labeled with a name on his list. The address checked out. He merely put the file aside and went on with the job. It was lumbering work, like a stake-out or a 24-hour shadow. You didn't stop to question what you were doing; it was just something that had to be done, usually to prove the "no" rather than discover the "yes."

When he finished the last file in the last cardboard carton, it was nearly 7:00 P.M. He had long ago finished his second sandwich and the remainder of his coffee. But he wasn't hungry; just thirsty. His nostrils and throat seemed caked with dust, but the radiator had never stopped clanking, hissing steam and water, and his shirt was plastered to armpits, chest, and back; he could smell his own sweat.

He packed carefully. Three files. Three of the people on Monica's cards had been involved in cases of "street justice." He tucked the files carefully in his brief case, added the empty thermos and wax paper wrappings from the sandwiches. He pulled on jacket and overcoat, put on his hat, took a final look around. If he ever came back to the Two-five-one, the first thing he'd do was have this room cleaned up. He turned off the light, stepped out into the hallway, made certain the spring lock clicked.

He walked past the drunk tank and detention cells. Two of the drunks were gone, and only one cell was occupied. There was no uniformed officer about, but he might have gone upstairs for coffee. Delaney walked up the rickety staircase and was surprised to feel his knees tremble from tiredness. Dorfman was standing near the outside door, talking to a civilian Delaney didn't recognize. When he passed, the Captain nodded, smiling slightly, and Dorfman nodded in return, not interrupting his conversation.

In his bedroom, Delaney stripped down to his skin as quickly as he could, leaving all his soiled clothing in a damp heap on the floor. He soaked in a hot shower and soaped his hands three times but was unable to get the grime out of the pores or from under his nails. Then he found a can of kitchen cleanser in the cabinet under the sink; that did the trick. After he dried, he used cologne and powder, but he still smelled the carbolic.

He dressed in pajamas, robe, slippers, then glanced at the bedside clock. Getting on . . . He decided to call Barbara, rather than wait until he went through the retrieved files. But when she answered the phone, he realized that she had drifted away. Perhaps it was sleep or the medication, perhaps the illness; he just didn't know. She kept repeating his name. Laughing: "Edward!" Questioning: "Edward?" Demanding: "Edward!" Loving: "Ed-d-w-ward . . ."

Finally he said, "Good-night, dear," hung up, took a deep breath, tried not to weep. In his study, moving mechanically, he mixed a heavy rye highball, then unpacked his briefcase. Flashlight back to the drawer in the kitchen cabinet. Crumpled wax paper into the garbage can. Thermos rinsed out, then filled with hot water and left to soak on the sink sideboard. Ring of keys into his top desk drawer, to be handed over to Lieutenant Dorfman. Delaney knew now, in some realization, he would never again command the Two-five-one.

And the three files stacked neatly in the center of his desk blotter. He got a square of paper towel, wiped off their surface dust, stacked them neatly again. He washed his hands, sat down behind his desk, put on his glasses. Then he just sat there and slowly, slowly sipped away half his strong highball, staring at the files. Then he leaned forward, began to read.

The first case was amusing, and the officer who had handled the beef, Detective second grade Samuel Berkowitz, had recognized it from the start; his tart, ironic reports understated and heightened the humor. A man named Timothy J. Lester had been apprehended shortly after throwing an empty garbage can through the plate glass window of a Madison Avenue shop that specialized in maternity clothes. The shop was coyly called Expectin'. Berkowitz reported the suspect was "apparently intoxicated on Jamesons"—a reasonable deducation since next door to "Expectin' " was a tavern called "Ye Olde Emerald Isle." Detective Berkowitz had also determined that Mr. Lester, although only 34, was the father of seven children and had, that very night, been informed by his wife that it would soon be eight. Timothy had immediately departed for "Ye Olde Emerald Isle" to celebrate, had celebrated, and on his way home had paused to toss the garbage can through the window of "Expectin'." Since Lester was, in Berkowitz' words, "apparently an exemplary family man," since he had a good job as a typesetter, since he offered to make complete restitution for the shattered window, Detective Berkowitz felt the cause of justice would best be served if Mr. Lester was allowed to pay for his mischievous damage and all charges dropped.

Captain Edward X. Delaney, reading his file and smiling, concurred with the judgment of Detective Berkowitz.

The second file was short and sad. It concerned one of the few women included on Monica Gilbert's list. She was 38 years old and lived in a smart apartment on Second Avenue near 85th Street. She had taken in a roommate, a young woman of 22. All apparently went well for almost a year. Then the younger woman met a man, they became engaged, and she announced the news to her roommate and was congratulated. She returned home the following evening to discover the older woman had slashed all her clothes to thin ribbons with a razor blade and had trashed all her personal belongings. She called the police. But after consultation with her fiancé, she refused to press charges, moved out of the apartment, and the case was dropped.

The third file, thicker, dealt with Daniel G. Blank, divorced, living alone on East 83rd Street. He had been involved in two separate incidents about six months apart. In the first he had originally been charged with simple assault in an altercation involving a fellow tenant of his apartment house who apparently had been beating his own dog. Blank had intervened, and the dog owner had suffered a broken arm. There had been a witness, Charles Lipsky, a doorman, who signed a statement that Blank had merely pushed the other man after being struck with a folded newspaper. The man had stumbled off the curb and fell, breaking his arm. Charges were eventually dropped.

The second incident was more serious. Blank had been in a bar, The Parrot on Third Avenue, and was allegedly solicited by a middle-aged homosexual. Blank, according to testimony of witnesses, thereupon hit the man twice, breaking his jaw with the second blow. While the man was helpless on the floor, Blank had kicked him repeatedly in the groin until he was dragged away and the police were called. The homosexual refused to sign a complaint, Blank's lawyer appeared, and apparently the injured man signed a release.

The same officer, Detective first grade Ronald A. Blankenship, had handled both beefs. His language, in his reports, was official, clear, concise, colorless, and implied no judgments.

Delaney read through the file slowly, then read it through again. He got up to mix another rye highball and then, standing at his desk, read it through a third time. He took off his glasses, began to pace about his chilly study, carrying his drink, sipping occasionally. Once or twice he came back behind his desk to stare at the Daniel Blank manila folder, but he didn't open the file again.

Several years previously, when he had been a Detective lieutenant, he had contributed two articles to the Department's monthly magazine. The first monograph was entitled "Common Sense and the New Detective." It was a very basic, down-to-earth analysis of how the great majority of crimes are solved: good judgment based on physical evidence and experience—the ability to put two and two together and come up with four, not three or five. It was hardly a revolutionary argument.

The second article, entitled "Hunch, Instinct, and the New Detective," occasioned a little more comment. Delaney argued that in spite of the great advances in laboratory analysis, the forensic sciences, computerized records and probability percentages, the new detective disregarded his hunches and instinct at his peril, for frequently they were not a sudden brainstorm, but were the result of observation of physical evidence and experience of which the detective might not even be consciously aware. But stewing in his subconscious, a rational and reasonable conclusion was reached, thrust into his conscious thought, and should never be allowed to wither unexplored, since it was, in many cases, as logical and empirical as common sense.

(Delaney had prepared a third article for the series. This dealt with his theory of an "adversary concept" in which he explored the Dostoevskian relationship between detective and criminal. It was an abstruse examination of the "sensual"—Delaney's word—affinity between hunter and hunted, of how, in certain cases, it was necessary for the detective to penetrate and assume the physical body, spirit, and soul of the criminal in order to bring him to justice. This treatise, at Barbara's gentle persuasion, Delaney did not submit for publication.)

Now, thinking over the facts included in the Daniel Blank file, Captain Delaney acknowledged he was halfway between common sense and instinct. Intelligence and experience convinced him that the man involved in the two incidents described was worth investigating further.

The salient point in the second incident was the raw savagery Blank had displayed. A normal man—well, an average man—might have handled the homosexual's first advance by merely smiling and shaking his head, or moving down the bar, or even leaving The Parrot. The violence displayed by Blank was excessive. Protesting too much?

The first incident—the case of the injured dog-owner—might not be as innocent as it appeared in Detective Blankenship's report. It was true that the witness, the doorman—what was his name? Delaney looked it up. Charles Lipsky—it was true that Lipsky stated that Blank had been struck with a folded newspaper before pushing his assailant. But witnesses can be bribed; it was hardly an uncommon occurrence. Even if Lipsky had told the truth, Delaney was amazed at how this incident fit into a pattern he had learned from experience; men prone to violence, men too ready to use their fists, their feet, even their teeth, somehow became involved in situations that were obviously not their fault, and yet resulted in injury or death to their antagonist.

Delaney called Monica Gilbert.

"Monica? Edward. I'm sorry to disturb you at this hour. I hope I didn't wake the children."

"Oh no. That takes more than a phone ring. What is it?"

"Would you mind looking at your card file and see if you have anything on a man named Blank. Daniel G. He lives on East Eighty-third Street."

"Just a minute."

He waited patiently. He heard her moving about. Then she was back on the phone.

"Blank, Daniel G.," she read. "Arrested twice for speeding. Guilty and fined. Do you want the make of car and license number?"

"Please."

He took notes as she gave him the information.

"Thank you," he said.

"Edward, is it—anything?"

"I don't know. I really don't. It's interesting. That's about all I can say right now. I'll know more tomorrow."

"Will you call?"

"Yes, if you want me to."

"Please do."

"All right. Sleep well."

"Thank you. You, too."

Two arrests for speeding. Not in itself significant, but within the pattern. The choice of car was similarly meaningful. Delaney was glad Daniel Blank didn't drive a Volkswagen.

He called Thomas Handry at the newspaper office. He had left for home. He called him at home. No answer. He called Detective Lieutenant Jeri Fernandez at his office. Fernandez had gone home. Delaney felt a sudden surge of anger at these people who couldn't be reached when he needed them. Then he realized how childish that was, and calmed down.

He found Fernandez' home phone number in the back of his pocket notebook where he had carefully listed home phone numbers of all sergeants and higher ranks in the 251st Precinct. Fernandez lived in Brooklyn. A child answered the phone.

"Hello?"

"Is Detective Fernandez there, please?"

"Just a minute. Daddy, it's for you!" the child screamed.

In the background Delaney could hear music, shouts, loud laughter, the thump of heavy dancing. Finally Fernandez came to the phone.

"Hello?"

"Captain Edward X. Delaney here."

"Oh. Howrya, Captain?"

"Lieutenant, I'm sorry to disturb you at this hour. Sounds like you're having a party."

"Yeah, it's the wife's birthday, and we have some people in."

"I won't keep you long. Lieutenant, when you were at the Two-five-one, you had a dick one named Blankenship. Right?"

"Sure. Ronnie. Good man."

"What did he look like? I can't seem to remember him."

"Sure you do, Captain. A real tall guy. About six-three or four. Skinny as a rail. We called him 'Scarecrow.' Remember now?"

"Oh yes. A big Adam's apple?"

"That's the guy."

"What happened to him?"

"He drew an Assault-Homicide Squad over on the West Side. I think it's up in the Sixties-Seventies-Eighties—around there. I know it takes in the Twentieth Precinct. Listen, I got his home phone number somewhere. Would that help?"

"It certainly would."

"Hang on a minute."

It was almost five minutes, but eventually Fernandez was back with Blankenship's phone number. Delaney thanked him. Fernandez seemed to want to talk more, but the Captain cut him short.

He dialed Blankenship's home phone. A woman answered. In the background Delaney could hear an infant wailing loudly.

"Hello?"

"Mrs. Blankenship?"

"Yes. Who is this?"

"My name is Delaney, Captain Edward X. Delaney, New York Police Depart—"

"What's happened? What's happened to Ronnie? Is he all right? Is he hurt? What—"

"No, no, Mrs. Blankenship," he said hurriedly, soothing her fears. "As far as I know, your husband is perfectly all right."

He could sympathize with her fright. Every cop's wife lived with that dread. But she should have known that if anything had happened to her husband, she wouldn't learn of it from a phone call. Two men from the Department would ring her bell. She would open the door and they would be standing there, faces twisted and guilty, and she would know.

"I'm trying to contact your husband to get some information, Mrs. Blankenship," he went on, speaking slowly and distinctly. This was obviously not an alert woman. "I gather he's not at home. Is he working?"

"Yes. He's on nights for the next two weeks."

"Could you give me his office phone number, please?"

"All right. Just a minute."

He could also have told her not to give out any information about her husband to a stranger who calls in the middle of the night and claims he's a captain in the NYPD. But what would be the use? Her husband had probably told her that a dozen times. A dull woman.

He got the number and thanked her. It was now getting on toward eleven o'clock; he wondered if he should try or let it go till morning. He dialed the number. Blankenship had checked in all right, but he wasn't on the premises. Delaney left his number, without identifying himself, and asked if the operator would have him call back.

"Please tell him it's important," he said.

" 'Important'?" the male operator said. "How do you spell that, Mr. Important?"

Delaney hung up. A wise-ass. The Captain would remember. The Department moved in involved and sometimes mysterious ways. One day that phone operator in that detective division might be under Delaney's command. He'd remember the high, lilting, laughing voice. It was stupid to act like that.

He started a new file, headed "Blank, Daniel G.," and in it he stowed the Blankenship reports, his notes on Blank's record of arrests for speeding, the make of car he drove and his license number. Then he went to the Manhattan telephone directory and looked up Blank, Daniel G. There was only one listing of that name, on East 83rd Street. He made a note of the phone number and added that to his file.

He was mixing a fresh rye highball—was it his second or third?—when the phone rang. He put down the glass and bottle carefully, then ran for the phone, catching it midway through the third ring.

"Hello?"

"This is Blankenship. Who's this?"

"Captain Edward X. Delaney here. I was—"

"Captain! Good to hear from you. How are you, sir?"

"Fine, Ronnie. And you?" Delaney had never before called the man by his first name, hadn't even known what it was before his call to Fernandez. In fact, he couldn't remember ever speaking to Blankenship personally, but he wanted to set a tone.

"Okay, Captain. Getting along."

"How do you like the new assignment? Tell me, do you think this reorganization is going to work?"

"Captain, it's great!" Blankenship said enthusiastically. "They should have done it years ago. Now I can spend some time on important stuff and forget the little squeals. Our arrest rate is up, and morale is real good. The case load is way down, and we've got time to think."

The man sounded intelligent. His voice was pleasingly deep, vibrant, resonant. Delaney remembered that big, jutting Adam's apple.

"Glad to hear it," he said. "Listen, I'm on leave of absense, but something came up and I agreed to help out on it."

He let it go at that, keeping it vague, waiting to see if Blankenship would pick up on it and ask questions. But the detective hesitated a moment, then said, "Sure, Captain."

"It concerns a man named Daniel Blank, in the Two-five-one. He was involved in two beefs last year. You handled both of them. I have your reports. Good reports. Very complete."

"What was that name again?"

"Blank, B-l-a-n-k, Daniel G. He lives on East Eighty-third Street. The first thing was a pushing match with a guy who was allegedly beating his dog. The second—"

"Oh sure," Blankenship interrupted. "I remember. Probably because his name is Blank and mine is Blankenship. At the time I thought it was funny I should be handling him. Two beefs in six months. In the second, he kicked the shit out of a faggot. Right?"

"Right."

"But the victim wouldn't sign a complaint. What do you want to know, Captain?"

"About Blank. You saw him?"

"Sure. Twice."

"What do you remember about him?"

Blankenship recited: "Blank, Daniel G. White, male, approximately six feet or slightly taller, about—"

"Wait, wait a minute," Delaney said hastily. "I'm taking notes. Go a little slower."

"Okay, Captain. You got the height?"

"Six feet or a little over."

"Right. Weight about one seventy-five. Slim build but good shoulders. Good physical condition from what I could see. No obvious physical scars or infirmities. Dark complexion. Sunburned, I'd say. Long face. Sort of Chinese-looking. Let's see—anything else?"

"How was he dressed?" Delaney asked, admiring the man's observation and memory.

"Dark suits," Blankenship said promptly. "Nothing flashy, but well-cut and expensive. Some funny things I remember. Gold link chain on his wrist watch. Like a bracelet. The first time I saw him I think it was his own hair. The second time I swear it was a rug. The second time he was wearing a real crazy shirt open to his *pipik*, with some kind of necklace. You know—hippie stuff."

"Accent?" Delaney nodded.

"Accent?" Blankenship repeated, thought a moment, then said, "Not a native New Yorker. Midwestern, I'd guess. Sorry I can't be more specific."

"You're doing great," Delaney assured him, elated. "You think he's strong?"

"Strong? I'd guess so. Any guy who can break another man's jaw with a punch has got to be strong. Right?"

"Right. What was your personal reaction to him? Flitty?"

"Could be, Captain. When they punish an obvious faggot like that, it's got to mean something. Right?"

"Right."

"I wanted to charge him, but the victim refused to sign anything. So what could I do?"

"I understand," Delaney said. "Believe me, this has nothing to do with that beef."

"I believe you, Captain."

"Do you know where he works, what he does for a living?"

"It's not in my reports?"

"No, it isn't."

"Sorry about that. But you've got his lawyer's name and address, haven't you?"

"Oh yes, I have that. I'll get it from him," Delaney lied. It was Blankenship's first mistake, and a small one. No use going to the lawyer; he'd simply refuse to divulge the information, then surely mention to Blank that the police had been around asking questions.

"That just about covers it," Delaney said. "Thanks very much for your help. What are you working on now?"

"It's a beaut, Captain," Blankenship said in his enthusiastic way. "This old dame got knocked off in her apartment. Strangled. No signs of forcible entry. And as far as we can tell, nothing stolen. A neighbor smelled it; that's how we got on to it. A poor little apartment, but it turns out the old dame was loaded."

"Who inherits?"

"A nephew. But we checked him out six ways from the middle. He's got an alibi that holds up. He was down in Florida for two weeks. We checked. He really was there. Every minute."

"Check his bank account, back for about six months or a year. See if there was a heavy withdrawal—maybe five or ten big ones."

"You mean he hired—? Son of a bitch!" Blankenship said bitterly. "Why didn't I think of that?"

"Stick around for twenty-five years," Delaney laughed. "You'll learn. Thanks again. If there's ever anything I can do for you, just let me know."

"I'll hold you to that, Captain," Blankenship said in his deep, throaty voice.

"You do that," Delaney said seriously.

After he hung up, he finished mixing his highball. He took a deep swallow, then grinned, grinned, grinned. He looked around at walls, ceiling, floor, furniture, and grinned at everything. It felt good. It had gone beyond his first article on common sense: the value of personally observed evidence and experience. It had even gone beyond the second article that extolled the value of hunch and instinct. Now he was in the realm of the third, unpublished article which Barbara had convinced him should never be printed. Quite rightly, too. Because in that monograph, exploring the nature of the detective–criminal relationship—his theory of the adversary concept—he had rashly dwelt on the "joy" of the successful detective.

That was what he felt now—*joy!* He worked at his new file—BLANK, Daniel G.—adding to it everything Detective Blankenship had reported, and not a thing, not one single thing, varied in any significant aspect from his original "The Suspect" outline. He gained surety as he amplified his notes. It was beautiful, beautiful, all so beautiful. And, just as he had written in his unpublished article, there was sensuous pleasure—was it sexual?—in the chase. So intent was he on his rapid writing, his reports, his new, beautiful file, that the phone rang five times before he picked it up. As a matter of fact, he kept writing as he answered it.

"Captain Edward X. Delaney here."

"Dorfman. There's been another one."

"Captain—*what?*"

"Lieutenant Dorfman, Captain. Sorry to wake you up. There's been another killing. Same type, with extras."

"Where?"

"Eighty-fifth. Between First and York."

"A man?"

"Yes."

"Tall?"

"Tall? I'd guess five-ten or eleven."

"Weight?"

There was silence, then Dorfman's dull voice: "I don't know what he weighed, Captain. Is it important?"

"Extras? You said 'Extras.' What extras?"

"He was struck at least three times. Maybe more. There are signs of a struggle. Christmas packages, three of them, thrown around. Scuff marks on the sidewalk. His coat was torn. Looks like he put up a fight."

"Identified?"

"A man named Feinberg. Albert Feinberg."

"Anything missing? Identification of any kind?"

"We don't know," Dorfman said wearily. "They're checking with his wife now. His wallet wasn't out like in the Lombard kill. We just don't know."

"All right," Delaney said softly. "Thank you for calling. Sounds like you could use some sleep, lieutenant."

"Yes, I could. If I could sleep."

"Where was it again?"

"Eighty-fifth, between First and York."

"Thank you. Good-night."

He looked at his desk calendar and counted carefully. It had been eleven days since the murder of Detective Kope. His research was proving out; the intervals between killings were becoming shorter and shorter.

He got out his Precinct map with the plastic overlay and, with a red grease pencil, carefully marked in the murder of Albert Feinberg, noting victim's name, date of killing, and place. The locations of the four murders formed a rough square on the map. On impulse, he used his grease pencil and a ruler to connect opposite corners of the square, making an X. It intersected at 84th Street and Second Avenue, right in the middle of the crossing of the two streets. He checked Daniel Blank's address. It was on 83rd Street, about a block and a half away. The map didn't say yes and it didn't say no.

He was staring at the map, nodding, and awoke fifteen minutes later, startled, shocked that he had been sleeping. He pulled himself to his feet, drained the watery remains of his final highball, and made his rounds, checking window locks and outside doors.

Then the bed, groaning with weariness. What he really wanted to do . . . what he wanted to do . . . so foolish . . . was to go to Daniel Blank . . . go to him right now . . . introduce himself and say, "Tell me all about it."

Yes, that was foolish . . . idiotic . . . but he was sure . . . well, maybe not sure, but it was a chance, and the best . . . and just before he fell asleep he acknowledged, with a sad smile, that all this shitty thinking about patterns and percentages and psychological profile was just that—a lot of shit. He was following up on Daniel Blank because he had no other lead. It was as simple and obvious as that. Occam's Razor. So he fell asleep.

4

His bedside alarm went off at 8:00 A.M. He slapped it silent, swung his legs out from under the blankets, donned his glasses, consulted a slip of paper he had left under the phone. He called Thomas Handry at home. The phone rang eight times. He was about to give up when Handry answered.

"Hello?" he asked sleepily.

"Captain Edward X. Delaney here. Did I wake you up?"

"Why no," Handry yawned. "I've been up for hours. Jogged around the reservoir, wrote two deathless sonnets, and seduced my landlady. All right, what do you want, Captain?"

"Got a pencil handy?"

"A minute . . . okay, what is it?"

"I want you to check a man in your morgue file."

"Who is he?"

"Blank, Daniel G. That last name is Blank, B-l-a-n-k."

"Why should he be in our morgue?"

"I don't know why. It's just a chance."

"Well, what has he done? I mean, has he been in the news for any reason?"

"Not to my knowledge."

"Then why the hell should we have him in the morgue?"

"I told you," Delaney said patiently, "it's just a chance. But I've got to cover every possibility."

"Oh Jesus. All right. I'll try. I'll call you around ten, either way."

"No, don't do that," the Captain said quickly. "I may be out. I'll call you at the paper around ten."

Handry grunted and hung up.

After breakfast he went into the study. He wanted to check the dates of the four murders and the intervals between them. Lombard to Gilbert: 22 days. Gilbert to Kope: 17 days. Kope to Feinberg: 11 days. By projection, the next murder should occur during the week between after Christmas and New Year's Day, and probably a few days after Christmas. He sat suddenly upright. Christmas! Oh God.

He called Barbara immediately. She reported she was feeling well, had had a good night's sleep, and ate all her breakfast. She always said that.

"Listen," he said breathlessly, "it's about Christmas . . . I'm sorry, dear. I forgot all about gifts and cards. What are we to do?"

She laughed. "I knew you were too busy. I've mailed things to the children. I saw ads in the newspapers and ordered by phone. Liza and John are getting a nice crystal ice bucket from Tiffany's, and I sent Eddie a terribly expensive sweater from Saks. How does that sound?"

"You're a wonder," he told her.

"So you keep saying," she teased, "but do you *really* mean it? Give Mary some money, as usual, and maybe you can get her something personal, just some little thing, like a scarf or handkerchief or something like that. And put the check in the package."

"All right. What about the cards?"

"Well, we have some left over from last year—about twenty, I think—and they're in the bottom drawer of the secretary in the living room. Now if you buy another three boxes, I'm sure it'll be enough. Are you coming over today?"

"Yes. Definitely. At noon."

"Well, bring the cards and the list. You know where the list is, don't you?"

"Bottom drawer of the secretary in the living room."

"Detective!" she giggled. "Yes, that's where it is. Bring the list and cards over at noon. I feel very good today. I'll start writing them. I won't try to do them all today, but I should have them finished up in two or three days, and they'll get there in time."

"Stamps?"

"Yes, I'll need stamps. Get a roll of a hundred. A roll is easier to handle. I make such a mess of a sheet. Oh Edward, I'm sorry . . . I forgot to ask. Did you find anything in the old files?"

"I'll tell you all about it when I see you at noon."

"Does it look good?"

"Well . . . maybe."

She was silent, then sighed. "I hope so," she said. "Oh, how I hope so."

"I do, too. Listen dear . . . what would you like for Christmas?"

"Do I have a choice?" she laughed. "I know what I'm going to get—perfume from any drugstore you find that's open on Christmas Eve."

He laughed too. She was right.

He hung up and glanced at his watch. It was a little past 9:00 A.M., later than he wanted it to be. He dug hurriedly through his pack of business cards and found the one he was looking for: Arthur K. Ames. Automobile Insurance.

Blank's apartment house occupied an entire block on East 83rd Street. Delaney was familiar with the building and, standing across the street, looking up, thought again of how institutional it looked. All steel and glass. A hospital or a research center, not a place to live in. But people did, and he could imagine what the rents must be.

As he had hoped, men and women were still leaving for work. Two doormen were constantly running down the driveway to flag cabs and, even as he watched, a garage attendant brought a Lincoln Continental to the entrance, hopped out and ran back to the underground garage to drive up another tenant's car.

Delaney walked resolutely up the driveway, turned right and walked down a short flight of steps to the underground garage. A light blue Jaguar came roaring by him, the garage man at the wheel. Delaney waited patiently at the entrance until the black attendant came trotting back.

"Good morning," he said proffering his business card. "My name is Ames, of Cross-Country Insurance."

The attendant glanced at the card. "You picked a bad time to sell insurance, man."

"No, no," Delaney said quickly, smiling. "I'm not selling anything. One of the cars we cover was involved in an accident with a nineteen-seventy-one Chevy Corvette. The Corvette took off. The car we cover was trashed. The driver's in the hospital. Happened over on Third Avenue. We think the Corvette might be from the neighborhood, so I'm checking all the garages around here. Just routine."

"A nineteen-seventy-one Corvette?"

"Yes."

"What color?"

"Probably dark blue or black."

"When did this happen?"

"Couple of days ago."

"We got one Corvette. Mr. Blank. But it couldn't be him. He hasn't had his car out in weeks."

"The police found glass at the scene and pieces of fiberglass from the left front fender."

"I'm telling you it couldn't be Mr. Blank's Corvette. There's not a scratch on it."

"Mind if I take a look?"

"Help yourself," the man shrugged. "It's back there in the far corner, behind the white Caddy."

"Thank you."

The man took a phone call, hopped into a Ford station wagon, began to back out into the center of the garage so he could turn around. He was busy, which was why Delaney had picked this time. He walked slowly over to the black Corvette. The license number was Blank's.

The door was unlocked. He opened it and looked in, sniffing. A musty, closed-window smell. There was an ice-scraper for the windshield, a can of defogger, a dusty rag, a pair of worn driving gloves. Between the two seats was tucked a gasoline station map that had been handled, unfolded and refolded several times. Delaney opened it far enough to look. New York State. With a route marked on it in heavy black pencil: from East 83rd Street, across town, up the West Side Highway to the George Washington Bridge, across to New Jersey, up through Mahwah into New York again, then north to the Catskill Mountains, ending at a town named Chilton. He reshuffled the map, put it back where he found it.

He closed the car door gently and started out. He met the attendant coming back.

"It sure wasn't that car," he smiled.

"I told you that, man."

Delaney wondered if the attendant would mention the incident to Blank. He thought it likely, and he tried to guess what Blank's reaction would be. It wouldn't spook him but, if he was guilty, it might start him thinking. There was an idea there, Delaney acknowledged, but it wasn't time for it . . . yet.

Back in his study, he looked up Chilton in his world atlas. All it said was "Chilton, N.Y. Pop. 3,146." He made a note about Chilton and added it to the Daniel Blank file. He looked at his watch. It wasn't quite ten, but close enough. He called Handry at his office.

"Captain? Sorry. No soap."

"Well . . . it was a long shot. Thank you very much for—"

"Hey, wait a minute. You give up too easily. We got other files of people. For instance, the sports desk keeps a file of living personalities and so does the theatre and arts section. Could your boy be in either?"

"Maybe in the sports file, but I doubt it."

"Well, can you tell me *anything* about him?"

"Not much. He lives in an expensive apartment house and drives an expensive car, so he must be loaded."

"Thanks a lot," Handry sighed. "Okay, I'll see what I can do. If I have something, I'll call you. If you don't hear from me, you'll know I didn't turn up a thing. Okay?"

"Yes. Sure. Fine," Delaney said heavily, feeling this was just a polite kiss-off.

He got over to the hospital as Barbara's noon meal was being served and he watched, beaming, as she ate almost all of it, feeding herself. She really was getting better, he told himself happily. Then he showed her the Christmas cards he had purchased, in three different price ranges; the most expensive for their "important" friends and acquaintances, the least expensive for—well, for people. And the twenty cards left over from last year, the list, the stamps.

Then he told her about Daniel Blank, stalking about the room, making wide gestures. He told her the man's history, what he had been able to dig up, what he suspected.

"What do you think?" he asked finally, eager for her opinion.

"Yes," she said thoughtfully. "Maybe. But you've really got nothing, Edward. You know that."

"Of course."

"Nothing definite. But certainly worth following up. I'd feel a lot better if you could tie him up with an ice ax purchase."

"I would too. But right now he's all I've got."

"Where do you go from here?"

"Where? Checking out everything. Charles Lipsky. The Parrot, where he had that fight. Trying to find out who he is and what he is. Listen, dear, I won't be over this evening. Too much to do. All right?"

"Of course," she said. "Are you sticking to your diet?"

"Sure," he said, patting his stomach. "I'm up only three pounds this week."

They laughed, and he kissed her on the lips before he left. Then they kissed again. Soft, clinging, wanting kisses.

He clumped down to the lobby, dug out his pocket notebook, looked up the number. Then he called Calvin Case from the lobby booth.

"How you coming?"

"All right," Case said. "I'm still working on the general mountaineering equipment sales checks, pulling those in the Two-five-one Precinct."

Delaney was amused at Case's "Two-five-one Precinct." His amateur was talking officialese.

"Am I doing any good?" Case wanted to know.

"You are," Delaney assured him. "I've got a lead. Name is Daniel Blank. Know him?"

"What's it?"

"Blank. B-l-a-n-k. Daniel G. Ever hear of him?"

"Is he a climber?"

"I don't know. Could be."

"Hey, Captain, there're two hundred thousand climbers in the country and more every year. No, I don't know any Daniel G. Blank. What does the G. stand for?"

"Gideon. All right, let me try this one on you: Ever hear of Chilton? It's a town in New York."

"I know. Up in the Catskills. Sleepy little place."

"Would a mountain climber go there?"

"Sure. Not Chilton itself, but about two miles out of town is a state park. A small one, but nice. Benches, tables, barbecues—crap like that."

"What about climbing?"

"Mostly for hiking. There are some nice outcrops. There's one good climb, a monolith. Devil's Needle. It's a chimney climb. As a matter of fact, I left two pitons up there to help whoever came after me to crawl out onto the top. I used to go up there to work out."

"Is it an easy climb?"

"Easy? Well . . . it's not for beginners. I'd say an intermediate climb. If you know what you're doing, it's easy. Does that help?"

"At this point everything helps."

Back home, he added the information Calvin Case had given him about Chilton and the Devil's Needle to the Daniel Blank file. Then he checked the address of The Parrot in Blankenship's report. He went through his pack of business cards, found one that read: "Ward M. Miller. Private Investigations. Discreet—Reliable—Satisfaction Guaranteed." He began to plan his cover story.

He was still thinking it out an hour later, so deeply engrossed with the deception he was plotting that the phone must have rung several times without his being aware of it. Then Mary, who had picked up the hall extension, came in to tell him Mr. Handry was on the phone.

"Got him," Handry said.

"What?"

"I found him. Your Daniel G. Blank."

"Jesus Christ!" Delaney said excitedly. "Where?"

Handry laughed. "Our business-finance keeps a personality file, mostly on executives. They get tons of press releases and public relations reports every year. You know, Joe Blow has been promoted from vice president to executive vice president, or Harry Hardass has been hired as sales manager at Wee Tots Bootery, or some such shit. Usually it's a one-page release with a small photo, a head-and-shoulders shot. You know what the business desk calls that stuff?"

"What?"

"The 'Fink File.' And if you got a look at those photos, you'd understand why. You wouldn't believe! They print about one out of every ten releases they get, depending on the importance of the company. Anyway, that's where I found your pigeon. He got a promotion a couple of years ago, and there's a photo of him and a few paragraphs of slush."

"Where does he work?"

"Ohhh no," Handry said. "You haven't a bloody chance. I'll have a Xerox made of the release and a copy of the photo. I'll bring them up to your place tonight if you'll tell me why you're so interested in Mr. Blank. It's the Lombard thing, isn't it?"

Delaney hesitated. "Yes," he said finally.

"Blank a suspect?"

"Maybe."

"If I bring the release and photo tonight, will you tell me about it?"

"There isn't much to tell."

"Let me be the judge of that. Is it a deal?"

"All right. About eight or nine."

"I'll be there."

Delaney hung up, exultant. Information *and* a photo! He knew from experience the usual sequence of a difficult case. The beginning was long, slow, muddled. The middle began to pick up momentum, pieces coming together, fragments fitting. The end was usually short, fast, frequently violent. He judged he was in the middle of the middle now, the pace quickening, parts clicking into place. It was all luck. It was all fucking luck.

The Parrot was no worse and no better than any other ancient Third Avenue bar that served food (steak sandwich, veal cutlet, beef stew; spaghetti, home fries, peas-and-carrots; apple pie, tapioca pudding, chocolate cake). With the growth of high-rise apartment houses, there were fewer such places every year. As he had hoped, the tavern was almost empty. There were two men wearing yellow hardhats drinking beer at the bar and matching coins. There was a young couple at a back table, holding hands, dawdling over a bottle of cheap wine. One waiter at this hour. One bartender.

Delaney sat at the bar, near the door, his back to the plate glass window. He ordered a rye and water. When the bartender poured it, the Captain put a ten-dollar bill on the counter.

"Got a minute?" he asked.

The man looked at him. "For what?"

"I need some information."

"Who are you?"

Delaney slid the "Ward M. Miller—Private Investigations" business card across the bar. The man picked it up and read it, his lips moving. He returned the card.

"I don't know nothing," he said.

"Sure you do," the Captain smiled genially. He placed the card atop the ten-dollar bill. "It's a matter of public record. Last year there was a fight in here. A guy kicked the shit out of a faggot. Were you on duty that night?"

"I'm on duty every night. I own the joint. Part of it anyways."

"Remember the fight?"

"I remember. How come you know about it?"

"I got a friend in the Department. He told me about it."

"What's it got to do with me?"

"Nothing. I don't even know your name, and I don't want to know it. I'm interested in the guy who broke the other guy's jaw."

"That sonofabitch!" the bartender burst out. "That guy should have been put away and throw away the key. A maniac!"

"He kicked the faggot when he was down?"

"That's right. In the balls. He was a wild man. It took three of us to pull him away. He would have killed him. I came close to sapping him. I keep a sawed-off pool cue behind the bar. He was a raving nut. How come you're interested in him?"

"Just checking up. His name is Daniel Blank. He's about thirty-six, thirty-seven—around there. He's divorced. Now he's got the hots for this young chick. She's nineteen, in college. This Blank wants to marry her, and she's all for it. Her old man is loaded. He thinks this Blank smells. The old man wants me to check him out, see what I can dig up."

"The old man better kick his kid's tail or get her out of the country before he lets her marry Blank. That guy's bad news."

"I'm beginning to think so," Delaney agreed.

"Bet your sweet ass," the bartender nodded. He was interested now, leaned across the bar, his arms folded. "He's a wrongo. Listen, I got a young daughter myself. If this Blank ever came near her, I'd break his arms and legs. He was in trouble with the cops before, you know."

Delaney took back his business card, moved the ten-dollar bill closer to the man's elbow.

"What happened?" he asked.

"He got in trouble with some guy who lives in his apartment house. Something about the guy's dog. Anyway, this guy got a busted arm, and this Blank was hauled in on an assault rap. But they fixed it up somehow and settled out of court."

"No kidding?" the Captain said. "First I heard about it. When did this happen?"

"About six months before he had the fight in here. The guy's a trouble-maker."

"Sure sounds like it. How did you find out about it—the assault charge I mean?"

"My brother-in-law told me. His name's Lipsky. He's a doorman in the apartment house where this Blank lives."

"That's interesting. You think your brother-in-law would talk to me?"

The bartender looked down at the ten-dollar bill, slid it under his elbow. The two construction workers down at the other end of the bar called for more beer; he went down there to serve them. Then he came back.

"Sure," he said. "Why not? He thinks this Blank stinks on ice."

"How can I get in touch with him?"

"You can call him on the lobby phone. You know where this Blank lives?"

"Oh sure. That's a good idea. I'll call Lipsky there. Maybe this Blank is shacking up or something and is playing my client's daughter along for kicks or maybe he smells money."

"Could be. Another drink?"

"Not right now. Listen, have you seen Blank since he got in that fight in here?"

"Sure. The bastard was in a few nights ago. He thought I didn't recognize him, the shit, but I never forget a face."

"Did he behave himself?"

"Oh sure. He was quiet. I didn't say word one to him. Just served him his drink and left him alone. He had some Christmas packages with him so I guess he had been out shopping."

Christmas packages. It could be the night Albert Feinberg was killed. But Delaney didn't dare press it.

"Thanks very much," he said, sliding off the stool. He started toward the door, then stopped and came back. The ten-dollar bill had disappeared.

"Oh," he said, snapping his fingers, "two more things . . . Could you call your brother-in-law and tell him I'm going to call him? I mean, it would help if I didn't just call him cold. You can tell him what it's all about, and there'll be a couple of bucks in it for him."

"Sure," the bartender nodded, "I can do that. I talk to him almost every day anyway. When he's on days, he usually stops by for a brew when he gets off. But he's on nights this week. You won't get him before eight tonight. But I'll call him at home."

"Many thanks. I appreciate that. The other thing is this: if Blank should stop in for a drink, tell him I was around asking questions about him. You don't have to give him my name; just tell him a private investigator was in asking questions. You can describe me." He grinned at the bartender. "Might put the fear of God in him. Know what I mean?"

"Yeah," the man grinned back, "I know what you mean."

He returned home to find a packet of Operation Lombard reports Mary had signed for. He left them on the hallway table, went directly to the kitchen, still wearing his stiff Homburg and heavy, shapeless overcoat. He was so hungry he was almost sick, and realized he had eaten nothing since breakfast. Mary had left a pot of lamb stew on the range. It was still vaguely warm, not hot, but he didn't care. He stood there in Homburg and overcoat, and forked out pieces of lamb, a potato, onions, carrots. He got a can of beer from the refrigerator and drank deeply from that, not bothering with a glass. He gulped everything, belching once or twice. After awhile he began to feel a little better; his knees stopped trembling.

He took off hat and coat, opened another can of beer, brought that and the Operation Lombard reports into the study. He donned his glasses, sat at his desk. He began writing an account of his interview with the bartender at The Parrot.

He filed away his account, then opened the package of Operation Lombard reports dealing with the murder of the fourth victim, Albert Feinberg. There were sketchy preliminary statements from the first uniformed patrolmen on the scene, lengthier reports from detectives, temporary opinion of the Medical Examiner (Dr. Sanford Ferguson again), an inventory of the victim's effects, the first interview with the victim's widow, photos of the corpse and murder scene, etc., etc.

As Lt. Dorfman had said, there were "extras" that were not present in the three previous homicides. Captain Delaney made a careful list of them:

1. Signs of a struggle. Victim's jacket lapel torn, necktie awry, shirt pulled from belt. Scuff marks of heels (rubber) and soles (leather) on the sidewalk.

2. Three Christmas packages nearby. One, which contained a black lace negligcc, bore the victim's fingerprints. The other two were empty—dummy packages—and bore no prints at all, neither on the outside wrapping paper nor the inside boxes.

3. Drops of blood on the sidewalk a few feet from where the victim's battered skull rested. Careful scrapings and analysis proved these several drops were not the victim's blood type and were presumed to be the killer's. (Delaney made a note to call Ferguson and find out exactly what blood types were involved.)

4. The victim's wallet and credit card case appeared to be intact in his pockets. His wife stated that, to her knowledge, no identification was missing. However, pinned behind the left lapel of the victim's overcoat and poking through the buttonhole, examiners had found a short green stem. The forensic men had identified it as genus *Rosa,* family *Rosaceae,* order *Rosales.* Investigation was continuing to determine, if possible, exactly what type of rose the victim had been sporting on his overcoat lapel.

He was going over the reports once again when the outside door bell rang. Before he answered it, he slid the Operation Lombard material and his own notes into his top desk drawer and closed it tightly. Then he went to the door, brought Thomas Handry back into the study, took his coat and hat. He poured a Scotch on the rocks for Handry, drained the warm dregs of his own beer, then mixed himself a rye and water, sat down heavily behind the desk. Handry slumped in the leather club chair, crossed his knees.

"Well . . ." Delaney said briskly. "What have you got?"

"What have *you* got, Captain? Remember our deal?"

Delaney stared at the neatly dressed young man a moment. Handry seemed tired; his forehead was seamed, diagonal lines that hadn't been there before now ran from the corners of his nose down to the sides of his mouth. He bit continually at the hard skin around his thumbnails.

"Been working hard?" Delaney asked quietly.

"Handry shrugged. "The usual. I'm thinking of quitting."

"Oh?"

"I'm not getting any younger, and I'm not doing what I want to do."

"How's the writing coming?"

"It's not. I get home at night and all I want to do is take off my shoes, mix a drink, and watch the boob tube."

Delaney nodded. "You're not married, are you?"

"No."

"Got a woman?"

"Yes."

"What does she think about your quitting?"

"She's all for it. She's got a good job. Makes more than I do. She says she'll support us until I can get published or get a job I can live with."

"You don't like newspaper work?"

"Not anymore."

"Why not?"

"I didn't know there was so much shit in the world. I can't take much more of it. But I didn't come here to talk about my problems."

"Problems?" the Captain said, surprised. "That's what it's all about. Some you have to handle. Some there's nothing you can do about. Some go away by themselves if you wait long enough. What were you worrying about five years ago?"

"Who the hell knows."

"Well . . . there you are. All right, here's what I've got . . ."

Handry knew about the Captain's amateurs, of the checkings of mailing lists and sales slips, of the setting up of Monica Gilbert's master file of names, the investigation of their criminal records.

Now the Captain brought him up-to-date on Daniel Blank, how he, Delaney, had found the year-old beef sheets in the Precinct house basement, the search of Blank's car, the interview with the bartender at The Parrot.

". . . and that's all I've got," he concluded. "So far."

Handry shook his head. "Pretty thin."

"I know."

"You're not even sure if this guy is a mountain climber."

"That's true. But he was on the Outside Life mailing list, and that map in his car could be marked to a place where he climbs in this area."

"Want to go to the D.A. with that?"

"Don't be silly."

"You don't even know if he owns an ice ax."

"That's true; I don't."

"Well, what I've got isn't going to help you much more."

He drew an envelope from his breast pocket, leaned forward, scaled it onto Delaney's desk. The envelope was unsealed. The Captain drew out a 4 × 5 glossy photo and a single Xerox sheet that he unfolded and smoothed out on his desk blotter. He tilted his desk lamp to cast a stronger beam, took up the photo. He stared at it a long time. There. You. Are.

It was a close-up. Daniel Blank was staring directly at the lens. His shoulders were straight and wide. There was a faint smile on his lips, but not in his eyes.

He seemed remarkably youthful. His face was smooth, unlined. Small ears set close to the skull. A strong jaw. Prominent cheek bones. Large eyes, widely spaced, with an expression at once impassive and brooding. Straight hair, parted on the left, but combed flatly back. Heavy brows. Sculpted and unexpectedly tender lips, softly curved.

"Looks a little like an Indian," Delaney said.

"No," Handry said. "More Slavic. Almost Mongol. Look like a killer to you?"

"Everyone looks like a killer to me," Delaney said, not smiling. He turned his attention to the copy of the press release.

It was dated almost two years previously. It was brief, only two paragraphs, and said merely that Daniel G. Blank had been appointed Circulation Director of all Javis-Bircham Publications and would assume his new duties immediately. He was planning to computerize the Circulation Department of Javis-Bircham and would be in charge of the installation of AMROK II, a new computer that had been leased and would occupy almost an entire floor of the Javis-Bircham Building on West 46th Street.

Delaney read through the release again, then pushed it away from him. He took off his heavy glasses, placed them on top of the release. Then he leaned back in his swivel chair, clasped his hands behind his head, stared at the ceiling.

"I told you it wouldn't be much help," Handry said.

"Oh . . . I don't know," Delaney murmured dreamily. "There are some things . . . Fix yourself a fresh drink."

"Thanks. You want some more rye?"

"All right. A little."

He waited until Handry was settled back in the club chair again. Then the Captain sat up straight, put on his glasses, read the release again. He moved his glasses down on his nose, stared at Handry over the rims.

"How much do you think the Circulation Director of Javis-Bircham earns?"

"Oh, I'd guess a minimum of thirty thousand. And if it ran to fifty, I wouldn't be a bit surprised."

"That much?"

"Javis-Bircham is a big outfit. I looked it up. It's in the top five hundred of all the corporations in the country."

"Fifty thousand? Pretty good for a young man."

"How old is he?" Handry asked.

"I don't know exactly. Around thirty-five I'd guess."

"Jesus. What does he do with his money?"

"Pays a heavy rent. Keeps an expensive car. Pays alimony. Travels, I suppose. Invests. Maybe he owns a summer home; I don't know. There's a lot I don't know about him."

He got up to add more ice to his drink. Then he began to wander about the room, carrying the highball.

"The computer," he said. "What was it—AMROK II?"

Handry, puzzled, said nothing.

"Want to hear something funny?" Delaney asked.

"Sure. I could use a good laugh."

"This isn't funny-haha; this is funny strange. I was a detective for almost twenty years before I transferred to the Patrol Division. In those twenty years I had my share of cases involving sexual aberrations, either as a primary or secondary motive. And you know, a lot of those cases—many more than could be accounted for by statistical averages—involved electronic experts, electricians, mechanics, computer programmers, bookkeepers and accountants. Men who worked with things, with machinery, with numbers. These men were rapists or Peeping Toms or flashers or child molesters or sadists or exhibitionists. This is my own experience, you understand. I have never seen any study that breaks down sex offenders according to occupation. I think I'll suggest an analysis like that to Inspector Johnson. It might prove valuable."

"How do you figure it?"

"I can't. It might just be my own experience with sex offenders, too limited to be significant. But it does seem to me that men whose jobs are—are mechanized or automated, whose daily relations with people are limited, are more prone to sex aberrations than men who have frequent and varied human contacts during their working hours. Whether the sex offense is due to the nature of the man's work, or whether the man unconsciously sought that type of work because he was already a potential sex offender and feared human contact, I can't say. How would you like to go talk to Daniel Blank in his office?"

Handry was startled. His drink slopped over the rim of the glass.

"What?" he asked incredulously. "What did you say?"

Delaney started to repeat his question, but the phone on his desk shrilled loudly.

"Delaney here."

"Edward? Thorsen. Can you talk?"

"Not very well."

"Can you listen a moment?"

"Yes."

"Good news. We think Broughton's on the way out. This fourth killing did it. The Mayor and Commissioner and their top aides are meeting tonight on it."

"I see."

"If I hear anything more tonight, I'll let you know."

"Thank you."

"How are you coming?"

"So-so."

"Got a name?"

"Yes."

"Good. Hang in there. Things are beginning to break."

"All right. Thank you for calling."

He hung up, turned back to Handry. "I asked how you'd like to go talk to Daniel Blank in his office."

"Oh sure," Handry nodded. "Just waltz in and say, 'Mr. Blank, Captain Edward X. Delaney of the New York Police Department thinks you axed four men to death on the east side. Would you care to make a statement?' "

"No, not like that," Delaney said seriously. "Javis-Bircham will have a publicity or public relations department, won't they?"

"Bound to."

"I'd do this myself, but you have a press card and identifications man. Identify yourself. Make an appointment. The *top* man. When you go see him, flash your buzzer. Say that your paper is planning a series of personality profiles on young, up-and-coming executives, the—"

"Hey, wait a minute!"

"The new breed of young executives who are familiar with computers, market sampling, demographic percentages and all that shit. Ask the public relations man to suggest four or five young, progressive Javis-Bircham executives who might fit the type your paper is looking for."

"Now see here—"

"Don't—repeat, *do not*—ask for Blank by name. Just come down hard on the fact that you're looking for a young executive familiar with the current use and future value of computers in business operations. Blank is certain to be one of the four or five men he suggests to you. Ask a few questions about each man he suggests. Then you pick Blank. See how easy it is?"

"Easy?" Handry shook his head. "Madness! And what if the Javis-Bircham PR man checks back with the finance editor of my paper and finds out no such series of articles is planned?"

"Chances are he won't. He'll be happy to get the publicity for Javis-Bircham, won't he?"

"But what if he does check? Then I'll be out on my ass."

"So what? You're thinking of quitting anyway, aren't you? So one of your problems is solved right there."

Handry stared at him, shaking his head. "You really are a special kind of bastard," he said in wonderment.

"Or," Delaney went on imperturbably, "if you like, you can give the finance editor on your paper a cover story. Tell him it's a police case—which it is—and if he asks questions, tell him it involves a big embezzlement or fraud or something like that. Don't mention the Lombard case. He'd probably cover for you if the

Javis-Bircham PR man called and say, yes, the paper was planning a series of articles on young, progressive executives. He'd do that for you, wouldn't he?"

"Maybe."

"So you'll do it?"

"Just one question: why the fuck should I?"

"Two answers to that. One, if Blank turns out to be the killer, you'll be the only reporter in the world who had a personal interview with him. That's worth something, isn't it? Two, you want to be a poet, don't you? Or some kind of writer other than a reporter or a rewrite man. How can you expect to be a good writer if you don't understand people, if you don't know what makes them tick? You've got to learn to get inside people, to penetrate their minds, their hearts, their souls. What an opportunity this is—to meet and talk to a man who might have slaughtered four human beings!"

Handry drained his drink in a gulp. He rose, poured himself another, stood with his back to Delaney.

"You really know how to go for the jugular, don't you?"

"Yes."

"Aren't you ever ashamed of the way you manipulate people?"

"I don't manipulate people. Sometimes I give them the chance to do what they want to do and never had the opportunity. Will you do it, Handry?"

There was silence. The reporter took a deep breath, then blew it out. He turned to face Delaney.

"All right," he said.

"Good," the Captain nodded. "Set up the appointment with Blank the way I've outlined it. Use your brains. I know you've got a good brain. The day before your interview is scheduled, give me a call. We'll have a meet and I'll tell you what questions to ask him. Then we'll have a rehearsal."

"A rehearsal?"

"That's right. I'll play Blank, to give you an idea of how he might react to your questions and how you can follow up on things he might or might not say."

"I've interviewed before," Handry protested. "Hundreds of times."

"None as important as this. Handry, you're an amateur liar. I'm going to make you a professional."

The reporter nodded grimly. "If anyone can, you can. You don't miss a trick, do you?"

"I try not to."

"I hope to Christ if I ever commit a crime you don't come after me, Iron Balls."

He sounded bitter.

After Handry left, Delaney sat at his study desk, staring again at the photo of Daniel Blank. The man was handsome, no doubt about it: dark and lean. His face seemed honed; beneath the thin flesh cover the bones of brow, cheeks and jaw were undeniably there. But the Captain could read nothing from that face: neither greed, passion, evil nor weakness. It was a closed-off mask, hiding its secrets.

On impulse, not bothering to analyze his own motive, he took out the Daniel G. Blank file, flipped through it until he found Blank's phone number and dialed it. It rang four times, then:

"Hello?"

"Lou?" Delaney asked. "Lou Jackson?"

"No, I'm afraid you've got the wrong number," the voice said pleasantly.

"Oh. Sorry."

Delaney hung up. It was an agreeable voice, somewhat musical, words clearly enunciated, tone deep, a good resonance. He stared at the photo again, matching what his eyes saw to what his ears had heard. He was beginning, just beginning, to penetrate Daniel Blank.

He worked on his records and files till almost 11:00 P.M., then judged the time was right to call Charles Lipsky. He looked up the apartment house number and called from his study phone.

"Lobby," a whiny voice answered.

"Charles Lipsky, please."

"Yeah. Talking. Who's this?" Delaney caught the caution, the suspicion in that thin, nasal voice. He wondered what doom the doorman expected from a phone call at this hour.

"Mr. Lipsky, my name is Miller, Ward M. Miller. Did your brother-in-law speak to you about me?"

"Oh. Yeah. He called." Now Delaney caught a note of relief, of catastrophe averted or at least postponed.

"I was hoping we might get together, Mr. Lipsky. Just for a short talk."

"Yeah. Well, listen . . ." Now the voice became low, conspiratorial. "You know I ain't supposed to talk to anyone about the tenants. We got a very strict rule against that."

Delaney recognized this virtuous reminder for what it was: a ploy to drive the price up.

"I realize that, Mr. Lipsky, and believe me, you don't have to tell me a thing you feel you shouldn't. But a short talk would be to our mutual advantage. You understand?"

"Well . . . yeah."

"I have an expense account."

"Oh, well, okay then."

"And your name will be kept out of it."

"You're sure?"

"Absolutely. When and where?"

"Well, how soon do you want to make it?"

"As soon as possible. Wherever you say."

"Well, I get off tomorrow morning at four. I usually stop by this luncheonette on Second and Eighty-fifth for coffee before I go home. It's open twenty-four hours a day, but it's usually empty at that hour except for some hackies and hookers."

Delaney knew the place Lipsky referred to, but didn't mention he knew it.

"Second Avenue and Eighty-fifth," he repeated. "About four-fifteen, four-thirty tomorrow morning?"

"Yeah. Around there."

"Fine. I'll be wearing a black Homburg and a double-breasted black overcoat."

"Yeah. All right."

"See you then."

Delaney hung up, satisfied. Lipsky sounded like a grifter, and penny ante at that. He jotted a note to have Thorsen check Department records to see if there was a sheet on Charles Lipsky. Delaney would almost bet there was.

He went immediately to bed, setting his alarm for 3:30 A.M. Thankfully, he fell asleep within half an hour, even as he was rehearsing in his mind how to handle Lipsky and what questions to ask.

The luncheonette had all the charm and ambience of a subway station. The walls and counter were white linoleum tiles, dulled with grease. Counter and table tops were plastic, scarred with cigarette burns. Chairs and counter stools were molded plastic, unpadded to reduce the possibility of vandalism. Rancid grease hung in the air like a wet sheet, and signs taped to the walls would have delighted a linguist: "Turky and all the tremens: $2.25." "Fryed Shrims—$1.85 with French pots and cold slaw." "Our eggs are strickly fresh."

Down at the end of the counter, two hookers, one white, one black, both in orange wigs, were working on plates of steak and eggs, conversing in low voices as fast as they were eating. Closer to the door, three cabbies were drinking coffee, trading wisecracks with the counterman and the black short order cook who was scraping thick rolls of grease off the wide griddle.

Delaney was early, a few minutes after four. When he entered, talk ceased, heads swivelled to inspect him. Apparently he didn't look like a holdup man; when he ordered black coffee and two sugared doughnuts, the other customers went back to their food and talk.

The Captain carried his coffee and doughnuts to a rear table for two. He sat where he could watch the door and the plate glass window. He didn't remove his hat but he unbuttoned his overcoat. He sat patiently, sipping the bitter coffee that had a film of oil glinting on the surface. He ate half a doughnut, then gave up.

His man came in about ten minutes later. Short, almost stunted, but heavy through the waist and hips, like an old jockey gone to seed. His eyes drifted, seemed to float around the room. The other customers glanced at him, but didn't stop eating or talking. The newcomer ordered a cup of light coffee, a piece of apple pie, and brought them over to Delaney's table.

"Miller?"

Delaney nodded. "Mr. Lipsky?"

"Yeah."

The doorman sat down opposite the Captain. He was still wearing his doorman's overcoat and uniform but, incongruously, he was wearing a beaked cap, a horseman's cap, in an horrendous plaid. He looked at Delaney briefly, but then his yellowish eyes floated off, to his food, the floor, the walls, the ceiling.

A grifter. Delaney was sure of it now. And seedy. Always with the shorts. On the take. A sheet that might include gambling arrests, maybe some boosting, receiving stolen property, bad debts, perhaps even an attempted shakedown. Cheap, dirty stuff.

"I ain't got much time," Lipsky said in his low, whiny voice. "I start on days again at noon." He shoveled pie into his surprisingly prim little mouth. "So I got to get home and catch a few hours of shuteye. Then back on the door again at twelve."

"Rough," Delaney said sympathetically. "Did your brother-in-law tell you what this is all about?"

"Yeah," Lipsky nodded, gulping his hot coffee. "This Blank is after some young cunt and her father wants to break it up. Right?"

"That's about it. What can you tell me about Blank?"

Lipsky scraped pie crust crumbs together on his plate with his fingers, picked them up, tossed them down his throat like a man downing a shot of liquor neat.

"Thought you was on an expense account."

Delaney glanced at the other customers. No one was observing them. He took his wallet from his hip pocket, held it on the far side of the table where only Lipsky could see it. He opened it wide, watched Lipsky's hungry eyes slide over and estimate the total. The Captain took out a ten, proffered it under the table edge. It was gone.

"Can't you do better than that?" Lipsky whined. "I'm taking an awful chance."

"Depends," Delaney said. "How long has Blank been living there?"

"I don't know exactly. I been working there four years, and he was living there when I started."

"He was married then?"

"Yeah. A big *zoftig* blonde. A real piece of push. Then he got divorced."

"Know where his ex-wife is living?"

"No."

"Does he have any woman now? Anyone regular who visits him?"

"Yeah. What does this young cunt look like? The one her father doesn't want her to see Blank?"

"About eighteen," Delaney said smoothly. "Long blonde hair. About five-four or five. Maybe one-twenty. Blue eyes. Peaches-and-cream complexion. Big jugs."

"Yum-yum," the doorman said, licking his lips. "I ain't seen anyone like that around."

"Anyone else? Any woman?"

"Yeah. A rich bitch. Mink coat down to her feet. About thirty, thirty-five. No tits. Black hair. White face. No makeup. A weirdo."

"Know her name?"

"No. She comes and she goes by cab."

"Sleep over?"

"Sure. Sometimes. What do you think?"

"That's interesting."

"Yeah? How interesting?"

"You're getting there," Delaney said coldly. "Don't get greedy. Anyone else?"

"No women. A boy."

"A boy?"

"Yeah. About eleven, twelve. Around there. Pretty enough to be a girl. I heard Blank call him Tony."

"What's going on there?"

"What the hell do you think?"

"This Tony ever sleep over?"

"I never seen it. One of the other doors tells me yes. Once or twice."

"This Blank got any close friends? In the building, I mean?"

"The Mortons."

"A family?"

"Married couple. No children. You want a lot for your sawbuck, don't you?"

Sighing, Delaney reached for his wallet again. But he looked up, saw a squad car roll to a stop just outside the luncheonette, and he paused. A uniformed cop got out of the car and came inside. The cabbies had gone, but the two hookers were picking their teeth, finishing their coffee. The cop glanced at them, then his eyes slid over Delaney's table.

He recognized the Captain, and Delaney recognized him. Handrette. A good man. Maybe a little too fast with his stick, but a good, brave cop. And smart enough not to greet a plainclothesman or superior officer out of uniform in public unless spoken to first. His eyes moved away from Delaney. He ordered two hamburgers with everything, two coffees, and two Danish to go. Delaney gave Charles Lipsky another ten.

"Who are the Mortons?" he asked. "Blank's friends."

"Loaded. Top floor penthouse. They own a store on Madison Avenue that sells sex stuff."

"Sex stuff?"

"Yeah," Lipsky said with his wet leer. "You know, candles shaped like pricks. Stuff like that."

Delaney nodded. Probably the Erotica. When he had commanded the 251st, he had made inquiries about the possibility of closing the place down and making it stick. The legal department told him to forget it; it would never hold up in court.

"Blank got any hobbies?" he asked Lipsky casually. "Is he a baseball or football nut? Anything like that?"

"Mountain climbing," Lipsky said. "He likes to climb mountains."

"Climb mountains?" Delaney said, with no change of expression. "He must be crazy."

"Yeah. He's always going away on weekends in the Spring and Fall. He takes all his crap with him in his car."

"Crap? What kind of crap?"

"You know—a knapsack, a sleeping bag, a rope, things you tie on your shoes so you don't slip."

"Oh yes," Delaney said. "Now I know what you mean. And an ax for chipping away ice and rocks. Does he take an ax with him on these trips?"

"Never seen it. What's this got to do with cutting him loose from the young cunt?"

"Nothing," Delaney shrugged. "Just trying to get a line on him. Listen, to get back to this woman of his. The skinny one with black hair. You know her name?"

"No."

"She come around very often?"

"She'll be there like three nights in a row. Then I won't see her for a week or so. No regular schedule, if that's what you're hoping." He grinned shrewdly at Delaney. Two of his front teeth were missing, two were chipped; the Captain wondered what kind of bet he had welshed on.

"Comes and goes by cab?"

"That's right. Or they walk out together."

"The next time you're on duty, if she comes or goes by cab, get the license number of the hack, the date, and the time. That's all I need—the date, the time, the license number of the cab. There's another tenner in it for you."

"And then all you got to do is check the trip sheets. Right?"

"Right," Delaney said, smiling bleakly. "You're way ahead of me."

"I could have been a private eye," Lipsky bragged. "I'd make a hell of a dick. Listen, I got to go now."

"Wait. Wait just a minute," Delaney said, making up his mind that moment. He watched the cop pay for the hamburgers, coffee, Danish and carry the bag out to his partner in the parked squad. He wondered idly if the cop insisted on paying because he, the Captain, was there.

"In your apartment house," Delaney said slowly, "you keep master keys? Or dupes to all the door locks on tenants' doors, locks they put on themselves?"

"Sure we got dupes," Lipsky frowned. "What do you think? I mean, in case of fire or an emergency, we got to get in—right?"

"And where are all these keys kept?"

"Right outside the assistant manager's office we got—" Lipsky stopped suddenly. His lips drew back from his chipped teeth. "If you're thinking what I think you're thinking," he said, "forget it. Not a chance. No way."

"Look, Mr. Lipsky," Delaney said earnestly, sincerely, hunching forward on the table. "It's not like I want to loot the place. I wouldn't take a cigarette butt out of there. All I want to do is look around."

"Yeah? For what?"

"This woman he's been sleeping with. Maybe a photo of them together. Maybe a letter from her to him. Maybe she's keeping some clothes up there in his closet. Anything that'll help my client convince his daughter that Blank has been cheating on her all along."

"But if you don't take anything, how . . ."

"You tell me," Delaney said. "You claim you could have been a private eye. How would you handle it?"

Lipsky stared at him, puzzled. Then his eyes widened. "Camera!" he gasped. "A miniature camera. You take pictures!"

Delaney slapped the table top with his palm. "Mr. Lipsky, you're all right," he chuckled. "You'd make a hell of a detective. I take a miniature camera. I shoot letters, photos, clothes, any evidence at all that Blank has been shacking up with this black-haired twist or even this kid Tony. I put everything back exactly where it was. Believe me, I know how to do it. He'll never know anyone's been in there. He leaves for work around nine and comes back around six. Something like that—correct?"

"Yeah."

"So the apartment's empty all day?"

"Yeah."

"Cleaning woman?"

"Two days a week. But she comes early and she's out by noon."

"So . . . what's the problem? It'll take me an hour. No more, I swear. Would anyone miss the keys?"

"Nah. That board's got a zillion keys."

"So there you are. I come into the lobby. You've already got the keys off the board. You slip them to me. I'm up and down in an hour. Probably less. I pass the keys back to you. You replace them. You're going on duty days starting today—right? So we make it about two or three in the afternoon. Right?"

"How much?" Lipsky said hoarsely.

Got him, Delaney thought.

"Twenty bucks," the Captain said.

"Twenty?" Lipsky cried, horrified. "I wouldn't do it for less than a C. If I'm caught, it's my ass."

Five minutes later they had agreed on fifty dollars, twenty immediately, thirty when Delaney returned the keys, and an extra twenty if Lipsky could get the license number of the cab used by Blank's skinny girl friend.

"If I get it," Lipsky said, "should I call your office?"

"I'm not in very much," Delaney said casually. "In this business you've got to keep moving around. I'll call you every day on the lobby phone. If you go back on nights, leave a message with your brother-in-law. I'll find out from him when to call. Okay?"

"I guess," Lipsky said doubtfully. "Jesus, if I didn't need the dough so bad, I'd tell you to go suck."

"Sharks?" the Captain asked.

"Yeah," Lipsky said wonderingly. "How did you know?"

"A guess," Delaney shrugged. He passed twenty under the table to the doorman. "I'll see you at two-thirty this afternoon. What's the apartment number?"

"Twenty-one H. It's on a tag attached to the keys."

"Good. Don't worry. It'll go like silk."

"Jesus, I hope so."

The Captain looked at him narrowly. "You don't like this guy much, do you?"

Lipsky began to curse, ripe obscenities spluttering from his lips. Delaney listened awhile, serious and unsmiling, then held up a hand to cut off the flow of invective.

"One more thing," he said to Lipsky. "In a few days, or a week from now, you might mention casually to Blank that I was around asking questions about him. You can describe me, but don't tell him my name. You forgot it. Just say I was asking personal questions, but you wouldn't tell me a goddamned thing. Got that?"

"Well . . . sure," Lipsky said, puzzled. "But what for?"

"I don't know," Captain Delaney said. "I'm not sure. Just to give him something to think about, I guess. Will you do it?"

"Yeah. Sure. Why not?"

They left the luncheonette together. There were early workers on the streets now. The air was cold, sharp. The sky was lightening in the east; it promised to be a clear day. Captain Delaney walked home slowly, leaning against the December wind. By the time he unlocked his door he could hardly smell the rancid grease.

The projected break-in had been a spur-of-the-moment thing. He hadn't planned that, hadn't even considered it. But Lipsky had tied Daniel Blank to mountain climbing: the first time that was definitely established. And that led to the ice ax. That damned ax! Nothing so far had tied Blank to the purchase or possession of an ice ax. Delaney wanted things tidy. Possession would be tidy enough; purchase could be traced later.

He wasn't lying when he told Lipsky he'd be in and out of Blank's apartment in an hour. My God, he could find an ice ax in Grand Central Station in that time. And why should Blank hide it? As far as he knew, he wasn't suspected. He owned rucksack, pitons, crampons, ice ax. What could be more natural? He was a mountaineer. All Delaney wanted from that break-in was the ice ax. Anything else would be gravy on the roast.

He wrote up his reports and noted, gratified, how fat the Daniel G. Blank file was growing. More important, how he was beginning to penetrate his man. Tony, a twelve-year-old boy pretty enough to be a girl. A thin, black-haired woman with no tits. Friends who owned a sex boutique. Much, much there. But if the ice ax didn't exist in Blank's apartment, it was all smoke. What would he do then? Start in again—someone else, another angle, a different approach. He was prepared for it.

He worked on his reports until Mary arrived. She fixed him coffee, dry toast, a soft-boiled egg. No grease. After breakfast, he went into the living room, pulled the shades, took off his shoes and jacket, unbuttoned his vest. He lay down on the couch, intending to nap for only an hour. But when he awoke, it was almost 11:30, and he was angry at himself for time wasted.

He went into the downstairs lavatory to rub his face with cold water and comb his hair. In the mirror he saw how he looked, but he had already felt it: blueish bags swelling down beneath his eyes, the greyish unhealthy complexion, lines deeper, wrinkled forehead, bloodless lips pressed tighter, everything old and troubled. When all this was over, and Barbara was well again, they'd go somewhere, groan in the sun, stuff until their skins were tight, eyes clear, memories washed, blood pure and pumping. And they'd make love. That's what he told himself.

He called Monica Gilbert.

"Monica, I'm going over to visit my wife. I was wondering if—if you're not busy—if you'd like to meet her."

"Oh yes. I would. When?"

"Fifteen minutes or so. Too soon? Would you like lunch first?"

"Thank you, but I've had a salad. That's all I'm eating these days."

"A diet?" he laughed. "You don't need that."

"I do. I've been eating so much since—since Bernie died. Just nerves, I guess. Edward . . ."

"What?"

"You said you'd call me about Daniel Blank, but you didn't. Was it anything?"

"I think so. But I'd like my wife to hear it, too. I trust her judgment. She's very good on people. I'll tell you both at the same time. All right?"

"Of course."

"Be over in fifteen minutes."

Then he called Barbara and told her he was bringing Monica Gilbert to meet her, the widow of the second victim. Barbara said of course. She was happy to talk to him and told him to hurry.

He had thought about it a long time—whether or not to bring the two women together. He recognized the dangers and the advantages. He didn't want Barbara to think, even to suspect, that he was having a relationship—even an innocent relationship—with another woman while she, Barbara, was ill, confined to a hospital room, despite what she had said about his marrying again if anything happened to her. That was just talk, he decided firmly: an emotional outburst from a woman disturbed by her own pain and fears of the future. But Barbara would enjoy company—that he knew. She really did like people, much more than he did. He could tell her of a man arrested for molesting women—there was one crazy case: this nut would sneak into bedrooms out in Queens, always coming through unlocked windows, and he would kiss sleeping women and then run away. He never put his hands on them or injured them physically. He just kissed them. When he told Barbara about it, she gave a troubled sigh and said, "Poor fellow. How lonely he must have been."—and her sympathies were frequently with the suspect, unless violence was involved.

Monica Gilbert needed a confidante as well. Her job was finished, her file complete. He wanted to continue giving her a feeling of involvement. So, finally, he had decided to bring them together.

It wasn't a disaster, as he had feared, but it didn't go marvelously well, as he had hoped. Both women were cordial, but nervous, guarded, reserved. Monica had brought Barbara a little African violet, not from a florist's shop but one she had nurtured herself. That helped. Barbara expressed her condolences in low tones on the death of Monica's husband. Delaney stayed out of it, standing away from Barbara's bed, listening and watching anxiously.

Then they began speaking about their children, exchanging photographs and smiling. Their talk became louder than sickroom tones; they laughed more frequently; Barbara touched Monica's arm. Then he knew it was going to be all right. He relaxed, sat in a chair away from them, listening to their chatter, comparing them: Barbara so thin and fine, wasted and elegant, a silver sword of a woman. And Monica with her heavy peasant's body, sturdy and hard, bursting with juice. At that moment he loved them both.

For awhile they leaned close, conversing in whispers. He wondered if they might be talking about women's ailments, women's plumbing—a complete mystery to him—or perhaps, from occasional glances they threw in his direction, he wondered if they might be discussing him, although what there was about him to talk about he couldn't imagine.

It was almost an hour before Barbara held out a hand to him. He came over to her bedside, smiling at both of them.

"Daniel Blank?" Barbara asked.

He told them about the interviews with the bartender, with Handry, with Lipsky. He told them everything except his plan to be inside Blank's apartment within two hours.

"Edward, it's beginning to take form," Barbara nodded approvingly. As usual, she went to the nub. "At least now you know he's a mountain climber. I suppose the next step is to find out if he owns an ice ax?"

Delaney nodded. She would never even consider asking him how he might do this.

"Can't you arrest him now?" Monica Gilbert demanded. "On suspicion or something?"

The Captain shook his head. "Not a chance," he said patiently. "No evidence at all. Not a shred. He'd be out before the cell door was slammed behind him, and the city would be liable for false arrest. That would be the end of that."

"Well, what can you do then? Wait until he kills someone else?"

"Oh . . ." he said vaguely, "there are things. Establish his guilt without a doubt. He's just a suspect now, you know. The only one I've got. But still just a suspect. Then, when I'm sure of him, I'll—well, at this moment I'm not sure what I'll do. Something."

"I'm sure you will," Barbara smiled, taking Monica's hand. "My husband is a very stubborn man. And he's neat. He doesn't like loose ends."

They all laughed. Delaney glanced at his watch, saw he had to leave. He offered to take Monica Gilbert home, but she wanted to stay awhile and said she'd leave when it was time to pick up her girls at school. Delaney glanced at Barbara, realized she wanted Monica's company a while longer. He kissed Barbara's cheek, nodded brightly at both, lumbered from the room. Outside in the hall, adjusting his Homburg squarely atop his head, he heard a sudden burst of laughter from inside the room, quickly suppressed. He wondered if they could be laughing at him, something he had done or said. But he was used to people finding him amusing; it didn't bother him.

He had never, of course, had any intention of taking a camera to Blank's apartment. What would a photograph of an ice ax prove? But he did take a set of locksmith's picks, of fine Swedish steel, fitted into individual pockets in a thin chamois case. Included in the set were long, slender tweezers. The case went into his inside jacket pocket. In the lefthand pocket he clipped a two-battery penlite. Into his overcoat pocket he folded a pair of thin black silk gloves. Barbara called them his "undertaker's gloves."

At 2:30, Captain Delaney walked steadily up the driveway, pushed through the lobby door. Lipsky saw him almost at once. His face was pale, sheeny with sweat. His hand dipped into his lefthand jacket pocket. Brainless idiot, Delaney thought mournfully. The whole idea had been to transfer the keys during a normal handshake. Well, it couldn't be helped now . . .

He advanced, smiling, holding out his right hand. Lipsky grabbed it with a damp palm and only then realized the keys were gripped in his left fist. He dropped Delaney's hand, transferred the keys, almost losing them in the process. Delaney plucked them lightly from Lipsky's nerveless fingers. The Captain slid them into his overcoat pocket, still smiling slightly, and said, "Any trouble, give me three fast rings on the intercom."

Lipsky turned even paler. It was a warning Delaney had deliberately avoided giving the doorman at the luncheonette; it might have queered the whole thing right then.

He sauntered slowly toward the elevator banks, turning left to face the cars marked 15–34. Two other people were waiting: a man flipping through a magazine, a woman with an overflowing Bloomingdale's shopping bag. A door slid open on a self-service elevator; a young couple with a small child came out. Delaney hung back a moment, then followed the other two into the elevator. The man punched 16, the woman pushed 21—Blank's floor. Delaney pressed 24.

Both men removed their hats. They rode up in silence. The magazine reader got off at 16. The woman with the shopping bag got off at 21. Delaney rode up to 24 and stepped out. He killed a few minutes pinpointing the direction of apartment H, assuming it was in the same location on every floor.

He came back to the elevators to push the Down button. Thankfully, the elevator that stopped for him a moment later was empty. He pushed 21, suddenly became aware of the soft music. He didn't recognize the tune. The door opened at 21. He pushed the Lobby button, then stepped out quickly before the doors closed.

The 21st Floor corridor was empty. He took off his fleece-lined leather gloves, stuffed them in an overcoat pocket, pulled on his "undertaker's gloves." As he walked the carpeted corridor, he scraped soles and heels heavily, hoping to remove whatever mud or dog shit or dust or dirt that had accumulated, possibly to show up in Blank's apartment. And he noted the peephole in every door.

He rang the bell of apartment 21-H twice, heard it peal quietly inside. He waited a few moments. No answer. He went to work.

He had no trouble with two of the keys, but the third lock, the police bar, took more time. His hands were so large that he could not slip his fingers inside the partly opened door to disengage the diagonal rod. He finally took the tweezers from his pick case and, working slowly and without panic, moved the bar up out of its slot. The door swung open.

He stepped inside, closed the door gently behind him but did not lock it. He moved through the apartment swiftly, opening closet doors, glancing inside, closing them. He peeked behind the shower curtain in the bathroom, went down on his knees to peer under the bed. When he was satisfied the apartment was unoccupied, he returned to the front door, locked it, set the police bar in place.

The next step was silly, but basic. But perhaps not so silly. He remembered the case of a dick two who had spent four hours tossing the wrong apartment. Delaney went looking for subscription magazines, letters . . . anything. He found a shelf of books on computer technology. Each one, on the front end paper, bore an engraved bookplate neatly pasted in place. A nude youth with bow and arrow leaping through a forest glade. "Ex Libris. Daniel G. Blank." Good enough.

He returned to the front door again, put his back against it, then began to stroll, to wander through the apartment. Just to absorb it, to try to understand what kind of a man lived here.

But did anyone live here? Actually breathe, sleep, eat, fart, belch, defecate in these sterile operating rooms? No cigarette butts, no tossed newspapers, no smells, no photos, personal mementoes, vulgar little geegaws, souvenirs, no unwashed glass or chipped paint or old burns or a cracked ceiling. It was all so antiseptic he could hardly believe it; the cold order and cleanliness were overwhelming. Furniture in black leather and chrome. Crystal ashtrays precisely arranged. An iron candelabra with each taper carefully burned down to a different length.

He thought of his own home: his, Barbara's, their family's.

Their home sang their history, who they were, their taste and lack of taste, worn things, used things, roots, smells of living, memories everywhere. You could write a biography of Edward X. Delaney from his home. But who was Daniel G. Blank? This decorator's showroom, this model apartment said nothing. Unless . . .

That heavy beveled mirror in the foyer, handsomely framed. That long wall in the living room bearing at least 50 small mirrors of various shapes, individually framed. A full-length mirror on the bedroom door. A double medicine cabinet, both sliding doors mirrored. Did that plethora of mirrors say anything about the man who lived there?

There was another sure tip-off, to anyone's life style: the contents of the refrigerator, kitchen cabinets, the bathroom cabinet. In the refrigerator, a bottle of vodka, three bottles of juice—orange, grapefruit, tomato. Salad fixings. Apples, tangerines, plums, peaches, dried apricots and dried prunes. In the cabinets, coffee, herbal teas, spices, health foods, organic cereals. No meats anywhere. No cheese. No coldcuts. No bread. No potatoes. But sliced celery and carrots.

In the bathroom, behind the sliding cabinet doors, he found the scented soaps, oils, perfumes, colognes, lotions, unguents, powders, deodorants, sprays. One bottle of aspirin. One bottle of pills, almost full, he recognized as Librium. One envelope of pills he could not identify. One bottle of vitamin B-12 pills. Shaving gear. He closed the doors with the tips of his gloved fingers. Was the toilet paper scented? It was. He glanced at his watch. About ten minutes so far.

Once again he returned to the entrance, trying to walk softly in case the tenant in the apartment might hear footsteps and wonder who was in Mr. Blank's apartment at this hour.

He switched on the overhead light, opened the door of the foyer closet.

On the top shelf: six closed hatboxes and a trooper's winter hat of black fur.

On the rod: two overcoats, three topcoats, two raincoats, a thigh-length coat of military canvas, olive-drab, fleece-lined, with an attached hood, a waist-length jacket, fur-lined, two lightweight nylon jackets.

On the floor: a sleeping bag rolled up and strapped, heavy climbing boots with ridged soles, a set of steel crampons, a rucksack, a webbed belt, a coil of nylon line, and . . .

One ice ax.

There it was. It was that easy. An ice ax. Delaney stared at it, feeling no elation. Perhaps satisfaction. No more than that.

He stared at it for almost a minute, not doubting his eyes but memorizing its exact position. Balanced on the handle butt. The head leaning against two walls in the corner. The leather thong loop from the end of the handle curved to the right, then doubled back upon itself.

The Captain reached in, picked it up in his gloved hand. He examined it closely. "Made in West Germany." Similar to those sold by Outside Life. He sniffed at the head. Oiled steel. The handle darkened with sweat stains. Using one of his lock picks, he gently prized the leather covering away from the steel shaft, just slightly. No stains beneath the leather. But then, he hadn't expected to find any.

He stood gripping the ax, loath to put it down. But it could tell him nothing more; he doubted very much if it could tell the forensic men anything either. He replaced it as carefully as he could, leaning it into the corner at the original angle, arranging the leather thong in its double-backed loop. He closed the closet door, looked at his watch. Fifteen minutes.

The living room floor was a checkerboard pattern, alternating black and white tiles, 18 inches square. Scattered about were six small rugs in bright colors and modern design. Scandinavian, he guessed. He lifted each rug, looked underneath. He didn't expect to find anything; he didn't.

He wasted a few minutes staring at that long mirrored wall, watching his image jerk along as he moved. He would have liked to search behind each mirror but knew it would take forever, and he'd never get them back in their precise pattern. He turned instead to a desk near the window. It was a slim, elegant spider of chrome and glass. One center drawer, one deep file drawer on the left side.

The top drawer was marvelously organized with a white plastic divider: paper clips (two sizes), sharpened pencils, stamps, built-in Scotch tape dispenser, scissors, ruler, letter opener, magnifying glass—all matching. Delaney was impressed. Not envious, but impressed.

There were three documents. One was a winter catalogue from Outside Life; the Captain smiled, without mirth. One, in a back corner, was obviously half a salary check, the half that listed taxes, pension payment, hospitalization, and similar deductions. Delaney put on his glasses to read it. According to his calculations, Blank was earning about $55,000 a year. That was nice.

The third document was an opened manila envelope addressed to Mr. Daniel G. Blank from something called Medical Examiners Institute. Delaney drew out the stapled report, scanned it quickly. Apparently, six months ago, Blank had undergone a complete physical checkup. He had had the usual minor childhood illnesses, but the only operation noted was a tonsillectomy at the age of nine. His blood pressure was just slightly below normal, and he had a 20 percent impairment of hearing in his left ear. But other than that, he seemed to be in perfect physical condition for a man his age.

Delaney replaced this document and then, recalling something, drew it out again. In his pocket notebook he made a notation of Blank's blood type.

The deep file drawer contained one object: a metal document box. Delaney lifted it out, placed it atop the desk, examined it. Grey steel. Locked, with the lock on top. White plastic handle in front. About 12 inches long, eight inches wide, four inches deep. He could never understand why people bought such boxes for their valuables. It was true the box might be fire-resistant, but no professional thief would waste time forcing or picking the lock; he'd just carry the entire box away by its neat plastic handle, or slip it into a pillowcase with his other loot.

Delaney took a closer look at the lock. Five minutes at the most, but was it worth it? Probably checkbooks, bank books, maybe some cash, his lease, passport, a few documents not valuable enough to put in his safe deposit box. Blank, he was certain, would have a safe deposit box. He was that kind of a man. He replaced the document box in the desk, closed the drawer firmly. If he had time, he'd come back to it. He glanced at his watch; almost 25 minutes.

He moved toward the bedroom. But he paused before an ebony and aluminum liquor cabinet. He could not resist it, and opened the two doors. Matching glassware on one side: Baccarat crystal, and beautiful. What was it Handry had asked? What does Blank do with his money? He could tell Handry now: he buys Baccarat crystal.

The liquor supply was curious: one gin, one Scotch, one rye, one bourbon, one rum, and at least a dozen bottles of brandies and cordials. Curiouser and curiouser. What did a grown man want with an ink-colored liqueur called Fleur d'Amour?

There was a technique to a good search; some dicks were better at it than others. It was a special skill. Delaney knew he was good at it, but he knew others who were better. There was an old detective—the Captain thought he was probably retired by now—who could go through a six-room house in an hour and find the cancelled stamp he was looking for, or a single earring, or a glassine envelope of shit. You simply could not hide anything with absolute certainty that it could never be found. Given enough time, enough men, anything could be found, anywhere. Swallow a metal capsule? Stick a microfilm up your ass? Put a microdot in a ground-out tooth and have it capped? Tattoo your skull and let the hair grow over? Forget it. Anything could be found.

But those methods were rare and exotic. Most people with something to hide—documents, money, evidence, drugs—hid it in their own home or apartment. Easy to check its safety. Easy to destroy fast in an emergency. Easy to get when needed.

But within their homes—as the cops good at tossing well knew—most people had two tendencies: one rational, one emotional. The rational was that, if you lived a reasonably normal life, you had visitors: friends and neighbors dropping in, sometimes unexpectedly. So you did not hide your secret in the foyer, living room, or dining room: areas that were occupied by others at various times, where the hidden object might, by accident, be uncovered or be discovered by a drunken and/or inquisitive guest. So you selected bathroom or bedroom, the two rooms in your home indisputedly *yours*.

The emotional reason for choosing bathroom *or* bedroom was this: they were intimate rooms. You were naked there. You slept there, bathed, performed your bodily functions. They were your "secret places." Where else would you conceal something secret, of great value to you alone, something you could not share?

Delaney went directly to the bathroom, removed the top of the toilet tank. An old trick but still used occasionally. Nothing in there except, he was amused to note, a plastic daisy and a bar of solid deodorant that kept Daniel Blank's toilet bowl sweet-smelling and clean. Beautiful.

He tapped the wall tiles rapidly, lifted the tufted bathmat from the floor and looked underneath, made a closer inspection of the medicine cabinets, used his penlite to tap the length of the shower curtain rod. All hollow. What was he looking for? He knew but would not admit it to himself. Not at this moment. He was just looking.

Into the bedroom. Under the rug again. A long wiggle under the bed to inspect the spring. A careful hand thrust between spring and mattress. Under the pillows. Then the bed restored to its taut neatness. Nothing in the Venetian blinds. Base of the lamp? Nothing. Two framed French posters on the walls. Nothing on their backs. The paper appeared intact. That left the wall-length closet and the two dressers in pale Danish wood. He looked at his watch. Coming up to forty minutes. He was sweating now; he had not removed hat or overcoat or taken anything from his pockets that he did not immediately replace.

He tried the closet first. Two wide, hinged, louvered doors that could be folded back completely. So he did, and gazed in astonishment. He himself was a tidy man, but compared to Daniel Blank he was a lubber. Delaney liked his personal linen folded softly, neatly stacked with fold forward, newly laundered to the bottom. But this display in Blank's closet, this was—was mechanized!

The top shelf, running the length of both closets, held linen: sheets, pillowcases, beach towels, bath towels, bathmats, hand towels, dish towels, washcloths, napkins, tablecloths, mattress covers, mattress pads, and a stack of heavy things whose function Delaney could only guess at, although they might have been dustcloths for covering furniture during an extended absence.

But what was so amazing was the precision with which these stacks had been arranged. Was it a militaristic cleaning woman or Blank himself who had adjusted these individual stacks, and then aligned all stacks as if with a stretched string? And the colors! No white sheets and pillowcases here, no dull towels and washcloths, but bright, jumping colors, floral designs, abstract patterns: an eye-jarring display. How to reconcile this extravagance with the white-and-black sterility of the living room, the architectural furniture?

On the floors of both closets were racks of shoes. In the left-hand closet, summer shoes—whites, sneakers, multicolors—each pair fitted with trees, encased in clear plastic bags. In the other closet, winter shoes, also with trees but not bagged. Practically all blacks these, mostly slip-ons, moccasin styles, two pair of buckled Guccis, three pairs of boots, one knee-high.

Similarly, hanging from the rod, summer clothing on the left, winter on the right. The summer suits were bagged in clear plastic, jackets on wooden hangers, trousers suspended from their cuffs on clamps. The uncovered winter suits were almost all black or midnight blue. There was a suede sports jacket, a tartan, a modest hound's tooth. Four pairs of slacks: two grey flannel, one tartan, one a bottle-green suede. Two silk dressing gowns, one in a bird print, one with purple orchids.

Delaney did the best he could in a short time, feeling between and under the stacks of linen, shaking the shoes heels downward, pressing between his palms the bottoms of the plastic bags that protected the summer suits. He went into the living room, removed a small metal mirror from its hook on the wall, and by stretching, using the mirror and his penlight, he was able to see behind the stacks of linen on the top shelf. It was, he admitted, a cursory search, but better than nothing. That's just what he found—nothing. He returned the mirror to its hook, adjusted it carefully.

That left the two dressers. They were matching pieces, each with three full drawers below and two half-drawers on top. He looked at his watch. About 46 minutes gone now. He had promised Lipsky an hour, no more.

He started on the dresser closest to the bedroom window. The first half-drawer he opened was all jewelry, loose or in small leather cases: tie pins, cufflinks, studs, tie tacks, a few things he couldn't immediately understand—a belt of gold links, for instance, and a gold link wristwatch band, three obviously expensive identification bracelets, two heavy masculine necklaces, seven rings, a hand-hammered golden heart strung on a fine chain. He cautiously pried under everything.

The other half-drawer contained handkerchiefs, and how long had it been since he had seen Irish linen laundered to a silken feel? Nothing underneath.

Top full drawer: hosiery, at least fifty pair, from black silk formal to knee-length Argyle-patterned knits. Nothing there.

Second and third full drawers: shirts. Obviously business shirts in the second: white and light blue in a conservative cut. In the third drawer, sports shirts, wilder hues, patterns, knits, polyesters. Again he thrust his hand carefully between and beneath the neat piles. His silk-covered fingers slid on something smooth. He drew it out.

It was, or had been originally, an 8 × 10 glossy photo of Daniel Blank taken in the nude. Not recently. He looked younger. His hair was thicker. He was standing with his hands on his hips, laughing at the camera. He had, Delaney realized, a beautiful body. Not handsome, not rugged, not especially muscular. But beautiful: wide shoulders, slender waist, good arms. It was impossible to judge his legs since the photograph had been cut across just above the pubic hair, by scissors, razor, or knife. Blank stood smiling at Delaney, hands on hips, prick and balls excised and missing. The Captain carefully slid the mutilated photo back beneath the knitted sports shirts.

He went to the second dresser now, feeling certain he would find little of significance, but wanting to learn this man. He had already observed enough to keep him pondering for weeks, but there might be more.

One half-drawer of the second dresser contained scarves: mostly foulard ascots, squares, a formal white silk scarf, a few patterned handkerchiefs. The second half-drawer contained a miscellany: two crushable linen beach hats, two pairs of sunglasses, a bottle of suntan lotion in a plastic bag, a tube of "Cover-All" sunscreen cream, and timetables of airline flights to Florida, the West Indies, Britain, Brazil, Switzerland, France, Italy, Sweden—all bound together with a rubber band.

The top full drawer was underwear. Delaney looked at the assortment, oddly moved. It was a feeling he had had before when searching the apartment of a stranger: secret intimacy. He remembered once sitting around in a squad room, just relaxing with two other detectives, gossiping, telling stories about their cases and experiences. One of the dicks was telling about a recent toss he had made of the premises of a hooker who had been beaten to death by one of her customers.

"My God," the cop said, "I handled all her underwear and that frilly stuff, her garter belt and that thing they pin their napkins on and blue baby-doll pajamas she had, and the smell of it all, and I damned near came in my pants."

The others laughed, but they knew what he meant. It wasn't only that she had been a whore with lacy things that smelled sexy. It was the secret sharing, entering into another's life as a god might enter—unseen, unsuspected, but penetrating into a human being and knowing.

That was something of what Captain Edward X. Delaney felt, staring at Blank's precise stacks of briefs, bikinis, shorts, stretch panties, trimmed garments in colors he could not believe were sold anywhere but in women's lingerie shops. But stolidly he felt beneath each stack after flipping them through, replaced everything meticulously, and went on.

The second full drawer was pajamas: jackets and pants in nylon, cotton, flannel. Sleep coats. Even a bright red nightshirt.

The bottom drawer was bathing suits—more than one man could use in a lifetime: everything from the tiniest of bikinis to long-legged surfing trunks. Three jockstraps, one no larger than an eyepatch. And in with it all, unexpectedly, six pairs of winter gloves: thin, black leather; rough cowhide, fleece-lined; bright yellow suede; grey formal with black stitching along the knuckles; etc. Nothing. Between items or underneath.

Delaney closed the final drawer, drew a deep breath. He looked at his watch again. Five minutes to go. He might stretch it a minute or two, but no more. Then, he was certain, he'd hear three frantic intercom rings from a spooked Charles Lipsky.

He could open that document case in the living room desk. He could take a look at the bottom kitchen cabinets. He could try several things. On impulse, nothing more, he got down on his hands and knees, felt beneath the bottom drawer of one of the dressers. Nothing. He crawled on hands and knees, felt beneath the other. Nothing. But as he felt about, the wood panel pressed slightly upward.

Now that was surprising. In chests of drawers as expensive and elegant as these appeared to be, he would have guessed a solid piece of wood beneath the bottom drawer, and between each pair of drawers another flat layer of wood. They were called "dust covers," he remembered. Good furniture had them. Cheaply made chests had no horizontal partitions between the bottom of one drawer and the open top of the one beneath.

He climbed to his feet, brushed his overcoat, knees, and trouser cuffs free of carpet lint. There was lint; he picked it off carefully, put it into a vest pocket. Then he opened a few dresser drawers at random. It was true; there were no wooden partitions between drawers; they were simply stacked. Well, it would only take a minute . . .

He pulled out the first full drawer of one dresser, reached in and felt the bottom surfaces of the two half-drawers above it. Nothing. He closed the first full drawer, opened the second and ran his fingers over the bottom surface of the first full drawer. Nothing. He continued in this fashion. It only took seconds. Seconds of nothing.

He started on the second dresser. Closed the drawer containing Blank's incredible underwear, opened the drawer containing pajamas, thrust his hand in to feel the undersurface of the drawer above. And stopped. He withdrew his hand a moment, wiped his silk-clad fingertips on his overcoat, reached in again, felt cautiously. Something there.

"Please, God," he said aloud.

Slowly, with infinite caution, he closed the pajama drawer and then drew out the one above it, the underwear drawer. He drew it halfway out of the dresser. Then, fearful there might be wood splinters on the runners, sawdust, stains, anything, he took off his overcoat and laid it out on Daniel Blank's bed, lining side up. Then he carefully removed the underwear drawer completely from the chest, placed it softly on his overcoat. He didn't look at his watch now. Fuck Charles Lipsky.

He removed the stacks of underwear, placing them on the other side of the bed in the exact order in which he removed them. Four stacks across, two stacks back to front. They'd be returned to the drawer in the same order. When the drawer was empty, he slowly turned it upside down and placed it on his opened overcoat. He stared at the taped envelope. He could appreciate Blank's reasoning: if the tape dried out and the envelope dropped, it could only drop into the next drawer down.

He pressed the envelope gently with his fingertips. Things stiffer than paper, and something hard. Leather maybe, wood or metal. The envelope was taped to the wooden bottom of the drawer on all its four sides. He put on his glasses again, bent over it. He used one of his lock picks, probed gently at the corners of the envelope where the strips of tape didn't quite meet.

He wanted to avoid, if possible, removing the four strips of tape completely. He finally determined, to his satisfaction, the top of the envelope. Using a pick, he lifted a tiny corner of the top tape. Then he switched to tweezers. Slowly, slowly, with infinite caution, he peeled the tape away from the wood, making certain he did not pull the tape away from the paper envelope. Tape peeled off the rough wood stickily; he tried to curl it back without tearing it or folding it. He heard, dimly, three sharp rings on the intercom, but he didn't pause. Screw Lipsky. Let him sweat for his fifty bucks.

When the top tape was free of the wood, he switched back to a locksmith's pick, slender as a surgeon's scalpel. He knew the envelope flap would be unsealed, he *knew* it! Well, it wasn't just luck or instinct. Why should Blank want to seal the envelope? He'd want to gloat over his goodies, and add more to them later.

Gently Delaney prized out the envelope flap, lifted it. He leaned forward to smell at the open envelope. A scent of roses. Back to the tweezers again, and he carefully withdrew the contents, laying them out on his overcoat lining in the order in which they had been inserted in the envelope: Frank Lombard's driver's license. Bernard Gilbert's ID card. Detective Kope's shield and identification. And four withered rose petals. From Albert Feinberg's boutonniere. Delaney turned them over and over with his tweezers. Then he left them alone, lying there, walked to the window, put his hands in his pockets, stared out.

It really was a beautiful day. Crisp, clear. Everyone had been predicting a mild winter. He hoped so. He'd had his fill of snow, slush, blizzards, garbage-decked drifts—all the crap. He and Barbara would retire to some warm place, some place quiet. Not Florida. He didn't enjoy the heat that much. But maybe to the Carolinas. Some place like that. He'd go fishing. He had never fished in his life, but he could learn. Barbara would have a decent garden. She'd love that.

God damn it, it wasn't the murders! He had seen the results of murder without end. Murders by gun, by knife, by strangling, by bludgeoning, by drowning, by stomping, by—by anything. You name it; he had seen it. And he had handled homicides where the corpse was robbed: money taken, fingers cut off to get the rings, necklaces wrenched from a dead neck, even shoes taken and, in one case, gold teeth pulled out with pliers.

He turned back to that display on his overcoat. This was the worst. He could not say exactly why, but this was an obscenity so awful he wasn't certain he wanted to live, to be a member of the human race. This was despoiling the dead, not for vengeance, want, or greed, but for—for what? A souvenir? A trophy? A scalp? There was something godless about it, something he could not endure. He didn't know. He just didn't know. Not right now. But he'd think about it.

He cleaned up fast. Everything back into the envelope with tweezers, in the exact order in which they had originally been packed. The envelope flap tucked under with no bend or crease. The top tape pressed down again upon the wood. It held. The drawer turned rightside up. Underwear back in neat stacks in the original order. Drawer slid into the dresser. He inspected the lining of his overcoat. Some wood dust there, from the drawer runners. He went into the bathroom, moistened two sheets of toilet paper at the sink, came back into the bedroom, sponged his overcoat lining clean. Back into the bathroom, used tissues into the toilet. But before he flushed, he used two more squares to wipe the sink dry. Then those went into the toilet also; he flushed all away. He would, he thought sardonically—and not for the first time—have made a hell of a murderer.

He made a quick trip of inspection through the apartment. All clean. He was at the front door, his hand on the knob, when he thought of something else. He went back into the kitchen, opened the lower cabinets. A plastic pail, detergents, roach spray, floor wax, furniture polish. And, what he had hoped to find, a small can of light machine oil.

He tore a square of paper towel from the roll hanging from the kitchen wall. Could this man keep track of pieces of toilet paper or sections of paper towel? Delaney wouldn't be a bit surprised. But he soaked the paper towel in the machine oil, folded it up, put it inside one of his fleece-lined gloves in his overcoat pocket. Machine oil can returned to its original position.

Then back to the outside door, unlocking, a quick peer outside at an empty corridor. He stepped out, locked up, tried the knob three times. Solid. He walked toward the elevators, stripping off his black silk gloves stuffing them away into an inside pocket. He rang the Down button and while he waited, he took three ten-dollar bills from his wallet, folded them tightly about the keys, held them in his right hand.

There were six other people in the elevator. They stood back politely to let him get on. He edged slowly toward the back. Music was playing softly. In the lobby, he let everyone else off first, then walked out, looked about for Lipsky. He finally saw him, outside, helping an old woman into a cab. He waited patiently until Lipsky came back inside. Lipsky saw him, and the Captain thought he might faint. Delaney moved forward smiling, holding out his right hand. He felt Lipsky's wet palm as keys and money were passed.

Delaney nodded, still smiling, and walked outside. He walked down the driveway. He walked home. He was thinking a curious thought: that his transfer to the Patrol Division had been a mistake. He didn't want administrative experience. He didn't want to be Police Commissioner. This was what he did best. And what he liked best.

He called Thorsen from his home. It was no time to be worrying about tapped phones, if that ever had any validity to begin with. But Thorsen did not return his call, not for 15 minutes. Delaney then called his office. The Deputy Inspector was "in conference" and could not be disturbed.

"Disturb him," Delaney said sharply. "This is Captain Edward X. Delaney. It's an emergency."

He waited a few moments, then:

"Jesus Christ, Edward, what's so—"

"I've got to see you. At once."

"Impossible. You don't know what's going on down here. All hell is breaking loose. It's the showdown."

Delaney didn't ask what "showdown." He wasn't interested. "I've got to see you," he repeated.

Thorsen was silent a minute. Then: "Will it wait till six o'clock? There's another meeting with the Commissioner at seven, but I'll be able to see you at six. Can it hold till then?"

Delaney thought. "All right. Six o'clock. Where?"

"Uptown. The seven o'clock meeting's at the Mansion. Better make it my house at six."

"I'll be there."

He pressed the phone prongs just long enough to break the connection, then dialed Dr. Sanford Ferguson.

"Captain Edward X. Delaney here."

"Neglect, neglect, neglect," Ferguson said sorrowfully. "You haven't called me for 'two more things' in weeks. Not sore at me, are you, Edward?"

"No," Delaney laughed, "I'm not sore at you."

"How you coming along?"

"All right. I read your preliminary report on the Feinberg kill, but I didn't see the final PM."

"Completed it today. The usual. Nothing new."

"The preliminary report said that blood found on the sidewalk was not the victim's type."

"That's correct."

"What type was it?"

"You're *asking* me? Edward, you're losing your grip. I thought you'd be telling me."

"Just a minute." Delaney took his notebook from his inside coat pocket. "All right, I'll tell you. AB-Rh negative."

There was a swift intake of breath. "Edward, you *are* getting somewhere, aren't you? You're right. AB-Rh negative. A rare type. Who has it?"

"A friend of mine," Delaney said tonelessly. "A close friend."

"Well, when you take him, make it clean, will you?" the Medical Examiner said. "I'm getting bored with crushed skulls. A single pop through the heart would be nice."

"Too good for him," Delaney said savagely.

Silence then. Finally: "Edward, you're not losing your cool, are you?" Ferguson asked, concern in his voice.

"I've never been colder in my life."

"Good."

"One more thing . . ."

"Now I know you're normal."

"I'm mailing you a sample of a light machine oil. It's a different brand from the one I gave you before. Will you try to get a match with oil in the tissue from Feinberg's wounds?"

"I'll try. Sounds like you're close, Edward."

"Yes. Thank you, doctor."

He looked at his watch. Almost two hours to kill before his meeting with Thorsen. He sat down at his study desk, put on his glasses, picked up a pencil, drew a pad toward him. He began to head the page "Report on—" then stopped, thinking carefully. Was it wise to have an account of that illegal breakin, in his handwriting? He pushed pad and pencil away, rose, began to pace around the room, hands jammed in his hip pockets.

If, for some reason he could not yet foresee, it came to a court trial or the taking of sworn depositions, it was Lipsky's word against his. All Lipsky could swear to was that he had passed the keys. He had not seen Delaney in Blank's apartment. He could not honestly swear to that, only that he had given Delaney the keys and *presumed* he was going to search the apartment. But presumptions had no value. Still, the Captain decided, he would not make a written report of the search. Not at this moment, at any rate. He continued his pacing.

The problem, he decided—the *essential problem*—was not how to take Blank. That had to wait for his meeting with Thorsen at six o'clock. The essential problem was Blank, the man himself, who he was, what he was, what he might do.

That apartment was a puzzle. It displayed a dichotomy (the Captain was familiar with the word) of personality difficult to decipher. There was the incredible orderliness, almost a fanatical tidiness. And the ultramodern furnishings, black and white, steel and leather, no warmth, no softness, no personal "give" to the surroundings.

Then there were the multihued linens, luxurious personal belongings, the excess of silk and soft fabrics, feminine underwear, the perfumes, oils, scented creams, the jewelry. That mutilated nude photograph. And, above all, the mirrors. Mirrors everywhere.

He went over to the cabinet, flipped through the Daniel G. Blank file, pulled out the thick report he had written after his interview with Dr. Otto Morgenthau. Delaney stood at his desk, turning pages until he found the section he wanted, where Morgenthau, having discussed causes, spoke about motives, how the mass murderer justified his actions to himself. The Captain had jotted short, elliptic notes:

"Elaborate rationalizations. No guilt. Killings necessary . . .

"1. Impose order on chaos. Cannot stand disorder or the unpredictable. Needs rules of institution: prison, army, etc. Finds peace, because no responsibility in completely ordered world.

"2. Graffiti artist. Make his mark by murder. I exist! Statement to world.

"3. Alienation. Cannot relate to anyone. Cannot feel. Wants to come close to another human being. To love? Through love to all humanity and secret of existence. God? Because (in youth?) emotion, feeling, love have been denied to him. Cannot find (feel) except by killing. Ecstasy."

Delaney reread these notes again, and recalled Dr. Morgenthau's warning that in dealing with multiple killers, there were no precise classifications. Causes overlapped, and so did motives. These were not simple men who killed from greed, lust or vengeance. They were a tangled complex, could not recognize themselves where truth ended and fantasy began. But perhaps in their mad, whirling minds there were no endings and no beginnings. Just a hot swirl, with no more outline than a flame and as fluid as blood.

He put the notes away, no closer to Dan's heart. The thing about Dan was—He stopped suddenly. Dan? He was thinking of him as "Dan" now? Not Blank, or Daniel G. Blank, but Dan. Very well, he would think of him as Dan. "A friend," he had told Dr. Ferguson. "A close friend." He had smelled his soap, handled his underwear, felt his silken robes, heard his voice, seen a photo of him naked. Discovered his secrets.

The trouble with Dan, the trouble with understanding Dan, was the question he had posed to Barbara: Was it possible to solve an irrational problem by rational means? He hadn't the answer to that. Yet. He glanced at his watch, hurriedly emptied his pockets of penlite, black silk gloves, case of lock picks. He wrapped the oil-soaked wad of paper towel in a square of aluminum foil, put it into an envelope addressed to Dr. Sanford Ferguson, and mailed it on his way to the home of Deputy Inspector Thorsen.

It was strange; he could smell cigar smoke on the sidewalk outside Thorsen's brownstone. He walked up the stoop; the smell was stronger. He hoped to hell Karen was visiting or up in her bedroom; she hated cigars.

He rang. And rang. Rang. Finally Thorsen pulled open the door.

"Sorry, Edward. Lots of noise."

Thorsen, he noted, was under pressure. The "Admiral" was hanging on tight, but the fine silver hair was unbrushed, blue eyes dimmed, the whites bloodshot, lines in his face Delaney had never seen before. And a jerkiness to his movements.

The door of the living room was closed. But the Captain heard a loud, angry babble. He saw a pile of overcoats, at least a dozen, thrown over hallway chairs. Civilian and uniform coats, civilian hats and cop hats. One cane. One umbrella. The air was hot and swirling—cigar smoke, and harsh. Thorsen didn't ask for his hat and coat.

"Come in here," he commanded.

He led Delaney down a short hall to a dining room, flicked on a wall switch. There was a Tiffany lampshade over the heavy oak dining table. Thorsen closed the door, but the Captain could still hear the voices, still smell the coarse cigars.

"What is it?" Thorsen demanded.

Delaney looked at him. He could forgive that tone; the man was obviously exhausted. Something was happening, something big.

"Ivar," he said gently—perhaps the second or third time in his life he had used the Deputy Inspector's given name—"I've found him."

Thorsen looked at him, not comprehending.

"Found him?"

Delaney didn't answer. Thorsen, staring at him, suddenly knew.

"Oh Jesus," he groaned. "Now of all times. Right now. Oh God. No doubt at all?"

"No. No doubt. It's absolute."

Thorsen took a deep breath.

"Don't—" he started to say, then stopped, smiled wanly at the Captain. "Congratulations, Edward."

Delaney didn't say anything.

"Don't move from here. Please. I want Johnson and Alinski in on this. I'll be right back."

The Captain waited patiently. Still standing, he ran his fingers over the waxed surface of the dining table. Old, scarred oak. There was something about wood, something you couldn't find in steel, chrome, aluminum, plastic. The wood had lived, he decided; that was the answer. The wood had been seedling, twig, trunk, all pulsing with sap, responding to the seasons, growing. The tree cut down eventually, and sliced, planed, worked, sanded, polished. But the sense of life was still there. You could feel it.

Inspector Johnson seemed as distraught as Thorsen; his black face was sweated, and Delaney noted the hands thrust into trouser pockets. You did that to conceal trembling. But Deputy Mayor Herman Alinski was still expressionless, the short, heavy body composed, dark, intelligent eyes moving from man to man.

The four men stood around the dining room table. No one suggested they sit. From outside, Delaney could still hear the loud talk going on, still smell the crude cigar smoke.

"Edward?" Thorsen said in a low voice.

Delaney looked at the other two men. Then he addressed himself directly to Alinski.

"I have found the killer of Frank Lombard, Bernard Gilbert, Detective Kope, and Albert Feinberg," he said, speaking slowly and distinctly. "There is no possibility of error. I know the man who committed the four homicides."

There was silence. Delaney looked from Alinski to Johnson to Thorsen.

"Oh Jesus," Johnson said. "That tears it."

"No possibility of error?" Alinski repeated softly.

"No, sir. None."

"Can we make a collar, Edward?" Thorsen asked. "Now?"

"No use. He'd be out in an hour."

"Run him around the horn?" Johnson said in a cracked voice.

Delaney: "What for? A waste of time. He'd float free eventually."

Thorsen: "Search warrant?"

Delaney: "Not even from a pet judge."

Johnson: "Anything for the DA?"

Delaney: "Not a thing."

Thorsen: "Will he sweat in the slammer?"

Delaney: "No."

Johnson: "Break-in?"

Delaney: "What do you think?"

Thorsen: "You left it?"

Delaney: "What else could I do?"

Thorsen: "But it was there?"

Delaney: "Three hours ago. It may be gone by now."

Johnson: "Witnesses to the break-in?"

Delaney: "Presumption only."

Thorsen: "Then we've got nothing?"

Delaney: "Not right now."

Johnson: "But you can nail him?"

Delaney (astonished): "Of course. Eventually."

Deputy Mayor Herman Alinski had followed this fast exchange without interrupting. Now he held up a hand. They fell silent. He carefully relighted a cold cigar he had brought into the room with him.

"Gentlemen," he said quietly, "I realize I am just a poor pole, one generation removed from the Warsaw ghetto, but I did think I had mastered the English language and the American idiom. But I would be much obliged, gentlemen, if you could inform me just what the fuck you are talking about."

They laughed then. The ice was broken—which was, Delaney realized, exactly what Alinski had intended. The Captain turned to Thorsen.

"Let me tell it my way?"

Thorsen nodded.

"Sir," the Captain said, addressing the Deputy Mayor directly, "I will tell you what I can. Some things I will not tell you. Not to protect myself. I don't give a damn. But I don't think it wise that you and these other men should have guilty knowledge. You understand?"

Alinski, smoking his cigar, nodded. His dark eyes deepened even more; he stared at Delaney with curious interest.

"I know the man who committed these homicides," the Captain continued. "I have seen the evidence. Conclusive, incontrovertible evidence. You'll have to take my word for that. The evidence exists, or did exist three hours ago, in this man's apartment. But the evidence is of such a nature that it doesn't justify a collar—an arrest. Why not? Because it exists in his apartment, his home. How could I swear to what I have seen? Legally, I have seen nothing. And if, by any chance, a sympathetic judge issued a search warrant, what then? Served on the man while he was home, he could stall long enough to destroy the evidence. Somehow. Then what? Arrest him on a charge—any charge? And run the risk of a false arrest suit? What for? Run him around the horn? That's probably some of our cop talk you didn't understand. It means collaring a suspect, keeping him in a precinct house detention cell, trying to sweat him—getting him to talk. He calls his lawyer. We're required to let him do that. His lawyer gets a release. By the time the lawyer shows up with the paper, we've moved him to another precinct house tank. No one knows where. By the time the lawyer finds out, we've moved him again. We waltz him 'around the horn.' It's an old routine, not used much these days, originally used when cops needed to keep an important witness in the slammer, or needed another day or two days or three days to nail the guy good. It wouldn't work here. Sweating him wouldn't work either. Don't ask me how I know—I just know. He won't talk. Why should he? He makes fifty-five thousand a year. He's an important business executive with a big corporation in the city. He's no street ponce with a snoot full of shit. We can't lean on him. He's got no record. He's got a good lawyer. He's got friends. He carries weight. Got it now?"

"Yes . . ." Alinski said slowly. "I've got it now. Thank you, Captain."

"Fifty-five thousand a year?" Inspector Johnson said incredulously. "Jesus H. Christ!"

"One thing," the Deputy Mayor said. "Inspector Johnson asked if you could nail him, and you said yes. How do you propose to do that?"

"I don't know," Delaney admitted. "I haven't thought it through yet. That's not why I came here tonight."

"Why did you come?"

"This crazy's coming up to another kill. I figure it should be in the week between Christmas and New Year's. But it may be sooner. I can't take the chance."

Strangely, no one asked him how he had estimated the killer's schedule. They simply believed him.

"So," Delaney went on, "I came here tonight for three men, plainclothes, on foot, and one unmarked car, with two men, to cover this guy tonight. I either get this cover or I'll have to dump what I have in Broughton's lap, let him own it, and take my lumps. Before, I just had a lead to offer him. Now I've got the guy he's bleeding for."

His demand came so suddenly, so abruptly, that the other three were startled. They looked at each other; the noise and smells from outside, men talking, arguing, smoking in the living room, seemed to invade this quiet place and envelop them all.

"Now," Thorsen said bitterly. "It would have to be tonight."

"You can do it," Delaney said stonily, staring at the Deputy Inspector. "I don't give a fuck where you get them. Bring them in from Staten Island. This guy has got to be covered. Tonight and every night until I can figure out how to take him."

Silence then, in the dining room, the four men standing. Only Delaney looked at Thorsen; the other men's eyes were turned downward, unseeing.

Was it a minute, or five, or ten? The Captain never knew. Finally Deputy Mayor Alinski sighed deeply, raised his head to look at Thorsen and Johnson.

"Would you excuse us?" he asked gently. "I would like to speak to Captain Delaney privately. For just a few moments. Would you wait outside, please?"

Wordlessly, they filed out, Johnson closing the door behind them.

Alinski looked at Delaney and smiled. "Could we sit down?" he asked. "It seems to me we have been standing much too long."

Delaney nodded. They took padded armchairs on opposite sides of the oak table.

"You don't smoke cigars?" Alinski asked.

"No more. Oh, occasionally. But not very often."

"Filthy habit," Alinski nodded. "But all enjoyable habits are filthy. I looked up your record. 'Iron Balls.' Am I right?"

"Yes."

"In my younger days I was called 'Bubble Head.' "

Delaney smiled.

"Good record," Alinski said. "How many commendations?"

"I don't know."

"You've lost count. Many. You were in the Army in World War Two. Military Police."

"That's correct."

"Yes. Tell me something, Captain: Do you feel that the military—the Army, Navy, Air Force—should be, at the top, under control of civilian authority—President, Secretary of Defense, and so forth?"

"Of course."

"And do you also believe that the Police Department of the City of New York should also, essentially, be under civilian control? That is, that the Commissioner, the highest ranking police officer, should be appointed by the Mayor, a civilian politician?"

"Yes . . . I guess I believe that," Delaney said slowly. "I don't like civilian interference in Department affairs anymore than any other cop. But I agree the Department should be subject to some civilian control authority, not be a totally autonomous body. Some form of civilian control is the lesser of two evils."

Alinski smiled wryly. "So many decisions in this world come down to that," he nodded. "The lesser of two evils. Thorsen and Johnson tell me you are an apolitical man. That is, you have very little interest in Department politics, in feuds, cliques, personality conflicts. Is that correct?"

"Yes."

"You just want to be left alone to do your job?"

"That's right."

The Deputy Mayor nodded again. "We owe you an explanation," he said. "It won't be a complete explanation because there are some things you have no need to know. Also, time is growing short. We must all be at the Mansion by seven. Well then . . .

"About three years ago it became apparent that there was a serious breach of security in the Mayor's inner circle. This is an informal group, about a dozen men—the Mayor's closest personal friends, advisors, various media experts, campaign contributors, labor leaders, and so forth—on whom he depends for advice and ideas. Meetings are held once a month, or more often when needed. Well, someone in that group was leaking. Newspapers were getting rumors they shouldn't get, and some individuals were profiting from plans still in the discussion stage, before the public announcement was made. The problem was dumped in my lap; one of my responsibilities is internal security. It wasn't hard to discover who was leaking—his name's of no importance to you."

"How did you do it?" Delaney asked. "I'm just interested in the technique you used."

"The most obvious," Alinski shrugged. "Various fictitious documents planted with every man in the Inner Circle. Only one was leaked. It was that easy. But before we kicked this bastard downstairs to a job inspecting monuments or potholes—you don't fire a man like that; the public scandal helps no one—I put him under twenty-four hour surveillance and discovered something interesting. Once a week he was having dinner with five men, always the same five men. They were meeting at one of their homes or in a hotel room or renting a private dining room in a restaurant. It was a curious group. Chairman of the Board of a downtown bank, real estate speculator, editor of a news magazine, a corporation VP, our squealer, and Deputy Commissioner Broughton. I didn't like the smell of it. What did those men have in common? They didn't even all belong to the same political party. So I kept an eye on them. A few months later, the six had grown to twelve, then to twenty. And they were entertaining occasional guests from Albany, and once a man from the Attorney General's office in Washington. By this time there were almost thirty members, dining together every week."

"Including the man you infiltrated," Delaney said.

Alinski smiled distantly but didn't answer. "It took me a while to catch on," he continued. "As far as I could determine, they had no name, no address, no letterhead, no formal organization, no officers. Just an informal group who met for dinner. That's what I called them in my verbal reports to the Mayor—the 'Group.' I kept watching. It was fascinating to see how they grew. They split into three divisions; three separate dinners every week: one of the money men; one of editors, writers, publishers, TV producers; one of cops—local, state, a few federal. Then they began recruiting. Nothing obvious, but a solid cadre. Still no name, no address, no program—nothing. But odd things began happening: certain editorials, hefty campaign contributions to minor league pols, pressure for or against certain bills, some obviously planned and extremely well organized demonstrations, heavy clout that got a certain man off on probation of a tax evasion rap that should have netted him five years. The Group was growing, fast. And the members were Democrats, Republicans, Liberals, Conservatives—you name it, they had them. Still no public announcements, no formal program, no statement of principles—nothing like that. But it came increasingly clear what they were after: an authoritarian city government, 'law and order,' let the cops use their sticks, guns for everyone. Except the blacks. More muscle in government. Tell people, don't ask them. Because people really want to be told, don't they? All they need or want is a cold six-pack and a fourth rerun of 'I Love Lucy.' "

Alinski glanced at his watch. "I've got to cut this short," he said. "Time's running out. But I get carried away. Half my family got made into soup at Treblinka. Anyway, Deputy Commissioner Broughton began to throw his weight around. The man is good; I don't deny it. Shrewd, strong, active. And loud. Above all, loud. So when Frank Lombard was killed, the Group's agit-prop division went to work. It was a natural. After all, Frank Lombard was a member of the Group."

Delaney looked at him, astounded. "You mean these four victims had something in common after all—a political angle? Were the other three members of the Group, too?"

"No, no," Alinski shook his head. "Don't get me wrong. Detective Kope couldn't have been a member because the Group doesn't recruit cops under the rank of lieutenant. And Bernard Gilbert and Albert Feinberg couldn't have been members because there are no Jews in the Group. No, Lombard's death was just a coincidence, a chance killing, and I guess the man you've found has never even heard of the Group. Not many people have. But Lombard's murder was a marvelous opportunity for the Group. First of all, he was a very vocal advocate of 'law and order.' 'Let us crush completely crime in our city streets.' Broughton saw his opportunity. He got command of Operation Lombard. With the political pressures the Group organized, he got everything he wanted—men, equipment, unlimited funds. You've met Broughton?"

"Yes."

"Don't underestimate him. He has the confidence of the devil. He thought he'd wrap up the Lombard murder in record time. Score one for his side, and an important step toward becoming the next Commissioner. But in case he didn't find Lombard's killer, the Group would be left with their thumbs up their assholes. So I asked Thorsen and Johnson who were the best detectives in New York. They named you and Chief Pauley. Broughton took Pauley. Thorsen and Johnson asked for you, and we went along with them."

"Who is 'we'?"

"Our Group," Alinski smiled. "Or call it our 'Anti-Group.' Anyway, here is the situation of this moment. At the meeting tonight, we think we can get Broughton dumped from Operation Lombard. No guarantee, but we think we can do it. But not if you go to him now and give him the killer."

"Fuck Broughton," Delaney said roughly. "I couldn't care less about his ambitions, political or otherwise. I won't go to him if you'll just give me my three plainclothesmen on foot and two in an unmarked car."

"But you see," Alinski explained patiently, "we cannot possibly do that. How could we? From where? You don't realize how big the Group has grown, how powerful. They are everywhere, in every precinct, in every special unit in the Department. Not the men; the officers. How can we risk alerting Broughton that we have the killer and want to put a watch on him? You know exactly what would happen. He would come galloping with sirens screaming, flashing lights, a hundred men and, when all the TV cameras were in place, he'd pull your man out of his apartment in chains."

"And lose him in the courts," Delaney said bitterly. "I'm telling you, at this moment you couldn't even indict this man, let alone convict him."

The Deputy Mayor looked at his watch again and grimaced. "We're going to be late," he said. He strode to the door, yanked it open. Thorsen and Johnson were waiting outside, in hats and overcoats. Alinski waved them into the dining room, then closed the door behind them. He turned to Delaney. "Captain," he said. "Twenty-four hours. Will you give us that? Just twenty-four hours. After that, if Broughton still heads Operation Lombard, you better go to him and tell him what you have. He'll crucify you, but he'll have the killer—and the headlines—whether or not the man is ever convicted."

"You won't give the guards?" Delaney asked.

"No. I can't stop you from going to Broughton right now, if that's what you want to do. But I will not cooperate in his triumph by furnishing the men you want."

"All right," the Captain said mildly. He pushed by Alinski, Thorsen, Johnson, and pulled open the door. "You can have your twenty-four hours."

He made his way through the hallway, crowded now with men pulling on hats and coats. He looked at no one, spoke to no one, although one man called his name.

Back in the dining room, Alinski looked at the two officers in astonishment. "He agreed so easily," he said, puzzled. "Maybe he was exaggerating. Perhaps there is no danger tonight. He certainly didn't fight very hard for the guards he wanted."

Thorsen looked at him, then looked out into the hallway where the others were waiting.

"You don't know Edward," he said, almost sadly.

"That's right," Inspector Johnson agreed softly. "He's going to freeze his ass off tonight."

He wasn't furious, wasn't even angry. They had their priorities, and he had his. They had the "Group" and "Anti-Group." He had Daniel G. Blank. It was interesting, listening to the Deputy Mayor, and he supposed their concern was important. But he had been in the Department a long time, had witnessed many similar battles between the "Ins" and the "Outs," and it was difficult for him to become personally involved in this political clash. Somehow the Department always survived. At the moment, his only interest was Dan, his close friend Dan.

He walked home rapidly, called Barbara immediately. But it was Dr. Louis Bernardi who answered the phone.

"What's wrong?" Delaney demanded. "Is Barbara all right?"

"Fine, fine, Captain," the doctor soothed. "We're just conducting a little examination."

"So you think the new drug is helping?"

"Coming along," Bernardi said blithely. "A little fretful, perhaps, but that's understandable. It doesn't worry me."

Oh you bastard, Delaney thought again. Nothing worries *you.* Why the hell should it?

"I think we'll give her a little something to help her sleep tonight," Bernardi went on in his greasy voice. "Just a little something. I think perhaps you might skip your visit tonight, Captain. A nice, long sleep will do our Barbara more good."

"Our Barbara." Delaney could have throttled him, and cheerfully.

"All right," he said shortly. "I'll see her tomorrow."

He looked at his watch: almost seven-thirty. He didn't have much time; it was dark outside; the street lights were on, had been since six. He went up to the bedroom, stripped down to his skin. He knew, from painful experience, what to wear on an all-night vigil in the winter.

Thermal underwear, a two-piece set. A pair of light cotton socks with heavy wool socks over them. An old winter uniform, pants shiny, jacket frayed at the cuffs and along the seams. But there was still no civilian suit as warm as that good, heavy blanket wool. And the choker collar would protect his chest and throat. Then his comfortable "cop shoes" with a pair of rubbers over them, even though the streets were dry and no rain or snow predicted.

He unlocked his equipment drawer in the bedroom taboret. He owned three guns: his .38 service revolver, a .32 "belly gun" with a two-inch barrel, and a .45 automatic pistol which he had stolen from the U.S. Army in 1946. He selected the small .32, slid it from its flannel bag and, flicking the cylinder to the side, loaded it slowly and carefully from a box of ammunition. He didn't bother with an extra gun belt. The gun was carried on his pants belt in a black leather holster. He adjusted it under his uniform jacket so the gun hung down over his right groin, aimed toward his testicles: a happy thought. He checked the safety again.

His identification into his inside breast pocket. A leather-covered sap slid into a special narrow pocket alongside his right leg. Handcuffs into his righthand pants pocket and, at the last minute, he added a steel-linked "come-along"—a short length of chain, just long enough to encircle a wrist, with heavy grips at both ends.

Downstairs, he prepared a thick sandwich of bologna and sliced onion, wrapped it in waxed paper, put it into his civilian overcoat pocket. He filled a pint flask with brandy; that went into the inside overcoat breast pocket. He found his fleece-lined earmuffs and fur-lined leather gloves; they went into outside overcoat pockets.

Just before he left the house, he dialed Daniel Blank. He knew the number by heart now. The phone rang three times, then that familiar voice said, "Hello?" Delaney hung up softly. At least his friend was home, the Captain wouldn't be watching an empty hole.

He put on his stiff Homburg, left the hall light burning, double-locked the front door, went out into the night. He moved stiffly, hot and sweating under his layers of clothing. But he knew that wouldn't last long.

He walked over to Daniel Blank's apartment house, pausing once to transfer the come-along to his lefthand pants pocket so it wouldn't clink against the handcuffs. The weighted blackjack knocked against his leg as he walked, but he was familiar with that feeling; there was nothing to be done about it.

It was an overcast night, not so much cold as damp and raw. He pulled on his gloves and knew it wouldn't be long before he clamped on the earmuffs. It was going to be a long night.

Plenty of people still on the streets; laden Christmas shoppers hurrying home. The lobby lights of Dan's apartment house were blazing. Two doormen on duty now, one of them Lipsky. They were hustling tips. Why not—it was Christmas, wasn't it? Cabs were arriving and departing, private cars were heading into the underground garage, tenants on foot were staggering up with shopping bags and huge parcels.

Delancy took up his station across the street, strolling up and down the length of the block. The lobby was easily observable during most of his to-and-from pacing, or could be glimpsed over his shoulder. When it was behind him, he turned his head frequently enough to keep track of arrivals and departures. After every five trips, up and down, he crossed the street and walked along the other side once, directly in front of the apartment house, then crossed back again and continued his back-and-forth vigil. He walked at a steady pace, not fast, not slow, stamping each foot slightly with every step, swinging his arms more than he would ordinarily.

He could perform this job automatically, and he welcomed the chance it gave him to consider once again his conversation with Thorsen, Johnson, Deputy Mayor Alinski.

What disturbed him was that he was not positive he had been entirely accurate in his comments regarding the admissibility of evidence and the possibility of obtaining a search warrant. Ten years ago he would have been absolutely certain. But recent court decisions, particularly those of the Supreme Court, had so confused him—and all cops—that he no longer comprehended the laws of evidence and the rights of suspects.

Even such a Philadelphia lawyer as Lieutenant Marty Dorfman had admitted his confusion. "Captain," he had said, "they've demolished the old guidelines without substituting a new, definite code. Even the DA's men are walking on eggs. As I see it, until all this gets straightened out and enough precedents established, each case will be judged on its own merits, and we'll have to take our chances. It's the old story: 'The cop proposes, the judge disposes.' Only now even the judges aren't sure. That's why the percentage of appeals is way, way up."

Well, start from the beginning . . . His search of Dan's apartment had been illegal. Nothing he saw or learned from that search could be used in court. No doubt about that. If he had taken away Dan's "trophies," it would have served no purpose other than to alert Blank that his apartment had been tossed, that he was under suspicion.

Now what about a search warrant? On what grounds? That Dan owned an ice ax of a type possibly used to kill four men? And, of course, of a type owned by hundreds of people all over the world. That blood of Dan's type had been found at the scene of the most recent homicide? How many people had that blood type? That he possessed a can of light machine oil that a thousand other New Yorkers owned? And all of these facts established only by an illegal break-in. Or tell the judge that Daniel G. Blank was a known mountaineer and was suspected of carrying two dummy Christmas packages the night Albert Feinberg was slain? Delaney could imagine the judge's reaction to a request for a search warrant on those grounds.

No, he *had* been correct. As of this moment, Dan was untouchable. Then why hadn't he taken the whole mess to Broughton and dumped it on him? Because

Alinski had been exactly right, knowing his man. Broughton would have said, "Fuck the law," would have come on like Gang Busters, would have collared Blank, got the headlines and TV exposure he wanted.

Later, when Blank was set free, as he was certain to be, Broughton would denounce "permissive justice," "slack criminal laws," "handcuffing the cops, not the crooks." The fact that Blank walked away a free man would have little importance to Broughton compared to the publicity of the suspect's release, the public outcry, the furtherance of exactly what the Group wanted.

But if Dan couldn't legally—

Delaney ceased pondering, his head crooked over his shoulder. There was a man standing in the lighted lobby, talking to one of the doormen. The man was tall, slender, wearing a black topcoat, no hat. Delaney stopped midstride, took a sham look at a nonexistent wristwatch, made a gesture of impatience, turned in his tracks, walked toward the lobby. He should apply for an Actors Equity card, he thought; he really should.

He came abreast of the lobby, across the street, just as Daniel Blank exited from the glass doors and stood a moment. It was undeniably him: wide shoulders, slim hips, handsome with vaguely Oriental features. His left hand was thrust into his topcoat pocket. Delaney glanced long enough to watch him sniff the night air, button up his coat with his right hand, turn up the collar. Then Blank walked down the driveway, turned west in the direction Delaney was moving across the street.

Ah there, the Captain thought. Out for a stroll, Danny boy?

"Danny Boy." The phrase amused him; he began to hum the tune. He matched Blank's speed, and when Dan crossed Second Avenue, Delaney crossed on his side, keeping just a little behind his target. He was good at tailing, but not nearly as good as, say, Lieutenant Jeri Fernandez, known to his squad as the "Invisible Man."

The problem was mainly one of physical appearance. Delaney was obvious. He was tall, big, stooped, lumbering, with a shapeless black overcoat, a stiff Homburg set squarely atop his heavy head. He could change his costume but not the man he was.

Fernandez was average and middle. Average height, middle weight, no distinguishing features. On a tail, he wore clothes a zillion other men wore. More than that, he had mastered the rhythm of the streets, a trick Delaney could never catch. Even within a single city, New York, people moved differently on different streets. In the Garment District they trotted and shoved. On Fifth Avenue they walked at a slower tempo, pausing to look in shop windows. On Park Avenue and upper eastside cross streets they sauntered. Wherever he tailed, Fernandez picked up the rhythm of the street, unconsciously, and moved like a wraith. Set him down in Brussels, Cairo, or Tokyo, the Captain was convinced, and Lieutenant Jeri Fernandez would take one quick look around and become a resident. Delaney wished he could do it.

But he did what he could, performed what tricks he knew. When Blank turned the corner onto Third Avenue, Delaney crossed the street to move up behind him. He increased his speed to tail from in front. The Captain stopped to look in a store window, watched the reflection in the glass as Blank passed him. Delaney took up a following tail again, dropping behind a couple, dogging their heels closely. If Blank looked back, he'd see a group of three.

Dan was walking slowly. Delaney's covering couple turned away. He continued in his steady pace, passing his quarry again. He was conscious that Blank was now close behind him, but he felt no particular fear. The avenue was well lighted; there were people about. Danny Boy might be crazy, but he wasn't stupid. Besides, Delaney was certain, he always approached his victims from the front.

Delaney walked another half-block and stopped. He had lost him. He knew it, without turning to look. Instinct? Something atavistic? Fuck it. He just knew it. He turned back, searched, cursed his own stupidity. He should have known, or at least wondered.

Halfway down the block was a pet shop, still open, front window brilliantly lighted. Behind the glass were pups—fox terriers, poodles, spaniels—all frolicking on torn newspaper, and gumming each other, pissing, shitting up a storm, pressing noses and paws against the window where at least half a dozen people stood laughing, tapping the glass, saying things like "Kitchy-koo." Daniel Blank was one of them.

He should have guessed, he repeated to himself. Even the dullest dick three learned that a high percentage of killers were animal lovers. They kept dogs, cats, parakeets, pigeons, even goldfish. They treated their pets with tender, loving care, feeding them at great expense, hustling them to the vet at the first sign of illness, talking to them, caressing them. Then they killed a human being, cutting off the victim's nipples or slicing open the abdomen or shoving a beer bottle up the ass. Captain Edward X. Delaney really didn't want to know the explanation of this predilection of animal lovers for homicide. It was difficult enough, after years of experience, to assimilate the facts of these things happening. The facts themselves were hard enough to accept; who had the time or stomach for explanations?

Then Blank moved off, crossed the street, dodging oncoming traffic. Delaney tailed him on his side of the avenue, but when Dan went into a large, two-window liquor store, the Captain crossed and stood staring at the shop's window display. He was not alone; there were two couples inspecting Christmas gift packages, wicker baskets of liqueurs, cases of imported wine. Delaney inspected them, too, or appeared to. His head was tilted downward just enough so that he could observe Daniel Blank inside the store.

Dan's actions were not puzzling. He took a paper from his righthand pocket, unfolded it, handed it to the clerk. The clerk glanced at it and nodded. The clerk took a bottle of Scotch from a shelf, showed it to Blank. The bottle was in a box, giftwrapped, a red plastic bow on top. Blank inspected it and approved. The clerk replaced the bottle on the shelf. Blank took several sealed cards from his pocket. They looked to Delaney, standing outside, like Christmas cards. The clerk ran off a tape on an electric adding machine, showed it to Blank. Dan took a wallet from his pocket, extracted some bills, paid in cash. The clerk gave him change. The clerk kept the sheet of paper and the envelopes. They smiled at each other. Blank left the store. It wasn't difficult to understand; Dan was sending several bottles of holiday-wrapped Scotch to several people, several addresses. He left his list and identical cards to be enclosed with each gift. He paid for the liquor and the delivery fee. So?

Delaney tailed him away from the store, south three blocks, east two blocks, north four blocks. Dan walked steadily, alertly; the Captain admired the way he moved: balls of feet touching before the heels came down. But he didn't dawdle, apparently wasn't inspecting, searching. Just getting a breath of air. Delaney was back and forth, across, behind, in front, quartering like a good pointer. Nothing.

In less than a half-hour, Dan was back in his apartment house, headed for the bank of elevators, and eventually disappeared. Delaney, across the street, took a swallow of brandy, ate half his bologna and onion sandwich as he paced, watching. He belched suddenly. Understandable. Brandy and bologna and onion?

Was Dan in for the night? Maybe, maybe not. In any event, Delaney would be there until dawn. Blank's stroll had been—well, inconclusive. It made sense, but the Captain had a nagging feeling of having missed something. What? The man had been under his direct observation for—oh, well, say 75 percent of the time he had been out on the street. He had acted like any other completely innocent evening stroller, out to buy some Christmas booze for his friends, doormen, acquaintances. So?

It did nag. Something. Delaney rewrapped his half-sandwich, continued his routine pacing. Now the thing to do was to take it from the start, the beginning, and remember everything his friend had done, every action, every movement.

He had first glimpsed him inside the lobby, talking to a doorman. Blank came outside, looked up at the sky, buttoned his coat, turned up the collar, started walking west. Nothing in all that.

He recalled it all again. The slow walk along Third Avenue, Blank's stop outside the pet shop, the way—

Suddenly there was a car pulling up alongside Delaney at the curb. A dusty, four-door, dark blue Plymouth. Two men in the front seat in civilian clothes. But the near man, not the driver, turned a powerful flashlight on Delaney.

"Police," he said. "Stop where you are, please."

Delaney stopped. He turned slowly to face the car. He raised his arms slightly from his body, turned his palms outward. The man with the flashlight got out of the car, his right hand near his hip. His partner, the driver, dimly seen, was cuddling something in his lap. Delaney admired their competence. They were professionals. But he wondered, not for the first time, why the Department invariably selected dusty three-year-old dark blue Plymouth four-doors for their unmarked cars. Every villain on the streets could spot one a block away.

The detective with the flashlight advanced two steps, but still kept a long stride away from Delaney. The light was directly in the Captain's eyes.

"Live in the neighborhood?" the man asked. His voice was dry gin, on the rocks.

"Yes," the Captain nodded.

"Do you have identification?"

"Yes," Delaney said. "I am going to reach up slowly with my left hand, open my overcoat, then my jacket. I am going to withdraw my identification from the inside right breast pocket of my jacket with my left hand and hand it to you. Okay?"

The detective nodded.

Delaney, moving slowly, meticulously, handed over his buzzer and ID card in the leather folder. It was a long reach to the detective. The flashlight turned down to the badge and photo, then up again to Delaney's face. Then it was snapped off.

"Sorry, Captain," the man said, no apology in his voice. He handed the leather back.

"You did just right," Delaney said. "Operation Lombard?"

"Yeah," the detective said, and asked no unnecessary questions. "You'll be around awhile?"

"Until dawn."

"We won't roust you again."

"That's all right," Delaney assured him. "What's your name?"

"You're not going to believe it, Captain, but it's William Shakespeare."

"I believe it," Delaney laughed. "There was a football player named William Shakespeare.

"You remember him?" the dick said with wonder and delight. "He probably had the same trouble I have. You should see the looks I get when I register at a motel with my wife."

"Who's your partner?"

The dick turned his flashlight on the driver. He was black, grinning. "A spook," the man on the sidewalk said. "Loves fried chicken and watermelon. Sam Lauder."

The black driver nodded solemnly. "Don't forget the pork chops and collard greens," he said in a marvelously rich bass voice.

"How long you two been partners?" Delaney asked.

"About a thousand years," the driver called.

"Naw," the sidewalk man said. "A year or two. It just *seems* like a thousand."

They all laughed.

"Shakespeare and Lauder," Delaney repeated. "I'll remember. I owe you one."

"Thanks, Captain," Shakespeare said. He got back in the car; they drove away. Delaney was pleased. Good men.

But to get back to Dan . . . He resumed his pacing, the lobby never out of his glance for more than 30 seconds. It was quiet in there now. One doorman.

After the stop at the pet shop, Dan had crossed to the liquor store, presented his Christmas list, paid for his purchases, then sauntered home. So what was bugging Delaney? He reached into his inner overcoat pocket for a swig of brandy from the flask. Reached into his outer pocket for a bit of sandwich. Reached—

Ah. Ah. Now he had it.

Blank had been talking to a doorman inside the lobby when Delaney first spotted him. Unbuttoned black topcoat, left hand thrust into topcoat pocket. Then Dan had come out under the portico, buttoning up his topcoat, turning up the collar with his right hand. No action from the left hand so far—correct?

Then the stroll. Both hands jammed into topcoat pockets. The walk, the tail, the stop at the pet shop—all that was nothing. But now Delaney, from under the brim of his wooden Homburg, is observing Blank inside the liquor store. The right hand dips into the righthand topcoat pocket and comes out with a folded list. The right hand unfolds it on the counter. The right hand holds it out to the clerk. The clerk offers a Christmaswrapped bottle of Scotch to Blank. Dan takes it in his right hand, inspects it, approves, hands it back to the clerk. Still no action from that left hand. It's dead. Right hand goes back into the topcoat pocket. Out come a half-dozen Christmas cards to be taped to the gifts of liquor. The right hand comes out again with a wallet. The tape is run off. Money paid. The change goes back into the righthand pocket of the topcoat. Left hand, where are you?

Captain Delaney stopped, stood, remembering and suddenly laughing. It was so beautiful. The details always were. What man would carry his Christmas list, Christmas cards and wallet in the outer pocket of his topcoat? Answer: no man. Because Delaney owned a handsome, custom-made, uniform overcoat that had flapped slits just inside the pocket openings so that he could reach inside to equipment on his gun belt without unbuttoning the overcoat. During World War II he had a lined trench coat with the same convenience, and for his birthday in 1953, Barbara had given him an English raincoat with the identical feature; it could be raining cats and dogs, but you didn't have to unbutton your coat, you just reached through those flapped slits for wallet, tickets, identification—whatever.

Sure. That's how Dan had paid for his liquor purchase. He had reached *through* his topcoat pocket for the list in his jacket pocket. *Through* his topcoat pocket to take the wallet off his hip. *Through* his topcoat pocket to find, somewhere, in some jacket or trouser pocket, the addressed and sealed Christmas cards to be taped to the bottles he was sending. Beautiful.

Beautiful not because this was how Daniel G. Blank was sending Christmas gifts, but because this was how Danny Boy was killing men. Slit pockets. Left hand in pocket, through the slit, holding the ice ax handle. Coat unbuttoned. Right hand swinging free. Then, at the moment of meeting, the quick transfer of the ax to the right hand—that innocent, open, swinging right hand—and then the assault. It was slick. Oh God, was it slick.

Delaney continued his patrol. He knew, he *knew,* Blank would not come out again this night. But that was of no consequence. Delaney would parade until dawn. It gave him time to think things out.

Time to consider The Case of the Invisible Left Hand. What was the solution to that? Two possibilities, Delaney thought. One: The left hand was through the slit of the topcoat pocket and was actually holding the ax under the coat by its handle or leather loop. But the Captain didn't think it likely. Dan's coat had been open when Delaney first saw him in the brightly lighted lobby. Would he risk the doorman or another tenant glimpsing the ax beneath his open coat? From then on, the topcoat was buttoned. Why would Dan carry an ice ax beneath a buttoned coat? He obviously wasn't on the prowl for a victim.

Possibility Two: The left hand was injured or incapacitated in some way. Or the wrist, arm, elbow, or shoulder. Danny Boy couldn't use it normally and tucked it away into the topcoat pocket as a king of sling. Yes, that was it and it would be easy to check. Thomas Handry could do it in his interview or, better yet, when Delaney called Charles Lipsky tomorrow, he'd ask about any sign of injury to Blank's left arm. The Captain planned to call Lipsky every day to ask if the doorman had been able to get the taxi license number of Dan's dark, skinny girl friend.

All Delaney's interest in a possible injury to Dan's left arm was due, of course, to the evidence of a scuffle, a fight, at the scene of the most recent homicide. Albert Feinberg had made his killer bleed a few drops on the sidewalk. He might have done more.

What time was it? Getting on toward midnight, Delaney guessed. On a long stakeout like this he very deliberately avoided looking at his watch. Start watching the clock, and you were dead; time seemed to go backwards. When the sky lightened, when it was dawn, then he could go home and sleep. Not before.

He varied his patrol, just to keep himself alert. Three up and-downs on the apartment side. Crossing at different corners. Stopping in the middle of the block to retrace his steps. Anything to keep from walking in a dream. But always watching the lobby entrance. If his friend came out again, he'd come through there.

He finished his sandwich but saved the remainder of the brandy for later. It must be in the low 40s or high 30s by now; he put on his earmuffs. They were cops' style, connected with a strip of elastic that went entirely around his head, and they fitted snugly. No metal band clamping them to his ears. That clamp could get so cold you thought your skull was coming off.

So what was this business about right hand, left hand, and slit pockets? He knew—no doubt at all—that Daniel Blank was guilty of four homicides. But what he needed was hard evidence, good enough to take to the DA and hope for an indictment. That was the reason for the Handry interview, and the follow-ups he'd have to make on Blank's girl friend, the boy Tony, the Mortons. They were leads that any detective would investigate. They might peter out—probably would—but one of them might, just might, pay off. Then he could nail Danny Boy and bring him to trial. And then?

Then Delaney knew exactly what would happen. Blank's smart, expensive lawyer would cop an insanity plea—"This sick man killed four complete strangers for no reason whatsoever. I ask you, Your Honor, were those the acts of a sane man?"—and Dan would be hidden away in an acorn academy for a period of years.

It would happen, and Delaney couldn't object too strongly; Blank *was* sick, no doubt of that. Hospitalization, in his case, was preferable to imprisonment. But still . . . Well, what was it he, Delaney, wanted? Just to get this nut out of circulation? Oh no. No. More than that.

It wasn't only Dan's motives he couldn't understand; it was his own as well. His thoughts about it were nebulous; he would have to do a lot more pondering. But he knew that never in his life had he felt such an affinity for a criminal. He had a sense that if he could understand Dan, he might better understand himself.

Later in the morning, the sky lightening now, Delaney continued his patrol, swinging his arms, stamping his feet because the brandy had worn off; it was goddamned cold. He got back to the problem of Daniel G. Blank, and to his own problems.

The truth came to him slowly, without shock. Well, it was *his* "truth." It was that he wanted this man dead.

What was in Daniel Blank, what was in him, what he hoped to demolish by putting Dan to death was evil, all evil. Wasn't that it? The idea was so irrational that he could not face, could not consider it.

He looked up to the sky again; it was once again black. It had been a false dawn. He resumed his patrol, flinging his arms sideways to smack his own shoulders, slapping his feet on the pavement, shivering in the darkness.

The phone awoke him. When he looked at the bedside clock it was almost 11:00 A.M. He wondered why Mary hadn't picked it up downstairs, then remembered it was her day off. And he had left a note for her on the kitchen table. He really hadn't been functioning too well when he came off that patrol, but he felt okay now. He must have slept "fast"—as they said in the Army; those four hours had been as good as eight.

"Captain Edward X. Delaney here."

"This is Handry. I got that interview set up with Blank."

"Good. When's it for?"

"The day after Christmas."

"Any trouble?"

"Noo . . . not exactly."

"What happened?"

"I did just what you said, contacted the Javis-Bircham PR man. He was all for it. So I went to see him. You know the type: a big laugh and lots of teeth. I showed him my press pass but he didn't even look at it. He'll never check with the paper. He can't believe anyone could con him. He's too bright—he thinks."

"So what went wrong?"

"Nothing went wrong . . . exactly. He suggested the names of four young, up-and-coming J-B executives—that's the way he kept referring to the corporation, J-B, like IBM, GE and GM—but none of the four names was Blank's."

"Did you tell him you wanted to interview a guy familiar with the uses and future of the computer in business?"

"Of course. But he didn't mention Blank. That's odd—don't you think?"

"Mmm. Maybe. So how did you handle it?"

"Told him I was particularly interested in AMROK II. That's the computer mentioned in that release about Blank I dredged out of the Fink File. Remember?"

"I remember. What did he say to that?"

"Well, then, he mentioned Blank, and agreed when I said I wanted to interview him. But he wasn't happy about it, I could tell."

"It might be personal animosity. You know—office politics. Maybe he hates Blank's guts and doesn't want him to get any personal publicity."

"Maybe," Handry said doubtedly, "but that's not the impression I got."

"What impression did you get?"

"Just a crazy idea."

"Let's have it," Delaney said patiently.

"That maybe Blank's stock is falling. That maybe he hasn't been doing a good job. That maybe the rumor is around that they're going to get rid of him. So naturally the PR man wouldn't want an article in the paper that says what a great genius Blank is, and a week later J-B ties a can to him. Sound crazy?"

Delaney was silent, thinking it over. "No," he said finally, "not so crazy. In fact, it may make a lot of sense. Can you have lunch today?"

"You paying?"

"Sure."

"Then I can have lunch today. Where and when?"

"How about that chophouse where we ate before?"

"Sure. Fine. Great ale."

"About twelve-thirty? In the bar?"

"I'll be there."

The Captain went to shave. As he scraped his jaw, he thought that Handry's impression might possibly be correct. Blank's little hobby could be affecting his efficiency during office hours; that wasn't hard to understand. He had been the corporation's fairhaired boy when that Fink File release was sent out. But now they weren't happy about his being interviewed by the press. Interesting.

Wiping away excess lather and splashing after-shave lotion on his face, Delaney decided he better brief Handry on the upcoming interview during lunch. The interview was scheduled for the day after Christmas. By that time Handry might be reporting the results to Broughton, if he wanted to. But Delaney was determined to do everything he possibly could right up to that 24-hour deadline Alinski had promised which, when the Captain left the house, was now only six hours away.

Handry ordered a broiled veal chop and draft ale. Delaney had a rye highball and steak-and-kidney pie.

"Listen," the Captain said to the reporter "we've got a lot to get through, so let's get started on it right away."

Handry stared at him. "What's up?" he asked.

"What's up?" Delaney repeated, puzzled. "What do you mean, 'What's up'?"

"We've been sitting here five minutes at the most. You've already looked at your watch twice, and you keep fiddling with the silverware. You never did that before."

"You should be a detective," Delaney growled, "and go looking for clues."

"No, thanks. Detectives lie too much, and they always answer a question with a question. Right?"

"When did I ever answer a question with a question?"

Handry shook with laughter, spluttering. Finally, when he calmed down, he said: "On the way over, just before I left the office, I met a guy at the water cooler. He's on the political side. City. He says there was a big meeting at the Mansion last night. Heavy brass. He says the rumor is that Deputy Commissioner Broughton is on the skids. Because of his flop with Operation Lombard. You know anything about that?"

"No."

"Doesn't affect you one way or another?"

"No."

"All right," Handry sighed. "Have it your own way. So, like you said, let's get started."

"Look," Delaney said earnestly, leaning forward across the table on his elbows. "I'm not conning you. Sure, there are some things I'm not telling you, but they're not mine to tell. You've been a great help to me. This interview with Blank is important. I don't want you to think I'm deliberately lying to you."

"All right, all right," Handry said, holding up a hand. "I believe you. Now, what I'd guess you'd like to know most from this Blank interview is whether or not he's a mountain climber, and if he owns an ice ax. Right?"

"Right," the Captain said promptly, not bothering to mention that he had already established these facts. It was necessary that Handry continue to believe that his interview was important. "Sure, I want to know what he does at Javis-Bircham, what his job is, how many people work for him, and so on. That has to be the bulk of the interview or he'll get suspicious. But what I *really* want is his personal record, his history, his background, the man himself. Can you get that?"

"Sure."

"You can? All right, let's suppose I'm Blank. You're interviewing me. How do you go about it?"

Handry thought a moment, then: "Could you tell me something about your personal life, Mr. Blank? Where you were born, schools you attended—things like that."

"What for? I thought this interview was about the installation of AMROK II and the possibilities for the computer in business?"

"Oh, it is, it is. But in these executive interviews, Mr. Blank, we always try to include a few personal items. It adds to the readability of the article and to make the man interviewed a real person."

"Good, good," Delaney nodded. "You've got the right idea. Play up to his ego. There are millions of readers out there who want to know about *him,* not just the job he does."

Their food and drinks arrived, and they dug in, but Delaney wouldn't pause.

"Here's what I need about him," he said, and took a deep swallow from his glass. "Where and when he was born, schools, military service, previous jobs, marital status. All right—let's take marital status. I'm Blank again. You ask questions."

"Are you married, Mr. Blank?" Handry asked.

"Is that important to the article?"

"Well, if you'd rather not . . ."

"I'm divorced. I guess it's no secret."

"I see. Any children?"

"No."

"Any plans for marriage in the near future?"

"I really don't think that has any place in your article, Mr. Handry."

"No. You're right. I guess not. But we have a lot of women readers, Mr. Blank—more than you'd guess—and things like that interest them."

"You're doing great," Delaney said approvingly. "Actually, he's got a girl friend, but I doubt if he'll mention her. Now let's rehearse the mountain climbing thing. How will you go about that?"

"Do you have any hobbies, Mr. Blank? Stamp collecting, skiing, boating, bird watching—anything like that?"

"Well . . . as a matter of fact, I'm a mountain climber. An amateur one, I assure you."

"Mountain climbing? That *is* interesting. Where do you do that?"

"Oh . . . here, in the States. And in Europe."

"Where in Europe?"

"France, Switzerland, Italy, Austria. I don't travel as much as I'd like to, but I try to include some climbing wherever I go."

"Fascinating sport—but expensive, isn't it, Mr. Blank? I mean, outside the travel. I'm just asking out of personal curiosity, but don't you need a lot of equipment?"

"Oh . . . not so much. Outdoor winter wear, of course. A rucksack. Crampons. Nylon rope."

"And an ice ax?"

"No," Delaney said definitely. "Don't say that. If Blank doesn't mention it, don't you suggest it. If he's guilty, I don't want to alert him. Handry, this stuff could be important, very important, but don't say anything or suggest anything that might make him think your conversation is anything but what it's supposed to be—an interview with a young executive who works with a computer."

"You mean if he suspects it's not what it seems, I may be in danger."

"Oh yes," the Captain nodded, digging into his meat pie. "You may be."

"Thanks a whole hell of a lot," Handry said, trying to keep his voice light. "You're making me feel much better about the whole thing."

"You'll do all right," Delaney assured him. "You take shorthand on these interviews?"

"My own kind. Very short notes. Single words. No one else can read it. I transcribe as soon as I get home or back to the office."

"Good. Just take it easy. From what you've said, I don't think you'll have any trouble with the personal history, the background. Or with the hobby of mountain climbing. But on the ice ax and his romantic affairs, don't push. If he wants to tell you, fine. If not, drop it. I'll get it some other way."

They each had another drink, finished their food. Neither wanted dessert, but Captain Delaney insisted they have espresso and brandy.

"That's a great flavor," Handry said, having taken a sip of his cognac. "You're spoiling me. I'm used to a tuna fish sandwich for lunch."

"Yes," Delaney smiled. "Me, too. Oh, by the way, a couple of other little things."

Handry put down his brandy snifter, looked at him with wonderment, shaking his head. "You're incredible," he said. "Now I understand why you insisted on the cognac. 'A couple of little things?' Like asking Blank if he's the killer, or putting my head in the lion's mouth at the zoo?"

"No, no," Delaney protested. "Really little things. First of all, see if you can spot any injury to his left hand. Or wrist, arm or elbow. It might be bandaged or in a sling."

"I don't get it."

"Just take a look, that's all. See if he uses his left arm normally. Can he grip anything in his left hand? Does he hide it beneath his desk? Just observe—that's all."

"All right," Handry sighed. "I'll observe. What's the other 'little thing'?"

"Try to get a sample of his handwriting."

Handry looked at him in astonishment. "You *are* incredible," he said. "How in Christ's name am I supposed to do that?"

"I have no idea," Delaney confessed. "Maybe you can swipe something he signed. No, that's no good. I don't know. You think about it. You've got a good imagination. Just some words he's written and his signature. That's all I need. If you can manage it."

Handry didn't answer. They finished their brandy and coffee. The Captain paid the check, and they left. Outside on the sidewalk, they turned coat collars up against the winter wind. Delaney put his hand on Handry's arm.

"I want the stuff we talked about," he said in a low voice. "I really do. But what I want most of all are your *impressions* of the man. You're sensitive to people; I know you are. How could you want to be a poet and not be sensitive to people, what they are, what they think, what they feel, who they hate, who they love? That's what I want you to do. Talk to this man. Observe him. Notice all the little things he does—bites his fingernails, picks his nose, strokes his hair, fidgets, crosses his legs back and forth—anything and everything. Watch him. And absorb him. Let him seep into you. Who is he and what is he? Would you like to know him better? Does he frighten you, disgust you, amuse you? That's really what I want—your *feeling* about him. All right?"

"All right," Thomas Handry said.

As soon as he got home, Delaney called Barbara at the hospital. She said she had had a very good night's sleep and was feeling much better. Monica Gilbert was there, they were having a nice visit, she liked Monica very much. The Captain said he was glad, and would come over to see her in the evening, no matter what.

"I send you a kiss," Barbara said, and made a kissing sound on the phone.

"And I send you one," Captain Edward X. Delaney said, and repeated the sound. What he had always considered silly sentimentality now didn't seem silly to him at all, but meaningful and so touching he could hardly endure it.

He called Charles Lipsky. The doorman was low-voiced and cautious.

"Find anything?" he whispered.

For a moment, Delaney didn't know what he was talking about, then realized Lipsky was referring to the previous afternoon's search.

"No," the Captain said. "Nothing. The girl friend been around?"

"Haven't seen her."

"Remember what I said; you get the license number and—"

"I remember," Lipsky said hurriedly. "Twenty. Right?"

"Yes," Delaney said. "One other thing, is anything wrong with Blank's left arm? Is it hurt?"

"He was carrying it in a sling for a couple of days."

"Was he?"

"Yeah. I asked him. He said he slipped on a little rug in his living room. His floors were just waxed. He landed on his elbow. And he hit his face on the edge of a glass table, so it was scratched up."

"Well," the Captain said, "they say most accidents happen in the home."

"Yeah. But the scratches are gone and he ain't wearing the sling no more. That worth anything?"

"Don't get greedy," Delaney said coldly.

"Greedy?" Lipsky said indignantly. "Who's greedy? But one hand washes the other—right?"

"I'll call you tomorrow," the Captain said. "You still on days?"

"Yeah. Until Christmas. Jesus, you know you was up there over an hour, and I buzzed you, and you—"

The Captain hung up. A little of Charles Lipsky went a long, long way.

He wrote up reports of his meeting with Thomas Handry and his conversation with the doorman. The only thing he deliberately omitted was his final talk with Handry on the sidewalk outside the restaurant. That exchange would mean nothing to Broughton.

It was past 4:00 P.M. when he finished putting it all down on paper. The reports were added to the Daniel G. Blank file. He wondered if he'd ever see that plump folder again. Alinski and the Anti-Group had about two more hours. Delaney didn't want to think of what would happen if he didn't hear from them. He'd have to deliver Blank's file to Broughton, of course, but *how* he'd deliver it was something he wouldn't consider until the crunch.

He went into the living room, slipped off his shoes, lay down on the couch, intending only to relax, rest his eyes, think of happier times. But the weariness he hadn't yet slept off, the two drinks and brandy at lunch—all caught up with him; he slept lightly and dreamed of the wife of a homicide victim he had interrogated years and years ago. "He was asking for it," she said, and no matter what questions he put to her, that's all she'd say: "He was asking for it, he was asking for it."

When he awoke, the room was dark. He laced on his shoes, walked through to the kitchen before he put on a light. The wall clock showed almost 7:00 P.M. Well, it was time . . . Delaney opened the refrigerator door, looked for a cold can of beer to cleanse his palate and his dreams. He found it, was just peeling back the tab when the phone rang.

He walked back into the study, let the phone ring while he finished opening the beer and taking a deep swallow. Then:

"Captain Edward X. Delaney here."

There was no answer. He could hear loud conversation of several men, laughter, an occasional shout, the clink of bottles and glasses. It sounded like a drunken party.

"Delaney here," he repeated.

"Edward?" It was Thorsen's voice, slurred with drink, weariness, happiness.

"Yes. I'm here."

"Edward, we did it. Broughton is out. We pooped him."

"Congratulations," Delaney said tonelessly.

"Edward, you've got to return to active duty. Take over Operation Lombard. Whatever you want—men, equipment, money. You name it, you've got it. Right?" Thorsen shouted; Delaney grimaced, held the phone away from his ear. He heard two or three voices shout, "Right!" in reply to Thorsen's question.

"Edward? You still there?"

"I'm still here."

"You understand? You back on active duty. Head of Operation Lombard. Whatever you need. What do you say?"

"Yes," Captain X. Delaney said promptly.

"Yes? You said yes?"

"That's what I said."

"He said yes!" Thorsen screamed. Again Delaney held the phone away, hearing the loud gabble of many voices. This was fraternity house stuff, and it displeased him.

"My God, that's great," the Deputy Inspector said in what Delaney was sure Thorsen thought was a sober and solemn voice.

"But I want complete control," the Captain said stonily. "Over the whole operation. No written reports. Verbal reports to you only. And—"

"Whatever you want, Edward."

"And no press conferences, no press releases, no publicity from anyone but me."

"Anything, Edward, anything. Just wrap it up fast. You understand? Show Broughton up for the stupid schmuck, he is. He gets canned and three days later you've solved it. Right? Shows up the bastard."

"Canned?" the Captain asked. "Broughton?"

" 'mounts to the same thing," Thorsen giggled. "Filed for retirement. Stupid sonofabitch. Says he's going to run for mayor next year."

"Is he?" Delaney said, still speaking in a dull, toneless voice. "Ivar, are you certain you've got this straight? I'll take it on, but only on the conditions that I have complete control, verbal reports only to you, pick my own men, handle all the publicity personally. Is that understood?"

"Captain Delaney," a quiet voice said, "this is Deputy Mayor Herman Alinski. I apologize, but I have been listening in on an extension. There is a certain celebration going on here."

"I can hear it."

"But I assure you, your conditions will be met. You will have complete control. Whatever you need. And nothing in the press or TV on Operation Lombard will come from anyone but you. Satisfactory?"

"Yes."

"Great!" Deputy Inspector Thorsen burbled. "The telex will go out immediately. We'll get out a press release right away—just so we can make the late editions—that Broughton has put in for retirement and you're taking over Operation Lombard. Is that all right, Edward? Just a short, one-paragraph release. Okay?"

"Yes. All right."

"Your personal orders have already been cut. The Commissioner will sign them tonight."

"You must have been very sure of me," Delaney said.

"I wasn't," Thorsen laughed, "and Johnson wasn't. But Alinski was."

"Oh?" Delaney said coldly. "Are you there, Alinski?"

"I am here, Captain," the soft voice came back.

"You were sure of me? That I'd take this on?"

"Yes," Alinski said. "I was sure."

"Why?"

"You don't have any choice, do you, Captain?" the Deputy Mayor asked gently.

Delaney hung up, just as gently.

The first thing the Captain did was finish his beer. It helped. Not only the tang of it, the shock of coldness in his throat, but it stimulated the sudden realization of the magnitude of the job he had agreed to, the priorities, big responsibilities and small details, and the fact that "first things first" would be the only guide that might see him through. Right now, the first thing was finishing a cold beer.

"You don't have any choice, do you, Captain?" the Deputy Mayor had asked gently.

What had he meant by that?

He switched on the desk lamp, sat down, put on his glasses, pulled the yellow, legal-lined pad toward him, began to doodle—squares, circles, lines. Rough diagrams, very rough, and random ideas expressed in arrowheads, lightning bolts, spirals.

First things first. First of the first was around-the-clock surveillance of Daniel G. Blank. Three plainclothesmen on foot and two unmarked cars of two men each should do it. Seven men. Working eight-hour shifts. That was 21 men. But a police commander with any experience at all didn't multiply his personnel requirements by three: he multiplied by four, at least. Because men are entitled to days off, vacations, sick leave, family emergencies, etc. So the basic force watching Danny Boy was 28, and Delaney wondered if he had been too optimistic in thinking he could reduce the 500 detectives assigned to Operation Lombard by two-thirds.

That was one division: the outside force shadowing Blank. A second division would be inside, keeping records, monitoring walkie-talkie reports from the Blank guards. That meant a communications set-up. Receivers and transmitters. Somewhere. Not in the 251st Precinct house. Delaney owed Lieutenant Dorfman that one. He'd get Operation Lombard out of there, establish his command post somewhere else, anywhere. Isolate his men. That would help cut down leaks to the press.

A third division would be research: the suspect's history, background, credit rating, bank accounts, tax returns, military record—anything and everything that had ever been recorded about the man. Plus interviews with friends, relatives, acquaintances, business associates. Cover stories could be concocted so Blank wasn't alerted.

(But what if he was? That blurry idea in the back of Delaney's mind began to take on a definite outline.)

A possible fourth division might investigate the dark, skinny girl friend, the boy Tony, the friends—what was their name? Morton. That was it. They owned the Erotica. All that might take another squad.

It was all very crude, very tentative. Just a sketching in. But it was a beginning. He doodled on for almost an hour, starting to firm it up, thinking of what men he wanted where, who he owed favors to. Favors. "I owe you one." "That's one you owe me." The lifeblood of the Department. Of politics. Of business. Of the thrusting, scheming, rude world. Wasn't that the rough cement that kept the whole rickety machine from falling apart? You be nice to me and I'll be nice to you. Charles Lipsky: "One hand washes the other—right?"

It was an hour—more than that—since his conversation with Thorsen. The Telex would now be clicked out in every precinct house, detective division, and special unit in the city. Captain Delaney went up to his bedroom, stripped down to his underwear and took a "whore's bath," soaping hands, face and armpits with a washcloth, then drying, powdering, combing his hair carefully.

He put on his Number Ones, his newest uniform, used, so far, only for ceremonies and funerals. He squared his shoulders, pulled the blouse down tautly, made certain his decorations were aligned. He took a new cap from a plastic bag on the closet shelf, wiped the shield bright on his sleeve, set the cap squarely atop his head, the short beak pulled down almost over his eyes. The uniform was a brutal one: choker collar, shielded eyes, wide shoulders, tapered waist. Menace there.

He inspected himself in the downstairs mirror. It was not egotism. If you had never belonged to church, synagogue or mosque, you might think so. But the costume was continuing tradition, symbol, myth—whatever you like. The clothing, decorations, insignia went beyond clothing, decorations, insignia. They were, to those of the faith, belief.

He decided against an overcoat; he wouldn't be going far. He went into the study just long enough to take the photo of Daniel G. Blank from the file and scrawl the man's address, but not his name, on the back. He slipped the photo into his hip pocket. He left his glasses on the desk. If possible, you did not wear eyeglasses when you exercised command, or exhibit any other signs of physical infirmity. It was ridiculous, but it was so.

He locked up, marched next door to the 251st Precinct house. The Telex had obviously come through; Dorfman was standing near the sergeant's desk, his arms folded, waiting. When he saw Delaney, he came forward at once, his long, ugly face relaxing into a grin. He held out a hand eagerly.

"Congratulations, Captain."

"Thank you," Delaney said, shaking his hand. "Lieutenant, I'll have this gang out of your hair as soon as possible. A day or two at the most. Then you'll have your house back."

"Thank you, Captain," Dorfman said gratefully.

"Where are they?" Delaney asked.

"Detectives' squad room."

"How many?"

"Thirty, forty—around there. They got the word, but they don't know what to do."

Delaney nodded. He walked up the old creaking stairway, past the commander's office. The frosted glass door of the detectives' squad room was closed. There was noise from inside, a lot of men talking at once, a buzz of confused sound, angry turbulence. The Captain opened the door, and stood there.

The majority were in plainclothes, a few in uniform. Heads turned to look at him, then more. All. The talk died down. He just stood there, looking coldly out from under the beak of his cap. They all stared at him. A few men rose grudgingly to their feet. Then a few more. Then more. He waited unmoving, watching them. He recognized a few, but his aloof expression didn't change. He waited until they were all standing, and silent.

"I am Captain Edward X. Delaney," he said crisply. "I am now in command. Are there any lieutenants here?"

Some of the men looked around uneasily. Finally, from the back, a voice called, "No, Captain, no lieutenants."

"Any detective sergeants?"

A hand went up, a black hand. Delaney walked toward the raised hand, men stepping aside to let him through. He walked to the back of the room until he was facing the black sergeant, a short, heavyset man with sculpted features and what appeared to be a closely-fitted knitted cap of white wool. He was, Delaney knew, called "Pops," and he looked like a professor of Middle English literature. Strangely enough, he had professorial talents.

"Detective sergeant Thomas MacDonald," Captain Delaney said loudly, so everyone could hear him.

"That's right, Captain."

"I remember. We worked together. A warehouse job over on the west side. About ten years ago."

"More like fifteen, Captain."

"Was it? You took one in the hip."

"In the ass, Captain."

There were a few snickers. Delaney knew what MacDonald was trying to do, and fed him his lines.

"In the ass?" he said. "I trust it healed, sergeant?"

The black professor shrugged. "Just one more crease, Captain," he said. The listening men broke up, laughing and relaxing.

Delaney motioned to MacDonald. "Come with me." The sergeant followed him out into the hallway. The Captain closed the door, shutting off most of the laughter and noise. He looked at MacDonald. MacDonald looked at him.

"It really was the hip," Delaney said softly.

"Sure, Captain," the sergeant agreed. "But I figured—"

"I know what you figured," the Captain said, "and you figured right. Can you work till eight tomorrow morning?"

"If I have to."

"You have to," Delaney said. He drew Blank's photo from his pocket, handed it to MacDonald. "This is the man," he said tonelessly. "His address is on the back. You don't have to know his name—now. It's a block-size apartment building. Entrance and exit through a lobby on East Eighty-third. One doorman this time of night. I want three men, plain, covering the lobby. If this man comes out, I want them close to him."

"How close?"

"Close enough."

"So if he farts, they can smell it?"

"Not that close. But don't let this guy out of their sight. Not for a second. If he spots them, all right. But I wouldn't like it."

"I understand, Captain. A crazy?"

"Something like that. Just don't play him for laughs. He's not a nice boy."

The sergeant nodded.

"And two cars. Two men each, in plain. At both ends of the block. In case he takes off. He's got a black Chevy Stingray in the underground garage, or he might take a cab. Got all that?"

"Sure, Captain."

"You know Shakespeare and Lauder?"

"The 'Gold Dust Twins?' I know Lauder."

"I'd like them in one of the cars. If they're not on duty, any good men will do. That makes seven men. You pick six more, three in plain and three in uniform, and have them stand by here until eight tomorrow morning. Everyone else can go home. But everyone back by eight tomorrow, and anyone else you can reach by phone or who calls in. Got it?"

"Where do you want me, Captain?"

"Right here. I've got to go out for an hour or so, but I'll be back. We'll have some coffee together and talk about that extra crease in your ass."

"Sounds like a jolly night."

Delaney looked at him a long time. They had started in the Department the same year, had been in the same Academy class. Now Delaney was a captain, and MacDonald was a sergeant. It wasn't a question of ability. Delaney wouldn't mention what it was, and MacDonald never would either.

"What's Broughton had you on?" he asked the sergeant finally.

"Rousting street freaks," MacDonald said.

"Shit," Delaney said disgustedly.

"My sentiments exactly, Captain," the sergeant said.

"Well, lay it all on," the Captain said. "I'll be back in an hour or so. Your men should be in position by then. The sooner, the better. Show them that photo, but you hang onto it. It's the only one I've got. I'll have copies run off tomorrow."

"Is he it, Captain?" Detective sergeant MacDonald asked.

Delaney shrugged. "Who knows?" he said.

He turned, walked away. He was at the staircase when the sergeant called softly: "Captain." He turned around.

"Good to be working with you again, sir," MacDonald said.

Delaney smiled faintly but didn't answer. He walked down the stairway thinking of Broughton's stupidity in using MacDonald to pull in street freaks. MacDonald! One of the best professors in the Department. No wonder those forty men had been sour and grumbling. It wasn't that Broughton hadn't kept them busy, but he had misused their individual abilities and talents. No one could take that for long without losing drive, ambition, even interest in what he was doing. And what was he, Delaney? What were his abilities and talents? He waved a hand in answer to the desk sergeant's salute as he walked out. He knew what he was. He was a cop.

He would have commandeered a squad car, but there was none around. So he walked over to Second Avenue, got a cab heading downtown. He walked into the hospital and, for once, the white tiled walls and the smell couldn't depress him. Wait until Barbara heard!

Then he pushed open the door of her room. There was a nurses' aide sitting alongside the bed. Barbara appeared to be sleeping. The aide motioned to him, beckoning him outside into the corridor.

"She's had a bad evening," she whispered. "Earlier it took two of us to hold her down, and we had to give her something. Doctor said it would be all right."

"Why?" the Captain demanded. "What is it? Is it the new drug?"

"You'll have to ask doctor," the aide said primly. Delaney wondered again, in despair, why they always just said "doctor." Never "the doctor." "You have to consult engineer." "You'll have to talk to architect." "You'll have to discuss that with lawyer." It made the same sense, and it all made no sense whatever.

"I'll sit with her awhile," Delaney told the aide. She was so young; he couldn't blame her. Who could he blame?

She nodded brightly. "Tell me when you leave. Unless she's asleep by then."

"She's not asleep now?"

"No. Her eyes are closed, but she's awake. If you need any help, ring the bell or call."

She walked away quickly, leaving him wondering what help he might need. He went softly back into the hospital room, still wearing his uniform cap. He pulled a chair over to Barbara's bedside, sat looking at her. She did seem to be sleeping; her eyes were shut tight, she was breathing deeply and regularly. But, while he watched, her eyelids flicked open, she stared at the ceiling.

"Barbara?" he called gently. "Darling?"

Her eyes moved, but her head didn't turn. Her eyes moved to look at him, into him, through him, not seeing him.

"Barbara, it's Edward. I'm here. I have so much to tell you, dear. So much has happened."

"Honey Bunch?" she said.

"It's Edward, dear. I have a lot to tell you. A lot has happened."

"Honey Bunch?" she said.

He found the books in the metal taboret alongside her bed. He took the top one, not even glancing at the title, and opened it at random. Not having his glasses, he had to hold the book almost at arm's length. But the type was large, there was good white space between the lines.

Sitting upright in his Number One uniform, gleaming cap squarely atop his head, the commander of Operation Lombard began reading:

"Honey Bunch picked her nasturtiums that morning and she gave away her first bouquet. That is always a lovely garden experience—to give away your first bouquet. Of course Honey Bunch gave hers to Mrs. Lancaster and the little old lady said that she would take the flowers home and put them in water and make them last as long as possible.

" 'Haven't you any garden at all?' asked Honey Bunch. 'Just a little one?'

" 'No garden at all,' replied the old lady sadly. 'This is the first year I can remember that I haven't had a piece of ground to do with as . . .' "

5

He slept when he could, but it wasn't much: perhaps four or five hours a night. But, to his surprise and pleasure, it didn't slow him down. Within three days he had it all organized. It was functioning.

He took Lieutenant Jeri Fernandez out of the Garment Center division he hated, put him in command of the squad shadowing Daniel Blank. Delaney let him select his own spooks; the "Invisible Man" almost wept with gratitude. It was exactly the kind of job he loved, that he did best. It was his idea to borrow a Consolidated Edison van and tear up a section of East 83rd Street near the driveway leading to Blank's apartment house. Fernandez' men wore Con Ed uniforms and hard hats, and worked slowly on the hole they dug in the pavement. It played hell with traffic, but the van was filled with communication gear and weapons, and served as Fernandez' command post. Delaney was delighted. Fuck the traffic jams.

For "Mr. Inside," the Captain requisitioned Detective first grade Ronald Blankenship, the man who had handled the two original beefs on Daniel Blank. Working together closely, Delaney and Blankenship transferred the command post of Operation Lombard from the 251st Precinct house to the living room of Delaney's home, next door. It wasn't as spacious as they would have liked, but it had its advantages; the communications men could run wires out the window, up to Delaney's roof, then across to tie in with the antennae on the precinct house roof.

Detective sergeant Thomas MacDonald, "Pops," was Delaney's choice to head up the research squad, and MacDonald was happy. He got as much pleasure from an afternoon of sifting through dusty documents as another man might get in an Eighth Avenue massage parlor. Within 24 hours his men had compiled a growing dossier on Daniel G. Blank, taking him apart, piece by piece.

Captain Delaney appreciated the unpaid labors of his amateurs, but he couldn't deny the advantages and privileges of being on active duty, in official command, with all the resources of the Department behind him, and a promise of unlimited men, equipment, funds.

Item: A tap was put on the home telephone of Daniel Blank. It was installed in the central telephone office servicing his number.

Item: The next day's call to Charles Lipsky had resulted in the time of departure and license number of a cab picking up Blank's dark-haired girl friend at his apartment house. Delaney told Blankenship what he wanted. Within three hours the license number had been traced, the fleet identified, and a dick was waiting in the garage for the driver to return. His trip sheet was checked, and the Captain had the address where the cab had dropped her off. One of Fernandez' boys went over to check it; it turned out to be a townhouse on East End Avenue. After consultation with the lieutenant, Delaney decided to establish surveillance: one plainclothesman around the clock. Fernandez suggested detailing a two-man team to comb the neighborhood, to learn what they could about that house.

"It's an expensive section," Delaney said thoughtfully. "Lots of VIP's around there. Tell them to walk softly."

"Sure, Captain."

"And lots of servants. You got a good-looking black who could cuddle up to some of the maids and cooks on the street?"

"Just the man!" Fernandez said triumphantly. "A big, handsome stud. He don' walk, he glides. And smart as a whip. We call him 'Mr. Clean.'"

"Sounds good," the Captain nodded. "Turn him loose and see what he can come up with."

He then put on his civilian clothes, went over to Blank's apartment house to slip Lipsky his twenty dollars. The doorman thanked him gratefully.

Item: An hour later, Blankenship handed him the trace on Charles Lipsky. As Delaney had suspected, the man had a sheet. As a matter of fact, he was on probation, having been found guilty of committing a public nuisance, in that he did "with deliberate and malicious intent," urinate on the hood of a parked Bentley on East 59th Street.

Item: Christopher Langley called to report he had completed a list of all retail outlets of the West German ice ax in the U.S. With his new authority, Delaney was able to dispatch a squad car to go up to Langley's, pick up the list, bring it back to the command post. The list was assigned to one of Detective sergeant MacDonald's research men and, on the phone, he struck gold with his first call. Daniel G. Blank had purchased such an ax five years ago from Alpine Haven, a mail order house in Stamford, Conn., that specialized in mountaineering gear. A man was immediately sent to Stamford to bring back a photostatic copy of the sales check made out to Daniel G. Blank.

Item: Fernandez' men, particularly "Mr. Clean," made progress on that East End Avenue townhouse. At least, they now had the names of the residents: Celia Montfort, Blank's dark, thin girl friend; her young brother Anthony; a houseman named Valenter; and a middle-aged housekeeper. The names were turned over to MacDonald; the professor set up a separate staff to check them out.

During these days and nights of frantic activity, in the week before Christmas, Captain Delaney took time out to perform several personal chores. He gave Mary her Christmas gift early and, in addition, two weeks' vacation. Then he brought in an old uniformed patrolman, on limited duty, waiting for retirement, and told him to buy a 20-cup coffee urn and keep it going 24 hours a day in the kitchen; to keep the refrigerator filled with beer, cold cuts, cheese; and have enough bread and rolls on hand so anyone in Operation Lombard coming off a cold night's watch, or just stopping by during the day to report, would be assured of a sandwich and a drink.

He ordered folding cots, pillows and blankets brought in, and they were set up in the living room, hallway, kitchen, dining room—any place except in his study. They were in use almost constantly. Men who lived out on Long Island or up in Westchester sometimes preferred to sleep in, rather than make the long trip home, eat, sleep a few hours, turn around and come right back again.

He also found time to call his amateurs, wish them a Merry Christmas, thank them, for their help and support and tell them as gently as he could, that their efforts were no longer needed. He assured them their aid had been of invaluable assistance in developing a "very promising lead."

He did this on the phone to Christopher Langley and Calvin Case. He took Monica Gilbert to lunch and told her as much as he felt she should know: that partly through her efforts, he had a good chance to nail the killer but, because of the press of work, he wouldn't be able to call her or see her as often as he'd like. She was understanding and sympathetic.

"But take care of yourself," she entreated. "You look so tired."

"I feel great," he protested. "Sleep like a baby."

"How many hours?"

"Well . . . as much as I can."

"And you have regular, nourishing meals, I'm sure," she said sardonically.

He laughed. "I'm not starving," he assured her. "With luck, this may be over soon. One way or another. Are you still visiting Barbara?"

"Almost every day. You know, we're so dissimilar, but we have so much in common."

"Do you? That's good. I feel so guilty about Barbara. I dash in and dash out. Just stay long enough to say hello. But she's been through this before. She's a cop's wife."

"Yes. She told me."

Her sad voice gave him a sudden, vague ache, of something he should have done but did not do. But he couldn't think about it now.

"Thank you for visiting Barbara and liking her," he said. "Did I tell you we're now grandparents?"

"Barbara did. *Mazel tov.*"

"Thank you. An ugly little boy."

"Barbara told me," she repeated. "But don't worry; within six months he'll be a beautiful little boy."

"Sure."

"Did you send a gift?"

"Well . . . I really didn't have time. But I did talk to Liza and her husband on the phone."

"It's all right. Barbara sent things. I picked them out for her and had them sent."

"That was very kind of you." He rubbed his chin, felt the bristle, realized he had neglected to shave that morning. That was no good. He had to present the image of a well-groomed, crisply uniformed, confident commander to his men. It was important.

"Edward," she said, in a low voice, with real concern, "are you all right?"

"Of course I'm all right," he said stonily. "I've been through things like this before."

"Please don't be angry with me."

"I'm not angry. Monica. I'm all right. I swear it. I could be sleeping more and eating better, but it's not going to kill me."

"You seem so—so wound up. This is important to you, isn't it?"

"Important? That I nail this guy? Of course it's important to me. Isn't it to you? He killed your husband."

She flinched at his brutality. "Yes," she said faintly, "it's important to me. But I don't like what it's doing to you."

He wouldn't think of what she had said, or what she had meant. First things first.

"I've got to get back," he said, and signaled for a check.

During that wild week he found time for two more personal jobs. Still not certain in his mind why he was doing it, he selected the business card of a certain J. David McCann, representative of something called the Universal Credit Union. Wearing his stiff Homburg and floppy civilian overcoat, he walked into the effete, scented showroom of the Erotica on Madison Avenue and asked to speak to Mr. or Mrs. Morton, hoping neither would recognize him as the former commander of the precinct in which they lived and worked.

He spoke to both in their backroom office. Neither glommed him; he realized that except for members of business associations, VIP's, community groups and social activists, the average New Yorker hadn't the slightest idea of the name or appearance of the man who commanded the forces of law and order in his precinct. An ego-deflating thought.

Delaney took off his hat, bowed, presented his phony business card, did everything but tug his forelock.

"I'm not selling anything," he said ingratiatingly. "Just a routine credit investigation. Mr. Daniel G. Blank has applied for a loan and given us your names as references. We just want to make sure you actually do know him."

Flo looked at Sam. Sam looked at Flo.

"Of course we know him," Sam said, almost angrily. "A very good friend."

"Known him for years," Flo affirmed. "Lives in the same apartment house we do."

"Mm-hmm," Delaney nodded. "A man of good character, you'd say? Dependable? Honest? Trustworthy?"

"A Boy Scout," Sam assured him. "What the hell's this all about?"

"You mentioned a loan," Flo said. "What kind of a loan? How big?"

"Well . . . I really shouldn't reveal these details," Delaney said in soft confidential tones, "but Mr. Blank has applied for a rather large mortgage covering the purchase of a townhouse on East End Avenue."

The Mortons looked at each other in astonishment. Then to Delaney's interest, they broke into pleased smiles.

"Celia's house!" Sam shouted, smacking his thighs. "He's buying her place!"

"It's on!" Flo screamed, hugging her arms. "They're really getting together!"

Captain Delaney nodded at both, snatched his business card back from Sam's fingers, replaced his Homburg, started from the office.

"Wait, wait, wait," Sam called. "You don't mind if we tell him you were here?"

"That you were checking up?" Flo asked. "You don't mind if we kid him about it?"

"Of course not," Captain Delaney smiled. "Please do."

On the second call he wore the same clothes, used the same business card. But this time he had to sit on his butt in an overheated outer office for almost a half-hour before he was allowed to see Mr. René Horvath, Personnel Director of the Javis-Bircham Corp. Eventually he was ushered into the inner sanctum where Mr. Horvath inspected the Captain's clothing with some distaste. As well he might; he himself was wearing a black raw silk suit, a red gingham plaid shirt with stiff white collar and cuffs, a black knitted tie. What Delaney liked most, he decided, were the black crinkle-patent leather moccasins with bright copper pennies inserted into openings on the top flaps. Exquisite.

Delaney went through the same routine he used with the Mortons, varying it to leave out any mention of a mortgage on a townhouse, saying only that Mr. Daniel G. Blank had applied for a loan, and that he, Mr. J. David McCann—"My card, sir"—and the Universal Credit Union were simply interested in verifying that Mr. Blank was indeed, as he claimed to be, employed by Javis-Bircham Corp.

"He is," the elegant Mr. Horvath said, handing back the soiled business card with a look that suggested it might be a carrier of VD. "Mr. Daniel Blank is presently employed by this company."

"In a responsible capacity?"

"Very responsible."

"I suppose you'd object to giving me a rough idea of Mr. Blank's annual income?"

"You suppose correctly."

"Mr. Horvath, I assure you that anything you tell me will be held in strictest confidence. Would you say that Mr. Blank is honest, dependable, and trustworthy?"

Horvath's pinched face closed up even more. "Mr. McClosky—"

"McCann."

"Mr. McCann, *all* J-B executives are honest, dependable and trustworthy."

Delaney nodded, replaced the Homburg on his big head.

"Thank you for your time, sir. I certainly do appreciate it. Just doing my job—I hope you realize that."

"Naturally."

Delaney turned away, but suddenly a squid hand was on his arm, gripping limply.

"Mr. McCann . . ."

"Yes?"

"You said Mr. Blank has applied for a loan?"

"Yes, sir."

"How large a loan?"

"That I am not allowed to say sir. But you've been so cooperative that I can tell you it's a very large loan."

"Oh?" said Mr. Horvath. "Hmm," said Mr. Horvath, staring at the bright pennies inserted into his moccasin tongues. "That's very odd. Javis-Bircham, Mr. McCann, has its own loan program for all employees, from cafeteria busboy to Chairman of the Board. They can draw up to five thousand dollars, interestfree, and pay it back by salary deductions over a period of several years. Why didn't Mr. Blank apply for a company loan?"

"Oh well," Delaney laughed merrily, "you know how it is; everyone gets caught by the shorts sooner or later—right? And I guess he wanted to keep it private."

He left a very perturbed Mr. René Horvath behind him, and he thought, if Handry's impression was right and Blank's position with the company was shaky, it was shakier now.

In that week before Christmas, while the Delaney's living room furniture was being pushed back to the walls, deal tables and folding chairs brought in, cots set up, and communications men were still fiddling with their equipment, including three extra telephone lines, a "council of war" was scheduled every afternoon at 3:00 P.M. It was held in the Captain's study where the doors could be closed and locked. Attending were Captain Delaney, Lieutenant Jeri Fernandez, Detective first grade Ronald Blankenship, and Detective sergeant Thomas MacDonald. Delaney's liquor cabinet was open or, if they preferred, there was cold beer or hot coffee from the kitchen.

The first few meetings were concerned mostly with planning, organization, division of responsibility, choice of personnel, chain of command. Then, as information began to come in, they spent part of their time discussing the "Time-Habit Charts" compiled by Blankenship's squad. They were extremely detailed tabulations of Daniel Blank's daily routine: the time he left for work, his route, time of arrival at the Javis-Bircham Building, when he left for lunch, where he usually went, time of arrival back at the office, departure time, arrival at home, when he departed in the evening, where he went, how long he stayed. By the end of the fourth day, his patterns were pretty well established. Daniel Blank appeared to be a disciplined and orderly man.

Problems came up, were hashed out. Delaney listened to everyone's opinion. Then, after the discussion, he made the final decision.

Question: Should an undercover cop, with the cooperation of the management, be placed in Daniel Blank's apartment house as a porter, doorman, or whatever? Delaney's decision: No.

Question: Should an undercover cop be placed in Javis-Bircham, as close to Blank's department as he could get? Delaney's decision: Yes. It was assigned to Fernandez to work out as best he could a cover story that might seem plausible to the J-B executives he'd be dealing with.

Question: Should a Time-Habit Chart be set up for the residents of that town-house on East End Avenue? Delaney's decision: No, with the concurring opinions of all three assistants.

"It's a screwy household," MacDonald admitted. "We can't get a line on them. This Valenter, the butler—or whatever you want to call him—has a sheet on molesting juvenile males. But no convictions. But that's all I've got so far."

"I don't have much more," Fernandez confessed. "The dame—this Celia Montfort—was admitted twice to Mother of Mercy Hospital for suicide attempts. Slashed wrists, and once her stomach had to be pumped out. We're checking other hospitals, but nothing definite yet."

"The kid seems to be a young fag," Blankenship said, "but no one's given me anything yet that makes a pattern. Like Pops said, it's a weird set-up. I don't think anyone knows what's going on over there. Nothing we can chart, anyway. She's in, she's out, at all hours of the day and night. She was gone for two days. Where was she? We don't know and won't until we put a special tail on her. Captain?"

"No," Delaney said. "Not yet. Keep at it."

Keep at it. Keep at it. That's all they heard from him, and they did because he seemed to know what he was doing, radiated an aura of confidence, never appeared to doubt that if they all kept at it, they'd nail this psycho and the killings would stop.

Daniel G. Blank. Captain Delaney knew his name, and now the others did, too. Had to. The men on the street, in the Con Ed van, in the unmarked cars adopted, by common consent, the code name "Danny Boy" for the man they watched. They had his photo now, reprinted by the hundreds, they knew his home address and shadowed his comings and goings. But they were told only that he was a "suspect."

Sometime during that week, Captain Delaney could never recall later exactly when, he scheduled his first press conference. It was held in the now empty detectives' squad room of the 251st Precinct house. There were reporters from newspapers, magazines, local TV news programs. The cameras were there, too, and the lights were hot. Captain Delaney wore his Number Ones and delivered, from memory, a brief statement he had labored over a long time the previous evening.

"My name is Captain Edward X. Delaney," he started, standing erect, staring into the TV cameras, hoping the sweat on his face didn't show. "I have been assigned command of Operation Lombard. This case, as you all know, involves the apparently unconnected homicides of four men: Frank Lombard, Bernard Gilbert, Detective Roger Kope, and Albert Feinberg. I have spent several days going through the records of Operation Lombard during the time it was commanded by former Deputy Commissioner Broughton. There is nothing in that record that might possibly lead to the indictment, conviction, or even identification of a suspect. It is a record of complete and utter failure."

There was a gasp from the assembled reporters; they scribbled furiously. Delaney didn't change expression, but he was grinning inwardly. Did Broughton really think he could talk to Delaney the way he had and not pay for it, eventually? The Department functioned on favors. It also functioned on vengeance. Run for mayor, would he? Lots of luck, Broughton!

"So," Captain Delaney continued, "because there is such a complete lack of evidence in the files of Operation Lombard while it was under the command of former Deputy Commissioner Broughton, I am starting from the beginning, with the death of Frank Lombard, and intend to conduct a totally new investigation into the homicides of all four men. I promise you nothing. I prefer to be judged by my acts rather than by my words. This is the first and last press conference I intend to hold until I either have the killer or am relieved of command. I will not answer any questions."

An hour after this brief interview, shown in its entirety, appeared on local TV news programs, Captain Delaney received a package at his home. It was brought into his study by one of the uniformed patrolmen on guard duty at the outside door—a 24-hour watch. No one went in or out without showing a special pass

Delaney had printed up, issued only to bona fide members of *his* Operation Lombard. The patrolman placed the package on Delaney's desk.

"Couldn't be a bomb, could it, Captain?" he asked anxiously. "You was on TV tonight, you know."

"I know," the Captain nodded. He inspected the package, then picked it up gingerly. He tilted it gently, back and forth. Something sloshed.

"No," he said to the nervous officer, "I don't think it's a bomb. But you did well to suggest it. You can return to your post."

"Yes, sir," the young patrolman said, saluted and left.

Handsome, Delaney thought, but those sideburns were too goddamned long.

He opened the package. It was a bottle of 25-year-old brandy with a little envelope taped to the side. Delaney opened the bottle and sniffed; first things first. He wanted to taste it immediately. Then he opened the sealed envelope. A stiff card. Two words: "Beautiful" and "Alinski."

The mood of the "war councils" changed imperceptibly in the three days before Christmas. It was obvious they now had a working, efficient organization. Danny Boy was blanketed by spooks every time he stepped outside home or office. Blankenship's bookkeeping and communications were beyond reproach. Detective sergeant MacDonald's snoops had built up a file on Blank that took up three drawers of a locked cabinet in Delaney's study. It included the story of his refusal to attend his parents' funeral and a revealing interview with a married woman in Boston who agreed to give her impressions of Daniel Blank while he was in college, under the cover story that Blank was being considered for a high-level security government job. Her comments were damning, but nothing that could be presented to a grand jury. Blank's ex-wife had remarried and was presently on an around-the-world honeymoon cruise.

During those last three days before Christmas, the impression was growing amongst Delaney's assistants—he could *feel* the mood—that they were amassing a great deal of information about Daniel G. Blank—a lot of it fascinating and libidinous reading—but it amounted to a very small hill of beans. The man had a girl friend. So? Maybe he was or was not sleeping with her brother, Tony. So? He came out occasionally at odd hours, wandered about the streets, looked in shop windows, stopped in at The Parrot for a drink. So?

"Maybe he's on to us," Blankenship. "Maybe he knows the decoys are out every night, and he's being tailed."

"Can't be," Fernandez growled angrily. "No way. He don' even *see* my boys. As far as he's concerned, we don' exist."

"I don't know what else we can do," MacDonald confessed. "We've got him sliced up so thin I can see right through him. Birth certificate, diplomas, passport, bank statements—everything. You've seen the file. The man's laid out there, bare-assed naked. Read the file and you've got him. Sure, maybe he's a psychopath, capable of killing I guess. He's a cold, smart, slick sonofabitch. But take him into court on what we've got? Uh-uh. Never. That's my guess."

"Keep at it," Captain Edward X. Delaney said.

Things slowed down on Christmas Eve. That was natural; men wanted to be home with their families. Squads were cut to a minimum (mostly bachelors or volunteers), and men sent home early. Delaney spent that quiet afternoon in his study, reading once again through his original Daniel G. Blank file and the great mass of material assembled by Pops and his squad who seemed to get their kicks sifting through dusty documents, military records, tax returns.

He read it all once more, sipping slowly from a balloon glass of that marvelous brandy Alinski had sent. He would have to call the Deputy Mayor to thank him, or perhaps mail a thank-you note, but meanwhile Alinski's envelope was added to the stack of unopened Christmas cards and presents that had accumulated in a corner of the study. He'd get to them, eventually, or take them over to Barbara when she was well enough to open them and enjoy them.

So he sipped brandy through a long Christmas Eve afternoon (the usual conference had been cancelled). As he read, the belief grew in him that the chilling of Danny Boy would come about through the man's personality, not by any clever police work, the discovery of a "clue," or by a sudden revelation of friend or lover.

Who was Daniel G. Blank? Who *was* he? MacDonald had said he was sliced thin, that he was laid out in that file bareassed naked. No, Delaney thought, just the facts of the man's life were there. But no one is a simple compilation of official documents, of interviews with friends and acquaintances, of Time-Habit schedules. The essential question remained: Who *was* Daniel G. Blank?

Delaney was fascinated by him because he seemed to be two men. He had been a cold, lonely boy who grew up in what apparently had been a loveless home. No record of juvenile delinquency. He was quiet, collected rocks and, until college, didn't show any particular interest in girls. Then he refused to attend his parents' funeral. That seemed significant to Delaney. How could anyone, no matter how young, do a thing like that? There was a callous brutality about it that was frightening.

Then there was his marriage—what was it Lipsky had called her? A big zaftig blonde—the divorce, the girl friend with a boy's body, then possibly the boy himself, Tony. And meanwhile the sterile apartment with mirrors, the antiseptic apartment with silk bikini underwear and scented toilet paper. And according to one of MacDonald's beautifully composed and sardonic reports, a fast climb up the corporate ladder.

Delaney went back to an interview one of MacDonald's snoops had with a man named Robert White who had been Blank's immediate superior at Javis-Bircham. He had, from all the evidence and statements available, been knifed and ousted by Daniel Blank. The interview with White had been made under the cover story that Blank was being considered for a high executive position with a corporation competing with J-B.

"He's a nice lad," Bob White had stated. ("Possibly under the influence of alcohol," the interrogating detective had noted carefully in his report.) "He's talented. Lots of imagination. Too much maybe. But he gets the job done: I'll say that for him. But no blood. You understand? No fucking blood."

Captain Delaney stared up at the ceiling. "No fucking blood." What did that mean? Who *was* Daniel G. Blank? Of such complexity . . . Disgusting and fascinating. Courage—no doubt about that; he climbed mountains and he killed. Kind? Of course. He objected when he saw a man hit a dog, and he kept sentimental souvenirs of the men he murdered. Talented and imaginative? Well, his previous boss had said so. Talented and imaginative enough to fuck a 30-year-old woman and her 12-year-old brother, but Delaney didn't suppose Bob White knew anything about *that!*

Who *was* Dan?

Captain Delaney rose to his feet, brandy glass in hand, about to propose a toast: "Here's to you, Danny Boy," when there was a knock on his study door. He sat down sedately behind his desk.

"Come in," he called.

Lieutenant Jeri Fernandez stuck his head through the opened door.

"Busy, Captain?" he asked. "Got a few minutes?"

"Of course, of course," Delaney gestured. "Come on in. Got some fine brandy here. How about it?"

"Ever know me to refuse?" Fernandez asked in mock seriousness, and they both laughed.

Then Delaney was in his swivel chair, swinging back and forth gently, holding his glass, and Fernandez was in the leather club chair. The lieutenant sipped the brandy, said nothing, but his eyes rolled to Heaven in appreciation.

"Thought you'd be home by now," the Captain said.

"On my way. Just making sure everything's copasetic."

"I know I've told you this before, lieutenant, but I'll say it again: tell your boys not to relax, not for a second. This monkey is fast."

Fernandez hunched over in the club chair, leaning forward, head lowered, moving the brandy snifter between his palms.

"Faster than a thirty-eight, Captain?" he asked in a voice so low that Delaney wasn't sure he heard him.

"What?" he demanded.

"Is this freak faster than a thirty-eight?" Fernandez repeated. This time he raised his head, looked directly into Delaney's eyes.

The Captain rose immediately, went to the study doors, closed them and locked them, then came back to sit behind his desk again.

"What's on your mind?" he asked quietly, looking directly at Fernandez.

"Captain, we been at this for—how long? Over a week now. Almost ten days. We got this Danny Boy covered six ways from Sunday. You keep calling him a 'suspect.' But I notice we're not out looking for other suspects, digging into anyone else. Everything we do is about this guy Blank."

"So?" Delaney said coldly.

"So," Fernandez sighed, looking down at his glass, "I figure maybe you know something we don' know, something you're not telling us." He held up a hand hastily, palm out. "This isn't a beef, Captain. If there's something we don' have to know, that's your right and privilege. Just thought—maybe—you might be sure of this guy but can't collar him. For some reason. No witnesses. No evidence that'll hold up. Whatever. But I figure you know it's him. *Know* it!"

The Captain resumed his slow swinging back and forth in his swivel chair. "Supposing," he said, "just *supposing,* mind you, that you're right, that I know as sure as God made little green apples that Blank is our pigeon, but we can't touch him. What do you suggest then?"

Fernandez shrugged. "Supposing," he said, "just *supposing* that's the situation, then I can't see us collaring Danny Boy unless we grab him in the act. And if he's as fast as you say he is, we'll have another stiff before we can do that. Right?"

Delaney nodded. "Yes," he said, "I've thought of that. So what's your answer?"

Fernandez took a sip of brandy, then looked up.

"Let me take him, Captain," he said softly.

Delaney set his brandy glass on the desk blotter, poured himself another small portion of that ambrosia, then carried the bottle over to Fernandez and added to his snifter. He returned to his swivel chair, set the bottle down, began to drum gently on his desk top with one hand, watching the moving fingers.

"You?" he asked Fernandez. "You alone?"

"No. I got a friend. The two—"

"A friend?" Delaney said sharply, looking up. "In the Department?"

The lieutenant was astonished. "Of course in the Department. Who's got any friends outside the Department?"

"All right," Delaney nodded. "How would you handle it?"

"The usual," Fernandez shrugged. "We go up to his apartment and roust him. He resists arrest and tries to escape, so we ice him. Clean and simple and neat."

The Captain sighed, shook his head. "It doesn't listen," he said.

"Captain, it's been done before."

"Goddamn it, don't try to tell me my business," Delaney shouted furiously. "I know it's been done before. But we do it your way, and we all get pooped."

He jerked to his feet, unbuttoned his uniform jacket, jammed his hands in his hip pockets. He began to pace about the study, not glancing at Fernandez as he talked.

"Look, lieutenant," he said patiently, "this guy is no alley cat with a snoot full of shit, that no one cares if he lives or dies. Burn a guy like that, and he's just a number in a potter's field. But Danny Boy is *somebody*. He's rich, he lives in a luxury apartment house, drives an expensive car, works for a big corporation. He's got friends, influential friends. Chill him, and people are going to ask questions. And we better have the answers. If it's done at all, it's got to be done *right*."

Fernandez opened his mouth to speak, but Delaney held up a hand. "Wait a minute. Let me finish. Now let's take your plan. You and your friend go up to brace him. How you going to get inside his apartment? I happen to know that guy's got more locks on his door than you'll find in a Tombs' cellblock. You think you'll knock, say, 'Police officers,' and he'll open up and let you in? The hell he will; he's too smart for that. He'll look at you through the peephole and talk to you through the locked door."

"Search warrant?" Fernandez suggested.

"Not a chance," Delaney shook his head. "Forget it."

"Then how about this: One of us goes up and waits outside his door, before he gets home from work. The other guy waits in the lobby until he comes in and rides up in the elevator with him. Then we got him in his hallway between us."

"And then what?" the Captain demanded. "You weight him right there in the corridor, while he's between you, and then claim he was trying to escape or resisting arrest? Who'd buy that?"

"Well . . ." Fernandez said doubtfully, "I guess you're right. But there's got to—"

"Shut up a minute and let me think," Delaney said. "Maybe we can work this out."

The lieutenant was silent then, sipping a little brandy, his bright eyes following the Captain as he lumbered about the room.

"Look," Delaney said, "there's a doorman over there. Guy named Charles Lipsky. He's got access to duplicate keys to every apartment in the building. They hang on a board outside the assistant manager's office. This Lipsky's got a sheet. As a matter of fact, he's on probation, so you can lean on him. Now . . . you hear on the radio that Danny Boy has left work and is heading home. You and your friend get the keys from Lipsky, go upstairs and get inside Blank's apartment. Then you relock the door from the inside. So when he comes home, unlocks his door and marches in, you're already in there."

"I like it," Fernandez grinned.

"When the time comes I'll draw you a floor plan so you'll know where to be when he comes in. Then you—"

"A floor plan?" the lieutenant interrupted. "But how—"

"Just don't worry about it. Don't even think about it. When the time comes, you'll have a floor plan. But you give him time to get inside before you show yourselves. Maybe even give him time to relock his door so he can't make a fast run for it. He's sure to relock once he's inside his apartment; that's the kind of a guy he is. *Then* you show yourselves. Now here's where it begins to get cute. Can you get hold of a piece that can't be traced?"

"Oh sure. No trouble."

"What is it?"

"A Saturday-night special."

The Captain took a deep breath, blew it out in an audible sigh.

"Lieutenant," he said gently, "Danny Boy makes fifty-five big ones a year, drives a Stingray, and wears silk underwear. Do you really think he's the kind of guy who'd own a piece of crap like that? What else can you get?"

The "Invisible Man" thought a moment, his teeth clenched.

"A nine-millimeter Luger," he said finally. "Brand-new. Right off the docks. Never been used. Still in the oiled envelope."

"What kind of grips."

"Wood."

"Yesss . . ." Delaney said thoughtfully. "He might own a gun like that. But the brand-new part is no good. It'll have to have at least three magazines fired through with a complete breakdown and cleaning between firings. Can you manage that?"

"No sweat, Captain."

"And it's got to be banged up a little. Not a lot. A few nicks on the grips. A little scratch here and there. You understand?"

"Like he's owned it for a long time?"

"Right. And took it on those mountain climbing trips of his to plink at tin cans or some such shit. Now here's something else: keep the box or envelope it came in, get the right cleaning tools and some oil-soaked rags. You know, the usual crap. This stuff you turn over to me."

"To *you,* Captain?"

"Yes, to me. All right, now you and your buddy are inside the apartment, and the door is locked. You've both got your service revolvers, and one of you has also got the used Luger. It's loaded. Full magazine. As soon as Danny Boy is inside his apartment, and has locked the door, you show. And for God's sake, have your sticks out. Don't relax for a second. Keep this guy covered."

"Don't worry, he'll be covered."

"Don't say a word to him, not a word. Just back him toward the bedroom door. You'll see where it is on that floor plan I'll draw for you. Now this is where you've got to work fast. As soon as he's in the bedroom doorway, or near it, facing you, weight him. Make it fast, and—this is important—make certain you both ice him. I don't know how good a friend this pal of yours is, but you've *both* got to do it. You understand?"

Fernandez smiled slyly. "You're a smart man, Captain."

"Yes. Now you're working fast. He's down, and for Christ's sake make certain he's gone."

"He'll have enough weight in him to sink him," the lieutenant assured him. "He'll be a clunk before he hits the floor."

"I'll take your word for it," Delaney grunted. "Now, the moment he's down, one of you—I don't care who it is—straddles his body, facing in the direction he was facing just before he bought it. And then—"

"And then we fire two or three shots from the Luger into the opposite wall," Fernandez said rapidly. "Where the two of us was just standing."

"Now you're catching it," the Captain said approvingly. "But it's got to be done fast—so that if anyone hears the shots, it's just a lot of shots, no pauses. No witness is going to remember how many shots were fired, when, or in what order. But just to play safe, the Luger should be fired into the opposite wall as soon as possible after you've iced him."

"I've got it," Fernandez smiled. "Two or three shots into the wall. Not too high. Like he really was firing at us."

"Right. Splinter a couple of mirrors if you can. That opposite wall is full of mirrors. Then what do you do?"

"Easy," Fernandez said. "Wipe the Luger clean. Put it in his hand and—"

"His *right* hand," Delaney cautioned. "He's right-handed. Don't forget it."

"I won't forget it. The Luger gets wiped clean and put in his right hand."

"Try it," Delaney said, "but don't get spooked if it doesn't work. It's tougher than you think to get a clunk's hand to grip a gun—even a fresh clunk. Just make sure you get a couple of good prints on it. They probably won't show on the wood grips, especially if they're checkered, but put them on the metal. Anywhere. The gun can even be on the floor, near his right hand. But a couple of good prints are what we need. What do you do next?"

"Let's see . . ." Fernandez thought deeply. He took a sip of his brandy. "Well, we've still got the keys to the guy's apartment."

"Right," Delaney said promptly. "So your friend has got to go down to the lobby and slip the keys back to Lipsky. Tell him to leave Danny Boy's apartment door open on the way out. Not open, but unlocked. And while he's doing that, what are you doing?"

"Me? Well, I guess I could start tossing—"

"Forget it," the Captain said. "Don't touch a goddamn thing. The first thing you do is call me on Blank's phone. I'll be waiting for your call. I'll collect a squad and be right over. But don't do a thing until I get there. Don't even sit down in a chair. Just stand there. If you get any flak from neighbors, just identify yourself, tell them more cops are on the way, and keep them out in the corridor. All right, I come in with a squad. You tell us what happened, and keep it as short as possible. I make the calls I have to make—the ME, lab, and so forth. *Then* we start a search, and *then* I'll plant the oily rag, the cleaning tools, the extra Luger magazines, and so forth. I don't know how I'll carry them up there, but I'll—"

"But why should *you* do it, Captain?" Fernandez protested. "We could take that stuff up there with us."

Delaney grinned cynically. "In cases like this, it's best that everyone be involved, as equally as possible. It's insurance. That's why I want you to make certain that both you and your friend feed Danny Boy the pills."

The lieutenant puzzled over this. Then his face cleared.

"Smart," he nodded. "So no one talks, ever, and knows none of the others is going to spill."

"Something like that," Delaney agreed, not smiling. "Mutual trust. Now here's the cover story: Operation Lombard determined that the weapon used in the four homicides was an ice ax. That's a tool used by mountain climbers. Danny Boy is a mountain climber. There's hard evidence for all this. We checked into purchasers of ice axes in the Two-five-one Precinct, where all the killings occurred, and you and your friend were given a list of ice ax owners to question. Just to put the icing on the cake, I'll give you two or three names and addresses to check out before you get to Danny Boy. Then you say you identified yourselves as police officers, he let you in, and you asked to examine his ice ax. He said it was in his bedroom and went in there to get it. It's really in the outside hall closet, but he went into the bedroom and came out with the Luger, blasting. But he missed. The two of you went for your sticks and iced him. How does it sound?"

The lieutenant shook his head admiringly. "You're a wonder, Captain," he said. "It sounds great, just great."

"And, with any luck, while I'm planting the Luger equipment, I'll turn up the evidence that will put the finger on Danny Boy but good. It was there a few weeks ago. If it's still there, believe me, no one will ask any questions. But even if he's destroyed it by now, it won't make any difference. He'll be wasted, and it'll all be over."

"Sounds perfect, Captain."

"No," Delaney said, "it's not perfect. There are some loose ends we'll have to take care of. For instance, this friend of yours—I'll have to meet him."

"You already know him."

"He's in Operation Lombard?"

"Yes."

"Good. That makes it easier. This was just a quick outline, lieutenant. The three of us will have to go over it again and again and again until we've got it just right and our timing set. Maybe we could even have a dry-run to work out any bugs, but essentially I think it's a logical and workable plan."

"I think it's a winner, Captain. Can't miss."

"It can miss," Delaney said grimly. "Anything can miss. But I think it's worth a chance."

"Then it's on, Captain? Definitely?"

Delaney took a deep breath, came back to sit behind his desk again. He sat erect in his swivel chair, put his big hands flat on the desk top.

"Well . . . maybe not definitely," he said finally. "I like it because it gives me another option, and I'm practically running out of those. I've got just one other idea that's been percolating in my brain. I tell you what: Go ahead and get the Luger. Fire it, clean it, and bang it up a little. But don't mention a word to your friend. If I decide to go ahead, I'll let you know. Got it?"

"Sure," Fernandez nodded. "I do what you said about the Luger but hold up on anything else until I get the word from you."

"Exactly."

They both rose to their feet. The lieutenant put out his hand; Delaney grasped it.

"Captain," Lieutenant Fernandez said seriously, "I want to wish a Merry Christmas and a very happy New Year to you and yours. I hope Mrs. Delaney is feeling much better real soon."

"Thank you, lieutenant," Delaney said. "The very merriest of Christmases to you and your family, and I hope the New Year brings you everything you want. It's a real pleasure working with you."

"Thank you, Captain," Fernandez said. "Likewise."

Delaney closed the door, came back into the study.

He sat down at his desk, wished he had a fresh Cuban cigar, and considered the plan he had discussed with Lieutenant Fernandez. It wasn't foolproof; such plans never were. There was always the possibility of the unexpected, the unimagined: a scream from somewhere, a sudden visitor, a phone call. Danny Boy might even charge the two police officers, going right into their naked guns. He was capable of such insanity.

But essentially, Delaney decided, it was a logical and workable program. It was a solution. There were a lot of loose ends: how would he carry the Luger tools and cleaning equipment up to the apartment when he answered Fernandez' call, where would he plant them (in the bedroom, obviously), what if the souvenirs were no longer taped to the bottom of the dresser drawer? A hundred questions would be asked, by newsmen and by his superiors. How had Operation Lombard determined that an ice ax was the weapon used in the four homicides? How had they latched onto Daniel Blank? There would be many, many such questions; he would have to anticipate them all and have his answers ready.

He looked at his watch. Almost 4:15; it was a long afternoon. He sighed, pulled himself to his feet, unlocked the study door to the living room, wandered in.

The two big transceivers were on plain pine planks, placed across sawhorses. A uniformed officer was seated in front of each instrument, hunched over a table microphone. A separate table, not as large, held the three new telephones. There was a uniformed officer on duty there, reading a paperback novel. Two men, stripped to their scivvies, were sleeping on cots alongside the wall. One was snoring audibly. Detective second grade Samuel Wilding—he was one of Blankenship's assistants—was seated at a card table making notes on a chart. Delaney raised a hand to him.

He stood a moment near the radios, hands clasped behind his back. He was probably, he thought regretfully, making the operators nervous. But there was no answer for that.

The room was quiet. No, not quiet; except for the low snoring, it was absolutely silent. Late afternoon darkness crept through open drapes, and with it came a—what? A sweetness, Captain Delaney admitted, laughing at himself, but it was a kind of sweetness.

The uniformed men had taken off their blouses. They were working at their desks in sweaters or T-shirts, but still wearing gun belts. Only Detective Wilding wore a jacket, and his was summer-weight, with lapels. So what was it? Delaney wondered. Why the sweetness? It came, he decided, from men on duty, doing their incredibly boring jobs, enduring. The fraternity. Of what? (Delaney: "A friend? In the Department?" Fernandez: ((astonished)): "Of course in the Department. Who's got any friends outside the Department?") A kind of brotherhood.

A phone rang on the deal desk. The officer on duty put aside his paperback, picked up the ringing phone. "Barbara," he said.

They had devised a radio and telephone code as simple and brief as they could make it. Not because Danny Boy might be listening in, but to keep away the short-wave nuts who tuned to police frequencies.

"Danny Boy"—Daniel G. Blank.

"Barbara"—the command post in Delaney's home.

"White House"—Blank's apartment house.

"Factory"—the Javis-Bircham Building.

"Castle"—the East End Avenue townhouse.

"Bulldog One"—the phony Con Ed van on the street outside the White House. It was Lieutenant Fernandez' command post.

"Bulldog Two, Three, Four, etc"—code names for Fernandez' unmarked cars and spooks on foot.

"Tiger One"—the man watching the Montfort townhouse. "Tiger Two" and "Tiger Three" were the street men sweeping the neighborhood.

Other than that, the Operation Lombard investigators used their actual names in transmissions, keeping their calls, in compliance with frequently repeated orders, informal and laconic.

When the phone rang, the officer who answered it said "Barbara." Then he listened awhile, turned to look at Detective Wilding. "Stryker at the Factory," he reported. "Danny Boy has his coat and hat on, looks like he's ready to leave." Stryker was the undercover man planted at Javis-Bircham. He was a tabulating clerk—and a good one—in Blank's department.

Detective Wilding nodded. He turned to a man at the radio. "Alert Bulldog Three." He looked at Delaney. "Okay for Stryker to cut out?"

The Captain nodded. The detective called to the man on the phone, "Tell Stryker he can take off. Report back the day after Christmas."

The officer spoke into the phone, then grinned. "That Stryker," he said to everyone listening. "He doesn't want to take off. He says they've got an office party going, and he ain't going to miss it."

"The greatest cocksman in the Department," someone said.

The listening men broke up. Captain Delaney smiled thinly. He leaned forward to hear one of the radio operators say, "Bulldog Three from Barbara. Got me?"

"Yes. Very nice." It was a bored voice.

"Danny Boy on his way down."

"Okay."

There was a quiet wait of about five minutes. Then: "Barbara from Bulldog Three. We've got him. Heading east on Forty-sixth Street. A yellow cab. License XB sixty-one—dash—forty-nine—dash—three—dash—one. Got it?"

"XB sixty-one—dash—forty-nine—dash—three—dash—one."

"Right on."

It was all low key; it was routine. The logs were kept carefully, and the 24-hour Time-Habit Charts were marked in. But nothing was happening.

Delaney stalked back into his study, put on his glasses, drew his yellow pad toward him. He jotted two lists. The first consisted of five numbered items:

1. Garage attendant.
2. Bartender at Parrot.
3. Lipsky.

4. Mortons.
5. Horvath at J-B.

The second list came slower, over a period of almost an hour. It finally consisted of four numbered items.

Delaney put it aside, rose, lumbered back into the living room. He went directly to Detective Samuel Wilding.

"When's Blankenship coming back on?" he demanded.

"Tomorrow at noon, Captain. We're splitting up because of Christmas."

Delaney nodded. "Tell him, or leave a note for him, that I want to be informed immediately of any change in Danny Boy's Time-Habit pattern. Got that?"

"Yes, sir."

"Informed immediately," the Captain repeated.

He marched through to his dining room and up to the lone man of Detective sergeant MacDonald's squad on duty. The man looked up, startled.

"When's MacDonald due back?" Delaney asked.

"Tomorrow at four in the afternoon, Captain. We're splitting—"

"I know, I know," Delaney said testily. "Christmas. I want to leave a message for him." The duty officer took up a pad and waited, pencil in hand. "Tell him I want a photograph of Detective Kope."

The officer's pencil hesitated.

"Kope? The guy who got chilled?"

"Detective third grade Roger Kope, homicide victim," Delaney said grimly. "I need a photograph of him. Preferably with his family. A photograph of the entire Kope family. Got that?"

He looked down at the officer's pad. It was covered with squiggles.

"You know shorthand?" he asked.

"Yes, sir. I took a course."

"Very good. It's valuable. I wish I knew it. But I guess I'm too old to learn now."

He started to explain to the officer that MacDonald would do best to send a man for the photo who had known Kope, who had been a friend of the family. But he stopped. The sergeant was an old cop; he'd know how to handle it.

He tramped back into his study, closed the doors. He looked at his watch. Almost 7:00 P.M. It was time. He looked at the list on his desk, then dialed the number of Daniel G. Blank. The phone rang and rang. No one answered. He walked back into the living room, over to the radio operator keeping the log.

"Danny Boy in the White House?" he asked.

"Yes, sir. No departure. About half an hour ago Tiger One called in. Princess left the Castle in a cab." ("Princess" was the code name for Celia Montfort.) "About ten minutes later Bulldog One reported her arrival at the White House. They're both still in there, as far as we know."

Delaney nodded, went back into his study, closing the door. He called Blank's number again. No answer. Maybe Danny Boy and the Princess were having a sex scene and weren't answering the phone. Maybe. And maybe they were at a Christmas Eve party. At the Mortons, possibly? Possibly. He went to the file cabinet, took out the thin folder on the Mortons that MacDonald's snoops had assembled. Their home phone number was there.

Delaney came back to his desk, dialed the number.

"Mortons' residence," a female voice answered, after the seventh ring.

In the background Delaney could hear the loud voices of several people, shouts, laughter. A party. He didn't grin.

"I'm trying to reach Mr. Daniel Blank," he said slowly, distinctly, "and I was given this number to call. Is he there?"

"Yes, he is. Just a minute, please."

He heard her call, "Mr. Blank! Phone!" Then that familiar voice was there, curious and cautious. Delaney knew what Danny Boy was wondering: how had anyone traced him to the Mortons' Christmas Eve party?

"Hello?"

"Mr. Daniel G. Blank?"

"Yes. Who is this?"

"Frank Lombard."

There was a sound at the other end of the phone: part moan, part groan, part gasp—something sick and unbelieving.

"Who?"

"Frank Lombard," Delaney said in a low, soft voice. "You know me. We've met before. I just wanted to wish you—"

But the connection went dead. Delaney hung up gently, smiling now. Then he put on overcoat and cap and went out into the dark night to find a drugstore that was still open so he could buy a bottle of perfume and take it to the hospital, a Christmas gift for his wife.

Part VIII

◎

1 Something was happening. What was happening? Something . . .

Daniel Blank thought it had started two weeks before. Or perhaps it was three; it was difficult to remember. But the garage attendant in his apartment house casually mentioned that an insurance examiner had been around, asking about Blank's car.

"He thought you had been in some kind of accident," the man said. "But he took one look at your car and knew you wasn't. I told him so. I told him you ain't had that car out in months."

Blank nodded and asked the man to wash the Stingray, check the battery, oil, gas. He thought no more about the insurance examiner. It had nothing to do with him.

But then, one night, he stopped in at The Parrot. The bartender served him his brandy, then asked if his name was Blank. When Daniel acknowledged it—a tickle of agitation there—the bartender told him a private detective had been in, asking questions about him. He couldn't recall the man's name, but he described him. Troubled now, Blank went back to the garage attendant; his description of the "insurance examiner" tallied with that of the bartender's "private detective."

Not two days later, doorman Charles Lipsky reported that a man had been around asking "very personal questions" about Daniel Blank. The man, Lipsky said, had not stated his name or occupation, but Lipsky could describe him, and did.

From these three descriptions Blank began to form a picture of the man dogging him. Not so much a picture as a silhouette. A dark, hulking figure, rough as a woodcut. Big, with stooped shoulders. Massive. Wearing a stiff Homburg set squarely atop his head, an old-fashioned, double-breasted, shapeless overcoat.

Then, with great glee, Flo and Sam Morton told him of the visit of the credit investigator, and Dan—you devil!—why hadn't you told your best friends about your plans to marry Celia Montfort and purchase her townhouse? He grinned bleakly.

Then that humbling, mumbling meeting with René Horvath, Javis-Bircham's

Director of Personnel. Blank finally got it straight that a credit investigator had been making inquiries; apparently Blank had applied for a "very large loan"—much larger than that offered by the J-B employees' loan program. Horvath had felt it his duty to report the investigator's visit to his superiors, and he had been assigned to ask Daniel Blank the purpose of the loan.

Blank finally got rid of the disgusting little creep, but not before eliciting a physical description of the "credit investigator." Same man.

He knew now his days at Javis-Bircham were numbered, but it wasn't important. The phony credit investigation would just be the last straw. But it wasn't important. He'd be fired, or allowed to resign, and given a generous severance payment. It wasn't important. He knew that during the last few months he simply hadn't been doing his job. He wasn't interested. It wasn't important.

What was important, right now, was the insurance examiner-private detective-credit investigator—a composite man who had become more than a silhouette, a vague image, but was now assuming a rotundity, a solidity, with heavy features and gross gestures, a shambling walk and eyes that never stopped looking. Who was he? God in a stiff Homburg and floppy overcoat?

Blank looked for him wherever he went, on the street, in bars and restaurants, at night, alone in his apartment. On the streets he would search the faces of approaching strangers, then whirl suddenly to see if that big, huddled man was lumbering along behind him. In restaurants, he strolled to the men's room, looking casually at patrons, walking into the kitchen "by accident," glancing into occupied phone booths, inspecting toilet cubicles. Where was he? At home, at night, the door locked, bolted, jammed tight, he would lie awake in the darkness and suddenly hear night noises: thumpings, creakings, a short snap. Then he would rise, put on all the lights, stalk through the apartment, wanting to meet him face to face. But he was not there.

Then, finally, it was Christmas Eve. Javis-Bircham would not fire him until after the holidays; he knew that. So he could accept happily an invitation to the Mortons' Christmas Eve party and ask Celia to join him. He would drink a little, laugh, put his arm around Celia's slender, hard waist, and surely the dark, thrusting shadow could not be there.

The call shattered him. For how could anyone know he was at the Mortons'? He approached the phone cautiously, picked it up as if expecting it to explode in his hand. Then that soft, insinuating voice said: "Frank Lombard. You know me. We've met before. I just wanted—"

Then he was out of there, leaving Celia behind him, saying goodnight to no one. The elevator took a decade; it was a generation before he got his door unlocked and locked again; it was a century before he had the drawer out, turned upside down on his bed. He inspected the taped envelope carefully but, as far as he could see, it had not been touched. He opened it; everything was there. He sat on his bed, fingering his mementoes, and became aware that he had wet his pants. Not a lot. But a few drops. It was degrading.

He stuffed the black velvet suit, white cashmere turtleneck sweater, and flowered panties into the bathroom laundry hamper. He peeled off the Via Veneto wig before getting under a shower as hot as he could stand it. When he soaped his bare skull, he felt the light fuzz and knew he'd soon need another shave.

He dried, smoothed on cologne, powdered, stuck the wig firmly back into place. Then he put on one of his silk robes, the crane design, and padded barefoot into the living room to pour himself a warm vodka and light one of his dried-lettuce cigarettes.

Then he realized the apartment doorbell was chiming had been for several rings. He stubbed his cigarette out carefully and drained his vodka before going into the hallway to peer at Celia Montfort through the peephole. He unlocked the door to let her in, bolted it again behind her.

"You're not ill, are you, Dan?"

"You don't talk in your sleep, do you?" he asked. Even in his own ears his laugh sounded wild and forced.

She stared at him, expressionless.

She sat on the living room couch, waited patiently while he opened a bottle of bordeaux, poured her a stemmed glass and for himself the glass still wet from the vodka he had finished. She sipped the wine cautiously.

"Good," she nodded. "Dry as dust."

"What? Oh yes. I should have bought more. The price has almost doubled. Did you tell anyone about me?"

"What are you talking about, Dan?"

"What I've done. Did you tell anyone?"

Her answer was prompt, but it was no answer at all: "Why should I do a thing like that?"

She was wearing a tube of black jersey, high at the neck, long-sleeved, hanging to her dull black satin evening pumps. About her neck was what appeared to be a six-foot rope of cultured pearls, wound tightly, around and around, so it formed a gleaming collar that kept her head erect, chin raised.

He had the sense—as he had at their first meeting—of never being able to recognize her, of forgetting what she looked like when she was out of his sight. The long, black, almost purple hair; drawn, witch-like face; slender, tapering hands; but the eyes—were they grey or blue? Were the lips full or flat? Was the nose Egyptian—or merely pinched? And the pallid complexion, bruised weariness, aura of corruption, of white flesh punished to a puddle—where did those fantasies come from? She was as much a mystery to him now as at their first meeting. Was it a thousand years ago?

She sat on the couch, composed, withdrawn, sipping her wine as he passed back and forth. He never took his eyes from her as he told her about the man who had been dogging him—the insurance examiner-private detective-credit investigator man—and the people this man had seen, the questions he had asked, what he had said.

As he talked, words spilling out so fast that he spluttered a few times and white spittle gathered in the corners of his mouth—well, as he chattered, he saw her cross her legs slowly, high up, at her thighs, hidden by her long dress. But from the bent knee, one ankle showed, a satin evening pump hung down. As he told her what had happened, that loose foot, that black shoe, began to bob up and down, lower leg swinging from the hidden knee, slow at first, nodding in a graceful rhythm, then moving faster in stronger jerks. Her face was still expressionless.

Watching Celia's bobbing foot, the leg from the knee down swinging faster under her long dress, he thought she must be masturbating, sitting there on his couch, naked thighs pressed tightly together beneath her gown. The rhythm of that jerking foot became faster and faster until when he told her about the telephone call he had just received at the Mortons, she began to pant, her eyes glazed, pearls of sweat to match her necklace formed on brow and upper lip. Then, eyes closed now, her entire body stiffened for a moment. He stopped talking to watch her. When she finally relaxed, shuddering, looked about with vacant eyes, uncrossed her legs, he thought she must have been sexually excited by his danger, but for what reason he did not know, could not guess.

"Could the man be Valenter?" he asked her.

"Valenter?" She took a deep sip of wine. "How could he know? Besides, Valenter is skinny, a scarecrow. You said this man following you about is heavy, lumbering. It couldn't be Valenter."

"No. I suppose not."

"How could this man—the one on the phone—know about Frank Lombard?"

"I don't know. Perhaps there was an eyewitness—to Lombard or one of the others—and he followed me home and got my address and then my name."

"For what reasons?"

"It's obvious, isn't it? He didn't go to the police, so it must be blackmail."

"Mmm, possibly. Are you frightened?"

"Well . . . disturbed." Then he told her about what he had been doing since he left the Mortons' apartment so abruptly: trying to make his mind into a blank blackboard, erasing thoughts as quickly as they appeared in chalk script.

"Oh no," she shook her head, and in her voice was an imploring tone he had never heard her use before, "you shouldn't do that. Open your mind wide. Let it expand. Let it shatter into a million thoughts, sensations, memories, fears. That's how you'll find perception. Don't erase your consciousness. Let it flower as it will. Anything is possible. Remember that: anything is possible. Something will come to you, something that will explain the man following you and the phone call. Open your mind; don't close it down. Logic won't help. You must become increasingly aware, increasingly sensitive. I have a drug at home. Do you want to use it?"

"No."

"All right. But don't shut yourself in, inside yourself. Be open to everything."

She stood, picked up the remainder of the wine.

"Let's go to your bedroom," she said. "I'll stay the night."

"I won't be any good."

Her free hand slid inside the opening of his robe. He felt her slim, cool fingers drift across his nakedness to find him, to hold him.

"We'll play with each other," she murmured.

And so they did.

2

On the day following Christmas, Captain Delaney worked all morning in his study, in his shirtsleeves—it was unseasonably warm, the house overheated—trying to prepare estimates of his manpower and vehicle requirements for the coming week. The holiday season complicated things; men wanted to spend time at home with their families. That was understandable, but it meant schedules had to be reshuffled, and it was impossible to satisfy everyone.

Delaney's three commanders—Fernandez, MacDonald, and Blankenship—had prepared tentative schedules for their squads, but had appended suggestions, questions, requests. From this tangled mess of men available for duty, men on vacation or about to go, sick leave, hardship cases, special pleadings (one of Fernandez' spooks had an appointment with a podiatrist to have his bunions trimmed), Delaney tried to construct a master schedule for Operation Lombard that would, at least, have every important post covered 24 hours a day but still leave enough "wiggle room" so last-minute substitutions could be made, and there would always be a few men playing poker for matchsticks in the radio room, available for emergency duty if needed.

By noon he had a rough timetable worked out; he was shocked at the number of men it required. The City of New York was spending a great deal of money to monitor the activities of Daniel G. Blank. That didn't bother Delaney; the City spent more money for more frivolous projects. But the Captain was concerned about how long Thorsen, Johnson, et al., would give him a free hand and a limitless budget before screaming for results. Not too long, he thought grimly; perhaps another week.

He pulled on jacket, civilian overcoat and hat, and checked out with the uniformed patrolman keeping an entrance-exit log at a card table set up just inside the outer door. Delaney gave him destination and phone number where he could be reached. Then he had one of the unmarked cars parked outside drive him over to the hospital. Another breach of regulations, but at least it gave the two dicks in the car a few minutes' relief from the boredom of their job: sitting and waiting.

Barbara seemed in a subdued mood, and answered his conversational offerings with a few words, a wan smile. He helped her with her noon meal and, that finished, just sat with her for another hour. He asked if she'd like him to read to her, but when she shook her head, he just sat stolidly, in silence, hoping his presence might be of some comfort, not daring to think of how long her illness would endure, or how it might end.

He returned home by cab, dutifully showed his Operation Lombard pass for entrance, even though the uniformed outside guard recognized him immediately and saluted. He was hungry for a sandwich and a cold beer, but the kitchen was crowded with at least a dozen noisy men taking a lunch-hour break for coffee, beer, or some of the cheese and cold cuts for which they all contributed, a dollar a day per man.

The old uniformed patrolman on kitchen duty saw the Captain walk through to his study. A few minutes later he knocked on the door to bring Delaney a beer and ham-and-Swiss on rye. The Captain smiled his thanks; it was just what he wanted.

About an hour later a patrolman knocked and came in to relay a request from Detective first grade Blankenship: could the Captain come into the living room for a minute? Delaney hauled himself to his feet, followed the officer out. Blankenship was standing behind the radio operators, bending over the day's Time-Habit log of Daniel Blank's activities. He swung around when Delaney came up.

"Captain, you asked to be informed of any erratic change in Danny Boy's Time-Habit Pattern. Take a look at this." Delaney leaned forward to follow Blankenship's finger pointing out entries in the log. "This morning Danny Boy comes outside the White House at ten minutes after nine. Spotted by Bulldog One. Nine-ten is normal; he's been leaving for work every day around nine-fifteen, give or take a few minutes. But this morning he doesn't leave. According to Bulldog One, he turns around and goes right back into the White House. He comes out again almost an hour later. That means he just didn't forget something—right? Okay . . . he gets a cab. Here it is: at almost ten a.m. Bulldog Two tails him. But he doesn't go right to the Factory. His cab goes around and around Central Park for almost forty-five minutes. What a meter tab he must have had! Then, finally, he gets to his office. It's close to eleven o'clock when Stryker calls to clock him in, almost two hours late. Captain, I realize this all might be a lot of crap. After all, it's the day after Christmas, and Danny Boy might just be unwinding. But I thought you better know."

"Glad you did," Delaney nodded-thoughtfully. "Glad you did. It's interesting."

"All right, now come over here and listen to this. It's a tape from Stryker, recorded about a half-hour ago. I wasn't here then so I couldn't talk to him. He asked the operator to put it on tape for me. Spin it, will you, Al?"

One of the operators at the telephone table started his deck recorder. The other men in the room quieted to listen to the tape.

"Ronnie, this is Stryker, at the Factory. How you doing? Ronnie, I just came back from lunch with the cunt I been pushing down here. A little bony, but a wild piece. At lunch I got the talk around to Danny Boy. He was almost two hours late getting to work. This cunt of mine—she's the outside receptionist in Danny Boy's department—she told me that just before I met her for lunch, she was in the ladies' john talking to Mrs. Cleek. That's C-l-e-e-k. She's Danny Boy's personal secretary. A widow. First name Martha or Margaret. White, female, middle thirties, five-three, one-ten or thereabouts, dark brown hair, fair complexion, no visible scars, wears glasses all the time. Well, anyway, in the can, this Mrs. Cleek tells my cunt that Danny Boy was acting real queer this morning. Wouldn't dictate or sign any letters. Wouldn't read anything. Wouldn't even answer any important phone calls. Probably a sack of shit, Ronnie—but I figured I better report it. If you think it's important, I can cozy up to this Cleek dame and see what else I can find out. No problem; she's hungry I can tell. Nice ass. Let me know if you want me to follow up on this. Stryker at the Factory, off."

There was silence in the radio room after the tape was stopped. Then someone laughed. "That Stryker," someone said softly, "all he thinks about is pussy."

"Maybe," Captain Delaney said coldly, speaking to no one man, speaking to them all, "but he's doing a good job." He turned to Blankenship. "Call Stryker. Tell him to cozy up to the Cleek woman and keep us informed—of anything."

"Will do, Captain."

Delaney walked slowly back into his study, heavy head bowed, hands shoved into his hip pockets. The altered Time-Habit Pattern and Danny Boy's strange behavior in his office: the best news he'd had all day. It might be working. It just might be working.

He searched for the sheet of yellow paper on which he had jotted his nine-point plan. It wasn't in his locked top desk drawer. It wasn't in the file. Where was it? His memory was really getting bad. He finally found the plan under his desk blotter, alongside the plus-minus list he used to evaluate the performance of men under his command. Before looking at the plan, he added the name of Stryker to the plus column of the performance list.

Peering at the plan closely through his reading glasses, he checked off the first six items: Garage attendant, Parrot bartender, Lipsky, the Mortons at Erotica, Visit to Factory, Lombard Christmas Eve call to Blank. The seventh item was "Monica's call to Blank." He sat back in his swivel chair, stared at the ceiling, tried to think out the best way to handle *that.*

He was still pondering his options—what *he* would say and what *she* would say—when the outside guard knocked on his study door and didn't enter until he heard Delaney's shouted, "Come in!" The officer said a reporter named Thomas Handry was on the sidewalk and claimed he had an appointment with the Captain.

"Sure," Delaney nodded. "Let him in. Tell the man at the desk to make certain he's logged in and out."

He went into the kitchen for some ice cubes. When he came back Handry was standing in front of the desk.

"Thanks for coming," Delaney smiled genially. "I had it marked down: 'Day after Christmas, Handry interviews Blank.' "

Handry sat in the leather club chair, then rose immediately, took two folded sheets from his inside breast pocket, tossed them onto Delaney's desk.

"Background stuff on this guy," he said, slumping back into his soft chair. "His job, views on the importance of the computer in industry, biography, personal life. But I imagine you've got all this by now."

The Captain took a quick look at the two typed pages. "Got most of it," he acknowledged. "But you've got a few things here we'll follow up on—a few leads."

"So my interview was just wasted time?"

"Oh Handry," Delaney sighed. "At the time I asked you to do this, I was on my own. I had no idea I'd be back on active duty with enough dicks to run all this down. Besides, all this background shit isn't so important. I told you that at the restaurant. I wanted your personal impressions of the man. You're sensitive, intelligent. Since I couldn't interview him myself, I wanted you to meet him and tell me what your reactions were. That *is* important. Now give me the whole thing, how it went, what you said and what he said."

Thomas Handry took a deep breath, blew it out. Then he began talking. Delaney never interrupted once, but leaned forward, cupping one ear, the better to hear Handry's low-voiced recital.

The newspaperman's report was fluid and concise. He had arrived precisely at 1:30 p.m., the time previously arranged for the interview by Javis-Bircham's Director of Public Relations. But Blank had kept him waiting almost a half-hour. It was only after two requests to Blank's secretary that Handry had been allowed into the inner office.

Daniel G. Blank had been polite, but cold and withdrawn. Also, somewhat suspicious. He had asked to inspect Handry's press card—an odd act for a business executive giving an interview arranged by his own PR man. But Blank had spoken lucidly and at length about the role played by AMROK II in the activities of Javis-Bircham. About his personal background, he had been cautious, uncommunicative, and frequently asked Handry what his questions had to do with the interview in progress. As far as the reporter could determine, Blank was divorced, had no children, had no plans to marry again. He lived a bachelor's life, found it enjoyable, had no ambitions other than to serve J-B as best he might.

"Very pretty," Delaney nodded. "You said he was 'withdrawn.' Your word. What did you mean by that?"

"Were you in the military, Captain?"

"Yes. Five years U.S. Army."

"I did four with the Marines. You know the expression 'a thousand-yard stare'?"

"Oh yes. On the range. For an unfocused vision."

"Right. That's what Blank has. Or had a few hours ago during the interview. He was looking at me, in me, through me, and somewhere beyond. I don't know what the hell he was focussing on. Most of these high-pressure business executives are all teeth, hearty handshake, sincere smile, focussing between your eyes, over the bridge of your nose, so it looks like they're returning your stare frankly, without blinking. But this guy was gone somewhere, off somewhere. I don't know where the hell he was."

"Good, good," Delaney muttered, taking quick notes. "Anything else? Physical peculiarities? Habits? Bite his nails?"

"No . . . But he wears a wig. Did you know that?"

"No," the Captain said in apparent astonishment. "A wig? He's only in his middle-thirties. Are you sure?"

"Positive," Handry said, enjoying the surprise. "It wasn't even on straight. And he didn't give a goddamn if I knew. He kept poking a finger up under the edge of the rug and scratching his scalp. Anything?"

"Mmm. Maybe. How was he dressed?"

" 'Conservative elegance' is the phrase. Black suit well-cut. White shirt, starched collar. Striped tie. Black shoes with a dull gloss, not shiny."

"You'd make a hell of a detective."

"You told me that before."

"Smell any booze on his breath?"

"No. But a high-powered cologne or after-shave lotion."

"That figures. Scratch his balls?"

"What?"

"Did he play with himself?"

"Jesus, no! Captain, you're wild."

"Yes. Did he look drawn, thin, emaciated? Like he hasn't been eating well lately?"

"Not that I could see. Well . . ."

"What?" Delaney demanded quickly.

"Shadows under his eyes. Puffy bags. Like he hasn't been sleeping so well lately. But all the rest of his face was tight. He's really a good-looking guy. And his handshake was firm and dry. He looked to be in good physical shape. Just before I left, when we were both standing, he handed me a promotion booklet Javis-Bircham got out on AMROK II. It slipped out of my hand. It was my fault; I dropped it. But Blank stooped and caught it before it hit the floor. The guy's quick."

"Oh yes," Delaney nodded grimly, "he's quick. All right, this is all interesting and valuable. Now tell me what you think about him, what you *feel* about him."

"A drink?"

"Of course. Help yourself."

"Well . . ." Thomas Handry said, pouring Scotch over ice cubes, "he's a puzzle. He's not one thing and he's not another. He's a between-man, going from A to B. Or maybe from A to Z. I guess that doesn't make much sense."

"Go on."

"He's just not *with* it. He's not *there.* The impression I got was of a guy floating. He's out there somewhere. Who the hell knows where? That thousand-yard stare. And it was obvious he couldn't care less about Javis-Bircham and AMROK II. He was just going through the motions; a published interview couldn't interest him less. I don't know what's on his mind. He's lost and floating, like I said. Captain, the guy's a balloon! He's got no anchor. He puzzles me and he interests me. I can't solve him." A long pause. "Can you?"

"Getting there," Captain Delaney said slowly. "Just beginning to get there."

There was a lengthy silence, while Handry sipped his drink and Delaney stared at a damp spot on the opposing wall.

"It's him, isn't it?" Handry said finally. "No doubt about it."

Delaney sighed. "That's right. It's him. No doubt about it."

"Okay," the reporter said, surprisingly chipper. He drained his glass, rose, walked toward the hallway door. Then, knob in hand, he turned to stare at the Captain. "I want to be in on the kill," he stated flatly.

"All right."

Handry nodded, turned away, then turned back again. "Oh," he said nonchalantly, "one more thing . . . I got a sample of his handwriting."

He marched back to Delaney's desk, tossed a photo onto the blotter. Delaney picked it up slowly, stared. Daniel G. Blank: a copy of the photo taken from the "Fink File," the same photo that was now copied in the hundreds and in the hands of every man assigned to Operation Lombard. Delaney turned it over. On the back, written with a felt-tipped pen, was: "With all best wishes. Daniel G. Blank."

"How did you get this?"

"The ego-trip. I told him I kept a scrapbook of photos and autographs of famous people I interviewed. He went for it."

"Beautiful. Thank you for your help."

After Handry left, Delaney kept staring at that inscription: "With all best wishes. Daniel G. Blank." He rubbed his fingers lightly over the signature. It seemed to bring him closer to the man.

He was still staring at the handwriting, trying to see beyond it, when Detective sergeant Thomas MacDonald came in sideways, slipping his bulk neatly through the hallway door, left partly open by Handry.

The black moved a step into the study, then stopped.

"Interrupting you, Captain?"

"No, no. Come on in. What's up?"

The short, squat detective came over to Delaney's desk.

"You wanted a photo of Roger Kope, the cop who got wasted. Will this do?"

He handed Delaney a crisp white cardboard folder, opening sideways. On the front it said, in gold script, "Holiday Greetings." Inside, on the left, in the same gold script, it read: "From the Kope family." On the right side was pasted a color photo of Roger Kope, his wife, three little children. They were posed, grinning self-consciously, before a decorated Christmas tree. The dead detective had his arm about his wife's shoulders. It wasn't a good photo: obviously an amateur job taken a year ago and poorly copied. The colors were washed out, the face of one of the children was blurred. But they were all there.

"It was all we could get," MacDonald said tonelessly. "They had about a hundred made up a month ago, but I guess Mrs. Kope won't send them this year. Will it do?"

"Yes," Delaney nodded. "Just fine." Then, as MacDonald turned to go, he said, "Sergeant, a couple of other things . . . Who's the best handwriting man in the Department?"

MacDonald thought a moment, his sculpted features calm, carved: a Congo mask or a Picasso sketch. "Handwriting," he repeated. "That would be Willow, William T., detective lieutenant. He works out of a broom-closet office downtown."

"Ever have any dealings with him?"

"About two years ago. It was a forged lottery ticket ring. He's a nice guy. Prickly, but okay. He sure knows his stuff."

"Could you get him up here? No rush. Whenever he can make it."

"I'll give him a call."

"Good. The next day or so will be fine."

"All right, Captain. What's the other thing?"

"What?"

"You said you had a couple of things."

"Oh. Yes. Who's controlling the men on the tap on Danny Boy's home phone?"

"I am, Captain. Fernandez set it up: technically they're his boys. But he asked me to take over. He's got enough on his plate. Besides, these guys are just sitting on their ass. They've come up with zilch. Danny Boy makes one or two calls a week, usually to the Princess in the Castle. Maybe to the Mortons. And he gets fewer calls. So far it's nothing."

"Uh-huh," Delaney nodded. "Listen, sergeant, would it be possible to make some clicks or buzzes the next time Danny Boy makes or gets a call?"

MacDonald picked up on it instantly. "So he thinks or knows his phone is tapped?"

"Right."

"Sure. No sweat; we could do that. Clicks, buzzes, hisses, an echo—something. He'll get the idea."

"Fine."

MacDonald stared at him a long time, putting things together. Finally: "Spooking him, Captain?" he asked softly.

Captain Delaney put out his hands, palms down on his desk blotter, lowered his massive head to stare at them.

"Not spooking," he said in a gentle voice. "I mean to split him. To crack him open. Wide. Until he's in pieces and bleeding. And it's working. I know it is. Sergeant, how do *you* know when you're close?"

"My mouth goes dry."

Delaney nodded. "My armpits begin to sweat something awful. Right now they're dripping like old faucets. I'm going to push this guy right over the edge, right off, and watch him fall."

MacDonald's smooth expression didn't change. "You figure he'll suicide, Captain?"

"Will he suicide . . ." Delaney said thoughtfully. Suddenly, that moment, something began that he had been hoping for. *He* was Daniel G. Blank, penetrating deep into the man, smoothing his body with perfumed oils, dribbling on scented powders, wearing silk bikini underwear and a fashionable wig, living in sterile loneliness, fucking a boy-shaped woman, buggering a real boy, and venturing out at night to find loves who would help him to break out, to feel, to discover what he was, and meaning.

"Suicide?" Delaney repeated, so quietly that MacDonald could hardly hear him. "No. Not by gunshot, pills, or defenestration." He smiled slightly when he pronounced the last word, knowing the sergeant would pick up the mild humor. Defenestration: throwing yourself out a window to smash to jelly on the concrete below. "No, he won't suicide, no matter how hard the pressure. Not his style. He likes risk. He climbs mountains. He's at his best when he's in danger. It's like champagne."

"Then what will he do, Captain?"

"I'm going to run," Delaney said in a strange, pleading voice. "I've *got* to run."

3

The second day after Christmas, Daniel Blank decided the worst thing—the *worst* thing—was committing these irrational acts, and *knowing* they were irrational, and not being able to stop.

For instance, this morning, completely unable to get to work at his usual hour, he sat stiffly in his living room, dressed for a normal day at Javis-Bircham. And between 9:00 and 11:00 a.m., he rose from his chair at least three times to check the locks and bolts on the front door. They were fastened—he *knew* they were fastened—but he had to check. Three times.

Then suddenly he darted through the apartment, flinging open closet doors, thrusting an arm between hanging clothes. No one there. He knew it was wrong to be acting the way he was.

He mixed a drink, a morning drink, thinking it might help. He picked up a knife to slice a wedge of lime, looked at the blade, let it clatter into the sink. No temptation there, none, but he didn't want the thing in his hand. He might reach up to wipe his eyes and . . .

What about the sandals? That was odd. He owned a pair of leather strap-sandals, custom-made. He still remembered the shop in Greenwich Village, the cool hands of the young Chinese girl tracing his bare feet on a sheet of white paper. He frequently wore the sandals at night, when he was home alone. The straps were loose enough so that he could slip the sandals onto his feet without unbuckling and buckling. He had been doing it for years. But this morning the straps had been unbuckled, the sandals there beside his bed with straps flapping wide. Who had done that?

And time—what was happening to his sense of time? He thought ten minutes had elapsed, but it turned out to be an hour. He guessed an hour, and it was 20 minutes. What was happening?

And what was happening to his penis? It was his imagination, of course, but it seemed to be shrinking, withdrawing into his scrotum. Ridiculous. And he no longer had his regular bowel movement a half-hour after he awoke. He felt stuffed and blocked.

Other things . . . Little things . . .

Going from one room to another and, when he got there, forgetting why he had made the trip.

Hearing a phone ring on a television program and leaping up to answer his own phone.

Finally, when he got to the office, things didn't go well at all. Not that he couldn't have handled it; he was thinking logically, he was lucid. But what was the point?

Near noon, Mrs. Cleek came in and found him weeping at his desk, head bent forward, palms gripping his temples. Her eyes blurred immediately with sympathy.

"Mr. Blank," she said, "what *is* it?"

"I'm sorry," he gasped, and then, saying the first thing that came into his mind: "A death in the family."

What caused his tears was this: do mad people know they are mad? That is, do they know they are acting abnormally but cannot help it? That was why he wept.

"Oh," Mrs. Cleek mourned, "I'm so sorry."

He got home, finally. He was as proud as a drunk who walks out of a bar without upsetting anything, steadfast, steps slowly through the doorway without brushing the frame, follows a sidewalk seam slowly and carefully homeward, never wavering.

It was early in the evening. Was it 6:00 p.m.? It might be eight. He didn't want to look at his watch bracelet. He wasn't sure he could trust it. Perhaps it might not be his own faulty time sense; it might be his wristwatch running wild. Or time itself running wild.

He picked up his phone. There was a curious, empty echo before he got a dial tone. He heard it ring. Someone picked up the phone. Then Blank heard two sharp clicks.

"Mith Montforth rethidenth," he heard Valenter say.

"This is Daniel Blank. Is Miss Montfort in?"

"Yeth, thir. I'll call—"

But then Daniel Blank heard a few more soft clicks, a strange hissing on the line. He hung up abruptly. Jesus! He should have known. He left the apartment immediately. What time *was* it? It didn't matter.

"He's tapping my phone," he said to Celia indignantly. "I definitely heard it. Definitely."

They were in that tainted room at the top of the house; city sounds came faintly. He told her he had followed her advice, had opened his mind to instinct, to all the primitive fears and passions that had come flooding in. He told her how he had been acting, the irrational fits and starts of his daily activities, and he told her about the clicks, hisses, and echo on the phone when he had called her.

"Do you think I'm going mad?" he demanded.

"No," she said slowly, almost judiciously, "I don't think so. I think that in the time I have known you, you have been moving from the man you were to the man you are to be. What that is, I don't believe either of us know for sure. But it's understandable that this growth be painful, perhaps even frightening. You're leaving everything familiar behind you and setting out on a journey, a search, a climb, that's leading . . . somewhere. Forget for a moment the man who has been following you and the phone call you received. These pains and dislocations have nothing to do with that. Dan, you're being born again, and you're feeling all the anguish of birth, being yanked from the safety of a warm womb into a foreign world. The wonder is that you've endured it as well as you have."

As usual, her flood of murmured words soothed and assured him; he felt as relaxed as if she was stroking his brow. She *did* make sense; it *was* true that he had changed since he met her, and was changing. The murders were part of it, of course—she was wrong to deny that—but they were not the cause but just one effect of the monumental upheaval inside him, something hot and bubbling there thrusting to the surface.

They made love slowly then, with more tenderness than passion, more sweetness than joy. In the eerie light of that single orange bulb he leaned close to see her for the first time, microscopically.

Her nipples, under his tongue's urging, engorged and, peering close, he saw the flattened tops with ravines and gorges, tiny, tiny, a topographic map. And threaded through the small breasts a network of bluish veins, tangled as a silken skein.

Along the line of curved hip sprouted a Lilliputian wheatfield of surprisingly golden hairs, and more at the dimpled small of her back. These tender sprouts tickled dry and dusty on his tongue. The convoluted navel returned his stare in a lascivious wink. Inside, prying, he found a sharp bitterness that tingled.

Far up beneath her long hair, at nape of neck, was swamp dampness and scent of pond lilies. He stared at flesh of leg and groin, so close his eyelashes brushed and she made a small sound. There was hard, shiny skin on her soles, a crumbling softness between her toes. It all became clear to him, and dear, and sad.

They fenced with tongues—thrust, parry, cut—and then he was tasting creamy wax from her ear and in her armpits a sweet liquor that bit and melted on his lips like snow. Behind her knees more blue veins meandered, close to a skin that felt like suede and twitched faintly when he touched.

He spread her buttocks; the rosebud glared at him, withdrawing and expanding—a time-motion film of a flower reacting to light and darkness. He put his erect penis in her soft palm, slowly guided her fingers to stroke, circle, gently probe the opening, their hands clasped so they might share. He touched his lips to her closed eyes, thought he might suck them out and gulp them down like oysters, seasoned with her tears.

"I want you inside me," she said suddenly, lay on her back, spread her knees wide, guided his cock up into her. She wrapped arms and legs about him and moaned softly, as if they were making love for the first time.

But there was no love. Only a sweetness so sad it was almost unendurable. Even as they fucked he knew it was the sadness of departure; they would never fuck again; both knew it.

She was quickly slick, inside and out; they grappled to hold tight. He spurted with a series of great, painful lunges and, stunned, he continued to make the motions long after he was drained and surfeited. He could not stop his spasm, had no desire to, and felt her come again.

She looked at him through half-opened eyes, glazed; he thought she felt what he did: the defeat of departure. In that moment he knew she had told. She had betrayed him.

But he smiled, smiled, smiled, kissed her closed mouth, went home early. He took a cab because the darkness frightened him.

If it was a day of departure and defeat for Daniel Blank, it was a day of arrival and triumph for Captain Edward X. Delaney. He dared not feel confident, lest he put the whammy on it, but it did seem to be coming together.

Paper work in the morning: requisitions, reports, vouchers—the whole schmear. Then over to the hospital to sit awhile with Barbara, reading to her from "Honey Bunch: Her First Little Garden." Then he treated himself to a decent meal in one of those west side French restaurants: *coq au vin* with a half-bottle of a heavy burgundy to help it along. He paid his bill and then, on the way out, stopped at the bar for a Kirsch. He felt good.

It was good; everything was good. He had no sooner returned to his home when Blankenship came in to display Danny Boy's Time-Habit Pattern. It was very erratic indeed: Arrived at the Factory at 11:30 a.m. Skipped lunch completely. Took a long zigzag walk along the docks. Sat on a wharf for almost an hour—"Just watching the turds float by" according to the man tailing him.

Report from Stryker: He had taken Mrs. Cleek to lunch, and she told him she had found Danny Boy weeping in his office, and he had told her there had been a death in the family. Danny Boy returned to the White House at 2:03 p.m.

"Fine," the Captain nodded, handing the log back to Blankenship. "Keep at it. Is Fernandez on?"

"Comes on at four, Captain."

"Ask him to stop by to see me, will you?"

After Blankenship left, Delaney closed all the doors to his study, paced slowly around the room, head bowed. "A death in the family." That was nice. He paused to call Monica Gilbert and ask if he could come over to see her that evening. She invited him for dinner but he begged off; they arranged that he would come over at 7:00 p.m. He told her it would only be for a few minutes; she didn't ask the reason. Her girls were home from school during the holiday week so, she explained, she hadn't been able to visit Barbara as much as she wanted to, but would try to get there the following afternoon. He thanked her.

More pacing, figuring out options and possibilities. He walked into the radio room to tell Blankenship to requisition four more cars, two squads and two unmarked, and keep them parked on the street outside, two men in each. He didn't want to think of the increase in manpower that entailed, and went back into his study to resume his pacing. Was there anything he should have done that he had not? He couldn't think of anything, but he was certain there would be problems he hadn't considered. No help for that.

He took out his plan and, alongside the final three items, worked out a rough time schedule. He was still fiddling with it when Lt. Jeri Fernandez knocked and looked in.

"Want me, Captain?"

"Just for a minute, lieutenant. Won't take long. How's it going?"

"Okay. I got a feeling things are beginning to move. Don' ask me how I know. Just a feeling."

"I hope you're right. I've got another job for you. You'll have to draw more men. Get them from wherever you can. If you have any shit with their commanders, tell them to call me. It's a woman—Monica Gilbert. Here's her address and telephone number. She's the widow of Bernard Gilbert, the second victim. There was a guard on her right after he was iced, so there may be a photo of her in the files and some Time-Habit reports. I want a twenty-four hour tap on her phone, two men in an unmarked car outside her house, and two uniformed men outside her apartment door. She's got two little girls. If she goes out with the girls, both the buttons stick with them, and I mean close. If she goes out alone, one man on her and one on the kids. Got all that?"

"Sure, Captain. A tight tail?"

"But I mean *tight*. Close enough to touch."

"You think Danny Boy'll try something?"

"No, I don't. But I want her and her children covered, around the clock. Can you set it up?"

"No sweat, Captain. I'll get on it right away."

"Good. Put your first men on at eight tonight. Not before."

Fernandez nodded. "Captain . . ."

"Yes?"

"The Luger's almost ready."

"Fine. Any problems?"

"Nope, not a one."

"You spending any money on this?"

"Money?" Fernandez looked at him incredulously. "What money? Some guys owed me some favors."

Delaney nodded. Fernandez opened the hallway door to depart, and there was a man standing there, his arm bent, knuckles raised, about to knock on the Captain's door.

"Captain Delaney?" the man asked Fernandez.

The lieutenant shook his head, jerked a thumb over his shoulder at the Captain, stepped around the newcomer and disappeared.

"I'm Captain Edward X. Delaney."

"My name is William T. Willow, Detective lieutenant. I believe you wanted to consult me."

"Oh yes," Delaney said, rising from his chair. "Please come in, lieutenant, and close the door behind you. Thank you for coming up. Please sit down over there. Sergeant MacDonald tells me you're the best man in your field."

"I agree," Willow said, with a sweet smile.

Delaney laughed. "How about a drink?" he asked. "Anything?"

"You don't happen to have a glass of sherry, do you, Captain?"

"Yes, I do. Medium dry. Will that be all right?"

"Excellent, thank you."

The Captain walked over to his liquor cabinet, and while he poured the drink, he inspected the handwriting expert. A queer bird. The skin and frame of a plucked chicken, and clad in a hairy tweed suit so heavy Delaney wondered how the man's frail shoulders could support it. On his lap was a plaid cap, and his shoes were over-the-ankle boots in a dark brown suede. Argyle socks, wool Tattersall shirt, woven linen tie secured with a horse's head clasp. Quite a sight.

But Willow's eyes were washed blue, lively and alert, and his movements, when he took the glass of sherry from Delaney, were crisp and steady.

"Your health, sir," the lieutenant said, raising his glass. He sipped. "Harvey's," he said.

"Yes."

"And very good, too. I would have been up sooner, Captain, but I've been in court."

"That's all right. No rush about this."

"What is it?"

Delaney searched in his top desk drawer, then handed Willow the photo Thomas Handry had delivered, with the inscription on the back: "With all best wishes. Daniel G. Blank."

"What can you tell me about the man who wrote this?"

Detective lieutenant William T. Willow didn't even glance at it. Instead, he looked at the Captain with astonishment.

"Oh dear," he said, "I'm afraid there's been a frightful misunderstanding. Captain, I'm a QD man, not a graphologist."

Pause.

"What's a QD man?" Delaney asked.

"Questioned Documents. All my work is with forgeries or suspected forgeries, comparing one specimen with another."

"I see. And what is a graphologist?"

"A man who allegedly is able to determine character, personality, and even physical and mental illness from a man's handwriting."

" 'Allegedly'," Delaney repeated. "I gather you don't agree with graphologists?"

"Let's just say I'm an agnostic on the matter," Willow smiled his sweet smile. "I don't agree and I don't disagree."

The Captain saw the sherry glass was empty. He rose to refill it, and left the bottle on the little table alongside Willow's elbow. Then the Captain sat down behind his desk again, regarded the other man gravely.

"But you're familiar with the theories and practice of graphology?"

"Oh my, yes, Captain. I read everything on the subject of handwriting analysis, from whatever source, good and bad."

Delaney nodded, laced his fingers across his stomach, leaned back in his swivel chair.

"Lieutenant Willow," he said dreamily, "I am going to ask a very special favor of you. I am going to ask you to pretend you are a graphologist and not a QD man. I am going to ask you to inspect this specimen of handwriting and analyze it as a graphologist would. What I want is your opinion. I do not want a signed statement from you. You will not be called upon to testify. This is completely unofficial. I just want to know what you think—putting yourself in the place of a graphologist, of course. It will go no further than this room."

"Of course," Willow said promptly. "Delighted."

From an inner pocket he whipped out an unusual pair of glasses: prescription spectacles with an additional pair of magnifying glasses hinged to the top edge. The lieutenant shoved on the glasses, flipped down the extra lenses. He held the Daniel Blank inscription so close it was almost touching his nose.

"Felt-tipped pen," he said immediately. "Too bad. You lose the nuances. Mmm. Uh-huh. Mmm. Interesting, very interesting. Captain, does this man suffer from constipation?"

"I have no idea," Delaney said.

"Oh, my, look at this," Willow said, still peering closely at Blank's handwriting. "Would you believe . . . Sick, sick, sick. And this . . . Beautiful capitals, just beautiful." He looked up at the Captain. "He grew up in a small town in middle America—Ohio, Indiana, Iowa—around there?"

"Yes."

"He's about forty, or older?"

"Middle-thirties."

"Well . . . yes, that could be. Palmer Method. They still teach it in some schools. Goodness, look at that. This is interesting."

Suddenly he jerked off his glasses, tucked them away, half-rose to his feet to flip the photo of Blank onto Delaney's desk, then settled back to pour himself another glass of sherry.

"Schizoid," he said, beginning to speak rapidly. "On one side, artistic, sensitive, imaginative, gentle, perceptive, outgoing, striving, sympathetic, generous. The capitals are works of art. Flowing. Just blooming. On the other side, lower case now, tight, very cold, perfectly aligned: the mechanical mind, ordered, disciplined, ruthless, without emotion, inhuman, dead. It's very difficult to reconcile."

"Yes," Delaney said. "Is the man insane?"

"No. But he's breaking up."

"Why do you say that?"

"His handwriting is breaking up. Even with the felt-tipped pen you can see it. The connections between letters are faint. Between some there are no connections at all. And in his signature, that should be the most fluid and assured of anyone's handwriting, he's beginning to waver. He doesn't know who he is."

"Thank you very much, Lieutenant Willow," Captain Delaney said genially. "Please stay and finish your drink. Tell me more about handwriting analysis—from a graphologist's point of view, of course. It sounds fascinating."

"Oh yes," the bird-man said, "it is."

Later that evening Delaney went into the living room to inspect the log. Danny Boy had returned to the White House at 2:03 p.m. At 5:28 p.m., he had called the Princess in the Castle, hung up abruptly after speaking only a few minutes and then, at 5:47 p.m., had taken a cab to the Castle. He was still inside as of that moment, reported by Bulldog Three.

Delaney went over to the telephone desk.

"Did you get a tape of Danny Boy's call to the Castle at five twenty-eight?"

"Yes, sir. The man on the tap gave it to us over the phone. Spin it?"

"Please."

He listened to Daniel Blank talking to the lisping Valenter. He heard the clicks, hisses, and echo they were feeding onto the tapped line. He smiled when Blank slammed down his phone in the middle of the conversation.

"Perfect," Delaney said to no one in particular.

He had planned his meeting with Monica Gilbert with his usual meticulous attention to detail, even to the extent of deciding to keep on his overcoat. It would make her think he could only stay a moment, he was rushed, working hard to convict her husband's killer.

But when he arrived at 7:00 p.m., the children were still awake, but in their nightgowns, and he had to play with them, inspect their Christmas gifts, accept a cup of coffee. The atmosphere was relaxed, warm, pleasant, domestic—all wrong for his purpose. He was glad when Monica packed the girls off to bed.

Delaney went back to the living room, sat down on the couch, took out the single sheet of paper he had prepared, with the speech he wanted her to deliver.

She came in, looking at him anxiously.

"What is it, Edward? You seem—well, tense."

"The killer is Daniel Blank. There's no doubt about it. He killed your husband, and Lombard, Kope, and Feinberg. He's a psycho, a crazy."

"When are you going to arrest him?"

"I'm not going to arrest him. There's no evidence I can take into court. He'd walk away a free man an hour after I collared him."

"I can't believe it."

"It's true. We're watching him, every minute, and maybe we can prevent another killing or catch him in the act. But I can't take the chance."

Then he told her of what he had been doing to smash Daniel Blank. When he described the Christmas Eve call as Frank Lombard, her face went white.

"Edward, you didn't," she gasped.

"Oh yes. I did. And it worked. The man is breaking apart. I know he is. A couple of more days, if I keep the pressure on, he's going to crack wide open. Now here's what I want you to do."

He handed her the sheet of dialogue he had written out. "I want you to call him, now, at his home, identify yourself and ask him why he killed your husband."

She looked at him with shock and horror. "Edward," she choked, "I can't do that."

"Sure you can," he urged softly. "It's just a few words. I've got them all written down for you. All you've got to do is read them. I'll be right here when you call. I'll even hold your hand, if you want me to. It'll just take a minute or so. Then it'll all be over. You can do it."

"I can't, I *can't!*" She turned her head away, put her hands to her face. "Please don't ask me to," she said, her voice muffled. "Please don't. Please."

"He murdered your husband," he said stonily.

"But even if—"

"And three other innocent strangers. Cracked their skulls with his trusty little ice ax and left them on the sidewalk with their brains spilling out."

"Edward, please . . ."

"You're the woman who wanted revenge, aren't you? 'Vengeance,' you said. 'I'll do anything to help,' you said. 'Type, run errands, make coffee.' That's what you told me. A few words is all I want, spoken on the phone to the man who slaughtered your husband."

"He'll come after me. He'll hurt the children."

"No. He doesn't hurt women and children. Besides, you'll be tightly guarded. He couldn't get close even if he tried. But he won't. Monica? Will you do it?"

"Why me? Why must I do it? Can't you get a policewoman—"

"To call him and say it's you? That wouldn't lessen any possible danger to you and the girls. And I don't want any more people in the Department to know about this."

She shook her head, knuckles clenched to her mouth. Her eyes were wet.

"Anything but this," she said faintly. "I just can't do it. I *can't.*"

He stood, looked down at her, his face pulled into an ugly smile.

"Leave it to the cops, eh?" he said in a voice he scarcely recognized as his own. "Leave it to the cops to clean up the world's shit, and vomit, and blood. Keep your own hands clean. Leave it all to the cops. Just so long as you don't know what they're doing."

"Edward, it's so cruel. Can't you see that? What you're doing is worse than what he did. He killed because he's sick and can't help himself. But you're killing him slowly and deliberately, knowing exactly what you're doing, everything planned and—"

Suddenly he was sitting close beside her, an arm about her shoulders, his lips at her ear.

"Listen," he whispered, "your husband was Jewish and you're Jewish—right? And Feinberg, that last guy he chilled, was a Jew. Four victims; two Jews. Fifty percent. You want this guy running loose, killing more of your people? You want—"

She jerked away from under his arm, swung from the waist, and slapped his face, an open-handed smack that knocked his head aside and made him blink.

"Despicable!" she spat at him. "The most despicable man I've ever met!"

He stood suddenly, looming over her.

"Oh yes," he said, tasting the bile bubbling up. "Despicable. Oh yes. But Blank, he's a poor, sick lad—right? Right? Smashed your husband's skull in, but it's Be Nice to Blank Week. Right? Let me tell you—let me tell you—" He was stuttering now in his passion to get it out. "He's dead. You understand that? Daniel G. Blank is a dead man. Right now. You think—you think I'm going to let him walk away from this just because the law . . . You think I'm going to shrug, turn away, and give up? I tell you, he's *dead!* There's no way, *no* way, he can get away from me. If I have to blow his brains out with my service revolver at high noon on Fifth Avenue, I'll do it. Do it! And wait right there for them to come and take me away. I don't care. The man is *dead!* Can't you get that through your skull? If you won't help me, I'll do it another way. No matter what you do, it doesn't matter, doesn't matter. He's gone. He's just gone."

He stood there quivering with his anger, trying to draw deep breaths through his open mouth.

She looked up at him timidly. "What do you want me to say?" she asked in a small voice.

He sat beside her on the couch, holding her free hand, his ear pressed close to the phone she held so he could overhear the conversation. The script he had composed lay on her lap.

Blank's phone rang seven times before he picked it up.

"Hello?" he said cautiously.

"Daniel Blank?" Monica asked, reading her lines. There was a slight quaver in her voice.

"Yes. Who is this?"

"My name is Monica Gilbert. I'm the widow of Bernard Gilbert. Mr. Blank, why did you kill Bernie? My children and I want—"

But she was interrupted by a wild scream, a cry of panic and despair that frightened both of them. It came wailing over the wire, loud enough to be painful in their ears, shrill enough to pierce into their hearts and souls and set them quivering. Then there was the heavy bumping of a dropped phone, a thick clatter.

Delaney took the phone from Monica's trembling hand, hung it up gently. He stood, buttoned his overcoat, reached for his hat.

"Fine," he said softly. "You did just fine."

She looked at him.

"You're a dreadful man," she whispered. "The most dreadful man I've ever met."

"Am I?" he asked. "Dreadful and despicable, all in one evening. Well . . . I'm a cop."

"I never want to see you again, ever."

"All right," he said, saddened. "Good-night, and thank you."

There were two uniformed men outside her apartment door. He showed them his identification, made certain they had their orders straight. Both had been given copies of Daniel Blank's photo. Outside the house, two plainclothesmen sat in an unmarked car. One of them recognized Delaney, raised a hand in greeting. Fernandez had done an efficient job; he was good on this kind of thing.

The Captain shoved his hands into his overcoat pockets and, trying not to think of what he had done to Monica Gilbert, walked resolutely over to Blank's apartment house and into the lobby. Thank God Lipsky wasn't on duty.

"I have a letter for Daniel Blank," he told the doorman. "Could you put it in his box? No rush. If he gets it tomorrow, it'll be okay."

Delaney gave him two quarters and handed over the Holiday Greetings from Roger Kope and Family, sealed in a white envelope addressed to Mr. Daniel G. Blank.

4

After that call from Monica Gilbert, Daniel Blank had dropped the phone and gone trotting through the rooms of his apartment, mouth open, scream caught in his throat; he could not end it. Finally, it dribbled away to moans, heaves, gulps, coughs, tears. Then he was in the bedroom, forehead against the full-length mirror, staring at his strange, contorted face, torn apart.

When he quieted, fearful that his shriek had been heard by neighbors, he went directly to the bedroom phone extension, intending to call Celia Montfort and ask one question: "Why did you betray me?" But there was an odd-sounding dial tone, and he remembered he had dropped the living room handset. He hung up, went back into the living room, hung up that phone, too. He decided not to call Celia. What could she possibly say?

He had never felt such a sense of dissolution and, in self-preservation, undressed, checked window and door locks, turned out the lights and slid into bed naked. He rolled back and forth until silk sheet and wool blanket were wrapped about him tightly, mummifying him, holding him together.

He thought, his mind churning, that he might be awake forever, staring at the darkness and wondering. But curiously, he fell asleep almost instantly: a deep, dreamless slumber, more coma than sleep, heavy and depressing. He awoke at 7:18 the next morning, sodden with weariness. His eyelids were stuck shut; he realized he had wept during the night.

But the panic of the previous day had been replaced by a lethargy, a nonthinking state. Even after going through the motions of bathing, shaving, dressing, breakfasting, he found himself in a thoughtless world, as if his overworked brain had said, "All right! Enough already!" and doughtily rejected all fears, hopes, passions, visions, ardors. Even his body was subdued; his pulse seemed to beat patiently at a reduced rate, his limbs were slack. Dressed for work, like an actor waiting for his cue, he sat quietly in his living room, staring at the mirrored wall, content merely to exist, breathing.

His phone rang twice, at an hour's interval, but he did not answer. It could be his office calling. Or Celia Montfort. Or . . . or anyone. But he did not answer, but sat rigidly in a kind of catalepsy, only his eyes wandering across his mirrored wall. He needed this time of peace, quiet, non-thinking. He might even have dozed off, there in his Eames chair, but it wasn't important.

He roused early in the afternoon, looked at his watch; it seemed to be 2:18. That was possible; he was willing to accept it. He thought vaguely that he should get out, take a walk, get some fresh air.

But he only got as far as the lobby. He walked past the locked mail boxes. The mail had been delivered, but he just didn't care. Late Christmas cards, probably. And bills. And . . . well, it wasn't worth thinking about. Had Gilda sent him a Christmas card this year? He couldn't remember. He hadn't sent her one; of that he was certain.

Charles Lipsky stopped him.

"Message for you, Mr. Blank," he said brightly. "In your box." And he stepped behind the counter.

Blank suddenly realized he hadn't given the doormen anything for Christmas, nor the garage attendant, nor his cleaning woman. Or had he? Had he bought a Christmas gift for Celia? He couldn't remember. Why did she betray him?

He looked at the plain white envelope Lipsky thrust into his hand. "Mr. Daniel G. Blank." That was his name. He knew that. He suddenly realized he better not take that short walk—not right now. He'd never make it. He knew he'd never make it.

"Thank you," he said to Lipsky. That was a funny name—Lipsky. Then he turned around, took the elevator back up to his apartment, still moving in that slow, lethargic dream, his knees water, his body ready to melt into a dark, scummed puddle on the lobby carpet if an elevator didn't come soon. He took a deep breath. He'd make it.

When the door was bolted, he leaned back against it and slowly opened the white envelope. Holiday Greetings from the Kope Family. Ah well. Why had she betrayed him? What possible reason could she have, since everything he had done had been at her gentle urging and wise tutelage?

He went directly to the bedroom, took out the drawer, turned it upside down on the bed, scattering the contents. He ripped the sealed envelope free. The souvenirs had been a foolish mistake, he thought lazily, but no harm had been done. There they were. No one had taken them. No one had seen them.

He brought in a pair of heavy shears from the kitchen and chopped Lombard's license, Gilbert's ID card, Kope's identification and leatherette holder, and Feinberg's rose petals into small bits, cutting, cutting, cutting. Then he flushed the whole mess down the toilet, watching to make sure it disappeared, then flushing twice more.

That left only Detective third grade Roger Kope's shield. Blank sat on the edge of the bed, bouncing the metal on his palm, wondering dreamily how to get rid of it. He could drop it down the incinerator, but it might endure, charred but legible enough to start someone thinking. Throw it out the window? Ridiculous. Into the river would be best—but could he walk that far and risk someone seeing? The most obvious was best. He would put the shield in a small brown paper bag, walk no more than two blocks or so, and push it down into a corner litter basket. Picked up by the Sanitation Department, dumped into the back of one of those monster trucks, squashed in with coffee grounds and grapefruit rinds, and eventually disgorged onto a dump or landfill in Brooklyn. Perfect. He giggled softly.

He pulled on gloves, wiped the shield with an oily rag, then dropped it into a small brown paper bag. He put on his topcoat; the bag went into the righthand pocket. Through the lefthand pocket he carried his ice ax, beneath the coat, though for what reason he could not say.

He walked over to Third Avenue, turned south. He paused halfway down the block, spotting a litter basket on the next corner. He paused to look in a shop window, inspecting an horrendous display of canes, walkers, wheelchairs, prosthetic devices, trusses, pads and bandages, emergency oxygen bottles, do-it-yourself urinalysis kits. He turned casually away from the window and inspected the block. No uniformed cops. No squad cars or anything that looked like an unmarked police car. No one who could be a plainclothes detective. Just the usual detritus of a Manhattan street-housewives and executives, hippies and hookers, pushers and priests: the swarm of the city, swimming in the street current.

He walked quickly to the litter basket at the corner, took out the small brown paper bag with the shield of Detective Kope inside, thrust it down into the accumulated trash: brown paper bags just like his, discarded newspapers, a dead rat, all the raw garbage of a living city. He looked about quickly. No one was watching him; everyone was busy with his own agonies.

He turned and walked home quickly, smiling. The simplest and most obvious was best.

The phone was ringing when he entered his apartment. He let it ring, not answering. He hung away his topcoat, put the ice ax in its place. Then he mixed a lovely vodka martini, stirring endlessly to get it as chilled as possible and, humming, took it into the living room where he lay full-length upon the couch, balanced his drink on his chest, and wondered why she had betrayed him.

After awhile, after he had taken a few sips of his drink, still coming out of his trance, rising to the surface like something long drowned and hidden, rising on a tide or cannon shot or storm to show itself, the phone rang again. He got up immediately, set his drink carefully and steadily on the glass cocktail table, went into the kitchen and selected a knife, a razor-sharp seven-inch blade with a comfortable handle.

Strange, but knives didn't bother him anymore; they felt good. He walked back into the living room, almost prancing, stooped, and with his sharp, comfortable knife, sawed through the coiled cord holding the handset to the telephone body. He put the severed part gently aside, intesting dangling.

With that severance, he cut himself loose. He felt it. Free from events, the world, all reality.

Captain Delaney awoke with a feeling of nagging unease. He fretted that he had neglected something, overlooked some obvious detail that would enable Danny Boy to escape the vigil, fly off to Europe, slide into anonymity in the city streets, or even murder once again. The Captain brooded over the organization of the guard, but could not see how the net could be drawn tighter.

But he was in a grumpy mood when he went down for breakfast. He drew a cup of coffee in the kitchen, wandered back through the radio room, dining room, hallways, and he did become aware of something. There were no night men sleeping on the cots in their underwear. Everyone was awake and dressed; even as he looked about, he saw three men strapping on their guns.

Most of the cops in Operation Lombard were detectives and carried the standard .38 Police Special. A few lucky ones had .357 Magnums or .45 automatics. Some men had two weapons. Some holstered on the hip; some in front, at the waist. One man carried an extra holster and a small .32 at his back. One man carried an even smaller .22 strapped to his calf, under his trouser leg.

Delaney had no objection to this display of unofficial hardware. A dick carried what gave him most comfort on a job in which the next opened door might mean death. The Captain knew some carried saps, brass knuckles, switchblade knives. That was all right. They were entitled to anything that might give them that extra edge of confidence and see them through.

But what was unusual was to see them make these preparations now, as if they sensed their long watch was drawing to a close. Delaney could guess what they were thinking, what they were discussing in low voices, looking up at him nervously as he stalked by.

First of all, they were not unintelligent men; you were not promoted from patrolman to detective by passing a "stupid test." When Captain Delaney took over command of Operation Lombard, all their efforts were concentrated on Daniel G. Blank, with investigations of other suspects halted. The dicks realized the Captain knew something they didn't know: Danny Boy was their pigeon. Delaney was too old and experienced a cop to put his cock on the line if he wasn't sure, of that they were certain.

Then the word got around that he had requested the Kope photo. Then the telephone men heard the taped replay, from the man tapping Danny Boy's phone, of the phone call from Monica Gilbert. Then the special guard was placed on the Gilbert widow and her children. All that was chewed over in radio room and squad car, on lonely night watches and long hours of patrol. They knew now, or guessed, what he was up to. It was a wonder, Delaney realized, he had been able to keep it private as long as he had. Well, at least it was his responsibility. His alone. If it failed, no one else would suffer from it. If it failed . . .

There was no report of any activity from Danny Boy at 9:00 a.m., 9:15, 9:30, 9:45, 10:00. Early on when the vigil was first established, they had discovered a back entrance to Blank's apartment house, a seldom-used service door that opened onto a walk leading to 82nd Street. An unmarked car, with one man, was positioned there, in full view of this back exit, with orders to report in every fifteen minutes. This unit was coded Bulldog 10, but was familiarly known as Ten-O. Now, as Delaney passed back and forth through the radio room, he heard the reports from Ten-O and from Bulldog One, the Con Ed van parked on the street in front of the White House.

10:15, nothing, 10:30, nothing. No report of Danny Boy at 10:45, 11:00, 11:15, 11:30. Shortly before 12:00, Delaney went into his study and called Blank's apartment. The phone rang and rang, but there was no answer. He hung up; he was worried.

He took a cab over to the hospital. Barbara seemed in a semi-comatose state and refused to eat her meal. So he sat helplessly alongside her bed, holding her limp hand, pondering his options if Blank didn't appear for the rest of the day.

It might be that he was up there, just not answering his phone. It might be that he had slipped through their net, was long gone. And it might be that he had slit his throat after receiving the Kope photo, and was up there all right, leaking blood all over his polished floor. Delaney had told Sergeant MacDonald that Danny Boy wouldn't suicide, but he was going by patterns, by percentages. No one knew better than he that percentages weren't certainties.

He got back to his brownstone a little after 1:00 p.m. Ten-O and Bulldog One had just reported in. No sign of Danny Boy. Delaney had Stryker called at the Factory. Blank hadn't arrived at the office. The Captain went back into his study and called Blank's apartment again. Again the phone rang and rang. No answer.

By this time, without intending to, he had communicated his mood to his men; now he wasn't the only one pacing through the rooms, hands in pockets, head lowered. The men, he noticed, were keeping their faces deliberately expressionless, but he knew they feared what he feared: the pigeon had flown.

By two o'clock he had worked out a contingency plan. If Danny Boy didn't show within another hour, at 3:00 p.m., he'd send a uniformed officer over to the White House with a trumped-up story that the Department had received an anonymous threat against Daniel Blank. The patrolman would go up to Blank's apartment with the doorman, and listen. If they heard Blank moving about, or if he answered his bell, they would say it was a mistake and come away. If they heard nothing, and if Blank didn't answer his bell, then the officer would request the doorman or manager to open Blank's apartment with the pass-keys "just to make certain everything is all right."

It was a sleazy plan, the Captain acknowledged. There were a hundred holes in it; it might endanger the whole operation. But it was the best he could come up with; it had to be done. If Danny Boy was long gone, or dead, they couldn't sit around watching an empty hole. He'd order it at exactly 3:00 p.m.

He was in the radio room, and at 2:48 p.m. there was a burst of static from one of the radio speakers, then it cleared.

"Barbara from Bulldog One."

"Got you, Bulldog One."

"Fernandez," the voice said triumphantly. "Danny Boy just came out."

There was a sigh in the radio room; Captain Delaney realized part of it was his.

"What's he wearing?" he asked the radioman.

The operator started to repeat the question into his mike, but Fernandez had heard the Captain's loud voice.

"Black topcoat," he reported. "No hat. Hands in pockets. He's not waiting for a cab. Walking west. Looks like he's out for a stroll. I'll put Bulldog Three on him, far back, and two sneaks on foot. Officer LeMolle, designated Bulldog Twenty. Officer Sanchez, designated Bulldog Forty. Got that?"

"LeMolle is Bulldog Twenty, Sanchez is Forty."

"Right. You'll get radio checks from them as soon as possible. Danny Boy is nearing Second Avenue now, still heading west. I'm out."

Delaney stood next to the radio table. The other men in the room closed in, heads turned, ears to the loudspeaker.

Silence for almost five minutes. One man coughed, looked apologetically at the others.

Then, almost a whisper: "Barbara from Bulldog Twenty. Read me?"

"Soft but good, Twenty."

"Danny Boy between Second and Third on Eighty-third, heading west. Out." It was a woman's voice.

"Who's Lemolle?" Delaney asked Blankenship.

"Policewoman Martha LeMolle. Her cover is a housewife—shopping bag, the whole bit."

Delaney opened his mouth to speak, but the radio crackled again.

"Barbara from Bulldog Forty. Make me?"

"Yes, Forty. Good. Where is he?"

"Turning south on Third. Out."

Blankenship turned to Delaney without waiting for his question. "Forty is Detective second grade Ramon Sanchez. Dressed like an orthodox Jewish rabbi."

So when Daniel G. Blank deposited the brown paper bag in the litter basket, the housewife was less than twenty feet behind him and saw him do it, and the rabbi was across the avenue and saw him do it. They both shadowed Danny Boy back to his apartment house, but by the time he arrived they had both reported he had discarded something in a litter basket, they had given the exact location (northeast corner, Third and 82nd; and, at Delaney's command, Blankenship had an unmarked car on the way with orders to pick up the entire basket and bring it back to the brownstone. Delaney thought it might be the ice ax.

At least twenty men crowded into the kitchen when the two plainclothesmen carried in the garbage basket and set it on the linoleum.

"I always knew you'd end up in Sanitation, Tommy," someone called. There were a few nervous laughs.

"Empty it," Delaney ordered. "Slowly. Put the crap on the floor. Shake out every newspaper. Look into every bag."

The two detectives pulled on their gloves. They began to snake out the sodden packages, the neatly wrapped bags, the dead rat (handled by the tip of its tail), loose garbage, a blood-soaked towel. The stench filled the room, but no one left; they had all smelled worse odors than that.

It went slowly, for almost ten minutes, as bags were pulled out, emptied onto the floor, and tied packages were cut open and unrolled. Then one of the dicks reached in, came out with a small brown paper bag, opened it, looked inside.

"Jesus Christ!"

The waiting men said nothing, but there was a tightening of the circle; Captain Delaney felt himself pressed closer until his thighs were tight against the kitchen table. Holding the bag by the bottom, the detective slowly slid the contents out onto the tabletop. Cop's shield.

There was something: a collective moan, a gasp, something of anguish and fear. The men peered closer.

"That's Kope's tin," someone cried, voice crackling with fury. "I worked with him. That's Kope's number. I know it."

Someone said: "Oh, that dirty cocksucker."

Someone said, over and over: "Motherfucker, motherfucker, motherfucker . . ."

Someone said: "Let's get him right now. Let's waste him."

Delaney had been bending over, staring at the buzzer. It wasn't hard to imagine what had happened: Daniel G. Blank had destroyed the evidence, the ID cards and rose petals flushed down the toilet or thrown into the incinerator. But this was good metal, so he figured he better ditch it. Not smart, Danny Boy.

"Let's waste him," someone repeated, in a louder voice.

And here was another problem, one he had hoped to avoid by keeping his knowledge of Daniel Blank's definite guilt to himself. He knew that when a cop was killed, all cops became Sicilians. He had seen it happen: a patrolman shot down, and immediately his precinct house was flooded with cops from all over the city, wearing plaid windbreakers and business suits, shields pinned to lapels, offering to work on their own time. Was there anything they could do? Anything?

It was a mixture of fear, fury, anguish, sorrow. You couldn't possibly understand it unless you belonged. Because it was a brotherhood, and corrupt cops, stupid cops, cowardly cops had nothing to do with it. If you were a cop, then *any* cop's murder diminished you. You could not endure that.

The trouble was, Captain Edward X. Delaney acknowledged to himself, the trouble was that he could understand all this on an intellectual level without feeling the emotional involvement these men were feeling now, staring at a murdered cop's tin. It wasn't so much a lack in him, he assured himself, as that he looked at things differently from these furious men. To him *all* murders, in sanity and without conscience, demanded judgment, whether assassinated President, child thrown from rooftop, drunk knifed to death in a tavern brawl, whatever, wherever, whomever. His brotherhood was wider, larger, broader, and encompassed all, all, all . . .

But meanwhile, he was surrounded by a ring of blood-charged men. He knew he had only to say, "All right, let's take him," and they would be with him, surging, breaking down doors. Daniel G. Blank would dissolve in a million plucking bullets, torn and falling into darkness.

Captain Delaney raised his head slowly, looked around at those faces: stony, twisted, blazing.

"We'll do it my way," he said, keeping his voice as toneless as he could. "Blankenship, have the shield dusted. Get this mess cleaned up. Return the basket to the street corner. The rest of you men get back to your posts."

He strode into his study, closed all the doors. He sat stolidly at his desk and listened. He heard the mutterings, shufflings of feet. He figured he had another 24 hours, no more. Then some hothead would get to Blank and gun him down. Exactly what he told Monica Gilbert he would do. But for different reasons.

About 7:30 p.m., he dressed warmly and left the house, telling the log-man he was going to the hospital. But instead, he went on his daily unannounced inspection. He knew the men on duty were aware of these unscheduled tours; he wanted them to know. He decided to walk—he had been inside, sitting, for too many hours—and he marched vigorously over to East End Avenue. He made certain Tiger One—the man watching the Castle—was in position and not goofing off. It was a game with him to spot Tiger One without being spotted. This night he won, bowing his shoulders, staring at the sidewalk, limping by Tiger One with no sign of recognition. Well, at least the kid was on duty, walking a beat across from the Castle and, Delaney hoped, not spending too much time grabbing a hot coffee somewhere or a shot of something stronger.

He walked briskly back to the White House and stood across the street, staring up at Blank's apartment house. Hopefully, Danny Boy was tucked in for the night. Captain Delaney stared and stared. Once again he had the irrational urge to go up there and ring the bell.

"My name is Captain Edward X. Delaney, New York Police Department. I'd like to talk to you."

Crazy. Blank wouldn't let him in. But that's all Delaney really wanted—just to talk. He didn't want to collar Blank or injure him. Just talk, and maybe understand. But it was hopeless; he'd have to imagine.

He knocked on the door of the Con Ed van; it was unlocked and opened cautiously. The man at the door recognized him and swung the door wide, throwing a half-assed salute. Delaney stepped inside; the door was locked behind him. There was one man with binoculars at the concealed flap, another man at the radio desk. Three men, three shifts; counting the guy in the hole and extras, there were about 20 men assigned to Bulldog One.

"How's it going?" he asked.

They assured him it was going fine. He looked around at the hot plate they had rigged up, the coffee percolator, a miniature refrigerator they had scrounged from somewhere.

"All the comforts of home," he nodded.

They nodded in return, and he wished them a Happy New Year. Outside again, he paused at the hole they had dug through the pavement of East 83rd Street, exposing steam pipes, sewer lines, telephone conduits. There was one man down there, dressed like a Con Ed repairman, holding a transistor radio to his ear under his hardhat. He took it away when he recognized Delaney.

"Get to China yet?" the Captain asked, gesturing toward the shovel leaning against the side of the excavation.

The officer was black.

"Getting there, Captain," he said solemnly, "Getting there. Slowly."

"Many complaints from residents?"

"Oh, we got plenty of those, Captain. No shortage."

Delaney smiled. "Keep at it. Happy New Year."

"Same to you, sir. Many of them."

He walked away westward, disgusted with himself. He did this sort of thing badly, he knew: talking informally with men under his command. He tried to be easy, relaxed, jovial. It just didn't work.

One of his problems was his reputation. "Iron Balls." But it wasn't only his record; they sensed something in him. Every cop had to draw his own boundaries of heroism, reality, stupidity, cowardice. In a dicey situation, you could go strictly by the book and get an inspector's funeral. Captain Edward X. Delaney would be there, wearing his Number Ones and white gloves. But all situations didn't call for sacrifice. Some called for a reasoned response. Some called for surrender. Each man had his own limits, set his own boundaries.

But what the men sensed was that Delaney's boundaries were narrower, stricter than theirs. Too bad there wasn't a word for it: coppishness, copicity, copanity—something like that. "Soldiership" came close, but didn't tell the whole story. What was needed was a special word for the special quality of being a cop.

What his men sensed, why he could never communicate with them on equal terms, was that he had this quality to a frightening degree. He was the quintessential cop, and they didn't need any new words to know it. They understood that he would throw them into the grinder as fast as he would throw himself.

He got to the florist's shop just as it was closing. They didn't want to let him in, but he assured them it was an order for the following day. He described exactly what he wanted: a single long-stem rose, to be placed, no greenery, in a long white florist's box and delivered at 9:00 the next morning.

"Deliver one rose?" the clerk asked in astonishment. "Oh, sir, we'll have to charge extra for that."

"Of course," Delaney nodded. "I understand. I'll pay whatever's necessary. Just make certain it gets there first thing tomorrow morning."

"Would you like to enclose a card, sir?"

"I would."

He wrote out the small white card: "Dear Dan, here's a fresh rose for the one you destroyed." He signed the card "Albert Feinberg," then slid the card in the little envelope, sealed the flap, addressed the envelope to Daniel G. Blank, including his street address and apartment number.

"You're certain it will get there by nine tomorrow morning?"

"Yes, sir. We'll take care of it. That's a lot of money to spend on one flower, sir. A sentimental occasion?"

"Yes," Captain Edward X. Delaney smiled. "Something like that."

5

The next morning Delaney awoke, lay staring somberly at the ceiling. Then, for the first time in a long time, he got out of bed, kneeled, and thought a prayer for Barbara, for his own dead parents, for all the dead, the weak, the afflicted. He did not ask that he be allowed to kill Daniel Blank. It was not the sort of thing you asked of God.

Then he showered, shaved, donned an old uniform, so aged it was shiny enough to reflect light. He also loaded his .38 revolver, strapped on his gunbelt and holster. It was not with the certainty that this would be the day he'd need it, but it was another of his odd superstitions: if you prepared carefully for an event, it helped hasten it.

Then he went downstairs for coffee. The men on duty noted his uniform, the bulge of his gun. Of course, no one commented on it, but a few men did check their own weapons, and one pulled on an elaborate shoulder holster that buckled across his chest.

Fernandez was in the kitchen, having a coffee and Danish. Delaney drew him aside.

"Lieutenant, when you're finished here, I want you to go to Bulldog One and stay there until relieved. Got that?"

"Sure, Captain."

"Tell your lookout to watch for a delivery by a florist. Let me know the minute he arrives."

"Okay," Fernandez nodded cheerfully. "You'll know as soon as we spot him. Something cooking, Captain?"

Delaney didn't answer, but carried his coffee back into the radio room. He set it down on the long table, then went back into his study and wheeled in his swivel chair. He positioned it to the right of the radio table, facing the operators.

He sat there all morning, sipping three black coffees, munching on the dry, stale heel of a loaf of Italian bread. Calls came in at fifteen-minute intervals from Bulldog One and Ten-O. No sign of Danny Boy. At 9:20, Stryker called from the Factory to report that Blank hadn't shown up for work. A few minutes later, Bulldog One was back on the radio.

Fernandez: "Tell Captain Delaney a boy carrying a long, white florist's box just went into the White House lobby."

Delaney heard it. Leaving as little as possible to chance, he went into his study, looked up the florist's number called, and asked if his single red rose had been delivered. He was assured the messenger had been sent and was probably there right now. Satisfied, the Captain went back to his chair at the radio table. The waiting men had heard Fernandez' report but what it meant, they did not know.

Sergeant MacDonald leaned over Delaney's chair.

"He's freaking, Captain?" he whispered.

"We'll see. We'll see. Pull up a chair, sergeant. Stay close to me for a few hours."

"Sure, Captain."

The black sergeant pulled over a wooden, straight-backed chair, sat at Delaney's right, slightly behind him. He sat as solidly as the Captain, wearing steel-rimmed spectacles, carved face immobile.

So they sat and waited. So everyone sat and waited. Quiet enough to hear a Sanitation truck grinding by, an airliner overhead, a far-off siren, hoot of tugboat, the bored fifteen-minute calls from Ten-O and Bulldog One. Still no sign of Danny Boy. Delaney wondered if he could risk a quick trip to the hospital.

Then, shortly before noon, a click loud enough to galvanize them, and Bulldog One was on:

"He's coming out! He's carrying stuff. A doorman behind him carrying stuff. What? A jacket, knapsack. What? What else? A coil of rope. Boots. What?"

Delaney: "Jesus Christ. Get Fernandez on."

Fernandez: "Fernandez here. Wearing black topcoat, no hat, left hand in coat pocket, right hand free. No glove. Knapsack, coil of rope, some steel things with spikes, jacket, heavy boots, knitted cap."

Delaney: "Ice ax?"

Barbara: "Bulldog One, ice ax?"

Fernandez: "No sign. Car coming up from garage. Black Chevy Corvette. His car."

Captain Delaney turned slightly to look at Sergeant MacDonald. "Got him," he said.

"Yes," MacDonald nodded. "He's running."

Fernandez: "They're pushing his stuff into the car. Left hand still in coat pocket, right hand free."

Delaney (to MacDonald): "Two unmarked cars, three men each. Start the engines and wait. You come back in here."

Fernandez: "He's loaded. Getting into the driver's seat. Orders?"

Delaney: "Fernandez to trail in Bulldog Two. Keep in touch."

Fernandez: "Got it. Out."

Captain Delaney looked around. Sergeant MacDonald was just coming back into the room.

MacDonald: "Cars are ready, Captain."

Delaney: "Designated Searcher One and Searcher Two. If we both go, I'll take One, you take Two. If I stay, you take both."

MacDonald nodded. He had taken off his glasses.

Fernandez: "Barbara from Bulldog Two. He's circling the block. I think he's heading for the Castle. Out."

Delaney: "Alert Tiger One. Send Bulldog Three to Castle."

Fernandez: "Bulldog Two. It's the Castle all right. He's pulling up in front.

We're back at the corner, the south corner. Danny Boy's parked in front of the Castle. He's getting out. Left hand in pocket, right hand free. Luggage still in car."

Bulldog Three: "Barbara from Bulldog Three."

Barbara: "Got you."

Bulldog Three: "We're in position. He's walking up to the Castle door. He's knocking at the door."

Delaney: "Where's Tiger One?"

Fernandez: "He's here in Bulldog Two with me. Danny Boy is parked on the wrong side of the street. We can plaster him."

Delaney: "Negative."

Barbara: "Negative, Bulldog Two."

Fernandez (laughing): "Thought it would be. Shit. Look at that . . . Barbara from Bulldog Two."

Barbara: "You're still on, Bulldog Two."

Fernandez: "Something don' smell right. Danny Boy knocked at the door of the Castle. It was opened. He went inside. But the door is still open. We can see it from here. Maybe I should take a walk up there and look."

Delaney: "Tell him to hold it."

Barbara: "Hold it, Bulldog Two."

Delaney: "Ask Bulldog Three if they're receiving our transcriptions to Bulldog Two."

Barbara: "Bulldog Three from Barbara. Are you monitoring our conversation with Bulldog Two?"

Bulldog Three: "Affirmative."

Delaney: "To Bulldog Two. Affirmative for a walk past Castle but put Tiger One with walkie-talkie on the other side of the street. Radio can be showing."

Fernandez: "Bulldog Two here. Got it. We're starting."

Bulldog Three: "Bulldog Three here. Got it. Fernandez is getting out of Bulldog Two. Tiger One is getting out, crossing to the other side of the street."

Delaney: "Hold it. Check out Tiger One's radio."

Barbara: "Tiger One from Barbara. How do you read?"

Tiger One: "T-One here. Lots of interference but I can read."

Delaney: "Tell him to cover. Understood?"

Barbara: "Tiger One, cover Lieutenant Fernandez on the other side of the street. *Coppish?*"

Tiger One: "Right on."

Delaney: "Bring in Bulldog Three."

Bulldog Three: "They're both walking toward us, slowly. Fernandez is passing the Castle, turning his head, looking at it. Tiger One is right across the street. No action. They're coming toward us. Walking slowly. No sweat. Fernandez is crossing the street toward us. He'll probably want to use our mike. Ladies and gentlemen, the next voice you hear will be that of Lieutenant Jeri Fernandez."

Delaney (stonily): "Get that man's name."

Fernandez: "Fernandez in Bulldog Three. Is the Captain there?"

Delaney bent over the desk mike.

Delaney: "Here. What is it, lieutenant?"

Fernandez: "It smells, Captain. The door to the Castle is half-open. Something's propping it open. Looks like a man's leg to me."

Delaney: "A leg?"

Fernandez: "From the knee down. A leg and a foot propping the door open. How about I take a closer look?"

Delaney: "Where's Tiger One?"

Fernandez: "Right here with me."

Delaney: "Both of you go back to Bulldog Two. Tiger One across the street, covering again. You take a closer look. Tell Tiger One to give us a continuous. Got that?"

Fernandez: "Sure."

Delaney: "Lieutenant . . ."

Fernandez: "Yeah?"

Delaney: "He's fast."

Fernandez (chuckling): "Don' give it a second thought, Captain."

Tiger One: "We're walking south. Slowly. Fernandez is across the street."

Delaney: "Gun out?"

Barbara: "Is your gun out, Tiger One?"

Tiger One: "Oh Jesus, it's been out for the last fifteen minutes. He's coming up to the Castle. He's slowing, stopping. Now Fernandez is kneeling on one knee. He's pretending to tie his shoelace. He's looking toward the Castle door. He's—Oh my God!"

Daniel Blank awoke in an antic mood, laughing at a joke he had dreamed but could not remember. He looked to the windows; it promised to be a glorious day. He thought he might go over to Celia Montfort's house and kill her. He might kill Charles Lipsky, Valenter, the bartender at The Parrot. He might kill a lot of people, depending on how he felt. It was that kind of a day.

It took off like a rocket: hesitating, almost motionless, moving, then spurting into the sky. That's the way the morning went, until he'd be out of the earth's pull, and free. There was nothing he might not do. He remembered that mood, when he was atop Devil's Needle, weeks, months, years ago.

Well, he would go back to Devil's Needle and know that rapture again. The park was closed for the winter, but it was just a chain-link fence, the gate closed with a rusty padlock. He could smash it open easily with his ice ax. He could smash anything with his ice ax.

He bathed and dressed carefully, still in that euphoria he knew would last forever.

So the chime at his outside door didn't disturb him at all.

"Who is it?" he called.

"Package for you, Mr. Blank."

He heard retreating footsteps, waited a few moments, then unbolted his door. He brought the long, white florist's box inside, relocked the door. He took the box to the living room and stared at it, not understanding.

Nor did he comprehend the single red rose inside. Nor the card. Albert Feinberg? Feinberg? Who was Albert Feinberg? Then he remembered that last death with longing; the close embrace, warm breath in his face, their passionate grunts. He wished they could do it again. And Feinberg had sent him another rose! Wasn't that sweet. He sniffed the fragrance, stroked the velvety petals against his cheek, then suddenly crushed the whole flower in his fist. When he opened his hand, the petals slowly came back to shape, moving as he watched, forming again the whole exquisitely shaped blossom, as lovely as it had been before.

He drifted about the apartment, dreaming, nibbling at the rose. He ate the petals, one by one; they were soft, hard, moist, dry on his tongue, with a tang and flavor all their own. He ate the flower down to the stem, grinning and nodding, swallowing it all.

He took his gear from the hallway closet; ice ax, rucksack, nylon line, boots, crampons, jacket, knitted watch cap. He wondered about sandwiches and a thermos—but what did he need with food and drink? He was beyond all that, outside the world's pull and the hunger to exist.

It was remarkable, he thought happily, how efficiently he was operating; the call to the garage to bring his car around, the call to a doorman—who turned out to be Charles Lipsky—to help him down with his gear. He moved through it all smiling. The day was sharp, clear, brisk, open, and so was he. He was in the lemon sun, in the thin blue sac filled with amniotic fluid. He was one with it all. He hummed a merry tune.

When Valenter opened the door and said, "I'm thorry, thir, but Mith Montfort ith not—" he smashed his fist into Valenter's face, feeling the nose crunch under his blow, seeing the blood, feeling the blood slippery between his knuckles. Then, stepping farther inside, he hit the shocked Valenter again, his fist going into the man's throat, crushing that jutting Adam's apple. Valenter's eyes rolled up into his skull and he went down.

So Daniel Blank walked easily across the entrance hall, still humming his merry tune. What was it? Some early American folksong; he couldn't remember the title. He climbed the stairs steadily, the ice ax out now, transferred to his right hand. He remembered the first time he had followed her up these stairs to the room on the fifth floor. She had paused, turned, and he had kissed her, between navel and groin, somewhere on the yielding softness, somewhere . . . Why had she betrayed him?

But even before he came to that splintered door, a naked Anthony Montfort darted out, gave Daniel one mad, frantic glance over his shoulder, then dashed down the hall, arms flinging. Watching that young, bare, unformed body run, all Blank could think of was the naked Vietnamese girl, burned by napalm, running, running, caught in pain and terror.

Celia was standing. She, too, was bare.

"Well," she said, her face a curious mixture of fear and triumph. "Well . . ."

He struck her again and again. But after the first blow, the fear faded from her face; only the triumph was left. The certitude. Was this what she wanted? He wondered, hacking away. Was this her reason? Why she had manipulated him. Why she had betrayed him. He would have to think about it. He hit her long after she was dead, and the sound of the ice ax ceased to be crisp and became sodden.

Then, hearing screams from somewhere, he transferred the ice ax to his left hand, under the coat, hidden again, and rushed out. Down the stairs. Over the fallen Valenter. Out into the bright, sharp, clear day. The screams pursued him: screams, screams, screams.

They were all on their feet in the radio room, listening white-faced to Tiger One's furious shouts, a scream from somewhere, "Fernandez is—", shots, roar of a car engine, squeal of tires, metallic clatter. Tiger One's radio went dead.

Captain Delaney stood stock-still for almost 30 seconds, hands on hips, head lowered, blinking slowly, licking his lips. The men in the room looked to him, waiting.

He was not hesitating as much as deliberating. He had been through situations as fucked-up as this in the past. Instinct and experience might see him through, but he knew a few seconds of consideration would help establish the proper sequence of orders. First things first.

He raised his head, caught MacDonald's eye.

"Sergeant," he said tonelessly, raised a hand, jerked a thumb over his shoulder, "on your way. Take both cars. Sirens. I'll stay here. Report as soon as possible."

MacDonald started out. Delaney caught up with him before he reached the hallway door, took his arm.

"In the outside toilet," he whispered, "in the cabinet under the sink. A pile of clean white towels. Take a handful with you."

The sergeant nodded, and was gone.

The Captain came back into the middle of the room. He began to dictate orders to the two radiomen and the two telephone men.

"To Bulldog Two, remain on station and assist."

"To Bulldog Three, take Danny Boy. Extreme caution."

Both cars cut in to answer; the waiting men heard more shots, curses, shouts.

"To downtown Communications. Operation Lombard top priority. Four cars New York entrance to George Washington Bridge. Detain black Chevy Corvette. Give them license number, description of Danny Boy. Extreme caution. Armed and dangerous."

"You and you. Take a squad. Up to George Washington Bridge. Siren and flasher. Grab a handful of those photos of Danny Boy and distribute them."

"To Communications. Officer in need of assistance. Ambulance. Urgent. Give address of Castle."

"To Deputy Inspector Thorsen: 'He's running. Will keep you informed. Delaney.' "

"To Assault-Homicide Division. Crime in progress at Castle. Give address. Urgent. Please assist Operation Lombard."

"To Bulldog Ten. Recall to Barbara with car."

"To Bulldog One. Seal Danny Boy's apartment in White House. Twenty-one H. No one in, no one out."

"To Stryker. Seal Danny Boy's office. No one in, no one out."

"You and you, down to the Factory to help Stryker. Take Ten-O's car when he arrives."

"To Special Operations. Urgently need three heavy cars. Six men with vests, shotguns, gas grenades, subs, the works. Three snipers, completely equipped, one in each car. Up here as soon as possible. Oh yes . . . cars equipped with light bars, if possible."

"You and you, pick up the Mortons, at the Erotica on Madison Avenue, for questioning."

"You, pick up Mrs. Cleek at the Factory. You, pick up the owner of The Parrot on Third Avenue. You, pick up Charles Lipsky, doorman at the White House. Hold all of them for questioning."

"To Communications. All-precinct alert. Give description of car and Danny Boy. Photos to come. Wanted for multiple homicide. Extreme caution. Dangerous and armed. Inform chief inspector."

Delaney paused, drew a deep breath, looked about dazedly. The room was emptying out now as he pointed at men, gave orders, and they hitched up their guns, donned coats and hats, started out.

The radio crackled.

"Barbara from Searcher One."

"Got you, Searcher One."

"MacDonald. Outside the Castle. Fernandez down and bleeding badly. Tiger One down. Unconscious. At least a broken leg. Bulldog Three gone after Danny Boy. Bulldog Two and Searcher Two blocking off the street. Send assistance. Am now entering Castle."

Delaney heard, began speaking again.

"To Communications. Repeat urgent ambulance. Two officers wounded."

"To Assault-Homicide Division. Repeat urgent assistance needed. Two officers wounded."

"Sir, Deputy Inspector Thorsen is on the line," one of the telephone operators interrupted.

"Tell him two officers wounded. I'll get back to him. Recall guard on Monica Gilbert and get men and car over here. Recall taps on Danny Boy's phone and Monica Gilbert's phone. Tell them to remove all equipment, clean up, no sign."

"Barbara from Searcher One."

"Come in, Searcher One."

"MacDonald here. We have one homicide: female, white, black hair, early thirties, five-four or five, a hundred and ten, slender, skull crushed, answering description of the Princess. White, male boy, about twelve, naked and hysterical, answering description of Anthony Montfort. One white male, six-three or four, about one-sixty or sixty-five, unconscious, answering description of houseman Valenter, broken nose, facial injuries, bad breathing. Need two ambulances and doctors. Fernandez is alive but still bleeding. We can't stop it. Ambulance? Soon, please. Tiger One had broken right leg, arm, bruises, scrapes. Ambulances and doctors, please."

Delaney took a deep breath, started again.

"To Communications. Second repeat urgent ambulance. One homicide victim, four serious injuries, one hysteria victim. Need two ambulances and doctors soonest."

"To Assault-Homicide. Second repeat urgent assistance. Anything on those cars Communications sent to block the George Washington Bridge?"

"Cars in position, sir. No sign of Danny Boy."

"Our men there with photos?"

"Not yet, sir."

"Anything from Bulldog Three?"

"Can't raise them, sir."

"Keep trying."

Blankenship came over to the Captain, looking down at a wooden board with a spring clamp at the top. He had been making notes. Delaney noted the man's hands were trembling slightly but his voice was steady.

"Want a recap, sir?" he asked softly.

"A tally?" Delaney said thankfully. "I could use that. What have we got left?"

"One car, unmarked, and four men. But the recalls should be here soon, and Lieutenant Dorfman next door sent over two men in uniform to stand by. He also says he's holding a squad car outside the precinct house in case we need it. The three cars from Special Operations are on the way."

"No sign of Danny Boy at the Bridge, sir. Traffic beginning to back up."

"What?" the other radio operator said sharply. "Louder. Louder! I'm not making you."

Then they heard the hoarse, agonized whisper:

"Barbara . . . Bulldog Three . . . cracked up . . . lost him . . ."

"Where?" Delaney roared into the mike. "God damn you, stay on your feet? Where are you? Where did you lose him?"

". . . north . . . Broadway . . . Broadway . . . Ninety-fifth . . . hurt . . ."

"You and you," Delaney said, pointing. "Take the car outside. Over to Broadway and Ninety-fifth. Report in as soon as possible. You, get on to Communications. Nearest cars and ambulance. Officers injured in accident. Son of a bitch!"

"Barbara from Searcher One."

"Got you, Searcher One."

"MacDonald. One ambulance here. Fernandez is all right. Lost a lot of blood but he's going to make it. The doc gave him a shot. Thanks for the towels. Another ambulance pulling up. Cars from Assault-Homicide. Mobile lab . . ."

"Hold it a minute, sergeant." Delaney turned to the other radio operator. "Did you check the cars on the Bridge?"

"Yes, sir. The photos got there, but no sign of Danny Boy."

Delaney turned back to the first radio. "Go on, sergeant."

"Things are getting sorted out. Fernandez and Tiger One (what the hell *is* his name?) on their way to the hospital. The way I make it, Danny Boy came running out of the Castle and caught Fernandez just as he was straightening up, beginning his draw. Swung his ax at the lieutenant's skull. Fernandez moved and turned to take it on his left shoulder, back, high up, curving in near the neck. Danny Boy pulled the ax free, jumped into his car. Tiger One rushed the car from across the street, firing as he ran. He got off there. Two hits on the car, he says, with one through the front left window. But Danny Boy apparently unhurt. He got started fast, pulled away, sideswiped Tiger One, knocked him down and out. The whole goddamned thing happened so *fast.* The men in Bulldog Two and Three were left with their mouths open."

"I know," Delaney sighed. "Remain on station. Assist Assault-Homicide. Guards on the kid and Valenter until we can get statements."

"Understood. Searcher One out."

"Any word from the Bridge?" Delaney asked the radio operator.

"No, sir. Traffic backing up."

"Captain Delaney, the three cars from Special Operations are outside."

"Good, Hold them. Blankenship, come into the study with me."

They went in; Delaney closed all the doors. He searched a moment, pulled from the bookshelves a folded road map of New York City and one of New York State. He spread the city map out on his desk, snapped on the table lamp. The two men bent over the desk. Delaney jabbed his finger at East End Avenue.

"He started here," he said. "Went north and made a left onto Eighty-sixth Street. That's what I figure. Went right past Bulldog Three who still had their thumbs up their asses. Oh hell, maybe I'm being too hard on them."

"We heard a second series of shots and shouts when we alerted Bulldog Three," Blankenship reminded him.

"Yes. Maybe they got some off. Anyway, Danny Boy headed west."

"To the George Washington Bridge?"

"Yes," the Captain said, and paused. If Blankenship wanted to ask any questions about why Delaney had sent blocking cars to the Bridge, now would be the time to ask them. But the detective had too much sense for that, and was silent.

"So now he's at Central Park," Delaney went on, his blunt finger tracing the path on the map. "I figure he turned south for Traverse Three and crossed to the west side at Eighty-sixth, went over to Broadway, and turned north. Bulldog Three said he was heading north. He probably turned left onto Ninety-sixth to get on the West Side Drive."

"He could have continued north and got on the Drive farther up. Or taken Broadway or Riverside Drive all the way to the Bridge."

"Oh shit," Captain Delaney said disgustedly, "he could have done a million things."

Like all cops, he was dogged by the unpredictable. Chance hung like a black cloud that soured his waking hours and defiled his dreams. Every cop lived with it: the meek, humble prisoner who suddenly pulls a knife, a shotgun blast that answers a knock on a door during a routine search, a rifle shot from a rooftop. The unexpected. The only way to beat it was to live by percentages, trust in luck, and—if you needed it—pray.

"We have a basic choice," Delaney said dully, and Blankenship was intelligent to note the Captain had said, "We have . . ." not "I have . . ." He was getting sucked in. This man, the detective reflected, didn't miss a trick. "We can send out a five-state alarm, then sit here on our keisters and wait for someone else to take him, or we can go get him and clean up our own shit."

"Where do you think he's heading, Captain?"

"Chilton," Delaney said promptly. "It's a little town in Orange County. Not ten miles from the river. Let me show you."

He opened the map of New York State, spread it over the back of the club chair, tilted the lampshade to spread more light.

"There it is," he pointed out, "just south of Mountainville, west of the Military Academy. See that little patch of green? It's Chilton State Park. Blank goes up there to climb. He's a mountain climber." He closed his eyes a moment, trying to remember details of that marked map he had found in Danny Boy's car a million years ago. Once again Blankenship was silent and asked no questions.

Delaney opened his eyes, stared at the detective. "Across the George Washington Bridge," he recited, delighted with his memory. "Into New Jersey. Onto Four. Then onto Seventeen. Over into New York near Mahwah and Suffern. Then onto the Thruway, and turn off on Thirty-two to Mountainville. Then south to Chilton. The Park's a few miles out of town."

"New Jersey?" Blankenship cried. "Jesus Christ, Captain, maybe we better alert them."

Delaney shook his head. "No use. The Bridge was blocked before he got there. He couldn't possibly have beat that block. No way, city traffic being what it is. No, he by-passed the Bridge. If he hadn't he'd have been spotted by now. But he's still heading for Chilton. I've got to believe that. How can he get across the river north of the George Washington Bridge?"

They bent over the state map again. Blankenship's unexpectedly elegant forefinger traced a course.

"He gets on the Henry Hudson Parkway, say at Ninety-sixth. Okay, Captain?"

"Sure."

"He gets up to the George Washington Bridge, but maybe he sees the block."

"Or the traffic backing up because of the search."

"Or the traffic. So he sticks on the Henry Hudson Parkway, going north. My God, he can't be far along right now. He may be across this bridge here and into Spuyten Duyvil. Or maybe he's in Yonkers, still heading north."

"What's the next crossing?"

"The Tappan Zee Bridge. Here. Tarrytown to South Nyack."

"What if we closed that off?"

"And he kept going north, trying to get across? Bear Mountain Bridge is next. He's still south of Chilton."

"And if we blocked the Bear Mountain Bridge?"

"Then he's got to go up to the Newburgh-Beacon Bridge. Now he's north of Chilton."

Delaney took a deep breath, put his hands on his waist. He began to pace about the study.

"We could block every goddamned bridge up to Albany," he said, speaking to himself as much as to Blankenship. "Keep him on the east side of the river. What the hell for? I want him to go to his hole. He's heading for Chilton. He feels safe there. He's alone there. If we block him, he'll just keep running, and God only knows what he'll do."

Blankenship said, almost timidly, "There's always the possibility he might have made it across the George Washington Bridge, sir. Shouldn't we alert Jersey? Just in case."

"The hell with them."

"And the FBI?"

"Fuck 'em."

"And the New York State cops?"

"Those shitheads? With their sombreros. You think I'm going to let those apple-knockers waltz in and grab the headlines? Fat chance! This boy is mine. You got your pad?"

"Yes, sir. Right here."

"Take some notes. No . . . wait a minute."

Captain Delaney strode to the door of the radio room, yanked it open. There were more men; the recalls were coming in. Delaney pointed at the first man he saw. "You. Come here."

"Me, sir?"

The Captain grabbed him by the arm, pulled him inside the study, slammed the door behind him.

"What's your name?"

"Javis, John J. Detective second grade."

"Detective Javis, I am about to give orders to Detective first grade Ronald Blankenship. I want you to do nothing but listen and, in case of a Departmental hearing, testify honestly as to what you heard."

Javis' face went white.

"It's not necessary, sir," Blankenship said.

Delaney gave him a particularly sweet smile. "I know it isn't," he said softly. "But I'm cutting corners. If it works, fine. If not, it's my ass. It's been in a sling before. All right, let's go. Take notes on this. You listen carefully, Javis.

"Do all this through Communications. To New Jersey State Police, to the FBI, to New York State Police, a fugitive alert on Danny Boy. Complete description of him and car. Photos to follow. Apprehend and hold for questioning. Exercise extreme caution. Wanted for multiple homicide. Armed and dangerous. Got that?"

"Yes, sir."

"A *general* alert. The fugitive can be anywhere. You understand?"

"Yes, sir. I understand."

"Phone calls from here to police in Tarrytown, Bear Mountain, Beacon. Same alert. But tell them, do not stop or interfere with suspect. Let him run. If he crosses their bridge, call us. Let him get across the river but inform us immediately. Tell them he's a cop-killer. Got that?"

"Yes, sir," Blankenship nodded, writing busily. "If he tries to cross at the Tappan Zee, Bear Mountain, or Newburgh-Beacon Bridges, they are to let him cross but observe and call us. Correct?"

"Correct," Delaney said definitely. He looked at Javis. "You heard all that?"

"Yes, sir," the man faltered.

"Good," Delaney nodded. "Outside and stand by."

When the door closed behind the detective, Blankenship repeated, "You didn't have to do that, Captain."

"Screw it."

"You're going after him?"

"Yes."

"Can I come?"

"No. I need you here. Get those alerts off. I'll take the three cars from Special Operations and more men. I don't know the range of the radios. If they fade, I'll check by phone. I'll call on my private line here." He put his hand on his desk phone. "Put a man in here. No out-going calls. Keep it clear. I'll keep calling. You keep checking with Tarrytown, Bear Mountain and Beacon, to see where he goes across. You got all this?"

"Yes," Blankenship said, still jotting notes. "I'm caught up."

"Bring MacDonald back to Barbara. The two of you start on the paperwork. You handle the relief end: schedules, manpower, cars, and so forth. MacDonald is to get the statements, the questioning of everyone we took in. Clean up all the crap. He'll know what to do."

"Yes, sir."

"If Deputy Inspector Thorsen calls, just tell him I'm following and will contact him as soon as possible."

Blankenship looked up. "Should I call the hospital, sir?" he asked. "About your wife?"

Delaney looked at him, shocked. How long had it been?

"Yes," he said softly. "Thank you. And about Fernandez, Tiger One, and Bulldog Three. I'd appreciate that. I'll check with you when I call in. Let's see . . . Is there anything else? Any questions?"

"Can I come with you, sir?"

"Next time," Captain Edward X. Delaney said. "Get on those alerts right now."

The moment the door closed behind Blankenship, Delaney was on the phone. He got information, asking for police headquarters in Chilton, New York. It took time for the call to go through, but he wasn't impatient. If he was right, time didn't matter. And if he was wrong, time didn't matter.

Finally, he heard the clicks, the pauses, the buzzing, then the final regular ring.

"Chilton Police Department. Help you?"

"Could I speak to the commanding officer, please?"

A throaty chuckle. "Commanding Officer? Guess that's me. Chief Forrest. What can I do for you for?"

"Chief, this is Captain Edward X. Delaney, New York Police Department. New York *City*. I've got—"

"Well!" the Chief said. "This *is* nice. How's the weather down there?"

"Fine," Delaney said. "No complaints. A little nippy, but the sun's out and the sky's blue."

"Same here," the voice rumbled, "and the radio feller says it's going to stay just like this for another week. Hope he's right."

"Chief," Delaney said, "I've got a favor I'd like to ask of you."

"Why, yes," Forrest said. "Thought you might."

Delaney was caught up short. This was no country bumpkin.

"Got a man on the run," he said rapidly. "Five homicides known, including a cop. Ice ax. In a Chevy Corvette. Heading—"

"Whoa, whoa," the Chief said. "You city fellers talk so fast I can't hardly make sense. Just slow down a mite and spell it out."

"I've got a fugitive on the run," Delaney said slowly, obediently. "He's killed five people, including a New York City detective. He crushed their skulls with an ice ax."

"Mountain climber?"

"Yes," the Captain said, beginning to appreciate Chief Forrest. "It's just a slim chance, but I think he may be heading for the Chilton State Park. That's near you, isn't it?"

"Was, the last time I looked. About two miles out of town. What makes you think he's heading there?"

"Well . . . it's a long story. But he's been up there to climb. There's some rock—I forget the name—but apparently he—"

"Devil's Needle," Forrest said.

"Yes, that's it. He's been up there before, and I figured—"

"Park closed for the winter."

"If he wanted to get in, how would he do it, Chief?"

"It's a small park. Not like the Adirondacks. Nothing like that. Chain-link fence all around. One gate with a padlock. I reckon he could smash the gate or climb the fence. No big problem. This fugitive of yours—he a crazy?"

"Yes."

"Probably smash the gate. Well, Captain, what can I do you for?"

"Chief, I was wondering if you could send one of your men out there. Just to watch. You understand? If this nut shows up, I just want him observed. What he does. Where he goes. I don't want anyone trying to take him. I'm on my way with ten men. All I want is him holed up."

"Uh-huh," Chief Forrest said. "I think I got the picture. You call the State boys?"

"Alert going out right now."

"Uh-huh. Kinda out of your territory, isn't it, Captain?"

Shrewd bastard, Delaney thought desperately.

"Yes, it is," he confessed.

"But you're bringing up ten men?"

"Well . . . yes. If we can be of any help . . ."

"Uh-huh. And you just want a watch on the Park gate. Out of sight naturally. Just to see where this crazy goes and what he does. Have I got it right?"

"Exactly right," Delaney said thankfully. "If you could just send one of your men out . . ."

There was a silence that extended so long that finally Captain Delaney said, "Hello? Hello? Are you there?"

"Oh, I'm here, I'm here. But when you talk about sending out one of my men, I got to tell you, Captain: there ain't no men. I'm it. Chief Forrest. The Chilton Police Department. I suppose you think that's funny, a one-man po-*leece* department calling hisself 'Chief.' I know what a big-city 'Chief' means."

"I don't think it's funny," Delaney said. "Different places have different titles and different customs. That doesn't mean one is any better or any worse than another."

"Sonny," Chief Forrest rumbled, "I'm looking forward to meeting you. You sound like a real bright boy. Now you get up here with your ten men. Meanwhile, I'll mosey out to the Park and see what I can see. It's been a slow day."

"Thank you, Chief," Delaney said gratefully. "But it may take some time."

"Time?" the deep voice laughed. "Captain, we got plenty of that around here."

Delaney made one more call, to Thomas Handry. But the reporter wasn't in, so he left a message. "Break it. Blank running. After him. Call Thorsen. Delaney." Having paid his debt, he hitched up his gun belt, hooked his choker collar. He went into the radio room, pointed at three men; they all headed out to the heavy, armed cars waiting at the curb.

Still high, the air in his lungs as sharp and dry as good gin, Daniel Blank came dashing down the inside staircase of Celia Montfort's home, leaped over the fallen Valenter, went sailing out into the thin winter sunlight, those distant screams pursuing him.

There was a man kneeling on the sidewalk between Blank and his car. This man saw Blank coming; his face twisted into an expression of wicked menace. He began to rise from his knee, one hand snaked beneath his jacket; Blank understood this man hated him and meant to kill him.

He performed his ax-transferring act as he rushed. He struck the man who was very quick and jerked aside so that the ax point did not enter his skull but crunched in behind his shoulder. But he went down. Daniel wrenched the ice ax free, ran to his car, conscious of shouts from across the avenue. Another man came dodging through traffic, pointing his finger at Blank. Then there were light, sharp explosions—snaps, really—and something smacked into and through the car body. Then there was a hole in the left window, another in the windshield, and he felt a stroke of air across his cheek, light as an angel's kiss.

The man was front left and seemed determined to yank open the door or point his finger again. Blank caught a confused impression of black features contorted in fear and fury. There was nothing to do but accelerate, knock the man aside. So he did that, heard the thud as the body went flying, but he didn't look back.

He turned west onto 86th Street, saw a double-parked car with three men scrambling to get out. More shouts, more explosions, but then he was moving fast down 86th Street, hearing the rising and dwindling blare of horns, the squeal of brakes as he breezed through red lights, cut to the wrong side of the street to avoid a pile-up, cut back in, increasing speed, hearing a far-off siren, enjoying all this, loving it, because he had cut that telephone line that held him to the world, and now he was alone, all alone, no one could touch him. Ever again.

He took Traverse No. 3 across Central Park, turned right on Broadway, went north to 96th Street, made a left to get onto the Henry Hudson Parkway, which everyone called the West Side Drive. He went humming north on the Drive, keeping up with the traffic, no faster, no slower, and laughed because it had all been such a piece of cake. No one could touch him; not even the two police squads screaming by him, sirens open, could bring him down or spoil the zest of this bright, lively, *new* day.

But there was some kind of hassle at the Bridge—maybe an accident—and traffic was backing up. So he just stayed on the Parkway, went winging north as traffic thinned out and he could sing a little song—what was it? That same folksong he had been crooning earlier—and tap his hands in time on the steering wheel.

North of Yonkers he pulled onto the verge, stopped, unfolded his map. He could take the Parkway to the Thruway, cross the Tappan Zee Bridge to South Nyack. Around Palisades Interstate Park to 32, take that to Mountainville. Then south to Chilton. Simple . . . and beautiful. Everything was like that today.

He was folding up his map when a police car pulled alongside on the Parkway. The officer in the passenger's seat jerked his thumb north. Blank nodded, pulled off the verge, fell in behind the squad car, but kept his speed down until the cops were far ahead, out of sight. They hadn't even noticed the holes in window, windshield, car body.

He had no trouble, no trouble at all. Not even any toll to pay going west on the Tappan Zee. If he returned eastward, of course, he'd have to pay a toll. But he didn't think he'd be returning. He drove steadily, a mile or two above the limit, and almost before he knew it, he was in and out of Chilton, heading for the Park. Now his was the only car on the gravel road. No one else anywhere. Wonderful.

He turned into the dirt road leading to the Chilton State Park, saw the locked gate ahead of him. It seemed silly to stop and hack off the padlock with his ice ax, so he simply accelerated, going at almost 50 miles an hour at the moment of impact. He threw his forearm across his eyes when he hit, but the car slammed through the fence easily, the two wings of the gate flinging back. Daniel Blank braked suddenly and stopped. He was inside. He got out of the car and stretched, looking about. Not a soul. Just a winter landscape: naked black trees against a light blue sky. Clean and austere. The breeze was wine, the sun a tarnished coin that glowed softly.

Taking his time, he changed to climbing boots and lined canvas jacket. He threw his black moccasins and topcoat inside the car; he wouldn't need those anymore. At the last minute he also peeled off his formal "Ivy League" wig and left that in the car, too. He pulled the knitted watch cap over his shaved scalp.

He carried his gear to Devil's Needle, a walking climb of less than ten minutes, over a forest trail and rock outcrops. It was good to feel stone beneath his feet again. It was different from city cement. The pavement was a layer, insulating from the real world. But here you were on bare rock, the spine of the earth; you could feel the planet turning beneath your feet. You were close.

At the entrance to the chimney, he put on his webbed belt, attached one end of the nylon line, shook out the coils of rope carefully, attached the other end to all his gear; rucksack, crampons, extra sweater, his ice ax. He put on his rough gloves.

He began to climb slowly, wondering if his muscles had gone slack. But the climb went smoothly; he gained confidence as he hunched and wiggled upward. Then he reached to grasp the embedded pitons, pulled himself onto the flat. He rested a moment, breathing deeply, then rose and hauled up his gear. He unbuckled his belt, dumped everything in a heap. He straightened, put hands on his waist, inhaled deeply, forcing his shoulders back. He looked around.

It was a different scene, a winter scene, one he had never witnessed before from this elevation. It was a steel etching down there: black trees spidery, occasional patches of unmelted snow, shadows and glints, all blacks, greys, browns, the flash of white. He could see the roofs of Chilton and, beyond, the mirror river, seemingly a pond, but moving, he knew, slowly to the sea, to the wide world, to everywhere.

He lighted one of his lettuce cigarettes, watched the smoke swirl away, enter into, disappear. The river became one with the sea, the smoke one with the air. All things became one with another, entered into and merged, until water was land, land water, and smoke was air, air smoke. Why had she smiled in triumph? Now he could think about it.

He sat on the bare stone, bent his legs, rested one cheek on his knee. He unbuttoned canvas jacket, suit jacket, shirt, and slid an ungloved hand inside to feel his own breast, not much flatter than hers. He worked the nipple slowly and thought she had been happy when her eyes turned upward to focus on that shining point of steel rushing downward to mark a period in her brain. She had been happy. She wanted the certitude. Everything she had told him testified to her anguished search for an absolute. And then, wearied of the endless squigglings of her quick and sensitive intelligence—so naked and aware it must have been as painful as an open wound—she had involved him in her plan, urging him on, then betraying him. Knowing what the end would be, wanting it. Yes, he thought, that was what happened.

He sat there a long time—the sky dulling to late afternoon—dreaming over what had happened. Not sorry for what had happened, but feeling a kind of sad joy, because he knew she had found her ultimate truth, and he would find his. So they both—but then he heard the sound of car engines, slam of car doors, and crawled slowly to the edge of Devil's Needle to peer down.

They came down the gravel road from Chilton, saw the sign: "One mile to Chilton State Park," then made their turn onto the dirt road. They pulled up outside the fence. The wings of the gate were leaning crazily. Inside was Daniel Blank's car. A big man, clad in a brown canvas windbreaker with a dirty sheepskin collar, was leaning against the car and watched them as they stopped. There was a six-pack of beer on the hood of the car; the man was sipping slowly from an opened can.

Captain Delaney got out, adjusted his cap, tugged down his jacket. He walked through the ruined gate toward Blank's car, taking out identification. He inspected the big man as he advanced. Six-four, at least; maybe five or six if he straightened up. At least 250, maybe more, mostly in the belly. Had to be pushing 65. Wearing the worn windbreaker, stained corduroy pants, yellow, rubber-soled work shoes laced up over his ankles, a trooper's cap of some kind of black fur. Around his neck the leather cord of what appeared to be Army surplus field glasses from World War I. About his waist, a leather belt blotched with the sweat of a lifetime, supporting one of the biggest dogleg holsters Delaney had ever seen, flap buttoned. On the man's chest, some kind of a shield, star or sunburst; it was difficult to make out.

"Chief Forrest?" Delaney asked, coming up.

"Yep."

"Captain Edward X. Delaney, New York Police Department." He flipped open his identification, held it out.

The Chief took it in a hand not quite the size and color of a picnic ham, and inspected it thoroughly. He passed it back, then held a hand out to Delaney.

"Chief Evelyn F. Forrest," he rumbled. "Pleased to make your acquaintance, Captain. I suppose you think 'Evelyn' is a funny name for a man."

"No, I don't think that. My father's name was Marion. Not so important, is it?"

"Nooo . . . unless you've got it."

"I see our boy got here," Delaney said, patting the fender of the parked car.

"Uh-huh," Forrest nodded. "He arrived. Captain, I've got a cold six-pack here. Would you like . . ."

"Sure. Thank you. Go good right now."

The Chief selected a can, pulled the tab, handed over the beer. They both raised their drinks to each other, then sipped. The Captain inspected the label.

"Never had this brand before," he confessed. "Good. Almost like ale."

"Uh-huh," Chief Forrest nodded. "Local brewery. They don't go into the New York City area, but they sell all they can make."

He had, Delaney decided, the face of an old bloodhound, the skin a dark purplish-brown, hanging in wrinkles and folds: bags, jowls, wattles. But the eyes were unexpectedly young, mild, open; the whites were clear. Must have been quite a boy about 40 years ago, the Captain thought, before the beer got to him, ballooned his gut, slowed him up.

"Look here, Captain," Forrest said. "One of your men got some into him."

The Chief pointed out a bullet hole in the body of the car and another through the left front window.

"Come out here," he continued, pointing to a star-cracked hole in the windshield.

Delaney stooped to sight through the entrance hole in the window and the exit hole in the windshield.

"My God," he said, "by rights it should have taken his brains right along with it, if he was in the driver's seat. The man's got the luck of the Devil."

"Uh-huh," Chief Forrest nodded. "Some of 'em do. Well, here's what happened . . . I get here about an hour before he does, pull off the gravel road into the trees, opposite to the turnoff to the Park. Not such good concealment, but I figure he'll be looking to his right for the Park entrance and won't spot me."

"That makes sense."

"Yep. Well, I'm out of my station wagon, enjoying a brew, when he comes barreling along, pretty as you please. Turns into this here dirt road, sees the locked gate, speeds up, and just cuts right through; hot knife through butter. Then he gets out of the car, stretches, and looks around. I got him in my glasses by now. Handsome lad."

"Yes, he is."

"He starts changing to his outdoor duds: a jacket, boots, and so forth. I got a turn when he ducks into the car with a full head of hair and comes out balder'n a peeled egg."

"He wears a wig."

"Uh-huh. I found it, back there in the car. Looks like a dead muskrat. Also his coat and city shoes. Then he pulls on a cap, packs up his gear, and starts for Devil's Needle. I come across the road then and into the Park."

"Did he spot you?"

"Spot me?" the Chief said in some amazement. "Why no. I still move pretty good, and I know the land around here like the palm of my hand. No, he didn't spot me. Anyways, he gets there, attaches a line to his belt and to his gear, and goes into the chimney. Makes the climb in pretty good time. After awhile I see his line going out, and he pulls up his gear. Then I see him standing on top of Devil's Needle. I see him for just a few seconds, but he's up there all right, Captain; no doubt about that."

"Did you see any food in his gear? Or a canteen? Anything like that?"

"Nope. Nothing like that. But he had a rucksack. Might have had food and drink in that."

"Maybe."

"Captain . . ."

"Yes, Chief?"

"That alert you phoned to the State boys . . . You know, they pass it on to all us local chiefs and sheriffs by radio. I was on my way out here when I heard the call. Didn't mention nothing about Chilton."

"Uh . . . well, I didn't mention Chilton to them. It was just a hunch, and I didn't want them charging out here on what might have been a wild-goose chase."

The Chief looked at him steadily a long moment. "Sonny," he said softly, "I don't know what your beef is with the State boys, and I don't want to know. I admit they can be a stiff-necked lot. But Captain, when this here is cleaned up, you're going back home. This is my home, and I got to deal with the State boys every day in the week. Now if they find out I knew a homicidal maniac was holed up on State property and didn't let them know, they'll be a mite put out, Captain, just a mite put out."

Delaney scuffed at the dirt with the toe of his city shoe, looking down. "Guess you're right," he muttered finally. "It's just . . ." He looked up at the Chief; his voice trailed away.

"Sonny," Forrest said in a kindly voice, "I been in this business a lot longer'n you, and I know what it means to be after a man, to track him for a long time, and to corner him. Then the idea of anyone but you takin' him is enough to drive you right up into the rafters."

"Yes," Delaney nodded miserably. "Something like that."

"But you see my side of it, don't you, Captain? I got to call them. I'll do it anyway, but I'd rather you say, 'All right.' "

"All right. I can understand it. How do you get them?"

"Radio in my wagon. I can reach the troop. I'll be right back."

The Chief moved off, up the dirt road, with a remarkably light stride for a man his age and weight. Captain Delaney stood by Blank's car, looking through the window at the coat, the shoes, the wig. They already had the shapeless, dusty look of possessions of a man long dead.

He should be feeling an exultation, he knew, at having snubbed Daniel Blank. But instead he felt a sense of dread. Reaction to the excitement of the morning, he supposed, but there seemed to be more to it than that. The dread was for the future, for what lay ahead. "Finish the job," he told himself, "Finish the job." He refused to imagine what the finish might be. He remembered what his Army colonel had told him: "The best soldiers have no imagination."

He turned as Chief Forrest came driving through the sprung gate in an old, dilapidated station wagon with "Chilton Police Department" painted on the side in flaking red letters. He pulled up alongside Blank's car. "On their way," he called to Delaney. "About twenty minutes or so, I reckon."

He got from behind the wheel with some difficulty, grunting and puffing, then reached back inside to haul out two more six-packs of beer. He held them out to Delaney.

"For your boys," he said. "While they're waiting."

"Why, thank you, Chief. That's kind of you. Hope it's not leaving you short."

Forrest's big belly shook with laughter. "That'll be the day," he rumbled.

The Captain smiled, took the six-packs over to his cars.

"Better get out and stretch your legs," he advised his men. "Looks like we'll be here awhile. The State boys are on their way. Here's some beer, compliments of Chief Forrest of the Chilton Police Department."

The men got out of the cars happily, headed for the beer. Delaney went back to the Chief.

"Could we take a close look at Devil's Needle?" he asked.

"Why sure."

"I've got three snipers with me, and I'd like to locate a spot where they could cover the entrance to the chimney and the top of the rock. Just in case."

"Uh-huh. This fugitive of yours armed, Captain?"

"Just the ice ax, as far as I know. As for a gun, I can't guarantee either way.

Chief, you don't have to come with me. Just point out the way, and I'll get there."

"Shit," Chief Forrest said disgustedly, "that's the first dumb thing you've said, sonny."

He started off with his light, flat-footed stride; Captain Delaney stumbled after him. They made their way down a faint dirt path winding through the skeleton trees.

Then they came to the out-crops. Captain Delaney's soles slipped on the shiny rocks while Chief Forrest stepped confidently, never missing his footing, not looking down, but striding and moving like a gargantuan ballet dancer to the base of Devil's Needle. When Delaney came up, breathing heavily, the Chief had opened his holster flap and was bending it back, tucking it under that sweat-stained belt.

Delaney jerked his chin toward the dogleg holster. "What do you carry, Chief?" he asked, one professional to another.

"Colt forty-four. Nine-inch barrel. It belonged to my daddy. He was a lawman, too. Replaced the pin and one of the grips, but otherwise it's in prime condition. A nice piece."

The Captain nodded and turned his eyes, unwilling, to Devil's Needle. He raised his head slowly. The granite shaft poked into the sky, tapering slightly as it rose. There were mica glints that caught the late afternoon sunlight, and patches of dampness. A blotter of moss here and there. The surface was generally smooth and wind-worn, but there was a network of small cracks: a veiny stone torso.

He squinted at the top. It was strange to think of Daniel G. Blank up there. Near and far. Far.

"About eighty feet?" he guessed aloud.

"Closer to sixty-five, seventy, I reckon," Chief Forrest rumbled.

Up and down. They were separated. Captain Delaney had never felt so keenly the madness of the world. For some reason, he thought of lovers separated by glass or a fence, or a man and woman, strangers, exchanging an eye-to-eye stare on the street, on a bus, in a restaurant, a wall of convention or fear between them, yet unbearably close in that look and never to be closer.

"Inside," he said in a clogged voice, and stepped carefully into the opening of the vertical cleft, the chimney. He smelled the rank dampness, felt the chill of stone shadow. He tilted his head back. Far above, in the gloom, was a wedge of pale blue sky.

"A one-man climb," Chief Forrest said, his voice unexpectedly loud in the cavern. "You wiggle your way up, using your back and feet, then your hands and knees as the rock squeezes in. He's up there with an ice ax, ain't no man getting up there now unless he says so. You've got to use both hands."

"You've made the climb, Chief?"

Forrest grunted shortly. "Uh-huh. Many, many times. But that was years ago, before my belly got in the way."

"What's it like up there?"

"Oh, about the size of a double bedsheet. Flat, but sloping some to the south. Pitted and shiny. Some shallow rock hollows. Right nice view."

They came outside, Delaney looked up again.

"You figure sixty-five, seventy feet?"

"About."

"We could get a cherry-picker from the Highway Department, or I could bring up a ladder truck from the New York Fire Department. They can go up a hundred feet. But there's no way to get a truck close enough; not down that path and across the rocks. Unless we build a road. And that would take a month."

They were silent then.

"Helicopter?" Delaney said finally.

"Yes," Forrest acknowledged. "They could blast him from that. Tricky in these downdrafts and cross-currents, but I reckon it could be done."

"It could be done," Captain Delaney agreed tonelessly. "Or we could bring in a fighter plane to blow him away with rockets and machineguns."

Silence again.

"Don't set right with you, does it, sonny?" the Chief asked softly.

"No, it doesn't. To you?"

"No. I never did hanker to shoot fish in a barrel."

"Let's get back."

On the way, they selected a tentative site for the snipers. It was back in a clump of firs, offering some concealment but providing a clear field of fire covering the entrance to the chimney and the top of Devil's Needle.

The State police had not yet arrived. Delaney's men were lounging in and out of the cars, nursing their beers. The three pale snipers stood a little apart from the others, talking quietly, hugging their rifles in canvas cases.

"Chief, I've got to make some phone calls. Do I go into Chilton?"

"No need. Right there." Forrest waved his hand toward the gate-keeper's cottage. He pointed out the telephone wire that ran on wooden poles back to the gravel road. "They keep that line open all winter. Highway crews plowing snow use it, and Park people who come in for early spring planting."

They walked over to the weathered wooden shack, stepped up onto the porch. Delaney inspected the hasp closed with a heavy iron padlock.

"Got a key?" he asked.

"Sure," the Chief said, pulling the massive revolver out of his holster. "Step back a mite, sonny."

The Captain backed away hastily, and Chief Forrest negligently shot the lock away. Delaney noted he aimed at the shackle, not the body of the lock where a bullet might do nothing but jam the works. He was beginning to admire the old man. The explosion was unexpectedly loud; echoes banged back and forth; Delaney's men rose uneasily to their feet. Two brown birds took off from the dry underbrush alongside the dirt road, went whirring off with raucous cries.

The Chief pushed the door open. The cabin smelled dusty and stale. An old, wood-based "cookie-cutter" phone was attached to the wall, operated by a little hand crank.

"Haven't seen one of those in years," Delaney observed.

"We still got a few around. The operator's name is Muriel. You might tell her I'm out here, in case she's got any words for me." He left Delaney alone in the shack.

The Captain spun the crank; Muriel came on with pleasing promptness. Delaney identified himself, and gave her the Chief's message.

"Well, his wife wants to know if she should hold supper," she said. "You tell him that."

"I will."

"You got the killer out there?" she asked sternly.

"Something like that. Can I get through to New York City?"

"Of course. What do you think?"

He called Blankenship first and reported the situation as briefly as he could. He told the detective to call Deputy Inspector Thorsen and repeat Delaney's message.

Then he called Barbara at the hospital. It was a harrowing call; his wife was weeping, and he couldn't find out the cause. Finally a nurse came on the phone and told the Captain his wife was hysterical; she didn't think the call should be continued. He hung up, bewildered and frightened.

Then he called Dr. Sanford Ferguson, and got him in his office.

"Captain Edward X. Delaney here."

"Edward! Congratulations! I hear you got him."

"Not exactly. He's on top of a rock, and we can't get to him."

"On top of a rock?"

"High. Sixty-five, seventy feet. Doctor, how long can a man live without food and water?"

"Food *or* water? About ten days, I'd guess. Maybe less."

"Ten days? That's all?"

"Sure. The food isn't so important. The water is. Dehydration is the problem."

"How long does it take to get to him?"

"Oh . . . twenty-four hours."

"Then what?"

"What you might expect. Tissue shrinks, strength goes, the kidneys fail. Joints ache. But by that time, the victim doesn't care. One of the first psychological symptoms is loss of will, a lassitude. Something like freezing to death. He'll lose from one-fifth to one-quarter of his body weight in fluids. Dizziness. Loss of voluntary muscles. Weakness. Can't see. Blurry images. Probably begin to hallucinate after the third day. The bladder goes. Just before death, the belly swells up. Not a pleasant way to die—but what is? Edward, is that what's going to happen?"

"I don't know. Thank you for your help."

He broke the connection, put in a call to Monica Gilbert. But when she recognized his voice, she hung up; he didn't try to call her again.

He came out onto the cottage porch and said to Forrest: "Your wife wants to know if she should hold supper."

"Uh-huh," the Chief nodded. "I'll let her know when I know. Captain, why don't—" He stopped suddenly, tilted his head. "Sireens," he said. "Coming fast. That'll be the troopers."

It was five seconds before Captain Delaney heard them. Finally, two cars careened around the curve into the Park entrance, skidded to a stop outside the fence, their sirens sighing slowly down. Four men in each car and, bringing up the rear, a beat-up Ford sedan with "Orange County Clarion" lettered on the side. One man in that.

Delaney came down off the porch and watched as the eight troopers piled out of their cars, put their hands on their polished holsters.

"Beautiful," he said aloud.

Then one man, not too tall, wider in the hips than the shoulders, stalked through the gate toward them.

"Oh-oh," Chief Forrest murmured. "Here comes Smokey the Bear."

The Captain took out his identification, watching the approaching officer. He was wearing the grey woolen winter uniform of the New York State Police, leather belt and holster gleaming wickedly. Squarely atop his head was the broad-brimmed, straight-brimmed, stiff-brimmed Stetson. He carried his chin out in front of him, a bare elbow, with narrow shoulders back, pigeon breast thrust. He marched up to them, stood vacant-faced. He glanced at Chief Forrest and nodded slightly, then stared at Delaney.

"Who are you?" he demanded.

The Captain looked at him a moment, then proffered his identification. "Captain Edward X. Delaney, New York Police Department. Who are you?"

"Captain Bertram Sneed, New York State Police."

"How do I know that?"

"Jesus Christ. What do I look like?"

"Oh, you look like a cop. No doubt about it; you're wearing a cop's uniform. But four men in cops' uniforms pulled the St. Valentine's Day Massacre. You just can't be too sure. Here's my ID. Where's yours?"

Sneed opened his trap mouth, then shut it suddenly with a snap of teeth. He opened one button of his woolen jacket, tugged out his identification. They exchanged.

As they examined each other's credentials, Delaney was conscious of men moving in, his men and Sneed's men. They sensed a confrontation of brass, and they wouldn't miss it for the world.

Sneed and Delaney took back their ID cards.

"Captain," Sneed said harshly, "we got a jurisdiction problem here."

"Oh?" Delaney said. "Is that our problem?"

"Yes. This here Park is State property, under the protection of the New York State Police Organization. You're out of your territory."

Captain Delaney put away his identification, tugged down his jacket, squared his cap away.

"You're right," he smiled genially. "I'll just take my men and get out. Nice to have met you, captain. Chief. Goodby."

He was turning away when Sneed said, "Hey, wait a minute."

Delaney paused. "Yes?"

"What's the problem here?"

"Why," Delaney said blandly, "it's a problem of jurisdiction. Just like you said."

"No, no. I mean what have we got? Where's this here fugitive?"

"Oh . . . *him*. Well, he's sitting on top of Devil's Needle."

Chief Forrest had fished a wooden match from his side pocket and inserted the bare end into the corner of his mouth. He appeared to be sucking on it, watching the two captains with a benign smile on his droopy features.

"Sitting on top of the rock?" Sneed said. "Shit, is that all? We got some good climbers in our outfit. I'll send a couple of men up there and we'll take him."

Delaney had turned away again, taken a few steps. His back was to Sneed when he halted, put his hands on his waist, then turned back again. He came close to Sneed.

"You shit-headed, wet-brained sonofabitch," he said pleasantly. "By all rights, I should take my men and go and leave you to stew in your own juice, you fucking idiot. But when you talk about sending a brave man to his death because of your stupidity, I got to speak my piece. You haven't even made a physical reconnaissance, for Christ's sake. That's a one-man climb, captain, and every man you send up there will get his skull crushed in. Is that what you want?"

Sneed's puppet face had gone white under the lash of Delaney's invective. Then red blotches appeared on his cheeks, discs of rouge, and his hands worked convulsively. Everyone stood in silence, frozen. But there was an interruption. A heavy white van turned into the entrance from the gravel road; heads turned to look at it. It was a mobile TV van from one of the national networks. They watched it park outside the gate. Men got out and began unloading equipment. Sneed turned back to Delaney.

"Well . . . hell," he said, smiling triumphantly, "so I won't send a man up. But the first thing tomorrow morning, I'll have a helicopter up there and we'll pick him off. Make a great TV picture."

"Oh yes," Delaney agreed. "A great TV picture. Of course, this man is just a suspect right now. He hasn't been convicted of *anything*. Hasn't even been tried. But you send your chopper up and grease him. I can see the headlines now: 'State Cops Machine-gun Suspect on Mountaintop.' Good publicity for your outfit. Good public relations. Especially after Attica."

The last word stiffened Captain Bertram Sneed. He didn't breathe, his arms hanging like fluked anchors at his side.

"Another thing," Delaney went on. "See that TV truck out there? By dawn, there'll be two more. And reporters and photographers from newspapers and magazines. It's already been on radio. If you don't get the roads around here closed off in a hell of a hurry, by morning you'll have a hundred thousand creeps and nuts with their wives and kiddies and picnic baskets of fried chicken, all hurrying to be in on the kill. Just like Floyd Collins in the cave."

"I got to make a phone call," Captain Sneed said hoarsely. He looked around frantically. Chief Forrest jerked a thumb toward the gate-keeper's cottage. Sneed hurried toward it. "You stay here a minute," he called back to Delaney. "Please," he added.

He got up on the porch, saw the smashed lock.

"Who blew open this door?" he cried.

"I did," Chief Forrest said equably.

"State property," Sneed said indignantly, and disappeared inside.

"O Lord, will my afflictions never cease?" the Chief asked.

"I shouldn't have talked to him like that," Delaney said in a low voice, his head bowed. "Especially in front of his men."

"Oh, I don't know, Captain," the Chief said, still sucking on his matchstick. "I've heard better cussing-outs than that. Besides, you didn't say nothing his men haven't been saying for years. Amongst theirselves, of course."

"Who do you think he's calling?"

"I know exactly who he's calling: Major Samuel Barnes. He's in command of Sneed's troop."

"What's he like?"

"Sam? Cut from a different piece of cloth. A hard little man, smart as a whip. Knows his business. Sam comes from up near Woodstock. I knew his daddy. Hy Barnes made the best applejack in these parts, but Sam don't like to be reminded of that. Smokey the Bear will explain the situation, and Major Sam will listen carefully. Sneed will complain about you being here, and he'll tell Sneed what you said about machinegunning that man from a chopper, and what you said about a mob of nuts descending on us tomorrow. Sneed will tell the Mayor *you* said those things, because he's too damned dumb to take credit for them hisself. Sam Barnes will think a few seconds, then he'll say, 'Sneed, you turd-kicking nincompoop, you get your fat ass out there and ask that New York City cop, just as polite as you can, if he'll stick around and tell you what to do until I can get on the scene. And if you haven't fucked things up too bad by the time I get there, you might—you just might—live to collect your pension, you asshole.' Now you stick around a few minutes, sonny, and see if I ain't exactly right."

A few moments later Captain Sneed came out of the cottage, pulling on his gloves. His face was still white, and he moved like a man who has just been kneed in the groin. He came over to them with a ghastly smile.

"Captain," he said. "I don't see why we can't cooperate on this."

"Cooperation!" the Chilton Chief cried unexpectedly. "That's what makes the world go 'round!"

They went to work, and by midnight they had it pretty well squared away, although many of the men and much of the equipment they had requisitioned had not yet arrived. But at least they had a tentative plan, filled it in and revised it as they went along.

The first thing they did was to establish a four-man walking patrol around the base of Devil's Needle, the sentries carrying shotguns and sidearms. The walkers did four hours on, and eight off.

Delaney's snipers established their blind in the fir copse, sitting crossed-legged atop folded blankets. They had mounted their scopes, donned black sweaters and pants, socks and shoes, jackets and tight black gloves. Each wore a flak vest on watch.

Squad cars were driven in as close as possible; their headlights and searchlights were used to illuminate the scene. Portable battery lanterns were set out to open up the shadows. Captain Delaney had called Special Operations and requisitioned a generator truck and a flatbed of heavy searchlights with cables long enough so the lights could be set up completely around Devil's Needle.

Captain Bertram Sneed was bringing in a field radio receiver-transmitter; the local power company was running in a temporary line. The local telephone company was bringing in extra lines and setting up pay phones for the press.

Major Samuel Barnes had not yet put in an appearance, but Delaney spoke to him on the phone. Barnes was snappish and all business. He promised to reshuffle his patrol schedules and send another twenty troopers over by bus as soon as possible. He was also working on the road blocks, and expected to have the Chilton area sealed off by dawn.

He and Delaney agreed on some ground rules. Delaney would be the on-the-spot commander with Sneed acting as his deputy. But Major Barnes would be nominal commander when the first report to the press was made, calling the siege of Devil's Needle a "joint operation" of New York State and New York City police. All press releases were to be okayed by both sides; no press conferences were to be held or interviews granted without representatives of both sides present.

Before agreeing, Captain Delaney called Deputy Inspector Thorsen to explain the situation and outline the terms of the oral agreement with the State. Thorsen said he'd call back; Delaney suspected he was checking with Deputy Mayor Alinski. In any event, Thorsen called back shortly and gave him the okay.

Little of what they accomplished would have been possible without the aid of Chief Evelyn Forrest. Laconic, unflappable, never rushing, the man was a miracle of efficiency, joshing the executives of the local power and telephone companies to get their men cracking.

It was Forrest who brought out a highway crew to open up the shut-off water fountains in the Park and set up two portable chemical toilets. The Chief also got the Chilton High School, closed for the Christmas holiday, to open up the gymnasium, to be used as a dormitory for the officers assigned to Devil's Needle. Cots, mattresses, pillows and blankets were brought in from the county National Guard armory. Forrest even remembered to alert the Chilton disaster unit; they provided a van with sides that folded down to form counters. They served hot coffee and doughnuts in the Park around the clock, the van staffed by lady volunteers.

Chief Forrest had offered Captain Delaney the hospitality of his home, but the Captain opted for a National Guard cot set up in the gate-keeper's cottage. But, the night being unexpectedly chill, he did accept the Chief's loan of a coat. What a garment it was! Made of grey herringbone tweed, it was lined with raccoon fur with a wide collar of beaver. It came to Delaney's ankles, the cuffs to his knuckles. The weight of it bowed his shoulders, but it was undeniably warm.

"My daddy's coat," Chief Forrest said proudly. "Made in Philadelphia in Nineteen-and-one. Can't buy a coat like that these days."

So they all worked hard, and Delaney had one moment of laughing fear when he thought of what fools they'd all look if it turned out that somehow Daniel G. Blank had already climbed down off his perch and escaped into the night. But he put that thought away from him.

Shortly after dark they started bullhorn appeals to the fugitive, to be repeated every hour on the hour:

"Daniel Blank, this is the police. You are surrounded and have no chance of escape. Come down and you will not be hurt. You will be given a fair trial, represented by legal counsel. Come down now and save yourself a lot of trouble. Daniel Blank, you will not be injured in any way if you come down now. You have no chance of escape."

"Do any good, you think?" Forrest asked Delaney.

"No."

"Well," the Chief sighed. "at least it'll make it harder for him to get some sleep."

By 11:30 p.m., Delaney felt bone-weary and cruddy, wanted nothing more than a hot bath and eight hours of sleep. Yet when he lay down on his cold cot without undressing, just to rest for a few moments, he could not close his eyes, but lay stiffly awake, brain churning, nerves jangling. He rose, pulled on that marvelous coat, walked out onto the porch.

There were a lot of men still about—detectives and troopers, power and telephone repairmen, highway crews, reporters, television technicians. Delaney leaned against the railing, observed that all of them, sooner or later, went wandering off, affecting nonchalance, but looking back in guilt, anxious to see if anyone had noted their departure, half-ashamed of what they were doing. He knew what they were doing; they were going to Devil's Needle to stand, stare up and wonder.

He did the same thing himself, drawn against his will. He went as far as the rock outcrops, then stepped back into the shadow of a huge, leafless sugar maple. From there he could see the slowly circling sentries, the sniper sitting patiently on his blanket, rifle cradled on one arm. And there were all the men who had come to watch, standing with heads thrown back, mouths open, eyes turned upward.

Then there was the palely illumined bulk of Devil's Needle itself, looming like a veined apparition in the night. Captain Delaney, too, lifted his head, opened his mouth, turned his eyes upward. Above the stone, dimly, he could see stars whirling their courses in a black vault that went on forever.

He felt a vertigo, not so much of the body as of the spirit. He had never been so unsure of himself. His life seemed giddy and without purpose. Everything was toppling. His wife was dying and Devil's Needle was falling. Monica Gilbert hated him and that man up there, that man . . . he knew it all. Yes, Captain Edward X. Delaney decided, that man now knew it all, or was moving toward it with purpose and delight.

He became conscious of someone standing near him. Then he heard the words.

". . . soon as I could," Thomas Handry was saying. "Thanks for the tip. I filed a background story and then drove up. I'm staying at a motel just north of Chilton."

Delaney nodded.

"You all right, Captain?"

"Yes. I'm all right."

Handry turned to look at Devil's Needle. Like the others, his head went back, mouth opened, eyes rolled up.

Suddenly they heard the bullhorn boom. It was midnight.

The bullhorn clicked off. The watching men strained their eyes upward. There was no movement atop Devil's Needle.

"He's not coming down, is he, Captain?" Handry asked softly.

"No," Captain Delaney said wonderingly. "He's not coming down."

6

He awoke the first morning on Devil's Needle, and it seemed to him he had been dreaming. He remembered a voice calling, "Daniel Blank . . . Daniel Blank . . ." That could have been his mother because she always used his full name. "Daniel Blank, have you done your homework? Daniel Blank, I want you to go to the store for me. Daniel Blank, did you wash your hands?" That was strange, he realized for the first time—she never called him Daniel or Dan or son.

He looked at his watch; it showed 11:43. But that was absurd, he knew; the sun was just rising. He peered closer and saw the sweep second hand had stopped; he had forgotten to wind it. Well, he could wind it now, set it approximately, but time really didn't matter. He slipped the gold expansion band off his wrist, tossed the watch over the side.

He rummaged through his rucksack. When he found he had neglected to pack sandwiches and a thermos, he was not perturbed. It was not important.

He had slept fully clothed, crampons wedged under his ribs, spikes up, so he wouldn't roll off Devil's Needle in his sleep. Now he climbed shakily to his feet, feeling stiffness in shoulders and hips, and stood in the center of the little rock plateau where he could not be seen from the ground. He did stretching exercises, bending sideways at the waist, hands on hips; then bending down, knees locked, to place his palms flat on the chill stone; then jogging in place while he counted off five minutes.

He was gasping for breath when he finished, and his knees were trembling; he really wasn't in very good condition, he acknowledged, and resolved to spend at least an hour a day in stretching and deep-breathing exercises. But then he heard his name being called again. Lying on his stomach, he inched cautiously to the edge of Devil's Needle.

Yes, they were calling his name, asking him to come down, promising he wouldn't be hurt. He wasn't interested in that, but he was surprised by the number of men and vehicles down there. The packed dirt compound around the gate-keeper's cottage was crowded; everyone seemed very busy with some job they were all doing. When he looked directly downward, he could see armed men circling the base of Devil's Needle, but whether they were protecting the others from him or him from the others, he could not say and didn't care.

He felt a need to urinate, and did so, lying on his side, peeing so the stream went over the edge of the rock. There wasn't very much, and it seemed to him of a milky whiteness, not golden at all. There was a clogged heaviness in his bowels, but the difficulties of defecating up there, what he would do with the excrement, how he would wipe himself clean, were such that he resisted the urge, rolled back to the center of the stone, lay on his back, stared at the new sun.

At no time had he debated with himself and come to a conscious decision to stay up there, to die up there. It was just something his mind grasped instinctively and accepted. He was not driven to it; even now he could descend if he wanted to. But he didn't. He was content where he was, in a condition of almost drowsy ease. And he was safe; that was important. He had his ice ax and could easily smash the skull of any climber who came after him. But what if one should come in the dark, wiggling his way silently upward to kill Daniel G. Blank as he slept?

He didn't think it likely that anyone would attempt a night climb, but just to make it more difficult, he took his ice ax and using it as a hammer, knocked loose the two pitons that aided the final crawl from the chimney to the top of Devil's Needle. The task took a long time; he had to rest awhile after the pitons were free. Then he slid them skittering across the stone, watched them disappear over the side.

Then they were calling his name again, a great mechanical booming: "Daniel Blank . . . Daniel Blank . . ." He wished they wouldn't do that. For a moment he thought of shouting down and telling them to stop. But they probably wouldn't. The thing was, it was disturbing his reverie, intruding on his isolation. He was enjoying his solitude, but it should have been a silent separateness.

He rolled over on his face, warming now as the watery sun rose higher. Beneath his eyes, close, close, he saw the rock itself, its texture. In all his years of mountain climbing and rock collecting, he had never looked at stone in that manner, seeing beneath the worn surface gloss, penetrating to the deep heart. He saw then what the stone was, and his own body, and the winter trees and glazed sun: infinite millions of bits, multicolored, in chance motion, a wild dance that went on and on to some silent tune.

He thought, for awhile, that these bits might be similar to the "bits" stored by a computer, recalled when needed to form a pattern, solve a problem, produce a meaningful answer. But this seemed to him too easy a solution, for if a cosmic computer did exist, who had programmed it, who would pose the questions and demand the answers? What answers? What questions?

He dozed off for awhile, awoke with that steel voice echoing, "Daniel Blank . . . Daniel Blank . . ." and was forced to remember who he was.

Celia had found her certitude—whatever it was—and he supposed everyone in the world was searching for his own, and perhaps finding it, or settling, disappointed, for something less. But what was important, what was important was . . . What was important? It had been right there, he had been thinking of it, and then it went away.

There was a sudden griping in his bowels, a sharp pain that brought him sitting upright, gasping and frightened. He massaged his abdomen gently. Eventually the pain went away, leaving a leaden stuffiness. There was something in there, something in him . . . He fell asleep finally, dimly hearing the ghost voice calling, "Daniel Blank . . . Daniel Blank . . ." It might be his imagination, he admitted, but it seemed to him the voice was higher in pitch now, almost feminine in timbre, dawdling lovingly over the syllables of his name. Someone who loved him was calling.

Was it the second day or the third? Well . . . no matter. Anyway, a helicopter came over, dipped, circled his castle, tilted. He had been sitting with his knees drawn up, head down on folded arms, and he raised his head to stare at it. He thought they might shoot him or drop a bomb on him. He waited patiently, dreaming. But they just circled him, low, three or four times; he could see pale faces at the windows, peering down at him. He lowered his head again.

They came back, every day, and he tried to pay no attention to them, but the heavy throbbing of the rotor was annoying. It was slow enough to have a discernible rhythm, a heartbeat in the sky. Once they came so low over him that the downdraft blew his knitted watch cap off the stone. It went sailing out into space, then fell into the reaching spines of winter trees. He watched it go.

One morning—when was it?—he knew he was going to defecate and could not control himself. He fumbled at his belt with weak fingers, got it unbuckled and his pants down, but was too late to pull down his flowered bikini panties, and had to void. It was painful. Later he got his pants off his feet—he had to take his boots off first—then pulled down the panties and shook them out.

He looked at his feces curiously. They were small black balls, hard and round as marbles. He flicked them, one by one, with his forefinger; they rolled across the stone, over the edge. He knew he no longer had the strength to dress, but he could tug off socks, jacket, and shirt. Then he was naked, baring his shrunken body to pale sun.

He was no longer thirsty, no longer hungry. Most amazing, he was not cold, but suffused with a sleepy warmth that tingled his limbs. He was, he knew, sleeping more and more until on the fourth day—or perhaps it was the fifth—he was not conscious of sleep as a separate state. Sleep and wakefulness became so thin that they were no longer oil and water, but one fluid, grey and without flavor, that ebbed and flowed.

The days passed, he supposed, and so did the nights. But where one ended and the other began, he did not know. Days and darkness, all boundaries lost, became part of that grey, flavorless tide, warm, milky at times, without odor now. It was a great placid sea, endless; he wished he had the strength to stand and see just once more that silver river that flowed to everywhere.

But he could not stand, could not even make the effort to wipe away a thin, viscous liquid leaking from eyes, nose, mouth. When he moved his hand upon himself, he felt pulped nipples, knobbed joints, wrinkles, folds of scratchy skin.

Pain had gone; will was going. But he held it tight, to think awhile longer with a slow, numbed brain.

"Daniel Blank . . . Daniel Blank . . . ," the voice called seductively. He knew who it was who called.

On the second day, an enterprising New York City newspaper hired a commercial helicopter; they flew over Devil's Needle and took a series of photos of Daniel Blank sitting on the rock, knees drawn up. The photograph featured on the newspaper's front page showed him with head raised, pale face turned to the circling 'copter.

Delaney was chagrined that he hadn't thought of aerial reconnaissance first and, after consultation with Major Samuel Barnes, all commercial flights over Devil's Needle were banned. The reason given to the press was that a light plane or helicopter approach might drive Blank to a suicide plunge, or the chopper's downdraft might blow him off the edge.

Actually, Captain Delaney was relieved by the publication of that famous photo; Danny Boy was up there, no doubt about it. At the same time, with the cooperation of Barnes, he initiated thrice-daily flights of a New York State Police helicopter over the scene. Aerial photographs were taken, portions greatly enlarged and analyzed by Air Force technicians. No signs of food or drink were found. As the days wore away and Blank spent more and more time on his back, staring at the sky, his physical deterioration became obvious.

Delaney went along on the first flight, taking a car north with Chief Forrest and Captain Sneed to meet Barnes at an Air Force field near Newburgh. It was his first face-to-face meeting with Sam Barnes. The Major was like his voice: hard, tight, peppery. His manner was cold, withdrawn, his gestures quick and short. He wasted little time on formalities, but hustled them aboard the waiting helicopter.

On the short flight south, he spoke only to Delaney. The Captain learned the State officer had consulted his departmental surgeon and was aware of what Delaney already knew: without food or liquid, Blank had about ten days to live, give or take a day or two. It depended on his physical condition prior to his climb, and to the nature and extent of his exposure to the elements. The Major, like Delaney, was monitoring the long-range weather forecasts daily. Generally, fair weather was expected to continue with gradually lowering temperatures. But there was a low-pressure system building up in northwest Canada that would bear watching.

They were all discussing their options when the 'copter came in view of Devil's Needle, then tilted to circle lower. Their talk died away; they stared out their windows at the rock. The cabin was suddenly cold as a crewman slid open the wide cargo door, and a police photographer positioned his long-lensed camera.

Captain Delaney's first reaction was one of shock at the small size of Daniel Blank's aerie. Chief Forrest had said it was "double bedsheet size," but from the air it was difficult to understand how Blank could exist up there for an hour without rolling or stumbling off the edge.

As the 'copter circled lower, the photographer snapping busily, Delaney felt a sense of awe and, looking at the other officers, suspected they were experiencing the same emotion. From this elevation, seeing Blank on his stone perch and the white, upturned faces of the men surrounding Devil's Needle on the ground, the Captain knew a dreadful wonder at the man's austere isolation and could not understand how he endured it.

It was not only the dangerous height at which he had sought refuge, lying atop a rock pillar that thrust into the sky, it was the absolute solitude of the man, deliberately cutting himself off from life and the living. Blank seemed, not on stone, but somehow floating in the air, not anchored, but adrift.

Only a few times before in his life had Delaney felt what he felt now. Once was when he forced his way into that concentration camp and saw the stick-men. Once was when he had taken a kitchen knife gently from the nerveless fingers of a man, soaked in blood, who had just murdered his mother, his wife, his three children, and then called the cops. The final time Delaney had helped subdue a mad woman attempting to crunch her skull against a wall. And now Blank . . .

It was the madness that was frightening, the loss of anchor, the float. It was a primitive terror that struck deep, plunged to something papered over by civilization and culture. It stripped away millions of years and said, "Look." It was the darkness.

Later, when copies of the aerial photos were delivered to him, along with brief analyses by the Air Force technicians, he took one of the photos and thumbtacked it to the outside wall of the gate-keeper's cottage. He was not surprised by the attention it attracted, having guessed that the men shared his own uncertainty that their quarry was actually up there, that any man would deliberately seek and accept this kind of immolation.

Captain Delaney also noted a few other unusual characteristics of the men on duty: They were unaccountably quiet, with none of the loud talk, boasting and bantering that usually accompanied a job of this type. And they were in no hurry, when relieved, to return to their warm dormitory in the high school gymnasium. Invariably, they hesitated, then wandered once again to the base of Devil's Needle, to stare upward, mouths open, at the unseen man who lay alone.

He discussed this with Thomas Handry. The reporter had gone out to the roadblocks to interview some of the people being turned back by the troopers.

"You wouldn't believe it," Handry said, shaking his head. "Hundreds and hundreds of cars. From all over the country. I talked to a family from Ohio and asked them why they drove so far, what they expected to see."

"What did they say?"

"The man said he had a week off, and it wasn't long enough to go to Disneyworld, so they decided to bring the kids here."

They were organized now: regular shifts with schedules mimeographed daily. There were enough men assigned to cover all the posts around the clock, and the big searchlights and generator truck were up from New York City so Devil's Needle was washed in light 24 hours a day.

Captain Delaney had a propane stove in his cottage now, and a heavy radio had been installed on the gate-keeper's counter. The radiomen had little to do and so, to occupy their time, had rigged up a loudspeaker, a timer, and a loop tape, so that every hour on the hour, the message went booming out mechanically: "Daniel Blank . . . Daniel Blank . . . come down . . . come down . . ." It did no good. By now no one expected it would.

Every morning Chief Forrest brought out bags of mail received at the Chilton Post Office, and Captain Delaney spent hours reading the letters. A few of them contained money sent to Daniel Blank, for what reason he could not guess. Blank also received a surprisingly large number of proposals of marriage from women; some included nude photos of the sender. But most of the letters, from all over the world, were suggestions of how to take Daniel Blank. Get four helicopters, each supporting the corner of a heavy cargo net, and drop the net over the top of Devil's Needle. Bring in a large group of "sincere religious people" and pray him down. Set up a giant electric fan and blow him off his rock. Most proposed a solution they had already rejected: send up a fighter plane or helicopter and kill him. One suggestion intrigued Captain Delaney: fire gas grenades onto the top of Devil's Needle and when Daniel Blank was unconscious, send up a climber in a gas mask to bring him down.

Captain Delaney wandered out that evening, telling himself he wanted to discuss the gas grenade proposal with one of the snipers. He walked down the worn path toward Devil's Needle, turned aside at the sniper's post. The three pale-faced men had improved their blind. They had dragged over a picnic table with attached benches. From somewhere, they had scrounged three burlap bags of sand—Chief Forrest had helped with that, Delaney guessed—and the bags were used as a bench rest for their rifles. The sniper could sit and be protected from the wind by canvas tarps tied to nearby trees.

The man on duty looked up as Delaney approached.

"Evening, Captain."

"Evening. How's it going?"

"Quiet."

Delaney knew that the three snipers didn't mix much with the other men. They were pariahs, as much as hangmen or executioners, but apparently it did not affect them, if they were aware of it. All three were tall, thin men, two from Kentucky, one from North Carolina. If Delaney felt any uneasiness with them, it was their laconism rather than their chosen occupation.

"Happy New Year," the sniper said unexpectedly.

Delaney stared at him. "My God, is it?"

"Uh-huh. New Year's Eve."

"Well . . . Happy New Year to you. Forgot all about it."

The man was silent. The Captain glanced at the scope-fitted rifle resting on the sandbags.

"Springfield Oh-three," Delaney said. "Haven't seen one in years."

"Bought it from Army surplus," the man said, never taking his eyes from Devil's Needle.

"Sure," the Captain nodded. "Just like I bought my Colt Forty-five."

The man made a sound; the Captain hoped it was a laugh.

"Listen," Delaney said, "we got a suggestion, in the mail. You think there's any chance of putting a gas grenade up there?"

The sniper raised his eyes to the top of Devil's Needle. "Rifle or mortar?"

"Either."

"Not mortar. Rifle maybe. But it wouldn't stick. Skitter off or he'd kick it off."

"I guess so," Captain Delaney sighed. "We could clear the area and blanket it with gas, but the wind's too tricky."

"Uh-huh."

The Captain strolled away and only glanced once at that cathedral rock. Was he *really* up there? He had seen the day's photos—but could he trust them? The uneasiness returned.

He went back to the cottage, found a heavy envelope of reports a man coming on duty from Chilton had dropped off for him. They were from Sergeant MacDonald, copies of all the interrogations and statements of the people picked up in the continuing investigation. Delaney walked out to the van, got a paper cup of black coffee, brought it back. Then he sat down at his makeshift desk, pulled the gooseneck lamp closer, put on his heavy glasses, began reading the reports slowly.

He was looking for . . . what? Some explanation or lead or hint. What had turned Daniel G. Blank into a killer? Where and when did it begin? It was the motive he wanted, he needed. It wasn't good enough to use words like nut, crazy, insane, homosexual, psychopath. Just labels. There had to be more to it than that. There had to be something that could be comprehended, that might explain why this young man had deliberately murdered five people. And four of them strangers.

Because, Delaney thought angrily, if there was no explanation for it, then there was no explanation for anything.

It was almost two in the morning when he pulled on that crazy coat and wandered out again. The compound around the cottage was brilliantly lighted. So was the packed path through the black trees; so was the bleak column of

Devil's Needle. As usual, there were men standing about, heads back, mouths gaping, eyes turned upward. Captain Delaney joined them without shame.

He opened himself to the crisp night, lightly moaning wind, stars that seemed holes punched in a black curtain beyond which shone a dazzling radiance. The shaft of Devil's Needle rose shimmering in light, smoothed by the glare. Was he up there? Was he *really* up there?

There came to Captain Edward X. Delaney such a compassion that he must close his mouth, bite his lower lip to keep from wailing aloud. Unbidden, unwanted even, he shared that man's passion, entered into him, knew his suffering. It was an unwelcome bond, but he could not deny it. The crime, the motive, the reason—all seemed unimportant now. What racked him was that lonely man, torn adrift. He wondered if that was why they all gathered here, at all hours, day and night. Was it to comfort the afflicted as best they might?

A few days later—was it three? It could have been four—late in the afternoon, the daily envelope of aerial photos was delivered to Captain Delaney. Daniel G. Blank was lying naked on his rock, spread-eagled to the sky. The Captain looked, took a deep breath, turned his gaze away. Then, without looking again, he put the photos back into the envelope. He did not post one outside on the cottage wall.

Soon after, Major Samuel Barnes called.

"Delaney?"

"Yes."

"Barnes here. See the photos?"

"Yes."

"I don't think he can last much longer."

"No. Want to go up?"

"Not immediately. We'll check by air another day or so. Temperature's dropping."

"I know."

"No rush. We're getting a good press. Those bullhorn appeals are doing it. Everyone says we're doing all we can."

"Yes. All we can."

"Sure. But the weather's turning bad. A front moving in from the Great Lakes. Cloudy, windy, snow. Freezing. If we're socked in, we'll look like fools. I say January the sixth. In the morning. No matter what. How do you feel about it?"

"All right with me. The sooner the better. How do you want to do it: climber or 'copter?"

" 'Copter. Agreed?"

"Yes. That'll be best."

"All right. I'll start laying it on. I'll be over tomorrow and we'll talk. Shit, he's probably dead right now."

"Yes," Captain Delaney said. "Probably."

The world had become a song for Daniel Blank. A song. Soonngg . . . Everything was singing. Not words, or even a tune. But an endless hum that filled his ears, vibrated so deep inside him that cells and particles of cells jiggled to that pleasant purr.

There was no thirst, no hunger and, best of all, there was no pain, none at all. For that he was thankful. He stared at a milky sky through filmed eyes almost closed by scratchy lids. The whiteness and the tuneless drone became one: a great oneness that went on forever, stretched him with a dreamy content.

He was happy he no longer heard his name shouted, happy he no longer saw a helicopter dipping and circling above his rock. But perhaps he had imagined those things; he had imagined so much: Celia Montfort was there once, wearing an African mask. Once he spoke to Tony. Once he saw a hunched, massive silhouette, lumbering away from him, dwindling. And once he embraced a man in a slow-motion dance that faded into milkiness before the ice ax struck, although he saw it raised.

But even these visions, all visions, disappeared; he was left only with an empty screen. Occasionally discs, whiter than white, floated into view, drifted, then went off, out of sight. They were nice to watch, but he was glad when they were gone.

He had a slowly diminishing apprehension of reality, but before weakness subdued his mind utterly, he felt his perception growing even as his senses faded. It seemed to him he had passed through the feel-taste-touch-smell-hear world and had emerged to this gentle purity with its celestial thrum, a world where everything was true and nothing was false.

There was, he now recognized with thanksgiving and delight, a logic to life, and this logic was beautiful. It was not the orderly logic of the computer, but was the unpredictable logic of birth, living, death. It was the mortality of one, and the immortality of all. It was all things, animate and inanimate, bound together in a humming whiteness.

It was an ecstasy to know that oneness, to understand, finally, that he was part of the slime and part of the stars. There was no Daniel Blank, no Devil's Needle, and never had been. There was only the continuum of life in which men and rocks, slime and stars, appear as seeds, grow a moment, and then are drawn back again into that timeless whole, continually beginning, continually ending.

He was saddened that he could not bring this final comprehension to others, describe to them the awful majesty of the certitude he had found: a universe of accident and possibility where a drop of water is no less than a moon, a passion no more than a grain of sand. All things are nothing, but all things are all. In his delirium, he could clutch that paradox to his heart, hug it, know it for truth.

He could feel life ebbing in him—*feel* it! It oozed away softly, no more than an invisible vapor rising from his wasted flesh, becoming part again of that oneness from whence it came. He died slowly, with love, for he was passing into another form; the process so gentle that he could wonder why men cried out and fought.

Those discs of white on white appeared again to drift across his vision. He thought dimly there was a moisture on his face, a momentary tingle; he wondered if he might be weeping with joy.

It was only snow, but he did not know it. It covered him slowly, soothing the roughened skin, filling out the shrunken hollows of his body, hiding the seized joints and staring eyes.

Before the snow ended at dawn, he was a gently sculpted mound atop Devil's Needle. His shroud was white and without stain.

Late on the night of January 5th, Captain Delaney met with Major Samuel Barnes, Chief Forrest, Captain Sneed, the crew of the State Police helicopter, and the chief radioman. They all crowded into the gate-keeper's cottage; a uniformed guard was posted outside the door to keep curious reporters away.

Major Barnes had prepared a schedule, and handed around carbon copies.

"Before we get down to nuts-and-bolts," he said rapidly, "the latest weather advisory is this: Snow beginning at midnight, tapering off at dawn. Total accumulation about an inch and a half or two. Temperatures in the low thirties to upper twenties. Then, tomorrow morning, it should clear with temperatures rising to the middle thirties. Around noon, give or take an hour, the shit will really hit the fan, with a dropping barometer, temperature going way down, snow mixed with rain, hail, and sleet, and winds of twenty-five gusting to fifty.

"Beautiful," one of the pilots said. "I love it."

"So," Barnes went on, disregarding the interruption, "we have five or six hours to get him down. If we don't, the weather will murder us, maybe for days.

This is a massive storm front moving in. All right, now look at your schedules. Take-off from the Newburgh field at nine ayem. I'll be aboard the 'copter. The flight down and the final aerial reconnaissance completed by nine-thirty ayem, approximate. Lower a man to the top of Devil's Needle via cable and horse collar by ten ayem. Captain Delaney, you will be in command of ground operations here. This shack will be home base, radio coded Chilton One. The 'copter will be Chilton Two. The man going down will be Chilton Three. Everyone clear on that? Sneed, have your surgeon here at nine ayem. Forrest, can you bring out a local ambulance with attendants and a body bag?"

"Sure."

"I think Blank is dead, or at least unconscious. But if he's not, the man going down on the cable will be armed."

Captain Delaney looked up. "Who's Chilton Three?" he asked. "Who's going down on the cable?"

The three-man helicopter crew looked at each other. They were all young men, wearing sheepskin jackets over suntan uniforms, their feet in fleece-lined boots.

Finally the smallest man shrugged. "Shit, I'll go down," he said, rabbity face twisted into a tight grin. "I'm the lightest. I'll get the fucker."

"What's your name?" Delaney asked him.

"Farber, Robert H."

"You heard what the Major said, Farber. Blank is probably dead or unconscious. But there's no guarantee. He's already killed five people. If you get down there, and he makes any threatening movement—anything at all—grease him."

"Don't worry, Captain. If he as much as sneezes, he's a dead fucker."

"What will you carry?"

"What? Oh, you mean guns. My thirty-eight, I guess. Side holster. And I got a carbine."

Captain Delaney looked directly at Major Barnes. "I'd feel better if he carried more weight," he said. He turned back to Farber. "Can you handle a forty-five?" he asked.

"Sure, Captain. I was in the fuckin' Marine Corps."

"You can borrow mine, Bobby," one of the other pilots offered.

"And a shotgun rather than the carbine," Delaney said. "Loaded with buck."

"No problem," Major Barnes said.

"You really think I'll need all that fuckin' artillery?" Farber asked the Captain.

"No, I don't," Delaney said. "But the man was fast. So fast I can't tell you. Fast enough to take out one of my best men. But he's been up there a week now without food or water. If he's still alive, he won't be fast anymore. The heavy guns are just insurance. Don't hesitate to use them if you have to. Is that an order, Major Barnes?"

"Yes," Barnes nodded. "That's an order, Farber."

They discussed a few more details: briefing of the press, positioning of still and TV cameramen, parking of the ambulance, selection of men to stand by when Blank was brought down.

Finally, near midnight, the meeting broke up. Men shook hands, drifted away in silence. Only Delaney and the radioman were left in the cabin. The Captain wanted to call Barbara, but thought it too late; she'd probably be sleeping. He wanted very much to talk to her.

He spent a few minutes getting his gear together, stuffing reports, schedules, and memos into manila envelopes. If all went well in the morning, he'd be back in Manhattan by noon, leading his little squad of cops home again.

He hadn't realized how tired he was, how he longed for his own bed. Some of it was physical weariness: too many hours on his feet, muscles punished, nerves pulled and strained. But he also felt a spiritual exhaustion. This thing with Blank had gone on too long, had done too much to him.

Now, the last night, he pulled on cap and fur-lined greatcoat, plodded down to Devil's Needle for a final look. It was colder, no doubt of that, and the smell of snow was in the air. The sentries circling the base of the rock wore rubber ponchos over their sheepskin jackets: the sniper was huddled under a blanket, only the glowing end of a cigarette showing in black shadow. Captain Delaney stood a little apart from the few gawkers still there, still staring upward.

The gleaming pillar of Devil's Needle rose above him, probing the night sky, ghostly in the searchlight glare. About it, he thought he heard a faintly ululant wind, no louder than the cry of a distant child. He shivered inside his greatcoat: a chill of despair, a fear of something. It would have been easy, at that moment, to weep, but for what he could not have said.

It might, he thought dully, be despair for his own sins, for he suddenly knew he had sinned grievously, and the sin was pride. It was surely the most deadly; compared to pride, the other six seemed little more than physical excesses. But pride was a spiritual corruption and, worse, it had no boundaries, no limits, but could consume a man utterly.

In him, he knew, pride was not merely self-esteem, not just egotism. He knew his shortcomings better than anyone except, perhaps, his wife. His pride went beyond a satisfied self-respect; it was an arrogance, a presumption of moral superiority he brought to events, to people and, he supposed wryly, to God.

But now his pride was corroded by doubt. As usual, he had made a moral judgment—was that unforgivable for a cop?—and had brought Daniel G. Blank to this lonely death atop a cold rock. But what else could he have done?

There were, he now acknowledged sadly, several other courses that had been open to him if there had been a human softness in him, a sympathy for others, weaker than he, challenged by forces beyond their strength or control. He could have, for instance, sought a confrontation with Daniel Blank after he had discovered that damning evidence in the illegal search. Perhaps he could have convinced Blank to confess; if he had, Celia Montfort would be alive tonight, and Blank would probably be in an asylum. The story this revealed would have meant the end of Captain Delaney's career, he supposed, but that no longer seemed of overwhelming importance.

Or he could have admitted the illegal search and at least attempted to obtain a search warrant. Or he could have resigned the job completely and left Blank's punishment to a younger, less introspective cop.

"Punishment." That was the key word. His damnable pride had driven him to making a moral judgment, and, having made it, he had to be cop, judge, jury. He had to play God; that's where his arrogance had led him.

Too many years as a cop. You started on the street, settling family squabbles, a Solomon in uniform; you ended hounding a man to his death because you knew him guilty and wanted him to suffer for his guilt. It was all pride, nothing but pride. Not the understandable, human pride of doing a difficult job well, but an overweening that led to judging him, then to condemning, then to executing. Who would judge, condemn, and execute Captain Edward X. Delaney?

Something in his life had gone wrong, he now saw. He was not born with it. It did not come from genes, education, or environment, any more than Blank's homicidal mania had sprung from genes, education, or environment. But circumstances and chance had conspired to debase him, even as Daniel Blank had been perverted.

He did not know all things and would never know them; he saw that now. There were trends, currents, tides, accidents of such complexity that only an unthinking fool would say, "I am the master of my fate." Victim, Delaney thought. We are all victims, one way or another.

But, surprisingly, he did not feel this to be a gloomy concept, nor an excuse for licentious behavior. We are each dealt a hand at birth and play our cards as cleverly as we can, wasting no time lamenting that we received only one pair instead of a straight flush. The best man plays a successful game with a weak hand—bluffing, perhaps, when he has to—but staking everything, eventually, on what he's holding.

Captain Delaney thought now he had been playing a poor hand. His marriage had been a success, and so had his career. But he knew his failures . . . he knew. Somewhere along the way humanity had leaked out of him, compassion drained, pity became dry and withered. Whether it was too late to become something other than what he was, he did not know. He might try—but there were circumstance and chance to cope with and, as difficult, the habits and prejudices of more years than he cared to remember.

Uncertain, shaken, he stared upward at Devil's Needle, shaft toppling, world tilting beneath his tread. He was anxious and confused, sensing he had lost a certitude, wandered from a faith that, right or wrong, had supported him.

He felt something on his upturned face: a light, cold tingle of moisture. Tears? Just the first frail snowflakes. He could see them against the light: a fragile lacework. At that moment, almost hearing it, he knew the soul of Daniel Blank had escaped the flesh and gone winging away into the darkness, taking with it Captain Delaney's pride.

Shortly before dawn the snowfall dissolved into a freezing rain. Then that too ceased. When Captain Delaney came out on the porch at 8:30 a.m., the ground was a blinding diamond pavé; every black branch in sight was gloved with ice sparkling in the new sun.

He wore his greatcoat when he walked over to the van for black coffee and a doughnut. The air was clear, chill, almost unbearably sharp—like breathing ether. There was a chiselled quality to the day, and yet the world was not clear: a thin white scrim hung between sun and earth; the light was muted.

He went back to the shack and instructed the radioman to plug in an auxiliary microphone, a hand-held model with an extension cord so he could stand out on the porch, see the top of Devil's Needle above the skeleton trees, and communicate with Chilton Two and Chilton Three.

The ambulance rolled slowly into the compound. Chief Forrest climbed out, puffing, to direct its parking. A stretcher and body bag were removed; the two attendants went back into the warmth of the cab, smoking cigarettes. Captain Sneed showed a squad of ten men where they were to take up their positions, handling his duties with the solemnity of an officer arranging the defense of the Alamo. But Delaney didn't interfere; it made no difference. Finally Forrest and Sneed came up to join the Captain on the porch. They exchanged nods. Sneed looked at his watch. "Take-off about now," he said portentously.

Chief Forrest was the first to hear it. "Coming," he said, raised his old field glasses to his eyes, searched northward. A few minutes later Captain Delaney heard the fluttering throb of the helicopter and, shortly afterward, looking where Forrest was pointing, saw it descending slowly, beginning a tilted circle about Devil's Needle.

The radio crackled.

"Chilton One from Chilton Two. Do you read me?" It was Major Samuel Barnes' tight, rapid voice, partly muffled by the throb of rotors in the background.

"Loud and clear, Chilton Two," the radioman replied.

"Beginning descent and reconnaissance. Where is Captain Delaney?"

"Standing by with hand-held mike. On the porch. He can hear you."

"Top of rock covered with snow. Higher mound in the middle. I guess that's Blank. No movement. We're going down."

The men on the porch shielded their eyes from sun glare to stare upward. The 'copter, a noisy dragonfly, circled lower, then slowed, slipping sideways, hovered directly over the top of the rock.

"Chilton One from Chilton Two."

"We've got you, Chilton Two."

"No sign of life. No sign of anything. Our downdraft isn't moving the snow cover. Probably frozen over. We'll start the descent."

"Roger."

They watched the chopper hanging almost motionless in the air. They saw the wide cargo door open. It seemed a long time before a small figure appeared at the open door and stepped out into space, dangling from the cable, a padded leather horse collar around his chest, under his arms. The shotgun was held in his right hand; his left was on the radio strapped to his chest.

"Chilton One from Chilton Two. Chilton Three is now going down. We will stop at six feet for a radio check."

"Chilton Two from Chilton One. Delaney here. We can see you. Any movement on top of the rock?"

"None at all, Captain. Just an outline of a body. He's under the snow. Radio check now. Chilton Three from Chilton Two: How do you read?"

They watched the man dangling on the cable beneath the 'copter. He swung lazily in slow circles.

"Chilton Two from Chilton Three. I'm getting you loud and clear." Farber's voice was breathless, almost drowned in the rotor noise.

"Chilton Three from Chilton Two. Repeat, how do you read me?"

"Chilton Two, I said I was getting you loud and clear."

"Chilton Three from Chilton Two. Repeat, are you receiving me?"

Captain Delaney swore softly, moved his hand-held mike closer to his lips.

"Chilton Three from Chilton One. Do you read me?"

"Christ, yes, Chilton One. Loud and clear. What the hell's going on? Do you hear me?"

"Loud and clear, Chilton Three. I'll get right back to you. Chilton Two from Chilton One."

"Chilton Two here. Barnes speaking."

"Delaney here. Major, we're in communication with Chilton Three. He can read us and we're reading him. He can hear you, but apparently you're not getting him."

"Son of a bitch," Barnes said bitterly. "Let me try once more. Chilton Three from Chilton Two, do you read me? Acknowledge."

"Yes, I read you, Chilton Two, and I'm getting fuckin' cold."

"Chilton Two from Chilton One. We heard Chilton Three acknowledge. Did you get it?"

"Not a word," Barnes said grimly. "Well, we haven't got time to pull him back up and check out the goddamn radios. I'll relay all orders through you. Understood?"

"Understood," Delaney repeated. "Chilton Three from Chilton One. You are not being read by Chilton Two. But they read us. We'll relay all orders through Chilton One. Understood?"

"Understood, Chilton One. Who's this?"

"Captain Delaney."

"Captain, tell them to lower me down onto the fuckin' rock. I'm freezing my ass off up here."

"Chilton Two from Chilton One. Lower away."

They watched the swinging figure hanging from the cable. Suddenly it dropped almost three feet, then brought up with a jerk, Farber swinging wildly.

"Goddamn it!" he screamed. "Tell 'em to take it fuckin' easy up there. They almost jerked my fuckin' arms off."

Delaney didn't bother relaying that. He watched, and in a few minutes the cable began to run out slowly and smoothly. Farber came closer to the top of Devil's Needle.

"Chilton Three from Chilton One. Any movement?"

"No. Not a thing. Just snow. Mound in the middle. Snow drifted up along one side. I'm coming down. About ten feet. Tell them to slow. Slow the fuckin' winch, goddamn it!"

"Chilton Two from Chilton One. Farber is close. Slow the winch. Slow, slow."

"Roger, Chilton One. We see him. He's almost there. A little more. A little more . . ."

"Chilton Three here. I'm down. Feet are down."

"How much snow?"

"About an inch to three inches where it's drifted. I need more fuckin' cable slack to unshackle the horse collar."

"Chilton Two, Farber needs more cable slack."

"Roger."

"Okay, Chilton One. I've got it unsnapped. Tell them to get the fuck out of here; they're damn near blowing me off."

"Chilton Two, collar unshackled. You can take off."

The 'copter tilted and circled away, the cable slanting back beneath it. It began to make wide rings about Devil's Needle.

"Chilton Three, you there?" Delaney asked.

"I'm here. Where else?"

"Any sign of life?"

"Nothing. He's under the snow. Wait'll I get this fuckin' collar off."

"Is he breathing? Is the snow over his mouth melted? Is there a hole?"

"Don't see anything. He's covered completely with the fuckin' snow."

"Brush it off."

"What?"

"Brush the snow away. Brush all the snow off him."

"With what, Captain? I got no gloves."

"With your hands—what do you think? Use your hands. Scrape the snow and ice away."

They heard Farber's heavy breathing, the clang of shotgun on rock, some muffled curses.

"Chilton One from Chilton Two. What's going on?"

"He's brushing the snow away. Farber? Farber, how's it coming?"

"Captain, he's naked!"

Delaney took a deep breath and stared at Forrest and Sneed. But their eyes were on Devil's Needle.

"Yes, he's naked," he spoke into the mike as patiently as he could. "You knew that; you saw the photos. Now clean him off."

"Jesus, he's cold. And hard. So fuckin' hard. God, is he white."

"You got him cleaned off?"

"I—I'm—"

"What the hell's wrong?"

"I think I'm going to be sick."

"So be sick, you shithead!" Delaney roared. "Haven't you ever seen a dead man before?"

"Well . . . sure, Captain," the shaky voice came hesitantly, "but I never touched one."

"Well, touch him," Delaney shouted. "He's not going to bite you, for Chrissakes. Get his face cleaned off first."

"Yeah . . . face . . . sure . . . Jesus Christ."

"Now what?"

"His fuckin' eyes are open. He's looking right at me."

"You stupid sonofabitch," Delaney thundered into the mike. "Will you stop acting like an idiot slob and do your job like a man?"

"Chilton One from Chilton Two. Barnes here. What's the problem?"

"Farber's acting up," Delaney growled. "He doesn't enjoy touching the corpse."

"Do you have to rough him?"

"No, I don't," Delaney said. "I could sing lullabies to him. Do you want that stiff down or don't you?"

Silence.

"All right," Barnes said finally. "Do it your way. When I get down, you and I will have a talk."

"Any time, anywhere," Delaney said loudly, and saw that Forrest and Sneed were staring at him. "Now get off my back and let me talk to this infant. Farber, are you there? Farber?"

"Here," the voice came weakly.

"Have you got him brushed off?"

"Yes."

"Put your fingers on his chest. Lightly. See if you can pick up a heartbeat or feel any breathing. Well . . . ?"

After a moment: "No. Nothing, Captain."

"Put your cheek close to his lips."

"What?"

"Put. Your. Cheek. Close. To. His. Lips. Got that?"

"Well . . . sure . . ."

"See if you can feel any breath coming out."

"Jesus . . ."

"Well?"

"Nothing. Captain, this guy is dead, he's fuckin' *dead.*"

"All right. Get the horse collar on him, up around his chest, under his arms. Make sure the shackle connection is upward."

They waited, all of them on the porch now straining their eyes to the top of Devil's Needle. So were all the men in the compound, sentries, snipers, reporters. Still and TV cameras were trained on the rock. There was remarkably little noise, Delaney noted, and little movement. Everyone was caught in the moment, waiting . . .

"Farber?" Delaney called into his mike. "Farber, are you getting the collar on him?"

"I can't," the voice came wavering. "I just can't."

"What's wrong now?"

"Well . . . he's all spread out, Captain. His arms are out wide to his sides, and his legs are spread apart. Jesus, he's got no cock at all."

"Screw his cock!" Delaney shouted furiously. "Forget his cock. Forget his arms. Just get his feet together and slip the collar over them and up his body."

"I can't," the voice came back, and they caught the note of panic. "I just can't."

Delaney took a deep breath. "Listen, you shit-gutted bastard, you volunteered for this job. 'I'll bring the fucker down,' you said. All right, you're up there. Now bring the fucker down. Get his ankles together."

"Captain, he's cold and stiff as a board."

"Oh no," Captain Edward X. Delaney said. "Cold and stiff as a board, is he? Isn't it a shame this isn't the middle of July and you could pick him up with a shovel and a blotter. You're a cop, aren't you? What the hell you think they pay you for? To clean up the world's garbage—right? Now listen, you milk-livered sonofabitch, you get working on those legs and get them together."

There was silence for a few moments. Delaney saw that Captain Bertram Sneed had turned away, walked to the other end of the porch. He was gripping the railing tightly, staring off in the opposite direction.

"Captain?" Farber's voice came faintly.

"I'm here. How you coming with the legs?"

"Not so good, Captain. I can move the legs a little, but I think he's stuck. His skin is stuck to the fuckin' rock."

"Sure it is," Delaney said, his voice suddenly soft and encouraging now. "It's frozen to the rock. Of course it would be. Just pull the legs together slowly, son. Don't think about the skin. Work the legs back and forth."

"Well . . . all right . . . Oh God."

They waited. Delaney took advantage of the pause to pull off his coat. He looked around, then Chief Forrest took it from him. The Captain realized he was soaked with sweat; he could feel it running down his ribs.

"Captain?"

"I'm here, son."

"Some of the skin on his legs and ass came off. Patches stuck to the fuckin' rock."

"Don't worry about it. He didn't feel a thing. Got his ankles together?"

"Yes. Pretty good. Close enough to get through the collar."

"Fine. You're doing just fine. Now move his whole body back and forth, side to side. Rock him so his body comes free from the stone."

"Oh Jesus . . ." Farber gasped, and they knew he was weeping now. They didn't look at each other.

"He's all shrunk," Farber moaned. "All shrunk and his belly is puffed up."

"Don't look at him," Delaney said. "Just keep working. Keep moving him. Get him loose."

"Yes. All right. He's loose now. He didn't lose much skin."

"Good. You're doing great. Now get that horse collar on him. Can you lift his legs?"

"Oh sure. Christ, he don't weigh a thing. He's a skeleton. His arms are still out straight to the sides."

"That's all right. No problem there. Where's the collar?"

"Working it upward. Wait a minute . . . Okay. There. It's in position. Under his arms."

"He won't slip through?"

"No chance. His fuckin' arms go straight out."

"Ready for the 'copter?"

"Jesus, *yes!*"

"Chilton Two from Chilton One."

"Chilton Two. Loud and clear. Barnes here."

"The collar is on the body. You can pick up."

"Roger. Going in."

"Farber? Farber, are you there?"

"I'm still here, Captain."

"The 'copter is coming over for the pickup. Do me a favor, will you?"

"What's that, Captain?"

"Feel around under the snow and see if you can find an ice ax. It's about the size of a hammer, but it has a long pick on one side of the head. I'd like to have it."

"I'll take a look. And do me a favor, Captain."

"What?"

"After they pick him up and land him, make sure they come back for me. I don't like this fuckin' place."

"Don't worry," Delaney assured him. "They'll come back for you. I promise."

He watched until he saw the helicopter throttling down, moving slowly toward the top of Devil's Needle. He walked back inside to place his microphone on the radioman's counter. Then he took a deep breath, looked with wonder at his trembling hands. He went outside again, down the steps, into the compound. The photographers were busy now, lens turned to the 'copter hovering over Devil's Needle.

Delaney stood in the snow, his cap squarely atop his head, choker collar hooked up. Like the others, his head was tilted back, eyes turned upward, mouth agape. They waited. Then they heard the powered roar of the rotors as the 'copter rose swiftly, tilted, circled, came heading toward them.

At the end of the swinging cable, Daniel Blank hung in the horse collar. It was snug under his outstretched arms. His head was flung back in a position of agony. His ankles were close together. His shrunken body was water-white, all knobs and bruises.

The helicopter came lower. They saw the shaved skull, the purpled wounds where skin had torn away. The strange bird floated, dangling. Then, suddenly, caught against the low sun, there was a nimbus about the flesh, a luminous radiation that flared briefly and died as the body came back to earth.

Delaney turned, walked away. He felt a hand on his shoulder, stopped, turned to see Smokey the Bear.

"Well," Captain Sneed grinned, "we got him, didn't we?"

Delaney shrugged off that heavy hand and continued to walk, his back to the thunder of the descending 'copter.

"God help us all," Captain Edward X. Delaney said aloud. But no one heard him.

Epilogue

In the months after the events recounted here:

Christopher Langley and the Widow Zimmerman were wed, in a ceremony attended with great pleasure by Captain Delaney. The happy newlyweds moved to Sarasota, Florida.

Calvin Case, with the assistance of a professional writer, produced a book entitled *Basic Climbing Techniques*. It had a modest but encouraging sale, and seems on its way to becoming a manual of Alpinism. Case is currently working on a second book, *The World's Ten Toughest Climbs*.

Anthony (Tony) Montfort rejoined his parents in Europe. The whereabouts of Valenter are presently unknown.

Charles Lipsky became involved in a criminal ring forging welfare checks and is currently being held for trial.

Samuel and Florence Morton opened the first of a chain of "health clubs" featuring mixed nude swimming. They are under indictment for "maintaining a public nuisance," but are free on bail pending trial.

Former Deputy Commissioner Broughton was defeated in the primary to select his party's candidate for mayor of New York City. He is attempting to form a new political party based on the promise of "law and order."

Former Lieutenant Marty Dorfman passed the examination for captain, and was appointed Legal Officer of the Patrol Division.

Lieutenant Jeri Fernandez, Sergeant MacDonald, and Detective Blankenship received commendations.

Reporter Thomas Handry, apparently giving up hopes of becoming a poet, was reassigned to his newspaper's Washington Bureau.

Dr. Sanford Ferguson was killed in an automobile accident early one morning when returning to his home from a visit to his mistress.

Deputy Mayor Alinski is still Deputy Mayor. Former Inspector Johnson and former Deputy Inspector Thorsen have both been promoted one rank.

Captain Edward X. Delaney was jumped to Inspector and made Chief of the Detective Division. About a month after the death of Daniel Blank, Barbara Delaney died from Proteus infection. After a year's period of mourning, Inspector Delaney married the former Monica Gilbert. Mrs. Delaney is pregnant.

THE SECOND DEADLY SIN

1

The studio was an aquarium of light; the woman and the girl blinked in the glare. Victor Maitland slammed the door behind them, locked it, put on the chain. The woman turned slowly to watch, unafraid.

"You didn't tell me your name, Mama," Maitland said.

"You din' tell me yours," she said, smiling, showing a gold tooth.

He stared at her a moment, then laughed.

"Right," he said. "What the fuck difference does it make?"

"You talk dirty, beeg boy," she said, still smiling.

"And think dirty and live dirty," he added.

She looked at him speculatively.

"You wanna draw me?" she asked archly. "Okay, I pose for you. I show you all I got. Everyteeng. Ten dahlair."

"Ten dollars? For how long?"

She shrugged. "All night."

He looked at the olive-tinted lard.

"No, thanks, Mama," he said. He jerked a thumb at the girl. "It's her I want. How old are you, honey?"

"Feefteen," the woman said.

"Don't you go to school?" he asked the girl.

"She don' go," Mama said.

"Let her talk," he said angrily.

The woman looked about cautiously, lowered her voice.

"Dolores ees—" She pointed a finger at her temple, made little circles. "A good girl, but not so smart. She don' go to school. Don' got job. How much you pay?"

"Good body?" he asked.

The woman got excited. She kissed the tips of her fingers.

"Beautiful!" she cried passionately. "Dolores ees beautiful!"

"Take off your clothes," he said to the girl. "I'll see if I can use you."

He strode to the front of the studio. He kicked the posing dais into place beneath the skylight. Warm April sunshine came splaying down. He jerked a crate around and poked through the litter on the floor until he found an

11 × 14-inch sketchpad and a box of charcoal sticks. When he looked up, the girl was still standing there; she hadn't moved.

"What the hell are you waiting for?" he yelled angrily. "Go on, get undressed. Take your clothes off."

The woman moved closer to the girl, rattled off a mutter of Spanish.

"Where?" she called to Maitland.

"Where?" he shouted. "Right here. Throw her shit on the bed. Tell her she can keep her shoes on; the floor is damp."

The woman spoke to the young girl again. The girl went over to the cot, began undressing. She took off her clothes placidly, looking about vacantly. She dropped her coat and dress in a pile on the cot. She was wearing soiled greyish cotton underwear. The straps were held up with safety pins. She unhitched the pins. She pulled her pants down. She stood naked.

"All right," Maitland called. "Come over here and stand on this platform."

Mama led the girl by the hand and helped her up on the dais. Then she stepped away, leaving the girl alone. Dolores was still looking off somewhere into space. She hadn't looked at Maitland since coming into the studio. She just stood there, arms straight down at her sides.

He walked around her. He walked around her twice.

"Jesus Christ," he said.

"I tol' you," the woman said proudly. "Beautiful, no?"

He didn't answer. He jerked the crate forward a few feet, propped the big sketchpad on a can of turpentine. He stood staring at the naked girl through squinched eyes.

"You got something to dreenk, beeg boy?" Mama asked.

"Beer in the icebox," he said. "She coppish English?"

"Some."

Maitland went close to the girl.

"Look, Dolores," he said loudly, "stand like this. Bend over, put your hands on your knees. No, no, bend from the hips. Look at me. Like this . . . Now stick out your ass. That's good. Now arch your back. Put your head up. Come on . . . like this. Put it up. Farther. Keep your legs stiff. That's it. Now try to stick your tits out."

"Wheeskey?" Mama asked.

"In the cupboard under the sink. Tits, Dolores! Here. Stick them out. Now you've got it. Don't move."

Maitland rushed back behind the crate and sketchpad. He picked up a stick of charcoal and attacked the white paper. He looked up at Dolores, looked down, and sketched rapidly—slash, slash, slash. He ripped off the sheet of paper, let it fall to the floor. Then he struck at the new sheet, swinging his arm from the shoulder.

He tore off that sheet, let it drop, began a fresh one. Halfway through the third sketch the charcoal stick broke. Maitland whirled and flung the remainder at the brick wall. He laughed delightedly. He strode to the naked girl, grabbed a buttock in one hand, shook it savagely.

"Gold!" he howled. "Pure gold!"

He went to the rear of the studio. Mama was sitting on the cot, bottle of whiskey in one hand, a smeared, half-filled glass in the other. Maitland grabbed the bottle from her, put it to his mouth. He took two heavy swallows and belched.

"Okay, Mama," he said. "She'll do. Five bucks an hour. Maybe two or three hours a day."

"No mahnkey beesness," the woman said severely.

"What?"

"No mahnkey beesness weeth Dolores."

Maitland roared with raucous laughter. "No monkey business," he agreed, spluttering. "Shit, I won't touch her."

"Mahnkey beesness costs more than five dahlair," the woman smiled a ghastly smile.

He let her finish her drink, and then got them out of there. The woman promised to bring Dolores around at eleven o'clock on Monday morning. Maitland locked and chained the door behind them. He went back to the crate, whiskey bottle in his fist. He drank while he looked at the drawings on the floor, nudging them with his toe. He squinted at the sketches, remembering how the girl looked, beginning to plan the first painting.

There was a knock at the studio door. Angry at the interruption, he yelled, "Who?"

A familiar voice answered, and Maitland scowled. He set the whiskey bottle on the crate. He went to the door, unlocked it, took off the chain. He pulled the door open, turned his back, walked away.

"You again!" he said.

The first knife thrust went into his back. High up. Alongside the spine. The blow was strong enough to drive him forward, face breaking, hands thrown up in a comical gesture of dismay. But he did not go down.

The blade was withdrawn and stuck again. And again. And again. Even after Victor Maitland was face down on the wide floor boards, life leaking, the blade was plunged. Fingers scrabbled weakly. Then were still.

2

His stepdaughters were bright, scornful girls, and ex–Chief of Detectives Edward X. Delaney enjoyed their company at lunch. He cherished them. He loved them. But my God, their young energy was wearing! And they shrieked; their laughter pierced his ears.

So when he kissed them a fond farewell at the entrance to their private school on East 72nd Street, Manhattan, it was with mingled tenderness and relief that he watched them scamper up the steps and into the safety of the school. He turned away, reflecting wryly that he had come to an age when he wanted everything *nice*. In his lexicon, "nice" meant quiet, cleanliness, order. Perhaps Barbara, his first wife, had been right. She said he had become a cop because he saw beauty in order, and wanted to maintain order in the world. Well . . . he had tried.

He walked over to Fifth Avenue and turned south, the shrill voices of the children still ringing in his ears. What he wanted at that precise moment, he decided, was an old-fashioned Irish bar, dim and hushed, all mahogany and Tiffany lampshades, all frosted glass and the smell of a century of beer. There were still such places in New York—fewer every year, but they did exist. Not, unfortunately, on upper Fifth Avenue. But there was a place nearby of quiet, cleanliness, order. A nice place . . .

The courtyard of the Frick Collection was an oasis, a center of tranquility in the raucous, brawling city. Sitting on a gleaming stone bench amongst that strong greenery was like existing in a giant terrarium set down in a hurricane. You knew the ugliness and violence raged outside; inside was calm and a renewing sense of the essence of things.

He sat there a long time, shifting occasionally on the hard bench, wondering once again if he had done the right thing to retire. He had held a position of prominence, power, and responsibility: Chief of Detectives, New York Police Department. Three thousand men under his command. An enormous budget that was never enough. A job to do that, considered in the context of the times and the mores, could never be more than a holding operation. Battles could be won, the war never. The important thing was not to surrender.

In a way, of course, he *had* surrendered. But it was his personal surrender, not the capitulation of the Department. He had resigned his prestigious post for a single reason: he could no longer endure the political bullshit that went along with his high-ranking job.

He knew, of course, the role politics played in the upper echelons of the Department before he accepted the position. Nothing unusual about that. Or even contemptible. The City was a social organization; it was realistic to expect a clash of wills, stupidity, strong ambitions, idealism, cynicism, devious plots, treachery, and corruption. Politics existed in the functioning of every social organization larger than two people.

It became unbearable to Chief Edward X. Delaney when it began to intrude on the way he did his job, on who he assigned where, how he moved his forces from neighborhood to neighborhood, his priorities, statements he made to the press, his relations with other city departments, and with State and Federal law enforcement agencies.

So he had filed for retirement, after long discussions with Monica, his second wife. They had agreed, finally, that his peace of mind was more important than the salary and perquisites of his office. The Department had, he thought ruefully, borne up extremely well under the news of his leaving. (He had "rocked the boat," it was whispered. He was "not a team player.") He had been given the usual banquet, handed a set of matched luggage and a pair of gold cufflinks, and sent on his way with encomiums from the Commissioner and Mayor attesting to his efficiency, loyalty, trustworthiness, and wholehearted cooperation. Bullshit to the last.

So there he was, the age of sixty looming, and behind him a lifetime as a cop: patrolman, detective third-grade, second, first, detective sergeant, lieutenant, precinct captain in the Patrol Division, and then back to the Detective Division as Chief. Not a bad professional career. Second in the history of the Department for total number of citations earned. Physical scars to prove his bravery. And a few changes in method and procedure that wouldn't mean much to civilians but were now a part of police training. It was he, for instance, who had fought for and won the adoption of new regulations specifying that a suspect's hands were to be handcuffed *behind* him. Not on a par with the discovery of gravity or atomic energy, of course, but important enough. To cops.

He would not admit to himself that he was bored. How could a man as rigidly disciplined and self-sufficient as he be bored? He and Monica traveled, a little, and he carefully avoided inflicting his company on the police of Fort Lauderdale, Florida, and La Jolla, California, knowing what a trial visiting cops (especially retired cops!) can be to a harried department, no matter how large the city.

At home, in their brownstone next to the 251st Precinct house (it had been *his* precinct), he took care not to get in Monica's way, not to follow her about like a lorn puppy as he had seen so many other retired men dog their wives' footsteps. He read a great deal, he visited museums, he wrote letters to Eddie Jr. and Liza, his children by his first wife. He treated Monica to dinner and the theatre, he treated his stepdaughters to lunch, he treated old Department friends to drinks, listened to their complaints and problems, offering advice only if asked. They called him after he retired. At first, many. Later, few.

And he walked a great deal, all over Manhattan, visiting neighborhoods he hadn't seen since he was a street cop, marveling every day how the city had changed, was changing—a constant flux that dazzled with its speed: a middle-class Jewish neighborhood had become Puerto Rican, a rundown tenement street had been refurbished by young married couples into smart converted brownstones, skyscrapers had become parking lots, factories had become parks, some streets had disappeared completely, one street that had been solidly fur wholesalers was now wall-to-wall art galleries.

But still . . . you could write so many letters, read so many books, walk so many city blocks. And then . . . ?

Get a job, Monica had suggested. In the security department of a store. Or start your own security company. Something like that. Could you be a private detective? A private eye? Like on TV?

No, he had laughed, kissing her. He couldn't be a private eye. Like on TV.

Finally, the afternoon drawing on, the elegant courtyard of the Frick Collection darkening, he rose and walked toward the entrance without visiting any of the galleries. He knew the paintings. El Greco's *St. Jerome* was one of his favorites, and there was a portrait in the long gallery that looked like Don Ameche. He liked that one, too. He walked out past the magnificent pipe organ on the stairway landing.

He had read or heard somewhere a story about old man Frick, the robber baron who had built this palace. It was said that after a stint of crushing labor unions and ruining competitors, Frick would return to this incredible home, put up his feet, and listen dreamily as his private organist played, "When you come to the end of a perfect day . . ."

Smiling at the image, Edward X. Delaney stopped at the cloakroom and surrendered his check.

He gave a quarter to the attendant who brought his hard, black homburg.

The man palmed the coin and said, "Thank you, Chief."

Delaney looked at him, surprised and pleased, but said nothing. He left the building, thinking, They *do* remember! He had walked almost a block before he acknowledged the man might have intended "chief" as "pal" or "fella." "Thank you, buddy." It might have been as meaningless as that. Still . . .

He walked south on Fifth Avenue, enjoying the waning May afternoon. Say what you would—at the right time, the right place, it was a fucking *beautiful* city. At this moment the sun lowering over Central Park, there was a golden glow on the towers, a verdant perfume from the park. The sidewalks of Fifth Avenue were clean. The pedestrians were well dressed and laughing. The squalling traffic was part of it. All growing. It had been there before he was born, and would be there when he was under. He found comfort in that, and thought it odd.

He walked down to 55th Street, lumbering his way through increasing crowds as he moved south. Shoppers. Tourists. Messengers. A chanting Hare Krishna group. A young girl playing a zither. Peddlers. Mendicants. Strollers. He spotted a few hookers, a few bad lads on the prowl. But mostly an innocent, good-natured crowd. Sidewalk artists (butterflies on black velvet), political and religious orators with American flags, one line of pickets with a precinct cop nearby, lazily swinging a daytime stick. Delaney was part of them all. His family, he was tempted to think. But that, he admitted, was fanciful and ridiculous.

He was a heavy, brooding man. Somewhat round-shouldered, almost brutish in appearance. Handsome in a thick, worn way, with grey hair cut *en brosse.* A solemn mien; he had a taste for melancholy, and it showed. His hands were fists. He had the trundling walk of an old street cop on patrol.

He wore a dark suit of dense flannel. A vest festooned with a clumpy gold chain that had been his grandfather's. At one end of the chain, a hunting case in a waistcoat pocket. It had belonged to his father and had stopped fifty years ago. Twenty minutes to noon. Or midnight. At the other end of the chain was a jeweled miniature of his detective's badge, given to him by his wife on his retirement.

Squarely atop his head was his black homburg, looking as if it had been cast in iron. He wore a white shirt with a starched collar. A maroon tie of silk rep. A white handkerchief in the breast pocket of his jacket, and another in his left trouser pocket. Both fresh. And ironed. His shoes were polished to a dull gloss, ankle-high, of black kangaroo leather. The soles were thick. When he was tired, he thumped as he walked.

He suddenly knew where he wanted to go. He crossed 55th Street and turned east.

"Chief!" a voice called.

He looked. There was no mistaking the car illegally parked at the curb: a dusty blue Plymouth. A white man was climbing out, grinning. A black, also smiling, sat behind the wheel, bending over to look up at Delaney.

"Haryah, Chief," the first man said, holding out his hand. "You're looking real good."

Delaney shook the proffered hand, trying to remember.

"Shakespeare," he said suddenly, "William Shakespeare. Who could forget that?"

"Right on," the detective laughed. "We were with you on Operation Lombard."

"And Sam Lauder," Delaney said. He leaned down to shake the hand of the black inside the car. 'You two still married?"

"You'd think so the way we fight," Lauder laughed. "How you been, Chief?"

"Can't complain," Delaney said cheerfully. "Well, I can—but who's to listen? How are you doing?"

"Made first," Shakespeare said proudly. "Sam, too. On your recommendation."

Delaney made a gesture.

"You had it coming," he said. He waved at Fifth Avenue, the elegant Hotel Knickerbocker, the last hotel in New York to have a billiard room. "What are you doing around here—slumming?"

"Nah," Shakespeare said. "It's a half-ass stakeout. Sam and me are on temporary assignment to the East Side hotel squad for the summer. Ever hear of a wrong guy named Al Kingston?"

"Al Kingston?" Delaney repeated. He shook his head. "No, I don't think I make him."

"Arthur King? Albert Kingdon? Alfred Ka—"

"Wait a minute, wait a minute," Delaney said. "Arthur King. That rings a bell. Hotel rooms and jewelry shops. Works alone or with a young twist. In and out so slick and so fast, no one could nail him."

"That's the cat," Shakespeare nodded. "Nabbed a dozen times, and it all added up to nit. Anyway, we got a flash from Miami that Al baby had been rousted and was believed heading our way. We picked him up at the airport and have been keeping tabs on him ever since. Loose tail. We just don't have the manpower."

"I know," Delaney said sympathetically.

"Anyway, this is his third visit to the Knickerbocker. We figure he's casing. When he comes out this time we're going to grab him and bounce him a little. Nothing heavy. Just enough to convince him to move on to Chicago or L.A. Anywhere."

"There's a service entrance," Delaney cautioned. "On Fifty-fourth. You got it covered?"

"Front and back," Shakespeare nodded. "Sam and me have been watching the lobby entrance. We won't miss him."

"Sure you will," Delaney said genially. "There's an arcade from the lobby that leads down the block to an outside drugstore. He could slip out through there as easy as Mary, kiss my ass."

"Son of a *bitch!*" William Shakespeare said bitterly, and began running.

Sam Lauder piled out of the car and went pounding after his partner. Delaney watched them go, feeling, he admitted, better than he should have. He was still smiling when he went into the small, secluded Hotel Knickerbocker bar.

It was a dark, paneled box of a room. The mahogany bar was about ten feet long, with six stools padded with black vinyl. There were a dozen small bistro tables placed around, each with two wire chairs, also padded with black vinyl. Behind the bar, covering the entire wall, was a mural from the 1930s, a vaguely Art Decoish montage of skyscrapers, jazz musicians, mustached men in nipped-waist tuxedos and blonde women in shimmery evening gowns—dancing to some maniacal beat. The mural was painted in white, black, and silver, with musical notes in fire-engine red floating across the surface. Along the top, in jerky lettering, was the legend: "Come on along and listen to—the lullaby of Broadway."

Delaney swung onto one of the stools. He was the only patron in the room. The big, paunchy bartender put down his *Daily News* and came over. He was wearing a white shirt with sleeve garters, a small, black leather bowtie clipped to the collar. He had a long white apron tied under his armpits. It covered him from chest to ankles. He smiled at Delaney, set out an ashtray, a wooden bowl of salted peanuts, a paper napkin with the hotel's crest printed on it.

"Good afternoon, sir," he said. "What can I do you for?"

"Good afternoon," Delaney said. "Do you have any ale or dark beer?"

"Dark Löwenbräu," the man said, staring at Delaney.

"That'll be fine."

The man stood there. He began snapping his fingers, still staring at Delaney.

"I seen you," he said. "I *seen* you!"

Delaney said nothing. The man kept staring, snapping his fingers.

"Delaney!" he burst out. "Chief Delaney! Right?"

Delaney smiled. "Right," he said.

"I knew the second you walked in you was somebody," the bartender said. "I knew I seen you in the paper, or on the TV." He wiped his hand carefully on his apron, then stuck it out. "Chief Delaney, it's a pleasure, believe me. I'm Harry Schwartz."

Delaney shook his hand.

"Not Chief anymore, Harry," he said. "I'm retired."

"I read, I read," Schwartz said. "Wear it in good health. But a President, he retires and he's still Mister President. Right? And a governor is a governor till the day he dies. Likewise a colonel in the army. He retires, but people will call him 'Colonel.' Right?"

"Right," Delaney nodded.

"So you're still Chief," the bartender said. "And me, when I retire, I'll still be Harry Schwartz."

He took a dark Löwenbräu from a tub of crushed ice, wiped the bottle carefully with a clean towel. He selected a glass from the back rack, held it up to the light to detect spots. Satisfied, he placed the glass in front of Delaney on the paper napkin. He uncapped the bottle, filled the glass halfway, allowing about an inch of white head to build. Then he set the bottle on a little paper coaster next to Delaney's hand. He waited expectantly until Delaney took a sip.

"All right?" Harry Schwartz asked anxiously.

"Beautiful," Delaney said, and meant it.

"Good," the bartender said. He leaned across the bar on folded arms. "So tell me, what have you been doing with yourself?"

It didn't come out like that, of course. It came out, "S' tell me, watcha bin doon witcha self?" Chief Delaney figured the accent for Manhattan, probably the Chelsea district.

"This and that," he said vaguely. "Trying to keep busy."

The bartender spread his hands wide.

"What else?" he said. "Just because you're retired don't mean you're dead. Right?"

"Right," Delaney said obediently.

"I thought all cops when they retire they go to Florida and play shuffleboard?"

"A lot of them do," Delaney laughed.

"My brother-in-law he was a cop," Harry Schwartz said. "You prolly wouldn't know him. Out in Queens. A good cop. Never took a nickel. Well, maybe a *nickel.* So he retires and moves to Arizona because my sister she's got asthma. Get her to a dry climate, the doc says, or she'll be dead in a year. So my brother-in-law, Pincus his name was, Louis Pincus, he retires early, you know, and moves Sadie to Arizona. Buys a house out there. Got a lawn, the whole schmear. It looked nice the house from the pictures they sent. A year later, a year mind you, Louie's out mowing that lawn and he drops." Harry Schwartz snapped his fingers. "Like that. The ticker. So he goes out there for Sadie's health, he drops dead, and to this day she's strong as a horse. That's life. Am I right?"

"Right," Delaney said faintly.

"Ah well," Harry Schwartz sighed, "waddya going to do? That's the way things go. Tell me something, Chief—what about these young cops you see nowadays? I mean with the sideburns, the mustaches, the hair. I mean they don't even *look* like cops to me, you know?"

They didn't look like cops to Edward X. Delaney either, but he'd never tell a civilian that.

"Look," he said, "a hundred years ago practically every cop in New York had a mustache. And most of them were big, bushy walrus things. I mean then you almost had to *have* a mustache to get a job as a cop. Styles change, but the cops themselves don't change. Except maybe they're smarter today."

"Yeah," Harry Schwartz said. "I guess you're right. Ready for another?"

"Please. That one just cut the dust. How about you? Have something with me?"

"Nah," Schwartz said. "Thanks, but not while I'm working. I ain't supposed to."

"Come on."

"Well . . . maybe I'll have a beer. I'll keep it under the counter. Many thanks."

He went through the ceremony again, opening a fresh bottle of imported beer for Delaney. Then he opened a bottle of domestic for himself, poured a glass. He looked around at the empty room cautiously, held up the glass quickly, and said, "To your health, Chief."

"To yours," Delaney replied.

They both sipped, and the bartender hid his glass expertly below the counter.

"If you got your health you got everything—right?" he said.

"Right."

"But it's a miserable job, ain't it? I mean being a cop?"

Edward X. Delaney looked down at his glass. He lifted it off the paper napkin. He set it on the polished bar top and began moving it around in small, slow circles.

"Sometimes," he nodded. "Sometimes it's the most miserable job on earth. Sometimes it's okay."

"That's what I figured," Schwartz said. "I mean you see a lot of shit—right? Then, on the other hand, you are also helping people which is okay."

Delaney nodded.

"I was thinking of becoming a cop," Schwartz reminisced. "I really was. I got out of Korea alive and I come back to New York, and I thought what should I do? And I thought maybe I should be a cop. I mean the pay isn't all that great—at least then it wasn't—but it was steady, you know, and the pension and all. But then I knew I really didn't have the balls to be a cop. I mean it takes balls, don't it?"

"Oh yes," Delaney said, wondering if Schwartz knew what they had called him in the Department—"Iron Balls" Delaney.

"Sure. Well, I figured what the hell, so I didn't. I mean like if someone shot at me, I'd probably piss my pants. I mean that. A hero I ain't. And as for shooting someone, I just couldn't."

"You shot at people in Korea, didn't you?"

"Nah. I was a cook."

"Well," Delaney sighed, "Shooting or being shot at is really a very small part of a cop's job. Most people don't realize that, but it's true. Only perhaps one percent or less of a cop's time is spent with a gun in his hand. Most cops put in thirty years on the force, retire, and never fire their guns off the range. The stuff you see in the papers and on TV, the dramatic stuff, happens now and then, sure. But for every shootout there's a thousand cops pounding the beat day after day, settling family squabbles, calling an ambulance for a heart case, getting drunks off the street, rousting junkies or hookers."

"Sure," Harry Schwartz said, "I know all that, and I agree one hundred percent. But still and all, let's face facts, they don't give cops that gun for nothing—right? I mean a cop might go year after year and nothing happens, and that gun could grow right into his holster for all the use it gets. Right? But still and all, the time might come—and bang! There he is and some nut is trying to kill him and he's got to kill that nut first. I mean it happens, don't it?"

"Yes. It happens."

"Still and all," Harry Schwartz said, "I bet you miss it. Right?"

"Right," Edward X. Delaney said.

The garbage had been collected that day and, as usual, the empty cans had been left on the curb. He brought them down in the little areaway below the front stoop and replaced the lids. He could have entered through the basement door, but it meant opening two padlocks and a chain on the outside iron grille, so he went up to the sidewalk again and climbed the eleven steps to the front door.

When he and Barbara had remodeled this old brownstone almost thirty years ago, they had been able to save and refurbish some of the original amenities, including the front door, which had to be, he figured, at least seventy-five years old. Unlocking it now, he admired it anew—polished oak with brass hardware, and set with a diamond-shaped judas of beveled glass.

He entered the lighted hall, double-locked the door, put the chain on.

"I'm home," he yelled.

"In here, dear," his wife called from the kitchen.

He hung his homburg on the hall rack and went down the long corridor, sniffing appreciatively.

"Something smells good," he said, coming into the big kitchen.

Monica turned, smiling. "Meal or cook?" she said.

"Both," he said, kissing her cheek. "What are we having?"

"Your favorite," she said. "Boiled beef with horseradish sauce."

He stopped suddenly, stared at her.

"All right," he said. "What did you buy?"

She turned back to the pots and pans, vexed, a little, but still smiling.

"Stop being a detective," she said. "It wasn't so much. New bedspreads for the girls' room."

"That's not so bad," he said. He took a stalk of celery from a platter of greens and sat heavily at the wooden kitchen table, munching. "How was your day?"

"Hectic. The stores were mobbed. The girls said they had a nice lunch and you drank two highballs."

"The dirty squealers," he said. "They home?"

"Yes. Upstairs. Getting a start on their homework. Edward, they give the kids a lot of homework at that school."

"It won't kill them," he said.

"And Ivar Thorsen called. He wants to see you."

"Oh? Did he say why?"

"No. He wants to come over tonight at nine. He said to call his office if you can't make it. If he doesn't hear from you, he'll figure it's all right to come over."

"All right with me. You? Have anything planned?"

"No. There's a program on Channel Thirteen I want to watch. About breast cancer."

"I'll take Thorsen," he said. "Can I set the table?"

"Done," she said. "We'll eat in fifteen minutes."

"I'll wash up then," he said, rising.

"And chase the kids down," she said, tasting the sauce.

He slid an arm around her soft waist. She came close to him, still holding a big wooden spoon.

"Did I tell you I love you?" he asked her.

"Not today, you haven't."

"Consider it told."

"Oh no you don't, buster," she said. "You don't get off that easy."

"I love you," he said, and kissed her lips. "Umm," he said. "Nothing like a horseradishy kiss. Going to have a beer with dinner?"

"I'll have a sip of yours."

"The hell you will," he said. "Have your own. With boiled beef, I want *all* of mine."

She made a rude gesture with the wooden spoon, and he left, laughing.

She had been Monica Gilbert, the widow of Bernard Gilbert, one of the victims of a psychopathic killer, Daniel Blank. Delaney had been a captain then, in command of a special task force that had taken Blank, and he had met Monica during the investigation of that case. A year after Barbara Delaney had died of proteus infection, the Chief had married Monica. She was twenty years younger than he.

Their evening meal was, as usual, dominated by the lively chatter of the girls. Mary and Sylvia were eleven and thirteen and, of course, knew everything. Most of the discussion involved plans for the summer, whether it would be best for the sisters to attend the same camp or different camps. They spoke learnedly of "sibling rivalry" and "intrafamilial competition." Chief Delaney listened gravely, asked serious questions, and only Monica was aware of his amusement.

Afterwards, Delaney helped clear the table, but left the rest to his wife and stepdaughters. He went upstairs to take off jacket and vest and put on a worn cardigan. He also took off his high shoes, massaged his feet, and slid them into old carpet slippers. He came down to the living room, stopping off in the kitchen to fill a hammered silver ice bucket. The dishwasher was grinding away, and Monica was just finishing tidying up. The girls had gone up to their room again.

"Can we afford it?" she asked anxiously. "Camp, I mean? It's expensive, Edward."

"You tell me," he said. "You're the financial expert in this family."

"Well . . . maybe," she said, frowning. "If you and I don't go anywhere."

"So? We'll stay home. Lock up, pull down the shades, turn on the air conditioner and make love all summer."

"Knocker," she scoffed. "Your back couldn't take it."

"Sure it could," he said equably. "As long as your pearls don't break."

She burst out laughing. He looked at her wryly.

It had happened the first time they went to bed together, about two months before they were married. He had taken her to dinner and the theatre. After, she had readily agreed to stop at his home for a nightcap before returning to her home in the same neighborhood, to her children, a baby-sitter.

She was a big-bodied woman, strong, with a good waist between heavy bosom and wide hips. Not yet matronly. Still young, still juicy. A look of limpid, almost ingenuous sensuality. All of her warm and waiting.

That night she wore a thin black dress. Not clinging, but when she moved, it touched her. About her neck, a choker of oversize pearls. When he kissed her, she pressed to him, clove to him, breast to breast, belly to belly, thigh to thigh. They stumbled, panting, up to his bedroom, where high drama became low farce.

She was lying on the bed crossways, naked except for those damned pearls. Spread out, pink and anxious. He stood at the bedside, crouched and swollen, and lifted her hips. She writhed up to embrace him. The string of pearls broke, spilling down onto the parquet floor. But they were both nutty with their lust and . . .

"You broke my pearls," wailed she.

"Fuck the pearls," roared he.

"No, me!" screamed she. *"Me!"*

But the beads were under his floundering feet, rolling, hurting, and he began skidding about, doing a mad schottische, a wild gavotte, an insane kadzotsky, until laughter defeated them both. So they had to change positions and start all over again, which wasn't all that bad.

Smiling at the memory, they went into the living room, where he mixed them each a rye highball. They sat contentedly, both slumped with legs extended.

Deputy Commissioner Ivar Thorsen arrived promptly at nine. Monica remained in the living room to watch her TV program. The two men went into the study and closed the door. Delaney emerged a moment later to fetch the bucket of ice. His wife was seated on the edge of her chair, leaning forward, arms on her knees, eyes on the screen. Delaney smiled and touched her hair before he went back into the study.

"What, Ivar?" he asked. "Rye? Scotch? Anything?"

"A little Scotch would be fine, Edward. Just straight. No ice, please."

They sat facing in old club chairs, the original leather dry and cracked. They raised their glasses to each other, sipped.

In the Department, Thorsen was called "Admiral," and looked it: fine, silvered hair, cutting blue eyes, a posture so erect he was almost rigid. He was slender, small-boned, fastidiously well groomed.

He had been Edward Delaney's mentor in the Department, his "rabbi," and a good one, for he had a talent for political infighting, an instinct for picking the winner in the ferocious conflicts that periodically racked city government. More, he *enjoyed* that world where government of law crashed against government of men. He stepped his way daintily through the debris, and was never soiled.

"How are things going?" Delaney asked.

Thorsen flipped a palm back and forth.

"The usual," he said. "You know about the budget cuts and layoffs."

"Rates up?"

"No, that's the crazy thing." Thorsen laughed shortly. "Fewer cops, but no great increase in crime. The unions thought there would be. So did I."

"So did I," Delaney nodded. "Glad to hear there isn't. Chief Bernhardt is doing a good job."

Bernhardt was Delaney's successor as Chief of Detectives. A career cop, he had commanded Brooklyn detectives before being brought to headquarters in Manhattan. His wife's father was on the board of a prestigious New York bank that held a vaultful of New York City and State notes and bonds. It didn't hurt.

"Good," Thorsen said, "but not great. But Bernhardt's got his problems, too. The cutbacks have hurt. That's why I'm here."

"Oh?"

"You read about a homicide about a month ago? Victor Maitland? The artist?"

"Sure. Down in Little Italy. I followed it. It fell out of the papers in a hurry."

"There was a lot of other hot news at the time," Thorsen said. "Thank God. Also, we didn't have anything. It's still open."

"Sounded like a B-and-E to me," Delaney said. "A guy with a snootful of shit breaks the door, this Maitland puts up a fight and gets the shiv."

"Could be," Thorsen said. "I don't know all the details, but his place had been ripped off twice before, and he had locks and a chain. They weren't forced. We figured he opened for someone he knew."

"Oh? Anything missing?"

"His wallet. But he never carried much cash. And he still had his credit cards on him. There was an expensive portable radio in the place. It wasn't touched."

"Ah?" Delaney said. "A faked heist? It's been done before. Who inherits?"

"No will. That'll give a lot of lawyers a lot of work. The IRS sealed everything. The guy was loaded. His last painting went for a hundred big ones."

"I've seen his stuff," Delaney said. "I like it."

"I do, too," Thorsen said. "So does Karen. She thinks he was the greatest thing since Rembrandt. But that's neither here nor there. We're dead on the case. No leads. It would be just another open file, but we're getting a lot of flak."

Delaney rose to freshen Thorsen's drink. He also dropped two more ice cubes into his rye-and-water.

"Flak?" he said. "Where from?"

"Ever hear of a guy named J. Barnes Chapin?"

"Sure. A politico. State senator. From upstate somewhere."

"That's right," Thorsen nodded. "His home base is Rockland County. Chapin has been in Albany since the year one. He swings a lot of clout. Right now, there's a bill up for a special State grant to New York City for law enforcement—cops, courts, prisons, the works. Chapin could tip the scale."

"So?"

"Chapin is—or was—Victor Maitland's uncle."

"Oh-ho."

"The funny thing is that Chapin couldn't care less who offed Maitland. From what we've learned, this Maitland was a Grade-A bastard. As the old saying goes, the list of suspects has been narrowed to ten thousand. Everyone hated his guts, including his wife and son. Everyone but his mother. A boy's best friend etcetera. She's a wealthy old dame who lives near Nyack. One daughter, Maitland's sister, lives with her. The mother's been driving Chapin crazy. He's her brother. And he's been driving us crazy. When are we going to find Victor Maitland's killer and get his sister off his back?"

Delaney was silent, staring at Thorsen. He took a slow sip of his drink. The two men locked eyes.

"Why me?" he asked quietly.

Thorsen hunched forward.

"Look, Edward," he said, "you don't have to quote me the numbers. I know the graph: if a homicide isn't solved in the first forty-eight hours, solution probability drops off to nit. It's a cold trail. Granted. And just between you, me, and the lamppost, finding the killer of Victor Maitland comes pretty far down on the Department's anxiety list."

"I understand."

"But we've got to go through the motions. To keep J. Barnes Chapin happy. So he can keep his sister happy. Convince her we're working on it."

"And keep Chapin on the City's side when that new bill comes up for a vote."

"Of course," Thorsen shrugged. "What else?"

"Again," Delaney said, "why me?"

Thorsen sighed, sat back, crossed his knees, sipped his drink.

"Great Scotch, Edward. What is it?"

"Glenlivet."

"Well, for one thing, Chapin asked for you. Yes, he did. In person. He remembers Operation Lombard. Second, we just don't have the manpower to waste on this thing. Edward, it's *cold.* You know it, we know it. It was probably a smash-and-grab like you said, and the cat is probably in Kansas City by now. Who the hell knows? No one's expecting you to break it. For Christ's sake, Edward, there's been a hundred unsolved homicides in the city since Maitland was greased. We can only do so much."

"What do you want from me?" Delaney asked stonily.

"Look into it. Just look into it. Edward, I know you're retired, but don't tell me you're all that busy. I won't buy it. Just look into it. We can cover your expenses. And we'll assign you one man on active duty to drive you around and flash his potsy whenever it's needed. You'll get copies of everything we've got—reports, photos, PM, the works. Edward, we don't *expect* anything. Just take a look at it."

"So you can tell Chapin the murder of his nephew is under active investigation?"

Thorsen smiled wanly.

"That's exactly correct," he said. "It's for the Department, Edward."

Delaney raised his arms and went through an elaborate mime of bowing a violin. Thorsen laughed.

"Iron Balls!" he said. "Well, what the hell, I thought it might interest you, might intrigue you. Get you out of Monica's hair. No?"

Delaney looked down at his glass, turning it in his hands.

"I'll sleep on it," he said. "Talk it over with Monica. All right? I'll call you in the morning, one way or the other."

"Sure," Thorsen said. "That's good enough for me. Fine. Think it over."

He drained his drink and stood up. Delaney started to rise, then suddenly Thorsen flopped back into his chair.

"There's one other thing," he said.

"Had to be," Delaney said sardonically.

"Remember a cop named Sam—Samuel Boone? About fifteen years ago?"

"Sure, I remember him," Delaney said. "He got blown away. I went to his funeral."

"Right. It was in the South Bronx. My precinct at the time. Jewish then. Now it's all Spic and Span. This Sam Boone was the best. I mean, the *best.* They loved him. On his birthday, old Jewish ladies would bring cakes and cookies to the precinct house. I swear it. He was out of Kentucky or Tennessee or West Virginia, or someplace like that. An accent you could cut with a knife, and the Jews on his beat taught him some Yiddish. They'd say, 'Samele, speak me some Yiddish,' and he'd say what they had taught him in that corn-pone accent of his, and they'd break up. Anyway, a car pulled into a one-way street, going the wrong way, and piled up against oncoming traffic. Sam was nearby and walked over. The car had Illinois plates or Michigan. Something like that. Knowing Sam, I figure he would have explained to the driver about our one-way streets, get him turned around, and send him on his way with a warning. He leans down to talk to the guy—and pow! pow! pow! Three in the face and chest. The guy had to be an idiot, an *idiot!* What's he going to do? He can't pull ahead; he's bumper to bumper with the on-coming cars. And he can't back up because of the traffic on the avenue. So he piles out of the car.

"Edward, I got there about ten minutes after it happened. The streets were crowded, lots of people on the sidewalks, and they saw Sam go down. I swear we had to *tear* this guy away from them. If someone had had a rope, he'd have been swinging. I've never seen people so infuriated. To this day it scares me to think about it. And of course the clincher is that this guy was facing a GTA back in Michigan, or Illinois, or whatever. Even if Sam had asked for his ID, which, knowing Sam, I doubt he'd have done, the guy faced three-to-five at most, and probably less. But he panicked, and I lost the best street cop in my precinct."

Delaney nodded somberly, rose to pour fresh drinks, add ice cubes to his glass. Then he sat down again opposite Thorsen.

"That's the way it goes," he said. "But what's that got to do with Maitland's murder?"

"Well . . ." Thorsen said. He drew a deep breath. "Sam had a son. Abner Boone. He joined the Department. I kept an eye on him. I figured I owed him. Abner Boone. He's a detective sergeant now. You know him, Edward?"

"Abner Boone?" Delaney said, frowning. "I remember him vaguely. About six-one. One-eighty. Sandy hair. Blue eyes. Long arms and legs. Nice grin. Slightly stooped. Looks like his ankles and wrists are sticking out of his clothes. White scar on the left neck. Wears glasses for reading. That the guy?"

"Remember him vaguely?" Thorsen mimicked. "I should have your memory! That's the guy. Edward, you know when the son of a slain patrolman joins the Force, we've got to keep an eye on him. Maybe the kid did it to get revenge, or to prove he's as good as his daddy was, or to prove he's a *better* man than his daddy was. It can be sticky. Anyway, I kept an eye on Abner Boone, and helped when I could. The kid did just great. Made detective sergeant, finally, and about two years ago they gave him one of those commando homicide squads that are supposed to help out the regular units when the workload piles up or when a big case comes along."

"How are they working out?" Delaney asked. "The special squads?"

"Still being evaluated," Thorsen said. "But I don't think they'll last. Too much jealousy from the regular units. That's natural. Anyway, this Abner Boone got this squad, and after a year or so, he had a good record. Some important busts and a lot of good assists. Then he started hitting the sauce. Hard. His squad covered for him for awhile. Then it couldn't be covered. I did what I could—counseling, doctors, psychiatrists, AA, the lot—but nothing worked. Edward, the kid is trying. I know he is. He's really *trying*. If he falls again, he's out."

"And this is the man you want to assign me on the Maitland case? A lush?"

Thorsen laughed shortly.

"You got it," he said. "I figured we can keep J. Barnes Chapin happy with an on-going investigation, even if it comes to zilch. At the same time, I can get Abner Boone out of the office on detached assignment, and maybe he can straighten himself out. It's worth the gamble. And even if he goes off again, who's to see? Except you."

Delaney looked at him with wonder. Perhaps, he thought, this was the secret of Thorsen's success. You manipulate people, but as you do, you tell them exactly why and how you are doing it. Bemused by the honesty, won by the candor in the ice-blue eyes, they agree to do what you want. It all sounds so reasonable.

"I'll sleep on it," he repeated.

Two hours later, he sat with Monica on the living room couch. The TV screen was dead. They were sipping decaf coffee. He told her exactly what Deputy Commissioner Ivar Thorsen had said. He had almost total recall.

"What do you think?" he finished.

"He's an alcoholic?" she asked.

"Abner Boone? Sounds like it from what Ivar said. Or on his way. But that's not important. If Boone fucks up, they'll give me someone else. The question is, should I do it?"

"Do you want to?"

"I don't know. In a way I do, and in a way I don't. I'd like a chance to stick Maitland's killer. A human being shouldn't be destroyed, and the killer walks away. That's not right. I know that sounds simple, but it's the way I feel. My God, if . . . Well . . . On the other hand, I'm retired, and it's the Department's migraine, not mine. Still . . . What do you think?"

"I think you should," she said.

"Want me out of your hair?" he said, smiling. "Out of the house? Working?"

"Nooo," she said slowly. "You're a pain in the ass at times." He looked up sharply. "But I think this is something you should do. But it's really up to you. It's your decision."

He motioned, and she came over to sit on his lap, a soft weight. He put an arm about her waist. She put an arm around his neck.

"Am I really a pain in the ass?" he asked.

"Sometimes," she nodded. "Sometimes I am too. I know. Everyone is. Sometimes. I really think you should do this thing, Edward. Ivar said he doesn't really expect results, but that was just to convince you to take the job, to challenge you. He really does think you can do it, and so does this Chapin. I don't like that man; he's such a reactionary. Do you think you can find Maitland's killer?"

"I don't know," he sighed. "It's a cold, cold trail."

"If anyone can, you can," she said, and that ended it as far as she was concerned. "Coming to bed?" she asked.

"In a while," he said.

She rose, kissed the top of his head, took their cups and saucers into the kitchen. He heard running water, then the sound of her footsteps going upstairs.

He sat another half-hour by himself, slumped, pondering. It was an injustice to Monica, but he thought of what Barbara, his first wife, would have counseled. He knew. Exactly what Monica urged. He was lucky with his women. It was odd how they felt, their lust for life, their passion for children and plants. They were right of course, he acknowledged. You nurtured it. The park. You breathed on it to keep it alive. You punished people who destroyed it. The spark . . .

He sighed again, stood up and stretched, began his rounds. First into the basement to test windows and doors. Then, moving upward, checks to make certain chains and locks were in place to keep out the darkness. Mary and Sylvia were sleeping placidly, secure. The whole house was secure. An island.

He undressed as quietly as he could, and slid into bed. But Monica was still awake. She turned to come into his arms. Warm and waiting.

3

The material on the Maitland case was delivered to the Delaney brownstone by an unmarked police car shortly before noon. It came jammed into three battered liquor cartons with a note from Deputy Commissioner Ivar Thorsen: "Sorry it's not in order, Edward—but you're good at that! Boone will call you tomorrow to set up a meet. Luck."

The Chief had the cartons brought into the study and piled on the floor next to his broad desk. He went into the kitchen and made himself two sandwiches: salami and sliced Spanish onion (with mayonnaise) on rye, and ham and cheese (with mustard) on a seeded roll. He took the sandwiches and an open bottle of Heineken back into the study, placed them carefully aside on a small end table, and set to work.

He went through the three cartons slowly and steadily, glancing briefly at each document before adding it to one of four loosely classified piles:

1. Official reports of the investigating officers.
2. Signed statements of those questioned, and photographs.
3. Photos of the victim alive and as a corpse *in situ,* and reports of the Medical Examiner.
4. Miscellaneous bits of paper, most of which were informal reactions of

detectives to those they had questioned, or suggestions for additional lines of inquiry.

Working methodically, stopping occasionally for a bite of sandwich, a gulp of beer, Delaney had all the records broken down by 3:30 P.M. He then went through each stack arranging it by date and time, switching a few documents from one pile to another, but generally adhering to his original division.

He put on his heavy reading glasses, pulled the green-shaded student lamp close. He sat down in his swivel chair and began with the photos and PM, since this was the smallest stack. Finished, he started on the pile of official reports. He was halfway through when Monica called him to dinner.

He washed up and joined the family in the dining room. He tried to eat slowly and join in the conversation. He made a few ponderous jokes. But he left the table early, declining dessert, and took a mug of black coffee back into the study with him. He completed the initial reading shortly after 9:00 P.M. He then began a second reading, slower this time, with a pad of yellow legal paper nearby on which he occasionally jotted brief notes and questions.

Monica brought him a thermos of coffee at 11:00 and announced she would watch TV for an hour and then go to bed. He smiled absently, kissed her cheek, went back to his reading. He completed the second review by 1:00 A.M. He then filed the material in folders in the bottom drawer of a metal cabinet equipped with a lock. He dug out his street map and street guide of Manhattan and located the scene of the killing, on Mott Street between Prince and Spring.

He knew the section; about twenty years previously, when he was a dick two, he had been assigned temporarily as a summer replacement for precinct detectives going on vacation. The neighborhood was practically 100 percent Italian then, part of Little Italy. Delaney remembered how, later in the year, he had enjoyed the Feast of San Gennaro on Mulberry Street, one of the city's big ethnic festivals.

He was assigned as partner to Detective first grade Alberto Di Lucca. Big Al was a jowly, pot-bellied, wine-swilling pasta fiend, and had introduced Delaney to the glories of Italian cooking. He had also taught him a lot of tricks of the trade.

In July of that year, there was a ripoff of a wholesale warehouse on Elizabeth Street. Four masked men, armed, forced their way in, tied up the night watchman, and drove off in a huge semitrailer loaded with imported olive oil. This, to Di Lucca, a man who worshipped *spaghetti all'olio,* was sacrilege.

"Now what you got to know," Di Lucca told Delaney, "is that we got a lot of bad boys in this precinct. But generally they go outside the neighborhood for their fun and games. It's like an unwritten law: you don't shit in the living room. Howsomever, in this case I think it was locals."

"How do you figure?" Delaney asked.

"Now take the watchman. Outsiders would have blasted him, cold-cocked him, or treated him rough. But no, this old man is asked politely to lie down on a pile of burlap bags, he's tied up, and a piece of tape put gently across his mouth. And before the gonnifs leave, they ask him is he comfortable? Can he breathe okay? They did everything but serve him breakfast in bed. I figure he knew them, and they knew him. Maybe he fingered the job. He's got a lot of relatives, a lot of young, hot-blooded nephews. One of them, Anthony Scorese, isn't nice. He runs with three pals: Vito Gervase, Robert Scheinfelt—a Wop, but you'd never know it from that name, right?—and a punk named Giuseppe something. I don't know his last name, but they call him Kid Stick. I think those four desperadoes pulled this job. Let's ask around and see if they're spending."

So Di Lucca and Delaney asked around, and sure enough the Fearsome Four had been spending. Not a lot, but enough to indicate they had come into sudden wealth: good wine and Strega with their meals, blonde broads from uptown, new alligator shoes.

"Now we're going to break them," Di Lucca told Delaney. "They swore undying allegiance to each other. On their mothers' graves. They'll die before they talk. They swore. Now watch this. I'm going to break these stupidos. I'll talk Italian to them, but later I'll tell you what they said."

Di Lucca questioned each of the suspects alone. He'd ask Anthony Scorese, for instance, where he was at the time of the heist. "In bed," Scorese said, then laughed. "I got a witness. This broad, she'll tell you."

"In bed with a broad?" Di Lucca said. He smiled enigmatically. "That ain't what Vito Gervase says."

He let it go at that, and moved to Gervase.

"I was out in Jersey at my uncle's place."

"So?" Di Lucca said softly. "That ain't what Scheinfelt says."

And so forth, over a period of two weeks. He worked on them, asking more questions, playing one against the other. They thought they knew what Di Lucca was doing, but they couldn't be sure. They began staring at each other. Then Di Lucca concentrated on Kid Stick, telling him that because of his youth, he'd probably get nothing more than probation if he cooperated. The Kid began to weaken, but it was Robert Scheinfelt who cracked first and made a deal.

"And that's how you do it," Di Lucca told Delaney. "Honor among thieves? My ass! They'd turn in their twin for a suspended sentence."

Now, staring at the street on the map, the street where Victor Maitland had been knifed to death, Delaney remembered Detective Alberto Di Lucca and wished he was still around with his house-by-house knowledge of the neighborhood. But Big Al had retired a long time ago, had returned to Naples, and had probably suffocated his heart with just one more helping of *costoletta di maiale alla napoletana.*

Delaney sighed, turned out the study lamp, started his security check. He wasn't depressed by what he had read, but he wasn't elated, either. The investigation of Maitland's murder had been a good one, he acknowledged. Thorough. Energetic. Imaginative. A lot of bells had been rung. A lot of pavements pounded. A lot of people questioned. A lot of records had been dug up and reviewed. It all added up to zero, to zip, to zilch. A cipher case.

The body had been discovered by Saul Geltman, owner of Geltman Galleries on Madison Avenue, and Victor Maitland's exclusive agent. Maitland had promised to be at the Galleries at three o'clock Friday afternoon to work with Geltman and an interior designer on plans for a new exhibition of Maitland's work. When he hadn't shown up by four, Geltman had called the Mott Street studio. No answer. He had then called Maitland's home on East 58th Street. He spoke to Alma Maitland, the artist's wife. She didn't know Maitland's whereabouts, but said he had mentioned he was meeting Geltman at the Galleries at three that afternoon.

Neither wife nor agent was particularly concerned about Maitland's absence. It was not the first time he had failed to keep an appointment. Apparently, he was a chronic liar, broke promises carelessly, often disappeared for a day or two at a time. When working in the Mott Street studio, he frequently took the phone off the hook or simply didn't answer calls. He slept there occasionally.

Saul Geltman stated that he continued trying to reach Maitland at his home and the studio all day Saturday, with no success. He also called a few acquaintances of Maitland's. None knew where the artist was. Finally, by noon on Sunday, Geltman was becoming worried. He cabbed down to the studio. The door was closed but unlocked. There were roaches in the blood. Geltman promptly vomited, then called 911, the police emergency number, from the studio phone.

A two-man precinct squad car was first to respond. They put in the call reporting an apparent homicide; police machinery began to grind. Within an hour, the tenement building was roped off. Upstairs, the fifth-floor studio was crowded with officers from the precinct, detectives from the homicide unit covering that area, a doctor from the Medical Examiner's office, lab technicians, photographers, the district attorney's man, and Sergeant Abner Boone and two men from his special commando homicide squad.

The autopsy report stated laconically that Victor Maitland had died of "exsanguination resulting from multiple stab wounds." In other words, the man had bled to death; internal cavities were full, and he was lying in a coagulated pool. The weapon was described as "a knife, a single-edged weapon approximately five or six inches in length, tapering to a fine point." Analysis of stomach contents revealed ingestion of a moderate amount of whiskey just prior to death, which occurred, the ME's surgeons estimated, between 10:00 A.M. and 3:00 P.M. on Friday. They refused to be more precise.

A double investigation was begun. On the assumption that the artist was killed by a thief, a mugger, one team of detectives began searching the files for similar attacks, began questioning neighbors and nearby shopkeepers, copied down license-plate numbers of parked cars in the vicinity, later to question their owners. Catch basins, sewers, garbage cans, and litter baskets in a ten-block area were searched for the weapon. Snitches were queried, police and court records were reviewed for recent releases of knife-wielding smash-and-grab experts.

A second team, working on the assumption that Victor Maitland had opened his locked door to someone he knew and was dirked by that someone, began looking into the painter's private life and personal affairs, questioning anyone they could find who knew Maitland and might, conceivably, have closed him out. Eventually, they concentrated their efforts on seven people.

Before limiting their inquiries to this group, detectives questioned a depressingly long list of artists, models, art dealers, art critics, prostitutes, drinking companions, and a few distant relatives, none of whom seemed particularly distressed by the sudden blanking of Victor Maitland, and made little effort to hide their indifference. Depending on the education and/or social status of the acquaintance questioned, the dead man was described as everything from "an offensive and disagreeable individual" to "a piece of shit."

But after a heavy investigation that lasted almost six weeks, after the expenditure of thousands of man-hours of slogging work, the Department was no closer to the solution of the crime than they had been when Saul Geltman made his call to 911. Everything was gone over three times. New detectives were brought in for a fresh look at the evidence collected. Researchers went back to Maitland's two-year hitch in the army, even to his school days, looking for a possible motive.

Nothing.

One of the homicide dicks summed up the feelings of all of them:

"What the hell," he said wearily. "Why don't we say the son of a bitch stabbed himself in the back, and forget about it?"

Monica Delaney devoted every Thursday to volunteer work at a local hospital. Before leaving the house, she delivered a written list of instructions to Chief Delaney: a timetable detailing when he was to put the roast in the oven, at what temperature, when he was to put the potatoes in the stove-top baker, when he was to take the Sara Lee chocolate cake from the freezer. He inspected the list solemnly, his glasses sliding down his nose.

"And I'll try to get the windows done," he told her.

She laughed, and stuck out her tongue at him.

He went into the study, sat down at his desk. He left the door open. He was alone in the house; he wanted to hear every unfamiliar and unexpected creak and thump.

He took a new manila file folder from a desk drawer. He had intended to write on the tab: "Killing of Victor Maitland." But he paused. Perhaps he should write: "Murder of Victor Maitland." There was a difference, he felt, between a murder and a killing. It went beyond the legal definition of First Degree: "With malice aforethought . . ."

Delaney tried to analyze his feeling, and decided that the difference he saw between the two was in the deliberation of the act. The soldier in war usually killed, he didn't murder. But an assassination was a murder, not a killing. Unless the assassin was hired. A fine line there that involved not only deliberation but passion. Cold passion.

If Victor Maitland had been offed because he resisted a thief, that would be a killing. If he had been stabbed to death by someone known to him, someone who had pondered and planned, for whatever reason, it would be a murder. Delaney shook his head ruefully. This decision was to color his whole approach to the case, he knew. He was hardly into it, and already he was faced with the very basic question that had flummoxed the Department. Finally, taking a deep breath, he wrote on the folder tab: "Murder of Victor Maitland," and let it go at that.

Inside the folder he placed two pages of notes and questions he had jotted down while reviewing the Department's records. Then he drew the legal pad to him and began listing the things he planned to do in his private investigation. He wrote them down in no particular order, just as they occurred to him.

When the list was as complete as he could make it, when he ran out of ideas, he began putting the items in the proper sequence. As important as the ideas themselves. He struggled with it, juggling, trying to construct the most logical order. That completed, he added the final sequence to the manila folder. It pleased him. This was *his* paper. Up to now, the Maitland case had consisted solely of other men's paper. The phone rang while he was preparing additional file folders, labeled VICTIM, AGENT, WIFE, MISTRESS, etc.

"Edward X. Delaney here," he said.

"Chief, this is Detective sergeant Abner Boone."

There was a pause, each waiting for the other to speak again. Finally . . .

"Yes, sergeant," Delaney said. "Thorsen said you'd call. When can we get together?"

"Whenever you say, sir."

The voice was slightly twangy, not quite steady. There was no slur, but the agitation was there, controlled but there.

Delaney's first impulse was to invite the man for dinner. With a standing rib roast and baked potatoes, there'd be plenty of food. But he had second thoughts. It would be wiser if his initial meeting with Boone was one-on-one. Then he could evaluate the man. Before introducing him to the family.

"Would this evening at nine inconvenience you, sergeant?" he asked. "At my home? Do you have anything planned?"

"No, sir. Nothing planned. Nine will be fine. I have your address."

"Good. See you then."

Delaney hung up and went to his file cabinet for the stacks of official reports and signed statements. He began to divide these into his new folders: VICTIM, AGENT, WIFE, MISTRESS . . .

He had a sandwich and a glass of milk at noon, went for a short walk along the streets of Two-five-one Precinct, smoking a cigar. He returned home in the early afternoon and continued his filing chores. This was donkey work, but most police work was. In fact, he found a curious satisfaction in this task of "putting things in order."

That's what a cop's job was all about, wasn't it? To restore and maintain order in a disordered world. Not only in society, but in the individual as well. Even in the cop himself. That was the reason for the multitude of forms, the constantly increasing mass of regulations. That was the reason for the formalistic, and sometimes ridiculous officialese. A cop never nabbed a crook. Not in a filed report or court testimony he didn't. He apprehended a suspect, or took a perpetrator into custody.

"Officer, when did you first encounter the accused?"

"I approached the defendant at nine-fifteen on the morning of April two, of this year, as he was exiting the premises of Boog's Tavern, located on Lexington Avenue and Ninetieth Street, City of New York, Borough of Manhattan. I identified myself as an officer of the law. I thereupon recited to this person his legal rights, as required, and placed him under arrest, charging him with the criminal act specified. I then accompanied the accused to the Two-five-one Precinct house, where he was duly incarcerated."

A touching search for precision in a lunatic world . . .

So Chief Edward X. Delaney worked away at his files, trying to create order from the murder of Victor Maitland.

The dinner was fine, the roast of beef blood-rare, the way Delaney liked it. Monica and the girls took their slices from the well-done ends; he liked his from the dripping middle. They had a California jug burgundy; Mary and Sylvia were each allowed one glass, cut half-and-half with water.

The girls went upstairs to their homework. Delaney helped Monica clear the table, put leftovers away, stack the dishwasher. Then they took second cups of coffee into the living room. He began telling her about the Maitland murder. He had learned a long time ago, when Barbara was alive, that it helped him to verbalize a case to an attentive listener. Even if the listener could offer no constructive suggestions, sometimes the questions—untrained, ingenuous—opened new paths of inquiry, or forced Delaney to re-examine his own thinking.

Monica listened intently, her eyes squinching with pain as he described what had happened to Victor Maitland. Remembering what had happened to her first husband, Bernard Gilbert . . .

"Edward," she said, when he had finished, "it could have been a robber, couldn't it?"

"A burglar."

"A burglar, a mugger . . . whatever."

"Could have been," he acknowledged. "What about the unlocked door? No sign of forced entry."

"Maybe he just forgot to lock the door."

"Maybe. But he had been ripped-off twice before. And he hated interruptions while he was painting. His wife and his agent both say he was paranoiac about it. He *always* locked up."

"Like you," she said.

"Yes," he smiled. "Like me. Also, he was stabbed several times. Someone spent a lot of time on that. A chance mugger might stab him once, or twice, but he probably wouldn't stand over him plunging the knife again and again. Once Maitland was down and obviously incapable of resistance, a thief would go to work stripping the place. All right, maybe the thief killed him so Maitland couldn't identify him later from mug shots. But if Maitland saw him, then he should have been facing him and the wounds would be in the front. Follow? I'm just going by percentages. Maitland's wallet was taken, true, but it could have been an attempt to make it look like a heist. There was an expensive portable radio that wasn't touched, and a box of snappers in plain view on a dresser top."

"What are snappers?"

"Ampules of amyl nitrite. You break them and sniff. Supposed to increase your sexual power. Want me to try them?"

"No, thanks, dear. I don't think I could take it."

"God bless you," he said. "Anyway, snappers—sometimes they're called poppers—are used legitimately to treat heart disorders. By prescription only. But of course they're sold on the street. Maitland had no record of heart trouble, and his doctor never prescribed amyl nitrite for him. The detectives on the case made a half-assed effort to find out where Maitland was buying, but came up with a big, fat naught. It's one of the things I want to go into more thoroughly."

"You think there's a drug angle?"

"Oh no. The PM said no evidence of habituation. No, I don't think drugs had any great importance in this. The snappers are just a loose end. But they might lead to something that leads to something. I don't like loose ends."

"You said the autopsy report said he had been drinking."

"Moderately, that morning. But I think he hit it pretty hard; his liver was enlarged. There was a half-empty bottle of whiskey in the studio, on a crate where he had been sketching. The bottle was dusted, but all they got were Maitland's prints, smudges, and a few partials of someone else. Not enough for a make. Ditto for a glass that was on the sink. It had held whiskey, the same brand that was in the bottle. Which tells us exactly nothing."

"Maybe the killer had a drink after—after he did what he did."

"Maybe," Delaney said dubiously, "but I doubt it. The bottle was at one end of the studio, the sink at the other. If the murderer had had a drink, bottle and glass would probably be close together. You said, '—after he did what he did.' *He.* How about a woman? Female killers frequently use knives. At least, more often than they do guns. Percentages again."

"I don't think a woman would stab him so many times."

"Why not?"

"I don't know . . . It just seems so—so awful."

"Man or woman, it was awful. All those stabs indicate hot blood, fury, or just an absolute need to make certain the man was dead. The strange thing is that whoever did it didn't kill him after all. Not right then. After a dozen stab wounds, he was still alive. He finally bled to death."

"Oh Edward . . ."

"I'm sorry," he said quickly, reaching out to touch her. "It upsets you. I shouldn't have started talking about it. I won't discuss it with you again."

"Oh no," she protested. "I want to hear about it. It's interesting. Fascinating, in a horrible kind of way. No, talk to me about it, Edward. Maybe I can help."

"You can, just by listening."

The doorbell chimed, and she rose to answer it.

"I still don't think it was a woman," she said firmly.

He smiled after her. He didn't think it was a woman either, but not for her reasons. He didn't think so because the PM had mentioned that several of the knife blows had been delivered with such force that the blade had penetrated completely, and the killer's knuckles had bruised the surrounding flesh. That indicated powerful thrusts, masculine power. Still, it might have been an extremely strong woman. Or an extremely enraged woman . . .

Chief Delaney's memory had been accurate: Detective Sergeant Abner Boone was a tall, thin, shambling man, with floppy gestures, and a way of tilting his head to one side when he spoke. His hair was more gingery than sandy. His skin was pale and freckled. He was, Delaney guessed, somewhere between thirty and thirty-five; it was difficult to judge. He had the kind of face that would change very little in sixty years. Then, suddenly, he would be an old man.

There was an awkward, farmerish quality in his manner, in the way he bowed slightly over Monica's hand and murmured shyly, "Pleased, ma'am." His grip was firm enough and dry enough when he shook Delaney's hand, but when he was seated in one of the cracked-leather club chairs in the study, he didn't seem to know what to do with his hands—or feet either, for that matter. He kept crossing and recrossing his ankles, and he finally thrust his hands into the pockets of his worn tweed jacket. To hide a tremor, Delaney guessed.

"Would you like something?" the Chief asked. "We have some rare roast beef. How about a sandwich?"

"No, thank you, sir," Boone said faintly. "Nothing to eat. But I'd appreciate coffee. Black, please."

"I'll get a thermos," Delaney said.

When he went into the kitchen, Monica was emptying the dishwasher, putting things away on the shelves.

"What do you think?" he asked her in a low voice.

"I like him," she said promptly. "He seems so innocent."

"Innocent!"

"Well, kind of boyish. Very polite. Is he married?"

He stared at her.

"I'll find out," he said. "If not, you can alert Rebecca. Matchmaker!"

"Why not?" she giggled. "Don't you want the whole world to be as happy as we are?"

"They couldn't endure it," he assured her.

Back in the study, he poured steaming coffee for both of them. Boone picked up his cup from the tray with both hands. Now the tremor was obvious.

"I suppose Deputy Commissioner Thorsen told you what the deal is?" Delaney started.

"Just that I'll be working under you on a continuing investigation of the Maitland thing. He said it's okay to use my own car; he'll cover me on expenses."

"Right," Delaney nodded. "What kind of car?"

"Four-door black Pontiac."

"Good. As long as it isn't one of those little sporty jobs. I like to stretch my legs."

"It's not very sporty," Boone smiled wanly. "Six years old. But pretty good condition."

"Fine. Now—" Delaney paused. "What do I call you? Boone? Abner? Ab? What did the men call you?"

"Mostly they called me Daniel."

Delaney laughed.

"Should have known," he said. "Well, I prefer sergeant, if it's all right with you?"

Boone nodded gratefully.

"I'll try to work regular hours," Delaney said. "But you may have to put in weekends. Better warn your wife."

"I'm not married," the sergeant said.

"Oh?"

"Divorced."

"Ah. Live alone?"

"Yes."

"Well, I'll want your address and phone number before you leave. How much time did you put in on the Maitland case?"

"My squad was in on it from the start," Boone said. "I got there right after the body was found. Then we were in on questioning the family, friends, acquaintances, and so forth."

"What was your take? Someone he knew?"

"Had to be. He was a big, hefty guy. And mean. He could have put up a fight. But he turned his back on someone he knew."

"No signs of a struggle?"

"None. The studio was a mess. I mean all cluttered. But the agent said it was always like that. It was the way Maitland lived. But no signs of a fight. No chairs knocked over or anything broken. Nothing like that. He turned his back, bought it, and went down. That simple."

"Woman?" Delaney asked.

"Don't think so, sir. But possible."

Delaney thought a moment.

"Your squad check the snappers?"

Boone was confused, twisting his fingers.

"Uh—ah—I really don't know about the snappers, Chief. I got taken off the case. Thorsen tell you? About my trouble?"

"He told me," Delaney said grimly. "He also told me that if you fuck-up once more, you're out."

Boone nodded miserably.

"When did it start?" Delaney asked. "The divorce?"

"No," Boone said. "Before that. The divorce was one of the results, not the cause."

"A lot of cops crawl into a bottle," Delaney said. "Pressures. The filth."

"The pressures I could take," Boone said, raising his head. "I took them for almost ten years. The filth got to me. What people do. To each other. To themselves. I was handling it—the disgust, I mean—then I caught a sex case. Two beautiful little girls. Sisters. Cut. Burned. Everything. It pushed me over the edge. No excuse. Just an explanation. The only choice was to get hard or to get drunk. I had to sleep."

"You're not a religious man?"

"No," Boone said. "I was a Baptist originally, but I don't work at it."

"Well, sergeant," Edward X. Delaney said coldly, "don't expect any sympathy from me. Or advice. You're a grown man; it's your choice. If you can't hack it, I'll have to tell Thorsen to give me someone else."

"I know that, sir."

"As long as you know it. Let's get back to the case . . . I've read the file, but I'll have some questions on your personal reactions as we go along. For instance, what's your take on Maitland?"

"Everyone says he was the greatest painter in the country, but an A-Number-One shit. Some evidence he beat his wife. His son hated him. Still does, I guess. Humiliated his agent in public. Always getting into brawls. I mean breaking up bars and restaurants. A mean drunk. Got beaten up himself several times. Things like insulting a woman who was with a guy bigger than Maitland. Crazy things. Like he *wanted* to be kicked to hell and gone. A hard guy to figure. I guess he had talent to burn, but he was one miserable human being."

"Miserable?" Delaney picked up on that. "You mean he himself was miserable, like sad, or he was a poor excuse for a human being?"

Boone pondered a moment.

"Both ways, I'd guess," he said finally. "A very complex guy. Before I got taken off the case, I bought a book of his paintings and went to see the ones in the Geltman Galleries and in the museums. I figured if I could get a handle on the guy, maybe it would help me find who offed him, and why."

Delaney looked at him with surprised admiration.

"Good iea," he said. "Learn anything?"

"No, sir. Nothing. Maybe it was me. I don't know much about painting."

"You still have that book? Of Maitland's paintings?"

"Sure. It's around somewhere."

"Can I borrow it?"

"Of course."

"Thank you. Tomorrow's Friday. The PM says he was knocked on Friday, between ten and three in the afternoon. Can you pick me up tomorrow morning around nine? I want to go down to that Mott Street studio and look around. And the neighborhood. We'll be there from ten to three, when it happened."

Abner Boone looked at him intently.

"Anything special, Chief?" he asked.

Delaney shook his head.

"Not a whisper," he said. "Just noodling. But we got to start somewhere."

He saw the sergeant brighten and straighten when he said "we."

Both men stood up. Then Boone hesitated.

"Chief, did they send you the inventory of Maitland's personal effects from the ME's office?"

"Yes, I got it."

"Spot anything unusual?"

"Nooo," Delaney said. "Did I miss something?"

"Not something that was on the list," Boone said. "Something that wasn't." Suddenly, unexpectedly, he blushed. His pale face reddened; the freckles disappeared. "The guy wasn't wearing any underwear."

Delaney looked at him, startled.

"You're sure?"

Boone nodded. "I checked it out with the guys who stripped the corpse at the morgue. No underwear."

"Odd. What do you make of it?"

"Nothing," Boone said. "I had a session with a Department shrink—I guess Thorsen told you about that—and just for the hell of it I asked him what about a guy who didn't wear underwear. He gave me the usual bullshit answer: it might be significant, and it might not."

Delaney nodded and said, "That's the trouble. In a case like this, it's a temptation to see all facts as of equal significance. They're not. But crossing off the meaningless stuff takes just as much time as tracking down what's important. Well, we've got plenty of time. The Department really doesn't expect a break on this. See you in the morning, sergeant."

Boone nodded, and they shook hands again. The sergeant seemed a little more cheerful, or a little less beaten. He left his address and phone number. Delaney saw him out, locked and chained the door behind him.

Monica was motionless in bed, but stirred when Delaney began undressing.

"Well?" she asked.

"Divorced," he reported.

"That's nice," she said drowsily. "I'll call Rebecca in the morning."

4

They parked on Houston Street and got out of the car.

"Aren't you going to show an 'Officer on Duty' card?" Delaney asked.

"Don't think I better, Chief," Abner Boone said. "The last time I displayed it, they stole my hubcaps."

Delaney smiled, then looked around slowly. He told Boone of the tour of duty he had served in this precinct twenty years ago.

"It was all Italian then," he said. "But I guess it's changed."

Boone nodded. "Some blacks. Lots of Puerto Ricans. But mostly Chinese moving up across Canal Street. Mulberry Street is still Italian though. Good restaurants."

"I remember," Delaney said. "I could eat those cannoli like there was no tomorrow."

They sauntered over to Mott Street, then turned south. The Chief looked up at the red-brick tenements.

"It hasn't changed all that much," he said. "The first day I was down here I got hit by airmail. You know what that is?"

"Sure." Boone grinned. "Flying garbage. They throw it out the windows into the street."

When he grinned, the boyishness Monica had noted became more evident. He had big, horsey teeth, but they didn't seem out of place in his long, smooth face. His eyes were pale blue, small and watchful. He walked in a kind of springy, loose-limbed lope, all the more youthful in contrast to Delaney's heavy, splay-footed trundle.

It was a warm, hazy May morning, beginning to heat up. But there was a dark cloud bank hovering over New Jersey; the air smelled of rain.

"Do you remember the weather for that Friday?" Delaney asked. "When Maitland died?"

"Clear, bright, but about ten degrees colder than it is now. It rained on Saturday. When we got there on Sunday, it was grey and overcast. Clammy."

Delaney stopped at Prince Street and looked around.

"Lots of traffic," he said. "Lots of activity."

"One of the problems," Boone said. "So busy that no one saw nothing. The precinct had Italian- and Spanish-speaking cops do the door-to-doors. No one offered anything. I don't think they were covering; they honestly didn't see. Probably one guy in and out in five minutes. Who's to notice?"

"No screams? No thumps or crash when Maitland fell?"

"There are ten apartments in his building. Everyone was at work or out shopping except for a deaf old lady on the third floor, a guy who works nights sleeping on the second, and the super and his wife in the basement. None of them heard anything, didn't see anything. They say."

"No lock on the outside door of the house?"

"Supposed to be, but it had been jimmied so many times, the super gave up trying to fix it. Anyone could have walked right up those stairs."

"What's the break-in rate on the street?"

Boone flipped a palm back and forth.

"About average, sir. Not the best, not the worst."

They crossed Prince Street, walking slowly, looking about.

"Why did he have his studio down here?" Delaney wondered. "He could have afforded something better than this, couldn't he? He had money."

"Oh, he had plenty of money," Boone nodded. "No doubt about that. And spent it as fast as he made it, according to his wife. We asked his agent the same thing—why he worked down here. The answers weren't logical, but I guess they make sense considering the kind of man he was. This was where he lived and worked when he first came to New York and was just getting started. This was where he did the first paintings that sold. He was superstitious and thought the place brought him luck. So he kept it as a studio after he got married and moved uptown. Also, it was off the beaten track. The guy was a loner. He hated the usual art-colony bullshit of Greenwich Village. He got sore when the galleries spread to SoHo, and more and more artists began taking lofts across Lafayette south of Houston, and even on the Bowery. He told his agent the shitheads were surrounding him, and if it got any worse, he'd have to find some place the art-fuckers hadn't discovered yet. That's Maitland's phrase: 'Art-fuckers.' Here, this is the house, Chief."

It was a grimy red-brick building exactly like dozens of others on the street. A stoop of nine grey stone steps leading up to an outer door. The first-floor apartments on either side had rusted iron grilles over their dusty windows.

"I know the layout," Delaney said. "And this wasn't in the file; I've seen hundreds of tenements like this. Two apartments on each floor. Railroad flats running front to back. The super's apartment in the basement. He can enter through that door in the areaway under the steps, but he usually keeps it locked and goes in through the hallway and down a flight of backstairs to the basement.

In addition to his apartment, the cellar's got the boiler, heater, fuse boxes, and so forth. Storage space. And a back door that opens out into a little paved courtyard. Maitland's studio on the fifth floor was one big room—the whole floor. Sink and tub, but toilet in a little closet on the top stairway landing. How's that?"

"You got it, sir," Boone said admiringly. "The door in the basement, the one to the backyard, is kept locked. It's got iron bars with a chain and padlock on it. It wasn't touched. Our guy didn't get out that way. Besides, the super and his wife were in their apartment. They said they'd have heard someone in the basement. They didn't."

"Let's go," Delaney said.

They trudged up the steps. The outer door was not only unlocked but unlatched; it swung open a few inches. Delaney paused to look at the names on the mailboxes.

"Mostly Italians," he noted. "One Spanish. One Chinese. One 'Smith' that could be anything."

The inner door was also unlocked, the handle missing.

"He said he'd replace it," Boone said.

"Maybe he did," Delaney said mildly. "Maybe someone busted the new one."

There were two short flights of stairs between floors. They went up slowly. They were on the third-floor landing when one of the doors jerked open to the length of its chain, and an angry woman poked her face out at them. She had a head of bright red hair wound around beer-can curlers. She was wearing a wrapper of hellish design she kept clutched to her scrawny neck.

"I seen you staring at the house," she accused them. "Watcha want? I'll call the cops."

"We *are* the cops, ma'am," Boone said softly. He showed the woman his ID. "Nothing to fret about. Just taking another look upstairs."

"You catch him yet?" the woman demanded.

"Not yet."

"Shit!" the woman said disgustedly, and slammed her door shut. They heard the sound of locks being turned and bolts being closed. They continued their climb.

"Where was she when we needed her?" Delaney growled.

They paused on the top landing, both of them breathing heavily. Delaney looked into the WC. Nothing but a stained toilet. The tank was up near the ceiling, flushed by pulling a wooden handle attached to a tarnished brass chain. There was one small window of frosted glass, cracked.

"Unheated," Delaney remarked. "In winter, a place like this could make it a pleasure to be constipated."

Boone looked at him, startled by the Chief's levity. They moved over to stand before the door of Victor Maitland's studio. There was a shiny new hasp and padlock. There was also a sign tacked to the door: THESE PREMISES HAVE BEEN SEALED BY THE INTERNAL REVENUE SERVICE, AN AGENCY OF THE U.S. GOVERNMENT. In smaller type, the sign detailed what an interloper might expect in the way of imprisonment, a fine, or both.

"Ah, hell," Boone said. "What's this about?"

"He died intestate," Delaney said. "No will. That means the IRS wants to make sure it gets its share of the goodies. Also, the IRS had a back claim he'd been fighting for years. Well . . . what do we do now?"

Boone glanced around.

"Uh, Chief . . ." he said in a low voice. "Uh, I got a set of picks. Okay?"

Delaney stared at him.

"Sergeant," he said, "you're looking better to me every minute. Sure okay."

Abner Boone took a flat pouch of black suede from his inside jacket pocket. He inspected the heavy padlock, then selected one of the picks—a long, thin sliver of stainless steel with a tiny hook at one end. Boone inserted the hook end into the keyhole of the padlock. He probed delicately, staring up at the ceiling. The pick caught. Boone turned his wrist slowly. The lock popped open.

"Very nice," Delaney said. "And the first time you've done it, too."

Boone smiled and put his picks away. He pushed the door open. They entered, closed the door behind them.

"Stand right here," Delaney commanded. "Take a good look around. See if it's all about the same as it was when the body was found. Anything out of place? Anything missing? Take your time."

He waited patiently while Boone inspected the interior of the studio. Sunshine was flooding through the overhead skylight. One of the panes of glass was broken and had been stuffed with a blue rag. There was a wire mesh over the skylight. But no ventilator. The room smelled musty, spoiled.

Delaney glanced at his watch.

"About ten-thirty," he said. "It must have looked like this six weeks ago. You said it was a bright, clear day, so he wouldn't be using the lamps. The sun is higher now, of course, but it should be just about as it was."

"I don't see anything missing or out of place," Boone said. "I have the feeling that glass on the drainboard was closer to the sink than it is now. They moved it after dusting. And the mattress on the cot was flipped. Old semen stains on the top side. Nothing fresh. Otherwise, it looks exactly the same to me."

"Were the windows open?"

"No, sir. Shut, like they are now."

"Radio on?"

"No. Switched off. That stuff at the far end, all his paints and brushes and rolls of canvas, all that mess, that's not in the original position because we went through it. But as far as I know, nothing was taken. We left it all right here."

"No paintings?"

"No. The agent said he had just finished a series and brought the last to the Geltman Galleries. There's a couple of rough sketches on the floor. The agent wanted to take them, but we wouldn't let him. He said they might have been Maitland's last work and belonged to the estate."

Delaney walked over to the chalked outline on the floor and stared down. The wood around it was stained a dark brown, almost black in patches.

"The outline about right?" he asked Boone.

"About. The right arm, here, wasn't exactly straight. More bent at the elbow. And the knees were bent a little. But he went down flat on his face and spread out."

Delaney knelt by the rude outline of the dead painter, staring at it through half-closed eyes.

"Was his face right down on the floor?"

"Turned a little to the left maybe, but mostly straight down."

"Do you know where he carried his wallet?"

"We figured right hip pocket. He had a comb in his left hip. His wife and agent confirmed."

The Chief stood up, dusting his knees.

"Smell?" he asked.

"Plenty," Boone said. "That was a warm, clammy weekend."

"No, no," Delaney said. "I mean, did anyone get down on him to smell him?"

Abner Boone was bewildered.

"No one I saw, Chief," he said. "What for?"

"Oh . . ." Delaney said vaguely. "You never know . . ."

He went over to the sink, inspecting the stained basin and the drainboard.

"The drain searched?"

"Sure. And the tub drain. And the toilet and the tank."

The old-fashioned bathtub, on claw feet, had a white enameled metal lid. Delaney lifted it to peer underneath, then crouched to look under the tub.

"Roaches," he reported.

"Plenty of those," Boone nodded. "All over. He wasn't exactly what you'd call Mister Clean."

Delaney walked slowly toward the front of the studio. He paused at the platform under the skylight.

"What's this thing?" he asked.

"The agent said it's a posing dais. The model got up there when Maitland was making drawings or paintings."

Delaney moved around the clutter on the floor, stopped, looked down.

"I can figure what most of this stuff is," he said. "But why the saw, nails, hammer? And that thing—that claw—what's that?"

"Geltman said Maitland stretched his own canvas. Bought it in rolls. Made a wood frame, then stretched the canvas over it and tacked it down. The claw helped him pull the canvas taut. Those little wooden wedges went into the inside corners of the frame to help keep the canvas tight."

"What's this black stuff near the wall? Black crumbs?"

"Pieces of a charcoal stick. The agent helped us identify all this shit. It seems Maitland used charcoal sticks for sketching. Most artists use pencils."

"Why all the little pieces?"

"It breaks easily. But there's a mark on the wall, up there, to your right. Looks like Maitland threw the stick at the wall. Geltman says he'd do something like that."

"Why?"

"He didn't know, unless Maitland's work wasn't going good and he got sore."

Delaney picked up the two sketches from the floor, handling them with his fingernails at the corners, and brought them closer to the front windows to examine them.

"There's a third drawing on the pad on the crate," Boone said. "Half-finished. And there's half a charcoal stick alongside it. The agent said it looked to him like Maitland was doing the third sketch, the charcoal stick broke in two, and Maitland threw the piece he was holding at the wall."

Delaney didn't reply. He was staring at the drawings, awed. Maitland had been putting a three-dimensional torso on two-dimensional paper, working with hard, bold strokes of his charcoal. There was no conventional shading; the line itself suggested the modeling of the flesh. But in two places he had made fast smudges with thumb or finger to suggest hollow and shadow.

The body was that of a young girl, juicy, bursting. You could almost feel the heat. She stood bent over in a distorted pose that bunched muscles, jutted breasts. Maitland had caught swoop of back, flare of hips, sweet curve of shoulder and arm. The face, in profile, was barely suggested; something vaguely Oriental about it. But the body, to the knees, leapt from the white paper. The black lines seemed alive, seemed to writhe. There was no doubt that a heart pumped, breath flowed, blood coursed.

"Jesus," Delaney said in a low voice. "I don't care what the guy was, he shouldn't be dead." Then, in a louder voice, he asked: "Did the agent know when these were done?"

"No, sir. Could have been that morning. Could have been a week before. He had never seen them before."

"Did he know the model?"

"Said not. Said the sketches looked to him like preliminary work, the kind of throwaway stuff Maitland might try with a new model. To see if he could catch what he wanted."

"Throwaway stuff? Not these. I'm going to take them. I'll return them to the estate. Eventually. Where's the third?"

"Here. Still on the crate."

Chief Delaney inspected the still life atop the rough crate: sketchpad propped on a can of turpentine, half a charcoal stick, bottle of whiskey. He looked from the whiskey to the studio entrance and back again. Then he tore the third drawing from the pad and flipped through the remaining pages to make certain there was nothing more. There wasn't. He carefully rolled the three sketches into a tight tube. Then he looked around.

"Can't think of anything else," he said. "Can you?"

"No, Chief. There was no address book. No books at all. A few old newspapers under the sink, some catalogues from art-supply stores. There're a few numbers written on the wall near the telephone. We checked them out. A neighborhood liquor store that delivers. Ditto for a delicatessen over on Lafayette. The number for an artist friend named Jake Dukker. He's in the file. That's all there was. No letters, no bills, nothing. A few pieces of old clothes in the chest of drawers. Most of his personal stuff he kept uptown in his apartment. Not that that was of any more help."

They put the padlock back on the door and trudged downstairs. The red-haired woman stuck her face out again.

"Well?" she demanded.

"Good day, madam," Edward X. Delaney said politely, lifting his homburg.

Out on the street Abner Boone said, "If the IRS comes around asking questions, she can make us."

"Conjecture," Delaney said, shrugging. "She didn't actually see us *in* the place. Don't worry; if necessary, Thorsen will scam it."

They strolled back to Houston Street in silence. Boone walked around his car, inspecting it. It hadn't been touched. They got in, and Delaney lighted a cigar. Boone found him a rubber band in the cluttered glove compartment to put around his roll of drawings. The sergeant had also brought the book of Maitland's paintings, in an old manila envelope. Delaney held it on his lap. He didn't open it.

They sat awhile in silence, their comfort with each other growing. Boone lighted a cigarette. His fingers were stained yellow.

"I'm trying to cut down," he told Delaney.

"Any luck?"

"No. Since I've been off the sauce, it's worse."

The Chief nodded, put his head back against the seat rest. He stared through the windshield at a noontime game of stickball being played in the middle of traffic on Houston Street.

"Let's play games, too," he said dreamily, not looking at Boone. "Try this on for size . . . Maitland picks up a young twist. On the street, in a bar, anywhere. Maybe he figures she really would make a good model—that body in the drawings is something—or maybe it's just his con to get a slab on the mat. Anyway, she shows up at the studio Friday morning. She strips. He does the sketches of her. I don't know what *he* thought of them; I think they're great. The charcoal stick breaks on the third drawing. Maitland throws the piece in his hand against the wall. Maybe he's sore it broke, maybe he's just feeling frisky. Who knows? He gives the bimbo a drink. Near the sink and cot. Those are her partials on the glass. Maybe they talk money. He boffs her or he doesn't boff her. She leaves. He locks the door, goes back to the crate with the bottle of whiskey, looks at his sketches. Knock-knock at the door. Who is it? Someone answers, a voice he recognizes. He puts the bottle on the crate, goes to the door, unlocks it. The door opens. The guy comes in. Maitland turns his back and walks away. *Finí.* How does it grab you?"

"Motive?"

"Jesus Christ, sergeant, I haven't even *begun* to think about that. I don't know enough. I'm just trying to figure what happened that Friday morning. The action. How does it listen?"

"Possible," Boone said. "It covers all the bases. They might have screwed around for an hour or two. The killing was some time between ten and three."

"Right."

"But there's no hard evidence to show her presence. Those sketches could have been done a week before Maitland was snuffed. There's no face powder, no bobby pins, no lipstick smears on the glass. Just that one safety pin."

Delaney jerked erect. Whirled. Stared at Boone.

"That what?" he said furiously.

"The safety pin, sir. On the floor near the cot. Wasn't it in the file?"

"No, goddamn it, it wasn't in the file."

"Should have been, Chief," Boone said softly. "One safety pin. Open. The lab boys took it to check it out. No different from zillions of others. Sold in a million stores."

"How long was it?"

Boone held thumb and forefinger apart.

"Like so. About an inch. No fibers or hairs on it. Nothing to indicate if Maitland used it or if it belonged to a broad."

"Shiny?"

"Oh yes. It had been used recently."

"Definitely a woman's," Delaney said. "What's Maitland going to do with it—hold up the underwear he wasn't wearing? No, a young piece was there that morning."

They were both silent on the long, slow ride uptown. Around Fourteenth Street, Delaney said, "Sergeant, I'm sorry I barked at you about that safety pin not being in the reports. I know it wasn't your fault."

Boone turned briefly to give him that boyish grin.

"Bark all you like, Chief," he said. "I've taken worse than that."

"Haven't we all," Delaney said. "Look, I've been thinking . . . I've been in this business a long time, and I know, I *know* there are a lot of things that don't go into the reports. An investigating officer can't put *everything* down in writing, or he'd spend his life behind a typewriter and have no time for investigating. Just the act of making out a report is a process of selection. The officer picks out what he thinks is meaningful, what's significant. He doesn't include in the record that the guy he was tailing was chewing gum, or the woman he questioned was wearing Chanel Number Five perfume. He leaves out all the innocuous crap. Or what he *thinks* is innocuous. You understand? He reports only what he thinks is important. Or really what he thinks his superior will think is important. Agree so far?"

"To a point," Boone said cautiously. "Sometimes an officer might include something that doesn't mean much to him, but it's so unusual, so odd or different that he figures the higher-ups should know about it."

"Then he's a good cop, because that's exactly what he should do. Even if nothing comes of it. And if it turns out to be hot, then he's off the hook, because he filed it. Right?"

"Right, sir. I agree with you there."

"But still," Delaney persisted, "a lot of stuff never gets put down. Little-bitty things. Most of it's nothing and never should be reported. But sometimes, very occasionally, if it had been reported, it would have helped break a case a lot sooner. I worked a homicide up in the Two-oh. A strangling in this big apartment house. Ten apartments on the floor. Naturally, the neighbors were questioned. No one heard a thing; the hallway had a thick carpet. One old dame mentioned that the only thing she heard was a dog sniffing under her door and making little whining sounds. But it doesn't mean anything, she tells the dick, because four people on that floor have dogs, and they're always taking them for walks. And the moron takes her word for it and doesn't put it in his report. Two weeks later we're at a standstill and start all over again. The old lady tells about the dog sniffing under her door again. This time it's in a report, and the lieutenant has me check all the people on that floor who own dogs. None of them took their dog for a walk at that time. But the guy who got strangled, he had a rough boyfriend, and *he* had a dog. Never went out without him. So one thing led to another, and we nailed him. If that miserable sniffing dog had been mentioned in an early report, we'd have saved a month of migraine. Now a lot of men were working on the Maitland thing, and I know there was stuff that's not in those records. I'm not blaming the men. I know their workload. But it's possible that some things they sluffed in the scramble to break this case would be a big help to you and me, now that we've got all the time in the world to look into every little thing with no one breathing down our necks."

Boone picked up on it at once.

"What do you want me to do, Chief?"

"You know most of the men who worked on the case—at least the heavies—and you can talk to them better than I could. Whenever we're not working together, I want you to go see these guys, or call them, and ask them if there was anything they remember that wasn't reported. I mean *anything!* Tell them they won't get their ass in a sling. You won't even tell me their names. That's the truth. I don't want to know their names. But see if you can get them to dredge their memories and come up with something they didn't report. Someone must have seen something or heard something. It doesn't have to be big. In fact, if it was big, it would probably be in the file. What I'm looking for are odds and ends, little inconsequential things. You understand, Sergeant?"

"Sure," Abner Boone said. "When do you want me to get started?"

"This afternoon. Will you drop me at home, please? I have enough to keep me busy for the rest of the day. You can start looking up the men who worked on the Maitland case. And while you're at it, drop by the labs, or call them, and find out why that safety pin wasn't mentioned in their analysis of physical evidence. Maybe it was, and I missed it. But I don't think so. I think it was a foul-up, and it scares me, because maybe it happened more than once and there are things I won't know about by reading the file. That's why I'm happy you're working with me."

Sergeant Boone was happy, too, and showed it.

"One more thing," Delaney said. "I intend to write up a report of this morning's visit to Maitland's studio. What I saw, what I found, what I took. I'll write a daily report of my investigation, just as if I was on active duty. I want you to write daily reports, too. You'll find they'll be a big help to keep things straight."

"All right, sir," Boone said doubtfully. "If you say so."

He let Delaney out in front of his brownstone. The Chief came around the car and leaned down to Boone's open window.

"Did Deputy Commissioner Thorsen tell you to keep him privately informed on the progress of my investigation?" he asked.

Boone lowered his head, blushed again, the freckles lost.

"I'm sorry, Chief," he mumbled. "I had no choice."

Delaney put a hand on the man's arm.

"Report to him," he told Boone. "Do just as he ordered. It's all right."

He turned and marched up the steps into the house. Boone watched the door close behind him.

Delaney hung his homburg on the hall rack, carried his drawings and book directly into the study, put them on his desk, and then came back into the hallway.

"Monica?" he called.

"Upstairs, dear," she called back. She came to the head of the stairway. "Did you have lunch?"

"No, but I'm not hungry. I think I'll skip. Maybe I'll just have a beer."

"If you want a sandwich, there's ham and cheese. But don't touch the beef; that's for tonight."

He went into the kitchen and opened the refrigerator door. He took out a can of beer, peeled off the flip-top. The bulk of the rib roast, the leftovers wrapped in aluminum foil, caught his eye. He stared at it, then resolutely shut the door. He went toward the study, hesitated, stopped. Out into the hallway. Peered up. No Monica. Back to the kitchen. Sharp carving knife. Swiftly took the beef out, peeled away the foil. There, pinned to the meat with a toothpick, a little note: "Only one sandwich. M." He laughed and made his one sandwich, taking it with the beer into the study.

He unrolled the sketches on his desk and weighted the corners so the paper would lose its curl. Then he took Sergeant Boone's book of the paintings of Victor Maitland from the envelope. He settled down in his swivel chair and put on his reading glasses. He flipped through the book quickly.

It was practically all black-and-white and full-color reproductions of Maitland's paintings on slick paper. The limited text consisted of a short introduction, a biography of the artist, a listing of his complete *oeuvre*, and an essay by an art critic analyzing Maitland's work. Chief Delaney was not familiar with the critic's name, but his professional record, stated in the introduction, was impressive. Delaney began to read.

He learned little from the biography that had not been included in the copies of the Department's records sent over by Deputy Commissioner Thorsen. The essay by the art critic, although attempting to be moderate and judicial in tone, added up to a paean. According to the writer, Victor Maitland had breathed fresh life into the techniques of the great Italian masters, had turned his back on the transient fads and fashions of contemporary art and, going his own way, had imbued the traditional, representational style of painting with a fervor, a passion that had not been seen for centuries.

There was much more of a technical nature that Edward X. Delaney could not completely comprehend. But it was not difficult to understand the critic's admiration, his *awe* at what Maitland had done. "Awe" was the word used in the text. Delaney responded to it because it was exactly what he had felt on first looking at those rough sketches in Maitland's studio. Not only awe at the man's talent, but wonder and a kind of dread in seeing beauty he had never known existed.

"At last," the critic concluded, "America has a painter of the first magnitude who devotes his art to the celebration of life."

But not for long, Delaney thought morosely. Then, standing, the better to view the illustrations in the oversized book, he began slowly to turn the pages engraved with the paintings of Victor Maitland.

He went through them twice, turned back a third time to a few that had particularly moved him. Then he closed the book softly, moved away from the desk. He saw his sandwich and beer, untouched. He took them to one of the club chairs, sat down, began to eat and drink slowly. The beer was warmish and flat by now, but he didn't care.

He was an untrained amateur when it came to the appreciation of art. He acknowledged this. But he loved painting and sculpture. And the cool, ordered ambience of museums, the richness of gilt frames, the elegance of marble pedestals. He had tried to educate himself by reading books of art history and art criticism. But he found the language so recondite that he wondered if it was not deliberately designed to obfuscate and confuse the uninitiated. But, he admitted, the fault might be his: an inability to grasp art theory, to follow the turgid logic of cubists, dadaists, abstractionists, and all the other art "schools" that followed one after another in such rapid and bewildering succession.

Finally, he was forced back to his own eye, his own taste: that much scorned cliché "I know what I like when I see it," sensing dimly that it served for the butcher who liked sunsets painted on black velvet as well as for the most ideological of art experts who wrote knowingly of asymmetrical tensions, ovular torpidity, and exogenous calcification.

Edward X. Delaney liked paintings that were recognizable. A nude was a nude, an apple an apple, a house a house. He found technique interesting and enjoyable; the folds of satin in the paintings of Ingres were a delight. But technique was never enough. To be truly satisfying, a painting had to *move* him, to cause a flopover inside him when he looked upon life revealed. A painting did not have to be beautiful; it had to be true. Then it was beautiful.

Munching his cold roast beef, sipping his tepid beer, he reflected that most of Victor Maitland's paintings were true. Delaney not only saw it, he felt it. There were a few still lifes, one or two portraits, several cityscapes. But Maitland had painted mostly the female nude. Young women and old women, girls and harridans. Many of the subjects were certainly not beautiful, but all of the paintings were bursting with that "celebration of life" the critic had noted.

But that was not what impressed Chief Delaney most about Maitland's work. It was the purpose of the artist, the use he made of his talent. There was something frantic there, something almost deranged. It was, Delaney thought, a superhuman striving to be aware of life and capture it with cold paint on rough canvas. It was a manic greed to know it all, own it all, and to display the plunder.

5

"I'm having lunch with Rebecca," Monica said.

"That's nice," Chief Delaney said, flapping a "commuter fold" into his copy of *The New York Times*.

"Then we might go shopping," Monica said.

"I'm listening, dear," he said, reading of the aborted plan of a Central American politico to sell 10,000 submachine guns to the Mafia.

"Then we'll probably come back here," Monica said. "For a cup of coffee. At three o'clock."

He put down his paper, stared at her.

"Do you know what you're doing?" he asked. "The man's a heavy drinker, a *very* heavy drinker."

"You said he's off it."

"*He* said he's off it. Do you really want to mate your best friend with an alcoholic?"

"Well, it surely wouldn't do any harm if they just met. By accident. It doesn't mean they have to get married tomorrow."

"I wash my hands of the entire affair," he said sternly.

"Then you'll bring him back here around three?" she asked.

He groaned.

Sergeant Abner Boone was parked in front of the Delaney home, reading the *Daily News*. When the Chief got into the car, Boone tossed the newspaper onto the back seat.

"Morning, Chief," he said.

"Morning," Delaney said. He gestured at the newspaper. "What's new?"

"Nothing much. They fished a car out of the East River. They opened the trunk, and lo and behold, there was old Sam Zuckerman, sent to his reward with an ice pick."

"Zuckerman? I don't make him."

"He owned a string of massage parlors on the West Side. I guess someone wanted to buy in, and Sam said no. We've been playing pitty-pat with him for years. We'd jail him and leave the door open because Sam would be out on the street in an hour. He must have spent a fortune on lawyers. But of course he had a fortune. Now Sam's gone to the great massage parlor in the sky."

"How did you make out?" Delaney asked.

Boone took out a small, black leather notebook and flipped the pages.

"About the safety pin . . ." he said. "The way I get it, the guy in the lab was making out the physical-evidence list. In the middle, he gets a call from the lieutenant of the homicide unit asking about the pin. The lab guy tells him it's an ordinary pin, no way to trace it, no fibers caught in it, no hair, nothing. They talk about the pin for a couple of minutes and hang up. Then the lab guy was interrupted. His words, and I quote: 'Then I was interrupted,' unquote. He didn't say whether he went to lunch, got a call from his wife, or went to the can, and I didn't push it. After the interruption, whatever it was, he continues typing out the list. But because the conversation with the lieutenant is fresh in his mind, he thought he had already included the safety pin. So, naturally, it got left out."

Delaney was silent. Boone looked sideways at him.

"It was just a human error, Chief."

"Is there any other kind?" Delaney asked sourly. "All right, we'll forget about it. Did you make any calls to the men who worked on the Maitland case?"

Boone sat quietly a moment, tapping his notebook on his knee, staring straight ahead.

"Chief," he said finally, "maybe I'm not the right guy for this job. I called three men who worked the case. I've known them for years. They were friendly, but cool. They all know the trouble I'm in, and they didn't want to be too buddy-buddy. You understand? Like I had a contagious disease, and they might catch it."

"I understand," Delaney said. "A natural reaction. I've seen it before."

"That's one thing," Boone said. "The other is that they all know I'm working with you on the Maitland thing. I don't think they'll be too happy to see us break it. They put in long hours, a lot of hard work, and came up with a horse collar. Then we come along—and bingo? It doesn't set so good. It would make them look like bums. So they're not too anxious to cooperate."

Delaney sighed.

"Well . . ." he said. "That, too, is a normal reaction. I guess. I should have anticipated. So you got nothing?"

"I called three. Nothing from two of them. In fact, they got a little sore. They said I was hinting their records weren't complete, that they had left something out. I tried to explain that it wasn't like that at all, that we just wanted the little useless junk that every cop runs across in an investigation. But they said there was nothing that wasn't in their reports. The third guy was more sympathetic. He understood what we were after, but he said he had nothing."

"So that's that," Delaney said resignedly.

"No, no," Boone protested. "There's more. That third guy called me back about an hour later. He said he had been thinking about what I said, and he remembered one thing he saw that he didn't put in his report. He was one of the guys who questioned Jake Dukker, Maitland's artist friend. This Dukker is a rich, fancy guy with a studio on Central Park South. He's even got a secretary. This dick goes up to question Dukker, and the secretary shows him into the studio and says Dukker will be with him in a few minutes. So while the guy is waiting, he looks around. The walls of Dukker's studio are covered with drawings and paintings, apparently all of them by friends of Dukker. And this dick sees a signed drawing by Victor Maitland in a frame with glass over it. But what he remembered was that the drawing had been torn. It had been torn down the middle, and then the two pieces had been torn across. But the four pieces had been put back together again with Scotch tape, and then framed. This cop I talked to didn't know what that meant, if anything. I don't either."

"I don't either," Chief Delaney said. "Not now. But it's exactly the kind of thing I was hoping to learn. Keep at it, sergeant; maybe we'll pick up some more bits and pieces."

"Will do."

"I called the widow and Saul Geltman, and set up appointments to see them today. Mrs. Maitland is first at ten this morning. It's on East Fifty-eighth. You know the address?"

"Sure. Chief, how come you called them first? Wouldn't it make more sense to walk in on them unexpectedly, so they have no time to set up a con?"

"Ordinarily it would," Delaney agreed. "But everyone involved in this case has been questioned a dozen times already. They've got their stories down pat. True or false. Let's get started."

Boone drove over to Second Avenue and turned south. Morning traffic was heavy; they seemed to hit a red light every block or so. But Delaney made no comment. He was engrossed in his own little black notebook, flipping pages.

"How did you handle the questioning?" he asked Boone.

"By the book. We sent three or four different guys for the first three or four sessions with each subject. Then those guys would get together with the lieutenant and compare notes. Then they'd figure which guy got the most, which guy had established the best relationship with the subject. That guy would go back for a final session, or more if needed."

"Who did you handle?"

"Me personally? I had one session with Mrs. Maitland, one with Geltman, and two with Belle Sarazen, the woman Maitland was screwing. Then I got taken off the case."

Chief Delaney didn't ask for Boone's reactions to these witnesses, and the sergeant didn't volunteer any.

The Maitland apartment was a duplex occupying the top two floors of what had originally been a private townhouse on East 58th Street between First Avenue and Sutton Place. It was an elegant building, with a uniformed doorman and tight security. Boone gave their names and showed his ID. They waited while the doorman announced their arrival over an intercom. When he got approval, he directed them to the single elevator at the side of the small lobby.

"Fourth floor rear, gents," he told them, but Delaney didn't move.

The doorman was big, fleshy, red-faced. His uniform might have fit him once, a few years ago. Now the jacket was straining at its brass buttons.

"We're investigating the Maitland murder," Delaney said.

"Still?" the man said.

"You knew him?" Delaney asked.

"Sure, I knew him," the doorman said. "Listen, I told this to a dozen cops. I answered a hundert questions."

"Tell *me,*" Delaney said. "What kind of a guy was he?"

"Like I told the others, an okay guy. A heavy tipper. Very heavy."

"Ever see him drunk?"

"Does a goat smell? Sure, I seen him drunk. Lots of times. He'd have a load on, and I'd help him out of the cab, into the elevator, up to his door. Then I'd ring the bell for him. The next day he'd always give me a little something."

"They have many friends, the Maitlands?" Delaney asked. "Guests? Did they entertain a lot?"

"Not so much" the doorman said. "Mrs. Maitland, she has lady friends. Once or twice a year maybe they'd have a party. Not like Jacobson on two. That guy never stops."

"Maitland ever bring a woman home with him?"

The doorman's jaw clamped, his beefy face grew redder.

"Come on," Delaney urged.

"Onct," the doorman whispered. "Just onct. The wife raised holy hell. A real bimbo he brought home. She came flying down out of here about five minutes after she came."

"When was this?"

"About a year ago. The only time since I been dooring here. Seven years come July."

"The son ever bring a girl home?"

"I never seen one. Maybe a couple would come in with him. Not a single girl."

"You smoke cigars?" Delaney asked.

"What?" the doorman said, startled. "Sure, I smoke cigars."

Delaney reached into his inside pocket, brought out a pigskin case, a Christmas gift from Monica. He took off the top, held the filled case out to the doorman.

"Have a cigar," he said.

The doorman took one daintily, with the tips of his fingers.

"Thanks," he said gratefully. "Would you believe it, it's the first time in my whole life a cop gave me something."

"I believe it," Delaney said.

Alma Maitland was waiting for them outside the door of her fourth-floor apartment.

"I was afraid you got lost," she said. Cold smile.

"The elevator was busy," Delaney said, taking off his homburg. "Mrs. Maitland? I am Chief Edward X. Delaney. This gentleman is Detective sergeant Abner Boone."

She offered a cool hand to each of them.

"I've already met Sergeant Boone," she said.

"Yes," Delaney said. His manner was weighty, almost pompous. His voice was orotund. "It is indeed good of you to see us on such short notice. We deeply appreciate it. May we come in?"

"Of course," she said, impressed by his solemnity. She led the way into the apartment, closing the door. "I thought we'd talk in the family room. It's cozier there."

If Mrs. Maitland considered her family room cozy, Delaney hated to think of what the rest of the apartment was like. The austere chamber into which Mrs. Maitland led them looked like a model room in a department store. It was so coldly designed, so precisely arranged, so bereft of any signs of human use that a cigarette ash or a fart seemed a blasphemy.

They sat in undeniably expensive and uncomfortable blonde wood armchairs. They placed their hats on a cocktail table that seemed to be a sheet of plate glass floating in space. There was a slight odor of lemon deodorant in the air. The room had all the warm charm of an operating theatre. Delaney had expected blazing Maitland paintings on the walls. He saw a series of steel etchings depicting London street cries.

"Mrs. Maitland," he said formally, "may I first express my sincere sympathy and condolences on the tragic death of your husband."

"Thank you," she murmured. "You're very kind."

"He was a great artist."

"The greatest," she said loudly, raising her head to look directly at him. "The obituary in the *Times* called him the greatest American painter of his generation."

She was, Delaney saw, a handsome woman, big-boned, with a straight spine and the posture of a drill sergeant. She sat in the middle of a couch upholstered in beige wool, sitting toward the edge, not relaxing against the back. Her hands were folded demurely in her lap. Her ankles were crossed, lady-like, both knees bent slightly to one side.

She wore a high-necked, long-sleeved dress of nubby black silk. Her stockings, or pantyhose, had a black tint. Black shoes. No jewelry. Little makeup. The only color that saved her from chiaroscuro was a great mass of burnished coppery hair, braided into a gleaming plait, wound around and around into a crown atop her head. With her erect carriage, the effect was queenly.

Her features seemed to Delaney to be beautiful without being attractive. Too crisp. Too precise. Too perfect in their sculpted smoothness. On a face like that, a pimple would be a godsend. But her complexion was an unflawed porcelain glaze. Big eyes like licked stones. An expression so serene it was blank. Beneath the black dress was a hint of generous bosom, bountiful hips. But the face, the posture, the demeanor, all denied humor. She would never leave a note to her husband toothpicked to a roast of beef.

"Mrs. Maitland," Chief Delaney began, "I regret the necessity of intruding further on your grief. But the investigation into your husband's death continues, and I am certain you will endure any inconvenience if it aids in bringing to justice the person or persons responsible for this vicious crime."

He had, quite deliberately, adopted the manner and language to which he thought she might respond. His instinct was correct.

"Anything," she said, lifting her chin. "Anything I can do."

"Mrs. Maitland, I have read your statements to the investigating officers who questioned you. Please let me review briefly what you told them, and when I have finished, you can tell me if it is accurate. On the Friday he was murdered, your husband left this apartment at approximately nine in the morning. He told you he was going to his studio, then had an appointment at the Geltman Galleries at three that afternoon, and should be home about six or seven that evening. You yourself left this apartment at approximately ten o'clock. You spent the morning shopping. You met a friend for lunch at one-thirty at Le Provençal on East Sixty-second Street. After lunch you cabbed back here. At about four that afternoon, Saul Geltman called to ask if you knew your husband's whereabouts. Do I have it right?"

"You do, Chief Delano," she said. "I pre—"

"Delaney," he said. "Edward X. Delaney."

"Pardon me," she said. Her voice was low-timbred, husky, but curiously dry. "Chief Delaney, I presume you have checked my story?"

"We have," he nodded gravely. "The doorman on duty confirmed your time of leaving. Your friend affirmed she had lunch with you at the time and place specified. The records of the restaurant bear this out. Unfortunately, we have not been able to find witnesses to your shopping from ten to one-thirty."

"I went to Saks, Bonwit's, Bergdorf's, and Gucci," she said. "But I didn't buy anything. I don't suppose anyone would remember me; the stores were crowded."

"No one did," he said. There was a short pause while he leaned toward her earnestly. "But, Mrs. Maitland, that could be entirely normal and understandable. You purchased nothing, tried on no clothing, made no special inquiries; it's quite natural that no one would have any special recollection of your presence in those stores. You didn't try on any clothing, did you?"

"No, I did not. I saw nothing I liked."

"Of course. Meet anyone you knew at any time between ten and one-thirty? A salesperson, an acquaintance, a friend?"

"No. No one."

"Make any telephone calls during that period?"

"No."

"Mail any letters?"

"No."

"Speak to anyone at all? Have any personal contact whatsoever?"

"No."

"I see. Please understand, Mrs. Maitland, all we're trying to do is clear up loose ends. It appears to me you acted in a perfectly normal manner. I trust you are not offended by the tone of these questions?"

"Not at all, Chief Delaney."

"Was your husband cheating on you?" he asked harshly.

If he had slapped her, the effect would not have been any more dramatic. She jerked back, her face reddened, her hands flew up.

"Believe me, Mrs. Maitland," he continued, once again in his smooth, almost unctuous voice, "it grieves me to pry into your personal life, your private relations with your husband. But surely you must see the necessity for it."

"My husband was the dearest, sweetest man who ever lived," she said stiffly, her lips white. "I assure you he was completely faithful. He loved me, and I loved him. He expressed his love frequently. By telling me and in—in other ways. Ours was a very happy marriage. A perfect marriage. Victor Maitland was a very great artist, and it was an honor to be his wife. Oh, I know the filthy gossip that has been circulated about him, but I assure you that he was as fine a husband and father as he was a painter. I assure you."

"And your son shares your feelings, Mrs. Maitland?"

"My son is young, Chief Delaney. He is presently going through an identity crisis. When he is older, and more experienced, he will realize what a giant his father was."

"Yes, yes. A giant. How true, Mrs. Maitland. Well put. And by the way, where is your son? I was hoping to meet him."

"Now? He's at school."

"Studying to be an artist, is he?"

"In a way," she said shortly. "Graphic design."

"But your husband *was* an artist, Mrs. Maitland. Specializing in the female nude. He was alone in his studio with naked models for long periods of time. Did that not disturb you?"

"Oh my!" she laughed, a tinny sound that clanged through the deodorized air. "You have some very middle-class ideas about the life style of artists, Chief Delaney. I assure you that to most artists, the naked female body is about as exciting as a bowl of fruit or an arrangement of flowers."

"Of course, of course."

"The body is just a subject, an object to them. Let me show you something. Don't get up. I'll bring it to you."

She jerked to her feet, rushed from the room. Sergeant Boone looked at Delaney with wonder.

"Wow," he said. "You're something else again, Chief. First the velvet glove, then the knuckle sandwich. You sure shook her."

"She needs shaking," Delaney growled. "She's playing a role. Did you catch it? While he was alive, she played the Betrayed Wife. Now that he's dead, she's playing the Bereaved Widow. Have you ever heard such shit in your life? Shh. She's coming."

She came striding into the room, thumbing through the pages of an oversized book. Delaney admired the way she moved: energetically, healthily, power in her thighs and shoulders. She found the page she wanted, reversed the book, held it out to Delaney. Boone rose and moved behind him to look over the Chief's shoulder.

It was a copy of the book of Maitland's paintings the sergeant had loaned to Delaney. It was open to a full-color plate. A nude lay on her side on a rough wood plank, her back to the viewer. The curve of raised shoulder, narrow waist, swell of hip, diminishing rhythm of leg flowed like water. It was not one of Delaney's favorite paintings in the book. The model was in repose. The best of Maitland's nudes were charged with vigor, caught in movement, captured in postures that surged, bursting. But now, looking at this particular reproduction that Mrs. Alma

Maitland had thrust into his hands, Chief Delaney saw only the flame of coppery hair spilling down from the model's head, across the rough wood plank, to the painting's border.

"Me!" Mrs. Maitland said proudly, raising her chin again. "I posed for that. Years ago. And many others. I was Victor's first model. So I assure you, Chief Delaney, when I tell you of artists and models, I know whereof I speak. I posed for many artists. Many. My body was considered classic. Classic!"

"Beautiful," Chief Delaney murmured. "Very beautiful indeed," and wondered why it was the only nude in the book in which the face was not shown.

He closed the book and put it aside. He took up his homburg and rose to his feet.

"Mrs. Maitland," he said, "I thank you for your valuable assistance, and only hope I have not caused you undue anguish."

"Not at all," she said, obviously glad to see him going.

"And I hope, as our investigation progresses, you will be kind enough to grant me additional time. Things do come up, you know, and we like to clear them up if we can. And as the one person closest to this great artist, we are depending on you for information no one else can furnish."

"I will be happy and eager to do anything I can to help you find the man who robbed the world of such a talent," she said solemnly.

Sergeant Abner Boone looked at the two of them in amazement. A couple of loonies.

Delaney started toward the door, then stopped.

"By the way, Mrs. Maitland, how did your husband get from here to his studio?"

"He usually took a cab. Sometimes he went by subway."

"Subway? Did he ride the subway frequently?"

"Occasionally. He said he liked to look at the faces."

"The doorman confirms that your husband left the building at approximately nine o'clock that Friday morning. But he did not ask the doorman to call a cab; he just walked westward. And we've been unable to find a cabdriver who dropped a fare at your husband's address on Mott Street. So perhaps he took the subway that morning. Did he tell you how he intended to spend the day?"

"No. I presumed he would be working."

"Mentioned no particular painting or model?"

"No."

"Did he call during the day?"

"The maid says he did not. Of course I wasn't here."

"Of course, of course."

Delaney paused, pondered a moment, staring at the brown carpeting.

"One more thing, Mrs. Maitland . . . What's your personal opinion of Saul Geltman?"

He looked up. Her face had tightened. Delaney fancied those slick stone eyes dried as he watched.

"I would rather not express an opinion of Mr. Geltman at the present time," Alma Maitland said coldly. "Suffice to say that I am currently consulting an attorney in an effort to get a complete and truthful accounting from Geltman Galleries as to monies paid and owed to me. I mean to my husband's estate."

"I see," Delaney said softly. "Thank you again, Mrs. Maitland."

When they left the apartment house, the doorman was standing outside, his hands clasped behind him. He nodded to the two men.

"Find the dear lady?" he asked.

"We found her," Delaney said. "Tell me something . . . You said that Maitland left that Friday morning about nine o'clock. What time did he usually leave in the morning?"

The doorman stared at him, then slowly, deliberately winked.

"As soon as he could," he said. "As soon as he could."

In the car, Sergeant Boone said, "Well?"

"She knew he was cheating," Delaney said. "Everyone knew he screwed anything that moved. But she's busy creating the giant, the Great Man, of spotless character and immaculate integrity. She's making a statue out of the guy."

"Did you believe what she said about artists and models?"

"Come on," Delaney said. "If you were an artist and had a naked piece of tush alone in a studio, would you consider it an object?"

"Yeah," Boone laughed. "A sex object. Chief, I followed most of your line except for the last question about Geltman. What was the reason for that?"

Delaney told him the story of old Detective Alberto Di Lucca down in Little Italy, and how he had broken the warehouse heist by pitting one suspect against another.

"I've used variations of that technique ever since," he told Boone. "With good results. I could have pushed it farther with Mrs. Maitland, but she gave us enough for starters. Now I'll ask Geltman what he thinks of her. Eventually we'll get them all biting each other, and maybe we'll learn something. What did you think of that painting Maitland did of her?"

"Nice ass," Abner Boone said.

"Yes," Chief Delaney said, "but he didn't show her face. Why didn't he show her face?"

"I don't know, Chief. She's a beautiful woman."

"Mmm."

"And strong."

"Oh, you caught that, too? Yes, a big, strong woman. Think she could be a killer?"

"Who couldn't?" Sergeant Boone said.

They had lunch at Moriarty's on Third Avenue, sitting in the front room. Boone looked around at the Tiffany lamps, the long mahogany bar.

"Nice place, Chief," he said.

"Nothing fancy," Delaney said. "Solid food, honest drinks. Order what you like; it's on the Department."

They both ordered steak sandwiches with home fries, Delaney had a Labatt's ale, Boone had an iced tea.

"She's the only one with a loose alibi," the sergeant said casually, scrubbing his face with his palms.

"Where were you last night?" Delaney asked.

"What?"

"Where were you last night?" Delaney repeated patiently.

"Why?"

"Just answer the question."

"I was home, sir."

"Alone?"

"Sure."

"What did you do?"

"Wrote some checks, watched some TV, read some magazines."

"Can you prove it?"

Sergeant Boone smiled crookedly.

"All right, Chief," he said. "You made your point."

"Alibis are about as much use as fingerprints," Chief Delaney said. "If they exist and can be checked out thoroughly, all well and good. But most of the time you get partials; they don't say yes, they don't say no. Maybe Alma really did go shopping. Except women usually meet, go shopping together, and then have lunch. Or they meet for lunch, and then go shopping together. She says she went shopping alone, met her friend for lunch, and then went home. It bothers me. I have the friend's name and address in the file. Will you check her out? Just ask why she didn't go shopping that Friday with Mrs. Maitland."

"Will do. Ah, here's our food . . ."

They had a leisurely lunch, trading Department gossip and occasionally exchanging stories of cases they had worked.

"Who collects in this Maitland thing, sir?" the sergeant asked.

"Good question. He didn't leave a will. I'll have to get an opinion on it from the Department's legal eagles. I think the widow takes all, after taxes. I know she's definitely entitled to half. I want to know if the son's entitled, too."

"You know we got copies of Maitland's bank accounts," Boone said, "and he didn't leave all that much. No safe-deposit boxes we could find. And apparently his only unsold paintings are up in the Geltman Galleries."

"Which reminds me," Delaney said, "we better get going. We can walk over; it isn't far."

The Geltman Galleries occupied the ground floor of a modern professional building on Madison Avenue. Enormous plate-glass windows, set back from the sidewalk, fronted one long room high enough to accommodate a half-balcony reached by a spiral iron staircase. Paintings and sculpture were customarily displayed on the main level, prints and drawings on the balcony. Offices and storage rooms were at the rear of the ground floor. Entrance to the Galleries was directly from the street.

When Chief Delaney and Sergeant Boone walked over after lunch, they found the high plate-glass windows covered from the inside with drapes of oyster-white burlap. A sign stated that the Geltman Galleries, temporarily closed, were being prepared for a memorial exhibit of the last works of Victor Maitland, paintings that had never been shown before. The sign urged visitors to return after June 10th, when "we will be proud to present the final creations of this premier American artist."

The street door was locked. A smaller notice, handwritten, stated that those with deliveries to make should enter through the building lobby and ring the bell on the Galleries' interior door. Delaney and Boone went into the lobby, to discover the side door open, workmen passing in and out, carrying plasterboard, lighting fixtures, boxes of eighteen-inch tiles of white and black vinyl. They followed the workmen inside, looked around at the bustling confusion: shouts, men hammering, a lad with a foulard kerchief knotted about his neck rushing about with a roll of blueprints under his arm. They stood irresolutely a moment, then a slat-thin young girl hurried up to them.

"We're closed," she said breathlessly. "The show doesn't open until—"

"I have an appointment with Mr. Geltman," Chief Delaney said. "My name is—"

"Please, no more interviews," she frowned. "No photos. Absolutely none. A press conference and reception will be held the evening of—"

"—Edward X. Delaney," he finished in heavy voice. "Chief, New York Police Department. I have an appointment at one o'clock with Saul Geltman."

"Oh," she said. "Oh. Wait right here, please."

She disappeared into the jumble. They waited stolidly, inspecting. The walls were being repainted from a delft blue to a flat white. The white and black tiles were being laid in a diagonal diamond pattern. Temporary partitions were being erected to break up the room into several compartments of varying widths. Lighting fixtures of a brushed-steel teardrop design were being attached to the walls.

"Must be costing a fortune," Boone said.

Delaney nodded.

The girl was back in a few minutes.

"This way, please," she said nervously. "Mr. Geltman is expecting you. Watch where you step; everything is in such a mess."

She led them toward the rear. They watched where they stepped and arrived at the back office without misadventure. She stayed outside, motioned them in, closed the door behind them. The man behind the desk, talking on the telephone, smiled at them and lifted a hand to beckon them forward. He continued speaking on the phone as he waved them to armless chairs arranged in front of his desk. The chairs, in black leather on chrome frames, looked like jet-plane ejection seats. But they were comfortable enough.

"Yes, darling," Saul Geltman was saying. "You better if you know what's good for you . . . Yes . . . Put it down in your little mauve book . . . June ninth from eight o'clock on . . . Of course . . . Darling, but everyone! . . . I can expect you then? Marvelous!" He made kissing sounds into the telephone.

The two detectives looked about the office. A square room painted dove grey. The most startling fixture was a window behind Geltman's desk. Through the window they saw waves breaking on a rocky coast. It took a second or two for their minds to adjust. It was a marvel of *trompe l'oeil.* An actual wooden window frame had been fixed to the wall. The panes were glass. There were curtains of white nylon ninon. The seacoast was a large phototransparency, lighted from behind. The effect was incredibly realistic. The icing on the cake was that the bottom half of the window had been slightly raised, and a concealed fan billowed the curtains.

Both men smiled; a whimsical trick, but a good one. There was nothing else on the office walls, no paintings, drawings, etchings. The furnishings were all white and black leather and vinyl on chrome and stainless-steel frames. The desk appeared to be pewter (over wood?) supported on a cast-iron base. The desk fittings—rocker blotter, pen set, letter opener, etc.—were antique mother-of-pearl. In one corner of the room was an ancient safe, at least a hundred years old, on big casters. It was painted black, delicately striped, the front decorated with an ornate American eagle, wings outspread. There were two tumblers and two polished brass handles.

"Black-and-white," Geltman said on the phone. "White walls . . . But you know Maitland's colors, darling; you just can't compete . . . Correct . . . Darling, leave it to Halston; he'll know what to do . . . Yes, *dear!* . . . See you then. Byeee."

He hung up and made a face at the two officers.

"Rich, lonely widows," he said ruefully. "The story of my life."

He bounded to his feet, hurried around the desk to them, hand outthrust. Then they saw how small he was.

"Don't get up, don't get up," he said rapidly, motioning them back. "Take you five minutes to fight your way out of those chairs. Sergeant Boone, nice to see you again. You must be Chief Delaney."

"Yes. Thank you for seeing us on such short notice. It's obvious you're very busy."

"Listen, Chief," Geltman said, rushing back behind his desk again, "I'll see you every day in the week and twice on Sunday, if you say so. Just as long as the cops haven't forgotten Victor Maitland."

"We haven't forgotten," Delaney said.

"Glad to hear it." Geltman pressed his forefingers together, tapped them against his lips a moment, then straightened up, sighing. "The poor guy."

"What kind of a man was he?" Delaney asked.

"What kind of a man?" Geltman repeated. He spoke quickly; occasionally spraying a mist of spittle. "As a human being, a terrible, frightening, mean, contemptible, cruel, heartless son of a bitch. As an artist, a giant, a saint, a god, the one real genius I've seen in this schlocky business in the last twenty years. A century from now you gentlemen and I will be nothing. Dust. But Victor Maitland will be something. His paintings in museums. Books on him. Immortal. Like David and Rubens. I really mean that."

"So you put up with his miserable personality because of his talent?" Delaney asked.

"No," Geltman smiled. "I put up with his miserable personality because of the money he made me. Fifteen years ago I had a hole-in-the-wall gallery on Macdougal Street in the Village. I sold a few crappy originals for bupkiss, but mostly I sold cheap reproductions. Van Gogh's sunflowers and Monet's water lilies. Then Victor Maitland entered my life, and today I'm in hock for almost a quarter of a million, I have three lawsuits pending against me, and my ex-wife is threatening to sue for non-support. Success—no?"

They laughed with him; it was hard not to.

He was a small man, made somehow larger by his vigor. He was in constant motion: slumping, straightening, twisting, gesturing, drumming his fingers on the desk top, crossing his knees to scratch his ankle, pulling an ear lobe, smoothing the brown-grey hair combed sideways across a broad skull.

He wore a beautifully tailored Norfolk suit of brown covert with a white turtleneck sweater of some sheeny knit. His little feet were shod in Gucci loafers, and Chief Delaney noted a bracelet of heavy gold links hanging loosely from one thin wrist.

His head seemed disproportionately large for his body, and his features seemed small for the head. Big face, but small eyes, nose, and mouth, like a pumpkin jackknifed with tiny openings. But the voice that came booming from this pleasantly ugly little man was warm, confiding, bubbling with good humor and laughter at himself.

"Not entirely correct," he told them, speaking so quickly he sometimes stuttered. "About putting up with Maitland's nastiness because of the money he made me. Half-correct, but not *all* correct. The bulk of my income came from him; I don't deny it. But I represent other artists. I do okay. If Maitland had left me, I wouldn't have starved. He got killed, but I'm still in business. The money I liked, I admit it. But something else . . . When I was a kid, I wanted to be a violinist." He held up a hand, palm out. "God's truth. Another Yehudi Menuhin I wanted to be. So I studied, I practiced; I practiced, I studied, and one day I was playing a Bach concerto, and I suddenly stopped, put the fiddle away, and I haven't touched it since. I don't mean I was bad, but I just didn't have it. At least I had sense enough to know; no one had to tell me. Studying isn't enough, and practicing isn't enough. If you haven't got it in the genes, you'll always be a second-rater, no matter how good you force yourself to be. Maitland had it in his genes. Not just talent—genius. Hey, genius and genes! Is that where the word comes from? I got to look it up. But Maitland had it, and it's too rare to let go of just because the guy insults you in public and treats you like dirt. I represent a lot of other artists. Good artists. But Maitland was the only genius I had, and probably ever will have. Well . . . you don't want to listen to me dribble on and on. What do you want to know?"

"No, no, Mr. Geltman," Delaney said. "Just keep talking. It may be a help. Tell us about your financial arrangements with Maitland. How did that work?"

"Money," Geltman said. He smoothed his hair again, leaned back in his chair. "You want to know about the money. First, let me tell you something about the art business. Like any other business, you buy low and you sell high. That's basic. But art—now I'm talking about original paintings, drawings, sculpture, and so forth—is different from other business. Why? Because Kellogg's makes umpteen million boxes of Corn Flakes every year, and all those boxes are identical and make a lot of money. Closer to home, a writer writes a book, and a million copies of that book are sold, if he's lucky. And a singer or even a violinist makes a recording and maybe a million copies are sold. But a painter? One. That's all.

One. Oh, maybe guys like Norman Rockwell and Andy Wyeth can make deals to sell reproductions, and drawings and etchings and lithographs can be reproduced in limited numbers. But now we're talking about oil paintings. Originals. One of a kind. Maybe the artist worked a year on it, maybe more. He wants to get paid for his work, his time, his talent. That's natural. Normal. But how many people in this country, in the world, buy original works of art? Original oil paintings and sculptures? Especially from artists who haven't made a reputation yet? Guess how many?"

"I couldn't guess," Delaney said. "Not many, I'd say."

"You'd say right," Saul Geltman said, clasping his hands behind his head. "Three thousand. Four thousand maybe. In the whole world. Who'll pay a good price for original art. That's where an agent comes in. A good agent. He knows those three or four thousand people. Not all of them, of course, but enough of them. You follow? The agent builds a reputation, too. The rich people who collect art, they trust him. Damned few of them trust their own taste, so they trust an agent. Maybe they want to buy art just for an investment—a lot of them do; I could tell you stories of profits you wouldn't *believe!*—or they want art to match their drapes, or maybe, just a few of them, like art the way I do. I mean they just *like* it. They want it in their homes. They want to see it every day. They want to *live* with it. A good agent knows all these kinds of art nuts. That's how he makes a living. That's the service he supplies to the artists he represents. Thirty percent. That's what I got on Victor Maitland." Geltman grinned cheerfully. "The bullshit buildup was so you wouldn't think it so much. I took thirty percent of the selling price. From a new artist I'd take on, it would be maybe fifty percent. Up or down, depending on the type of thing the guy does, what the critics say, how much work he turns out, and so forth."

"Thirty to fifty percent," Delaney repeated. "Is that normal for most galleries?"

Geltman flipped his hands up in the air.

"Maybe a little more, maybe a little less. With the rents we got on Madison Avenue, I'd say thirty to fifty is about right."

"And what determines the selling price of a painting?" Chief Delaney asked.

"Oh-ho," Saul Geltman said, jerking forward suddenly. "Now you've opened a whole new can of worms. Is the guy known? Has he had any good reviews from the critics? Is he turning out the stuff like sausages or does he really sweat them out? Have any museums bought him? Has he got something to say? Has he got a new way of saying it? Has someone important bought him? Has he got a good gallery behind him? Has he got a following who'll buy anything he does? And on and on and on. It's not one thing; it's a lot of things. I charge what I think the traffic will bear, after considering all those factors."

"I read Maitland sold for a hundred thousand," Delaney said. "What made him so special? I happen to like his work, but what made it worth that much?"

"Yes, I sold *Study in Blue* for a hundred," Geltman said. "He brought it in, I made one phone call, sold it sight unseen. So I made thirty G's on one phone call. But it took me twenty years to learn who to call . . ."

He spun in his swivel chair until he was facing the fake seacoast. He stared at the unmoving waves. The breeze ruffled his hair.

"To answer your question," he said, speaking to the wall. "What made him worth big money . . . Victor was a throwback. A dinosaur. He knew what was going on in painting in this country in the Fifties and Sixties. Abstract Expressionism, Pop-Art, Minimal, Op-Art, Less-Is-More, Flat, all the avant-garde idiocies. But Maitland paid no attention to it. He went his way. Traditional. Representational. If he painted a tit, it was a *tit.* And you'd be surprised how many people want paintings they can recognize, paintings that tell a story, *beautiful* paintings. And Maitland could paint beautiful. A marvelous colorist. A marvelous draftsman. A marvelous anatomist."

"But it can't be wholly a matter of technique," Delaney said. "It was something more."

"Oh, yes," Geltman nodded. "Much, much more. Without trying to intellectualize what Maitland did, I think it's obvious that he, in a way, spiritualized sensuousness. Or maybe a better way of putting it would be to say that he conceptualized physical passion. So you can look at his nudes and feel no more lust than you would on viewing the Venus de Milo."

"Can *I?*" Delaney said dryly.

Geltman laughed shortly.

"Well, let's say *I* can," he said. "To me, there's nothing carnal in Maitland's work. I see his paintings as essentially sexless. They're more the idea of sex, the visual representation of a conception. But I admit, that's my personal reaction. You might see something entirely different."

"I do," Delaney assured him.

"That's one of Maitland's greatest gifts," Geltman nodded. "He's everything to everyone. He gives you back what you bring to his art and confirms your secret dreams."

He swiveled to face them, his eyes wet.

"What can I tell you?" he said, his voice clogged. "I was so ambivalent about him. I hated his guts. But if I had the money, I'd buy everything he did, buy it for myself, line my apartment walls with it, lock the door, and just sit there and stare."

Chief Delaney flipped through his notebook. The tears didn't impress him one way or the other. He remembered an accused ax murderer who had literally banged his head against the wall in horror and despair of being charged with such a disgusting crime. Which he had committed, of course.

"Mr. Geltman," he said, "I know you've been questioned several times before. I just want to review briefly your movements from Friday, the day Maitland was killed, until you discovered the body on Sunday. All right?"

"Sure," Geltman said. "Shoot." Then he added hastily, "Except maybe that isn't the right thing to say to a cop!"

Delaney ignored the weak joke.

"According to our records, you said you had an appointment with Maitland on Friday. He was to meet you and an interior designer here at three o'clock to go over plans for the installation of a new exhibition."

"Correct. Now it's a memorial show. The interior designer is that fag running around out there dressed like a cowboy."

"Let me finish, please. Then we can go back and pick up any additions or changes you'd like to make."

"Sorry."

"Let's start with that Friday. You arrived here at the Galleries about nine, maybe a little before. Talked to your staff, sent out for coffee—and, did a little business on the phone. Went through the morning mail. At about ten, you walked around the corner to your attorney's office, Simon and Brewster. Your lawyer is J. Julian Simon. You had an appointment with him at ten. You were with him till about one-thirty. You didn't go out for lunch; the two of you sent out for sandwiches around twelve-thirty. Roast beef on whole wheat."

"With sugar-free Dr. Peppers," Geltman said solemnly. Delaney paid no heed.

"You and Simon discussed personal matters—taxes, the lawsuits pending against you, and so forth. Until one-thirty. Approximately. You returned directly here. Busy with mail, phone calls, business in general. The interior designer showed up at three, on schedule, but no Maitland. You didn't worry; he was usually late."

"Invariably."

"But by four o'clock, you were concerned. The interior designer had another appointment, couldn't wait. You called Maitland's Mott Street studio. No answer. You called his home. His wife didn't know where he was. You made five more calls on Friday, and, you estimate, at least a dozen on Saturday. Now you were also calling Maitland's friends and acquaintances. No one knew where he was. No one had heard from him. On Sunday morning you called his home again. They hadn't heard from him. You called his studio again. No answer. So you cabbed down and found him. At about one-twenty Sunday afternoon. Any additions, corrections, comments?"

"No," Geltman said shortly, his face pale. "That's about it."

"*About* it?"

"No, no. That *is* it. How it happened. Jesus, just remembering . . . Of course, you've checked it out?"

"Of course. Your staff saw you here Friday morning between nine and ten. Your lawyer says he was with you from ten to one-thirty. Your staff and customers saw you here from one-thirty to six that evening. The people you say you called said you did call. We even found the hackie who took you down to Mott Street on Sunday. Yes, we checked it out. I just hoped you might have something to add."

"No," Saul Geltman shook his head. "I have nothing to add."

"All right . . . Now let's get back to your financial dealings with Maitland," Chief Delaney said. "I'm trying to get a picture of how it worked. Suppose Maitland finished a new painting in his Mott Street studio. Would you send for it, or would he bring it up here?"

"Usually he brought it up here in a cab. Then we'd talk about it."

"You gave him your opinion of it?"

"Oh, God, no!" Geltman said, coming alive again. "I wouldn't dare! With Maitland, I had a standard comment for his stuff: I'd say, 'Victor, it's the best thing you've ever done.' Then maybe we'd discuss how it should be framed if it was going into a show, or if we should leave it unframed, on the stretcher."

"Stretcher?"

"That's the interior frame, made of wood, over which the canvas is stretched and tacked down. Maitland made his own stretchers."

"Then what would happen, after you discussed the framing?"

"I'd enter the painting in the book. I keep a ledger for every artist I represent. I keep telling them they should keep a journal themselves: a list of their paintings, when started and when completed, title, size, brief description, and so forth. A great help if there's ever any question about the provenance or a forgery. But most artists are lousy businessmen and don't keep complete records. Maitland didn't. So when he'd bring in a new painting, I'd have a color Polaroid taken of it. I'd paste that in his ledger, with the date it was delivered, the title, the size in centimeters, and so on. When it was sold, I'd enter date of sale, name and address of buyer, amount received, and the number and date of the check I mailed to Maitland. Here, let me show you . . ."

Geltman bounced to his feet, strode to his antique safe, worked the combination on both dials, swung open the heavy door. There was another locked door within, this one sheet steel opened with a key. The agent took out a large buckram ledger with red leather corners. He carried it back to his desk. Chief Delaney and Sergeant Boone fought their way out of their deep chairs and stood on either side of Geltman, dwarfing the diminutive agent.

"Here's one we called *Red Poppies.* Delivered March third, nineteen seventy-one. The Polaroid shot. The size. Date of sale. Amount. Check. Go ahead, take a look. That's how I handle all my merchandise."

"Who set the selling price?"

"I did. But with Maitland, I always checked with him first before making the deal."

"Did he ever object? Want more?"

"That happened a few times. I never argued with him. Once he wanted to hold out for more, and we did get more. The other times he settled for what I recommended."

Delaney flipped through the book, one painting per page, glancing mostly at the selling prices.

"He did all right," he noted. "A gradual increase. He starts out at one hundred bucks and ends up with a hundred big ones."

"Yes, but look at these," Geltman said, turning to the back of the book. "His new work that'll be in the show. Unsold. Look at this one. Magnificent! I'll get two hundred for that, I know. At least."

"And after these are gone?" Delaney asked. "No more Maitlands?"

"Well, that I can't say for sure," Geltman said cautiously. "You know, most artists are nuts. They're *nuts!* They do paintings and squirrel them away. For a rainy day. In case they get sick and can't work. Or maybe just something to leave the wife and kiddies. Their inheritance."

"You think Maitland did that?"

"I don't know," Geltman said, troubled. "He never said. Once I came right out and asked him, but he just laughed. So I don't really know."

"I'm surprised Mrs. Maitland is letting you have this show," Delaney said. "Letting you sell his last work."

"Surprised?" Geltman said. "Why should you be surprised?"

"She told us she was suing you," Delaney said, looking at him.

Geltman laughed, went behind his desk to flop into his swivel chair.

"She'll have to get in line," he said cheerfully. "Wives and widows of artists—the curse of my profession. If you can call it a profession. They all think we're screwing their poor, impractical husbands. Well, there's the ledger. I told Alma she's welcome to bring her lawyer in and examine it any time she wants. I have all the canceled checks I gave Maitland. What she is afraid of finding, of course, and what she *will* find, is that he was doing paintings he wasn't telling her about. The checks were given to him in person or mailed to his Mott Street studio. She didn't know anything about it—but she suspected. He was spending that money himself."

"On what?" Delaney asked.

"Wine, women, and song. But very easy on the song."

Delaney and Boone lowered themselves cautiously into their reclining chairs again.

"Mr. Geltman," Delaney asked, "what's your personal opinion of Mrs. Maitland?"

"Dear Alma? I knew her in the Village, you know. Twenty years ago. She tried her hand at painting for awhile, but gave it up. She was terrible. Just terrible. Much worse than me on my violin. So she decided to make her contribution to art by modeling. I admit she had an incredible body. Big. Junoesque. Maillol would have loved her. But you know what we called her in the Village then? The Ice Maiden. She wouldn't screw. She-would-not-screw. I often wondered if she was a closet lez. So Maitland married her, that being the only way he could make her without her filing a rape charge."

"She told us she was his first model."

"Bullshit!" Saul Geltman said explosively. "He had plenty of models before she came along. And he layed them all: young, old, fat, thin, beautiful, ugly—he didn't care. The man was a stallion. And after he married Alma, he told everyone she was the worst lay of the lot."

"Hardly a gentleman."

"No one ever accused Victor Maitland of *that!*"

"Why did they stay married?"

"Why not? He had someone to cook his meals and mix his paints, to run down to the store for a jug, and nurse him through his hangovers. Also, he had a free model. She had the type of body he liked. It was a good deal for him."

"What about her?" Delaney asked. "What did she get out of it?"

Geltman leaned back, clasped his hands behind his head, stared at the ceiling.

"You've got to remember that the Ice Maiden was a very beautiful woman. Very. A lot of men were in love with her. Or thought they were. I might have thought so myself. Once. She loved that. Loved having men wildly in love with her. The center of attraction at any party. The professional virgin. I think it gave her a sense of power: all of us sniffing around with hard-ons. She didn't believe there was any man who didn't love her. She just took it for granted."

"Did Maitland love her?"

"Come on, Chief; you know better than that. He probably told her he did. He'd tell a woman *anything* to get in her pants. And he was beginning to sell, so I guess she figured he was a good catch. So of course he made her miserable. He made everyone miserable. She just couldn't believe he didn't come home nights because he was out drinking or shafting someone older and uglier than she was. She wanted all of him. I mean *all* of him. But I'll tell you something funny. Well . . . maybe not so funny. If he had been a good husband and didn't cheat and swore off the booze, she still wouldn't have been satisfied. She'd have wanted more of him and more and more and more, until she had him all. Then, I think, she would have turned to someone else."

"A barracuda," Sergeant Abner Boone said suddenly, and then blushed when the other two looked at him in surprise.

"Exactly, sergeant," Geltman said gently. "A beautiful barracuda. But Victor wasn't having any. He knew her greed, but he wasn't about to be devoured. At least, that's the way I figure it."

"Interesting," Delaney said noncommittally. He snapped his notebook shut, struggled out of that damned chair again. Sergeant Boone followed suit. "Thank you very much, Mr. Geltman, for giving us so much of your valuable time. I hope you'll be willing to see us again if it's necessary."

"I told you, any time at all. Can I ask a question now?"

"Of course."

"Those three drawings that were in the studio—what happened to them?"

"They're in my possession at the present time," Delaney said. "They'll be returned to Mrs. Maitland eventually."

"What did you think of them?" Geltman asked.

"I thought they were very good."

"More than that," the agent said. "I've seen some of his preliminary work before. I've sold some of it: drawings, studies for paintings. But those are something special. Rough, fast, strong. Something primitive there."

"Have any idea when they were done?"

"No. Recently, I'd guess. Maybe just before he was killed."

"You said you didn't recognize the model."

"No, I didn't. Very young. Looked Spanish to me. Well . . . Puerto Rican or Cuban. Latin."

"Spanish?" Delaney said. "I thought Oriental."

"The body was too full to be Oriental, Chief. I'd say a Latin-type. But maybe Italian or Greek."

"Interesting," Delaney said again. He moved toward the door. "Thank you once more, Mr. Geltman."

"Say!" the agent said, snapping his fingers. "I'm having a big reception here before the opening. A combination press party and just plain party. A kind of wake, I guess. A lot of important people. The beautiful people. Oy! And important customers, of course. How would you and the sergeant like to come? At eight o'clock on June ninth. Bring your wives. Or girlfriends. Plenty to eat and drink. How about it?"

Chief Delaney turned slowly to smile at the agent.

"That's kind of you, Mr. Geltman," he said softly. "I'd like very much to come." He looked at Boone. The sergeant nodded.

"Good, good, good," Saul Geltman said, rubbing his palms together. "I'll make certain you get invitations. And look, wear your uniforms if you like. Maybe then I won't lose so many ashtrays!"

They walked back to Boone's car, parked on Lexington Avenue.

"Reticent little fellow, isn't he?" the sergeant said sardonically.

"Oh I don't know," Delaney said. "It helped. We learned a lot."

"Did we, sir?" Boone said.

In the car, Delaney glanced at his watch.

"My God," he groaned. "Almost three. Where does the time go? Can you get me home?"

"Sure, Chief. Ten minutes."

On the ride uptown, Delaney said, "You're going to check with more of the men who worked on the Maitland case? To see if they remember anything not in the reports?"

"Right," Boone said. "But I'm running out of names of guys I know. Could you give me some more from the file?"

"Of course. Come in with me when we get home. I also want to give you the name and address of Mrs. Maitland's friend. The one she had lunch with. To ask why the two of them didn't go shopping together."

"Will do."

Just before they parked near Delaney's brownstone, the Chief said, "You know, he's not as frail as he looks. I hefted that ledger. It's heavy, but he handled it like a feather. And did you catch the way he swung that safe door open? It must be six inches of steel. He didn't have any trouble."

"Maybe the door was well balanced and well oiled, Chief."

"Not on those old safes," Delaney said. "No way. It took muscle."

They spent a few moments in Delaney's study while Sergeant Boone copied names and addresses in his notebook, and the Chief flipped through *his* notebook, fretting over cryptic jottings he had made during the interviews with Alma Maitland and Saul Geltman.

"More questions than answers," he grumbled. "We'll have to see these people again. But I prefer to see all the principals first, before we start the second round."

Boone looked up.

"What Geltman said about his financial condition," he said. "The money he owed, the lawsuits, and so on . . . . Was that legit?"

"Apparently," Delaney said. "It's in the file. But maybe not as bad as he put it. He's got some heavy loans. But those lawsuits are piddling stuff. One guy is suing because he wants to return a painting that his wife didn't like, and Geltman won't give him his money back. He seems to have a good income, but his bank balances don't reflect it. You'd think a man who can make thirty G's by picking up a phone would have *something* tucked away, but it looks like Mr. Geltman is suffering from a bad case of the shorts. I wonder where it goes? The next time we see him, let's try to schedule it in his apartment. I'd like to see how he lives."

"Chief—" Boone started, then stopped.

"What were you going to say?"

"You think he's a flit?"

Delaney looked at him curiously.

"Why do you say that?"

"A lot of little things," Boone frowned. "None of them significant in themselves—but maybe they add up. He's so fucking *neat*. The bracelet. Calling the interior designer a fag. There was no need for that. Except to prove his own masculinity, figuring we'd think that way, too. He's got an ex-wife, he said. The way he touches himself. He said he might have loved Alma Maitland. Then he added, 'Once.' And that fake window. That's flitty."

"You're good," Delaney said. "You really are. Good eye, good memory."

Boone blushed with pleasure.

"But I don't know," Delaney said doubtfully. "As you say, each item is innocent. But maybe they do add up. Then we've got to ask ourselves, 'So what?' "

"Maybe he was in love with Maitland and couldn't stand the thought of the guy alley-catting around."

"Original idea. Another possibility. That's the trouble with this thing: all smoke, nothing solid. We'll see Jake Dukker and Belle Sarazen tomorrow. That leaves only Maitland's son, and his mother and sister up in Nyack. After we talk to all of them, we'll sit down and try to—"

There was a brisk rap-rap on the closed study door. Then it was opened, Monica Delaney stuck her head in . . .

"Hullo, dear," she said to her husband. "Rebecca and I just—Why, Sergeant Boone! How nice to see you again!"

She came swiftly into the room. Abner Boone jerked to his feet, took the proffered hand, almost bowed over it.

"Pleasure, ma'am," he murmured.

Chief Delaney carefully avoided smiling as he watched the effect of his wife's formidable charm on the sergeant. It was strictly no contest.

"Edward," Monica said brightly, turning to him. "Rebecca and I have been shopping, and she came back with me for a cup of coffee. We stopped at the Eclair and bought some of those petits fours you love. Why don't you and the sergeant take a minute off and have coffee with us? Just in the kitchen. Informal."

"Sounds good to me," Delaney said, picking up his cue dutifully. "You, sergeant?"

"Just fine," Boone nodded.

The poor fish, Delaney thought. He hasn't got a chance.

They sat around the kitchen table on wooden chairs, and laughed at Monica's droll description of the trials and tribulations of shopping in crowded department stores.

"And," she concluded, "I know you'll be happy to hear, dear, we didn't buy a thing. Did we, Becky?"

"Not a thing," Rebecca Hirsch vowed.

She was a shortish, plump, jolly woman, with soft eyes set in a cherubic face. Her complexion seemed so limpid and fine that a finger's touch might bruise it. She wore her black, glistening hair parted in the middle, falling unfettered to below her shoulders. Her body was undeniably chubby, but wrists and ankles were slender, hands and feet delicate. She moved with robust grace.

She was wearing a tailored suit, but even beneath the heavy material, bosom and hips were awesome. There was a rosy glow to her, and if not especially beautiful, there was comfort in her prettiness and no guile in her manner. Her voice was light, somewhat flutey, but her laugh was hearty enough. Delaney found much enjoyment in chivying her. Not maliciously, but only to see those button eyes suddenly flash, the innocent mien change to outraged indignation.

The talk bubbled. Nothing of an artist bleeding to death in a Mott Street tenement. Just the weather, the latest cosmic pronouncements of Mary and Sylvia Delaney, Rebecca's continuing feud with the superior of a private day-care center where she worked four days a week, the high cost of flounder filets, and the problems of getting tickets to Broadway theatrical hits.

"The problem is," Rebecca Hirsch said seriously, "the problem is that it's practically impossible to do anything on impulse these days. You decide in the evening that you'd like to go to a Broadway show or see a first-run movie. But then you discover you've got to buy tickets weeks in advance for the show or stand in line for three hours to see the movie. Don't you agree, Sergeant Boone?"

"Uh," he said.

"Or going somewhere," Monica Delaney said quickly. "A trip or vacation. The *planning!*"

"Yes," Chief Delaney nodded solemnly. "The planning . . ."

His wife looked at him blandly.

"You were going to say, dear?" she asked.

"Just agreeing," he said equably. "Just agreeing."

After awhile, the coffee finished, the petits fours demolished, Rebecca Hirsch rose to her feet.

"Gotta go," she sang. "One dog, two cats, three African violets, and a mean-tempered parakeet to feed. Monica, Edward, thank you for the feast."

"Feast!" Monica scoffed. "A nosh."

"The calories!" Rebecca said. "Sergeant Boone, nice to have met you."

"I'm leaving too," he said. "I have a car outside. Can I drop you anywhere?"

They left together. Monica and Edward Delaney waved from the stoop. Inside, the door closed, she turned to him proudly.

"See?" she said triumphantly.

That evening, after dinner, alone in his study, Chief Edward X. Delaney carefully wrote out complete reports of his day's activities: the questioning of Mrs. Maitland and Geltman. He wrote slowly, in the beautifully legible Palmer method he had been taught. Twice he rose to mix a rye highball, but most of the time he sat heavily in one position as he doggedly put the interviews down on paper, consulting his notebook occasionally for exact quotes, but generally relying on his memory for the substance, mood and undertone of the meetings.

When he had finished, he read over what he had written, made several minor corrections, and appended lists of additional questions to ask at further interviews. Then he filed the reports away in the proper folders, and pondered the usefulness of asking Sergeant Boone for copies of his reports. He decided not to, for the time being. He went up to bed.

Shortly after midnight, the bedside phone shrilled, and Delaney was instantly awake. He grabbed it off the hook before the second ring was finished, then moved cautiously, trying not to disturb Monica.

"Edward X. Delaney here," he said in a low voice.

"Chief, this is Boone. Sorry to disturb you at this hour. I hope you're still awake. I'd hate to think—"

"What is it?" Delaney asked, wondering if Boone was sober.

"I spoke to four guys who worked the Maitland case. Got nothing from them, but at least they were reasonably friendly. But that's not why I'm calling. I finally got through to Susan Hemley. She's the friend of Mrs. Maitland. The friend who had lunch with her that Friday."

"I know."

"The reason I'm calling so late is that she had a date and just got home. And the reason she didn't go shopping that Friday morning with Alma Maitland is that she couldn't. She's got a job. She's a working girl."

"Simple solution," Delaney sighed. "We should have thought of it."

"Not so simple," Abner Boone said. "Just for the hell of it, I asked her where she worked. Are you ready for this? At Simon and Brewster, attorneys-at-law, on East Sixty-eighth Street. She's the personal secretary of J. Julian Simon, Saul Geltman's lawyer."

There was silence.

"Chief?" Boone said. "Are you there?"

"I'm here. I heard. Any ideas?"

"None. Total confusion. You?"

"Let's talk about it in the morning. Thank you for calling, sergeant."

He hung up and rolled carefully back under the covers. But Monica stirred.

"What is it?" she murmured.

"I don't know," he said.

6

Sergeant Boone apologized for his late call the previous night.

"It could have waited, Chief," he admitted. "It wasn't all that important. But I got excited. It's the first *new* thing we've turned up. It wasn't in the file, was it?"

"No," Delaney said. "No, it wasn't. I looked this morning, in case I had missed it."

They were seated in Boone's car, parked in front of the Chief's brownstone. Both men had their black notebooks open.

"I stayed awake half the night trying to figure it," the sergeant said. "Then I thought, what the hell, the two were just friends, that's all. Why shouldn't Mrs. Maitland be friendly with the secretary of Geltman's lawyer? That's probably how they met. But then I remembered how hostile Mrs. Maitland sounded when you mentioned Geltman's name. So maybe she was using the secretary as a private pipeline, to keep track of what the little guy was up to. What do you think?"

"That could be," Delaney nodded. "Except the two had lunch at Le Provençal on East Sixty-second Street. That's not far from the Geltman Galleries. If Mrs. Maitland was playing footsie with this Susan Hemley, maybe even paying her for information, wouldn't she have picked some place for lunch where there was no danger of running into Geltman?"

"I suppose so," Boone sighed. "Right now, it makes no sense at all, no matter how you figure it."

"One thing's certain," Delaney said grimly. "We're going to have a talk with J. Julian Simon and the Hemley woman."

"Today?"

"If we have time. Belle Sarazen first, at ten o'clock. Then Jake Dukker at two this afternoon. We'll see how it goes. You know where the Sarazen woman lives?"

"Yes, *sir!*" Boone said. Then he grinned. "Wait'll you see her place. A Persian whorehouse."

He pulled out slowly into traffic and headed north to Eighty-fifth Street, to take a traverse across Central Park to the West Side. There was a fine, warm mist in the air, but they had the windows open. The sun glowed dimly behind a grey scrim; it looked like it might burn through by noon.

"The file was skimpy on Belle Sarazen," Delaney remarked. "Seemed to me everyone was walking on eggs. You said you questioned her twice. What was your take?"

"Remember the Canfield case?" Abner Boone asked. "In Virginia? About ten, fifteen years ago?"

"Canfield?" Delaney repeated. "Wasn't he the heir to tobacco money who got his head blown off? His wife said she thought she was blasting an intruder?"

"That's the one. Our Belle was the gal behind the twelve-gauge. Buckshot. Spread him all over the bedroom wall. She was Belle Canfield then. Youngish wife, oldish husband. He was an heir all right, but they kept him out of the tobacco business. Heavy drinker and heavy gambler. There had been attempts to break in; no doubt about that. In fact, he had bought her the shotgun for protection and taught her how to use it. Still, she knew he was out with the boys that night and pulled the trigger without even asking, 'Is that you, darling?' The coroner's jury—or whatever they have down there—called it 'a tragic accident,' and she waltzed away with almost two mil."

"And the county prosecutor retired to the French Riviera one year later."

"I don't know about that," Boone laughed, "but the Canfields practically *owned* that county and were kissin' cousins to half the money in Virginia. The Sarazens weren't money, but they were family: one of the oldest in the state. Belle sold the old plantation and the horses and moved to Paris. She cut a wide swath through Europe. French poets, English race drivers, Italian princes, and Spanish bullfighters. And I think there was a Polish weightlifter in there somewhere. The money lasted for five years and three marriages. Then she came back to the States and married a Congressman."

"Now I remember!" Delaney said. "Burroughs of Ohio. The guy who dropped dead while making a speech against socialized medicine."

"Right! But while he was alive, Belle was the most popular hostess in Washington. The scandal mags said John Kennedy, quote, Enjoyed her hospitality, unquote. Anyway, after the Congressman conked, she came up to New York. Still has a lot of political friends."

"Oh-ho," Delaney nodded. "I'm beginning to understand why the file was so cautious. But she doesn't use any of her married names; that's probably why I didn't make her."

"No, now she's just plain Belle Sarazen, a little ole gal from Raccoon Ford, V-A. But she's still flying high, wide, and handsome. One of Saul Geltman's Beautiful People. The Jet Set. Gives lavish parties. In big with the art and museum crowd. Contributes to the Democrats. Models for charity fashion shows and for fashion magazines, and sometimes for artists and photographers."

"She must be pushing forty," Delaney said. "At least."

"At least," Boone agreed. "But she's got the body of an eighteen-year-old. You'll see."

"Where does the money come from?" Delaney asked. "For these lavish parties and political contributions?"

"I think she hustles," Boone said, then laughed when he glanced sideways and saw Delaney's startled expression. "No con, Chief. I asked her directly. I said, 'What is the main source of your income, Miss Sarazen?' And she said, 'Men give me gifts.' So naturally, I said, 'Money gifts?' And she said, 'Is there any other kind?' Maybe she was putting me on, but I doubt it. She just doesn't give a damn."

"Did Maitland give her money?"

"According to her, yes. Plenty. Did they have sex together? Yes. Did she love him? God, no, she said, he was a savage. But she thought he was amusing. Her word: 'amusing.' "

"Yes, I read that in your report. Where did you pick up the other stuff on her? The background stuff?"

"From her scrapbooks. She's got three fat scrapbooks of newspaper clippings about herself. And magazine articles. Photos with famous people. Letters from politicians and royalty. She let me go through them as long as I wanted."

"Anything from Maitland? Or about Maitland?"

"Not a thing, sir. And I looked carefully."

"I'm sure you did, sergeant. It must be that building—the highrise across from Lincoln Center. Listen, I noticed in our interviews with Mrs. Maitland and Geltman that you hardly opened your mouth. Don't be afraid to speak up. If you think of something I haven't covered, ask it."

"I'd rather let you carry the ball, sir. First of all, they're liable to be more intimidated by a chief than a sergeant. And also, I'm studying your interrogation technique."

"My technique?" Delaney said, smiling. "Now *I'm* amused."

The door to the twenty-ninth-floor penthouse was opened by a Filipino manservant wearing livery of an unusual color: a blue-grey with an undertint of red. Not lilac or purple or violet, but something of all three. Looking around at the Persian whorehouse, Delaney saw the identical shade had been used on the painted walls, the curtains and drapes, the upholstered furniture, even the hassocks, pillows, and picture frames. The effect was that of a purpled grotto, a monochromatic cave that tinged skin and even seemed to color the air.

"I tell Miss Sarazen you are here, gentlemens," the butler said, almost lisping "Mith Tharathen," but not quite.

He disappeared into an inner room. They stood uneasily, hats in hand, looking about the stained chamber.

"Is the whole place like this?" Delaney whispered.

"No," Boone whispered back. "Every room a different color. The bedroom is blood-red. I had to use the can; it's dead black. The one I used was. She said that the place has three bathrooms."

"Hustling must be good," Delaney murmured.

The Filipino was back in a moment, to lead them down a hallway with walls covered with framed autographed photos. He ushered them into a bedroom, closed the door behind them. Here, again, was a one-color room: blood-red walls, curtains, drapes, bedspread, carpet, furniture—everything. The only striking exceptions were the white leotard, silvered hair, and chammy skin of the woman exercising near wide French doors. They led to a tiled terrace that provided a view, in the distance, of Central Park and the towers of the East Side.

"Sit down anywhere, darlings," she called to them, not interrupting her slow, steady movements. "There's champagne and orange juice on the cocktail table. Push the intercom button by the bedside table for anything stronger—or weaker."

They sat cautiously in fat armchairs with plump red cushions, facing the French doors. Daylight was behind the woman. There was a nimbus about her, a glow; it was difficult to make out her features.

She was seated on the floor, legs spread wide, flat out. She was bending from the hips, touching right hand to bare left toes, then left hand to bare right toes, the free arm windmilling high in the air. She wore a skin-tight white leotard, cut high to the hipbones, tight over the crotch. A soft mound there. The garment was sleeveless, strapped—a tanktop.

The body was that of a dancer, long-legged, hard, with flat rump, muscled thighs, sinewy arms, small breasts (nipples poking), and a definite break between ribcage and waist. Her exercise was strenuous—both men realized they could not have done it—but she had not huffed or gasped when she spoke, and Delaney saw no sweat stains on the leotard.

The silvery hair was fine, cut short and parted on the left. It was combed and brushed sideways, like a boy's haircut. It lay absolutely flat against her well-shaped skull: no wave, no curl, no loose tips or bounce to it. A helmet of hair, as tight and gleaming as beaten metal.

She ended her toe-touching, folded her legs, bent forward and rose to her feet without using her hands for support. Chief Delaney heard Sergeant Boone's low groan of envy.

"I want to thank you, Miss Sarazen," Delaney said mechanically, "for seeing us on such short notice."

She stood erect, feet about eighteen inches apart, clasped her hands over her head as high as she could reach. She began to bend slowly to each side alternately, hips level, her upper torso coming down almost to the horizontal.

"Call me Belle, sweet," she said. "All my friends call me Belle. Even the Scarecrow calls me Belle. Don't you, Scarecrow?"

Boone turned to Delaney with a sickly smile.

"I'm the Scarecrow," he said. "Yes, Belle," he said to her.

"I hope we're going to be friends," she said, still bending steadily. "I so want to be friends with the famous Edward X. Delaney."

"Not so famous," he said tonelessly.

"Famous enough. I'm a fan of yours, you know. I imagine I know things about you that even you've forgotten."

"Do you?" he asked, uncomfortable, realizing he was losing the initiative.

"Oh yes," she said. "The Durkee case is my favorite."

He was startled. The Durkee case had happened twenty years ago. It had certainly been in the New York papers, but he doubted if anyone in Raccoon Ford, or in all of Virginia for that matter, had read of it.

Ronald Durkee, a Queens auto mechanic, had gone fishing in Long Island Sound early one Saturday morning, despite threatening weather and small-craft warnings. When he had not returned by midnight, his distraught young wife reported his absence to the police. Durkee's boat was found floating overturned a few hundred yards offshore. No sign of Ronald Durkee.

The missing man had twenty thousand in life insurance, was in deep to the loansharks, and was known to be a strong swimmer. When the wife applied almost immediately for the insurance, Delaney figured it for attempted fraud. He broke it by convincing the wife that her missing husband had a girlfriend, even producing a fraudulent photograph to show her.

"This is the woman, Mrs. Durkee. Pretty, isn't she? We think he ran off with her, I'm sorry to say. Apparently he was seeing her on his lunch hour and after work. He did come home late from work occasionally, didn't he? We have statements from her neighbors. They identified your husband. He visited her frequently. I hate to be the one to tell you this, Mrs. Durkee, but we think he's gone off with her. Florida, probably. Too bad, Mrs. Durkee. Well, they say the wife is the last to know."

And so on. After a week of this, she broke, and Delaney picked up Ronald Durkee in a motel near LaGuardia Airport where he had grown a mustache and was patiently waiting for his wife to show up with the insurance money. Delaney wasn't particularly proud of his role in the case, but you worked with what you had.

It had resulted in a lot of newspaper stories, and his name had become known. A year later he was promoted to lieutenant.

"The Durkee case?" he said. He could not bring himself to address her as Belle. "That was long before you came to New York. You must have been checking into my background."

"As you checked into mine, dearie," she said. Her voice was lilting, laughing, with just a hint of soft Virginia drawl. "You did, didn't you?"

"Of course. You seem to make no secret of it."

"Oh, I have no secrets at all," she said. "From anyone."

She began reaching high overhead, then bending deeply from the hips to touch the floor. But not with her fingertips; her palms. He could see then what a slender, whippy body she had. No excess anywhere. He recalled with pleasure a line from an old movie he had enjoyed. Spencer Tracy looking at Katharine Hepburn: "Not much meat on her, but what there is, is cherce."

"Then you know I killed my husband," Belle Sarazen said casually. "My first husband. Four husbands ago. A tragic accident."

"Yes, I know of it."

"Tell me, Edward X. Delaney," she said mockingly, "if you had been investigating that, what would you have done?"

"My usual routine," he said coldly, tiring of her flippancy. "First, I would have checked to see if your husband really was out drinking with the boys that night. Or was he with another woman? Or if not that night, then any other night? Was there another woman in his life, or more than one other woman, that would make you jealous enough to blow away an intruder without yelling, 'Who's there?' or screaming or maybe just firing your shotgun into the ceiling to scare him away?"

"What time is it?" she asked suddenly.

Abner Boone glanced at his watch.

"Almost ten-thirty, Belle," he said.

"Close enough," she said. "That's my daily hour devoted to the carcass."

She stopped exercising. Came toward them. Turned on a floor lamp (with a blood-red shade). Bent forward to shake the Chief's hand.

"Edward X. Delaney," she said. "A pleasure. Scarecrow, good to see you again. I have this pitcher of champagne and orange juice waiting for me. A reward for my labors. Somewhat flat, which is good for little girls in the morning. Anything for you boys? Coffee?"

"That would be appreciated," Delaney said. "You, sergeant?"

Boone nodded. They watched her push a button and speak into a small intercom on the bedside table. No one said anything until the manservant entered bearing a silver tray with coffee pot, sugar bowl and creamer, two cups, saucers, spoons. She poured for them. They both refused sugar and cream. Delaney leaned forward to examine the tray.

"Handsome," he said. "Very old, isn't it?"

"So I understand," she said carelessly. "Daddy said it belonged to Thomas Jefferson—but who knows? Listen to Virginians, and Thomas Jefferson must have owned six thousand silver serving trays."

She folded down onto the floor at their feet. Went down without putting a hand out to aid her. She sat in the Lotus Position, back straight, knees bent and legs crossed so tightly that each foot rested on the opposite thigh, soles turned almost straight up. She sipped from a champagne glass that had not lost a drop during her descent.

"Yoga," she said. "Ever try it?"

"Not me," Delaney said. "You, sergeant?" he asked solemnly.

"No sir."

"Keeps the spine flexible," she said. "Puts pow in the pelvis. Improves performance." She winked at them.

Delaney could see her triangular face clearly now. High cheekbones—Indian blood there?—tight skin, somewhat slanted eyes widely spaced. Open, astonished eyes. Thin lips extended a bit above the skin line with rouge to give the impression of soft fullness. Hard chin. Small ears revealed by the short, flat silvered hair. Thin nose, patrician, with oval nostrils. Not a wrinkle, mark, or imperfection. She felt Delaney's stare.

"I work at it," she said laconically.

"You succeed," he assured her, and meant it.

"You want to know about Victor Maitland," she said, more of a statement than a question. "Again?"

"Not really," Chief Delaney said. "I want to know about Jake Dukker. What's your personal opinion of him?"

He noted, with some satisfaction, her small start of surprise. He had her off-balance.

"Jake Dukker," she repeated. "Well, Jake is an artist."

"We know that."

"Very facile, very competent. You cops are lucky he never decided to become a forger. Jake can copy *anyone's* style. Rembrandt, Picasso, Andy Warhol . . . you name it."

"Could he copy Victor Maitland?"

"Of course he could. If he wanted to. But why should he? Jake does very well indeed doing his own thing."

"Which is?"

"Whatever's selling. Superficial stuff. Very trendy. As soon as something shows signs of making money, Jake gets in on it. Abstracts, Calligraphy, Pop-Art, Op-Art, Photo-Realism—he's been into it all. You know what he's doing now? You'll never guess. Not in a million years. A nude of me painted on aluminum foil. Ask him to show it to you. Fan-tas-tic. It's not finished yet, but it's already sold."

"Who bought it?" Sergeant Boone asked quickly.

"A friend of mine," she said, taking a sip of her drink. "A very important man."

"Do you model frequently?" Delaney asked.

She nodded. "Mostly nudes. I enjoy it. Painters and photographers." She looked down at her body, stroked her small, hard breasts, ribs, waist, hips, her bare thighs. "Not a bad bod for a thirty-five-year-old chippy—right, men? I have this friend who wants to make a plaster cast of my body. The whooole thing. But I'm not sure I want to. I understand it gets hot as hell while that plaster is hardening. Is that right?"

"I wouldn't know," Chief Delaney said. "Did you ever model for Victor Maitland?"

"No," she said. "Never. I wasn't his type. His type of model, I mean. He liked the zoftigs. Big tits, big ass. He said I was the Venus of the Computer Age. That's what Jake Dukker is going to call his aluminum-foil nude of me: *Venus of the Computer Age.*"

"Could Dukker have killed Maitland?" Delaney asked directly.

Again he rocked her. He decided this was the way to do it: keep her off-balance, switch from one topic to another before she could get set. If he followed a logical train of thought, she'd be two questions ahead of him.

"Jake?" she said. "Jake Dukker kill Maitland?"

That was what people did when they wanted time to think: they repeated the question.

"Maybe," she said. "They were friends, but Victor had something Jake will never have. It drove him ape."

"What was that?"

"Integrity," she said. "Old-fashioned word, but I'll bet you just dote on old-fashioned words, Edward X. Delaney. Jake is the better painter. Listen, I know painting, I really do. God knows I've screwed enough artists. Jake is better than Maitland was. Technically, I mean. And as fast. But Victor didn't give one good goddamn what was in fashion, the fads, what was selling. I tell you this, and I know for a fact: if Victor Maitland had never sold a painting in his life, he wouldn't have changed his style, wouldn't have stopped doing what he wanted to do, what he had to do. Jake isn't like that at all, and can never be. He hated Victor's integrity. *Hated* it! At the same time he wanted it, wanted it so bad it drove him right up a wall. I know it. He told me once and started crying. Jake likes to be spanked."

That stopped them. They didn't know if she meant it literally or metaphorically. Delaney decided not to press it.

"Sergeant Boone tells me you admitted you were intimate with Victor Maitland."

" 'Intimate with Victor Maitland,' " she mimicked. "You sound like daddy. I always did have a thing for older men. All my shrinks have told me I'm a father-fucker at heart. Sure, I balled Victor. I wish he had bathed more often, but sometimes that can be fun, too. What a savage!"

"And he paid you?"

"He gave me gifts, yes," she said, unconcerned.

"Money?"

"Mostly. Once a small painting, which I sold for ten thousand."

"You didn't like it?"

"The painting? I loved it. A little still life. A single poppy in a crystal bud vase. But I liked those long, green still lifes even better."

"Did you tell Maitland you had sold his painting?"

"Of course."

"What was his reaction?"

"He thought it was funny as hell. He said I got more for it than Geltman would have."

"Apparently Maitland was a generous man."

"He wasn't cheap," she acknowledged.

Delaney rubbed his chin, squinting through the French doors. The mist was burning away. He could see fuzzy shadows forming on the tiled terrace.

"Did you ever procure women for Maitland?" he asked.

There was a moment of silence, brief, heavy.

"Procure," she said. "I don't like that word. I suggested models for him occasionally. Girls I thought he could use. His type."

"He paid you for this—this service?"

"Of course. Don't worry, Edward X. Delaney; I declared it all on my tax return. I'm clean."

"I'm sure you are," he said blandly. "Let's get on to the Friday he was killed. You said you left here about ten-thirty and went to your yoga class for an hour."

"Yoga and meditation," she said. "For twenty minutes we sit naked on the floor and go, 'Ooom.' "

"After that you went to Jake Dukker's studio on Central Park South. Did you pose for the aluminum-foil nude then?"

"No, Jake was setting up for a photo session. He's a photographer, too, you know, and a good one. Mostly fashion. He's in *Vogue* and *Town & Country* all the time. I sat around kibitzing until they broke for lunch."

"That was at twelve? Or thereabouts?"

"Thereabouts."

"And then?"

"Then Jake and I went upstairs to his apartment. He's got a duplex, you know. Jake made lunch for us. He thinks he's a great gourmet cook. He's lousy. I lived in Paris, and I *know*. He made an herb omelet that was barely edible. But he had a nice chilled Spanish white. I filled up on that."

"And did you have relations?"

She looked at him blankly.

"Sexual relations," he said. "While you were up in his apartment? Before, during, or after lunch?"

"You know," she said, "you're not going to believe this, but I don't remember. I really don't."

"I believe you," he said. "After all, it was six weeks ago."

She laughed her trilling laugh, up and down the scale.

"Oh, Edward X. Delaney," she said. "You're a sly one, you are. All right, I remember that awful herb omelet, but I don't remember if we screwed. Probably not."

"Why 'Probably not'?"

"Because his assistants and the fashion models were waiting for him downstairs. And the models get paid by the hour. Jake is all business."

"Even in his painting?"

"You better believe it, buster. If the Hudson River School ever comes back into style, Jake will be sitting out there on the Palisades, painting the river and trees and clouds and Indians in canoes."

"So then, after lunch, you and Dukker went downstairs to the studio, and he resumed shooting that photography assignment at about one-thirty. Is that correct?"

"That's correct."

"How late did you stay?"

"Oh, for another hour or so. I had an appointment at the hairdresser's."

"How many models were involved in this photography session at Dukker's?"

"I don't remember."

"One?"

"No, two or three, I guess."

"Perhaps four? Or five?"

"There could have been," she said. "Is it important?"

"What were they modeling?"

"Lingerie."

"Why did you attend? Photography shootings are usually boring, aren't they?"

She shrugged. "I just dropped by to kill a few hours. Before my appointment."

"It wasn't to take a look at the models, was it? For your friends? The important men?"

At first he thought he had cracked her. He watched her head jerk back. Thin lips peeled away from wet teeth. He thought he heard a faint hiss. But she held herself together. She smiled bleakly.

"Edward X. Delaney," she said. "Good old Edward X. Delaney. I don't run a call-girl ring, you know."

"I do know that," he said. "You wouldn't be involved in anything as obvious and vulgar as that."

He was conscious of Boone stirring restlessly in the chair alongside him. He turned to him.

"Sergeant?" he said. "Anything?"

"Belle," Abner Boone said, "you said you provided Maitland with models."

"Occasionally," she said tightly. "And I didn't *provide* them; I *suggested* girls to him."

"Ever suggest a very young girl?" Boone pressed on. "Maybe Puerto Rican? Or Italian? A Latin type?"

She thought a moment, frowning.

"Can't recall anyone like that," she said. "Recently?"

"Say a few weeks before he died. Maybe a month."

"No," she said definitely. "I didn't send Victor a girl for at least six months. Who is she?"

Boone looked at Delaney. The Chief saw no reason not to tell Belle Sarazen why they were interested. He described the three drawings they had found in Maitland's studio. He said it was believed they had been done shortly before Maitland's death. Maybe on the morning he had been killed.

"Where are they now?" she said. "The drawings?"

"I have them," Delaney said.

"Bring them around," she suggested. "I'll take a look. Maybe I can identify her. I know most of the girls Victor used, and a lot more besides."

"I may do that," Delaney said. He rose to his feet, putting his notebook away, and Sergeant Boone did the same. They thanked Belle Sarazen for her cooperation, and asked if they might return if more questions came up.

"Any time," she said. "I'll be right here."

She rang for the Filipino to show them out. They were at the bedroom door when she called Delaney's name. He stopped and turned slowly to face her.

"You don't really think I knew it was my husband when I fired the shotgun, do you?" she asked. Her smile was flirtatious, almost coy.

His smile was just as meaningless.

"We'll never know, will we?" he said.

They sat in Boone's car, comparing notes and blowing more smoke.

"There's nothing in the file about her and drugs," Delaney said. "No record of busts. But a woman like that, living a life like that, has *got* to be on. I'd be willing to bet she's feeding her nose. Maybe she was the source of the poppers they found in Maitland's studio."

"Could be," Boone said. "And maybe dealing a little with her important friends. You were a mite rough on her, Chief. Think we'll get any flak?"

Delaney considered a moment.

"We might," he acknowledged. "She could be humping the entire Board of Estimate, and I wouldn't be a bit surprised. If I get a call from Thorsen tonight, I'll know we made a dent. How do you figure her motive?"

"For wasting Maitland?"

"No, no. For living. The way she does."

"Money hungry," Boone said promptly. "Anything for a buck."

"I don't agree," Delaney said, just as promptly. "That might do for Saul Geltman. By the way, did you catch the way he referred to the art he sells as 'the merchandise'? But I don't think it holds for the Sarazen woman. Money, sure; she needs it. We all need it. But as a means to an end; not money for the sake of piling it up."

"What, then?"

"Here's how I see her: a spunky kid from a good family that's seen better days. Marries a wealthy, older man. Big house, horses, mistress of the manor—the whole enchilada. Now she *is* someone. But he strays, and she's got pride and a temper. So she blows Canfield away, with a lot of publicity, her name and picture in the papers. She likes that. Off she goes to Paris and starts spending, feeling pretty good, a tough, smart twist who got away with murder. But Europe is full of jackals, tougher and smarter, and in five years the money is gone, and who cares about Belle Sarazen from Raccoon Ford, Virginia? If she stays in Europe, she'll be peddling her ass in flea markets. So she comes home and marries Congressman Burroughs. Now she's someone again: the Washington hostess with the mostest. Big parties. Entertaining the President. It doesn't cost Burroughs that much. I know how D.C. works; she'd have no trouble getting lobbyists and PR men to pick up the tab if she could collect the right guests and maybe provide some push-push on a crucial vote. Then Burroughs conks, and she's lost her power base. Washington is full of Congressional widows. So she moves to New York and gets in with the art and museum crowd. Keeps up her old friendships with politicos. Helps them out with high-class girls and maybe some dust when needed. Lends her apartment for their fun and games. Takes gifts for these services, money gifts, and gets high-level protection in return. More important to her—she's on all the society pages: party-thrower, woman-about-town, model for famous artists and fashion photographers; she's still *someone.*"

"But *why?*" Boone wanted to know.

"If not fame, then notoriety," Delaney said somberly, almost speaking to himself. "As long as the world knows Belle Sarazen exists. Those scrapbooks are the tip-off. She's got to reassure herself about who she is. Some people are like that. They have such a low opinion of themselves that to endure, they've got to create another image in other people's eyes. She's a mirror woman. Now she can look in the mirror and see a sexy beauty with a face that looks like it hasn't been lived in, and a body that doesn't stop. The scrapbooks tell her who she is. But if it wasn't for the publicity, if it wasn't for the world's reaction to her, she'd look in the mirror and there would be nothing there. That's why she'll do almost anything for those important friends. She's got to hang onto the movers and shakers. To prove *she's* important, too. The poor doxy."

"Chief, you really think she knew it was Canfield when she blasted?"

"Of course. She gave herself away when she said the Durkee case was her favorite. We broke that one by working on a jealous wife, a woman who thought she had been scorned. Belle could identify with that; she had been a scorned woman herself."

"But could she have chopped Maitland?"

"I think so—if he was threatening her self-esteem, her vision of herself. And obviously she has the strength."

"Or for kicks," Boone said wonderingly. "Maybe she did it just for kicks."

"She's capable of that, too," Delaney said stonily. "She got away with it once. After they've done that, they think they can keep kicking God's shins."

"Listen, Chief," the sergeant said hesitantly. "Sounds to me that with the girls and the important friends, she's in a good position for some polite blackmail."

Delaney shook his head.

"Not our Belle," he said. "I told you she's not money hungry. All she wants is to call Senators by their first names."

They had time before their meeting with Jake Dukker, and they talked about lunch.

"Something quick," Delaney said. "And light. You have your big meal at night, don't you?"

"Usually," Boone said. "The doc's got me on a high-protein diet. Mostly I cook at home. Easy stuff like steaks, fish, hamburgers, and so forth."

"How are you doing?" Delaney asked, staring straight ahead.

"On the drinking?" Boone said calmly. "All right, so far. There isn't a minute I don't want it, but I've been able to lay off. Keeping busy on this Maitland thing helps."

"Does it bother you when you're with someone, and the other man orders a drink? Like yesterday, when I had an ale at lunch, and you had iced tea?"

"No, that doesn't bother me," the sergeant said. "What bothers me is when people joke about it. You know, friends and comics on TV who make jokes about how much they drink, and funny stories about drunks, and all. I don't think it's funny anymore. For awhile there I was working at getting through the next hour without a drink. Now I work at getting through a whole day without a drink, so I guess that's an improvement."

Delaney nodded. "I know it sounds stupid to say it, but you've got to do it yourself. No one can do it for you, or even help."

"Oh, I don't know, Chief," Abner Boone said slowly. "You've helped."

"I have?" Delaney said, pleased. "Glad to hear it."

He didn't ask how.

The sun was at full blast now, the sky rapidly clearing, a nice breeze coming from the west. They decided to park somewhere near Columbus Circle, buy hotdogs from a street vendor, and maybe some cold soda, and have their lunch on a bench in Central Park. Then they could walk over to Jake Dukker's studio.

They pulled into a No Parking zone near the Circle, and Boone put the OFFICER ON DUTY card behind the windshield, hoping for the best. They found a vendor near the Maine Monument, and each bought two hotdogs, with sauerkraut, pickles, relish, mustard, and onions, and a can of wild-cherry soda. Delaney insisted on paying. They carried their lunch, bundled in paper napkins, into the park and finally discovered an empty bench stuck off on a small hillock covered with scrawny grass.

They ate leaning forward, knees spread, to avoid the drippings. The opened cans of soda were set on the bald ground.

"The way I see it," Sergeant Boone said, mouth full, "Sarazen and Dukker have got a mutual alibi for ninety minutes. We got statements from Dukker's assistants and from the models placing Sarazen and Dukker in the downstairs studio before twelve and after one-thirty. But for ninety minutes the two of them were upstairs, alone together. They say."

"You think one is covering for the other?"

"Or they were both in on it together. Look, Chief, those times are approximate. You know how unreliable witnesses are when it comes to exact time. Maybe they were out of the studio for more than ninety minutes. Maybe as much as two hours."

"Keep talking. It listens."

"They probably didn't take a cab. We checked thousands of trip sheets and followed up on every drop in the vicinity of the Mott Street studio between ten and three that Friday. But suppose they had a private car waiting. I think one of them, or both, could get down to Mott Street from Dukker's place and back in ninety minutes, or maybe a little more."

"That's assuming they didn't have to go through the downstairs studio to get out. Is there a door to the outside from the upstairs floor? The apartment?"

"That I don't know, sir. Something we'll have to check. Assuming there is, they leave the studio at twelve, go upstairs, pop out the door, go downstairs and head for their car. Or even—how's this?—they drive over to Lex and Fifty-ninth, by private car or cab, and take the downtown IRT subway. There's a local stop on Spring Street, less than two blocks from Maitland's studio. By taking the subway, they eliminate the risk of getting stuck in traffic. And I think they could make the round trip in ninety minutes to two hours, allowing five or ten minutes for killing Maitland."

"I don't know," Delaney said doubtfully. "It's cutting it thin."

"Want me to time it, sir?" Boone asked, getting a little excited about his idea. "I'll drive from Dukker's place to Maitland's studio and back, and then I'll try the same trip by subway. And time both trips."

"Good idea," Delaney nodded. "Make both between ten and three on a Friday, when the traffic and subway schedule will be approximately the same as they were then."

"Will do," Boone said happily.

They were silent awhile, working on their dripping hotdogs. When they used up the paper napkins, both used their handkerchiefs to wipe their smeared faces and fingers.

"Well, let's go brace Jack Dukker," Delaney said. "We can walk over . . ."

The building, tall, narrow, sooty, was one of the oldest on Central Park South. It had been designed for artists' studios, for painters, sculptors, musicians, singers. Ceilings were high, rooms spacious, walls thick. Floor-to-ceiling windows provided a steady north light and afforded a fine view of Central Park, an English farm set down in the middle of the steel and concrete city.

Jake Dukker occupied a duplex on the fourth and fifth floors. The lower level had been converted to a reception area, working studio, models' dressing room, a photographic darkroom, prop room and storage area, a lavatory, and a tiny kitchenette with refrigerator, sink, stove and a small machine that did nothing but produce ice cubes, chuckling at intervals as cubes spilled into a storage tray.

The studio was all efficiency: rolls of seamless paper and canvas, a battery of flood and spotlights with high-voltage cables, a stage, posing dais, overhead illumination of a theatrical design, mirrors, sets, stainless-steel and white-cloth reflectors, easels, a working table littered with paints, palettes, mixing pots . . . The walls were covered with framed paintings, prints, etchings, lithographs, drawings. Most of them signed.

The fifth floor, reached by an interior spiral staircase, provided living quarters for the artist: one enormous chamber with enough sofas, chairs, and floor pillows to accommodate an interdenominational orgy. Two bedrooms, two bathrooms, a spacious, well-equipped kitchen—copper-bottomed pans and pots hanging from the walls, a gargantuan spice rack—and a dining area with a glass-topped table long enough to seat twelve.

The living quarters were jangling with color, a surprisingly comfortable and attractive mix of the owner's short-lived enthusiasms: Bauhaus, Swedish Modern, Art Deco, New York Victorian, Art Nouveau, and such soupy examples of modern furnishings as iron tractor seats on pedestals and rough wooden cocktail tables that were originally the reels for telephone cable.

The owner of this hodgepodge was also a jumble of trendy fashions. He wore faded blue jeans cinched with a wide leather belt and tarnished brass buckle inscribed with the Wells Fargo insignia. Negating these symbols of rugged masculinity were the soft, black ballet slippers he wore on his long, slender feet. His overblouse was Indian tissue cotton, cut to the pipik, embroidered across the shoulders with garlands of roses, and boasting loose sleeves full enough to inspire a gypsy to make his violin cry. In the cleavage of this transparent shirt, a sunburst medallion swung from a clunky gold chain.

The man himself was tall and lanky, his slender grace somewhat marred by a well-fed paunch, half a bowling ball that strained the leather belt and threatened to eclipse Wells Fargo. He didn't move so much as strike a quick succession of poses, feet turned so, arms akimbo, head tilted, shoulder thrust, knee bent artfully. He was a stop-motion film, click, click, click, each shutter advance showing a different arrangement of features and limbs. But there was no flow.

The nubile receptionist told the officers to go into the studio. As Jake Dukker came forward to meet them, two cameras hanging from leather thongs about his neck, the first things Chief Delaney saw were the Stalin mustache, a bushy, bristly growth, and the glowering eyes, swimming and seemingly unfocussed. The nose was a sharp beak, the teeth as square and chiseled as small tombstones, faintly stained. The caved cheeks were pitted and shadowed; he had not shaved well. Black hair, cut in Mod style, full, brushed, and sprayed, covered his ears. Like Saul Geltman, he wore a gold bracelet. Unlike Geltman, there was nothing spruce, neat, or particularly clean about his person. But that, Delaney charitably decided, might have been due to the hot studio lights.

After the introductions, Dukker said, "Just finishing up. A few more shots. Take a look around. Don't trip on the cables."

At the center of the raised stage, posed against a roll of seamless purple paper, a young model with a teenager's body stood with her back to the lights and reflectors manned by Dukker's two assistants. She wore the bottom half of a bright red bikini; her upper back was bare. Atop her head was an enormously wide-brimmed white straw hat with a violet ribbon band. She assumed a hip-sprung pose, both arms to one side, hands perched on the handle of a closed pink parasol.

Jake Dukker lifted one of his cameras, a Nikon, and moved into position, crouching . . .

"More ass, honey," he called. "Magnificent. Lean onto the umbrella. Sensational. Profile to me. That's it. Sexy smile. Wonderful. Weight on that leg. More ass. Beautiful. Here we go . . ."

The girl held her pose, and Dukker was up, down, leaning, stretching, moving forward, moving back, clicking, winding. He switched quickly from one camera to another, adjusted his setting, continued his gymnastics with hardly a pause, snap, snap, snap, until finally he straightened up, arched his shoulders back, lifted his chin high to stretch his neck.

"That's it," he called to his assistants. "Kill it."

All the burning lights went off. One of the assistants came forward to take the cameras from Dukker. The model relaxed, took off her hat, shook her blonde hair free. She turned to face forward, showing little breasts with surprisingly large brown aureoles.

"Okay, Jake?" she asked.

"Incredible, honey," he said. "Sexy but pure. Gretchen will have your check."

"Anything coming up?" she asked.

"Me," he said, showing his teeth. "Cover up; it's the cops. Don't call us, sweetie, we'll call you. And stop eating. Five more pounds and you're dead."

He turned to Delaney and Boone, his pitted face glistening with sweat.

"A paperback cover," he explained. "No tits, but it's okay to titillate."

He grabbed up a soiled towel and wiped his face and hands.

"The place is air conditioned," he said, "but you'd never know it when the lights are on."

"You work hard, Mr. Dukker," Delaney said.

"The name of the game," Dukker said. "I do everything; fashion, book covers, record slips, paintings, magazine illustrations, posters, ads. You name it; I do it. A guy called me this morning and wants me to do a pack of playing cards. Can you believe it?"

"Pornographic?" Chief Delaney asked.

Dukker was startled.

"Close," he said, trying to smile. "Mighty close. I turned him down. Want to look around? Before we go upstairs?"

"Just for a minute," Delaney said, moving to inspect the framed art on the walls. "You have some beautiful things here. You know all these artists?"

"All of them," Dukker said. "Lousy friends and rotten enemies. Take a look at that one. The drawing over by the window, the one in the thin gold frame. That should interest you."

Obediently, Delaney and Boone found the sketch and stood before it. It had been torn twice, the four pieces patched with transparent tape and pressed behind glass. In the corner, a scrawled but legible signature: Victor Maitland.

"An original Maitland," Delaney said.

It was a hard, quick sketch of a running woman. In profile. Bulge of naked breast and ass caught in one fast S-stroke, a single charcoal line. A suggestion of high-stepping knees, hair flaming, the whole bursting with life, motion, young charm, vigor, a bright gaiety.

"No, sir," Jake Dukker said. They turned to look at him. "A *signed* Maitland. An original Dukker!" Then when he saw their expressions, he showed his teeth again, a pirate. "Come over here," he commanded. "I'll explain."

They followed him to a corner of the studio, a three-sided closure lined with pegboard. Pinned to the walls were photographic prints and contact sheets, sketches, clippings from newspapers and magazines, sheets of type fonts, illustrations of photo distortions, and color samples of paper and fabric. The small room was dominated by a tilt-top drawing table with a long T-square, jars of pens, pencils, chalks, pastels, plastic triangles and French curves, liquid-cement pot, a battered watercolor tin, and overflowing ashtrays everywhere.

Behind the drawing table, facing a window, was a sturdy workbench. Clamped to the bench was a curious device, a prism at the end of a jointed chrome arm. It was positioned between a vertical and a horizontal drawing board.

"See that?" Dukker said. "It's called a camera lucida. Commonly known as a 'luci.' A kind of visual pantograph. Suppose you want to do a drawing of a nude. So you photograph a nude, the body and pose you want. Make an eight-by-ten print. Pin the print on the vertical board. Put your drawing paper flat on the horizontal board. Then you look through that prism at the end of the jointed arm. You see the photo image and at the same time you see the flat drawing paper. You can trace the photo with pen, pencil, chalk, charcoal, pastel stick, whatever. Absolute, realistic likeness."

They looked at him, and he laughed.

"Don't knock it," he said. "Takes too much time and work to do it the old-fashioned way, with sittings and all. Even if the artist or illustrator had the talent to do it. And most of them don't. Anyway, one night I was tracing a photo of a family group on my luci when Maitland shows up drunk as a skunk. He starts giving me a hard time about what a mechanic I am. I'm not an artist. I can't draw my way out of a wet paper bag. I'm a disgrace. And so forth and so on. Really laying it on me."

Dukker stopped suddenly, staring at the empty drawing board. His eyes squinched up, as if he was staring at something pinned there. Then he sighed and continued . . .

"Finally I got fed up, and I said, 'You son of a bitch, I've had all the horseshit I'm going to take from you. I'm twice the draftsman you'll ever be, and to prove it, I'm going to do an original Victor Maitland that any art expert in the world will swear is genuine.' He laughed, but I grabbed a pad, a charcoal stick, and I knocked out that sketch you see there, the nude running. Victor was a fast worker, but I'm faster. I'm the best. It took me less than three minutes. Then I showed it to him. He looked at it, and I thought he was going to kill me. I really was scared. His face got pale as hell, and his hands started shaking. I really thought he was going to get physical; it never did take much to set him off. I started looking around for something to hit him with. I'd never go up against that crazy bastard with my bare fists; he'd cream me."

Dukker paused to scratch at the tight denim across his crotch, looking up thoughtfully at the ceiling.

"Then he tore my drawing in four pieces and threw them at me. Then I put some more booze into him, and later that night we patched my drawing together with tape, and he signed it. Then he thought it was a big joke. It really is my drawing, but he admitted he wasn't ashamed to put his name to it. Shit, it's better than a lot of things he did. And I didn't trace a photograph either. I just knocked it off. He wasn't so great. I could have been . . . Everyone thinks . . . Well, let's go upstairs and relax. I got another shooting in an hour or so. Got to keep going. Can't stop."

Before he led them up the spiral staircase, he grabbed up a maroon beret from the littered work table and jammed it rakishly over one eye. They watched him put it on, but said nothing. They were cops; human nuttiness didn't faze them.

Upstairs, he asked if they'd like a drink. When they declined, he insisted on making a fresh pot of coffee for them. He made it in an unusual glass container with a plunger arrangement that shoved a strainer of ground coffee down through hot water.

"You'll love this," he assured them. "Better than drip. And the coffee is my own blend of mocha, Java, and Colombian that I buy in the bean at this marvelous little place on the Lower East Side. I grind it fresh every morning. Full-bodied, with a subtle bouquet."

Chief Delaney thought it was possibly the worst cup of coffee he had ever drunk. And he could tell from Boone's expression that his opinion was shared. But they sipped politely.

They were seated somewhat nervously on a short crimson velvet couch shaped like human lips. Jake Dukker slouched opposite them in a soft leather chair shaped like a baseball mitt.

"So . . ." he said. "What can I do for you?"

They took out their notebooks. Chief Delaney reviewed the record of the artist's activities on the Friday that Victor Maitland had been killed. Dukker's receptionist and assistants had come to work around 9:00 A.M. They had set up for the fashion assignment. The models appeared around 10:00, and shooting commenced about thirty minutes later. Belle Sarazen showed up around 11:30. At noon, she and Jake Dukker had come upstairs for lunch.

"A divine omelet," Dukker interjected.

They had gone back downstairs around 1:30, and Belle Sarazen left the studio about an hour later, maybe a little less. Shooting was completed slightly before 3:00 P.M., and the models departed. Dukker remained in his apartment until seven that evening, when he went to a dinner party with friends in Riverdale, driving up.

"Your own car?" Delaney asked.

Dukker nodded. "A waste of money really. I usually take cabs. Trying to park in midtown Manhattan is murder. Most of the time I keep it garaged. On West Fifty-eighth Street. Want the name and address of the garage?"

"No, thank you, Mr. Dukker," Delaney said. "We have that information. What about Belle Sarazen?"

"What about her?"

"Were you intimate with her?"

Dukker took a long swallow of his coffee and grimaced.

"Oh God, yes," he said. "Like half of New York. Belle distributes her favors regardless of race, creed, color, or national origin."

"She says you hated Victor Maitland," Delaney said tonelessly.

Dukker jerked erect, some of his drink slopping over onto his jeans.

"She said *that?*" he said. "I don't believe it."

"Oh yes," Delaney nodded. He looked down at his notebook. "Said you hated him because you envied Maitland's integrity. Her word—'integrity'—not mine."

"The bitch," Dukker said, relaxing back into the baseball mitt. "Envied maybe. Yes, I suppose I did. Hated? I don't think so. Certainly not enough to kill him. I cried when I heard he was dead. I didn't want him dead. You can believe that or not, but I really took it hard."

"Well, that's something different," Delaney said. "You're the first person we've talked to who was close to Maitland who's expressed any kind of sorrow. Except possibly his agent, Saul Geltman."

"His *agent?*" Dukker said. Unexpectedly he laughed. "Is that what you call him?"

"He was Maitland's agent, wasn't he?"

"Well . . . yes, I suppose so," Dukker said, still smiling. "But they don't like to be called 'agents.' 'Art dealer' is the term they prefer."

"We had a long discussion with Geltman about art agents," Delaney said stubbornly. "How much they make, their duties and responsibilities, and so forth. Never once did Geltman object to being called Maitland's agent."

"Maybe he didn't want to rub you the wrong way," Dukker shrugged. "But I assure you that art *dealer* is what they want to be called. Like a garbageman likes the title of sanitation engineer."

"Do you have an agent, Mr. Dukker?" Sergeant Boone asked. "Or an art dealer?"

"Hell, no," Dukker said promptly. "What for? I sell directly. People come to me; I don't have to look for customers. Why should I pay thirty percent of my gross to some leech who can't do anything for me I can't do myself? Listen, my stuff sells itself. I'm the best."

"So you told us," Delaney murmured. "To get back to Belle Sarazen, can you tell us anything about her relationship with Victor Maitland?"

"Hated him," Dukker said immediately. He put his drink aside, half-finished. He slumped lower in his leather baseball mitt, laced his fingers across his pot belly. "Hated his guts. Vic hated phonies, you see. Hated sham and hypocrisy in any way, shape or form. And Belle is the biggest phony going."

"Is she?" Delaney said.

"You bet your sweet ass," Dukker said enthusiastically, rubbing his bristly jaw. "Listen, Vic Maitland was a rough guy. I mean, if he thought you were talking shit, he'd tell you so. Right out. No matter who was listening. I remember once Belle had a big party at her place. A lot of important people. Maitland showed up late. Maybe he hadn't been invited. Probably not. But he'd hear about parties and come anyway. He didn't care. He knew they really didn't want him there because he got into trouble all the time. I told you, he'd get physical. He'd deck art critics and throw things. Food. Drinks at people he didn't like. Stuff like that. Anyway, Belle was having this fancy party, and Vic showed up. Drunk, as usual. But keeping his mouth shut. Just glaring at all the beautiful people. Then Belle started talking about what a big shot she had been in Washington. You know, entertaining the President and dancing with ambassadors and playing tennis with Senators and teaching yoga to Congressmen's wives. All that crap. Everyone was listening to Belle brag, not wanting to interrupt. After all, she swings a lot of clout. Then Maitland broke in. In a loud voice. Everyone heard him. He called Belle the World's Greatest Blower. He said she had blown off her husband's head, had blown a fortune in Europe, and had ended up blowing the Supreme Court."

Delaney and Boone smiled down at their notebooks.

"He broke up the place," Dukker grinned, remembering. "We couldn't stop laughing. He was such a foulmouthed bastard, really dirty, but at the same time he was funny. Outrageous. Sometimes."

"How did Belle Sarazen take this?" Delaney asked.

"Tried to laugh it off," Dukker shrugged. "What else could she do? But she was burning, I could see. Hated him right then. Could have killed him. I knew she'd never forget it."

"Why did Maitland do it? Say those things?"

"Why? I told you why. Because he couldn't stand phonies. Couldn't stand sham and hypocrisy."

"Well . . ." Delaney sighed, "sometimes people use complete honesty as an excuse for sadism."

Jake Dukker looked at him curiously.

"Right on, Chief," he said. "There was that, too. In Maitland's personality. He liked to hurt people. No doubt about it. He called it puncturing their ego balloons, but there was more to it than that. At least I think there was. He could get vicious. Wouldn't leave anyone a shred of illusion or self-esteem. Like he did to Belle that night. You can hate someone like that, someone who strips all your pretense away and leaves you naked."

The two officers were busy scribbling in their notebooks.

"You said the Sarazen woman swings a lot of clout," Delaney said, not looking up. "What did you mean by that?"

"Well . . . you know," Dukker said. "Political influence. She really does know some important people. Knows where the bodies are buried. Also, she's a powerhouse in the New York art world. She can promote a gallery show for some shlocky little cartoonist. Or get her rich friends to buy some guy's stuff. Great on publicity and promotion. Throws parties. Knows everyone. She can be valuable to artists. To dealers. To collectors."

"You think she knows what's good?" Delaney asked. "I mean, does she have good taste in art?"

Jake Dukker burst out laughing.

"Good taste?" he spluttered. "Belle Sarazen? Come on! She'll find some kid in the Village with a long schlong, and she'll bring his stuff to me and say, 'Isn't he fan-tas-tic? Isn't he great?' And I'll say, 'Belle, the kid just hasn't got it. He's from stinksville.' A month later the kid will have a show in a Madison Avenue gallery, and a month after *that* he'll be dead, gone, and no one will ever hear of him again. Which is all to the good because he didn't have anything in the first place. All Belle's doings. She picked the guy up, gave him a gallery show, and dropped him just as quick. After showing him a few positions even the Kama Sutra doesn't include. Then she's on to someone else, and the original guy is back in the Village, eating Twinkies, and wondering what the hell hit him. Art is just one big game to Belle."

"But you like her?" Delaney asked, staring at Dukker without expression. "You like Belle Sarazen?"

"Belle?" Dukker repeated. "Like her? Well . . . maybe I do. Like goes to like.

We're both a couple of phonies. I could have been . . . well, what the hell's the use of talking about it. Belle and me, we know who we are, and what we are."

"But Victor Maitland wasn't a phony?" Abner Boone said softly.

"No," Dukker said defiantly. "He was a lot of rotten things, but he wasn't a phony. The miserable shit. He wasn't too happy, you know. He was driven, too. He was as greedy as all of us. But for different things."

"What things?" Delaney asked.

"Oh . . . I don't know," Dukker said vaguely. "He was a hell of a painter. Not as good as me. Technically, I mean. But he had something I never had. Or maybe I had it and lost it. I'll never know. But he was never as good as he wanted to be. Maybe that's why he worked so hard, so fast. Like someone was driving him."

There was silence a few moments while Delaney and Boone flipped through their notebooks. From downstairs they heard voices and the clatter of props and equipment as Dukker's assistants set up for the next shooting.

"Mr. Dukker," Delaney said, "did you ever provide or suggest models for Maitland?"

"Models? Once or twice. Mostly he found his own. Big, muscular women. Not the type I dig."

"Did you suggest anyone to him recently? A very young girl? Puerto Rican or Latin-type?"

Dukker thought a moment.

"No," he shook his head. "No one like that. No one at all in the last six months or so. Maybe a year. Why?"

Chief Delaney told him of the sketches found in Maitland's studio. Dukker was interested.

"Bring them around," he suggested. "I'd like to see them. Maybe I can identify the girl. I use a lot of models. For photography and illustration. Painting, too, of course. Though I'm doing less and less of that. The big money's in advertising photography. And I'm beginning to get into film. Commercials. Lots of dinero there."

He lurched suddenly to his feet, the maroon beret jerking to the back of his head.

"Got to get downstairs," he said briskly. "Okay?"

The two cops looked at each other. Delaney nodded slightly. They snapped notebooks shut, stood up.

"Thank you for being so cooperative, Mr. Dukker," Delaney said. "We appreciate that."

"Any time at all," the artist said, waving, expansive. "You know, you've got an interesting face, Chief. Very heavy. I'd like to sketch it some time. Maybe I will—when you come back with those Maitland drawings."

Delaney nodded again, not smiling.

"Can we leave from up here?" Sergeant Boone asked casually. "Or do we have to go downstairs to get out?"

"Oh no," Dukker said, "you can leave from here. That door over there. Leads to the fifth-floor landing and elevator."

"Just one more thing," Chief Delaney said. "Belle Sarazen told us you were doing a painting of her. A nude on aluminum foil."

"Belle talks too much," Dukker said crossly. "It'll get around and everyone will be doing it before I'm finished."

"Could we see it?" Delaney asked. "We won't mention it to anyone."

"Sure. I guess so. Why not? Come on—it's downstairs."

They were waiting for Dukker in the studio—the receptionist with a sheaf of messages, the assistants behind their lights, a model perched on a high stool. She was wearing a sleazy flowered kimono, chewing gum, and flipping the pages of *Harper's Bazaar*. Behind her, on the stage, the assistants had put together a boudoir scene: a brocaded chaise longue, a tall pier glass on a swivel mount, a dresser covered with cosmetics, a brass bedstead with black satin sheets.

"Hi, Jake, honey," she called as Dukker came down the stairs. "Were you serious? Is this really for a deck of playing cards?"

Dukker didn't answer. The officers couldn't see his face. He led them to a stack of paintings leaning against a wall. He flipped through for the one he wanted, slid it out, set it on a nearby easel. They moved close to inspect it.

He had glued aluminum foil to a Masonite panel, and prepared the surface to take tempera. The background was ebony black, which lightened to a deep, deep Chinese red in the center, a red as glossy as old lacquer ware. Belle Sarazen was posed in the center portion, on hands and knees, on what appeared, dimly, to be a draped bench.

She had, Delaney thought, almost the position of a hound on point: back arched and rigid, head up and alert, arms stiff, thighs straining forward. The artist had not used skin tones, but had allowed the aluminum foil, unpainted, to delineate the flesh. Modeling and shadows of the body were suggested with quick slashes of violet, the sharp features of the face implied rather than detailed.

The painting was a startling tour de force. There was no questioning the artist's skill or the effectiveness of his novel technique. But there was something disquieting in the painting, something chill and spiritless. The woman's hard-muscled body hinted of corruption.

That effect, Delaney decided, was deliberately the artist's, achieved by tightly crumpling the foil. Dukker had then smoothed it out before gluing it to the board. But the skin, the unpainted foil, still bore a fine network of tiny wrinkles, hundreds of them, that gave the appearance of crackle, as if the flesh had been bruised by age, punished by use, damaged by too-frequent handling. He could not understand why Belle Sarazen was so proud of a portrait that seemed to show her a moment before she fell apart, splintered into a dusty pile of sharp-edged fragments.

"Very nice," he told Dukker. "Very nice indeed."

He and Boone walked slowly back to their parked car. They stared at the sidewalk, brooding . . .

"The garage checked, Chief?" Boone asked.

"Yes," Delaney said. "The only record they had was when he took his car out at seven that evening. But check them again."

"Will do," the sergeant said. "You know, these people worry me."

"Worry you?"

"Yes, sir," Boone said, frowning. "I'm not used to the type. Most of the stuff I caught up to now involved characters with sheets. Addicts. Double offenders. Professionals. You know? I haven't had an experience dealing with people like this. I mean, they *think*."

"They also sleep," Delaney said stonily. "And they eat, they crap, and one of them killed. What I'm trying to say is that one of them is guilty of a very primitive act, as stupid and unthinking as a muscle job by some punk with a skinful of shit. Don't let the brains worry you. We'll get him. Or her."

"You think the killer fucked-up somewhere along the line?"

"I doubt it," Delaney said. "I'm just hoping for chance. An accident. Something they couldn't possibly foresee and plan for. I know a guy named Evelyn Forrest. He's the Chief in Chilton, New York, a turnaround in the road up near the Military Academy at West Point. Forrest is Chilton's one-man police department. Or was. An old cop gone to beer. I hope he's still alive.

"Anyway, this Forrest told me about a cute one he caught. This retired professor, his second wife, and his stepdaughter bought an old farmhouse with some land near Chilton. The professor is writing a biography of Thoreau, but he's got time to make it with the stepdaughter. So he decides to snuff the wife and make it look like an accident. He's got a perfect situation: On their land they've got this small apple orchard, and the local kids and drifters are always sneaking in to swipe apples. Lots of apples. Not off the ground; right off the trees. So this professor buys a twenty-gauge with birdshot, and every time they see or hear someone swiping their apples, they run out yelling and spray the orchard with their shotgun. Far enough away so no one gets hurt. Just to scare the kids.

"So the professor with the hots for the stepdaughter, he sets up the murder of his wife very carefully. Everything planned. A half-buried rock under one of the apple trees, a rock that anyone could trip over. Takes his wife out there for a stroll late one afternoon. Blows her away when she's at the rock. He's wearing gloves. Puts the shotgun in her hands for prints. Runs back to the house. Hides the gloves. Screams on the phone for help. His wife tripped, the shotgun hit the ground and blew, she's got no chest, and what a horrible, horrible accident it is. This Chief Forrest went out to look around. He thought it smelled, but there was no way he could shake the professor's story. Until a local farmer brought his scared kid around to Forrest to tell his version. The kid had seen the whole thing. He was up in that tree swiping apples. So much for careful planning . . ."

That evening, the girls staying the night with friends for something called a Pillow Party, Monica and Edward X. Delaney had a lonely kitchen dinner. She tried for awhile; then, knowing his moods, she gave up trying to make conversation and said nothing when he excused himself to go into the study and close the door.

He felt his age: lumpy and ponderous. And somewhat awkward. His clothes were damp and heavy on his skin. His joints creaked. He seemed to be pressing down into his swivel chair, all of him dull and without lift. He had a sudden vision of a young girl leaning on a pink parasol. The tanned skin of her naked back. He shook his massive head, and doggedly began writing out detailed reports of the interviews with Belle Sarazen and Jake Dukker.

When they were finished, and filed away, he took the three drawings found in Victor Maitland's studio and fixed them to his wall map of the 251st Precinct, mounted on corkboard. He used pushpins to attach them over the map, then tilted his desk lamp so they were illuminated. He sat behind his desk and stared at the sketches.

Youth. Vigor. All juice, all bursting. Caught in the hard, quick lines of a frantic artist who wanted it all. Wanted to own it all, and show it. Maitland was driven, Jake Dukker had said. Delaney could believe that. In all these interviews, from all this talk, these words, he was beginning to see most clearly the man who was dead. The painter, the artist, Victor Maitland. That gifted hand moldering now, but not so long ago eager and grasping. A filthy human being he might have been. Malicious, besotted, maybe sadistic. But there was no law that said only saints could be talented.

The trouble was, Delaney brooded, the trouble was that he was beginning to feel sympathy. Not only for the victim—that was natural enough—but for all the others involved in the murder. One of whom, he was convinced, had plunged the blade. The trouble was that he liked them—liked Mrs. Maitland, Saul Geltman, Belle Sarazen, Jake Dukker. And, he suspected, when he met Maitland's son, and his mother and sister, he'd like them, too. Feel compassion.

"They *think,*" Sergeant Boone had said. But it was more than that. They were spunky, bright, *wanting* human beings, touching in their hungers and illusions. There was not one he could hate. Not one he could hope would prove to be a killer and deserving of being boxed and nailed.

His sympathy disturbed him. A cop was not paid to be compassionate. A cop had to see things in black and white. *Had* to. Explanations and justification were the work of doctors, psychiatrists, sociologists, judges, and juries. They were paid to see the shades of grey, to understand and dole out ruth.

But a cop had to go by Yes or No. Because . . . well, because there had to be a rock standard, an iron law. A cop went by that and couldn't allow himself to murmur comfort, pat shoulders, and shake tears from his eyes. This was important, because all those other people—the ruth-givers—they modified the standard, smoothed the rock, melted the law. But if there was no standard at all, if cops surrendered their task, there would be nothing but modifying, smoothing, melting. All sweet reasonableness. Then society would dissolve into a kind of warm mush: no rock, no iron, and who could live in a world like that? Anarchy. Jungle.

He drew his yellow legal pad to him, put on his heavy reading glasses, began making notes. Things he must do to find the murderer of Victor Maitland.

It was getting on to midnight when the desk phone rang. The Chief picked it up with his left hand, still scribbling at his notes.

"Edward X. Delaney here," he said.

"Edward, this is Ivar . . ."

Deputy Commissioner Thorsen chatted a few moments, asking after the health of Monica and the girls. Then he inquired casually, "How's Boone making out?"

"All right," Delaney said. "I like him."

"Glad to hear it. Off the booze, is he?"

"As far as I know. He's completely sober when I see him."

"Any signs of hangovers?"

"No. None." Delaney didn't appreciate this role; he wasn't Boone's keeper, and didn't relish reporting on the man's conduct.

"Any progress, Edward?"

"On the case? Nothing definite. I'm just learning what went on, and the people involved. It takes time."

"I'm not leaning on you, Edward," Thorsen said hastily. "Take all the time you want. No rush."

There was a moment of silence then. Delaney knew what would come next, but refused to give the man any help.

"Ah . . . Edward," Thorsen said hesitantly, "you questioned the Sarazen woman today?"

"Yes."

"She a suspect?"

"They're all suspects," Delaney said coldly.

"Well, ah, we have a delicate situation there, Edward."

"Do we?"

"The lady has some important friends. And apparently she feels you were a little rough on her."

Delaney didn't reply.

"Were you rough on her, Edward?"

"She probably thought so."

"Yes, she did. And called a few people to complain. She said . . ." Thorsen's voice trailed away.

"You want me off the case?" Delaney said stonily.

"Oh God, no," Thorsen said quickly. "Nothing like that. I just wanted you to be aware of the situation."

"I'm aware of it."

"And you'll treat her—"

"I'll treat her like everyone else," Delaney interrupted.

"My God, Edward, you're a hard man. I can't budge you. Listen, if that lady is guilty, I'll be delighted to see her hung by the heels and skinned alive. I'm not asking you to cover up. I'm just asking that you use a little discretion."

"I'll do things my own way," Delaney said woodenly. "This is the kind of bullshit that made me retire. I don't have to take it now."

"I know, Edward," Thorsen sighed. "I know. All right . . . do it your own way. I'll handle the flak. Somehow. Anything you need? Cooperation from the Department? Files or background stuff? Maybe another man or two?"

"Not at the moment, Ivar," Delaney said, thawing now, grateful. "But thanks for the offer."

"Well . . . keep at it. Give me a call if anything turns up, or if you need anything. Forget what I said—about handling the Sarazen woman with chopsticks."

"I already have," Delaney said.

"Iron Balls!" Thorsen laughed, and hung up.

Delaney sat a moment, staring at the dead phone in his hand. Then his eyes rose slowly. Almost against his will, his gaze sought those drawings pinned to the wall. The victim's final statement. His last words . . .

Delaney hung up and, on impulse, looked up the phone number of Victor Maitland's Mott Street studio. It was an unlisted number, but had been included in the police reports of the homicide.

Then he dialed the number. It rang and rang. He listened a long time. But of course there was no answer.

7

"Dinner will be at seven sharp," Monica Delaney said firmly. "I expect you and Sergeant Boone to be back by then."

"We're just going out of the county, not out of the country," Chief Delaney said mildly. "We'll be back long before seven. What are you having?"

"London broil and new potatoes."

"What kind of London broil?" he demanded.

"A nice piece of flank steak."

"Good. That's the best flavor. Want me to pick up anything on our way back?"

"No—well, we're low on beer. Or will you have wine?"

"Either. But I'll pick up some beer—just in case."

"He doesn't object if other people drink, does he?"

"I asked him, and he said he didn't."

"All right, dear. Have a good trip. And a *very* light lunch."

"I promise," he said. "I know a good inn near Dobbs Ferry. They serve excellent London broil and new potatoes."

She laughed and poured them their second cups of breakfast coffee.

Sergeant Abner Boone was waiting for him outside. All the car windows were rolled down; Boone was fanning himself with a folded newspaper.

"Going to be a hot one, sir," he said cheerfully. "Seventy-three already."

Delaney nodded, tossed his homburg onto the back seat. Both men took out their notebooks and went through the morning ritual of comparing notes.

"I checked Dukker's garage," Boone said. "No record of him taking his car out before the evening. So then, just for the hell of it, I talked to the doorman of Belle Sarazen's apartment house. She doesn't own a car—or if she does, she doesn't garage it there. I don't think she does; I ran a vehicle check, and she's got no license. The doorman said that sometimes she rents from a chauffeured-limousine service. He remembered the name, and I checked them out. No record of her hiring a car on that Friday. I suppose she could have used another service. Want me to run down the list, Chief?"

"No," Delaney said. "Hold off. It's a long shot."

"Well, they still might have used the subway," Boone said stubbornly. "I'll run a time trial tomorrow."

"You still think they're it?"

"A possible," Boone nodded. "Either one, or both together. Give them two hours, and they could have made it down to Mott Street and back."

"All right," Delaney said. "Keep hacking away at it until you're satisfied. I'm not saying you're wrong. Thorsen called last night. The Sarazen woman beefed to her important friends."

"Was Thorsen sore?"

"Not very. He'll schmaltz it over for us. He's good at that."

"One more thing," Boone said, consulting his notes. "I talked to a few more guys who worked the case. One of them had gone up to Nyack to check out the mother and sister. They said they were both home that Friday from ten to three. They couldn't prove it, and he couldn't disprove it. They've got a housekeeper, but it was her day off. No one saw them there; no one saw them leave."

"They own a car?"

"Yeah. A big, old Mercedes-Benz. Both mother and sister drive. But what this dick remembered, what wasn't in his report, was when he was leaving, the mother grabbed him by the arm and said something like, 'Find the killer of my son. It's very important to me.' This guy thought that was kind of funny. 'Very important to *me*,' she said. It stuck in his mind."

"Yes," Delaney nodded. "An odd way of putting it. Of course, she may have meant it to mean avenging the Maitland family name, or some such shit. Well, let's talk to the lady. How do you figure on going?"

"I thought we'd take the FDR, across the George Washington to Palisades Parkway, and then 9W into Nyack. Okay, sir?"

"Fine with me."

"I'm going to take off my jacket and get comfortable," the sergeant said. "You, Chief?"

"I'm comfortable," Delaney said.

When Boone removed his lightweight plaid sports jacket and leaned over to put it on the back seat, Delaney saw he was carrying a .38 Colt Detective Special in a black short-shank holster high on his hip. The two cops talked guns while Boone was maneuvering through city streets over to the FDR.

As they crossed the George Washington Bridge, traffic thinned, they could relax and enjoy the trip. It was warming up, but a cool river breeze was coming through the open windows and the air was mercifully free of pollution. They could see the new apartment houses on the Jersey side rising sharply into a clear, blue sky. There was some slow barge traffic on the river. A few jetliners droned overhead. Nice day . . .

"Chief, was your father a cop?" Abner Boone asked.

"No," Delaney said, "he was a saloon-keeper. Had a place on Third near Sixty-eighth, then opened another place on Eighty-fourth, also on Third. I used to work behind the stick in the afternoons when I was going to nightschool."

"My father was a cop," Boone said.

"I know," Delaney said. "I went to his funeral."

"You did?" Boone said. He seemed pleased. "I didn't know that."

"I was a sergeant then and brought over a squad from the Two-three."

"I was sure impressed," Boone said. "They even had cops from Boston and Philadelphia. The Mayor was there. He gave my mother a plaque."

"Yes," Delaney said. "Your mother living?"

"No, she's gone. I've got some cousins down in Tennessee, but I haven't seen them for years."

"You and your wife didn't have any children?"

"No," Boone said, "we didn't. I'm glad. Now."

They rode awhile in silence. Then Delaney said, "I want you to do something on this Maitland thing, but I don't want you to get sore."

"I won't get sore," Boone said. "What is it, Chief?"

"Well, first of all I want to question Maitland's son—what's his name? Theodore. They call him Ted. I want to question him myself. Alone."

"Well, sure, Chief," Boone said. He kept his eyes on the road. "That's okay."

But Delaney knew he was hurt.

"The way I figure is this," he explained. "From the files, and from what his mother said, I think the kid is a wise-guy. The kind of snotnose who calls cops 'pigs' or 'fuzz.' I figured if we both go up against him, he'll feel we're leaning on him. Pushing him around. But if I go up against him alone, all sweetness and light, playing the understanding older man, the father he never had, maybe he'll crack a little."

Boone glanced at him briefly, with wonderment.

"Makes sense," he said. "But I wouldn't have thought of it."

"In return," Delaney said, "I want you to brace that Susan Hemley alone. How did she sound on the phone? Young? Old?"

"Youngish," Boone said. "But very sure of herself. Deep voice. Good laugh."

"Well, here's what you do," Delaney said. "I'll meet the Maitland kid tomorrow. Alone. You do the time trials on the subway from Dukker's place to the Mott Street studio. Either before or after, go up to the office of Simon and Brewster and see this Susan Hemley. Your scam is that you dropped by to set up an appointment for you and me to talk to her boss, J. Julian Simon. Any day next week, morning or afternoon, at his convenience."

"I get it," Boone said, feeling better. "You want me to romance her—right?"

"If you can," Delaney nodded. "See what she's like. If she gives a little, ask her to have lunch. I think it's a one-on-one situation, and we'll get more if you go in alone. If you can make lunch, don't push it. You know—just idle talk. Did she know Maitland, and wasn't it awful what happened to him, and so forth. You know the drill. You can listen, can't you?"

"I'm a good listener," Boone said.

"Fine. That's all I want you to do. Don't drag anything out of her. Just make friends."

"What if she asks about the case?"

"Play it cozy. Tell her nothing, but make it sound like something. Tell her Maitland wasn't wearing any underwear. That'll make her think she's getting the inside poop that wasn't in the newspapers. Also, later we'll try to find out if she told Mrs. Maitland about the underwear. That'll be a tip-off on how intimate the two women are, just what that relationship is. But keep it hush-hush with the Hemley woman. Very confidential. You lean on her and say, 'I want you to promise not to breathe a word of this to anyone, but—' She'll get all excited, and maybe she'll start trading you secret for secret. Think you can handle it?"

Boone took a deep breath, blew it out heavily.

"Oh, I can handle it," he said. "But I'll tell you one thing, Chief: if I ever waste someone, I hope you don't catch the squeal."

They stopped in Nyack to ask directions, and shortly after noon they cruised slowly by the Maitland home and grounds, taking a good gander.

The grounds were an impressive size: a wide expanse of lawn leading up from the road, bordered by a thick stand of oaks, maples, a few firs. The driveway from the road was graveled, led under a side portico, and then to the wide doors of a smaller building that looked as if it had been built as a barn, then converted to a garage. An old black Mercedes-Benz was parked under the side portico.

The house itself was a rambling structure, two stories high, with a widow's walk facing the river. The building was sited atop a small hill with good drainage; trees at the rear had been cut away to provide a splendid river view.

The main entrance had four wooden pillars going up the entire height of the house to support a peaked portico. There were dormers, small minarets, plenty of gingerbread around porticos, windows, doors, and a screened-in porch overhanging a bank that sloped steeply to the river. At one side, close to the trees, was a gazebo that looked unused.

"I'd guess seventy-five years old," Delaney said. "Maybe a hundred. It looks like it started with that main house in the center, and the wings were added later. But the barn is original."

"She's supposed to have money," Boone said, "but it sure doesn't look like it. At least she's not spending much on upkeep."

The lawn badly needed mowing, the trees should have been trimmed, and the undergrowth cut away. Several windows of the gazebo were broken. The graveled driveway had bald patches. The flowerbeds close to the house grew in wild, untended profusion, choked with weeds. The house itself, and the barn, were peeling, a weather-beaten grey, almost silver in spots.

"Seedy," Delaney said. "The house looks sound, but it would take a crew a month to get this place in shape. But nothing could spoil that view. Well, let's go . . ."

They drove slowly up the driveway and parked in front of the three-step entrance. Sergeant Boone put on his jacket before they walked up to the front door. The paint was cracked, the brass knocker tarnished. Chief Delaney rapped sharply, twice.

The door was opened immediately. The tall woman who glowered at them was gaunt, almost emaciated. Rawboned and sunburned. A big-featured farm face. There were stained carpet slippers on her feet, the heelbacks bent under so the slippers were actually scuffs. The shiny black dress had soiled ruching at throat and cuffs. The woman was wearing a cameo brooch on her flat bosom and, unexpectedly, a man's gold digital wristwatch.

"Yes?" she said. Her voice was harsh, peremptory.

"Mrs. Maitland?" Chief Delaney asked.

"No," the woman said. "You the po-leece?"

"Yes, ma'am," Delaney said softly, trying to smile. "Mrs. Maitland is expecting us."

"This way," the woman commanded. "They on the poach."

Delaney couldn't place the accent. Possibly tidewater Virginia, he thought.

She held the door open just wide enough for Delaney and Boone to slip through, one at a time. They waited while she locked and bolted the door. Then they followed her as she flap-flapped across the uncarpeted parquet floor, down a long, narrow hallway to the river side of the house. The officers, looking around, caught a quick glance of dark, heavy furniture, dried flowers under glass bells, dusty velvet drapes, antimacassars, ragged footstools, gloomy walls of dull mahogany paneling and stained wallpaper. A fusty smell, with vagrant scents of cats, a heavy perfume, furniture polish.

The hallway debouched into a screened porch overlooking the river. Hinged windows had been opened inward and secured with cheap hooks and eyebolts. The porch, which had the appearance of having been added after the main house was built, was approximately twenty feet long and eight feet deep. It was furnished with a ratty collection of wicker furniture, once white, with faded chintz cushions. There was a frazzled rag rug on the planked floor. A small portable TV set was on one of the chairs, a fat, sleepy calico cat on another.

The two women on the porch had their armchairs drawn up near a sagging wicker table. On it was a black japanned tray with a pitcher of what appeared to be lemonade, surrounded by four tall, gracefully tapered glasses decorated with raised designs of enamel flowers, each glass different. Delaney guessed the lemonade set to be authentic Victoriana.

Neither woman rose to greet the visitors.

"Mrs. Maitland?" Delaney asked pleasantly.

"I," the older woman said, "am Dora Maitland."

She held out her hand in a kiss-my-ring gesture. Delaney came forward to clasp the firm hand briefly.

"Chief Edward X. Delaney, New York Police Department," he said. "A pleasure, ma'am."

"And *this,*" Mrs. Maitland said, a lepidopterologist pointing out a rare specimen, "is my daughter, Emily."

The younger woman held out her hand obediently. This time, Delaney found the hand plump, soft, moist.

"Miss Maitland," he said. "My pleasure. May I present my associate, Detective Sergeant Abner Boone."

Boone went through the hand-shaking ceremony, murmuring something unintelligible. Then the two officers stood awkwardly.

"Please to pull up chairs, gentlemen," Mrs. Maitland said sonorously. "I suggest those two chairs in the corner. I pray you, do not disturb the cat. I fear she is in heat and somewhat ill-tempered. I have had this pitcher of lemonade prepared. I imagine you are thirsty after your long drive."

"Very welcome, ma'am," Delaney said, as the two cops carried the unexpectedly heavy wicker chairs to the table. "A close day."

"Martha," Mrs. Maitland said imperiously, "will you serve, please."

"I got the sheets to do," the gaunt woman whined. She had been standing in the doorway; now she turned abruptly and flap-flapped away.

"So hard to get good help these days," Mrs. Maitland said imperturbably. He hadn't, Delaney reflected, heard that line in twenty years. "Emily," she commanded her daughter, "pour."

The younger woman heaved immediately to her feet.

"Yes, Mama," she said.

She was wearing a sleeveless caftan with a mandarin collar. But even this paisley-printed tent could not hide the obesity, the billows of breast and hip. Her bare arms belonged on a butcher's block, and three chin rolls bulged above the high collar. Even her fingers were fat; puffy toes swelled through strap sandals.

But she had the flawless skin of many fat women, and if her face at first glance seemed girlish and vacant, it was also pleasant and without malice. As she poured the lemonade, she spilled a few drops and said, "My land!" and colored with almost pretty confusion. Delaney guessed her age at about thirty-two, and wondered what her life might be like, with that balloon body, stuck out here ten miles from nowhere.

When she handed him his glass of lemonade, he looked closely at her brown eyes and saw, he fancied, a shrewd intelligence, which startled him. And for all her excessive weight her movements were sure and graceful. Almost dainty. Her voice too was light, younger than her years, with a warm, flirty undertone. When she handed a glass to Boone, she smiled nicely and said, "There you are, sergeant!" and Delaney noted she contrived to have their fingers briefly touch.

The lemonade had been freshly squeezed, lightly sugared, and well chilled. It was delicious, and Chief Delaney told Mrs. Maitland so. She inclined her head regally.

He then admired the view, watching a cruise boat move slowly upriver from New York to Bear Mountain between wooded shores. "Magnificent," Delaney commented, and Mrs. Maitland said, "Thank you," as if she had designed it.

Then, amenities at an end, she said crisply, "Chief Delaney, what exactly is being done to find the murderer of my son?"

"Ma'am," Delaney said, leaning forward to deliver what he later described to Boone as "the bullshit speech," and looking directly in the woman's eyes, "I assure you the full and complete resources of the New York Police Department are presently engaged in the search for your son's killer. Nothing is being left undone to find the person or persons responsible. Sergeant Boone and I have been relieved of all other duties to concentrate wholly on this case, and the enormous manpower and technical know-how of the Department are available to us. Believe me, speaking for Sergeant Boone and myself, the search for your son's murderer has Number One priority. The case is open and very active indeed."

His eagerness seemed to impress Mrs. Maitland. It took her a few moments to realize Chief Delaney had really said nothing at all.

"But what is being *done?*" she demanded. "Is anyone suspected?"

"We have several promising leads," Delaney said. "Very promising. I wish I could tell you more, Mrs. Maitland, but I cannot without slandering possibly innocent people. But I assure you, we are getting close."

"And you think you will find the killer?"

"I believe we have an excellent chance."

"And when will an arrest be made?"

"Soon," he said softly. "It is a very difficult case, Mrs. Maitland. I cannot recall working on a more difficult or more important case. Can you, sergeant?"

"Never," Boone said promptly. "A very tough case. Very complex."

"Complex," Delaney cried. "Exactly! Which is why we have come up from New York to see you and your daughter, Mrs. Maitland. In hopes that you may provide information that will help resolve those complexities."

"We have already been questioned," she said edgily. "And we signed statements. We told all we knew."

"Of course you did," he soothed. "But that was soon after the death of your son. When you were both, quite understandably, numb with grief and shock and horror. But now, with the passage of time, perhaps you can recollect some important information you didn't recall at that time."

"I don't see what possible—"

"Oh Mama," the daughter said, smiling prettily, showing teeth as shiny and small as white peg corn, "why don't we just answer Chief Delaney's questions and get it over with?"

Her mother whirled on her furiously.

"You shut your mouth!" she said. Then she turned to the officers. "More lemonade, gentlemen? Please help yourselves."

Sergeant Boone rose to do the honors, topping off the ladies' glasses first.

"Thank you, sir," Emily Maitland said pertly.

During this pause, with the sergeant moving about, Delaney had the opportunity to examine Dora Maitland more closely.

It was a face, he decided, that belonged on a cigar box. The skin was dusty ivory, eyes dark and flashing, lips carmine, and hair pouring in curls of jet black to below her shoulders. It *had* to be a wig, and yet it suited her exotic appearance so perfectly that Delaney wondered if it might not be her own hair, darkened, oiled, and fashioned into those glossy ringlets by the hairdresser's art.

He guessed her age at about sixty; face and hair denied it, but the hands were the tip-off. She wore lounging pajamas, not too clean, of bottle-green silk. The blouse was styled like a man's shirt, with an open collar that showed a magnificent, unwrinkled throat and hinted at shoulders just as luscious. She was fleshy enough, but without her daughter's corpulence.

Both men were conscious of her musky scent. Even more conscious of the mature voluptuousness of her ungirdled body. Her feet were bare; toenails painted the same red as fingernails and lips. Just below one corner of her mouth was a small black mole, although it could have been a velvet *mouche.*

She moved infrequently and had the gift of natural repose, not unlike the cat sleeping carelessly on a nearby chair. She exuded a very primitive sensuality, no less impressive because it was partly the product of artifice. Her physical presence was as deliberately mannered as Cleopatra's on her barge, and just as confident. Such a role, essayed by even a younger woman of less talent and smaller natural gifts, might inspire laughter. Neither officer had any desire to laugh at Dora Maitland; they were convinced.

"Very well, Chief Delaney," she said. "What is it you wish to know?"

Her voice was low-pitched, throaty, with a tendency to raspiness. She had not lighted a cigarette since they arrived, but Delaney thought hers the voice of a heavy smoker.

He took out his notebook, and Sergeant Boone followed suit. Delaney slid on his heavy reading glasses.

"Mrs. Maitland," he started, "you have stated that on the day your son was killed, you and your daughter were here, in this house, during the period from ten in the morning until three in the afternoon. Is that correct?"

"Yes."

"And on that Friday, the housekeeper was not present because it was her day off?"

"That's correct."

"The housekeeper is Martha, the lady who let us in?"

"Yes."

"During that time period, did you have any visitors?"

"No."

"Did you make or receive any phone calls?"

"I don't recall. I don't think so. No, I didn't make any calls or receive any. Emily, did you?"

"No, Mama."

"Did you go anywhere in your car?" Delaney asked. "Shopping, perhaps? To visit? Or just for a ride?"

"No, we went nowhere on that Friday. I had a dreadful headache, and I believe I spent most of the day lying down. Isn't that right, Emily?"

"Yes, Mama. I brought lunch to your room."

"Now I would like both of you to listen to my next question carefully," Delaney said solemnly, "and think very carefully before you answer. Do either of you know or suspect anyone who for whatever reason, real or fancied, disliked or hated Victor Maitland enough to murder him?"

The two women looked at each other a moment.

"I'm sure there were people who disliked or even hated my son," Dora Maitland said finally. "He was a very successful artist in a very competitive field, and there are always those who are jealous of talent. I know something of this, you see. I was on the stage before I married Mr. Maitland, and achieved quite some success and was myself the object of very bitter jealousy, cruel gossip, and all sorts of vile rumors. But one learns to expect this in the creative arts. People without talent become so frustrated that their jealousy sometimes drives them to malicious cruelty. I'm certain my son suffered many such attacks."

"But do you know of anyone specifically who was capable of killing him, or who threatened him with physical harm?"

"No, I do not. Emily?"

"I don't know anyone, Mama."

"Your son never mentioned anyone threatening him?"

"No, he did not," Dora Maitland said.

"You saw your son frequently?"

There was the barest of pauses before she said, "Not as frequently as I would have wished."

"And how often did your son visit you, Mrs. Maitland?"

Again a brief pause, then, "As often as he could."

"How often? Once a week? Once a month? Less often or more often?"

"I really don't see what this has to do with finding my son's murderer, Chief Delaney," she said coldly.

He sighed and leaned toward her, the sincere confidant.

"Mrs. Maitland, I am not trying to cause you pain, or to pry into the relationship between you and your son. After all, it was a normal, loving mother-son relationship. Was it not?"

"Of course it was," she said.

"Of course it was," he repeated. "He loved you and you loved him. Isn't that correct?"

"Yes."

"Miss Maitland, would you care to comment?"

"What Mama says is right," the younger woman said.

"Of course," Delaney nodded. "So when I ask how often your son visited you, it is not to doubt that relationship; it is only to establish a pattern of his movements. Who he saw, and when. Where he traveled and how often. Did he come up here once a month, Mrs. Maitland?"

"Less," she said shortly.

"Once a year?"

"Perhaps," she said. "When he could. He was a very busy, successful artist."

"Of course," Delaney said. "Of course." He took off his glasses, gazed out at the murky river flowing slowly to the sea. "A very successful artist," he said musingly. "Did you know that your son had sold a single painting for a hundred thousand dollars?"

"I read of it," she said tonelessly.

"Think of it!" Delaney said. "A hundred thousand for one painting!" Then he turned suddenly to stare at her. "Did he send any of that money to you, Mrs. Maitland?"

"No."

"Did he ever contribute to your support? Ever make any effort to share his financial success with his mother?"

"He never gave us a cent," Emily Maitland burst out, and they all turned to look at her. She colored, giggled, took a sip of lemonade. "My land!" she said. "I got all carried away. But it is true—isn't it, Mama?"

"I never asked him for anything," Mrs. Maitland said. "I am not without my own resources, Chief Delaney. I'm sure that if I had been in need, Victor would have offered help gladly and generously."

"I'm sure he would have," Delaney murmured. "You are well provided for, Mrs. Maitland?"

"Comfortable," she said. "The late Mr. Maitland . . . " She let her voice trail away.

"When did your husband die, Mrs. Maitland?" Sergeant Boone asked quietly.

"Oh . . ." she said. "Quite some time ago."

"Twenty-six years in November," Emily Maitland said.

"From illness?" Boone persisted.

"No," Dora Maitland said.

"My father committed suicide," Emily said. "Mama, don't look at me so. My land, they'll find out anyway. My father hanged himself in the barn."

"Yes," Dora Maitland said. "In the barn. Which is why we never use it. The doors are nailed shut."

Delaney busied himself with his notebook, looking down, saying, "Just a few more questions, ladies, and then we'll be finished. For the time being. Now I am going to mention several names. Please tell me if you know these individuals or ever heard your son speak of them. The first is Jake Dukker. D-u-k-k-e-r. An artist."

"I never heard of him," Dora Maitland said. "Emily?"

"No, Mama."

"Belle Sarazen. S-a-r-a-z-e-n."

Dora Maitland shook her head.

"I never heard Vic speak of her," Emily Maitland said, "but I've read about her. Isn't she that beautiful thin blonde lady who gives all the big parties? She sponsors charity bazaars, and she poses naked for artists and photographers."

"Emily!" Dora Maitland said. "Where did you read such things?"

"Oh Mama, it's in all the newspapers and magazines. And she's been on TV talk shows."

Dora Maitland muttered something that no one could catch.

"Yes, that's the lady," Delaney nodded.

"Lady!" Mrs. Maitland said explosively.

"You never heard your son mention her name?"

"No. Never."

"Nor you, Miss Maitland?"

"No."

"How about Saul Geltman? G-e-l-t-m-a-n. Your son's agent, or art dealer. Do you know him, or of him?"

"Saul? Of course I know him," Dora Maitland said. "A dear, sweet little man. He has been up here to visit us."

"Oh?" Delaney said. "Frequently?"

"No. Not frequently. On occasion."

"How frequently?"

"Perhaps two or three times a year. Maybe more often."

"More often than your son," Delaney said. It was a statement, not a question.

"Oh Mama," Emily said with a light, little laugh. "You'll have the officers thinking Saul Geltman came to visit us." She turned to him, smiling. "He didn't, of course. Saul has friends in Tuxedo Park he visits frequently. He drives up from New York and on his way stops by here to say hello. He never stays long."

"Do you know the names of his friends in Tuxedo Park?" Boone asked casually.

Emily Maitland considered a moment before she answered.

"No, sergeant, I don't believe he ever did mention their names. Just some nice boys, he said, who gave a lot of parties. I remember once I teased him about why he never asked me to the parties. But he said I'd probably be bored. I expect he was right."

Delaney nodded and, watching Dora Maitland, said, "The final name on the list is Alma Maitland, your son's widow. I wondered if you could tell us something about your daughter-in-law, Mrs. Maitland?"

She looked at him with basalt eyes.

"Tell you what?" she asked huskily.

"Well, let's start with your personal relations with her. Are you friendly?"

"Friendly enough. Hardly what you'd call close. She goes her way, and we go ours."

"I gather she did not accompany her husband when he visited you here?"

"You gather correctly." A harsh bark of laughter. "But don't get the wrong idea, Chief Delaney. There is no argument between Alma and me. No open warfare."

"More of an armed truce?" he suggested.

"Yes," she agreed. "Something like that. Hardly an unusual state of affairs between mother-in-law and daughter-in-law."

"That's true," he assented. "Would you mind telling me the cause of your, ah, disagreement?"

"I didn't think much of the way she was raising Ted, and I told her so. The boy needed discipline and wasn't getting it. We have spoken very little since."

"But we always get Christmas cards from her, Mama," Emily said mischievously, and her mother glared.

"One final question, Mrs. Maitland," Chief Delaney said. "When your son visited you here, how did he come up? By train or bus? Or did he drive?"

"He drove," she said.

"Oh?" Delaney said. "I understood he didn't own a car. Well, perhaps he rented one."

"No," she said. "On the few trips he made, he borrowed Saul Geltman's car."

"It's a station wagon, Mama," Emily said.

"Is it?" her mother said. "I know very little about cars."

Delaney stood up slowly, tucked notebook and spectacles away, moved to the doorway. Sergeant Boone joined him.

"Mrs. Maitland," the Chief said with grave courtesy, "Miss Maitland, we thank you both for your hospitality and patience. Your cooperation has been a very great help."

"I don't see how," Dora Maitland said.

Delaney ignored that.

"One final favor . . ." he said. "If we may impose on you a few moments longer, would you object if we looked about your lovely grounds a bit? It's not often we get out of the city, and it's such a pleasure to breathe clean air and see this beautiful, peaceful place. Could we see a little more of it before we go back to the streets?"

He had, unwittingly, ignited her with his reference to "this beautiful, peaceful place." She came alive, insisted on donning webbed sandals and conducting the officers on a tour. They paired off, Mrs. Maitland with Delaney, Emily with Sergeant Boone, and wandered off onto the grounds. The housekeeper was nowhere to be seen, but a radio was blasting country music in one wing of the house.

Dora Maitland showed Chief Delaney the cluttered flower beds of peonies, irises, and lilies; a gnarled oak she claimed to be 150 years old; a broken birdbath half-hidden in the undergrowth; the tangle of wild ground cover on the bank sloping down to the river; a small, sandstone plaque set into the brick foundation of the house on which the legend "T.M. 1898" could be dimly discerned.

"My husband's father, Timothy Maitland, began building this house that year," she explained to Delaney. "He died of TB before it was finished. His wife, my mother-in-law, completed the main building, added the wings, and did much of the landscaping herself. My husband and I added the gazebo, installed the driveway, and made many modern improvements inside. Of course it all needs work, as you can see. I had planned to restore everything to its original beauty, but Victor died, and I'm afraid I lost all my ambition. But I feel my strength and resolve coming back more each day, and I intend to go through with it. It's really a dream, you see. Oh, Chief Delaney, you should have seen this place when I was a young bride carried over the threshold. One of the finest, loveliest homes in this area, with a view that no place in Rockland County could equal. A velvety lawn. Everything spanking clean and neat. The river glittering. The air. The sky. Birds and flowers. Like you, I came from the city streets, and this place seemed paradise to me. I am determined to make it a paradise once again. Oh yes. Everything is here. I have not sold off an acre of land. You would not *believe* the taxes! And the house is structurally sound. I intend to make it just as lovely as it was when I first saw it."

"I'm sure you shall," he murmured.

She clutched him urgently by the sleeve.

"You will find him, won't you?" she whispered, desperation in her voice. "The killer, I mean?"

"I'll do my best," he said. "I promise you that."

They moved around to the front of the house again. Emily and Sergeant Boone were strolling between the garage and the gazebo. She was talking brightly, although Delaney could not hear what was being said. But the sergeant was stooping slightly, head lowered, listening intently.

Dora Maitland and Delaney waited at the entrance for the other two to come up. Mrs. Maitland clasped her hands to her bosom dramatically, raised her eyes to the pellucid sky.

"What a divine day!" she exclaimed rapturously.

Delaney could believe she had once been on the stage.

Finally, bidding goodbye to the ladies, the two officers went through the handshaking ceremony again, nodding and smiling. They then drove down the graveled driveway.

"Did you see the doors?" Delaney asked.

"Yes, sir," Boone said. "They're nailed shut all right."

"You were correct about Geltman," Delaney said. "He is a flit."

"And she's a lush," Boone said stolidly.

"You're sure?"

"It takes one to know one," Boone said matter-of-factly.

"What were the tip-offs?"

"That huskiness—from whiskey, not from smoking."

"Her fingers were nicotine-stained," Delaney noted.

"But she didn't dare light up; we'd have seen the tremble. And she didn't move. Like her head was balanced and might roll off. I know the feeling. And she gripped the arms of her chair, again to hide the shakes. Drank two full glasses of lemonade to put out the fire."

"You think she had a few before we came?"

"No," Boone said, "or she'd have been looser. She wanted to be absolutely sober, even if it hurt. She didn't want to risk blabbing."

"She did with me," Delaney said. "At the end."

"When she figured the danger was over," Boone said. "Take my word for it, Chief; she's on the sauce."

"She's what used to be called 'a fine figure of a woman,'" Delaney said.

"Still is, as far as I'm concerned," the sergeant said. "A great pair of lungs. Sir, can we stop for some food?"

"God, yes!" Delaney said. "I'm starved. But leave room for dinner tonight, or my wife will make my life miserable. It's London broil and new potatoes, by the way."

"I'm sold," Boone said. "Want me to pick up Rebecca?"

"No need," Delaney said. "She's coming over early to help Monica."

They stopped at the first luncheonette they hit. It was crowded and noisy, but they had lucked onto a gem; their ham-and-scrambled were good. They strolled out to the car replete, Boone sucking on a mint-flavored toothpick. Delaney got behind the wheel.

The Chief drove cautiously until he got the feel of the car. After they were over the bridge, he relaxed, held it slightly below the legal limit, and stayed in the right-hand lane, letting the speed merchants zip by.

"What did you get from the girl?" he asked Boone. "Although I don't know why I call her 'girl.' About thirty-two, I figure."

"Thirty-five," Boone said. "She volunteered that. Which probably means thirty-eight. Did you catch Mama's reference to more discipline for her grandson? That's the way I see it: plenty of discipline for Victor and Emily. But Victor wouldn't take it, and split. Emily stayed under Mama's thumb."

"I'm not so sure," Delaney said slowly. "The girl's got moxie; she's not beaten. Maybe the drinking is a recent thing, and Mama is losing control. Why did the old man do the Dutch? Did you get that?"

"He owned a lumberyard. Construction material. Stuff like that. Very successful. A big wheel in county politics. But he kept thinking he could draw to an inside straight. Also horses and local crap games. It all went. So he kicked the bucket, literally, and all the lawyers could salvage were the house and grounds, plus enough income from blue-chips to keep the two women going. Nothing from Victor baby. They're not starving, far from it, but they're not rolling either."

"Funny," Delaney said. "Thorsen thought she was a rich old twist."

"Emily said that's what everyone thinks. But they're not. Just getting by."

"With a housekeeper," Delaney reminded him. "Hardly poverty. Dora boasted of never selling off an acre. That land must be worth a mint. But she keeps coming up with the taxes and hanging on."

"For what?" Boone said.

"Her dream," Delaney said. "To restore it all the way it was. A paradise. Birds and flowers. She's got to have it."

"No," Boone said "that's not what I meant. What is she hanging on *for?* A windfall? Like an inheritance?"

"Ah," Delaney said. "Good question. A shrewd lady. Did you catch that business of how she was a victim of malicious gossip when she was on the stage? I'll bet she was! All that bullshit was just to disarm us if we went digging. Well, it was a profitable morning."

"Was it, sir?" Boone asked. "How?"

"A lot of things we have to do now. We'll have to come up here again. At least one more time. We'll come on a Friday, when the housekeeper is off. We'll get her full name and address from the local postman, or somehow. I want you to check her out."

"Me?"

"How did you make her accent? I figured Virginia."

"Farther south than that, Chief," Boone said. "Maybe Georgia."

"That's why I want you to check her out. You're a good old boy. You've got the accent."

"I do?" Boone said. "I didn't think I had."

"Sure you do," Delaney said genially. "Not much, but it's there. And you can force it without faking."

"You want to know how often Victor Maitland and Saul Geltman visited?" Boone guessed.

"Right," Delaney nodded. "That for starters. And anything else you can glom. Like Dora's drinking and does fat Emily have any larcenous boyfriends."

"What else?"

"I'll handle the bank account. I don't know what it'll take; maybe a court order, or maybe just a letter or call from Thorsen to the locals will do. We've got to walk on eggs here. After all, Dora's brother is J. Barnes Chapin, and the last thing in the world we want is for him to get his balls in an uproar. But I've got to see those bank records."

"Chief, you really think Dora or Emily or both drove that great big old Mercedes down to New York that Friday and nixed the son? For the loot?"

"It's possible. He didn't leave any will, but maybe the mother would share. That's another thing I've got to check out. But even if they didn't do it themselves, a hefty bank withdrawal in, say, the last six months would be a red flag."

Boone pondered a moment.

"She hired someone?"

"Could be," Delaney said. "Happens all the time."

"Jesus Christ, Chief, she's his *mother!*"

"So?" Delaney said coldly. "It used to be that seventy-five percent of all homicides were committed by relatives, friends, or acquaintances of the victim. Things have changed in the past five years; the number of 'stranger-murders' has increased. But family and friends still do about two-thirds of the killing. It's basic. If you catch a homicide, you look at the family first."

Abner Boone sighed. "That's depressing," he said.

Delaney glanced at him sideways.

"Sometimes, sergeant," he said. "I think you may be an idealist. We work with what we've got. We'd be morons to disregard percentages. And I think both Dora and Emily are big enough and strong enough to have done it. At first, I didn't think it was a woman. My wife doesn't think so. But I'm beginning to wonder. How much strength does it take to push in a shiv?"

"More than I've got," Sergeant Boone said.

They were in the city, heading downtown on Columbus Avenue, when Delaney pulled over, double-parking.

"I'll just be a minute," he said, and went into a bodega to buy a cold six-pack of Ballantine ale. When he returned, Boone asked him to wait a minute, and dashed across the street to a florist. He came back with a bunch of small white mums wrapped in green tissue paper.

"For your wife," he said.

"You didn't have to do that," Delaney said, pleased.

They had to park in a restricted area in front of the 251st Precinct house, but Boone's car was known to the local cops by now, and wouldn't be plastered or hauled away. Just to make sure, the sergeant put the "Officer on Duty" card behind his windshield.

The women were in the kitchen, flushed and laughing. Partly due to a pitcher of martinis Monica had prepared. Delaney helped himself to a double over ice, and added a slice of lemon peel. Boone had a small bottle of tonic water poured over ice and a squeezed wedge of lime.

The two men were willing to sit around the kitchen shmoozing, but the ladies chased them out. They went into Delaney's study, slumped into the worn club chairs gratefully, stretched out their legs. They sat awhile in comfortable silence.

"I remember a homicide I worked, oh, maybe twenty years ago," Delaney said finally. "It looked to be an open-and-shut. This young kid, maybe about twenty-five, around there, said he killed his father. The kid had been in Korea and smuggled in a forty-five. The old man was a terror. Always beating on the old lady. A long record of physical assaults. She filed complaints, but never pushed a prosecution. The son took it just so long, he said, then blasted away. Holy Christ, you should have seen that room. They had to replaster the walls. A full magazine had been fired, and the father took most of them. I mean, he was *pieces*. The son waltzed into the precinct house and slammed the pistol down on the desk. The duty sergeant almost fainted. The son admitted everything. But it didn't add up. The kid had been an MP. And no dummy. He knew how to handle that Colt. He wouldn't have sprayed. One pill would have done it."

"The mother," Boone said somberly.

"Sure," Delaney nodded. "The son was covering for her. That's what everyone thought. And who could blame her? After taking all that abuse. And what would she get? No one's going to put an old lady in the slammer for blowing away a husband who talks to her with his fists. What would she get? A slap on the wrist. Probation, probably. Everyone knew it; everyone was satisfied."

Delaney stopped and sipped his martini. Boone looked at him, puzzled. The Chief's expression revealed nothing.

"So?" Boone said. "What's the point, sir?"

"The point?" Delaney said, almost rumbling, his chin down on his chest. "The point is that I couldn't buy it. I went digging. The kid had a chance to buy in on a garage, and the old man wouldn't lend him the dough. He had it, but he wouldn't give his son a chance. 'I worked hard for every penny I got. You go out and dig ditches—whatever.' That kind of shit. Plenty of arguments, hot arguments. So finally the son blew him away in a fury, but not so furious that he didn't make it look like the old lady had done it, knowing she'd get home free. It was the son all along. He figured we'd think he was covering. I told you he was no dummy."

"Son of a bitch," Boone said slowly. "So what happened?"

"I dumped it in the lieutenant's lap," Delaney said. "He could have killed me. He was all set to charge the old lady and see her walk. Now it was his decision on charging the kid. Finally he decided to go with the old lady. He buried my paper and told me he was doing it, and I could have his balls if I wanted them. I didn't. He was a good cop. Well, maybe not so good, but he was human. So he buried my paper on the kid, the old lady got charged, and like everyone expected, she walked. There was some insurance money, and the kid invested in his garage and lived happily ever after. Kept his nose clean; never strayed from the arrow. So where was justice in that case?"

"Just the way it came out," Boone said stoutly. "A no-goodnik gets wasted, a wife gets out of a miserable marriage, and the son gets a start on a clean life."

"Is that how you see it?" Delaney asked, raising his eyes to stare at Abner Boone. "There hasn't been a day since that case twenty years ago that I haven't regretted not pushing it. I should have racked up that kid, and if my lieutenant got in the way, I should have racked him up, too. Sergeant, that kid murdered a human being. No one should do that and get away with it. It's not right. I've made my share of mistakes, and letting that kid off the hook was one of them."

Boone was silent awhile, staring across at the brooding figure slumped wearily in the club chair.

"Are you sure of that, sir?" he said softly.

"Yes," Delaney said. "I'm sure."

Boone sighed, took a deep swallow of his tonic water.

"How did you break it?" he asked. "How did you figure it wasn't the abused wife who blasted the old man?"

"She couldn't have done that," Delaney said. "She loved him."

Then after a moment, the Chief said, "Why did I tell you that story? Oh . . . now I remember. I was wondering if anyone loved Victor Maitland."

Rebecca Hirsch flung open the door, stood posed, a dish towel folded over one arm.

"Gentlemen," she announced, "dinner is served."

They laughed, dragged themselves to their feet, went into the dining room. The table was set for six, with candles yet, and Sergeant Boone's flowers in a tall vase in the center. Chief Delaney sat at one end, Monica at the other, with Mary and Rebecca on one side and Sylvia and Sergeant Boone on the other.

They started with an appetizer of caviar that everyone knew was lumpfish, and didn't care. This with sour cream, chopped onions, capers, and a lemon wedge. A salad of oiled endive and cherry tomatoes. The London broil with new potatoes, plus fresh stringbeans and a bowl of hot spinach leaves with bacon chunks.

Edward X. Delaney stood up to carve, and said, "Who wants the drumstick?" Monica and Rebecca Hirsch writhed with laughter, and the Chief looked at his wife suspiciously.

"Did you tell Rebecca I'd say that?" he accused.

It was a good meal, a good evening. Two, three, even four conversations went on at once. The London broil was pronounced somewhat chewy but flavorsome. Everyone had seconds, which pleased the cook. The salad disappeared, as did a chilled bottle of two-year-old Beaujolais. Potatoes, stringbeans, and spinach were consumed dutifully, and by the time the key-lime pie was brought in, the diners had lost their initial momentum and were beginning to dawdle.

The girls kissed Monica, Rebecca, and their stepfather good night, shook hands solemnly with Sergeant Boone, giggling, and took their wedges of pie and glasses of milk upstairs to their room. Delaney moved around the table, pouring coffee. He paused to lean down and kiss his wife's cheek.

"Wonderful meal, dear," he said.

"Just great, Mrs. Delaney," Boone said enthusiastically. "Can't remember a better one."

"I'm glad you enjoyed it," she smiled happily. "Where did you boys have lunch?"

"A greasy spoon," Boone said.

"You shouldn't eat at places like that," Rebecca said severely. "Instant heartburn. If not ulcers."

Now she and Boone were sitting across from each other. When their eyes met, they looked casually away. She called him "Sergeant," and he avoided addressing her directly by name. Their manner with each other was polite, coolly friendly.

Son of a bitch, Delaney thought suddenly; they've been to bed.

Abner Boone had suffered through cocktails and wine—drinking only water during dinner—and Delaney couldn't see torturing him further by inhaling a snifter of cognac. So he sipped his coffee with every evidence of satisfied benignity, silent as he listened to Boone and the women discuss the best way to roast a goose.

Talk was quiet, almost subdued, although no one felt constraint. But there was no need for chatter. Each hoped the others felt equally content: a good meal, a surcease of wanting. The peace that comes when covetousness vanishes, even temporarily.

"Rebecca," Chief Delaney said, almost lazily, "is your mother living?"

"Oh yes," she said. "In Florida. Thank God."

"Why 'Thank God'?" he asked. "Because she's living or because she's living in Florida?"

She laughed and hung her head, the beautiful long hair falling forward to hide her face. Then she threw back her head suddenly, the hair flinging back into place. Sergeant Boone stirred restlessly in his chair.

"I shouldn't have said that," she confessed, "but she's a bit much. A professional mother. When she lived in New York, she drove me up a wall. Even from Florida, I still get the nudging. What to eat, what to wear, how to act."

"She wants to run your life?" Delaney asked.

"Run it? She wants to *own* it!"

Monica turned to look at him.

"Edward, why the interest in Rebecca's mother?"

He sighed, wondering what he should and should not say. Still, they were women and their insights might be useful. He'd use anyone, and not apologize for it.

"This thing Sergeant Boone and I are working on . . ." he said. "We ran into an interesting situation today. A mother-and-daughter relationship . . ."

He described, as accurately as he could, Dora and Emily Maitland, their ages, physical appearance, the clothes they wore, the house they lived in, their voices, manner, and behavior.

"Is that an accurate description, would you say, sergeant?" he asked Boone when he finished.

"Yes, sir, I'd say so. Except you seemed to see more—more spirit in the girl than I did. I thought the mother was the heavy."

"Mmm," Delaney said. Then, without telling Monica and Rebecca that the two women under discussion were suspects in a murder investigation (although surely Monica guessed it), he asked them directly, looking back and forth, "How do you see a relationship like that? Specifically, why is the daughter still hanging around? Why didn't she take off? And does mother dominate daughter or vice versa?"

"Take off where?" Monica Delaney demanded. "With what? Mama controls the money, doesn't she? What's the daughter going to do—come to New York and walk Eighth Avenue? The way you describe her, I don't think she'd make out. Is she trained for anything? Can she hold down a job?"

"Then why didn't she leave home fifteen years ago and learn to support herself?" Rebecca asked. "Maybe she likes it there. The nice, safe cocoon."

"That's my point, too," Sergeant Boone said. "Chief, if she had as much chutzpah as you—"

"Hoo-hah!" Rebecca cried. "Chutzpah. Listen to the knacker!"

Boone blushed, smiling.

"Well . . . you know," he said lamely. "If the girl had as much courage as you think, Chief, she'd have split years ago."

"Maybe she's afraid," Monica said.

"Afraid?" Delaney said. "Of what?"

"Of the world," his wife said. "Of life."

"You said she's overweight," Rebecca said. "That could be from loneliness. Believe me, I know! You're miserable, so you eat. Stuck out there in the country with a crazy mother—or am I being redundant?—what else is there to do but eat? She wants something else, something better. The Is-this-all-there-is-to-life syndrome? But like Monica said, she's afraid. Of change. And every year it gets harder to make the break."

"Or maybe she's waiting for Mama to die," Monica said. "That happens sometimes. But also, sometimes it takes so long that by the time it *does* happen, the daughter has become the mother. If you know what I mean."

"I know what you mean," Delaney nodded, "but I'm not sure you're right. This girl isn't dead. I mean, inside she isn't dead. She still feels things. She's got urges, wants, desires. My question is why hasn't she done something about getting what she wants?"

"Maybe she has," Rebecca said. "Maybe she's working on her ambitions right now, and you don't know anything about it."

"That's possible," Delaney acknowledged. "Very possible. Another explanation might be that she's lazy. I know that sounds simple, but sometimes we credit people with more complex motives than they're capable of feeling. Maybe this girl is just bone-lazy, and likes that slow, sluggish life she's living out there."

"Do you believe that, sir?" Boone asked.

"No," Delaney said, "I don't. There's something there. Something. No idiot she. She's not just a lump. Going by the book, I'd have to say the mother is running her. But I can't get rid of the feeling that maybe she's running the mother."

"That would be a switch," Rebecca said.

"But understandable," Delaney said. "How's this: At first the mother was the honcho. The iron fist and strict discipline for her children. Then, as she grows older, the vigor fades. The mother weakens; the daughter senses it. The mother seems to be living in the past, more every year. There's a power vacuum. The daughter moves in. Slowly. A little at a time. Remember, there's no man around the house. As the old lady's energy gets less and less, the daughter gets more and more. The mother is weary of trying to make ends meet, trying to live in style. All she wants are her dreams of the past. She can't cope with today. Like there's an X-quantity of resolve there, and less for the mother means more for the daughter. Like an hourglass. The sand runs from one container to another. The mother loses, the daughter gains. Well . . ." He laughed briefly. "It's fanciful, but that's the way I see it."

"The mother wants her dream," Boone said. "The house restored. The grounds prettied up. Just the way everything was when she was a bride. Okay. Admitted. But what does the daughter want?"

"Escape," Delaney said.

They looked at him with strange expressions.

"Edward," his wife said, "is this the way detectives work? Trying to guess why people do what they do?"

"Not usually," he said. "Usually we work with physical evidence. Hard facts. Percentages, timing, weapons, testimony of witnesses, things you can look at, hold in your hand, or put under a microscope. But sometimes when none of this exists, or not enough to break a case, you've got to turn to people. As you said, why they do what they do. You try to put yourself in their place. What drives them? What do they want? Everyone *wants*. But some people can't control it. Then want becomes need. And need—I mean a real greedy need—the kind that haunts you night and day—that's motive enough for any crime."

His listeners were all silent then, disturbed. Delaney looked at the sergeant. Boone jerked immediately to his feet.

"Getting late!" he sang cheerily. "Busy day tomorrow. Got to get going."

There was the usual confusion of departure: "More pie?" "Oh no!" "Coffee?" "Not a thing!" Then Rebecca Hirsch and Abner Boone left together. Delaney locked up and came back to help his wife clear the dining room table, straighten up, load the dishwasher, store away leftovers.

"They're making it, aren't they?" he asked casually.

"Yes," she nodded.

"I hope she doesn't get hurt," he said.

His wife shrugged. "She's a grown woman, Edward. She can take care of herself."

8

It was not the first time Detective sergeant Abner Boone had mused on how similar police work was to theatre. Undercover cops were closest, of course, with their costumes, makeup, accents, and fictitious identities. But detectives were into theatre too, and so were uniformed street cops. You soon learned the value of feigning emotions, of delivering speeches in other men's words, of acting roles best suited for the situation.

"Now, now," a street cop says soothingly, patting the shoulder of a frenzied husband. "I know exactly how you feel. Haven't I been through the same thing m'self? I know, I know. But bashing her head in will do you no good. Just give me the brick like a good lad. I know, I tell you. I know exactly how you feel."

"I know you're not involved," the dick says shamefacedly. "Look, I don't even like the idea of bothering you. A girl of your intelligence and good looks. You're too good for the likes of him; that's easy to see. But I've got to ask these questions, you know. I don't *want* to, but it's my job. Now then . . . was he *really* with you when the shop was ripped off?"

Not always sympathetic, of course. When a heavy is needed, one is supplied . . .

"You're nailed, cheese-brain. Signed, sealed, and delivered. No way out of this. Three-to-five in the slammer, and you'll be a faggot in a week. Locked in with all those horny studs. You'll be gang-banged the first night. That's what it's like, pal. And your wife on the outside, looking around for company. You dig? Your life is over, kiddo. But tell me who else was in on it, and maybe we can work a deal. There are ways . . ."

And so forth. The roles fitted to circumstances. So Abner Boone dressed with extra care that Friday morning. No brassy slacks and screaming jacket, but a conservative suit of tan poplin, with white shirt and black knit tie. Something that wouldn't spook a woman who worked as legal secretary to an attorney. He also shaved carefully and used his best cologne. Zizanie. And he powdered his armpits. There wasn't much he could do with his short, gingery hair, but at least it was clean.

He folded his jacket neatly onto the back seat of his car, then drove downtown to Central Park South and double-parked outside the studio of Jake Dukker. The doorman wandered over, and Boone had to flash his tin. He waited patiently, smoking his third cigarette of the morning, until his watch showed exactly ten o'clock. Then he started up.

He drove east to Park Avenue and turned south. He planned to take it all the way down to what used to be called Fourth Avenue, and was now Park Avenue South. Then he figured to cut over to Broadway on 14th Street, and take that south to Spring Street, then over to Mott and Victor Maitland's studio. There were a dozen other routes, but one was as good, or bad, as another.

He obeyed all traffic regulations, didn't jump any lights, and when he got caught in jams, he didn't press it. It took forty-three minutes to reach the Mott Street studio, and Boone made a careful record in his notebook. He sat in front of Maitland's studio for exactly ten minutes, smoking another cigarette placidly, then started back. He arrived in front of Dukker's place on Central Park South at precisely 11:53. The northbound traffic had been heavy, and he had been caught in a three-minute jam at 42nd Street. Still, he had made the round-trip in one hour and fifty-three minutes, allowing ten minutes for the chopping of Victor Maitland. Jake Dukker or Belle Sarazen, or both, could have done the same on that Friday. At least he had proved it was possible in under two hours. He wondered if Chief Delaney would be pleased or disappointed. Probably neither. Just another fact to add to the file.

Boone then drove east and north, and found a parking space a block away from the offices of Simon & Brewster on East 68th Street. He put on his jacket, locked the car, and popped a chlorophyll tablet into his mouth. He walked over to the lawyer's office, his back held deliberately straight, trying to compose his features into the picture of a pleasant, boyish officer of the law, eager and ingratiating.

She was sitting alone in the outer office, typing with blinding speed on an electric IBM. She kept working a moment after he came in and halted before her big, glass-topped desk. He had time to make her as a tall, skinny blonde with no chest. None at all. Then she stopped typing and looked up.

"Miss Hemley?" he smiled. "Susan Hemley?"

"Yes?" she said, cocking her head to one side, puzzled.

"I spoke to you on the phone the other night," he smiled. "Detective sergeant Abner Boone."

He unfolded his ID and handed it over. She took it and examined it carefully, something people rarely did.

"You've come to arrest me?" she asked archly.

"Sure," he smiled. "For attracting a police officer. Actually, this is just a social visit, Miss Hemley. To thank you for your cooperation. And to try to set up an appointment with Mr. Simon. For my boss, Chief Edward Delaney."

"A chief," she said. "Oh my. Sounds important."

"Not really," he smiled. "Just a few routine questions to get the record straight."

"The Maitland murder?" she asked in a hushed voice.

He nodded, still smiling. "Any morning or afternoon next week at Mr. Simon's convenience."

"Just a minute, sergeant," she said. "Let me check."

She rose and moved to an inner door, knocked once, entered, closed the door behind her. Boone was grateful; his face felt stretched. She was back in a moment. He saw she moved loosely, with a floppy grace. Thin as a pencil, with good, long legs. A smooth, unmarked face. An eggshaped head. The blonde hair was in short, tight curls. Black, horn-rimmed glasses were, somehow, sexy. He thought she would be a terror in bed. Yelping. Kicking hell out of the sheets.

"How's for Tuesday morning at ten?" she asked.

"Fine," he said, smiling again. "We'll be here."

He began to move away, hesitated, turned back to her.

"One more favor," he smiled. "Where can a hungry cop get a good lunch in this neighborhood?"

Twenty minutes later they were seated opposite each other on the upper level of a Madison Avenue luncheonette.

"I'm afraid they don't serve drinks," she apologized.

"No problem," he assured her. "Order what you like. We'll let the City pay for it. You're a taxpayer, aren't you?"

"Am I ever!" she said, and they both laughed.

He watched his manners, and they got along swimmingly. They talked about the subject of most interest to both of them: her. He hadn't exaggerated when he had told Delaney he knew how to listen; he did, and before the iced tea and sherbet were served, he had her background: Ohio, business college, a special training in legal stenography, eleven years' experience in law offices. Which would make her, he figured, about thirty-seven to thirty-eight, around there. Good salary, good vacation and fringe benefits, a small office, but a relaxed place to work. J. Julian Simon was a pleasure. Her words: "That man is a pleasure." Boone assumed she meant to work for.

"How about you?" she asked finally. "You're working on the Maitland case?"

He nodded, looked down at the table, moved things about.

"I know you can't talk about it," she said.

He looked up at her then.

"I'm not supposed to," he said. "But . . ."

He glanced about carefully, was silent while a waitress cleared a neighboring table.

"We're getting close," he whispered.

"Really?" she whispered back. She hunched her chair forward, put elbows on the table, leaned to him. "The last story I read in the papers said the police had no leads."

"The papers," he scoffed. "We don't tell them everything. You understand?"

"Of course," she said eagerly. "Then there's more?"

He nodded again, looked about carefully again, leaned forward again.

"Did you know him?" he asked. "Victor Maitland? Did you ever meet him?"

"Oh yes," she said. "Several times. At the office. And once at a party in Mr. Geltman's apartment."

"Oh?" Boone said. "At the office? Was Mr. Simon his lawyer too?"

"Not really," she said. "He just came up once or twice with Mr. Geltman. I don't think he had a personal attorney. Once he said to Mr. Simon, 'The first thing we do, let's kill all the lawyers.' I don't think that was a very nice thing to say."

"No," Boone said, "it wasn't. But I guess Maitland wasn't a very nice guy. No one seems to have liked him."

"I certainly didn't," she said stoutly. "I thought he was rude and nasty."

"I know," he said sympathetically. "That's what everyone says. I guess his wife put up with a lot."

"She certainly did. She's such a lovely woman."

"Isn't she?" he agreed enthusiastically. "I met her, and that's exactly what I thought: a lovely woman. And married to that animal. Did you know—" Here he lowered his voice, leaned even closer. Susan Hemley also leaned to him, until their heads were almost touching. "Did you know—well, this wasn't in the papers. You've got to promise not to breathe a word of it to anyone."

"I promise," she said sincerely. "I won't say a word."

"I trust you," he said. "Well, when they found him, dead, he wasn't wearing any underwear."

She jerked back, eyes widening.

"Nooo," she breathed. "Really?"

He held up a hand, palm out.

" 'Struth," he said. "So help me. We don't know what it means yet, but he definitely wasn't wearing any underwear."

She leaned forward again.

"I told you he was nasty," she said. "That proves it."

"Oh yes," he said. "You're right. We know he was very nasty to Mr. Geltman."

"He certainly was," she said. "You should have heard how Maitland talked to Saul. And in public. In front of everyone. He was so nasty."

"And to think Geltman was in your office at the time Maitland was killed," Boone said, shaking his head. "Makes you think. Maybe if Geltman hadn't been there, we'd have suspected him. But he was there all right. Wasn't he?"

"Oh sure," she said, nodding her head so violently that the blonde curls bounced. "I saw him come in. And I spoke to him a minute or two before he went into Mr. Simon's office."

"About ten o'clock that was," Boone said reflectively. "And then you saw him come out around one-thirty in the afternoon. Right?"

"Oh no," she said. "At one-thirty I was at lunch with Alma. Alma Maitland. Don't you remember?"

"Of course," Boone said, snapping his fingers. "How could I forget? Well, anyway, the other people in the office saw him come out. Didn't they?"

"Nooo," she said slowly. "Just Mr. Simon. Mr. Brewster was in court all that day, and the clerk, Lou Broniff, was out with the flu."

"Well," he said, "Mr. Simon told us when he left, and that's good enough."

"It certainly is," she said. "Mr. Simon is a fine man. A pleasure."

"Mr. Geltman spoke very highly of him," Boone lied casually.

"I should think so," she laughed. "They've been friends for years. I mean they're more than lawyer and client. They play handball together. After all, they're both divorced."

"Very buddy-buddy," Boone observed, enjoying this.

"They certainly are. Mr. Geltman is such a nice little man. He really says funny things. I like him."

"I do, too," Boone agreed. "A lot of personality. Too bad he and Mrs. Maitland don't seem to get along."

"Oh, that," Susan Hemley said. "It's really just a little misunderstanding. Maitland was doing some paintings and making Geltman sell them and not telling his wife about them. I told Alma it wasn't Saul's fault. After all, he had to sell what Maitland brought him, didn't he? That was his job, wasn't it? And what Maitland did with the money was none of Saul's business, was it? If Maitland didn't tell his wife how much he was making, she really shouldn't blame Mr. Geltman."

"I agree with you," Boone said. "And you told Alma Maitland that?"

"I certainly did. But she seems to think there was more to it than that."

"More to it than that?" Boone asked. "I don't understand. What did she mean by that?"

"Goodness!" Susan Hemley cried. "Look at the time! I've got to get back to the office. Thank you so very much for the lunch, sergeant. I really enjoyed it. I hope to see you again."

"You will," he smiled once more. "Tuesday morning at ten o'clock. With Chief Delaney."

He returned to Jake Dukker's studio on Central Park South. It was now almost two P.M., not precisely corresponding to the hour of the murder but close enough, he felt, for a time trial by subway.

He found a parking space on the north side of 59th Street, locked his car, checked his watch. He decided to walk to the subway station on Lexington

Avenue rather than wait for a cab. He walked rapidly, threading his way through the throngs, occasionally stepping down into the gutter to make better time. Like a man with murder on his mind, he dashed across streets against the lights, not heeding the blasting horns and screamed insults of the hackies.

In the 59th Street IRT station he waited almost four minutes for a downtown express. He changed to a local at 14th Street, took that to Spring, got off and walked quickly over to Maitland's Mott Street studio. He looked at his watch; forty-six minutes since leaving Dukker's place.

He then strolled around the block, using up the ten minutes allotted for the murder of Victor Maitland. Then he started back by the same route. This time he had a long wait for the local, and suffered the vexation of seeing two express trains thunder by on the inside track. Once aboard the local, he decided to stay with it to 59th Street. The train jerked to a halt for almost five minutes, somewhere between 14th and 23rd. It was one of those inexplicable New York subway delays for which no explanation is ever given the sweltering passengers.

He hurried off the train and out of the station at 59th, shouldering his way through the crowds, and dashed westward across town to Dukker's studio. He arrived under the canopy, puffing, his poplin suit sweated through. He looked at his watch. One hour and forty-nine minutes for the round trip. He could hardly believe it. He had made better time by walking and taking the subway than by driving the entire distance. It certainly proved his theory was plausible: Dukker or Sarazen could have made that trip, fixed Maitland and returned without their absence noted by the models and assistants in the downstairs studio. It would mean, of course, the two of them were in on it together.

Satisfied, jacket off, tie and collar jerked open, he drove home to East 85th Street. He lived in a relatively new high-rise apartment house. The rent and underground garage fee kept him constantly on the edge of bankruptcy, but he had lacked the resolve to move after his divorce. He would have *had* to move to a cheaper place if Phyllis had demanded alimony. But fortunately, she was into Women's Lib, took a five-thousand cash settlement, most of the furniture, and they shook hands. It was all civilized. And so awful he could never think of it without wanting to weep.

He collected his mail, bills and junk, and rode alone up to his eighteenth-floor apartment. It was sparsely furnished after Phyllis cleaned it out, but he still had a couch, chair, and cocktail table in the living room. The bedroom was furnished with bed, chest of drawers, and a card table he used for a desk, with a folding bridge chair. Rebecca Hirsch had brought over a little oak bedside table and some bright posters for the living-room walls. They helped. Rebecca kept talking about curtains and drapes, and he supposed he'd get around to them eventually. Right now, the venetian blinds sufficed.

He flipped on the air-conditioner, and stripped down to his shorts. He got a can of sugar-free soda from the fridge and sat down at the bedroom card table to write out a report while the interview with Susan Hemley was fresh in his mind. He typed out the report rapidly on an old Underwood that his ex-wife had left behind.

After he finished with the Hemley meet, he typed up a record of his two time trials, consulting his notebook to get the times exactly right. Then he added everything to his personal file on the Maitland homicide, wondering, not for the first time, if anyone would ever read it, or even consult it. But Delaney had told him to make daily reports, so he made daily reports. He owed the Chief that.

He took a tepid shower, dried in front of the air-conditioner, and felt a lot better. He started on his second pack of cigarettes and thought, fleetingly, of an iced Gibson. He opened another can of diet soda.

He checked his wallet and made a quick calculation of how much he could spend daily until the next payday. And he made a mental list of which creditors he could stiff, which he could stall, and who had to be paid at once. He knew how easy it was for a cop to get a loan, but he didn't want to start stumbling down that path.

Finally, he called Rebecca Hirsch. She sounded happy to hear from him, and said she could offer a tunafish salad if he could stand it. He told her he had been dreaming of a tunafish salad all day and would be right over. After dinner, he said, they could take a drive, or see a movie, or watch TV, or whatever.

She said she would prefer whatever.

9

On the same Friday morning that Detective sergeant Abner Boone began his time trials, Chief Edward X. Delaney was in his study planning the day's activities. He jotted down a list of "Things to do," and folded the note into his jacket pocket. He unpinned the three Maitland sketches from the map board, rolled them up, slid a rubber band around them. Then he called to Monica that he wouldn't be home for lunch, and started out. He carefully double-locked the outside door behind him.

His first stop was at a Second Avenue printing shop that also made photostats. Delaney ordered three 11 × 14 stats of each Maitland sketch. The clerk examined the nude drawings, then looked up with a wise-ass grin that faded when he saw Delaney's cold stare. He promised to have the photostats ready at noon.

The Chief then began walking slowly downtown to East 58th Street; his appointment with Theodore Maitland was at 11:00. Delaney had been doing so much riding in Boone's car recently, he figured the exercise would do him good. For awhile he tried inhaling deeply and slowly for a count of twelve, holding the breath for the same time, then exhaling slowly for another twelve-count. That regimen lasted for two blocks, and he didn't feel any better for it. He resumed his normal breathing and ambled steadily southward, observing the bustling life of the morning city and wondering when he was going to get a handle on the Maitland case: a break, a lead, an approach, anything that would give him direction and purpose.

He knew from experience that the first hours and days of an investigation were hardest to endure. Disparate facts piled up, evidence accumulated, people lied or spoke the truth—but what the hell did it all mean? You had to accept everything, keep your wits and nerve, let the mess grow and grow until you caught a pattern; two pieces fit, then more and more. It was like the traffic jam he saw at Second Avenue and 66th Street. Cars stalled every which way. Horns blaring. Red-faced drivers bellowing and waving. Then a street cop got the key car moving, the jam broke, in a few minutes traffic was flowing in a reasonably orderly pattern. But when was he going to find the key to the Maitland jam? Maybe today. Maybe tomorrow. And maybe, he thought morosely, he already had it and couldn't recognize it.

Mrs. Alma Maitland was nowhere to be seen, for which Delaney was grateful. A Puerto Rican maid ushered him into that cold "family room," where he sat on the edge of the couch, homburg on his knees. He waited for almost five minutes, guessing this was the son's form of hostility, and willing to endure patiently.

He had seen photos of Victor Maitland, of course, and was surprised at the close resemblance when the son finally stalked into the room. The same husky body, burly shoulders. Heavy head thrust forward. Coarse, reddish hair. The glower. Big hands with spatulate fingers. A thumping tread. The young face was marked by thick, dark brows, sculpted lips. Older, it might be a gross face, seamed, the mouth thinned and twisted. But now it had the soft vulnerability of youth. Hurt there, Delaney decided, and anger. And want.

He rose, but Ted Maitland made no effort to greet him or shake hands. Instead, he threw himself into one of the blonde wood armchairs, slumped down, began biting furiously at the hard skin around a thumbnail. He was wearing blue jeans with a red gingham shirt open almost to his waist. The inevitable necklace of Indian beads. Bare feet in moccasins. A bracelet of turquoise chips set in hammered silver.

"I don't know why I'm even talking to you," the boy said petulantly. "Only because Mother asked me. I've gone over this shit a hundred times with a hundred other cops."

Delaney was shocked by the voice: high-pitched, straining. He wondered if the kid was close to breaking. His movements and gestures had the jerky, disconnected look the Chief had seen just before a subject tried to climb barbed wire or began screaming and couldn't stop.

So he sat down slowly, set his hat aside slowly, spoke slowly in a low, quiet, and what he hoped was an intimate tone.

"I know you have, Mr. Maitland," he said. "And I'm sorry to put you through this once again. But reading or even hearing reports is never good enough. It's always best to go right to the source. A one-on-one, man-to-man conversation. Less chance of misinterpretation. Don't you agree?"

"What difference does it make if I do or don't agree?" Theodore Maitland demanded. His eyes were on his bitten thumb, on the rug, the ceiling, the walls, the air. Anywhere but on Delaney. He would not or could not meet his eyes.

"I know what you've been through," the Chief soothed. "I really do. And this shouldn't take long. Just a few questions. A few minutes . . ."

The boy snorted and crossed his knees abruptly. He was, Delaney thought, a handsome lad in a bruised, masculine way—his father's son—and he wondered if the kid had a girlfriend. He hoped so.

"Mr. Maitland—" he started, then stopped. "Would you object if I called you Ted?" he asked gently. "I won't if you don't want me to."

"Call me anything you damn please," the boy said roughly.

"All right," Delaney said, still speaking slowly, softly, calmly. "Ted it is. Just let me run through, very briefly, your movements on the day your father was killed, and let's see if I've got it straight. Okay, Ted?"

Maitland made a sound, neither assent nor objection, uncrossed his legs, crossed them in the other direction. He turned in his armchair so one shoulder was presented to Delaney.

"You left here about nine-thirty that Friday morning," the Chief said. "Took the downtown IRT at Fifty-ninth Street. A local. Got off at Astor Place. Had classes at Cooper Union from ten to twelve. At noon you talked awhile with classmates out on the steps, then bought a couple of sandwiches and a can of beer and went over to eat your lunch in Washington Square Park. You were there until about one-thirty. Then you returned to Cooper Union in time for lectures from two o'clock to four. Then you returned directly home. Here. Is that correct?"

"Yes."

"You ate lunch in the park alone?"

"I said I did."

"Meet anyone you know, Ted?"

Maitland whirled to glare at him.

"No, I didn't meet anyone I know," he almost shouted. "I ate lunch alone. Is that a crime?"

Chief Delaney held up both hands, palms out.

"Whoa," he said. "No crime. No one's accusing you of anything. I'm just trying to get your movements straight. Yours and everyone else's who knew your father. That makes sense, doesn't it? No, it's no crime to eat alone in the park. And I don't even question that you didn't meet anyone you knew. I just walked down here from Seventy-ninth Street, and I didn't meet anyone I knew. It's natural and normal. Usually eat lunch alone, Ted?"

"Sometimes. When I feel like it."

"Frequently?"

"Two or three times a week. Why?" he demanded. "Is it important?"

"Oh Ted," Delaney said lightly, "in an investigation like this, everything is important. What are you studying at Cooper Union?"

"Graphic design," Maitland muttered.

"Decoration and printing?" Delaney asked. "Things like that?"

"Yeah," the boy grinned sourly. "Things like that."

"Proportion?" Delaney asked. "Visual composition? The history and theory of art? Layout and design?"

Ted Maitland met his eyes for the first time.

"Yes," he said grudgingly. "All that. How come a cop knows that?"

"I'm an amateur," Delaney shrugged. "I don't know a lot about art, but—"

"But you know what you like," the boy hooted.

"That's right," Delaney said mildly. "For instance, I like your father's work. What do you think of it, Ted?"

"Ridiculous," Maitland said. Scornful laugh. "Old-fashioned. Square. Dull. Out-of-date. Antique. Bloated. Emotional. Juvenile. Melodramatic. Reactionary. Is that enough for you?"

"Saul Geltman says your father was a great draftsman, a great anatomist, a great—"

"Saul Geltman!" Maitland interrupted angrily, almost choking. "I know *his* type!"

"What type is that?" Delaney asked.

"You don't know a thing about art in modern society," the boy said disdainfully. "You're stupid!"

"Tell me," Delaney said. "I want to learn."

Theodore Maitland turned to face him squarely. Leaned forward, arms on knees. Dark eyes aflame. Face wretched with his intensity. Quivering to get it out. Shaking with his fury.

"An upside-down pyramid. You understand? Balanced on its point. And above, all the shits like Saul Geltman. The dealers. Curators. Critics. Rich collectors. Hangers-on like Belle Sarazen. Trendy sellouts like Jake Dukker. Publishers of art books and reproductions. Rip-off pirates. Smart-asses who go to the previews and charity shows. The whole stinking bunch of them. The art lovers! Sweating to get in on the ground floor. Find a new style, a new talent, and ride it. Then sell out, take your profit, and go on to the next ten-day wonder. Leeches! All of them! And you know what that upside-down pyramid is balanced on? Supported by? Way down there? The creative artist. Oh yes! At the bottom of the heap. But the point of the whole thing. The guy who spends his talent because that's all he's got. He's the one who provides the champagne parties, the good life for the leeches. Yes! The poor miserable slob trying to get it down on paper or canvas, or in wood or metal. And they laugh at him. They do! They do! Laugh at him! Well, my father gave it to them. He gave it to them good! He saw them for the filth they are. Parasites! They were afraid of him. I mean literally afraid! But he was so good they couldn't ignore him, couldn't put him down. He could shit on them, and they had to take it. Because they knew what he had. What they'd never have. What they wanted and would never have. My father was a genius. A genius!"

Chief Delaney looked at him in astonishment. There was no mistaking the boy's fervor. It burned in his eyes. Showed in his clenched fists, trembling knees.

"But you told me you didn't like your father's work," Delaney said.

Ted Maitland jerked backward into his chair, collapsed, spread arms and legs wide. He looked at Delaney disgustedly.

"Ahh, Jesus!" he said, shaking his head. "You haven't understood a word I've said. Not a word. Dumb cop!"

"Let me try," Delaney said. "You might not like your father's work, his style, the paintings he did, but that has nothing to do with his talent. *That* you recognize and admire. What he did with his talent isn't what you like at all. Not your style. But no one can deny his genius. Certainly not you. Is that about right?"

"Yes," Maitland said. A voice so low Delaney could barely hear him. "That's about right . . . about right . . ."

"And you?" Delaney asked gently. "Do you have your father's talent?"

"No."

"Will you? Could you? I mean if you study, work . . ."

"No," the boy said. "Never. I know. And it's killing me. I want . . . Ahh, fuck it!"

He jumped to his feet, turned away, almost ran from the room. Delaney watched him go, made no effort to stop him. He sat on the couch a few moments, staring at the empty doorway. Everyone wanting. Either what they could not have, or more of what they had. The poor, greedy lot of them. Talent, money, fame, possessions, integrity—the prizes hung glittering just above their grasping fingers as they leapt, strained, grabbed air and fell back, sobbing . . .

The Chief stood and was moving toward the door when Alma Maitland came sweeping into the room, head up, fists balled: an avenging amazon. He had a moment to admire the mass of coppery hair piled high, the fitted suit of russet wool, the luxuriousness of her body and the glazed perfection of her skin.

Then she confronted him, stood close, directly in his path. For a second he thought she meant to strike him.

"Mrs. Maitland . . ." he murmured.

"What did you do to Ted?" she demanded loudly. "What did you *do* to him?"

"I did nothing to him," Delaney said sternly. "We discussed his movements on the day his father was killed. We talked about art and Ted's feelings about his father's work. If that was enough to upset him, I assure you it was none of my doing, madam."

She shrunk suddenly, shoulders drooping, head bowed. She held a small handkerchief in her fingers, twisting it, pulling it. Delaney looked at her coldly.

"Is the boy getting professional help?" he asked. "Psychologist? Psychiatrist?"

"No. Yes. He goes—"

"Psychiatrist?"

"He really doesn't—"

"How often?"

"Three afternoons a week. But he's showing—"

"How long has this been going on?"

"Almost three years. But his analyst said—"

"Has he ever become violent?"

"No. Well, he does—"

"To his father? Did he ever attack his father or fight with him?"

"You're not giving me time to answer," she cried frantically.

"The truth takes no time," he snapped at her. "Do you want me to ask the maid? The doorman? Neighbors? Did your son ever attack his father?"

"Yes," she whispered.

"How often?"

"Twice."

"During the past year?"

"Yes."

"Violently? Was one or both injured?"

"No, it was just—"

"Mrs. Maitland!" he thundered.

She was a step away from an armchair, and collapsed into it, huddling, shaking and distraught. But he observed that it had been a graceful fall, and even in the chair her posture of distress was pleasingly composed, knees together and turned sideways, ankles neatly crossed. The bent head with its gleaming plait revealed a graceful line of neck and shoulder. Victor Maitland, he reflected, wasn't the only artist in the family.

"Well?" he said.

"Once they fought," she said dully. "Victor knocked him down. It was horrible."

"And once . . . ?" he insisted.

"Once," she said, her voice raddled, "once Ted attacked him. Unexpectedly. For no reason."

"Attacked him? With his fists? A weapon?"

She couldn't answer. Or wouldn't.

"A knife," Delaney said. Declaration, not question.

She nodded dumbly, not showing him her face.

"What kind of a knife? A hunting knife? A carving knife?"

"A paring knife," she muttered. "A little thing. From the kitchen."

"Was your husband wounded?"

"A small cut," she said. "In his upper arm. Not deep. Nothing really."

"Was a doctor called?"

"Oh no. No. It was just a small cut. Nothing. Victor wouldn't see a doctor. I—I put on disinfectant and—and put a bandage on. With tape. Really, it was nothing."

"What is your doctor's name? Your family physician. And where is his office?"

She told him, and he made a careful note of it.

"Does your son own a knife? Hunting knife, a switchblade, pocket knife? Anything?"

"No," she said, shaking her head. "He had a—like a folding knife. Swiss. Red handle. But after he became—became—disturbed, I took it away from him."

"Took it away from him?"

"I mean I took it out of his dresser drawer."

"Where is it now?"

"I threw it away. Down the incinerator."

He stood, feet firmly planted, staring unblinking at the top of her head. He drew a deep breath and exhaled in a sigh.

"All right," he said. "I believe you."

She raised her head then, looked at him. He saw no sign of tears.

"He didn't," she said. "I swear to you, Ted didn't. He worshipped his father."

"Yes," Delaney said stonily, "so he told me."

He turned away and moved to the door. Then paused and turned back.

"One more thing, Mrs. Maitland," he said. "Did you know any of the models your husband used?"

She looked at him, bewildered.

"The girls or women your husband used in his paintings," Delaney said patiently. "Did you know any of them personally? By name?"

She shook her head. "Years ago I did. But not recently. Not in the past five years or so."

"A young girl? Very young. Puerto Rican perhaps, or Italian. Latin-type."

"No, I know no one like that. Why do you ask?"

He explained about the three charcoal sketches of the young model found in Victor Maitland's studio.

"They belong to you, of course," he said. "Or rather to your husband's estate. I wanted you to know they are presently in my possession and will be returned to the estate when our investigation is completed."

She nodded, apparently not caring. He made a small bow to her, and left.

He lumbered over to Third Avenue and turned uptown. In this busy shopping district—big department stores, smart shops, fast-food joints jammed with noonday crowds—he pondered proper Latin. Was it *qui bono* or *cui bono?* He decided on the latter.

Cui bono? The first question of any homicide dick: Who benefits? He had a disturbed son envious of his father's talent. A sexless wife furious at her husband's cheating. An art dealer scorned and humiliated in public. An artist friend jealous of the victim's integrity. A quondam mistress hating his contempt. A mother and sister deserted and left to flounder.

Some very highfalutin motives for murder—but *cui bono?*

Edward X. Delaney ambled northward, considering the possibility of failure by limiting his investigation to these seven suspects. But the Department's investigators had checked out all Maitland's known drinking companions, models, neighbors, prostitutes, even distant relatives and old army buddies. Zilch. So Delaney was left with the seven. *Cui bono?*

He picked up the photostats, paid, and asked for a receipt. He was keeping a careful list of all his expenses, to be submitted to the Department. He didn't expect salary, but he'd be damned if he'd pay for the pleasure of assisting the NYPD.

The house was empty when he returned. But there was a little note from Monica attached to the refrigerator door with a magnetic disk: "Gone supermarketing. You need new shirts. Buy some."

He smiled. It was true the collars on some of his shirts were frazzled. He remembered when men had their collars turned when they got in that condition. Their wives did it, or the shirts were taken to local tailors who had signs posted: WE TURN COLLARS. Put up a sign like that today, and no one would know what the hell you were talking about.

He took a can of cold ale to his study. He took off his jacket and draped it across the back of his swivel chair. But he didn't loosen his tie or roll up his cuffs. He repinned Maitland's charcoal sketches to the map board and slid the photostats in a lower desk drawer. He planned to show them to Jake Dukker and Belle Sarazen, hoping for a make.

He took a swallow of ale, then dialed the office of Deputy Commissioner Ivar Thorsen. He wasn't in, but Delaney spoke to his assistant, Sergeant Ed Galey, and explained what he wanted: an opinion from the Department's legal staff on how Victor's Maitland's estate would be divided under the laws of inheritance and succession of New York State.

"The man left no will," Delaney told Galey. "But there's a wife and eighteen-year-old son. Also a mother and sister. I want to know who gets what. Understand?"

"Got it, Chief," Galey said. "I'm making notes. Wife and son, eighteen years old. Mother and sister. How do they split?"

"Right," Delaney said. "That's it."

"The sister a minor?"

"No," Delaney said, thankful he was talking to a sharp cop, "she's in her thirties. How soon do you think I can get it?"

"It'll be a couple of days, at least. But we'll try to light a fire under them."

"Good. Thank you. One more thing, sergeant—is that Art Theft and Forgery Squad still in existence?"

"Far as I know. It's a little outfit. Two or three guys. They work out of Headquarters. Want the extension?"

"Yes, please."

"Hold on."

In a minute, Sergeant Galey was back with the phone number and the name of the commanding officer, Lieutenant Bernard Wolfe.

Delaney made a note, thanked him, and hung up. Two more swallows of ale. Then he called the Art Theft and Forgery Squad. The line was busy. More ale. Busy signal again. More ale. He finally got through, but the lieutenant wasn't there. He left his name and number and asked that Wolfe call him as soon as possible.

He drained off the ale and began writing out a report of his conversations with Theodore and Alma Maitland. He had almost finished when the phone rang, and he continued writing as he picked it up.

"Chief Edward X. Delaney here."

"Chief, this is Lieutenant Bernard Wolfe. Art Squad. I understand you called me?"

"Yes, lieutenant, I did. I'm working on the Victor Maitland homicide in a semi-official capacity."

"So I heard."

"Department grapevine?"

"Not so much the Department as the art-business grapevine. It's a small world, Chief; the word gets around."

"I imagine it does," Delaney said. "And I figure you know a lot about that small world. I think you could be a big help to me, lieutenant, and I was hoping we could get together."

"Be glad to," Wolfe said. "You say when and where."

Delaney started to make a date, then remembered that Sergeant Boone was arranging a meeting with J. Julian Simon.

"Suppose I call you Monday morning and we'll set a definite time and place," he said. "I'll call about ten. Will that be all right?"

Wolfe said that would be fine, and they hung up.

10

On Monday morning, Boone arrived, as usual, at nine A.M. Delaney went out in his shirtsleeves to invite the sergeant into the house.

"I thought we'd spend the day getting caught up," he told Boone. "Paperwork and so forth. And plan where we go from here."

"Fine with me, Chief," Boone nodded. "I brought along my notes on what happened on Friday."

They went into Delaney's study, and in a few minutes Monica brought in cups and a thermos of coffee, and a plate of miniature cinnamon doughnuts. She chatted a few minutes with Sergeant Boone, then left the two men together.

The first thing Delaney wanted to know was about the appointment with J. Julian Simon. Boone said it was set for ten o'clock the following morning, and the Chief made a careful note of it.

Then, both drinking black coffee and munching on their doughnuts, Boone told about his two time trials from Dukker's place to Victor Maitland's Mott Street studio. Delaney made notes as Boone reported. Neither man felt it necessary to comment on the significance of the trials.

At ten, Chief Delaney called Lieutenant Bernard Wolfe of the Art Theft and Forgery Squad and made a luncheon appointment for noon on Tuesday, at Keen's English Chop House on West 36th Street.

"Ever been there?" he asked Boone, after he had hung up.

"Never have, sir."

"Great mutton chops, if you can eat mutton at noon."

"What do you figure on getting from Wolfe?"

"Nothing specific. Maybe some useful background on the New York art scene. And maybe he can mooch around for us and pick up something on Maitland. At this stage I'll take anything—rumors, tips, gossip, whatever. All right, you go first; how did you make out with the Hemley woman?"

Boone had good recall and, consulting his notes only a few times, delivered an accurate report on his lunch and conversation with Susan Hemley. After he had finished, the two men sat in silence a few moments, staring holes in the air.

"Interesting," Delaney said finally. "She told you that Mrs. Maitland thought, quote, There was more to it than that, unquote. And when you pressed her on it, she suddenly had to get back to the office. What was your impression? Did she know and was scamming? Or did she really not know, and had to get back? Which?"

"I don't know," Boone said, troubled. "I've thought about it since, and I can't make a hard assessment."

"Guess."

"I'd guess she didn't know what Alma Maitland was talking about."

"All right. Let's accept that for now. How about Geltman's alibi? She saw him go in around ten, but she didn't see him come out at one-thirty?"

"That's right, Chief. She was at lunch with Alma Maitland, or on her way to lunch."

"And no one else in the office saw Geltman come out?"

"Right again. The office was empty. Everyone was out. So Geltman really has a one-man alibi: J. Julian Simon."

"How's this . . ." Delaney said. "It's not far from Simon's office to Le Provençal, where Hemley lunched with Alma Maitland. So let's say she leaves the office about one-fifteen. The moment she's gone, the coast is clear and Geltman ducks out, goes downtown and knocks Maitland. No, no, no. Scratch that. It doesn't listen. The Geltman staff and customers saw him back in the galleries at one-thirty, so he couldn't have done that."

"Son of a bitch!" Boone said bitterly, and when Delaney stared at him, the sergeant blushed.

"Sorry, sir," he said. "The Simon and Brewster offices are halfway down a long corridor from the elevator. A wood-paneled door leading to the outer office. That's where Susan Hemley has her desk. She said she talked a few minutes with Geltman that Friday morning, then he went into Simon's inner office. That's where she went to set up our appointment. But like a fool, I didn't check."

Delaney blinked twice, then smiled.

"A private entrance," he said. "From Simon's inner office out to the corridor. It isn't unusual to have a setup like that. So lawyers can duck out if there's someone in the outer office they don't want to see. Like a process server or a cop with a warrant."

"Right!" Boone said. "If Simon has a corridor door from his private office, Geltman could arrive at ten, and lam right out again. That would give him all the time in the world to get down to Mott Street, fix Maitland, and either return to Simon's office or go directly back to his Galleries. Sorry I missed that door, Chief."

"No harm done. We can check on it tomorrow. And Hemley said Simon and Geltman are old friends?"

"Yep. Play handball together."

"Cute. Playing ball together. Well . . . we'll see. What kind of a woman is this Hemley? Pretty?"

"Attractive enough. Not beautiful. Very thin. Not too young. Short, blonde, curly hair. No tits or ass. Good legs. Good voice. Not too much in the brains department."

"Sexy?"

Boone thought a moment.

"I'd say yes. Something there. Like if she let herself go, she'd be hell on wheels."

"If Geltman was right about maybe Alma Maitland being a lez, would there be that between them?"

Boone considered again, then sighed.

''Might be,'' he said. ''A possibility. I just can't say. What man could?''

''Certainly not me,'' Delaney rumbled. ''But did she come on with you? You know, man-woman stuff? Make a play? Angling for another date?''

''Nooo,'' Boone said slowly. ''Not really. Polite and friendly, but nothing heavy. Maybe I didn't turn her on. All I can do is tell you my feeling, that if I had invited her to an orgy, she'd have giggled and said, 'Sure!' ''

''Well, I'll meet her tomorrow morning and see how my take compares with yours. Now let me tell you about my little soiree with Ted and Alma Maitland.''

He reported to Boone everything that had happened during the interrogations of the two. The sergeant listened intently, making occasional notes but not interrupting. When Delaney finished, Boone looked up from his notebook, excited.

''Wow,'' he said. ''That's something. And all new. The business of Ted's violence wasn't in the tub, was it, sir?''

''No. Not a word.''

''Can we get the psychiatrist to talk?''

''No way. He'll clam. And legally.''

''So Ted boy was having his lunch alone in Washington Square Park. He says. You realize what that means, Chief? Alma says she was shopping alone. Sarazen and Dukker claim they were with each other, but they could have pulled it. Even the mother and sister could have driven down from Rockland in plenty of time for the fun. And Saul Geltman's half-ass alibi depends on J. Julian Simon, his old handball buddy. Beautiful. They're all guilty. What do we do now?''

''What we do now,'' Edward X. Delaney said, ''is construct a time chart. Names listed in a vertical column. Times in a horizontal line. So we can see at a glance where each of the seven was at any fifteen-minute period between nine o'clock that Friday morning and, say, five that afternoon. Or where they say they were. I have some graph paper around here somewhere; that'll get us started.''

They had hardly begun their time chart when Monica called them to lunch. She had set it out in the dining room, but it was a do-it-yourself sandwich luncheon. Sour rye, dark pumpernickel, fluffy challeh. Salami, bologna, braunschweiger, turkey. Tomatoes, radishes, cukes, slices of Spanish onion. Herring in sour cream. Olives. Kosher dills. German potato salad and cold baked beans. Dark beer for Delaney and iced tea for Boone. Monica sat with them, picked, and wouldn't let them talk business. So they could do nothing but eat and eat.

After, they helped her clear the table, wash up, get the leftovers put away.

''Just right,'' Delaney said, kissing her cheek. ''Hit the spot.''

''Great, Mrs. Delaney,'' Sergeant Boone said. ''I don't have food like that very often.''

He thought she murmured, ''You could,'' but he wasn't certain.

Then the two men went back into the study and got to work on the time chart. When they had finished, they had a handsome graph that showed the movements of the suspects almost minute by minute during the day of the murder. And, in colored pencil, it revealed whether the suspect's whereabouts were merely claimed or confirmed by one or more witnesses.

It proved nothing, of course; they didn't expect it would. But it did give them a visual image of all the action, and after it was pinned to the map board, alongside Maitland's charcoal sketches, they gazed at it with approval. It seemed to bring everything into focus.

The Chief went into the kitchen, and brought back a can of beer for himself and a bottle of tonic water for Boone. Then they sat staring at the time chart again and began blowing smoke, trying out scenarios on each other.

''I worked a case—'' they both said at the same time. Then both stopped, and both laughed.

"You first," Chief Delaney said.

"It wasn't much, sir," Boone said. "This was just after I made dick three. The precincts had their own detective squads then, and I was working the Two-oh. There was this fancy jewelry shop on Broadway, mostly good antique stuff, and the guy was losing stock. Regularly. Maybe one or two pieces a week. There was just him and his wife in the store, so we figured it had to be boosting. There was no cleaning guy, no signs of forced entry. We put on an inside stakeout, a man in the backroom looking through a peephole while customers were in the store. But no one was lifting. A real mindblower. One day this jeweler is on the Fifth Avenue bus, going downtown, and he sees this beautiful young twist sitting across from him. And she's wearing one of his missing pieces. He said it had to be; it was a brooch of rubies shaped like a rose. He said it was Victorian, and he didn't think there was another in the world like it. Anyway, he played it smart and didn't say anything to the young twist, but he followed her home, and then he called us. Well, to make a long story short, we found out the ruby brooch had been a gift to the young twist from her boyfriend. And where did he get it? From the jeweler's wife. Can you believe it? The boyfriend was a real nogoodnik, a gigolo-type, and was playing the old lady along for what he could get from her. I had to tell the jeweler; not the easiest thing I've ever done. But the point I'm trying to make is this: if it hadn't been for the chance meeting of the jeweler and the young twist on that Fifth Avenue bus, I doubt if we'd ever have broken it, until that jeweler was picked clean, down to the bare walls. It was an accident, a one-in-a-million break."

Delaney nodded. "My story is something like that, but the break was due more to the bad guy's stupidity than to accident. This was an extortion thing. The guy wasn't asking for much: five hundred in small bills. Peanuts considering the rap he was risking. He'd write these letters demanding the five hundred bucks or he'd throw acid on the mark's wife or kids. Nice. God knows how many paid up before one of the victims had the sense and balls to call us. And would you believe it, the extortion letter had been sent by metered mail. I guess the nut figured to save postage by mailing the letter from the office where he worked. We went to the postal inspectors, and it took one day to locate the meter from the number on the postmark, and a four-day stakeout to nab the guy who put the letter through the meter. He was trying it again. I remember he said he needed the money because he was studying at Delehanty—this was when they had civil-service courses—on how to get into the Police Academy. I don't think he ever made it. Well, you're figuring we'll get a break by chance, and I'm hoping for the same thing, but maybe from the stupidity of the killer."

Abner Boone grinned at him.

"Chief, that's figuring we're smarter than the bad guys."

"Any time you start doubting that, sergeant," Edward X. Delaney said seriously, "you better get into another line of work."

11

On Tuesday morning, the Chief sat in Boone's car outside the Delaney brownstone, listening to the sergeant report on his unsuccessful efforts to jog the memories of detectives who worked the original Maitland investigation.

"A cipher," Boone said gloomily. "They all say everything they saw, heard, or learned was in their reports. I'm afraid we draw zilch on this, Chief."

"I still think it was a good idea," Delaney said stubbornly. "Anyone left to contact?"

"Two," the sergeant said. "I'll try them tonight. One's just back from vacation, and the other's on a stakeout, and his loot won't tell me where. Down to Simon's office now?"

"Sure," Delaney said. "First we'll see if a corridor door—" He stopped suddenly, and said, "Wait a minute."

He got out of the car and went back into the house, into the kitchen. Monica was sitting on a high stool near the counter, sipping a third cup of morning coffee, making out her day's shopping list, and listening to WQXR on the kitchen transistor. She looked up when he came in.

"Forget something, dear?" she asked.

"Masking tape," he said. "I know we've got some of it somewhere."

"The end drawer," she said. "With the fuses, batteries, flashlight, hammer, screwdriver, pliers, Scotch tape, rubber bands, Elmer's glue, candles, Band-Aids, old corks, paint brushes, a can of—"

"All right, all right," he laughed. "I promised to straighten it out, and I will."

He found the roll of masking tape and tore off a piece about an inch long. Then he took a sheet from Monica's small scratchpad and pressed the tape onto it lightly.

"What are you doing?" she asked curously.

"Tricks of the trade," he advised loftily. "I don't tell you everything."

He kissed her quickly and left again.

"I couldn't care less," she yelled after him.

Back in the car, he showed Sergeant Boone his little sheet of paper with the square of masking tape lightly affixed.

"An old B-and-E artist taught me this trick," he explained. "Suppose you have a lot of panes of frosted glass. You want to identify one of them. In his case, it was the one he wanted to cut. When the light comes through, they all look alike. So if you can get inside, you put a little square of masking tape down in one corner. No one notices it. But when you're outside, with the light coming through, you can easily pick out the pane you want. If J. Julian Simon has a corridor door from his private office, we'll pull the gimmick in reverse. I'll show you how it works."

Boone took his word for it and drove downtown to the offices of Simon & Brewster. They finally found a metered space, three blocks away, parked, and walked back.

The attorneys' offices were on the sixth floor of a modern, ten-story office building. Clean lobby, no doorman, self-service elevator. Chief Delaney looked around, then inspected the register on the wall.

"Lawyers, art dealers, three foundations," he noted. "A trade magazine. A guy who repairs violins. Odds and ends. Not much traffic, I'd guess."

The elevator was small, but efficient enough. Silent. They stepped out at the sixth floor. They still hadn't seen anyone. Boone motioned down the corridor. He paused outside the walnut-paneled door bearing the golden legend: SIMON & BREWSTER, ATTORNEYS-AT-LAW. He looked at Delaney questioningly. The Chief waved him farther along the tiled hallway, then halted. He put his lips close to Boone's ear.

"When Susan Hemley went into Simon's inner office," he whispered, "which direction did she go?"

Boone thought a moment, turning, trying to orient himself. He pointed on down the corridor. They moved that way, to a frosted glass doorway with nothing on it but a number in gilt figures. They walked beyond it and found another door exactly like it, but with a higher number. Delaney looked at Boone, but the sergeant shrugged helplessly.

The Chief went back to the first frosted glass door and, standing to one side so his shadow would not be seen from inside, he unpeeled the little square of masking tape from its paper carrier. He stuck it lightly and deftly to the glass, at eye-height, next to the frame.

"Bright light out here," he said to Boone. "If that's the door to Simon's private office we should be able to see the tape from inside. For identification. So we don't get it mixed up with a door to a john or a storeroom. Let's go . . ."

He led the way and took off his straw skimmer when he entered the office. It was June 1st.

"Here we are, Miss Hemley," Boone smiled. "Right on time."

"You certainly are," she said. "A little early, in fact. Mr. Simon's on the phone. I'll tell him you're here as soon as he gets off."

"Miss Hemley, I'd like you to meet Chief Delaney. Chief, Miss Susan Hemley."

She held out her hand, and Delaney took it and bent over it in a bow that was almost courtly.

"Miss Hemley," he said. "Happy to meet you. Now I can understand the sergeant's enthusiasm."

"Oh Chief!" she said. "This is such a—a *thing* for me. I've read all about you. Your cases. You're famous!"

"Oh," he said, making a gesture. "The papers . . . You understand, I'm sure. They exaggerate. How long have you worked for Mr. Simon?"

"Almost six years," she said. "He's such a pleasure."

"So I understand," he said. "Well, our business shouldn't take long. We'll be out of your lovely hair before you know it."

Her hand rose mechanically, fingers poked at the tight blonde curls. Eyes glittered behind the black horn-rims.

"It's the Maitland case, isn't it?" she said breathlessly.

He nodded gravely, put a forefinger solemnly to his closed lips.

"I understand," she whispered. "I won't say a word."

A light went out on her six-button telephone. She caught it at once.

"He's off," she said. "I'll tell him you're here."

She rose and moved lithely to the door of Simon's inner office. Her full skirt whipped about her good legs. She knocked once, opened the door, entered, closed the door behind her. A ballet.

"You were right," Delaney murmured to Boone. "It's there."

She came back to them in a moment.

"Mr. Simon will see you now, gentlemen," she said brightly.

She ushered them in and closed the door gently, regretfully. The man behind the desk rose and came forward smiling, hand outstretched.

"Chief," he said. "Sergeant. I'm J. Julian Simon."

They shook hands, and Delaney remembered what Lincoln had said about men who "part their name in the middle."

Simon, moving smoothly and confidently, got them seated on a tufted, green leather chesterfield. Then he pulled over a castered armchair in the same leather and sat down facing them. He offered cigarettes in a silver case. When they declined, he returned the case to his inside jacket pocket without lighting a cigarette for himself. He leaned back, crossed his knees casually.

"Gentlemen," he said, "how may I help you?"

He was a shining man, so polished that a steely glow seemed to surround him. Silvery hair brushed to a mirror gleam. A white mustache exquisitely trimmed and waxed. A pink-and-white complexion massaged to health. Teeth too good to be true. Eyes like disks of sky. Fingernails alight with clear polish. Gold wrist-watch, tie clasp, and rings, one set with a square diamond, a tiny ice cube.

And the clothes! A suit of hard grey sharkskin with soaring lapels. Shirt of water blue. A tie that appeared to have been clipped from a sheet of chromium. Black moccasins with tassels as bushy as a shaving brush, the leather so glossy it seemed to have been oiled.

And his manner as artfully finished as his appearance. A resonant voice that flowed, deeply burbling. A laugh that boomed. Gestures as smooth, slow, and ornate as those of a deep-sea diver. Earnestness in his gaze. Sincerity in his brilliant smile. Elegance in the lift of a white eyebrow or the casual droop of a crossed foot. Altogether, a marvelous product.

"Sorry to bother you again with questions on the Maitland case, counselor," the Chief said, "but we just can't walk away from it."

"Of course not," the lawyer trumpeted. "We all want the crime solved and justice meted out."

"A beautiful office you have here," the Chief said, looking around. A glass door was set into an embrasure beyond the couch. It could not be seen clearly from where they sat.

"Thank you, Chief Delaney," Simon said complacently. He looked with satisfaction at his paneled walls, open bookcases, and framed Spy prints. "Nothing like oak and leather to impress the clients—what?"

The laugh boomed out, and they smiled dutifully.

"I suppose you want to know about Saul Geltman," the lawyer said, "since it's my only connection with the case. As I have heretofore stated, he entered my office, here, at approximately ten o'clock on the morning I've been told Victor Maitland was killed. Saul and I are both busy men, and we had postponed our conference too many times."

"You handle all his legal affairs, sir?" Sergeant Boone asked. "The Galleries too?"

"I do indeed," Simon nodded. "Also, his tax situation and estate planning. And I occasionally offer advice on his investment program, although I admit he sometimes doesn't take it!" Mouth snapped open, china teeth shone. "So we had a lot to discuss when we finally did get together that Friday morning. To reiterate, he arrived at approximately ten A.M. We discussed various matters, and around noon I called out for sandwiches and soft drinks. Which reminds me: I am derelict in my duties as host. I have a small but well-equipped bar here. May I offer you gentlemen anything?"

"Thank you, no," Delaney said. "But we appreciate the thought. Then after lunch you returned to your discussions?"

"Well, actually we talked as we ate, of course. The conference continued until about one-thirty when Saul left and, I understand, returned to the Geltman Galleries. And that's all I can tell you, gentlemen."

"He left at exactly one-thirty, counselor?" Delaney asked.

"Oh, not precisely." Simon waved such exactitude away: a matter of no importance. "Five minutes either way. To the best of my remembrance."

"Counselor, was Mr. Geltman out of your sight at any time on that Friday between ten and one-thirty?"

"Approximately," the lawyer admonished him.

"Approximately," Delaney agreed.

"No, he was not out of my sight between the approximate hours of ten and one-thirty that Friday. Oh, wait!" He snapped his finger crisply. "He did go into the john. Back there." He jerked a thumb over his shoulder, gesturing at a solid wooden door set into the wall between oak bookcases. "But he was only gone two or three minutes."

"Other than that, he was in your sight every minute during the period specified?"

"He was."

"Thank you very much," Chief Delaney said suddenly, clapped his notebook shut, rose abruptly. "You've been very cooperative, and we appreciate it."

Sergeant Boone stood up, and so did J. Julian Simon. The lawyer seemed surprised at the unexpected end of the questioning, pleasantly surprised. He beamed, grew more expansive, did everything but throw his arms about the cops' shoulders.

"Always happy to help out New York's Finest," he caroled.

"When the lunch came, did Miss Hemley bring it in?" Delaney demanded sharply.

"What?" Simon said, shaken. "I don't understand."

"You ordered sandwiches for you and Geltman. When your order was delivered, did Susan Hemley bring it into your office?"

"Why—ah—no, she didn't."

"Then the delivery man from the deli brought it in?"

"No, that's not the way it happened at all," Simon said, regaining his poise. "Miss Hemley called me on the intercom and said the delivery boy was outside with the lunch. So I went out, paid him, and brought the lunch back in here. But I fail to see—"

"It's nothing," Delaney assured him. "I'm an old woman; I admit it. I like to have every little detail straight, exactly how everything happened. Now I know. It certainly is a handsome office you have here, counselor."

He wandered about a moment, Sergeant Boone following him. The Chief inspected the caricatures on the walls, stroked the oak bookcases, touched the marble top of a small sideboard. And glanced toward the glass door. As did Sergeant Boone. They both saw the little square of masking tape clearly, outlined against the lighted corridor.

There were thanks and handshakes all around. More handshakes and farewells when they left Susan Hemley in the outer office. In the empty corridor, Delaney motioned Boone to stay where he was. Then he moved back to the frosted glass door and, standing to one side again, peeled the tape away. He came back to Boone, rolling the tape into a little ball between his fingers. He dropped it into his side pocket.

"Destroying the evidence," he said. "A felony."

There was a passenger in the elevator when it came down, so they didn't speak. Out on the street, walking toward their parked car, Delaney said, "I don't think he was lying about how the lunch got into the inner office, but just to make sure, check the delicatessen where it came from. Find out if the delivery boy saw Geltman. Also Susan Hemley. Did she take the sandwiches into the inner office, or did it happen as Simon told us? And if it did, did she see Geltman while the door was open? Maybe you better have another lunch with her."

"Can't I do it on the phone, Chief?" Boone asked.

Delaney looked sideways at him, surprised.

"Don't you like her?" he asked.

"She scares me," the sergeant confessed.

"Go on, have lunch with her," Delaney smiled. "She's not going to bite you."

"I'm not so sure," Boone said mournfully.

They sat awhile in the parked car, windows down, waiting for the car to cool. They were silent, going over the permutations and combinations.

"He could have made it out to the corridor," Boone offered finally. "Without Hemley seeing him."

"Could have," Delaney agreed. "Risky but possible. So we scratch another alibi. Now none of them is home free."

Boone nodded gloomily.

"Sergeant," Delaney said, almost dreamily, "I'm a bigot."

Boone turned to look at him.

"What, sir?"

"I am," the Chief insisted. "I have two great unreasoning prejudices. First, I hate Brussels sprouts. And second"—he paused dramatically—"I don't trust men who wear pinkie rings."

"Oh, that," Boone grinned.

"Yes," Delaney said. "That. Run him through Records, will you? Maybe he's got a sheet."

"J. Julian Simon?" Boone said incredulously. "A sheet?"

"Oh yes," Delaney nodded. "Maybe."

"Wow," Abner Boone said, looking at the overhead racks of customers' clay pipes. "This place must be a thousand years old."

"Not quite," Delaney said. "But it didn't open yesterday either."

They were in Keen's English Chop House, waiting for Lieutenant Bernard Wolfe to arrive. The Chief had rated a booth in the main dining room. When the ancient waiter had asked, "A little something, gentlemen?" the Chief had ordered a dry Gibson up, and looked to Boone.

"Just tomato juice for me," the sergeant said stolidly.

"A Virgin Mary," the waiter nodded wisely. "Also known as a Bloody Shame."

Boone grinned at him.

"You're so right," he said.

"If this place ever closes," Delaney said, looking around, "I'm dead. I mean, I'm not talking about the Pavillon and Chauveron and places like that. All gone. But I was never in them. I'm talking about places like Steuben's Tavern and the Blue Ribbon and Connollys on Twenty-third Street. Good, solid eating establishments. All gone. Beveled glass, Tiffany lamps, a mahogany bar. Enrico and Paglieri down in the Village. Moscowitz and Lupowitz over on Second Avenue. The food! You wouldn't believe. Real cops' restaurants when you wanted to spread. Things like boiled beef and horseradish sauce, a nice corn beef and cabbage, venison in season. Once I had wild-boar chops at Steuben's. Can you imagine? Honest drinks. Waiters who knew what it was all about. It's going, sergeant," he ended sorrowfully. "This place is one of the best and the last. If it disappears, where the hell are you going to get mutton in Manhattan?"

"Beats me, sir," Boone said solemnly, and Delaney laughed.

"Yes," he said, "I do get carried away. But it's hard to see the old places die. Although I suppose some good new places are coming along. The blessing of this city. It keeps rejuvenating itself. Well . . . here's our drinks. Now, where's Wolfe?"

And there he was, standing by their booth—but they couldn't believe it.

Tall, slender as a whip, with a devil's black beard and mustache. A suit of bottle-green velvet with nipped waist and flaring tails. A puce shirt, open collar, knotted scarf of paisley silk about a muscled throat. A dark, flashing man, lean, with hard eyes and a soft smile. All of him sharp as a blade, coldly handsome, a menace to every woman on earth and half the men. He took their startled looks, threw his head back, flashing the California whites.

"Don't let the threads fool you," he said. "My working uniform. At home in Brooklyn I wear dirty chinos and basketball sneakers. You must be Chief Delaney. I'm Loot Bernie Wolfe. Don't get up."

They shook hands all around, and he slid in next to Boone. The waiter appeared at his elbow, and he ordered a kir. He seemed to live with that raffish smile.

"Great," he said, looking around at the smoky walls and faded memorabilia. "I'll have a suckling pig on toast. Would you believe the last time I was in here was when I proposed?"

"How long have you been married?" Delaney asked.

"Who's married?" Wolfe asked. "But we're still intimate. On and off."

He kept it up through lunch—rare steak sandwiches for all, with pewter tankards of musty ale for Delaney and Wolfe—and they enjoyed his fresh, bouncy talk. He told them a cute one he had just closed.

"This East Side goniff with a penthouse, apparently plenty of dineros—well, he's into this and that. You know, import-export, plays the commodities market, etcetera. Suddenly, he's got the shorts. Who knows? Maybe he invested in a buggy-whip company or something. Anyway, he can't come up with the scratch, and he's hurting. The banks won't touch him, and he's leery of the sharks. Now this guy has got a nice collection of Matisse and Picasso drawings. Absolutely legit. Authenticated. Loaned out to at least three museum shows. No doubt about them; they're kosher. And insured for a hundred big ones. But that's not enough for him; he needs more to tide him over. Now you've got to know that modern drawings, simple black lines on white paper, are the easiest things in the world to fake. Photograph them. Trace them. Any which way. I mean a good forgery of a Rembrandt, say, that's something. A forgery of a Picasso scrawl, a plumber could do it. All right, so our bad guy hires himself a crew of flatnoses to rip off his own collection. The whole thing is snatched. The heist takes place while the guy is having a dinner party. Four people eating by candlelight, and these nasty pascudyniks bust in, show their heaters, strip the walls and take off. Witnesses—right? He figures that's a hundred G's for him on the insurance. And he knows the drawings will never be recovered because he's told the slobs in the ski masks to burn the shit. And it is shit, because what they took were fakes he had made. The real stuff is being peddled in Geneva—that's in Switzerland. So the guy plans to make it on the insurance plus what he makes on the sale of the real stuff in Europe. Coppish? All right, class, how did teacher break it?"

He grinned at them, back and forth, and both Delaney and Boone pondered.

Finally, the sergeant said, "You got a flash from Geneva that the real drawings were being pushed over there?"

"Nah," Lieutenant Bernard Wolfe said. "International cooperation isn't that good yet. But we're working on it. Maybe if a da Vinci had been glommed, they'd have been alerted. But not on a portfolio of modern drawings. How about you, Chief?"

"They guys in the ski masks tried to unload the fakes over here instead of burning them?"

"Right!" Wolfe said. "They got paid five thou for the ripoff. But then they got to thinking—which was a mistake because they were schmucks. They figured, why settle for the five G's? They could contact the insurance company and collect maybe another ten or twenty. The insurer would be happy to pay that for recovery. So that's what they did. A meet was arranged, and the insurance guy showed up with an art expert to make sure he was buying the true-blue stuff. The expert took one look and laughed. So the insurance company walked and tipped me. One thing led to another, and we busted all their asses. So how can I help you on the Maitland thing?"

They were having coffee and dessert by then. American coffee and fresh strawberries for Delaney and Boone, espresso and a kirsch for Wolfe.

"This art scene," the Chief said fretfully. "We don't know enough about it. It's a whole new world. Saul Geltman, Maitland's dealer—by the way, do you know him?"

"Sure do," Wolfe said cheerfully. "Nice little guy. Take off your rings before you shake hands with him."

"Oh-ho," Delaney said. "Like that, is it? Well, anyway, Geltman told us something of how dealers work with artists. Something about the art-gallery business. What I was hoping to get from you was more about the business of painting from the artist's point of view. How the money angle works."

"The money," Wolfe nodded. "What makes the world go 'round. From an artist's point of view? Okay. An unsuccessful artist, he's going to starve. You're not interested in that. A successful artist, his troubles are just beginning. Let's take a guy like Maitland, who makes it. Ten, fifteen years ago he's selling for peanuts. Today his stuff is pulling maybe two hundred thou. Fine, but what happens to the early stuff he was selling for walking-around money when no one knew who he was? I'll tell you what happens to it: the smartasses who bought it for kreplach, *they* made the lekach. Buy for a hundred, sell for a thousand. Profits like you wouldn't believe. And the artist gets nothing of that. Not a cent. Is that right? Of course it isn't right. Profiting like that on another man's work. It sucks."

"I agree," Delaney nodded. "Don't the artists scream?"

"Sure they do," Wolfe said. "For all the good it does them. Buy low, sell high. There's no law against it. It's the Eleventh Commandment. Now they're beginning to really *do* something about it. They say when you buy a guy's painting, you should sign an agreement that if you sell for profit in the future, the artist shares. Like ten or twenty percent of the profit. And the guy who buys the painting from the original buyer, if he also eventually sells, he's also got to share his profit with the artist. And so on."

"Makes sense to me," Boone said.

"Of course it makes sense," Wolfe said indignantly. "The present system is ridiculous. The artist sweats out the work; he should get at least a *share* of the bonanza if he hits. But the dealers and galleries and museums are fighting it. The old story: money, moola, mazuma. It'll cut into their take if the artists share. A crock of shit, I tell you. An artist who sold a painting for five hundred bucks ten years ago reads in the paper that it just went for half a mil—how do you think that makes him feel?"

"Is that what happened to Maitland?" Delaney asked.

"Sure," Wolfe said. "Exactly what happened to Maitland. I met him once. He was a six-ply bastard, but he was right on this thing. It drove him up the wall. Could I have another shot, Chief? All this talking is drying me out."

"Of course," Delaney said. "The Department's treat. Another kirsch?"

"No," Wolfe said. "I think I'll go back to the musty ale again. It goes down good. You're not drinking, sergeant?"

"Not today," Boone smiled.

"Good man," Wolfe said. "I spend half my time at exhibition previews and cocktail parties. They booze up a storm. Rots the liver. But it's all for the Department—right?"

Fresh ales were brought for Delaney and Wolfe. The lieutenant took a deep draft, then bent over the table toward the Chief. His black mustache had an icing of white foam.

"Okay," he said. "A successful artist like Victor Maitland gets fucked that way: the early paintings he sold for nothing end up getting traded for zillions, and he doesn't share. But there's another way he gets screwed. Let's take a young artist just starting out. He works his ass off. He's got so much drive and so many hot ideas, he hates to sleep. If he's lucky, he's selling maybe one out of every ten paintings. The others pile up—right? In his studio, the basement, the attic, homes of friends—wherever. Maybe he gives them away just to get rid of them. And a lot of these young artists barter paintings for meals and a place to work. So the years pass, the artist gets a wife and kids, and his stuff begins to sell. The prices go up, up, up. Meanwhile, he's still got the old things that no one wanted. But he keeps them around because that's all he's got to leave to his family. In case he drops dead, it's their inheritance. So one day he does drop dead, and he leaves his wife a few bucks and a studio full of his old paintings. Now this is where the screwing comes in: the U.S. Government, wearing its IRS hat, steps in to evaluate the dead artist's estate. They say all his old paintings have to be appraised at current market value, regardless of when they were painted. In other words, a very early Maitland is worth a hundred G's if the last few Maitlands sold on the open market for a hundred G's. So that's how they figure the estate tax. And New

York State figures *their* bite on what the IRS estimates. Sometimes the poor widow goes broke trying to pay those estate taxes, and sometimes she has to sell off the entire collection to make good. Just another sweet example of how society shits on the artist. Well . . . any of this any use to you?''

''Very useful, lieutenant,'' Delaney said. ''You've given us a lot to think about. But tell me this . . . you say when the artist becomes famous and starts to sell at higher prices, he still has a lot of his early, unsold stuff around. So why doesn't he sell that, too, as prices go up? Why not get the cash instead of leaving the stuff to his estate?''

''A lot of reasons,'' Wolfe said. ''Maybe his style has changed completely, and the old stuff looks like crap to him, and he's ashamed of it. Maybe his dealer tells him to keep it off the market. Listen, scarcity is one factor in the price a dealer can ask. If there's a warehouse of the guy's work available, the price drops. If only a few pieces are up for sale, the price goes up and stays up. Why do you think Picasso had so many unsold paintings when he died? Also, a lot of artists know from nothing about estate taxes; they're lousy businessmen. The poor schlemiel thinks he's leaving a tidy nest egg for the wife and kiddies, not knowing how it's going to be reduced by taxes. And also, maybe the artist does a painting that comes out so right, that he likes so much, that he doesn't ever want to sell it. He puts it on his wall and looks at it. Maybe he'll even make little changes in it as the years go by. Lighten a tint here, heavy a shadow there. But he'll keep it for years, maybe never put it up for sale at all. Look, Chief, when you're talking about artists, you're dealing with a bunch of nuts. Don't expect logical behavior from them, or even common sense. They ain't got it. If they had sense, they'd be truck drivers or shoe salesmen. It's a tough racket, and most of them fall by the wayside.''

''The reason I asked you why the successful artist didn't sell his old stuff,'' Delaney explained, ''is because there were no paintings in Victor Maitland's studio when the body was found.''

Lieutenant Bernard Wolfe was shocked. He jerked back from the table, looking in astonishment from Delaney to Boone.

''No paintings?'' he repeated. ''Nothing started? No canvases half-done? Nothing on his easel? No stacks of finished paintings? Nothing hung up for the varnish to dry. None of his own stuff on the walls?''

''No paintings,'' Delaney said patiently. ''Not a one.''

''Jesus Christ,'' Wolfe said. ''I can't believe it. I've been in a million artists' studios, and every one was jammed with paintings in all stages. The only thing I can figure is that someone cleaned Maitland out. Maybe the guy who whacked him. He should have had at least *one* painting there. He had the reputation of being a fast worker. But *nothing?* That smells.''

''We did find three charcoal sketches,'' Sergeant Boone said. ''Geltman claims they were probably preliminary drawings of a new model Maitland was trying out.''

''Could be,'' Wolfe nodded. ''They do that sometimes: knock off a few quick sketches of a fresh girl to see if she's simpatico.''

''That's another thing,'' the Chief said. ''Do you know many models?''

''My share,'' Wolfe grinned. ''Want me to look at the drawings to see if I can make her?''

''Would you? We'd appreciate it.''

''Be glad to. Just tell me where and when. I'm in and out of the office all the time, but you can always leave a message.''

Delaney nodded, and called for the bill. He paid, and they all rose and moved to the door. Out on the sidewalk, they shook hands with the lieutenant and thanked him for his help. He waved it away, and thanked them for the lunch.

''And look into that business of no paintings in the studio,'' he said.

* * *

The evening was still young, not yet midnight, and perhaps they thought to talk lazily awhile, or maybe even go downstairs again for a late snack. In any event, the room was still lighted, and they lay awake, temporarily sated, when the bedside phone shrilled.

He cleared his throat and answered.

"Edward X. Delaney here."

It was Rebecca Hirsch, her words tumbling in a torrent, voice screechy, stretched, almost breaking. He tried to interrupt, to slow her down, but she was too distraught to pause. Began weeping, didn't answer his questions. Finally he just let her rattle, until sobs stopped her. He could reckon then what had happened, was happening.

Abner Boone had called her almost an hour previously, obviously drunk. It was a farewell call; he said he was going to blow his brains out with his service revolver. Rebecca had been in bed, had dressed hastily, hurried over in a cab. Boone was falling-down drunk, bouncing off the walls drunk. He had an almost full bottle, and was drinking from that. Gibbering. When she tried to grab the whiskey from him, he had rushed into the bathroom and locked the door. He was still in there, wouldn't come out, wouldn't answer her.

"All right," Delaney said stonily. "Stay there. If he comes out, don't try to take the bottle. Speak quietly to him. And keep out of his way. I'll be right over. Meanwhile, look around. Everywhere. For another bottle. And for a gun. I'll be there as soon as I can."

He hung up and got out of bed. He told Monica what had happened as he dressed. Her face grew bleak.

"You were right," she said.

"I'll send Rebecca back here," he said. "In a cab. Watch for her. I may spend the night there. I'll call you and tell you what's happening."

"Edward, be careful," she said.

He nodded, and unlocked his equipment drawer in the bedside table. His guns were in there, with cartridges and cleaning tools. A gun belt. Two holsters. Handcuffs. A steel-linked "come-along." A set of lock picks. But the only thing he took was a leather-covered sap, about eight inches long. It stuck out of his hip pocket, but the tail of his jacket covered it. He relocked the drawer carefully.

"Come down with me and put the chain on when I leave," he told Monica. "Open it only for Rebecca. Get some hot coffee into her, and maybe a shot of brandy."

"Be careful, Edward," she repeated.

Outside, he paused until he heard the chain clink into place. Then he debated how he could make the best time, cab or walking. He decided on a cab, strode over to First Avenue as quickly as he could. He waited for almost five minutes, then stepped into the path of an on-coming hack showing Off-duty lights. It squealed to a halt, the bumper a foot away. The furious driver leaned out.

"Cancha—" he began bellowing.

"Five to East Eighty-fifth Street," Delaney said, waving the bill.

"Get in," the driver said.

At Boone's apartment house, there was a night doorman on duty, sitting behind a high counter. He looked up as Delaney stalked in.

"Yes?" he said.

"Abner Boone's apartment."

"I need your name," the doorman said. "I gotta ring up first. Rules."

"Delaney."

The doorman picked up his phone, dialed a three-digit number.

"A Mr. Delaney to see Mr. Boone," he said.

He hung up and looked at the Chief.

"A woman answered," he said suspiciously.

"My daughter," Delaney said coldly.

"I don't want no trouble," the doorman said.

"Neither do I," Delaney said. "I'll waltz her out of here nice and quiet, and you never saw a thing."

The doorman's hand folded around the proffered sawbuck.

"Right," he said.

When he got off the elevator, Rebecca was waiting in the corridor, hands wrestling. She didn't look good to him: greenish-white, hair dank and scraggly, pupils dilated, lips bitten. He knew the signs.

"Yes, yes," he said softly. He slid an arm gently about her shoulders. "All right now. All right."

"I didn't," she stammered. "He wouldn't. I couldn't."

"Yes, yes," he repeated in a monotone, drew her into the apartment, closed the door behind him. "He's still in there?"

She nodded dumbly. She began to shake, her entire soft body trembling. He stood apart from her, but touched her with his hands: patted her shoulders, stroked her arms, pressed her hands lightly.

"Yes, yes," he intoned. "All right. All right now. It's going to be all right. Deep breath. Come on, take a deep breath. Another. That's it. That's fine."

"He can't—" she choked.

"Yes," he said. "Yes. Of course. Now come on over here and sit down. Just for a minute. Lean on me. That's right. That's it. Now just breathe deeply. Catch your breath. Good. Good."

He sat beside her a few moments until breathing eased, trembling stopped. He brought her a glass of water from the kitchen. She gulped frantically, water spilling down her chin. He went through the bedroom to the bathroom door. He pressed his ear against the thin wooden paneling. He heard mumbling, a few incoherent words. He tried the knob gently; the door was still locked.

He went back, sat down beside her. He took her hands again.

"Rebecca?" he said. "Better?"

She nodded.

"Good," he said quietly. "That's good. You're looking better, too. Did you find another bottle?"

She shook her head violently, hair flying.

"A gun?"

The headshake again.

"All right. Now I'm going to do something, but I need your help. Do you think you can help me?"

"What?" she said. "Will he—"

"We've got to get the whiskey away from him," he explained patiently, looking into her eyes. "And his gun. You understand?"

She nodded.

"I'm going to break in. As suddenly and quickly as I can. I'll try to get the bottle first. He may resist. You know that, don't you, Rebecca?"

Again she nodded.

"If I get hold of the bottle, I'll hand it to you or toss it to you. Then I'll take care of the gun. But your responsibility is the bottle. Grab it any way you can and run. Take it to the kitchen sink and empty it. Don't worry if it falls. Just make sure it's emptied, in the sink, on the floor, out the window—I don't care. Just get rid of the booze. Can you do that, Rebecca?"

"I—I think I can. You won't—won't hurt him, will you?"

"I don't want to," he said. "But you just worry about dumping the whiskey. All right?"

"All right," she whispered. "Please don't hurt him, Edward. He's sick."

"I know," he said grimly. "And he's going to be sicker. Think you can handle it now? Good. Let's go."

He led her to the bathroom door, a hand under her elbow. He positioned her behind him, to his right. He managed to transfer the leather-covered sap to his righthand jacket pocket. He didn't think she saw it.

He glanced at her, hoped she'd do. He stood directly in front of the bathroom door.

"This is Chief Edward X. Delaney," he called in a loud, harsh voice. "Come out of there, Boone."

There was mumbling. Then a slurred, "G'fuck y'self."

"This is Chief Edward—" Delaney began again, then raised his right knee high, almost to his chin, and drove his right foot against the door, just above the lock and knob. There was a splintering crack, the door sprung wide, smacked the tiled wall, began to bounce back. But by then Delaney was inside, moving fast.

Abner Boone, sitting hunched over on the closed toilet seat, bottle close to his mouth, couldn't react fast enough. Delaney grabbed the bottle away with a wide swipe, tossed it behind him, heard it thump to the bedroom rug, heard Rebecca's gasp. He didn't glance back.

Boone was raising his head in a drunk's delayed response, features changing comically to surprise, outrage. Delaney, swinging an arm from the shoulder, hit the sergeant across the face with an open palm. It smacked the man's head around, left him quivering, face reddening.

"Cocksucker," Delaney said, without expression.

He stepped quickly back through the doorway into the bedroom. Waited tensely. Knees slightly bent. Sap held in his right hand, behind him. He heard water running in the kitchen. Heard Rebecca's loud sobs.

Boone came out with a rush, a roar of fury. Hands reaching. Delaney leaned to one side. Feet firmly planted. As Boone fell past, the Chief put the sap alongside his skull. Not a blow, but a tap. Just laying it on. Almost nestling it on. The street cop's gentling stroke: not enough to split the skin, concuss, or break the bone. A matter of experience. It made the knees melt, the eyes turn up. Boone dropped face down onto the bedroom rug.

The Chief stooped swiftly, found the sergeant's gun. He yanked it from the short holster, slid it into his own jacket pocket. Then he put his sap away. His pocket, out of sight. Rebecca came from the kitchen, carrying an empty whiskey bottle foolishly. She saw Boone stretched out, face down. She wailed.

"Is he—" she coughed.

"Passed out," Delaney said crisply. He took the empty bottle from her limp hand, tossed it onto the couch. "You did fine. Just fine. Do you have any money?"

"What?" she said.

"Money," he repeated patiently. "Where's your purse?"

They found her purse on the floor, alongside the couch. She had some singles and a five.

"Take a cab back to Monica," Delaney instructed her. "Wait downstairs in the lobby until the doorman gets you a cab. Give him a dollar. Got that? Take the cab to Monica. She's waiting for you. All clear?"

"Is he—? Will he—?"

"Understand what I just said? Take a cab. Monica is waiting for you."

She nodded, dazed again. He hung the purse on her arm, pushed her gently toward the door. When she was gone, he locked up behind her, put on the chain. Came back and searched for another bottle, another gun. Found nothing. Boone was beginning to stir. Mutter. Make thick, gulping sounds.

Delaney called Monica, gave her a brief report. He told her to watch for Rebecca and to call him if she didn't arrive within twenty minutes. Then he let down all the venetian blinds, closed them. He stripped to his shorts. Boone was heaving in deep retches. He took him by the neck: collar of shirt and collar of jacket. He dragged him across the bedroom floor back into the bathroom, the sergeant's toes making rough furrows in the rug. He lifted and dumped him face down into the tub. Boone's head, arms, shoulders, upper torso were inside the tub. Balanced on the rim on his waist. Hips and legs outside the tub.

Immediately he began to vomit. Food, liquid, bile. It came out of him in a thick flood. Bits of spaghetti. Meatballs. Slime. The stench was something, but Delaney was a cop; he had smelled worse.

He turned on the shower, adjusted it to a hard, cool spray. He let it splay over Boone's head and shoulders. It washed the vomit down to the drain, which almost immediately clogged. The slurry began to back up. Delaney took hold of Boone's right wrist. The hand hung limply. Using the nerveless fingers as a soft claw, he brushed at the clogged drain until the liquid ran out. It didn't sicken him.

He turned off the shower, dragged Boone back to the bedroom rug. Let him drain a minute, then turned him over. Now the sergeant was hacking and coughing. But his tracheal passage seemed reasonably clear; he was breathing in harsh, grating sobs.

Delaney kneeled beside him and wrestled him out of his sodden clothes. It took a long time, and the Chief was grunting and sweating by the time he got Boone down to his stained briefs. He levered him onto the bed, atop a crumpled sheet and light wool blanket. It seemed to him Boone was breathing okay, but muttering occasionally, twisting, head whipping side to side.

Delaney went into the kitchen, found some paper napkins. He cleaned up the solid vomitus in the bathroom tub as best he could, and flushed the mess down the toilet. He looked in at Boone. No change. So Delaney took a hot shower in his underwear, soaping everything. He wrung out his underwear, hung it on a towel rack. He rubbed himself dry with one of Boone's towels, then knotted it about his thick waist and padded barefoot back into the bedroom. Boone was snoring, mouth open, fretful line between his eyebrows.

Delaney called Monica again, and they talked awhile. She had Rebecca calmed and lying down in the spare bedroom. He told her everything was under control, and he'd be home in the morning. They spoke briefly, sadly, and both said, "I love you" before they hung up. It was necessary.

Still wearing the knotted towel, he checked the apartment again. Everywhere. He could find no more whiskey nor another gun. There were small containers of after-shave lotion and rubbing alcohol. He poured both down the sink, and dropped the empty bottles into the kitchen garbage can. He also looked for money, but found only Boone's wallet in the hip pocket of his damp trousers. It held eighteen dollars in fives and singles. Delaney slid the wallet under a cushion of the living room couch.

Boone was still sleeping restlessly in the bedroom. Snoring, twitching, turning. Delaney left him there, found a linen cupboard with a scant supply of unpressed sheets and pillowcases. He put a sheet over the living-room couch, an empty pillowcase over the couch arm. He covered himself with another sheet. Before he settled down, he slid his leather-covered sap and Boone's revolver under the couch, within easy reach. Then he put his head on the hard couch arm. He could hear Boone in the bedroom. Stertorous breathing, gasps, moans. An occasional cough. A sob.

Delaney dozed. Light sleep. Awake. Light sleep. Alert. Then, much later, he heard Boone moving, groaning. Delaney reached for the sap, swung his feet onto the floor. He padded gently over to the bedroom door, peeked in. In dim nightlight he could see Boone sitting on the edge of the bed. He was fumbling with pencil and pad on the bedside table, muttering to himself. He wrote something with the exaggerated attention, the tongue-out care of a drunk. Still muttering. Then fell back into bed, began to snore again.

Delaney went in silently, lifted Boone's lower legs and feet onto the wrinkled sheet, covered him with the wool blanket. The man stank stalely. Delaney took the scratchpad back to the bathroom, switched on the light. He read what Boone had scrawled. As far as he could make out, it read: "Mon two clean." Delaney put it aside, turned off the light. He stumbled back to the lumpy couch. He went through the motions of settling down to sleep.

He woke early the next morning, stared wrathfully about at strange surroundings. He remembered the operatic night with disgust, and was thankful things had not been worse. He rose groggily and looked in on Boone. The sergeant was sleeping in the center of the bed, head bowed, spine curved, knees drawn up in the fetal position.

Delaney went into the bathroom. He rubbed cold water on his face, felt the bristle. He looked in the mirror. White. An old man's beard. Boone's shaving gear was in the medicine cabinet, but the Chief didn't use it. He squeezed some toothpaste onto his forefinger and scrubbed his teeth. And he used Boone's comb and brush.

He went into the kitchen. The spareness of supplies and equipment dismayed him. What a way for a man to live! An expensive apartment with sticks of furniture, and nothing in the refrigerator but a hunk of store cheese, an opened package of dried bologna, and two bruised tomatoes.

Delaney found a jar of instant coffee in the cupboard above the sink. He made himself a cup, not bothering to boil water but using hot water right out of the tap.

He was sitting there, sipping slowly, brooding grumpily, when Boone came in. The sergeant was wearing a threadbare robe. His feet were bare. Neither man said anything nor looked at the other. Boone did what Delaney had done: made a cup of coffee with water from the tap. He also took a little bottle from the cupboard over the sink and popped two aspirin, dry. Then he sat down at the rickety table, facing Delaney.

Boone couldn't lift the full cup. He leaned forward and slurped up a few mouthfuls of the hot brew. Then, the level of coffee well below the rim, he picked up the cup slowly, using both trembling hands. He moved it cautiously to his lips, his head bending far down to meet it.

"You prick," Chief Delaney said tonelessly. "You shit-eating son of a bitch. Bastardly piss-hole. You rotten, no-good motherfucker. You can crawl into a bottle and pull the cork in after you for all I care. But when you hurt a good woman who believed in you, a woman I like and admire, then it becomes my business. And what you've done to my wife. We invited you to our home. You ate at our table. And Ivar Thorsen, who stuck his neck out for you. Not once, but a dozen times. And you shit on all of us, you filthy cocksucker."

Then Boone looked up at him. Eyes dulled and swollen. Bits of white matter in the corners. Smutty shadows below.

"Forget it," he said. Voice thready, he almost coughed. "You're just blowing off. You don't understand."

"Tell me then."

"If I don't count, then no one counts."

"Oh?" Delaney said. "Like that, is it?"

"Yes."

"Why don't you count?"

"I just don't. I'm nothing."

"You say," Delaney said furiously. And, not knowing how to refute this without praising a man he had just damned, said nothing more.

They both sat in silence. After awhile Delaney made himself another cup of coffee. When he was seated again, Boone rose and did the same thing. This time he was able to get the cup to his lips.

"Am I out?" he asked hoarsely.

"It's up to Thorsen."

"You going to tell him?"

"Of course. I'm not going to cover for you. I'll tell him just how it was."

"He'll take your recommendation," Boone said hopefully. "In or out."

Delaney didn't reply.

"If I told you it won't happen again," the sergeant said, "would you believe me?"

"No."

"I don't blame you," Boone said miserably. "I'd be lying. I can't make a promise like that."

Delaney looked at him pityingly.

"What in Christ's name set you off?"

"I called one of the dicks who worked the Maitland thing. He had just come off a long stakeout, and he and two of his buddies were unwinding in a Yorkville joint. Not too far from here. I figured it was a good chance to talk to him, so I walked over. They were drinking boilermakers, but no one was juiced. Yet. So I sat in a booth with them. It's been a long time; I had forgotten how good that can be; four cops sitting around drinking, blowing smoke, and kidding. After awhile they noticed I wasn't drinking and said I was spoiling the party. I'm not blaming them. No one twisted my balls. So I had a beer. The best I've ever tasted. Ice-cold. Moisture running down the bottle. Creamy head on the glass. That tart, malty taste. After awhile I was drinking boilermakers with them. Then we were all zonked. I don't remember getting home. I remember Rebecca being here."

"You called her," Delaney said.

"I suppose I did," Boone said sadly. "And I remember, vaguely, your being here. Did I call you?"

"No. Becky did."

"Most of it's a blackout," Boone confessed. "Jesus!" he said, and touched his head tenderly behind his ear. "I got a lump. Sore as hell. I must have fallen."

"No," Delaney said, "You didn't fall. I sapped you."

"Sapped me?" the sergeant said. "Well, I guess I needed it."

"You did," Delaney said grimly.

He rose, stalked into the living room, came back with the scrap of paper. He thrust it at Boone.

"What the hell's this?" he demanded. "You wrote it last night. After I got you into bed. You passed out, then got up, scribbled this thing and went back to sleep. 'Mon two clean.' What does that mean?"

Abner Boone stared at the piece of paper. Then he covered his eyes with his hand.

" 'Mon two clean,' " he repeated, then looked up. "Yes. Right. I remember now. When I first got there, before we were all gibbering like apes, I asked the dick who worked the Maitland case if there was anything not in his reports. Anything he heard, saw or found. Or guessed. He said no, nothing. Then, almost five minutes later, he snapped his fingers and said there was something. A little thing. The clunk was discovered on Sunday—right? So naturally they put up sawhorses and sealed off the house. The local precinct sent over a couple of street cops to keep the rubbernecks away. Then, on Monday, they were letting tenants in and out, but Maitland's studio was still off-limits. Some of the lab guys were working in there, and there was a precinct cop on the landing to guard the door."

Sergeant Boone got up, went to the sink, drank off two glasses of water as fast as he could gulp them. He brought a third glassful over to the table and sat down again.

"A couple of days later—the dick who told me the story says maybe it was Wednesday or Thursday; he can't remember—the precinct cop who had been guarding the door of Maitland's studio on Monday came to him and said that on Monday morning two women started up the last flight of stairs to Maitland's studio. He asked them what they wanted. The older woman said they were looking for cleaning work to do—you know, dusting, vacuuming, washing windows, and so forth. The cop told them they couldn't come up; the guy who lived there was dead. So they split."

" 'The older woman'?" Delaney said. "Then there was a younger one. How young? What were the ages, approximately?"

"The dick didn't know," Boone said. "He just said the cop had mentioned two dames, and the older one did the talking."

"Accent?"

"He didn't know."

"White? Black? Spanish? What?"

"The dick didn't know. The cop didn't say."

"Why did the cop wait two or three days before he told the detective about this?"

"He said he thought at first it was nothing. That the two women really were looking for cleaning work. Then, when he heard the investigation was getting nowhere, he thought it might possibly be something."

"Smart cop."

"Sure, Chief," Boone nodded. "And also, the cop probably figured if he told a detective, then he was off the hook. Then it was the dick's problem, not his."

"Right. Did the dick remember the cop's name?"

"No. Never saw him before or after. Says he was a black. That's all he remembers."

"Did he try to check it out? Find the women?"

"No. He thought it was nothing. Just what the older woman said: they were looking for cleaning work to do."

"All right," Delaney said, "now here's what you do: Go down to the Mott Street precinct and check their rosters. Get the name, home address, and badge number of the cop who was on guard duty at Maitland's studio that Monday morning. Don't try to brace him. I want to be there. Just identify him. Then go back to Maitland's Mott Street address. Go during the day, and also in the evening, when most of the tenants will be home from work. Ask them if anyone came around looking for cleaning work to do. During the week Maitland was burned, or any other time before or after. Call me at home tonight. Got all that?"

"Yes, sir," Sergeant Boone said, "Chief, does this mean I'm still in?"

"For today," Delaney said. "Until I have a chance to report to Deputy Commissioner Thorsen. You shithead!"

By the time he had showered, shaved, donned blessedly fresh linen and his favorite flannel slacks (double pleats at the waist), Monica was just putting the finishing touches to his late breakfast: scrambled eggs, onions and lox, toasted bagels with cream cheese, and coffee that didn't taste as if it came out of the tap.

She sat at the oak kitchen table with him, nibbling on half his bagel, sipping coffee. She told him of her problems with Rebecca the previous night.

"She wanted to call every five minutes," Monica said. "She was afraid you'd hurt him. You didn't, did you, Edward?"

"Not enough," he growled.

"Well, she's over there now. She went as soon as I told her you were coming back—to see if he's all right."

"He's all right," Delaney assured her. "And she's a fool. There's no guarantee he won't do it again. He admitted that himself."

"Did you give him back his gun?"

"Yes. He's a cop on active duty and needs it. It makes no difference; if he's intent on suicide, he'll find a way, gun or no gun. Rebecca should stay away from him. Just drop him. He's bad news."

"What are you going to do about him?"

"I don't know. If I bounce him and ask Thorsen to get me another man, he'll flush Boone down the drain."

"Everyone deserves a second chance, Edward."

His head snapped up; he stared at her.

"Is that so?" he said. "Do you really believe that? Ax-murderers and mutliple rapists? Guys who blow up airliners and kill infants? They all deserve a second chance?"

"Will you stop that?" she said angrily. "Abner isn't in that class, and you know it."

"I'm just trying to point out that 'Everyone deserves a second chance' is not valid in all cases. It sounds nice and Christian, but I wouldn't care to see it become the law of the land. Besides, Boone has had a second chance, and a third, and a fourth, and so on. Thorsen has given him his second chance, and then some!"

"You haven't," Monica said softly. "Was what he did really so bad? It didn't interfere with his job, did it?"

"No," he said shortly, "but if he does it again, it might."

"You're disappointed in him," she said. And when she saw his expression, she added hastily, "And I am, too. But can't you keep him on, Edward? I know—I think—I feel that if you dump him now, it would be the end of him. Really the end. No hope left."

"I'll think about it," he said grudgingly.

He moved his chair back a bit so he could cross his legs. He lighted a cigar to enjoy with his final cup of coffee. He blew a plume of smoke into the air, then looked at Monica. She was staring moodily into her cup.

Morning sunshine glinted from her shiny hair. He saw the sweet curve of throat and cheek. Solid body planted. Her flesh alive and firm. All of her assertively womanly. The strength!

Then he looked about the warm, fragrant kitchen. Worn things gleaming. Crumbs on the counter. A full larder. All the dear, familiar sights of the best room in the house. The hearth. The drawbridge up, moat flooded.

She saw something in his face and asked, "What are you thinking about?"

"An empty refrigerator," he said, and rose to kiss her.

Abner Boone had showered and shaved, scowling at his hollowed eyes and caved-in cheeks. He dressed, checked his ID and revolver, and started from the apartment. When he opened the outside door, there was Rebecca Hirsch, her hand raised to knock. They stared at each other, her hand falling slowly to her side.

"I just—" she said huskily, then caught her breath. "I just want to see if you're all right."

"I'm all right," he nodded. "Come in."

He held the door wide for her. She came in hesitantly, sat at one end of the couch. He sat across the room.

"You're going out?" she said. "Maybe I better go."

"It can wait," he said. "I want to talk to you. I'm sorry about last night. 'Sorry.' Whatever that means. Rebecca, I don't think we should see each other any more."

"You don't want to see me?"

"I didn't say that. But it's not going to work. Last night proved it."

"Why do you do it, Ab?"

"Lots of reasons. I told the Chief it was because of the filth I see as a cop. That's one reason. It's true. Losing my wife is another reason. That's true, too. Want to hear another reason? I like whiskey. And beer and wine. I like the taste. I like what alcohol does for me."

"What does it do for you?"

"Dulls anxieties. Makes everything seem a little better. Two ways: either there's hope, or it doesn't make any difference if there isn't any hope. Either way, it helps. Can you understand that?"

"No," she said. "I don't understand."

"I know you don't," he said. "I don't expect you to or blame you. It's my fault; I know that."

"What about AA?" she said. "Medicine? Counseling? Therapy?"

"Had 'em all," he said stonily. "I just can't hack it. You better walk."

"There's a way," she said.

He shook his head. "I don't think so. I'm one short step away from a pint of muscatel in a brown paper bag. Shuffling along."

"Jesus!" she gasped. "Don't say that!"

"It's true. Get out while you can."

They sat staring at each other, two species, so different. She with the gloss of unwounded health, he with the pallor of defeat.

"If you could love me . . ." she tried.

"Redeemed by the love of a good woman?" He smiled sadly. "You're something, you are."

"I didn't say that," she said angrily. "You already have my love. You must know that. And it didn't keep you from . . . No, what I meant was your loving me. And knowing you'll lose me if—if it happens again. That might work—if you could love me."

"It wouldn't be hard," hc said gallantly.

"You say," she scoffed. "But I think it might be. For you. It wouldn't come easily. You'd have to work at it."

He looked at her curiously.

She flung back her hair, smoothed it from her temples with both palms.

"Oh yes," she said. "My motives are purely selfish. But then, if it kept you from drinking, if it saved your job, your motives would be selfish too, wouldn't they?"

"You're a Jewish Jesuit," he said.

"Am I?" she said. "Not really. Just a woman who knows what she wants and is trying to get it. I lay awake last night thinking about it. It's worth a try. Don't you think it's worth a try?"

He was silent.

She said: "Unless the idea of absolute doom is so attractive to you?"

He shook his head wildly. "I don't like it. I swear I don't. It frightens me."

"Well then?"

"All right," he nodded. "With the understanding that you walk whenever you want to. Okay?"

"Okay," she said.

"One more thing," he said. "Don't, please don't, plead with the Chief for me. If he cans me, he cans me, and that's it."

"I understand," she said gravely.

"You see," he said with a flimsy grin, "I don't want the woman I love begging."

She smiled for the first time, eyes glistening.

"See?" she said. "It's working already."

They went down in the elevator together, making plans. When they separated on the street, he kissed her fingers and she touched his cheek.

12 When Delaney climbed into Boone's car on the following morning, carrying the Maitland charcoal sketches rolled up, the two men carefully avoided looking at each other.

"Morning, sir," the sergeant said.

"Morning," the Chief said. "Feels like rain."

"The radio says partly cloudy," Boone offered.

"My bunion says rain," Delaney stated, and that was that. "Let's get caught up . . ."

Both men opened their notebooks.

"Two items," Delaney said. "About Maitland dying without a will, the Department legal eagles gave me the usual bullshit: maybe this, maybe that. But under New York State law, the widow gets two thousand in cash or property and one-half of what's left. The balance of the estate, after taxes, goes to the surviving child—in this case, Ted Maitland."

"So Alma Maitland is the big winner?" Boone asked.

"Apparently," Delaney nodded. "But the bank accounts and a few piddling investments and the apartment on East Five-eighth—that's a co-op—all together don't add up to much over a hundred grand. The big asset in the estate are those unsold paintings in Saul Geltman's show. By the way, here's your invitation. They came yesterday afternoon. Each ticket admits two."

Boone took the card and ran fingertips over the printing.

"Nice," he said. "Geltman's laying out the loot."

"You're taking Rebecca?" Delaney asked.

Boone nodded.

"Monica will call her," the Chief said. "We'll all go somewhere for dinner, and then go over to the Galleries together. All right with you?"

"Sure. How much do you figure those paintings will add to the estate?"

"Didn't Geltman say one would go for a quarter of a mil? Even if he was hyping us, the lot of them should go for a mil, minimum."

"That's a better motive than a hundred grand," Boone observed.

"Oh yes," Delaney agreed. "Maybe that's what the killer figured on: the paintings would automatically increase in value once Maitland had conked. Of course, the IRS will take a nice slice of the pie, and so will the State, but there should be enough left over to keep Alma Maitland off welfare."

"You figure her?" the sergeant asked.

"Capable," Delaney rumbled. "Eminently capable. So is Ted Maitland. As of now, they're the ones with the money motive. I also called Thorsen's office about getting to see Dora Maitland's bank records up in Nyack. Thorsen wants to avoid a court order, if possible. All it'll do is get J. Barnes Chapin sore, and keeping him happy is the point of this whole shmear. So Thorsen is going to work through some local Nyack pols he knows. Maybe they can get the bank to cooperate. I'll be in and out of there, make a few notes, and no one will be the wiser."

The sergeant was silent. The Chief knew what he was thinking: Had Delaney talked to Thorsen? Had he blown the whistle on Boone? Delaney said nothing about it. Let him sweat awhile. Do him good.

"All right," the Chief said finally, "what did you get?"

"A lot," Boone said, flipping the notebook pages. "Some of it interesting. I checked the deli that sent up those sandwiches when Saul Geltman was having his conference with J. Julian Simon. The guy who made the delivery said it happened just like Simon told us: The lawyer came out of the inner office, paid, and took the lunch back inside. The delivery guy didn't see anyone in the office but Simon and Susan Hemley. I called her and made a date for lunch. To find out if she saw Geltman in the inner office when Simon came out to get the sandwiches."

"Or at any other time from ten to one-thirty," Delaney added.

"Right," Boone nodded, making a note.

"Anything else?"

"Yes, sir. Something else. The interesting part. Your prejudice against pinkie rings paid off. J. Julian Simon has a sheet."

"Knew it," Delaney said with satisfaction. "What was he doing—fronting a baby farm?"

"Not quite; no, sir. It goes back twenty years. Twenty-four to be exact. The bus companies in Manhattan and the Bronx were getting hit on a lot of accident claims. More than normal. All of a sudden it seemed like their drivers were a bunch of rumdums, knocking pedestrians down right and left."

"Fallaways," Delaney said.

"Correct," Boone said. "The insurance companies handling the liability got together and ran a joint computer tape. About twenty-five percent of the claims were coming through J. Julian Simon and two doctors he had on the string. Plus a crew of repeat tumblers, of course. The guys with trick knees and backs who can show the right X-rays. So they closed Simon down, and he almost got disbarred. Reading the old reports I got the feeling that a shmear changed hands somewhere along the way. Anyway, he kept his license. And lo and behold, there he is in his oak-and-leather office off Madison Avenue, sporting ten big ones in dental work, and probably wearing silk undershorts with 'The Home of the Whopper' printed on them."

"Well, well," Delaney said, smiling coldly. "A shyst. Who'd have thunk it?"

"You did, sir," Boone said. "You figure he's still playing games?"

"The percentages say yes," the Chief said. "Some bad guys reform and walk the arrow. But don't take it to the bank. Most of them develop a taste for the nasty. All right, one bad mark for Lawyer Simon. How did you make out downtown?"

"I talked to every tenant in that Mott Street building. Not one of them had a cleaning woman. Not one knew of anyone coming around looking for cleaning work. Before, during or after the time Maitland was hit. They all looked at me like I was some kind of a nut. That's a poor neighborhood, Chief. Who can afford cleaning women?"

"That's what I figured," Delaney nodded. "The older woman was thinking fast on that Monday morning and scammed the cop. Did you make him?"

"I got him," Boone said, looking at his notebook. "Here he is . . . Jason T. Jason. His buddies called him Jason Two because there's another Jason, Robert Jason, in the precinct. Jason Two is a black, a big guy, three years in the Department, two citations, some solid arrests and good assists. This week he's on foot. Today he's got the eight to four."

"Good," Delaney said. "Let's buy him lunch."

"This place used to be called Ye Old Canal Inn," the Chief said, looking around the bustling restaurant. "And before that, I don't know what it was called. But there's been a tavern or restaurant on this spot since the early days of New York, when Canal Street was uptown. By the way, there really is a canal here. Underground now. A cheeseburger for me, with home fries and slaw. Black coffee."

He had told the others to order what they liked; the Department was picking up the tab. But they followed his lead. Jason T. Jason was sitting across the booth table from Delaney and Boone. The black cop was big enough to fill half the booth.

"You look like you could handle two burgers," Sergeant Boone told him. "Or three."

"Or four," Jason grinned. "But I'm trying to cut down. You see the latest memo on overweight cops? My sergeant gives me a month to drop twenty pounds. I'm trying, but it ain't easy."

He was almost six-four, Delaney figured, and was pushing 250 at least. His skin was a deep cordovan with a soft, powdery finish. A precisely trimmed mustache ran squarely across his face, cheek to cheek. Dark, dancing eyes. Full lips that turned outward. Hands like smoked hams, and the feet, the Chief noted, had to be bigger than his own size thirteens.

The bulk of the man was awesome. Revolver, walkie-talkie, and equipment dangled from him like tiny baubles on a Christmas tree. If he's got the will to go with the weight, Boone mused, the best thing a bad guy braced by that man-mountain could do would be to throw up his hands and scream, "I surrender! I surrender!"

"Football?" Delaney asked.

"Nah," Jason T. Jason said. "I was big enough but not fast enough. I tried out, but the coach said, 'Jase, you run too long in the same place.' Chief, is my ass in a sling on the Maitland thing?"

"Just the opposite," Delaney assured him. "You did exactly right to tell the homicide dick. If anyone screwed up, he did—for not following up on it. But you can't really blame him either; he probably had a hundred other leads to follow, and figured it was nothing."

"It may still be nothing, Jason," Boone put in. "We just don't know. But we'd like to prove it out one way or another."

"Here's our food," Delaney said. "Want to wait until we finish?"

"I better eat and talk," Jason said. "I get itchy when I'm not on the street."

"I know the feeling," Delaney nodded. "Listen, if you want the rest of your tour off, I can square it with your lieutenant."

"No, no," Jason said. "This won't take long. There's not that much to tell. All right, let's see now . . . That Monday morning they pulled me off patrol and put me to guarding the door to Maitland's studio. Eight to four."

"The sawhorses were down around the house?" Boone asked.

"Right," Jason Two said. "Down and gone. I was posted on the top landing, right outside the door. The lab guys were inside taking up the drains, vacuuming dust samples, and stuff like that. Man it was something! They were even taking scrapings from inside the toilet. Anyway, a little before eleven I was out on the landing."

"Sure of the time?" Delaney said.

"Absolutely. Had just looked at my watch to see how close noon was. Two guys in a squad had promised to bring me sandwiches and a coffee at noon. So at about eleven, these two women came up the stairs. They got halfway up to the landing, where the stairs turn, when they see me standing on top, and they stop."

"Surprised to see you there?" the Chief asked.

"Yeah, surprised."

"Frightened?"

Jason T. Jason took an enormous bite of his cheeseburger and chewed a moment, thinking about it.

"Frightened, yeah," he said. "But I don't think that counts. I'm a big black guy, Chief, wearing a cop's suit and swinging a stick. I scare a lot of people. It helps," he smiled.

"I'll bet it does," Boone said. "What were they? White? Black? Spanish?"

"Spanish," Jason Two said promptly. "Take it to the bank. But whether they were Puerto Rican, Cuban, Dominican Republic, or whatever, I couldn't say. But definitely Spanish. Bright clothes—red and pink and orange. Like that."

Only he was eating now; both Delaney and Boone were taking notes. Jason T. Jason seemed to enjoy his importance.

"Descriptions?" the Chief asked.

"The older woman, say about fifty, fifty-five, she's a butterball. Maybe a hundred-forty. Short. Say five-two or three. I'm looking down at them, you know, it's hard to figure from above. Also, this was like two months ago."

"You're doing fine," Delaney assured him.

"She does the talking, and then I'm positive she's Spanish. Also, she has like a whorey look. But she's so old and fat, maybe she hustles the Bowery. Stringy hair dyed a bright red. The other one is a kid. I figure her from twelve to fifteen. In that range. Maybe five-seven or five-eight. One-twenty. Good body from what I could see. Long black hair hanging loose down her back."

"Pretty?" Boone asked.

"Yeah, pretty," the cop said. "Get her cleaned up, the hair fixed, some decent clothes and makeup, and she'd be fucking beautiful. Sorry, Chief."

"I've heard the word before," Delaney said, writing busily. "How did the talk go?"

"You want me to hold a minute so you can eat?" Jason Two asked.

"No, no," Delaney said. "Don't worry about us. You just keep rolling. What did you say and what did they say?"

"Only the older woman talked. The kid didn't open her mouth. I asked them what the hell they were doing there. The woman said they were going through the house, all the houses in the neighborhood, knocking on doors, looking for cleaning work to do."

"Did she say that immediately after you asked her what she was doing?"

The question came from Chief Delaney. Jason T. Jason stopped eating, frowned, trying to remember.

"I can't rightly recall," he said.

"Guess," Boone said.

"I'd guess maybe she hesitated for a beat or two before she answered."

"You didn't figure she was scamming you?"

"Not then I didn't. Later, when I got to thinking about it, I figured she might have been lying. You know, I been a cop for three years now, and I'm just beginning to realize that everyone lies to cops. I mean *everyone!* Even when they don't have to, when there's no point in it. It's automatic. Is it like that in plainclothes, too?"

"If they know you're a cop, it's exactly like that," Delaney nodded. "So they said they were looking for cleaning work. What did you say then?"

"I said there was no work for them on the top floor and to get their ass out of there. The woman said she was told a guy lived on the top floor, and she wanted to ask him. I told her he was fucking dead, and unless she wanted to mop up a puddle of old blood, she better disappear. Maybe I shouldn't have told her that, but I didn't want to stand there arguing with her. Anyway, it worked. She didn't say another word. The two of them turned around and went back downstairs."

"Ever see them again?" Boone asked.

"No," Jason Two said. "Never."

"Anything else you can tell us about them?" Delaney asked. "Their appearance? Any little thing?"

"Let's see . . ." Jason T. Jason said, finishing his cole slaw. "The old woman had a gold tooth. In front. That any help?"

"Could be," Delaney said. "Anything else?"

"The young girl," the cop said. "Something about her. Something funny . . ."

"Funny?" Boone said.

"Not funny ha-ha," Jason said, "but funny-strange. She had like a vacant expression. Kept staring up into the air like she was spaced out."

"Drugs?" Boone asked.

"I don't think so. More like she was maybe retarded or a little flaky. Like something wasn't right there. I mean, she didn't say word one so it was hard to tell. But I got the feeling she was out of it. Off somewhere."

"Recognize them if you see them again?" Delaney asked.

"Is the pope Catholic?" Jason T. Jason said.

"Good," the Chief said. He tore a blank page from his notebook, scribbled down his telephone number and Boone's. "Here are our phone numbers. Keep an eye out on the street. If you make them, call one of us. Or leave a message."

"You want me to hold them?"

"No, no, don't do that. But tail them until they hole up in a restaurant or store or movie or their home. Whatever. Then call us. Don't worry if it takes you off your beat. I'll square it at the precinct."

"Will do," the cop nodded. He took the page, folded it into his wallet. "I better hit the pavement. Nice talking to you gents. I hope something comes of it."

"So do we," Boone said. He and Delaney half rose to shake hands with Jason Two. "Many thanks. You've been a big help."

"Anything else I can do, give me a shout."

They watched him move away. He had to go through the outer door sideways.

"Good cop," Delaney said. "Observant. And he remembers."

"How would you like to be a mugger or purse-snatcher?" Boone said. "You make your hit, you've got the loot, you're running hell-for-leather, you come scrambling around a corner, and there's Jason T. Jason."

"I wouldn't like that," Chief Delaney said. "My God, they're growing them big these days! Well, let's eat. Want a hot coffee?"

They ordered fresh coffees, but ate their cold cheeseburgers and home fries without protest.

"Think the young girl was the model in those Maitland sketches?" Boone asked.

"It fits," Delaney nodded. "How's this: Our first scenario was correct; Maitland picks up a young, fresh twist on Friday. But she's not alone. The woman sounds too old to be her mother, but maybe she's a relative or friend."

"Or madam," the sergeant offered. "Jason said she looked like a hooker. Maybe she's peddling the young kid's ass."

"Could be," the Chief said. "So they go up to the studio on Friday. The girl strips down, and Maitland makes his drawings."

"While the older woman has a drink and leaves her partials on the glass and bottle."

"Right. Maitland likes what he draws, and makes a date to use the girl at eleven on Monday morning. That listens, doesn't it?"

"Does to me," Boone said. "The older woman wouldn't have shivved him on Friday, would she? Because he tried to screw the girl?"

"No way," Delaney said, shaking his head. "They'd never have come back on Monday if that had happened. No, I think when the two of them left the studio on Friday, Maitland was breathing. They were probably the last ones to see him alive."

"Except for the killer," Boone said.

"Except for the killer," Delaney nodded. "I'd like to find those two women. Maybe they saw something. Maybe the guy we're looking for was coming up the stairs on that Friday while they were going down."

"Not much chance of finding them, Chief," Boone sighed. "Unless Jason T. Jason hits it lucky and spots them on the street."

"Stranger things have happened," Chief Delaney said. "You finished? Let's get uptown. We'll brace Alma Maitland first."

* * *

Once again they were ushered into that cheerless family room, which, today, smelled faintly of oiled machinery. They hadn't yet seated themselves when Alma Maitland came sweeping in, hatted, tugging on white gloves.

"Really, Chief Delaney," she said angrily. "I was just going out. This is very inconvenient."

He stared at her coldly.

"Inconvenient, ma'am?"

She caught the implication; her face whitened, lips pressed.

"Of course I want to help," she said. "As much as I can. But you might have called."

Both the cops looked at her without expression. A proved technique: say nothing and let them yammer on and on. Sometimes they dug themselves deep simply because they could not endure the silence.

"Besides, I told you everything I know," she said, lifting her chin.

"Did you?" Delaney said, and was silent again.

Finally, with a pinching of features, a small sound of exasperation, she asked them to be seated. They took the couch, sitting almost shoulder to shoulder, a bulwark. She sat in an armchair, in her ladylike position: spine frozen, ankles crossed, knees turned, gloved hands folded demurely in her lap.

"You don't get along with your mother-in-law and sister-in-law, do you?" Delaney said suddenly. It came out more flat statement than question.

"Did they say that?" she demanded.

"I'm asking you," Delaney said.

"We're not close," she admitted. A tinselly laugh. "We both prefer it that way."

"And your late husband? How close was he to his mother and sister?"

"Very close," she said stiffly.

"Oh?" the Chief said. "He only saw them once or twice a year."

"Nonsense," she said sharply. "He saw them at least once a month. Sometimes once a week. They were always coming down to have lunch or dinner with him."

Neither Delaney nor Boone showed surprise.

"And you didn't attend these lunches and dinners, Mrs. Maitland?" the sergeant asked.

"I did not."

"Did they ever visit his Mott Street studio?"

"I have no idea."

"He never told you they did?"

"No, never. What's all this about?"

Delaney asked: "Did your husband ever contribute to the living expenses of his mother and sister? To your knowledge?"

She laughed scornfully. "I doubt that very much. My husband rarely spent any money that did not contribute to his own pleasure."

"Belle Sarazen considered him a very generous man."

"I'm sure she would," Alma Maitland said furiously. "While I scrimped and saved to make ends meet."

Delaney looked around the room.

"Hardly poverty," he said mildly enough. "Mrs. Maitland, are you aware that unless other claims are filed, you and your son will probably be the sole beneficiaries of your husband's estate?"

"Estate!" she cried. "What estate? This apartment that can't even be sold in today's market for what we paid for it? Bank accounts that will barely cover outstanding bills?"

"The unsold paintings . . ." Boone murmured.

"Oh yes!" she said, with something close to despair in her voice. "And how much of that will be left after Saul Geltman takes his share, and all the tax departments take theirs? I assure you, my husband did not leave me a wealthy woman. Far from it!''

Delaney looked at her closely.

''You have an independent income?'' he guessed.

''Some,'' she said grudgingly. ''It's no business of yours, but I suppose you could find out—if you haven't already. My father left me some municipal bonds. He, at least, knew a man's responsibility.''

''What does that income amount to?'' Delaney asked. ''As you said, we can always find out.''

''About twenty thousand a year,'' she said.

''Did your husband know of this income?''

''Of course he did.'' She paused, then sighed. ''Twenty years ago it seemed a fortune. Today it's nothing.''

''Somewhat more than nothing,'' Delaney said dryly, ''but I won't argue the point. Mrs. Maitland, I have here the three sketches found in your husband's studio. I know you told me you knew none of his recent models, but I'd like you to take a look at these in case you may be able to identify the girl. I admit the face is just suggested, but there may be enough there.''

He rose and, with Sergeant Boone's help, unrolled the drawings and held up each of the three for Alma Maitland's inspection.

''They're very good,'' she said softly.

''Aren't they?'' Delaney said. ''Recognize the girl?''

''No. Never saw her or anyone like her before. When will you be finished with these? They're part of the estate, you know.''

''I'm well aware of that, madam. They'll be returned when our investigation is completed.''

''And when will that be?'' she demanded.

He didn't answer, but rolled up the drawings again and secured them with a rubber band. He signaled Boone, and the two moved toward the door. Then the Chief paused and turned back.

''Mrs. Maitland,'' he said, ''one more thing . . . Don't you think it odd that the only work of your husband we found in his studio were these three drawings?''

''Odd?'' she said, puzzled. ''Why odd?''

''You told us you were a model; you must have been in many artists' studios. We've been told that most painters usually have many works on hand. Unsold paintings. Half-finished works. Old things they don't want to sell. And so forth. Yet all we found in your husband's studio were these three sketches. Don't you think that odd?''

''No, I don't,'' she said. ''My husband was a very successful artist. After he became famous, he sold off all his old work. He was not a sentimentalist; he kept nothing around to remind him of the old days. And his style changed very little; his early work was as good as his most recent paintings. As soon as he finished a new canvas, it was brought to Saul Geltman for sale. Whether I was told of it or not,'' she added bitterly.

''I see,'' Delaney said thoughtfully. ''Thank you for your time. Do you plan to attend the preview of your husband's memorial show at the Geltman Galleries?''

''Of course,'' she said, surprised.

''Your son, also?''

''Yes, we'll both be there. Why?''

''We hope to see you then,'' Delaney said politely. ''Good day, Mrs. Maitland.''

They drove over to Jake Dukker's studio, and the Chief said to Boone:

''What Jason T. Jason said about everyone lying to the cops—that's true. But there's something else he's going to learn: no one ever volunteers any information either. I'm talking about Dora and Emily Maitland up in Nyack. They said

Victor visited them a couple of times a year. They answered my question. But you see the inadequacy of interrogation? If you don't ask the right questions, you find yourself farting around in leftfield. I came away with the impression that Victor was a cold-hearted bastard of a son who wanted as little as possible to do with his mother and sister. Didn't you get that feeling?"

"Absolutely," Boone said.

"Because I didn't ask how often did you *see* Victor. Instead I asked how often did he visit Nyack. Now Alma claims they came down frequently for lunches and dinners with son Victor, and it was one big happy family. Son of a bitch! It's my fault."

"No harm done, Chief," the sergeant said.

"Yes, harm done," Delaney said wrathfully. "Not just because Dora and Emily scammed us, but because now they'll think us pointy-heads and try it again on something else. Well, we shall see. We shall certainly, fucking-ay-right, see!"

They drove on a few minutes in silence, and then Abner Boone asked, somewhat timidly, "What she said about her independent income—twenty thousand a year. You think that's important?"

"No," Delaney said, still fuming. "All it proves is that Victor Maitland was as greedy as the whole slick, avaricious, grasping lot of them. Now we know why he married the Ice Maiden."

In the old elevator, rising with wheezing stubbornness to Jake Dukker's studio, Delaney said: "The second round. Bust in on them without warning. Keep them off balance. Alma reacted fast. You really think she was going out?"

"Wasn't she?" Boone said.

"I'd bet no," the Chief said. "Heard we were there, grabbed up a hat and gloves, and sallied forth. Not an intelligent woman, but shrewd. Let's see how Jake baby reacts."

He reacted as if a visit from police officers investigating a homicide was an everyday occurrence. Came out into the reception area to greet them friendlily, said he was finishing up a photography session and would be with them in a few minutes, offered them coffee, and disappeared. He was wearing a black leather jumpsuit decorated with gleaming metal studs. The pitted cheeks glistened with sweat, and his handshake slid.

True to his word, he welcomed them into the studio ten minutes later. The assistants were dismantling a set that apparently was designed to reproduce a middle-class, suburban living room. No models were present, but they heard dogs barking from somewhere.

"Flea spray," Dukker explained. "A print campaign. Don't get Fido's fleas in your upholstery. Use Fidoff. The hounds were easier to work with than the models. Let's go upstairs and relax."

He led the way up the spiral staircase, and offered them the lip-shaped couch again. They settled for more conventional chairs. Once again Dukker collapsed into the overstuffed baseball mitt.

"How are you coming?" he asked cheerily. "Anything new?"

They looked at him. He sat slumped far down, fingers laced across his bowling-ball belly. The black leather jumpsuit glistened, and so did his face and bare forearms. He smiled at them genially, showing his stained teeth.

"We timed it from here to Maitland's Mott Street studio," Delaney told him. "You could have made it."

The smile held, but all the mirth went out of it. Then it was just stretched mouth and wet teeth, framed by the droopy Stalin mustache.

"I told you I was up here with Belle Sarazen," Dukker said hoarsely.

"So you say," Boone shrugged. "So she says. Means nothing."

"What do you mean it means nothing?" Dukker said indignantly. "Do you really think—"

"She says you like to be spanked," Delaney said. "Is that also the truth?"

"And that you envied him," Boone said. "Hated him because he did his own thing, and you chased the buck."

"The bitch!" Jake Dukker shouted, jerking forward to the edge of his chair. "Are you going to listen—Let me tell you that she—I can't believe that you actually think I—Well, she sold him drugs—did she tell you that? I know it for a fact. Snappers. Poppers. She kept him supplied. Oh yes! For a fact. And she's got the goddamned nerve to—"

He stopped suddenly, fell back suddenly into the baseball mitt, put his knuckles to his mouth.

"I didn't," he mumbled. "I swear to God I didn't. I couldn't have killed him. *Couldn't* have."

"Why not?" Boone said.

"Well, because," Jake Dukker said. "I'm just not like that."

The two cops looked at each other. A unique alibi.

"We figure maybe you were in on it together," Chief Delaney said in a gentle, musing voice. "You both had reasons. Crazy reasons, but neither of you has what I'd call your normal, run-of-the-mill personality. You both come up here for lunch on that Friday. The models and assistants are downstairs. You duck out that doorway, take the elevator down, either drive or take the subway downtown, put Maitland's lights out, and come back. You could have managed it."

"Easy," Boone said. "I timed it. Myself."

"I don't believe this," Jake Dukker said, shaking his head from side to side. "I-do-not-believe-this. Jesus."

"It's possible," Edward X. Delaney smiled. "Isn't it? Come on, admit it; it's possible."

"You're going to arrest me?" Dukker said.

"Not today," Delaney said. "You asked us what's new. We're telling you—that we discovered you could have done it. Possibly. That's what's new."

They regarded him gravely as he gradually calmed, quieted, stopped gnawing his knuckles. He tried a smile. It came out flimsy.

"I get it," he said. "Just throwing a scare—right?"

They didn't answer.

"Nothing to it—right?"

"You ever go down to Maitland's studio?" Sergeant Boone asked. "Ever?"

"Well, sure," Dukker said nervously. "Once or twice. But not for months. Maybe not in a year."

"He have any paintings there?" Delaney demanded. "In the studio?"

"What?" Dukker said. "I don't understand."

They were coming at him so fast, from so many angles, he couldn't get set.

"In Maitland's studio," Delaney repeated. "Did he have paintings stacked against the walls? Like you have. Unsold stuff. Things he was working on. Old paintings."

"No," Dukker said. "Not much. He sold everything he did. He didn't keep things around. Geltman moved his stuff fast."

"And you said he was fast," Boone said. "A fast worker. He sold everything?"

"Sure he did. He could—"

"You on anything?" Delaney asked. "Pot? Pills? Or stronger? From Belle Sarazen?"

"What? Hell, no! A little grass now and then. Not from her."

"But she deals?" Boone said.

"I don't know. For sure. I swear I don't. But I hear things."

"You seemed sure enough about the poppers," Delaney said. "Why to Maitland? Was he hooked?"

"Jesus Christ, no! Just to give him a lift. You start a painting, you've got to be up."

"Not for sex?"

"Vic? No way! He was a goddamned stud. A stud!"

"You have a sheet?" Boone asked. "A criminal record?"

"Are you kidding?"

"We can find out. We're asking politely."

"Traffic tickets. Like that. And . . ."

"And?" Delaney said.

"A party. A drug bust. They let us all go. I don't even know if they kept our names. But I'm telling you. See, I'm telling you."

"Fingerprinted?"

"No. I swear I wasn't."

"You pay Belle Sarazen for the illicit fornication?" Boone asked. "For the spanking? Whipping, maybe?"

"Never! Never!"

"But you had a working relationship," Delaney said. "Right? She'd take a look at your models. Maybe for dates with her important friends. And maybe she'd provide models for you. For dirty playing cards. It worked both ways. And she posed for you. That aluminum-foil painting. A friend of hers bought it. You split the take—right? Real friends. Real cozy. Girls. Drugs on demand. Maybe even boys—who knows? All kinds of swell stuff. Orgies, maybe? Skin shows? The whole bit. Rich, freaky people. Plenty of cash. Something like that. Right?"

"I swear . . ." the artist whispered. "I swear . . ."

"Mr. Dukker," Chief Delaney said formally, "I wonder if you'd do us a favor?"

"What? What? Well . . . sure."

"Take a look at these drawings. The ones we found in Maitland's studio. See if you recognize the girl."

He and Boone held the sketches up before the dazed and shattered Dukker. He looked at them with dulled eyes.

"The son of a bitch," he muttered. "He was so good. He didn't have to think. From the eye to the hand. Nothing in between. Instantaneous."

"You recognize the girl?"

"No. Never saw her before."

"Let's go downstairs," Delaney said. "Okay?"

On the lower level, the Chief went over to the corner drawing table. He spread out the sketches, weighted down the corners so they lay flat.

"You said you were as good as Maitland," he told Dukker. "You said you could imitate his style. You got a Maitland drawing on your wall. So good that he got sore when he saw it. But then he signed it. Now what I want you to do is look at these three drawings and complete the girl. As Victor Maitland would. Just the face. He suggested the shape and features. You fill in the details."

"Jesus Christ," Jake Dukker said, "you don't want much, do you? There's hardly anything to go by."

"Do what you can," Delaney said. "We know you'll be happy to cooperate."

The artist found an 11 × 14 sketchpad, searched around and picked up a soft carpenter's pencil. He glanced at the three drawings and began to sketch. Hesitantly at first, then with more confidence. They watched him, fascinated. He limned the girl's face with bold outline strokes, then began to fill it in. Hollows. Shadows. Fullness. Glint of eyes. Angle of chin and bulge of brow.

"Son of a bitch!" he said enthusiastically. "A beauty! This is how Vic would have done her. Young. Maybe like fourteen. Around there. Innocent. And dumb. Nothing but beauty. That's it. That's her. There you are."

Less than three minutes, Delaney estimated. And he had the portrait of a young, beautiful, empty-eyed girl. A flood of dark hair spilling down. Sensual mouth. Lips parted to show glistening teeth. High cheekbones. All of her bursting with youth, but vacant. Untouched.

He took the three Maitland sketches and Dukker's drawing, and rolled them carefully together.

"Thank you very much," he said. "We'll be seeing you again."

"Soon," Sergeant Boone added.

They left Jake Dukker slack-jawed and shaken. In the elevator, going down, Delaney said, "We're beginning to work pretty good together."

"Just what I was thinking, Chief," Boone grinned. "He's going to call Belle Sarazen now, and scream at her."

"Oh yes," Delaney nodded. "The animals are nipping and clawing at each other. I think we have most of what we need right now."

Boone looked at him, astounded.

"You mean you've . . . ?"

"Got it figured?" Delaney said, amused. "No way. I'm just saying I think we've got the main pieces. Putting them together is something else again. Sarazen will be on her guard. I'll play the heavy; you play the friend. We'll dazzle her with our footwork."

"I like this," Abner Boone said.

"It has its moments," Edward X. Delaney said. "Filthy people! Messy lives!"

The Filipino houseboy showed no surprise when he opened the door and saw them planted there. "Thith way, gentlemens," he said.

He led the way to a small room, almost a corridor between the blood-red bedroom and a bathroom that seemed to be all varicose marble and gold fixtures. The passageway held a massage table and, on a track just below the ceiling, a battery of lighted ultraviolet lamps. They cast a cold blue-white glow that filled the chamber and made it look like a fish tank.

The massage table was covered with a flowered sheet. Belle Sarazen lay face down, her cheek resting on her forearms. She was apparently naked; a pink towel was spread over her rump. She wore black goggles: two disks of semi-opaque glass the size of half-dollars, held together by an elastic.

A similar pair of protective goggles was worn by the muscular young man bending over the table, kneading the muscles of her upper arms and shoulders with long, powerful strokes. He was dressed in white sneakers, white duck trousers, a white T-shirt that had obviously been altered to display his brawny torso. He had the bulging biceps and deltoids of a weightlifter. His flaxen hair was artfully arranged in a cap of Greek curls, with divine bangs that dangled over his forehead.

"Halloo, darlings!" Belle Sarazen sang cheerily, not raising her head. "Don't come into the room or you're liable to go blind or become impotent or something. This gorgeous hunk of meat is Bobbie. Bobbie, say hello to these nice gentlemen, members of New York's Finest."

Bobbie turned his blank goggles toward them and showed a mouthful of teeth as square and white as sugar cubes.

"Take a walk, Bobbie," Chief Delaney said gruffly. "Do your nails or something."

A tambourine laugh came from Belle Sarazen.

"Run along, Bobbie," she advised. "Go play games with Ramon. But don't leave. This won't take long. Will it, Edward X. Delaney?"

He didn't answer.

The goggled Bobbie departed, not forgetting to inflate his massive chest and ripple his triceps as he pushed by the two officers. They stood at the bedroom entrance, outside the glow of the suntan lamps. Belle Sarazen's head was toward them, but they couldn't see her face. Just the long, oiled back. Roped muscles of thighs and calves. Within her reach was a small table and a tall glass of something orange with chunks of fresh fruit floating in bubbles.

"Poor Jake," she murmured. "He called me, you know. I'm afraid you upset him dreadfully."

"You were selling poppers to Maitland," Delaney said wrathfully.

"Selling?" she said. "Nonsense. He was up here frequently. He might have taken a few from my medicine cabinet."

"You have a prescription for those?" Delaney demanded.

"Of course, dear," Belle Sarazen said lazily. "I can give you the name of my doctor. If you care to check."

"Goddamned right I'll check," Delaney thundered.

"Hey, Chief," Boone said nervously. "Take it easy."

"Oh, let him bellow, Scarecrow," she said. "He'll huff and he'll puff, but he won't blow my house down."

"You could have made it to Maitland's studio from Jake Dukker's place," Delaney told her. "We timed it. You and Dukker could have skinned out to the elevator, gone down to Mott Street and zonked Maitland. You come back the same way, and no one downstairs in the studio is any the wiser."

"Now why would I do a silly thing like that, Edward X. Delaney?"

"Because you hated his guts," he yelled at her. "He called you a whore in public. You've got the kind of ego that couldn't take that. And maybe he—"

"Chief," Sergeant Boone said urgently, "for God's sake, cool it. We don't—"

"No, by God!" Delaney said. "I'm going to pin her. Maybe Maitland was ready to blow the whistle on her sweet little rackets. The call girls, the drugs, the sex shows, the whole bit. That would be motive enough."

"Listen here," Belle Sarazen said, raising her head, beginning to lose her flippancy. "What right have you—"

"Oh yes," Delaney nodded. "Dukker told us plenty. Things he didn't tell you he told us. We know all about the models and your important friends. And Bobbie? That muscle-bound butterfly! Is he in on it, too? I'll bet he is! We've got—"

"Guessing," she said sharply. "You and your dirty little mind. You're just guessing."

"How often did Maitland come up here?" Delaney demanded. "Once a week? Three times? Every day? We can check the doorman, so don't lie about it."

"I have no reason to lie," she said, her voice getting colder and thinner. "Victor Maitland was a personal friend of mine. A very special friend. Is it a crime to have friends visit?"

"He gave you money?"

"He gave me gifts, yes. I've already told you that."

"Gifts!" Delaney said. "That's good, that is! Maybe you raised the rates. Maybe he wanted to end it. Maybe he—"

"Chief, Chief," Boone groaned. "Take it easy. Please! We've got no evidence. You're just spit-balling. There's no way we can—"

"I don't care," Delaney shouted. "She killed once and walked. She's not going to do it in my city. She's guilty as hell. If not murder, then procuring and the drug thing. I'm going to rack her up. I swear, I'm going to hang her ass!"

Now Belle Sarazen had raised the upper part of her torso to stare at her tormentor with blank, goggled eyes. She propped herself on her forearms. They could see her small, muscled breasts, like hard shields with shiny pink bosses.

"You just try!" she spat at him. "Just try! I'll make you the laughing stock of New York. I'll sue, and believe me I can afford the best lawyers in the country. By the time I've finished with you, you'll be lucky to have your pension left. I'll drain you dry!"

"You're finished," he screamed at her. "Can't you get that through your scrambled brain? It's all over for you, kiddo. You're finished and down the drain."

He thrust the roll of Maitland drawings into Boone's hands, spun around, stalked off. They heard his thumping footsteps and, far off, the slam of the outside door. Belle Sarazen stared at Abner Boone through her black goggles.

"Wow!" he said. "I've never seen him like that before."

She grunted, got off the table, wrapping the big towel around her, covering herself from breasts to upper thighs. She switched off the sunlamps. She ripped away her goggles.

"The son of a bitch!" she said. "That fucking cocksucker! I'll have his balls!"

"I want to apologize, Miss Sarazen," Boone said earnestly. "He's not going to do those things he said. He's been under so much pressure lately . . . Please, I wish you'd forget what happened."

"Forget?" She laughed—or tried to. It caught in her throat. "No way, baby! Mister Chief Edward X. Delaney has no idea how much clout I can swing in Fun City. He's dead and doesn't know it."

She pushed by him, went into the bedroom. She fell into a blood-red armchair, hooked a knee over one of the arms, foot swinging crazily. She began sucking frantically on a thumb, a maniacal baby with a long-nailed pacifier.

"Look, Miss Sarazen," Sergeant Boone pleaded. "He's retired. You know that. You can't touch him. But I'm on active duty. You go to your important friends, and I'm the one they'll come down on. I'll be walking a beat in Richmond. You know that. I think he was way out of line. Is it right my career should be ruined because he blew his cork? Look, I'm on your side. We've got nothing on you. Not a thing. He was just shooting off at the mouth."

Finally, the hooked leg stopped its mad jerking, the thumb came from her lips with a *plop!* sound. She smiled at him.

"Scarecrow," she said, "I like you. Get me that glass from the other room."

Obediently, he brought her the glass of fruit chunks floating in bubbles. She sipped it slowly, reflectively. He sat down cautiously, bent forward, hands clasped in supplication.

"Is that the truth?" she asked. "You've got nothing on me?"

"The truth," Boone vowed. "All gossip and hearsay. Even what Jake Dukker told us about you. I mean the drugs and girls and all. How can we use that? He's in on it, too, isn't he?"

"Is he ever!" she said.

"Well, there you are," the sergeant said, sitting back. "Now you know he's not going to make any kind of a signed statement or testify if it means his own ass, too. Right?"

"Right," she said, nodding. "Jake's a weak sister; I've known that all along. If push comes to shove, he'll clam up. I have ways of making sure he does."

"Of course," Boone said encouragingly. "And what Delaney said about Maitland paying you for the sex—hell, that's your personal business. No one's going to court with that."

"Vic paid me for sex?" Belle Sarazen said. She moved her head back and laughed. A genuine, deep laugh that made the towel about her middle billow in and out. "That'd be the day when Victor Maitland paid for a fuck. No way, Scarecrow! No, Vic and I had a little business deal going. You might say we were partners. It was all strictly business."

"Well, I'm certainly glad to hear that," Boone said, smiling. "I didn't think you were that kind of a woman, Belle. In spite of what Delaney said."

"That bastard," she growled.

"As long as it was just business," the sergeant said, with a deep sigh of relief. "What kind of a business were you two in?"

"I helped him out a few deals," she shrugged. "I have some rich friends. All over the country. Everywhere. Here and in Europe."

"Oh, I see," Boone nodded, still smiling. "You mean you helped his career? His reputation? Helped him sell his paintings?"

"Something like that," she said.

"Nothing wrong with that," Boone said. "Perfectly legit. I imagine you must know a lot of people in the art world."

"Everyone, baby. *Everyone.*"

"I mean, like rich collectors?"

"You better believe it. Top-dollar collectors."

"Well, you could certainly be a big help to any artist," Boone said enthusiastically. "But I thought Saul Geltman handled all of Maitland's stuff?"

"Well, he did and he didn't," Belle Sarazen said vaguely. "There's more than one way to skin a cat. Listen, Scarecrow, are you sure what Delaney said—all that bullshit about procuring and drugs and all—that *was* bullshit, wasn't it? He hasn't got anything to take to the DA, does he?"

"Don't worry," the sergeant assured her. "It's all smoke. It's just that he wants to break this thing so bad he can taste it. Listen, just between you, me and the lamp post, were you really with Jake Dukker every minute from, say, noon till two o'clock on the Friday Maitland was killed? The reason I ask is because right now, Jake's our Number One suspect."

She stared at him a long moment, clinking the rim of the glass against her gleaming teeth. She stared at him, but he could see she wasn't looking at him. Her gaze was unfocussed, going through him, off into the distance.

Finally, she sighed, drained her glass. She picked out a piece of fresh pineapple and began to chew on it. He waited patiently.

"I couldn't swear to it in a court of law," she said dreamily. "I might have fallen asleep up there. I really don't know what he did while I was asleep. I really couldn't say."

"Thank you, Belle," he said humbly. "Thank you very much. Now just one more thing . . . I've got the three sketches we found in Maitland's studio. Would you take a look at them and see if you recognize the model?"

"Sure," she said, straightening up. "Let's have a look."

He slid off the rubber band and handed the drawings to her. She went through them slowly.

"Nice," she said. "I could sell these with one phone call."

"I'm afraid not," he said. "They belong to the estate."

"What a body. Yum-yum. What's this one—the finished head?"

"Jake Dukker did that one. What he thought the girl looked like, done the way he thought Maitland would have done it. Recognize the girl?"

"No. Never saw her before. Wish I could help you—you've been sweet—but I can't. Sorry."

"Just a long shot," he shrugged, rolling up the drawings again. "Well, I'll be on my way."

"Send Bobbie in on your way out," she commanded him. "You bastards interrupted my massage. Bobbie finishes me off with a mink glove. Ever get rubbed down with mink, Scarecrow?"

"No," he said, getting to his feet, "I never have."

"Well . . ." she said speculatively, looking at him, "you keep on being sweet to me and telling me what's going on, and you never know . . ."

Chief Delaney was waiting patiently in the car, slumped down. He was smoking a cigar, his straw hat tilted down over his eyes. He pushed it back when Boone got behind the wheel.

"How did you make out?" he asked.

"Not bad, Chief," Boone said. "You got her so sore, I could play the Father Confessor."

"What did you get?"

"First of all, she doesn't recognize the girl in the sketches. Says she never saw her before. On the drug and prostitution things, she and Dukker are in on it together. Like we figured. But they've probably knocked off while we're sniffing around."

"Only temporarily," Delaney said.

"Sure," Boone agreed. "Also, she's ready to throw Dukker to the wolves. Says now she might have fallen asleep up in his place and couldn't testify that he was there all the time."

"Oh-ho," the Chief said. "Isn't she a nice lady? That's what Dukker gets for telling us about the poppers."

"But the big thing is this: Maitland wasn't paying for her tush. She says. She claims they were in business together. I couldn't get her to spell it out, but it sounded like maybe she was getting her rich friends to buy Maitland's paintings, and she was taking a slice."

Delaney thought about that a moment.

"Fucking Saul Geltman?" he asked.

"That's how it adds up to me, Chief. She said she knows well-heeled collectors all over the country and in Europe. Maybe they were cutting out Geltman."

"Could be," Delaney nodded. "We'll have to check to see if Maitland and Geltman had any kind of an exclusive contract or signed agreement. Look, sergeant, we know Maitland was selling paintings he wasn't telling his wife about. It's very possible he was also selling paintings he didn't tell Geltman about."

"That would give Saul baby motive enough," Boone noted. "Or . . ."

"Or what?" Delaney said.

"This is a wild one, Chief."

"Go ahead, try it."

"Well, this is just a scenario . . . We know Jake Dukker can forge Maitland's style. My God, he proved it to us. Now suppose—"

"I got it," Delaney interrupted. "Maybe Dukker was producing fake Maitlands. Sarazen was peddling them to her rich collector friends, and Maitland found out. So they clipped his wick."

"Right," Boone said.

"It's all jazz," the Chief said. "But I'll ask Lieutenant Wolfe to see if he can find someone, somewhere, who owns a Maitland painting that wasn't sold through Saul Geltman. That would confirm that either Maitland was selling his own stuff on the sly, or Dukker was pushing fakes. Good work, sergeant."

"Thank you, sir."

"And now," Delaney said, sighing, "I suppose I can expect a call from Deputy Commissioner Thorsen expressing the displeasure of all her important friends at the rude way I treated Belle Sarazen."

"No, I don't think so," Abner Boone said. "I told her you had nothing on her, and if she screamed, I'd be the only one who'd get the shaft. I don't think she'll yelp."

"I owe you one," Delaney said.

Boone wanted to say, "We're even," but said nothing.

On the evening following the interrogations of Jake Dukker and Belle Sarazen, Monica and the Chief relaxed in the study with after-dinner rye highballs while he delivered a précis of his day's activities. She sat slouched in the worn leather club chair, her shoeless feet parked up on his desk. He sat in his swivel chair behind the desk, occasionally consulting his notebook and reports as he told her what had been learned.

He followed up the account of Jason T. Jason's encounter with the two Spanish women by showing Monica the drawing Jake Dukker had made of the young model's face, based on the Maitland sketches. Monica guessed the girl's age as fifteen or sixteen. She asked the Chief if he intended to circulate copies of the drawing to the city's precincts, in hopes of locating the girl.

Delaney rose to pin the drawing to his map board alongside the Maitland sketches. He told her that he and Boone had discussed that possibility, but decided against it for the time being, since they had nothing more than a wild hope that the two women might be helpful in identifying the killer. If other, more promising leads fizzled, then Jason T. Jason would be set to work with a police artist, and drawings of both women would be circulated in hopes of locating them.

The Chief described the Mutt and Jeff technique he and Boone had used with Belle Sarazen. He thought the results had justified what they had done, although he admitted it probably meant Boone would have to handle Sarazen by himself in the future. Monica said Sarazen sounded like a dreadful woman, and Delaney told her she'd probably get a chance to meet the lady herself at Saul Geltman's pre-show party. In fact, the Chief said, he hoped Monica would try to meet all the principals in the case at that party; he wanted her take on them.

Monica asked if he really thought Belle Sarazen had sufficient motive for killing Victor Maitland. Would a jury, for instance, believe that a woman had knifed a man to death because he insulted her in public? Monica didn't think so.

Delaney said there might be an additional motive in those "business dealings" Belle Sarazen claimed she had with Maitland. But even if no further motive was uncovered, he still believed Sarazen was capable of killing to revenge a real or even fancied slight to her amour propre. He said Monica's doubts were based on the fact that she assumed Sarazen was a rational human being who acted in a reasonable manner. The truth was, he said, she was an unstable personality who had lived an incoherent life, with a history of irrational acts.

He said, almost as much to himself as to Monica, that one of the hardest things for a cop to learn was that people frequently acted in ways that not only contravened the laws of society, but of intelligence and good, gutter common sense. Cops sometimes failed, Delaney said, because they looked for reason and logic in what was too often an unreasonable and illogical world. They could not grasp the essential *nuttiness* of the human situation. The Chief told Monica of a homicide he had worked in Greenwich Village when he was a lieutenant . . .

This kid had come out of the midwest. A college kid, good family, money. He wanted to get into the theatre, and his parents agreed to bankroll him for two years. So he came to New York, signed up for courses in an acting school, began to make the rounds.

The freedom in the Village in the 1960s almost literally exploded his mind. Drugs. Sex. Whatever he wanted. He couldn't handle it. Trying to reconstruct it later, the cops could nail some of it and guess the rest. The kid never did get hooked on the hard stuff, but he was dropping acid and bombed out of his gourd most of the time on pills and booze. He moved into a loft with five or six others, men and women. Different cast every night, but the play never changed. He was fucking everything that moved and being used the same way himself. He had to experience everything: that was the road to revelation and great art. After awhile, he couldn't even judge the quality of pleasures.

One night he strangled the young girl he was sodomizing. It could have been another man or a child; that night it happened to be a woman. After they got him dried out and off the pills, they asked him why he had done it. He looked at them, puzzled. He didn't know. He actually didn't know. The victim was almost a stranger to him. It had just occurred to him to kill her, to experience that, and so he had done it.

It was the freedom, Delaney said somberly to Monica. It was partly the drugs, he agreed, but mostly it was the freedom. Complete, without any restraint. There were no rules, no laws, no prohibitions. Moral anarchy. The kid was really surprised, Delaney said, when he finally realized he was going to be punished for what he had done. He couldn't understand it. It didn't seem to him all that big a deal.

The Chief told Monica that it frequently happened that way with people who couldn't handle freedom. They didn't know self-discipline. They acted only on whim, impulse. They couldn't sacrifice the pleasure of today for the satisfaction of tomorrow.

He thought that might be what was happening to Belle Sarazen. She lived in a world of easy money, easy thrills. No rules, no laws, no prohibitions. Total liberty, and a greed for kicks. It was, Delaney acknowledged, a difficult motive to present to a jury. They looked for neater reasons: vengeance, hate, lust, jealousy. It was hard to convince reasonable people that someone could kill casually, without motive. But it did happen. It was happening more and more often.

So motive was important, he told Monica, but not so important as to make an experienced cop rule out motiveless crime. Sarazen sold drugs and bodies; that was evident. Was it such a quantum leap from that to pushing a knife into someone who annoyed you? Especially when you believe nothing is wrong, everything is right?

Monica shivered, and hugged herself. She asked her husband if that meant Belle Sarazen was the leading suspect. He said no, that what he said about her could also be said about Jake Dukker. And Alma Maitland, Ted Maitland, and Saul Geltman had firmer, more conventional motives.

And the mother and sister? Monica wanted to know. Did they also have motives?

Delaney said that none were presently apparent, but that didn't mean none existed.

Monica sighed, and after awhile she asked if his working lifetime as a cop, in dealing with things like the Maitland homicide—which, he had to admit, had a depressing sordidness about it—if dealing with the baseness of people had not soured him on the human race.

He thought a long time, and finally said he didn't think it had. He had learned, he told her, not to expect too much from people, and thus avoided being constantly disappointed. Abner Boone, on the other hand, Delaney said, was a closet romantic. And this was probably the cause of his drinking. Boone said it was the "filth" of police work, but he really meant the evil of human beings. He expected so much good and found so little.

Edward X. Delaney said he expected little, and sometimes was pleasantly surprised. And so he kept his sanity. And it was also important, he added stoutly, that his own life, his personal life, be ordered and coherent. That was a cop's salvation.

Monica said she hoped Rebecca Hirsch could help Abner Boone achieve that. The Chief said he hoped so, too. Then they each had another rye highball, talked about summer camp for the girls, and argued drowsily about whether or not onions should be grated into potato pancakes.

13

They ordered coffee and dessert, then Chief Delaney rose and excused himself. Sergeant Boone followed immediately. Monica and Rebecca Hirsch watched their men troop away, the Chief lumbering, Boone bouncing after him.

"Has he been behaving?" Monica asked.

"So far," Rebecca said.

"You can never trust him," Monica said severely. Then she smiled sadly. "I'm beginning to talk like Edward."

Rebecca covered Monica's hand with hers. "That's all right. We know it. We take it a day at a time."

Monica freed her hand, glanced at her watch.

"Worried about the girls?" Rebecca asked.

"It's the first time they've been alone at night. They've got to learn sometime. But I think I'll give them a call to say good night. When the men come back."

In the lavatory, Delaney and Boone relieved themselves at adjoining urinals.

"I had lunch with the Hemley woman," Boone said in a low voice. "She never saw Geltman after he entered the office about ten o'clock. When Simon came out to pay for the sandwiches, he closed the door to his private office behind him."

"Tricky business," Delaney said.

"You think the two of them have the balls for something like that?"

"Sure," the Chief said equably. "The risk wasn't all that big."

"And I got a call from Jason T. Jason," Boone went on as they zipped up and began washing their hands. "He's been spending a few hours a day of his own time, in plainclothes, wandering around looking for the Spanish woman and the girl."

"Good for him."

"He thinks they might have come from east of the Bowery. Maybe around Orchard Street. A lot of Puerto Ricans around there, he says. I think he was hinting maybe we could get him detached from patrol to spend all his time looking for the women."

"Well . . . not yet," Delaney said. "He's ambitious, isn't he? Nothing wrong with that. I'll get a list of Maitland's hangouts from the file, and we'll have Jason Two check them out. Maybe Maitland met the woman in a bar, or near one. Will Susan Hemley be at the party tonight?"

"She said yes."

"Does Rebecca know you had lunch with her?"

"Yes, sir. I told her."

"That's good," Delaney said. Faint smile. "I wouldn't want her to misunderstand if Hemley says something. If Emily Maitland shows up, and you get a chance to talk to her, mention casually that we know about all the times she and her mother came down from Nyack for lunches and dinners with Victor."

Boone stared at him a moment before they went out to rejoin the ladies.

"I get it," he said finally. "You want to know if they took the bus or train or if they drove down in that big, old Mercedes."

"Right," Delaney said. "You're beginning to think like me."

When the Chief saw the crush of people inside the Geltman Galleries, with more arriving every minute, he turned to the others and said: "If we get separated in the crowd, suppose we all meet right here on the sidewalk at midnight. That'll give us more than two hours. Should be long enough to see everything."

They all agreed, and plunged into the mob.

Delaney saw the Mephistophelian features of Lieutenant Bernard Wolfe. The detective was wearing a collarless suit of black velvet, ruffled mauve shirt, glittering studs, and cufflinks that looked like glass eyes. He bent low over Monica's hand.

"Watch this guy," Chief Delaney advised his wife with heavy good humor. "He's dangerous."

"I can believe it," she said, staring at the lieutenant with admiration. "And I thought all cops bought their clothes at Robert Hall."

"The costume's a scam," Wolfe grinned at her. "Actually, I'm a brown shoes and white socks guy."

"I'll bet," she scoffed.

"You know all these people?" Delaney asked, maneuvering to keep from being jostled away.

"Most of them," Wolfe nodded. "Want to meet anyone?"

"Not at the moment," Delaney said. "If you can get Geltman alone for a minute, will you ask him if Belle Sarazen ever helped him find buyers for Maitland's paintings? Keep it casual. And keep me out of it."

"Consider it done," Wolfe said. "Mrs. Delaney, there's food and a bar in the back. Bring you something?"

"I'll come with you," she said. "I'm supposed to circulate. Orders."

"Your husband trusts you?" the lieutenant said, turning his raffish smile on Delaney.

"Yes, he does," Monica said. "Damn it."

"Edward X. Delaney!" came the gurgling laugh, and the Chief turned slowly to face Belle Sarazen. She was sleek as a steel rod, silvery hair flat and gleaming, whippy body molded in a metallic sheath that could have been sprayed on.

"What's the *X* stand for?" she demanded.

"Marks the spot," he said, the "joke" he had repeated all his life without humor or even lightness.

"You two boys whipsawed me, didn't you?" she said, showing her Chiclet teeth.

He inclined his head.

"Clever," she said, looking at him curiously now. "And I fell for it. I thought I was smarter than that."

"So did I," he said.

She laughed and clutched his arm to her hard breasts.

"Want to meet anyone?" she asked.

"No, thanks," he said. "But I'd like to see the paintings."

"The paintings?" A burlesque leer of cynical disbelief. "Who comes to these things to look at paintings?"

"Mrs. Maitland," Sergeant Boone said. "Nice to see you again. May I present Rebecca Hirsch?"

The women looked at each other.

"My son, Ted," Alma Maitland said. "Miss Hirsch. Sergeant Boone of the New York Police Department."

Ted Maitland stared at them, not speaking.

"We're trying to see the paintings," Boone said. "But the crowd . . ."

"What do you think of them?" Rebecca asked Ted Maitland.

He glared at her with something close to hatred.

"You wouldn't understand," he said.

Chief Delaney bulled his way toward the wall. Finally, the mob thrust him close. He was pressed into one of the small, three-sided alcoves. Three paintings. Each, he noted, signed carefully at the bottom righthand corner: VICTOR MAITLAND, 1978. The signature surprised him. Not the flamboyant script he expected, but neat, bookkeeper's handwriting in black print. Name and date. Almost legalistic in its precision and legibility.

Three views of what was obviously the same model: front, back and profile. Exhibited together, the effect was of seeing her in the round, of grasping all. A heavily fleshed, auburn-haired woman. Sulky eyes. Sullen mouth. Tension of fury in clenched fists, muscled thighs. She jutted from the canvas, challenging.

"Look at the impasto," someone said. "A hundred bucks' worth of paint there."

"It'll be crackled in a year," someone said. "He never would let it dry properly. Take the money and run."

"Dynamic dysphoria," someone said. "The furious Earth Mother. The son of a bitch could draw. But strictly exogenous. I can resist it—and her."

"You better, dearie," a woman said. Brittle laugh. "They'd have to peel you off the ceiling."

Delaney half-listened. He stared at the defiant nude. He heard the mumbles of smart talk. He saw only life caught and held in vibrant colors that jangled the eye and forced him to see what he had never seen before.

"You like?" Jake Dukker asked, thrusting his head around to peer into Delaney's face. "I know the model. Bull dyke."

"Is she?" Delaney said. "She's beautiful. He caught the anger."

"And the box," Dukker laughed. "Look at that castrating box. You find the girl yet? The young girl in the drawings?"

"No," Delaney said. "Not yet."

"I saw you come in with Delaney," Belle Sarazen said. "You his wife?"

"Yes. Monica Delaney. You must be Belle Sarazen."

"Oh, you know?"

"My husband described you. He said you were very beautiful."

"Well, aren't you nice, sweetie. And did he tell you all about me?"

"Very little, I'm afraid. My husband never discusses his cases with me."

"Too bad. I imagine it could be exciting being in bed with a cop. Listening to him talk."

"It's exciting even if he doesn't talk."

"See you around, kiddo."

"Nice to see you again, Miss Maitland," Abner Boone said. "Is your mother here, too?"

"Around somewhere," Emily Maitland said breathlessly. "My land, isn't this just fascinating? I love it!"

"Love the paintings?"

"Those, too. Vic was such a naughty boy! But this crowd! The famous people! Have you ever seen such beautiful people?"

"Men or women?" he asked.

"All of them," she sighed. "So grand and skinny."

"Did you drive down?" the sergeant asked, wishing she had not worn that shattering flowered muumuu.

"Oh yes," she said, looking about with wide, shining eyes. "We always drive down."

"When you had lunch and dinner with your brother?" he pressed. "You drove?"

"Oh look!" she breathed. "That gorgeous man in the velvet suit and ruffled shirt. The devil!"

"Would you like to meet him?" Boone asked. "I know him. I'll introduce you."

"Would you?" she gasped. "Maybe he'll let me take him home to Nyack and keep him under a belljar."

Abner Boone looked at her.

"Having a good time, dear?" Edward X. Delaney asked. "Did you get a drink? Some caviar?"

"I'm doing fine," Monica assured him. "I know what you mean about his paintings, Edward. They're very strong, aren't they? They're sort of . . ."

"Of what?" he asked.

"A little crazy?" she said cautiously.

"Yes," he agreed. "A little crazy. He wanted to know it all, have it all, and show it. That way he could own it."

She wasn't sure what he meant.

"I met Belle Sarazen," she said.

"And . . . ?"

"Very sexy. Very hard. Bitchy."

"Could she kill?"

Monica looked at him queerly.

"I think so," she said slowly. "She's very unhappy."

"No," he said. "Just greedy. Will you do me a favor?"

"Of course. What?"

"See that young fellow over there? Under the spiral staircase? Alone? That's Ted Maitland. Victor's son. Go talk to him. Tell me what you think."

"Could he . . . ?"

"You tell me."

"Talked to Saul," Lieutenant Wolfe said, grinning. The crowd shoved him tightly against Delaney.

"Oh?" Delaney said, smiling broadly in return. Two friends laughing, enjoying a joke.

"He says he works with Sarazen, like half the dealers on Madison Avenue. She finds buyers. Here and in Europe. Takes ten percent."

"From the dealer or the artist?"

"You kidding? The artist, of course. No dealer's going to reduce his take."

"So they worked together on Maitland's stuff?"

"Occasionally. He says."

"Mooch around, will you, lieutenant? Maybe she and Maitland were cutting him out."

"Oh-ho. Like that, was it?"

"Could be."

"I'll see what I can dig. By the way, I may run away with your wife."

"I'd mind," Delaney said. "Great cook. Come up for dinner?"

"You say when."

Boone put his back against the wall. He held his glass of gingerale chest-high, stared with a vacant smile. Guests pushed by, stepped on his toes, slopped his drink. He paid no attention; he was watching Saul Geltman and the Maitlands, mother and daughter. The agent had the two women crowded into a corner. He was speaking rapidly, gesturing. Emily was listening intently, head lowered. Dora seemed out of it, leaning back, swaying, eyes closed.

To the sergeant, it looked as if Geltman were trying to sell them something. He was almost spluttering in his eagerness to convince. He took hold of Dora's shoulder, shook it gently. Her eyes opened. Geltman moved closer and spoke directly into her face. Her hand, clenched into a fist, rose slowly. For a moment, Boone thought she was going to hit the agent: punch him in the mouth or club him on the head. But Emily Maitland grabbed her mother's arm, soothed her, took hold of the menacing hand. She pried the fist open, straightening the fingers, smiling, smiling, smiling . . .

"Chief!" a harried Saul Geltman said. "Glad you could make it. You've met Mrs. Dora Maitland? Victor's mother?"

"I've had that pleasure," the Chief said, bowing. "A pleasure again, ma'am. A beautiful show. Your son's paintings are magnificent."

" 'Nificent," she nodded solemnly.

Zonked, Delaney thought. Boone was right: she's on the sauce.

"Pardon me a moment," Saul Geltman said. "The critics. Photographers. It's going well, don't you think?"

He turned away. Delaney grabbed his arm, pulled him back.

"One quick question," he said. "Did you have a contract with Maitland?"

Geltman looked at him, puzzled. Then his face cleared, and he laughed.

"No contract," he said. "Not even a handshake. He could have walked away any time he wanted to. If he thought I wasn't doing a good job. Sometimes artists jump from dealer to dealer. The second-raters looking for instant success. Gotta run . . ."

He disappeared. Delaney steadied Mrs. Maitland with a firm hand under her elbow. He steered her skillfully, got her against a wall. A waiter passed, and Delaney lifted a glass of something from his tray. He folded Dora Maitland's fingers around it. She stared at it blearily.

"Scotch?" she said.

"Whatever," he said. "How I enjoyed my visit to your lovely home."

She raised those dark, brimming eyes and tried to focus. Lurched closer. The oiled ringlets swung around his face. He caught the musky scent.

"You'll see," she said in a curdled voice. "Like it was. When I get the money . . ."

"Oh?" he said lightly. "Well, I can imagine all the improvements you'll make. When you get the money. But won't it be very costly to restore the house and grounds?"

"Don' you worry," she said, patting his arm with floating fingers. "Plenty of—"

"There you are, Mother!" Emily Maitland said brightly. "I was wondering where you'd got to. Chief Delaney, how nice to see you again. Land, but isn't it hot? How I'd like a glass of that nice fruit punch. Chief? Please?"

"My pleasure," Chief Delaney said, and moved toward the bar. But when he returned with the glass of punch, the Maitland women were gone. He looked about, searching for them.

"If you can't find a customer, I'll take that," Susan Hemley said. She plucked the glass from Delaney's fingers. "Remember me? Susan Hemley? You liked my hair."

"How could I ever forget?" he said gallantly. "Enjoying yourself?"

"A lot of fags," she said. "You and the sergeant are the only straight men in the place."

"You're very kind," he said, without irony. "And the paintings? What do you think of them?"

"Alma says . . ." she giggled, then tried again. "Alma thinks they're vulgar and dirty. All that skin. Alma thinks they're like, you know, porn."

"Does she?" he smiled. "So that's what Alma thinks. What do you think?"

"Live and let live," she shrugged.

"My sentiments exactly," he told her. "I'm sorry to hear Mrs. Maitland doesn't approve of her husband's work. She modeled for him, didn't she?"

"A long time ago," Susan Hemley said. "She's changed."

"Now she doesn't like the nudes?"

"Well, she does and she doesn't," Susan Hemley said vaguely. "Doesn't like all the bare ass. But still, they do sell, don't they? And who can argue with money?"

"Not me," he assured her.

"You were kidding, weren't you?" Jake Dukker asked Sergeant Abner Boone.

"Kidding? About what?"

"What you and the Chief said. Me a suspect."

"Oh, that," Boone said. "No, we weren't kidding. Sarazen claims she went upstairs with you at noon all right. On that Friday. But then she fell asleep. She says. So she can't swear you were there until one-thirty or two. She doesn't know what you were up to."

Dukker's face blanched. The pits of his cheeks became black pimples. His mouth opened and closed.

"She . . ." he tried.

"Oh yes," Boone said, nodding. "She can't remember a thing."

He smiled and moved away.

"I talked to Ted Maitland," Monica said. "At least I tried to."

"And?" the Chief asked.

"Nothing. All he did was grunt. Did you notice the bandage?"

"What bandage?"

"Ah-ha" Monica said triumphantly. "I'm a better detective than you are."

"Did I ever deny it?" he said. "What bandage?"

"On Ted's wrist."

"Which wrist? Or both?"

"On his left wrist. Under his cuff."

"So," Delaney said, with a bleak smile. "The boy's got a thing for sharp edges."

"Maybe it was an accident," Monica said.

"Maybe it was guilt," the Chief said. "I'll ask Ted and Alma about it, but I know what I'll get from them. Zilch."

The pot didn't disturb him; he had smelled marijuana before. And the swirls of perfume and whiffs of deodorant-masked sweat he could identify and accept. It was something else: a smell that was not a scent, but in the air, permeating the hard chatter he heard, the gargled laughter.

Perhaps it was the way they disregarded Victor Maitland's paintings, or debated their cash value with cold eyes. He glimpsed the lorn figure of Theodore Maitland standing near a keen J. Julian Simon, and he remembered what the boy had said: the upsidedown pyramid of the art world. All this glitter and the clang of coin sprouting from the lonely talent of a doomed creative artist who was, at the bottom, secretly derided. If they could, if it was possible, they would prefer that art could be produced by means other than individual pain. A factory perhaps. A computer. Anything they could understand and control. But wild genius daunted them; to accept it demeaned their own brutal lives. They lived off another man's talent and travail, and despised him for it to hide their own empty envy and want.

That was what he smelled: the greed of the contemptuous leeches. Their scorn hung in the air, and they turned their backs to those tortured, blazing paintings on the walls. They knew everything, but they knew nothing. This loud, brazen, laughing crowd reminded him so much of the drunken throng that gathered beneath the hotel ledge and turned white faces and wet lips upward, screaming, "Jump! Jump!"

Delaney and Boone, standing apart, exchanged what they had learned.

"We've got to get back to Nyack," the Chief said. "Dora's counting on money. 'Plenty of money,' she said. Where? From whom? She doesn't inherit."

"They drove down," Boone said. "For those lunches and dinners. Emily didn't say so, but I know. God, what a mess.

"No," Delaney said, "not a mess. Just a disorder. No pattern at all. What we've—"

But then a woman screamed. Commotion. The crowd surged toward the bar. More screams. Shouts. Then laughter. Cries.

"What the hell," Delaney said. "Let's take a look."

The press of heated bodies was thick, jammed. They pushed, shoved, slid by, working their way to the bar. Voices were high, everyone gabbling, excited, eyes shining.

"He hit her," a man said happily. "Slammed her in the chops. She fell into the punch bowl. I saw it. Beautiful."

Boone grabbed his shoulder.

"Who?" he said harshly. "Who hit who?"

"Whom," the man said. "Jake Dukker hit Belle Sarazen. Right in the chops. I saw it. Knocked her ass over tea kettle. Loverly! Great party!"

Delaney put a hand on Boone's arm.

"Let's stay out of it," he said, his lips close to the sergeant's ear.

"My doing," Boone grinned. "I told him she had thrown him to the wolves."

"Good," Delaney nodded. "Maybe we'll visit them both again. Just to listen. Let's find our women and go home. I've had enough."

"See the paintings, Chief?" Boone asked.

"Some. I'll come back in a few days when I can really look. Alone."

They sat awhile in Boone's car, discussing the evening's events, reporting on what they had seen and what they had heard. Chief Delaney and the sergeant listened intently as Monica and Rebecca Hirsch exchanged opinions on people they had met, subjective reactions to appearance, manner, dress, and style.

"What about Alma Maitland?" Delaney asked. "The widow?"

"What about her?" Monica said.

The Chief tried to phrase it delicately.

"Is she—ah—interested in—ah—well . . . women?"

The two women looked at each other and burst out laughing.

Monica took her husband's hands in hers.

"What an old foof you are," she said. "Sometimes. Is she a lesbian? Is that what you want to know?"

"Yes," he said gratefully.

Monica thought a moment.

"Could be," she said. "Becky, did you get any reaction?"

"I'd say she is," Rebecca nodded. "She may not know it, but she is. And Saul Geltman is gay; that's obvious. Belle Sarazen is a cruel bitch. I'm glad she got slugged. Jake Dukker is a complete nut. But it's Ted Maitland who really scares me."

"Why is that?" Boone asked.

"Repressed violence," Rebecca said promptly. "He's right on the edge. Did you notice his fingernails? Bitten down to the quick."

"Did either of you get to meet the mother and daughter?"

"I didn't," Rebecca said.

"I met the daughter," Monica said. "A lonely girl. But underneath all that flab there's drive and ambition."

"Dreams?" Delaney asked.

"Definitely," his wife said. "Big expectations. She kept looking at the way other women were dressed and said, 'I like that. I'm going to get that.' And I asked her when, and she said, 'Soon.' She knows what she wants."

"Interesting evening," the Chief said. "Let's go home. How about you folks coming in with us for coffee-and?"

"And what?" Rebecca asked. "I fell off my diet too far tonight."

"And nothing," Monica said. "No, wait, I have a pound cake in the freezer."

"Good enough," Delaney said. "Toasted pound cake; I can endure that. We'll take our shoes off, and the postmortems will continue."

They had to park almost a block away. They strolled back to the Delaney brownstone, the two men together in front, the women following, all of them chatting.

The men trudged up the stone steps of the stoop, still talking, Chief Delaney taking out his keys. He stopped suddenly. Two steps from the top. Boone, not watching, bumped into him. He began to murmur an apology, then stopped. He saw it, too.

The front door, the fine old oak door, was open a few inches. The light that had been left on in the hallway streamed through. Around the lock and knob, the door was scarred, crushed, splintered. A piece had been broken away and lay on the landing.

"Stay here," Delaney said to Boone.

The Chief went back down to the sidewalk. The two women were just coming up. Delaney stopped them. He stood directly in front of Monica, took hold of her upper arms.

"Listen to me," he said in a cold, dead voice. "Do exactly what I tell you."

"Edward, what—"

"Just listen. The house has been broken into. The door is smashed open."

"The girls!" she wailed. He gripped her tighter.

"I want you and Rebecca to walk slowly next door to the precinct house. Don't run. Don't scream or yell. Go into the station. Identify yourself to the desk sergeant. Tell him what's happened. Tell him to send some men, anyone he can spare. Got that?"

She nodded dumbly.

"Tell the sergeant that Boone and I will be inside. That's very important. We'll both be inside. Be sure the desk sergeant and the men he sends know that. I don't want them to come in blasting. You understand, Monica?"

Again she nodded. Rebecca stepped closer to her. Delaney stood back. The two women linked arms. The Chief gave his wife a tight smile.

"All right," he said. "Now go."

She hesitated a moment.

"It's all right," he assured her. "Now go get help."

The women turned. Delaney watched them walk steadily, with measured step, back toward the precinct house. Then he rejoined Abner Boone. They moved up slowly, silently to the top landing. They stood at the hinged side of the jimmied door.

"You carrying?" Boone whispered.

Delaney shook his head.

The sergeant slid his revolver from the hip holster beneath his suit jacket.

"Back way out?" he asked in a low voice.

"Dead end," Delaney said. "Courtyard. No way."

Boone nodded, pushed the safety off, crouched.

"You stay here," he commanded. "I'll go in fast and low. Keep away from the open door, sir."

Delaney didn't answer. Boone set himself. Bent lower. Pushed off with a thrust of his thighs. Hit the door with a shoulder. It flung wide, banged the opposite wall, began to bounce back.

By then the sergeant was in. Down. On the floor. Rolling. Ending up against the entrance-hall wall. Gun held in both hands. Propped up. Pointing.

Nothing. No sound. No movement.

"I'm coming," Delaney called. "Upstairs. Along the hall. Second door on the right. My gun's there. You lead. I'll follow. Ready? Let's go!"

They went with a rush, Boone scrambling to his feet. Dashing up the staircase. Delaney pounding after him. Down the hall. To the half-open bedroom door.

Boone rolled in again. Ready. In a few seconds Delaney reached around from the hallway. Snapped on the light. Took a quick glance around. Nothing. He had his keys out. Unlocked his equipment drawer in the bedside table. Took his loaded S&W .38 Chief's Special. A belly gun. Two-inch barrel. Flicked off the safety.

"You," he said to Boone, "take downstairs and the basement. Put all the lights on and leave them on. I want everything—closets, behind drapes, under couches . . . the works. Be careful of the men coming in from the precinct."

The sergeant nodded and was gone.

Delaney stalked down the hallway to the girls' bedroom, following his gun. He was stiffly erect, making an enormous target. He didn't care. His stomach was sour with fury and sick fear. He tasted copper.

The light was on in their bedroom. He stepped through the doorway, gun first, without crouching. Then, that moment, he would kill, and he knew it.

The room was vacant. The bed was mussed, blankets and sheets scattered. The Chief turned slowly. He went down on one knee to peer under the bed. He swept the drapes aside. He went into the bathroom. Empty.

He came back into the bedroom. There was a sound from the closet. A small, mewing cry. He stood to one side. He gripped the knob, flung the door wide. He shoved his gun forward.

They were down on the floor. Mary and Sylvia. Cowering behind hanging clothes. They were hugging each other, weeping. They looked up at him, eyes wide and blinking.

He groaned, dropped to his knees. He gathered them into his arms, weeping with them. Hugging them. Kissing them. They all, the three of them, wept together, rubbing wet cheeks, all talking at once, sobbing. Holding each other. Patting. Stroking.

He heard the sound of feet pounding up the staircase, along the hall. And Monica's despairing scream, "Edward! Edward!"

"Here!" he yelled, laughing and holding the girls to him. "We're here. It's all right. It's all right."

An hour later, the entire house had been twice searched thoroughly. No evidence of the intruder had been found. The precinct men departed, shaking their heads dolefully at the chutzpah of a B&E artist who selected a home next door to a station house.

Chief Delaney had insisted on making his own individual search, into every corner of every room, the attic, the basement, the back courtyard. As fear waned, cold fury grew. Worst of all was the disgust, knowing your home, your sanctuary, your private and secret place had been invaded, pillaged. It was a stranger putting his hands upon your body, feeling you, prying you out. And, hard to understand, there was shame there. As if, somehow, you had connived in your own despoiling.

The girls, once they had been calmed, petted, and clucked over, told a strange story. They were in bed, asleep, had heard nothing. But then the light in their bedroom had been switched on; a man stood in the doorway. He was wearing a mask, a knitted ski mask. Mary thought he was tall. Sylvia thought he was short. They agreed he was wearing a raincoat and carrying something. An iron bar. But it was flattened on one end.

The intruder ordered them into the closet. He said he would remain in their room, and if they came out of the closet or made any noise, he would kill them. Then he slammed the closet door. They huddled, terrified and weeping, not daring to move.

Monica and Rebecca, outraged, got the girls back into bed. They sat with them in the lighted bedroom. Chief Delaney and Sergeant Boone went back to the kitchen, nerves twanging. It was then almost two A.M. They had their delayed coffee and cake, lifting cups with trembling hands. They discussed the *Why?* For apparently nothing had been stolen. The things in plain view—transistor radio, portable TV set, silver service—had not been disturbed. Nothing touched, nothing taken.

Rebecca Hirsch, white-faced, came into the kitchen and heard the last part of their discussion.

"Maybe he got scared away," she suggested nervously. "He broke in, and put the girls in the closet. Then some cops came out of the station house, or he saw a squad car pull up, or he heard a siren. So he just walked away."

"It could have happened that way," Sergeant Boone said slowly, looking at Delaney. "An addict with an itch and no sense."

"That's probably what it was," the Chief said, with more confidence than he felt. "A hophead trying to make the price of a fix. He just picked the first place he came to. Our bad luck. He springs the door. Then he gets spooked and takes off. Without hurting the girls. Our good luck. Then he moves on to some other place. I'll check tomorrow. Maybe some other house on the block got hit."

None of them believed it.

Rebecca was silent. She sat huddled, shrunk in on herself, tight hands clasped between her knees. Delaney didn't like her color.

"I think a brandy would go good," he said heartily. "A wee bit of the old nasty."

Rebecca lifted her head. "I'll take some up to Monica. And warm milk for the girls."

The Chief rose, went into the study. Then he saw it. The third time he had been in this room in the last hour, and he saw it for the first time. He went back into the kitchen and got the others. Insisted on shepherding them into the study. Pointed toward his empty map board.

"That's what it was," he said. "The three Maitland sketches we found in his studio. The Jake Dukker drawing of the young model. That's what he came for. That's what he got."

"Jesus Christ," Abner Boone said.

14

Chief Delaney sat reading the *Times* in his study on Saturday morning, waiting patiently for nine o'clock, when, he figured, he could decently call Deputy Commissioner Ivar Thorsen at home. But his own phone rang fifteen minutes before the hour.

"Edward X. Delaney here."

"Edward, this is Ivar. I just heard what happened. My God, right next door to a police station! Are you all right? Monica? The girls?"

"Everyone's all right, Ivar. Thank you. No one was hurt."

"Thank God for that. What did they get?"

Delaney told him. There was a silence for a moment. Then . . .

"How do you figure that, Edward?"

"It could have been just for the intrinsic value of Maitland's last drawings. But I doubt that; they took Dukker's sketch, too. I think it was the killer, or someone hired by the killer. Has Boone been reporting to you, Ivar?"

A brief silence again, then: "Yes, he has, Edward. I didn't want to bother—"

"That's all right. At least I don't have to fill you in. The break-in happened during the preview of Maitland's last show at the Geltman Galleries. They were all there—everyone connected with the case. But it was a mob scene, Ivar. Any one of them could have skinned out, cabbed up here, grabbed the drawings, and returned within half an hour. Or hired someone to do it."

"Risky, Edward. Next door to a precinct house?"

"Sure, risky. So it must have been important. I think what we were hoping for happened: that Spanish woman and the young girl saw the killer on Friday. Either near the studio or actually in the house, maybe on the stairs. The killer sees the sketches, remembers the women, and figures maybe they can finger him. So he grabs the drawings, thinking that'll end any chance we have of finding the witnesses. But he doesn't know about the photostats I had made, or Officer Jason, who saw the women on Monday."

"Who knew about the sketches?" Thorsen asked.

"All of them did," Delaney said. "Except Dora and Emily Maitland, and they could have been told about them."

"Talking about Dora and Emily . . ." Thorsen said. "I've got something for you. It *could* be something. It could be nothing. Our contact with J. Barnes Chapin called. Dora's in the hospital. Emily found her this morning lying at the bottom of a cliff. In the back of their house."

"I know the place. A steep slope down to the river."

"Fell or pushed, the deponent knoweth not. Anyway, the lady's got a busted arm, a torn ligament in her knee, and sundry cuts and bruises."

"She had a snootful when I saw her at Geltman's bash."

"Edward, that must have been a very wet party."

"It was."

"So she fell?"

"Not necessarily," Delaney said, remembering the scene Boone had reported witnessing between Saul Geltman, Dora and Emily Maitland. "Maybe someone gave her a gentle nudge."

Thorsen sighed. "I'll ask the Nyack blues to look into it. So where do we go from here?"

"I was going to call you," Delaney said. "Here's what we need . . ."

He spoke steadily for almost five minutes, carefully explaining the reasons for his requests. When he finished, Thorsen agreed to everything.

Jason T. Jason would be detached from patrol duty and assigned to the Maitland investigation. His first task would be to work with a police artist in creating likenesses of the Spanish woman and the young girl he had seen. Reproductions of the drawings would be circulated to all Manhattan precincts with a "Hold for questioning" request.

"And to the newspapers and TV stations?" Thorsen asked. "It would help, Edward. Prove to J. Barnes Chapin that we're working on the case and getting close."

Delaney thought a moment.

"Yes," he said finally. "The danger is that the killer will get to the women before we do. Goodbye witnesses. But I'm willing to risk that for spooking the killer and maybe panicking him into doing something stupid. He hasn't made any mistakes yet, as far as I can see. Let's give him, or her, a chance. What's happening with the Nyack banks?"

"I've been working on it, Edward, I really have. But these things take time; you know that. I hope to have some word on Monday."

"Good enough. If they won't cooperate, we'll have to get a court order, and screw J. Barnes Chapin."

"It's that important?"

"Yes," Chief Delancy said stonily, "it's that important."

"All right, Iron Balls," Thorsen sighed. "It's not the first time I've crawled out on a limb for you."

"Never sawed it off, have I?"

"No," Thorsen laughed. "Not yet you haven't. How's Boone getting along?"

"Fine."

"Staying sober?"

There was the briefest of pauses before Delaney said, "Far as I know."

The moment Thorsen got off the phone, the Chief called Abner Boone and briefed him on what was happening.

"You handle Jason Two," he told the sergeant. "Get him to a police artist first thing Monday morning. Take along that set of photostats I gave you. If the artist can't come up with good likenesses, take the stats to Jake Dukker and have him do another drawing."

"He should be willing to cooperate," Boone said.

"I'd say so," Delaney said dryly. "Even if he was the guy who grabbed the original Maitland sketches. He doesn't know we have photostats. If you go to him, watch his face when you show him the copies; I'll be interested in his reactions."

"Will do," Boone said. "Anything else?"

"Better make sure Jason Two knows how to operate. By Monday morning, I'll have a list of Maitland's hangouts. You can stop by and pick it up on your way downtown. I think that's about all."

"Chief, should Jason Two flash his tin or work undercover?"

"I'll leave that to you," Delaney said. "And to him. Whichever you feel will get the best results. And try to figure how we're going to get the home address of Martha, the Maitlands' housekeeper up in Nyack. If all goes well, we'll be heading that way next Friday."

All that being accomplished, Edward X. Delaney carefully clipped from the morning *New York Times* the news story on the preview of the Victor Maitland Memorial Show. The headline read: SLAIN ARTIST REMEMBERED AT GALA. There was a small photo of Saul Geltman and a large photo of Belle Sarazen. She had been photographed standing next to a Maitland oil. The contrast between her hard, silvery slimness and the lush nude made an eye-catching picture. The caption referred to "Belle Sarazen, well-known patroness of the arts . . ." Chief Delaney grunted.

Monica and the girls were out, shopping at Bloomingdale's for last-minute items before Mary and Sylvia departed for summer camp on Monday. The windows were open wide; a warm breeze billowed through. It promised a shining day in early June, one of those rare marvels: big sky, washed clouds, a smoky sun, air smelling green and eager.

Savoring his quiet solitude, wondering if it was too early for a chilled beer and deciding it was, Edward X. Delaney carried the original file folders of the official Maitland investigation to his desk, sat down, prepared to draw up a list of the bars, restaurants, cabarets, and other public places known to have been frequented by the victim. Then Jason T. Jason could . . .

But, as had happened to him before on other cases, he found himself reading once again every document in the file. Not that he had any great hope of happening upon a revelation he had previously missed; it was just that official paper fascinated him. The most laconic police document was an onion, Chief Delaney decided, a goddamned onion. The layers peeled away, and the thing got smaller and smaller until you were left with a little white kernel you could hold between thumb and forefinger. And what was that? The truth? Don't count on it. Don't take it to the bank.

His eyes skimmed the autopsy report for the third time. And in the "Incidental Notes"—a heading that invited inattention—he read about an enlarged liver; evidence of a broken arm, healed normally; some old lung lesions, healed normally; perhaps a heart murmur in Victor Maitland's youth, healed normally. And, almost as an afterthought, the PM noted casually: "Possible polymyositis."

Delaney blinked, reading that and set the report aside.

He had filled six personal pocket notebooks since he began the Maitland investigation (and he assumed Sergeant Boone had done the same). In his methodical way, Delaney had Scotch-taped a précis of each notebook to the inside of the front cover so he wouldn't have to paw through the lot to find a particular fact or statement he wanted. So it didn't take him long to find the notebook that contained his second interrogation of Alma Maitland, and the name of the Maitlands' family physician.

Dr. Aaron Horowitz, Delaney had written, followed by "dwn blk," which in Delaney shorthand meant that the doctor's office was down the block from the Maitland apartment on East 58th Street.

He looked up Dr. Aaron Horowitz's number in the Manhattan telephone directory, using a magnifying glass to read it. He dialed and, as he expected, this being a Saturday, was connected with an answering service. When the operator asked him if he cared to leave a message, Delaney had no qualms at all in telling her it was an emergency, a matter of life-or-death, a police matter, and please have Dr. Horowitz call him at once.

He just had time to settle back, peel the cellophane wrapper from his first cigar of the day, and pierce it, when his phone shrilled. He thought even the ring was angry, but perhaps that was an after-the-fact reaction—after he heard the voice of Dr. Aaron Horowitz.

"What the hell is this?" the doctor screamed, after Delaney identified himself. "What's this 'emergency' shit? This 'life-or-death' shit? What the hell you pulling here?"

"Doctor, doctor," Delaney said, as soothingly as he could. "It *is* an emergency, a matter of life-or-death, a police matter. It concerns a patient of yours. His name is—"

"You got your brains in your ass?" Dr. Horowitz demanded. "The doctor-patient relationship is privileged. You didn't know that? I won't tell you a word about any patient of mine."

Chief Delaney took a deep breath. "This is a *dead* patient," he yelled at Dr. Horowitz. "You got no fucking privilege, no fucking right to deny information to the police about a deceased patient."

"Who says so?" the doctor shouted.

"The courts say so," Delaney thundered, and then launched into a brilliant flight of fantasy. "In case after case—the most recent being Johnson versus the State of New York—the courts have held that a medical practitioner has no right, by statute or by precedent, to withhold vital information regarding a deceased patient from police officers discharging their legal duty."

It was amazing how easily educated men could be conned.

"What patient you talking about?" Dr. Aaron Horowitz said grudgingly. He was no longer yelling.

"Victor Maitland."

"Oh . . . him."

"Yes, him," Delaney said sternly. "All I want is five minutes of your time. Can't you spare five minutes from your golf game?"

"Golf game!" Dr. Horowitz said bitterly. "Very funny. I'm laughing all over. For your information, my dear Chief Delaney, I am at Roosevelt Hospital, and I got a kid who's going. From what? Nobody knows from what. Meningitis maybe. Some golf game!"

"If I come over now," Delaney said, "can you spare me five minutes?"

"Can't it wait till Monday?"

"No," Delaney said, "it can't. Five minutes is all I need. I'll be there in half an hour."

"If you're coming, how can I stop you?" Horowitz said.

Delaney took that for acquiescence. He slammed down the phone, grabbed up reading glasses and notebook, and was on his way.

In addition to a normal dislike of all hospitals, Edward X. Delaney had special reason for aversion to Roosevelt: it was the hospital where his first wife, Barbara, had languished and died. It was, he admitted, irrational to hold a building accountable for that, but it was the way he felt. He knew that if, God forbid, he was ever stricken on the steps of Roosevelt Hospital, his first words to those who ran to aid him would be, "Take me to Mount Sinai, goddammit!"

He finally located Dr. Aaron Horowitz in the surgeons' lounge, a small cheerless room with a television set, a couch and two armchairs covered with orange plastic, a card table and four folding chairs, and not much else.

Dr. Horowitz turned out to be a small man, about a head shorter than Delaney, but as old, if not older. He had a pinched, disillusioned face. He wore steel-rimmed spectacles. There was a horseshoe of white hair around his scalp, but it was mostly bare skin, tan and freckled. He was wearing a white surgical gown. A mask hung loosely around his neck. He didn't offer to shake hands, and Delaney stood well away from him, across the room.

"You got some fucking nerve," the doctor said wrathfully. "What the hell's so important about Victor Maitland it couldn't wait for Monday?"

"You ever treat him for a knife wound?" Delaney asked. "In the arm?"

"No. Is that the emergency, the matter of life-or-death?"

"There's more," Delaney said. "The autopsy report said 'Possible polymyositis.' "

" 'Possible,' " Horowitz sneered. "That's good. I like that."

"You knew about it?" Delaney asked.

"Knew about it? Of course I knew about it. The man was my patient, wasn't he?"

"What is it—polymyositis?" Delaney asked. "Like bursitis or arthritis?"

"Oh sure," Horowitz said. "Just like it. Like death is like fainting."

Delaney stared at him a moment, not comprehending.

"Death?" he said. "You mean it's fatal?"

"In Victor Maitland it was terminal. Or would have been if someone hadn't killed him first."

Delaney took a small step backward.

"Terminal?" he repeated hoarsely. "You're sure?"

Dr. Aaron Horowitz threw up his hands in disgust.

"Why don't you have the Board investigate me?" he jeered. "Am I sure? What kind of a shit-ass question is that? You want to see Maitland's file? You want to read the tests? How the corticosteroid therapy failed? You want the opinions of two other—"

"All right, all right," Delaney said hastily. "I believe you. How long did he have it?"

Horowitz thought a moment.

"About five years maybe," he said. "I'd have to check his file to be sure."

"How long would he have to live?"

"He should have been dead a year ago. The man had the constitution of an ox."

"How long would he have lived if he hadn't been killed? Just a guess, Doctor. You won't be asked to testify. I'm not taking any of this down."

"A guess? Maybe another year. Two, three at the most. This isn't an exact science, you know. Everyone's different."

"Did he know it? Did you tell him?"

"That he was dying? Sure, I told him."

"How did he react?"

"He laughed."

Delaney stared at the doctor.

"He laughed?"

"That's right. What's so unusual? Some people cry, some break down, some don't do anything. Everyone's different. Maitland laughed."

"Did he ever tell anyone else he was dying?"

"Now how in hell would I know that?"

"But you never told anyone else? His wife, for instance?"

"I told no one. Just Maitland. Your five minutes are up."

"All right, Doctor," Chief Delaney said. "Thank you for your time." He turned to go, had the corridor door opened when he paused, turned back. "How's that kid you mentioned?" he asked.

"Died about twenty minutes ago."

"I'm sorry," Delaney said.

"Zol dich chapen beim boych!"

"Zol vaksen tsibelis fun pipik!" Edward X. Delaney said to an amazed Dr. Aaron Horowitz.

The Chief went directly to a lobby phone booth and looked up the number of Saul Geltman. The art dealer was home and, Delaney could tell, wasn't overjoyed to hear from a cop on a bright, sunshiny June afternoon. But he agreed to see him, asked him to come up. It turned out Geltman lived way over east, in one of the new high-rise apartment buildings overlooking the East River and Brooklyn beyond. Delaney took a cab and finally got to smoke the cigar he had prepared an hour ago. The cab interior was plastered with signs that read: PLEASE DO NOT SMOKE. DRIVER ALLERGIC. But Delaney lighted up anyway, and the driver didn't say anything. Which was wise, considering the Chief's mood.

Delaney had told Sergeant Boone he wanted to see Saul Geltman's apartment, believing there was no better way to judge a man's character than to get a look at his home. It was a secret place where a man, if he wished, could take off the mask he presented to the world. It revealed his tastes, idiosyncrasies, needs and wants, strengths and weaknesses. If a man had a lot of books, that told you something about him. The titles of the books he owned told you more. And *no* books told you even more.

But the presence or absence of a private library was an obvious clue to a man's personality. Chief Delaney sincerely believed you could better judge by the pictures on his walls, the carpets on the floor, ashtrays on the desk. And if all these things had been selected by his wife or an interior decorator—well, that too revealed something, didn't it?

But more than rugs, paintings, ashtrays, or books, Delaney was interested in the ambience of a man's home. Was it cold and contrived, or warm and cheery? Was it cluttered as the man's own mind or as serene as his soul? The Chief never ceased marveling at how many criminals lived in hotels, furnished rooms, and motels, their rootless lives mirrored by their transient surroundings. And like most cops, Delaney had seen old cons who lived in square chambers with a cot, dresser, chair. Not because they couldn't afford better, but because they were attempting to reproduce the institutional life for which they subconsciously yearned and to which they inevitably returned.

The home of art dealer Saul Geltman was on the east side of the seventeenth floor of the high-rise apartment house. The building itself was constructed of glazed brick tinted a light green, with horizontal bands of picture windows. The lobby was small, spare, tiled, with a single piece of abstract stainless-steel sculpture as the sole decoration.

The living room of Geltman's apartment, Delaney estimated, had to be forty by twenty. It was all windows on the east side, with glass doors at each end opening onto a terrace as long as the room itself, but only half as deep. There were two bedrooms, two bathrooms, a combined kitchen and dining area separated by a serving counter with a butcher's-block top. All the rooms were well proportioned, airy, smiling. The ceilings were higher than Delaney had expected; the floors were parquet.

But it was the manner in which this joyous apartment had been furnished that delighted the Chief. There was an eclectic selection of antiques, leaning heavily to lightwood French provincial. A plenitude of gleaming copper, brass, and pewter ornaments. A zinc-covered dining table set on a cast-iron base. Polished carved oak caryatids supporting a black marble sideboard. Worn Persian and Turkish rugs on the parquetry. Chair fabrics and drapes in a pleasantly clashing rainbow of plaids, candy stripes, and rich, nubbly wools.

And all spotless, glittering, almost overwhelming in its comfortable perfection. It stopped just short of being a department-store model apartment. Delaney did not miss the "careless elegance" of tossed art magazines on the pitted teak cocktail table, the carefully arranged informality of the bookcase, with a few art books tilted, a few lying on their sides, but the entire display ordered in such a manner that it pleased the eye, and the Chief wondered if there could be any art without artifice.

"Beautiful," he said to Saul Geltman, who had shown him through with great enthusiasm, giving the age (and frequently the cost) of each antique, pointing out amusing bric-a-brac, calling Delaney's attention to a seventeenth-century desk reputed to have six secret drawers—although Geltman had found only five—and a set of eighteenth-century carved walnut bookends which, joined together, proved to be an old man buggering a goat.

"Not bad for a poor kid from Essex Street, huh?" Geltman laughed. "Now all I got to do is pay for it!"

"You decorated the place yourself?" Delaney asked.

"Every stick I personally selected," the little art dealer said proudly. "Every fabric, every rug, ashtrays—the lot. I'm still working on it. I see something I got to have, I buy it, bring it up, get rid of something. Otherwise this place would be a warehouse."

"Well, you've done wonders," the Chief told him. "There isn't a single thing here I wouldn't like to have in my home."

"Really?" Geltman said, glowing. "You really mean that?"

"Absolutely," Delaney said, wondering at the other man's need for reassurance. "Excellent taste."

"Taste!" Geltman cried, looking about with shining eyes. "Yes! Well, I couldn't play the fiddle, and I can't paint, so I suppose whatever creative talent I have came out here." He looked down, let his fingertips drift softly across the top of a charming pine commode, the drawers and doors fitted with hammered brass hardware. "I love this place," Geltman murmured. "Love it. Sounds silly, I know, but—" He stopped suddenly, straightened up, smiled at Delaney. "Well," he said briskly, rubbing his palms together, "what can I get you to drink? Wine? Whiskey? What?"

"Do you have any beer?" the Chief asked.

"Beer. Of course I have beer. Heineken. How's that?"

"Just fine, thank you."

"Sit anywhere. I'll be right back."

Delaney selected a high-backed wing chair at the rear of the room, facing the expanse of glass. He settled himself and, for the first time, saw there were two men on the terrace, seated in chairs of white wire at a white cast-iron table. The Chief was startled. He had not seen them before, nor had Geltman mentioned that he had guests.

The two men, youths actually, were almost identically clad in short-sleeved knitted white shirts, trousers of white duck, white sneakers. They lounged indolently in their chairs, not facing each other but turned so they could watch the river traffic below.

There was a bottle of rosé wine on the white table, sparkling in the sunlight. As Delaney watched, both youths raised crystal glasses slowly to their lips and sipped. Viewed through sheer ecru curtains, the scene had the feel of an Edwardian garden party, peaceful and haunting, frozen in an old sepia photograph, faded, emulsion cracking, corners bent or missing, but the moment in time and place caught like a remembered dream: languid youth, sunshine over all, a breeze that would kiss forever and a day that would never die.

"I'm sorry," he said when Geltman came back, "I didn't know you had company."

"Oh, just two local boys," Geltman said lightly. "Stopped by to raid my wine cellar."

He had brought the opened bottle of beer on a silver salver, along with a glass of a tulip design. The glass had been chilled; frost coated the sides.

"You do it with an electric gadget," Geltman laughed. "Instant frosting. Silly, but it looks nice."

"Tastes better too," Delaney said, pouring his beer. "Nothing for you?"

"Not at the moment. Well, what can I do for you, Chief? More questions?"

The little man sat on the arm of a club chair, facing Delaney at an angle. Geltman's back was to the windows, his face in shadow. He was wearing bags of light grey flannel, a turtleneck sweater of white wool. His cordovan moccasins gleamed wickedly. The bracelet of heavy gold links was much in evidence, catching the light, but Delaney saw none of the nervous vigor the dealer had displayed in his gallery. No slumping, straightening, twisting, gesturing. No drumming of fingers or smoothing the thin, brown-grey hair across his skull. Saul Geltman seemed composed, at peace. Because, Delaney supposed, he was in his own home.

"More questions, yes," the Chief said. "But first I'd like to thank you for having us to your party. We enjoyed it."

"I'm glad you did." Geltman grinned. "See the *Times* story this morning? Wonderful! Of course Belle and Jake Dukker misbehaved, but an art show isn't counted a success without at least one fight. Did you get to see the paintings? In that mob?"

"Not as much as I wanted to. I'd like to come back."

"Of course. Any time. They'll be there for a month, at least. We're charging admission. For a charity. But ask for me at the door."

Delaney waved the suggestion away.

"Are the paintings selling?" he asked.

"Marvelously," Geltman nodded. "Most of them are sold. Only a few left, and they'll go soon enough."

Delaney looked around the elegant room.

"You don't have any Maitlands?" he observed, half-question, half-statement.

"Can't afford him," the dealer laughed. "Besides, it's bad business to have artists you represent in your own home. Buyers suspect you'd save the best for yourself. Which is true, of course."

Delaney held his frosted glass to the light, admiring the dark, glowing amber of the beer. He took a deep, satisfying swallow. Then he held the stemmed glass in both hands, tinked the edge of the glass gently against his teeth.

"You knew he was dying?" he asked.

Then he heard, for the first time, soft laughter from the terrace. The two youths, wine glasses in hand, were standing at the railing, looking down at something on the East River.

When he looked back, he saw Geltman had slid from his perch on the chair arm. Now he was in the chair, sitting sideways, his legs hooked over the opposite arm.

"Yes," he told Delaney, "I knew."

"You didn't tell us," the Chief said flatly.

"Well . . ." Geltman sighed, "it's not the kind of thing you like to talk about. Also, I couldn't see how it could possibly help you find the guy who did it. I mean, how could it help?"

Delaney took another sip of beer. From now on, he decided, he would frost his glasses.

"It might help," he said. "It just might. I'm not saying it would help explain other people's actions, but it might help explain Maitland's."

Geltman stared at him a moment, then shook his head. "I'm afraid I don't understand."

"The doctor says that when he told Maitland he had a fatal illness, Maitland laughed. I believe that. It's in character with what we've learned about the man. But I don't care how hard he was, how cynical, what a lush. Hearing a thing like that would change his life. The life he had left. It *had* to. He'd do things he wouldn't otherwise do. Make plans maybe. Or try to jam as much into his remaining days as he could. *Something.* It would result in something. The man was human. Just ask yourself how you'd react if you got heavy news like that. Wouldn't it affect the way you'd live out your days?"

"I suppose so," Geltman said in a low voice. "But I knew about it, and I didn't see any change in him. He was still the same crude, mean son of a bitch he had always been."

"When did you learn about the illness?"

"About five years ago, I think it was. Yes, about then."

"He told you himself?"

"Yes."

"Did he tell anyone else, to your knowledge? His wife, for instance? His son?"

"No," Geltman said. "He told me I was the only one he was telling. He swore me to secrecy. Said if I told anyone, and he learned about it, he'd cut my balls off. And he'd have done it, too."

"Did you tell anyone?" Delaney asked.

"Jesus, no!"

"His mother? His sister? Anyone?"

"I swear I didn't, Chief. It's just not the sort of thing you go around blabbing about."

"No," Delaney said, "I suppose not. You say you saw no change in his conduct? His personality?"

"That's right. No change."

"He didn't, to your knowledge, make any special plans? Men sentenced to death usually tidy up, put their affairs in order."

"He didn't do anything special. Not to my knowledge."

"Well," Delaney sighed, finishing his beer, "he certainly didn't seem to make any effort to leave his wife and son well provided for. They inherit, but not much."

"They'll do all right," Geltman said shortly. "With the sale of the last paintings. Even after taxes, they'll come out with half a million. At least. I'm not shedding any tears for them. Another beer, Chief?"

"No, thank you. That just hit the spot."

He looked out onto the terrace again. The languid youths were draped again in their white wire chairs, lounging comfortably. As Delaney watched, one of them, a golden-haired boy, tilted his head back and, holding the wine glass high above him, let the last few drops of wine spill into his mouth and onto his face. The other youth laughed.

"It was some muscle disorder," Delaney said. "As I understand it."

"Yes," Geltman said.

"It didn't affect his painting? For five years?"

"Not noticeably," the art dealer said.

"What does that mean?"

"The buyers didn't notice," Geltman said. "The critics didn't. But Maitland did. And I did."

"How? How did it affect his painting?"

"He said there was a—well, not pain, but a stiffness. That's how he described it—a stiffness. In his hands, arms, shoulders. So he took something that seemed to help."

"Poppers? Snappers?"

"Yes."

"From Belle Sarazen?"

"I don't know where he got them."

"But they helped?"

"That's what Vic told me. He said they loosened him up. You can see it in his last paintings. The stuff he did in, oh, the last year or two. They were looser, the line not as sharp, the colors harsher, brighter. It's a subtle thing. I think only Vic and I could see it. No one else saw any change. They were still the same old Maitlands. Still as wonderful, still as evocative, as stirring."

"Yes," Edward X. Delaney said. "Stirring."

He heaved himself to his feet, cleared his throat.

"I thank you, Mr. Geltman," he said. "For seeing me. The hospitality."

"My pleasure," the little man said. He thrust himself up from the chair, slid over the arm to land agilely on the balls of his feet. "Hope it helped. Getting anywhere, are you?"

"Oh yes," Chief Delaney said. "Definitely."

"Good," Geltman said. "Glad to hear it."

They moved to the entrance hall. Delaney turned back to look around that fabulous room one more time.

"A kind of dream," he said.

"Yes," Saul Geltman said wonderingly, looking at Delaney. "That's exactly what it is—a kind of dream."

Then the Chief glanced out to the terrace. The two youths were standing again, at the railing. Their long, fine hair whipped in the breeze like flame. One had his arm around the other's waist.

Again, Delaney had the impression of a remembered photograph. White-clad youths against a china-blue sky. A tomorrow that would never come. No future at all. But an endless now, caught and held.

"Beautiful, isn't it?" Saul Geltman said softly.

Edward X. Delaney turned to him, smiling faintly. He quoted: " 'Golden lads and girls all must, as chimney sweepers, come to dust.' "

He left then, as Saul Geltman was trying to compose some kind of response, his face slack and struggling.

15

By Wednesday of the following week, copies of a police artist's sketches of the Spanish woman and the young model had gone out to all Manhattan precincts. They had also been distributed to newspapers and TV stations. The *Daily News* had given them a nice display on page 4, under a two-column head: NEW LEAD IN MAITLAND SLAYING. And the drawings had been shown on the evening news programs of channels 2 and 7, with a phone number that any citizen with information could call.

In addition, Jason T. Jason had been taken off patrol and assigned full-time to the Maitland investigation. He was enthusiastic about his new job and, according to Sergeant Boone, was spending about eighteen hours a day checking out the list of Maitland's known hangouts and just wandering the streets of the Lower East Side, showing pocket-size reproductions of the police sketches to pushcart vendors, bartenders, beauty-parlor operators, shop owners, street peddlers, pimps, prosties, hustlers, bums—anyone who might have seen one or both of the women.

Also during this week, Abner Boone ran another time check and proved to his satisfaction, and that of Chief Delaney, that it would have been no problem for Ted Maitland to get from Cooper Union to the Mott Street studio, zap his father, and return to Cooper Union in time for his two o'clock lecture.

Boone was also able to determine the last name of Martha, the housekeeper of Dora and Emily Maitland up in Nyack. Her last name was Beasely. The sergeant discovered this by calling the Maitland home. The first time he called, Emily Maitland answered and Boone hung up. The second time, a harsh, twangy voice said, "Maitland residence."

Boone said, "I'm trying to locate Martha Jones. Is this Martha?"

"Well, it's Martha," the housekeeper said, "but my name ain't Jones; it's Beasely."

"Sorry to bother you," Abner Boone said, and hung up. He then checked the Nyack telephone directory and got Martha Beasely's home address.

On Thursday, Deputy Commissioner Thorsen phoned Delaney and told him that Mrs. Dora Maitland's Nyack bank had agreed to cooperate; the Chief could examine her account. But it was all on the qt, and Delaney was to speak only to an assistant vice-president who would be present during his examination to make certain Delaney did not alter or remove the records. The Chief readily agreed to that.

So, all in all, it was a busy, productive week—lots of phone calls, meetings, writing of reports and new time charts—and as they drove up to Nyack on Friday morning, Chief Delaney and Sergeant Boone sourly agreed they were not one step closer to finding the killer of Victor Maitland. Though neither would admit discouragement, they weren't exactly bubbling over with optimism either.

"Still," Delaney said, "you never know when a break's going to come, or from what direction. I had a partner once in the One-eight Precinct. He had worked the homicide of a young woman raped and strangled in her apartment. All the leads petered out. They chewed on it for weeks and months, and then the file got pushed to the back of the tub. You know how it is: there's so much new stuff coming along, you just can't give any time to the old. So more than a year later, the NYPD gets a letter from a woman out in Ohio, Michigan, Indiana—some place like that. She had signed up for the Peace Corps, got sent to Africa, caught some kind of a fever, and was sent home. Now this Peace Corps girl had her mail forwarded to her in Africa—right? And she was a good girlfriend of this girl who got knocked off in New York. And while she's in Africa, a letter is forwarded to her from this girl who got zonked. This letter is all little jokes about a new guy she's met, he's got a red beard, his name is David and how nice he is, and all that, and she's got to close this letter and mail it fast because this David is coming over for dinner. This letter, which the Peace Corps woman had saved and sent to the New York cops, was dated the day the girl got snuffed. The Peace Corps woman didn't know her friend had been killed till she got back to this country. So the dicks go to the old file and find a married guy named David—he's got a red beard, too—who worked in the dead girl's office. They broke him, and that was that. But that's how a break came along that no one counted on."

"We should be so lucky," Boone said mournfully.

"We will be," Edward X. Delaney said confidently. "Our cause is just."

And Sergeant Boone didn't know if he was kidding or not; one of these days he was going to ask the Chief for a blueprint of his sense of humor.

On the drive up, they talked a lot about Victor Maitland's fatal illness. The sergeant couldn't get over it.

"Everyone talks about what a stud he was and how he was pronging everything in sight," Boone said. "And now we find he was dying, and knew it. Chief, you think that's why he was so busy in the sack? Trying to cram in as much as he could before he passed?"

"No," Delaney said, "I don't think so. His reputation as a stallion goes way back. Remember what Saul Geltman said about him in Greenwich Village twenty years ago? He was getting more than his share even then. No, I don't think getting the death sentence from Doc Horowitz turned him on. But I'll bet my bottom dollar that it set him off some other way. Sergeant, it's impossible to hear news like that and not have it affect your life style *some* way."

"But Geltman told you no," Boone reminded him. "Said Maitland didn't change at all."

"Geltman," Delaney said broodingly. "I like that little guy. I really do. But there's something about him . . ." The Chief held his open hand a few inches from his temple, palm cupped, fingers spread. He turned the whole hand a short way, as if he were turning a big dial. "Something just a little off up there. Something too much."

"The young boys on the balcony?"

"No. Well . . . that's part of it maybe. But his apartment. The beautiful things he owns. The *things!* He loves them. You should have seen him touch them. Did everything but kiss the tables. I've never seen such a passion for things. They were magnificent, I admit it. But still, they were just things. When he's as old as I am, he'll realize you spend the first half of your life accumulating things, and the second half getting rid of them. I think if I had broken his crystal tulip glass, he'd have cried."

"Things never turned me on," the sergeant said.

"No?" Delaney said. "I never would have guessed it from the luxury of your apartment."

Boone grinned, but resolved to visit his local Woolworth's and buy some decent glasses.

The sergeant dropped Delaney off in front of the bank. The Chief told him to take his time finding and talking to Martha Beasely. When he was finished, he could pick Delaney up at the bank or, if he wasn't there, to try the tavern across the street. The bar had a big sign in the window reading: YES, WE HAVE COORS!

The assistant vice-president of the bank turned out to be young, wistful, with a blonde mustache that didn't quite make it. He ensconced Delaney in one of the small, private rooms in the safe-deposit vault. On the desk was a stack of folded computer printouts, two small reels of microfilm in labeled boxes, and a microfilm-reading device.

"Know how to work this thing?" he asked the Chief.

"Sure," Delaney said. "Start. Stop. Advance. Rewind. I can handle it."

"Right," the banker said. "Well . . . uh . . ."

Then he asked a few eager questions about police work. ("Must be a fascinating life. Tell me, do you . . . ?") But when he realized this New York City cop was going to answer only in grunts, or not at all, he finally gave up, disregarded the agreement, and said, "Just tell the man outside when you're finished." Then he departed, leaving behind the faint scent of Canoe.

Chief Delaney closed the door and locked it. He put on his reading glasses, took off his jacket, and settled down in a tubular steel chair with a meagerly padded seat cushion. He laid out notebook and pen. He started on the stack of computer printouts, and had worked barely fifteen minutes when he knew he wasn't going to need notebook or pen. Zilch.

The printout was a record of Mrs. Dora Maitland's checking and saving accounts for the previous six months. The microfilm carried similar information for the past seven years. When Chief Delaney realized he was going to find no startling revelations, he began going faster and faster, flipping microfilm through the electric viewer almost as fast as he could press the Advance button. He finished everything in a little more than an hour.

Dora Maitland had a savings account that began with a total of slightly more than six thousand dollars and was gradually reduced by small withdrawals (usually fifty or a hundred dollars) to a current total of slightly less than four thousand dollars. The withdrawals showed no periodic pattern. During the period covered by the records, no deposits other than accumulated interest had been made.

The records of the checking account did show patterns but they seemed entirely innocent to Delaney. For instance, there were quarterly deposits of precisely the same sum: $117.50. That was probably a stock dividend. And regular semi-annual deposits of $375 were probably municipal-bond coupons.

There were weekly checks written in the amount of $125, which, the Chief guessed, could be Martha Beasely's salary. And there were odd-cents sums for electricty, telephone and, he assumed, living expenses.

There was a check written annually for more than two thousand dollars, and Delaney thought that was the property tax. He could find no monthly schedule of disbursements large enough to be mortgage payments, so he assumed the Maitland home was free and clear.

When he had finished, he sat there a few moments, shoulders drooping, staring balefully at the unmarked page of his notebook. What he had been hoping for, of course, were large deposits or withdrawals. A single big withdrawal, for instance, might indicate payment to a hired hiller. Hefty checks drawn at regular intervals sometimes signaled payments to a blackmailer. But what Delaney was particularly looking for was a record of big deposits. It would then be a reasonable assumption that Victor Maitland, a very successful artist, was contributing handsomely to the support of his mother and sister, with whom he was on friendly terms. But apparently Dora and Emily had been telling the truth. Victor gave them nothing. At least the bank accounts revealed nothing.

From all indications, Dora and Emily Maitland were getting by—but just. They owned their home and grounds, but their total net worth—their cash worth—rarely ran over five thousand dollars, according to these records. It just didn't make sense when the loving son was selling paintings at 100 G's, and Edward X. Delaney didn't believe it for a minute. Something smelled—and it wasn't Canoe.

The Chief told the vault attendant he was leaving, and tramped across the sun-baked street to the tavern. It was a hot, steamy afternoon, and he carried his jacket and straw skimmer. The bar was just as desolate as Delaney's mood—a big, empty barn of a place, reeking of stale beer and a creosote disinfectant, with sawdust on the floor and a piebald cat yawning around. There were two silent customers at the bar, slumped over their beers, and a bartender just as silent. He was sucking on a toothpick, staring out the flyblown window and waiting patiently for the end of the world.

The Chief ordered a Budweiser. He paid for it and took bottle and glass to a back booth. The place was dim enough, and cool, and quiet. He drank the beer slowly, taking little sips, sitting stolidly and avoiding unnecessary movement.

What angered him, he knew, was that he felt he was being tricked and made a fool of. Someone of intellect was toying with him. Whichever way he turned, that path had been anticipated and blocked. All his training, experience, all his crafts and instincts brought to nothing by a guy who had probably killed *for the first time!* That's what hurt most: a beginner, a goddamned amateur, and he had Edward X. Delaney snookered. In such a smoldering mood, he could understand why cops used their fists and saps. The frustration curdled the stomach and rubbed nerve ends raw.

He was on his second beer when Abner Boone came lounging in. He took off his sunglasses, glanced around, spotted Delaney and nodded. He stopped at the bar for a Coke, gulped it down, ordered another. He brought that one to the Chief's booth and slid in opposite him.

"Jesus," he said, "feels like ninety. And high humidity. Been waiting long?"

"Not so long," Delaney said. "I was thinking about food, but I'm not really hungry. You?"

"I can skip," the sergeant said. "Right now I just want to cool off. My shirt's sticking."

"Take off your jacket," Delaney suggested.

"Ahh, I'm carrying," Boone said. "Someone will spot the heat and call the locals. I'll be all right." He dug his notebook from his inside pocket. "I hope you did better than I did, Chief."

"I did shit!" Delaney said, so vehemently that Boone looked up in surprise.

Delaney told the sergeant what he had discovered—or what he had not discovered.

"All negative," he said. "The only thing it proves, or apparently proves, is that Maitland was making no contributions to his mother and sister. And they already told us that."

"Could Dora have an account in another bank? Or Emily? Or maybe safe-deposit boxes loaded with cash?"

Delaney shook his head. "Thorsen checked all that out first thing. This was the only bank. How did you make out with Martha Beasely?"

"More questions than answers," Boone said, flipping through his notebook. "That's what snows me about this thing: every time we do something we get more problems. For instance, Martha Beasely claims she's been working for the Maitlands for almost four years. And in all that time she never even saw Victor Maitland or Saul Geltman. Knew they existed and visited occasionally because Dora and Emily talked about them. But Martha Beasely never laid eyes on them. Now how do you figure that?"

"Easy," Delaney said, straightening up, leaning forward, interested now. "Maitland and Geltman made sure they only came up on Martha's day off, or maybe at night, when she wasn't there."

"But *why?*"

"That's something else again. I don't know that, sergeant. But I'll bet they timed their visits so the housekeeper wouldn't see them. What else?"

"A lot of nothing. Dora hits the bottle, just like we figured. She takes a lot of naps, but some afternoons she can't stand up. Emily never goes out by herself as far as the Beasely woman knows. No dates. No boyfriends coming around. No phone calls except from old family friends."

"Well . . ." Delaney sighed, "that's that."

"No, sir," Sergeant Boone said. "Not quite. Something else. Another question. This Beasely woman was very tight at first. Suspicious. Wouldn't open up. But then I told her it had to do with Victor Maitland's tax troubles, that he claimed he was supporting his mother and sister, and we didn't think he did. Then she opened up and started complaining about how much money she made at the Maitlands—or how little. Says she makes a bill and a quarter for five and a half days. Does the cleaning and laundry, and usually cooks lunch for all of them. She says they've got less money than she has, so Victor couldn't have been supporting them. Then I said that was a big house with lots of grounds to take care of—you know, laying it on thick with the good-old-boy accent—and she said Emily and Dora had to take care of the grounds themselves because they can't afford a man to come in once a month to do it. Anyway, just talking away—this Martha Beasely is a widow and a gabber when she gets going—she said Emily is pretty good at mowing that big lawn, cutting down dead branches, odd repair jobs around the house, and stuff like that. I said something about that was a fair piece of lawn to keep mowed, and she said about two years ago they bought a second-hand power mower, which Emily learned how to use. And she mentioned that Emily keeps the power mower and a lot of other garden stuff, rakes and tools and junk, in that old barn."

"Oh-ho," Delaney said.

"Right," Boone nodded. "My ears perked up, I asked her how come? I said they had told us the doors of that barn had been nailed shut years ago because their old man had hanged himself in there, and I had *seen* them nailed shut. This Beasely woman said yes, the wide front doors were nailed shut and even locked with a rusty old padlock. But there was another door, a narrow back door, and inside was like a little shed where they kept the power mower and garden tools. Sorry I missed that other door, Chief."

"That's all right," Delaney said. "Maybe Emily wanted you to miss it."

"Well, why the hell would they make a big sentimental thing about nailing shut the doors of a place where the old man did the Dutch, and then have a back door that's open? Doesn't make any sense, does it, sir?"

"Nooo," the Chief said slowly. "Not much. Is that back door unlocked?"

"Beasely says yes. Says she's been in there once or twice. Nothing in there but the power mower, rakes and so forth, a can of gasoline, some old buckets, a tarp, and so forth. Old, rusty shit like that. But still . . ."

"Yes . . . still," Delaney nodded. "I wouldn't give it a second thought except that they made sure we knew about the nailed doors. They didn't even have to mention it. Who cares? Not us, because it didn't have anything to do with our investigation. Did it?" He thought a few moments, then finished his beer. "You're sure you're not hungry?" he asked Boone.

"I can wait till we get back to the city."

"Where are you parked?"

"Right around the corner."

"Well, let's do this . . . I'll drive, and we'll go out to the Maitland place. I'll drop you off just before we get to their driveway. You stay in those trees for a few minutes. I'll drive up to the house. I want to see Dora and Emily anyway, to ask them if they knew Victor was dying from polymyositis. Geltman said they didn't know. But maybe he was lying, or maybe he didn't know they knew. Anyway, I'll keep the two of them busy inside the house for, oh say fifteen minutes. That long enough for you?"

"Sure," Abner Boone said. "I can make it. I'll keep the barn between me and house, so in case they glance out the windows or from the porch they won't spot me. You'll pick me up on the road?"

"Right," Delaney said. "The same place I drop you. The housekeeper didn't say how big that storage place was, did she?"

"No. She just called it a tool shed. Like it was, at most, maybe ten feet by ten feet. Probably smaller."

Delaney thought a moment, eyes squinched, trying to remember.

"That barn's got to be at least fifty by thirty," he said.

"At least," Boone nodded.

"So there's a lot of space inside there left over," Delaney said. "Now I'm curious."

"Me, too," Sergeant Boone said.

On their way out to the Maitland place, Delaney driving, Boone said, "You don't happen to have a set of lock picks, do you, sir?"

"I own a set, but I haven't got them with me," the Chief said.

"I didn't bring mine either," the sergeant said. "A fine couple of dicks we are. Well, I've got a screwdriver, pliers, and a short jimmy in the trunk. I'll have to make do."

Delaney pulled off the road just before they got to the turnoff to the Maitland place. Trees screened them from the house. Abner Boone got out, and borrowed the keys long enough to open the trunk and take out his tools. Then the two cops compared watches.

"Let's make it about fifteen to twenty minutes," Delaney said. "About that. But take all the time you need; I'll wait for you."

"I should be able to do it in that," Boone agreed. "If I'm not out in half an hour tops, send in the Marines."

Delaney nodded, started up the car, drove slowly ahead. He glanced in the rearview mirror. The sergeant had disappeared. The Chief turned into the Maitland driveway.

He felt sure they were home—the big, black Mercedes was parked in the driveway—but he banged that tarnished brass knocker again with no result. He was beginning to wonder if they had strolled away somewhere when the door was opened a crack, a bright eye surveyed him, then the door was opened wide.

"My land!" Emily Maitland said. "It's Chief Delaney. Now this *is* a pleasant surprise!"

She stood in the open doorway, bare feet spread and firmly planted on the warm floor boards. She was wearing a caftan of tissue-thin Indian cotton. He was aware that she was naked beneath the semi-transparent cloth. Glimpsed dark shadows of oval aureoles and triangular pubic hair. But most of all, he saw the obese, randy body, thighs bursting, quivering melon breasts, all of her seemingly exploding outward, straining the seams of the flimsy garment she wore. And balanced on everything, the puffy throat, chin rolls, a bland, innocent face scarred by shrewd, glittering eyes.

"Miss Maitland," Delaney said, smiling genially, "it's good to see you again. Forgive me for not calling you first, but something important came up, and I decided to drive up at once in hopes of catching you at home."

"Of course," she said vaguely, looking over his shoulder. "And where is Sergeant Boone?"

"Oh, he's taking a day off," the Chief said. "Even cops need a rest now and then. May I come in?"

"Land!" she said. "Here we are tattling on the stoop! Of course, you come right in, Chief Delaney. Mama's a bit indisposed today, but I'm sure she'll be happy to see you. Mama, look who's here!"

She led him into a dim, musty parlor, where Dora Maitland reclined on a Victorian loveseat, the upholstery a faded maroon velvet, worn and shiny. Delaney could hardly make her out in the gloom: just another rococo whatnot and knickknack, fitting in perfectly with the antimacassars, bell jars and dried flowers, china figurines, feather fronds and ornate paperweights, mahogany paneling and stained wallpaper, dust and murk—an archeological dig, an age lost, a culture gone.

She was wearing a peignoir of satin, the weave showing its age. One arm, in a soiled plaster cast, was cradled in a canvas sling. A knee was heavily bandaged, the surrounding flesh puffed and discolored. The pulpy body lay flaccid, spread. But resting on a suede pillow was that incredible cigar-box head: the flood of glossy black ringlets, skin of dusty ivory, flashing eyes and carmined lips half-pursed in a promised kiss.

"How nice," she murmured drowsily, holding out a limp hand. "How nice."

Chief Delaney touched those soft, hot fingers, then, without waiting for an invitation, sat in a sprung armchair from which he could see, dimly, Dora on the couch and Emily standing nearby. The daughter had picked up a sphere of glass in which a simulated snowfall floated. She bounced it back and forth in her plump hands, almost caressing the hard globe, feeling it, stroking it, her eyes on Delaney.

"Forgive me this intrusion," he said solemnly, his own voice sounding to him like a recording. "Sorry about your accident, Mrs. Maitland. At least that's what the Nyack cops called it—an accident. But I'm not here to talk about that. Did you—either of you or both of you—know your son and brother was dying of a fatal illness?"

There were a few seconds of breathy silence. Then:

"My land!" said Emily Maitland.

"What?" said Dora Maitland.

"Whatever do you mean, Chief Delaney?" Emily asked. "A fatal illness?"

"Oh yes," he nodded. "Polymyositis. A muscle disorder. I have spoken to his doctor. I don't like being the one to tell you this, but Victor Maitland was dying. Should have been dead a few years ago. In any event, he hadn't long to live. A year or two at the most."

He was staring at Dora Maitland and saw, through the dusk, her face gradually tighten, slowly congeal. Tears welled and ran from her eyes, leaving smudged tracks down her cheeks.

"Victor," she choked. "My baby."

"I'm sorry," Delaney said humbly. "But it's true. Did either of you know?"

They shook their heads, two porcelain dolls, the round heads wagging back and forth.

"He never told you? Never mentioned it?"

Again the wagging.

"Oh Mama," Emily said. She set aside the crystal paperweight, put her hands lightly on her mother's shoulders. "Isn't that just awful? Land, I don't know what to say? Do you, Mama?"

"Emily, my medicine," Dora Maitland said with great dignity. "Sir, would you care for . . . ?"

"Oh no," Delaney said hastily. "Nothing for me. Thank you."

He was watching Dora and didn't see where the glass came from, the full glass that appeared like magic in Emily's hand. Probably on the floor, tucked under the loveseat when I came in, Delaney thought. He watched Emily hand the drink to Dora, pressing her mother's fingers around the glass. A colorless liquid. Gin or vodka. No ice. She could be sipping water.

"You think it has something to do with my son's murder?" Dora Maitland asked, the voice low-pitched, husky, not quite raspy but as furred as the worn velvet couch.

"It might," Chief Delaney said, wanting to stretch this charade to fifteen to twenty minutes. "It might not. Victor's wife never mentioned his illness?"

"We saw her so seldom," Emily said. "She never said a word, no."

"And Saul Geltman? Never told you about it?"

"Saul? Saul knew about it?"

"Yes, he knew."

"No, Saul didn't tell us about it."

Delaney nodded. He looked around the cluttered room. "I'm surprised you don't have any of your son's paintings, Mrs. Maitland. He never gave you any?"

"He gave us two," Emily Maitland said. "Portraits. Of Mama and me. They're hanging in our bedrooms." She giggled. "The one of me's a nude," she said.

"Ah," Delaney said. "And when did he do those?"

"My land, it must have been years ago," Emily said. "Twenty years ago. At least. He was just starting."

"To paint?" Delaney asked.

"To sell," Emily said. "Vic drew things and painted since he was seven years old. But he just started to sell twenty years ago."

"Well," Delaney said, "they're worth a lot more now."

"I should think so," Dora Maitland nodded, and couldn't stop nodding. "A lot more now."

Delaney glanced at his watch, rose to his feet.

"Thank you, ladies. Sorry to have troubled you."

"Land," Emily Maitland said. "No trouble at all."

"Maybe it's all for the best," Dora Maitland muttered.

The Chief didn't know what she meant, and didn't ask. Emily saw him to the door.

"Say hello to Sergeant Boone for me." She smiled mischievously.

"I'll surely do that, Miss Maitland," Chief Delaney said seriously.

He walked down the steps, heard the door close behind him. He stood at Boone's car while he slowly lighted a cigar. Then he took off his jacket, got in, started up. The car was an oven: no air stirring at all. He drove out to the main road, stopping across from the point where he had dropped Boone. But there was no sign of the sergeant. Delaney cut the engine, puffed calmly, waited.

About five minutes later, Abner Boone appeared among the trees on the other side of the road. He lifted a hand to Delaney, then came slouching across the pavement. He opened the back door, tossed the tools onto the floor. He stripped off his jacket. His shirt was soaked through. Sweat sheened on his face and glistened in the gingery hair on the backs of his hands.

"Like a sauna in there," he said to Delaney. "I'm demolished."

He got in and Delaney started up. Boone found a rag in the glove compartment, and tried to wipe some of the grime from his palms.

"They knew about Maitland's illness," the Chief said. "Claimed they didn't, but they were lying. How did you do?"

"About like Martha Beasely described it," the sergeant said. "There's a path from the gravel driveway to this back door. The path's been used a lot: grass beaten down, practically bare earth. The door itself is unlocked. Made of vertical planks with an inside Z-shaped frame. Looks as old as the barn itself. Original issue. Inside is this shed, like Martha Beasely said. About six by four. I paced it off. Goes up to the eaves. A lot of junk in there. The power mower, garden tools, a five-gallon can of gas, a box of hand tools, most of them rusty. Pieces of pipe, an old, cracked sink. Stuff like that. Mostly junk."

"Earth floor?"

"No, it's planked. But earth right below. No cellar or foundation. The floor's just a few inches above the ground. I got the screwdriver down in a crack between two of the planks and poked around. Just dirt."

"And that's all?" Delaney asked. "Just that tool shed?"

"No," Sergeant Boone said, turning sideways to look at the Chief. "There's more. There's an old tarp hanging on the back wall. A greasy piece of canvas just hooked over a couple of nails. Like it was hung up to dry. There's a door behind the tarp."

"A door," Delaney nodded, with some satisfaction. "Behind the tarp. Hidden."

"Right," Boone said. "A modern door. A flush door. Solid, I'd say; not hollow. Hinged from the other side."

"Locked?"

"Oh yes. A good tumbler lock. Maybe a Medeco. But no door knob. No handle at all. Just that lock. You spring that and push the door open."

"You couldn't spring it?"

"No way. Not with a screwdriver and pliers. I figured you didn't want me to jimmy the door."

"You figured right. Got any idea what's behind the locked door?"

"No, sir. No cracks. No tracks. Nothing. So I put the tarp back the way it was, came out, and closed the outside door. Now get this . . . I'm around the back of the barn, looking around. High up, right under the peak of the roof, there's a small window that's been boarded up. It's like fifteen, maybe eighteen feet from the ground. No way to get to it. And even if I had had a ladder, it was really sealed tight. Heavy planks nailed across it every which way. So while I'm staring at it, I hear a click, and then there's a low hum."

Delaney took his eyes off the road long enough to glance at Boone. "What the hell?" he said.

"Right," the sergeant nodded. "Just what I thought. So then I went back into the shed, pulled the tarp aside again, and put my ear on the door. I could hear it better: a low, steady hum. A drone. Like machinery."

"I can't believe it," the Chief said wonderingly.

"How do you think I felt?" Abner Boone said. "At first I thought I was hearing things. But then there was a click again, and the humming stopped. Just like that. Then I knew. An air conditioner."

"Jesus Christ," Delaney said.

"Had to be," the sergeant said. "Working on a thermostat. The temperature inside gets too high, and it kicks on automatically. So then I went outside again to see if I could find where the damned thing vents. That's what took me so long. I finally found it. There's a half-moon hole in the ground for runoff from the roof gutter. It's lined with rocks. Old, old, old. Anyway, the vent grille has been set into that. Below ground level but open to the air. Neat. If it drips, who's to notice? In fact, you'd never see the vent at all unless you went looking for it."

"An air conditioner," Delaney said, shaking his head. "What the hell they got in there—a meat market? The walls lined with hams and sides of beef?"

"Who the hell knows?" Boone said wearily.

"We'll never get a warrant," Delaney said.

"No way, sir," the sergeant agreed.

"Think you could pick that lock?"

"I could give it the old college try. I guess we'll have to, won't we?"

"I guess we will," Chief Delaney nodded. "We've got no choice."

They stopped at a gas station on the way back to New York, and Abner Boone washed up and tried to scrub a grease stain from the knee of his slacks, with no success. Then he took the wheel, and they drove into Manhattan without exchanging half a dozen words, both frowning because of what they were thinking. Once Delaney said, "He had to do something," but Boone didn't reply, and the Chief said nothing more.

Monica was out when they arrived at the Delaney brownstone. The Chief poked around in the refrigerator, and brought out bread, mustard, cold cuts, cheese, a jar of kosher dills, and an onion. He and Boone made their own sandwiches, two for each, and carried them into the study balanced on squares of paper toweling; no plates, nothing to wash up but a couple of forks and knives. The Chief took a can of Ballantine ale, and Boone had a bottle of tonic water. No glasses.

They ate slowly, in silence, still ruminating, their eyes turned downward and blinking.

"Look," Chief Delaney said, beginning to work on his second sandwich—salami and onion on pumpernickel—"let's do this . . ." He tore a sheet from his yellow legal pad and pushed it across the desk to Abner Boone. He put a pencil alongside it. "You write what you think are the three biggest question marks in this mess. I mean besides who wasted Maitland. The three things that bug you the most. I'll do the same. Then we'll read each other's list and see if we're thinking along the same lines."

"Only three questions?" Boone said. "I can think of a hundred."

"Just three," Delaney said. "The three you think are most important. Most significant."

"I'm game," the sergeant said, picking up the pencil as Delaney took out his pen.

The Chief's list of the three most puzzling aspects of the case read as follows:

1. Why were no paintings found in Mott Street studio?
2. Where's the big money coming from that Dora and Emily Maitland are counting on?
3. Why didn't Victor Maitland, knowing he was dying, change his life style or make special plans?

Delaney looked up, but Boone was staring into space, pondering. So the Chief worked on his sandwich while the sergeant began writing again. Finally he nodded he was finished. They exchanged lists, and Delaney read what Boone had written:

1. What's in the Maitlands' barn?
2. Why didn't Maitland contribute to support of mother and sister?
3. Why did Victor Maitland and Saul Geltman arrange Nyack visits so Martha Beasely wouldn't see them?

"Jesus Christ," Abner Boone said disgustedly, "we're not even worrying along the same lines."

Chief Delaney raised his eyes slowly, stared at the sergeant a moment. Then he took his own list back, placed it alongside Boone's, read them both again. Then he raised his eyes again.

"Sure we are," he said softly. "We're both on the same track. Closer than you think. Look at this . . ."

He took a pair of scissors from his top desk drawer. He trimmed the excess paper from the bottom of his and Boone's lists and dropped the scraps neatly into the wastepaper basket concealed in the well of his desk. Then carefully, slowly, he scissored each list into three parts. Now he had six slips of paper, six individual questions. He placed them in a single column and began to move them around.

Interested, Abner Boone rose, moved behind Delaney, bent over his shoulder. He watched the Chief try the six questions in various sequences. Then Delaney got them in an order that pleased him, sat back staring at them.

"Well?" he asked Boone, not looking at him.

The sergeant shook his head.

"I still don't get it," he said.

"Read them again," the Chief urged.

Now the list read:

1. Why didn't Maitland contribute to support of mother and sister?
2. Why didn't Victor Maitland, knowing he was dying, change his life style or make special plans?
3. Why were no paintings found in Mott Street studio?
4. Why did Victor Maitland and Saul Geltman arrange Nyack visits so Martha Beasely wouldn't see them?
5. Where's the big money coming from that Dora and Emily Maitland are counting on?
6. What's in the Maitlands' barn?

Boone straightened up. He put his hands on his hips, bent backward until his spine cracked, stretched, took a deep breath.

"Chief," he said, "are you thinking what I'm thinking?"

"I sure am," Delaney said, trying not to sound excited. "I've got to make some phone calls . . . You sit down. Or make yourself another sandwich. Or open another—no, wait. There's a job you've got to do while I phone."

He went to his bookcase, got the oversized art volume of the works of Victor Maitland, the book Boone had loaned him. He showed the sergeant the section listing the artist's *oeuvre*.

"This book was published six months ago," Delaney said, "and probably written at least six months before that. So the list won't be right up to the minute. But it should tell us if we're thinking straight."

"What you want is the number of known paintings Maitland did every year—right?" Boone asked.

"Right!" Delaney said. He wanted to clap the sergeant on the shoulder, but didn't. "The list starts twenty years ago, when he began to sell. You get on the numbers, and I'll call Jake Dukker."

He had no trouble getting Dukker's studio, but the receptionist told him the artist was busy in a shooting session and couldn't come to the phone.

"What's he doing—photographing pornographic confirmation cards?" Delaney said. "You tell Jake baby this is Chief Edward X. Delaney, New York Police Department, and if he doesn't get his tuchas to the phone, there'll be a man in blue up there in— Oh hello, Mr. Dukker. Forgive me for bothering you, but I know how anxious you are to cooperate. Just one short question this time: How long did it take Victor Maitland to do a painting?"

Abner Boone raised his head from his counting to listen to Delaney's conversation.

"I know, I know . . . Look, you told us he was a fast worker, Belle Sarazen told us he was a fast worker, Saul Geltman told us he was a fast worker. All right—how fast? . . . Uh-huh . . . I understand . . . And if he was pushing it? . . . Yes . . . I get it . . . But on an average, what would you say? . . . Yes . . . So that could be at least fifty a year? . . . Yes . . . No, I'm not going to make you swear to it; it's just for my own information . . . And you're faster?" Delaney winked at the listening Abner Boone. "I understand completely, Mr. Dukker. Thank you very much for your kind cooperation."

He hung up and made some quick notes on his pad while talking to the sergeant.

"Says it depends on the artist," he said rapidly. "Some can spend a year on a single canvas. Maitland worked fast, like everyone told us. Twenty or thirty a year. Easily. One a week if he pushed it. Maybe even more, Dukker says. Didn't even let the layers of paint dry properly. Jake baby says Maitland could do a painting overnight on a bet, but let's figure an average of one a week to be on the conservative side. How you doing?"

"Give me a couple of more minutes," Boone said. "It looks good."

Delaney waited patiently while the sergeant counted the number of known paintings Maitland produced each year. Finally, Boone pushed the book away and studied his list.

"All right," he said, "here's how it stands: Beginning when the list starts, he did about twenty a year, then thirty, then more, and more, until he's doing like fifty paintings a year. This is on the average. Then, five years ago—"

"When he learns he's dying," Delaney put in.

"Right. About five years ago, suddenly it goes to twelve, ten, fourteen, eleven paintings a year. His annual production fell way off."

"The hell it did," the Chief said. "If anything, he began working harder and faster. If he turned out fifty paintings a year, say, for the past five years, and you subtract the number of known paintings listed in that book, how many paintings are unaccounted for?"

"About two hundred," Boone said, staring at his list. "Jesus, two hundred missing paintings!"

"Missing, my ass," Delaney said. "They're in the Maitlands' barn. That explains the air conditioner, doesn't it?"

"I'll buy that," Boone nodded. "Now give me the why."

Delaney grabbed for his Manhattan telephone directory.

"I'm going to call Internal Revenue Service information," he told the sergeant. "You get on the phone in the hallway and listen in. I don't want to have to repeat the conversation; it'll probably be a long one."

Boone took his second sandwich and what was left of his bottle of tonic into the hallway. Delaney dialed IRS information and was answered by a recorded message telling him all the information lines were busy, and would he please wait. He hung up, dialed again, and got the same message. Went through it again, and on the third try decided to wait. He held the phone almost five minutes, and then a growly voice came on, saying, "Information. Can I help you?"

"I'd like some information on gift taxes," the Chief said.

"What do you want to know?" the voice growled.

"How much can I give to relatives—or to anyone—without paying taxes on it?"

"An individual can give three thousand a year to as many donees as he wants."

"And the donor doesn't have to pay any tax on that, and the donee receiving the gift doesn't?"

"Right," the growler said.

"Look," Delaney said, "that's for money. Cash. What about things—like, oh say sterling silver, antiques, stamps, coins, paintings—stuff like that?"

"The same holds true. The value of the annual gifts cannot exceed three thousand if they're to be tax-free."

Delaney was getting interested. Like most cops, he was intrigued by how the system could be fiddled.

"Suppose I sell something to a relative or friend," he suggested, "for, say, a hundred dollars, and it's really worth five thousand. Then what?"

"Then you're in the soup," the voice growled. "If we find out about it. Gifts of *anything*—antiques, stamps, coins, paintings, whatever—are evaluated at current market value at the time of the gift. We hire expert appraisers. If the sale price is obviously out of line, then the person who fakes the purchase has to pay tax on the value over three thousand."

"If you find out about it," Delaney reminded him.

"If we find out—right," the growler said. "You want to take a chance of being racked up on tax fraud, go right ahead; be my guest."

"Let me ask you another question," Delaney said. "All right?"

"Sure. This is more interesting than most of the stuff I get."

"Let me give you a for-instance. Suppose I own ten acres of land. Now the value of that land is three thousand dollars, and I sign the land over to my son, say. That's okay, right?"

"If the value of the land is legitimate, it's okay. It would mean that surrounding land, similar acres, are going for that price. Then, sure, that would be a legal gift, tax-free."

"All right, let's say it's legal. I've got proof those ten acres are worth three thousand. They're a gift I make to my son. Tax-free. But then, about ten years later, or fifteen, or twenty, oil is discovered on that land, and suddenly those acres are worth a million dollars. What then? Was it still a legal gift?"

There was silence on the other end of the phone. Then:

"That's a good one. First time I've had that thrown at me. Look, I got to admit the tax laws about gifts are murky. We know a lot of people get away with murder, and there's nothing we can do about it. Mostly because we never hear about it, never learn about it. But to get back to your question . . . you give land to your son legitimately worth three thousand. Right?"

"Right."

"Then, years later, oil is discovered on that land, and it greatly appreciates in value. Have I got it correct?"

"Yes, correct."

"Then it's your son's good luck. That's the way I interpret the regulations. I may be wrong, but I don't think I am. When you gave that land to your son, you didn't know there was oil on it, did you?"

"No, I didn't."

"No hanky-panky? There were no acres around it or near it producing oil?"

"No. None."

"Then, like I said, it's your son's good luck. The gift is legitimate. We'll take our cut from the sale of the oil."

"Thank you very much," Chief Delaney said.

"Thank *you,*" the voice growled. "A welcome relief from old dames wanting to know if they can deduct the cost of dogfood for their poodles."

Delaney hung up. Abner Boone came walking in from the hallway. He was frowning.

"It's tax fraud, isn't it?" he asked.

"That's how I see it," Delaney nodded. "Sit down. Relax. Let me give you a scenario. A lot of it's smoke, but I think it makes sense."

Delaney leaned back in his swivel chair. He lighted a cigar, put his hands behind his head, stared at the ceiling. Boone slumped in the cracked club chair, cigarettes and matches in his lap.

"All right," the Chief said, "let's go . . . Interrupt me any time you think I'm flying too high, or you have something to add.

"Let's start about six years ago. Victor Maitland's stuff is beginning to bring really high prices, and he's turning out like fifty paintings a year. Now this is supposition, but maybe Geltman's getting a little itchy. Sure, he's making a lot of money off Maitland, but maybe the dealer's worried that the artist is doing too many paintings too fast. Remember what Geltman said about scarcity being a factor in the price of art? But let's skip that for the moment. Six years ago, everything's coming up roses for Victor Maitland.

"Then, suddenly, Doc Horowitz tells him he's dying. He's got maybe three years. Wham, bang, and pow! Maitland laughed, according to Horowitz, but don't tell me news like that wouldn't shake a man. Maitland's first reaction is that now he's got to work harder and faster in the days he's got left. Because he really is an obsessed creative artist, and he wants to know it all, own it all, and prove it on canvas. But then he starts thinking—working harder and faster for whom? The IRS? He's already paying heavy income taxes, and if he works more and sells more, he pays more. Save up his paintings to leave to his heirs? Then the IRS and New York State take an enormous inheritance tax."

"Lieutenant Wolfe told us how Maitland felt about that," Boone observed.

"Correct. So Maitland goes to Geltman and tells him his problem, and Geltman takes him to see J. Julian Simon. I figure it's got to be a lawyer who figured out this whole cockamamie scheme. It's got shyst written all over it. After all, they're going to risk tax fraud, a Federal rap. But Simon figures out ways to reduce the risk to practically nil."

"Who benefits?" the sergeant asked.

"*Cui bono?*" the Chief smiled. "I asked myself that a long time ago, and didn't have the answer. Maitland wanted his mother and sister to benefit. Maybe he hadn't been giving them anything. Maybe he'd been tossing them nickels. But he knows they're just getting by, and that the old Maitland homestead in Nyack is going to rack and ruin. Now that he's dying, he gets an attack of the guilts. He wants his mother and sister to benefit, and screw the IRS; they're taking plenty on his income taxes. That's how I think Maitland would figure it."

"What about his wife and son?"

"Fuck 'em. That's what Maitland would think, and probably said to Geltman: Fuck 'em. The wife has twenty grand a year of her own, doesn't she? She's not going to starve. And Victor figures he'll leave enough cash and legitimate paintings in the Geltman Galleries to give his son a start. The kid gets about half the estate after taxes, remember. No, Maitland wants his mother and sister to be the big winners."

"Then Dora and Emily were in on it?"

"Had to be; it was their barn being used for storage. I guess they felt sorry about Victor dying and all—maybe that's why Dora's on the sauce—but they were consoled by all those beautiful paintings piling up in the barn. Their inheritance. This is how I figure they worked it:

"Say Maitland did a minimum of fifty paintings a year after he learned he was dying. Ten or fifteen of those would go to the Geltman Galleries to be sold normally. An artificial scarcity, so the price of Maitlands kept climbing. The other twenty-five or more paintings were put in the barn. Brought up there by Maitland or Geltman when Martha Beasely wasn't around to see them unload the station wagon."

"And when Dora and Emily came down for lunch or dinner," Boone said, "they took paintings back with them. In the Mercedes."

"Right," Delaney nodded. "And if the IRS ever found them, Dora and Emily and Saul Geltman would claim those paintings had been done twenty years ago, when Maitlands were selling for a hundred bucks. Listen, the guy's style never changed that anyone could notice. And you heard what the IRS man said on the phone. At a hundred bucks, a fair market value twenty years ago, Maitland could give thirty paintings to his mother and thirty to his sister every year, and still keep within the legal gift limit. How could the Feds prove the paintings had been done in 1978, when Maitlands were selling for a hundred G's and more?"

"They'd have to keep a record," Boone said slowly. "Some kind of a ledger like the one Geltman showed us for the legitimate sales."

Delaney pointed a finger at him.

"That's it," he said. "You've got it. Double-entry bookkeeping. The art dealer's got an illustrated record book proving the painting was done in 1958 and given to Dora or Emily as a gift. All as phony as a three-dollar bill, of course, but the IRS would have a hell of a time fighting it."

"Why didn't Victor let Dora and Emily sell off some of the paintings while he was alive? They'd have to pay taxes on their profit, but they could get started on renovating that old place."

"Because Geltman convinced them that the prices of Maitland paintings were going up, up, up, and the longer they held on, the more they'd eventually make. And when Maitland conked, the price of his paintings would go through the roof. Just the way it happened. Listen, J. Julian Simon and Saul Geltman worked this out very carefully. And, for their reward, I suppose Geltman had an arrangement with Dora and Emily. When Victor Maitland died, the stored paintings would be sold off slowly, ten or twenty a year, to keep the price up. Geltman would handle the sales, perfectly legitimately, and take like fifty percent."

"From which he'd pay J. Julian Simon his share for setting up the scam."

"That's the way I figure it," Delaney nodded.

"That's it," Boone said. "That's got to be it."

"Sure," Edward X. Delaney said. "Except for one thing. Who slammed Victor Maitland?"

16

Jason T. Jason felt like a detective, even if he didn't have the rank. Like most young men and women who join the cops, wherever, this was what he thought police work was all about: prowling around in plainclothes, asking questions, solving homicides. Three years' duty on uniformed patrol had dimmed the vision, but never quite obliterated it. And now it was coming true.

At the suggestion of Sergeant Abner Boone, and with the aid of his wife, Jason Two dressed like your normal denizen of the lower depths for his role as detective. He wore a fuzzy maroon fedora with a brim four inches wide, pinned up on one side with a rhinestone as big as the Ritz and a long feathered plume waving in the air.

His jacket was fringed buckskin over a ruffled purple shirt open to the waist. Around his neck hung an enormous silver medallion on a beaded necklace. His skintight jeans were some kind of black, shiny stuff, like leather, and his yellow boots had platform soles and three-inch heels.

His wife said this costume made Jason T. Jason look like the biggest, raunchiest pimp in New York, and she made him wear a raincoat over it when he got into and out of their car in front of their Hicksville, Long Island, home. His two young sons thought their father's outfit was the most hilarious thing they had ever seen, and he had to crack them a few times before they'd stop yelling, "Hey, Ma, superstud is home!"

Jason T. Jason enjoyed every minute of his assignment. He liked people, and found it easy to gossip with them and relate to their problems. He wasn't self-conscious about his enormous size, and discovered that, perhaps because of it, there were many who liked to be seen talking to him or drinking with him. It made them proud, as if they were in the company of a celebrity.

He found he was putting in a twelve-hour day on the new job, sometimes more, but he talked it over with Juanita, his wife, and they decided he'd push it. The opportunity was one most patrol officers would give their left nut for, and if he helped break the case, he'd get a commendation at least, and an on-the-spot promotion to dick three wasn't unheard of.

He had had the usual basic training at the Academy, and had learned more in the three years on patrol, of course, but nothing in his background had prepared him for this job. He told Juanita he probably would be making a mess of it if it weren't for the counsel and assistance of Abner Boone. The sergeant taught him the tricks of the trade.

For instance, Boone told him, suppose you're tailing a guy for some reason, and you want to find out his name. You see him go up and talk to another guy for a few minutes, then move off. So you go up to this other guy, but you don't flash your tin and demand, "What was the name of the man you were just talking to?" Do that, and the chances are the guy will stiff you, or lie. But if you come up smiling and say, "Hey, man, was that Billy Smith you were just talking to?" then the chances were pretty good the guy might say, "Billy Smith? Hell, no, that was Jack Jones."

Similarly, Boone said, when Jason T. Jason went into a bar on the Lower East Side, he shouldn't march in, flash his potsy at the bartender, show the police artist's sketch of the Spanish woman, and demand, "Have you seen this woman?" Even if the guy had, he was going to clam after that treatment.

The better way, the sergeant told Jason Two, was to amble into the bar, order a beer, sip it slowly, and when the bartender wasn't busy, ask lazily, "Mary been around lately?" And if the bartender said, "Mary? I don't know no Mary," then Jason was to say, "Sure, man, she comes in here all the time. Here, I got this little drawing of her." The bartender might still clam, but he might say, "Oh her. Her name ain't Mary, it's Lucy." Or June, or Sue, or whatever.

"It's all in knowing how to manipulate people," Abner Boone told the black cop. "A good detective's got a thousand tricks to make people tell things they don't want to tell, or do things they don't want to do. You've got to study human nature and what makes people tick. I always figured you can catch more flies with honey than you can with vinegar, but I know a lot of dicks don't feel that way. Just the opposite; they come on strong. You've got to find the way that suits you best and gets the best results for you."

Jason told Juanita he thought Boone's way suited him best; it really made him uncomfortable to lean on people. So he ambled all over the Lower East Side, smiling, chatting up a storm with bartenders and shopkeepers. Some of them guessed he was a cop, but never came right out and asked. His costume and manner must have been convincing because once, on Norfolk Street at high noon, a pretty young hooker, white, sidled up to him and said she wouldn't mind joining his stable. Jason told this story to his wife, thinking she'd be amused. She wasn't.

He made some progress, but not much. Using Boone's system, he had wandered into a Forsythe Street greasy spoon and casually asked the Puerto Rican waitress, "Mary been around lately?" It worked just as the sergeant said it might, and the waitress identified the drawing of the woman as "Mama Perez," first name unknown, who came in occasionally with the young girl in the second sketch. This girl, introduced as Mama's niece, was named Dolores, last name unknown.

Sergeant Boone ran "Mama Perez" through records, and came up with nothing. There were more than 750 Perezes listed in the Manhattan telephone directory, and they weren't about to start on *that* unless absolutely necessary.

So Jason T. Jason continued his daily rounds, becoming a familiar figure around Orchard and Rivington and Delancey streets. But now he could ask casually, "Seen Mama Perez lately?" He went as far west as the Bowery and as far east as Roosevelt Drive. Sometimes he worked nights and the early-morning hours, and he went into hairy places. But perhaps because of his size, he never got mugged. There was one night, under the Williamsburg Bridge, when he thought four young punks were going to try to take him. But he sauntered slowly away whistling, and sweating, and they faded off when he came into a lighted section.

The worst experience he had during this period was not with the shtarkers of the Lower East Side, but with Sergeant Abner Boone.

Boone came down to join Jason occasionally, usually at night, to make the rounds with him for a few hours and teach him more tricks. Boone wore dirty sneakers and khaki jeans, and a stained nylon Windbreaker. He didn't wear any socks, and some shirt buttons were missing. No one looked at him twice.

Jason noticed that when he and Boone went into a bar together, the sergeant would always order a draft beer, and then let it just sit there, getting flat, the head disappearing.

The first time this happened, Jason Two said, "Not drinking?" And Boone smiled tightly and said, "Not tonight." It happened two or three more times; Boone never touched his beer. Finally, Jason, who had a huge thirst and a huge capacity, took to saying, "Mind if I finish that?" When Boone nodded, Jason would drain his glass, too, before they departed.

When Jason T. Jason had his worst experience, he and Boone had been covering Bowery booze joints where you could get a double shot for fifty-five cents, but most of the customers wisely stuck to bottled beer. Jason Two and the sergeant came off the Bowery at Grand Street and started meandering eastward. They turned the corner onto Eldridge Street, where Jason's car was parked, and there was a squad car pulled into the curb at an angle, the roof lights still flashing. Both cops were out of it and working, although there wasn't much for them to do except try to keep the gathering crowd moving.

It looked like two old winos had gone at each other with broken bottles. This was surprising; old winos rarely had enough strength to twist the cap from a pint of muscatel. But maybe it was a grudge or a vendetta. In any event, they had sliced up each other thoroughly—there was an eyeball lying on the sidewalk—and it was obvious one of the winos was dead and the other, a flag of slashes, was breathing in thick, wheezy gasps in a diminishing rhythm.

The young cops who had caught the squeal didn't know what to do. They had radioed for help, but there was no way to stop the dying man's bleeding or to bandage him, unless they could swaddle him up like a mummy. Blood ran across the sidewalk, over the curb, into the gutter. A gush, a river, a flood of blood. The smell was thick on the hot night air. Boone hadn't caught one of these in a long time; he had almost forgotten that blood smelled.

He started walking away, fast, and Jason Two had to hurry to catch up to him. Boone wheeled into the first open bar he came to and ordered a boilermaker. He put the shot down with a flick of his wrist and a single gulp, swilled the beer, and ordered another before Jason even had time to swing his bulk aboard a bar stool.

Oh-oh, the black cop thought. I got trouble.

He did, too. Within an hour, Sergeant Abner Boone was falling-down drunk and talking stupidly. Following one of Boone's own tips—"Never argue with a drunk, a nut, an armed guy, or a woman"—Jason agreed with everything the sergeant said, and tried to get him out of there. But Boone wouldn't go, insisted on ordering another drink. Suddenly he stopped babbling, became silent and morose. He staggered off to the can.

While he was gone, Jason debated what he should do. He had never faced a situation like this before. He had gotten pissy-assed drunk with fellow cops, and usually helped one or more of them home, all of them boisterous and roaring. But Boone was Jason's superior officer, and he didn't even know where the sergeant lived. He wondered if he should call Chief Edward X. Delaney and explain the situation, but decided that wouldn't be right. He didn't know what to do.

Boone seemed to be staying in the can a long time, and Jason Two thought he might have passed out in there. But when Jason went in, he saw Boone hadn't passed out; the sergeant was sitting in a pool of urine and vomit, his back against the filthy tiled wall, and he was trying to eat his gun. His forefinger stroked slowly at the trigger. Jason T. Jason almost fainted.

He got the revolver away from Boone and began slapping his face to bring him around. After awhile, the sergeant started weeping, and covered his face with his hands—whether to hide his tears or so he couldn't be slapped anymore, Jason didn't know. But he got Boone up on his feet, propped in a corner, and he wiped the sergeant off with wet paper towels as best he could.

Then Jason bent down from the waist and pulled Boone forward over his shoulder. He straightened up easily, holding the sergeant with one arm, and carried him out of the can, out of the bar, down Eldridge Street to Jason's car. He had a copy of that afternoon's *Post* in the car, and he had the foresight to cover the back seat with newspaper before he dumped Boone in there. The sergeant was completely out now. He was a mess, dirty and stinking.

Jason Two searched his sticky pockets with the tips of his fingers and found out where Boone lived. But he didn't know if the sergeant was married. If he was, Jason didn't want to deliver him to his wife in that condition. Sighing, Jason T. Jason realized the only thing he could do was to deliver Abner Boone in that condition to *his* wife. Juanita wasn't going to like it, but Jason didn't see where he had any choice. So he drove Sergeant Boone home to Hicksville, Long Island.

His wife wasn't happy about receiving an unexpected, smelly, and unconscious guest at that hour. But after Jason Two told her what had happened, she nodded grimly and helped him get Boone undressed, showered off, and under a blanket on the couch in the half-basement that Jason was still hoping to finish one of these days. The only time his wife *really* got sore was when she was washing out Boone's filthy clothes, and Jason said, "That's really white of you, hon."

Because the sergeant had tried to eat his gun, Officer Jason T. Jason decided to sit up with him till morning, fearing Boone might wake up and try to hurt himself again. But the sergeant slept right through, groaning and grinding his teeth. He awoke sick and sober, looked around, saw Jason sitting nearby.

"Thanks," Abner Boone said huskily, holding his head.

Jason didn't say anything. A week later Sergeant Boone sent Mrs. Juanita

Jason about fifty bucks' worth of roses with a timid note of apology and thanks. And he sent Jason's two boys authentic-looking plastic Colt .44 revolvers that shot soap bubbles.

"That's what he should have," Juanita said.

Sergeant Boone never came down to the Lower East Side again to make the rounds with Jason T. Jason. But he spoke to Jason every day on the phone, listened to his reports, offered advice and encouragement. Neither of them ever mentioned that night again.

So Jason Two continued his rounds alone, paying particular attention to the places on the list Boone had given him: the known hangouts of Victor Maitland. During his prowling, the black cop broke up one knife fight, collared one purse-snatcher, and reassured one old lady who was convinced her neighbor was beaming cancer rays at her through their adjoining wall. Other than that, his assignment was uneventful—just the way he wanted it. He was confident that, given time, he would find Mama Perez and Dolores. But he feared Chief Delaney would get impatient with his lack of progress and ship him back to uniformed patrol.

He tried to change his routes and hours every day, and on the Friday night of his third week of searching, he planned to cover the section between Canal and Delancey, from the Bowery to Essex. Around midnight, he was ambling north on Ludlow Street, past a dark brick building that looked like a garage or warehouse. There was a gloomy alley alongside it, shadowed where the street light failed to penetrate.

Movement in the alley caught his eye. He slowed, stopped, then moved a few steps closer. He glimpsed a swirl of light-colored fabric, a woman's dress, and his heart stopped its frantic pounding.

"Hey there, baby!" he called cheerily.

She came out a little farther into the light.

" 'Allo, beeg boy," she said. "Wanna have fon?"

Then she smiled, and he saw the gleam of a gold tooth.

17

They spent a lot of time planning it, and even more debating its necessity. On the same Friday night Jason T. Jason was jiving Mama Perez in a Ludlow Street alley, Chief Edward X. Delaney and Sergeant Abner Boone were driving up to Nyack, still discussing the advisability of what they were about to do.

"We could have slipped Martha Beasely a finiff," Boone said. "To tip us off when Dora and Emily are out."

"Look," Delaney said, "if Dora and Emily are involved in icing Maitland, and it comes out that we pulled an illegal search, then they take a walk and we're left with bubkes. It's risky enough as it is, but we'd be stupidos to bring the Beasely woman into it."

"I'm still not sure it's worth it, Chief," Boone fretted.

"It's worth it if we find something that ties in with the kill. Right now, I admit, all we got is presumption of tax fraud. I couldn't care less. It's a matter for the Feds, and we'll tip them when the time is right. But a homicide takes precedence, and I don't think this tax scam exists in a vacuum. I think it's got something to do with why Maitland got the shiv. Also, to tell you the truth, it's just curiosity; I want to make sure we're guessing right. Besides, look at it this way, if Dora and Emily catch us breaking and entering, they're not going to squeal; it would just point the IRS to the treasure trove that much sooner."

"But what if the local blues show up?" Boone said mournfully. "Or the State cops?"

"We'll handle that when we have to," Delaney said. He glanced at Boone, puzzled by the sergeant's uncertainty. Boone had shown up for work a week previously with a spoiled complexion, shadowed eyes, and a breath smelling so strongly of mint that it had to be a coverup. The Chief was convinced Boone had fallen off the wagon again. He seemed sober enough now, but twitchy. "Want to drop me off at the Maitland place?" the Chief asked him. "I'll go in alone, and you stand lookout."

"Nah," the sergeant said. "I'll come along. If only to see how well I learned my lessons."

Boone was referring to a three-hour crash course he had taken under the tutelage of Detective first grade Sammy ("The Pick") Delgado. Sammy, who worked mostly safe and loft heists, was reputed to be the best cracksman in the New York Police Department. He had initiated Sergeant Boone into the arcane skill of the two-handed pick, a delicate operation in which two needle-thin picks are operated simultaneously to spring a good tumbler lock. Sammy just loved watching TV shows in which the dick or private eye opened a solid lock with a plastic credit card.

In the back of Boone's car was the equipment they thought they'd need: a big battery lantern, two penlights, a Polaroid camera with flash, several squares of black cloth about napkin-size, two jimmies, a few other tools, and a first-aid kit they hoped wouldn't be needed. Both cops were armed; both carried their kits of lock picks, plus a small can of oil and a nozzled tube of liquid graphite.

"All we need are ski masks," Boone observed.

They had timed their arrival for 1:00 A.M. Drove slowly past the Maitland home and saw no lights in the house itself, though low-wattage bulbs burned in converted carriage lamps on both sides of the outside door. They U-turned on the road, drove past again, and pulled up so far off the verge that branches scraped the car roof and windows. Boone switched off the engine and lights. They sat silently for almost ten minutes, until their eyes became accustomed to the darkness. During that period only one car passed on the river road.

Finally, Delaney said quietly, "You wait here. I want to check the Mercedes. Fifteen minutes."

He slid out of the car cautiously. Boone was surprised at how lightly and quietly the big man moved. There was a three-quarter moon, but clouds were heavy enough to dim the light. Delaney disappeared into black shadows. Boone sat stolidly, aching for a cigarette.

The Chief was back in ten minutes, appearing with startling suddenness at Boone's window.

"It's parked," he whispered. "They're in. Let's go."

Both men were wearing dark slacks, shirts, sweaters, shoes. They carried tools and equipment in two burlap bags, swaddled in the squares of black cloth to prevent clinking. Boone went first, one of the penlights switched on and held low; a small circle of dim light jerked along at his feet.

They were city cops, not woodsmen; they could not avoid snapping dried twigs on the ground and blundering into branches. But they moved slowly, stopping frequently to snap off the light, stand and listen. They made a wide circle to keep the barn between themselves and the house. It was a humid night, but a cool river breeze helped. The smells were unfamiliar: rank earth, a brief stench of some live animal, the odor of sappy things, an occasional thick, sweet smell of flowers. Once they heard the rush and scamper of a small beast running. It spooked them.

They came up alongside the barn. Boone turned the penlight aside briefly to show Delaney the rock-lined drain pit and the air-conditioner vent. Neither man spoke. They waited for clouds to obscure the moon completely before they slipped around the corner. The sergeant led the way into the shed, the Chief following close behind, one hand on Boone's shoulder.

They closed the outside door softly behind them, made a quick sweep of the shed with the watery penlight beam, then set to work. They took the canvas tarp from the wall and hung it across the ill-fitting outside door so light would not escape through the chinks. Then they moved close to the hidden door and went into the drill they had planned.

Chief Delaney held a square of black cloth between the lock and the house, to provide additional masking. He held the penlight in his mouth, gripping it lightly in his teeth, more firmly with his lips. Boone found the tube of liquid graphite, gave the key opening a little squirt, and selected two picks from the kit in his hip pocket. They were long needles, one pointed, one with a tiny paddle head.

He inserted the pointed lock pick into the keyhole, began to probe gently, staring up into the darkness. ("No use staring at the lock," Sammy Delgado had said. "Your eyesight will fuzz. It's all in the touch, all in the feel.") But Boone touched nothing, felt nothing. He swabbed around gently, trying to catch a tumbler. But the pick kept slipping in his sweaty hands. He left it there, sticking from the lock, stooped and rubbed fingers and palms on the dusty floorboards. Then he went back to his probing, blinking nervously. Finally, he shook his head in the gloom. Delaney dropped one corner of the masking cloth, took the penlight from his mouth, switched it off. He moved his head closer to Boone's.

"Want me to try?" he whispered.

"Not yet. Let me rest a minute and get rid of the shakes. Then I'll try a hook."

They stood there in the blackness, both trying to breathe deeply. The shed held the day's heat and the must of years. It stuffed their nostrils, clotted their eyes. They smelled themselves, and each other.

"All right," Boone said in a low voice. "I need the light down here for a second."

Delaney held the penlight to illuminate the sergeant's dusty hands fumbling at his pick kit. He replaced the pointed pick, withdrew one with a tiny hook at the end. They went back to their original positions, Boone probing now with the hooked pick, frowning thoughtfully up into the darkness. He felt the pick catch.

"Got one," he breathed.

He slid the paddle-tipped pick into the keyhole alongside the hook. Now he was working with both hands, the paddle searching for clearance as the hook turned a tumbler.

It took almost half an hour, and they stopped to rest and listen three times. But finally the paddle pick slid firmly in; they both heard the satisfying click. Boone slowly turned his wrists until both elbows were pointing upward as Delaney pressed a knee softly but firmly against the door. The final click was louder as the tang pulled back. They stopped, sweating, listened again. Then Delaney nudged the door open.

The light was switched off. Both sat on the floor for a few minutes. Delaney kept his hand carefully on the sill of the opened door, to prevent it from swinging shut. They felt a waft of cool air pouring from the interior.

"Let's go," Boone said.

They got to their feet, picked up their burlap bags. The sergeant pushed the door open slowly.

"Wait," Delaney said.

He wedged a wrapped screwdriver and pliers into place across the lower inside hinge so the door was immobilized. They moved cautiously: a slow-motion film.

The first thing they did was to check the inside of the door. There was a knob, and when Boone satisfied himself that it worked the long tang, he withdrew his picks and slid them back into his kit. Delaney removed the hinge obstruction, and closed the door softly behind them. They were in.

"A felony," the Chief said.

"The door fits tightly," Boone said. "Okay for the lantern?"

"Sure," Delaney said. "Here, I've got it."

He unwrapped the black cloth, stuffed it back into the burlap bag. He straightened up, held the lantern waist-high, snapped it on. A powerful beam probed straight ahead, so bright that their eyes squinted. Then widened. They saw it all.

The interior of the old barn had been insulated, and rough wooden racks built almost to the roof. A sturdy ladder leaned against a wall. A heavy air conditioner was emplaced in a corner. There was a wooden kitchen table, a single wooden chair. And nothing more. Except the paintings.

They were everywhere. On the racks. On the floor. Leaning against the walls. Not in stacks, canvas against canvas, but singly, apart, to dry and gleam. In the glare of the lantern, burning faces stared at them, eyes blazed, mouths mocked.

Delaney and Boone stood frozen, awed by the liquid fire of color that poured over them. They had a sense of shame, of having invaded a church, violated a holy place. There were a few still lifes, landscapes, portraits. But most of the paintings were nudes, bursting Victor Maitland nudes, strangling with their ripeness, gorgeous tints of cream and crimson. Shadows of violet. Hidden parts, secret nooks. Arms reaching, eager legs grasping.

"Jesus Christ," Boone whispered.

They stood and stared, stared, stared. The Chief moved the lantern beam slowly about. In the shifting illumination, now bright, now gloom, they saw swollen limbs quiver, move languorously. They choked in a sea of flesh, drowning. Bodies came writhing off canvas to embrace, entwine, suffocate with breath of steam and hair of flame.

Delaney flicked off the lantern, and they heard themselves breathing heavily.

"Too much," the Chief said in the darkness. "All together like this. Too strong. Too much to take."

"What do you figure?" Abner Boone said hoarsely. "About two hundred of them?"

"Say two hundred," Delaney said. "Say a minimum of a hundred grand a painting."

"Say twenty million," Boone said. "In a wooden barn. I can't believe it. Let's lift ten or so, Chief, and take off for Rio."

"Don't think I haven't thought of that," Delaney said. "Except I know I could never bring myself to fence them. Let's take another look. Use the penlight this time."

The weak light was a relief; they were no longer dazzled, befuddled. They moved to the nearest painting, a dark, rope-bodied nude, torso twisted, hip sprung, legs and arms like serpents, and a wicked smile that challenged. Boone moved the circle of light to the lower righthand corner. They saw that neat bookkeeper's signature, Victor Maitland, followed by the date: 1958.

"Son of a bitch," Delaney said. "Try another."

They went from painting to painting. All were dated 1957, 1958, 1959, a few 1960. None more recent.

"Beautiful," Boone said. "Not only a fake record in Geltman's safe, but a fake date right there on the painting. The IRS will have a sweet job proving they were done a year ago."

"They thought of everything," Delaney marveled. "It had to be J. Julian Simon. *Had* to be. It smells of the legal mind at work. Let's get some shots. Just to prove this harem exists."

Boone held the lantern, turned on for added illumination while Delaney shot a pack of color Polaroid with flash. The colors of the prints weren't as rich as the oils of the paintings, but the overall shots were impressive: a crowded mint of art.

They gathered up all their equipment, stowed it into the burlap bags. They inspected the floor carefully to make certain they were leaving no track of their presence.

They went out slowly, cautiously, guided by the beam of a penlight, now weak and flickering. Boone wiped the inside knob before he stepped through to the shed. He closed the door by inserting a hooked pick into the keyhole, then pulling the door to him until the tang snicked into place. They quickly hung the greasy tarp back in its original position. They waited a few moments in darkness, listening. Then they moved silently outside.

They both glanced toward the Maitland house. Even as they did, a light came on in an upstairs window. They didn't rush, but they didn't dawdle either. Around the corner, down the side, into the trees. Twenty minutes later they were headed back to New York, both of them smoking furiously.

"What do we do now?" Boone asked. "Brace Geltman?"

"What for?" Delaney asked. "It's just a tax rap. He won't scare. J. Julian Simon maybe. He's the key to Geltman's alibi. But why should he talk? Shit, shit, and shit. Maybe Belle Sarazen."

"Why her?"

"Possible motive. Oh God, I don't know, sergeant. Just fishing."

"Maybe the wife found out about the tax scam and got sore. Because those paintings wouldn't be included in the estate, in her inheritance."

"Another possibility," Delaney sighed. "We've got plenty of those. Want me to drive awhile?"

"No. Thank you, sir. I'm fine. Steadying down now. How the B-and-E guys get the balls to do that, I'll never know."

"I suppose it gets easier with experience."

"I don't want to find out," Boone said. "Stop for coffee-and, if we can find a place that's open?"

"Let's go straight in. You stop by; Monica left a fresh pot and some cinnamon buns for us in the kitchen."

"Sounds good," the sergeant said, and began driving faster.

It was past three A.M.; the Chief expected Monica had been asleep for hours. But when they pulled up in front of the Delaney brownstone, the living-room lights were on; he saw the figure of his wife standing at the curtains, peering out.

"Now what the hell?" he growled.

They went up the stairs with some trepidation, hands hovering near gun butts. But Monica unlocked the door for them, safe, eager to tell her story.

Jason T. Jason had called several times. He had also tried calling Abner Boone's apartment. He told Mrs. Delaney he would call every fifteen minutes, on the quarter-hour, until the Chief returned home, and Jason could talk to him.

"Did he say what it was?"

"No, he just said it was important, and he had to report to you or Abner as soon as possible. He's very polite."

The two cops looked at each other.

"In trouble?" Delaney suggested.

"Or he's found Mama Perez," Boone said. "One or the other."

"Well . . ." Delaney looked at his watch. "About ten minutes before he calls again."

"The coffee's warm," Monica said. "I'll just turn up the light. The two of you wash up. You look like you've been digging."

They sat around the kitchen table, sipping their coffee, munching their cinnamon buns. Monica refused to go to bed; she wanted to hear what had happened.

Delaney was telling her about that incredible cache of paintings when the phone rang. He picked up the kitchen extension. He had already set out paper and pencil, ready to take notes.

"Edward X. Delaney here," he said. "Yes, Jason . . . So I understand . . . We've both been out . . . Yes . . . Good. Excellent. Where? . . . Right . . . Between what streets? . . . You're sure she's in for the night? . . . All right, hang on a moment . . ."

He covered the receiver with his palm, turned to the others, smiling coldly.

"Got her," he said. "Orchard Street, just south of Grand. Top floor of a tenement. Apparently she's a hooker, but Jason says she's in for the night. If not, he'll tail her."

"I better get down there," Abner Boone worried. "He won't know what to do."

"Yes," Delaney nodded, "you better go. Send Jason home. If he wants to go. But he sounds excited. I'll join you in the morning, and we'll brace her then. Call here every hour on the hour."

He got back on the phone and asked Jason Two his exact location. He jotted down a few notes.

"Stay right there," he ordered. "Sergeant Boone is on his way. If she leaves the house, you follow and try to keep in touch with me here. Have you eaten tonight? . . . All right, we'll take care of it. Good work, Jason."

He hung up, looked at his notes with grim satisfaction.

"You'll find him on the corner of Orchard and Grand," he told Boone. "He'll be watching for you. For God's sake, don't lose her. If you need more men, call me here."

"We won't lose her, sir," Boone promised.

"Has he eaten?" Monica asked. "Jason?"

"No. Not since yesterday afternoon."

"I'll make some sandwiches," she said.

"Good," the Chief said gratefully. "Big, thick sandwiches. He's a big man. And we have that quart thermos. Sergeant, take that with coffee. You'll never find any place open at this hour."

They equipped Boone with coffee, sandwiches, extra cigarettes, all the dimes they had in the house, for phone calls, and sent him on his way.

"Mrs. Delaney," he muttered, before he left, blushing, head lowered, "could you call Rebecca for me and explain? Why I can't—uh—see her?"

"I'll call, Abner," she promised.

"Call her where?" Delaney asked after Boone had departed.

"His apartment," Monica said shortly. "They're living together now."

"Oh?" the Chief said, and they took their coffee mugs into the study. He showed her the Polaroid color shots he had taken in the Maitland barn.

"I can't believe it," she said, shaking her head.

"I saw it, and I can't believe it," he told her. "Overwhelming. All that color. All those nudes. What a thing. It shook me."

"What will you do now, Edward?"

"Get photographs together of everyone connected with the case. I think I have most of them in the file. J. Julian Simon I don't have. And maybe Ted Maitland. I'm not sure; I'll have to check. Then tomorrow we'll show them to Mama Perez and ask her who she saw at Maitland's studio that Friday morning."

"You think she'll tell you?"

"Oh, she'll tell us," he said. "One way or another."

18

Like most cops, he was superstitious, and so he considered it a good omen that he was able to find photographs of all the principals in the folders of the Maitland file. The photos of J. Julian Simon and Ted Maitland had been taken with a telephoto lens by a police photographer at Victor Maitland's funeral. They were grainy enlargements, but clear enough for identification.

He put all the photos in a manila envelope, and added a set of photostats of the three sketches found in Maitland's studio. At the last minute he also added the clippings of the *New York Times* article describing the Maitland gala at the Geltman Galleries. The article included photos of Belle Sarazen and Saul Geltman.

The Chief had everything prepared by the time Abner Boone called at nine A.M. on Saturday morning. The sergeant and Jason T. Jason had the Perez tenement under surveillance. Mama was still up in her sixth-floor apartment. They had investigated a paved rear courtyard, but the only exit from that was by a narrow walkway alongside the building. It emerged on Orchard Street, so Boone didn't think there was any way for Mama to leave the building without their seeing her.

"Unless she goes across the roofs," the Chief said.

Delaney told the sergeant to stay right where he was, that he'd join them within an hour. He figured he'd take the subway down, then thought the hell with it, and stopped the first empty cab he saw. He was keeping a careful account of his expenses and, even with cabs and gas for Boone's car, they seemed modest enough to the Chief. In any event, the expenses were Thorsen's problem, not his.

He sat in the back of Boone's car, the two active-duty cops in the front seat, while they told him what they had turned up—which wasn't much. Mama's real first name was Rosa, though everyone on the street called her Mama. Apparently she was a hooker—Jason Two confirmed that—but Boone guessed she was drawing some kind of public assistance; even in that neighborhood the successful prosties were younger and flashier.

They had also collected a few facts about Dolores. The young girl wasn't related to Mama Perez. Her full name was Dolores Ruiz, and she was the daughter of Maria Ruiz, who lived on the sixth floor, right next to Rosa Perez. Maria Ruiz apparently didn't have any man. She worked long hours, cleaning office buildings, and Mama Perez befriended Dolores during the day: took her shopping, to the movies, etc. Dolores, the neighbors said, wasn't right in the head.

"Does the Perez woman peddle the girl's ass?" Delaney asked them.

Jason said he didn't think so. During his chat with Mama in the Ludlow Street alley, he had politely rejected her proposition but hinted broadly that he might be interested in a younger girl. She hadn't taken the bait.

The three sat there, aware of the noisy, bustling street but staring at the entrance of Mama Perez' tenement. It was an ugly grey building, the front stones chipped and covered with graffiti, most of it in Spanish. Overflowing garbage cans almost blocked the sidewalk. There was a pack of scrofulous cats darting up and down the stoop, into and out of the narrow alley, and even prowling across the rusty fire escape bolted to the front of the tenement. As they watched, sidewalk vendors began setting up their folding tables and arranging their stocks of plastic sunglasses and sleazy T-shirts.

"Well," the Chief said finally, "let's go have a talk with Mama."

"How do you want us to handle it, sir?" Boone asked. "Come on strong?"

"No," Delaney said. "I don't think we'll have to do that. Nothing physical anyway. Jason, did she make you as a cop?"

"No way, Chief."

"Well . . . come up with us just the same. It'll blow your cover, but she'll realize we've got her on soliciting, at least, and that'll give us an edge."

The three got out, and Boone locked the car carefully.

"I hope I'll still have wheels when we get back," he said mournfully.

The entrance and hallways of the walk-up tenement were about what they expected: scummed tile floors, walls with the rough, puckered look of fifty years' painting, the outside coats chipped away in places to show multicolored pits—green, pink, blue, brown, green, blue—like archeological digs revealing the layers of ages. Electric bulbs were broken, landing windows cracked, the wooden banisters carved with dozens of initials or just whittled carelessly. And the smell. It hung in the air like a mist, as if someone had sprayed this place and the fog would never disappear or even diminish.

There had been no names in the slots of the broken bells, but the bank of mailboxes—some of them with jimmied lids—showed R. Perez in apartment 6-D. It also showed M. Ruiz in 6-C. On the second floor, Delaney checked the tin letters nailed to apartment doors and found that D was the farthest to the rear. They continued their slow climb upward, stepping aside to let children clatter down, laughing and screaming, and once to allow the slow descent of a painfully pregnant woman dragging along two smeary-faced tots.

They paused in the sixth-floor hallway to catch their breath, then moved back to stand alongside the door marked D. The tin letter was missing; the D had been scrawled on the green paint with a black Magic Marker. Boone put his ear close, listened a moment, then looked at the others and nodded. Delaney motioned them clear, so no one was standing directly in front of the door. Then he reached out and rapped sharply.

No answer. He knocked again, louder. They heard movement, the scuff of dragged steps.

"Who?" a woman's voice called.

"Board of Education," Delaney said loudly. "About Dolores Ruiz."

They heard the sound of locks being opened, a chain unhooked. The door opened. Jason T. Jason immediately planted one of his enormous feet on the sill.

The woman looked down at that protruding foot, then up to the face of Jason Two. Then she looked slowly at Delaney and Boone.

"Sonnenbitch," she said bitterly. "You got badges?"

Boone and Jason flashed their ID. She didn't seem to notice that Delaney showed her nothing.

"Can we come in, Mama?" the Chief asked pleasantly.

"You got a warrant?" she demanded.

"A warrant?" Delaney said. He looked at the other two men, then back to Rosa Perez. "Why should we have a warrant? This isn't a bust, Mama. We don't want to toss your place. Just talk, that's all. A few questions."

"About what?" she said suspiciously.

Delaney dug the photostats of the Maitland sketches from his envelope. He held them up for the woman to see.

"About these," he said.

She stared, and her punished face softened. She almost smiled.

"Beautiful," she said. "No?"

"Very beautiful," Delaney nodded. "May we come in and talk about them?"

Grudgingly, she stepped aside, swinging the door open wider. The three men filed in. The Chief took a quick look around. A one-room apartment. A box. About thirteen by thirteen, he guessed. A narrow closet with a cloth curtain pulled aside. A kitchenette hardly larger than the closet: sink, cabinet, two-burner gas stove, a small, yellowed refrigerator. There was one window in the room, a closed door opposite. Delaney glanced at the door, looked at Jason, motioned with his head. The cop took three steps, stood to one side, opened the door slowly, peered inside cautiously. Then he closed the door.

"Small bathroom," he said. "Sink, tub, toilet, cabinet. And another door on the other side."

"Another door?" Delaney said thoughtfully. He turned to Mama Perez. "You share the bathroom with Maria and Dolores Ruiz?"

She nodded.

"Sure," he said. "Originally this was all one apartment, but the landlord broke it up into two for more money—right?"

Again she nodded.

"Mama, can we sit down?" he asked her. "We want to talk—just a friendly talk—but it may take a few minutes."

She told the story without hesitation, speaking fluently. They listened gravely and never interrupted her.

On that Friday morning, she had taken Dolores Ruiz out to Orchard Street to buy the girl a pair of summer sandals. This crazy man had rushed up to them on the street and grabbed Mama's arm. He said he was an artist and wanted to paint pictures of Dolores. He would pay if Dolores posed for him. In the nude. Mama could be there while he worked, to protect Dolores' honor. But he wanted to see Dolores' body, to see if it was as good as he thought it was.

So they all piled into a cab, and he took them to the Mott Street studio. Dolores undressed, and the crazy man did three drawings and said he wanted Dolores to pose for him. He said he'd pay five dollars an hour, so they agreed to come back on Monday morning. Then they went away. They came back Monday morning at eleven, and found out the man was dead. Later she learned he had been murdered. She read it in the newspapers and saw it on TV. And that's all that happened.

There was a short silence after she finished. They believed every word she had said. Then . . .

"Did you have a drink?" Sergeant Boone asked. "In the studio?"

"Yes. Wan."

"Did Maitland have a drink?" Delaney asked.

"He drank," she nodded. "From the boatal. Crazy man."

"When Dolores undressed," the Chief said, "did she have a safety pin somewhere on her clothes? Did she drop it?"

Rosa Perez shrugged. "Maybe. I don't know."

"Maitland was alive when you left the studio?" Boone asked.

She turned her head slowly, looked at him shrewdly.

"You tink I keel heem?"

"Was he alive?" Boone repeated.

"He was alive," Mama Perez nodded. "Why should I keel heem?"

"Is Dolores here?" Chief Delaney said. "Now? In her apartment?"

The woman straightened slowly. The stone eyes focussed on him.

"What you want weeth Dolores?"

"Just to see her, ask her a few questions."

Mama Perez shook her head.

"Dolores she don' onnerstan'."

"Get her," Delaney said.

She sighed, rose to her feet. She was wearing a cheap cotton wrapper, a thin, flowered shift. She smoothed the cloth down over her bulging hips in a gesture that was coquettish, almost girlish.

"You hurt Dolores," she said casually, "I keel you."

"No one's going to hurt Dolores," the Chief told her. "Jason, go with her."

Rosa Perez went to the bathroom door, Jason right on her heels. She went through the bathroom, knocked on the far door. Delaney and Boone heard a chatter of Spanish.

They sat waiting. The summer sun streamed through the big window. The little apartment, right under the roof, was suddenly a hotbox, steaming. Chief Delaney rose, stalked to the window, pulled it open. He had to struggle with it; the heavily painted frame was swollen. But he finally got it open wide. He leaned far out, hands propped on the low sill. He looked down. Then he came back into the room, closed the window halfway.

"Six stories straight down to the cement courtyard," he reported to Boone. "You'd think she'd have a window guard—one of those iron grilles you screw on. If this kid—"

"Dolores," Mama Perez said. "Beautiful, no?"

They looked at the vacant-faced girl standing near the doorway to the bathroom. Her arms hung straight down at her sides. She was barefoot. She was wearing a pink rayon slip. They saw what Victor Maitland had seen. The youth. Ripe youth. Ready. And long, glistening black hair. Empty perfection in that mask-face. Eyes of glass. Erupting flesh.

"Hello, Dolores," Delaney said, smiling. "How are you?"

She didn't answer, didn't even look at him.

Delaney took the photostats of the Maitland sketches to her and held them up.

"You, Dolores," he said, still smiling.

She looked at the drawings but saw nothing. Her face showed nothing. She scratched one arm placidly.

"Ask her to sit down," the Chief said to Mama Perez.

The woman muttered something in Spanish. The girl walked slowly to the unmade bed, sat down gently. She moved like bird flight, as pure and sure. She was complete. She composed space.

"You sit down, too, Mama," Delaney said. "A few more questions."

"More?"

"Just a few."

He and Rosa Perez took their seats again. Boone and Jason T. Jason stood at opposite walls.

"We've been looking for you," Chief Delaney said. "You and Dolores. Drawings of you were in the newspapers and on TV. You saw them?"

For the first time she hesitated. Delaney saw she was calculating how the truth might hurt her.

"I saw," she said finally.

"But you didn't come forward. You didn't come to us to ask why we wanted to find you."

"Why should I?" she asked.

"Right," he said equably. "Why should you? Well, Mama, we wanted to find you to ask you about someone you and Dolores may have seen that Friday morning."

"Someone we seen?" she said. "We seen lots of peoples that morning."

"In the building where Maitland's studio is," Delaney said patiently. "On the stairs maybe. Or coming up the outside steps. Somewhere close."

Rosa Perez shook her head.

"I don' remember," she said. "So long ago. I don' remember."

"Let me help you," Delaney said. He took all the photographs and newspaper clippings from his manila envelope. He arranged them neatly on the Formica-topped table, all facing Mama Perez.

"Take a look," he urged her. "A good long look. Take your time. Did you see any of these men or women near Maitland's studio that Friday morning?"

She glanced quickly at the photos, then shook her head again.

"I don' remember," she said.

"Sure you do," Chief Delaney said quietly. "You're a smart woman. You notice things. You remember things. Take another look at them."

"I don' remember."

Delaney sighed. He stood up, but he left the photographs lying there.

"All right, Mama," he said. "But we weren't the only ones looking for you."

She stared at him blankly.

"The killer is looking for you too," Delaney said. "He must have seen the newspaper stories and the TV, just like you did. He's afraid you saw him and will recognize him. So he's looking for you. He doesn't know we have Officer Jason there, who actually saw you and Dolores on Monday morning. So we found you first. But he'll keep looking. The killer."

"So?" she said, shrugging. "How he's going to find me?"

Delaney looked at her with admiration. She hadn't yet lost her nerve.

"I'm going to tell him," he said.

He watched her face pull tight under the thick makeup. Eyes widened. Lips stretched back to show sharp, cutting teeth. The gold incisor gleamed.

"You?" she gasped.

"Oh, not directly," Delaney said. "But the newspapers have been after us. And the TV stations. They're interested. They want to know: Have you found the woman and girl? We ran the drawings for you; have you found them? So now I'll have to tell them, yes, we found the woman and the girl, thanks to you. And this is their address."

She understood. He didn't have to spell it out for her.

"You do that?" she asked tentatively.

"Oh yes," he said. "I would."

"You are not a nice man," she said.

"No," he agreed. "I'm not."

She flared suddenly into a screamed stream of Spanish that he could only guess was curses, a flood of invective spat at him.

"I don' care!" she yelled in English. "I don' care! Let heem come! Let heem keel me!"

He waited until she was screamed out, until she calmed, sank back in her chair, glaring at him, still muttering. He could afford to wait; he had the key to her.

"Not you," he said. "Not only you. Dolores, too. He'll hurt Dolores."

She stared fiercely at him a moment longer before she crumpled. She never did weep. But the hand that went out was trembling, the finger wavering that pointed to the newspaper photograph of Saul Geltman.

"Thees wan," she said in a low voice. "On the stairs. Me and Dolores, we were coming down. He was going up. We saw heem. He saw us. Thees ees the man."

They were back in Boone's car, watching Orchard Street fill up with street vendors and the Saturday afternoon shopping crowd, streaming down from all over New York for bargains. Delaney sat in the back seat again, an unlighted cigar in his fingers.

"Can I ask you a question, Chief?" Jason T. Jason said, without turning around.

"Ask away," Delaney said expansively. "Any time."

"If she hadn't identified anyone in the photos, would you have given her address to the papers? Like you told her you would?"

"Sure. After putting a twenty-four-hour guard on her. Use her as bait. Smoke him out."

"Wow," Jason Two said. "I learn something new every day. Well, anyway, we got him."

Abner Boone made a sound.

"Something, sarge?" Jason asked innocently.

"We haven't got him."

"Haven't got him?" the black cop said indignantly. "She fingered him as being on the scene of the crime at the right time. I can testify to that."

"Oh sure," Boone said. "That and half a buck gets you on the subway."

"It's no good, Jason," Delaney amplified. "Suppose we take that to the DA's office and ask them to seek an indictment of Saul Geltman for Murder One. Okay, they say, what have you got on him? We say, we got an old Puerto Rican whore who saw him near the scene of the crime about the time it was committed. Okay, they say, what else have you got? That's all, we say. Then they fall on the floor holding their ribs and laughing before they kick our ass out of their office. Jason, we have no *case.* You can't convict a man of homicide because he was in the neighborhood about the time the killing took place. Where's the weapon? What's the motive? Where's the legal proof? The sergeant's right; we've got nothing."

Jason looked back and forth, Delaney to Boone, frowning.

"You mean this dude is going to walk?"

"Oh no," Delaney said. "I didn't say that. He's not going to walk. He probably thinks he is, but he's wrong."

"Still," Abner Boone said, turning sideways in the driver's seat to look at Delaney, "he must be having some wet moments. Here's how I see it:

"Geltman goes down to Mott Street on Friday morning to burn Maitland. On the stairs, going up to the studio, he meets Mama and Dolores. He sees them, they see him. Maybe Mama even hustles him right there; she's got the balls for it. But the important thing is that he's got no way of knowing they just came down from Victor Maitland's studio. Right, Chief?"

"Right."

"Okay. So Saul baby goes up, ices Maitland, and skins out. He goes through his little scam as the anxious agent and then, on Sunday, he returns to the studio, allegedly discovers the body, and calls the cops. Now it gets cute. When the blues come, they find the three drawings Maitland did of Dolores. Geltman is there and recognizes the girl he met on the stairs on Friday. He wants the drawings, but we won't give them to him. I know; I was there. So he goes home sweating, hoping nothing will come of those damned drawings because he's afraid the girl may identify him, not knowing she's a wet-brain."

"Then you and I come around asking questions about the girl," the Chief said.

"Right!" Boone said. "Now he's really shitting. Those fucking sketches could cook him if we found the girl. So he thinks fast—hand it to him—and invites us to his show. You particularly, Chief."

"Sure," Delaney nodded. "To get me out of the house so he can lift the drawings."

"Which he does," Boone continued. "Hell, he could be missing from that mob scene for an hour, and no one would realize he was gone."

"Or he could have hired a smash-and-grab lad," Delaney suggested.

"Easily," Boone nodded. "Maybe one of his golden boys. Anyway, now he's got the sketches and he figures he's home free and can relax. But then, a couple of days later, he picks up the paper and lo! there's the police drawings of Mama and Dolores. He must have had a cardiac arrest right then. Imagine how he felt! Thought it was a piece of cake, and now he finds out the cops know about Mama and Dolores. And that's the mood he's in right now. Is that about the way you see it, Chief?"

"Just right," Edward X. Delaney approved. "I figure that's about the way it happened. But I don't think he's all that spooked. Listen, this is one cool monkey. When I went up to his apartment unexpectedly, he didn't turn a hair. My God, those Maitland drawings were probably right there, in one of his beautiful cabinets."

"Wouldn't he keep them in the office safe?" Boone asked.

"Oh no," Delaney said. "Too many people in and out of the place. Too dangerous. That marvelous apartment is his secret place, his dream. He'll have them there. And won't destroy them, as he should, any more than Mama Perez would spit on her velvet hanging of Jesus on the Cross. They're beautiful things, holy things."

"Search warrant?" Boone asked.

"Mmm . . . maybe," the Chief said slowly. "But not yet."

Jason T. Jason had listened closely to this exchange, had followed most of it.

"How we going to nail him?" he asked.

"I don't know," Delaney confessed. "He's got an alibi we've got to break. And I'd like to see a motive. You can convict without establishing motive—but it helps. Especially when you've got damned little else."

"Funny," Abner Boone said, shaking his head. "Saul Geltman. You know, I like the little guy."

"I do, too," Chief Delaney said. "So?"

Boone had no answer to that.

"Sergeant," Delaney said, "think you can stay awake for a few more hours?"

"Sure, Chief. No sweat."

"I'm going to call Deputy Commissioner Thorsen and ask for more men. Round-the-clock surveillance of Mama Perez."

"Could we pull her in as a material witness?" Boone asked him.

"Maybe," Delaney said. "But it would tip our hand, and she's no good to us in the slammer. A loose tail should be enough. Just to make sure she doesn't skip."

"What about Geltman, sir? Want him covered, too?"

"No. He's not going to run. Unless he spots a tail, and that might panic him. Surveillance of Mama will be enough for starters. You brief the new men when they show up. I'll try to have the first one down here in an hour or so."

"What do you want me to do, sir?" Jason T. Jason asked anxiously, fearing his brief career as a detective was drawing to a close.

"Go home and get some sleep," Delaney told him. And then when he saw the man's expression, he said, "Report to Sergeant Boone on Monday morning. In plainclothes. That means a business suit, not that Superfly outfit."

Jason T. Jason smiled happily.

19

He had prepared a "Things to do" list, and even a time-sequence chart, but on Monday morning all his carefully plotted plans went awry.

He got through to Bernie Wolfe on the first call, but the lieutenant was unable to help him.

"I'm due in court in an hour, Chief," he explained. "Testimony on a Chagall-forgery case. One of my men is out sick, and my other guy is in Brooklyn, digging into the cutting of some Winslow Homer etchings from a library's file copies of the old *Harper's Weekly*. It's happening more and more."

"Look, lieutenant," Delaney said desperately, "what I need is poop on how the loss of income from Maitland's work will affect the Geltman Galleries. Can Saul continue in business with the other artists he handles, or will he go broke? I figure the best answer to that would come from his competitors on Madison Avenue."

"Or Fifty-seventh Street," Wolfe added.

"Right. Could we do this: if I send Sergeant Boone and another guy to meet you in court, could you give them the names of, oh say a dozen art dealers they could check today and try to get a rundown on Geltman's financial problems?"

"Of course," Wolfe assured him. "That's easy."

"Good. I'll have Boone call you and set up a meet."

"By the way, Chief, I've been mooching around a little. I got nothing hard, but there's some vague talk that you could buy a Maitland painting without going through Geltman Galleries."

"Uh-huh," Delaney said. "Now that's interesting. Many thanks, lieutenant. I'll have Boone call you. And don't forget to call when you can make dinner."

Then he had to wait for the sergeant's hourly report.

"We still got Mama Perez in sight," Boone said cheerfully. "She tumbled to the stakeout and blew her cork. But one of the new men speaks Spanish, and we got her calmed down. Told her the cover was for her protection, and for Dolores'."

"Good," Delaney said promptly. "That could be a plus. How's Jason working out?"

"Fine," Boone said. "Very eager. Chief, he's faster than he said he was. He and I were coming back to his car from breakfast, and there was a punk working on the front window with a bent coat hanger. He saw us and took off, Jason Two pounding along right behind him. Must have chased the kid two blocks, but he caught him. That Jason can run."

"What did he do to the punk?"

"Frisked him, then kicked his ass and turned him loose."

"Sound judgment," Delaney said. "Got good men on Mama Perez today?"

"Oh sure. Old-timers. Not too fast, but they know the job."

"Then here's what I want you and Jason to do . . ."

He instructed Abner Boone to call Lieutenant Wolfe and arrange to meet him in court. To get a list of art dealers and to check them out on the finances of Geltman Galleries.

"Competitors are usually happy to gossip about a rival," he told Boone. "Take Jason with you, and the two of you divide up the list. Cover as many dealers as you can. Brief Jason on the case so he knows what's going on. I'll be out most of the day, but you'll be able to get me here later this afternoon. If I'm not in, Monica probably will be, so you and Jason come over and wait for me."

"Yes, sir," the sergeant said. "You think we'll nail him, Chief?"

"Sure we will," Delaney said, with more confidence than he felt.

Then, going down his list, he called the office of J. Julian Simon. Susan Hemley answered, and he forced himself to chat casually with her for a few minutes. Finally . . .

"Think I could see the big man this morning, Susan?" he asked.

"Oh no, Chief," she said. "He didn't come in. He's due in court this morning."

"My God," he groaned. "Is *everyone* going to court this morning?"

"Beg pardon?"

"No, no. Nothing. Listen, do you think he'll be in at all today?"

She said Simon expected to be back by three or four in the afternoon at the latest. Delaney told her he'd take a chance and show up around that time in hopes the counselor could give him a few minutes. He was very respectful.

Then yielding to circumstances, he resolved to revise his schedule and barge in on Belle Sarazen without notice. But first he made some peculiar preparations.

He went to the odds-and-ends drawer in the kitchen cabinet and rummaged until he found what he sought: a small waxed-paper envelope containing a few faucet washers. It wasn't an authentic glassine envelope, but he thought it would serve the purpose. He dumped the washers into the cluttered drawer, then filled the envelope with a teaspoonful of confectioner's sugar. He folded the tab over twice and secured it with a little square of Scotch tape.

He slid the packet into the side pocket of his seersucker jacket. He wondered if he should carry a gun, but decided against it. He set his sailer squarely atop his head and sallied forth, lumbering over to First Avenue to get a cab, and resisting the desire for a morning cigar.

Either the doorman recognized him from previous visits, or something in the Chief's manner convinced him that stopping this big, vaguely menacing man would be unwise. In any event, Delaney went directly to the elevator bank without being questioned. As usual, the Filipino houseman, Ramon, answered his ring.

"Yeth?"

"Miss Sarazen in?"

"Ith she expecting the gentlemens?"

"Why don't you ask her?" Delaney said.

Ramon hesitated, then finally allowed Delaney to enter.

"Pleath to wait," he said, and disappeared.

But Delaney didn't stay in the hallway. He went immediately into the monochromatic living room, the one decorated in the blue-grey-violet shade he could not identify. He looked about swiftly, took the little envelope of sugar from his pocket, and slipped it under the plump seat cushion of a softly upholstered armchair. Then he took up his position at a caned straight chair facing it. He stood stolidly, hat in hand, and waited.

She came sailing in, barefoot, a white robe billowing out behind her. It was closed from neck to hem with a wide industrial zipper. Suspended from the tab was an English bobby's whistle.

It was evident she had come directly from bath or shower. The fine, silvered hair was wet and plastered flat. The skin of her face shone; her body exuded a damp, sweetly soapy scent. But he had little time to admire her; she was not pleased to see him, and her attack began immediately.

"Now look," she said angrily. "I'm getting sick and tired of this crap. I want—"

"What crap?" he asked.

"This hassling," she said hotly. "I want—"

"What hassling?" he said. "I'm not hassling you."

"Well, what the hell are you doing here, then?"

"Look, Miss Sarazen," he said, as calmly as he could, "I just have a question or two I'd like to ask. Is that hassling?"

"I've been talking to some smart lawyer friends of mine," she told him. "Very important people. And they tell me I don't have to answer another goddamn question. If you want to arrest me, then go ahead, and I'll stand on my rights. But I'm not going to answer any more questions."

"Sure you are," he said gently. "You really are, Miss Sarazen. Because you're an intelligent woman and know what's best for you. Couldn't we sit down—just for a moment? It won't take long, I promise you."

She stared at him. He saw her indecision, and knew she was teetering; it could go either way.

"You help me," he said, "and I'll help you."

"How could you help me?" she scoffed.

"Sit down," he urged. "Let me tell you about it."

She made a sound of disgust, but fell back into the plump armchair where he had hoped she would sit. She hooked one knee over the arm; a bare foot jerked up and down irritably.

He sat on the edge of the caned chair, leaning forward, his straw hat clasped between his knees. His manner was solemn, intent—a solicitor advising a client of the grave consequences of her foolish acts.

"These smart friends of yours . . ." he said. "I suppose they're important men. In business and politics and society. But when they tell you not to cooperate with cops, they're giving you bad advice, Belle. You don't mind if I call you Belle, do you?"

She made an impatient gesture.

"You see, Belle, they know the law all right. And they assume that cops have to follow it. That's true—up to a point. Most cops do follow the law and police regulations. Your smart friends know this and take advantage of it."

"You bet your ass they do," she nodded. "That's why I listen to what they tell me."

He sat back, relaxed, crossed his knees. He held his skimmer on his lap, his hands clasped across it.

"Well, Belle," he said, almost dreamily, "there are laws without end, and police regulations without end. Books and books of them. But now I'm going to let you in on a secret. Most cops—those who have been around for awhile—go by another book. Although you can't really call it a book because it's never been written down. What it is is a large collection of tips, tricks, hints, procedures, techniques, and so forth. Stuff that one cop tells another cop. Listen, we're all on the front line, and the only way we can survive is to exchange information, trade secrets, learn from each other. And some of the stuff was bought with blood. Not necessarily how to break the law, but how to get around it. You follow?"

She didn't answer, but he thought he saw interest; he was getting to her.

"Some of the stuff cops talk about when they get together are little things," he continued. "Like how a pusher delivered horse in a metal capsule stuck up his ass. Or how to check inside the boot of a guy you're frisking; some of these dudes carry a blade in there. Or how to puncture the taillight of a car you're following, so the rear end shows one red light and one white and is easier to spot. Or how an undercover cop should wear mirrored sunglasses, so he can stop to polish them and use the glasses like a rearview mirror to make sure no one's on his tail. Little tricks like that. Cop talk. Nothing illegal about that, is there?"

Almost against her will, she was listening to him, fascinated. The bare foot stopped jerking up and down. She straightened in her chair, leaning back comfortably, but watching him and listening.

"And we talk cases, too, of course," he went on. "Unsolved cases, and cases that were broken, and how they were broken. Shop talk. That's all it is, Belle: shop talk. Whenever cops get together. In a bar, in a restaurant, at law school, in their homes. It always gets around to shop talk. And police conventions? You wouldn't believe! For instance, I remember I went to a police convention once in Atlantic City. After the formal program during the day was finished, we all got together at night and exchanged cases. Ways to beat the bad guys. Well, there was this one fellow there from a town in Texas. Not a small town, I guess, but not so big either. This guy—let's call him Mike—told us about a cute one he was involved in down there. There was this bentnose in their town, a crud with a long drug sheet pushing a lot of shit to school kids. A couple of the kids OD'd, and Mike knew the source was this bad guy. Knew it, but couldn't prove it. So he decided to take him. He got himself a glassine envelope of horse. You know cops can usually lay their hands on some smack, stuff taken in a raid and never turned in."

"And then I suppose he planted it and arrested the pusher for possession," she said, really intrigued now.

"No," Delaney said. "The cop, this Mike, had a better idea. He waited for the pusher to come home. Then he unloaded his revolver and set it loosely in his holster, the strap unsnapped. He had a backup squad of two other cops. They were in the hall and on the stairs, outside. So Mike broke into the pusher's apartment. 'Where's your warrant?' the crud screams. 'Right here,' Mike says, waving a folded sheet of paper at him. You'd be surprised how even these so-called smart guys can be conned. So Mike shoves him around a little and then tosses the place. Naturally he finds the envelope with the shit in it. While all this is going on, Mike keeps walking around in front of the bad guy, the unloaded gun practically falling out of his holster. You should have heard him tell the story; it was hilarious. He said he kept throwing his hip at the pusher, but the guy wouldn't take the bait. Then, when Mike found the horse and laughed and told the pusher he was going to take him in, and the crud would get twenty years at least, *then* he went for Mike's gun, grabbed it from the holster, said Mike wasn't taking him anywhere, and ducked out the door. And of course the backup guys saw him come running out waving a gun, and they blew him away. They reloaded Mike's gun before they called the brass. So it all ended happily."

She looked at him curiously.

"Why are you telling me all this?" she asked.

"Well," the Chief said thoughtfully, "I was trying to convince you that your smart, important friends don't have all the answers. You see, Belle, if you ever get into trouble, serious trouble, these pals of yours will drop away like the leaves of October. Most of them are married men—right? With responsible jobs and good reputations. You don't really think they're going to put their cocks on the line for you if you get into serious trouble, do you? You'll call, and they'll be in conference, or out of town, or in Mexico on vacation. Believe me, Belle, don't count on them if you get in serious trouble."

"Serious trouble," she repeated. "You keep saying, 'Serious trouble.' What serious trouble could I get in?"

"Oh . . ." he said, gesturing loosely, "like if I said goodbye to you, walked out of here, called the narcotic guys and told them a gabber had informed me that you had a stash of horse up here. The narcs would come galloping and tear this place apart."

"What do I care?" she laughed. "I wouldn't touch heroin. They'd find nothing."

"Sure they would," he said softly. "Under the cushion you're sitting on."

She stared at him, not understanding at first. Then her face whitened; she grew old. She jerked to her feet, flung the seat cushion aside, grabbed up the little envelope. She looked down at it in her hand, raised her head, looked at him.

"You bastard," she breathed. "You bastard!"

"Belle," he laughed. "Oh Belle!"

He stood up, placed his hat carefully on his chair. He walked to her, plucked the envelope from her shaking fingers. He ripped off the top, dumped the white powder into his other palm, licked it clean.

"Powdered sugar," he told her. "Just a demonstration. That you and your important friends don't know all the tricks, Belle. Not all of them. Cops have their little ways, too."

"Powdered sugar?" she said dully.

"That's right," he smiled. "But of course you don't know if I've planted other envelopes of the real stuff in other places, do you?"

He had locked her eyes with his, and she could not look away.

"What do you want to know?" she asked hoarsely.

"That's better," he said. "Now sit down and relax, and let's not have any more crap about your smart lawyer friends."

He replaced her seat cushion. He took her by the elbows and helped her sit down. Then he went back to his caned chair.

"Feeling all right?" he inquired solicitously.

She nodded jerkily.

"Good," he said briskly. "This won't take long now. What kind of business dealings were you having with Victor Maitland?"

She started hesitantly, but he spurred her with sharp, stern questions, and her story didn't take long. About six months before he was killed, Victor Maitland had come to her and asked if she could sell his paintings in the U.S. and abroad. She said sure, and she wanted 35 percent. He said screw that; he was paying Saul Geltman that commission, and if that was her price, what did he need her for? So they finally settled for 20 percent on sales under $100,000, and 15 percent on those over.

"Maitland was to okay the price before the sale?" Delaney asked.

"Of course," Belle Sarazen said.

"So the only one you were shafting was Saul Geltman?"

"Vic said he didn't have a contract with him," she said defensively.

"Apparently he didn't," Delaney nodded. "Go on . . ."

So she had put the word out among her important friends in this country and Europe, and she sold everything Maitland brought her.

"Don't worry," she told the Chief. "I declared my take on my income-tax return."

"I'm sure you did," he said gravely. "How many paintings did you sell?"

"About ten before he was killed," she said. "We were cleaning up."

"Wasn't Maitland worried that Saul Geltman would find out?"

"Worried?" she laughed. "Vic? No way, darling. That guy didn't worry about anything—except getting enough loot to live the way he wanted to. He did say the buyers should agree to keep their purchases secret and not lend the paintings for shows for at least five years."

"And they agreed?"

"Of course. Listen, Vic was selling at bargain-basement rates. Much less than they'd have to pay if they went through Geltman."

"Oh-ho," Delaney said. "I'm beginning to see why your business was so good. You were his discount operation."

"Right," she agreed.

"You said the only thing Maitland worried about was getting the money to live the way he wanted to. Belle, what did he do with his money? Where did it all go?"

"Taxes took like half."

"I know, but still . . ."

"Liquor," she said. "Parties."

He looked at her, not believing.

"How much liquor can you buy?" he said. "How many parties? You said you sold ten paintings. Say the average price was fifty G's. That's half a cool mil. Say your commish was twenty percent. That leaves him four hundred thousand. Say he paid his legitimate tax on that—which I doubt—and it ran as high as fifty percent. That still leaves him two hundred thousand, just through you, not counting his take from Geltman Galleries. Are you trying to tell me he spent two hundred thousand dollars on booze and parties?"

She was silent a few moments. Then the bare foot began jerking nervously again. She started smoothing her damp hair with her palm.

"You won't believe this," she said.

"At this stage," he said, "I'll believe anything."

"Well, he didn't want anyone to know," she said. "About the money, I mean. He was giving most of it away."

"Giving it away? To whom?"

"Young artists. In the Village, SoHo, downtown, Brooklyn. Here, there, everywhere. He wandered all over the city. Going to little galleries. To guys' lofts. Studios. When he found someone he thought had talent, he'd stake them. Put them on salary. That's where all his money was going."

"Jesus Christ," Delaney said. "I don't believe it."

"You better believe it," she nodded. "It's the truth. I know some of the artists he bankrolled. Want to meet them?"

"No," he said slowly, "I'll take your word for it. Did Geltman know about this?"

"I don't know. I doubt it."

"His wife?"

"No way. He didn't tell her *anything.*"

"Let's get back to the paintings you were selling for him. Did Geltman find out?"

"Oh sure," she said. "He'd have to—eventually. The art scene's a tight little world. Everyone knows everyone else. People talk. There are no secrets for long."

She said that Saul Geltman had gone to London to attend an art auction at Sotheby's. At a party, he had heard a man bragging about a Maitland he had just bought at a bargain price. Geltman got himself invited to the guy's apartment to see it. He took one look and knew it hadn't come through his gallery. He came back to New York, and he and Maitland had a knock-down, drag-out fight. Geltman said not only was Maitland depriving him of his rightful commission, but he was depressing the price of Maitland paintings all over the world. The artist had told Belle Sarazen of his bitter argument with Saul Geltman.

" 'Fuck him,' " she quoted Maitland as saying. " 'Geltman's taken care of. For the rest of his life. Where does he get off complaining that I'm selling my own work? I don't need him. I don't need anyone!' "

"So you continued selling Maitland's paintings?" the Chief asked her.

"Sure, I did," she said. "It wasn't *illegal,* was it?"

"No," he said, "it wasn't illegal. Tell me this, Belle—did you happen to notice the dates on the paintings Maitland brought to you to sell? When were they done?"

"They were all early stuff," she said. "Painted twenty years ago. In 1957 and '58. Like that. But just as good as his newer things. You couldn't tell the difference."

"There wasn't any," he said.

She looked at him, puzzled. "That's what I said."

He nodded and got up slowly, preparing to leave. He didn't want to hear any more. He had heard enough. But he turned at the door.

"Belle," he said, "why didn't you tell us all this a long time ago? When we first came up here?"

She lifted her chin.

"I didn't want to get involved," she said.

He sighed resignedly, and turned again to leave. This time she stopped him.

"Edward X. Delaney," she said, "you didn't plant any other envelopes around here, did you? With the real junk?"

"Why Belle," he said, with a curdy smile, "you don't think I'd do anything *illegal,* do you?"

He would never get to the end of people—never. He came to this chastening realization during a slow, ruminative walk through Central Park, from Belle Sarazen's apartment to the East Side. He ambled ponderously, leaning forward a bit, his straw hat tipped to shield his eyes from the burning June sun.

What surprised Edward X. Delaney, what shocked him, was the discovery of what the doomed Victor Maitland was doing with his wealth. To hear suddenly that this gross, brawling, vicious man was capable of such anonymous generosity was equivalent, Delaney reflected mournfully, to learning that Attila the Hun had endowed a home for unwed mothers.

He had lunch on the terrace at the Central Park Zoo. Had a hotdog and a beer, then went back in for another frank and beer. He ate and drank slowly, hearing the trumpeting and screeching and howling of caged animals. It seemed a good place to put it all together, give it form and sequence—this story of craving humans.

Victor Maitland had died, Delaney decided, because he lived too long. It was true. If he had lived only three or four years, as Dr. Horowitz had predicted, the tax fraud would have gone like silk, Saul Geltman would be assured of a good annual income from those paintings stored in the barn, Alma and Ted would have been left a comfortable legacy from the final sale, Dora and Emily would have restored the old homestead, and everyone would have lived happily ever after. If Victor Maitland had died . . .

But the son of a bitch didn't die, wouldn't die. Not the way he was supposed to. He lived, and lived, and lived. And there were all those beautiful paintings drying in the Nyack barn. What the hell. Might as well turn a few of them into ready cash and have some fun before he conked. Maitland might think that way, Delaney guessed. There were so many finished paintings; selling off ten or twenty or more wouldn't make all that difference.

Except to Saul Geltman. It made a lot of difference to Saul. He was trying to keep the price high for Maitland's paintings. So he fed them into the market carefully. And the barn paintings were as much his inheritance as Dora's and Emily's. He could live twenty years on his commissions from those. What was it Maitland had told Belle Sarazen? "Fuck him. He's taken care of. For the rest of his life."

Then Geltman learned about the secret sales, and it all began to come apart. No commissions for him on the secret sales. Worse, it was bringing the market price down. How could he depend on scarcity when anyone could go to the Sarazen woman and get a discount Maitland? And the artist *lived!* The bastard *lived!* And was working and grinding out more and more paintings. It was time to turn off the faucet. Yes, Delaney reckoned, Geltman must have figured just that: it was time to turn off the faucet. Victor Maitland's death would solve everything.

The Chief walked into the offices of Simon & Brewster, all beaming geniality. But the lubricious Susan Hemley was absent from her desk. In her place was a stiff, bespectacled young man with a grey complexion. The desk was bare; the young man sat as if nailed to the chair, hands clasped so tightly atop the desk blotter that knuckles showed white.

"Yes?" he asked coldly. "May I help you?"

"Is Miss Hemley in?"

"No."

"Mr. Simon? I called for an appointment. My name is Chief Edward X. Delaney."

"Chief?"

"New York Police Department."

"Oh. Just a moment."

He rose jerkily to his feet, crossed to Simon's door, knocked in a rough manner. He entered without pausing and slammed the door behind him. He was out again in a moment, scowling.

"Mr. Simon will be with you shortly. Take a chair."

They sat in silence, trying not to stare at each other.

"Are you also an attorney?" Delaney asked finally.

"No," the young man said angrily. "I was hired as a paralegal assistant."

It was evident that his conception of paralegal employment did not include serving as a receptionist. Delaney had the feeling that if he offered sympathy, the young man would either start screaming or burst into tears. So the Chief sat without speaking, straw hat balanced on his knees, and endured the long, silent wait, guessing this was J. Julian Simon's little oneupmanship ploy.

Eventually, twenty minutes later, the man himself came bustling from his inner office, hand outstretched, perfect teeth gleaming.

"Sorry to keep you waiting," he smiled, and offered no apology.

"I'm in no hurry," Delaney said equably. " 'The mills of the gods . . .' and so forth and so forth."

As usual, Simon looked as though he had been oiled and polished. A day spent in court had not dulled his knife-edge creases, disturbed his elaborately coiffed hair, or tangled his perfectly groomed mustache. Today the shirt was light blue polka dots on white, the tie knitted maroon silk, the suit itself a shiny navy linen with white buttons and lapels like vertical stabilizers.

He ushered the Chief into his private office, sat him down, inquired solicitously as to his health, adjusted the drapes to block more of the late-afternoon sunlight, and offered a drink. When it was politely declined, he mixed himself a Rob Roy at his handsome bar with all the care of a mad scientist distilling the elixir of life. It was not, Delaney judged, Simon's first Rob Roy of the day.

"Five hours in court," the attorney boomed. "Endless delays. Boring, boring, boring. But you know all that, I'm sure."

"Cops know all about waiting," Delaney agreed. "It's part of the job. But eventually, I've noted, things get done. If you have the patience."

"Of course, of course," Simon said. He took a sip of his drink, said, "Aah!" and settled back more comfortably into his leather swivel chair. "Is this an official visit, Chief?"

"Not exactly," Delaney said. "I guess you might say it's a courtesy call."

"Oh?" Simon said, puzzled.

"Counselor, as a member of the bar, you're an officer of the court. That's true, isn't it?"

"Yes, of course."

"And I'm acting in the capacity of an officer of the law. So you might say we're on the same side. Don't you agree?"

Simon nodded, watching the Chief carefully now.

"So I felt it only right," Delaney continued, "that I come to you directly and give you the facts before taking official action."

Simon finished the Rob Roy in a gulp. He rose, stalked to the bar, busied himself stirring another. His back was turned to Delaney. When he spoke, his mellifluous voice had lost its honeyed drip.

"What's this all about, Delaney?" he demanded.

"Are you a friend of Saul Geltman?"

The lawyer brought his drink back to the desk, sat down heavily in the swivel chair. He raised the glass but didn't sip; he stared at Delaney over the rim.

"You know I am," he said.

"Do you *want* to be a friend of his?"

"What the hell is that supposed to mean?"

"I'm trying to discover just how far out on a limb you'll crawl for him. Who ate the sandwiches?"

"What?" Simon said, bewildered. "What are you talking about?"

"The sandwiches you ordered for lunch," Delaney explained patiently. "For you and Geltman. On that Friday. Who ate them? He wasn't here for lunch. Did you eat them all? Throw the extras away? Or did he come back for his later?"

"I have told you again and again that—"

"You've told me shit," Delaney said harshly. "What kind of sandwiches were they, counselor?"

"Delaney, what's this with the sandwiches?"

"What kind were they? Tunafish? Egg salad? Meat? What?"

"Well, if you must know, they were roast beef on whole wheat bread with diet soda."

"What did you have for lunch last Tuesday, counselor?"

"Last Tuesday?" Simon said. "Who can remem—"

He stopped suddenly, too late. Delaney grinned at him.

"Right," he nodded. "Can't remember what you had for lunch last Tuesday. Who can? I can't. But you remember perfectly that more than two months ago you had roast beef on whole wheat bread with diet soda. Geltman volunteered the same information. Unasked, by the way. That's the trouble with amateurs: they talk too much. Now, counselor, as an expert in cross-examination, wouldn't you say that the fact that both you and Saul Geltman remember exactly what you had for lunch two months ago suggests rehearsal, if not collusion?"

J. Julian Simon rose to his feet, somewhat unsteadily.

"This conversation is at an end," he said thickly. "I'll thank you to leave."

Delaney also stood up. He unbuttoned his jacket, raised his tails high. He turned slowly, so Simon could see his shirted torso.

"Look," he said, "I'm not wired. Frisk me if you like. No bugs, no transmitter, no recorder. This talk is just between you and me, counselor."

"No more talk," Simon said.

"For your own good," Delaney urged, rebuttoning his jacket and sitting down again. "In your own interest. Don't you want to hear what I've got?"

Simon suddenly seemed drained. That ruddy complexion, nourished by a thousand facials and hours under the sunlamp, became as soft and puckered as a deflated balloon. He fell rather than sat back in his chair.

"Sure you want to hear," Delaney went on grimly. "So you'll know what you're up against if you decide to be Saul Geltman's friend. He comes in here around ten that Friday morning. You close and lock the door to the outer office. Look, now I'm Saul Geltman . . ."

The Chief rose, strode quickly to the frosted-glass door leading to the outside corridor. He pushed the button release on the lock. He opened the door, stepped halfway through, then turned to wave at J. Julian Simon.

"Bye-bye," he said merrily.

Then he came back inside, relocked the door, took his seat again.

"No one saw Saul Geltman in this office after he arrived at ten o'clock," he went on. "Not Susan Hemley, not even the guy from the deli who brought the lunch. No one. We checked."

"I did," Simon said hoarsely. "He was here all the time."

"Was he? Stick with that story, counselor, and your ass is up for grabs. A subpoena. Testimony before a grand jury. Questions. About your business, taxes, your record. Publicity. Your picture on the six o'clock news holding a copy of the *Wall Street Journal* in front of your face. Is that what you want, counselor? Are you willing to go through all that for the sake of your friendship with Saul Geltman?"

"The man is my client. You have no right to—"

"No right?" Delaney thundered. "No right? Don't give me that crap, you lousy shyster. You think we don't have your sheet? You think we don't know how close you came to disbarment? Don't talk to me about privileged lawyer-client relationships. I'm not talking about your client now, I'm talking about you, about obstruction of justice, perjury, and accessory to homicide. How's that for openers?"

"You're guessing," Simon cried. "Guessing! You've got nothing. You come in here and—"

"I've got an eyewitness," Chief Delaney said triumphantly. "An eyewitness who saw Geltman near Victor Maitland's studio the morning he was killed. At a time you say he was up here eating roast beef on whole wheat and drinking diet soda with you. An eyewitness, counselor! Think of it! A responsible citizen, pillar of the community, who picked Saul Geltman's picture out of a dozen others and will swear he was there at that time. Plus supporting physical evidence. Is your friendship worth it? *Think,* man! Use your goddamned brain! Now's the time. You can work a deal; you know that. Get out of the way of the landslide, Mr. Simon. It's coming. You can't stop it. And if you repeat that stupid statement of yours under oath, you'll be swept away. You and your Spy caricatures and your oak bookcases and all this swell stuff—all gone. Nothing left."

Edward X. Delaney rose abruptly to his feet.

"An eyewitness," he repeated softly. "Who saw him. Think of that! Well, you give the problem a lot of thought, counselor, a lot of careful consideration. If you decide you'd like to amend your statement, that you made a mistake and maybe Saul Geltman did step out of your office for an hour or two, why just give me a call. I'm in the book. Take your time. Think it over carefully. I'm in no hurry. I'm a patient man. I learned how by cooling my heels in lawyers' offices. Take care, counselor. See you around."

He left a shaken, slack-jawed J. Julian Simon slumped behind his leather-topped desk, holding his cocktail glass in trembling fingers. Delaney left the office building quickly, crossed to the north side of East 68th Street. He walked a half-block westward, toward Fifth Avenue, and stood partly concealed by trees and parked cars, but in a position where he could observe the entrance to the building he had just left.

He reckoned it would take at least ten minutes for J. Julian Simon to start his adrenaline flowing with another Rob Roy, to call Saul Geltman at the Galleries on Madison Avenue, and to summon him with the news that the sky was falling. But it was almost twenty minutes before the little art dealer came scurrying around the corner, almost trotting in his haste. He rushed into the building, and Edward X. Delaney, smiling, wended his way slowly homeward, lighting a cigar. He didn't, he acknowledged, know exactly what the hell he was doing; he had no definite plan. Yet. But he wanted Saul Geltman scared witless. It could do no harm.

When he entered his brownstone, he found Monica, Abner Boone, and Jason T. Jason seated around the kitchen table, laughing, and sharing a bowl of potato chips. Monica was drinking a martini, Boone a bottle of club soda, and Jason Two was working on a can of beer. They all looked up as he came clumping in.

"Hullo, dear," Monica said. "What have you been doing all day?"

"Threatening people," he said cheerfully. "Thirsty work. Don't I get a reward?"

"The pitcher's in the icebox," she said. "Lemon peel already cut."

"Perfect," he nodded, and poured himself a martini over ice and added a twist. Then he pulled up a chair to join them, and looked at Boone. "How did it go, sergeant?"

"Good enough, sir. I think. Between us, we hit eleven dealers. Four of them wouldn't say one way or another. Didn't know or wouldn't talk. The other seven said that without Maitland, Saul Geltman is down the drain."

"Two of my guys said he's got no one heavy enough to pay the freight on Madison Avenue, Chief," Jason put in. "High-rent district. They said he might be able to stay in business downtown, but not on Mad. Ave. Unless he comes up with another Maitland."

"Chief," Boone said, "you remember we asked him the same question the first time we talked to him. He said that the death of Maitland would hurt him, but not all that much, that he'd survive."

"Sure he would," Delaney said. "With twenty million dollars' worth of Maitland's stuff in the Nyack barn. Here's what I got . . ."

He gave them brief accounts of his meetings with Belle Sarazen and J. Julian Simon. They listened intently, silent and fascinated. When he finished, Monica got up to pour herself another drink, freshen her husband's glass, and put another can of beer before Jason Two.

"Then he's guilty, Edward?" she asked. "No doubt about it?"

"No doubt about it," he said. "Proving it is something else again."

"Uh, Chief," Jason said. "Sounds to me like we got motive now. And opportunity, if this lawyer guy chickens out on the alibi. No weapon, I admit. But enough to rack him up. No?"

Chief Delaney looked at Boone.

"What do you think, Sergeant?"

Abner Boone shook his head angrily.

"No way," he said. "I don't see it. Indictment maybe. Possibly. But I'll bet the DA won't prosecute. Too thin."

"Thin?" Jason T. Jason cried. "My God, it seems to me the man's tied in knots."

"No, Jason," Delaney said. "Sergeant Boone's right. We'd never get a conviction on the basis of what we've got. Look, everyone thinks a Not Guilty verdict means innocence. Not necessarily. Sometimes it just means the prosecutor hasn't proved his case beyond a reasonable doubt. Usually in cases like that, the DA doesn't even go to trial. He wants to show a good conviction rate. Prosecuting an obviously weak case is a waste of time for him, the taxpayers, everyone."

"Look, Jase," Boone said to the disappointed cop, "everything we've got so far is circumstantial. That's not too bad; most homicide prosecutions are based on circumstantial evidence. How often do you get an eyewitness to a killing? But we've got nothing that will stand up in court."

"Right," Delaney nodded. "Belle Sarazen's report of the heavy argument between Maitland and Geltman is hearsay. Not admissible. And if J. Julian Simon decides to repeat his lie under oath, who do you think the jury's going to believe—a slick Madison Avenue lawyer or a been-around hooker ready for Social Security?"

"You mean Saul Geltman is going to get away with this?" Monica said indignantly.

"Ah," Chief Delaney said. "We shall see. Geltman knows now that we have an eyewitness placing him at the murder scene at the right time. Let's figure he saw those police drawings in the newspapers and on TV, so he knows we were looking for her. And he knows what a danger she represents to him because he saw Mama Perez and Dolores near Maitland's studio that Friday morning."

"So?" Monica said.

"So," Edward X. Delaney said dreamily, "let's help him find her."

But Deputy Commissioner Ivar Thorsen wasn't enthusiastic when Delaney spelled it out for him on the phone that evening.

"Sounds like entrapment to me, Edward," he said.

"For God's sake," Delaney said, "entrapment is legal junk. It all depends on whether the judge got laid the night before. We're not luring him into committing a crime; we're giving him a choice. If he's really innocent—which he isn't—he'll laugh at us and walk away. Maybe even report it to the cops. But if he's guilty—which he is—he'll take the bait. Ivar, this guy is sweating; I know he is. He'll bite."

"The cost . . ." Thorsen groaned.

"Not so much," Delaney said. "One or two tech men working a day or so. We'll keep the equipment simple. I've got enough personnel with Boone and Jason and the guys watching Mama Perez. What do you say?"

"A helluva risk to the Perez woman."

"She'll be protected."

"If it goes sour, it's my neck."

"I know that, Ivar," Delaney said patiently. "Want me to go ahead on my own, and we'll pretend this conversation never took place?"

"No," Thorsen said. "Thanks for the offer, but it wouldn't work. You need my okay to draw the equipment. And you need that to nail him—right?"

"Right. Well? Are you in?"

There was silence for a few moments. Delaney waited.

"Look, Edward," Thorsen said finally, "let's do this: make the approach first. If he bites, I'll authorize what you need. If he doesn't go for it, then all bets are off and the bastard walks. Agreed?"

"After what he did to Mary and Sylvia?" Edward X. Delaney said. "Never."

20

They were dawdling over their lunch coffee. Chief Delaney was reading an early edition of the *Post,* smiling over a story about a Chicago cat-burglar who had tried to squeeze through an iron-barred gate and got his head caught. He had to call the cops to pry him free. Monica, chin in hand, was listening to the kitchen radio.

"Piano Sonata Number Two," she said dreamily. "Prokofiev."

"Sam Prokofiev?" Delaney asked, not looking up. "Used to play third base for the Cincinnati Reds?"

"That's the man."

"Fast hands," he murmured. "But he couldn't hit."

Then he looked up. They stared at each other solemnly.

The news came on at 2:00 P.M., and Delaney put his paper aside. The first items dealt with a flood in Ohio, a famine in Pakistan, and the indictment of a California Congressman for malfeasance and misfeasance.

"And mopery," the Chief muttered.

Then the announcer said:

"The body of a middle-aged man was removed from the ruins of a luxury apartment on the upper East Side of Manhattan early this morning following a three-alarm fire that routed almost a hundred tenants of the building and caused extensive fire and water damage. The dead man has been tentatively identified as J. Julian Simon, a prominent attorney . . . In Italy, sources close to the—"

Delaney reached across the table, clicked off the radio.

"Did he say . . . ?" Monica faltered.

"That's what he said," Delaney snapped. "J. Julian Simon. Sometimes I'm too fucking smart by half," he added savagely.

He had his hand on the kitchen phone when it shrilled under his fingers. He jerked it off the hook.

"Edward X. Delaney here," he said furiously.

"Edward," Ivar Thorsen said breathlessly, "did you hear the—"

"I heard," the Chief said angrily. "God damn it to hell! It's my fault, Ivar."

"Then you think—"

"*Think,* shit! The little bastard knocked off his old handball buddy when he started to come apart. Now all we got is Simon's original statement, and Geltman's still got his alibi. He thinks! Ivar, you've got to handle this. I haven't the clout. Where's the body now?"

"I don't know, Edward. On the ME's slab, I suppose."

"Will you call and tell them to carve the roast very, very carefully? Especially look for knife wounds, particularly in the back."

"All right," Thorsen said faintly.

"Or evidence of drugging or heavy drinking. Then call your contact at the Fire Department, and put a bee in his ear. Victim was involved in hanky-panky, foul play suspected, and so forth and so on. Was the fire deliberately started? Evidence of arson? Tell them to go over that apartment with a comb."

"Will do, Edward."

"Get back to me as soon as you've got anything. Please, Ivar?"

He banged the phone back on the hook. He couldn't look at Monica.

"Edward," she started, "it isn't your—"

"He's gone," he said loudly. "He's just gone."

She thought he meant J. Julian Simon—but he didn't. He stamped into the study, slammed the door behind him. He threw himself into his swivel chair. He held out his hands before him, saw them trembling. It was, he knew, the rage of humiliation. It was his bruised ego that was suffering. Snookered and made a fool of, again. He wondered just how much of his successful career had stemmed from an exaggerated sense of his own talents and shrewdness. Well, he reflected ruefully, little Saul Geltman was giving him a lesson in humility.

He tried to put the man together. It was a crossword puzzle with too many clues. Geltman was this, he was that. He was cruel, he was tender. He was profound, he was frivolous. Edward X. Delaney, struggling with reports, notes, memories, couldn't get a handle on the man. The "handle" he was looking for was motivation.

He had been a cop long enough to know that only rarely did people act with singleness of purpose. Motives were usually jungles, a complexity of drives and incentives. A son who fed an arsenic sandwich to his aged, ailing father might say, "I did it to ease his pain," and believe it. Dig a little deeper, and you found that the killer was in hock to the shys and needed his legacy to keep his kneecaps from being splintered; that he had the hots for a young twist who demanded he show some green before she said Yes; that his sick father was a whining, incontinent, spiteful invalid. But it was also true that the victim was in extreme and constant pain. So?

Delaney's analysis of Saul Geltman was interrupted by a call from Ivar Thorsen. The Deputy Commissioner was excited.

"Edward? They were way ahead of us. They'd already found them. Multiple stab wounds in the back. Similar to the MO on Maitland. It was definitely a homicide, according to the ME who did the autopsy. He happens to be the guy who did Maitland, and he says it could be the same knife. I've alerted the Fire Department. Their investigators are already there."

"That's fine, Ivar," Delaney said heavily. "But nothing to the press on this. *Nothing!* Let that midget think he's scammed us. Can you send some men around with photos of Geltman? Maybe someone saw him at the scene—doorman, neighbors, anyone. It's a long shot, but we've got to go through the motions."

The Deputy Commissioner said he'd take care of it, but it wouldn't be easy; the manpower cuts were hurting.

"I know," Delaney said consolingly, "but it's only for a few days. A week at the most."

Thorsen was silent for a beat or two.

"Think you can wrap it up by then?" he asked casually.

"One way or another," Delaney said, deliberately enigmatic. "Did Boone tell you about the tax fraud?"

Thorsen said he had, and that he supposed they'd have to tip the IRS eventually. He wondered what effect that would have on the sympathies of J. Barnes Chapin, learning that the NYPD had blown the whistle on his sister.

"It could be a plus if you handle it right," Delaney told him. "Have a meet with Chapin and lay it out for him. Tell him we'll hold off tipping the Feds if he can convince his sister to get religion and spill her guts about the whole con—how it was set up, who was involved, and so forth. Tell Chapin the IRS probably won't even charge Dora and Emily; they'll be so happy to find that treasure house of Maitland paintings. It'll mean that Dora and Emily inherit zilch, and Alma and Ted Maitland become wealthy, but that's the way the cream curdles. At least Chapin's sister and niece won't go to the slammer. In return, he should be happy to cooperate on that bill you want passed."

"Edward, you should have been a politician," Thorsen said.

"God forbid."

"Well, I like it. And I think it'll work."

"Hold off talking to Chapin until I give you the go-ahead."

"Will do. Anything else?"

"Could you come up with, say a few hundred dollars from the discretionary fund? You know, the money put aside for gabbers and dope buys?"

"A couple of hundred? What for?"

"Don't you trust me, Ivar?"

"Sure I do, Edward. For a hundred, tops."

"All right," Delaney laughed. "I'll try to get by on that. It's for Mama Perez. I'll lay it out of my own pocket, and you make good. Agreed?"

"Agreed."

Then Edward X. Delaney went back to his analysis of the character of art dealer Saul Geltman. He made a list of possible motives and, on the basis of what he knew or guessed about the man, gave each motive a value rating of one to ten. Then he eliminated minor or superficial goads that might drive a man to murder. What he was left with was the obvious and simple spur of greed.

The problem with covetousness—for money, physical possessions, power—was that it was an open-ended motive; there was no end to it. A man compelled by a desire for revenge, for example, might kill, and that would finish it. Act committed, need satisfied. But there was no end to greed. It fed upon itself. More never led to satiety; more led to more. In a way, it was an addiction. "Yes," says the multimillionaire, "I have a lot of money. But I don't have *all* of it!"

In Geltman's case, Delaney decided, greed was driving him to acts he had never imagined. Obsessed with a passion for more, with a fear of losing what he had already gained, he had surrendered to his addiction, whirling down into a maelstrom of deceit, treachery, murder. All the while stroking his zinc-covered dining table, sipping fine cognac from a Baccarat snifter, and murmuring, "Mine, mine, mine!"

The Chief was still at his musings when Monica came into the study bearing two rye highballs. She gave her husband his, then perched on the edge of the desk next to him, her good legs dangling.

"God bless you, child," he said, taking an appreciative sip, stroking her bare calf. "I'll remember who offered aid in my hour of need."

"What's the need?" she asked. "What are you doing?"

"Trying to understand why Saul Geltman is Saul Geltman, and not Edward X. Delaney, say, or even Jake Dukker. Here's a philosophical question for you: Which is worse—to want all the good things of life and never get them, or to get them and then lose them?"

She considered a moment, her glass at her lips.

"You understand the question?" he asked.

"Oh, I understand it," she said. "I'm just trying to decide. I guess it would be worse to want things and never get them."

"Why?"

"Because if you had them and then lost them, at least you could console yourself with the thought that, for awhile, you had it all and were happy. But not having, *never* having, would just be constant frustration."

"Mmm," he pondered. "That's your personal reaction."

"Of course," she said. "That's what you wanted, wasn't it?"

"Yes. No. Actually, I was wondering how Saul Geltman would answer that question."

"Saul Geltman," she said. "I still can't believe it. That nice little man."

"Oh, everyone speaks very highly of him," Delaney said with heavy sarcasm. "One of the nicest guys I ever met had just murdered his mother, father, two sisters, a brother, and the family dog. With a hammer yet. While they slept. I don't think Geltman would agree with your answer. Just the opposite. I told you once, it's when want turns to need that the trouble starts."

She looked at him.

"I want you," she said.

He looked at her.

"I need you," he said.

"Then let the trouble start," she said, sliding off the desk and taking him by the hand.

"In the middle of the afternoon?" he said.

"Why not?"

"Depraved," he said, shaking his big head.

But he rose immediately to his feet and followed her upstairs.

21

His first intention was to approach Rosa Perez by himself and try to sell her on his scheme. But he finally decided to brace her with Sergeant Boone and Officer Jason in attendance. They were all three big men; while they would not threaten physical harm, their massive presence would have a psychological effect. He had used it before: a suspect surrounded by looming and glowering giants, unconsciously intimidated, imagination creating the fear—and eager cooperation.

But Mama wasn't having any.

"You tink I'm nuts?" she said indignantly.

Patiently, Delaney went through his prepared speech. What they were asking was really a very small thing: a single phone call to Saul Geltman for starters. She was to say she was the eyewitness who had seen him near Maitland's studio the morning of the murder. She was also to tell Geltman she had made a tentative identification to the cops, but maybe she could change her mind. After all, she was a very poor woman. Etc., etc.

Then, if Geltman sounded interested, she was to set up a meet with him in her apartment. Delaney would take it from there. And that's all there was to it.

Mama said no.

Delaney told her that putting Geltman in the slammer was the only way she could guarantee her own safety, since the art dealer was sure to come gunning for her. When that had no effect, the Chief reminded Rosa that Geltman had also seen Dolores, and for the sake of the girl's safety, the phone call should be made.

She waffled a bit on that, but then stoutly decided that she and Dolores and Dolores' mother would move, and Geltman would never find them. So Delaney offered her fifty dollars to make the call. The gold tooth gleamed, but Mama still refused. And she remained adamant even after the ante was raised to a hundred dollars, and Delaney swore she would be in no physical danger.

"We'll be in the next room watching everything during the meet," he assured her. "He makes one cute move, and we smear him. Dolores won't even be here. You're a strong woman; you can hold off one puny little guy for a few seconds, can't you? I'll bet you've handled bigger bums than him and never got hurt. And there's that yard for your trouble. A cool hundred dollars for a few minutes alone with this guy. Mama, he's practically a *midget!* What do you say?"

She was tempted, they could all see that, but she wouldn't commit herself. She was a small, bulky woman with eyes as bright as berries, a wise mouth, tartish voice, a manner that alternated between street twist and saucy virgin.

Chief Delaney, stymied, noted her frequently coquettish manner. Seeing behind that damaged face, he realized she must have been a beauty forty years ago, and she remembered.

"Your picture in all the papers, Mama," he said softly. "If you help us. Television interviews. Rosa Perez Helps Capture Killer. Everyone will see you. Everyone will know who you are. You'll be someone. Someone, Mama. Rosa Perez. Famous."

"On TV?" she asked slowly, and he knew he had her.

It was decided the phone call would be made from the Chief's brownstone. Both Boone and Jason owned small tape recorders. The sergeant's had a suction-cup attachment for telephone use. He'd tape the call from the hallway extension with Jason standing by with his recorder as backup. Delaney and Rosa Perez would place the call from the study.

They spent an entire afternoon on rehearsals. Mama was not an educated woman, but her parents had not raised her to be a fool, and she had added street wit and a shrewd understanding of human foibles. Delaney prepared a script for her to follow, but soon discarded the text and let her speak her own argot. They tossed questions at her—things they thought Saul Geltman might ask—and, after an initial hesitation, she began to answer all their queries with just the right mixture of bravado and cupidity. Delaney thought she'd do very well indeed.

After the rehearsal, on the ride uptown, Jason Two said, "What a bimbo! I think she's really enjoying this."

"She's the center of attention," Delaney said, "and that pleases her. We'll go with the call tomorrow afternoon about three o'clock. He should be back from lunch by then."

"If he goes for it, Chief," Boone asked, "and he makes the meet, what have we got? You figuring on aggravated assault or assault with a deadly weapon?"

"Hopefully," Delaney nodded. "If not that, we'll have another link with the Maitland kill at least. But I'm betting he'll show with his trusty blade, all charged up to off her."

"He won't pay the blackmail?" Jason said.

"He's not that stupid," Delaney said. "He'll guess it's just the first installment, and he's got to silence her permanently. That's how I'd figure if I was him."

"You think he's got the balls to take her?" Boone said.

"He did it twice," Delaney said somberly. "It gets easier."

The call was set for Thursday afternoon. The Chief had planned it that way so Monica would be absent on her weekly stint as a hospital volunteer; he preferred she not be aware of his use of Rosa Perez as bait. Jason T. Jason was assigned the task of chauffeuring Mama uptown in his car. Boone and Delaney met early in the brownstone to arrange chairs, and set up and test the small tape recorders.

Jason arrived on schedule a little after two o'clock. Delaney was touched to see that Mama Perez had dolled up for the occasion. She was wearing a shiny purple dress with an embroidered bib of seed pearls, only a few of which were missing. She carried a white plastic handbag with a black poodle painted on one side. Her platform soles gave her an additional three inches of height; the straps wound about fat calves bulging under rose-tinted stockings or pantyhose. The makeup was thick and startling: green eyeshadow, patches of pink rouge, and puckered Cupid's-bow lips.

"You look terrific," Delaney assured her.

"You like?" she said delightedly, then shrugged casually. "Is nothing."

She asked for a drink, and he promptly brought her a double whiskey with water on the side, having no doubts that she could handle it. Sergeant Boone and Jason went into the hall to man their equipment. Delaney had Rosa Perez sit in the swivel chair behind the study desk. He pulled a straight chair close to her where he could listen to the conversation by leaning forward, his ear pressed to the receiver. He was prepared to break the connection if she crossed him.

A few minutes before three o'clock, he dialed the number of Geltman Galleries and handed the phone to Mama Perez. She hitched forward on the padded chair, her back straight, looking very serious and intent.

"Geltman Galleries," a woman's voice said.

"Meester Geltman," Mama Perez said.

"May I ask who's calling?"

"He don' know me. Tell heem eet's about Victor Maitland."

"Victor Maitland? Perhaps I can help you. What is it—"

"Meester Geltman," Rosa repeated sternly. "Is important. You jus' tell heem."

"Just a moment, please."

They waited. Delaney nodded encouragingly at Mama Perez and made an O sign with thumb and forefinger. She flashed her gold tooth in a surprisingly impish smile.

They heard clicks on the phone as the call was switched. Then . . .

"Saul Geltman speaking. Who is this, please?"

"You don' know me," Mama Perez said. "I seen your peecture een the paper. But I seen you before that."

"Oh?" Geltman said easily. "What was that—"

"Sure I seen you," she went on quickly. "On the stairs. Victor Maitland's studio. On Friday morning. The day he was keeled."

"I don't know what you're talking about," Geltman said.

"You know," Mama Perez said. "You know. I seen you there, an' you seen me. Right, Meester Geltman?"

"I haven't the slightest—"

"I tol' the cops I taught it was you," she continued. "I peeked your peecture out. But maybe eet wasn't you. Maybe I make a meestake. Eet was a long time ago. I only seen you a meenute. So I could maybe make a meestake. You onnerstan', Meester Geltman?"

There was silence a moment. They heard his breathing. Then he said, "Wait a minute; I'll be right back." Then they heard the scrape of a chair on the floor, footsteps, the sound of a door being closed, footsteps, the creak of the chair as he sat down again.

"Would you give me your name, please?" he asked pleasantly.

"No," Mama Perez said. "You don' need to know. I'm jus' a poor woman, Meester Geltman. A *poor* woman. You onnerstan'?"

"I think I do," he said, his voice still steady. "Did the cops put you up to this?"

"The cops?" Mama repeated. She laughed scornfully. "Focking cops! I speet on the cops!"

She spoke that rehearsed line with such genuine vehemence that even Delaney was convinced. He figured that either Geltman would believe, or the whole scam would die right there.

"What do you want?" Saul Geltman asked, and the Chief took a deep breath, guessing the art dealer was hooked.

"I wan' five tousan'," she said. "I wanna go back to Puerto Rico. I wanna get out of thees steenking seety an' nevair come back."

"Five thousand dollars?" Saul Geltman said. "That's a lot of money."

"Not so much moaney. Not eef I go away an' nevair come back. You onnerstan', Meester Geltman?"

"I think I do. What about the young girl who was with you?"

"My daughter. She goes back weeth me. We nevair come back. Nevair."

"And what happens if the cops find you in Puerto Rico?"

Mama Perez laughed again. "In Puerto Rico? Nevair, Meester Geltman. But eef they do, then we don' remember. We don' remember who we seen near Victor Maitland's studio that Friday morning he was keeled. We forget. For five tousan' we forget."

"Well . . . uh . . ." Geltman said cautiously, "maybe we could discuss it. Come to some arrangement to our mutual benefit."

"Five tousan'," Rosa Perez said definitely. 'Een cash. No check. Cash money. Small beels."

"You've figured this out very carefully, haven't you?"

"Oh sure."

"And have you figured out how the money is to be delivered to you?"

Delaney put a finger to his lips, shook his head. Mama nodded and said nothing on the phone.

"I asked how the money was to be delivered," Geltman repeated. "Have you thought of that?"

"N-n-no," Rosa Perez stammered. "You mail eet to me?"

"Mail five thousand cash?" Geltman said. "I don't think that would be smart, do you?"

"No. Maybe not so smart."

"Of course not," he said smoothly. "I can see you're an intelligent woman. Why don't we meet somewhere, and I'll hand over the package in person?"

"Where we meet?" she said suspiciously.

"Oh, I can think of half a dozen places," he said. "Central Park, Grand Central Station, and so forth. But the problem is privacy. We really want privacy for our little transaction, don't we? You live in Manhattan?"

"Oh sure. Downtown."

"You live alone?"

"Oh sure. Jus' me an' my daughter."

"Not your husband?"

"My hosbon' he don' leeve weeth us. He's gone."

"I see. Well, why don't I deliver the package to you where you live? You give me your name and address, and I'll bring it to you. How's that?"

"Well . . . I don' know . . ."

"It's the best way," he assured her. "Then we'll have privacy—right?"

"I don' like eet," she said. "Maybe I come to where you leeve?"

"No," he said. "Definitely not. It's got to be at your place or the deal is off."

"Well," she said dubiously, "all ri'. But no mahnkey beesness."

"It's the best way," he repeated. "I'll just drop off the package and be on my way. And you'll be on your way to Puerto Rico. How does that sound?"

"All ri', I guess," she said. "Today?"

"Not today," he said. "I can't get the money today. It's after three; the banks are closed. How about tomorrow?"

"Tomorrow I work," she told him. "Saturday?"

"Fine," he said. "I'll have it by then. Noon on Saturday? How's that?"

"Hokay," she said. "Eet sounds hokay. Five tousan' een small beels."

"You'll get it," he said confidently. "Now what's your name and where do you live?"

She gave him the address on Orchard Street, and told him to come to Apartment 6-D, Rosa Perez.

"Fine," he said heartily. "Your daughter will be there?"

"Oh sure."

"Good. Thank you for calling. I'll see you at noon Saturday."

He hung up. Mama Perez replaced the receiver gently. Edward X. Delaney leaned forward and kissed her cheek.

"You're beautiful, Mama," he said.

Sergeant Boone and Jason T. Jason came in beaming from the hallway, carrying their tape recorders.

"Got every blessed word," Boone said happily.

22

Chief Delaney had them all wait around until he got through to Ivar Thorsen. He played the tape over the phone and then, at the Deputy Commissioner's request, ran it through again.

"All right, Edward," Thorsen said, after the second hearing, "you can have what you want. Let's get this over with."

"Sure," Delaney said. "I'll keep you informed on what's happening. I think you better plan to be in your office on Saturday so I—"

"I always am," Thorsen said ruefully.

"—so I can reach you afterward," Delaney went on. "You might be thinking about a press statement."

"You're awfully confident," the Deputy Commissioner said.

"That's right," the Chief acknowledged, "I am. I think it would be best if you kept me out of it. The publicity I mean. Let the Department take the credit. You know—'A cooperative effort of all concerned.' That kind of shit."

"I understand."

"Can we get a search warrant for his home and office? To look for the Maitland sketches and the weapon?"

"I don't see why not—with that tape."

"We won't use it until noon on Saturday. Also—say on Friday night—you might call J. Barnes Chapin and give him the bad news about his sister's tax scam."

"I'm not looking forward to that."

"Take my word for it, Ivar, he'll thank you for the advance notice and owe you one."

"When are you tipping the IRS?"

"I'm not; you are. Goodwill for the Department. I suggest you hold off until Saturday morning. That'll give Chapin time to find a lawyer for Dora and Emily Maitland. Let's see, what else . . . ? Well, I guess that about covers it. If there's anything more I need, I'll let you know."

"I'm sure you will," Thorsen said. "Congratulations, Edward."

"Jesus!" Delaney cried. "Not so soon! You'll put the whammy on it."

He hung up and turned to the others.

"It's going down," he told them. "Let's get organized . . ."

The first thing he ordered was closer surveillance of Rosa Perez.

"This monkey may get an attack of the smarts," he said, "and decide to show up a few hours or even a day early. I wouldn't like that."

So they moved the plainclothesman inside Mama's building, and sat him on a milk crate in the back of the ground-floor lobby, where he could observe anyone entering from the front or the rear door from the concrete courtyard. And they made certain the trap to the roof in the sixth-floor ceiling was bolted from the inside.

Rosa was a problem; she refused to stay put in her own apartment. So Jason Two was assigned as her personal bodyguard. He accompanied her on shopping trips to drugstore and bodega, and even went drinking beer with her on Thursday night. The other cops started calling him Papa Perez, which he didn't think was so funny.

Arrangements were made for Dolores and Maria Ruiz to stay with relatives on Friday and Saturday, and Maria agreed to let her apartment be used temporarily by the police. She gave her permission after a long, sparkling argument with Mama Perez. Chief Delaney could understand a few words and phrases in Spanish, but he couldn't follow that loud, fiery exchange. It sounded to him mostly like threats and curses, but Jason told him later it was really a friendly business discussion; they were deciding how to divide Mama's hundred-dollar bounty.

The tech man selected by Sergeant Abner Boone arrived early Friday morning, and Delaney told him what was needed. The electronics specialist made a survey of the Perez and Ruiz apartments, took some measurements, and departed. He was back by noon with a van loaded with equipment. Boone helped him upstairs with his gear, and they set to work.

It was decided to leave the cloth curtain of the narrow closet pulled aside. It revealed a rod of hanging dresses and coats, shoes on the floor, a shelf above with odds and ends: a carroty wig on a plastic form, a cigar box of sewing materials, a small overnight bag, three hats, some assorted junk. To this collection they added a small, round vanity mirror held upright on a brass easel. But the mirror was two-way glass, and behind it they concealed a miniature TV camera with wide-angle lens and a sensitive omnidirectional microphone. The tech figured they'd be able to pick up all of the one-room apartment except for the bathroom and the near corner of the kitchenette.

The flat cable was run down the inside of the closet and out a hole drilled through the base close to the floor. The linoleum was then lifted to conceal the cable between floor covering and baseboard. It continued in similar manner across one end of the bathroom and through a hole drilled in the far wall at the floor.

Inside the Ruiz apartment, the cable was connected to both a videotape machine and a small black-and-white TV monitor with an eight-inch screen. A transmitter provided backup protection by sending a simultaneous signal to another monitor and videotape recorder in the electronics van parked across Orchard Street. The van, with antennae on the roof, was painted white with blue signs on both sides: BIG APPLE TELEVISION REPAIR & SERVICE: YOUR SATISFACTION IS OUR REWARD.

It took most of Friday to install the equipment in the Perez and Ruiz apartments, and it was almost midnight before it was working to the satisfaction of the specialist. Men observing the monitors in the Ruiz apartment and in the parked van had a reasonably clear TV picture of activity in Mama Perez' apartment, and the sound was loud and clear. The videotape recorders picked up both.

Chief Delaney treated everyone to coffee when the task was completed. They discussed job assignments, and the electronics specialist promised to bring along a buddy on Saturday to handle the equipment in the van while he took care of the hardware in the Ruiz apartment. The Chief said he wanted Boone and Jason upstairs. The plainclothesmen who had been on surveillance would cover the entrance of the tenement from across the street and warn by walkie-talkie when Saul Geltman arrived. Delaney asked everyone to show up by eight A.M. for final tests and run-throughs.

Then Sergeant Boone drove him home. During the ride they discussed how they would handle it:

The door of the bathroom on the Perez side would be left open, so Geltman could glance in there if he was suspicious of being mouse-trapped. The bathroom door on the Ruiz side would be locked. If Geltman asked about it, Mama Perez would explain that it led to the adjoining apartment, but no one was home there. After Geltman was settled in the Perez apartment, the Ruiz door would be quietly unlocked. The turnbolt had already been oiled, and Delaney was satisfied it could be opened slowly and quietly without alerting Geltman.

In case of emergency—and both Delaney and the sergeant knew that "emergency" meant a Geltman assault on Mama Perez—Jason T. Jason would go in first, fast, followed by Boone and Delaney, all armed. In addition, once Saul Geltman was inside the Perez apartment, the surveillance men across the street would move over to take backup positions on the sixth-floor landing and on the stairs.

They went over it two or three times, trying "what ifs" on each other, and planning their response to a variety of possible situations. By the time Boone pulled up in front of the Delaney brownstone, they figured they had done as much plotting as they could. The rest depended on chance and luck.

Before they parted, the Chief offered his hand to a surprised Sergeant Boone. They shook once, a hard up-and-down pump.

He knew Monica would still be awake, and called upstairs to let her know he was home. Then he made his security rounds before he turned off the downstairs lights and tramped up to the bedroom. Monica had been reading in bed, covered only with a sheet, but her glasses were pushed up and her novel was face down when he entered the room. He went over to kiss her cheek.

"You smell like a goat," she smiled.

"Don't I though?" he said. "I'm tired and dusty and grumpy. A hot shower for me."

"Did you eat, dear?"

"Sure I did."

"What did you have?"

"Pizza for lunch and chili for supper."

"My God," she said, "your stomach will be rumbling all night."

"I suppose so," he agreed. "But I really enjoyed it."

"Edward, do you realize that I've hardly *seen* you for the past two days?"

"I realize," he said.

"Well . . . tell me: what's going on? What have you been doing? The Geltman thing?"

"Let me get my shower first."

They kept a bottle of brandy and two small snifters on the shelf of his clothes closet. When he came from the shower, tying the drawstring of his pajama pants, he saw that Monica had left the bed long enough to pour each of them a good snort. She was back under the sheet, but sitting up, her heavy, tight breasts exposed. She was warming her glass between her palms. His drink was on the bedside table.

"Oh my," he said happily. "Oh my, oh my, oh my."

He sat on the edge of the bed and touched the brandy to his lips, taking a sip so small the liquid seemed to evaporate on his tongue. He realized, almost with a shock, that he was content. He put a hand on the sheet covering his wife's hard thigh.

"I love you," he said.

"No romance, buster," she said sternly. "Just talk. What have you been doing?"

He hadn't wanted to tell her, hoped he wouldn't have to, knowing it might diminish him in her eyes. But he could not plead "top secret" or "official business." Not to her. So he sighed and spelled it out, going through it rapidly but making no effort to conceal the fact that he was using Mama Perez as bait, and no matter how detailed and careful their plans, there was still a good possibility the woman would be hurt. Or worse . . .

"If Geltman tries to take her," he said, "Jason will be right there, on top of him. Boone says he's fast. But still . . ."

Monica was silent, thoughtful, her lips on the rim of her glass, but not sipping.

"Was it your idea, Edward?"

"Yes. I suppose you think I'm some kind of a monster."

She smiled. "Some kind."

She never ceased to surprise him.

"Then you think it's worth the risk?"

"Will it put Geltman away?" she asked.

"Oh, it'll put him away all right. Or help to. I can't let him walk, Monica. I'd never forgive myself if I let him off the hook."

"I know," she said, almost sadly. "God's surrogate on earth."

"Oh Jesus," he said, "I don't see myself that way at all. Not anymore. It's a personal thing. Like he slapped my face, or hurt someone I loved."

She looked at him, astonished.

"Edward, you never even *knew* Maitland."

"What difference does that make?"

"What if he hadn't been an artist whose work you admire? What if he had been a shoemaker, say, or a butcher?"

"No difference at all," he said doggedly.

"I believe you," she sighed. "I just wish I could understand you. Completely."

"And I you," he said. "I can never get to the end of you."

"Maybe it's best this way," she said.

"Sure it is. Like Maitland's paintings. I can't understand the attraction. Can't analyze it. But I can feel it. Respond to it. Know it provides something I want. Like you."

"Like you," she said. "Tired?" she asked.

"Oh yes. Beat."

"Maybe we'll finish our drinks, you get into bed, and we'll just hold each other."

He looked at her. She looked at him.

"We can start that way," he said.

23

Delaney was dressing the following morning when the phone rang. It was Boone. He apologized for calling so early. The sergeant wondered if maybe they should put a tail on Saul Geltman, in case he decided to run. The Chief considered it a moment, then decided against it.

"If he spots a tail, all bets are off," he told Boone. "We'll just have to believe he plans to make the meet with Mama Perez at noon, as planned."

The sergeant agreed that was probably best, and confessed he was getting antsy. The Chief said that was understandable, he was too, but last-minute changes of plans had soured many a good setup, and he wanted this scam to go down as rigged. He told Boone that if he wanted to keep busy, and stop fretting about possible fluffs, to check on the search warrant Commissioner Thorsen had promised. If it had been issued, the sergeant was to select two good men to make the toss—but not before noon.

Then the Chief finished dressing, and strapped on his short-barreled belly gun. He slipped the packet of Polaroid shots of the Maitland barn into his jacket pocket. At the last minute he also took his handcuffs, wrapping them in his handkerchief so they wouldn't jangle.

He had only grapefruit juice, a slice of unbuttered toast, and two cups of black coffee for breakfast.

"Very good," Monica approved. "You're getting heavy as a bear. Ask me; I know."

"Let's have no lascivious tittle-tattle at breakfast," he said. "How did you sleep?"

"Fine. How about you?"

"Went out like a light."

"So did I," she said. "Too bad the light didn't. It was still burning this morning."

They both laughed, and then, as they ate, they discussed a trip they were planning for the Fourth of July weekend. They were going to rent a car, leave early, drive up to the girls' camp in New Hampshire, and spend the entire three days with them.

"How about Rebecca and Boone?" Delaney said suddenly. "Should we ask them to come along?"

"That would be fun," Monica said. "But we'll be staying at a motel. It won't embarrass you, will it?"

"My God, Monica," he said grouchily, "you must think I'm an old fuddy-duddy."

"Not at all," she said. "You're the youngest fuddy-duddy I know."

He smiled, humor restored, and put his empty dishes in the sink.

"I better go," he said. "Expect me when you see me."

They embraced briefly, and she kissed his chin.

"Take care," she said lightly.

On Orchard Street, already beginning to fill up with shoppers, he made the rounds of electronics van, surveillance team, and the Perez and Ruiz apartments. He found everyone present except for Abner Boone, who had called and said he'd be there by eleven o'clock.

Delaney then took Mama Perez aside, sat her down, and went over with her once again what she was to say and how she was to act. On his instructions, she was wearing one of her oldest dresses, a shapeless sack of faded rayon. Her feet were thrust into worn mules, and she had removed most of her heavy makeup. To him, she looked old, weary, vulnerable. He hoped that was the way Saul Geltman would see her.

Abner Boone arrived, reported the warrant had been obtained, and two dicks were standing by to toss Geltman's apartment and office at noon.

"They'll get in," the sergeant assured Delaney. "They're good men; they'll con the super."

Then they ran a noise-level test, with Jason T. Jason acting the part of Saul Geltman. The problem was to adjust the volume of sound on the TV monitor in the Ruiz apartment so it was loud enough for them to hear, but not so loud that it would carry through the wall between apartments, and Geltman would hear his own voice booming back at him. They cut it down as low as they could, so they had to put their heads close to the set, but nothing could be heard in the Perez apartment.

They took a final look around to make certain there was no track of their presence. Then they filed into the Ruiz apartment, leaving Mama Perez alone. Delaney was the last to leave.

"When this is over," he told her, "win, lose, or draw, I'm buying you a half-gallon of the best whiskey I can find."

"Ooh," she said, eyes widening. "You stay tonight, help me dreenk eet?"

He laughed and patted her veined cheek. If she was fearful, he could see no sign of it. He went into the Ruiz apartment. The bathroom door was locked. They settled down to wait. They watched Mama on the monitor. She moved slowly about her apartment, made a cup of coffee, sat down to drink it and leaf through a Spanish magazine. When she took her empty cup to the sink, they saw her pause before one of her painted plaster saints. Her lips moved, and she crossed herself. No one smiled. They waited in silence.

They remained silent as their watches showed 11:30, 11:45, 12:00, 12:15. At 12:20, Jason T. Jason muttered, "Come on. Come *on!*"

At 12:26 the walkie-talkie Sergeant Boone was holding crackled into life, and the surveillance man across the street said, "He's coming. North to south. Alone."

They pushed closer to the TV monitor.

"Stopping," the walkie-talkie reported. "Looking around. Looking at the building. Going up the steps. He's in."

Boone put his lips close to the mike, pressed the Send button.

"Give him five minutes," he whispered. "Then move across to backup. Got it?"

"Got it. Will do. Out."

Delaney looked at the others: Boone, Jason, the electronics man.

"No movement," he warned in a low voice. "Strangle before you cough or sneeze."

They all nodded. Eyes on the TV screen. Waiting . . .

They heard the knock on the door of the Perez apartment. Watched Mama start, freeze, then move slowly to the door.

"Who?" she called.

They didn't hear the reply, but Mama turned the lock, slipped the chain, opened the door. Her body blocked their view, but they heard the voice.

"Rosa Perez?"

"Yesss. You Meester Geltman?"

"I am indeed. May I come in?"

"Oh sure. Come in."

She stood aside then. Saul Geltman sauntered into the room. He was carrying a small, paper-wrapped package. He looked around. Mama Perez closed the door but, following Delaney's instructions, didn't lock or chain it.

"Nice place you've got here," Geltman said tonelessly, staring about.

He glanced at the open closet, the kitchenette, peered through the open door of the bathroom.

"You share the bathroom?" he asked lightly.

"Oh sure. But nex' door, they ain't home."

He walked slowly into the bathroom. Now he was off screen, but they heard him try the bathroom door to the Ruiz apartment.

"Is locked," Mama said.

"So I see," Geltman said.

He came back into the main room, still looking around.

"And where is your daughter?" he asked pleasantly.

"At the bodega," Mama Perez said. "Shopping. She come back soon. Feefteen meenutes maybe. Half an hour."

"Good," he said. "I'd like to meet her. May I sit down?"

"Oh sure. Anywhere."

They watched Geltman look at the furniture. He started to sit in the upholstered armchair, then changed his mind.

"I'll bet that's *your* chair," he smiled winningly.

He selected one of the tubular aluminum chairs. He pulled it free of the table, turned it to face the armchair. He gestured.

"After you, Mrs. Perez," he said gallantly.

He waited until she was seated in the armchair. Then he sat down gracefully in the straight chair. He put the package on the table. He crossed his knees negligently.

In the Ruiz apartment, Chief Delaney touched Officer Jason's arm, pointed toward the bathroom door. The big black nodded, rose slowly to his feet. He moved lightly, cautiously to the door. He put his fingers on the turnbolt, looked back at Delaney. The Chief put up his hand, signaling Jason to wait.

"Do you mind if I smoke?" Saul Geltman asked.

"Hokay," Mama nodded. "Is hokay."

"Will you join me?"

"Oh sure."

Geltman rose to proffer a silver case. While he was going through the business of lighting their cigarettes, Delaney nodded to Jason. He opened the lock easily, slowly. They watched the screen. Apparently Geltman heard nothing. Jason tiptoed back to his original position.

Geltman lounged back casually, smoking his cigarette with an elegance so exaggerated that the watching cops realized, for the first time, how wound-up he was, how tight and anxious. On the black-and-white TV monitor he appeared to be wearing a loosely cut black suit, white shirt, black tie, black shoes. He looked, Delaney thought, like a miniature undertaker, and he wondered where Geltman was carrying a weapon, if he had one.

"Well now," the art dealer said. "We seem to have a problem, don't we?"

"Problem?" Mama said. "*You* got a problem. I got no problem."

"Yes, of course," he said with a clenched smile. "That's very true. Tell me, did you go to the police or did they find you?"

Rosa lowered her head, and they didn't catch her reply in the Ruiz apartment.

"I wonder how they did that?" Geltman said. "Well . . . no matter. I still don't understand how they managed to get drawings of you and your daughter. Do you?"

"He hired my daughter," Mama said. "The artist. To pose for heem. I went back weeth her on Monday. A cop was there. He seen us."

"Oh-ho. I understand. Bad luck. For me, I mean," he added hastily.

Mama jerked her chin toward the package on the table.

"You breeng the moaney?" she asked.

"Of course. As I promised."

"Five tousan'? Small beels?"

"Just as you requested. When will you and your daughter leave for Puerto Rico?"

"Soon. Maybe nex' week."

"And you say you'll never return?"

"Nevair," she vowed.

He nodded. Holding his cigarette butt, one hand cupped underneath, he looked around for an ashtray. Rosa Perez stood up, moved to the kitchenette. For a moment her back was turned to Geltman, and Delaney tensed. But the little art dealer didn't move. Mama came back with a saucer, and they stubbed out their cigarettes. The Chief found he was gripping his own knees tightly. He forced himself to spread his hands limply.

"When did the police ask you to identify my photograph?" Geltman asked.

He's stalling, Delaney decided. What for? Hasn't the blood for it? Waiting for Dolores? What?

"Couple days ago," Mama Perez said. "They show me a lot of peectures. 'Who was the man you seen?' they ask me."

"And you picked out my picture?"

She nodded.

"You're certain it was me you saw, Mrs. Perez?"

Again she nodded. "But I tol' them I ain't sure."

"Very smart of you," he smiled. "Very intelligent. Well, I'm glad you called and we got together. Mutual benefit, you might say."

He reached out, pushed the package slowly across the table toward her.

"Open it," he said harshly. "Count it."

She stood, moved to the table, took up the package. Saul Geltman also stood. He stretched. All his movements easy, nonchalant. He slid his hands into his trouser pockets.

Delaney grabbed Jason's arm, jerked, nodded. Jason glided across the floor, stood at the bathroom door, his hand lightly on the knob. He stared back at Delaney. The Chief pointed at Boone. The sergeant moved up behind Jason. He slid his revolver from the hip holster. He thumbed off the safety. He, too, stared back at Delaney. Both cops had a strained, stretched look, lips drawn back from glistening teeth.

On the screen, Mama Perez was fumbling with the package. It was tightly wrapped with Scotch tape. She struggled to tear it open.

Saul Geltman was now directly behind her, a few feet away. He spread his feet a little wider. He braced himself. His hands came slowly from his pockets. Delaney saw the gleam.

"Go!" he shouted. "Take him!"

Boone had been right: Jason was fast. The black flung back the bathroom door. Went hurtling through. Boone dashed after. Both men roaring. Geltman caught. Stoned by sound. Head pulled. Neck stretched. Face twisted. Mama Perez suddenly bowed. Stooping. Back tensed for the knife held high, twinkling in sunlight.

Jason didn't go for the knife hand. No punch, no blow, no karate chop. He simply ran into Geltman, a full body block. Charged into him and tried to keep running, knees pumping high, feet slipping on the polished linoleum.

Geltman bounced off him. Just smashed away. Hair and knife flying, arms and legs every which way. His limp body, boneless, landed half on the bed, half off. Slowly, slowly, slipped onto the floor, and Jason clamped one big foot on the back of his neck.

"Stay here," Delaney snapped at the tech. "Keep the tape rolling."

He lumbered into the Perez apartment. Jason was jerking a dazed Saul Geltman to his feet. Boone put the muzzle of his revolver to Geltman's teeth. Mama Perez had retreated from the action. She was facing them, back against the wall. Hissing faintly. Delaney pulled out his handkerchief. Handcuffs clattered to the floor. He ignored them, but picked up the knife carefully by the tip, using the wadded handkerchief. He placed the knife on the table, alongside the torn package. One corner was ripped open; he could see the stack of cut newspaper.

Sergeant Boone holstered his revolver. He took a come-along grip on one of Geltman's arms. Jason clamped the other. The art dealer looked about wildly, hair and clothes in disarray. Delaney thought everything was under control when Mama Perez came off the wall.

"Sonnenbitch!" she screamed. "Bestid!"

She came leaping across the room, hands clawed, and jumped on Geltman before they could block her. It looked as if she were trying to shin up his body, one leg crooked around his, one knee slamming at his groin, a hand tearing at his throat, fingers raking at his eyes. While she screamed, screamed, screamed. Spanish and English. Curses, oaths, obscenities, execrations.

Delaney got an arm about her thick waist from behind. Boone and Jason tugged Geltman in the other direction. But they could not peel Rosa Perez away. She clung to Geltman, pounding on his skull with her fist, spitting in his face. Clawing, biting, butting him with her head. The five of them stood swaying, one tight group, pressed tightly together, staggering to keep their balance.

Delaney turned his face toward the door. "Brady!" he yelled desperately.

In a few seconds the backup man came dashing in from the hallway, revolver held out in front of him. The man posted on the stairs was hard on his heels. They holstered their guns and joined in, prying Mama's fingers loose, one by one, bending them back, then twisting her arms behind her as Delaney strained mightily at her waist, and Boone kicked one of her legs loose.

Finally, huffing, sweating, cursing furiously, they got the maddened woman off Geltman and dragged her away.

"Jesus Christ!" Delaney panted. "Take her in the other room and sit on her!"

The backup men hustled Mama Perez, still kicking and spitting, into the Ruiz apartment. The Chief followed them in there.

"Got enough tape?" he asked the tech man.

"Plenty, Chief. All you'll need."

"Good. Keep it rolling till I tell you to disconnect."

He went back into the Perez apartment, closing both bathroom doors behind him. They sat Saul Geltman down in a straight-backed aluminum chair facing the big window. Sergeant Boone took the other tubular chair. Delaney sat in the armchair, and Jason T. Jason stood with his back against the door.

All four of them were breathing heavily, limp and exhausted in that hot-box of a room under the roof. Boone and Jason loosened their ties, unbuttoned their collars. No one spoke for several minutes. Then Saul Geltman attempted to dust himself off.

"I have a comb in my hip pocket," he said. "Can I reach for it?"

The Chief nodded. The art dealer took out a little black comb and straightened his hair. Then he took out his handkerchief, dabbed delicately at the shallow scratches on his face.

"I'm bleeding," he said.

"I'm sorry about that, Mr. Geltman," Delaney said without irony, "but you really can't blame her."

"I want to call a lawyer," Geltman said. "I know my rights."

"I'm afraid you don't," the Chief said gently. "You're not entitled to a phone call until you've been booked. You haven't even been arrested yet. Am I correct, sergeant?"

"That's correct, sir. When we arrest him, we read him his rights."

"That's how it's done," Delaney said, spreading his hands. "I thought we could just sit here a few minutes, relax, get our breath back. Just talk a little. Talk about why you assaulted that poor woman with a knife."

"I didn't assault her," Geltman said indignantly. "I just took the knife out to help her open a package."

"Assault with a deadly weapon," Delaney said tonelessly.

"It's your word against mine," Geltman said.

"Well . . . no," the Chief said. "Not quite. Look at this . . ."

He rose, stepped to the open closet. Geltman turned his head to watch him reach up and push aside the small, round mirror.

"A TV camera," he explained to the little man. "Picks up image and sound. Records it on videotape. It's still running."

"Shit," Saul Geltman said.

"Yes," Delaney said.

"Well, then, you were tapping my phone. That's how you knew I'd be here. And the phone tap was illegal."

The Chief sighed. "Oh, Mr. Geltman, do you really think we'd do that? No, she called from a private phone. We had the owner's permission to tape the call."

"I'd like a glass of water," Geltman said.

"Sure," Delaney said. "Jason?"

Geltman was given not one but two glasses of water. He drained both greedily, wiped his lips with his soiled handkerchief. He looked around. He seemed punished but not defeated. There was a spark in his eye. He tried for a smile and settled for a smirk.

"Miserable place," he said with a theatrical shudder. "How people can live like this . . ."

"I've seen worse," Delaney shrugged. "Didn't you tell me you came from Essex Street? You must have lived in an apartment something like this."

"A long time ago," Geltman said in a low voice. "A long time . . ."

"Uh-huh," Delaney nodded. "Well, that's really what I wanted to talk to you about: how you live now. And how you're going to live. You don't have to admit anything. I'm not asking for a confession. I just want you to take a look at these, please."

He took the Polaroid photos from his jacket pocket, leaned forward, handed them to Geltman. The art dealer looked at the top one, shuffled through the pack hurriedly, then shriveled back into his chair. His face had gone slack. He tossed the photos listlessly onto the table.

"So that's all over," Delaney said briskly. "The IRS was notified this morning, and I imagine they're up there right now, taking inventory. They'll pump Dora and Emily, of course. My guess is that Dora will sing first; she's the weak reed. She'll implicate you and Simon."

Geltman made a gesture, a hopeless flap of his hand.

"I don't mean to suggest you'll go to jail for tax fraud," Delaney said. "You might, but I don't think the Feds will prosecute. They'll be happy enough when they add up the estate. Oh, you might get a fine and probation, and a personal audit, of course. But I doubt if anyone will draw jail time for this. It means the end of Dora's and Emily's dreams, naturally, but then it makes millionaires of Alma and Ted. I don't derive any particular satisfaction from that, do you?"

"No," Geltman said shortly.

"And talking about the end of dreams," the Chief continued, "there goes your guaranteed future, doesn't it? I think you've sold your last Maitland painting, Mr. Geltman."

The art dealer made no reply. For a moment or two no one spoke. Then . . .

"My God, it's hot in here," Edward X. Delaney said. He rose, strode to the big window, struggled with it a moment, then threw it wide open. He leaned far out, hands propped on the sill, drew a deep breath. He looked down. He came back into the room, dusting his hands, leaving the window open. "Six floors straight down to a cement courtyard," he reported. "You'd think they'd have a guard on a window like that. Well, anyway we'll get a breath of air."

He sat in the armchair again, leaned back, laced his fingers across his middle. He looked at Saul Geltman reflectively.

"Now let's talk about the murder of Victor Maitland," he said. "Premeditated murder because the man that killed brought a knife along. He didn't kill in a sudden flash of passion with whatever weapon came to hand; he brought his weapon with him. That's premeditation in any court in the land."

"I didn't kill him," Geltman said tightly.

"Sure you did," Delaney said. "You know it; we know it. I thought, just from simple curiosity, you'd like to know what we've got. Well, for starters, we've got motive. Your discovery that Maitland was sneaking paintings from the barn and peddling them secretly through Belle Sarazen. They were his paintings, and he could do anything he wanted with them. But to your way of thinking, those paintings were as much your inheritance as Dora's and Emily's, and the dying Victor Maitland was robbing you. Crazy. Not only that, but he was depressing the price of Maitlands by shoveling out more and more paintings. Right, Mr. Geltman? So you had a big fight with him about it, and he told you to go fuck yourself. Right, Mr. Geltman?"

"Conjecture," the art dealer said. "Just conjecture."

" 'Conjecture,' " Delaney repeated, amused. "A legal term. You played a lot of handball with your late pal J. Julian Simon, didn't you, Mr. Geltman? By the way, do you notice I call you 'Mr. Geltman' and not 'Saul'? That's not going by the book. It's cop psychology to use first names when talking to a suspect. It diminishes them, robs them of dignity. Like stripping a man naked before you question him. But I wouldn't do that to you, Mr. Geltman; I have too much respect for your intelligence."

"Thank you," he said faintly, and sounded sincere.

"All right," Delaney said, slapping his knees. "So much for motive. A few rough spots here and there, but I think a little more digging will fill it out nicely. Now we come to opportunity. I suppose Lawyer Simon told you that we tumbled to your little con of skipping out his back door into the corridor. You must have done that, you see, because Rosa Perez and Dolores saw you near Victor Maitland's studio at a time when Simon said you were in his office."

"It's his statement against what they claim," Geltman said hotly.

"His *statement,*" Delaney said. "Too bad he isn't alive to testify in court, isn't it?"

"I was shocked when I heard he was dead."

Delaney stared at him reflectively a few moments, then sighed.

"You weren't thinking too straight, Mr. Geltman," he said softly. "Getting a little frantic, were you? The bloodhounds nipping at your heels, and your dear chum having an attack of the runits about facing a perjury rap. So you had to take him out—right? Wait, wait," Delaney said, holding up a hand. "Just let me finish. It hasn't been announced yet, but we know Simon didn't die in that fire. Surprise! He was a clunk before he fried. Lung analysis proved that. And the Medical Examiner found the multiple stab wounds in his back. And the fire laddies think whiskey was used to make sure the whole place went up in a *poof!* They found the empty bottles. A terrible waste! Oh yes, we know how Simon died, Mr. Geltman. We have men flashing your photograph to tenants in Simon's building, cab drivers, everyone in the neighborhood. Sooner or later we'll find *someone* who saw you at or near the scene. So if I were you, I wouldn't count too much on your late buddy's statement to alibi you for the Maitland kill."

Saul Geltman had sought to interrupt this breezy recital. As it progressed, his eyes widened, mouth opened. He slipped farther down in his chair like a man hammered. He stared at Delaney, stricken.

"Well," the Chief said briskly, "that takes care of opportunity. Now we come to the weapon . . ."

He rose, stepped to the table, bent far over the knife. His nose was almost touching it. Then he put on his glasses and bent over it again.

"Nice," he said. "French. High-carbon steel. Holds a good edge a long time. It might have been used to slice Maitland and Simon; the length and width of the blade fit the description of the wounds in the autopsy reports. I'll tell you, I'd never use a knife like that to murder someone, Mr. Geltman. First of all, the blade is too thin. It might hit a rib on the first jab and snap. Also, no matter how you wash it, you can never get a wood-handled knife clean. Tell him, sergeant."

"The wood handle is riveted to the blade," Boone explained. "But no matter how much you scrub, blood has soaked in between wood handle and steel. The lab guys pop the rivets, take off the wood, and examine the steel tang for blood seepage. Then they take tiny particles from the inside of the wood handles and examine *them* for blood. They can tell if it's animal or human. If it's human, they can usually determine the type. And tell if it matches Simon's or Maitland's."

"That's how it's done," Delaney nodded. "That's how it will be done on this knife."

"I didn't do it," Geltman muttered.

Delaney started back to his chair, replacing his glasses in his breast pocket. Then he returned to examine the knife again.

"You know," he said, "this is what cooks call a boning knife. It looks to me like it's part of a matched cutlery set. Very nice and very expensive. Sergeant, I think we better send those detectives back to Mr. Geltman's apartment again to pick up the other knives in the set and put them all through the lab."

Geltman was bewildered.

"Detectives?" he said. "Back to my apartment again?"

"Oh, I didn't mention that," Delaney said, snapping his fingers lightly. "We got a search warrant. To toss your apartment and office. They're looking for those three sketches we lifted from Maitland's studio—and you lifted from my home. Think they'll find them, Mr. Geltman?"

"I'm not going to say another word," the art dealer said.

"You put my daughters in a closet, you fucker!" Delaney screamed at him.

Geltman closed his mouth firmly, clenched his jaws. He crossed his legs and began to drum slowly with his fingers on the top knee. He refused to meet Delaney's eyes, but stared out the open window, seeing a rooftop, a wide patch of blue sky, a puff of cloud floating lazily.

"Motive, opportunity, weapon," Chief Delaney went on inexorably. "And now, on top of that, we've got you on attempted subornation. Got it on tape. And on top of *that,* assault with a deadly weapon. How does it sound to you, Mr. Geltman?"

No answer. Delaney let the silence build awhile, frowning slightly, looking down at his flexing hands. Jason shifted his weight from foot to foot at the door. Sergeant Boone sat perfectly still, eyes never leaving the art dealer.

"I'll be honest with you, Mr. Geltman," Delaney said finally. "I don't think the DA will go for a Murder One conviction."

Geltman started, uncrossed his knees. Then he did stare at Chief Delaney, leaning forward a little in his eagerness.

"I think you'll get a smart lawyer who'll do some plea bargaining and advise you to plead guilty to a lesser charge. Murder Two, maybe. If he's a *very* smart lawyer, he might even get you a manslaughter rap. The point is, no matter how you slice it, you're going to do time, Mr. Geltman. No way out of that. Jason, you want to make a guess?"

"Fifteen to twenty-five, Chief," Jason boomed.

"Sergeant?"

"Eight to ten," Boone said.

"My guess is somewhere between," Delaney said thoughtfully. "About ten to fifteen before you're up for parole. Fifteen years, Mr. Geltman. Great Meadows, I suppose. Or maybe Attica. A hard place like that."

Saul Geltman made a sound, a small sound deep inside him. His stare slid off Delaney, lifted, moved across the ceiling, stopped at the square of summer sky outside the open window.

"Ten to fifteen," Delaney nodded. "A smart lawyer could get you that. A smart, *expensive* lawyer. Your gallery will go, of course. You couldn't have kept that without Maitland anyway; we know that. And that beautiful apartment of yours. All your lovely things. You know, Mr. Geltman, I think that was the most magnificent home I've ever seen. Truth. I remember so much about it: those soft-toned rugs, that elm's-burl highboy, the polished wood and gleaming brass. The way everything seemed to go together. You were right: it was a dream, a beautiful dream. All gone now, of course. I suppose the IRS will sell the stuff at auction to pay your fine. Or you'll have to sell it to pay for your defense. Other people will own those lovely things. But your beautiful home will be broken up, the dream destroyed."

His voice had taken on a curious singsong quality, an almost musical cadence. Far away he could hear, dimly, street sounds: vendors' chants, traffic, blare of horns, shouts and cries. But the other men in the room heard only the soft drone of Delaney's voice, words that painted pictures and mesmerized them.

"All gone," the Chief repeated. "The beauty, the softness, the rich comfort of it all. Very different from where you're going, Mr. Geltman. For fifteen years. You'll be in a ten-by-ten concrete cell with two other guys and a pisspot. And those guys! Animals, Mr. Geltman. Rough studs who'll have you serving them hand and foot. Literally hand and foot, if you get my meaning. Food you can hardly stomach. A routine so boring that your imagination shrivels as your hope withers. Because every day is exactly like every other day—*exactly*, Mr. Geltman—and those fifteen years might as well be fifty years, or a hundred years, or a thousand, that's how far away the end of them will seem to you. But all that's not the worst part of prison, Mr. Geltman. Not to a man of your intelligence and sensibility and taste. Remember when we talked in your gallery about Maitland's work, and you said you thought his paintings were the idea or conception of sensuality? Well, prison is the conception of ugliness. It is complete greyness, greyness in walls and clothing and even in food. And eventually the greyness in the skin of old cons, and a greyness of the soul. Dismal, gloomy. No bright colors there. No music. No real laughter or song. No beauty anywhere. Just hard, grey ugliness that seeps and presses all around. To a man like you, it means—"

It happened so quickly, so suddenly, that viewing the videotape later, a board of inquiry agreed it could not have been prevented.

Saul Geltman jerked to his feet as if plucked up by the hand of God.

He tilted forward, saved himself from falling by taking three running steps to the open window.

He went out like a man doing a header from the high board, arms extended, head tucked down.

His toes didn't even tick the sill.

He cleared it, and he sailed.

They heard the noise when he hit.

Boone flinched. Jason shuddered. Edward X. Delaney had heard that sound before, and slowly closed his eyes.

"Oh my God!" Boone groaned. He leapt to his feet, rushed to the window. He propped his hands on both sides, leaned out cautiously, looked down. He turned back to the room, face blanched.

"They'll need a blotter," he reported.

Chief Delaney opened his eyes, stared at the ceiling.

"Well," he said to no one, "he didn't walk after all, did he?"

It was late in the afternoon before everything was done that had to be done. Deputy Commissioner Ivar Thorsen took command of the investigation, received signed statements of all involved, impounded the videotapes, issued a report to the newspapers, granted a short interview to TV cameramen.

The three Maitland sketches were found in Geltman's apartment. Rosa Perez was slipped her hundred-dollar baksheesh, and Delaney didn't forget her half-gallon. Mama selected dark rum. The television equipment was removed, and the Perez and Ruiz apartments were restored, as completely as possible, to their original state.

The body of Saul Geltman was removed to the morgue in a blue plastic body-bag. Sawdust was scattered on the stained indentation in the concrete courtyard.

Abner Boone offered to drive Delaney home, and the Chief accepted gratefully. It took them awhile to get free of downtown traffic, but once they got on Third Avenue, they began to make good time, Boone driving at a speed to hit all the greens.

"By the way," Delaney said, "over the Fourth of July weekend, Monica and I are going to rent a car and drive up to New Hampshire to visit the girls. We wondered if you and Rebecca would like to come along."

"Like to very much," Boone said promptly. "Thank you, sir. I'll ask Rebecca; I'm sure she'll go for it. But why rent a car? We can take mine."

"I'll tell you," Delaney said dreamily, "all my life I've wanted to drive a Rolls-Royce, and I never have. I thought I'd surprise Monica and rent a great, big black Rolls. She'll get a kick out of it, the kids will flip and it'll be a treat for me. It's about an eight-hour trip, I figure, so I thought we could pack a hamper and have lunch on the road. You know, cold fried chicken and potato salad. Stuff like that."

"Sounds wonderful," the sergeant laughed. "Count us in. A Rolls-Royce, huh? Would you believe I've never been in one?"

"I haven't either," Delaney smiled. "Now's our chance."

Then they were silent. Past 34th Street, traffic lightened, and Boone relaxed at the wheel.

"Chief . . ." he started.

"Yes?"

"When you were talking to Geltman before he jumped . . . I mean about his beautiful home, and how lousy prison life was . . ."

"Yes?"

"I thought you were . . ."

"You thought I was what?"

"Ahh, hell," Abner Boone said, staring straight ahead. "I guess I was imagining things."

"Sure you were," Edward X. Delaney said genially, lighting a cigar.

THE THIRD DEADLY SIN

1

Some days lasted forever; some were never born. She awoke in a fury of expectation, gone as soon as felt; the world closed about. Once again life became a succession of swan pecks.

Zoe Kohler, blinking, woke holding a saggy breast, soft as a broken bird. The other wrist was clamped between her thighs. She was conscious of the phlegmy light of late winter, leaking through drawn blinds.

Outside, she knew, would be a metal day, no sun, and a sky that pressed. The air would smell of sulfur. She heard traffic drone and, within the apartment house, the dull thumps of morning doors. In the corner of her bedroom a radiator hissed derisively.

She stared at the ceiling and sensed herself anxiously, the auguries of her entrails: plump organs, a living pulse, the whispering course of tainted blood. A full bladder pressed, and deeper yet she felt the heavy ache that would become biting cramps when her menses began.

She pushed the covers aside, swung her feet out of bed. She moved cautiously; something might twist, something might snap. She sat yawning, hugging herself, bending forward.

"Thursday," she said aloud to the empty room. "March thirteenth."

Her voice sounded cracked, unused. She straightened up, cleared her throat, tried again:

"Thursday. March thirteenth."

That sounded better. A huskiness, but strong, definite. Almost masculine.

Naked, she stood up, stretched, knuckled her scalp. For an instant she swayed, and grabbed the headboard of the bed for support. Then the vertigo passed; she was steady again.

"Like a dizzy spell," she had said to Dr. Stark. "I feel like I might fall."

"And how long does this last?" he inquired. He was shuffling papers on his desk, not looking at her. "A few minutes?"

"Less than that. Just a few seconds."

"How often?"

"Uh . . . occasionally."

"Just before your period?"

She thought a moment.

"Yes," she said, "that's right. Before the cramps begin."

Then he looked up.

"Nothing to worry about," he assured her.

But she did worry. She did not like that feeling of disorientation, however brief, when she was out of control.

She padded into the kitchen to switch on the electric percolator, prepared the night before. Then into the bathroom to relieve herself. Before she flushed the toilet, she inspected the color of her urine. It appeared to be a pale gold, but perhaps a little cloudy, and she wondered if she should call Dr. Stark.

Back to the bedroom for five minutes of stretching exercises, performed slowly, almost languidly. She bent far over, knees stiff, to put her palms flat on the floor. She reached far overhead, flexing her spine. She twisted her torso side to side, arms extended. She moved her head about on her neck. She thrust pelvis and buttocks forward and back in a copulative movement she had never seen in any exercise manual but which, she was convinced, lessened the severity of her menstrual cramps.

She returned to the bathroom, brushed her teeth, massaged her gums. She stepped on the scale. Still 124. Her weight hadn't varied more than three pounds since the day she was married.

Because her period was approaching, she took a hotter shower than usual. She lathered with a soap advertised to contain a moisturizing cream that would keep her skin soft and supple. She believed this to be true.

She soaped her body thoroughly and carefully, although she had showered before going to bed the previous night. While she was drying herself with one of the blue-striped towels stolen from the hotel where she worked, she looked down and regretted her smooth, hairless legs for reasons she could not comprehend.

And while looking down, inspecting, saw, yes, the glint of two gray pubic hairs, the first she had ever found. She uttered a sound of dismay, took manicure scissors from the medicine cabinet and clipped them away. She stared at the kinked hairs lying in her palm. Silver wires.

In the bedroom, she turned on the bedside radio, tuned to WQXR. The weather report was not encouraging: overcast, chance of showers, temperature in the high thirties. The announcer's voice sounded something like Kenneth's, and she wondered if her alimony check would arrive on time.

She dressed swiftly. White cotton bra and panties. Not too sheer pantyhose in a mousy color. Low-heeled brogues. White turtleneck sweater, tweed skirt with wide, crushed leather belt. Her makeup was minimal and palish. She spent as little time as possible before the mirror. Her short brown hair needed only a quick comb.

In the cabinet over the sink in the kitchen, Zoe Kohler kept her medicines and vitamins and minerals, her pills and food supplements, painkillers and tranquilizers: a collection much too large for the bathroom cabinet.

Taped to the inside of the kitchen cabinet door was a typed schedule of what items should be taken each day of the month: some daily, some every other day, some semiweekly, some weekly, some biweekly, some monthly. New drugs were occasionally added. None was ever eliminated.

She poured a full glass of cold grapefruit juice, purchased in quart bottles. On this Thursday morning, March 13th, sipping and swallowing, she downed vitamins A, C, E, and B-12, iron and zinc tablets, her birth control pill, a Midol tablet, the capsule for her disease, half a choline tablet, two Anacin, an alfalfa pill, a capsule said to be rich in lecithin, and another of kelp, a single Librium, and an antacid tablet which she was supposed to let melt in her mouth but which she chewed up and swallowed.

She then had a slice of unbuttered whole wheat toast with her first cup of black, decaffeinated coffee. She put an ice cube in the coffee to cool it quickly so she could gulp it down. With her second cup of coffee, also with an ice cube, she smoked a filter-tip advertised as having the lowest tar content of any cigarette in the world.

She rinsed the breakfast things in the sink and left them there for washing in the evening. The kitchen was a walk-through, and she exited into the living room, moving a little faster now, a little more purposefully.

She took a coat from the foyer closet. It was a chesterfield in black wool with a gray velvet collar. She checked the contents of her black leather shoulder bag: keys, wallet, this and that, a small can of Mace, which was illegal in New York City but which had been obtained for her by Everett Pinckney, and her Swiss Army folding pocket knife, a red-handled tool with two blades, a file, an awl, a tiny pair of scissors, and a bottle opener.

She peered through the peephole of the outside door. The corridor appeared empty. She unbolted the door, took off the chain, turned the lock and eased the door open cautiously. The hallway was empty. She double-locked the door behind her, rang for the elevator, and waited nervously.

She rode down to the lobby by herself, moved quickly to the outside doors and the sidewalk. Leo, the doorman, was shining the brass plaque that listed the names of the five doctors and psychiatrists who had offices on the ground floor.

"Morning, Miz Kohler," Leo said.

She gave him a dim smile and started walking west toward Madison Avenue. She strode rapidly, with a jerky step, looking neither to the right nor the left, not meeting the eyes of pedestrians who passed. But they did not give her a second glance. In fact, she knew, not even a first.

The Hotel Granger, a coffin on end, was pressed between two steel and glass skyscrapers on Madison Avenue, between 46th and 47th streets. The entrance to the hotel, framed by stained marble columns, seemed more like the portal to an obsolete gentlemen's club where members dozed behind *The Wall Street Journal* and liveried servants brought glasses of sherry on silver salvers.

The reality was not too different. The Granger dated from 1912, and although occasionally refurbished, nothing had been "modernized" or "updated." In the gloomy cocktail lounge, one still rang a bell to summon service, plastic and chromium were abjured, and over the entire main floor-lobby, desk, lounge, dining room, and executive offices—lay the somber, sourish smell of old carpeting, musty upholstery, and too many dead cigars.

For all of that, the Granger was a successful hostelry, with most of its 283 rooms and suites leased on an annual basis to midtown corporations for the use of executives staying overnight in the city, or for the convenience of out-of-town visitors. Those accommodations available to transients were frequently reserved a year in advance, for the rooms were large and comfortable, the service genial, the rates moderate, and the dining room was said to possess the third-best wine cellar in New York.

The Granger also offered the last hotel billiard room in the city, although there was only one table, and the faded, green felt was torn.

In its almost seventy-year history, the Granger, like all hotels, had its share of tragedy and violence. Heart attacks. Strokes. Two murders. Eight suicides, three of which were leaps from upper floors.

In 1932, a guest had choked to death on a fishbone in the dining room.

In 1949, two gentlemen sharing a suite on the 8th floor had taken an overdose of barbiturates and died, naked, in each other's arms.

In 1953, in a particularly messy incident, an enraged husband had smashed open the door of Room 1208 where his wife and her lover were singing "God Bless America" in bed. The husband had not harmed either, but had dived headfirst from the nearest window, hurtling to his death on Madison Avenue, badly damaging the frosted glass marquee.

In 1968, there had been a shoot-out in a large 3rd-floor corporation suite. One man had been killed, one injured, and a room-service waiter present in the suite had suffered the indignity of a bullet wound in his nates.

The management, of course, had immediately canceled the lease, since a morality clause was an important part of all long-term agreements with the Hotel Granger.

But despite these isolated occurrences, the Granger was essentially a quiet, staid, conservative establishment, catering to old, familiar guests, and frequently their children and grandchildren. The Security Section was not large, and most of its efforts were devoted to quietly evicting drunks and derelicts who wandered in from Madison Avenue, politely asking obvious hookers to move from the cocktail lounge, and keeping a record of lost-and-found articles, a task that bedevils every metropolitan hotel.

Zoe Kohler, having walked uptown from her East 39th Street apartment, entered the Hotel Granger at 8:46 A.M. She nodded at the doorman, the bellhops, the day shift coming on duty behind the reservation desk.

She went through a door marked "Employees Only," down a short corridor to a small suite of offices housing the Security Section. As usual, Barney McMillan, who worked the 1:00 to 9:00 A.M. shift, was asleep on the leather couch in Everett Pinckney's office. She shook him awake. He was a fleshy man, not too clean, and she found it distasteful to touch him.

"Wha'?" he said.

"Get up," she said. "You're supposed to be on duty."

"Yeah," he said, sitting up, yawning, tasting his tongue. "How about some coffee, babe?"

She looked at him.

"No," she said stiffly.

He looked at her.

"How about some coffee, Zoe?"

"That's better," she said. "A Danish?"

"Why not? Prune—or whatever they've got."

"Any excitement?" she asked.

"Nah," he said. "A couple of drunks singing on the ninth floor. That was about it. Quiet night. Just the way I like it."

She hung her coat away in an open closet. She put her purse in the bottom drawer of her desk, and extracted a japanned tray from the wide top drawer. She went out the way she had come, through the lobby and cocktail lounge, into a side corridor that led to the kitchen.

They were busy with breakfast in there, serving in the dining room and making up room orders, and no one spoke to her. No one looked at her. Sometimes she had a fantasy that she was an invisible woman.

She poured two black coffees for Mr. Pinckney and herself. Barney McMillan liked his with two sugars and two creams. The Danish and strudel didn't look especially appetizing, so she selected a jelly doughnut for Barney. He'd eat anything.

She carried her loaded tray back to the Security Section offices. Everett Pinckney had arrived; he and McMillan were sitting on opposite sides of Pinckney's desk, their feet up. They were laughing loudly, but cut it short and took their feet down when Zoe entered. Mr. Pinckney said good morning and both thanked her politely for their morning coffee.

When she went back to her own office, she heard their laughter start up again. She suspected they might be laughing at her, and looked down to make certain her sweater and skirt were not stained, her belt was properly buckled, her pantyhose without runs. She could see nothing amiss, but still . . .

She sat primly at her desk in the windowless office, sipping her coffee. She listened to the drone of talk of the two men and the bustling sounds of the hotel about her. She wondered if she *was* invisible. She wondered if she did exist.

Zoe Kohler was neither this nor that: not short, not tall; not fair, not dark; not thin, not plump. She lacked the saving grace of a single extreme.

In their final argument, just before Kenneth had stormed out of the house, he had shouted in fury and frustration: "You're not definite! You're just not *there!*"

Her lusterless hair was cut in a short bob: a straight line of bangs across her brow, a center part with thick wings falling just below her ears. She had not changed that style since college. Her hair fitted as precisely as a good wig and was all of a piece, no tendrils or curls, as if it could be lifted off, revealing the pale scalp of a nun or collaborator.

Her face was triangular, dwindling to a pointed chin. The eyes were the same shade of brown as her hair, and without fire or depth. The eyeballs were slightly distended, the lashes a lighter brown and wispy.

Her lips were not pinched. Clever makeup could have softened them—but for what?

At work, in public, her features seemed immobile, set. She rarely smiled—and then it was gone, a flicker. Some thought her serious, solemn, dull. All were wrong. No one knew.

She would soon be thirty-seven, and though she exercised infrequently, her body remained young, with good muscle tone. Her stomach was reasonably flat, buttocks taut. Her thighs were not slack, and there was a sweet indentation between ribcage and hips.

Dr. Stark assured her that, other than the controllable disorder and menstrual cramps, she was in excellent health.

She knew better. She was unloved and incapable of inspiring respect. Was that not an illness?

Dim she may have been, even blank, for there was nothing robust, vital, or assertive in the role she played. The dowdy clothes. The sensible shoes. The subdued eyes, the quick, tremulous smile.

That was the lark, you see. It was all a grand hustle. Now, after so many years, she was swindling the world. She was making her mark.

Barney McMillan left, giving her a wave as he passed her office.

"Ta-ta," he said.

She planned her work for the day: drawing up the Security Section's employment schedule for the following week, writing letters to departed guests who had left personal property in their rooms, filing petty cash vouchers with the bookkeeping department.

It was, she acknowledged, hardly enough to keep her busy for eight hours. But she had learned to pace herself, to appear constantly busy, to maintain a low profile so that no executive might become curious enough to question her value to the Hotel Granger.

She felt no guilt in taking advantage of this sinecure; her take-home pay was less than $200 a week. She was able to live comfortably only because of her alimony and the yearly checks of $3,000 each from her mother and father. She had a modest savings account, a checking account, and a small portfolio of tax-exempt municipal bonds.

She did not waste money, but neither did she deny herself. Anyone who might glimpse the gowns concealed in the back of her closet, or the lingerie hidden in the bottom drawer of her dresser, would agree to that: she did not deny herself—what she wanted and what she needed.

Everett Pinckney stopped by. Because there was no extra chair in her tiny office, he put one thin haunch on the edge of her desk and perched there, looking down at her.

He was a tall, jointed man, balding, a bony crown rising from a horseshoe of gray hair. His bare scalp was freckled and there was a sprinkle across his nose and cheekbones.

His eyes seemed constantly teary, his lips moist. He had the largest ears Zoe Kohler had ever seen: slices of drooping veal. His voice was hoarse and raspy, which was odd because he had a Boston accent, and one expected a tone more elegant and precise.

He wore vested suits with small bowties and, occasionally, in his lapel, a fake flower made of feathers. His cracked shoes were always polished to a high gloss. If he was a man on the way down, there was no bitterness or self-pity in him.

It hadn't taken Zoe long to realize she had been hired by an alcoholic. You could not judge from his manner or speech, for he moved steadily, if slowly, and his words were never garbled. But even in the morning he exuded a faint but perceptible odor: sour, piercing, musty. Whiskey had soaked into his cells, into the lining of his stomach, and bubbled up to seep from the pores of his skin.

He was never obviously drunk, but she had heard the drawer of his desk slide open, the clink of bottle against glass, the closing of the desk drawer: a steady and never-ending series of sounds that got him through the day in what Zoe imagined to be a constant glow, a buzz, a dulling of whatever gnawed at him so that he could function and face the world with equanimity and charm.

And he *was* charming, with a crooked smile, endless patience, and sympathy that seemed without limit. He was invariably cheerful, always obliging, and knew how to endure fools. Zoe had heard gossip of a bedridden wife and a son who had gone bad, but she had never asked, and Everett Pinckney had volunteered no information about his life outside the Hotel Granger.

Nor did he ever question Zoe about her private life. They respected each other's pain. It brought them closer than confessions and confidences.

"Sergeant Coe called me last night," Pinckney told her. "At home. His wife is pregnant."

"Again?" Zoe Kohler said.

"Again," he said, smiling. "So he'd like all the work he can get. Naturally. You're going to make out next week's schedule today?"

She nodded.

"Can you use him?"

That was the way Everett Pinckney was. He didn't *tell* her to find work for Sergeant Coe, although he had every right to. But the employment schedule of the Security Section was one of her duties, so he asked her.

"Could he fill in for Joe Levine?" she asked.

"I'm sure he could."

"I'll check with him before I show you the schedule."

"Fine. Thank you, Zoe."

Pinckney, Barney McMillan, and Joseph T. Levine, the three security officers, worked eight hours a day. Each had two days off a week (Pinckney, the chief, on Saturday and Sunday). To fill in on their days off, or during vacations or illness, temporary security guards were employed.

Most of the temps were moonlighting New York policemen and detectives. The Security Section had a list of a dozen or so officers who might be available, and had little trouble keeping a man on duty around the clock.

Pinckney told Zoe Kohler he was going to check at the desk and then he was going to inspect the new locks on the steel doors leading to the roof.

"Be back in about an hour," he said.

She nodded.

He slid off her desk. He stood a moment, not departing, and she looked up inquiringly.

"Zoe . . ." he said.

She waited.

"You're all right?" he asked anxiously. "You're not ill? You seem a little, uh, subdued."

His concern touched her briefly.

"I'm fine, Mr. Pinckney," she said. "It's that time of the month again."

"Oh, *that,*" he said, relieved. Then, with a harsh bark of laughter, "Well, I have to shave every morning."

He smiled, and was gone.

Yes, he shaved every morning. But you didn't get back pains and cramps from shaving, she should have told him. You didn't see the dark, gummy stains. You didn't imagine the ooze and flow. The constant crucifixion.

The longer she lived, the more vulgar life seemed to her. Not society or culture, but life itself. Breathing, eating, excreting, intercourse, bleeding.

Animal. Crude. Disgusting. Those were the words she used.

She worked slowly, steadily all morning, head bent over her desk, a silent drudge. She didn't look up when Everett Pinckney returned from his tour of inspection. She heard him in his office: desk drawer opened, clink of glass, drawer slammed shut.

She was not bored with her job. To be bored, she would have had to think about it, be conscious of it. But she moved mechanically, her hands, eyes, and a snippet of brain sufficient for the task. The rest of her was away and floating.

At 12:30 she took her japanned tray and went into the kitchen. One of the chefs fixed her a tunafish salad plate with lettuce, tomato and cucumber slices, a single large radish cut fancily to resemble a flower. She carried the food and a pot of hot tea back to her office.

Pinckney never ate lunch.

"Got to keep this down," he would say, patting his sunken stomach.

But she heard the sliding of his desk drawer . . .

She ate her lunch sitting erect in her stenographer's chair, her spine not touching the back. The cramps were intensifying, the pain in the lumbar region beginning to glow. It seemed centered just above the sacrum, but internal. The pain was a sun, spreading its rays.

She picked delicately at her salad, taking small bites, masticating thoroughly. She sipped her tea. When she had finished the food, she lighted a cigarette and poured a second cup of tea.

She kept a small pharmacopoeia in the middle drawer of her desk. She washed down two Anacin, a Midol and a vitamin C tablet. Then she patted her lips lightly with the linen napkin and brought the used dishes back to the scullery.

It was a rackety, steaming room, manned by two youths, a black and a Puerto Rican in sweat-soaked T-shirts. They worked at top speed, scraping plates into garbage cans, filling racks with china, glassware, cutlery, pushing the racks into a huge washing machine.

They looked up when she came in, gave her scurvy glances. The Puerto Rican winked and shouted something in Spanish. The black roared with laughter and slapped his thigh. She emptied her tray, turned, and walked out. Their laughter followed her.

She called Sergeant Coe at his precinct, but he wasn't on duty. She called him at home. Mrs. Coe answered, and Zoe identified herself.

"Oh yes," Mrs. Coe said anxiously. "Can you hang on a sec? He's working in the basement. I'll call him right away."

When the sergeant came on the phone, breathless, Zoe informed him that she had him down for Joe Levine's shift, 5:00 P.M. to 1:00A.M., on Monday and Tuesday nights.

"Great," he said. "Many thanks."

"If for any reason you are unable to make it," she said formally, "please let us know as soon as possible."

"I'll be there," he assured her. "Thanks again."

She took the employment schedule into Mr. Pinckney's office and stood by his desk as he read it.

"I checked with Sergeant Coe," she said. "He told me he'll be able to fill in for Joe Levine."

"Good," Pinckney said. "It looks fine to me, Zoe. You can type it up. Copies to the desk, front office, and bookkeeping."

He said that every week.

"Yes, Mr. Pinckney," she said.

She had just started typing the roster when her phone rang, an unusual occurrence.

"Hotel Granger," she said. "Security Section. May I help you?"

"You sure can, sweetie," a woman's voice said briskly. "Come to a great cocktail party Harry and I are throwing this afternoon."

"Maddie!" Zoe Kohler said happily. "How *are* you?"

"Full of piss and vinegar," Madeline Kurnitz said. "How they hanging, kiddo?"

The two women chatted awhile. Mostly, Maddie chatted, rapidly and loudly, and Zoe listened, smiling and nodding at the phone.

It seemed to her she had been listening to Madeline Kurnitz all her life. Or at least since she had shared a room with her and two other girls at the University of Minnesota. That had been in 1960–1963, and even then Maddie had been gabbling a blue streak.

"A four-year vacation from the realities of life," was her judgment on the value of a college education, and her scholastic career reflected this belief. It was one long party studded with dates, escapades, affairs, unexplained absences, threats of expulsion, and an endless parade of yearning boys and older men that awed her roommates.

Maddie: "Listen, the only reason we're all here is to snare a husband. Right? So why don't they teach us something useful—like moaning. The only reason I got all these guys calling is that I've learned how to moan realistically while screwing. That's all a woman has to know to be a success: how to moan. This place should have a course called Moaning 101–102. Then the second year's course could be called Remedial Moaning."

Maddie: "Look, there are men, and there are husbands. If you were male, would you want to be a husband? The hell you would. You'd want to charge through life banging everything in sight. Men fuck, husbands have sex. Men smell, husbands use fou-fou. Men drink whiskey, husbands drink beer. Men are hung, husbands have hernias. Shit, I don't want a husband, I want a *man.*"

The three roommates, from small towns in Minnesota, Wisconsin, and Iowa, listened to these pronouncements with nervous giggles. It wasn't the way *they* had been brought up. Maddie, from New York City, was a foreigner.

They worshiped her, because she was smart, funny, generous. And she passed along the men she didn't want or had tired of. In return, they loaned her lecture notes, coached her, covered up her absences, and finally got her through the four years to a BA degree.

She didn't show up for graduation, having taken off for Bermuda with a Yalie. But her diploma was mailed to her.

When Zoe Kohler came to New York from Winona, Minnesota, after her divorce, her first phone call was to Maddie. She was now Madeline Kurnitz with her own number in the directory. Harold Kurnitz was her fourth husband, and Maddie took Zoe under her wing as an experienced combat soldier might comfort, advise, and share his know-how with a raw recruit.

Maddie: "A divorce is like falling off a horse. You've got to get right back up and ride again or you'll be spooked for life."

"I don't think I want to marry again," Zoe said timidly.

Maddie: "Bullshit."

She had done her best—cocktail parties, dinner, blind dates—but finally she realized Zoe Kohler had been telling the truth: she didn't want to marry again, not at that point in her life.

Maddie (wrathfully): "That doesn't mean you can't *screw*, for God's sake. No wonder you have cramps. If I go two days without a bang, I sneeze and dust comes out my ears."

Now, listening to Maddie natter on about all the beautiful people who would be at her cocktail party ("A zillion horny studs!"), Zoe Kohler caught some of her excitement and said she'd come over from work, just for a few minutes, but she had to get home early.

Maddie: "That's what they all say, kiddo. But they come and they stay and they drink up all our booze. There's a guy I want you to meet . . ."

"Oh no," Zoe said. "Not again."

"Just meet him," Maddie urged. "That's all. Just shake his paw and say, 'How ja do.' Is that so awful?"

"No," Zoe said faintly, "I guess not."

Maddie finally got off the phone and Zoe went back to typing the Security Section roster for the following week. She guessed that she had been invited to the cocktail party at the last minute because Maddie had realized that she would have a preponderance of male guests and not enough women. So she was calling friends and acquaintances frantically, trying to redress the balance.

Zoe wasn't offended. That was the way she reccived the few invitations that came her way. At the last minute. To even up a dining table or take the place of a reneging guest. She was never first choice.

The empty afternoon wasted away. She distributed copies of the Security Section's employment schedule. She typed up four letters to departed guests who had left personal property in their rooms, and took the letters to Everett Pinckney for his signature. She delivered petty cash vouchers to the bookkeeping department.

She spoke briefly and coolly to the other Hotel Granger employees she dealt with, and they replied in kind. She had rebuffed their attempts at friendship, or even lighthearted companionship. She preferred to do her job swaddled in silence.

Back in her office, she spent the last hour at her desk, idly leafing through the current issue of a weekly trade magazine devoted to the hotel business in New York City. It contained articles on current occupancy rates, conventions scheduled for the coming months, predictions on the summer tourism season.

The most interesting section, to Zoe, was that dealing with hotel security matters. Frequently the names and addresses (undoubtedly fictitious) and physical descriptions of deadbeats were given. Numbers of stolen credit cards were listed. Crimes committed in hotels, especially swindles and cons, were detailed.

A regular column titled "Wanted" gave names, aliases, and descriptions of known criminals—robbers, burglars, prostitutes, pimps, professional gamblers, etc.—working New York hotels. In addition, unsolved hotel crimes were listed, with the name and phone number of the New York Police Department officer investigating the crime.

The last item in the column read:

"Homicide at the Grand Park on February 15th. Victim of stabbing: George T. Puller, 54, white male, of Denver, Colo. Anyone with information relating to this crime please contact Detective Sergeant Abner Boone, KL5-8604."

That notice had been in the magazine for the past three weeks. Zoe Kohler wondered if Detective Sergeant Abner Boone was still seated by the phone, waiting . . .

* * *

Madeline and Harold Kurnitz lived in a high-rise on East 49th Street. The apartment house was just like Maddie: loud, brash, glittering. Five people crowded into the self-service elevator behind Zoe Kohler. She huddled back in a corner, watching them. They were laughing, their hands on each other. Zoe guessed they were going to the party. They were.

The door of the seven-room duplex was open. Sound surged out into the hall. In the foyer a uniformed maid took hats and coats, hung them away on a temporary rack, and handed out numbered checks. That was the way Maddie did things.

The party was catered, with two bartenders working behind counters and liveried waiters passing trays of hors d'oeuvres and California champagne. Maddie was lost in the throng, but her husband stood near the doorway to greet guests.

He was a big, hairy man, tufts sprouting from his ears. Zoe knew he was in yarn, fabrics, linings—something like that. "The rag business," Maddie called it. He had a slow, dry manner, ironic, amused and amazed that he found himself married to a jangling, outgoing, capricious woman.

Zoe liked him, and kissed his cheek. He seemed very solid to her, very protective, as he steered her to the nearest bar and ordered a glass of white wine for her.

"You remembered, Harry," she said.

"Of course I remembered," he said, smiling. "Of all Maddie's friends, I like you the best. I wish you'd see more of her. Maybe you can calm her down."

"No one can calm Maddie down."

"That's true," he said happily. "She's something, isn't she? Isn't she something?"

He moved away to greet more guests. Zoe put her back against the bar, looked around. A typical Maddie stand-up party: crushed, smoky. A hi-fi was blasting from somewhere. People were shrieking. She smiled, smiled, smiled. No one spoke to her.

She had never seen so many beautiful men. Some were elegant in three-piece Italian suits, gold aglitter at cuffs and wrists. Some were raffish, with embroidered Greek shirts opened low, medallions swinging against furred chests. Some, many, she supposed, were homosexuals. It didn't matter; they were all beautiful.

White, flashing teeth. Wicked eyes. Jaws bearded or shaved blue. Twirled mustaches. Hair slicked, blown-dry, coiffed, or deliberately tangled. Wet mouths in motion. Hands waving: long, slender fingers. Sprung hips. Sculpted legs and, here and there, jeans tight enough to show a bulge.

She thought of their fuzzed thighs. The satiny buttocks. Coil of tendon, rope of muscle. Most of all, their strength. Physical strength. The power there.

That was what had astounded her about Kenneth. He was not a stalwart man, but when he first gripped her on their wedding night, she had cried out in shock and surprise. The force! It frightened her.

And that—that thing. That reddish, purplish, knobbed thing poking out, trembling in the air. A club. It was a club, nodding at her.

She looked dazedly around the crowded room and saw the clubs, straining.

"Zoe!" Maddie screamed. "Baby! Why aren't you mingling? You've got to *mingle!*"

A bouncy ragamuffin of a woman with a snarl of long black hair liberally laced with gray. Silver wires didn't bother *her.* She couldn't be slowed by age or chastened by experience. She plunged vigorously through life, kicking up her heels.

Her face was a palette of makeup: black eyebrows like carets, shadowed eyes with fake lashes as thick as feather dusters. A whitened face with a bold, crimsoned mouth. Sharp teeth, feral teeth.

Her plump, unbound body capered; everything jounced, bobbed, swung. Diamonds sparkled at throat, ears, wrists, fingers. Her smart frock of black crepe was stained with a spilled drink. She smoked a thin cigar.

"He's around here somewhere," she shouted, grasping Zoe's arm. "David something. How are you, kiddo? He's wearing some kind of a cheesy velvet suit, but on him it looks good. My God, you're pale. David something. A mustache from here to there, and he smells of pot. You've *got* to take care of yourself, sweetie. Now get out there and *mingle.* You can't miss him. David something. Oh God, he's gorgeous. A young Clark Gable. If I see him, I'll grab him and find you. They say he's hung like Man-o'-War."

Then she was gone, diving into the mob. Zoe turned her back to the party, pressed against the bar, asked for another glass of white wine. She would sip it slowly, then slip away. No one would miss her.

This city had a rude vigor she could not countenance. It swirled her, and she felt adrift. Things were always at high tide, rising and rubbing. Noise, dirt, violence. The scream of sex everywhere. She could not endure the rawness.

A shoulder touched her; she pulled away, and looked at him.

"I beg your pardon," he said, smiling timidly. "Someone bumped me."

"That's all right," she said.

He looked at what she was drinking.

"White wine?" he asked.

She nodded.

He asked the bartender for a glass of white wine.

"Quite a party," he said to Zoe.

She nodded again. "Noisy," she said.

"Isn't it. And crowded and stuffy. My name is Ernest Mittle. I work in Mr. Kurnitz's office."

"Zoe Kohler," she said, so softly that he didn't hear and asked her to repeat it. "Zoe Kohler. I'm a friend of Maddie Kurnitz."

They shook hands. His clasp was tender, his smile fragile.

"I've never been here before," he offered. "Have you?"

"A few times."

"I guess it's a beautiful apartment—without the people."

"I don't know," she confessed. "I've only been here for parties. It's always been crowded."

She thought desperately of something more to say. She had been taught to ask men questions about themselves: their work, ambitions, hobbies—whatever. Get them talking about themselves, and they would think you interesting and clever. That's what her mother had told her—several times.

But the best she could do was: "Where are you from?"

"Wisconsin," he said. "A small town. Trempealeau. I'm sure you've never heard of it."

She didn't want to tell him; she wanted him to think her a Manhattan sophisticate. But then her smile flickered, and she said:

"Yes, I've heard of it. I'm from Winona."

He turned to her with the delighted astonishment of a small boy.

"Winona!" he cried. "Neighbor!"

They moved a little closer: explorers caught in a dance of savages.

"Listen," he said excitedly, "are you here with anyone?"

"Oh no. No."

"Could we go someplace and have a drink together? Some quieter place? You're the first person I've met in New York who even heard of Trempealeau. I'd really like to talk to you."

"All right," she said.

No one noticed them leave.

In the lobby, he stopped her with a light hand on her arm, then jerked it away convulsively.

"Uh," he said, "I was wondering . . . Could we have dinner together? I know a little Italian place not far from here. If we're going to have a glass of wine, we might as well . . ."

His wispy voice trailed off. She stared at him a moment.

He was no David something in a velvet suit, smelling of pot. He was Ernest Mittle, a dusty young man who would always be an outlander in the metropolis.

There he stood, stooped, eager, as anxious to please as a cocker spaniel. The cheap tweed overcoat was too tight in the shoulders and strained at its buttons. About his neck was a plaid wool muffler. He was hatless, but carried a pair of clumpy, fleece-lined gloves.

He seemed inoffensive and washed-out to Zoe Kohler. Faded eyebrows, blond lashes, eyes of milky blue. His complexion was fair, his haircut an atrocity that left his pink ears naked, isolated by clipper and razor.

But still . . . His smile was warm and hopeful. His small teeth were even and white. He was as tall as she, and if he straightened up, he would have been taller. But he seemed to crouch inside himself, hiding.

She was ever so careful. He appeared harmless, not pushy in the New York manner, but she knew as well as anyone the dangers that awaited the lone woman in the cruel city. Mugging. Burglary. Rape. Violent death. It was in the newspapers every day. And on TV in color. The chalked outline. The congealing blood.

"Well . . . all right," she said finally. "Thank you. But I have to get home early. By nine at the latest. Uh, I'm expecting a phone call."

"Fine," he said happily. "Let's go. It's not far; we can walk it in a few minutes."

She knew the restaurant. She had been there twice before, by herself. Each time she had been seated at the same small table near the door to the restrooms. The food was good, but the service had been execrable, although she had left generous tips.

This time, with a man, she was escorted by a smiling maitre d' to a comfortable corner table. A waiter came bustling to assist in removing her coat. A table candle in a ruby globe was lighted. Glasses of white wine were brought, menus proffered.

They both ordered veal piccata, spaghetti, and salad. They each had two more glasses of wine with their food. Service was prompt and flawless. They agreed the dinner was a success.

And she did enjoy it. Ernest Mittle was well-mannered, solicitous of her wants: "More bread? Butter? Ready for another wine? Dessert? No? Then surely espresso and a brandy? Fine!"

She had an uneasy feeling that he could ill afford this splendid meal, but he seemed delighted to be dining with her. When their brandies were served, she murmured something about paying her share, but he grandly waved the suggestion away and assured her that it was *his* pleasure. He sounded sincere.

During dinner, their early conversation had been about their childhood in Winona and Trempealeau: the hayrides and sleighrides, skating on the river, hunting and the taste of fried squirrel, illicit applejack, and days so cold that schools were closed and no one dared venture forth from home.

They spoke of college days (he had attended the University of Wisconsin at Madison). He had visited Minneapolis, both had been to Chicago. Once he had gone to New Orleans for Mardi Gras, and once she had been as far west as Denver. They agreed that one day they would journey to Europe, the West Indies, and perhaps Japan.

She learned more about him:

He was thirty-five, almost two years younger than she. He had never been married, or even engaged. He lived alone in a small studio apartment in the Gramercy Park area. He had a small circle of friends and acquaintances, mostly business associates.

He entertained rarely, went to the movies, theater, and ballet infrequently. He was taking courses at the New School in computer technology. His current job with Harold Kurnitz's company was in a small section called Inventory Control, and he hoped some day to persuade Mr. Kurnitz to computerize the entire operation.

All this came pouring forth with little prompting from Zoe. Ernest Mittle seemed happy to talk about himself, and it suddenly occurred to her that he might very well be as lonely as she.

When they came out of the restaurant a little before 8:00 P.M., the sky was blotchy. A moldy wind gusted off the East River, and the air smelled rawly of snow.

"We'll get a cab," Ernest Mittle said, pulling on his clumsy gloves.

"Oh, that's not necessary," she said. "I can get a bus right across the street."

"Where do you live, Zoe?"

She hesitated a moment, then: "East Thirty-ninth Street. Near Lexington."

"But you'll have to walk from the bus stop. Alone. I don't like that. Look, it's only about ten short blocks. Why don't we walk? It's still early, and there are a lot of people around."

"You don't have to do that. I'll just go on—"

"Come on," he said exuberantly, taking her arm. "In Minnesota and Wisconsin, this is a nice spring evening!"

So they set off, walking briskly southward. He adjusted his stride to her, assisted her up and down curbs, led her carefully around dog droppings and sidewalk obstructions, including a man slumped in a doorway, his legs extended. He was drinking from a bottle in a brown paper bag.

"That used to upset me," Ernest said. "When I first came to New York. But you get so you hardly notice it."

Zoe nodded. "Once I saw a well-dressed man lying on the sidewalk on Fifth Avenue. People were just walking around him."

"Was he drunk or dead or what?"

"I don't know," she confessed. "I just walked around him, too. That happened almost eight years ago, and it still bothers me. I should have done something or tried to do something."

"You know what New Yorkers say: 'Don't get involved.' "

"I know," she said. "Still . . ."

"Zoe, I've been babbling about myself all evening, but you've hardly said a word about yourself. Do you work?"

"Oh yes. In the Security Section of the Hotel Granger."

"That sounds interesting," he said politely.

"Not really," she said, and then perhaps it was the wine and brandy, but she began speaking of herself, she who was usually so secret.

She told him she had been married for three years, and was divorced. She told him she now lived alone, and the moment she heard her own words, she regretted them. A divorced woman living alone; she knew how men reacted to *that*.

She told him that she lived a very quiet life, read a lot, watched TV. She admitted that New York frightened her at times. It was so big, so dirty and noisy, so uncaring. But she had no desire to return to the Midwest, ever.

"I know what you mean," he said. "It's everything bad you can think of, but it's—exciting. And fascinating. Things are always happening. Unexpected things. Nothing unexpected happens much in Trempealeau."

"Or Winona," she said.

"It's a kind of love-hate relationship. With New York, I mean."

"Love-hate," he said wonderingly. "Yes, that's very true."

They turned onto her block, and she began to worry. It had been a pleasant evening, better than she had expected—but what now? Would he demand a good-night kiss? Would he insist on seeing her to her apartment door? Would he suddenly turn angry and importunate?

But when she halted outside the lobby entrance, he stopped too, drew off a glove, and proffered a white hand.

"Thank you, Zoe," he said smiling. "It's been a fine evening. I really enjoyed it."

"Thank *you,*" she said, surprised and shaking his soft hand. "The dinner was wonderful."

"Can we do it again?" he asked anxiously. "Can I call you?"

"Of course," she said. "I'd like that. I'm in the book."

"I'll call," he vowed, and she hoped he meant it.

She stopped to get her mail, including, thankfully, her alimony check. At the elevator, she turned to look back at the sidewalk. Ernest Mittle was still standing there. He waved. She waved back, but didn't feel safe until she was upstairs, inside her own apartment, the door locked, bolted, and chained.

She turned on all the lights and walked cautiously through the rooms, peering into closets and under the bed.

She made certain the venetian blinds were tightly closed. She was convinced there was a man across the street who stood in a darkened room with binoculars, watching her windows. She had never actually seen him, but his shades were always up and occasionally she had glimpsed flashes of white and moving shadows.

She went directly to her medicine supply in the kitchen, and swallowed a vitamin C pill, a B-complex capsule, and a magnesium tablet. Her premenstrual cramps had become increasingly severe, and she wanted to take a Darvon. But in view of what lay ahead, she settled for a Midol and two Anacin.

Dr. Stark could not understand her monthly cramps. She was on the Pill, and that usually eliminated or alleviated the symptoms. A complete examination had revealed no physiological cause, and Stark had suggested that the cramps might have a psychological origin.

He had offered to recommend a counselor, psychologist, or psychiatrist. Zoe had indignantly rejected his advice.

"There's nothing wrong with me," she said hotly.

"*Something* is wrong," he replied, "if what should be a normal, natural, healthy function causes you so much pain."

"I've had bad cramps all my life," she told him. "Ever since I began to bleed."

He looked at her queerly.

"It's your decision," he said.

She started the tub, then returned to the bedroom to undress. When she was naked, she palpated her breasts tenderly. That morning they had been soft, saggy. Now they seemed enlarged, harder, the nipples semi-erect. But at least she felt no sensation of bloat and could see no indication that her ankles had swollen.

She poured perfumed oil into the tub and eased into water as hot as she could endure. She lay motionless, melted, the back of her neck on the tub rim. She closed her eyes and soaked blissfully. The cramps seemed to diminish.

After a while she roused, and began to lather herself with scented soap that she bought from a Madison Avenue apothecary. It cost $2.75 a cake, and smelled subtly of frangipani. She cleansed herself thoroughly, her ears, vulva, rectum, and between her toes.

She did not masturbate.

Zoe opened the tub drain and stood cautiously. She turned on the shower and rinsed the suds away. She sniffed at her armpits, but smelled only the flowery fragrance of the imported soap. She dried thoroughly and inspected herself for more gray pubic hairs, but found none.

She returned to the bedroom. She turned on the bedside radio, switching from WQXR to a station that featured hard rock. Sitting on the edge of the bed, listening to the driving music, she painted her toenails and fingernails a glossy vermilion. Then she walked about the room, waving her hands in the air to dry the polish and moving her body in time to the music.

Taking care not to smudge her nails, she opened the bottom drawer of her dresser and lifted out stacks of sensible underwear and earth-colored pantyhose. In the back of the drawer were concealed her treasures. Her precious things.

She selected a brief brassiere and a bikini of sheer black nylon with small appliquéd leaves that concealed the nipples and pudendum. The lingerie came on with a whisper, weightless and clinging. She applied Aphrodisia behind her ears, within her armpits, on the inside of her thighs.

In the back of the bedroom closet, behind the rack of practical, everyday clothes, were her secret costumes. They hung in plastic bags from hooks screwed into the wall. There were five gowns, all expensive, all new. The red silk had been worn once. The others had never been used.

She donned a sheath of black crepe. When the side zipper was closed, the dress clung like paint. A second skin. Décolletage revealed the swell of her hardened breasts. Her slender waist was accented, the lyre of her hips. In back, firm buttocks pressed.

Then, seamed black silk hose with rosetted garters. Evening sandals of thin straps with three-inch spike heels, the tallest she could manage. She wore no jewels, but around her left wrist she fastened a fine chain supporting a legend of gold letters. It read: WHY NOT?

She combed her short brown hair quickly. Then went into the living room, to the closet. In the back, concealed, was her trenchcoat and a large patent leather shoulder bag. In the bag, wrapped in tissue, was a black nylon wig and a makeup kit.

She spent a few moments transferring things from her workaday bag: cigarettes, matches, Swiss Army pocket knife, the small can of Chemical Mace, keys, coins, wallet with slightly more than forty dollars. Before she transferred the wallet, she removed all her identification cards and hid them on the top shelf of the closet.

Then she shrugged into the trenchcoat and buttoned it up to her neck. She buckled the belt loosely so the coat hung like a sack. Slinging her shoulder bag, she sallied forth leaving all the lights in the apartment burning.

Bathing and dressing had taken almost an hour. Never once during that time had she looked in a mirror.

The night doorman was behind the desk and tipped his cap to her as she passed. She teetered over to Third Avenue on her high heels. She looked about nervously for Ernest Mittle, but he was long gone.

There were sudden swirls of light, powdery snow, and she had to wait almost five minutes for an uptown cab. She told the driver to take her to Central Park West and 72nd Street.

"The Dakota?" he asked.

"That corner," she said crisply. "It's close enough."

"Whatever you say, lady," he said, and then drove in silence, for which she was thankful.

She gave him a generous tip when he let her off. She stood on the windswept corner, lighting a cigarette slowly and not moving in any direction until the cab pulled away, and she saw its taillights receding west on 72nd Street.

Then she, too, headed west, walking rapidly, her heels clicking on a sidewalk already dusted with snow. Men passed, but she did not raise her eyes. She bent against the wind, clutching her shoulder bag with both hands. But she was not cold. She glowed.

The Filmore was a residential hotel. Downstairs, one flight from the sidewalk, was a dim restaurant featuring a "continental menu." The restaurant seemed to be languishing, but the connecting bar, brightly lighted, had several customers, most of them watching a TV set suspended on chains from the ceiling.

Zoe Kohler had been there once before. It suited her needs perfectly.

She sat at the bar in her trenchcoat, holding her bag on her lap. She ordered a glass of white wine and finished it quickly. Very calm. Making certain she looked at none of the single men. The bartender was not the one who had been on duty during her previous visit.

"Where is the ladies' room, please?" she asked, just as she had before.

"Back there through the hotel entrance," he said, pointing. "You go up the stairs and through the lobby. It's to your right."

"Thank you," she said, paid for her wine and left a tip. Not too large a tip, she judged, and not too small. He'd never remember her. No one ever did.

The lavatory was tiled in white with stained fixtures of cracked porcelain. Disinfectant stung the nose. There was a middle-aged woman at one of the sinks, inspecting herself in the streaked mirror, moving her head this way and that. She turned when Zoe came in.

"Hullo, dearie," she said brightly, smiling.

Zoe nodded and walked down the row of five toilet stalls, glancing under the doors. They all appeared to be unoccupied. She went into the last stall, closed the door and latched it. She waited patiently for two or three minutes, then heard the outside door open and close.

She exited cautiously. The restroom seemed to be empty, but to make certain, she opened the doors of all the stalls and checked. Then she went over to one of the sinks and began working swiftly. Finally, finally, she looked at her image.

She removed the wig from her shoulder bag, shook it out, pulled it on. The nylon was black and glossy, with feathered curls across her brow and thick, rippling waves that fell almost to her shoulders. She smoothed it into place, turning this way and that, just as the middle-aged woman had.

Satisfied, she began applying makeup. She darkened her brows, mascaraed her lashes, brushed on silvery-blue eye shadow, powder, rouge, a deep crimson lipstick with an outer layer of moist gloss.

She worked quickly, and within fifteen minutes the transformation was complete. Even in the dulled mirror she looked vibrant, alive. She was a warm, sensuous woman, eager for joy. Glittering eyes challenged and promised.

She opened her coat to snug the wool crepe dress down over her hips, wiggling slightly to make certain it fit without a wrinkle. She tugged the neckline lower, took a deep breath and, in the mirror, showed her teeth.

Then she wrapped the unbuttoned trenchcoat about her, cinched the belt tight, and turned up the collar in back. Her neck and the top of her bosom were exposed.

She examined herself. She licked her lips.

She exited through the hotel lobby, bag swinging from her shoulder. Men in the lobby stared at her. Men passing on the sidewalk outside stared at her. She lighted a cigarette, smoking with outsize, theatrical movements.

She waited under the marquee for a cab, humming.

The Hotel Pierce, Manhattan's newest hostelry, occupied the entire blockfront on Sixth Avenue between 56th and 57th streets. It had 1,200 rooms, suites, penthouses, banquet rooms, meeting rooms, a convention hall, a nightclub on the roof.

Below the main lobby floor was a concourse with three dining rooms, a coffee and snack bar, gift shops and boutiques, the offices of travel agents and a stockbroker, a bookstore, men's and women's clothing shops, and four cocktail lounges. "You can live your life at the Pierce" was the advertised boast.

Zoe Kohler had selected the Pierce because she knew it was currently hosting three conventions; the concourse cocktail lounges were sure to be crowded. She chose the El Khatar, a bar with a vaguely Moorish theme, walls hung with silken draperies, waitresses dressed as belly dancers.

She stood a moment just inside the entrance, looking around as if expecting to be met. When the hatcheck girl came forward, she surrendered her trenchcoat and made her way slowly to the bar, peering about in the dimness, still acting the role of a lady awaiting her escort.

Most of the small tables were occupied by couples and foursomes. The bar was crowded: singles, doubles, groups. There were a few seated women, but men were standing two and three deep, reaching over shoulders to take refills from perspiring bartenders in fezzes.

The room was terribly overheated, smoky, smelling vilely of cheap incense. Shriek of conversation. Shouts of laughter. Tinny blare of piped Eastern music. Zoe wondered how long she might endure this swamp of raw noise.

She stood a moment near the bar, chin up, spine straight.

A red-faced man, hair tousled, tie askew, spluttering with laughter at something his companion had just said, made a sudden lurch backward and bumped her roughly.

"Whoops!" he said, catching her arm as she staggered. "Beg your pardon, lady. Any harm done?"

"No, no," she said, giving him a rueful smile, rubbing her arm. "It's all right."

"Not all right," he protested. "I'm sorry as hell. Buy you a drink? Then you'll forgive me?"

"Thank you," she said, still smiling, "but I'll pay for it. But I'd appreciate it if you could order a glass of white wine for me. I can't get near the bar."

She fumbled in her bag. He made a grand gesture.

"Put your money away, sweetie," he said. "This is on the house—my house!"

He and his friend found this a remarkably humorous sally. They heaved with merriment, bending over their drinks. In a few minutes, Zoe had her glass of wine.

"Come join us," the red-faced man urged. "Me and my pal here have been boring each other all night. He's a sex fiend, but I'll protect you from him!"

More loud guffaws.

"Sounds like a lot of fun," Zoe said, "but I'm waiting for my boyfriend. Maybe some other time."

"Any time at all," the friend said, speaking for the first time. His lickerish eyes traveled slowly down the length of her body to her strapped sandals, then up again. "You name the time, and I'll be there, I guarantee!"

They were still laughing, nudging each other with elbows when, smiling faintly, she moved away from them, down the bar. She didn't want two men. She wanted one man.

Searching, she saw a woman seated at the bar gathering up purse and gloves. Her escort, standing alongside, had just received his bill and was counting money onto the bar.

Sidling swiftly through the press, protecting her glass of wine with a cupped hand, and saying, "Pardon. Pardon. Pardon," Zoe Kohler succeeded in claiming the barstool a second after the woman slid off.

"Got it all warm for you, honey," the brassy blonde said. Then she took a closer look at Zoe, and said, "Good luck!"

"Yes," Zoe said. "Thanks." And turned swiftly away.

To her right was a noisy group of five men engaged in a loud debate on professional football teams. It was the single man seated to her left who interested Zoe. He was staring straight ahead, hunched over what appeared to be a martini-rocks. He was apparently oblivious to the hubbub around him.

"Pardon me, sir," Zoe Kohler said, leaning toward him. "Could you tell me what time it is, please?"

He turned his head slowly to look at her, then glanced down at his gold wristwatch.

"Almost eleven-fifteen," he said.

"Thank you, sir," she said, then swung partly around on her barstool to search the room with anxious eyes. As she swung, her knees brushed his fat thigh.

"What's the matter?" the man said. "He didn't show up?"

She swung back, then turned her head to face him, looking into his eyes.

"What makes you think it's a man?" she said. "Maybe I'm waiting for my girlfriend."

"No way," he said, his eyes lowering to her bosom. "A beautiful woman like you, it's got to be a man. And he's a fool for being late."

"Well," she said, giggling, "to tell you the truth, it's me that's late—by about an hour!"

Five minutes later, he had become more animated, had bought a round of drinks, and they knew all about each other—all they wanted to know.

His name was Fred (no last name offered), and he was in New York to attend a convention of electrical appliance marketing managers in that very hotel. He was from Akron, Ohio, and couldn't wait to get back. Zoe judged him to be in his early fifties.

She was Irene (no last name offered), and she was originally from Minneapolis. She had come to New York seeking a career as model and actress. But now she was executive assistant to an independent TV producer who made commercials and educational films.

They had swung around to face each other. Their knees rubbed.

"Why are you sitting here alone?" Zoe asked. "A convention and all that. Why aren't you out with the boys, tearing up the town?"

"Oh, I was," he said. "Earlier. But then things got a little raunchy. They wanted to go down to Greenwich Village and see the freaks. That's not my idea of a good time. So I cut out."

"What's your idea of a good time?" she challenged, but when she saw the flicker of fear in his eyes, she wondered if she was moving too fast.

"Oh," he said, looking down, "you know . . . A nightcap, and then up to my room to watch TV. I'm really a very quiet guy."

"You say," she scoffed. "You quiet ones are the worst. Hell on wheels when you get rolling."

He laughed, chest swelling with pride.

"Well . . ." he said, "maybe. I guess I've sowed my share of wild oats."

He was heavy, heavy. His florid face was pudgy, neck thick, torso soft. Collops flapped at the corners of his mouth. He had the sandpaper cough of a heavy smoker. In addition to the gold wristwatch, he wore gold cufflinks, a pearl tie tack, a pinkie ring set with a square diamond. He was not drunk, exactly, but he was on his way: a little dazed, beginning to slur.

He ordered another round of drinks. She reached for her wine, and he grabbed her wrist and turned the chain so he could read the words: WHY NOT?

He raised his eyes to stare at her.

"Why not?" he said hoarsely.

She leaned close to him, her cool cheek against his hot, sweated jowl. She whispered into his ear:

"I told you that you quiet ones are hell on wheels. Can we go to your room? Have a little party?"

He nodded dumbly.

They drained their drinks. He paid his bill from a thick wallet. They pushed their way through the throng. She gave him her coat check and he paid to reclaim her trenchcoat.

"I left my coat in my room," he said. "I'm on the thirtieth floor."

"Way up in the sky," she said.

"That's right, girlie," he said, staggering and catching her arm to steady himself. "Way up with the birdies."

"It's your own room?" she said in a low voice. "Or do you have a roommate?"

"It's all mine," he mumbled. "Yours and mine."

They had to jam their way into a crowded elevator filled with laughing, yelling, drunken convention-goers. Another couple got off on the 30th floor, but turned down the long corridor in the opposite direction. Fred led the way around one turn to Room 3015.

He halted before the flush door.

"Take a look at this door, Irene," he demanded. "Tell me what you see. Or don't see!"

She knew immediately what it was—she had read about it in the hotel trade magazine—but she could not deny him his moment of triumph.

"It just looks like an ordinary door to me," she said, shrugging.

"No keyhole!" he said. "Just that thing . . ."

He pointed to a narrow, metal-rimmed slot directly under the knob. Then he took a white plastic card from his jacket pocket. It was no larger than a credit card.

"Magnetic," he explained to Zoe. "The printed code is between two pieces of solid plastic. You can't see it. And no way for your friendly neighborhood locksmith to copy it. Not yet there isn't."

"That's wonderful," she said.

"Great security," he said. "Practically eliminates break-ins. Who can pick a lock that doesn't show?"

He fumbled a bit, then got the plastic card inserted into the slot. The bolt slid back, he turned the knob, opened the door and stood aside.

"Welcome to my castle," he said.

The room was certainly larger, cleaner, and more attractively furnished than the rooms at the Hotel Granger. But it had the impersonality of all hotel rooms: everything designed to repel cigarette burns and glass stains, to require minimal maintenance. Pictures were bolted to the walls; the base of the TV set was anchored to the floor.

"Make yourself at home," Fred said. "I gotta see a man about a dog."

He went into the bathroom, closed the door. Zoe moved slowly and cautiously. She removed her coat, folded it once, placed it carefully on the polished bureau near the door. She sat down slowly in a high-backed armchair. She touched no surface.

She heard the toilet flush. In a moment he came out of the bathroom, smoothing strands of rusty hair across his white scalp.

"Well now," he said heartily, "let's get this show on the road. How about a shot of the world's best brandy? I never travel without it."

"You know what they say about alcohol?" she said archly. "It increases the desire and decreases the performance."

"Lotta bullshit," he said. "You won't have any complaints, little lady."

"Well . . . maybe just a sip."

"Atta girl. This'll put lead in your pencil—if you had a pencil!"

They both laughed immoderately. She watched him take a pint bottle from the top dresser drawer. He poured her a small drink in a water glass and a larger one for himself.

When he brought the drink over to her, she was deliberately busy with a compact mirror, poking at her wig. So he set the glass on the endtable next to the armchair. Then he sat on the edge of the bed. He turned to face her.

"Say," he said, "you wouldn't mind if I smoked a cigar, would you?"

"Of course not, honey," she said. "I just love the smell of a good cigar."

"You sure, babe?" he said doubtfully. "My wife doesn't."

"I do," she assured him. "Go right ahead."

So he stripped the cellophane from a cigar and lighted up, puffing contentedly. He took the pillows from under the bedspread, propped them against the headboard. He removed his jacket and vest, took off his shoes. He loosened his tie, unbuttoned his collar. The fleshy neck, reddened, bulged free.

Then he sat back against the pillows, his feet up, ankles crossed. He held his cigar in one hand, brandy in the other.

"Oh boy, oh boy, oh boy," he sighed. "This is the life. Daddy told me there would be nights like this, but he didn't tell me how few and far between. Hey, sweetheart, why don't you make yourself more comfortable?"

"I thought you'd never ask," she said, giggling.

She stood, moved closer to the bed. She locked his eyes, but when she began to draw the side zipper of her dress slowly downward, his gaze followed that movement. The brandy and cigar were forgotten. He watched everything she did.

She pulled the dress over her head, being careful not to dislodge her wig. She smiled at his expression, turned, walked away with an exaggerated wiggle. She folded the dress atop her trenchcoat.

She turned to face him, hip-sprung, hands on her waist. She sucked in her stomach, thrust her bosom forward. She tilted her head to one side.

"You like?" she said coquettishly.

"Wow," he said shakily. "Oh wow, you're really something. Old Fred really grabbed the brass ring tonight. Come here."

She stood next to the bed. He put his brandy on the bedside table. He touched the band of smooth white skin between bikini and stocking top. She turned back and forth, letting him stroke.

"You're driving me crazy," she said throatily.

She leaned over the bed, her face close to his. He reached up to touch the wig. She drew back.

"Why don't you take off all those clothes?" she whispered. "I have to go make wee-wee and then I'll come back to you. I'll do anything you want. And I mean *anything.*"

He made a grunting sound and reached for her. But she laughed, moved away. She picked up her shoulder bag, went to the bathroom door, turned. He was staring at her. She waggled her fingers at him, disappeared inside.

She locked the door, worked swiftly. She took off sandals, garters, stockings, lingerie. She relieved herself. When she flushed the toilet, she used two sheets of toilet paper to press the tank lever, then watched as the tissue went swirling away.

She opened her bag, made her preparations. Then she just waited, staring at her image in the medicine cabinet mirror. After a while she recognized herself.

She stayed in there until she heard his call:

"Irene? What's keeping you?"

She unlocked the door, opened it a crack, peeked out. He had turned off the overhead light, turned on the bedside lamp. The bedspread and blankets had been thrown off. He was lying back. The sheet was pulled up to his waist. His naked torso was haired and puffy. His plump breasts made almond-shaped shadows. He was smoking his cigar.

She draped one of the hotel bath towels over her right forearm and hand. She switched off the bathroom light.

"Ready or not," she said lightly, "here I come."

He turned to stare at her naked body moving into the cone of lamplight.

"Ah Jesus," he breathed.

She went around to the right side of the bed, away from the table and the lamp. She bent over him, smiling tenderly.

He turned to the left to put his cigar in the ashtray. She lowered her arm, let the towel fall away.

Handling the Swiss Army knife like a dagger, she plunged the big blade into the left side of his fat neck and sawed back toward her.

He made a sound, a gargle, and his heavy body leaped compulsively from the bed. Blood spouted in streams, gobbets, a flood that sprayed the air with a crimson fog. It soaked the bed, dripped onto the floor.

Zoe Kohler threw back the sheet, exposing his pulpy abdomen, veined legs, his flaccid penis and testicles, half-hidden in a nest of grayish-brown hair, tangled.

With bloodied, slippery hand, she drove the knife blade again and again into his genitals. No triumph or exultation in her face. Not grinning or yowling, but intent and businesslike. Saying aloud with each stab, "There. There. There."

2

Former Chief of Detectives Edward X. Delaney had two methods of eating sandwiches.

Those he categorized as "dry" sandwiches—such as roast beef on white or what he termed an interracial sandwich, ham on bagel—were eaten while seated at the kitchen table. The top was spread with the financial section of the previous day's *New York Times.*

The meal finished, crumbs and newspaper were crumpled up and dumped into the step-on garbage can under the sink.

"Wet" sandwiches—such as potato salad and pastrami on rye, with hot English mustard, or brisling sardines with tomato and onion slices slathered with mayonnaise—were eaten while standing bent over the sink. Finished, Delaney ran the hot water and flushed the drippings away.

Both methods of dining were anathema to the Chief's wife, Monica. She never ceased in her efforts to persuade him to adopt more civilized eating habits, even if it was only a midday snack.

Delaney tried to explain to her, as patiently as he could, that he had spent thirty years of his life with the New York Police Department, most of them in the Detective Division. He had become addicted to sandwiches since, considering the long, brutal hours the job demanded, sandwiches consumed while working were usually the only sustenance available.

"But you're retired now!" she would cry.

"Habits are habits," he would reply loftily.

Actually, he loved sandwiches. One of the recurring fantasies of his increasingly onerous retirement was the dream that he might one day compile a slim volume, *Chief Delaney's Sandwich Book.* Who had a better right? Who but he had discovered the glory of cold pork and thinly sliced white radish on pumpernickel?

On the evening of March 19th, Monica Delaney, with the assistance of Mrs. Rebecca Boone, wife of Detective Sergeant Abner Boone, was preparing a buffet for fourteen members of her women's group. The dinner was to be preceded by a psychologist's lecture followed by a general discussion. Then the buffet would be served.

"We're having avocado and cottage cheese salad," Monica said firmly. "Bibb lettuce, cherry tomatoes, cucumbers, little green peppers. There's plenty for you.

And if you don't like that, there's a cheese-and-macaroni casserole ready to pop in the oven, or the cold chicken left over from last night."

"Don't you worry about me," he advised. "I ate so much yesterday, I'd really like to take it easy tonight. I'll just make a sandwich and take that and a bottle of beer into the den. I assure you, I am not going to starve."

In his methodical way, he began his preparations early, before Rebecca Boone arrived and the women got busy in the kitchen. He inspected the contents of the refrigerator, and built two sandwiches from what was available.

One was white meat of chicken with slices of red onion and little discs of pitted black olives. With a small dollop of horseradish sauce. The second was a crude construction of canned Argentine corned beef, the meat red and crumbly, with cucumber slices. On rye. He wrapped both sandwiches in aluminum foil, and thrust them in the back of the refrigerator to chill.

When Rebecca arrived, and soon after that the front doorbell began to ring, Edward X. Delaney hastily retrieved his sandwiches, took a bottle of cold Löwenbräu Dark, and hustled out of the kitchen. He retired to his den, closing the heavy door firmly behind him.

The desk in the study was covered with papers, receipts, letters, vouchers, open notebooks. For the past two weeks, Delaney had been spending a few hours each day working on his federal income tax return. Actually, the Chief was doing the donkey work, assembling totals of income, expenses, deductions, etc. The final return would be prepared by Monica, his second wife.

Monica was the widow of Bernard Gilbert, a victim of Daniel Blank, a random killer Delaney had helped apprehend. The multiple homicides had been brought to an end right there in the room where Delaney was now seated, headquarters for Operation Lombard.

A year after his first wife, Barbara, had died of kidney infection, the Chief had married Monica Gilbert. He had two children, Edward Jr. and Elizabeth, both now married, Liza with twin boys. Monica had two young girls, Mary and Sylvia, now away at boarding school, preparing for college.

Monica's first husband, Gilbert, had been a CPA and tax accountant, and she had taken courses to enable her to assist him in what had started as a kitchen business. She had kept up with annual changes in the tax laws. Delaney was happy to leave to her the task of preparing the final return that each year seemed to become longer and more complex.

Since he didn't want to disturb the papers on his desk, Delaney drew up a wheeled typewriter table. He removed his old Underwood, setting it on the floor with an effort that, he was pleased to note, didn't elicit a grunt.

He then lifted the leaves of the table, locked them in position, and spread the wide surface with newspaper. He unwrapped his sandwiches, uncapped the beer, and settled down in his worn swivel chair.

He took a bite of the corned beef sandwich. Washed it down with a swallow of dark beer. *Then* he grunted.

He donned his reading glasses and set to work, oblivious to the sounds of talk and laughter in the living room outside his door. When you had worked as long as he had in a crowded detective squad room, you learned the trick of closing your ears. You can shut your mouth and your eyes; why not your ears?

He worked steadily, doggedly. He added up their total annual income, for Monica had brought to their marriage an annuity her deceased husband had set up, plus investments in a modest stock portfolio that yielded good dividends although prices were down.

Edward X. Delaney had a generous pension, income from investments in high-yield, tax-exempt New York City bonds which—thank God—had not defaulted, and he had applied for early Social Security. Between them, husband and wife, they were able to live comfortably in a wholly owned refurbished brownstone right next to the 251st Precinct house.

Still, a combined income that would have allowed them to live in comparative luxury ten years ago was now being cruelly eroded by inflation. It had not yet seriously affected their way of life, since neither was profligate, but it was worrisome.

Delaney, going over his check disbursements, saw how much had gone in cash gifts to Eddie Jr., to Liza, and to Liza's children. And how much had gone to clothing and educating Mary and Sylvia. He did not regret a penny of it, but still . . . By the time the two younger girls were ready for college, in a few years, the cost of a university education would probably be $50,000 or more. It was discouraging.

He finished the corned beef sandwich. And the beer. He listened carefully at the door to the living room. He heard the voice of a woman he believed to be the lecturing psychologist.

Judging the time was right, he darted out the door leading to the kitchen. Moving as quietly as he could, he grabbed another beer from the refrigerator, a can of Schlitz this time, and hurried back to his study. He pushed his glasses atop his head. He popped the beer, took a swallow. Took a bite of the chicken sandwich.

He sat slumped, feet up on the corner of his desk. He thought about the children, all the children, Monica's and his. And he thought sadly of the one child they had together, an infant son who died from a respiratory infection after three months of fragile life. The coffin had been so small.

After a while, munching slowly and sipping his beer, he heard the sounds of conversation and vociferous debate coming from the living room. He guessed the lecture was over, the general discussion period was concluding, and soon the avocado and cottage cheese salad would be served. He had been wise to avoid *that!*

The door to the living room opened suddenly. A young woman started in. She saw him, drew back in alarm and confusion.

"Oh!" she said. "I'm sorry. I thought this was . . ."

He lumbered to his feet, smiling.

"Perfectly all right," he said. "What you're probably looking for is out in the hallway, near the front door."

"Thank you," she said. "Sorry to disturb you."

He made a small gesture. She closed the door. He sat down again, and to reassure himself, to convince himself, he tested his skills at observation. He had seen the woman for possibly five seconds.

She was, he recited to himself, a female Caucasian, about thirty-five years old, approximately five feet, six inches tall, weight 120, blondish hair shoulder-length, triangular face with long, thin nose and pouty lips. Wearing gold loop earrings. A loose dress of forest-green wool. Digital watch on her left wrist. Bare legs, no stockings. Loafers. A distinctive lisp in her voice. A Band-Aid on her right shin.

He smiled. Not bad. He could pick her out of a lineup or describe her sufficiently for a police artist to make a sketch. He was still a cop.

God, how he missed it.

He sat brooding, wondering not for the first time if he had made an error in resigning his prestigious position as Chief of Detectives and opting for retirement. His reason then had been the political bullshit connected with the job.

Now he questioned if the political pressures in such high rank were not a natural concomitant. The fact that he could not endure them might have been a weakness. Perhaps a stronger man could have done all he did while resisting the tugs, threats, and plots of a city government of ambitious men and women. And when he could not resist, then compromising to the smallest degree compatible with survival.

Still, he was—

His reverie was interrupted by a light, tentative tap on the door leading to the kitchen.

"Come in," he called.

The door opened.

Edward X. Delaney struggled to his feet, strode across the room, shook the other man's proffered hand.

"Sergeant!" he said, smiling happily.

A few minutes later, Detective Sergeant Abner Boone was seated in a cracked leather club chair. Delaney moved his swivel chair so he could converse with his visitor without the desk being a barrier between them.

The Chief had made a quick trip to the busy kitchen to bring back a bucket of ice and a bottle of soda water for the sergeant, who was an alcoholic who had not touched a drop in two years. Delaney mixed himself a weak highball, straight rye and water.

"I dropped by to pick up Rebecca," Boone explained, "but they're still eating. I hope I'm not disturbing you, sir."

"Not at all," the Chief said genially. He motioned toward his littered desk. "Tax returns. I've had enough for one night. Tell me, what's the feeling about the new PC?"

For about fifteen minutes the two men talked shop, gossiping about Departmental matters. Most of the information came from Boone: who had been promoted, who transferred, who retired.

"They're putting the dicks back in the precincts," he told Delaney. "The special squads just didn't work out."

"I read about it," the Chief said, nodding. "But they're keeping some of the squads, aren't they?"

"A few. That's where I am now. It's a major crime unit working out of Midtown North."

"Good for you," Delaney said warmly. "How many men have you got?"

Boone shifted uncomfortably. "Well, uh, a month ago I had five. Right now I have twenty-four, and they're bringing in a lieutenant tomorrow morning."

The Chief was startled, but tried not to show it. He looked at Boone curiously. The man seemed exhausted, sallow loops below his eyes. His body had fallen in on itself, shrunken with fatigue. He looked in need of forty-eight hours of nothing but sleep and hot food.

Boone was tall, thin, with a shambling walk and floppy gestures. He had gingery hair, a pale and freckled complexion. He was probably getting on to forty by now, but he still had a shy, awkward, farmerish manner, a boyish and charming smile.

Delaney had worked with him on the Victor Maitland homicide and knew what a good detective he was when he was off the booze. Boone had a slow but analytical and thorough mind. He accepted the boredom and frustrations of his job without complaint. When raw courage was demanded, he could be a tiger.

The Chief inspected him narrowly. He noted the slight tremor of the slender fingers. It couldn't be booze. Rebecca had married him only after he had vowed never to touch the stuff again. Delaney couldn't believe that Boone would risk what was apparently a happy marriage.

"Sergeant," he said finally, "I've got to tell you: you look like death warmed over. What's wrong?"

Boone set his empty glass on the rug alongside his chair. He sat hunched over, forearms on his bony knees, his long hands clasping and unclasping. He looked up at Delaney.

"We've got a repeater," he said. "Homicide."

The Chief stared at him, then took a slow sip of his highball.

"You're sure?" he asked.

Boone nodded.

"Only two so far," he said, "but it's the same MO; no doubt about it. We've kept a lid on it so far, but it's only a question of time before some smart reporter puts the two together."

"Two similar killings?" Delaney said doubtfully. "Could be coincidence."

The sergeant sighed, straightened up. He lit a cigarette, holding it in tobacco-stained fingers. He sat back, crossed and recrossed his gangly legs.

"Maybe we're antsy," he acknowledged. "But ever since that Son of Sam thing, everyone in the Department's been super-alert for repeat homicides. We should have been onto the Son of Sam killings earlier. It took Ballistics to tip us off. Now maybe we're all too eager to put together two unconnected snuffings and yell, 'Mass killer!' But not in this case. These two are identical."

Chief Edward X. Delaney stared at him, but not seeing him. He felt the familiar tingle, the excitement, the challenge. More than that, he felt the anger and the resolve.

"Want to tell me about it?" he asked Boone.

"Do I ever!" Boone said fervently. "Maybe you'll see something we've missed."

"I doubt that very much," Delaney said. "But try me."

Detective Sergeant Abner Boone recited the facts in a rapid staccato, toneless, as if reporting to a superior officer. It was obvious he had been living with this investigation for many long hours; his recital never faltered.

"First homicide: February fifteenth, this year. Victim: male Caucasian, fifty-four years old, found stabbed to death in Room 914 of the Grand Park Hotel. Naked body discovered by chambermaid at approximately 9:45 A.M. Victim had throat cut open and multiple stab wounds in the genitals. Cause of death according to autopsy: exsanguination. That first throat slash didn't kill him. Weapon: a sharp instrument about three inches long."

"Three inches!" Delaney cried. "My God, that's a pocket knife, a jackknife!"

"Probably," Boone said, nodding. "Maximum width of the blade was about three-quarters of an inch, according to the ME who did the cut-'em-up."

The sergeant picked up his glass from the floor, began to chew on the ice cubes. Now that he was talking, he seemed to relax. His speech slowed, became more discursive.

"So the chambermaid knocks and goes in to clean," he continued. "She's an old dame who doesn't see too good. She's practically alongside the bed, standing in the blood, when she sees him. She lets out a scream and faints, right into the mess. A porter comes running. After him come two hotel guests passing in the corridor. The porter calls the security man, using the room phone of course, and ruining any prints. The security man comes running with his assistant, and he calls the manager who comes running with *his* assistant. Finally someone has enough brains to call 911. By the time the first blues got there, there's like maybe ten people milling about in the room. Instant hysteria. Beautiful. I got there about the same time the Crime Scene Unit men showed up. They were furious, and I don't blame them. You could have galloped the Seventh Cavalry through that room and not done any more damage."

"These things happen," Delaney said sympathetically.

"I suppose so," Boone said, sighing, "but we sure weren't overwhelmed with what you might call clues. The victim was a guy named George T. Puller, from Denver. A wholesale jewelry salesman. His line was handmade silver things set with turquoise and other semiprecious stones. He was in town for a jewelry show being held right there at the Grand Park. It was his second night in New York."

"Forced entry?"

"No sign," Boone said.

He explained that Room 914 was equipped with a split-lock—half spring-latch and half dead-bolt. The door locked automatically when closed, but the dead-bolt could only be engaged by a turn of the key after exiting or by a thumb knob inside.

"When the chambermaid came in," Boone said, "the spring-latch was locked, but not the dead-bolt. That looks like the killer exited and just pulled the door closed."

Delaney agreed.

"No signs of fiddling on the outside of the lock," Boone went on. "And the Crime Scene Unit took that mother apart. No scratches on the tumblers, no oil, no wax. So the chances are good the lock hadn't been picked; George T. Puller invited his killer inside."

"You went through the drill, I suppose," the Chief said. "Friends, business acquaintances? Personal enemies? A feud? Business problems? A jealous partner?"

"*And* hotel guests," the sergeant said wearily. "*And* hotel staff. *And* bartenders and waiters in the cocktail lounge and dining room on the lobby floor. A lot of 'Well, perhaps . . .' and 'Maybes . . .' But it all added up to zip. With the jewelry show and all, the hotel was crowded that night. The last definite contact was with two other salesmen in the jewelry show hospitality suite. That was about seven P.M. Then the three men split. Puller told the others he was going to wander around, find a place that served a good steak, and turn in early. They never saw him again.

"The CSU found a lot of prints, but mostly partials and smears. They're still working on elimination prints. My God, Chief, in that hotel room you've got to figure all the people who crowded in there after the body was discovered, plus the hotel staff, plus people who stayed in the room before Puller checked in. Hopeless. But we're still working on it."

"You've got no choice," Delaney said stonily.

"Right. One other thing: The Crime Scene Unit took the bathroom apart. They found blood in the bathtub drain. Not enough for a positive make, but the Lab Services Unit thinks it's the victim's blood. Same type and also, the victim was on Thorazine, and it showed up in the blood taken from the drain."

"Thorazine? What the hell was he taking that for?"

"You're not going to believe this, but he had bad attacks of hiccups. The Thorazine helped. Anyway, it's almost certain it was his blood in the drain, and no one else's. There was no way he was going to get from that bed to the bathroom, take a shower, and then go back to bed to bleed to death. So it had to be the killer—right? Covered with blood. Takes a shower to wash it off. Then makes an exit."

"No hairs in the drain? Hairs that didn't belong to the victim?"

"Nothing," Boone said mournfully. "We should be so lucky!"

"A damp towel?" the Chief asked.

Boone smiled, for the first time.

"You don't miss a thing, do you, sir? No, there was no damp towel. But one of the hotel's bath towels was missing. I figure the killer took it along."

"Probably," Delaney said. "A smart apple."

Sergeant Boone, intent again, serious, leaned forward.

"Chief," he said, "I think I've given you everything I had on the Puller homicide in the first couple of days. If you had caught the squeal, how would you have handled it? The reason I ask is that I'm afraid I blew it. Well, maybe not blew it, but spent too much time charging off in the wrong direction. How would you have figured it?"

Edward X. Delaney was silent a moment. Then he got to his feet, went over to the liquor cabinet. He mixed himself another highball, using the last of the ice in the bucket.

"Another club soda?" he asked Boone. "Coffee? Anything?"

"No, thanks, sir. I'm fine."

"I'm going to have a cigar. How about you?"

"I'll pass, thank you. Stick to these."

Boone shook another cigarette from his pack. The Chief held a light for him, then used the same wooden match for his cigar.

From the living room and hallway, they heard the sounds of departing guests: cries and laughter, the front door slamming. Monica Delaney opened the door to the kitchen and poked her head in.

"They're leaving," she announced, "but it'll take another hour to clean up."

"Need any help?" the Chief asked.

"What if I said, 'Yes'?"

"I'd say, 'No.' "

"Grouch," she said, and withdrew.

Delaney sat down heavily in his swivel chair. He tilted back, puffing his cigar, staring at the ceiling.

"What would I have done?" he asked. "I'd have figured it just as you probably did. Going by percentages. A salesman in New York for a convention or sales meeting or whatever. He goes out on the town by himself. He finds that good steak he was looking for. Has a few drinks. Maybe a bottle of wine. More drinks."

Boone interrupted. "That's what the stomach contents showed."

"He wanders around," Delaney continued. "Visits a few rough joints. Picks up a prostitute, brings her back to his room. Maybe they had a fight about money. Maybe he wanted something kinky, and she wouldn't play. She's got a knife in her purse. Most hookers carry them. He gets ugly, and she offs him. That's the way I would have figured it. Didn't you?"

Abner Boone exhaled a great sigh of relief.

"Exactly," he said. "I figured the same scenario. A short-bladed knife—that's a woman's weapon. And the killer had to be naked when Puller was killed. Otherwise, why the shower and missing towel? So I started the wheels turning. We picked up a zillion hookers, as far west as Eleventh Avenue. We alerted all our whore and pimp snitches. Hit every bar in midtown Manhattan and flashed Puller's photograph. Zilch. Then I began to wonder if we weren't wasting our time. Because of something I haven't told you. Something I didn't find out myself for sure until three days after the body was found."

"What's that?"

"Puller wasn't rolled. He had an unlocked sample case in the room with about twenty G's of silver and turquoise jewelry. Nothing taken. He had a wallet filled with cash and credit cards. All still there. We went back over his movements since he left Denver. His wife and partner knew how much he was carrying. We figured how much he would spend in one day and two nights in New York. It came out right. It was all there. He wasn't rolled."

Edward X. Delaney stared a moment, then shook his massive head from side to side.

"It doesn't listen," he said angrily. "A prostie would have taken him. For *something.* She didn't panic because she was smart enough to shower away his blood before she left. So why didn't she fleece him?"

The sergeant threw his hands in the air.

"Beats the hell out of me," he said bitterly. "It just doesn't figure. And there's another thing that doesn't make sense: there was no sign of a struggle. Absolutely none. Nothing under Puller's fingernails. No hairs other than his on the bed. The guy was fifty-four, sure, but he was heavy and muscular. If he had a fight with a whore, and she comes after him with a shiv, he's going to do *something*—right? Roll out of bed, smack her, throw a lamp—*something.* But there is no evidence he put up any resistance at all. Just lay there happily and let her slit his throat. How do you figure *that?*"

"Wasn't unconscious, was he?"

"The Lab Services Unit did the blood alcohol level and says he was about half-drunk, but unconsciousness would be highly improbable."

Then both men were silent, staring blankly at each other. Finally . . .

"You mentioned his wife," Delaney said. "Children?"

"Three," Boone said.

"Shit."

Boone nodded sadly.

"Anyway, Chief, they gave me more men, and we've really been hacking it. Out-of-town visitor in New York for a sales meeting gets stiffed in a midtown hotel. You can imagine the flak the Commissioner has been getting—from the hotel association and tourist bureau right up through a Deputy Mayor."

"I can imagine," Delaney said.

"All right," the sergeant said, "that was the first killing. Listen, Chief, are you sure I'm not disturbing you? I don't want to bore you silly with my problems."

"No, no, you're not boring me. Besides, our other choice is to go out and help Rebecca and Monica clean up the mess. You want to do that?"

"God forbid!" Boone said. "I'll just keep crying on your shoulder. Well, the second homicide was six days ago."

"How many days between killings?" the Chief said sharply.

"Uh . . . twenty-seven, sir. Is that important?"

"Might be. Same MO?"

"Practically identical. The victim's name was Frederick Wolheim, male Caucasian, fifty-six, stabbed to death in Room 3015 of the Hotel Pierce, that new palace on Sixth Avenue. Naked, throat slit, multiple stab wounds in the genitals. This time the victim died from that first slash. The killer got the carotid and the jugular. Blood? You wouldn't believe! A swimming pool. The—"

"Wait a minute," Delaney interrupted. "Those stab wounds in the genitals—vicious?"

"Very. The ME counted at least twenty in each case, and then gave up and called them 'multiple.' Delivered with force. A few wounds in the lower groin showed bruise marks indicating the killer's knuckles had slammed into the surrounding skin."

"I'm aware of what bruise marks indicate," Edward X. Delaney said.

"Oh," Boone said, abashed. "Sorry, sir. Well, this time everything went off all right. I mean, as far as protecting the murder scene. Wolheim was supposed to deliver a speech at a morning meeting of marketing managers of electrical appliances. It was a convention being held at the Pierce. When he didn't show up on time, the guy who had organized the program came up to his room looking for him. He got the chambermaid to open the door. They took one look, slammed the door, and called hotel security. The security man took one look, slammed the door, and called us. When my crew got there, and the Crime Scene Unit showed up, it was virgin territory, untouched by human hands. The security guy was standing guard outside the door."

"Good man," Delaney said.

"Ex-cop," Boone said, grinning. "But it wasn't all that much help. The Hotel Pierce is new, just opened last November, so the print problem was a little easier. But the CSU found nothing but Wolheim's prints and the chambermaid's. So the killer must have been very careful or smeared everything. Before he died, the victim had been drinking a brandy. His prints were on the glass and on the bottle on the dresser. There was another glass with a small shot of brandy on a table next to an armchair. Wolheim's prints on that. No one else's."

"The door?" the Chief asked.

"Here's where it gets cute," Boone said. "No keyhole showing on the outside."

He explained how the new electric locks worked. The door was opened by the insertion of a coded magnetic card into an outside slot. When closed, the door locked automatically. It was even necessary to insert the card into an inside slot when exiting from the room.

"A good security system," he told Delaney. "It's cut way down on hotel B-and-E's. They don't care if you don't turn in the card when you leave because the magnetic code for the lock is changed when a guest checks out, and a new card issued. No way for a locksmith to duplicate the code."

"There must be a passcard for all the rooms," the Chief said.

"Oh sure. Held by the Security Section. The chambermaids have cards only for the rooms on the floor they service."

"Well," Delaney said grudgingly, "it sounds good, but sooner or later some wise-ass will figure out how to beat it. But the important thing is that the killer couldn't have left Wolheim's room without putting the card in the slot on the inside of the door. Have I got that right?"

"Right," Boone said, nodding. "The card had apparently been used to open the door, then it was tossed on top of a bureau. It's white plastic that would take nice prints, but it had been wiped clean."

"I told you," the Chief said with some satisfaction. "You're up against a smart apple. Any signs of a fight?"

"None," Boone reported. "The ME says Wolheim must have died almost instantly. Certairly in a second or two after his throat was ripped. Chief, I saw him. It looked like his head was ready to fall off."

Delaney took a deep breath, then a swallow of his highball. He could imagine how the victim looked; he had seen similar cases. It took awhile before you learned to look and not vomit.

"Anything taken?" he asked.

"Not as far as we could tell. He had a fat wallet. Cash and travelers checks. Credit cards. All there. A gold wristwatch worth at least one big one. A pinkie ring with a diamond as big as the Ritz. Untouched."

"Son of a bitch!" Delaney said angrily. "It doesn't make sense. Anything from routine?"

"Nothing, and we've questioned more than 200 people so far. That Hotel Pierce is a city, a *city!* No one remembers seeing him with anyone. His last contact was with some convention buddies. They had dinner right there in the hotel. Then his pals wanted to go down to the traps in Greenwich Village, but Wolheim split. As far as we've been able to discover, they were the last to see him alive."

"Was he married?"

"Yes. Five children. He was from Akron, Ohio. The cops out there broke the news. Rather them than me."

"I know what you mean." Delaney was silent a moment, brooding. Then: "Any connection between the two men—Puller and Wolheim?"

"We're working on that right now. It doesn't look good. As far as we can tell, they didn't even know each other, weren't related even distantly, never even met, for God's sake! Went to different schools. Served in different branches of the armed forces. If there's a connection, we haven't found it. They had nothing in common."

"Sure they did."

"What's that?"

"They were both men. And in their mid-fifties."

"Well . . . yeah," Boone acknowledged. "But Chief, if someone is trying to knock off every man in his mid-fifties in Manhattan, we got real trouble."

"Not *every* man," the Chief said. "Out-of-towners in the city for a convention, staying at a midtown hotel."

"How does that help, sir?"

"It doesn't," Delaney said. "But it's interesting. Did the Crime Scene Unit come up with anything?"

"No unidentified prints. But they took the bathroom apart again. This time there were traces of the victim's blood in the trap under the sink, so I guess the killer didn't have to take a shower. Just used the sink."

"Towel missing again?"

"That's right. But the important thing is that they found hairs. Three of them. One on the pillow near the victim's head. Two on the back of the armchair. Black hairs. Wolheim had reddish-gray hair."

"Well, my God, that's *something.* What did the lab men say?"

"Nylon. From a wig. Too long to be from a toupee."

Delaney blew out his breath. He stared at the sergeant. "The plot thickens," he said.

"Thickens?" Boone cried. "It curdles!"

"It could still be a hooker."

"Could be," the sergeant agreed. "Or a gay in drag. Or a transvestite. Anyway, the wig is a whole new ballgame. We've got pretty good relations with the gays these days, and they're cooperating—asking around and trying to turn up something. And of course we have some undercover guys they don't know about. And we're covering the black leather joints. Maybe it was a transvestite, and the victims didn't know it until they were in bed with a man. Some of those guys are so beautiful they could fool their mother."

Edward X. Delaney pondered awhile, frowning down into his empty highball glass.

"Well . . ." he said, "maybe. Was the penis cut off?"

"No."

"In all the homosexual killings I handled, the cock was hacked off."

"I talked to a sergeant in the Sex Crimes Analysis Unit, and that's what he said. But he doesn't rule out a male killer."

"I don't either."

Then the two men were silent, each looking down, busy with his own thoughts. They heard Rebecca Boone laughing in the kitchen. They heard the clash of pots and pans. Comforting domestic noises.

"Chief," Sergeant Boone said finally, "what do you think we've got here?"

Delaney looked up.

"You want me to guess? That's all I can do—guess. I'd guess it's the start of a series of random killings. Motive unknown for the moment. The more I think about it, the more reasonable it seems that your perp is a male. I never heard of a female random killer."

"You think he'll hit again?"

"I'd figure on it," Delaney advised. "If it follows the usual pattern, the periods between killings will become shorter and shorter. Not always. Look at the Yorkshire Ripper. But usually the random killer gets caught up in a frenzy, and hits faster and faster. Going by the percentages, he should kill again in about three weeks. You better cover the midtown hotels."

"How?" Boone said desperately. "With an army? And if we alert all the hotels' security sections, the word is going to get around that New York has a new Son of Sam. There goes the convention business and the tourist trade."

Edward X. Delaney looked at him without expression.

"That's not your worry, sergeant," he said tonelessly. "Your job is to nab a murderer."

"Don't you think I know that?" Boone demanded. "But you've got no idea of the pressure to keep this thing under wraps."

"I've got a very good idea," the Chief said softly. "I lived with it for thirty years."

But the sergeant would not be stopped.

"Just before I came over here," he said angrily, "I got a call from Deputy Commissioner Thorsen, and he . . ." His voice trailed away.

Delaney straightened up, leaned forward.

"Ivar?" he said. "Is he in on this?"

Boone nodded, somewhat shamefacedly.

"Did he tell you to brief me on the homicides?"

"He didn't exactly *tell* me, Chief. He called to let me know about the lieutenant who was taking over. I told him I was beat, and I was taking off. I happened to mention I was coming over here to pick up Rebecca, and he suggested it wouldn't do any harm to fill you in."

Delaney smiled grimly.

"If I did anything wrong, sir, I apologize."

"You didn't do anything wrong, sergeant. No apologies necessary."

"To tell you the truth, I need all the help on this I can get."

"So does Deputy Commissioner Thorsen," Delaney said dryly. "Who's the loot coming in?"

"Slavin. Marty Slavin. You know him?"

Delaney thought a moment.

"A short, skinny man?" he asked. "With a mean, pinched-up face? Looks like a ferret?"

"That's the guy," Boone said.

"Sergeant," the Chief said solemnly, "you have my sympathy."

The door to the living room burst open. Monica Delaney stood there, hands on her hips, challenging.

"All right, you guys," she said. "That's enough shop talk and 'Remember whens . . .' for one night. Coffee and cake in the living room. Right now. Let's go."

They rose smiling and headed out.

At the door, Sergeant Abner Boone paused.

"Chief," he said in a low voice, "any suggestions? Anything at all that I haven't done and should do?"

Edward X. Delaney saw the fatigue and worry in the man's face. With Lieutenant Martin Slavin coming in to take over command, Boone had cause for worry.

"Decoys," the Chief said. "If they won't let you alert the hotels, then put out decoys. Say between the hours of seven P.M. and midnight. Dress them like salesmen from out of town. Guys in their early fifties. Loud, beefy, flashing money. Have them cruise bars and hotel cocktail lounges. Probably a waste of time, but you never can tell."

"I'll do it," the sergeant said promptly. "I'll request the manpower tomorrow."

"Call Thorsen," Delaney advised. "He'll get you what you need. And sergeant, if I were you, I'd get the decoy thing rolling before Slavin shows up. Make sure everyone knows it was your idea."

"Yes. I'll do that. Uh, Chief, if this guy hits again like you figure, and I get the squeal, would you be willing to come over to the scene? You know—just to look around. I keep thinking there might be something we're missing."

Delaney smiled at him. "Sure. Give me a call, and I'll be there. It'll be like old times."

"Thank you, Chief," Boone said gratefully. "You've been a great help."

"I have?" Delaney said, secretly amused, and they went in for coffee and cake.

Chief Edward X. Delaney inspected the living room critically. It had been tidied in satisfactory fashion. Ashtrays had been cleaned, footstools were where they belonged. His favorite club chair was in its original position.

He turned to see his wife regarding him mockingly.

"Does it pass inspection, O lord and master?" she inquired.

"Nice job," he said, nodding. "You can come to work for me anytime."

"I don't do windows," she said.

The oak cocktail table had been set with coffeepot, creamer, sugar, cups, saucers, dessert plates, cutlery. And half a pineapple cheesecake.

"Ab," Rebecca Boone said, "the coffee is decaf, so you won't have any trouble sleeping tonight."

He grunted.

"And the cheesecake is low-cal," Monica said, looking at her husband.

"Liar," he said cheerfully. "I'm going to have a thin slice anyway."

They helped themselves, then settled back with their coffee and cake. Delaney was ensconced in his club chair, Sergeant Boone in a smaller armchair. The two women sat on the sofa.

"Good cake," the Chief said approvingly. "Rich, but light. Where did you get it?"

"Clara Webster made it," Monica said. "She insisted on leaving what was left."

"How did the meeting go?" Boone asked.

"Very well," Monica said firmly. "Interesting and—and instructive. Didn't you think so, Rebecca?"

"Absolutely," Mrs. Boone said loyally. "I really enjoyed the discussion after the lecture."

"What was the lecture about?" Boone said.

Monica Delaney raised her chin, glanced defiantly at her husband.

"The Preorgasmic Woman," Monica said.

"Good God!" the Chief said, and the two women burst out laughing.

"Monica told me you'd say that," Rebecca explained.

"Oh she did, did she?" Delaney said. "Well, I think it's a natural, normal reaction. What, exactly, is a Preorgasmic Woman?"

"It's obvious, isn't it?" Monica said. "It's a woman who has never had an orgasm."

"A frigid woman?" Boone said.

"Typical male reaction," his wife scoffed.

" 'Frigid' is a pejorative word," Mrs. Delaney said. "A loaded word. Actually, 'frigid' means being averse to sex, applying to both men and women. But the poor men, with their fragile little egos, couldn't stand the thought of there being a sexless male, so they've used the word 'frigid' to describe only women. But our speaker tonight said there is no such irreversible condition in men or women. They're just preorgasmic. Through therapy training, they can achieve orgasmic sexuality."

"And assume their rightful place in society," Chief Delaney added with heavy irony.

Monica refused to rise to the bait. She was aware that he was proud of her activities in the feminist movement. They might have discussions that sometimes degenerated into bitter arguments. But Monica knew that his willingness to debate was better than his saying, "Yes, dear . . . Yes, dear . . . Yes, dear," with his nose stuck in the obituary page of *The New York Times.*

And he *was* proud of her. Following the death of their infant son, she had gone into such a guilt-ridden depression that he had despaired of her sanity and tried to steel himself to the task of urging her to seek professional help.

But she was a strong woman and had pulled herself up. The presence of her two young girls helped, of course; their needs, problems, and demands could not be met if she continued to sit in a darkened room, weeping.

And after they went away to school, she had found an outlet for her physical energy and mental inquisitiveness in the feminist movement. She embarked on a whirlwind of meetings, lectures, symposiums, picketings, petition-signing, letter-writing, and neighborhood betterment.

Edward X. Delaney was delighted. It gave him joy to see her alive, flaming, eager to advance a cause in which she believed. If she brought her "job" home with her, it was no more than he had done when he was on active duty.

He had discussed all his cases with Monica and with Barbara, his first wife. Both had listened patiently, understood, and frequently offered valuable advice.

But admiring Monica's ardor for the feminist cause didn't mean he had to agree with all the tenets she espoused. Some he did; some he did not. And he'd be damned if he'd be reticent about expressing his opinion.

Now, sitting across from his wife as she chatted with the Boones, he acknowledged, not for the first time, how lucky he had been with the women in his life.

Monica Delaney was a heavy-bodied woman, with a good waist between wide shoulders and broad hips. Her bosom was full, her legs tapered to slender ankles. There was a soft sensuality about her, a physical warmth. Her ardor was not totally mental.

Thick black hair, with a sheen, was combed back from a wide, unlined brow and fell almost to her shoulders. She made no effort to pluck her solid eyebrows, and her makeup was minimal. She was a big, definite woman, capable of tenderness and tears.

Watching his wife's animation as she talked to the Boones, Edward X. Delaney felt familiar stirrings and wished his guests gone. Monica turned her head suddenly to look at him. As usual, she caught his mood. She winked.

"Tell me, Chief," Rebecca said in her ingenuous way, "what do you *really* think of the women's movement?"

He kept his eyes resolutely averted from Monica, and addressed his remarks directly to Rebecca.

"What do I *really* think?" he repeated. "Well, I have no quarrel with most of the aims."

"I know," she said, sighing resignedly. "Equal pay for equal work."

"No, no," he said quickly. "Monica has taught me better than that. Equal pay for *comparable* work."

His wife nodded approvingly.

"And what do you object to?" Rebecca asked pertly.

He marshaled his thoughts.

"Not objections," he said slowly. "Two reservations. The first is no fault of the feminist movement. It's a characteristic of all minority or subjugated groups that desire to be treated as individuals, not stereotypes. No argument there. But to achieve that aim, they must organize. Then, to obtain political and economic power, they must project as—as monolithic a front as they can. The blacks, Chicanos, Indians, Italian-Americans, women—whatever. To wield maximum power, they must form a group, association, bloc, and speak with a single, strong voice. Again, no argument.

"But by doing that, they become—or at least this is their public image—less individuals and more stereotypes. They become capitalized Women, Blacks, and so forth. There is a contradiction there, a basic conflict. Frankly, I don't know how it can be resolved—if it can. If the answer is fragmentation, allowing the widest possible expressions of opinion within the bloc, then they sacrifice most of the social, political, and economic power which was the reason for their organizing in the first place."

"Do you think I'm a feminist stereotype?" Monica said hotly.

"No, I do not," he replied calmly. "But only because I know you, am married to you, live with you. But can you deny that since the current women's movement started—when was it, about fifteen years ago?—a stereotype of the feminist has been evolving?"

Monica Delaney slammed her palm down on the top of the cocktail table. Empty coffee cups rattled on their saucers.

"You're infuriating!" she said.

"That's true," he said equably.

"What's the second thing?" Rebecca Boone said hastily, thinking to avert a family squabble. "You said you had two objections to the feminist movement. What's the second?"

"Not objections," he reminded her. "Reservations. The second is this:

"Women in the feminist movement are working to achieve equality of opportunity, equal pay, and the same chances for advancement offered to men in business, government, industry, and so forth. Fine. But have you really thought through what you call 'equality' might entail?

"Look at poor Sergeant Boone there—dead to the world." The sergeant grinned feebly. "I'd guess he's been working eighteen hours a day for the past six weeks. Maybe grabbing a catnap now and then. Greasy food when he can find the time to eat. Under pressures you cannot imagine.

"Rebecca, have you seen him as often as you'd like in the last six weeks? Have you had a decent dinner with him? Gone out to a show? Or just a quiet evening at home? Have you even known where he's been, the dangers he's been facing? My guess would be that you have not.

"You think your husband enjoys living this way? But he's a professional cop, and he does the best he can. Would you like a comparable job with all its demands and stress and strain and risk? I don't believe it.

"What I'm trying to say is that I don't believe that feminists fully realize what they're asking for. You don't knock down a wall until you know what's behind it. There are dangers, drawbacks, and responsibilities you're not aware of."

"We're willing to accept those responsibilities," Rebecca Boone said stoutly.

"Are you?" the Chief said with gentle sarcasm. "Are you really? Are you willing to charge into a dark alley after some coked-up addict armed with a machete? Are you willing to serve in the armed forces in combat and go forward when you know your chances of survival are practically nil?

"On a more prosaic level, are you willing to work the hours that a fast-track business executive does? Willing to meet the demands of bosses and workers, make certain your schedules are met, stay within budget, turn a profit—and risk peptic ulcers, lung cancer, alcoholism, and keeling over from a coronary or cerebral hemorrhage at the age of forty?

"Look, I'm not saying all men's jobs are like that. A lot of men can handle the pressures of a top-level position and go home every night and water the petunias. They die in bed at a ripe old age. But just as many crack up, mentally or physically. The upper echelons of the establishment to which women aspire produce a frightening percentage of broken, impotent, or just burned-out men. Is that the equality you want?"

Rebecca Boone was usually a placid dumpling of a woman. But now she exhibited an uncharacteristic flash of anger.

"Let *us* be the judge of what makes us happy," she snapped. "That's what the movement is all about."

Just as surprising, Monica Delaney didn't react with scorn and fury to her husband's words.

"Edward," she said, "there's a lot of truth in what you said. It's not *all* true, but there's truth in it."

"So?" he said.

"So," she said, "we recognize that when women achieve their rightful position in the upper levels of the establishment, they will be subject to the same strains, stresses, and pressures that men endure. But does it have to be that way? We don't think so. We believe the system can be changed, or at least modified, so that success doesn't necessarily mean peptic ulcers, coronaries, and cerebral hemorrhages. The system, the highly competitive, dog-eat-dog system, isn't carved on tablets of stone brought down from a mountain. It was created by men. It can be changed by liberated men—and women."

He stared at her.

"And when do you figure this paradise is going to come about?"

"Not in our lifetime," she admitted. "It's a long way down the road. But the first step is to get women into positions of power where they can influence the future of our society."

"Bore from within?" he said.

"Sometimes you're nasty," she said, smiling. "But the idea is right. Yes. Influence the system by becoming an integral part of it. First comes equality. Then liberation. For both women and men."

Sergeant Abner Boone rose shakily to his feet.

"Listen," he said hoarsely, "this is really interesting, and I'd like to stay and hear some more. But I'm so beat, I'm afraid I'll disgrace myself by falling asleep. Rebecca, I think we better take off."

She went over, took his arm, looked at him anxiously.

"Sure, hon," she said, "we'll go. I'll drive."

Chief Delaney went for hats and coats. The women kissed. The men shook hands. Farewells were exchanged, promises to get together again as soon as possible. The Delaneys stood inside their open front door, watched as the Boones got into their car and drove off, waving.

Then the Chief closed the front door, double-locked and chained it. He turned to face his wife.

"Alone at last," he said.

She looked at him.

"You covered yourself with glory tonight, buster," she said.

"Thank you," he said.

She glared, then burst out laughing. She took him into her strong arms. They were close, close. She drew back.

"What would I do without you?" she said. "I'll stack the dishes; you close up."

He made the rounds. He did it every night: barring the castle, flooding the moat, hauling up the drawbridge. He started in the attic and worked his way down to the basement. He checked every lock on every door, every latch on every window. This nightly duty didn't seem silly to him; he had been a New York cop.

When he had finished this chore, he turned off the lights downstairs, leaving on the outside stoop light and a dim lamp in the hallway. Then he climbed the stairs to the second-floor bedroom. Monica was turning down the beds.

He sat down heavily in a fragile, cretonne-covered boudoir chair. He bent over, began to unlace his thick-soled, ankle-high shoes of black kangaroo leather, polished to a high gloss. He didn't know of a single old cop who didn't have trouble with his feet.

"Was it really a good meeting?" he asked his wife.

"So-so," she said, flipping a palm back and forth. "Pretty basic stuff. The lecture, I mean. But everyone seemed interested. And they ate. My God, did they eat! What did you have?"

"A sandwich and a beer."

"Two sandwiches and two beers. I counted. Edward, you've got to stop gorging on sandwiches. You're getting as big as a house."

"More of me to love," he said, rising to his bare feet, beginning to strip off his jacket and vest.

"What does that mean?" she demanded. "That when you weigh 300 pounds I won't be able to contain my passion?"

They both undressed slowly, moving back and forth, to the closet, their dressers, the bathroom. They exchanged disconnected remarks, yawning.

"Poor Abner," he said. "Did you get a close look at him? He's out on his feet."

"I wish Rebecca wouldn't wear green," she said. "It makes her skin look sallow."

"The cheesecake was good," he offered.

"Rebecca said she's lucky if she sees him three hours a day."

"Remind me to buy more booze; we're getting low."

"You think the cheesecake was as good as mine?"

"No," he lied. "Good, but not as good as yours."

"I'll make you one."

"Make *us* one. Strawberry, please."

He sat on the edge of his bed in his underdrawers. Around his thick neck was a faded ring of blue: a remembrance of the days when New York cops wore the old choker collars. He watched his wife become naked.

"You've lost a few pounds," he said.

"Does it show?" she said, pleased.

"It does indeed. Your waist . . ."

She regarded herself in the full-length mirror on the closet door.

"Well . . ." she said doubtfully, "maybe a pound or two. Edward, we've got to go on a diet."

"Sure."

"No more sandwiches for you."

He sighed.

"You never give up, do you?" he said wonderingly. "You'll never admit defeat. Never admit that you're married to the most stubborn man in the world."

"I'll keep nudging you," she vowed.

"Lots of luck," he said. "Have you heard from Karen Thorsen lately?"

"As a matter of fact, she called yesterday. Didn't I tell you?"

"No."

"Well, she did. Wants to get together with us. I told her I'd talk to you and set a time."

"Uh-huh."

Something in his tone alerted her. She finished pulling the blue cotton nightgown over her head. She smoothed it down, then looked at him.

"What's it about?" she said. "Does Ivar want to see you?"

"I don't know," he said. "All he has to do is pick up the phone."

She guessed. She was so shrewd.

"What did you and Abner talk about—a case?"

"Yes," he said.

"Can you tell me about it?"

"Sure," he said.

"Wait'll I cream my face," she said. "Don't fall asleep first."

"I won't," he promised.

While she was in the bathroom, he got into his flannel pajama pants with a drawstring top. He sat on the edge of his bed, longing for a cigar but lighting one of Monica's low-tar cigarettes. It didn't taste like anything.

He was a rude, blocky man who lumbered when he walked. His iron-gray hair was cut *en brosse.* His deeply lined, melancholy features had the broody look of a man who hoped for the best and expected the worst.

He had the solid, rounded shoulders of a machine-gunner, a torso that still showed old muscle under new fat. His large, yellowed teeth, the weathered face, the body bearing scars of old wounds—all gave the impression of a beast no longer with the swiftness of youth, but with the cunning of years, and vigor enough to kill.

He sat there solidly, smoking his toy cigarette. He watched his wife get into bed, prop her back against the headboard. She pulled sheet and blanket up to her waist.

"All right," she said. "Tell."

But first he went to his bedside table. It held, among other things, his guns, cuffs, a sap, and other odds and ends he had brought home when he had cleaned out his desk at the old headquarters building on Centre Street.

It also contained a bottle of brandy and two cut-glass snifters. He poured Monica and himself healthy shots.

"Splendid idea," she said.

"Better than pills," he said. "We'll sleep like babies."

He sat on the edge of her bed; she drew aside to make room for him. They raised their glasses to each other, took small sips.

"Plasma," he said.

He then recounted to her what Sergeant Boone had told him of the two hotel murders. He tried to keep his report as brief and succinct as possible. When he described the victims' wounds, Monica's face whitened, but she didn't ask him to stop. She just took a hefty belt of her brandy.

"So," he concluded, "that's what Boone's got—which isn't a whole hell of a lot. Now you know why he was so down tonight, and so exhausted. He's been going all out on this for the past month."

"Why haven't I read anything about it in the papers?" Monica asked.

"They're trying to keep a lid on it—which is stupid, but understandable. They don't want a rerun of the Son of Sam hysteria. Also, tourism is big business in this town. Maybe the biggest, for all I know. You can imagine what headlines like HOTEL KILLER ON LOOSE IN MANHATTAN would do to the convention trade."

"Maybe Abner will catch the killer."

"Maybe," he said doubtfully. "With a lucky break. But I don't think he'll do it on the basis of what he's got now. It's just too thin. Also, he's got another problem: they're bringing in Lieutenant Martin Slavin to take command of the investigation. Slavin is a little prick. An ambitious conniver who always covers his ass by going strictly by the book. Boone will have his hands full with him."

"Why are they bringing in someone over Boone? Hasn't Abner been doing a good job?"

"I know the sergeant's work," the Chief said, taking a sip of brandy. "He's a good, thorough detective. I believe that he's done all that could be done. But they've got—what did he tell me?—about twenty-five men working on this thing now, so I guess they feel they need higher rank in command. But I do assure you, Slavin's not going to break this thing. Unless there's another homicide and the killer slips up."

"You think there will be another one, Edward?"

He sighed, looked down at his brandy glass. Then he stood, began to pace back and forth past the foot of her bed. She followed him with her eyes.

"I practically guarantee it," he said. "It has all the earmarks of a psychopathic repeater. The worst, absolutely the worst kind of homicides to solve. Random killings. Apparently without motive. No connection except chance between victim and killer."

"They don't know each other?"

"Right. The coming together is accidental. Up to that time they've been strangers."

Then he explained things to her that he didn't have to explain to Sergeant Boone.

"Monica, when I got my detective's shield, many, many years ago, about seventy-five percent of all homicides in New York were committed by relatives, friends, acquaintances, or associates of the victims.

"The other homicides, called 'stranger murders,' were committed by killers who didn't know their victims. They might have been felony homicides, committed during a burglary or robbery, or snipings, or—worst of all—just random killing for the pleasure of killing. There's a German word for it that I don't remember, but it means death lust, murder for enjoyment.

"Anyway, in those days, when three-quarters of all homicides were committed by killers who knew their victims, we had a high solution rate. We zeroed in first on the husband, wife, lover, whoever would inherit, a partner who wanted the whole pie, and so forth.

"But in the last ten years, the percentage of stranger murders has been increasing and the solution rate has been declining. I've never seen a statistical correlation, but I'd bet the two opposing curves are almost identical, percentage-wise; as stranger murders increase, the solution rate decreases.

"Because stranger murders are bitches to break. You've got nothing to go on, nowhere to start."

"You did," she said somberly. "You found Bernard's killer."

"I didn't say it couldn't be done. I just said it's very difficult. A lot tougher than a crime of passion or a murder that follows a family fight."

"So you think there's a chance they'll catch him—the hotel killer?"

He stopped suddenly, turned to face her.

"Him?" he said. "After what I told you, you think the murderer is a man?"

She nodded.

"Why?" he asked her curiously.

"I don't know," she said. "I just can't conceive of a woman doing things like that."

"A short-bladed knife is a woman's weapon," he told her. "And the victims obviously weren't expecting an attack. And the killer seems to have been naked at the time of the assault."

"But *why?*" she cried. "Why would a woman do a thing like that?"

"Monica, crazies have a logic all their own. It's not our logic. What they do seems perfectly reasonable and justifiable to them. To us, it's monstrous and obscene. But to them, it makes sense. *Their* sense."

He came over to sit on the edge of her bed again. They sipped their brandies. He took up her free hand, clasped it in his big paw.

"I happen to agree with you," he said. "At this point, knowing only what Sergeant Boone told me, I don't think it's a woman either. But you're going by your instinct and prejudices; I'm going by percentages. There have been many cases of random killings: Son of Sam, Speck, Heirens, Jack the Ripper, the Boston Strangler, the Yorkshire Ripper, Black Dahlia, the Hillside Strangler—all male killers. There have been multiple murders by women—Martha Beck in the Lonely Hearts Case, for instance. But the motive for women is almost always greed. What I'm talking about are random killings with no apparent motive. Only by men, as far as I know."

"Could it be a man wearing a long black wig? Dressed like a woman?"

"Could be," he said. "There's so much in this case that has no connection with anything in my experience. It's like someone came down from outer space and offed those salesmen."

"The poor wives," she said sadly. "And children."

"Yes," he said. He finished his brandy. "The whole thing is a puzzle. A can of worms. I know how Boone feels. So many contradictions. So many loose ends. Finish your drink."

Obediently, she drained the last of her brandy, handed him the empty snifter. He took the two glasses into the bathroom, rinsed them, set them in the sink to drain. He turned off the bathroom light. He came back to Monica's bedside to swoop and kiss her cheek.

"Sleep well, dear," he said.

"After *that?*" she said. "Thanks a lot."

"You wanted to hear," he reminded her. "Besides, the brandy will help."

He got into his own bed, turned off the bedside lamp.

"Get a good night's sleep," Monica muttered drowsily. "I love you."

"I love you," he said, and pulled sheet and blanket up to his chin.

He went through all the permutations and combinations in his mind: man, woman, prostitute, homosexual, transvestite. Even, he considered wildly, a transsexual. That would be something new.

He lay awake, wide-eyed, listening. He knew the moment Monica was asleep. She turned onto her side, her breathing slowed, became deeper, each exhalation accompanied by a slight whistle. It didn't annoy him any more than his own grunts and groans disturbed her.

He was awake a long time, going over Boone's account again and again. Not once did he pause to wonder why the investigation interested him, why it obsessed him. He was retired; it was really none of his business.

If his concern had been questioned, he would have replied stolidly: "Well . . . two human beings have been killed. That's not right."

He turned to peer at the bedside clock. Almost 2:30 A.M. But he couldn't let it go till tomorrow; he had to do it *now*.

He slid cautiously out of bed, figuring to get his robe and slippers from the closet. He was halfway across the darkened room when:

"What's wrong?" came Monica's startled voice.

"I'm sorry I woke you up," he said.

"Well, I *am* up," she said crossly. "Where are you going?"

"Uh, I thought I'd go downstairs. There's a call I want to make."

"Abner Boone," she said instantly. "You never give up, do you?"

He said nothing.

"Well, you might as well call from here," she said. "But you'll wake him up, too."

"No, I won't," Delaney said with certainty. "He won't be sleeping."

He sat on the edge of his bed, switched on the lamp. They both blinked in the sudden light. He picked up the phone.

"What's their number?" he asked.

She gave it to him. He dialed.

"Yes?" Boone said, picking up after the first ring. His voice was clogged, throaty.

"Edward X. Delaney here. I hope I didn't wake you, sergeant."

"No, Chief. I thought I'd pass out, but I can't get to sleep. My brain is churning."

"Rebecca?"

"No, sir. She'd sleep through an earthquake."

"Sergeant, did you check into the backgrounds of the victims? The personal stuff?"

"Yes, sir. Sent a man out to Denver and Akron. If you're wondering about their homosexual records, it's nil. For both of them. No sheets, no hints, no gossip. Apparently both men were straight."

"Yes," Delaney said, "I should have known you'd look into that. One more thing . . ."

Boone waited.

"You said that after the second homicide, the Crime Scene Unit found two black hairs on the back of an armchair?"

"That's correct, sir. And one on the pillow. All three were black nylon."

"It's the two they found on the armchair that interest me. Did they take photographs?"

"Oh, hell yes. Hundreds of them. And made sketches. To help the cartographer."

"Did they photograph those two hairs on the armchair before they picked them up?"

"I'm sure they did, Chief. With a ruler alongside to show size and position."

"Good," Delaney said. "Now what you do is this: Get that photograph of the exact position of the two hairs on the armchair. Take a man with you from the Lab Services Unit or the Medical Examiner's office. Go back to the murder scene and find that armchair. Measure carefully from the point where the hairs were found to the seat of the chair. Got that? Assuming the hairs came from the killer, you'll get a measurement from the back of his head to the base of his spine. From that, the technicians should be able to give you the approximate height of the killer. It won't be exact, of course; it'll be a rough approximation. But it'll be *something.*"

There was silence a moment. Then:

"Goddamn it!" Boone exploded. "Why didn't I think of that?"

"You can't think of everything," Delaney said.

"I'm supposed to," Boone said bitterly. "That's what they're paying me for. Thank you, sir."

"Good luck, sergeant."

When he hung up, he saw Monica looking at him with wonderment.

"You're something, you are," she said.

"I just wanted to help him out."

"Oh sure."

"I really am sorry I woke you up," he said.

"Well," she said, "so it shouldn't be a total loss . . ."

She reached for him.

3

Zoe Kohler had read the autobiography of a playwright who had suffered from mental illness. He had been confined for several years.

He said it was not true that the insane thought themselves sane. He said that frequently the mad knew themselves to be mad. Either they were unable to fight their affliction, or had no desire to. Because, he wrote, there were pleasures and beauties in madness.

The phrase "pleasures and beauties" stuck in her mind; she thought of it often. The pleasures of madness. The beauties of madness.

On the afternoon after her second adventure (that was what Zoe Kohler called them: "adventures"), Everett Pinckney came into her office at the Hotel Granger. He parked his lank form on the edge of her desk. He leaned toward her; she smelled the whiskey.

"There's been another one," he said in a low voice.

She looked at him, then shook her head.

"I don't understand, Mr. Pinckney."

"Another murder. A stabbing. This one at the Pierce. Just like that one at the Grand Park last month. You read about that?"

She nodded.

"This one was practically identical," he said. "Same killer."

"How awful," she said, her face twisting with distaste.

"It looks like another Son of Sam," he said with some relish.

She sighed. "I suppose the newspapers will have a field day."

"They're trying to keep the connection out of the papers. For the time being. Not good news for the hotel business. But it's got to come out, sooner or later."

"I suppose so," she said.

"They'll catch him," he said, getting off her desk. "It's just a question of time. How are you feeling today?"

"Much better, thank you."

"Glad to hear it."

She watched him shamble from her office.

"Him," he had said. "They'll catch *him.*" They thought it was a man; that was comforting. But what Pinckney had said about the newspapers—that was exciting.

She looked up the telephone number of *The New York Times.* It was an easy number to remember. She stopped at the first working phone booth she could find on her way home that night.

She tried to speak in a deep, masculine voice, and told the *Times* operator that she wanted to talk to someone about the murder at the Hotel Pierce. There was a clicking as her call was transferred. She waited patiently.

"City desk," a man said. "Gardner."

"This is about that murder last night at the Hotel Pierce," she said, trying to growl it out.

"Yes?"

"It's exactly like the one last month at the Grand Park Hotel. The same person did both of them."

There was silence for a second or two. Then:

"Could you give me your name and—"

She hung up, smiling.

She recalled, as precisely as she could, her actions of the previous night after she had waved goodbye to Ernest Mittle outside her apartment house door. She concentrated on the areas of risk.

When she had exited again, the doorman had hardly given her a glance. He would not remember the black-seamed hose, the high-heeled shoes. The cab-driver would never remember the woman he had driven to 72nd Street and Central Park West. And even if he did, what had that to do with a midnight murder at the Hotel Pierce?

No one in the ladies' room of the Filmore had seen her don wig and apply makeup. She had left from the hotel exit; the bartender could not have noted the transformation. The driver of the taxi that had taken her to a corner three blocks from the Pierce had hardly looked at her. They had exchanged no conversation.

The cocktail lounge, El Khatar, had been thronged, and there had been women more flamboyantly dressed than she. There had been another couple in the crowded elevator who had gotten off on the 30th floor. But they had turned away in the opposite direction, talking and laughing. Zoe Kohler didn't think she and Fred had been noticed.

Within the room, she had been careful about what she touched. After he was gone (she did not use the word "dead"; he was just gone), she was surprised to see that she was blood-splattered only from the elbows down.

She had stared at the blood a long time. Her hands and forearms dripping the bright, viscid fluid. She sniffed it. It had an odor. Not hers, but it did smell.

Then she had gone into the bathroom to wash the crimson stains away. Rinsing and rinsing with water as hot as she could endure. And then letting the hot water run steadily to cleanse the sink and drain while she dried her arms and hands. She went back to the bedroom to dress, not glancing at what lay on the bed.

Then, returning to the bathroom, she had turned off the water and used the damp towel to wipe the faucet handles, the inside doorknob and later, the white plastic card Fred had tossed atop the bureau near the outside door.

Before she left, she had removed her wig and makeup, scrubbing her face with the towel. Wig and towel went into her shoulder bag. She took a final look around and decided there was nothing she should have done that she had not.

The descending elevator was crowded and no one had looked at her: a pale-faced, mousy-haired woman wearing a loose-fitting trenchcoat buttoned up to the chin. Of course no one looked at her; she was Zoe Kohler again, the invisible woman.

She had walked over to Fifth Avenue and taken a cab downtown to 38th Street and Fifth. She walked from that corner to her apartment house. She felt no fear alone on the street. Her life could have ended at that moment and it would have been worthwhile. That was how she felt.

Locked and chained inside her own apartment, she had showered (the third time that day). She replaced all her secret things in their secret places. She pushed the damp towel deep into the plastic bag in her garbage can, to be thrown into the incinerator in the morning.

She hadn't been aware of her menstrual cramps for hours and hours. But now she began to feel the familiar pains, gripping with increasing intensity. She inserted a tampon and swallowed a Midol, two Anacin, a vitamin B-complex capsule, a vitamin C tablet, and ate half a container of blueberry yogurt.

Just before she got into bed, she shook a Pulvule 304 from her jar of prescription Tuinal and gulped it down.

She slept like a baby.

During the month that followed, Zoe Kohler had the sense of her ordered life whirling apart. She was conscious of an accelerated passage of time. Days flashed, and even weeks seemed condensed, so that Fridays succeeded Mondays, and it was an effort to recall what had happened between.

Increasingly, the past intruded on the present. She found herself thinking more and more of her marriage, her husband, mother, father, her girlhood. She spent one evening trying to remember the names of friends who had attended her 13th birthday party, and writing them down.

The party had been a disaster. Partly because several invited guests had not shown up, nor bothered to phone apologies. And partly because her periods had started on that day. She had begun to bleed, and was terrified. She thought it would never stop, and saw herself as an emptied sack of wrinkled white skin.

Ernest Mittle phoned her at home a week after their meeting. She hadn't expected him to call, as he had promised—men never did—and it took her a moment to bring him to mind.

"I hope I'm not disturbing you," he said.

"Oh no," she said. "No."

"How are you, Zoe?"

"Very well, thank you. And you?"

"Just fine," he said in his light, boyish voice. "I was hoping that if you didn't have any plans for tomorrow night, we might have dinner and see a movie, or something."

"I'm sorry," she said quickly. "I do have plans."

He said he was disappointed and would try again. They chatted awkwardly for a few minutes and then hung up. She stared at the dead, black phone.

"Don't be too eager, Zoe," her mother had instructed firmly. "Don't let men get the idea that you're anxious or *easy.*"

She didn't know if it was her mother's teaching or her own lack of inclination, but she wasn't certain she wanted to see Ernest Mittle again. If she did, it would just be something to do.

He did call again, and this time she accepted his invitation. It was for Saturday night, which she took as a good omen. New York men dated second or third choices during the week. Saturday night was for favorites: an occasion.

Ernest Mittle insisted on meeting her in the lobby of her apartment house. From there, they took a cab to a French restaurant on East 60th Street where he had made a reservation. The dining room was warm, cheerfully decorated, crowded.

Relaxing there, smoking a cigarette, sipping her white wine, listening to the chatter of other diners, Zoe Kohler felt for a moment that she was visible and belonged in the world.

After dinner, they walked over to 60th Street and Third Avenue. But there was a long line before the theater showing the movie he wanted to see. He looked at her, dismayed.

"I don't want to wait," he said. "Do you?"

"Not really," she said. And then, without considering it, she added: "Why don't we go back to my apartment and watch TV, or just talk?"

Something happened to his face: a quick twist. But then he was the eager spaniel again, anxious to please, his smile hopeful. He seemed constantly prepared to apologize.

"That sounds just fine," he said.

"I'm afraid I have nothing to drink," she said.

"We'll stop and pick up a couple of bottles of white wine," he said. "All right?"

"One will be plenty," she assured him.

They had exhausted remembrances of their youth in Minnesota and Wisconsin. They had no more recollections to exchange. Now, tentatively, almost fearfully, their conversation became more personal. They explored a new relationship, feinting, pulling back, trying each other, ready to escape. Both stiff with shyness and embarrassment.

In her apartment, she served the white wine with ice cubes. He sat in an armchair, his short legs thrust out. He was wearing a vested tweed suit, a tattersall shirt with a knitted tie. He seemed laden and bowed with the weight of his clothing, made smaller and frail. He had tiny feet.

She sat curled into a corner of the living room couch, her shoes off, legs pulled up under her gray flannel jumper. She felt remarkably at ease. No tension. He did not frighten her. If she had said, "Go," he would have gone, she was certain.

"Why haven't you married?" she asked him suddenly, thinking he might be gay.

"Who'd have me?" he said, showing his small white teeth. "Besides, Zoe, there isn't the pressure to marry anymore. There are all kinds of different life-styles. More and more single-person households every year."

"I suppose," she said vaguely.

"Are you into the women's movement?"

"Not really," she said. "I don't know much about it."

"I don't either," he said. "But what I've read seems logical and reasonable."

"Some of those women are so—so loud and crude," she burst out.

"Oh my, yes," he said hurriedly. "That's true."

"They just—just *push* so," she went on. "They call themselves feminists, but I don't think they're very feminine."

"You're so right," he said.

"I think that, first and foremost, women should be ladies. Don't you? I mean, refined and gentle. Low-voiced and modest in her appearance. That's what I was always taught. Clean and well-groomed. Generous and sympathetic."

"I was brought up to respect women," he said.

"That's what my mother told me—that men will always respect you if you act like a lady."

"Is your mother still alive?" he asked.

"Oh yes."

"She sounds like a wonderful woman."

"She is," Zoe said fervently, "she really is. She's over sixty now, but she's very active in her bridge club and her garden club and her book club. She reads all the best-sellers. And she's in charge of the rummage sales at the church. She certainly does keep busy.

"What I mean is that she doesn't just sit at home and do housecleaning and cook. She has a life of her own. That doesn't mean she doesn't take care of Father; she does. But goodness, he's not her *entire* life. She's a very independent woman."

"That's marvelous," Ernest said, "that she finds so much of interest to do."

"You should see her," Zoe said. "She looks much younger than her age. She has her hair done every week, a blue rinse, and she dresses just so. She's got wonderful taste in clothes. She's immaculate. Not a hair out of place. She's a little overweight now, but she stands just as straight as ever."

"Sounds like a real lady," he said.

"Oh, she is. A real lady."

Then Ernest Mittle began to talk about *his* mother, who seemed to be a woman much like Zoe had described. After a while she heard his voice as a kind of drone. She was conscious of what he was saying. She kept her eyes fixed on his face with polite interest. But her thoughts were free and floating, the past intruding.

She had lived in New York for about a year. Then, shriveled with loneliness, had ventured out to a highly publicized bar on Second Avenue that advertised: "For discriminating, sophisticated singles who want to get it on and get it off!" It was called The Meet Market.

She had given a great deal of thought to how she would dress and how she would comport herself. She would be attractive, but not in a brazen, obvious way. She would be alert, sparkling, and would listen closely to what men said, and speak little. Friendly but not forward. She would not express an opinion unless asked.

She had worn a black turtleneck sweater cinched with a wide, crushed leather belt. Her long wool skirt fitted snugly but not immodestly. Her pantyhose were sheer, and she wore pumps with heels that added an inch to her five-foot, six-inch height.

She tried a light dusting of powder, a faint blush of rouge and lipstick. Observing the effect, she added more. Her first experiment with false eyelashes was not a success; she got them on crooked, giving her a depraved, Oriental look. Finally, she stripped them away and darkened her own wispy lashes.

The Meet Market had been a shock. It was smaller than she had envisaged, and so crowded that patrons were standing outside on the sidewalk. They were drinking beers and shouting at each other to be heard above the din of the jukebox just inside the door.

She edged herself nervously inside and was dismayed to see that most of the women there, the singles and those with escorts, were younger than she. Most were in their late teens and early twenties, and were dressed in a variety of outlandish costumes, brightly colored, that made her look like a frump.

It took her fifteen minutes to work her way to the bar, and another five minutes to order a glass of beer from one of the busy, insolent bartenders. She was bumped continually, shouldered, jostled back and forth. No one spoke to her.

She stood there with a fixed smile, not looking about. Life surged around her: shouts of laughter, screamed conversation, blare of jukebox, obscene jesting. The women as lewd as the men. Still she stood, smiling determinedly, and ordered another glass of beer.

"Sorry, doll," a man said, knocking her shoulder as he reached across to take drinks from the bartender.

She turned to look. A husky young man, dark, with a helmet of greasy ringlets, a profile from a Roman coin. He wore an embroidered shirt unbuttoned to the waist. About his muscled neck were three gold chains. Ornate medallions swung against the thick mat of hair on his chest.

He had a musky scent of something so cloying that she almost gagged. His teeth were chipped, and he needed a shave. There were wet stains on the shirt beneath his armpits.

He doesn't care, she had thought suddenly. He just doesn't care.

She admired him for not caring.

She stayed at the bar, drinking the watery beer, and watched the strange world swirl about her. She felt that she had strayed into a circus. Everyone was a performer except her.

She had seen that most of the women were not only younger than she, but prettier. With ripe, bursting bodies they flaunted without modesty.

Zoe saw blouses zipped down to reveal cleavage. Tanktops so tight that hard nipples poked out. Sheer shirts that revealed naked torsos. Jeans so snug that buttocks were clearly delineated, some bearing suggestive patches: SMART ASS. BOTTOMS UP. SEX POT.

She had arrived at The Meet Market shortly after 11:30 P.M. The noise and crush were at their worst an hour later. Then, slowly, the place began to empty out. Contacts were made; couples disappeared. Still Zoe Kohler stood at the bar, drinking her flat beer, her face aching with her smile.

"Wassamatta, doll?" the dark young man said, at her elbow again. "Get stood up?"

He roared with laughter, putting his head back, his mouth wide. She saw his bad teeth, a coated tongue, a red tunnel.

He took another drink from the bartender, gulped down half of it without stopping. A rivulet of beer ran down his chin. He wiped it away with the back of his hand. He looked around at the emptying room.

"I missed the boat," he said to Zoe. "Always looking for something better. Know what I mean? Then I end up with Mother Five-fingers."

He laughed again, in her face. His breath smelled sour: beer, and something else. He clapped her on the shoulder.

"Where you from, doll?" he said.

"Manhattan," she said.

"Well, that's *something,*" he said. "Last night I connected with a *real* doll, and she's from Queens and wants to go to her place. My luck—right? No way am I going to Queens. North of Thirty-fourth and south of Ninety-sixth: that's my motto. I live practically around the corner."

"So?" she said archly.

"So let's go," he said. "Beggars can't be choosers."

She had never decided if he meant her or himself.

He lived in a dreadful one-room apartment in a tenement on 85th Street, off Second Avenue. The moment they were inside, he said, "Gotta piss," and dashed for the bathroom.

He left the door open. She heard the sound of his stream splashing into the bowl. She put her palms over her ears and wondered dully why she did not run.

He came out, stripping off his shirt, and then stepping out of his jeans. He was wearing a stained bikini no larger than a jockstrap. She could not take her eyes from the bulge.

"I got half a joint," he said, then saw where she was looking. He laughed. "Not here," he said, pointing. "I mean good grass. Wanna share?"

"No, thank you," she said primly. "But you go right ahead."

He found the butt in a dresser drawer, lighted up, inhaled deeply. His eyelids lowered.

"Manna from Heaven," he said slowly. "You know what manna is, doll?"

"A food," she said. "From the Bible."

"Right on," he said lazily. "But they didn't call it womanna, did they? Manna. You give good head, doll?"

"I don't know," she said truthfully, not understanding.

"Sure you do," he said. "All you old, hungry dames do. And if you don't know how, I'll teach you. But that comes later. Let's get with it. Off with the uniform, doll."

It was more of a cot than a bed, the thin mattress lumpy, sheet torn and blotched. He would not let her turn off the light. So she saw him, saw herself, could only block out what was happening by closing her eyes. But that was not enough.

He smelled of sweat and the awful, musky scent he was wearing. And he was so hairy, so hairy. He wore a singlet of black wire wool that covered chest, shoulders, arms, black, legs. His groin was a tangle. But his buttocks were satiny.

"Oh," she had cried out. "Oh, oh, oh."

"Good, huh?" he said, grunting with his effort. "You like this . . . and this . . . and this? Oh God!"

Moaning, just as Maddie Kurnitz had advised. And Remedial Moaning. Zoe Kohler did as she had been told. Going through the motions. Threshing about. Digging nails into his meaty shoulders. Pulling his hair.

"So good!" she kept crying. "So *good!*" Wondering if she had remembered to turn off the gas range before she left her apartment.

Then, as he kept pumping, and she heaved up to meet him, she recalled her ex-husband Kenneth and his fury at her mechanical response.

"You're just not *there!*" he had complained.

Finally, finally, the hairy thing lying atop her and punishing her with its weight, finished with a sob, and almost immediately rolled away.

He lighted the toke again, a roach now that he impaled on a thin wire.

"That was something," he said. "Wasn't that something?"

"The best I've ever had," she recited.

"You made it?"

"Of course," she lied. "Twice."

"What else?" he said, smiling complacently. "Haven't had any complaints yet."

"I've got to go," she said, sitting up.

"Oh no," he said, pushing her back down. "Not yet. We've got some unfinished business."

Something in his tone frightened her. Not menace; he was not threatening her. It was the brute confidence.

Kenneth had suggested it once, but she had refused. Now she could not refuse. He clamped her head between his strong hands and guided her mouth.

"Now you're getting it," he instructed her. "Up. Down. That's it. Around. Right there. The tongue. It's all in knowing how, doll. Take it easy with the teeth."

Later, on her way home in a cab, she had realized that she didn't even know his name and he didn't know hers. That was some comfort.

"More wine?" she asked Ernest Mittle. "Your glass is empty."

"Sure," he said, smiling. "Thank you. We might as well finish the bottle. I'm really enjoying this."

She rose, staggered just briefly, giddy from the memory, not the wine. She brought more ice cubes from the kitchen.

They sat at their ease. Remarkably alike. Mirror images. With their watery coloring, pinched frames, their soft, wistful vulnerability, they could have been brother and sister.

"This is better than standing on line to see a movie," he said. "It was probably no good anyway."

"Or going to some crowded party," she said. "Everyone getting drunk as fast as they can—like at Maddie's."

"I suppose you go out a lot?"

"I really do prefer a quiet evening at home," she said. "Like this."

"Oh yes," he agreed eagerly. "One gets tired of running around. I know I do."

They stared at each other, blank-eyed liars. He broke first.

"Actually," he said in a very low voice, "I don't go out all that much. Very rarely, in fact."

"To tell you the truth," she said, not looking at him, "I don't either. I'm alone most of the time."

He looked up, intent. He hunched forward.

"That's why I enjoy seeing you, Zoe," he said. "I can talk to you. When I do go to a party or bar, everyone seems to shout. People don't talk to each other anymore. I mean about important things."

"That's very true," she said. "Everyone seems to shout. And no one has good manners either. No common courtesy."

"Yes!" he said excitedly. "Right! Exactly the way I feel. If you try to be gentle, everyone thinks you're dumb. It's all push, rush, shove, walk over anyone who gets in your way. I, for one, think it's disgusting."

She looked at him with admiration.

"Yes," she said, "I feel the same way. I may be old-fashioned, but—"

"No, no!" he protested.

"But I'd rather sit home by myself," she went on, "with a good book or something tasteful on educational TV—I'd rather do that than get caught up in the rat race."

"I couldn't agree more," he said warmly. "Except . . ."

"Except what?" she asked.

"Well, look, you and I work in the most frantic city in the world. And I wonder—I've been thinking a lot about this lately—that in spite of the way I feel, if it isn't getting to me. I mean, the noise, the anger, the frustration, the dirt, the violence. Zoe, they've got to be having *some* effect."

"I suppose," she said slowly.

"What I mean," he said desperately, "is that sometimes I feel I can't cope, that I'm a victim of things I can't control. It's all changing so fast. Nothing is the same. But what's the answer? To drop out and go live in the wilderness? Who can afford that? Or to try to change things? I don't believe an individual can do anything. It's just—just forces."

He drew a deep breath, drained off his wine. He laughed shakily.

"I'm probably boring you," he said. "I'm sorry."

"You're not boring me, Ernest."

"Ernie."

"You're not boring me, Ernie. What you said is very interesting. You really think we can be influenced by our environment? Even if we recognize how awful it is and try to—to rebel against it?"

"Oh yes," he said. "Definitely. Did you take any psychology courses?"

"Two years."

"Well, then you know you can put rats in a stress situation—loud noise, overcrowding, bad food, flashing lights, and so forth—and drive them right up the wall. All right, admittedly human beings have more intelligence than rats. We have the ability to know when we *are* in a stress situation, and can make a conscious effort to endure it, or escape it. But I still say that what is going on about us today, in the modern world, is probably affecting us in ways we're not even aware of."

"Physically, you mean? Affecting us physically?"

"That, of course. Polluted air, radiation, bad water, junk food. But what's worse is what's happening to *us*, the kind of people we are. We're changing, Zoe. I know we are."

"How are we changing?"

"Getting harder, less gentle. Our attention span is shortening. We can't concentrate. Sex has lost its significance. Love is a joke. Violence is a way of life. No respect for the law. Crime *does* pay. Religion is just another cult. And so forth and so on. Oh God, I must sound like a prophet of doom!"

She went back to what fascinated her most.

"And feeling this way," she said, "knowing all this, you still feel that *you* are being changed?"

He nodded miserably.

"The other night," he said, "I was eating my dinner in front of the TV set. Franks and beans. With a can of beer. I was watching the evening news. They had films from the refugee camps in Thailand. The Cambodians.

"I sat there eating and drinking, and saw kids, babies, with pipe-stem arms and legs, and swollen bellies, flies on their eyes. I sat there eating my franks and beans, drinking my beer, and watched people dying. And after a while I discovered I was crying."

"I know," she said sympathetically. "It was terrible."

"No, no," he said in anguish. "That wasn't why I was crying—because it was so terrible. I was crying because I wasn't feeling anything. I was watching those pictures, and I knew they were true, and those people really were dying, and I didn't feel a thing. I just ate my franks and beans, drank my beer, and watched a TV show. But I didn't *feel* anything, Zoe. I swear, I didn't feel *anything*. That's what I mean about this world changing us in ways we don't want to be changed."

Suddenly, without warning, his eyes brimmed over, and he began to weep. She watched him helplessly for a moment, then held her arms out to him.

He stumbled over to collapse next to her on the couch. She put an arm about his thin shoulders, drew him close. With her other hand she smoothed the fine flaxen hair back from his temples.

"There," she said in a soft, crooning voice. "There, Ernie. There. There."

In the days following Zoe Kohler's phoned tip to *The New York Times*, she searched the newspaper with avid interest. But nothing appeared other than a few brief follow-ups on the slaying of Frederick Wolheim at the Hotel Pierce.

Soon, even this case disappeared from the paper. Zoe was convinced a cover-up was in effect. As Everett Pinckney had said, it wasn't good for the hotel business. Hotels advertised in newspapers. The economy of the city was based to a large extent on tourism. So the newspapers were silent.

But on March 24th, a two-column article appeared in the *Times'* Metropolitan Report. Headlined: KILLER SOUGHT IN TWO HOMICIDES, it reviewed the murders of George T. Puller and Frederick Wolheim, pointing out the similarities, and said the police were working on the theory that both killings were committed by the same person. The motive was unknown.

The *Times'* article reported that the investigation was under the command of Detective Lieutenant Martin Slavin. He had stated: "We are exploring several promising leads, and an arrest is expected shortly." A special phone number had been set up for anyone with information on the crimes.

The *Times* did not mention the Son of Sam killings, but the afternoon *Post* and the evening's *Daily News* were not so restrained. The *Post* headline was: ANOTHER SON OF SAM? The *News* bannered their page 4 report with: COPS CALL 'DAUGHTER OF SAM' A POSSIBILITY.

Both papers suggested the police were afraid that the Puller and Wolheim murders might be just the first of a series of psychopathic, motiveless slayings. Both papers repeated Lieutenant Slavin's statement: "We are exploring several promising leads, and an arrest is expected shortly."

After a brief initial shock, Zoe Kohler decided she had nothing to fear from Slavin's optimistic prediction; it was intended to reassure New Yorkers that everything that could be done was being done, and this menace to the public safety would soon be eliminated.

More worrisome was the *Daily News'* reference to "Daughter of Sam." But a careful reading of the story indicated that the police were merely investigating the possibility that a prostitute had been responsible for both murders. Midtown whores and their pimps were being rousted and questioned in record numbers.

So, Zoe Kohler felt, nothing had been discovered that really threatened her. It was, she admitted, becoming increasingly exciting. All those policemen running around. Millions of newspaper readers titillated and frightened. She was becoming someone.

Her exhilaration was dampened two days later when Everett Pinckney came into her office with a notice that had been hand-delivered by the police to the chiefs of security in every hotel in midtown Manhattan.

It was, in effect, a WANTED poster, asking the security officers to aid in apprehending the killer of George T. Puller and Frederick Wolheim. It was believed the murderer made contact with the victims in the bars, cocktail lounges, or dining rooms of hotels, especially those hosting conventions, sales meetings, or large gatherings of any type.

The description of the person "wanted for questioning" was sparse. It said only that the suspect could be male or female, approximately five-five to five-seven, wearing a wig of black nylon.

"Not much to go on," Pinckney said. "If we grabbed every man and woman wearing a black nylon wig, we'd really be in the soup. Can you imagine the lawsuits for false arrest?"

"Yes," Zoe said.

"Well," Mr. Pinckney said, studying the notice, "the two murders happened around midnight. I'll make sure Joe Levine sees this when he comes on at five tonight. Then I'll leave it on my desk. If I miss Barney McMillan in the morning, will you make sure he sees it?"

"Yes, sir," she said.

When he was gone, she sat upright at her desk, spine rigid, her back not touching her chair. She clasped her hands on the desktop. Knuckles whitened.

The black nylon wig didn't bother her. That was a detail that could be remedied. But how had they come up with the correct height?

She went over and over her actions during her two adventures. She could recall nothing that would give the police an accurate estimation of her height. She had a shivery feeling that there was an intelligence at work of which she knew nothing. Something or someone secret who *knew*.

She wondered if it might be a medium or someone versed in ESP, called in by the police to assist in their investigation. "I see a man or woman with—yes, it's black hair. No, not hair—it's a wig, a black nylon wig. And this person is of average height. Yes, I see that clearly. About five-five to five-seven. Around there."

That might have been how it was done. Zoe Kohler nodded, convinced; that was how.

On Thursday night, she went down to Wigarama on 34th Street. She tried on a nylon, strawberry blond wig, styled just like her black one. She looked in the mirror, pulling, tugging, poking it with her fingers.

"It'll make you a new woman, dearie," the salesclerk said.

"I'm sure it will," Zoe Kohler said, and bought it.

Madeline Kurnitz called and insisted they meet for lunch. Zoe was wary; a lunch with Maddie could last more than two hours.

"I really shouldn't," she said. "I'm a working woman, you know. I usually eat at my desk."

"Come on, kiddo," Maddie said impatiently. "You're not chained to the goddamned desk, are you? Live a little!"

"How about right here?" Zoe suggested. "In the hotel dining room?"

"How tacky can you get?" Maddie said disgustedly.

When she showed up, twenty minutes late, she was wearing her ranch mink, so black it was almost blue, over a tight sheath of brocaded satin. The dress had a stain in front; a side seam gapped. She couldn't have cared less.

She led the way grandly into the Hotel Granger dining room.

A wan maitre d' approached, gave them a sad smile.

"Two, ladies?" he said in sepulchral tones. "This way, please."

He escorted them to a tiny table neatly tucked behind an enormous plaster pillar.

Maddie Kurnitz opened her coat and put a soft hand on his arm.

"You sweet man," she said, "couldn't we have a table just a *wee* bit more comfortable?"

His eyes flicked to her unholstered breasts. He came alive.

"But of course!" he said.

He conducted them to a table for four in the center of the dining room.

"Marvelous," Maddie caroled. She gave the maître d' a warm smile. "You're a perfect dear," she said.

"My pleasure!" he said, glowing. "Enjoy your luncheon, ladies."

He helped Maddie remove her mink coat, touching her tenderly. Then he moved away regretfully.

"I made his day," Maddie said.

"How do you do it?" Zoe said. She shook her head. "I'd never have the nerve."

"Balls, luv," Maddie advised. "All it takes is balls."

As usual, her hair seemed a snarl, her makeup a blotch of primary colors. Her feral teeth shone. Diamonds glittered. She dug into an enormous snakeskin shoulder bag and came out with a crumpled pack of brown cigarillos. She offered it to Zoe.

"No, thank you, Maddie. I'll have one of my own."

"Suit yourself."

Maddie twirled a cigarillo between her lips. Instantly, a handsome young waiter was hovering over her, snapping his lighter. She grasped his hand to steady the flame.

"Thank you, you beautiful man," she said, smiling up at him. "May we have a drink now?"

"But of course, madam. What is your pleasure?"

"I'd tell you," she said, "but it would make you blush. For a drink, I'll have a very dry Tanqueray martini, straight up, with two olives. Zoe?"

"A glass of white wine, please."

The waiter scurried off with their order. Maddie looked around the crowded room.

"Never in my life have I seen so many women with blue hair," she said. "What's the attraction here—free Geritol?"

"The food is very good," Zoe said defensively.

"Let me be the judge of that, kiddo." She regarded Zoe critically. "You don't look so bad. Not so good, but not so bad. Feeling okay?"

"Of course. I'm fine."

"Uh-huh. Have a good time at our bash the other night?"

"Oh yes. I meant to thank you before I left, but I couldn't find you. Or Harry."

"Never did meet David something, did you? The guy I told you about?"

"No," Zoe said, "I never met him."

"You're lucky," Maddie said, laughing. "He was picked up later that night with a stash of coke on him. The moron! But you didn't leave alone, did you?"

Zoe Kohler hung her head.

The waiter came bustling up with their drinks and left menus alongside their plates.

"Whenever you're ready, ladies," he said.

"I'm always ready," Maddie said, "but we'll order in a few minutes."

They waited until he moved away.

"How did you know?" Zoe asked.

"My spies are everywhere," Maddie said. "What's his name?"

"Ernest Mittle. He works for your husband."

Madeline Kurnitz spluttered into her martini.

"Mister Meek?" she said. "That nice little man?"

"He's not so little."

"I know, sweetie. He just *looks* little. Didn't try to get into your pants, did he?"

"Oh Maddie," she said, embarrassed. "Of course not. He's not like that at all."

"Didn't think so," Maddie said. "Poor little mouse."

"Could we order, Maddie? I really have to get back to work."

Zoe ordered a fresh fruit salad.

Maddie would have the fresh oysters. Bluepoints weren't her favorite, but they were the only kind available. On each oyster she wanted a spoonful of caviar topped with a sprinkling of freshly ground ginger.

Then she would have thin strips of veal sautéed in unsalted butter and Marsala wine, with a little lemon and garlic. Cauliflower with bacon bits would be nice with that, she decided. And a small salad of arugula with sour cream and chives.

The ordering of her luncheon took fifteen minutes and required a conference of maître d', headwaiter, and two waiters, with a busboy hovering in the background. All clustered about Maddie, peered down her neckline, and conversed volubly in rapid Italian. Other diners observed this drama with bemusement. Zoe Kohler wished she were elsewhere.

Finally their meals were served. Maddie sampled one of her oysters. The waiters watched anxiously.

"Magnifico!" she cried, kissing the tips of her fingers.

They relaxed with grins, bowed, clapped each other on the shoulder.

"So-so," Maddie said to Zoe Kohler in a low voice. "The oysters are a bit mealy, but those dolts were so sweet, I didn't have the heart . . . Want to try one?"

"Oh no! Thank you."

"Still popping the pills, kiddo?"

"I take vitamins," Zoe said stiffly. "Food supplements."

Maddie finished the oysters, sat back beaming.

"Not bad," she admitted. "Not the greatest, but not bad. By the way," she added, "this is on me. I should have told you; maybe you'd have ordered a steak."

"We'll go Dutch," Zoe said.

"Screw that. I have a credit card from Harry's company. This is a business lunch in case anyone should ask." She laughed.

She had another martini while waiting for her veal. Zoe had another glass of white wine. Then their entrees were served.

"Beautiful," Maddie said, looking down at her plate. "You've got to order for color as well as taste. Isn't that a symphony?"

"It looks nice."

Maddie dug in, sampled a slice of veal. She closed her eyes.

"I'm coming," she said. "God, that's almost as good as a high colonic." She attacked her lunch with vigor. "Sweetie," she said, while masticating, "I never asked you about your divorce. Never. Did I?"

"No, you never did."

"If you don't want to talk about it, just tell me to shut my yap. But I'm curious. Why the hell did you and what's-his-name break up?"

"Kenneth."

"Whatever. I thought you two had the greatest love affair since Hitler and Eva Braun. That's the way your letters sounded. What happened?"

"Well . . . ah . . ." Zoe Kohler said, picking at her salad, "we just drifted apart."

"Bullshit," Madeline Kurnitz said, forking veal into her mouth. "Can I guess?"

"Can I stop you?" Zoe said.

"No way. My guess is that it was the sex thing. Am I right?"

"Well . . . maybe," Zoe said in a low voice.

Maddie stopped eating. She sat there, fork poised, staring at the other woman.

"He wanted you to gobble ze goo?" she asked.

"What?"

"Chew on his schlong," Maddie said impatiently.

Zoe looked about nervously, fearing nearby diners were tuned in to this discomfiting conversation. No one appeared to be listening.

"That was one of the things," she said quietly. "There were other things."

Maddie resumed eating, apparently sobered and solemn. She kept her eyes on her food.

"Sweetie," she said, "were you cherry when you got married?"

"Yes."

"After all I told you at school?" Maddie said, looking up angrily. "I tried to educate you, for God's sake. Stupid, stupid, stupid! Well, how was it?"

"How was what?"

"The wedding night, you idiot. The first bang. How was it?"

"It wasn't the greatest adventure I've ever had," Zoe Kohler said dryly.

"Did you make it?"

"He did. I didn't, no."

Maddie stared long and thoughtfully at her.

"Have you ever made it?"

"No. I haven't."

"What? Speak up. I didn't hear that."

"No, I haven't," Zoe repeated.

They finished their food in silence. Maddie pushed her plate away, belched, relighted the butt of her cigarillo. She looked at Zoe with narrowed eyes through a plume of smoke.

"Poor little scut," she said. "Sweetie, I know this wonderful woman who treats women like—"

"There's nothing wrong with me," Zoe Kohler said hotly.

"Of course there isn't, luv," Maddie said soothingly. "But it's just a shame that you're missing out on one of the greatest pleasures of this miserable life. This woman I know holds classes. Small classes. Five or six women like you. She explains things. You have discussions about what's holding you back. She gives you exercises and things to do by yourself at home. She's got a good track record for helping women like you."

"It's not me," Zoe Kohler burst out. "It's the men."

"Uh-huh," Maddie said, squashing the cigarillo butt in an ashtray. "Let me give you this woman's name."

"No," Zoe said.

Maddie Kurnitz shrugged. "Then let's have some coffee," she suggested. "And some rich, thick, fattening dessert."

She was conscious of other things happening to her. Not only the acceleration of time, and the increasing intrusion of the past into the present so that memories of ten or twenty years ago had the sharp vividness of the *now*. She was also beginning to see reality in magnified close-ups, intimate and revealing.

She had seen the pores in Maddie's nose, the nubby twist of Mr. Pinckney's tweed suit, the fine grain of the paper money in her purse. But not only the visual images. All her senses seemed more alert, tender and receptive. She heard new sounds, smelled new odors, felt textures that were strange and wonderful.

All of her was becoming more perceptive, open and responsive to stimuli. It seemed to her that she could hear the sounds of colors and taste the flavor of a scent. She twanged with this new sensitivity. She saw herself as raw, touched by life in marvelous and sometimes frightening ways.

She wondered that if this growing awareness increased, she might not develop X-ray vision and the ability to communicate with the dead. A universe was opening up to her, unfolding and spreading like a bloom. It had never happened to anyone before, she knew. She was unique.

It had all started with her first adventure, a night of fear, anguish and resolve. Then, when it was over, she was flooded with a warm peace, an almost drunken exaltation. When she had returned home, she had stared at herself in a mirror and was pleased with what she saw.

It seemed to her that, for self-preservation, she could not, should not stop. She was rational enough to recognize the dangers, to plan coldly and logically. But logic was limited. It was not an end in itself, a way of life. It was a means to an end, to a transfigured life.

The gratification was not sexual. Oh no, it was not that, although she loved those men for what they had given her. But she did not experience an orgasm or even a thrill when she—when those men went. But she felt a thawing of her hurts. The adventures were a sweet justification. Of what, she could not have said.

"It's God's will," her mother was fond of remarking.

If a friend sickened, a coffee cup was broken, or a million foreigners died in a famine—"It's God's will," her mother said.

Zoe Kohler felt much the same way about what she was doing. It was God's will, and her newfound sensibility was her reward. She was being allowed to enter a fresh world, reborn.

Dr. Oscar Stark, an internist, had his offices on the first floor of his home, a converted brownstone on 35th Street just east of Park Avenue. It was a handsome five-story structure with bow windows and a fanlight over the front door said to have been designed by Louis Tiffany.

The suite of offices consisted of a reception room, the doctor's office, two examination rooms, a clinic, lavatories, storage cubicles, and a "resting room."

All these chambers had the high, ornate ceilings, wood paneling, and parquet floors installed when the home was built in 1909. The waiting room and the doctor's office were equipped with elaborate, marble-manteled fireplaces. There were window seats, wall niches, and sliding oak doors.

Dr. Stark and his wife of forty-three years had found it impossible to reconcile this Edwardian splendor with the needs of a physician's office: white enameled furniture, stainless steel equipment, glass cabinets, and plastic plants. Regretfully, they had surrendered to the demands of his profession and moved their heavy antiques and gloomy paintings upstairs to the living quarters.

Dr. Stark employed a receptionist and two nurses, both RNs. His waiting room was invariably occupied, and usually crowded, from 9:00 A.M. to 7:00 P.M. These hours were not strictly adhered to; the doctor sometimes saw patients early in the morning, late in the evening, and on weekends.

Zoe Kohler had a standing appointment for 6:00 P.M. on the first Tuesday of every month. Dr. Stark had tried to convince her that these monthly visits were not necessary.

"Your illness doesn't require it," he had explained with his gentle smile. "As long as you keep on the medication faithfully, every day. Otherwise, you're in excellent health. I'd like to see you twice a year."

"I'd really prefer to get a checkup every month," she said. "You never can tell."

He shrugged his meaty shoulders, brushed cigar ashes from the lapels of his white cotton jacket.

"If it makes you feel better," he said. "What is it, exactly, you'd like me to do for you every month?"

"Oh . . ." she said, "the usual."

"And what do you consider the usual?"

"Weight and blood pressure. The lungs. Urine and blood tests. Breast examination. A pelvic exam. A Pap test."

"A Pap smear every month?" he cried. "Zoe, in your case it's absolutely unnecessary. Once or twice a year is sufficient, I assure you."

"I want it," she said stubbornly, and he had yielded.

He was a short, blunt teddy bear of a man in his middle sixties. An enormous shock of white hair crowned his bullet head like a raggedy halo. And below, ruddy, pendulous features hung in bags, dewlaps, jowls, and wattles. All of his thick face sagged. It waggled when he moved.

His hands were wide and strong, fingers fuzzed with black hair. He wore carpet slippers with white cotton socks. Unless a patient objected, he chain-smoked cigars. More than once his nurse had plucked a lighted cigar from his fingers as he was about to start a rectal examination.

He was, Zoe Kohler thought, a sweet old man with eyes of Dresden blue. He did not frighten her or intimidate her. She thought she might tell him anything, *anything*, and he would not be shocked, angered, or disgusted.

On the first Tuesday of that April, the first day of the month, Zoe Kohler arrived at Dr. Stark's office a few minutes early for her 6:00 P.M. appointment. Mercifully, there were only two other patients in the waiting room. She checked in with the receptionist, then settled down with a year-old copy of *Architectural Digest*. It was 6:50 before Gladys, the chief nurse, came into the reception room and gave Zoe as pleasant a smile as she could manage.

"Doctor will see you now," she said.

Gladys was a gorgon, broad-shouldered and wide-hipped, with a faint but discernible mustache. Zoe had once seen her pick up a steel cabinet and reposition it as easily as if it had been a paper carton. Dr. Stark had told her that Gladys was divorced and had a twelve-year-old son in a military academy in Virginia. She lived alone with four cats.

A few moments later Zoe Kohler was seated in Dr. Stark's office, watching him light a fresh cigar and wave the cloud of smoke away with backhand paddle motions.

He peered at her genially over the tops of his half-glasses.

"So?" he said. "Feeling all right?"

"Fine," she said.

"Regular bowel movements?"

She nodded, lowering her eyes.

"What about your food?"

"I eat well," she said.

He looked down at the opened file Gladys had placed on his desk.

"You take vitamins," he noted. "Which ones?"

"Most of them," she said. "A, B-complex, C, E, and some minerals."

"Which minerals?"

"Iron, zinc, magnesium."

"And? What other pills?"

"My birth control pill," she said. "The blood medicine. Choline. Alfalfa. Lecithin and kelp."

"And?"

"Sometimes a Librium. Midol. Anacin. Occasionally a Darvon for my cramps. A Tuinal when I can't sleep."

He looked at her and sighed.

"Oy gevalt," he said. "What a stew. Believe me, Zoe, if you're eating a balanced diet the vitamins and minerals and that seaweed just aren't needed."

"Who eats a balanced diet?" she challenged.

"What about the choline? Why choline?"

"I read somewhere that it prevents premature senility."

He leaned back and laughed, showing strong, yellowed teeth.

"A young woman like you," he chided, "worrying about senility. Me, *I* should be worrying. Try to cut down on the pills. All right?"

"All right," she said.

"You promise?"

She nodded.

"Good," he said, pushing a buzzer on his desk. "Now go with Gladys. I'll be along in a minute."

In the examination room, she took off all her clothes and put them on plastic hangers suspended from the top edge of a three-paneled metal screen. She draped a sheet about herself. Gladys came in with an examination form fastened to a clipboard.

Zoe stepped onto the scale. Gladys moved the weights back and forth.

"One twenty-three," she announced. "How do you do it? One of my legs weighs one twenty-three. Better put on your shoes, dear; the floor is chilly."

She handed Zoe a wide-mouthed plastic cup.

"The usual contribution, please," she said, motioning toward the lavatory door.

Zoe went in there and tried. Nothing. In a few moments Gladys opened the door a few inches.

"Having trouble?" she asked. "Run some warm water on your hands and wrists."

Zoe did as directed, and it worked. She came back into the examination room bearing half a cup of warm urine. She had filled the cup but, embarrassed, had poured half of it down the sink. She handed the cup to Gladys without looking at her.

Dr. Stark came in a few moments later. He set his cigar carefully aside. Zoe sat in an armless swivel chair of white-enameled steel. The doctor sat on a swivel stool facing her. His bulk overflowed the tiny seat.

"All right," he said, "let's get this critical operation going."

The nurse handed a stethoscope to Stark. He motioned Zoe to drop the sheet. She slid it from her shoulders, held it gathered about her waist.

He warmed the stethoscope on his hairy forearm for a moment, then applied the metal disk to Zoe's chest, sternum, ribcage.

"Deep breath," he said. "Another. Another."

She did as he commanded.

"Fine, fine, fine," he said. He spun her chair around and moved the plate over her shoulders, back. He rapped a few times with his knuckles. "All the machinery is in tiptop condition," he reported.

He hung the stethoscope around his neck and reached to Gladys without looking. The nurse had the sphygmomanometer ready and waiting. Stark wrapped the cuff about Zoe's upper arm and pumped the bulb. Gladys leaned down to take the readings.

"A little high," the doctor noted. "Just a tiny bit. Nothing to worry about. Now let's do the Dracula bit."

Gladys handed him the syringe and needle. She swabbed the inside of Zoe's forearm. Zoe looked away. She felt Dr. Stark's strong fingers feeling deftly along her arm. He found a vein; the needle went in unerringly. He had a light, butterfly touch. Still she felt the needle pierce, her body penetrated. Her tainted blood drained away.

In a few moments, the doctor pressed her arm, withdrew the needle and full syringe. He handed it to Gladys. The nurse set it aside, applied a small, round adhesive patch to the puncture in Zoe's arm.

"Now for the fun part," Dr. Oscar Stark said.

He hitched his wheeled stool closer and stared critically at Zoe Kohler's naked bosom through his half-glasses. He began to palpate her breasts. She hung her head. Through half-closed eyes she watched his furred fingers moving over her flesh. Like black caterpillars.

He used the flats of his wide fingertips, moving his hand in a small circle to feel the tissue under the skin. He examined each breast thoroughly, probing to the middle of her chest and under her arms. He finished by squeezing each nipple gently to detect exudation. By that time, Zoe Kohler had her eyes tightly shut.

"A-Okay," Stark said. "You can wake up now. Do you examine your breasts yourself, Zoe?"

"Uh . . . no, I don't."

"Why not? I showed you how."

"I, ah, rather have it done by a doctor. A professional."

"Uh-huh. Do you jog?"

"No."

"Good. You'd be surprised at how many women I'm getting with their boobs down to their knees. If you start to jog, make sure you wear a firm bra. All right, let's ride the iron pony."

Gladys assisted her onto the padded examination table, adjusted the pillow under her head. She placed Zoe's heels in the stirrups, smoothed the sheet to cover her body down to the waist. Dr. Stark, propelling himself with his feet, wheeled over to place himself between Zoe's legs. The nurse helped him into rubber gloves.

He leaned close, peering. He examined the vulva, using one hand to open the entrance to the vagina. He pushed back the clitoral hood. Then he reached sideways, and the nurse smacked a plastic speculum into his palm.

"Tell me if it hurts," the doctor said. "It shouldn't; it's your size."

He inserted the speculum slowly and gently, pressing with one finger on the bottom wall of her vagina to guide the instrument. Once inserted, the handle was turned to spread and lock the blades. They locked with an audible click. Zoe was expecting the sound, but couldn't resist twitching when she heard the crack.

"All right?" Dr. Stark asked.

"Fine," she said faintly.

She stared at the ceiling, biting on her lower lip. She felt no pain. Only the humiliation.

"Relax," he said. "It'll help if you try to relax. You're all rigid. Take deep breaths."

She tried to relax. She thought of blue skies, fair fields, calm waters. She breathed deeply.

"Spatula," the doctor said in a low voice.

She felt nothing, but knew he was getting the Pap smear, the plastic spatula scraping cells from her cervix. Part of Zoe Kohler ravaged and removed from her.

Stark and the nurse worked swiftly, efficiently. In a moment, the spatula was withdrawn, the speculum closed. She understood it was being withdrawn. Something, a stretched fullness, was subsiding.

Then Dr. Oscar, that sweet, sweet teddy bear of a man, was standing between her legs.

"Don't tense up," he cautioned.

He inserted two gloved fingers into her vagina slowly, pressing the walls apart as he went. He placed his other hand flat on her groin. Fingers pressed gently upward, palm downward.

"Pain?" he asked.

"No," she gasped.

"Tenderness?"

"No."

He began to probe her abdomen, feeling both sides, the center, down toward the junction of her thighs.

"Pain here?"

"No."

"Anything here?"

"No."

"Here?"

"No."

"Just another minute now."

She waited, knowing what was coming.

Slowly, easily, he inserted one gloved finger, coated with a jelly, into her rectum. Between that finger and the one still within her vagina, he felt the muscular wall separating the two passages as the fingertips of his other hand pressed deep into her groin.

She had been staring wide-eyed at the ceiling. She was determined not to cry. It was not the pain; she felt no pain. A twinge now and then, a sensation of being stretched, opened to the foreign world, but no pain. So why did she have to fight to hold back her tears? She did not know.

Slowly, easily, gently, fingers and hands were withdrawn. Dr. Stark stripped off his gloves. He slapped her bare knee lightly.

"Beautiful," he said. "Not a thing wrong. You're in great shape. Get dressed and stop by my office."

He reclaimed his cigar and lumbered out.

Gladys helped her off the table. Her legs were trembling. The big nurse held her until her knees steadied.

"Okay?" she asked.

"Fine. Thank you, Gladys."

"There are tissues in the bathroom if you have any jelly on you. You can go right into the doctor's when you're dressed."

She put on her clothes slowly. Drew a comb through her hair. She felt drained and, somehow, satisfied and content.

Dr. Stark was slumped behind his desk, his glasses pushed up atop that cloud of snowy hair. He rubbed his lined forehead wearily.

"Everything looks normal," he reported to Zoe. "We'll have the reports of the lab tests in three days. I don't anticipate anything unusual. If there is, I'll call. If not, I won't."

"Can I call?" she asked anxiously. "If I don't hear from you? In three or four days?"

"Sure," he said equably. "Why not?"

He put the short stub of his cigar aside. He yawned, showing those big, stained teeth. Then he laced his fingers comfortably across his thick middle. He regarded her kindly.

"Regular periods, Zoe?"

"Oh yes," she said. "Twenty-six or -seven or -eight days. Around there."

"Good," he said. "When's the next?"

"April tenth," she said promptly.

"Still have the cramps?"

"Yes."

"When do they start?"

"A day or two before."

"Severe?"

"They get worse. They don't stop until I begin to bleed."

He made an expression, a wince, then shook his head.

"I told you, Zoe, I can't find any physical cause. I wish you'd take my advice and see, uh, a counselor."

"Everyone wants me to see a shrink!" she burst out.

He looked up sharply. "Everyone?"

She wouldn't look at him. "A friend."

"And what did you say?"

"No."

He sighed. "Well, it's your body and your life. But you shouldn't have to suffer that. The cramps, I mean."

"They're not so bad," she said.

But they were.

At about 8:30 that evening, Dr. Oscar Stark pushed a button fixed to the doorjamb of his office. It rang a buzzer upstairs in the kitchen and alerted his wife that he'd be up in ten or fifteen minutes, ready for dinner.

He had already said goodnight to his receptionist and nurses. He took off his white cotton jacket. He washed up in one of the lavatories. He donned a worn velvet smoking jacket, so old that the elbows shone. He wandered tiredly through the first floor offices, turning off lights, making certain the drug cabinet was locked, trying doors and windows.

He climbed the broad staircase slowly, pulling himself along with the banister. Once again he vowed that he would retire in two years. Sell the practice and the building. Spend a year breaking in the new man.

Then he and Berthe would leave New York. Buy a condominium in Florida. Most of their friends had already gone. The children had married and left. He and Berthe deserved some rest. At peace. In the sun.

He knew it would never happen.

That night Berthe had prepared mushroom-and-barley soup, his favorite, and a pot roast made with first-cut brisket. His spirits soared. He had a Scotch highball and lighted a cigar.

"It was a hard day?" his wife asked.

"No better or worse than usual," he said.

She looked at him narrowly.

"That Zoe Kohler woman?" she said.

He was astonished. "You know about her?"

"Of course. You told me."

"I did?"

"Twice," she said, nodding. "The first Tuesday of every month."

"Oh-ho," he said, looking at her lovingly. "Now I understand the mushroom-and-barley soup."

"The first Tuesday of every month," Berthe said, smiling. "To revive you. Oscar, you think she . . . Well, you know, some women enjoy . . . You told me so."

"Yes," he said seriously, "that's so. But not her. For her it's painful."

"Painful? It hurts? You hurt her?"

"Oh no, Berthe. No, no, no. You know me better than that. But I think it's a kind of punishment for her. That's how she sees it."

"Punishment for what? Has she done something?"

"Such a question. How would I know?"

"Come, let's eat."

They went into the dining room. It was full of shadows.

"I don't think she's done something," he tried to explain. "I mean, she doesn't want punishment because she feels guilty. I think she feels unworthy."

"My husband the psychologist."

"Well, that's what I think it is," he repeated stubbornly. "She comes every month for an examination she doesn't need and that she hates. It's punishment for her unworthiness. That's how she gets her gratification."

"Sha," his wife said. "Put your cigar down and eat your soup."

The cramps were bad. None of her pills helped. The pain came from deep within her, in waves. It wrenched her gut, twisted her inside. It was a giant hand, clawing, yanking this way and that, turning her over. She wanted to scream.

She left work early on Wednesday night, April 9th. Mr. Pinckney was sympathetic when she told him the cause.

"Take tomorrow off," he said. "We'll manage."

"Oh no," she said. "I'll be all right tomorrow."

She went directly home and drew a bath as hot as she could endure. She soaked for an hour, running in more hot water as the tub cooled. She searched for telltale stains, but the water remained clear; her menses had not yet started.

She swallowed an assortment of vitamins and minerals before she dressed. She didn't care what Dr. Stark said; she was convinced they were helping her survive. And she sipped a glass of white wine while she dressed. The cramps had diminished to a dull, persistent throbbing.

She regretted the necessity of going up to the Filmore on West 72nd Street to put on makeup and don her new strawberry blond wig. But she didn't want to risk the danger of having her neighbors and doorman see her transformed.

Also, there was a risk of going directly from her apartment house to the Hotel Coolidge. The cabdriver might remember. A circuitous route was safer.

She had selected the Coolidge because the hotel trade magazine, in its directory of conventions and sales meetings, had listed the Coolidge as hosting two conventions and a political gathering on the night of April 9th. It was an 840-room hotel on Seventh Avenue and 50th Street. Close enough to Times Square to get a lot of walk-in business in its cocktail lounges and dining rooms.

She wore fire-engine-red nylon lingerie embroidered with small hearts, sheer pantyhose with a reddish tint, her evening sandals with their "hookers' heels." The dress, tightly fitted, was a bottle-green silk so dark it was almost black. It shimmered, and was skimpy as a slip, suspended from her smooth shoulders by spaghetti straps.

Two hours later she was seated alone at a small banquette in the New Orleans Room of the Hotel Coolidge. Her trenchcoat was folded on the seat beside her. She was smoking a cigarette and sipping a glass of white wine. She did not turn her head, but her eyes were never still.

It was a small, dimly lighted room, half-filled. A three-piece band played desultory jazz from a raised platform in one corner. It was all relatively quiet, relaxed. Zoe Kohler wondered if she might do better in the Gold Coast Room.

Most of the men who entered were in twos and threes, hatless and coatless, but bearing badges on the lapels of their suit jackets. They invariably headed directly for the bar. There were a few couples at the small tables, but not many.

Shortly after 11:00 P.M., a single man came to the entrance of the New Orleans Room. He stood a moment, looking about.

Come to me, Zoe Kohler willed. *Come to me.*

He glanced in her direction, hesitated, then moved casually toward the wall of banquettes.

Lover, she thought, not looking at him.

He slid behind the table next to hers. She pulled her shoulder bag and trenchcoat closer. The cocktail waitress came over and he ordered a bourbon and water. His voice was a deep, resonant baritone.

He was tall, more than six feet, hunched, and almost totally bald. He wore rimless spectacles. His features were pleasant enough, his cheeks somewhat pitted. The backs of his hands were badly scarred. He wore the ubiquitous name-badge on his breast pocket. Zoe caught a look at it. HELLO! CALL ME JERRY.

They sat at their adjoining tables. She ordered another glass of wine, he another bourbon. They did not speak nor look in each other's direction. Finally . . .

"I beg your pardon," he said, leaning toward her.

She turned to look coldly at him. He blushed, up into his bald head. He seemed about to withdraw.

"Uh, I, ah, uh, wondered if I could ask you a personal question?"

"You may ask," she said severely. "I may or may not answer."

"Uh," he said, gulping, "that dress you're wearing . . . It's so beautiful. I want to bring my wife a present from New York, and she'd look great in that." He added hastily, "Not as good as you do, of course, but I wondered where you bought it, and if . . ." His voice trailed away.

She smiled at him.

"Thank you—" She peered closer at his badge as if seeing it for the first time. "Thank you, Jerry, but I'm sorry to tell you that the shop where I bought it has gone out of business."

"Oh," he said, "that's too bad. But listen, maybe you can suggest a store where I can buy something nice."

Now they had turned to face each other. He kept lifting his eyes from her shoulders and cleavage, and then his eyes would slide down again.

They talked awhile, exploring. He was from Little Rock, Arkansas, and was regional manager for a chain of fast-food restaurants that sold chicken-fried steaks and was about to go the franchise route.

She touched the scars on the backs of his hands.

"What happened?" she asked. "A war wound?"

"Oh no," he said, laughing for the first time. He had a nice, sheepish laugh. "A stove caught fire. They'll heal. Eventually."

"My name's Irene," she said softly.

He bought them two more rounds of drinks. By that time, she had moved her coat and shoulder bag to her other side, and he was sitting beside her, at her table. She pressed her thigh against his. He drew his leg hastily away. Then it came back.

The New Orleans Room had filled up, every table taken. Patrons were standing two and three deep at the bar. The jazz trio was playing with more verve, music blasting. The distracted waitresses were scurrying about. Zoe Kohler was reassured; no one would remember her.

"Noisy in here," Jerry said, looking about fretfully. "We can't rightly talk."

"Where are you staying, Jerry?" she asked.

"What?" he said. "Snow again; I don't get your drift."

She put her lips close to his ear. Close enough to touch. She repeated her question.

"Why, uh, right here in the hotel," he said, shaken. "The fourteenth floor."

"Have anything to drink in your room?"

"I got most of a pint of sippin' whiskey," he said, staring at her. "Bourbon."

She put her lips to his ear again.

"Couldn't we have a party?" she whispered. Her tongue darted.

"I've never done anything like this before," he said hoarsely. "I swear, I never have."

There was one other couple in the automatic elevator, but they got off on the ninth floor. Jerry and Irene rode the rest of the way alone.

"Notice they got no thirteenth floor?" he said nervously. "It goes from twelve to fourteen. I guess they figure no one would want a room on the thirteenth. Bad luck. But I'm on the fourteenth which is really the thirteenth. Makes no nevermind to me."

She put a hand on his arm.

"You're sweet," she said.

"No kidding?" he said, pleased.

Inside his room, the door locked, he insisted on showing her wallet photographs of his wife, his home, his Labrador retriever, named Boots. Zoe looked at what she thought were a dumpy blonde, a naked development house with no landscaping, and a beautiful dog.

"Jerry, you're a very lucky man," she said, handling the photos by the edges.

"Don't I know it!"

"Children?"

"No," he said shortly. "No children. Not yet."

She thought he was in his late thirties, maybe forty. No children. That was too bad. But his widow would remarry. Zoe was sure of it; she had that look.

He rummaged in his open suitcase and came up with an almost full pint bottle of bourbon.

"Voila!" he said, pronouncing it "viola." Zoe didn't know if he was making a joke or not.

"I think I'll skip," she said. "All that white wine has got me a tiny bit tipsy. But you go right ahead."

"You're sure?"

"I'm sure."

He poured a small shot into a water glass. His hand was trembling; the bottle neck rattled against the rim of the glass.

"Listen," he said, not looking at her, "I told you I've never done anything like this before, and that's God's own truth. I got to be honest with you; I don't know whether you . . ."

He looked at her helplessly.

She went over to him, held him by the arms, smiled up at him.

"I know what you're wondering," she said. "You're wondering if I want money and if you should pay me before or after. Isn't that so?"

He nodded dumbly.

"Jerry," she said gently, "I'm not a professional, if that's what you think. I just enjoy being here with you. If a man wants to give me a little gift later because he's had such a good time . . ."

"Oh sure, Irene," he said swallowing. "I understand."

"You've got a radio?" she said briskly. "Turn on the radio. Let's get this show on the road."

He turned on the bedside radio. The station was playing disco.

"Wow," she said, snapping her fingers, "that's great. Do you like to dance?"

He took a gulp of bourbon.

"I'm not very good at it," he said.

"Then I'll dance by myself," she said.

She began to move about the room, dipping, swaying, her hips moving. Her arms were extended overhead, fingers still snapping. She bowed, writhed, twisted, twirled. Her heels caught in the heavy shag rug. A shoulder strap slipped off and hung loose.

He sat on the edge of the bed, touching the bourbon to his lips, and watched her with wondering eyes.

"Too many clothes," she said. In time to the music, she sashayed over to him, turned her back, and motioned. "Open me up," she commanded.

Obediently, he drew her back zipper down. It hissed. She slid off the remaining strap, let her dress fall, stepped out. She tossed it onto a chair.

She stood there a moment, facing him, in her heart-flecked lingerie, reddish pantyhose, high heels. They stared at each other. Then the music changed to a tango. She began to swoop and glide about the room.

"I swear to God," he said, his voice a croak, "this is the damndest thing that ever happened to me. Irene, you are one beautiful lady. I just can't believe it."

"You better believe it," she said, laughing. "It's true."

She continued dancing for him until the music ended. An announcer came on, talking about motor oil. Zoe Kohler took off her sandals, wiggled out of her pantyhose. Jerry was staring at the floor.

"Jerry," she said.

He raised his head, looked at her.

"You like?" she said, posing with hands on her waist, weight on one leg. She cocked her head quizzically.

He nodded. He looked frightened and miserable. She went over to him, stood close, between his legs. She pressed his head between her palms, pulled his face into her soft, scented belly.

"You get out of all those clothes, honey," she said throatily. "I have to go make wee-wee. Be back in a minute."

She took her shoulder bag and headed for the bathroom. She glanced back, but he wasn't looking at her. He was staring at the floor again.

She made her usual preparations, thinking that he was a difficult one. He didn't come on. He was troubled. He had no confidence. That wasn't fair.

She came out of the bathroom naked, towel draped over her right forearm and hand. "Here I am!" she said gaily.

He wasn't lying naked under the sheet. He had taken off only his jacket and vest, had loosened his tie and opened his collar. He was still sitting on the edge of the bed, hunched over, elbows on knees. He was turning his glass around and around in his scarred hands. Now it was filled with whiskey, almost to the brim.

When he heard her voice, he turned to look over his shoulder.

"Good lord a'mighty," he said with awe.

She came over to the bed, on the other side. She kneeled behind him. With her left hand, she pulled him gently back until he was leaning against her, pressing her breasts, stomach, thighs.

"Jerry," she said, "what's wrong?"

He groaned. "Irene, this is no good. I just can't do it. I'm sorry, but I can't. Listen, I'll give you money. I hate wasting your time like this. But when I think of my little girl waiting at home for me, I just can't. . ."

"Shh, shh," she said soothingly. She put the soft palm of her left hand on his brow and drew his head back toward her, between her breasts. "Don't think about that. Don't think about a thing."

She let the towel fall free. She plunged the point of the knife blade below his left ear and pulled it savagely to the right, tugging when it caught.

His body leaped convulsively off the bed. Glass fell. Drink spilled. He went flopping to the floor, limbs flailing.

That wasn't what surprised her. The shock was the fountain of blood, the giant spurt, the wild gush. It had gone out so far that gobbets had hit the wall and were beginning to drip downward.

She watched those trickles for a brief moment, fascinated. Then she scrambled across the bed and stood astride him, bent over. He was still threshing, limbs twitching, eyelids fluttering.

He was clothed, but it made no difference. She didn't want to see that knobbed thing, that club. She drove the blade through his clothing into his testicles, with the incantation, "There. There. There."

After a while she straightened up, looked about dully. Nothing had changed. She heard, dimly, traffic sounds from Seventh Avenue. An airliner droned overhead. Someone passed in the outside corridor; a man laughed. Next door, a toilet flushed.

She looked down at Jerry. He was gone, his life soaked into the carpet. The bedside radio was still playing. Disco again. She went into the bathroom for sheets of toilet paper before she handled the radio knob, stopping the music.

She was so careful.

---

4 Edward X. Delaney found himself obsessed with the puzzle of the two hotel deaths. He tried to turn his mind to other concerns, to keep himself busy. Inevitably, his thoughts returned to the murder of the two men: how it was done, why it was done, who might have done it.

Sighing, he surrendered to the challenge of the mystery, put his feet on his desk, smoked a cigar, and stared at the far wall.

Everything in his cop's instinct and experience told him it was the work of a criminal psychopath, a crazy, a nut. It was almost hopeless to try to imagine a motive. But it didn't seem to be greed; nothing had been stolen.

On impulse, he searched through the pages of an annual diary and appointment book, looking for the section that listed phases of the moon. There was no connection between the full moon and the dates of the slayings. He slammed the desk drawer in disgust.

The problem was, there was no brilliantly deductive way to approach a case in which a random killer selected victims by chance and murdered for apparently no reason. There was no handle, nowhere to start.

Because, Delaney told himself, he had nothing better to do, he wrote out dossiers of the two victims, trying to recall everything Sergeant Abner Boone had told him. Then he headed a third sheet: Perpetrator.

He pored over the known facts about the two victims, trying to find a link, a connection. He found nothing other than what he had mentioned to Boone: they were both middle-aged men, visitors to New York, staying at midtown hotels. That, he knew, meant next to nothing. But in his meticulous way, he made a careful note of it.

The sheet of paper devoted to the killer had few notations:

1. Could be male or female.
2. Wears black nylon wig.
3. Clever; careful; crafty if not intelligent.

Just writing all this down gave him a certain satisfaction. It brought a solution no closer, he knew, but it was a start in bringing order and form to a chaotic enigma. It was the only way he knew to apply logic to solving a crime born of abnormal motives and an irrational mentality.

He was back in his study again, on the morning of March 21st, ruminating about the case.

He was playing with the idea that perhaps the two victims, George T. Puller and Frederick Wolheim, had, at some time in their business careers, employed the same man, and had fired this man, for whatever reasons.

Then, years later, the discharged employee, his resentment turned to homicidal fury, had sought out his two former employers and slashed them to death. A fanciful notion, the Chief acknowledged, but not impossible. In fact, not far-fetched at all.

He was still considering this possibility and how it might be checked out when his phone rang. He reached for it absently.

"Edward X. Delaney here," he said.

"Chief, this is Boone," the sergeant said. "I thought you'd like to know . . .

I did what you said: took a Crime Scene Unit man back to the room at the Hotel Pierce where Wolheim was chilled. We took measurements on that armchair where the two black nylon hairs were found."

"And?"

"Chief, it was approxiimate. I mean, when you sit in that chair, it has a soft seat cushion that depresses. You understand? So it was tough getting an exact measurement from the back of the head to the tailbone."

"Of course."

"Anyway," Boone went on, "we did what we could. Then there was no one in the Lab Services Unit or ME's office who could help. But one of the assistant ME's suggested we call a guy up at the American Museum of Natural History. He's an anthropologist, supposed to be a hotshot on reconstructing skeletons from bone fragments."

"Good," Delaney said, pleased with Boone's thoroughness. "What did he say?"

"I gave him the measurement and he called back within an hour. He said his estimate—and he insisted it was only a guess—was that the person who sat in that chair was about five feet five to five feet seven."

There was silence.

"Chief?" Boone said. "You still there?"

"Yes, sergeant," Delaney said slowly, "I'm still here. Five-five to five-seven? That could be a smallish man or a tallish woman."

"Right," the sergeant said. "But it's *something,* isn't it, Chief? I mean, it's more than we had before."

"Of course," Edward X. Delaney said, as heartily as he could. He didn't want to say how frail that clue was; the sergeant would know that. "How are you getting along with Slavin?"

"Okay," Boone said, lowering his voice. "So far. He's been making us recheck everything we did before he came aboard. I guess I can understand that; he doesn't want to be responsible for anything that happened before he took command."

"Uh-huh," Delaney said, thinking that Slavin was a fool to waste his men's time in that fashion and to imply doubt of their professional competence.

"Chief, I'd like to ask you a favor . . ."

"Of course. Anything."

"Could I call you about the investigation?" the sergeant asked, still speaking in a muffled voice. "Every once in a while? To keep you up on what's going on and ask your help on things?"

That would be Deputy Commissioner Ivar Thorsen's suggestion, the Chief knew. "Sergeant, why don't you call Delaney every day or so? You're friends, aren't you? Keep him up on the progress of the investigation. See if he has any ideas."

Which meant that Thorsen didn't entirely trust the expertise of Lieutenant Martin Slavin.

"Call me any time you like, sergeant," Edward X. Delaney said. "I'll be here."

"Thank you, sir," Boone said gratefully.

Delaney hung up. On the dossier headed Perpetrator, he added:

4. Approx. 5-5 to 5-7.

Then he went into the kitchen and made a sandwich of sliced kielbasa and Jewish coleslaw, on sour rye. Since it was a "wet" sandwich, he ate it standing over the sink.

There was one person Edward X. Delaney was eager to talk to—but he wasn't sure the old man was still alive. He had been Detective Sergeant Albert Braun, assigned to the office of the District Attorney of New York County. But he had retired about fifteen years ago and Delaney lost track of him.

Braun had joined the New York Police Department with a law degree at a time when the force was having trouble recruiting qualified high school graduates. During his first five years, he served as a foot patrolman and continued his education with special studies at local universities in criminal law, forensic science and, his particular interest, the psychology of criminal behavior.

During his early years in the Department, he had won the reputation of being a dependable, if unspectacular, street cop. His nickname during this period of service was "Arf," from Little Orphan Annie's dog. That hound wasn't a bulldog, but Albert Braun was—and that's how he got the canine monicker.

Delaney remembered that it was said of Braun that if he was assigned to a stakeout in front of a house, and told, "Watch for a male Caucasian, five-eleven, 185 pounds, about fifty-five, grayish hair, wearing a plaid sport jacket," you could come back two years later and Arf would look up and say, "He hasn't shown up yet."

Finally, Albert Braun's background, erudition, and intelligence were recognized. He earned the gold shield of a detective, received rapid promotions, and ended up a sergeant in the Manhattan DA's office where he remained until his retirement.

Long before that, he was recognized as the Department's top expert in the history of crime. He possessed a library of more than 2,000 volumes on criminology, and his knowledge of old cases, weapons, and criminal methodology was encyclopedic.

He had been consulted many times by police departments outside New York City and even by foreign police bureaus and Interpol. In addition, he taught a popular course on investigative techniques to detectives of the NYPD and was a frequent guest lecturer at John Jay College of Criminal Justice.

Delaney remembered that Braun had never married, and lived somewhere in Elmhurst, in Queens. The Chief consulted his personal telephone directory, a small, battered black book that contained numbers so ancient that instead of a three-digit prefix some bore designations such as Murray Hill-3, Beekman-5, and Butterfield-8.

He found Albert Braun's number and dialed. He waited while the phone rang seven times. He was about to hang up when a woman came on the line with a breathless "Yes?"

"Is this the Albert Braun residence?" Delaney asked.

"Yes, it is."

He didn't want to ask anything as crude as, "Is the old man still alive?" He tried, "Is Mr. Braun available?"

"Not at the moment," the woman said. "Who's calling, please?"

"My name is Edward X. Delaney. I'm an old friend of Mr. Braun. I haven't seen or spoken to him in years. I hope he's in good health?"

"Not very," the woman said, her voice lowering. "He fell and broke his hip about three years ago and developed pneumonia from that. Then last year he had a stroke. He's recovering from that, somewhat, but he spends most of his time in bed."

"I'm sorry to hear it."

"Well, he's doing as well as can be expected. A man of his age."

"Yes," Delaney said, wanting to ask who she was and what she was doing there. She answered his unspoken question.

"My name is Martha Kaslove. *Mrs.* Martha Kaslove," she added firmly. "I've been Mr. Braun's housekeeper since he fell."

"Well, I'm glad he's not alone," the Chief said. "I had hoped to talk to him, but under the circumstances I won't bother him. I'd appreciate it if you'd tell him I called. The name is Edward X.—"

"Wait a minute," she said. "You knew him when he was a policeman? Before he retired?"

"Yes, I knew him well."

"Mr. Braun doesn't have many visitors," she said sadly. "None, in fact. He doesn't have any family. Oh, neighbors stop by occasionally, but it's really to visit with me, not him. I think a visit from an old friend would do him the world of good. Would you be willing to . . . ?"

"Of course," Delaney said promptly. "I'll be glad to. I'm in Manhattan. I could be there in half an hour or so."

"Good," she said happily. "Let me ask him, Mr. Laney."

"*De*laney," he said. "Edward X. Delaney."

"Hang on just a minute, please," she said.

He hung on for several minutes. Then Mrs. Kaslove came back on the phone.

"He wants to see you," she reported. "He's all excited. He's even putting clothes on and he wants me to shave him."

"Wonderful," the Chief said, smiling at the phone. "Tell him I'm on my way."

He made sure he had his reading glasses, notebook, two ballpoint pens, and a sharpened pencil. He pulled on his heavy, navy-blue melton overcoat, double-breasted. He set his hard black homburg squarely atop his big head. Then he went lumbering over to a liquor store on Second Avenue where he bought a bottle of Glenlivet Scotch. He had it gift-wrapped and put in a brown paper bag.

He stopped an empty northbound cab, got in, closed the door. He gave Albert Braun's address in Elmhurst.

The driver turned around to stare at him. "I don't go to Queens," he said.

"Sure you do," Edward X. Delaney said genially. "Or we can go to the Two-five-one Precinct House, just a block away. Or, if you prefer, you can take me downtown to the Hack Bureau and I'll swear out a complaint there."

"Jesus Christ!" the driver said disgustedly and slammed the cab into gear.

They made the trip in silence, which was all right with Delaney. He was rehearsing in his mind the questions he wanted to ask Albert Braun.

It was a pleasant house on a street of lawns and trees. In spring and summer, Delaney thought, it would look like a residential street in a small town, with people mowing the grass, trimming hedges, poking at flower borders. He had almost forgotten there were streets like that in New York.

She must have been watching for him through the front window, for the door opened as he came up the stoop. She filled the doorway: a big, motherly woman with twinkling eyes and a flawless complexion.

"Mr. Delaney?" she said in a warm, pleasing voice.

"Yes. You must be Mrs. Kaslove. Happy to meet you."

He took off his homburg. They shook hands. She ushered him into a small entrance hall, took his hat and coat, hung them away in a closet.

"I can't tell you how he's looking forward to your visit," she said. "I haven't seen him so alive and chirpy in months."

"If I had known . . ."

"Now you must realize he's been a very sick man," she rattled on, "and not be shocked at the way he looks. He's not bedridden, but when he gets up, he uses a wheelchair. He's lost a lot of weight and the left side of his face—you know—from the stroke . . ."

Delaney nodded.

"An hour," she said definitely. "The doctor said he can sit up an hour at a time. And try not to upset him."

"I won't upset him," the Chief said. He held up his brown paper bag. "Can he have a drink?"

"One weak highball a day," she said firmly. "You'll find glasses in his bathroom. Now I'm going to run out and do some shopping. But I'll be back long before your hour is up."

"Take your time," Delaney said, smiling. "I won't leave until you get back."

"His bedroom is at the head of the stairs," she said, pointing. "On your right. He's waiting for you."

The Chief took a deep breath and climbed the stairs slowly, looking about. It was a cheerful, informal home. Patterned wallpaper. Lots of chintz. Bright curtains. Some good rugs. Everything looked clean and shining.

The man in the bedroom was a bleached skeleton propped up in a motorized wheelchair parked in the middle of the floor. A crocheted Afghan covered his lap and legs and was tucked in at the sides. A fringed paisley shawl was draped about his bony shoulders. He wore a starched white shirt, open at the neck to reveal slack, crepey skin.

His twisted face wrenched in a grimace. Delaney realized that Albert Braun was trying to grin at him. He stepped forward and picked up the man's frail white hand and pressed it gently. It felt like a bunch of grapes, as soft and tender.

"How are you?" he asked, smiling.

"Getting along," Braun said in a wispy voice. "Getting along. How are *you*, Captain? I thought you'd be in uniform. How are things at the precinct? The usual hysteria, eh?"

Delaney hesitated just a brief instant, then said, "You're right. The usual hysteria. It's good to see you again, Professor."

"Professor," Braun repeated, his face wrenching again. "You're the only cop I ever knew who called me 'Professor.' "

"You *are* a professor," Delaney said.

"I was," Braun said, "I was. But not really. It was just a courtesy, an honorary title. It meant nothing. Detective Sergeant Albert Braun. That's who I was. That meant something."

The Chief nodded understandingly. He held out the brown paper bag. "A little something to keep you warm."

Braun made a feeble gesture. "You didn't have to do that," he protested. "You better open it for me, Captain. I don't have much strength in my hands these days."

Delaney tore the wrappings away and held the bottle close to the man in the wheelchair.

"Scotch," Braun said, touching the bottle with trembling fingers. "What makes the heart grow fonder. Let's have one now for old times' sake."

"I thought you'd never ask," Delaney said, and left the old man cackling while he went into the bathroom to mix drinks. He poured himself a heavy shot, tossed it down, and stood there, gripping the sink as he felt it hit. He thought he had been prepared, but the sight of Albert Braun had been a shock.

Then he mixed two Scotch highballs in water tumblers, a weak one for the Professor, a dark one for himself. He brought the drinks back into the bedroom. He made certain Braun's thin fingers encircled the glass before he released it.

"Sit down, Captain, sit down," the old man said. "Take that armchair there. I've got the cushions all broke in for you."

Edward X. Delaney sat down gingerly in what seemed to him to be a fragile piece of furniture. He hoisted his glass.

"Good health and a long life," he toasted.

"I'll drink to good health," Braun said, "but a long life is for the birds. All your friends die off. I feel like the Last of the Mohicans. Say, whatever happened to Ernie Silverman? Remember him? He was with the . . ."

Then they were off and running—twenty minutes of reminiscences, mostly gossip about old friends and old enemies. Braun did most of the talking, becoming more garrulous as he touched the watery highball to his pale lips. Delaney didn't see him swallowing, but noted the level of liquid was going down.

Then the old man's glass was empty. He held it out in a hand that had steadied.

"That was just flavored water," he said. "Let's have another with more kick to it."

Delaney hesitated. Braun stared at him, face mangled into a gargoyle's mask. All his bones seemed to be knobby, pressing out through parchment skin. Feathers of grayish hair skirted his waxen skull. Even his eyes were filmed and distant, gaze dulled and turned inward. Black veins popped in his sunken temples.

"I know what Martha told you," Braun said. "One weak drink a day. Right?"

"Right," Delaney said. Still he hesitated.

"She keeps the booze downstairs," the skeleton complained. "I can't get at it. I'm eighty-four," he added in a querulous tone. "The game is up. You think I should be denied?"

Edward X. Delaney made up his mind. He didn't care to analyze his motives.

"No," he said, "I don't think you should be denied."

He took Braun's glass, went back to the bathroom. He mixed two more Scotch-and-waters, middling strong. He brought them into the bedroom, and Braun's starfish hand plucked the glass from his hand. The old man sampled it.

"That's more like it," he said, leaning back in his wheelchair. He observed Delaney closely. The cast over his eyes had faded. He had the shrewd, calculating look of a smart lawyer.

"You didn't come all the way out here to hold a dying man's hand," he said.

"No. I didn't."

"Old 'Iron Balls,' " Braun said affectionately. "You always did have the rep of using anyone you could to break a case."

"That's right," Delaney agreed. "Anyone, anytime. There *is* something I wanted to ask you about. A case. It's not mine; a friend's ass is on the line and I promised I'd talk to you."

"What's his name?"

"Abner Boone. Detective Sergeant. You know him?"

"Boone? Boone? I think I had him in one of my classes. Was his father a street cop? Shot down?"

"That's the man."

"Sure, I remember. Nice boy. What's his problem?"

"It looks like a repeat killer. Two so far. Same MO, but no connection between the victims. Stranger homicides. No leads."

"Another Son of Sam?" Braun said excitedly, leaning forward. "What a case that was! Did you work that one, Captain?"

"No," Delaney said shortly, "I never did."

"I was retired then, of course, but I followed it in the papers and on TV every day. Made notes. Collected clippings. I had a crazy idea of writing a book on it some day."

"Not so crazy," Delaney said. "Now this thing that Boone caught is—"

"Fascinating case," Albert Braun said slowly. His head was beginning to droop forward on the skinny stem of his neck. "Fascinating. I remember the last lecture I gave at John Jay was on that case. Multiple random homicides. The motives . . ." His loose dentures clacked.

"Yes, yes," Delaney said hurriedly, wondering if he was losing the man. "That's what I wanted to talk to you about—the motives. And also, has there ever been a female killer like Son of Sam? A woman who commits several random homicides?"

"A woman?" the old man said, raising his head with an effort. "It's all in my lecture."

"Yes," Delaney said, "but could you tell me now? Do you remember if there was ever a case like Son of Sam when a woman was the perp?"

"Martha Beck," Braun said, trying to recall. "A woman in Pennsylvania—

what was her name? I forget. But she was a baby-sitter and knew the victims. All kids. A woman at a Chicago fair, around the turn of the century, I think. I'd have to look it up. She ran a boardinghouse. Killed her boarders. Greed, again." His face tried to make a grin. "Ground them up into sausages."

"But *stranger* homicides," Delaney insisted. "Any woman involved in a series of killings of *strangers?*"

"It's all in my last lecture," Albert Braun said sadly. "Two days later I fell. The steps weren't even slippery. I just tripped. That's how it ends, Captain; you trip."

He held out his empty glass. Delaney took it to the bathroom, mixed fresh highballs. When he brought the drinks back to the bedroom, he heard the outside door slam downstairs.

Braun's head had fallen forward, sharp chin on shrunken chest.

"Professor?" the Chief said.

The head came up slowly.

"Yes?"

"Here's your drink."

The coiled fingers clamped around.

"That lecture of yours," Delaney said. "Your last lecture. Was it written out? Typed?"

The head bobbed.

"Would you have a copy of it? I'd like to read it."

Albert Braun roused, looking at the Chief with eyes that had a spark, burning.

"Lots of copies," he said. "In the study. Watch this . . ."

He pushed the controls in a metal box fixed to the arm of his wheelchair. He began to move slowly toward the doorway. Delaney stood hastily, hovered close. But Braun maneuvered his chair skillfully through the doorway, turned down the hallway. The Chief moved nearby, ready to grab the old man if he toppled.

But he didn't. He steered expertly into the doorway of a darkened room and stopped his chair.

"Switch on your right," he said in a faint voice.

Delaney fumbled, found the wall plate. Light blazed. It was a long cavern of a room, a study-den-library. Rough, unpainted pine bookshelves rose to the ceiling. Bound volumes, some in ancient leather covers. Paperbacks. Magazines. Stapled and photocopied academic papers. One shelf of photographs in folders.

There was a ramshackle desk, swivel chair, file cabinet, typewriter on a separate table. A desk lamp. A wilted philodendron.

The room had been dusted; it was not squalid. But it had the deserted look of a chamber long unused. The desktop was blank; the air had a stale odor. It was a deserted room, dying.

Albert Braun looked around.

"I'm leaving all my books and files to the John Jay library," he said. "It's in my will."

"Good," Delaney said.

"The lectures are over there in the lefthand corner. Third shelf up. In manila folders."

Delaney went searching. He found the most recent folder, opened it. At least a dozen copies of a lecture entitled "Multiple Random Homicides: History and Motives."

"May I take a copy?" he asked.

No answer.

"Professor," he said sharply.

Braun's spurt of energy seemed to have depleted him. He raised his head with difficulty.

"May I take a copy?" Delaney repeated.

"Take all you want," Braun said in a peevish voice. "Take everything. What difference does it make?"

The Chief took one copy of Detective Sergeant Albert Braun's last lecture. He folded it lengthwise, tucked it into his inside jacket pocket.

"We'll get you back to your bedroom now," he said.

But there in the doorway, looming, was big, motherly Mrs. Martha Kaslove. She looked down with horror at the lolling Albert Braun and snatched the glass from his nerveless fingers. Then she looked furiously at Edward X. Delaney.

"What did you do to him?" she demanded.

He said nothing.

"You got him drunk," she accused. "You may have killed him! You get out of here and never, never come back. Don't try to call; I'll hang up on you. And if I see you lurking around, I'll call the cops and have you put away, you disgusting man."

He waited until she had wheeled Albert Braun back to his bedroom. Then Delaney turned off the lights in the study, went downstairs, and found his hat and coat. He called a taxi from the living room phone.

He went outside and stood on the sidewalk, waiting for the cab. He looked around at the pleasant, peaceful street, so free of traffic that kids were skateboarding down the middle of the pavement. Nice homes. Private lives.

He was back in Manhattan shortly after 3:30 P.M. In the kitchen, taped to the refrigerator door—she knew how to communicate with him—was a note from Monica. She had gone to a symposium and would return no later than 5:30. He was to put the chicken and potatoes in the oven at precisely 4:00.

He welcomed the chore. He didn't want to think of what he had done. He was not ashamed of how he had used a dying man, but he didn't want to dwell on it.

There were six chicken legs. He cut them into pieces, drumsticks and thighs, rinsed and dried them. Then he rubbed them with olive oil, sprinkled on toasted onion flakes, and dusted them with garlic and parsley salt. He put the twelve pieces (the thighs skin side down) in a disposable aluminum foil baking pan.

He washed and dried the four Idaho potatoes. He rubbed them with vegetable oil and wrapped them in aluminum foil. Monica and he could never eat four baked potatoes, but the two left over would be kept refrigerated, sliced another day, and fried with butter, chopped onions, and lots of paprika. Good homefries.

He set the oven for 350 degrees and put in chicken and potatoes. He searched in the fridge for salad stuff and found a nice head of romaine. He snapped it into single long leaves, washed them, wrapped them in a paper towel. Then he put them back into the refrigerator to chill. He and Monica liked to eat romaine leaf by leaf, dipped into a spicy sauce.

He made the sauce, a tingly mixture of mayonnaise, ketchup, mustard, Tabasco, salt, pepper, garlic powder, and parsley flakes. He whipped up a bowl of the stuff and left it to meld.

He was not a good cook; he knew that. He smoked too much and drank too much; his palate was dulled. That was why he overspiced everything. Monica complained that when he cooked, sweat broke out on her scalp.

He had accomplished all his tasks in his heavy, vested sharkskin suit, a canvas kitchen apron knotted about his waist. Finished, he untied the apron, took an opened can of Ballantine ale, and went into his study.

He settled down, took a sip of the ale, donned his reading glasses. He began to read Detective Sergeant Albert Braun's last lecture. He read it twice. Between readings, he went into the kitchen to turn the chicken, sprinkling on more toasted onion flakes and garlic and parsley salt. And he opened another ale.

Multiple Random Homicides
History and Motives
by Albert Braun, Det. Sgt., NYPD, Ret.

"Good evening, ladies and gentlemen . . .

"The homicide detective, in establishing the guilt or innocence of a suspect must concern himself—as we have previously discussed—with means, opportunity, and motive. The criminal may choose his weapon and select his opportunity. His motive cannot be manipulated; he is its creature. And it is usually motive by which his crime succeeds or fails.

"What are we to make of the motive of New York's current multiple murderer—an individual described in headlines as 'The .44 Caliber Killer' or 'Son of Sam'? The former title refers to the handgun used to kill six and wound seven—to date. The latter is a self-awarded nickname used by the killer in taunting notes to the police and press and, by extension, to all of us.

"The detective's mind at work: He calls himself 'Son of Sam.' Invert to Samson, who lost his potency when his long hair was shorn. Then we learn the victims had long hair. A connection here? A clue? No, I do not believe so. Too tenuous. But it illustrates how every possibility, no matter how farfetched, must be explored in attempting to establish the criminal's motive or plural motives.

"In researching the murky drives of the wholesale killer, the detective goes to the past history of similar crimes, and finds literature on the topic disturbingly scant. Rape, robbery, even art forgery have been thoroughly studied, analyzed, charted, computerized, dissected, skinned, and hung up to dry.

"But where are the psychologists, criminologists, sociologists, and amateur aficionados of murder most foul when it comes to resolving the motives of those who kill, and kill again, and again, and again . . . ?

"Good reason for this, I think. Cases of mass homicide are too uncommon to reveal a sure pattern. Each massacre is different, each slaughter unique. Where is the link between Jack the Ripper, Charles Manson, Unruh, the Black Dahlia, Speck, the Boston Strangler, Panzram, William Heirens ('Stop me before I kill again!'), Zodiac (never caught, that one), the rifleman in the Texas tower, the Los Angeles 'Trash Bag' butchers, the homosexual killers in Houston, the executioner of the California itinerant workers? What do all these monsters have in common?

" 'They were all quite mad,' you say. An observation of blinding brilliance rivaled only by John F. Kennedy's 'Life is unfair.'

"No, the puzzling denominator is that they are all male. Where are the ladies in this pantheon of horror? Victims frequently, killers never. Oh, there was Martha Beck, true, but she 'worked' with a male paramour and slaughtered from corruptive greed. Shoddy stuff.

"We are not here concerned with greed as a motive for multiple homicide. Nor shall we muse on familial tensions which erupt in the butchery of an entire Nebraska family or Kentucky clan, including in-laws and, oddly enough, usually the family dog.

"What concerns us this evening is a series of isolated murders, frequently over a lengthy period of time, the victims unrelated and strangers to the slayer. Let us also eliminate political and military terrorism. What remains of motive? It is not enough to intone, 'Paranoiac schizophrenic,' and let it go at that. It may satisfy a psychologist, but should not satisfy the homicide detective since labels are of no use to him in solving the case.

"What, then, should the detective look for? What possible motives for random slayings may exist that will help him apprehend the perpetrator?

"Pay attention here; watch your footing. We are in a steamy place of reaching vines, barbed creepers, roots beneath and swamp around. Beasts howl. Motives intertwine and interact. Words fail, and the sun is blocked. Poor psychologists. Poor sociologists. No patterns, no paths. But shivery shadows—plenty of those.

"First, *maniacal lust.* Oh yes. This staple of penny dreadfuls did exist, does exist and, if current statistics on rape are correct, seems likely to increase tomorrow. It might—and that was the first of many 'mights' you will hear from me tonight—it might account for the barbarities of Jack the Ripper, the Boston Strangler, the Black Dahlia, Heirens, Speck, and others whose names, fortunately, escape me. I have a good memory for old lags, con men, outlaws and safecrackers. When it comes to recalling mass killers, my mind fuzzes over. It is, I think, an unconscious protective mechanism. The horror is too bright; it shines a light in corners better left in gloom.

"Sexual frenzy: passion becomes violence through hatred, impotence, a groaning realization of the emptiness of sex without love. Water results; blood is wanted. Then blood is needed, and the throat-choked slayer seeks the ultimate orgasm. And aware—oh yes, aware!—and weeping for himself—never for his victim; his own anguish fills him—he scrawls in lipstick on the bathroom mirror, 'Stop me before I kill again!' As if anyone could rein his demented desire or want to. Leave that to the hangman's noose. It is stated that capital punishment does not deter. It will deter *him*.

"Second, *revenge*. It might serve for Jack the Ripper, the Boston Strangler, Unruh, the killer of those California farmhands, the homosexual executioner in Houston—ah, it might serve for the whole scurvy lot, including the latest addition, Son of Sam.

"Revenge, as a motive, I interpret as hatred of a type of individual or a class of individuals who, in the killer's sick mind, are deserving of death. All women, all blacks, all homosexuals, the poor, the mighty, or attractive young girls with long brown hair.

"When the New York Police Department compared ballistics reports and came to the stunned conclusion that it was up against a repeat killer, one of the first theories advanced involved the long hair of the victims. It was suggested that the murderer, having been spurned or humiliated by a girl with flowing tresses, vowed vengeance and is intent on killing her over and over again.

"More recent reports demolish this hypothesis. Males have been shot (one was killed), and not all the female victims had brown, shoulder-length hair. One was blonde; others had short coiffures.

"But still, revenge as a motive has validity. It has been proposed that Jack the Ripper executed and mutilated prostitutes because one had infected him with a venereal disease. A neat theory. Just as elegant, I believe, is my own belief: that he was the type of man who compulsively sought the company of whores (there are such men) and killed to eradicate his own weakness, eliminate his shame.

"I told you we are in a jungle here, and nowhere does the sun shine through. We are poking around the dark, secret niches of the human heart, and our medical chart resembles antique maps with the dread legends 'Terra incognita' and 'Here be dragons.'

"Third, *rejection*. Closely allied to revenge, but rejection not by individual or class but by society, the world, life itself. 'I didn't ask to be born,' the killer whines, and the only answer can be, 'Who did?' Is Son of Sam of this rejected brotherhood?

"There was once a mass killer named Panzram. He was an intelligent man, a thinking man, but a bum, a drifter, scorned, abused, and betrayed. He rejected, scorned, and abused in turn. And he slew, so many that it seemed he wanted to kill not people but life itself. Wipe out all humanity, then all things that pulse, and leave only a cinder whirling dead through freezing space.

"*That* was total rejection: rejection of the killer by society, and of society by the killer. Has no one ever turned his back on you, or you to him? We are dealing here not with another planet's language that no one speaks on ours. The vocabulary is in us all, but we dast not give it tongue.

"The flip side of rejection, real or fancied, is the need to assert: 'I *do* exist. I am I. A person of consequence. You must pay attention. And to make certain you do, I shall kill a baker's dozen of those lumps who look through me on the street.

Then you will recognize who I am.' Is that what Unruh was thinking as he strolled along the New Jersey street, shooting passersby, drivers of cars, pausing to reload, stopping in stores to pot a few more?

" 'I am I. World, take notice!' first, rejection; then, need to prove existence. Murder becomes a mirror.

"Finally, *punk rock, punk fashion, punk souls.* Not 'Small is better than big,' but 'Nothing is better than something.' So, what's new? Surely there were a few wild-eyed Neanderthals rushing about the caves, screaming, 'Down with up!'

"We can afford a low-kilowat smile at combat boots worn with gold lamé bikinis, at the splintered dissonance of punk rock, at the touching fervor with which punkists assault the establishment. We can smile, oh yes, knowing how quickly their music, fashions, language, and personal habits will be preempted, smoothed, glossed, gussied-up, and sold tomorrow via thirty-second commercials at highly inflated prices.

"But there are a few punk souls whose nihilism is so intense, who are so etched by negativism and riddled by despair, that they will never be preempted. Never! Anarchy was not invented yesterday; the demons of Dostoevski have been with us always. To the man who believes 'Nothing is evil,' it is but one midget step to 'Everything is good.'

"The nihilist may murder to prove himself superior to the tribal taboo (the human tribe): 'Thou shalt not kill.' Or he may slay to prove to his victims the fallacy and ephemerality of their faith. In either case, the killer is acting as an evangelist of anarchy. It is not enough that *he* not believe; he must convert—at the muzzle of a revolver or the point of a knife.

"Because the hell of punk souls is this: if *one* other person in the world believes, he is doomed. And so the spiritual anarchist will kill before he will acknowledge that he has spent his life in thin sneers while other, more ignorant and less cynical men have affirmed, and accepted the attendant pain with stoicism and resolve.

"The acrid stink of nihilism followed Charles Manson and his merry band on all their creepy-crawlies. And a charred whiff of spiritual anarchy rises from the notes and deeds of Son of Sam. But I do not believe this his sole goad. Two or more motives are interacting here.

"And that is the thought I wish to leave with you tonight. The motives of mass killers are rarely simple and rarely single. We are not earthworms. We are infinitely complex, infinitely chimerical organisms. In the case of multiple random killings, it is the task of the homicide detective to pick his way through this maze of motives and isolate those strands that will, hopefully, enable him to apprehend the murderer.

"Any questions?"

There was nothing wrong with the dinner. The chicken was crisp and tasty. The baked potatoes, with dabs of sweet butter and a bit of freshly ground pepper, were light and fluffy. The sauce for the romaine leaves was not too spicy. And there was a chilled jug of California chablis on the table.

But the meal was spoiled by Monica's mood. She was silent, morose. She picked at her food or sat motionless for long moments, fork poised over her food.

"What's wrong?" Delaney asked.

"Nothing," she said.

They cleaned the table, sat silently over coffee and small anise biscuits.

"What's wrong?" he asked again.

"Nothing," she said, but he saw tears welling in her eyes. He groaned, rose, bent over her. He put a meaty arm about her shoulders.

"Monica, what *is* it?"

"This afternoon," she sniffled. "It was a symposium on child abuse."

"Jesus Christ!" he said. He pulled his chair around next to hers. He sat holding her hand.

"Edward, it was so *awful,"* she said. "I thought I was prepared, but I wasn't."

"I know."

"They had a color film of what had been done to those kids. I wanted to die."

"I know, I know."

She looked at him through brimming eyes.

"I don't know how you could have endured seeing things like that for thirty years."

"I never got used to it," he said. "Never. Why do you think Abner Boone cracked up and started drinking?"

She was shocked. "Was that it?"

"Part of it. Most of it. Seeing what people are capable of. What they do to other people—and to children."

"Do you suppose he told Rebecca? Why he started drinking?"

"I don't know. Probably not. He's ashamed of it."

"Ashamed!" she burst out. "Of feeling horror and revulsion and sympathy for the victims?"

"Cops aren't supposed to feel those things," he said grimly. "Not if it interferes with doing your job."

"I think I need a brandy," she said.

After the brandy, and after they had cleaned up the kitchen, they both went into the study. Monica sat behind the desk. The lefthand stack of drawers was hers, where she kept her stationery, correspondence, notepaper, appointment books, etc. She began to write letters to the children: Eddie Jr., Liza, Mary, and Sylvia.

When she was finished, Delaney would append short notes in his hand. Usually things like: "Hope you are well. Weather here cold but clear. How is it there?" The children called these notes "Father's weather reports." It was a family joke.

While Monica wrote out her long, discursive letters at the desk, Edward X. Delaney sat opposite her in the old club chair. He slowly sipped another brandy and read, for the third time, the last lecture of Albert Braun, Det. Sgt., NYPD, Ret.

What Braun had to say about motives came as no surprise. During thirty years in the Department, most of them as a detective, Delaney had worked cases in which all those motives were involved, singly or coexistent.

The problem, he decided, was one that Braun had recognized when he had made a brief reference to labels satisfying the criminologist or psychologist, but being of little value to the investigating detective.

An analogy might be made to a man confronting a wild beast in the woods. An animal that threatens him with bared fangs and raised claws.

In his laboratory, the biologist, the *scientist,* would be interested only in classifying the beast: family, genus, species. Its external appearance, bone structure, internal organs. Feeding and mating habits. From what previous animal forms it had evolved.

To the man in the forest, menaced, all this would be extraneous if not meaningless. All he knew was the fear, the danger, the threat.

The homicide detective was the man in the woods. The criminologist, psychologist, or sociologist was the man in the laboratory. The lab man was interested in causes. The man in the arena was interested in events.

That was one point Delaney found not sufficiently emphasized in Braun's lecture. The other disappointment was lack of any speculation on *why* women were conspicuously missing from the rolls of multiple killers.

Braun had made a passing reference to Martha Beck and other females who had killed many from greed. But a deep analysis of why random murderers were invariably male was missing. And since Braun's lecture had been delivered, the additional cases of the Yorkshire Ripper and the Chicago homosexual butcher had claimed headlines. Both murderers were men.

Delaney let the pages of the lecture fall into his lap. He took off his reading glasses, massaged the bridge of his nose. He rubbed his eyes wearily.

"Another brandy?" he asked his wife.

She shook her head, without looking up. He regarded her intently. In the soft light of the desk lamp, she seemed tender and womanly. Her smooth skin glowed. The light burnished her hair; there was a radiance, almost a halo.

She wrote busily, tongue poking out one cheek. She smiled as she wrote; something humorous had occurred to her, or perhaps she was just thinking of the children. She seemed to Edward X. Delaney, at that moment, to be a perfect portrait of the female presence as he conceived it.

"Monica," he said.

She looked up inquiringly.

"May I ask you a question about that child abuse symposium? I won't if it bothers you."

"No," she said, "I'm all right now. What do you want to know?"

"Did they give you any statistics, national statistics, on the incidence of child abuse cases and whether they've been increasing or decreasing?"

"They had all the numbers," she said, nodding. "It's been increasing in the last ten years, but the speaker said that's probably because more doctors and hospitals are becoming aware of the problem and are reporting cases to the authorities. Before, they took the parents' word that the child had been injured in an accident."

"That's probably true," he agreed. "Did they have any statistics that analyzed the abusers by sex? Did more men than women abuse children, or was it the other way around?"

She thought a moment.

"I don't recall any statistics about that," she said. "There were a lot of cases where both parents were involved. Even when only one of them was the, uh, active aggressor, the other usually condoned it or just kept silent."

"Uh-huh," he said. "But when just one parent or relative was the aggressor, would it more likely be a man or a woman?"

She looked at him, trying to puzzle out what he was getting at.

"Edward, I told you, there were no statistics on that."

"But if you had to guess, what would you guess?"

She was troubled.

"Probably women," she admitted finally. Then she added hastily, "But only because women have more pressures and more frustrations. I mean, they're locked up all day with a bunch of squalling kids, a house to clean, meals to prepare. While the husband has escaped all that in his office or factory. Or maybe he's just sitting in the neighborhood tavern, swilling beer."

"Sure," Delaney said. "But it's your guess that at least half of all child abusers are women—and possibly a larger proportion than half?"

She stared at him, suddenly wary.

"Why are you asking these questions?" she demanded.

"Just curious," he said.

On the morning of March 24th, Delaney walked out to buy his copy of *The New York Times* and pick up some fresh croissants at a French bakery on Second Avenue. By the time he got back, Monica had the kitchen table set with glasses of chilled grapefruit juice, a jar of honey, a big pot of black coffee.

They made their breakfasts, settled back. He gave her the Business Day section, began leafing through the Metropolitan Report.

"Damn it," she said.

He looked up. "What's wrong?"

"Bonds are down again. Maybe we should do a swap."

"What's a swap?"

"The paper-value of our tax-exempts are down. We sell them and take the capital tax loss. We put the money back into tax-exempts with higher yields. We can write the loss off against gains in our equities. If we do it right, our annual income from the new tax-exempts should be about equal to what we're getting now. Maybe even more."

He was bewildered. "Whatever you say," he told her. "Oh God, look at this . . ."

He showed her the article headlined: KILLER SOUGHT IN TWO HOMICIDES.

"That's Abner's case," he said. "The hotel killings. The newspapers will be all over it now. The hysteria begins."

"It had to happen sooner or later," she said. "Didn't it? It was only a question of time."

"I suppose," he said.

But when he took the newspaper and a second cup of coffee into the study, the first thing he did was look up the phone number of Thomas Handry in his private telephone directory. Handry was a reporter who had provided valuable assistance to Delaney during Operation Lombard.

The phone was picked up after the first ring. The voice was terse, harried . . .

"Handry."

"Edward X. Delaney here."

A pause, then: "Chief! How the hell are you?"

"Very well, thank you. And you?"

They chatted a few minutes, then Delaney asked:

"Still writing poetry?"

"My God," the reporter said, "you never forget a thing, do you?"

"Nothing important."

"No, I've given up on the poetry. I was lousy and I knew it. Now I want to be a foreign correspondent. Who knows, next week I may want to be a fireman or a cop or an astronaut."

Delaney laughed. "I don't think so."

"Chief, it's nice talking to you after all these years, but I've got the strangest feeling that you didn't call just to say hello. You want something?"

"Yes," Delaney said. "There was an article on page three of the Metropolitan Report this morning. About two hotel murders."

"And?"

"No byline. I just wondered who wrote it."

"Uh-huh. In this case three guys provided information for the story, including me. Three bylines would have been too much of a good thing for a short piece like that. So they just left it off. That's all you wanted to know?"

"Not exactly."

"I didn't think so. What else?"

"Who made the connection? Between the two killings? They were a month apart, and there are four or five homicides every day in New York."

"Chief, you're not the only detective. Give us credit for little intelligence. We studied the crimes and noted the similarities in the MOs."

"Bullshit," Delaney said. "You got a tip."

Handry laughed. "Remember," he said, "you told me, I didn't tell you."

"Phone or mail?" Delaney asked.

"Hey, wait a minute," the reporter said. "This is more than idle curiosity. What's your interest in this?"

Delaney hesitated. Then: "A friend of mine is on the case. He needs all the help he can get."

"So why isn't he calling?"

"Fuck it," Delaney said angrily. "If you won't—"

"Hey, hold it," Handry said. "I didn't say I wouldn't. But what do I get out of it?"

"An inside track," Delaney said, "that you didn't have before. It may be something and it may add up to zilch."

Silence a moment.

"All right," the reporter said, "I'll gamble. Harvey Gardner took the call. About a week ago. We've been checking it out ever since."

"Did you talk to Gardner about it?"

"Of course. The call came in about five-thirty in the evening. Very short. The caller wouldn't give any name or address."

"Man or woman?"

"Hard to tell. Gardner said it sounded like someone trying to disguise their voice, speaking in a low growl."

"So it could be a man or a woman?"

"Could be. Another thing . . . Gardner says the caller said, 'The same person did both of them.' Not, 'It's the same killer' or 'The same guy did both of them,' but 'The same *person* did both of them.' What do you think?"

"I think maybe you wouldn't make a bad cop after all. Thanks, Handry."

"I expect a little quid pro quo on this, Chief."

"You'll get it," Delaney promised. "Oh, one more thing . . ."

"There had to be," Handry said, sighing.

"I may need some research done. I'll pay, of course. Do you know a good researcher?"

"Sure," Thomas Handry said. "Me."

"You? Nah. This is dull, statistical stuff."

"I'll bet," the reporter said. "Listen, I've got the best sources in the world right here. Just give me a chance. You won't have to pay."

"I'll think about it," Delaney said. "Nice talking to you."

"Keep in touch," Handry said.

The Chief hung up and sat a moment, staring at the phone. "The same person did both of them." The reporter was right; there was a false note there in the use of the word "person."

It would have to be the killer who called in the tip, or a close confederate of the killer. It seemed odd that either would say, "The same person . . ." That was a prissy way of putting it. Why didn't they say "guy" or "man" or "killer"?

He sighed, wondering why he had called Handry, why he was becoming so involved in this thing. He was a private citizen now; it wasn't his responsibility. Still . . .

There were a lot of motives involved, he decided. He wanted to help Abner Boone. His retirement was increasingly boring; he needed a little excitement in his life. There was the challenge of a killer on the loose. And even a private citizen owed an obligation to society, and especially to his community.

There was one other factor, Delaney acknowledged. He was getting long in the tooth. Why deny it? When he died, thirty years of professional experience would die with him. Albert Braun would leave his books and lectures to instruct detectives in the future. Edward X. Delaney would leave nothing.

So it seemed logical and sensible to put that experience to good use while he was still around. A sort of legacy while he was alive. A living will.

Detective Sergeant Abner Boone called on the morning of March 26th. He asked if he could stop by for a few moments, and Delaney said sure, come ahead; Monica was at a feminist meeting where she was serving as chairperson for a general discussion of government-financed day-care centers.

The two men had talked almost every day on the phone. Boone had nothing new to report on the killer who was now being called the "Hotel Ripper" in newspapers and on TV.

Boone did say that Lieutenant Martin Slavin was convinced that the murderer was not a prostitute, since nothing had been stolen. Most of the efforts of the cops under his command were directed to rousting homosexuals, the S&M joints in the Village, and known transvestites.

"Well," Delaney said, sighing, "he's going by the percentages. I can't fault him for that. Almost every random killer of strangers has been male."

"Sure," Boone said, "I know that. But now the Mayor's office has the gays yelling, plus the hotel associations, plus the tourist people. It's heating up."

But when Sergeant Abner Boone appeared on the morning of March 26th, he was the one who was heated up.

"Look at this," he said, furiously, scaling a flyer onto Delaney's desk. "Slavin insisted on sending one of these to the head of security in every midtown hotel."

Delaney donned his glasses, read the notice slowly. Then he looked up at Boone.

"The stupid son of a bitch," he said softly.

"Right!" the sergeant said, stalking back and forth. "I pleaded with him. Leave out that business about the black nylon wig, I said. There's no way, *no* way, we'll be able to keep that out of the papers if every hotel in midtown Manhattan knows about it. So it gets in the papers, and the killer changes his wig—am I right? Blond or red or whatever. Meanwhile, all our guys are looking for someone in a black wig. It just makes me sick!"

"Take it easy, sergeant," Delaney said. "The damage has been done; nothing you can do about it. Did you make your objections to Slavin in the presence of witnesses?"

"I sure did," Boone said wrathfully. "I made certain of that."

"Good," Delaney said. "Then it's his ass, not yours. Getting many false confessions?"

"Plenty," the sergeant said. "Every whacko in the city. Another reason I wanted to keep that black nylon wig a secret. It made it easy to knock down the fake confessions. Now we've got nothing up our sleeve. What an asshole thing for Slavin to do!"

"Forget it," Delaney advised. "Let him hang himself. You're clean."

"I guess so," Boone said, sighing. "I don't know what to tell our decoys now. Look for *anyone* in *any* color wig, five-five to five-seven. That's not much to go on."

"No," Delaney said, "it's not."

"We checked out that suggestion you gave me. You know—both victims employing the same disgruntled guy and firing him. We're still working on it, but it doesn't look good."

"It's got to be done," Delaney said stubbornly.

"Sure. I know. And I appreciate the lead. We're grabbing at anything. *Anything.* Also, I remembered what you said about the time between killings becoming shorter and shorter. So I—"

"Usually," Delaney reminded him. "I said *usually.*"

"Right. Well, it was about a month between the Puller and Wolheim murders. If there's a third, God forbid, I figure that going by what you say—what you *suggest,* it may be around April third. That would be three weeks after the Wolheim kill. So I'm alerting everyone for that week."

"Won't do any harm," Edward X. Delaney said.

"If there is another one," Boone said, "I'll give you a call. You promised to come over—remember?"

"I remember."

But April 3rd came and went, with no report of another hotel homicide.

Delaney was troubled. Not because events had proved him wrong; that had happened before. But he was nagged that this case wasn't following any known pattern. There was no handle on it. It was totally different.

But wasn't that exactly what Albert Braun had said in his last lecture? "Cases of mass homicide are too uncommon to reveal a sure pattern. Each massacre different, each slaughter unique."

Early on the morning of April 10th, about 7:30, Delaney was awake but still abed, loath to crawl out of his warm cocoon of blankets. The phone shrilled. Monica awoke, turned suddenly in bed to stare at him.

"Edward X. Delaney here," he said.

"Chief, it's Boone. There's been another. Hotel Coolidge. Can you come over?"

"Yes," Delaney said.

He got out of bed, began to strip off his pajamas.

"Who was that?" Monica asked.

"Boone. There's been another one."

"Oh God," she said.

Delaney came off the elevator on the 14th floor and looked to the left. Nothing. He looked to the right. A uniformed black cop was planted in the middle of the corridor. He was swinging a nightstick from its leather thong. Beyond him, far down the long hallway, Abner Boone and a few other men were clustered about a doorway.

"I'd like to see Sergeant Boone," Delaney told the cop. "He's expecting me."

"Yeah?" the officer said, giving Delaney the once-over. He turned and yelled down the corridor, "Hey, sarge!" When Boone turned to look, the cop hooked a thumb at Delaney. The sergeant nodded and made a beckoning motion. The cop moved aside. "Be my guest," he said.

Delaney looked at him. The man had a modified Afro, a neat black mustache. His uniform fit like it had been custom-made by an Italian tailor.

"Do you know Jason T. Jason?" he asked.

"Jason Two?" the officer said, with a splay of white teeth. "Sure, I know that big mother. He a friend of yours?"

Delaney nodded. "If you happen to see him, I'd appreciate it if you'd give him my best. The name is Delaney. Edward X. Delaney."

"I'll remember," the cop said, staring at him curiously.

The Chief walked down the hallway. Boone came forward to meet him.

"Sorry I'm late," Delaney said. "I couldn't get a cab."

"I'm glad you're late," the sergeant said. "You missed a mob scene. Reporters, TV crews, a guy from the Mayor's office, the DA's sergeant, Deputy Commissioner Thorsen, Chief Bradley, Inspector Jack Turrell—you know him?—Lieutenant Slavin, and so on and so on. We had everyone here but the Secretary of State."

"You didn't let them inside?"

"You kidding? Of course not. Besides, none of them wanted to look at a stiff so early in the morning. Spoil their breakfast. They just wanted to get their pictures taken at the scene of the crime and make a statement that might get on the evening news."

"Did you tell Slavin I was coming over?"

"No, sir, but I mentioned it to Thorsen. He said, 'Good.' So if Slavin comes back and gives us any flak, I'll tell him to take it up with Thorsen. We'll pull rank on him."

"Fine," Delaney said, smiling.

He looked around the corridor. There were two ambulance men with a folding, wheeled stretcher and body bag, waiting to take the corpse away. There were two newspaper photographers, laden with equipment. The four men were sitting on the hallway floor, playing cards.

The Chief looked inside the opened door. The usual hotel room. There were two men in there. One was vacuuming the rug. The other was dusting the bedside radio for prints.

"The Crime Scene Unit," Boone explained. "They'll be finished soon. The guy with the vacuum cleaner is Lou Gorki. The tall guy with glasses is Tommy Callahan. The same team that worked the Puller and Wolheim kills. They're sore."

"Sore?"

"Their professional pride is hurt because they haven't come up with anything solid. They want this guy so bad they can taste it. This time they rigged up that little canister vacuum cleaner with clear plastic bags. They vacuumed the bathroom, took the bag out and labeled it. Did the same thing to the bed. Then the furniture. Now Lou's doing the rug."

"Good idea," Delaney said. "What have you got on the victim?"

Sergeant Abner Boone took out his notebook, began to flip pages . . .

"Like Puller and Wolheim," he said. "With some differences. The clunk is Jerome Ashley, male Caucasian, thirty-nine, and—"

"Wait a minute," Delaney said. "He's thirty-nine? You're sure?"

Boone nodded. "Got it off his driver's license. Why?"

"I was hoping there might be a pattern—overweight men in their late fifties."

"Not this guy. He's thirty-nine, skinny as a rail, and tops six-one, at least. He's from Little Rock, Arkansas, and works for a fast-food chain. He came to town for a national sales meeting."

"Held where?"

"Right here at the Coolidge. He had an early breakfast date with a couple of pals. When he didn't show up and they got no answer on the phone, they came looking. They had a porter open the door and found him."

"No sign of forced entry?"

"None. Look for yourself."

"Sergeant, if you say there's no sign, then there's no sign. A struggle?"

"Doesn't look like it. But some things are different from Puller and Wolheim. He wasn't naked in bed. He had taken off his suit jacket, but that's all. He's on the floor, alongside the bed. His glasses fell off. His drink spilled. The way I figure it, he was sitting on the edge of the bed, relaxed, having a drink. The killer comes up behind him, maybe pulls his head back, slices his throat. He falls forward onto the floor. That's what it looks like. There's blood on the wall near the bed."

"Stab wounds in the genitals?"

"Plenty of those. Right through his pants. The guy's a mess."

The Crime Scene Unit men moved toward the door carrying their kit bags, cameras, the vacuum cleaner.

"He's all yours," Callahan said to Boone. "Lots of luck."

"Lou Gorki, Tommy Callahan," the sergeant said, introducing them. "This is Edward X. Delaney."

"Chief!" Gorki said, thrusting out his hand. "This is great! I was with you on Operation Lombard, with Lieutenant Jeri Fernandez."

Delaney looked at him closely, shaking his hand.

"Sure you were," he said. "You were in that Con Ed van, digging the street hole."

"Oh, that fucking hole!" Gorki said, laughing, happy that Delaney remembered him. "I thought we'd be down to China before that perp broke."

"See anything of Fernandez lately?" Delaney asked.

"He fell into something sweet," Gorki said. "He's up in Spanish Harlem, doing community relations."

"Who did he pay?" Delaney said, and they all laughed. The Chief turned to Callahan. "What have we got here?" he asked.

The two CSU men knew better than to question why he was present. He was Boone's responsibility.

"Bupkes is what we've got," Callahan said. "Nothing really hot. The usual collections of latents and smears. We even dusted the stiff for prints. It's a new, very iffy technique. Might work on a strangulation. We came up with nil."

"Any black nylon hairs?" Boone said. "Or any other color?"

"Didn't see any," Callahan said. "But they may turn up in the vacuum bags."

"One interesting thing," Gorki said. "Not earth-shaking, but interesting. Want to take a look?"

The two technicians led the way to the corpse alongside the bed. It was uncovered, lying on its side. But the upper torso was twisted, face turned upward. The throat slash gaped like a giant mouth, toothed with dangling veins, arteries, ganglia, muscle, stuff. Unbroken spectacles and water tumbler lay nearby.

To the Chief, the tableau had the frozen, murky look of a nineteenth-century still life in an ornate frame. One of those dark, heavily varnished paintings that showed dead ducks and hares, bloody and limp, fruit on the table, and a bottle and half-filled glass of wine. A brass title plate affixed to the frame: AFTER THE HUNT.

He surveyed the scene. It appeared to him that the murder had happened the way Boone had described it: the killer had come up behind the victim and slashed. A dead man had then fallen from the edge of the bed.

He bent to examine darkened stains in the rug.

"You don't have to be careful," Callahan said. "We got samples of blood from the stiff, the rug, the wall."

"Chances are it's all his," Gorki said disgustedly.

"What's this stain?" Delaney asked. He got down on his hands and knees, sniffed at a brownish crust on the shag rug.

"Whiskey," he said. "Smells like bourbon."

"Right," Gorki said admiringly. "That's what we thought. Where his drink spilled . . ."

Delaney looked up at Boone.

"I've got thirty men going through the hotel right now," the sergeant said. "It's brutal. People are checking in and out. Mostly out. Nobody knows a thing. The bartenders and waitresses in the cocktail lounges don't come on till five tonight. Then we'll ask them about bourbon drinkers."

"Here's what we wanted to show you," Gorki said. "You'll have to get down close to see it. This lousy shag rug fucked us up, but we got shots of everything that shows."

The other three men got down on their hands and knees. The four of them clustered around a spot on the rug where Gorki was pointing.

"See that?" he said. "A footprint. Not distinct, but good enough. The shag breaks it up. Tommy and I figure the perp stood over the stiff to shove the knife in his balls. He stepped in the guy's blood and didn't realize it. Then he went toward the bathroom. The footprints get fainter as he moved, more blood coming off his feet onto the rug."

On their hands and knees, the four of them moved awkwardly toward the bathroom, bending far over, faces close to the rug. They followed the spoor.

"See how the prints are getting fainter?" Callahan said. "But still, enough to get a rough measurement. The foot is about eight-and-a-half to nine inches long."

"Shit," Delaney said. "That could be a man or a woman."

They looked at him in surprise.

"Well . . . yeah," Gorki said. "But we're looking for a guy—right?"

Delaney didn't answer. He bent low again over the stained rug. He could just barely make out the imprint of a heel, the outside of the foot, a cluster of toes. A bare foot.

"The size of the footprint isn't so important," Callahan said. "It's the distance between prints. The stride. Get it? We measured the distance between footprints. That gives us the length of the killer's step. The Lab Services guys have a chart that shows average height based on length of stride. So we'll be able to double-check that professor up at the museum to see if the perp really is five-five to five-seven."

"Nice," Delaney said. "Very nice. Any stains on the tiles in the bathroom?"

"Nothing usable," Gorki said, "but we took some shots just in case. Nothing in the sink, tub, or toilet drains."

The four men were still kneeling on the rug, their heads raised to talk to each other, when they became conscious of someone looming over them.

"What the fuck's going on here?" an angry voice demanded.

The four men lumbered to their feet. They brushed off their knees. The Chief stared at the man glowering at him. Lieutenant Martin Slavin looked like a bookkeeper who had flunked the CPA exam.

"Delaney!" he said explosively. "What the hell are you doing here? You got no right to be here."

"That's right," Delaney said levelly. He started for the door. "So I'll be on my way."

"Wait a sec," Slavin said, putting out a hand. His voice was high-pitched, strained, almost whiny. "Wait just one goddamned sec. Now that you're here . . . What did you find out?"

Delaney stared at him.

Slavin was a cramped little man with nervous eyes and a profile as sharp as a hatchet. Bony shoulders pushed out his ill-fitting uniform jacket. His cap was too big for his narrow skull; it practically rested on his ears.

Appearances are deceiving? Bullshit, Edward X. Delaney thought. In Slavin's case, appearances were an accurate tipoff to the man's character and personality.

"I didn't find out anything," Delaney said. "Nothing these men can't tell you."

"You'll have our report tomorrow, lieutenant," Lou Gorki said sweetly.

"Maybe later than that," Tommy Callahan put in. "Lab Services have a lot of tests to run."

Slavin glared at them, back and forth. Then he turned his wrath on Delaney again.

"You got no right to be here," he repeated furiously. "This is my case. You're no better than a fucking civilian."

"Deputy Commissioner Thorsen gave his okay," Sergeant Boone said quietly.

The four men looked at the lieutenant with expressionless eyes.

"We'll see about that!" Slavin almost screamed. "We'll goddamned well see about that!"

He turned, rushed from the room.

"He'll never have hemorrhoids," Lou Gorki remarked. "He's such a perfect asshole."

Sergeant Boone walked Delaney slowly back to the elevators.

"I'll let you know what the lab men come up with," he said. "If you think of anything we've missed, please let me know. I'd appreciate it."

"Of course," Delaney said, wondering if he should tell Boone about the phoned tip to the *Times* and deciding against it. Handry had admitted that in confidence. "Sergeant, I hope I didn't get you in any trouble with Slavin."

"With a rabbi like Thorsen?" Boone said, grinning. "I'll survive."

"Sure you will," Edward X. Delaney said.

He decided to walk home. Over to Sixth Avenue, through Central Park, out at 72nd Street, and up Fifth Avenue. A nice stroll. He stopped in the hotel lobby to buy a Montecristo.

A soft morning in early April. A warming sun burning through a pearly haze. In the park, a few patches of dirty snow melting in the shadows. The smell of green earth thawing, ready to burst. Everything was coming alive.

He strode along sturdily, topcoat open and flapping against his legs. Hard homburg set squarely. Cigar clenched in his teeth. Joggers passed him. Cyclists whizzed by. Traffic whirled around the winding roads. He savored it all—and thought of Jerome Ashley and his giant mouth.

It was smart, Delaney figured, for a detective to go by the percentages. Every cop in the world did it, whether he was aware of it or not. If you had three suspects in a burglary, and one of them was an ex-con, you leaned on the lag, even if you knew shit-all about recidivist percentages.

"It just makes common fucking sense," an old cop had remarked to Delaney.

So it did, so it did. But the percentages, the numbers, the patterns, experience—all were useful up to a point. Then you caught something new, something different, and you were flying blind; no instruments to guide you. What was it the early pilots had said? You fly by the seat of your pants.

Edward X. Delaney wasn't ready yet to jettison percentages. If he was handling the Hotel Ripper case, he'd probably be doing exactly what Slavin was doing right now: looking for a male killer and rounding up every homosexual with a rap sheet.

But there were things that didn't fit and couldn't be ignored just because they belonged to no known pattern.

Delaney stopped at a Third Avenue deli, bought a few things, carried his purchases home. Monica was absent at one of her meetings or lectures or symposiums or colloquies. He was happy she was active in something that interested her. He was just as happy he had the house to himself.

He had bought black bread, the square kind from the frozen food section. A quarter-pound of smoked sable, because sturgeon was too expensive. A bunch of scallions. He made two sandwiches carefully: sable plus scallion greens plus a few drops of fresh lemon juice.

He carried the sandwiches and a cold bottle of Heineken into the study. He sat down behind his desk, put on his reading glasses. As he ate and drank, he made out a dossier on the third victim, Jerome Ashley, trying to remember everything Sergeant Boone had told him and everything he himself had observed.

Finished with sandwiches and beer, he read over the completed dossier, checking to see if he had omitted anything. Then he looked up the number of the Hotel Coolidge and called.

He told the operator that he was trying to locate Sergeant Abner Boone, who was in the hotel investigating the crime on the 14th floor. He asked her to try to find Boone and have him call back. He left his name and number.

He started comparing the dossiers of the three victims, still hoping to spot a common denominator, a connection. They were men from out of town, staying in Manhattan hotels: that was all he could find.

The phone rang about fifteen minutes later.

"Chief, it's Boone. You called me?"

"On the backs of the stiff's hands," Delaney said. "Scars."

"I saw them, Chief. The assistant ME said they looked like burn scars. Maybe a month or so old. Mean anything?"

"Probably not, but you can never tell. Was he married?"

"Yes. No children."

"His wife should know how he got those scars. Can you check it out?"

"Will do."

After Boone hung up, Edward X. Delaney started a fresh sheet of paper, listing the things that bothered him, that just didn't fit:

1. A short-bladed knife, probably a jackknife.
2. No signs of struggles.
3. Two victims with no records of homosexuality found naked in bed.
4. Hairs from a wig.
5. Estimated height from five-five to five-seven.
6. Phoned tip that could have been made by a man or woman.

He reread this list again and again, making up his mind. He thought he was probably wrong. He hoped he was wrong. He called Thomas Handry at the *Times.*

"Edward X. Delaney here."

"There's been another one, Chief."

"So I heard. When I spoke to you a few weeks ago, you said you'd be interested in doing some research for me. Still feel that way?"

Handry was silent a moment. Then . . .

"Has this got anything to do with the Hotel Ripper?" he asked.

"Sort of," Delaney said.

"Okay," Handry said. "I'm your man."

5

Zoe Kohler returned home after her adventure with Jerry. She slid gratefully into a hot tub, putting her head back. She thought she could feel her entrails warm, unkink, become lax and flaccid. All of her thawed; she floated defenseless in amniotic fluid.

When the tub cooled, she sat up, prepared to lather herself with her imported soap. She saw with shock that the water about her knees and ankles was stained, tinged a light pink. Thinking her period had started, she touched herself tenderly, examined her fingers. There was no soil.

She lifted one ankle to the other knee, bent forward to inspect her foot. Between her toes she found clots of dried blood, now dissolving away. There were spots of blood beneath the toes of the other foot as well.

She sat motionless, trying to understand. Her feet were not wounded, nor her ankles cut. Then she knew. It was Jerry's blood. She had stepped into it after he—after he was gone. The blood between her toes was his stigmata, the taint of his guilt.

She scrubbed furiously with brush and washcloth. Then she rinsed again and again under the shower, making certain no stain remained on her skin. Later, she sat on the toilet lid and sprayed cologne on her ankles, feet, between her toes. "Out, damned spot!" She remembered that.

She dried, powdered, inserted a tampon, clenching her teeth. Not against the pain; there was no pain. But the act itself was abhorrent to her: a vile penetration that destroyed her dignity. That little string hanging outside: the fuse of a bomb.

All her life, as long as she could remember, she had been daunted by the thought of blood. As a child, with a cut finger or skinned knee, it had been incomprehensible that her body was a bag, a sack, filled with a crimson viscid fluid that leaked, poured, or spurted when the bag was punctured.

Later, at that dreadful birthday party when her menses began, she was convinced she was going to die.

"Nonsense," her mother had said irritably. "It just means you're not a girl anymore; you're a woman. And you must bear the cross of being a woman."

"The cross." That called up images of the crucified Christ, bleeding from hands and feet. To Him, loss of blood meant loss of life. For her, loss of blood meant loss of innocence, punishment for being a woman.

The cramps began with her early periods and increased in severity as she grew older. In a strange way, she welcomed the pain. It was expiation for her guilt. That dark, greasy monthly flow was her atonement.

She donned her flannel nightgown, went into the kitchen for her vitamins and minerals, capsules and pills. She took a Tuinal and went to bed. An hour later, she was still wide-eyed. She rose, took another sleeping pill, and tried again.

This time she slept.

Harry Kurnitz was having a cocktail party and dinner for employees of his textile company. Maddie called to invite Zoe.

"Harry does this once a year," she said. "He claims it's cheaper than giving raises. Anyway, it's always a big, noisy bash, lots to eat, and people falling-down drunk. All the executives make passes at their secretaries. That's why Harry has it on a Friday night. So everyone can forget what asses they made of themselves by Monday morning. Ernest Mittle will be there, so I thought you'd like to come."

"Thank you, Maddie," Zoe Kohler said.

Ernest had been calling twice a week, on Wednesday and Saturday nights at 9:00 P.M. They talked a long time, sometimes for a half-hour. They nattered about their health, what they had been doing, odd items in the news, movie reviews . . .

Nothing important, but the calls had assumed a growing significance for Zoe. She looked forward to them. They were a lifeline. Someone was out there. Someone who cared.

Once he said:

"Isn't it awful about the Hotel Ripper?"

"Yes," she said. "Awful."

Zoe went to the party directly from work. Harry Kurnitz had taken over the entire second floor of the Chez Ronald on East 48th Street, and Zoe walked, fearing she would be too early.

But when she arrived, the big room was already crowded with a noisy throng. Most of them were clustered about the two bars, but several were already seated at the tables. At the far end of the room, a trio was playing disco, but there was no one on the minuscule dance floor.

Madeline and Harry Kurnitz stood at the doorway, greeting arriving guests. They both embraced Zoe and kissed her cheek.

"Jesus Christ, kiddo," Maddie said, inspecting her, "you dress like a matron at the House of Detention."

"Come on, Maddie," her husband protested. "She looks fine."

"I didn't have time to go home and change," Zoe said faintly.

"That's just the point," Maddie said. "You go to work looking like *that?* You and I have to go shopping together; I'll tart you up. I told Mister Meek you'd be here tonight. He lit up like a Christmas tree." She gave Zoe a gentle shove. "Now go find him, luv."

But Ernest Mittle found her. He must have been waiting, for he came forward carrying two glasses of white wine.

"Good evening, Zoe," he said, beaming. "Mrs. Kurnitz told me you'd be here. She said, 'Your love goddess is coming.' "

"Yes," Zoe said, smiling briefly, "that sounds like Maddie. How are you, Ernie?"

"I've got the sniffles," he said. "Nothing serious, but it's annoying. Would you like to move around and meet people, or should we grab a table?"

"Let's sit down," she said. "I'm not very good at meeting people."

They took a table for four near the wall. Ernest seated her where she could observe the noisy activity at the bars. He took the chair next to her.

"I don't want to get too close," he said. "I don't want you catching my cold. It was really bad for a couple of days, but it's better now."

"You should take care of yourself," she chided. "Do you take vitamin pills?"

"No, I don't."

"I'm going to make out a list for you," she said, "and I want you to buy them and take them regularly."

"All right," he said happily, "I will. Well . . . here's to us."

They hoisted their glasses, sipped their wine.

"I thought it was going to be the flu," he said. "But it was just a bad cold. That's why I haven't asked you out. But I'm getting better now. Maybe we can have dinner next week."

"I'd like that."

"Listen," he said, "would you like to come to my place for dinner? I'm not the world's greatest cook, but we can have, say, hamburgers and a baked potato. Something like that."

"That would be nice," she said, nodding. "I'll bring the wine."

"Oh no," he said. "I'm inviting you; I'll have wine."

"Then I'll bring dessert," she said. "Please, Ernie, let me."

"All right," he said, with his little boy's smile, "you bring the dessert. A small one."

"A small one," she agreed. She looked around. "Who are all these people?"

He began to point out and name some of the men and women moving about the room. It was soon apparent that he had a taste for gossip and the wit to relate scandalous stories in an amusing manner. Once he used the word "screwing," stopped abruptly, looked at her anxiously.

"I hope you're not offended, Zoe?"

"No, I'm not offended."

Ernest told her about office affairs, the personal peccadilloes of some of his co-workers, rumors about others. He pointed out the office lothario and the office seductress—quite ordinary looking people. Then he hitched his chair a little closer, leaned toward Zoe.

"I'll tell you something," he said in a low voice, "but you must promise not to repeat it to a soul. Promise?"

She nodded.

"See that tall man at the end of the bar in front of us? At the right end?"

She searched. "Wearing glasses? In the gray suit?"

"That's the one. He's Vince Delgado, Mr. Kurnitz's assistant. Can you see the woman he's talking to? She's blond, wearing a blue sweater."

Zoe craned her neck to get a better look.

"She's sort of, uh, flashy, isn't she?" she said. "And very young."

"Not so young," he said. "Her name is Susan Weiner. Everyone calls her Suzy. She's a secretary on the third floor. That's our Sales Department."

Zoe watched Vince Delgado put his arm about Susan Weiner's waist and pull her close. They were both laughing.

"Are they having an affair?" she asked Ernest Mittle.

"She is," he said, eyes bright with malice, "but not with Vince. Mr. Kurnitz."

She looked at him. "You're joking?"

He held up a hand, palm outward.

"I swear. But Zoe," he added nervously, "you've got to promise not to repeat this. Especially to Mrs. Kurnitz. Please. It could mean my job."

"I won't say a word." She turned again to stare at the blonde in the blue sweater. "Ernie, are you sure?"

"It's all over the office," he said, nodding. "They think no one knows. Everyone knows."

Zoe finished her wine. Mittle rose immediately, took their glasses, headed for the bar.

"Refill time," he said gaily.

While he was gone, Zoe watched the woman at the bar. She seemed very intimate with Vince Delgado, putting a hand on his arm, smiling at something he said, touching his face lightly, affectionately. They acted like lovers.

Zoe saw them take their drinks, walk over to one of the vacant tables. Susan Weiner was short but full-bodied. Almost chubby. She had a heavy bosom for a woman of her size. Her hair was worn in frizzy curls. Zoe Kohler thought she looked cheap. She looked available. Soft and complaisant.

Ernest came back with two more glasses of wine.

"I still can't believe it," Zoe said. "She looks so involved with the man she's with."

"Vince?" he said. "He's the 'beard.' That's what they call the other man who pretends to be the lover. He and Suzy and Mr. Kurnitz go out to lunch together, or dinner, or work late. If they're seen, everyone's supposed to think she's with Vince. She's not married, and he's divorced. But she's really with Mr. Kurnitz. Everyone in the office knows it."

"That's so—so sordid," she burst out.

He shrugged.

"What does he see in her?" she demanded.

"Suzy? She's really a very nice person. Pleasant and cheerful. Always ready to do someone a favor."

"Apparently."

"No, you know what I mean. I think if you met her, you'd like her. Zoe, I hope you won't breathe a word of this to Mrs. Kurnitz."

"I won't say anything. I wouldn't hurt her like that. But she'll probably find out, eventually."

"Probably. He just doesn't seem to care. Mr. Kurnitz, that is."

"Ernie, why do men do things like that?"

"Oh, I don't know . . . Mrs. Kurnitz comes on strong; you know that. She's loud and brassy and sort of throws herself around. I know she's a lot of fun, but that can be wearing all the time. Maybe Mr. Kurnitz wants someone a little quieter and more submissive."

"And she's younger than Maddie."

"Yes. That, too."

"It's just not fair," Zoe Kohler said.

"Well . . ." he said, sighing, "I guess not. But that's the way things are."

"I know," she said dully. "That's why I'm divorced."

He put a hand over hers.

"I hope I haven't upset you, Zoe. I guess I shouldn't have told you."

"That's all right," she said. "It just makes me feel so sad and old-fashioned. When I got married, I thought it would be forever. I never even thought of divorce. I mean, I didn't think, Well, if this doesn't work out, we can always split up. I really thought it would be till death do us part. I was such a simp."

"These things happen," he said, but she would not be comforted.

"It's just so awful," she said. "I can't tell you how ugly it is. People get married and, uh, sleep together for a year or two. Then they wave goodbye and go somewhere else and sleep with someone else. Like animals."

"It doesn't have to be that way," he said in a low voice, looking down at their clasped hands. "Really it doesn't Zoe."

Dinner was served at seven o'clock: roasted Rock Cornish hens with wild rice, baby carrots, and a salad of escarole and Bibb lettuce. Baked Alaska for dessert. Bottles of wine on every table and, with coffee, a selection of brandies and liqueurs.

Harry Kurnitz made a short, funny speech, and his employees applauded mightily. Then the trio started playing disco again; several couples got up to dance. Guests who lived in the suburbs thanked host and hostess and departed.

"Would you care to dance, Zoe?" Ernest Mittle asked politely. "I'm not very good with that kind of music, but . . ."

"Oh no," she said. "Thank you, but I can't dance to that at all. I'd like to, but I don't know how. Would you be angry if I left early? I ate so much, I'd really like to get home and just relax."

"Me, too," he said. "I think my cold is coming back; I'm all stuffed up. I have an inhaler at home; maybe that will help."

"Take some Anacin or aspirin," Zoe advised, "and get into bed."

"I will."

"Be sure to cover up and keep warm. Will you call me tomorrow?"

"Of course."

"I'll have a list of vitamins all made out and what strength to buy. I'll give it to you over the phone. You must promise to take them faithfully, every day."

"I will. Really I will."

They thanked Madeline and Harry Kurnitz for a pleasant evening and slipped away. They reclaimed their coats and hats downstairs. Ernest wanted to tip the hatcheck girl, but she told him that Mr. Kurnitz had taken care of everything.

Mittle said he wasn't feeling so great, and he was going to take a cab home. He would drop Zoe at her apartment house on his way downtown. Would that be all right? She said it would be fine.

The cab was unheated and Zoe saw he was shivering. She pulled his plaid muffler snugly about his throat and turned up the collar of his overcoat. She made him promise to drink a cup of hot tea the moment he got home.

He held the cab until he saw her safely inside her apartment house lobby. She turned to wave. She hoped he would take the hot tea and aspirin, and get into bed and stay covered up. She worried about him.

There were three letters in her mailbox: bills from Con Edison and New York Telephone, and a squarish, cream-colored envelope with her name and address written in a graceful script. Postmarked Seattle. She didn't know anyone in Seattle.

Inside her apartment, door bolted and chained, she turned on the living room lamp, hung away her coat and knitted hat. She glanced out the bedroom window before she lowered the venetian blind and switched on the bedside lamp. She thought she glimpsed movement in the apartment across the street. That man was watching her windows again.

She let the blind fall with a clatter and pulled the drape across. She sat on the edge of the bed and looked at the squarish, cream-colored envelope. She sniffed at it, but it was not scented. The cursive script read simply: "Zoe Kohler." No Miss, or Mrs., or Ms.

She opened the envelope flap slowly, picking it loose. It seemed a shame to tear such thick, rich-looking stationery. Within the envelope was a smaller envelope. Then she knew what it was. A wedding announcement.

Mr. and Mrs. Arnold Foster Clark
request the pleasure of your company
at the marriage of their daughter
Evelyn Jane
to Mr. Kenneth Garwin Kohler,
on Saturday, the tenth of May, at eleven o'clock
St Anthony's Church
Pine Crest Drive, Rockville, Washington
Reception immediately following the ceremony.
R.S.V.P. 20190 Locust Court, Rockville, Washington

Zoe Kohler read this joyous message several times. Her fingertips drifted lightly over the raised type. She folded the small piece of tissue paper that protected the printed copy, folded it and folded it until it was a tiny square, so minute that she could have swallowed it.

The last she had heard of Kenneth, he was living in San Francisco. That's where his alimony checks were postmarked. Now here he was marrying Evelyn Jane Clark in Rockville, Washington.

She read the invitation again. St. Anthony's Church. Did that mean the bride was a Catholic? Marrying a divorced man? Had Kenneth taken instruction or agreed to raise the children in the Catholic faith? Would Evelyn Jane go to San Francisco to live or would the newly married couple make their home in Rockville? Or Seattle?

Pondering these absurd questions kept her mind busy for a few moments. But soon, soon, she had to let herself recognize the enormity of what he had done. Mailing his wedding invitation to her was a malicious gloat. "I have found the woman you could never be. Now I shall be happy."

It would have been simple, kind, *human* to tell her nothing of his marriage. He was legally free; he could do as he pleased; it was no concern of hers. Sending her an announcement was an act of viciousness, of hatred.

Suddenly she was weary. Physically exhausted, her joints watery. And mentally wrung-out and depleted. Energy gone, resolve vanished. She sat hunched over on the edge of the bed, feeling worn-out and empty. The wedding invitation slipped from her fingers, fluttered to the floor.

Her depression had started when Ernest told her about Harry Kurnitz and that secretary. Zoe did not know why that saddened her. Maddie had been married previously, and so had Harry. A divorce would not be cataclysmic. Just another failure.

And now here was a message artfully printed on rich stationery to remind her of yet another failure: her own. She searched her memory frantically for a success in her life, but could find none.

"*Must* you empty the ashtray every time I put out a cigarette?" Kenneth had complained. "I'll be smoking all night. Can't you wait to clean the goddamned ashtray until we go to bed?"

And . . .

"Jesus, Zoe, do you have to wear that dull sweater again? It's like a uniform. All the other women at the party will be wearing dresses. You're the youngest frump I've ever seen."

And . . .

"You're not falling asleep, are you? I'd hate to come, and hear you snoring. Pardon me all to hell if I'm keeping you awake."

Always complaining, always criticizing. And she never condemned him or blamed him for anything. *Never!* Though there was plenty she could have said:

"*Must* you leave your dirty socks and underwear on the bathroom floor? Someone has to pick it up, and that someone is me."

And . . .

"Did you have to put your hands on every woman at the party? Do you think I didn't notice? Do you know the kind of reputation you're getting?"

And . . .

"Why do you persist when you know I don't enjoy it? I just go through the motions and hope you'll get it done quickly."

But she had never said those things. Because she had been brought up to believe that a good wife must endure and work hard to make her marriage a success, to keep a clean, comfortable home for her husband. Prepare his meals. Listen to his problems sympathetically. Bear his children. And all that . . .

Until one day, ignoring all her efforts, rejecting her martyrdom, he had shouted in fury and frustration, "You're not definite! You're just not *there!*" and had stormed out. And was now marrying Evelyn Jane Clark.

Zoe Kohler understood that men were different from women in many ways. Their physical strength frightened her. They swaggered through life, demanding. Violence excited them. Secretly, they were all war lovers. They preferred the company of other males. Gentleness was weakness.

Their physical habits appalled her. Even after bathing they had a strong masculine odor, something deep and musky. They chewed cigars, sniggered over dirty pictures, smacked their lips when they ate, drank, or fucked something pleasurable. They broke wind and laughed. Her father had.

She did not hate men. Oh no. But she saw clearly what they were and what they wanted. Every man she had ever known had acted as if he would live forever. They were without humility. They were so sure, so *sure.* Their confidence stifled her.

Worst of all was their hearty bluffness: voice too loud, smile too broad, manner too open. Even the sly, devious ones adopted this guise to prove their masculinity. Maleness was a role, and the most successful men were the most accomplished players.

She picked the wedding invitation from the floor and set it aside. She might send a gift and she might not. She would think about it. Would a gift shame Kenneth, make him realize the spitefulness of what he had done? Or would a gift confirm what he undoubtedly believed, that she was a silly, brainless, shallow woman who still loved him?

She undressed slowly. She showered, not looking at herself in the medicine cabinet mirror. She pulled on her old flannel robe, slipped her feet into tattered mules.

It was still early, barely ten o'clock, and there were things she could do: write checks for her bills, listen to WQXR or watch Channel 13, read a book.

She did none of these things. She took the Swiss Army knife from her purse. She had already washed it in hot water, dried it carefully. She had inspected it, then oiled the blades lightly.

Now she took the knife into the kitchen. She opened the largest blade. Her electric can opener had a knife sharpening attachment. She put a razor edge on the big blade, touching it to the whirling stone lightly, taking care to sharpen both sides of the steel.

To test its keenness, she took the knife into the bedroom, and with short, violent slashes, cut the wedding announcement of Evelyn Jane Clark and Kenneth Garvin Kohler into thin slivers.

On Saturday, April 26th, at about 6:00 P.M., Zoe Kohler left her apartment house and walked east to Second Avenue. She was carrying a bakery box containing four tarts, two strawberry and two apple, she had purchased that afternoon and kept fresh in her refigerator.

It was a balmy spring evening, sky clear, the air a kiss. Her depression of the previous week had drifted away with a breeze flowing from the south, bringing a scent of growing things and a resurgence of hope. The setting sun cast a warm and mellow light, softening the harsh angles of the city.

She took a downtown bus, got off at 23rd Street, and walked down to Ernest Mittle's apartment on East 20th Street. As always, she was bemused by the infinite variety of New York, the unexpected appearance of a Gothic church, Victorian townhouse, or a steel-and-glass skyscraper.

He lived in a five-story converted brownstone. It seemed to be a well-maintained building, the little front yard planted with ivy, the cast-iron fence freshly painted. Most of the windowsills displayed boxes of red geraniums. The brass mailboxes and bell register in the tiny vestibule were highly polished.

Mittle was listed in Apartment 3-B, and he buzzed the lock a few seconds after Zoe rang his bell. She climbed stairs padded with earth-colored carpeting. The walls were covered with flowered paper in a rather garish pattern. But they were cheerful and unmarked by graffiti.

Ernest was standing outside his open door, grinning a welcome. He leaned forward eagerly to kiss her cheek and ushered her proudly into his apartment. The first thing she saw was a vase of fresh gladiolus. She thought he had bought the flowers because of her, to mark her visit as an occasion. She was touched.

They looked at each other and burst out laughing. They had agreed on the phone not to dress up for this dinner. Zoe was wearing a gray flannel skirt, dark brown turtleneck sweater, and moccasins. Ernest was wearing gray flannel slacks, a dark brown turtleneck sweater, and moccasins.

"His-and-hers!" she said.

"Unisex!" he said.

"Here's our dessert," she said, proffering the bakery box. "Guaranteed no-cal."

"I'll bet," he scoffed. "Zoe, come sit over here. It's the most comfortable chair in the place—which isn't saying much. I thought that, for a change, we might have a daiquiri to start. Is that all right?"

"Marvelous," she said. "I haven't had one in years. I wish I knew how to make them."

"So do I," he said, laughing. "I bought these ready-mixed. But I tried a sip while I was cooking, and I thought it was good. You tell me what you think."

While he busied himself in the tiny kitchenette, Zoe lighted a cigarette and looked around the studio apartment. It was a single rectangular room, but large and of good proportions, with a high ceiling. It was a front apartment with two tall windows overlooking 20th Street.

The bathroom was next to the kitchenette, which was really no more than an alcove with small stove, refrigerator, sink, and a few cabinets. A wooden kitchen table was in the main room. It bore two plastic placemats and settings of melamine plates and stainless steel cutlery.

There were two armchairs, a convertible sofa, cocktail table. There was no overhead lighting fixture, just two floor lamps and two table lamps, one on a small maple desk. Television set. Radio. A filled bookcase.

Ceiling and walls were painted a flat white. There were two framed reproductions: van Gogh's *Bedroom at Arles* and Winslow Homer's *Gulf Stream*. On the desk were several framed photographs. The sofa and armchairs were covered with a brown batik print and the same fabric was used for the drapes.

What Zoe Kohler liked best about this little apartment was its clean tidiness. She did not think Ernest had rushed about, transforming it for her visit. It would always look like this: books neatly aligned on their shelves, sofa cover pulled taut, desk and lamps dusted—everything orderly. Almost precise.

Ernest brought the daiquiris in on-the-rocks glasses. He sat in the other armchair, pulling it around so that he faced her. He waited anxiously as she sipped her drink.

"Okay?" he asked.

"Mmm," she said. "Just right. Ernie, have you been taking your vitamins?"

"Oh yes. Regularly. I don't know whether it's the placebo effect or what, but I really do feel better."

She nodded, and they sat a moment in silence, looking at each other. Finally:

"I didn't get any nibbles or anything like that," he said nervously. "I was going to have hamburgers and baked potatoes—remember?—but I decided on a meal my mother used to make that I loved: meatloaf with mashed potatoes and peas. And I bought a jar of spaghetti sauce you put on the meat and potatoes. It's really very good—if everything turns out right. Anyway, that's why I didn't get any nibbles; I figured we'd have enough food, and cheese and olives and things like that would spoil our appetites. My God," he said, trying to laugh, "I'm chattering along like a maniac. I just want everything to be all right."

"It will be," she assured him. "I love meatloaf. Does it have chopped onions in it?"

"Yes, and garlic-flavored bread crumbs."

"That's the way my mother used to make it. Ernie, can I help with anything?"

"Oh no," he said. "You just sit there and enjoy your drink. I figure we'll eat in about half-an-hour. That'll give us time for another daiquiri."

He went back to his cooking. Zoe rose and, carrying her drink, wandered about the apartment. She looked at the framed reproductions on the walls, inspected his books—mostly paperback biographies and histories—and examined the framed photographs on the desk.

"Your family?" she called.

"What?" he said, leaning out of the kitchenette. "Oh yes. My mother and father and three brothers and two sisters and some of their children."

"A big family."

"Sure is. My father died two years ago, but Mother is still living. All my brothers and sisters are living and married. I now have five nephews and three nieces. How about that!"

She went over to the kitchenette and leaned against the wall, watching him work. He did things with brief, nimble movements: stirring the sauce, swirling the peas, opening the oven door to peer at the meatloaf. He seemed at home in the kitchen. Kenneth, she recalled, couldn't even boil water—or boasted he couldn't.

"Once more," Ernest said, pouring a fresh daiquiri into her glass and adding to his. "Then we'll be about ready to eat. I have a bottle of burgundy, but I'm chilling it. I don't like warm wine, do you?"

"I like it chilled," she said.

"Do you have any brothers or sisters, Zoe?" he asked casually.

"No," she said, "I'm an only child."

She watched him mash and then whisk the potatoes with butter and a little milk, salt, pepper.

"You said you can't cook," she commented. "I think you're a very good cook."

"Well . . . I get by. I've lived alone a long time now, and I had to learn if I didn't want to live on just bologna sandwiches. But it's not much fun cooking for one."

"No," she said, "it isn't."

It turned out to be a fine meal. She kept telling him so, and he kept insisting she was just being polite. But he was convinced when she took seconds on everything and ate almost half of the small loaf of French bread. And also did her share in finishing the bottle of burgundy.

"That was a marvelous dinner, Ernie," she said, sitting back. "I really enjoyed it."

"I did, too," he said, with his elfin grin. "A little more pepper in the meatloaf would have helped. Coffee and dessert now or later?"

"Later," she said promptly. "Much later. I ate like a pig. Can I help clean up?"

"Oh no," he said. "I'm not going to do a thing. Just leave everything right where it is. Let's relax."

They sat at the littered table, lighted cigarettes. Ernie brought out a pint bottle of California brandy and apologized because he had no snifters. So they sipped the brandy from cocktail glasses, and it tasted just as good.

She said, "It must be nice to grow up in a big family."

"Well . . ." He hesitated, touching the end of his cigarette in the ashtray. "There are some good things about it and some not so good. One of the things

I hated was the lack of privacy. I mean, there was just no space you could call your own—not even a dresser drawer."

"I had my own bedroom," she said slowly.

"That would have been paradise. I shared a bedroom with one of my brothers until I went away to college. And then I had *three* roommates. It wasn't until I graduated and came to New York that I had a place of my own. What luxury! It really was a treat for me."

"Do you still feel that way?"

"Most of the time. Everyone gets lonely occasionally, I guess. I remember that even when I was living at home with my brothers and sisters, sometimes I'd be lonely. In that crowd! Of course, all my brothers were bigger. I was the runt of the litter. They played football and basketball. I was nowhere as an athlete, so we didn't have a lot in common."

"What about your sisters?" Zoe asked. "I always wished I had a sister. Did you have a favorite?"

"Oh yes," he said, smiling. "Marcia, the youngest. The baby of the family. We had a lot in common. We used to walk out of town, sit in a field and read poetry to each other. Do you know what Marcia wanted to do? She wanted to be a harpist! Isn't that odd? But of course there was no one in Trempealeau to teach her to play the harp, and my folks couldn't afford to send her somewhere else to school."

"So she never learned?"

"No," he said shortly, pouring them more brandy, "she never did. She's married now and lives in Milwaukee. Her husband is in the insurance business. She says she's happy."

"I suppose we all have dreams," Zoe Kohler said. "Then we grow up and realize how impossible they were."

"What did you dream, Zoe?"

"Nothing special. I was very vague about it. I thought I might teach for a few years. But I guess I'd thought I'd just get married and have a family. That seemed to be the thing to do. But it didn't work out."

"You told me about your mother. What is your father like?"

"Dad? Oh, he's still a very active man. He has a car agency and owns half a real estate firm, and he's in a lot of other things. Belongs to a dozen clubs and business associations. He's always being elected president of this and that. I remember he was away at meetings almost every night. He's in local politics, too."

"Sounds like a very popular man."

"I guess. I hardly saw him. I mean, I knew he was there, but he really wasn't. Always rushing off somewhere. Every time he saw me, he'd kiss me. He smelled of whiskey and cigars. But he was very successful, and we had a nice home, so I really can't complain. What was your father like?"

"Tall and skinny and kind of bent over when he got older. I think he worked himself to death; I really do. He always had two jobs. He had to with that family. Came home late and fell into bed. All us boys had jobs—paper routes and things like that. But we didn't bring home much. So he worked and worked. And you know, I never once heard him complain. Never once."

They sat in sad silence for a few minutes, sipping their brandies.

"Zoe, do you think you'll ever get married again?"

She considered that. "I don't know. Probably not—as of this moment."

He looked at her. "Were you hurt that much?"

"I was destroyed," she cried out. "Demolished. Maddie Kurnitz can hop from husband to husband. I can't. Maybe that's my fault. Maybe I'm some kind of foolish romantic."

"You're afraid to take another chance?"

"Yes, I'm afraid. If I took another chance, and *that* didn't work out, I think I'd kill myself."

"My God," he said softly, "you're serious, aren't you?"

She nodded.

"Zoe, none of us is perfect. And relationships aren't perfect."

"I know that," she said, "and I was willing to settle for what I had. But he wasn't. I really don't want to talk about it, Ernie. It was all so—so ugly."

"All rightee!" he sang out, slapping the table. "We won't talk about it. We'll talk about cheerful things and have dessert and coffee and laugh up a storm."

She reached out to stroke his hair.

"You're nice," she said, looking into his eyes. "I'm glad I met you."

He caught her hand, pressed it against his cheek.

"And I'm glad I met you," he said. "And I want to keep on seeing you as much as I can. Okay?"

"Okay," she said. "Now . . . strawberry or apple tart? Which are you going to have?"

"Strawberry," he said promptly.

"Me, too," she said. "We like the same things."

They had dessert and coffee, chattering briskly about books and movies and TV stars, never letting the conversation flag. Then they cleared the table and Ernest washed while Zoe dried. She learned where his plates and cups and saucers and cutlery were stored.

Then, still jabbering away, they sat again in the armchairs with more brandy. He told her about his courses in computer technology, and she told him about the unusual problems of hotel security officers. They were both good listeners.

Finally, about eleven o'clock, feeling a bit light-headed, Zoe said she thought she should be going. Ernest said he thought they should finish the brandy first, and she said if they did, she'd never go home, and he said that would be all right, too. They both laughed, knowing he was joking. But neither was sure.

Ernie said he'd see her home, but she refused, saying she'd take a taxi and would be perfectly safe. They finally agreed that he'd go out with her, see her into a cab, and she'd call the moment she was in her own apartment.

"If you don't phone within twenty minutes," he said, "I'll call out the Marines."

They stood and she moved to him, so abruptly that he staggered back. She clasped him in her arms, put her face close to his.

"A lovely, lovely evening," she said. "Thank you so very much."

"Thank you, Zoe. We'll do it again and again and again."

She pressed her lips against his: a dry, warm, firm kiss.

She drew away, stroked his fine hair.

"You are a dear, sweet man," she said, "and I like you very much. You won't just drop me, will you, Ernie?"

"Zoe!" he cried. "Of course not! What kind of a man do you think I am?"

"Oh . . ." she said confusedly, "I'm all mixed up. I don't know what to think about you."

"Think the best," he said. "Please. We need each other."

"We do," she said throatily. "We really do."

They kissed again, standing and clasped, swaying. It was a close embrace, more thoughtful than fervid. There was no darting of tongues, no searching of frantic fingers. There was warmth and intimacy. They comforted each other, protective and reassuring.

They pulled away, staring, still holding to each other.

"Darling," he said.

"Darling," she said. "Darling. Darling."

He went about turning off lamps, checking the gas range, taking a jacket from a pressed wood wardrobe. Zoe went into the bathroom. Because the door was so flimsy and the apartment so small, she ran the faucet in the sink while she relieved herself.

Then she rinsed her hands, drying them on one of the little pink towels he had put out. The bathroom was as clean, tidy, and precisely arranged as the rest of his apartment.

She looked at herself in the medicine cabinet mirror. She thought her face was blushed, glowing. She felt her cheeks. Hot. She touched her lips and smiled.

She examined her hair critically. She decided she would have it done. A feather-cut perhaps. Something youthful and careless, to give her the look of a gamine. And a rinse to give it gloss.

Zoe Kohler brought morning coffee into Mr. Pinckney's office. He was behind his desk. Barney McMillan was lolling on the couch. She had brought him a jelly doughnut.

''Thanks, doll,'' he said; then, with a grin, ''Whoops, sorry. Thank you, Zoe.''

She gave him a frosty glance, went back to her own office. She could hear the conversation of the two men. As usual, they were talking about the Hotel Ripper.

''They'll get him,'' McMillan said. ''Eventually.''

''Probably,'' Mr. Pinckney agreed. ''But meanwhile the hotels are beginning to hurt. Did you see the *Times* this morning? The first cancellation of a big convention because of the Ripper. They better catch him fast or the summer tourist trade will be a disaster.''

''Come to Fun City,'' McMillan said, ''and get your throat slit. The guy must be a real wacko. A *fegelah,* you figure?''

''That's the theory they're going on, according to Sergeant Coe. They're rousting all the gay bars. But just between you, me, and the lamppost, Coe says they're stymied. They had a police shrink draw up a psychological profile, but you know how much help those things are.''

''Yeah,'' McMillan said, ''a lot of bullshit. What they really need is one good fingerprint.''

''Well . . .'' Mr. Pinckney said judiciously, ''prints are usually of limited value until they pick up some suspects to match them with. You know, there hasn't been a single arrest. Not even on suspicion.''

''But that guy in command—what's his name? Slavin?—he keeps putting out those stupid statements about 'promising leads' and 'an arrest expected momentarily.' It's gotten to be a joke.''

''If he doesn't show some results soon,'' Mr. Pinckney said, ''he'll find himself guarding a vacant lot in the Bronx. The hotel association has a lot of clout in this town.''

Then the two men started discussing next week's work schedule, and Zoe Kohler began flipping through her morning copy of *The New York Times.* The story on the Hotel Ripper was carried on page 3 of the second section, the Metropolitan Report.

The murder of Jerome Ashley, the third victim, had been front-page news in all New York papers for less than a week. Then, as nothing new developed, follow-up stories dropped back farther and farther.

That morning's *Times* had nothing to add to the story other than the mention of the first cancellation of a large convention directly attributable to the crimes of the Hotel Ripper. The story repeated the sparse description of the suspect: five-feet-five to five-feet-seven, wearing a black nylon wig.

But below the news account was an article bylined by Dr. David Hsieh, identified by the *Times* as a clinical psychologist specializing in psychopathology, and author of a book on criminal behavior entitled *The Upper Depths.*

Zoe Kohler read the article with avid interest. In it, Dr. Hsieh attempted to extrapolate the motives of the Hotel Ripper from the available facts, while admitting that lack of sufficient data made such an exercise of questionable validity.

It was Dr. Hsieh's thesis that the Hotel Ripper was driven to his crimes by loneliness, which was why he sought out hotels with their dining rooms, cocktail lounges, conventions, etc. "Places where many people congregate, mingle, converse, eat and drink, laugh and carry on normal social intercourse denied to the Ripper.

"Solitude can be a marvelous boon," Dr. Hsieh continued. "Without it, many of us would find life without savor. But there is this caveat: solitude must be by choice. Enforced, it can be as corrosive as a draft of sulfuric. To be wisely used, it must be sought and learned. And the danger of addiction lingers always. A heady thing, solitude. An elixir, a depressant. One man's triumph, another man's defeat. The Hotel Ripper cannot handle it.

"Solitude decays; mold appears; loneliness makes its sly and cunning infection. Loneliness rots the marrow, seeps through shrunken veins into the constricted heart. The breath smells of ashes, and men become desperate. The police call them 'loners,' making no distinction between those who eat alone, work alone, live alone and sleep alone by choice or through the grind of circumstances. Some desire it; some do not. The Hotel Ripper does not.

"There is a fatal regression at work here. It goes like this: Solitude. Loneliness. Isolation. Alienation. Aggression. In the penultimate stage, the happiness of others becomes an object of envy; in the final, an object of rage. 'Why should they . . . ? When I . . . ?' The Hotel Ripper is a terminal case."

Zoe Kohler put the newspaper aside and stared off into the middle distance. Try as she might, she could not recognize herself in the portrait drawn by Dr. David Hsieh.

Something new was happening to her. She had heretofore never sought to deny her responsibility for what had been done to those three men. She had planned her adventures carefully, carried them out with complete awareness of what she was doing, and reviewed her actions afterward.

She, Zoe Kohler, was the Hotel Ripper. She had not disavowed it. Never. Not for a minute. Indeed, she had gloried in it. Her adventures were triumphs. And the notoriety she had earned had been exciting.

But now she was beginning to feel a curious disassociation from her acts. She felt cleft, tugged apart. She could not reconcile the lustful images of the Hotel Ripper with the gentle memories of a woman who said, "Darling. Darling. Darling."

On May 6th, a few minutes before 6:00 P.M., Zoe Kohler entered the office of Dr. Oscar Stark. There were two patients in the reception room, which usually meant a wait of thirty minutes or so. But it was almost an hour before Gladys beckoned. The nurse led her directly to the examination room.

Zoe was weighed, then went into the lavatory with the wide-mouthed plastic cup. She handed the urine sample to Gladys and sat down, sheet-draped. Dr. Stark came bustling in a few minutes later, trailing a cloud of smoke. He set his cigar carefully aside.

"Well, *well,*" he said, staring at Zoe. "What have we here? A new hairdo?"

"Yes," she said, blushing. "Sort of."

"I like it," he said. "Very fetching. Don't you like it, Gladys?"

"I told her I did," the nurse said. "I wish I could wear a feather-cut. It's so youthful."

"Maybe I should get one," the doctor said.

He pulled up his wheeled stool in front of Zoe, warmed the stethoscope on his hairy forearm. She let the sheet drop to her waist. He began to apply the disk to her naked chest and ribcage.

"Mmp," he said. "You didn't run over here from your office, did you?"

"No," Zoe said seriously, "I've been in the waiting room for almost an hour."

He nodded, then felt her pulse, something he rarely did. He took the examination form and clipboard from Gladys and made a few quick notes. The nurse bent over him and pointed out something on the chart. The doctor blinked.

Gladys wheeled up the sphygmomanometer. Stark wrapped the cuff about Zoe's arm and pumped the bulb. The nurse leaned down to take the reading.

"Let's try that again," Stark said and repeated the process. Gladys made more notes.

The doctor sat a moment in silence, staring at Zoe, his face expressionless. Then he took the blood sample and set the syringe aside.

"Gladys," he said, "that big magnifying glass—you know where it is?"

"Right here," she said, opening the top drawer of a white enameled taboret.

"What would I do without you?" he said.

He hitched the wheeled stool as close to Zoe as he could. He leaned forward and began to examine her through the magnifying glass. He inspected her lips, face, neck, and arms. He peered at the palms of her hands, the creases in her fingers, the crooks of her elbows. He scrutinized aureoles and nipples.

"What are you doing that for?" Zoe asked.

"Just browsing," he said. "I'm a very kinky man. This is how I get my kicks. Zoe, do you shave your armpits?"

"Yes."

"Uh-huh. Open the sheet, please, and spread your legs."

Obediently, eyes lowered, she pulled the sheet aside and exposed herself. He tugged gently at her pubic hair, then examined his fingers. He had come away with a few curly hairs. He inspected them through the magnifying glass."

"Why did you do that?" she asked faintly.

He looked at her kindly. "I'm stuffing a pillow," he said, and Gladys laughed.

He handed the glass back to the nurse and began breast palpation. The pelvic examination followed. Ten minutes later, Zoe Kohler, dressed, was seated in Dr. Stark's office, watching him light a fresh cigar.

He blew a plume of smoke at the ceiling. He pushed his half-glasses atop his halo of white hair. He stared at Zoe, shaking his big head slowly. His pendulous features swung loosely.

"What am I going to do with you?" he said.

She was startled. "I don't understand," she said.

"Zoe, have you been under stress recently?"

"Stress?"

"Pressure. On your job? Your personal life? Anything upsetting you? Getting tense or excited or irritable?"

"No," she said, "nothing."

He sighed. He had been a practicing physician for more than thirty years; he knew very well how often patients lied. They usually lied because they were embarrassed, ashamed, or frightened. But sometimes, Stark suspected, a patient's lies to his doctor represented a subconscious desire for self-immolation.

"All right," he said to Zoe Kohler, "let's go on to something else . . . Are you on a diet? Trying to lose weight?"

"No. I'm eating just the same as I always have."

"You weigh almost four pounds less than you did last month."

Now she was shocked. "I don't understand that," she said.

"I don't either. But there it is."

"Maybe there's been some mistake," she said. "Maybe when Gladys—"

"Nonsense," he said sharply. "Gladys doesn't make mistakes. All right, here's what you've got . . . Your pulse is too rapid, your heart sounds like you just ran the hundred-yard dash, and your blood pressure is way up. It's still in the normal range, but very high-normal, and I don't like it. These are all signs of incipient hypertension—all the more puzzling because low blood pressure is a characteristic of your disease. That's why I asked if you've been under nervous or emotional stress."

"Well, I haven't."

"I'll take your word for it," he said dryly. "But it presents us with a small problem. A slight dilemma, you might say. You're still taking your salt tablets?"

"Yes. Two a day."

"Do you have any craving for additional salt?"

"No, not particularly."

"Well, that's something. The menstrual cramps continue?"

She nodded.

"Better, about the same, or worse?"

"About the same," she said. "Maybe a little worse last month."

"You're due—when?"

"In a few days."

He set his cigar aside. He leaned back in his chair, laced his fingers across his heavy stomach. His china-blue eyes regarded her gravely. When he spoke, his voice was flat, toneless, without emphasis.

"If you were under stress," he said, "it might account for the higher blood pressure. That would be, uh, of some concern in a woman with your condition. Increased stress—even a tooth extraction—results in higher cortisol secretion in the normal individual. But your adrenal cortex is almost completely destroyed. So if you are under stress of any kind, we should increase your cortisone intake to bring your levels up to normal."

"But I'm *not* under stress!" she insisted.

He ignored her.

"Also, while under stress, a higher amount of sodium chloride is required so that your body does not become dehydrated. You haven't been vomiting, have you?"

"No."

"Well, we'll have to wait for the blood and urine tests to come back from the lab before we know definitely that we have a cortisol deficiency. I saw minor signs of skin discoloration, which is usually a sure tip-off. A decrease in armpit and pubic hair is another indication. And there's that weight loss . . ."

"But you're not sure?" she said.

"About the cortisol deficiency? No, I'm not sure. It's the high blood pressure that puzzles me. Cortisol deficiency should be accompanied by lower blood pressure. The small problem I mentioned, the slight dilemma, is this: Ordinarily, for patients with high blood pressure, a reduced- or salt-free diet is recommended. But the nature of your disease demands that you continue to supplement your diet with sodium chloride. So what do we do? For the time being, I suggest an increased cortisone dosage. What are you taking now?" He flipped down his glasses, searched through her file on his desk. "Here it is—twenty-five milligrams once a day. Is that correct?"

"Yes."

"When do you take it?"

"In the morning. With breakfast."

"Any stomach upset?"

"No."

"Good. I'm going to suggest you take another dose in the late afternoon. That will give you fifty milligrams a day. You may not need it, but it won't do any harm. Try to take the second dose with milk or some antacid preparation. Sometimes the cortisone affects the stomach if it's taken without food. You understand all that?"

"Yes, doctor. But I'm running short of cortisone. I need another prescription."

He pulled a pad toward him and began scribbling.

"While you're at it," Zoe Kohler said casually, "could I have another prescription for Tuinal?"

He looked up suddenly.

"You're suffering from insomnia?"

"Yes. Almost every night."

"Try a highball just before you go to bed. Or an ounce of brandy."

"I've tried that," she said, "but it doesn't help."

"Another dilemma," he mourned. "Ordinarily, with insomnia, I'd reduce the cortisone dosage. But in view of your weight loss and the other factors, I'm going to increase it until the lab tests come in and we know where we are."

"And what about the salt pills?"

He drummed his blunt fingers on the desktop, frowning. Then . . .

"Continue with the salt. Two tablets a day. Zoe, I don't want to frighten you. I've explained to you a dozen times that if you take your medication faithfully—and you must take it for the rest of your days, just like a diabetic—there is no reason why you can't live a long and productive life."

"Well, I've been taking my medication faithfully," she said with some asperity, "and now you say something's wrong."

He looked at her strangely but said nothing. He completed the two prescriptions and handed them to her. He suggested she call in four days and he'd tell her the results of the blood test and urinalysis.

"Please," he said, "try not to worry. It might be hard not to, but worry will only make things worse."

"I'm not worried," she said, and he believed her.

After she had gone, he sat a moment in his swivel chair and relighted his cigar. He thought he knew the reason for the higher blood pressure. She was under stress, moderate to severe, but certainly acute enough to require an increase in corticosteroid therapy.

She had lied to him for her own good reasons. He wondered to what possible pressures this quiet, withdrawn, rather emotionless woman might be a victim. It wasn't unusual for female patients with her disorder to experience a weakening of the sex drive. But in Zoe Kohler's case, he suspected, the libido had been atrophied long before the onset of her illness.

So if it wasn't sexual frustration, or an emotional problem, it had to be some form of psychic stress that was demanding a higher cortisol level, burning up calories, and setting her blood pounding through her arteries. He felt like a detective searching for a motive when he should be acting like a physician seeking the proper therapy for a disorder that, untreated, was invariably fatal.

Sighing, he dug through Zoe Kohler's file for the photocopies he had made at the New York Academy of Medicine when Zoe had first consulted him. She had just come to New York and had brought along her medical file from her family doctor in Winona.

Stark thought that Minnesota sawbones had done a hell of a job in diagnosing the rare disease before it had reached crisis proportions. It was a bitch of an illness to recognize because many of the early symptoms were characteristic of other, milder ailments. But the Minnesota GP had hit it right on the nose and prescribed the treatment that saved Zoe Kohler's life.

Dr. Oscar Stark found the photocopies he sought. The main heading was "Diseases of the Endocrine System." He turned to the section dealing with "Hypofunction of Adrenal Cortex."

He began to read, to make certain he had forgotten nothing about the incidence, pathogenesis, symptoms, diagnosis, and treatment of Addison's disease.

* * *

Her menstrual cramps began on the evening of May 7th, twenty-four hours after her visit to Dr. Stark. In addition to the low-back twinges and the deep, internal ache, there was now an abdominal pain that came and went.

She felt so wretched on the evening of May 8th, a Thursday, that she took a cab home from work, although the night was clear and unseasonably warm. After she undressed, she probed her lower abdomen gingerly. It felt hard and swollen.

She took her usual dosage of vitamins and minerals. And she gulped down a Darvon and a Valium. She wondered what physiological effect this combination of painkiller and tranquilizer might have.

She soon discovered. Soaking in a hot tub, sipping a glass of chilled white wine, she felt the cramps ease, the abdominal pain diminish. She felt up, daring and resolute.

She had been watching the hotel trade magazine for notices of conventions, sales meetings, political gatherings. It appeared to her that the activities of the Hotel Ripper had not yet seriously affected the tourist trade in New York. Occupancy rates were still high; desirable hotel rooms were hard to find.

The Cameron Arms Hotel on Central Park South looked good to her. During the week of May 4–10, it was hosting two conventions and a week-long exhibition and sale of rare postage stamps. When she had looked up the Cameron Arms in the hotel directory, she found it had 600 rooms, banquet and dining rooms, coffee shop, and two cocktail lounges, one with a disco.

Lolling in the hot tub, she decided on the Cameron Arms Hotel, and pondered which dress she should wear.

But when she stepped from the tub, she felt again that familiar weakness, a vertigo. Her knees sagged; she grabbed the sink for support. It lasted almost a minute this time. Then the faintness passed. She took a deep breath and began to perfume her body.

It took her more than an hour to dress and apply makeup. It seemed to her she was moving in a lazy glow; she could not bring her thoughts to a hard focus. When she tried to plan what she was about to do, her concentration slid away and dissolved.

An odd thought occurred to her in this drifting haze: she wondered if her adventures were habit-forming. Perhaps she was venturing out this night simply because it was something she always did just prior to her period. It was not dictated by desire or need.

She drank two cups of black decaf coffee, but no more wine and no more pills. By the time she was ready to leave, close to 9:00 P.M., her mindless euphoria had dissipated; she felt alert, sharp, and determined.

She wore a sheath of plummy wool jersey with a wide industrial zipper down the front from low neckline to high hem. Attached to the tab of the zipper was a miniature police whistle.

She transferred belongings to the patent leather shoulder bag, making certain she had her knife and the small aerosol can of Chemical Mace. As usual, she removed all identification from her wallet.

She was wearing her strawberry blond wig. Around her left wrist was the gold chain with the legend: WHY NOT?

An hour later she strode briskly into the crowded lobby of the Cameron Arms Hotel, smoking a cigarette and carrying her trenchcoat over her arm. She noticed men turning to gawk, and knew she was desired. She felt serenely indifferent and in control.

She looked in at the cocktail lounge featuring the disco, but it was too noisy and jammed. She walked down the lobby corridor to the Queen Anne Room. It appeared crowded, but dim and reasonably quiet. She went in there.

It was a somewhat gloomy room, with heavy upholstery, fake marquetry, and vaguely Oriental decoration and drapes. All the tables and banquettes were occupied by couples and foursomes. But there were vacant stools at the bar.

Zoe Kohler went into her act. She looked about as if expecting to be met. She asked the hatcheck girl the time as she handed over her trenchcoat. She made her way slowly to the bar, still peering about in the semidarkness.

She ordered a glass of white wine from a bartender dressed like an English publican of an indeterminate period: knickers, high wool hose, a wide leather belt, a shirt with bell sleeves, a leather jerkin. The cocktail waitresses were costumed as milkmaids.

She sat erect at the bar, sipping her wine slowly, looking straight ahead. On her left was a couple arguing in furious whispers. The barstool on her right was empty. She waited patiently, supremely confident.

She had just ordered a second glass of wine when a man slid onto the empty stool. She risked a quick glance in the mirror behind the bar. About 45, she guessed. Medium height, thick at the shoulders, florid complexion. Well-dressed. Blondish hair that had obviously been styled and spray-set.

His features were heavy, almost gross. She thought he looked like an ex-athlete going to fat. When he picked up his double Scotch (he had specified the brand), she saw his diamond pinkie ring and a loose chain of gold links about his hairy wrist.

The Queen Anne Room began to fill up. A party of three raucous men pushed in for drinks on the other side of the single man. He hitched his barstool closer to Zoe to give them room. His shoulder brushed hers. He said, "Pardon me, ma'am," giving her a flash of white teeth too perfect to be natural.

"Getting crowded in here," he offered a moment later.

She turned to look at him. He had very small, hard eyes.

"The conventions, I suppose," she said. "The hotel must be full."

"Right," he said, nodding. "I made my reservation months ago, or I never would have gotten in."

"Which convention are you with?"

"I'm not with any," he said, "exactly. But I came up for the meeting of the Association of Regional Airline Owners and Operators. Here . . ."

He dug into his jacket pocket, brought out a business card. He handed it to Zoe, then flicked a gold cigarette lighter so she could read it.

"Leonard T. Bergdorfer," he said. "From Atlanta, Georgia. I'm a broker. Mostly in sales of regional airlines, feeder lines, freight forwarders, charter outfits—like that. I bring buyers and sellers together. That's why I'm at this shindig. Pick up the gossip: who wants to sell, who wants to buy."

"And have a little fun with the boys?" she asked archly.

"You're so right," he said with a thin smile. "That's the name of the game."

"From Atlanta, Georgia," she said, handing back his card. "You don't talk like a southerner."

He laughed harshly.

"Hell, no, I'm no rebel. But Atlanta is where the money is. I'm from Buffalo. Originally. But I've lived all over the U.S. of A. Where you from, honey?"

"Right here in little old New York."

"No kidding? Not often I meet a native New Yorker. What's your name?"

"Irene," she said.

He had a suite on the eighth floor: living room, bedroom, bath. There was a completely equipped bar on wheels, with covered tubs of ice cubes. Liquor, wine, and beer. Bags of potato chips, boxes of pretzels, jars of salted peanuts.

"Welcome to the Leonard T. Bergdorfer Hospitality Suite," he said. "Your home away from home."

She looked around, wondering if anyone in the Queen Anne Room or on the crowded elevator would remember them. She thought not.

"All the booze hounds are at a banquet right now," he said. "Listening to a fat-ass politician give a speech on the deregulation of airfares. Who needs that bullshit?"

This last was said with some bitterness. Zoe suspected he had not been invited.

"But it'll break up in an hour or so," he went on, "and then you'll see more freeloaders up here than you can count. Stick around, Irene; you'll make a lot of friends."

She was uneasy. It wasn't going the way she had planned.

"I better not," she said. "You boys will want to talk business. I'll have a drink and be on my way."

"You don't want to be like that, honey," he said with his thin smile, "or Poppa will spank. Be friendly. I'll make it worth your while. Now then . . . let me have your coat. We'll have a drink and a little fun before the thundering herd arrives."

He hung her coat in a closet, returned to the bar. He busied himself with bottles and glasses, his back to her.

I could take him now, she thought suddenly. But it wouldn't be—wouldn't be complete.

"You married, sweetie?" he asked over his shoulder.

"Divorced. What about you, Lenny?"

"Still a bachelor," he said, coming toward her with the drinks. "Why buy a cow when milk is so cheap—right?"

She took the wine from him. When she sipped, she made certain she implanted lipstick on the rim so she could identify the glass later.

"What's this for?" he asked, fingering the small whistle hanging from the tab of her zipper.

"In case I need help," she said, smiling nervously.

"You don't look like a woman who needs help," he said with a coarse laugh. "Me, maybe. Not you, babe."

He pulled the zipper down to her waist. The dress opened.

"Hey-hey," he said, eyes glittering. "Look at the goodies. Not big, but choice." He caught up her wrist, read the legend on her bracelet. "Well . . . why not? Let's you and me go in the bedroom and get acquainted before anyone else shows up."

He grabbed her upper arm in a tight grip. He half-led, half-pulled her into the bedroom. He released her, shut the bedroom door. He set his drink and hers on the bedside table. He began to take off jacket and vest.

"Wait, Lenny, wait," Zoe said. "What's the rush? Can't we have a drink first?"

"No time," he said, pulling off his tie. "This will have to be a quickie. You can drink all you like later."

He stripped to his waist rapidly. His torso was thick, muscular. None of the fat she had imagined. His chest, shoulders, arms were furred. He sat down on the bed and beckoned, making flipping motions with his hands.

"Come on, come on," he said. "Get with it."

When she hesitated, he stood again, took one stride to her. He ripped her zipper down its full length. The front of her dress fell apart. He embraced her, hands and arms inside the opened dress, around her naked waist. He pressed close, grinding against her.

"Oh yeah," he breathed. "Oh yeah. This is something like."

His face dug into her neck and shoulder. She felt his tongue, his teeth.

"Wait," she gasped. "Wait just a minute, Lenny. Give a girl a chance. I've got to get my purse."

He pulled away, looked at her suspiciously.

"What for?" he demanded.

"You know," she said. "Female stuff. You get undressed. I'll just be a sec."

"Well, hurry it up," he growled. "I'm getting a hardon like the Washington Monument. All for you, baby."

She ran into the living room. She saw at once that she could easily escape. Grab up shoulder bag and coat, duck out the corridor door. He was half-undressed; he wouldn't follow. She could be long gone before he was able to come after her.

But she wanted to stay, to finish what she had to do. He deserved it. It was the timing that bothered her, the risk. He was expecting guests. Could she complete her job and be out of the suite before the others arrived?

Softly, she locked and chained the corridor door. She went back to the bedroom with her shoulder bag. He was pulling down his trousers and undershorts. His penis was stiffening, empurpled. It was rising, nodding at her. A live club. Ugly. It threatened.

"Be right with you," she said and went into the bathroom. Closed and locked the door. Leaned back against it, breathing rapidly. Zipped up her dress, tried to decide what to do next.

"Come on, come on," he shouted, trying the locked door, then pounding on it. "What the hell's taking you so long?"

She would never be able to lull him, get behind him. Unless she submitted to him first. But that wasn't the way it was supposed to be. That would spoil everything.

She opened the knife, placed it on the edge of the sink. Took the can of Mace from her purse. Gripped it tightly in her right hand.

"All set, Lenny!" she cried gaily.

She unlocked the door with her left hand. He slammed it open. He was close, glowering. He reached for her.

She sprayed the gas directly into his face. She kept the button depressed and, as he staggered back, followed him. She held the hissing container close to his eyes, nose, mouth.

He coughed, sneezed, choked. He bent over. His hands came up to his face. He stumbled, fell, went down on his back. He tried to suck in air, breathing in great, hacking sobs. His fingers clawed at his weeping eyes.

She leaned over him, spraying until the can was empty.

She ran back to the bathroom, hurriedly soaked a washcloth in cold water. Held it over her nose and mouth. Picked up the knife, returned to the bedroom.

He was writhing on the floor, hands covering his face. He was making animal sounds: grunts, groans. His hairy chest was pumping furiously.

She bent over him. Dug the blade in below his left ear. Made a hard, curving slash. His body leaped convulsively. A fountain of blood. She leaped aside to avoid it. Hands fell away from his face. Watery eyes glared at her and, as she watched, went dim.

The gas was beginning to affect her. She gasped and choked. But she had enough strength to complete the ritual, stabbing his naked genitals again and again, with a mouthed, "There. There. There."

She fled to the bathroom, closed the door. She took several deep breaths of clear air. She soaked the washcloth again, wiped her eyes, cleaned her nostrils. She inspected her arms, dress, ankles, the soles of her shoes. She could find no bloodstains.

But her right hand and the knife were wet with his blood. She turned on the hot water faucet in the sink. She began to rinse the blood away. It was then she noticed the knife blade was broken. About a half-inch of the tip was missing.

She stared at it, calculating the danger. If the blade tip wasn't near him, lying on the rug, then it was probably lost in the raw swamp of his slashed throat, broken off against bone or cartilage. She could not search for it, could not touch him.

She began moving quickly. Finished rinsing hand and knife. Dried both with one of his towels. Put towel, knife, and emptied Chemical Mace can into her shoulder bag. Strode into the bedroom. The gas was dissipating now.

Leonard T. Bergdorfer lay sprawled in a pool of his own blood. Zoe looked about, but could not see the knife blade tip.

She picked up her glass from the bedside table, drained the wine. The empty glass went into her shoulder bag, too. She turned back to wipe the knobs of the bathroom door and the faucet handles with the damp washcloth. She did the same to the knobs of the bedroom door.

She put on her coat in the living room. She unlocked and opened the hallway door a few inches, peeked out. Then she wiped off the lock, chain, and doorknob with the washcloth, and tucked it into her bag. She opened the door wide with her foot, stepped out into the empty corridor. She nudged the door shut with her knee.

She was waiting for the Down elevator when an ascending elevator stopped on the eighth floor. Five men piled out, laughing and shouting and hitting each other. Men were so physical.

They didn't even glance in her direction, but went yelling and roughhousing down the corridor. They stopped in front of Bergdorfer's suite. One of them began knocking on the door.

Then the Down elevator stopped at the eighth floor, the doors slid open, and Zoe Kohler departed.

6

On April 18th, the night Zoe Kohler was sipping white wine at Harry Kurnitz's party at the Chez Ronald on East 48th Street, Edward X. Delaney was dining with reporter Thomas Handry at the Bull & Bear Restaurant, a block away.

Handry was a slender, dapper blade who looked younger than his forty-nine years. His suits were always precisely pressed, shoes shined, shirts a gleaming white. He was one of the few men Delaney had known who could wear a vest jauntily.

The only signs of inner tensions were his fingernails, gnawed to the quick, and a nervous habit of stroking his bare upper lip with a knuckle, an atavism from the days when he had sported a luxuriant cavalry mustache.

"You're picking up the tab?" he had demanded when he arrived.

"Of course."

"In that case," Handry said, "I shall have a double Tanqueray martini, straight up with a lemon twist. Then the roast beef, rare, a baked potato, and a small salad."

"I see nothing to object to there," Delaney said, and to the hovering waiter, "Double that order, please."

The reporter regarded the Chief critically.

"Christ, you never change, never look a day older. What did you do—sell your soul to the devil?"

"Something like that," Delaney said. "Actually, I was born old."

"I believe it," Handry said. He put his elbows on the table, scrubbed his face with his palms.

"Rough day?" the Chief asked.

"The usual bullshit. Maybe I'm just bored. You know, I'm coming to the sad conclusion that nothing actually new ever happens. I mean, pick up a newspaper of, say, fifty or a hundred years ago, and there it all is: poverty, famine, wars, accidents, earthquakes, political corruption, crime and so forth. Nothing changes."

"No, it doesn't. Not really. Maybe the forms change, but people don't change all that much."

"Take this Hotel Ripper thing," Handry went on. "It's just a replay of the Son of Sam thing, isn't it?"

But then the waiter arrived with their drinks and Delaney was saved from answering.

They had ale with their roast beef and, later, Armagnac with their coffee. Then they sat back and Delaney accepted one of Handry's cigarettes. He smoked it awkwardly and saw the reporter looking at him with amusement.

"I'm used to cigars," he explained. "I keep wanting to chew the damned thing."

They had a second cup of coffee, stared at each other.

"Got anything for me?" Handry said finally.

"A story?" Delaney said. "An exclusive? A scoop?" He laughed. "No, nothing like that. Nothing you can use."

"Let me be the judge of that."

"I can give you some background," the Chief said. "The powers-that-be aren't happy with Lieutenant Slavin."

"Is he on the way out?"

"Oh, they won't can him. Kick him upstairs maybe."

"I'll check it out. Anything else?"

Delaney considered how much he could reveal, what he would have to pay to get the cooperation he needed.

"That last killing . . ." he said. "Jerome Ashley . . ."

"What about it?"

The Chief looked at him sternly.

"This is not to be used," he said. "N-O-T. Until I give you the go-ahead. Agreed?"

"Agreed. What is it?"

"They found nylon hairs on the rug in Ashley's hotel room."

"So? They've already said the killer wears a black nylon wig."

"These nylon hairs were a reddish blond."

The reporter blinked.

"Son of a bitch," he said slowly. "He switched wigs."

"Right," Delaney said, nodding. "And could switch again to brown, red, purple, green, any color of the goddamned rainbow. That's why nothing's been released on the strawberry blond hairs. Maybe the killer will stick to that color if nothing about it appears in the newspapers or on TV."

"Maybe," Handry said doubtfully. "Anything else?"

"Not at the moment."

"Slim pickings," the reporter said, sighing. "All right, let's hear about this research you want."

Edward X. Delaney took a folded sheet of typing paper from his inside jacket pocket, handed it across the table. Thomas Handry put on heavy, horn-rimmed glasses to read it. He read it twice. Then he raised his head to stare at the Chief.

"You say this has something to do with the Hotel Ripper?"

"It could."

The reporter continued staring. Then . . .

"You're nuts!" he burst out. "You know that?"

"It's possible I am," the Chief said equably.

"You really think . . . ?"

Delaney shrugged.

"Gawd!" Handry said in an awed voice. "What a story that would make. Well, if your game plan was to hook me, you've succeeded. I'll get this stuff for you."

"When?"

"Take me at least a week."

"A week would be fine," Delaney said.

"If I have it before, I'll let you know."

"I need all the numbers. Percentages. Rates."

"All right, all right," the reporter said crossly. "I know what you want; you don't have to spell it out. But if it holds up, I get the story. Agreed?"

Delaney nodded, paid the bill, and both men rose.

"A nightcap at the bar?" the Chief suggested.

"Sure," the reporter said promptly. "But won't your wife be wondering what happened to you?"

"She's taking a course tonight."

"Oh? On what?"

"Assertiveness training."

"Lordy, lordy," Thomas Handry said.

He went over the dossiers on the three victims again and again. He was convinced there was something there, a connection, a lead, that eluded him.

Then, defeated, he turned his attention to the hotels in which the crimes had taken place, thinking there might be a common denominator there. But the three hotels had individual owners, were apparently just unexceptional midtown Manhattan hostelries with nothing about them that might motivate a criminal intent on revenge.

Then he reviewed again the timing of the killings. The first had occurred on a Friday, the second on a Thursday, the third on a Wednesday. There seemed to be a reverse progression in effect, for what possible reason Delaney could not conceive. But if the fourth killing happened on a Tuesday, it might be worth questioning.

He never doubted for a moment that there would be a fourth murder. He was furious that he was unable to prevent it.

Sergeant Abner Boone called regularly, two or three times a week. It was he who had informed Delaney that strawberry blond hairs had been found on the rug in the third victim's hotel room. It had still not been decided whether or not to release this information to the media.

Boone also said that analysis of the bloody footprints on Jerome Ashley's rug had confirmed the killer's height as approximately five feet five to five feet seven. It had proved impossible to determine if the prints were made by a man or woman.

The sergeant reported that the scars on Ashley's hands were the result of burns suffered when a greasy stove caught fire. Boone didn't think there was any possible connection with the murder, and the Chief agreed.

Finally, the investigation into the possibility that all three murdered men were victims of the same disgruntled employee seeking vengeance had turned up nothing. There was simply no apparent connection between Puller, Wolheim, and Ashley.

"So we're back to square one," Boone said, sighing. "We're still running the decoys every night in midtown, and Slavin is pulling in every gay with a sheet or reported as having worn a wig at some time or other. But the results have been zip. Any suggestions, Chief?"

"No. Not at the moment."

"At the moment?" the sergeant said eagerly. "Does that mean, sir, that you may have something? In a while?"

Delaney didn't want to raise any false hopes. Neither did he want to destroy Boone's hope utterly.

"Well . . . possibly," he said cautiously. "A long, long shot."

"Chief, at this stage we'll take anything, no matter how crazy. When will you know?"

"About two weeks." Then, wanting to change the subject, he said, "You're getting the usual tips and confessions, I suppose."

"You wouldn't believe," the sergeant said, groaning. "We've even had four black nylon wigs mailed to us with notes signed: 'The Hotel Ripper.' But to tell you the truth, if we weren't busy chasing down all the phony leads, we'd have nothing to do. We're snookered."

Delaney went back to his dossiers and finally he saw something he had missed. Something everyone had missed. It wasn't a connection between the three victims, a common factor. That continued to elude him.

But it was something just as significant. At least he thought it might be. He checked it twice against his calendar, then went into the living room to consult one of his wife's books.

When he returned to the study, his face was stretched. The expression was more grimace than grin, and when he made a careful note of his discovery, he realized he was humming tonelessly.

He wondered if he should call Sergeant Boone and warn him. Then he decided too many questions would be asked. Questions to which he did not have the answers.

Not that he believed a warning would prevent a fourth murder.

Thomas Handry called early on the morning of April 28th.

"I've got the numbers you wanted," he said.

There was nothing in his voice that implied the results were Yes or No. Delaney was tempted to ask, right then and there. But he didn't. He realized that, for some curious reason he could not analyze, he was more fearful of a Yes than a No.

"That's fine," he said, as heartily as he could.

"I didn't have time to do any adding up," Handry continued. "No compilation, no summary. You'll have to draw your own conclusions."

"I will," Delaney said. "Thank you, Handry. I appreciate your cooperation."

"It's my story," the reporter reminded him.

The Chief wondered what that meant. Was it a story? Or just an odd sidebar to a completely different solution?

"It's your story," he acknowledged. "When and where can I get the research?"

There was silence a moment. Then:

"How about Grand Central Station?" Handry said. "At twelve-thirty. The information booth on the main concourse."

"How about a deserted pier on the West Side at midnight?" Delaney countered.

The reporter laughed.

"No," he said, "no cloak-and-dagger stuff. I have to catch a train and I'm jammed up here. Grand Central would be best."

"So be it," Delaney said. "At twelve-thirty."

He was early, as usual, and wandered about the terminal. He amused himself by trying to spot the plainclothes officers on duty and the grifters plying their trade.

He recognized an old-time scam artist named Breezy Willie who had achieved a kind of fame by inventing a device called a "Grab Bag." It was, apparently, a somewhat oversized black suitcase. But it had no bottom and, of course, was completely empty.

Breezy Willie would select a waiting traveler with a suitcase smaller than the Grab Bag, preferably a suitcase with blue, tan, or patterned covering. The traveler had to be engrossed in a book, timetable, or newspaper, not watching his luggage.

Willie would sidle up close, lower the empty shell of the Grab Bag over the mark's suitcase, and pull a small lever in the handle. Immediately, the sides of the Grab Bag would compress tightly, clamping the suitcase within.

The con man would then lift the swag from the floor, move it ten or fifteen feet away and wait, reading his own newspaper. Willie never tried to run for it.

When the mark discovered his suitcase was missing, he'd dash about frantically, trying to locate it. Breezy Willie would get only a brief glance. He looked legit, and *his* suitcase was obviously black, not the mark's blue, tan, or patterned bag. When the excitement had died down, the hustler would stroll casually away.

The Chief moved close to Breezy Willie, whose eyes were busy over the top edge of his folded newspaper.

"Hullo, Willie," he said softly.

The knave looked up.

"I beg your pardon, sir," he said. "I'm afraid you've made a mistake. My name is—"

Then his eyes widened.

"Delaney!" he said. "This is great!"

He proffered his hand, which the Chief happily took.

"How's business, Willie?" he asked.

"Oh, I'm retired now."

"Glad to hear it."

"Going up to Boston to visit my daughter. She's married, y'know, with three kids, and I figured I'd—"

"Uh-huh," the Chief said.

He bent swiftly and picked up Breezy Willie's Grab Bag with one finger under the handle. He swung the empty shell back and forth.

"Traveling light, Willie?" He laughed and set the Grab Bag down again. "Getting a little long in the tooth for the game, aren't you?"

"That's a fact," the rascal said. "If it wasn't for the ponies, I'd have been playing shuffleboard in Florida years ago. I heard you retired, Chief."

"That's right, Willie."

"But just the same," Breezy Willie said thoughtfully, "I think I'll mosey over to Penn Station. I may visit my daughter in Baltimore, instead."

"Good idea," Delaney said, smiling.

They shook hands again and the Chief watched the scalawag depart. He wished all the bad guys were as innocuous as Breezy Willie. The jolly old pirate abhorred violence as much as any of his victims.

Then he spotted Thomas Handry striding rapidly toward him. The reporter was carrying a weighted Bloomingdale's shopping bag.

"I like your luggage," Delaney said, as Handry came up.

"It's all yours," he said, handing it over. "About five pounds of photocopies. Interesting stuff."

"Oh?"

Handry glanced up at the big clock.

"I've got to run," he said. "Believe it or not, I'm interviewing an alleged seer up in Mt. Vernon. She says she saw the Hotel Ripper in a dream. He's a six-foot-six black with one eye, a Fu Manchu mustache, and an English accent."

"Sounds like a great lead," Delaney said.

The reporter shrugged. "We're doing a roundup piece on all the mediums and seers who think they know what the Hotel Ripper looks like."

"And no two of them agree," the Chief said.

"Right. Well, I've got a train to catch." He hesitated, turned back, gestured toward the bag. "Let me know what you decide to do about all this."

"I will," Delaney said, nodding. "And thank you again."

He watched Handry trot away, then picked up the shopping bag and started out of the terminal. He hated carrying packages, especially shopping bags. He thought it might be a holdover from his days as a street cop: a fear of being encumbered, of not having his hands free.

It was a bright, blowy spring day, cool enough for his putty-colored gabardine topcoat, a voluminous tent that whipped about his legs. He paused a moment to set his homburg more firmly. Then he set out again, striding up Vanderbilt to Park Avenue.

He turned his thoughts resolutely away from what he was carrying and its possible significance. He concentrated on just enjoying the glad day. And the city.

It was his city. He had been born here, lived here all his life. He never left without a sensation of loss, never returned without a feeling of coming home. It was as much domicile as his brownstone; New Yorkers were as much family as his wife and children.

He saw the city clear. He did not think it paradise, nor did it daunt him. He knew its glories and its lesions. He accepted its beauties and its ugliness, its violence and its peace. He understood its moods and its fancies. He was grateful because the city never bored.

There he was, trundling north on Park Avenue, sunlight splintering off glass walls, flags snapping, men and women scuttling about with frowning purpose. He felt the demonic rhythm of the city, its compulsive speed and change. It was always going and never arriving.

The city devoured individuals, deflated the lofty, allowed dreams to fly an instant before bringing them down. New York was the great leveler. Birth, life, and death meant no more than a patched pothole or a poem. It was simply *there,* and the hell with you.

Edward X. Delancy wouldn't have it any other way.

He had made no conscious decision to walk home, but as block followed block, he could not surrender. He looked about eagerly, feeding his eyes. Never before had the city seemed to him so shining and charged. It had the excitement and fulfillment of a mountaintop.

And the women! What a joy. Men wore clothes; women wore costumes. There they were, swirling and sparkling, with wind-rosied cheeks, hair flinging back like flame. Monica had called him an old fogy, and so he was. But young enough, by God, to appreciate the worth of women.

He smiled at them all, toddlers to gammers. He could not conceive of a world without them, and gave thanks for having been lucky enough to have found Barbara, and then Monica. What a weasel life it would have been without their love.

Treading with lightened step, he made his way uptown, glorying in the parade of womankind. His face seemed set in an avuncular grin as he saw and loved them all, with their color and brio, their strut and sway.

Look at that one coming toward him! A princess, not much older than his stepdaughter Sylvia. A tall, smashing beauty with flaxen hair down to her bum. A face unsoiled by time, and a body as pliant and hard as a steel rod.

She strode directly up to him and stopped, blocking his way. She looked up at him with a sweet, melting smile.

"Wanna fuck, Pop?" she said.

The roiling was too much; he hadn't the wit to reply. He crossed to the other side of Park Avenue, lumbering now, his big feet in heavy, ankle-high shoes slapping the pavement. He climbed tiredly into the first empty cab that came along and went directly home, clutching the Bloomingdale's shopping bag.

Later, he was able to regain some measure of equanimity. He admitted, with sour amusement, that the brief encounter with the young whore had been typical of the city's habit of dousing highfalutin' dreams and romantic fancies with a bucketful of cold reality tossed right in the kisser.

He ate a sandwich of cold corned beef and German potato salad on dill-flavored rye bread while standing over the sink. He drank a can of beer. Resolution restored, he carried Handry's research into the study and set to work.

At dinner that night, he asked Monica what her plans were for the evening. "Going out?" he said casually.

She smiled and covered one of his hands with hers.

"I've been neglecting you, Edward," she said.

"You haven't been neglecting me," he protested, although he thought she had.

"Well, anyway, I'm going to stay home tonight."

"Good," he said. "I want to talk to you. A long talk."

"Oh-oh," his wife said, "that sounds serious. Am I being fired?"

"Nothing like that," he said, laughing. "I just want to discuss something with you. Get your opinion."

"If I give you my opinion, will it change yours?"

"No," he said.

The living room of the Delaney home was a large, high-ceilinged chamber dominated by a rather austere fireplace and an end wall lined with bookshelves framing the doorway to the study. The room was saved from gloom by the cheerfulness of its furnishings.

It was an eclectic collection that appeared more accumulated than selected. Chippendale cozied up to Shaker; Victorian had no quarrel with Art Deco. It was a friendly room, the old Persian carpet time-softened to subtlety.

Everything had the patina of hard use and loving care. The colors of drapes and upholstery were warm without being bright. Comfort created its own style; the room was mellow with living. Nothing was intended for show; wear was on display.

Delaney's throne was a high-back wing chair covered in burnished bottle-green leather and decorated with brass studs. Monica's armchair was more delicate, but just as worn; it was covered with a floral-patterned brocade that had suffered the depredations of a long-departed cat.

The room was comfortably cluttered with oversized ashtrays, framed photographs, a few small pieces of statuary, bric-a-brac, and one large wicker basket that still held a winterly collection of pussy willows, dried swamp grasses, and eucalyptus.

The walls held an assortment of paintings, drawings, cartoons, posters, etchings, and maps as varied as the furniture. No two frames alike; nothing dominated; everything charmed. And there always seemed room for something new. The display inched inexorably to the plaster ceiling molding.

That evening, dinner finished, dishes done, Monica moved to her armchair, donned half-glasses. She picked up knitting needles and an Afghan square she had been working on for several months. Delaney brought in all his dossiers and the Handry research. He dropped the stack of papers alongside his chair.

"What's all that?" Monica asked.

"It's what I want to talk to you about. I want to try out a theory on you."

"About the Hotel Ripper?"

"Yes. It won't upset you, will it?"

"No, it won't upset me. But it seems to me that for a cop not on active duty, you're taking a very active interest."

"I'm just trying to help out Abner Boone," he protested. "This case means a lot to him."

"Uh-huh," she said, peering at him over her glasses. "Well . . . let's hear it."

"When the first victim, George T. Puller, was found with his throat slashed at the Grand Park Hotel in February, the men assigned to the case figured it for a murder by a prostitute. It had all the signs: An out-of-town salesman is in New York for a convention, has a few drinks, picks up a hooker on the street or in a bar. He takes her to his hotel room. They have a fight. Maybe he won't pay her price, or wants something kinky, or catches her pinching his wallet. Whatever. Anyway, they fight and she kills him. It's happened a hundred times before."

"I suppose," Monica said, sighing.

"Sure. Only there were no signs of a fight. And nothing had been stolen. A prostitute would at least have nicked the cash, if not the victim's jewelry, credit cards, and so forth."

"Maybe she was drugged or doped up."

"And carefully wiped away all her fingerprints? Not very probable. Especially after the second murder in March. A guy named Frederick Wolheim. At the Hotel Pierce. Same MO. Throat slashed. No signs of a struggle. Nothing stolen."

"The paper said the victims were mutilated," Monica said in a small voice.

"Yes," Delaney said flatly. "Stabbed in the genitals. Many times. While they were dying or after they were dead."

His wife was silent.

"Black nylon hairs were found," Delaney continued. "From a wig. Now the prostitute theory was dropped, and it was figured the killer was a homosexual, maybe a transvestite."

"Women wear wigs, too. More than men."

"Of course. Also, the weapon used, a short-bladed knife, probably a pocket knife, is a woman's weapon. It could still figure as a female, but the cops were going by probabilities. There's no modern history of a psychopathic female murderer who selected victims at random and killed for no apparent reason. Lots of male butchers; no female."

"But why does it have to be a homosexual? Why not just a man?"

"Because the victims were found naked. So Lieutenant Slavin started hassling the gays, rousting their bars, pulling in the ones with sheets, criminal records. The results have been nil. After the third murder, it was determined the killer was five-five to five-seven. That could be a shortish man."

"Or a tall woman."

"Yes. No hard evidence either way. But the hunt is still on for a male killer."

She looked up at him again.

"But you think it's a woman?"

"Yes, I do."

"A prostitute?"

"No. A psychopathic woman. Killing for crazy reasons that maybe don't even make sense to her. But she's forced to kill."

"I don't believe it," Monica said firmly.

"Why not?"

"A woman couldn't do things like that."

He had anticipated a subjective answer and had vowed not to lose his temper. He had prepared his reply:

"Are you saying a woman would not be capable of such bloody violence?"

"That's correct. Once maybe. A murder of passion. From jealousy or revenge or hate. But not a series of killings of strangers for no reason."

"A few weeks ago we were talking about child abuse. You agreed that in half the cases, and probably more, the mother was the aggressor. Holding her child's hand over an open flame or tossing her infant into scalding water."

"Edward, that's different!"

"How different? Where's the crime of passion there? Where's the motive of jealousy or revenge or hate?"

"The woman child abuser is under tremendous pressure. She was probably abused herself as a child. Now she's locked into a life without hope. Made into a drudge. The poor child is the nearest target. She can't hold her husband's hand over a flame, as she'd like to, so she takes out all her misery and frustration on her child."

He made a snorting sound. "A very facile explanation, but hardly a justification for maiming an infant. But forget about motives for a minute. Right now I'm not interested in motives. All I'm trying to do is convince you that women are capable of mindless, bloody violence, just like men."

She was silent, hands gripping the needles and wool on her lap. Her lips were pressed to thinness, her face stretched tight. Delaney knew that taut look well, but he plunged ahead.

"You know your history," he said. "Women haven't always been the subdued, demure, gentle, *feminine* creatures that art and literature make them out to be. They've been soldiers, hard fighters, cruel and bitter foes in many tribes and nations. Still are, in a lot of places on the globe. It used to be that the worst thing that could happen to a captured warrior was to be turned over to the women of the conquering army. I won't go into the details of his fate."

"What's your point?" she snapped.

"Just that there's nothing *inherent* in women, nothing in their genes or instincts that would prevent them from becoming vicious killers of strangers if they were driven to it, if they were victims of desires and lusts they couldn't control. As a matter of fact, I would guess they'd be more prone to violence of that kind than men."

"That's the most sexist remark I've ever heard you make."

"Sexist," he said with a short laugh. "I was wondering how long it would take you to get around to that. The knee-jerk reaction. Any opinion that even suggests women might be less than perfect gets the 'sexist' label. Are you saying that women really are the mild, ladylike, ineffectual Galateas that you always claimed men had created by prejudice and discrimination?"

"I'm not saying anything of the kind. Women haven't developed their full potential because of male attitudes. But that potential doesn't include becoming mass killers. Women could have done that anytime, but they didn't. You said yourself that was the reason the police are looking for a male Hotel Ripper. Because there's no precedent for women being guilty of such crimes."

He looked at her thoughtfully, putting a fingertip to his lips.

"I just had a wild thought," he said. "It's got nothing to do with what we've been talking about, but maybe men did their best to keep women subjugated because they were afraid of them. Physically afraid. Maybe it was a matter of self-preservation."

"You're impossible!" she cried.

"Could be," he said, shrugging. "But to get back to what I was saying, will you agree women have the emotional and physical capabilities of being mass killers? That there is nothing in the female psyche that would rule against it? There *have* been women who killed many times, usually from greed, and they have always been acquainted with their victims. Now I'm asking you to make one small step from that and admit that women would be capable of killing strangers for no apparent reason."

"No," she said definitely, "I don't believe they could do that. You said yourself there are no prior cases. No Daughters of Sam."

"Right," he agreed. "The percentages are against it. That's why, right now, Slavin and Boone and all their men are looking for a male Hotel Ripper. But I think they're wrong."

"Just because you believe women are capable of murder?"

"That, plus the woman's weapon used in the murders, plus the absence of any signs of a fight, plus the fact that apparently heterosexual victims were found naked, plus the wig hairs, plus the estimated height of the killer. And plus something else."

"What's that?" she said suspiciously.

"One of the things I checked when Boone told me about the first two murders was the day of the month they had been committed. I thought there might be a connection with the full moon. You know how crime rates soar when the moon is full."

"Was there a connection?"

"No. And the third killing had no connection either. Then I looked at the intervals between the three murders. Twenty-six days between the first and second, and between the second and the third. Does that suggest anything to you?"

She didn't answer.

"Sure it does," he said gently. "Twenty-six days is a fair average for a woman's menstrual period. I checked it in your guide to gynecology."

"My God, Edward, you call that evidence?"

"By itself? Not much, I admit. But added to all the other things, it begins to make a pattern: a psychopathic female whose crimes are triggered by her monthly periods."

"But killing strangers? I still don't believe it. And you keep saying the percentages are against it."

"Wait," he said, "there's more."

He leaned down, picked up a stack of papers from the floor. He held them on his lap. He donned his reading glasses, began to flip through the pages.

"This may take a little time," he said, looking up at her. "Would you like a drink of anything?"

"Thank you, no," she said stiffly.

He nodded, went back to his shuffling until he found the page he wanted. Then he sat back.

"The probabilities are against it," he agreed. "I admit that. Going by experience, Slavin is doing exactly right in looking for a male killer. But it occurred to me that maybe the percentages are wrong. Not wrong so much as outdated. Obsolete."

"Oh?"

If she was curious, he thought mournfully, she was hiding it exceedingly well.

He looked at her reflectively. He knew her sharp intelligence and mordant wit. He quailed before the task of trying to elicit her approval of what he was about to propose. At worst, she would react with scorn and contempt; at best, with amused condescension for his dabblings in disciplines beyond his ken.

"I've heard you speak many times of the 'new woman,'" he started. "I suppose you mean by that a woman free, or striving to be free, of the restraints imposed by the oppression of men."

"And society," she added.

"All right," he said. "The oppression by individual men and a male-oriented society. The new woman seeks to control and be responsible for her own destiny. Correct? Isn't that more or less what the women's liberation movement is all about?"

"More or less."

"Feminism is a revolution," he went on, speaking slowly, almost cautiously. "A social revolution perhaps, but all the more significant for that. Revolutions have their excesses. No," he said hastily, "not excesses; that was a poor choice of words. But revolutions sometimes, usually, have results its leaders and followers did not anticipate. In any upheaval—social, political, artistic, whatever—sometimes the fallout is totally unexpected, and sometimes inimical to the original aims of the revolutionaries.

"When I was puzzling over the possibility of the Hotel Ripper being female, and trying to reconcile that possibility with the absence of a record of women committing similar crimes, it occurred to me that the new woman we were speaking about might be 'new' in ways of which we weren't aware.

"In other words, she might be more independent, assertive, ambitious, courageous, determined, and so forth. But in breaking free from the repression of centuries, she may also have developed other, less desirable traits. And if so, those traits could conceivably make obsolete all our statistics and percentages of what a woman is capable of."

"I presume," Monica said haughtily, "you're talking about crime statistics and crime percentages."

"Some," he said, "but not all. I wanted to learn if modern women had changed, were changing, in any ways that might make them predisposed to, uh, self-destructive or antisocial behavior."

"And what did you find out?"

"Well . . ." he said, "I won't claim the evidence is conclusive. I'm not even sure you can call it evidence. But I think it's persuasive enough to confirm—in my own mind at least—that I'm on the right track. I asked Thomas Handry—he's the reporter; you've met him—to dig out the numbers for me in several areas. I took the past fifteen years as the time period in which to determine if the changes I suspected in women had actually taken place."

"Why the past fifteen years?"

He looked at her stonily. "You know why. Because that period, roughly, is the length of time the modern feminist movement has been in existence and has affected the lives of so many American women. And men too, of course."

"You're blaming everything that's happened to women in the past fifteen years on women's liberation?"

"Of course not. I know other factors have been influential. But a lot of those factors, in turn, have been partly or wholly the result of feminism. The huge increase in the women's work force, for instance. Now do you or do you not want to hear what Handry discovered?"

"I'd feel a lot better if your research had been done by a woman."

He gave her a hard smile. "She would have found the same numbers Handry did. Let's start with the most significant statistics . . ."

He began speaking, consulting pages on his lap, letting them flutter to the floor as he finished with them.

"First," he said, "let's look at drugs . . . Statistics about illegal drugs are notoriously inaccurate. I'm talking now about marijuana, cocaine, and heroin. It's almost impossible to get exact tallies on the total number of users, let alone a breakdown by sex and age. But from what reports are available, it appears that men and women are about equal in illicit drug use.

"When we turn to legal drugs, particularly psychoactive drugs prescribed by physicians, we can get more accurate totals. They show that of all prescriptions issued for such drugs, about 80 percent of amphetamines, 67 percent of tranquilizers, and 60 percent of barbiturates and sedatives go to women. It is estimated that at least two million women have dependencies—addiction would be a better word—on prescription drugs. More than half of all women convicted of crimes have problems with prescription drug abuse. Twice as many women as men use Valium and Librium. Fifty percent more women than men take barbiturates regularly. They're a favored method of suicide by women."

"There's a good reason for all that," Monica said sharply. "When you consider the frustrations and—"

"Halt!" Delaney said, showing a palm. "Monica, I'm a policeman, not a sociologist. I'm not interested in the causes. Only in things as they are, and the effect they may have on crime. Okay?"

She was silent.

"Second," he said, consulting more pages, "the number of known female alcoholics has doubled since World War Two. Alcoholics Anonymous reports that in the past, one in ten members was a woman. Today, the ratio of women to men is about one to one. Statistics on alcoholism are hard to come by and not too accurate, but no one doubts the enormous recent increase of female alcoholics."

"Only because more women are coming forward and admitting their problem. Up to now, there's been such social condemnation of women drinkers that they kept it hidden."

"And still do, I imagine," he said. "Just as a lot of men keep *their* alcoholism hidden. But that doesn't negate all the testimony of authorities in the field reporting a high incidence of female alcoholism. Women make the majority of purchases in package liquor stores. Whiskey makers are beginning to realize what's going on. Now their ads are designed to attract women drinkers. There's even a new Scotch, blended expressly for women, to be advertised in women's magazines."

"When everyone is drinking more, is it so unusual to find women doing their share?"

"*More* than their share," he answered, with as much patience as he could muster. "Read the numbers in these reports Handry collected; it's all here. Third, deaths from lung cancer have increased about 45 percent for women and only about 4 percent for men. The lung cancer rate for women, not just deaths, has tripled."

"And pray, what does that prove?"

"For one thing, I think it proves women are smoking a hell of a lot more cigarettes, for whatever reasons, and suffering from it. Monica, as far as I'm concerned, alcohol and nicotine are as much drugs as amphetamines and barbiturates. You can get hooked on booze and cigarettes as easily as you can on uppers and downers."

She was getting increasingly angry; he could see it in her stiffened posture, the drawn-down corners of her mouth, her narrowed eyes. But having come this far, he had no intention of stopping now.

"All right," she said in a hard voice, "assuming more women are popping pills, drinking, and smoking—what does that prove?"

"One final set of numbers," he said, searching through the remaining research. "Here it is . . . Women constitute about 51 percent of the population. But all the evidence indicates they constitute a much higher percentage of the mentally ill. One hundred and seventy-five women for every 100 men are hospitalized for depression, and 238 women for every 100 men are treated as outpatients for depression."

"Depression!" she said scornfully. "Hasn't it occurred to you that there's a good explanation for that? The social roles—"

"Not only depression," he interrupted, "but mania as well. They're called 'affective disorders' and it's been estimated that more than twice as many women as men suffer from them."

"As a result of—"

"Monica!" he cried desperately. "I told you I'm not interested in the causes. If you tell me that drug addiction—including alcohol and nicotine—and poor mental health are due to the past role of women in our culture, I'll take your word for it. I'm just trying to isolate certain current traits in women. The 'new women.' I'm not making a value judgment here. I'm just giving you the numbers. Percentages have no conscience, no ax to grind, no particular point to make. They just exist. They can be interpreted in a hundred different ways."

"And I know how *you* interpret them," she said scathingly. "As a result of the women's liberation movement."

"Goddamn it!" he said furiously. "Are you listening to me or are you not? The only interest I have in these numbers is as a statistical background to my theory that the Hotel Ripper is a woman."

"What the hell is the connection?"

He drew a deep breath. He willed himself to be calm. He tried to speak reasonably. She seemed to be missing the point—or perhaps he was explaining it badly.

"Monica, I'm willing to admit that the things I've mentioned about women today may be temporary aberrations. They may be the result of the social upheavals and the rapidly changing role of women in the last few years. Maybe in another ten or fifteen years, women will have settled into their new roles and learned to cope with their new problems. Then their mental health will improve and their drug dependency decrease.

"But I'm only concerned with the way things are *today*. And I think women today are capable of making irrelevant all the existing criminal data dealing with females. Those numbers were accurate for yesterday, not today. The new women make them obsolete.

"I think enough hard evidence exists to justify believing the Hotel Ripper is a woman. I asked Handry to do this research in hopes that it might provide statistical background to reinforce that belief. I think it does.

"Monica, we have shit-all evidence of what the killer looks like. We know she's about five-five to five-seven and wears wigs. That's about it. But we can guess at other things about her. For instance, she's probably a young woman, say in the area of eighteen to forty, because she's strong enough to rip a man's throat and she's young enough to have menstrual periods.

"We also know she's smart. She plans carefully. She's cool and determined enough to carry through a vicious murder and then wash bloodstains from her body before leaving the scene. She makes certain she leaves no fingerprints. Everything indicates a woman of above average intelligence.

"This research gives us additional clues to other things she may be. Quite possibly she's addicted to prescription drugs, alcohol, or nicotine—or a combination of two or all three. The chances are good that she suffers from depression or mania, or both.

"All I'm trying to do is put together a profile. Not a psychological profile—those things are usually pure bullshit. I'm trying to give the killer certain personal and emotional characteristics that will give us a more accurate picture of the kind of woman she is."

"You think she's a feminist?" Monica demanded.

"She may be; she may not be. I just don't know and can't guess. But I do believe the great majority of women in this country have been affected by the women's liberation movement whether they are active in it or not."

Monica was silent a moment, pondering. She stared down, her eyes blinking. Then she asked the question Delaney had hoped to avoid. But, he admitted wryly, he should have known she'd go to the heart of the matter.

She looked up, directly at him. "Did Handry research current crime statistics?"

"Yes, he did."

"And?"

"The arrest rate is up for women. Much higher than that for men."

"What about murder?" she asked.

He had to be honest. "No, there's no evidence that murder by women is increasing. But their arrests for robbery, breaking-and-entering, and auto theft are increasing at a higher rate than for men. And much higher for larceny-theft, embezzlement, and fraud. Generally, women's crimes against property are increasing faster than men's, but not in the category of violent crimes such as murder and manslaughter."

"Or rape," she added bitterly.

He said nothing.

"Well?" she questioned. "If you think your research is justification for the Hotel Ripper being a woman, wouldn't there be some evidence of murder by women being on the increase?"

"I would have thought so," he admitted.

"You *hoped* so, didn't you?" she said, looking at him narrowly.

"Come on, Monica," he protested. "It's not giving me any great satisfaction to know the Hotel Ripper is a woman."

She sniffed and rose, gathering up her knitting things.

"You don't *know* any such thing," she said. "You're just guessing. And I think you're totally wrong."

"I may be," he acknowledged.

"Are you going to tell Boone about your wild idea?"

"No. Not yet. But I'm going to call him and warn him about May seventh to May ninth. If I'm right, then there will be another killing or attempted killing around then."

She swept grandly from the room.

"You're making a damned fool of yourself!" she flung over her shoulder.

After the door slammed behind her, he kicked fretfully at the pages of research discarded on the carpet.

"Won't be the first time," he grumbled.

On the morning of May 9th, a little before 9:00 A.M., Monica and Edward X. Delaney were seated at the kitchen table, having a quiet breakfast. They were sharing a pan of eggs scrambled with lox and onions.

Since their heated debate on the significance of Thomas Handry's research, their relation had been one of careful politesse:

"Would you care for more coffee?"

"Thank you. Another piece of toast?"

"No more, thank you. Would it bother you if I turned on the radio?"

"Not at all. Would you like a section of the newspaper?"

It had been going on like that for more than a week, neither willing to yield. But on that morning, the Chief decided it had continued long enough.

He threw down his newspaper, slammed his hand on the table with a *crack* that made Monica jump.

"Jesus Christ!" he said explosively. "What are we—a couple of kids? What kind of bullshit is this? Can't we disagree without treating each other like strangers?"

"You're so damned bullheaded," she said. "You can never admit you're wrong."

"I admit I *might* be wrong," he said. "On this thing. But I haven't been proved wrong—yet. You think I'm wrong? All right, how about a bet? Put your money where your mouth is. How much? Five, ten, a hundred? Whatever you say."

"It's too serious a matter to bet money on," she said loftily.

"All right, let's make a serious bet. The windows are filthy. If I'm proved wrong, I'll wash every goddamned window in the house. If I'm proved right, you wash them."

She considered that a moment.

"Every window," she insisted. "Including basement and attic. Inside and out."

"I agree," he said and held out his big paw. They shook hands.

"Turn the radio on," she ordered.

"Pour me some more coffee," he commanded.

Things were back to normal. But they both froze when they heard the first news item.

"The body of a murdered man was discovered in a suite at the Cameron Arms Hotel on Central Park South last night around midnight. The victim has been identified as Leonard T. Bergdorfer, an airline broker from Atlanta, Georgia. A police spokesman has definitely linked the slaying with the series of Hotel Ripper murders. The death of Bergdorfer is the fourth. No further details are available at this hour."

Monica and Edward stared at each other.

"The Windex is in the cupboard under the sink," he said slowly.

She began to cry, silently, tears welling down her cheeks. He rose to put a heavy arm about her shoulders, pull her close.

"It's so awful," she said, her voice muffled. "So awful. We were joking and making bets, and all the time . . ."

"I know," he said, "I know."

"You better tell Abner," she said. "About what you think."

"Yes," he said, "I guess I better."

He went into the study, sat down heavily behind the desk. He had his hand on the phone, but then paused, pondering.

He could not understand why he had not been informed. The newscaster had said the body was discovered around midnight.

Delaney would have expected Sergeant Boone to call him as soon as it had been verified as a Ripper killing.

Perhaps Boone had been commanded by Lieutenant Slavin to stop discussing the case with Delaney. Or perhaps enough evidence had been found to wrap up the investigation with no more help from a retired cop. Or maybe the sergeant was just too busy to report. Anything was possible.

He called Boone at home, at Midtown North, and at the Cameron Arms Hotel. No success anywhere. He left messages at all three places, asking the sergeant to call him back as soon as possible.

He started a new dossier: a sheet of paper headed: "Leonard T. Bergdorfer, midnight May 8, from Atlanta, Georgia. Fourth victim. Body found at Cameron Arms Hotel." Then he went back into the kitchen to listen to the ten o'clock news. Monica was gathering a pail of water, clean rags, Windex, a roll of paper towels.

"You don't have to do the windows," he told her, smiling. "It was just a stupid joke. We'll have someone come in and do them. Besides, it looks like rain."

"No, no," she said. "I lost the bet. Also, I think I'd like to keep busy with physical work today. Therapy. Maybe it'll keep me from thinking."

"Well . . . just do the insides," he said. "Stop when you get tired."

The news broadcast added a few more facts. The victim had come to New York to attend a convention at the Cameron Arms Hotel. His body was discovered by friends who stopped by his suite for a drink and found the door unlocked.

There were indignant statements from a Deputy Mayor, from travel agents, from the president of the hotel association. All called for quick apprehension of the Hotel Ripper before tourist trade in New York dwindled to nothing.

Edward X. Delaney waited all morning in his study, but Sergeant Abner Boone never called back. The Chief concluded that his aid was no longer being sought. For whatever reason, he was being ignored.

He pulled on his raincoat, homburg, took an umbrella from the hall closet. He yelled upstairs to Monica that he was going out and would be back shortly. He waited for her shouted reply before he left, double-locking the front door behind him.

It wasn't a hard rain. More of a thick, soaking mist that fell steadily from a steely sky. And it was unpleasantly warm. There were puddles on the sidewalks. The gutters ran with filth. The day suited Delaney's mood perfectly.

His pride was hurt; he acknowledged it. He had cooperated with Boone and, through him, with Deputy Commissioner Ivar Thorsen. He had made suggestions. He had warned of the May 7–9 time period.

The only thing he hadn't passed along was his theory that the Hotel Ripper was a woman. Not a prostitute, but a psychopathic female posing as one. And he hadn't told Boone about that simply because it *was* a theory and needed more evidence to give it substance.

He thought the timing of the murder of Leonard T. Bergdorfer made it more than just a hypothesis. But if they didn't want his help, the hell with them. It was no skin off his ass. He was an honorably retired cop, and for all he cared the Department could go take a flying fuck at a rolling doughnut.

That's what he told himself.

He walked for blocks and blocks, feeling the damp creep into his feet and shoulders. His umbrella soaked through, his ungloved hands dripped, and he felt as steamed as if the city had become an enormous sauna with someone pouring water on heated rocks.

He stopped at an Irish bar on First Avenue. He had two straight whiskies, which brought more sweat popping but at least calmed his anger. By the time he started home, he had regained some measure of serenity, convinced the Hotel Ripper case was past history as far as he was concerned.

He was putting his sodden homburg and raincoat in the hall closet when Monica came out of the kitchen.

"Where have you been?" she demanded.

"Taking a stroll," he said shortly.

"Ivar Thorsen is in the study," she said. "He's been waiting almost an hour. I gave him a drink."

Delaney grunted.

"You're in a foul mood," Monica said. "Just like Ivar. Put your umbrella in the sink to drip."

He stood the closed umbrella in the kitchen sink. He felt the shoulders of his jacket. They were dampish but not soaked. He passed a palm over his iron-gray, brush-cut hair. Then he went into the study.

Deputy Commissioner Thorsen stood up, drink in hand.

"Hullo, Ivar," the Chief said.

"How the hell did you know there'd be a killing last night?" Thorsen said loudly, almost shouting.

Delaney stared at him. "It's a long story," he said, "and one you're not likely to hear if you keep yelling at me."

Thorsen took a deep breath. "Oh God," he said, shaking his head, "I must be cracking up. I'm sorry, Edward. I apologize."

He came forward to shake the Chief's hand. Then he sat down again in the armchair. Delaney freshened his glass with more Glenlivet and poured himself a healthy shot of rye whiskey. They held their glasses up to each other before sipping.

Deputy Commissioner Ivar Thorsen was called "The Admiral" in the NYPD, and his appearance justified the nickname. He was a small, slender man with posture so erect, shoulders so squared, that it was said he left the hangers in the jackets he wore.

His complexion was fair, unblemished; his profile belonged on postage stamps. His white hair, worn short and rigorously brushed, had the gleam of chromium.

His pale blue eyes seemed genial enough, but subordinates knew how they could deepen and blaze. "It's easy enough to get along with Thorsen," one of his aides had remarked. "Just be perfect."

"How's Karen?" Delaney asked, referring to the deputy's beautiful Swedish wife.

"She's fine, thanks," Thorsen said. "When are you and Monica coming over for one of her herring smorgasbords?"

"Whenever you say."

They sat in silence, looking at each other. Finally . . .

"You first or me first?" Thorsen asked.

"You," Delaney said.

"We've got problems downtown," the Admiral announced.

"So what else is new? You've always got problems downtown."

"I know, but this Hotel Ripper thing is something else. It's as bad as Son of Sam. Maybe worse. The Governor's office called today. The Department is taking a lot of flak. From the politicians and the business community."

"You know how I feel about the Department."

"I know how you *say* you feel, Edward. But don't tell me a man who gave as many years as you did would stand idly by and not do what he could to help the Department."

"Fiddle music," Delaney said. " 'Hearts and Flowers.' "

Thorsen laughed. "Iron Balls," he said. "No wonder they called you that. But forget about the Department's problems for a moment. Let's talk about your problems."

Delaney looked up in surprise. "I've got no problems."

"You say. I know better. I've seen a lot of old bulls retire and I've watched what happens to them after they get out of harness. A few of them can handle it, but not many."

"I can handle it."

"You'd be surprised how many drop dead a year or two after putting in their papers. Heart attack or stroke, cancer or bleeding ulcers. I don't know the medical or psychological reasons for it, but studies show it's a phenomenon that exists. When the pressure is suddenly removed, and stress vanishes, and there are no problems to solve, and drive and ambition disappear, the body just collapses."

"Hasn't happened to me," Delaney said stoutly. "I'm in good health."

"Or other things happen," the Admiral went on relentlessly. "They can't handle the freedom. No office to go to. No beat to pound. No shop talk. Their lives revolved around the Department and now suddenly they're out. It's like they were excommunicated."

"Bullshit."

"Some of them find a neighborhood bar that becomes their office or squad room or precinct. They keep half-bagged all day and bore their new friends silly with lies about what great cops they were."

"Not me."

"Or maybe they decide to read books, visit museums, go to shows—all the things they never had time for before. Fishing and hunting. Gardening. Hockey games. And so forth. But it's just postponing the inevitable. How many books can you read? How many good plays or movies are there? How many hockey games? The day arrives when they wake up with the realization that they've got nothing to do, nowhere to go. They may as well stay in bed. Some of them do."

"I don't."

"Or become drunks or hypochondriacs. Or start following their wives around, walking up their heels. Or start resenting their wives because the poor women don't spend every waking minute with them."

Delaney said nothing.

Thorsen looked at him narrowly. "Don't tell me you haven't felt any of those things, Edward. You've never lied to me in your life; don't start now. Why do you think you were so willing to help Boone? So eager to get his reports on the Hotel Ripper case? To make out those dossiers I saw on your desk? Oh yes, I peeked, and I make no apology for it. Maybe you're not yet in the acute stage, but admit it's starting."

"What's starting?"

"The feeling that you're not wanted, not needed. No reason to your life. No aims, no desires. Worst of all is the boredom. It saps the spirit, turns the brain to mush. You're a wise man, Edward; I'd never deny it. But you're not smart enough to handle an empty life."

Delaney rose slowly to his feet, with an effort. He poured more whiskey. Glenlivet for Thorsen, rye for himself. He sat down heavily again in the swivel chair behind the desk. He regarded the Deputy Commissioner reflectively.

"You're a pisser, you are," he said. "You want something from me. You know you've got to convince me. So you try the loyalty-to-the-Department ploy. When that doesn't work, you switch without the loss of a single breath to the self-interest approach. Now I've got to do as you want if I hope to avoid dropping dead, becoming a lush, annoying my wife, or having my brain turn to mush."

"Right!" the Admiral cried, slapping his knee. "You're exactly right. It's in your own self-interest, man. That's the strongest motive of them all."

"You admit you're manipulating me—or trying to?"

"Of course. But it's in your own best interest; can't you see that?"

Delaney sighed. "Thank God you never went into politics. You'd end up owning the world. What is it, precisely, you want of me, Ivar?"

The sprucely dressed deputy set his drink aside. He leaned forward earnestly, hands clasped.

"Slavin has got to go," he said. "The man's a disaster. Releasing that black nylon wig story to the media was a blunder. We're beefing up the Hotel Ripper squad. Another hundred detectives and plainclothesmen for a start, and more available as needed. We'll put Slavin in charge of administration and scheduling of the task force. He's good at that."

"And who's going to be in command?"

Thorsen sat back, crossed his knees. He adjusted the sharp crease in his trouser leg. He picked up his drink, took a sip. He stared at Delaney over the rim of the glass.

"That's what I was doing all morning," he said. "A meeting downtown. It started at about three A.M., and went through to eleven. I've never drunk so much black coffee in my life. Everyone agreed Slavin had to go. Then we started debating who the CO should be. It had to be someone high up in the Department, to send a signal to the politicians and businessmen and public that we're giving this case top priority."

"Cosmetics," Delaney said disgustedly. "The image."

"Correct," Thorsen said levelly. "When you don't know where you're going, you rush around busily. It gives the impression of action. What more could we have done? Any suggestions?"

"No."

"So we needed a top man in command. It couldn't be the Chief of Detectives. He's got a full plate even without the Hotel Ripper. He can't drop everything and concentrate on one case. Besides, we figured we needed higher brass. Someone close to the PC. No one was willing to volunteer."

"Can't say I blame them," the Chief admitted. "Too much risk for the ambitious types. Failure could break them. End their careers."

"Right. Well, we finally got one guy who was willing to stick out his neck."

"Who's the idiot?"

The Admiral looked at him steadily. "Me," he said. "I'm the idiot."

"Ivar!" Delaney cried. "For God's sake, *why?* You haven't worked an active case in twenty years."

"Don't you think I know that? I recognized the dangers of taking it on. If I flop, I might as well resign. Nothing left for me in the Department. I'd always be the guy who bungled the Hotel Ripper case. On the other hand, if I could possibly pull it off, I'd be the fair-haired boy, remembered when the Police Commissioner's chair became vacant."

"And that's what you want?"

"Yes."

"Well . . ." Delaney said loyally, "the city could do a lot worse."

"Thank you, Edward. But it wasn't just wishful thinking on my part. When I agreed to take it on, I had an ace in the hole."

"Oh? What was that?"

"*Who* was that. You."

Delaney banged his hand down on the desktop in disgust.

"Jesus Christ, Ivar, you gambled on getting me to go along?"

Thorsen nodded. "That's what I gambled on. That's why I'm here pulling out all the stops to persuade you to help me, help the Department, help yourself."

Delaney was silent, staring at the composed man in the armchair, the small foot in the polished moccasin bobbing idly up and down. Thorsen endured his scrutiny with serenity, slowly sipping his drink.

"There's one stop you didn't pull, Ivar."

"What's that?"

"Our friendship."

The deputy frowned. "I don't want to put it on that basis, Edward. You don't owe me. Turn me down and we'll still be friends."

"Uh-huh. Tell me something, Ivar—did you instruct Sergeant Boone not to call me about that killing last night, figuring to give me a taste of what it would feel like to be shut out of this thing?"

"My God, Edward, do you think I'd be capable of a Machiavellian move like that?"

"Yes."

"You're perfectly right," Thorsen said calmly. "That's exactly what I did for the reason you guessed. And it worked, didn't it?"

"Yes, it worked."

"You've got cops' blood," the Admiral said. "Retirement didn't change that. Well . . . how about it? Will you agree to work with me? Serve as an unofficial right-hand man? You won't be on active duty, of course, but you'll know everything that's going on, have access to all the papers—statements, photographs, evidence, autopsy reports, and so on. Boone will act as our liaison."

"Ivar, what do you expect of me?" Delaney asked desperately. "I'm no miracle man."

"I don't expect miracles. Just handle it as if you were on active duty, assigned to the Hotel Ripper case. If you fail, it's my cock that's on the block, not yours. What do you say?"

"Give me a little time to—"

"No," Thorsen said sharply. "I haven't got time. I need to know now."

Delaney leaned back, laced his hands behind his head. He stared at the ceiling. Maybe, he thought, the reason for Ivar Thorsen's success in threading his way through the booby-trapped upper echelons of the New York Police Department was his ability to use people by persuading them that they had everything to gain from his manipulation.

Knowing that, the Chief still had to admit that Thorsen's sales pitch wasn't all con. There was enough truth in what he had said to consider his proposal seriously.

But not once had he mentioned a motive that cut more ice with Delaney than all the dire warnings of how retirement would flab his fiber and muddle his brain. It was a basic motive, almost simple, that would have sounded mawkish if spoken.

Edward X. Delaney wanted to stop the Hotel Ripper because killing was wrong. Not just immoral, antisocial, or irreligious. But *wrong.*

"All right, Ivar," he said. "I'm in."

Thorsen nodded, drained his glass. But when Delaney started to rise, to pour him more Glenlivet, the deputy held his hand over his glass.

"No more, thank you, Edward. I've got to go back downtown again."

"Tell me about the killing last night."

"I don't know too much about it. You'll have to get the details from Boone. But I gather it was pretty much like the others, with a few minor differences. The victim was naked, but his body was found on the floor between the bed and the bathroom. The bed hadn't been used."

"Throat slashed?"

"Yes."

"Genitals stabbed?"

"Yes."

"How old was he?"

"Middle forties. One odd thing—or rather two odd things. The body was discovered by a gang of pals who barged in for a drink. They said there was a sweet odor in the bedroom where the body was found."

"A sweet odor? Perfume?"

"Not exactly. One of the guys said it smelled to him like apple blossoms. The other odd thing was that the victim's face was burned. First-degree burns. Reddening but no blistering or charring."

"Tear gas," Delaney said. "It smells like apple blossoms in low concentrations and it can cause burns if applied close to the skin."

"Tear gas?" Thorsen said. "How do you figure that?"

"I don't. Unless the killer couldn't get behind the victim, like the others were slashed, and gassing was the only way to handle him."

"Well, they'll find out what it was in the P.M. We've been promised the report tomorrow morning. Now . . . let's get back to my original question: How the hell did you know there'd be a killing last night?"

"I didn't *know*. I guessed. And I didn't specify last night; I warned Boone about May seventh to ninth. Did you put on more men?"

"Yeah," Thorsen said sourly. "As a matter of fact, we had a decoy in the Cameron Arms Hotel last night while it was going down."

"Shit," Delaney said.

"He was in a disco, figuring that would be the logical place for the killer to make contact. It didn't work out that way. Edward, we can't cover every bar, cocktail lounge, disco, dining room, and hotel lobby in midtown Manhattan. That would take an army."

"I know. Still, it burns my ass to be so close and miss it."

"You still haven't told me how you figured it might happen last night."

"It's a long story. You better have another drink."

The Admiral hesitated just a moment.

"All right," he said finally. "After what I've gone through in the last twelve hours, I've earned it."

Delaney repeated everything he had previously related to Monica: how he had slowly come to believe the Hotel Ripper might be a woman; the research he had done; and how some of it substantiated his theory.

And how the implied circumstances of the murders lent further credence: the absence of any signs of struggles; the heterosexual victims found naked; the attacks (except for the last) all made from the rear, the victims apparently not expecting sudden violence.

Midway through his recital, Delaney took two cigars from his desk humidor. Still talking, he rose and leaned forward to hand one to the Admiral, then held a match for him. He sat down again and, puffing, resumed his discourse.

He argued that only presuming the perpetrator was a woman wearing a wig—not a prostitute, but a psychopath—could all the anomalies of the murders be explained.

"She kills at regular intervals," he concluded. "In, say, twenty-five to twenty-seven-day cycles."

"During her periods?"

"Probably. Maybe a few days before or a few days after. But every month."

"Well . . ." Thorsen said with a rueful smile, "that gives us an age approximation: twelve to fifty!"

"What do you think, Ivar? About the whole idea?"

Thorsen looked down at his drink, swirling the whiskey around slowly in the glass. "Not exactly what I'd call hard evidence. A lot of shrewd guesses. And a lot of smoke."

"Oh hell yes. I admit it. But have you got any better ideas?"

"I haven't got *any* ideas. But on the basis of what you've told me, you want us to—"

"I don't want you to do a goddamned thing," Delaney said furiously. "You asked me for my ideas and I gave them to you. If you think it's all bullshit, then I—"

"Whoa, whoa!" the deputy said, holding up a hand. "My God, Edward, you've got the shortest fuse of any man I know. I don't think it's all bullshit. I think you've come up with the first new idea anyone has offered on this mess. But I'm trying to figure out what to do about it. Assuming you're right, where do we go from here?"

"Start all over again," Delaney said promptly. "They've been checking out escaped mental patients and psychos, haven't they?"

"Of course. All over the country."

"Sure they have—male crazies, and probably just homosexual male crazies. We've got to go back and do it all over again, looking for psychopathic women, escaped or recently released. And pull out all the decoys from gay bars and send them to straight places. These killings have nothing to do with homosexuals. And go back through our records again, looking for women with a sheet including violent crimes. There's a hell of a lot that can be done once you're convinced the killer is female. It turns the whole investigation around."

"You think this should be released to the media?"

Delaney pondered that a long time.

"I don't know," he admitted finally. "They're going to find out sooner or later. But publicity might frighten the killer off."

"Or spur her on to more."

"That's true. Ivar, I'd suggest keeping this under wraps as long as possible. Just to give us a little time to get things organized. But it's not my decision to make."

"I know," the Admiral said mournfully, "it's mine."

"You volunteered," the Chief said, shrugging. "You're now the commanding officer. So command."

"I'd feel a lot better about this, Edward, if you could be more positive about it. If you could tell me that, yes, you absolutely believe that the killer is definitely a woman."

"My gut instinct tells me so," Delaney said solemnly, and both men burst out laughing.

"Well," Thorsen said, rising, "I've got to get going. I'll spread the news—at least to the people who count."

"Ivar, there's no need for the media to know I'm working with you."

"I agree. But some of the brass will have to know, and some of the politicos. And Sergeant Boone, of course. Call him tomorrow morning. I'll have a system set up by then on how he's to liaise with you."

"Fine."

"Edward, I want to tell you how happy I am that you've decided to help out."

"You're a supersalesman."

"Not really. You can't sell something to someone who really doesn't want to buy. Not to someone as stubborn as you, anyway. But having you with me makes all the difference in the world. May I use your phone?"

"Of course. Want me to step outside?"

"No, no. I want you to hear this."

Thorsen dialed a number, waited a moment.

"Mary?" he said. "It's Ivar Thorsen. Put himself on, will you? He's expecting my call."

While he waited, the Deputy Commissioner winked at Delaney. Then . . .

"Timothy?" he said. "Ivar Thorsen here. All right, Timmy, I'll take the job."

He hung up and turned to the Chief.

"You bastard!" Delaney gasped. "You've got to be the biggest son of a bitch who ever came down the pike."

"So I've been told," the Admiral said.

After he had shown Thorsen out, Delaney wandered back into the kitchen. Monica was readying a veal roast for the oven, laying on thin strips of fat salt pork. The Chief took a celery stalk from the refrigerator crisper. He leaned against the sink, chomping, watching Monica work.

"I told Ivar I'd help him out on the Hotel Ripper case," he offered.

She nodded. "I thought that was probably what he wanted."

"He's in command now. I'll be working through Abner Boone."

"Good," she said unexpectedly. "I'm glad you'll be busy on something important."

"Have I been getting in your hair?"

She gave him a quick, mischievous grin. "Not any more than usual. You told Ivar you think it's a woman?"

"Yes."

"Did he agree?"

"He didn't agree and he didn't disagree. We'll check it out. He'll want to move cautiously. That's all right; his reputation and career are on the line. He wants to be Police Commissioner some day."

"I know."

"You know? How do you know?"

"Karen told me."

"And you never told me?"

"I thought you knew. Besides, I don't tell you everything."

"You don't? I tell you everything."

"Bullshit," she said, and he kissed her.

7

It wasn't so much a weakness as a languor. Her will was blunted; her body now seemed in command of all her actions. An indolence infected her. She slept long, drugged hours, and awoke listless, aching with weariness.

Each morning she stepped on the bathroom scale and saw her weight inexorably lessening. After a while she stopped weighing herself; she just didn't want to know. It was something beyond her control. She thought vaguely it was due to her loss of appetite; food sickened her: all that *stuff* going into her mouth . . .

Her monthly had ended, but the abdominal cramps persisted. Sometimes she felt nauseated; twice she vomited for no apparent reason. She had inexplicable attacks of diarrhea followed by spells of constipation. The incidents of syncope increased: more of them for longer periods.

It seemed to her that her body, that fleshy envelope containing her, was breaking up, flying apart, forgetting its functions and programs, disintegrating into chaos. It occurred to her that she might be dying. She ran into the kitchen to take a Valium.

She looked down at her naked self. She felt skin, hair, softness of fat and hardness of bone. Undeniably she was still there; warm and pulsing. Pinched, she felt hurt. Stroked, she felt joy. But deep inside was rot. She was convinced of it; there was rot. She knew more wonder than fear.

She functioned; she did what she had to do. Dropped the broken knife down a sewer grating. Wrapped the empty Mace can in a bundle of garbage and tossed it into a litter basket two blocks from her home. Inspected her body and clothing for bloodstains. She did all these things indolently, without reasoning why.

She bathed, dressed, went to work each day. Chatted with Ernest Mittle on the phone. Had lunch with Maddie Kurnitz. It was all a dream, once removed from reality. Anomie engulfed her; she swam in a foreign sea.

Once she called Sergeant Coe to ask if he was available for moonlighting. Coe's wife answered the phone and Zoe said, "This is Irene—" stopped, dazed, then said, "This is Zoe Kohler."

Something was happening to her. Something slow, gradual, and final. She let it take her, going to her fate without protest or whimper. It was too late, too painful to change. There was comfort in being a victim. Almost a pleasure. Life, do with me what you will.

On May 10th, a Saturday, she met Ernest Mittle at the entrance to Central Park at Fifth Avenue and 59th Street. It was only a few blocks from the Cameron Arms Hotel. They exchanged light kisses and, holding hands, joined the throng sauntering toward the menagerie and children's zoo.

It was more summer than spring. A high sky went on forever; the air was a fluffy softness that caressed the skin. The breeze was scarcely strong enough to raise kites; the fulgent sun cast purplish shadows.

People on the benches raised white, meek faces to the blue, happy with the new world. Coats and sweaters were doffed and carried; children scampered. Bells and flutes could be heard; the greening earth stirred.

"Oh, what a day!" Ernest exulted. "I ordered it just for us. Do you approve, Zoe?"

"It *is* nice," she said, looking about. "Like being born again."

"Would you like an ice cream? Hot dog? Peanuts?"

"No, nothing right now, thank you."

"How about a balloon?" he said, laughing.

"Yes, I'd like a balloon. A red one."

So he bought her a helium-filled balloon and carefully tied the end of the string to the handle of her purse. They strolled on, the little sun bobbing above them.

A carnival swirled about: noise, movement, color. But they felt singularly alone and at peace, a universe of two. It seemed to them the crowd parted to allow passage, then closed behind them. They were in a private space and no one could intrude.

There were other couples like them, hand in hand, secret and serene as they. But none of them, as Ernest pointed out, had a red balloon. They laughed delightedly at their uniqueness.

They stared at a yak, watched a tiger pace, heard an elephant trumpet, saw the cavortings of sea lions, listened to the chattering of baboons, and were splashed by a diving polar bear. Even the caged animals seemed pleased by that blooming day.

Finally, wearying, they bought beers and sandwiches and carried them out of the zoo to a patch of greensward where the sounds of carnival and the cries of animals were muted.

They sat on the warm earth, Zoe's back against the trunk of a gnarled plane tree. They sipped their beers, nibbled their sandwiches. A fat squirrel came close to inspect them, but when Zoe tossed a crust, it darted off. Two pigeons fought over the crust, divided it, waited hopefully for more, then flew away.

Dappled light melted through the foliage above them. The world was solid beneath them. The air was awash with far-off cries and the faint lilt of music. They could see joggers, cyclists, horse-drawn carriages move along a distant road. A freshening wind brought the sweet smell of growing things.

Ernest Mittle lay supine, his head on Zoe's lap, eyes closed. She stroked his hair absently, looking about and feeling they were alone on earth. The last. The only.

"I wish we could stay here forever," she murmured. "Like this."

He opened his eyes to look up at her.

"Never go home," he said softly. "Never go to work again. No more subways and buses and traffic. No more noise and dirt. No violence and crime and cruelty. We'll just stay here forever and ever."

"Yes," she said wonderingly. "Just the two of us together."

He sat up, took her hand, kissed her fingertips.

"Wouldn't that be fine?" he said. "Wouldn't that be grand? Zoe, I've never felt so good. Never been so happy. Why can't it last?"

"It can't," she said.

"No," he said, "I suppose not. But you're happy, aren't you? I mean right this minute?"

"Oh yes," she said. "Happier than I've ever been in my life."

He lay back again; she resumed smoothing the webby hair back from his temples.

"Did you have a lot of boyfriends, Zoe?" he asked quietly. "I mean when you were growing up."

"No, Ernie," she said, just as dreamily. "Not many."

On a lawn, beneath a tree, blue shadows mottling, they were in the world but not of it. Locked in lovers' isolation. Away from the caged and uncaged animals, and somehow protected from them by their twoness.

"My mother was strict," she said in a memory-dulled voice. "So strict. The boy had to call for me and come inside for inspection. I had to be home by eleven. Midnight on weekends, but eleven during the week."

He made a sound of sympathy. Neither moved now, fearing to move. It was a moment of fragile balance. They knew they were risking revealment. Opening up—a sweet pain. They inched cautiously to intimacy, recognizing the dangers.

"Once I went out with a boy," she said. "A nice boy. His car broke down so I couldn't get home in time. My mother called the police. Can you imagine that? It was awful."

"It's for your own good, my dear," he said in a high-pitched feminine voice.

"Yes. That's what she said. It was for my own good. But after that, I wasn't very popular."

They were silent then, and content with their closeness. It seemed to them that what they were doing, unfolding, could be done slowly. It might even cost a lifetime. All the safer for that. Knowing was a process, not a flash, and it might never end.

"I was never popular," he said, a voice between rue and hurt. "I was small. Not an athlete or anything like that. And I never had enough money to take a girl to the movies. I didn't have any real girlfriends. I never went steady."

It was so new to them—this tender confession. They were daunted by the strange world. Shells were cracking; the naked babes peered out in fear and want. They understood there was a price to be paid for these first fumblings. Involvement presaged a future they could not see.

"I never went steady either," she said, determined not to stop. "Very few boys ever asked me out a second time."

"What a waste," he said, sighing. "For both of us. I didn't think any girl could be interested in me. I was afraid to ask. And you . . ."

"I was afraid, too. Of being alone with a boy. Mother again. Don't do this. Don't do that. Don't let a boy—you know . . . get personal."

"We were robbed," he said. "Both of us. All those years."

"Yes. Robbed."

Silence again. A comfortable quiet. The wind was freshening, cooling. She looked down at him, cupped his pale face in her palms. Their eyes searched.

"But you married," he said.

"Yes, I did."

She bent, he craned up. Their soft lips met, pressed, lingered. They kissed. They kissed.

"Oh," he breathed. "Oh, oh."

She traced his face, smiling sadly. She felt his brow, cheeks, nose, lips. He closed his eyes, and lightly, lightly, she touched the velvet eyelids, made gentle circles. Then she leaned again to press her lips softly.

She straightened up. She shivered with a sudden chill.

His eyes opened, he looked at her with concern.

"Cold?"

"A little," she said. "Ernie, maybe we should think about leaving."

"Sure," he said, scrambling to his feet.

He helped her up, picked twigs from her skirt, brushed bits of bark from the back of her tweed jacket.

"What should we do with the balloon?" he asked.

"Let's turn it loose," she said. "Let it fly away."

"Right," he said, and untied the string from her purse.

He handed it to her and let her release it. The red balloon rose slowly. Then, caught by the strengthening wind, it went soaring away. They watched it fly up, pulled this way and that, but sailing higher and higher, getting smaller and smaller until it was lost in the sky.

They wandered slowly back to the paved walkway.

"Something I've wanted to ask you, Zoe," he said, looking at the ground. "Is Kohler your married name or your maiden name?"

"My married name. It was on all my legal papers and driver's license and so forth. It just seemed too much trouble to change everything. My maiden name is Spencer."

"Zoe Spencer," he said. "That's nice. Zoe is a very unusual name."

"I think it's Greek," she said. "It means 'life.' It was my mother's idea."

"What's her name?" he asked.

"Irene," she said.

Dr. Oscar Stark's receptionist had Zoe's home and office telephone numbers in her file. On the afternoon of May 13th, the doctor called Zoe at the Hotel Granger and asked how she was feeling.

She told him she felt better since her period had ended, but sometimes she felt torpid and without energy. She reported nothing about her nausea, the continued loss of weight, the increasing incidents of syncope.

He asked if she was taking the doubled cortisone dosage and the salt tablets. She said she was and, in answer to his questions, told him she suffered no stomach upset from intake of the steroid hormone and experienced no craving for additional salt.

He then said that he had received the results of her latest blood and urine tests. They seemed to indicate a slight cortisol deficiency. Dr. Stark said it was nothing to be concerned about, but nothing to disregard either. He instructed her to take her medication faithfully, and he would reevaluate the situation after her office visit on June 3rd.

Meanwhile, he wanted Zoe to stop by and pick up a new prescription. It would be left with his receptionist, so Zoe would not have to wait.

The prescription would be for two items. The first was an identification bracelet that Stark wanted Zoe to wear at all times. It would give her name and Stark's name and telephone number. It would also state that Zoe Kohler suffered from an adrenal insufficiency, and in case of an emergency such as injury or fainting she was to be injected with hydrocortisone.

The hydrocortisone would be in a small labeled kit that Zoe was to carry in her purse at all times. The solution was contained in a packaged sterile syringe, ready for use.

Dr. Stark repeated all this and asked if Zoe understood. She said she did. He assured her the bracelet and kit were merely a precautionary measure and he doubted if they'd ever be used. He was having them made up at a medical supply house down on Third Avenue. Zoe would have to pay for them, but a check would be acceptable.

She copied the name and address he gave her.

On the following day, during her lunch hour, she picked up the prescription at Dr. Stark's office, then cabbed down to the medical supply house and purchased the bracelet and kit. When she returned to the Hotel Granger, she put them in the back of the bottom drawer of her desk. She never looked at them again.

On the night of May 16th, Zoe was alone at home. She had just showered and was wearing her old flannel robe and frayed mules. She was curled on the couch, filing her nails, wondering about the slight discoloration in the folds of her knuckles, and watching *Rebecca* on TV.

A little before ten o'clock her phone rang and the doorman reported that Mrs. Kurnitz was in the lobby and wanted to come up. Zoe told him to let her in and went to the door to wait.

Maddie came striding down the corridor from the elevator. She had a soiled white raincoat over her shoulders like a cape, empty sleeves flapping out behind her. Her makeup was a mess, smudged and runny. Zoe thought she had been weeping.

"Maddie," she said, "what are—"

"You got anything to drink?" Maddie demanded. "Beer, whiskey, wine? Or cleaning fluid, lye, hemlock? I don't give a good goddamn."

Zoe got her inside and locked the door. Maddie flung her coat to the floor. Zoe picked it up. Maddie tried to light a cigarette and broke it with trembling fingers. She dropped that on the floor, too, and Zoe picked it up. Maddie finally got a cigarette lighted and collapsed onto the couch, puffing furiously.

"I have some vodka," Zoe said, "and some—"

"Vodka is fine. A *biiig* vodka. On the rocks. No mix. Just more vodka."

Zoe went into the kitchen to pour Maddie's drink and a glass of white wine for herself. Because her supply of Valium was getting low, she took two Librium before she went back into the living room.

Maddie drained half the vodka in two throat-wrenching gulps. Zoe turned off the TV set and sat down in an armchair facing her visitor.

"Maddie," she said, "what on earth is—"

"That bastard!" Maddie cried. "That cocksucker! I should have kicked him in the balls."

"Who?" Zoe said bewilderedly. "Who are you talking about?"

"Harry. That asshole husband of mine. He's been cheating on me."

"Oh, Maddie," Zoe said sorrowfully, "are you sure?"

"Sure I'm sure. The son of a bitch told me himself."

She seemed halfway between fury and tears. Zoe had never seen her so defeated. Heavy breasts sagged, fleshy body spread. All of her appeared slack and punished. Chipped fingernails and smeared lipstick. Gaudy had become seedy.

She lighted a new cigarette from the butt of the old. She looked about vaguely.

"First time I've been up here," she said dully. "Christ, you're neat. Clean and neat."

"Yes," Zoe said. Then, when Maddie finished her vodka, she went into the kitchen again and brought back the bottle. She watched Maddie fill her glass, bottle clinking against the rim.

"It's not the cheating I mind," Maddie said loudly. "You know I play around, too. He can screw every woman in New York for all I care. We had this understanding. He could play, and I could play, and neither of us cared, and no one got hurt."

"Well then?" Zoe said.

"He wants to marry the bitch," Maddie said with a harsh bark of laughter. "Some stupid little twit in his office. He wants to divorce me and marry her. Did you ever?"

Zoe was silent.

"I met her," Maddie went on. "She was at that party you went to. A washed-out blonde with tits like funnels. A body that doesn't end and a brain that never starts. Maybe that's what Harry wants: a brainless fuck. Maybe I threaten him. Do you think I threaten him?"

"I don't think so, Maddie."

"Who the hell knows. Anyway, I'm out and she's in. God, what a bummer. What hurts is that he knows how much a divorce is going to cost him—I'm going to take the fillings right out of his teeth—but he still wants it. Like he'll pay anything to get rid of me. I even suggested we stick together and he could set her up on the side—you know? I wouldn't care. But no, he wants a clean break. That's what he said: 'a clean break.' I'd like to cleanly break his goddamned neck!"

"Uh, Maddie," Zoe said timidly, "I can understand your being upset, but you've been divorced before."

"I know, sweetie, I know. That's why I'm so down. I'm beginning to worry. What's wrong with me? Why can't I hold a guy? It lasts two or three years and then it falls apart. I get bored with him, or he gets bored with me, and off we go to the lawyers. Shit!"

"But you love—"

"Love?" Maddie said. "What the fuck is love? Having laughs together and moaning in the hay? If that's what love is, then I love Harry. A great sense of humor and a stallion in the sack. Generous with money. I had no complaints there. And he never bitched. Then *whammo!* Out of a clear blue sky he dumps on me."

"Is she younger?"

"Not all that much. If she was like nineteen or twenty, I could understand it. I'd figure he was going through a change of life and had to prove he could still cut the mustard with a young chick. But she's got to be thirty, at least, so what the hell does he see in her? I'm drinking all your booze, kiddo."

"That's all right. Take as much as you want."

"Harry dumps on me and I dump on you. I'm sorry. But I had to talk to a woman. I don't have any close women friends. A lot of guys, but all good-time Charlies. They don't want to listen to my troubles. And they're not going to be overjoyed to hear I'm getting unhitched. Zapping a married woman is fun and games, and no problems. When you haven't got a husband, a lot of men steer clear. Too much risk."

"Is there anyone you . . .?"

"Anyone I can snare on the rebound? No one in the picture right now. Another thing that scares me. Let's face it, luv, we're both getting long in the tooth. You've kept your body, but the rare beef and bourbon are catching up with me. Plus more than my share of one-night stands. I look like an old broad; I know it."

Zoe murmured something about going on a diet, cutting down on the drinking, buying some new clothes. But Madeline Kurnitz wasn't listening. She was staring off into the middle distance, the glass of vodka held near her lips.

"I've got to be married," she said. "Don't ask me why, but I've *got* to be. What the hell else can I do in this world? I wouldn't know how to earn a living if my life depended on it. I'm too old to peddle my ass, and just the idea of spending eight hours a day in some stinking office is enough to give me the up-chucks. I don't know how you do it."

"It's not so bad."

"The hell it isn't. While other women are having lunch at the Plaza and buying out Bonwit's . . . I couldn't stand that."

Zoe went to the kitchen again and brought back the bottle of white wine and a bowl of ice cubes for Maddie. They sat in silence for a few moments, sipping their drinks. Maddie kicked off her shoes, pulled up her feet, began picking reflectively at the silver polish on her toenails.

"You know, sweetie, my whole life has revolved around men. It really has. I mean I've depended on them. My daddy spoiled me rotten, and then I went from husband to husband like there was no tomorrow. And what have I got to show for it? A dead father and four flopped marriages. I suppose the women liberationists would say it's my fault, I should have done something with my life. Been more independent and all that horseshit. But Goddamnit, I like men. I like to be with men. Why the hell should I work my tuchas to a frazzle when there was always a guy ready to pick up the tab?"

"You'll find someone new."

"Yeah? I wish I could believe it. I'll take enough out of Harry's hide so that money won't be a problem. For a while at least. But I just can't live alone. I can't stand to be by myself. You can handle it, but I can't."

"Sometimes you have no choice," Zoe said.

"That's what scares me," Maddie said. "No choice. Thank God I never had any kids. Life is shitty enough without worrying about brats. Did you ever want to have kids, Zoe?"

"Once maybe. Not anymore."

"That fucking Harry sure pulled the plug on me. He's got me feeling sorry for myself—something I've never done before. That lousy turd. God, I'm going to miss him. Two years ago, for my birthday, he bought me a purple Mercedes-Benz convertible with my initials on the door."

"What happened to it?"

"I totaled it on the Long Island Expressway. I was drunk or I would have killed myself. But that's the way he was. Anything I wanted. He spoiled me rotten like my father. Oh Jesus, baby, I must be boring you senseless."

"Oh no, Maddie. I'm glad you came to me. I just wish there was some way I could help."

"You've done enough just listening to me. I don't know what—"

Suddenly Madeline Kurnitz was weeping. She cried silently, tears welling from her eyes and straggling down her powdered cheeks. Zoe went over to the couch, sat next to her, put an arm across her shoulders.

"God, God," Maddie wailed, "what am I going to do?"

Zoe Kohler didn't know. So she said, "Shh, shh," and held the other woman until she stopped crying. After a while, Maddie said, "Shit," blew her nose, took her bag and went into the bathroom.

She came out about ten minutes later, hair combed, makeup repaired. Her eyes were puffy but clear. She gave Zoe a rueful smile.

"Sorry about that, luv," she said. "I thought I was all cried out."

"Maddie, would you like to stay the night? You can take the bed and I'll sleep out here on the couch. Why don't you?"

"No, kiddo, but I appreciate the offer. I'll have one more drink and then I'll take off. I better get home before that shithead changes the locks on the doors. I feel a lot better now. What the hell, it's just another kick in the ass. That's what life is all about—right?"

She sat again on the couch, put more ice in her glass, filled it with vodka. She stirred it with a forefinger, then sucked the finger. She bowed her head, looked up at Zoe.

"Seeing as how it's hair-down time," she said, "how about the sad story of your life? You never did tell me what happened between you and—what was his name? Ralph?"

"Kenneth. And I told you. Don't you remember, Maddie? At that lunch we had at the hotel?"

"You mean the sex thing? Sure, I remember. You never got your rocks off with him. But there's got to be more to it than that."

"Oh . . . it was a lot of things."

"Like what?"

"Silly things."

"Other people's reasons for divorce always sound silly. First of all, how did you meet the guy?"

"He was with an insurance company and was transferred to their agency in Winona. He handled all my father's business policies, and Daddy brought him home for dinner one night. He called me up for a date and we started going out. Then we began getting invited to parties and things as a couple. Then he asked me to marry him."

"Handsome?"

"I thought so. Very big and beefy. He could be very jolly and charming when there were other people around. But about six months after we were married, he quit the insurance company and my father hired him as a kind of junior partner. Daddy was getting old, slowing down, and he wanted someone to sort of take over."

"Oh-ho. And did your husband know this when he asked you to marry him?"

"Yes. I didn't know it at the time, but later, during one of our awful arguments, he told me that was the only reason he married me."

"Nice guy."

"Well . . . a handsome man says you're beautiful, and he's in love with you, and you believe it."

"Not me, kiddo. I know all he wants is to dip Cecil in the hot grease."

"I believed him. I guess I should have known better. I'm no raving beauty; I know that. I'm quiet and not very exciting. But I thought he really did love me for what I am. I know I loved him. At first."

Maddie looked at her shrewdly.

"Zoe, maybe you just loved him for loving you—or saying he did."

"Yes. That's possible."

They were subdued then, pondering the complexities of living, the role played by chance and accident, the masks people wear, and the masks beneath the masks.

"When did the fights start?" Maddie asked.

"Almost from the start. We were so different, and we couldn't seem to change. We couldn't compromise enough to move closer to each other. He was so—so *physical.* He was loud and had this braying laugh. He seemed to fill a room. I mean, I could be alone in the house, and he'd come in, and I'd feel crowded. He was always touching me, patting me, slapping my behind, trying to muss my hair right after I had it done. I told you they were silly things, Maddie."

"Not so silly."

"He was just—just all over me. He suffocated me. I got so I didn't even want to breathe the air when he was in the house. The air seemed hot and choking and smelled of his cologne. And he was so messy. Leaving wet towels on the bathroom floor. Throwing his dirty underwear and socks on the bed. I couldn't stand that. He'd have dinner, belch, and just walk away, leaving me to clean up. I know a wife is supposed to do that, but he took it for granted. He was so sure of himself. I think that's what I hated most—his superior attitude. I was like a slave or something, and had no right to question what he did or where he went."

"He sounds like a real charmer. Did he play around?"

"Not at first. Then I began to notice things: women whispering about him at parties, his going out at night after dinner. To see customers, he said. Once, when I took his black suit to the cleaner's, there was a book of matches in his pocket. It was from a roadhouse out of town. It didn't, ah, have a very good reputation. So I guess he was playing around. I didn't care. As long as he left me alone."

"Oh, Zoe, was it that bad?"

"I tried, Maddie, really I did. But he was so heavy, and strong, and sort of—sort of uncouth."

"Wham, bam, thank you, ma'am?"

"Something like that. And also, he wanted to do it when he was drunk or all sweated up. I'd ask him to take a shower first, but he'd laugh at me."

"Hung?"

"What?"

"Was he hung? A big whang?"

"Uh, I don't know, Maddie. I don't have much basis for comparison. He was, uh, bigger than Michelangelo's *David.*"

Madeline Kurnitz laughed. How she laughed! She bobbed with merriment, slopping her drink.

"Honey, *everyone* is bigger than Michelangelo's *David.*"

"And he wanted to do disgusting things. I told him I wasn't brought up that way."

"Uh-huh."

"I told him if he wanted to act like an animal, I was sure he could find other women to accommodate him."

"That wasn't so smart, luv."

"I was past the point of worrying if what I said was smart. I just didn't want anything more to do with him. In bed, I mean. I would have kept on being married to him if he just forgot all about sex with me. Because I felt divorce would be a failure, and my mother would be so disappointed in me. But then he just walked out of the house, quit his job with my father, and left town. Lawyers handled the divorce and I never saw him again."

"Know what happened to him?"

"Yes. He went out to the West Coast. He got married again. About a week ago."

"How do you know that?"

"He sent me an invitation."

Maddie exhaled noisily. "Another prick. What a shitty thing to do."

"I was going to send a gift. Just, you know, to show him I didn't care. But I, ah, tore up the invitation and I don't have the address."

"Screw him. Send him a bottle of cyanide. All men should drop dead."

"Oh, Maddie, I don't know . . . I guess some of it, a lot of it, was my fault. But I tried so hard to be a good wife, really I did. I cooked all his favorite foods and I was always trying new recipes I thought he'd like. I kept the house as clean as a pin. Everyone said it was a showplace. We had all new furniture, and once he got angry and ripped all the plastic covers off. That's the way he was. He'd put his feet on the cocktail table and use the guest towels. I think he did those things just to annoy me. He swore a lot—dreadful words—and wouldn't go to church.

He wanted me to wear tight sweaters and low-cut things. I told him I wasn't like that, but he could never understand. He even wanted me to wear more makeup and have my hair tinted. So I guess I just wasn't the kind of woman he should have married. It was a mistake from the start."

"Oh, sweetie, it's not the end of the world. You'll find someone new."

"That's what I told you," Zoe said, smiling.

"Yeah," Maddie said, with a twisted grin, "ain't that a crock? Two old bags drinking up a storm and trying to cheer each other up. Well . . . what the hell; tomorrow's another day. You still seeing Mister Meek?"

"I wish you wouldn't call him that, Maddie. He's not like that at all. Yes, I'm still seeing him."

"Like him?"

"Very much."

"Uh-huh. Well, maybe he's more your type than Ralph."

"Kenneth."

"Whatever. You think he's interested in getting married?"

"We've never discussed it," Zoe said primly.

"Discuss it, discuss it," Maddie advised. "You don't have to ask him right out, but you can kind of hint around about how he feels on the subject. He likes you?"

"He says he does."

"Well, that's a start." Maddie yawned, finished her drink, stood up and began to gather her things together. "I've got to get going. Thanks for the booze and the talk. You were right there when I needed you, honey, and I love you for it. Let's see more of each other."

"Oh yes. I'd like that."

After Maddie left, Zoe Kohler locked and bolted the outside door. She plumped the cushions on couch and armchair. She returned the bottles to the kitchen, washed the glasses and ashtrays. She took a Tuinal and turned off the lights. She peeked through the venetian blind but could see no sign of the watcher across the street.

She got into bed. She lay on her back, arms down at her sides. She stared at the ceiling.

Those things she had told Maddie—they were all true. But she had the oddest feeling that they had happened to someone else. Not her. She had been describing the life of a stranger, something she had heard or read. It was not her life.

She turned onto her side and drew up her knees beneath the light blanket and sheet. She clamped her clasped hands between her thighs.

He was probably trying to get his new wife to do those disgusting things. Maybe she was doing them. And enjoying them.

It was all so common and coarse . . .

There was a luncheonette near 40th Street and Madison Avenue that Zoe Kohler passed on her way to and from work. It opened early in the morning and closed early in the evening. The food, mostly sandwiches, soups, and salads, was all right. Nothing special, but adequate.

On her way home, the evening of May 21st, Zoe stopped at the luncheonette for dinner. She had a cheeseburger with French fries, which she salted liberally. A cup of black coffee and a vanilla custard.

She sat by herself at a table for two and ate rapidly. She kept her eyes lowered and paid no attention to the noisy confusion churning about her. She left a fifteen percent tip, paid her check at the cashier's counter, and hurried out.

She went directly home. Her alimony check was in the mailbox and she tucked it into her purse. In her apartment, door carefully locked, bolted, and chained, she drew the blinds and changed into a cotton T-shirt and terry cloth shorts.

She took out mops, brooms, vacuum cleaner, cans of soap and wax, bottles of detergent, brushes, dustpan, pail, rags, sponges, whisks. She tied a scarf about her hair. She pulled on rubber gloves. She set to work.

In the bathroom, she scrubbed the tub, sink, and toilet bowl with Ajax. Washed the toilet seat with Lysol. Removed the bathmat from the floor, got down on her knees, and cleaned the tile with a brush and Spic and Span.

It had not been a good day. On the street, she had been pushed and jostled. In the office, she had been treated with cold indifference. Everyone in New York had a brusque assurance that daunted her. She wondered if she had made a mistake in coming to the city.

Emptied the medicine cabinet of all her makeup, perfume, medical supplies, and soap. Took out the shelves, washed them with Glass Plus and dried them. Replaced everything neatly, but not before wiping the dust from every jar, bottle, box, and tin.

The very size of the city demeaned her. It crumbled her ego, reduced her to a cipher by ignoring her existence. New York denied her humanness and treated her as a thing, no more than concrete, steel, and asphalt.

Shined the mirror of the medicine cabinet with Windex. Changed the shower curtain. Brought in a clean bathmat. Hung fresh towels, including two embroidered guest towels, although the old ones had not been used.

In the city, people paid to hear other people sing and watch other people feel. Passion had become a spectator sport supported by emotional cripples. Love and suffering were knacks possessed by the talented who were paid to display their gifts.

Emptied the wastebasket and put in a fresh plastic liner. Flushed Drano down the sink and tub drains. Changed the Vanish dispenser in the toilet tank that caused blue water to rush in with every flush. Sprayed the whole bathroom with lemon-scented Glade. Washed fingerprints from the door with Soft Scrub. Turned off the light.

Still, the anonymity of life in New York had its secret rewards. Where else but in this thundering chaos could she experience her adventures? If the city denied her humanity, it was big enough and uncaring enough to tolerate the frailties, vices, and sins of the insensate creatures it produced.

In the bedroom, she changed all the linen, replacing mattress cover, top and bottom sheets, and pillowcases. Made up the new bed with taut surfaces and sharp hospital corners. Turned down the bed, the top sheet overlapping the wool blanket by four inches.

Why had she sought adventures, and why did she continue? She could not frame a clear and lucid answer. She knew that what she was doing was monstrous, but that was no rein. The mind may reason, but the body will have its own. Who can master his appetites? The blood boils, and all is lost.

Dusted the dresser, bureau, and bedside table with Pride. Not only the top surfaces, but the front, sides, and legs as well. Cleaned the telephone with Lysol. Washed and polished the mirror with Windex. Wiped the ashtrays clean and dusted the bulbs in the lamps.

During her adventures, she quit the gallery for the stage. Never had she felt so alive and vindicated, never so charged with the hot stuff of animal existence. It was not that she donned a costume, but that she doffed a skin and emerged reborn.

Used her Eureka canister vacuum cleaner on the wall-to-wall carpeting, moving furniture when necessary. Dusted the slats of the venetian blinds. Cleaned fingerprints from the doorjambs. Lubricated the hinges of the closet with 3-in-One Oil.

Why her desire to live should have taken such a desperate form she could not have said. There were forces working on her that were dimly glimpsed. She felt herself buffeted, pushed this way and that, by powers as impersonal as the crush on city streets. The choice was hers, but so limited as to be no choice at all.

Rearranged all her clothing into precisely aligned stacks, piles, racks. Put a crocheted doily under the empty glass vase on the bedside table. Replaced the Mildewcide bags in the closet. Added more lavender sachets to the dresser and bureau drawers. Looked around. Turned off the lights.

She smiled at the theatricality of her existence. She relished the convolutions of her life. It was a soap opera! Her life was a soap opera! All lives were soap operas. At the end, just before the death rattle, a whispered, "Thank you, Proctor and Gamble."

In the kitchen, she took everything from the cupboards, cabinets, and closets. Washed the interiors with Mr. Clean. Dusted every item before putting it back. Wiped the doors. Applied Klean 'n Shine to get rid of fingerprints.

Who *was* she? The complexities defeated her. It seemed to her that she lived a dozen lives, sometimes two or more simultaneously. She turned different faces to different people. Worse, she turned different faces to herself.

Used Fantastik on the range top and refrigerator. Scrubbed away grease and splatters with Lestoil. Cleaned the stainless steel with Sheila Shine. Took all the food out of the refrigerator. Washed the interior. Put in a new open package of Arm & Hammer baking soda. Replaced the food.

Age brought not self-knowledge but a growing fear of failure to solve her mystery. Who she was, her essence, seemed to be drifting away, the smoke thinning, a misty figure lost. Her life had lost its edges; she saw herself blurred and going.

Used Bon Ami on the sink. Polished the faucets. Poured a little Drano down the drain. Threw away a sliver of hand soap and put out a fresh bar of Ivory. Replaced the worn Brillo pad. Hung fresh hand towel and dish towel.

She wished for a shock to bring her into focus. A fatal wound or a conquering emotion. Something to which she could give. She thought surrender might save her and make her whole. She felt within herself a well of devotion untapped and unwanted.

Mopped the tiled floor with soapy water. Dry-mopped it. Mopped again with Glo-Coat. Waited until it dried, then waxed it again with Future. Looked around at the sparkle.

She wondered if love could be at once that emotion and that wound. She had never thought of herself as a passionate woman, but now she saw that if chance and accident might conspire, she could be complete: a new woman of grace and feeling.

In the living room, she dusted with an oiled rag. Used Pledge on the tabletops. Wiped the legs of tables and chairs. Plumped pillows and cushions. Put fresh lace doilies under ashtrays and vases.

To Madeline Kurnitz, love was pleasure and laughter. But surely there was more. It might be such a rare, delicate thing, a seedling, that only by wise and willing nurture could it grow strong enough to make a world and save a soul.

Wiped picture frames and washed the glass. Ran a dry mop along baseboards. Washed fingerprints from doors and jambs. Polished a lamp with Top Brass. Cleaned the light bulb. Straightened the kinked cord.

If such a thing should happen to her, if she knew the growth, her body would heal of itself, and all the empty places in her life would be filled. She dreamed of that transfiguration and lusted for it with an almost physical want.

Vacuumed the wall-to-wall carpeting. Moved furniture to clean underneath. Replaced the furniture so the legs set precisely on the little plastic coasters. Used a vacuum cleaner attachment to dust the drapes. Another attachment on the couch and chair cushions. Another attachment to clean the ceiling molding.

Her vision soared; with love, there was nothing she might not do. The city would be created anew, she would have no need for adventures, and she would recognize herself and be content. All that by the purity of love.

Straightened the outside closet. Shook out and rehung all the garments, including her hidden gowns. Dusted the shelves. Wiped off the shoes and replaced them on the racks. Fluffed her wigs. Dusted the venetian blinds. Sprayed the whole room with Breath o' Pine.

Her penance done, she put away all the brooms, mops, vacuum cleaner, cans of soap and wax, bottles of detergent, brushes, dustpan, pail, rags, sponges, and whisks. She undressed in the bedroom while her bath was running. She went into the kitchen, swallowed several vitamin and mineral pills, capsules of this and that. A Valium. A salt tablet.

She started to pour a glass of wine, but changed her mind before opening the bottle. Instead, she poured vodka on the rocks. A big one. Like Maddie. She took that into the bathroom with her.

She eased cautiously into the hot tub. Added scented oil to the water. She floated, sipping her iced vodka. Her weariness became a warm glow. She looked down at her wavering body through half-closed eyes.

"I love you," she murmured aloud, and wondered who she addressed: Kenneth, Ernest Mittle, or herself. She decided it didn't matter; the words had a meaning of their own. They were important. "I love you."

Ernest Mittle arrived promptly at noon on Sunday, May 25th. He brought an enormous bunch of daffodils, so large that Zoe could fill vases in the living room and bedroom, with a few stalks left over for the kitchen. The golden yellow brought sunlight into her dark apartment.

She had prepared a Sunday brunch of Bloody Marys, scrambled eggs with Canadian bacon, hot biscuits, a watercress salad, and a lemon ice for dessert. She also served chilled May wine with a fresh strawberry in each glass.

They sat at the seldom used dining table, a small oval of mahogany with four ladder-back chairs set before the living room window. The china and plated silver service had been wedding gifts. Zoe had bought the crystal salad bowl and napery after she moved to New York.

Ernest complimented her enthusiastically on everything: the shining apartment, the dining table prepared just so, the excellence of the food, the fruity, almost perfumed flavor of the wine.

"Really," Zoe said, "it's nothing."

They were at ease with each other, talking animatedly of their jobs, summer clothes they were thinking of buying, TV shows they had seen.

They spoke as old friends, for already they were learning each other's habits, likes and dislikes, prejudices and fancies. And they were building a fund of mutual memories: the dinner at the Italian restaurant, the Kurnitz party, the meatloaf Ernest had made, the balloon in Central Park.

Each recollection was in itself insignificant, but made meaningful by being shared. They knew this pleasant brunch would be added to their bank of shared experience, and seemed all the more precious for that. An occasion to be savored and recalled.

After the brunch, Ernest insisted on helping Zoe clear the table. In the kitchen, she washed and he dried, and it seemed the most natural thing in the world. He even replaced all the clean dishes and cutlery in their proper racks in the correct cupboards.

Then they moved to the living room. The May wine was finished, but Zoe served vodka-and-tonics, with a wedge of fresh lime in each. She brought her little radio in from the bedroom, and found a station that was featuring Mantovani.

The dreamy music played softly in the background. They sprawled comfortably, sipping their iced drinks. They smiled at each other with satiety and ease. It seemed to them they recaptured the mood they had felt in the park: they owned the world.

"Will you be getting a vacation?" he asked casually.

"Oh yes. Two weeks."

"When are you taking it?"

"I haven't decided yet. They're very good about that. I can take off in June, July, or August."

"Me, too," he said. "I get two weeks. I usually go home for a few days. Sometimes a week."

"I do, too."

"Zoe . . ." he said.

She looked at him questioningly.

"Do you think . . . Would it be possible for us to go somewhere together? For a week, or maybe just a weekend? Don't get me wrong," he added hastily. "Not to share a room or anything like that. I just thought it might be fun to be together this summer for a while in some nice place."

She pondered a moment, head cocked.

"I think that's a fine idea," she said. "Maybe somewhere on Long Island."

"Or New England."

"There's a woman in the hotel who arranges tours and cruises and things like that. I could ask her to recommend some nice place."

"No swinging resorts," he said. "Where we'd have to dress up and all."

"Oh no," she said. "A quiet place on the beach. Where we can swim and walk and just relax."

"Right!" he said. "With good food. And not too crowded. It doesn't have to be supermodern with chrome and glitter and organized activities."

"Nothing like that," she agreed. "Maybe just an old, family-run tourist home or motel. Where no one would bother us."

"And we could do whatever we want. Swim and walk the beach. Collect shells and driftwood. Explore the neighborhood. I'd like that."

"I would, too," she said. She took their glasses into the kitchen and brought them fresh drinks. "Ernie," she said, sitting alongside him on the couch and taking his hand, "what you said about our not sharing a room—I was glad you said that. I suppose you think I'm some kind of a prude?"

"I don't think anything of the sort."

"Well, I'm not. It's just that going away together would be such a—such a new thing for us. And sharing a room would just make it more complicated. You understand?"

"Of course," he said. "That's exactly what I think. Who knows—if we're together for three days or a week, I might drive you batty."

"Oh no," she protested. "I think we'll get along very well and have a good time. I just don't think we should, you know, start off knowing we were going to sleep together. I'd be very nervous and embarrassed."

He looked at her with admiration.

"Just the way I feel, Zoe. We're so much alike. We don't have to rush anything or do anything that might spoil what we've got. Don't you feel that way?"

"Oh, I do, Ernie, I do! You're so considerate."

She had turned to look at him. He seemed a quiet, inoffensive man, no more exciting than she. But she saw beauty in his clear features and guileless eyes. There was a clean innocence about him, an openness. He would never deceive her or hurt her; she knew that.

"I don't want you to think I'm sexless," she said intently.

"Zoe, I could never think that. I think you're a very deep, passionate woman."

"Do you?" she said. "Do you really? I'm not very modern, you know. I mean, I don't hop around from bed to bed. I think that's terrible."

"It's worse than terrible," he said. "It just reduces everyone to animals. I think sex has to be the result of a very deep emotional need, and a desire for honest intimacy."

"Yes," she said. "And physical love should be gentle and tender and sweet."

"Correct," he said, nodding. "It should be something two people decide to share because they really and truly love each other and want to, uh, give each other pleasure. Happiness."

"Oh, that's very true," she said, "and I'm so glad you feel that way. It's really valuable, isn't it? Sex, I mean. You just don't throw it around all over the place. That cheapens it."

"It makes it nothing," he said. "Like, 'Should we have another martini or should we go to bed?' It really should mean more than that. I guess I'm a romantic."

"I guess I am, too."

"You know what's so wonderful, dear?" he said, twisting around to face her. "It's that with both of us feeling this way, we found each other. With the millions and millions of people in the world, we found each other. Don't you think that's marvelous?"

"Oh yes, darling," she breathed, touching his cheek.

"Just think of the odds against it! I know I've never met a woman like you before."

"And I've never met a man like you."

He kissed her palm.

"I'm nothing much," he said. "I know that. I mean, I'm not tall and strong and handsome. I suppose someday I'll be making a good living, but I'll never be rich. I'm just not—not ruthless enough. But still, I don't want to change. I don't want to be greedy and cruel, out for all I can get."

"Oh no!" she cried. "Don't change, Ernie. I like you just the way you are. I don't want you different. I couldn't stand that."

They put their drinks aside. They embraced. It seemed to them they were huddling, giving comfort to each other in the face of catastrophe. As survivors might hold each other, in fear and in hope.

"We'll go away together this summer, darling," she whispered. "We'll spend every minute with each other. We'll swim and walk the beach and explore."

"Oh yes," he said dreamily. "Just the two of us."

"Against the world," Zoe Kohler said, kissing him.

Something was happening. Zoe Kohler read it in the newspapers, heard it on radio, saw it on TV. The search for the Hotel Ripper had been widened, the investigating force enlarged, the leads being followed had multiplied.

More important, the police were now discussing publicly the possibility that the killer was a woman. The "Daughter of Sam" headline was revived. Statements were issued warning visitors to midtown Manhattan of the dangers of striking up acquaintance with strangers, men or women, on the streets, in bars and cocktail lounges, in discos and restaurants.

The search for the slayer took on a new urgency. The summer tourist season was approaching; the number of canceled conventions and tours was increasing. Newspaper editorialists quoted the dollar loss that could be expected if the killer was not quickly caught.

Surprisingly, there was little of the public hysteria that had engulfed the city during the Son of Sam case. One columnist suggested this might be due to the fact that, so far, all the victims had been out-of-towners.

More likely, he added, familiarity with mass murder had dulled the public's reaction. The recent Chicago case, with more than a score of victims, made the Hotel Ripper of minor interest. There now seemed to be an intercity competition in existence, similar to the contest to build the highest skyscraper.

But despite the revived interest of the media in the Hotel Ripper case, Zoe could find no evidence that the police had any specific information about the killer's identity. She was convinced they were no closer to solving the case than they had been after her first adventure.

So what happened to her on the afternoon of May 28th came as a numbing shock.

Mr. Pinckney had originally obtained the Chemical Mace for her as a protection against muggers and rapists. She did not want to risk telling him it had been used, lying about the circumstances, and asking him to supply another container. So she said nothing. The Mace wasn't an absolute necessity; a knife was.

She had purchased her Swiss Army pocket knife at a cutlery shop, one of a chain, in Grand Central Station. This time she determined to buy a heavier knife at a different store of the same chain. During her lunch hour, she walked over to Fifth Avenue and 46th Street.

An enormous selection of pocket knives, jackknives, and hunting knives was offered. Zoe waited patiently at the counter while the customer ahead of her made his choice. She was bemused to see that he picked a Swiss Army knife, but with more blades than the one she had owned.

While the clerk was writing up the sales check, he said, "Could I have your name and address, sir? We'd like to send you our mail-order catalog. Absolutely no charge, of course."

The customer left his name and address. Then it was Zoe's turn.

"I'd like a pocket knife as a gift for my nephew," she told the clerk. "Nothing too large or too heavy."

He laid out several knives for her inspection. She selected a handsome instrument with four blades, a horn handle, and a metal loop at one end for clipping onto a belt or hanging from a hook.

She paid for her purchase in cash, deciding that if the clerk asked for her name and address, she would give him false identity. But he didn't ask.

"I heard you offer to send that other customer your mail-order catalog," she said as the clerk was gift-wrapping her knife.

"Oh, we don't have a catalog," he said. He looked around carefully, then leaned toward her. "We're cooperating with the police," he whispered. "They want us to try and get the name and address of everyone who buys a Swiss Army knife. And if we can't get their names, to jot down a description."

Zoe Kohler was proud of her calmness.

"Whatever for?" she asked.

The clerk seemed uncomfortable. "I think it has something to do with the Hotel Ripper. They didn't really tell us."

Walking back to the Hotel Granger, the new knife in her purse, Zoe realized what must have happened: the police had identified the knife used from the tip of the broken blade found at the Cameron Arms Hotel.

But nothing had been published about it in the newspapers. Obviously the police were keeping the identification of the weapon a secret. That suggested there were other things they were keeping secret as well. Her fingerprints, perhaps, or something she had dropped at the scene, or some other clue that would lead them inevitably to her.

She should have felt dismayed, she knew, and frightened. But she didn't. If anything, she felt a sense of heightened excitement. The exhilaration of her adventures was sharpened by the risk, made more intense.

She imagined the police as a single malevolent intelligence with a single implacable resolve: to bring her down. To accomplish that, they would lie and deceive, work in underhanded and probably illegal ways, use all the powers at their command, including physical force and violence.

It seemed to her the police were fit representatives of a world that had cheated her, debased her, demolished her dreams and refused to concede her worth as a woman or her value as a human being.

The police and the world wanted nothing but her total extinction so that things might go along as if she had never been.

The evening of June 4th . . .

Zoe Kohler, alert, erect, strides into the crowded lobby of the Hotel Adler on Seventh Avenue and 50th Street. She pauses to scan the display board near the entrance. Under Current Events, it lists a convention of orthopedic surgeons, a banquet for a labor leader, and a three-day gathering of ballroom dancing teachers.

The hotel directory she had consulted listed the Adler's two restaurants, a "pub-type tavern," and a cocktail lounge. But Zoe is accosted before she can decide on her next move.

"See anything you like?" someone asks. A male voice, assured, amused.

She turns to look at him coolly. A tall man. Slender. A saturnine smile. Heavy, drooping eyelids. Olive skin. Black, gleaming hair slicked back from a widow's peak. The long fingers holding his cigarette look as if they have been squeezed from tubes.

"I don't believe we've met," she says frostily.

"We have now," he says. "You could save my life if you wanted to."

She cannot resist . . .

"How could I do that?"

"Have a drink with me. Keep me from going back into that meeting."

"What are you?" she challenges. "An orthopedic surgeon, a labor leader, or a ballroom dancing teacher?"

"A little of all three," he says, the smile never flickering. "But mostly I'm a magician."

He takes a silver dollar from his pocket, makes it flip-flop across his knuckles. It disappears into his palm. It reappears, begins the knuckle dance again. Zoe Kohler watches, fascinated.

"Now you see it," he says, "now you don't. The hand is quicker than the eye."

"Is that the only trick you know?" she asks archly.

"I know tricks you wouldn't believe. How about that drink?"

She doesn't think he is a police decoy. Too elegantly dressed. And a cop would not make the first approach—or would he?

"Where are you from?" she asks.

"Here, there, and everywhere," he says. "I've got a name you could never pronounce, but you can call me Nick. What's yours?"

"Irene," she says. "I'll have one drink with you. Only one."

"Of course," he says, plucking the silver dollar from her left ear. "Let's go, Irene."

But the cocktail lounge and the tavern are jammed. People wait on line. Nick takes her elbow in a tight grip.

"We'll go upstairs," he says, "to my room."

"One drink," she repeats.

He doesn't answer. His confidence daunts her. He pulls her along. But she cannot stop, cause a scene. No identity in her purse. But a knife with a sharpened blade.

His room looks as if he had moved in five minutes ago. Nothing to mark his presence but an unopened suitcase on a luggage rack.

He locks and chains the door behind them. He takes her coat and bag, throws them onto a chair.

"You want to see more tricks?" he says. "How about this?"

He unzips his fly, digs, pulls out his penis. It is long, dark, slender. Uncircumcised. He strokes it.

"Nice?" he says, his sardonic smile unwavering. "You like this trick?"

"I'm going," she says, reaching for her coat and bag.

He moves quickly between her and the door.

"What are you going to do?" he says. "Scream? Go ahead—scream."

She fumbles in her bag. He is there, and plucks it from her hands. She cannot believe anyone can move that swiftly. He is a blur.

He takes out her wallet, flips through it.

"No ID," he says. "That's smart."

He picks out the closed knife, dangles it by the steel loop.

"What's this for?" he asks. "Cleaning your toenails?"

He laughs, drops the knife back into the bag. He tosses it aside.

"You know the old saying," he says roguishly. "When rape is inevitable, relax and enjoy it."

"Why me?" she cries desperately.

He shrugs. "Just to pass the time. Something to do. You want to get undressed like a lady or do you want your pretty dress ripped?"

"Please," she says, "what about a drink? You promised me a drink."

"I lied," he says, grinning. "I'm always doing that."

He begins undressing. He stays between her and the door. He takes off his jacket, unknots his tie, unbuttons his shirt. He drops all his clothes onto the floor.

"Come on," he says. "Come *on.*"

She takes off her clothes slowly, fingers trembling. She looks about for a weapon. A heavy ashtray. A table lamp. Anything.

"No way," he says softly, watching her. "No *way.*"

She takes off shoes, dress, pantyhose. She drapes them over the back of a chair. When she looks up, he is naked. His penis is beginning to stiffen. He touches it delicately.

"Try it," he says. "You'll like it."

He takes one quick stride to her. He clamps his hands on her shoulders. His strength frightens her. She cannot fight that power.

He pulls the strapless bra to her waist. He pinches her nipples. He strips her panties down, lifts her away from them.

"Bony," he says, "but okay. The nearer the bone, the sweeter the meat."

He presses her down. His hands on her shoulders are a weight she cannot resist. Her knees buckle. She flops onto the rug.

"I don't want to mess the bed," he says. "The floor is best. Harder. More resistance. Know what I mean?"

It is a whirl, beyond her control. Things flicker. She is swept away, protests stifled. Her puny blows on his head, arms, chest, mean nothing. He laughs throatily.

She squirms, moving by inches toward her discarded shoulder bag. But he pins her with his weight, a hard knee prying between her clamped thighs. He makes thick, huffing sounds.

She continues to writhe, and he strikes her. The open-palmed slap stings, flings her head aside. Her eyes water, ears roar. His teeth are on her throat. His body twists, pressing, pressing . . .

"What the hell is this?" he says, finding her tampon. He makes a noise of disgust. He yanks it out roughly, tosses it aside.

Then she does what she has to do, telling herself it is the only way she might survive.

Her body stills. Her punches stop. Untaloned, she begins to stroke his shoulders, his back. She moans.

"Yeah," he breathes. "Oh yeah . . ."

Her thighs ache. She thinks he will split her apart, rip her, leave steaming guts on the carpet. She feels hot tears, tastes bile.

He ramps and plunges, crying out in a language she does not recognize. His hands beneath her, gripping cruelly, pull her body up in a strained arch.

Eyes shut tightly, she sees pinwheels, whirling discs, melting blood. She wraps herself about him, feeling cold, cold. She endures the pain; within she is untouched and plotting.

His final thrusts pound her, bruise. Her moans rise in volume to match his cries. When he collapses, shuddering, sobbing, she shakes her body in a paroxysm. She flings her arms wide—and her fingertips just touch the leather of her discarded shoulder bag.

She opens her eyes to slits. He props himself up, stares down at her, panting.

"More!" she pleads. "More!"

"Wait'll I turn you over," he says, glee in his voice. "It's even better."

He pulls away from her savagely; she feels she is being torn inside out. He rolls onto his back, lies supine, chest heaving.

She turns onto her side, onto hip and shoulder, pulling herself a few inches closer to her purse. Digs toes and feet into the rug, moving herself with cautious little pushes.

"Oh, that was so wonderful," she tells him. "So marvelous. What a lover you are. I've never had a man like you before."

He closes his eyes with satisfaction. He reaches blindly, finds her vulva, squeezes and twists roughly.

"Good, huh?" he says. "The greatest, huh?"

Moving slowly, watching his closed eyes carefully, her right hand snakes into the shoulder bag, comes out with the knife.

"Ohh . . . I feel so good," she murmurs quietly.

Stretches up her left arm. Above her head, she opens the big, sharpened blade. She eases it into position so it will not click when it locks. She brings her arms gradually down to her sides. Her right hand, gripping the knife, is concealed behind her.

She sits up, pulling herself closer to him. She puts her left hand on his hairless chest, toys with his nipples.

"When can we do it again?" she whispers. "I want more, Nick."

"Soon," he says. "Soon. Just give me a chance to—"

His closed eyelids flutter. Immediately she raises the knife high, drives the blade to the hilt into his abdomen, a few inches below the squinched navel.

She twists the knife, yanks it free, raises it for another blow.

But he reacts almost instantly. He rolls over completely, away from her. He springs to his feet. He stands swaying, hands clasped to his belly.

He looks down at the blood welling from between his fingers. He raises his head slowly. He stares at her.

"You stuck me," he says wonderingly. "You *stuck* me."

He lurches toward her, claws reaching. She scrambles out of his way. She stumbles to her feet. A floor lamp goes over with a crash. One of his grasping hands comes close. She slashes it open with a backhanded swipe.

Roaring with rage and frustration, he blunders toward her unsteadily. Blood pours down his groin, his legs, drips from his flaccid penis. His slit hand, flinging, sends drops of blood flying.

An endtable is upset. An armchair is knocked over. Someone bangs on the adjoining wall. "Stop that!" a woman shouts. Still he comes on, mouth open and twisted. No sounds now but harsh, bubbling breaths. And in his eyes, terror and fury.

She trips over his discarded clothing. Before she can recover, he is on her, grappling close. His blood-slick hand finds her wrist, presses down, turns.

In a single violent movement, the naked blade edge sweeps across her right thigh, opens it up six inches above the knee. She feels the burn. Hot and icy at once.

He tries to force her down, to lean her to the floor. But his strength is leaking out, pouring, dripping, leaving pools and puddles and dribblings.

She squirms from his clutch. She whirls and begins plunging the knife into his arms, belly, face, shoulders, neck. Shoving it in, twisting it out, striking again.

She dances about him, meeting his lunges and stumbles with more blows. His life escapes from a hundred ragged wounds. His head comes lower, arms drag, shoulders sag.

He totters, goes down suddenly onto his knees. He tries, shuddering, to raise his bloodied head. Then falls, slaughtered, thumping to the floor. He rolls over once. His reddened, sightless eyes stare meekly at the ceiling.

She bends over him, hissing, and completes the ritual: throat opened wide, a blade to the clotted genitals again and again.

She straightens up, sobbing for breath, looking with dulled eyes at the butchery. His blood is smeared on her hands, arms, breasts, stomach. Worse, she feels the warm course of her own blood on leg, knee, shin, foot. She looks down. How bright it is! How sparkling!

In the bathroom, she stands naked on the tiled floor. She wipes her body clean of his blood with a dampened towel. She washes the knife and her hands with hot, soapy water. Then, using a washcloth tenderly, she cleans and examines her wound.

It is more than a scratch and less than a slash. No arteries or veins appear to be cut, but it bleeds steadily, running down to form a stain and then a shallow puddle on the tile.

She winds toilet paper around and around her thigh, making a bandage that soon soaks through. Over this, she wraps a hand towel as tightly as she can pull it. She limps back into the bedroom to retrieve Nick's necktie. She uses that to bind the towel tightly to her thigh.

She dresses as quickly as she can, leaving off her pantyhose, jamming them into her bag. She wipes her fingerprints from the sink faucets. She makes no attempt to mop up her own blood—an impossible task—and leaves the sodden towels on the floor of the bathroom.

She dons her coat, slings her shoulder bag. At the last minute, she picks up her discarded tampon from the floor. It is not stained. She puts it into her purse. She takes a final look around.

The punctured man lies slack on the floor, wounds gaping. All his magic is gone, soaking into the rug. He is emptied. Of confidence, brute strength, surging life.

She took a cab from the hotel and was back in her apartment a little after 11:00 P.M. She had worn her trenchcoat, although it was much too warm a night for it. But she feared the towel about her leg might soak through her dress.

It had; the front of her gown was stained with blood. She stripped, gently unwound the towel, pulled the wet paper away. The flow had lessened, but the thin line still oozed.

She washed it with warm, soapy water, dried it, wiped it with Q-Tips dipped in hydrogen peroxide. Then she fastened a neat bandage of gauze pads and adhesive tape. The wound throbbed, but nothing she could not endure.

Only after the bandage was secured did she go into the kitchen and, standing at the sink, drink off a double shot of iced vodka almost as quickly as she could gulp. Then she held out her right hand. The fingers were not trembling.

She took Anacin, Midol, vitamins, minerals, a salt tablet, a Darvon. She poured a fresh drink, took it back to the bathroom. She washed her face, armpits, and douched with a vinegar-water mixture. She wiped herself dry and inserted a fresh tampon. It was painful; her vagina felt stretched and punished.

Then she went into the bedroom, sat down slowly on the edge of the bed. She felt bone-weary, all of her sore, rubbed, and pulsing. Not with pain but with a kind of rawness. She felt opened and defenseless. A touch would bring a scream.

Already her adventure was fading, losing its hard, sharp outlines. She could not limn it in her memory. She had chaotic recollections of noise, violence, and the spray of hot blood. But it had all happened to someone else, in another time, another place.

She went back into the kitchen and washed down a Tuinal with the last of her second drink. She pulled on her batiste cotton nightgown with the neckline of embroidered rosebuds. She padded through her apartment to check the bolted door and turn off the lights.

She opened the bedroom window, but made certain the shade was fully drawn. The sheets felt cool and comforting, but the blanket was too warm; she tossed it aside.

As she lay awake, drugged, heart fluttering, waiting for sleep, she tried to recall those moments when she had been convinced that love would be her soul's salvation.

8

On May 10th, the Saturday afternoon Zoe Kohler and Ernest Mittle were flying a red balloon in Central Park, Edward X. Delaney sat in a crowded office in Midtown North with Sergeant Abner Boone and other officers. They were discussing the murder of Leonard T. Bergdorfer at the Cameron Arms Hotel.

Present at the conference, in addition to Delaney and Boone, were the following:

Lieutenant Martin Slavin, who had been relegated to a strictly administrative role in the operations of the task force assembled to apprehend the Hotel Ripper . . .

Sergeant Thomas K. Broderick, an officer with more than twenty years' service in the Detective Division, most of them in midtown Manhattan . . .

Detective First Grade Aaron Johnson, a black, with wide experience in dealing with the terrorist fringes of minority groups and with individual anarchists . . .

Detective Second Grade Daniel ("Dapper Dan") Bentley, who specialized in hotel crimes, particularly robberies, gem thefts, confidence games, etc. . . .

Detective Lieutenant Wilson T. Crane, noted for his research capabilities and expertise in computer technology . . .

Sergeant Boone opened the discussion by recapping briefly the circumstances of Leonard Bergdorfer's death . . .

"Pretty much like the others. Throat slashed. Multiple stab wounds in the nuts. This time the body was found on the floor. Take a look at the photos. The bed wasn't used. The autopsy shows no, uh, sexual relations prior—"

BENTLEY: "Sexual relations? You mean like my sister-in-law?"

(Laughter)

BOONE: "He hadn't screwed at least twenty-four hours prior to his death. Like the others."

CRANE: "Prints?"

BOONE: "The Latent Print Unit is still at it. It doesn't look good. Two things that may help . . . The tip of a knife blade was found embedded in the victim's throat. It's a little more than a half-inch long. Lab Services is working on it now. There's no doubt it's from the murder weapon. Probably a pocket knife, jackknife, or clasp knife—whatever you want to call it."

JOHNSON: "How long was the blade do they figure?"

BOONE: "Maybe three inches long."

JOHNSON: "Sheet! A toothpick."

BOONE: "Victim suffered first-degree burns of the face, especially around the eyes and nose. The Medical Examiner's office blames phenacyl chloride used in CN and Chemical Mace. The burning indicates a heavy dose at close range."

BRODERICK: "Enough to knock him out?"

BOONE: "Enough to knock him down, that's for sure. As far as the victim's background goes, we're still at it. No New York sheet. He was from Atlanta, Georgia. They're checking. Ditto the Feds. Probably nothing we can use. And that's about it."

CRANE: "Was the Mace can found?"

BOONE: "No. The killer probably took it along. What's the law on Mace? Anyone know?"

SLAVIN: "Illegal to buy, sell, own, carry, or use in the State of New York. Except for bona fide security and law enforcement officers."

BENTLEY: "Black market? Johnson?"

JOHNSON: "You asking me 'cause I'm black?"

(Laughter)

JOHNSON: "There's some of it around. In those little purse containers for women to carry. There's not what you'd call a thriving market on the street."

BOONE: "Well, at the moment, the Mace and the knife blade tip are all we've got that's new. Before we start talking about what to do with them, I'd like you to listen to ex-Chief of Detectives Edward X. Delaney for a few minutes. The Chief is not on active duty. At the urging of Deputy Commissioner Ivar Thorsen and myself, he has agreed to serve as, uh, a consultant on this investigation. Chief?"

Delaney stood, leaning on his knuckles on the battered table. He loomed forward. He looked around slowly, staring at every man.

"I'm not here to give you orders," he said tonelessly. "I'm not here to ride herd on you. I've got no official status at all. I'm here because Thorsen and Boone are old friends, and because I want to crack this thing as much as you do. If I have any suggestions on how to run this case, I'll make them to Thorsen or Boone. They can pick up on them or not—that's their business. I just want to make sure you know what the situation is. I'd like my presence here to be kept under wraps as long as possible. I know it'll probably get out eventually, but I don't need the publicity. I've already got my pension."

They smiled at that, and relaxed.

"All right," he said, "now I want to tell you who I think the Hotel Ripper is . . ."

That jolted them and brought them leaning forward, waiting to hear.

He told them why he thought the killer was a woman. Not a prostitute, but a psychopathic female. He went over all the evidence he had presented to Monica and to Thorsen. But this time he remembered to include the additional detail that the person who tipped off the *Times* could have been a woman.

He said nothing about Thomas Handry's research, nothing about the statistics showing the increased evidence of alcoholism, drug addiction, and mental disturbance among women.

These men were professional policemen; they weren't interested in sociological change or psychological motivation. Their sole concern was evidence that could be brought into court.

So he came down heavily on the known facts about the murders, facts that could be accounted for only by the theory he proposed. They were facts already known to everyone in that room, except for his suggestion that the timing of the killings was equivalent to a woman's menstrual period.

But it was the first time they had heard these disparate items fitted into a coherent hypothesis. He could see their doubt turn to dawning realization that the theory he offered was a fresh approach, a new way of looking at old puzzles.

"So what we're looking for," Delaney concluded, "is a female crazy. I'd guess young—late twenties to middle thirties. Five-five to five-seven. Short hair, because she has no trouble wearing wigs. Strong. Very, very smart. Not a street bum. Probably a woman of some education and breeding. Chances are she's on pills or booze or both, but that's pure conjecture. She probably lives a reasonably normal life when she's not out slashing throats. Holds down a job, or maybe she's a housewife. That's all I've got."

He sat down suddenly. The men looked at one another, waiting for someone to speak.

BOONE: "Any reactions?"

SLAVIN: "There's not a goddamned thing there we can take to the DA."

BOONE: "Granted. But it's an approach. A place to start."

JOHNSON: "I'll buy it."

BENTLEY: "It listens to me. It's got to be a twist—all those straight guys stripping off their pants."

CRANE: "It doesn't fit the probabilities for this type of crime."

DELANEY: "I agree. In this case, I think the probabilities are wrong. Not wrong, but outdated."

BRODERICK: "I'll go along with you, Chief. Let's suppose the killer is a woman. So what? Where do we go from there?"

BOONE: "First, go back and check the records again. For women with a sheet that includes violent crimes. Check the prisons for recent releases. Check the booby hatches for ditto, and for escapees. Go through all our nut files and see if anything shows up."

CRANE: "My crew can handle that."

BOONE: "Second, the knife blade . . . Broderick, see if you can trace the knife by analysis of the metal in the blade."

DELANEY: "Or the shape. Ever notice how pocket knife blades have different shapes? Some are straight, some turn up at the point, some are sharpened on both edges."

BRODERICK: "That's nice. There must be a zillion different makes of pocket knives for sale in the New York area."

BOONE: "Find out. Third, Johnson you take the business with the Mace. Who makes it, how it gets into New York. Is it sold by mail order? Can you get a license to buy it? Anyone pushing it on the street? And so forth."

BENTLEY: "And me?"

BOONE: "Pull your decoys out of the gay bars. Concentrate on the straight places, and mostly the bars and cocktail lounges in midtown hotels. And show photos of the victims to bartenders and waitresses. See if you can pick up a trail."

BENTLEY: "We've already done that, sarge."

BOONE: "So? Do it again."

DELANEY: "Wait a minute . . ."

They all turned to look at him but the Chief was silent. Then he spoke to Detective Bentley.

DELANEY: "Your squad showed photos of all the victims around in hotel bars and cocktail lounges?"

BENTLEY: "That's right, Chief."

DELANEY: "And you came up with zilch?"

BENTLEY: "Correct. That's understandable; most of the places were mobbed. What waitress would remember one customer's face?"

DELANEY: "Uh-huh. Boone, who was the victim with the badly scarred hands?"

BOONE: "The third. Jerome Ashley, at the Hotel Coolidge."

DELANEY: "Go back to the Coolidge. Don't show Ashley's photo. At first. Ask if any waitress or bartender remembers a customer with badly scarred hands. If they do, *then* show his photo."

BENTLEY: "Got it. Beautiful."

BOONE: "Any more questions?"

CRANE: "Are we releasing this to the media? About the Ripper being a woman?"

BOONE: "Thorsen says no, not at the moment. They'll decide on it downtown."

BRODERICK: "No way we can keep it quiet. Too many people involved."

BOONE: "I agree, but it's not our decision to make. Anything else?"

BENTLEY: "What color wig are my decoys looking for?"

BOONE: "Probably strawberry blond. But it could be any color."

BENTLEY: "Thank you. That narrows it down."

Laughing, the men rose, the meeting broke up. Delaney watched them go. He was satisfied with them; he thought they knew their jobs.

More than that, he was gratified by the way they had accepted, more or less, his theory as a working hypothesis. He knew how comforting it was in any criminal case to have a framework, no matter how bare. The outline, hopefully, would be filled in as the investigation proceeded.

But to start out with absolutely nothing, and still have nothing three months later, was not only discouraging, it was enervating; it drained the will, weakened resolve, and made men question their professional ability.

Now, at least, he had given them an aim, a direction. Policemen, in many ways, are like priests. No experienced cop believes in justice; the law is his bible. And Delaney had given them hope that, in this case at least, the law would not be flouted.

"Want to stay around, Chief?" Sergeant Boone asked. "Maybe you can suggest some improvements on how we're organized."

"Thanks," Delaney said, "but I better climb out of your hair and let you get to work. I think it would be smart if I stayed away from here as much as possible. Keep resentment to a minimum."

"No one resents your helping out, Chief."

Delaney smiled and waved a hand.

On his way out of Midtown North, he looked in at busy offices, squad and interrogation rooms. Most of his years of service had been spent in precinct houses older than this one, but the atmosphere was similar. The smell was identical.

He knew that most of the bustle he witnessed had nothing to do with the Hotel Ripper case; it was the daily activity of an undermanned precinct that patrolled one of the most crowded sections of Manhattan, usually the only part of New York City visited by tourists.

It would have been helpful, and probably more efficient, if the entire Hotel Ripper task force could have been accommodated in one suite of offices, or even one large bullpen. But they had to make do with the space available.

As a result, only Boone and his command squad and Slavin and his bookkeepers worked out of Midtown North. Johnson and Bentley, and their crews, were stationed in Midtown South. Broderick's men had desks in the 20th Precinct, and Lieutenant Crane's research staff had been given temporary space downtown at 1 Police Plaza.

Still, the organization creaked along, twenty-four hours a day, with three shifts of plainclothesmen and detectives turning up to keep the investigation rolling. Delaney didn't want to think about the scheduling problems involved—that was Slavin's headache.

And the paperwork! It boggled the mind. Daily reports, status updates, requests for record checks, and pleas for additional manpower were probably driving Sergeant Boone right up the wall. Delaney suspected he was sleeping on a cot in his office—when he had a chance to grab a few hours.

The Chief walked across town on 54th Street, musing on the size of the machine that had been set in motion to stop a single criminal and what it was costing the city. He didn't doubt for a moment that it was necessary, but he wondered if adding more men, and more, and more, would bring success sooner. Would doubling the task force break the case in half the time? Ridiculous.

He guessed that the size of the operation must be a matter of some pride and satisfaction to the murderer. Most mass killers had a desire for recognition of the monstrousness of their crimes. They wrote to the newspapers. They called TV and radio stations. They wanted attention, and if it came at the cost of slashed corpses and a terrorized city—so be it.

He lumbered along the city street, crowded this Saturday afternoon in spring, and looked with new eyes at the women passing by. He was as adept at observing himself as others, and he realized that his way of looking at women had changed since he became convinced that the Hotel Ripper was female.

His feelings about women had already undergone one revolution, spurred by Monica's interest in the feminist movement. But now, seeing these strange, aloof creatures striding along on a busy New York street, he was conscious of another shift in his reactions to the female sex.

He could only recognize it as a kind of wariness. It was an awareness that, for him at least, women had suddenly revealed a new, hitherto unsuspected dimension.

There was a mystery there, previously shrugged off, like most males, with the muttered comment: "Just like a woman." With no one, ever, defining exactly what was meant by that judgment, except that it was inevitably uttered in a condemnatory tone.

But now, attempting to analyze the mystery, he thought it might be nothing more complex than granting to women the humanity granted to men—with all its sins and virtues, ideals and depravities.

If one was willing to accord to women equality (superiority even!) in all the finer instincts and nobilities of which men were capable, was it such a wrench or so illogical to acknowledge also that they were capable of men's faults and corruptions?

It was a nice point, he decided, and one he would certainly enjoy debating with Monica. The first time he caught her in a forgiving mood . . .

He took an uptown bus on Third Avenue and arrived home a little before 4:00 P.M. Monica was asleep on the living room couch, a book open on her lap, reading glasses down on her nose. He smiled and closed the door quietly when he went into the kitchen.

Moving stealthily, he opened the refrigerator door and considered the possibilities. He decided on a sandwich of anchovies, egg salad, and sliced tomato on a seeded roll. Rather than eat it while leaning over the sink, he put it on a sheet of waxed paper and carried it, along with an opened beer, into the study.

While he ate and drank, he added a few additional facts to the dossier of Leonard T. Bergdorfer. Then he shuffled the files of all four victims and tried to add to his list of commonalities.

The days of the week when the crimes were committed seemed to have no connection. Nor did the precise time of day. The exact location of the hotels, other than being in midtown Manhattan, suggested no particular pattern. The victims apparently had nothing in common other than being out-of-town males.

He threw his lists aside. Perhaps, he thought, he was deceiving himself by believing there was a link between the four killings that was eluding him. Maybe because he *wanted* a link, he had convinced himself that one existed.

An hour later, when Monica came into the study yawning and blinking, he was still staring morosely at the papers on his desk. When she asked him what he was doing, he replied, "Nothing." And that, he reflected sourly, was the truth.

* * *

There were days when he wanted to be the lowliest of plainclothesmen, assigned to ringing doorbells and asking questions. Or a deskbound researcher, poring over stacks of yellowed arrest records, looking for a name, a number, anything. At least those men were *doing* something.

It seemed to him that his role in the Hotel Ripper case was that of the "consultant" Boone had mentioned. He was the kindly old uncle whose advice was solicited, but who was then shunted aside while younger, more energetic men took over the legwork and the on-the-spot decision making.

He could not endure that inactivity. An investigation was precisely that: tracking, observing, studying, making a systematic examination and inquiry. A criminal investigation was a *search,* and he was being kept from the challenge, the excitement, the disappointments and rewards of *searching.*

Deputy Commissioner Ivar Thorsen had been right; he had cop's blood; he admitted it. He could not resist the chase; it was a pleasure almost as keen as sex. Age had nothing to do with it, nor physical energy. It was the mystery that enticed; he would never be free from the lust to reveal secrets.

His opportunity for action came sooner than expected . . .

On Friday morning, May 16th, the Delaneys sat down to breakfast at their kitchen table. The Chief looked with astonishment at the meal Monica had prepared: kippers, scrambled eggs, baked potatoes, sauteed onions.

"What," he wanted to know, "have you done to justify serving a magnificent breakfast like this?"

She laughed guiltily.

"It's the last meal you'll get from me today," she said. "I'm going to be busy. So I thought if you start out with a solid breakfast, it might keep you from sandwiches for a few hours. You're putting on weight."

"More of me to love," he said complacently, and dug into his food with great enjoyment. They ate busily for a while, then he asked casually, "What's going to keep you busy all day?"

"The American Women's Association is having a three-day convention in New York. I signed up for today's activities. Lectures and a film this morning. Then lunch. Seminars and a general discussion this afternoon. Then dinner tonight."

"You'll take a cab home?"

"Of course."

"Make the driver wait until you're inside the door."

"Yes, Daddy."

They ate awhile in silence, handing condiments back and forth. Delaney liked to put the buttered onions directly on his steaming potato, with a little coarsely ground black pepper.

"Where is the convention being held?" he asked idly. "Which hotel?"

"The Hilton."

He paused, holding a forkful of kipper halfway to his mouth. He gazed up in the air, over her head.

"How do you know the convention is at the Hilton?" he asked slowly.

"I got a notice in the mail. With an application blank."

"But there was no notice in the papers?"

"I didn't see any. Today is the first day. There may be stories tomorrow."

He took his bite of kipper, chewed it thoughtfully.

"But there was nothing in the papers about it?" he asked again. "No advance notice?"

"Edward, what *is* this?"

Instead of answering, he said, "What other conventions are being held at the Hilton today?"

"How on earth would I know that?"

"What conventions are being held at the Americana right now?"

"Edward, will you please tell me what this is all about?"

"In a minute," he said. "Let me finish this banquet first. It really is delicious."

"Hmph," she said, with scorn for this blatant effort to placate her. But she had to wait until he had cleaned his plate and poured each of them a second cup of black coffee.

"You don't know what conventions are at the Hilton," he said, "except for the one you're attending. I didn't know there were *any* conventions at the Hilton today. Neither of us know what conventions are being held right now at the Americana or any other New York hotel. Why should we know? We're not interested."

"So?"

"So for weeks now I've been looking for a link between the Hotel Ripper homicides. Something that ties them all together. Something we've overlooked."

She stared at him, puzzling it out.

"You mean there were conventions being held at all the hotels where the murders were committed?"

He stood, moved heavily around to her side of the table. He leaned down to kiss her cheek.

"My little detective," he said. "Thank you for a great breakfast and thank you for the lead. You're exactly right; the killings were at hotels where conventions were being held. And this was as early as the middle of February. Not precisely the height of the convention season in New York. But the killer picked hotels with conventions, sales meetings, big gatherings. Why not? She wants lots of people around, lots of single, unattached men. She wants crowds in the lobbies and dining rooms and cocktail lounges. She wants victims ready for a good time, maybe already lubricated with booze. So she selects hotels with conventions. Does that make sense?"

"It makes sense," Monica said. "In an awful way. But how does she know which hotels are having conventions?"

"Ah," he said, "good question. I've never seen a list in the daily papers. Have you?"

"No."

"But it must exist somewhere. The city's convention bureau or tourist bureau or some municipal office must keep track of these things. I know they make an effort to bring conventions to the city. Maybe they publish a daily or weekly or monthly list. And maybe the hotel association does, too. Anyway, the killer knows where the conventions are and heads for them."

"It doesn't sound like much of a clue to me," Monica said doubtfully.

"You never can tell," he said cheerfully. "You just never know. But if you do nothing, you have no chance to get lucky."

He helped Monica clean up and waited until she had departed for her first meeting at the New York Hilton. By that time he had figured out exactly how he was going to handle it.

He locked the front door, went into the study, and phoned Midtown Precinct South. He asked for Detective Second Grade Daniel Bentley, the expert on Manhattan hotels.

"Hello?"

"Bentley?"

"Yeah. Who's this?"

"Edward X. Delaney here."

"Oh, hiya, Chief. Don't tell me we got her?"

"No," Delaney said, laughing. "Not yet. How's it going?"

"Okay. I can't cover every bar and cocktail lounge, but I'm putting at least one man in every big hotel between Thirty-fourth and Fifty-ninth, river to river, between eight and two every night. You know we had a guy at the Cameron Arms when Bergdorfer was offed?"

"Yes, I heard that."

"So much for decoys," Bentley said mournfully. "But maybe next time we'll luck out."

Delaney paused, reflecting how everyone took it for granted that there would be a next time.

"About that Jerome Ashley kill at the Coolidge," Detective Bentley went on. "We checked with the bartenders and waitresses in the cocktail lounges. No one remembers a guy with scarred hands. But two of the waitresses on duty that night don't work there anymore. We're tracking them down. Nothing comes easy."

"It surely doesn't. Bentley, I wonder if you can help me."

"Anything you say, Chief."

"I'd like to talk to a hotel security officer. Preferably an ex-cop. Are there any working in hotels now?"

"Oh hell yes. I know of at least three. Guys who took early retirement. The pay's not bad and the work isn't all that hard, except maybe in the big hotels. Why do you ask? Anything cooking?"

"Not really. I just wanted to find out how hotel security works. Maybe we can convince them to beef up their patrols or put on extra guards to help us out."

"Good idea. Here are the guys I know . . ."

He gave Delaney the names of three men, one of which the Chief recognized.

"Holzer?" he asked. "Eddie Holzer? Was he in Narcotics for a while?"

"Sure, that's the one. You know him?"

"Yes. I worked with him on a couple of things."

"He's at the Hotel Osborne. It's not a fleabag, but it's not the Ritz either."

"I'll give him a call. Many thanks, Bentley."

"Anytime, Chief."

He hung up, wondering why he had lied—well, maybe not lied, but misled Detective Bentley as to the reason why he wanted to talk to a hotel security officer. He told himself that he just didn't want to bother a busy investigating officer with a slim lead and probably a dead-end search.

But he knew it wasn't that.

He looked up the number of the Hotel Osborne and called. He was told that Mr. Holzer wouldn't be at his desk until noon.

He had no sooner hung up than the phone rang. It was Ivar Thorsen. He said he was heading for a meeting and wanted to get Delaney's thinking on two subjects . . .

"This is with the brass and their public relations men from the offices of the Mayor, the Commissioner, and the Chief of Operations," he said. "About what we give to the media. First of all, do we release the business about the Hotel Ripper switching to a strawberry blond wig? Second, do we say we are definitely looking for a female killer? What do you think, Edward?"

Delaney pondered a moment. Then . . .

"Take the second one first . . . There's no way we can keep it quiet that we're looking for a woman. But fuzz the issue. Say the killer can be a man or a woman; we're looking for both."

"You still think it's a woman?"

"Of course. But I could be wrong; I admit it. The brass will want an out—just in case. Cover yourself on this one."

"All right, Edward; that makes sense. What about the wig?"

"Ivar, you've got to be definite on that. If the reporters print it was a blond wig, the killer will just switch to another color. That's what happened when Slavin fucked up."

"But if we don't warn tourists about a killer wearing a strawberry blond wig, aren't we endangering them?"

"Probably," Delaney said grimly. "But the decoys have got to have *something* to look for. We can't have her switching colors on us again."

"Jesus," Thorsen breathed, "if the papers find out, they'll crucify us."

"We've got to take the chance," the Chief urged. "And if the reporters dig it up, we can always say we didn't want the killer to go to another color—which is the truth."

"But meanwhile we're not warning the tourists."

"Deputy," Delaney said, his voice suddenly thick with fury, "do you want to stop this maniac or don't you?"

"All right, all right," Thorsen said hastily. "I'll try to get them to do it your way. I should be out of the meeting and uptown by late this afternoon. Can you meet me at Midtown North at, say, about four o'clock? I'll tell you how I made out and Boone can bring us up to date."

"I'll be there," Delaney said and hung up.

He was a little ashamed of himself for getting shirty with Ivar. He knew what the Admiral was up against: superior officers concerned with the image of the Department and the public relations aspects of this highly publicized case.

It was bullshit like that—image, public relations, politics—that had persuaded Edward X. Delaney it was time for him to retire from the New York Police Department. With his stubbornness, temper, and refusal to compromise, he knew he could never hope for higher rank.

"If you want to get along, you go along." That was probably true in every human organization. But being true didn't make it right. Delaney admitted he was a maverick, always had been. But he consoled himself with the thought that it was the mavericks of the world who got things done. Not the yes-men and the ass-kissers.

All *they* got for their efforts, he thought morosely, were success, wealth, and admiration.

Detective Bentley had been right; the Osborne wasn't much of a hotel. It could have been called the Seedy Grandeur. Located on 46th Street east of Seventh Avenue, it had a stone façade so gray and crumbled that it seemed bearded.

It was the type of Times Square hotel that had once hosted Enrico Caruso, Lillian Russell, and Diamond Jim Brady. Now it sheltered Sammy the Wop, Gage Sullivan, Dirty Sally, and others of hazy pasts and no futures.

Standing in the center of that chipped and peeling lobby, Delaney decided the odor was compounded of CN, pot, and ancient urinals. But the place seemed bustling enough, all the men equipped with toothpicks and all the women with orange hair. Tout sheets were everywhere.

Eddie Holzer was studying one, marking his choices. His feet were parked atop his splintered desk and he was wearing a greasy fedora. He held a cracked coffee cup in one trembling hand. Delaney guessed it didn't contain coffee.

Holzer glanced up when Delaney paused in the opened door.

"Chrissake," he said, lurching to his feet, "look what the cat drug in. Harya, Chief."

They shook hands, and Holzer brushed magazines and old newspapers off a straight chair. Delaney sat down cautiously. He looked at the other man with what he hoped was a friendly smile.

He knew Holzer's record, and it wasn't a happy one. The ex-detective had worked out of the Narcotics Division, and eventually the big money had bedazzled him. He had been allowed to retire before the DA moved in, but everyone in the Department knew he was tainted.

Now here he was, Chief of Security in a sleazy Times Square hotel, marking up a tipsheet and sipping cheap booze from a coffee cup. For all that, Delaney knew the man had been a clever cop, and he hoped enough remained.

They gossiped of this and that, remembering old times, talking of who was retired, who was dead. The Department put its mark on a man. He might be out for years and years, but he'd be in for the rest of his life.

Finally the chatter stopped.

Holzer looked at the Chief shrewdly. "I don't figure you stopped in by accident. How'd you find me?"

"Bentley," Delaney said.

"Dapper Dan?" Holzer said, laughing. "Good cop."

He was a florid, puffy man, rapidly going to flab. His face was a road map of capillaries, nose swollen, cheeks bloomy. Delaney had noted the early-morning shakes; Holzer made no effort to conceal them. If he was a man on the way down, it didn't seem to faze him.

The Chief wasn't sure how to get started, how much to reveal. But Holzer made it easy for him.

He said: "I hear you're helping out on the Hotel Ripper thing."

Delaney looked at him with astonishment. "Where did you hear that?"

Holzer flipped a palm back and forth. "Here and there. The grapevine. You know how things get around."

"They surely do," Delaney said. "Yes, I'm helping out. Deputy Commissioner Thorsen is an old friend of mine. I hunted you down because I—because we need your help."

He had pushed the right button. Holzer straightened up, his shoulders went back. Light came into his dulled eyes.

"You need *my* help?" he said, not believing. "On the case?"

Delaney nodded. "I think you're the man. You're a hotel security chief."

"Some hotel," Holzer said wanly. "Some security chief."

"Still . . ." Delaney said.

He explained that all the Ripper slayings had occurred at hotels in which conventions were being held. He was convinced the killer had prior knowledge of exactly where and when conventions and sales meetings and large gatherings were taking place.

Eddie Holzer listened intently, pulling at his slack lower lip.

"Yeah," he said, "that washes. I'll buy it. So?"

"So how would someone know the convention schedule in midtown Manhattan? It's not published in the papers."

Holzer thought a moment.

"These things are planned months ahead," he said. "Sometimes years ahead. To reserve the rooms, you understand. Someone in the Mayor's office would know. The outfit trying to bring new business to the city. The tourist bureau. Maybe there's a convention bureau. The Chamber of Commerce. Like that."

"Good," Delaney said, not mentioning that he had already thought of those sources. "Anyone else?"

"The hotel associations—they'd know."

"And . . . ?"

"Oh," Holzer said, "here . . ."

He bent over with some effort, rooted through the stack of magazines and newspapers he had swept off Delaney's chair. He came up with a thin, slick-paper magazine, skidded it across the desk to the Chief.

"New York hotel trade magazine," he said. "Comes out every week. It lists all the conventions in town."

"This goes to every hotel?" Delaney asked, flipping through the pages.

"I guess so," Holzer said. "It's a freebie. The ads pay for it. I think it goes to travel agencies, too. Maybe they send it out of town to big corporations—who knows? You'll have to check."

"Uh-huh," Delaney said. "Well, it's a place to start. Eddie, can I take this copy with me?"

"Be my guest," Holzer said. "I never look at the goddamned thing."

The Chief stood, held out his hand. The other man managed to get to his feet. They shook hands. Holzer didn't want to let go.

"Thank you, Eddie," Delaney said, pulling his hand away. "You've been a big help."

"Yeah?" Holzer said vaguely. "Well . . . you know. Anything I can do . . ."

"Take care of yourself," Delaney said gently.

"What? Me? Sure. You bet. I'm on top of the world."

Delaney nodded and got out of there. In the rancid lobby, a man and a woman were having a snarling argument. As the Chief passed, the woman spat in the man's face.

"Aw, honey," he said sadly, "now why did you want to go and do that for?"

Pierre au Tunnel was Delaney's favorite French restaurant on the West Side. And because it was Friday, he knew they would be serving bouillabaisse. The thought of that savory fish stew demolished the memory of Monica's scrumptious breakfast.

He walked uptown through Times Square, not at all offended by the flashy squalor. For all its ugliness, it had a strident vitality that stirred him. This section was quintessential New York. If you couldn't endure Times Square, you couldn't endure change.

But there were some things that didn't change; Pierre au Tunnel was just as he remembered it. The entrance was down a flight of stairs from the sidewalk. There was a long, narrow front room, bar on the right, a row of small tables on the left. In the rear was the main dining room, low-ceilinged, walls painted to simulate those of a tunnel or grotto.

It was a relaxed, reasonably priced restaurant, with good bread and a palatable house wine. Most of the patrons were habitues. It was the kind of neighborhood bistro where old customers kissed old waitresses.

The luncheon crowd had thinned out; Delaney was able to get his favorite table in the corner of the front room. He ordered the bouillabaisse and a small bottle of chilled muscadet. He tucked the corner of his napkin into his collar and spread the cloth across his chest.

He ate his stew slowly, dipping chunks of crusty French bread into the sauce. It was as good as he remembered it, as flavorful, and the hard, flinty wine was a perfect complement. He ordered espresso and a lemon ice for dessert and then, a little later, a pony of Armagnac.

Ordinarily, lunching alone at this restaurant, he would have amused himself by observing his fellow diners and the activity at the bar. But today, with the hotel trade magazine tucked carefully at his side, he had other matters to occupy him.

His original intention had been to take a more active role in the investigation. He had hoped that he alone might handle the search for persons with access to a list of current conventions in New York.

He saw now that such an inquiry was beyond his capabilities, or those of any other single detective. It would take a squad of ten, twenty, perhaps thirty men to track down all the sources, to make a list of all New Yorkers who might have access to a schedule of conventions.

It was a dull, routine, interminable task. And in the end, it might lead to nothing. But, he reflected grimly, it had to be done. Sipping his Armagnac, he began to plan how the men selected for the job should be organized and assigned.

He arrived at Midtown Precinct North a little after 3:30 P.M. Deputy Commissioner Ivar Thorsen was already present, and Delaney met with him and Abner Boone in the sergeant's office. Thorsen told them of the results of his meeting with the police brass.

"You got everything you wanted, Edward," he said. "I'll hold a press conference tomorrow. The official line will be that new leads are enlarging the investigation—which is true—and we are now looking for either a female or male perpetrator. Nothing will be released about the killer switching to a strawberry blond wig."

"Good," Boone said. "They picked up more blond hairs when they vacuumed Bergdorfer's suite at the Cameron Arms. What about the knife blade tip? And the Mace?"

"We'll keep those under wraps for the time being," Thorsen said. "We can't shoot our wad all at once. If the screams for action become too loud, we'll give them the investigation into the knife, and later into the tear gas. The PR guys were insistent on that. It looks like a long job of work, and we've got to hold something back to prove we're making progress."

Delaney and Boone both sighed, the Machiavellian manipulations of public relations beyond their ken.

"Edward," Thorsen went on, "we're keeping a lid on your involvement in the case for the time being."

"Keep it on forever as far as I'm concerned."

"Sergeant, all inquiries from the media will be referred to me. I will be the sole, repeat, *sole* spokesman for the Department on this case. Is that understood?"

"Yes, sir."

"Make certain your men understand it, too. I don't want any unauthorized statements to the press, and if I catch anyone leaking inside information, he'll find himself guarding vacant lots in the South Bronx so fast he won't know what hit him. Now . . . I don't suppose you have any great revelations to report, do you?"

"No, sir," Boone said, "nothing new. We're just getting organized on the knife and tear gas jobs. Lieutenant Crane's research hasn't turned up anything."

"I have something," Delaney said, and they looked at him.

He told them of his belief that the killer had prior knowledge of the location and dates of conventions held in midtown Manhattan. He listed the sources of such information and showed them the hotel trade magazine he had been given by Eddie Holzer.

"It's got to be someone connected with the hotel or convention business in some way," he argued. "We'll have to compile a list of everyone in the city who has access to the convention schedule."

Thorsen was aghast.

"My God, Edward!" he burst out. "That could be thousands of people!"

"Hundreds, certainly," Delaney said stonily. "But it's got to be done. Sergeant?"

"I guess so," Boone said glumly. "You want men *and* women listed?"

"Yes," Delaney said, nodding. "Just to cover ourselves. No use in doing the job twice. What do you figure—twenty or thirty more detectives?"

"At least," the sergeant said.

Thorsen groaned. "All right," he said finally, "you'll get them. Who's going to handle it?"

"I'll get it organized and rolling," Sergeant Boone said. "We better call in Slavin on the scheduling."

Delaney left them discussing the exact number of men needed and the office space that would be required. He walked uptown from the precinct house until he found a telephone booth in working order.

He called Thomas Handry.

He told the reporter there would be a press conference held at police headquarters the following day. An expanded investigation would be announced and it would be stated that the killer could be either a man or a woman. Delaney said nothing about the blond wig, the knife blade tip, or the Chemical Mace.

"So?" Handry said. "What's so new and exciting? An expanded investigation—big deal."

"What's new and exciting," Delaney explained patiently, "is that actually the investigation is zeroing in on a female killer."

A moment of silence . . .

"So that research convinced you?" Handry said. "And you convinced them?"

"Half-convinced," Delaney said. "Some of them still think I'm blowing smoke."

He then went over the evidence that had persuaded him the Hotel Ripper was female. He ended by telling Handry that the timing of the homicides matched a woman's menstrual periods.

"Crazy," the reporter said. "You're sure about all this?"

"Sure I'm sure. I'm giving you this stuff in advance of the press conference for background, not for publication. I owe you one. Also, I thought you might want to prepare by digging out old stories on women killers."

"I already have," Handry said. "It wasn't hard to figure how your mind was working. I started looking into the history of mass murders. A series of homicides in which the killer is a stranger to the victims. One criminologist calls them 'multicides.' "

"Multicides," Delaney repeated. "That's a new one on me. Good name. What did you find?"

"Since 1900, there have been about twenty-five cases in the United States, with the number of victims ranging from seven to more than thirty. The scary thing is that more than half of those twenty-five cases have occurred since 1960. In other words, the incidence of multicides is increasing. More and more mass killings by strangers."

"Yes," Delaney said, "I was aware of that."

"And I've got bad news for you, Chief."

"What's that?"

"Of those twenty-five cases of multicide since 1900, only one was committed by a woman."

"Oh?" Delaney said. "Did they catch her?"

"No," Handry said.

Monica came out of the bathroom, hair in curlers, face cold-creamed, a strap of her nightgown held up with a safety pin.

"The Creature from Outer Space," she announced cheerfully.

He looked at her with a vacant smile. He had started to undress. Doffed his dark cheviot jacket and vest, after first removing watch and chain from waistcoat pockets. The clumpy gold chain had been his grandfather's. At one end was a hunter that had belonged to his father and had stopped fifty years ago. Twenty minutes to noon. Or midnight.

At the other end of the chain was a jeweled miniature of his detective's badge, given to him by his wife on his retirement.

Vest and jacket hung away, he seated himself heavily on the edge of his bed. He started to unlace his ankle-high shoes of black kangaroo leather, polished to a high gloss. He was seated there, one shoe dangling from his big hands, when Monica came out of the bathroom.

He watched her climb into bed. She propped pillows against the headboard, sat up with blanket and sheet pulled to her waist. She donned her Benjamin Franklin glasses, picked up a book from the bedside table.

"What did you eat today?" she demanded, peering at him over her glasses.

"Not much," he lied effortlessly. "After that mighty breakfast this morning, I didn't need much. Skipped lunch. Had a sandwich and a beer tonight."

"One sandwich?"

"Just one."

"What kind?"

"Sliced turkey, cole slaw, lettuce and tomato on rye. With Russian dressing."

"That would do it," she said, nodding. "No wonder you look so remote."

"Remote?" he said. "Do I?"

He bent to unlace his other shoe and slide it off. He peeled away his heavy wool socks. Comfortable shoes and thick socks: secrets of a street cop's success.

When he straightened up, he saw that Monica was still staring at him.

"How is the case going?" she asked quietly.

"All right. It's really in the early stages. Just beginning to move."

"Everyone's talking about the Hotel Ripper. At the meetings today, it came up again and again. In informal conversations, I mean; not in lectures. Edward, people make jokes and laugh, but they're really frightened."

"Of course," he said. "Who wouldn't be?"

"You still think it's a woman?"

"Yes."

He stood, began to take off tie and shirt. Still she had not opened her book. She watched him empty his trouser pockets onto the bureau top.

"I wasn't going to tell you this," she said, "but I think I will."

He stopped what he was doing, turned to face her.

"Tell me what?" he said.

"I asked people I met if they thought the Hotel Ripper could be a woman. My own little survey of public opinion. I asked six people: three men and three women. All the men said the killer couldn't possibly be a woman, and all the women I asked said it could be a woman. Isn't that odd?"

"Interesting," he said. "But I don't know what it means—do you?"

"Not exactly. Except that men seem to have a higher opinion of women than women do of themselves."

He went to shower. He brushed his teeth, pulled on his pajamas. He came out, turned off the overhead light in the bedroom. Monica was reading by the bed-lamp. He got into his bed, pulled up the blanket. He lay awake, hands behind his head, staring at the ceiling.

"Why would a woman do such a thing?" he asked, turning his head to look at her.

She put down her book. "I thought you weren't interested in motives."

"Surely I didn't say that. I said I wasn't interested in *causes*. There's a difference. Every cop is interested in motives. Has to be. That's what helps solve cases. Not the underlying psychological or social causes, but the immediate motive. A man can kill from greed. That's important to a cop. What caused the greed is of little consequence. What immediate motive could a woman have for a series of homicides like this? Revenge? She mutilates their genitals. Could she have been a rape victim?"

"Could be," Monica said promptly. "It's reason enough. But it doesn't even have to be rape. Maybe she's been used by men all her life. Maybe they've just screwed her and deserted her. Made her feel like a thing. Without value. So she's getting back at them."

"Yes," he said, "that listens; it's a possibility. There's something sexual involved here, and I don't know what it is. Could she be an out-and-out sadist?"

"No," Monica said, "I don't think so. Physical sadism amongst women isn't all that common. And sadists prefer slow suffering to quick death."

"Emotional?" he said. "Could it be that? She's been jilted by a man. Betrayed. The woman scorned . . ."

"Mmm . . ." his wife said, considering. "No, I don't believe that. A woman might be terribly hurt by one man, but I can't believe she'd try to restore her self-esteem by killing strangers. I think your first idea is right: it's something sexual."

"It could be fear," he said. "Fear of sex with a man."

She looked at him, puzzled.

"I don't follow," she said. "If the killer is afraid of sex, she wouldn't go willingly to the hotel rooms of strange men."

"She might," he said. "To be attracted by what we dread is a very human emotion. Then, when she gets there, fear conquers desire."

"Edward, you make her sound a very complex woman."

"I think she is."

He went back to staring at the ceiling.

"There's another possibility," he said in a low voice.

"What's that?"

"She simply enjoys killing. *Enjoys* it."

"Oh Edward, I can't believe that."

"Because you can't feel it. Any more than you can believe that some people derive pleasure from being whipped. But such things exist."

"I suppose so," she said in a small voice. "Well, there's a fine selection of motives for you. Which do you suspect it is?"

He was silent for a brief time. Then . . .

"What I suspect is that it is not a single motive, but a combination of things. We rarely act for one reason. It's usually a mixture. Can you give me *one* reason why the Son of Sam did what he did? So I think this killer is driven by several motives."

"The poor woman," Monica said sadly.

"Poor woman?" he said. "You sympathize with her? Feel sorry for her?"

"Of course," she said. "Don't you?"

He had wanted to play a more active role in the investigation, and during the last two weeks of May he got his chance.

All the squad officers involved in the case came to him. They knew Deputy Commissioner Thorsen was in command, transmitting his orders through Sergeant Boone, but they sought out Edward X. Delaney for advice and counsel. They knew his record and experience. And he was retired brass; there was nothing to fear from him . . .

"Chief," Detective Aaron Johnson said, "I got the word out to all my snitches, but there's not a whisper of any tear gas being peddled on the street."

"Any burglaries of army posts, police stations, or National Guard armories? Any rip-offs of chemical factories?"

"Negative," Johnson said. "Thefts of weapons and high explosives, but no record of anyone lifting tear gas in cans, cartridges, generators, or whatever. The problem here, Chief, is that the Lab Services Section can't swear the stuff was Chemical Mace. But if it was carried in a pocket-size aerosol dispenser, it probably was. So where do we go from here?"

"Find out who makes it and who packages it. Get a list of distributors and wholesalers. Trace it to retailers in this area. Slavin says it's against the law for a New Yorker to buy the stuff, but it must be available to law enforcement agencies for riot control and so forth. Maybe prisons and private security companies can legally buy it. Maybe even a bank guard or night watchman can carry it—I don't know. Find out, and try to get a line on every can that came into this area in the past year."

"Gotcha," Johnson said.

"Chief," Sergeant Thomas K. Broderick said, "look at this . . ."

He dangled a small, sealed plastic bag in front of Delaney. The Chief inspected it curiously. Inside the bag was a half-inch of gleaming knife blade tip. On the upper half was part of the groove designed to facilitate opening the blade with a fingernail.

"That's it?" Delaney asked.

"That's it," Broderick said. "Fresh from Bergdorfer's slashed throat. We got a break on this one, Chief. Most pocket knives in this country are made with blades of high-grade carbon steel. The lab says this little mother is drop-forged Swedish stainless steel. How about that!"

"Beautiful," the Chief said. "Did you trace it?"

Broderick took a knife from his pocket and handed it to the Chief. It had bright red plastic handles bearing the crest of Switzerland.

"Called a Swiss Army knife," the detective said. "Or sometimes Swiss Army Officers' knives. They come in at least eight different sizes. The largest is practically a pocket tool kit. This is a medium-sized one. Open the big blade."

Obediently, Delaney folded back the largest blade. The two men bent over the knife, comparing the whole blade with the tip in the plastic bag.

"Looks like it," the Chief said.

"Identical," Broderick assured him. "The lab checked it out. But where do we go from here? These knives are sold in every good cutlery and hardware store in the city. And just to make the cheese more binding, they're also sold through mail order. Dead end."

"No," Delaney said, "not yet. Start with midtown Manhattan. Say from Thirty-fourth Street to Fifty-ninth Street, river to river. Make a list of every store in that area that carries this knife. The chances are good the killer will try to replace her broken knife with a new one just like it. Have your men visit every store and talk to the clerks. We want the name and address of everyone who buys a knife like this."

"How is the clerk going to do that? If the customer pays cash?"

"Uh . . . the clerks should tell the customer he wants the name and address for a free mail order catalogue the store is sending out. If the customer doesn't go for that scam and refuses to give name and address, the clerk should take a good look and then call you and give the description. Leave your phone number at every store; maybe they can stall the customer long enough for you or one of your men to get there. Tell the clerks to watch especially for young women, five-five to five-seven. Got it?"

"Got it," Broderick said. "But what if we come up with bupkes?"

"Then we'll do the same thing in all of Manhattan," Delaney said without humor. "And then we'll start on Brooklyn and the Bronx."

"It looks like a long, hot summer," Detective Broderick said, groaning.

"Chief," Lieutenant Wilson T. Crane said, "we've got sixteen possibles from Records. These are women between the ages of twenty and fifty with sheets that include violent felonies. We're tracking them all down and getting their alibis for the night of the homicides. None of them used the same MO as the Hotel Ripper."

"Too much to hope for," Delaney said. "I don't think our target has a sheet, but it's got to be checked out. What about prisons and asylums?"

"No recent releases or escapes that fit the profile," Crane said. "We're calling and writing all over the country, but nothing promising yet."

"Have you contacted Interpol?"

The lieutenant stared at him.

"No, Chief, we haven't," he admitted. "The FBI, but not Interpol."

"Send them a query," Delaney advised. "And Scotland Yard, too, while you're at it."

"Will do," Crane said.

"Chief," Detective Daniel Bentley said, "we went back to the bars at the Hotel Coolidge and asked if anyone remembered serving a man with scarred hands. No one did. But two of the cocktail waitresses who worked in the New Orleans Room the night Jerome Ashley was offed, don't work there anymore. We traced one. She's working in a massage parlor now—would you believe it? She doesn't remember any scarred hands. The other waitress went out to the Coast. Her mother doesn't have an address for her, but promises to ask the girl to call us if she hears from her. Don't hold your breath."

"Keep on it," Delaney said. "Don't let it slide."

"We'll keep on it," Bentley promised.

"Chief," Sergeant Abner Boone said, "I think we've got this thing organized. The hotel trade magazine gave us a copy of their mailing list. We're checking out every hotel in the city that got a copy and making a list of everyone who might have had access to it. I've got men checking the Mayor's office, Chamber of Commerce, hotel associations, visitors' bureau, and so forth. As the names come in, a deskman is compiling two master lists, male and female, with names listed in alphabetical order. How does that sound?"

"You're getting the addresses, too?"

"Right. And their age, when it's available. Even approximate age. Chief, we've got more than three hundred names already. It'll probably run over a thousand before we're through, and even then I won't swear we'll have everyone in New York with prior knowledge of the convention schedule."

"I know," Delaney said grimly, "but we've got to do it."

From all these meetings with the squad commanders, he came away with the feeling that morale was high, the men were doing their jobs with no more than normal grumbling.

After three months of bewilderment and relative inaction, they had finally been turned loose on the chase, their quarry dimly glimpsed but undeniably *there*. No man involved in the investigation thought what he was doing was without value, no matter how dull it might be.

It was not the first time that Edward X. Delaney had been struck by the contrast between the drama of a heinous crime and the dry minutiae of the investigation. The act was (sometimes) high tragedy; the search was (sometimes) low comedy.

The reason was obvious, of course. The criminal acted in hot passion; the detective had only cold resolve. The criminal was a child of the theater, inspired, thinking the play would go on forever. But along came the detective, a lumpish, methodical fellow, seeking only to ring down the curtain.

On May 30th, all the detectives met at Midtown Precinct North. If Delaney's hypothesis was correct—and most of them now believed it was, simply because no one had suggested any other theory that encompassed all the known facts—the next Hotel Ripper slaying would take place, or be attempted, during the week of June 1–7, and probably during midweek.

It was decided to assign every available man to the role of decoy. With the aid of the hotels' beefed-up security forces, all bars and cocktail lounges in large midtown Manhattan hotels would be covered from 8:00 P.M. until closing.

The lieutenants and sergeants worked out a schedule so that a "hot line" at Midtown North would be manned constantly during those hours. In addition, a standby squad of five men was stationed at Midtown South as backup, to be summoned as needed. The Crime Scene Unit was alerted; one of their vans took up position on West 54th Street.

Monica Delaney noted the fretfulness of her husband during the evenings of June 1–3. He picked up books and tossed them aside. Sat staring for an hour at an opened newspaper without turning a page. Stomped about the house disconsolately, head lowered, hands in his pockets.

She forbore to question the cause of his discontent; she knew. Wisely, she let him "stew in his own juice." But she wondered what would happen to him if events proved his precious theory wrong.

On the night of June 4th, a Wednesday, they were seated in the living room on opposite sides of the cocktail table, playing a desultory game of gin rummy. The Chief had been winning steadily, but shortly after 11:00 P.M., he threw his cards down in disgust and lurched to his feet.

"The hell with it," he said roughly. "I'm going to Midtown."

"What do you think you can do?" his wife asked quietly. "You'll just be in the way. The men will think you're checking up on them, that you don't trust them to do their jobs."

"You're right," he said immediately and dropped back into his chair. "I just feel so damned useless."

She looked at him sympathetically, knowing what this case had come to mean to him: that his expertise was valued, that his age was no drawback, that he was needed and wanted.

There he sat, a stern, rumpled mountain of a man. Gray hair bristled from his big head. His features were heavy, brooding. With his thick, rounded shoulders, he was almost brutish in appearance.

But she knew that behind the harsh façade, a more delicate man was hidden. He was at home in art museums, enjoyed good food and drink, and found pleasure in reading poetry—although it had to rhyme.

More important, he was a virile, tender, and considerate lover. He adored the children. He did not find tears or embraces unmanly. And, unknown to all but the women in his life, there was a core of humility in him.

He had been born and raised a Catholic, although he had long since ceased attending church. But she wondered if he had ever lost his faith. There was steel there that transcended personal pride in his profession and trust in his own rightness.

He had once confessed to her that Barbara, his first wife, had accused him of believing himself God's surrogate on earth. She thought Barbara had been close to the truth; there were times when he acted like a weapon of judgment and saw his life as one long tour of duty.

Musing on the contradictions of the man she loved, she gathered up the cards and put them away.

"Coffee?" she asked idly. "Pecan ring?"

"Coffee would be nice," he said, "but I'll skip the cake. You go ahead."

She was heating the water when the phone shrilled. She picked up the kitchen extension.

"Abner Boone, Mrs. Delaney," the sergeant said, his voice at once hard and hollow. "Could I speak to the Chief, please?"

She didn't ask him the reason for his call. She went back into the living room. Her husband was already on his feet, tugging down vest and jacket. They stared at each other.

"Sergeant Boone," she said.

He nodded, face expressionless. "I'll take it in the study."

She went back into the kitchen and waited for the water to boil, her arms folded, hands clutching her elbows tightly. She heard him come out of the study, go to the hallway closet. He came into the kitchen carrying the straw skimmer he donned every June 1st, regardless of the weather.

"The Hotel Adler," he told her. "About a half-hour ago. They've got the hotel cordoned, but she's probably long gone. I'll be an hour or two. Don't wait up for me."

She nodded and he bent to kiss her cheek.

"Take care," she said as lightly as she could.

He smiled and was gone.

When he arrived at Seventh Avenue and 50th Street, the Hotel Adler was still cordoned, sawhorses holding back a gathering crowd. Two uniformed officers stood in front of the closed glass doors listening to the loud arguments of three men who were apparently reporters demanding entrance.

"No one gets in," one of the cops said in a remarkably placid voice. "But no one. That's orders."

"The public has a right to know," one of the men yelled.

The officer looked at him pityingly. "Hah-hah," he said.

The Chief plucked at the patrolman's sleeve. "I am Edward X. Delaney," he said. "Sergeant Boone is expecting me."

The cop took a quick glance at a piece of scrap paper crumpled in his hand. "Right," he said. "You're cleared."

He held the door open for Delaney. The Chief strode into the lobby, hearing the howls of rage and frustration from the newsmen on the sidewalk.

There was a throng in the lobby being herded by plainclothesmen into a single file. The line was moving toward a cardtable that had been set up in one corner. There, identification was requested, names and addresses written down.

This operation was being supervised by Sergeant Broderick. When Delaney caught his eye, the sergeant waved and made his way through the mob to the Chief's side. He leaned close.

"Fifth floor," he said in a low voice. "A butcher shop. An old couple next door heard sounds of a fight. The old lady wanted to call the desk and complain; the old geezer didn't want to make trouble. By the time they ended the argument and decided to call, it was too late; a security man found the stiff. I swear we got here no more than a half-hour after it happened."

"Decoys?" Delaney asked.

"Two," Broderick said. "A hotel man in the pub, one of our guys in the cocktail lounge. Both of them claim they saw no one who looked like the perp."

The Chief grunted. "I better go up."

"Hang on to your cookies," Broderick said, grinning.

The fifth floor corridor was crowded with uniformed cops, ambulance men, detectives, the DA's man, and precinct officers. Delaney made his way through the crush. Sergeant Boone and Ivar Thorsen were standing in the hallway, just outside an open door.

The three men shook hands ceremoniously, solemn mourners at a funeral. Delaney took a quick look through the door.

"Jesus Christ," he said softly.

"Yeah," Boone said, "a helluva fight. And then the cutting. The ME says not much more than an hour ago. Two, tops."

"I'm getting too old for this kind of thing," Thorsen said, his face ashen. "The guy's in ribbons."

"Any doubt that it was the Ripper?"

"No," Boone said. "Throat slashed and nuts stabbed. But the doc says he might have been dead when that happened."

"Any ID?"

Sergeant Boone flipped the pages of his notebook, found what he was seeking. "Get a load of this," he said. "His paper says he was Nicholas Telemachus Pappatizos. How do you like that? Home address was Las Vegas."

"The hotel security chief made him," Thorsen said. "Known as Nick Pappy and Poppa Nick. Also called The Magician. A small-time hood. Mostly cons and extortion. We're running him through Records right now."

Delaney looked through the doorway again. The small room was an abattoir. Walls splattered with gobbets of dripping blood. Rug soaked. Furniture upended, clothing scattered. A lamp smashed. The drained corpse was a jigsaw of red and white.

"Naked," Delaney said. "But he did put up a fight."

The three men watched the Crime Scene Unit move about the room, dusting for prints, vacuuming the clear patches of carpet, picking up hairs and shards of glass with tweezers and dropping them into plastic bags.

The two technicians were Lou Gorki and Tommy Callahan, the men Delaney had met in Jerome Ashley's room at the Hotel Coolidge. Now Gorki came to the door. He was carrying a big plastic syringe that looked like the kind used to baste roasts. But this one was half-filled with blood. Gorki was grinning.

"I think we got lucky," he announced. He held up the syringe. "From the bathroom floor. It's tile, and the blood didn't soak in. And we got here before it had a chance to dry. I got enough here for a transfusion. I figure it's the killer's blood. *Got* to be. The clunk was sliced to hash. No way was he going to make it to the bathroom and bleed on the tile. Also, we got bloody towels and stains in the sink where the perp washed. It looks good."

"Tell the lab I want a report on that blood immediately," Thorsen said. "That means before morning."

"I'll tell them," Gorki said doubtfully.

"Prints?" Boone asked.

"Doesn't look good. The usual partials and smears. The faucet handles in the bathroom were wiped clean."

"So if she was hurt," Delaney said, "it wasn't so bad that she didn't remember to get rid of her prints."

"Right," Gorki said. "That's the way it looks. Give us another fifteen minutes and then the meat's all yours."

But it was almost a half-hour before the CSU men packed up their heavy kits and departed. Deputy Commissioner Thorsen decided to go with them to see what he could do to expedite blood-typing by the Lab Services Section. In truth, Thorsen looked ill.

Then Delaney and Boone had to wait an additional ten minutes while a photographer and cartographer recorded the scene. Finally they stepped into the room, followed by Detectives Aaron Johnson and Daniel Bentley.

The four men leaned over the congealing corpse.

"How the hell did she do that?" Johnson said wonderingly. "The guy had muscles; he's not going to stand there and let a woman cut him up."

"Maybe the first stab was a surprise," Bentley said. "Weakened him enough so she could hack him to chunks."

"That makes sense," Boone said. "But how did she get cut? Gorki says she bled in the bathroom. No signs of a second knife—unless it's under his body. Anyone want to roll him over?"

"I'll pass," Johnson said. "I had barbecued ribs for dinner."

"They may have fought for her knife," Delaney said, "and she got cut in the struggle. Boone, you better alert the hospitals."

"God *damn* it!" the sergeant said, furious at his lapse, and rushed for the phone.

Delaney hung around until the ambulance men came in and rolled Nicholas Telemachus Pappatizos onto a body sheet. There was no knife under the body. Only blood.

The other detectives went down to the lobby to assist in the questioning. Delaney stayed in the room, wandering about, peeking into the bathroom. He saw nothing of significance. Perhaps, he thought, because he was shaken by the echoes of violence. Tommy Callahan came back and continued the Crime Scene Unit investigation.

He pushed the victim's discarded clothing into plastic bags and labeled them. He collected toothbrush, soap, and toilet articles from the bathroom and labeled those. Then he popped the lock on the single suitcase in the room and began to inventory the contents.

"Look at this, Chief," he said. "I better have a witness that I found this . . ."

Using a pencil through the trigger guard, he fished a dinky, chrome-plated automatic pistol from the suitcase. He sniffed cautiously at the muzzle.

"Clean," he said. "Looks like a .32."

"Or .22," Delaney said. "Gambler's gun. Good for maybe twenty feet, but you'd have to be Deadeye Dick to hit your target. Find anything else?"

"Two decks of playing cards. Nice clothes. Silk pajamas. He lived well."

"For a while," Delaney said.

He left the death room and took the elevator to the lobby. The crowd had thinned, but police were still quizzing residents and visitors. Out on the sidewalk, the mob of noisy newspapermen had grown. In the street, two TV vans were setting up lights and cameras.

Delaney pushed through the throng and crossed the avenue. He turned to look back at the hotel. If she came out onto Seventh, she could have taken a bus or subway. But if she was wounded, she probably caught a cab. He hoped Sergeant Boone would remember to check cabdrivers who might have been in the vicinity at the time.

He walked over to Sixth Avenue and got a cab going uptown. He was home in ten minutes, double-locked and chained the door behind him. It was then almost 2:00 A.M.

"Is that you, Edward?" Monica called nervously from upstairs.

"It's me," he assured her. "I'll be right up."

He hung his skimmer away, then went through his nightly routine: checking the locks on every door and window in the house, even those in the vacant children's rooms. Not for the first time did he decide this dwelling was too large for just Monica and him.

They could sell the building at a big profit and buy a small cooperative apartment or a small house in the suburbs. It made sense. But he knew they never would, and he supposed he would die in that old brownstone. The thought did not dismay him.

He left a night-light burning in the front hallway, then climbed the stairs slowly to the bedroom. He was not physically weary, but he felt emptied and weak. The sight of that slaughterhouse had drained him, diminished him.

Monica was lying on her side, breathing deeply, and he thought she was asleep. She had left the bathroom light on. He undressed quickly, not bothering to shower. He switched off the light, moved cautiously across the darkened room, climbed into bed.

He lay awake, trying to rid his mind of the images that thronged. But he kept seeing the jigsaw corpse and shook his head angrily.

He heard the rustle of bedclothes. In a moment Monica lifted his blanket and sheet and slipped in next to him. She fitted herself to his back, her knees bending with his. She dug an arm beneath him so she could hold him tightly, encircled.

"Was it bad?" she whispered.

He nodded in the darkness and thought of what Thorsen had said: "I'm getting too old for this kind of thing." Delaney turned to face his wife, moved closer. She was soft, warm, strong. He held on, and felt alive and safe.

After a while he slept. He roused briefly when Monica went back to her own bed, then drifted again into a deep and dreamless slumber.

When the phone rang, he roused slowly and reached to fumble for the bedside lamp. When he found the switch, he saw it was a little after 6:00 A.M. Monica was sitting up in bed, looking at him wide-eyed.

He cleared his throat.

"Edward X. Delaney here."

"Edward, this is Ivar. I wanted you to know as soon as possible. They've run the first part of the blood analysis. You were right. Caucasian female. Congratulations."

"Thank you," Delaney said.

9

Zoe Kohler came out of the hairdresser's, poking self-consciously at her new coiffure. Her hair had been shampooed, cut and styled, and treated with a spray guaranteed to give it gloss and weight while leaving it perfectly manageable.

Now it was shorter, hugged her head like a helmet, with feathery wisps at temples and cheeks. It was undeniably shinier, though it seemed to her darker and stiffer. The hairdresser had assured her it took ten years off her life, and then tried to sell her a complete makeup transformation. But she wasn't yet ready for that.

She walked slowly toward Madison Avenue, still limping slightly although the cut in her thigh was healing nicely. Everett Pinckney had asked her about the limp. She told him that she had turned her ankle, and that satisfied him.

She passed a newsstand and saw the headlines were still devoted to the murder at the Hotel Adler. She had not been surprised to read that the victim had a police record. One columnist called him a "nefarious character." Zoe Kohler agreed with that judgment.

Two days after the homicide, the police had announced that the Hotel Ripper was definitely a woman. The media had responded enthusiastically with enlarged coverage of the story and interviews with psychologists, feminists, and criminologists.

At least three female newspaper columnists and one female TV news reporter had made fervent pleas to the Hotel Ripper to contact them personally, promising sympathetic understanding and professional help. One afternoon tabloid had offered $25,000 to the Ripper if she would surrender to the paper and relate her life story.

Even more amazing to Zoe Kohler was a casual mention that in a single day, the New York Police Department had received statements from forty-three women claiming to be the killer. All these "confessions" had been investigated and found to be false.

Zoe had asked Mr. Pinckney how the police could be so certain that the Hotel Ripper was a woman. He said they obviously had hard evidence that indicated it. Bloodstains, for instance. They could do wonderful things with blood analysis these days.

Barney McMillan, who was present during this conversation, slyly suggested that another factor might have been the results of the autopsy which could show if the victim had sexual intercourse just before he was killed.

"He probably died happy," McMillan said.

Zoe Kohler wasn't particularly alarmed that the police investigation was now directed toward finding a female murderer. And she had read that plainclothesmen were now being stationed in hotel cocktail lounges in midtown Manhattan. She thought vaguely that it might be necessary to seek her adventures farther afield.

She had been fortunate so far, mostly because of careful planning. She was exhilarated by the fearful excitement she had caused. More than that, the secret that she alone knew gave her an almost physical pleasure, a self-esteem she had never felt before.

All those newspaper stories, all those television broadcasts and radio bulletins were about *her*. What she felt came very close to pride and, with her new hairdo and despite her limp, she walked taller, head up, glowing, and felt herself queen of the city.

She paused on Madison Avenue to look in the show windows of a shop specializing in clothing for children, from infants to ten-year-olds. The prices were shockingly high for such small garments, but the little dresses and sweaters, jeans and overalls, were smartly designed.

Zoe stared at the eyelet cotton and bright plaids, the crisp party dresses and pristine nightgowns. All so young, so—so innocent. She remembered well that she had been dressed in clean, unsoiled clothing like that: fabrics fresh against her skin, stiff with starch, rustling with their newness.

"You must be a little lady," her mother had said. "And look at these adorable white gloves!"

"You must keep yourself clean and spotless," her mother had said. "Never run. Try not to become perspired. Move slowly and gracefully."

"A little lady always listens," her mother had said. "A little lady speaks in a quiet, refined voice, enunciating clearly."

So Zoe avoided mud puddles, learned the secrets of the kitchen. She did her homework every night and was awarded good report cards. All her parents' friends remarked on what a paragon she was.

"A real little lady." That's what the adults said about Zoe Kohler.

Seeing those immaculate garments in a Madison Avenue shop brought it all back: the spotlessness of her home, the unblemished clothing she wore, the purity of her childhood. Youth without taint . . .

On the evening of June 14th, a Saturday, Zoe had dinner with Ernest Mittle in the dining room of the Hotel Gramercy Park. They were surprised to find they were the youngest patrons in that sedate chamber.

Zoe Kohler, glancing about, saw Ernest and herself in twenty years, and found comfort in it. Well-groomed women and respectable men. Dignity and decorum. Low voices and small gestures. How could some people reject the graces of civilization?

She looked at the man sitting opposite and was content. Courtesy and kindness were not dead.

Ernest was wearing a navy blue suit, white shirt, maroon tie. His fine, flaxen hair was brushed to a gleam. Cheeks and chin were so smooth and fair that they seemed never to have known a razor.

He appeared so slight to Zoe. There was something limpid about him, an untroubled innocence. He buttered a breadstick thoroughly and precisely and crunched it with shining teeth. His hands and feet were small. He was almost a miniature man, painted with a one-hair brush, refined to purity.

After dinner they stopped at the dim bar for a Strega. Here was a more electric ambience. The patrons were younger, noisier, and there were shouts of laughter. Braless women and bearded men.

"What would you like to do, Zoe?" Ernest asked, holding her hand and stroking her fingers lightly. "A movie? A nightclub? Would you like to go dancing somewhere?"

She considered a moment. "A disco. Ernie, could we go to a disco? We don't have to dance. Just have a glass of wine and see what's going on."

"Why not?" he said bravely, and she thought of her gold bracelet.

An hour later they were seated at a minuscule table in a barnlike room on East 58th Street. They were the only customers, although lights were flashing and flickering and music boomed from a dozen speakers in such volume that the walls trembled.

"You wanted to see what's going on?" Ernest shouted, laughing. "Nothing's going on!"

But they were early. By the time they finished their second round of white wine, the disco was half-filled, the dance floor was filling up, and newcomers were rushing through the entrance, stamping, writhing, whirling before they were shown to tables.

It was a festival! a carnival! What costumes! What disguises! Naked flesh and glittering cloth. A kaleidoscope of eye-aching colors. All those jerking bodies frozen momentarily in stroboscopic light. The driving din! Smell of perfume and sweat. Shuffle of a hundred feet. The thunder!

Zoe Kohler and Ernest Mittle looked at each other. Now they were the oldest in the room, smashed by cacophonous music, assaulted by the wildly sexual gyrations on the floor. It wasn't a younger generation they were watching; it was a new world.

There a woman with breasts swinging free from a low-cut shirt. There a man with genitals delineated beneath skin-tight pants of pink satin. Bare necks, arms, shoulders. Navels. Hot shorts, miniskirts, vinyl boots. Rumps. Tits and cocks.

Grasping hands. Sliding hands. Grinding hips. Opened thighs. Stroking. Gasps and shiny grins. Flickering tongues and wild eyes. A churn of heaving bodies, the room rocking, seeming to tilt.

Everything tilting . . .

"Let's dance," Ernest yelled in her ear. "It's so crowded, no one will notice us."

On the floor, they were swallowed up, engulfed and hidden. They became part of the slough. Hot flesh poured them together. They were in a fevered flood, swept away.

They tried to move in time to the music, but they were daunted by the flung bodies about them. They huddled close, staggering upright, trying to keep their balance, laughing nervously and holding each other to survive.

For a moment, just a moment, they were one, knees to shoulders, welded tight. Zoe felt his slightness, his soft heat. She did not draw away, but he did. Slowly, with difficulty, he pulled her clear, guided her back to their table.

"Oh wow," he said, "what a crush! That's madness!"

"Yes," she said. "Could I have another glass of wine, please?"

They didn't try to dance again, but they didn't want to leave.

"They're not so much younger than we are," Zoe said.

"No," he agreed, "not so much."

They sat at their table, drinking white wine and looking with amusement, fear, and envy at the frenzied activity around them. The things they saw, flashing lights; the things they heard, pounding rhythm—all stunned them.

They glanced at each other, and their clasped hands tightened. Never had they felt so alone and together.

Still, still, there was an awful fascination. All that nudity. All that sexuality. It lured. They both felt the pull.

Zoe saw one young woman whirling so madly that her long blond hair flared like flame. She wore a narrow strip of shirred elastic across her nipples. Her jeans were so tight that the division between buttocks was obvious . . . and the mound between her thighs.

She danced wildly, mouth open, lips wet. Her eyes were half-closed; she gasped in a paroxysm of lust. Her body fought for freedom; she offered her flesh.

"I could do that," Zoe Kohler said suddenly.

"What?" Ernest shouted. "What did you say? I can't hear you."

She shook her head. Then they sat and watched. They drank many glasses of wine. They felt the heat of the dancers. What they witnessed excited them and diminished them at once, in a way they could not understand.

Finally, long past 1:00 A.M., they rose dizzily to their feet, infected by sensation. Ernest had just enough money to pay the bill and leave a small tip.

Outside, they stood with arms about each other's waist, weaving slightly. They tasted the cool night air, looked up at stars dimmed by the city's blaze.

"Go home now," Ernest muttered. "Don't have enough for a cab. Sorry."

"Don't worry about it, dear," she said, taking his arm. "I have money."

"A loan," he insisted.

She led him, lurching, to Park Avenue. When a cab finally stopped, she pushed Ernest into the back seat, then climbed in. She gave the driver her address.

"Little high," Ernest said solemnly. "Sorry about that."

"Silly!" she said. "There's nothing to be sorry for. I'll make us some black coffee when we get home."

They arrived at her apartment house. He tried to straighten up and walk steadily through the lobby. But upstairs, in her apartment, he collapsed onto her couch and looked at her helplessly.

"I'm paralyzed," he said.

"Just don't pass out," she said, smiling. "I'll have coffee ready in a jiff. Then you'll feel better."

"Sorry," he mumbled again.

When she came in from the kitchen with the coffee, he was bent far forward, head in his hands. He raised a pale face to her.

"I feel dreadful," he said. "It was the wine."

"And the heat," she said. "And that smoky air. Drink your coffee, darling. And take this . . ."

He looked at the capsule in her palm. "What is it?"

"Extra-strength aspirin," she said, proffering the Tuinal. "Help prevent a hangover."

He swallowed it down, gulped his coffee steadily. She poured him another cup.

"Ernie," she said, "it's past two o'clock. Why don't you sleep here? I don't want you going home alone at this hour."

"Oh, I couldn't—" he started.

"I insist," she said firmly. "You take the bed and I'll sleep out here on the couch."

He objected, saying he already felt better, and if she'd lend him a few dollars, he'd take a cab home; he'd be perfectly safe. But she insisted he stay, and after a while he assented—but only if she slept in her own bed and he bunked down on the sofa. She agreed.

She brought him a third cup of coffee. This one he sipped slowly. When she assured him a small brandy would help settle his stomach, he made no demur. They each had a brandy, taking off their shoes, slumping at opposite ends of the long couch.

"Those people . . ." he said, shaking his head. "I can't get over it. They just don't care—do they?"

"No, I suppose not. It was all so—so ugly."

"Yes," he said, nodding, "ugly."

"Not ugly so much as coarse and vulgar. It cheapens, uh, sex."

"Recreational sex," he said. "That's what they call it; that's how they feel about it. Like tennis or jogging. Just another diversion. Isn't that the feeling you got, watching them? You could tell by the way they danced."

"All that bare flesh!"

"And the way they moved! So suggestive."

"I, ah, suppose they have—they make—they go to bed afterwards. Ernie?"

"I suppose so. The dancing was just a preliminary. Did you get that feeling?"

"Oh yes. The dancing was definitely sexual. Definitely. It was very depressing. In a way. I mean, then making love loses all its importance. You know? It means about as much as eating or drinking."

"What I think," he said, looking directly at her, "is that sex—I mean just physical sex—without some emotional attachment doesn't have any meaning at all."

"I couldn't agree more. Without love, it's just a cheap thrill."

"A cheap thrill," he repeated. "Exactly. But I suppose if we tried to explain it to those people, they'd just laugh at us."

"I suppose they would. But I don't care; I still think we're right."

They sat a moment in silence, reflectively sipping their brandies.

"I'd like to have sex with you," he said suddenly.

She looked at him, expressionless.

"But I never would," he added hastily. "I mean, I'd never ask you. Zoe, you're a beautiful, exciting woman, but if we went to bed together, uh, you know, casually, it would make us just like those people we saw tonight."

"Animals," she said.

"Yes, that's right. I don't want a cheap thrill and I don't think you do either."

"I don't, dear; I really don't."

"It seems to me," he said, puzzling it out, "that when you get married, you're making a kind of statement. It's like a testimonial. You're signing a legal document that really says it's not just a cheap thrill, that something more important is involved. You're pledging your love forever and ever. Isn't that what marriage means?"

"That's what it's supposed to mean," she said sadly. "It doesn't always work out that way."

She pushed her way along the couch. She sat close to him, put an arm about his neck. She pulled him close, kissed his cheek.

"You're an idealist," she whispered. "A sweet idealist."

"I guess I am," he said. "But is what I want so impossible?"

"What do you want?"

"Something that has meaning. I go to work every day, come home and fry a hamburger. I watch television. I'm not complaining; I have a good job and all. But there must be more than that. And I don't mean a one-night stand. Or an endless series of one-night stands. There's got to be more to life than that."

"You want to get married?" she asked in a low voice, remembering Maddie's instructions.

"I think so. I think I do. I've thought a lot about it, but the idea scares me. Because it's so final. That's the way I see it anyway. I mean, it's for always, isn't it? Or should be. But at the same time the idea frightens me, I can't see any substitute. I can't see anything else that would give me what I want. I like my job, but that's not enough."

"An emptiness," she said. "A void. That's what my life is like."

"Yes," he said eagerly, "you understand. We both want something, don't we? Meaning. We want our lives to have meaning."

The uncovering that had started that afternoon in Central Park had progressed to this; they both felt it. It was an unfolding, a stripping, that neither wanted to end. It was a fearful thing they were doing, dangerous and painful.

Yet it had become easier. Intimacy acted on them like an addictive drug. Stronger doses were needed. And they hardly dared foresee what the end might be, or even if there was an end. Perhaps their course was limitless and they might never finish.

"There's something I want," she said. "*Something.* But don't ask me what it is because I don't know, I'm not sure. Except that I don't want to go on living the way I do. I really don't."

He leaned forward to kiss her lips. Twice. Tenderly.

"We're so alike," he breathed. "So alike. We believe in the same things. We want the same things."

"I don't know what I want," she said again.

"Sure you do," he said gently, taking her hand. "You want your life to have significance. Isn't that it?"

"I want . . . ," she said. "I want . . . What do I want? Darling, I've never told this to anyone else, but I want to be a different person. Totally. I want to be born again, and start all over. I know the kind of woman I want to be, and it isn't me. It's all been a mistake, Ernie. My life, I mean. It's been all wrong. Some of it was done to me, and some of it I did myself. But it's my life, and so it's all my responsibility. Isn't that true? But when I try to understand what I did that I should not have done, or what I neglected to do, I get the horrible feeling that the whole thing was beyond my . . ."

But as she spoke, she saw his eyelids fluttering. His head came slowly down. She stopped talking, smiled, took the empty brandy glass from his nerveless fingers. She smoothed the fine hair, stroked his cheek.

"Beddy-bye," she said softly.

He murmured something.

She got him into the bedroom, half-supporting him as he stumbled, stockinged feet catching on the rug. She sat him down on the edge of the bed and kneeled to pull off his socks. Small, pale feet. He stroked her head absently, weaving as he sat, eyes closed.

She tugged off his jacket, vest, tie, shirt. He grumbled sleepily as she pushed him back, unbelted and unzipped his trousers, peeled them away. He was wearing long white drawers, practically Bermuda shorts, and an old-fashioned undershirt with shoulder straps.

She yanked and hauled and finally got him straightened out under the covers, his head on the pillow. He was instantly asleep, didn't even stir when she bent to kiss his cheek.

"Good night, darling," she said softly. "Sleep well."

She washed the coffee things and the brandy glasses. She swallowed down a salt tablet, assorted vitamins and minerals, drank a small bottle of club soda. After debating a moment, she took a Tuinal.

She went into the bathroom to shower, her third that day. The wound on her thigh was now just a red line, and she soaped it carefully. She lathered the rest of her body thickly, wanting to cleanse away—what?

She dried, powdered, used spray cologne on neck, bosom, armpits, the insides of her thighs. She pulled on a long nightgown of white batiste with modest inserts of lace at the neckline.

She crawled into bed cautiously, not wanting to disturb Ernie. But he was dead to the world, breathing deeply and steadily. She thought she saw a smile on his lips, but couldn't be sure.

Maddie had instructed her to determine Ernest's attitude toward marriage, and she had done it. She thought that if she were a more positive woman, more aggressive, she might easily lead him to a proposal. But at the moment that did not concern her.

What was a puzzlement was her automatic response to Maddie's advice. She had obeyed without question, although she was the one intimately involved, not Maddie. Yet she had let the other woman dictate her conduct.

It had always been like that—other people pushing her this way and that, imposing their wills. Her mother's conversation had been almost totally command, molding Zoe to an image of the woman she wanted her daughter to be.

Even her father, by his booming physical presence, had shoved her into emotions and prejudices she felt foreign to her true nature.

And her husband! Hadn't he sought, always, to remake her into something she could not be? He had never been satisfied with what she was. He had never accepted her.

Everyone, all her life, had tried to change her. Ernest Mittle, apparently, was content with Zoe Kohler. But could she be certain he would remain content? Or would the day come when he, too, would begin to push, pull, haul, and tug?

It came to her almost as a revelation that this was the reason she sought adventures. They were her only opportunity to try out and to display her will.

She knew that others—like the Son of Sam—had blamed their misdeeds on "voices," on hallucinatory commands that overrode their inclinations and volition.

But her adventures were the only time in Zoe Kohler's life when she listened to her own voice.

She turned onto her side, moved closer to Ernie. She smelled his sweet, innocent scent. She put one arm about him, pulled him to her. And that's how she fell asleep.

During the following week, she had cause to remember her reflections on how, all her life, she had been manipulated.

The newspapers continued their heavy coverage of the Hotel Ripper investigation. Almost every day the police revealed new discoveries and new leads being pursued.

Zoe Kohler began to think of the police as a single intelligence, a single person. She saw him as a tall, thin individual, sour and righteous. He resembled the old cartoon character "Prohibition," with top hat, rusty tailcoat, furled umbrella. He wore an expression of malicious discontent.

This man, this "police," was juiceless and without mercy. He was intelligent (frighteningly so) and implacable. By his deductive brilliance, he was pushing Zoe Kohler in ways she did not want to go. He was maneuvering her, just like everyone else, and she resented it—resented that anyone would tamper with her adventures, the only truly private thing in her life.

For instance, the newspapers reported widened surveillance of all public places in midtown Manhattan hotels by uniformed officers and plainclothesmen.

Then a partial description of the Hotel Ripper was published. She was alleged to be five-seven to five-eight in very high heels, was slender, wore a shoulder-length wig, and carried a trenchcoat.

She also wore a gold link bracelet with the legend: WHY NOT? Her last costume was described as a tightly fitted dress of bottle-green silk with spaghetti straps.

These details flummoxed Zoe Kohler. She could not imagine how "police" had guessed all that about her—particularly the gold bracelet. She began to wonder if he had some undisclosed means of reading her secret thoughts, or perhaps reconstructing the past from the aura at the scene of the crime.

That dour, not to be appeased individual, who came shuffling after her told the newspaper and television reporters that the Hotel Ripper probably dressed flashily, in revealing gowns. He said her makeup and perfume would probably be heavy. He said that, although she was not a professional prostitute, she deliberately gave the impression of being sexually available.

He revealed that the weapon used in the first four crimes was a Swiss Army knife, but it was possible a different knife was used in the fifth killing. He mentioned, almost casually, that it was believed the woman involved was connected, somehow, with the hotel business in Manhattan.

It was astounding! Where was "police" getting this information? For the first time she felt quivers of fear. That dried-up, icily determined old man with his sunken cheeks and maniacal glare would give her no rest until she did what he wanted.

Die.

She thought it through carefully. Her panic ebbed as she began to see ways to defeat her nemesis.

On June 24th, a Tuesday, Zoe Kohler was awakened by a phone call at about 2:15 A.M.

At first she thought the caller, a male, was Ernest Mittle since he was sniffling and weeping; she had witnessed Ernie's tears several times. But the caller, between chokes and wails, identified himself as Harold Kurnitz.

She was finally able to understand what he was saying: Maddie Kurnitz had attempted to commit suicide by ingesting an overdose of sleeping pills. She was presently in the Intensive Care Unit of Soames-Phillips—and could Zoe come at once?

She showered before dressing, for reasons she could not comprehend. She told herself that she was not thinking straight because of the shocking news. She gave the night doorman a dollar to hail a cab for her. She was at the hospital less than an hour after Harry called.

He met her in the hallway on the fifth floor, rushing to her with open arms, his face wrenched.

"She's going to make it!" he cried, his voice thin and quavery. "She's going to make it!"

She got him seated on a wooden bench in the brightly lighted corridor. Slowly, gradually, with murmurs and pattings, she calmed him down. He sat hunched over, deflated, clutching trembling hands between his knees. He told her what had happened . . .

He said he had returned to the Kurnitz apartment a little before 1:30 A.M.

"I had to work late at the office," he mumbled.

He had started to undress, and then for some reason he couldn't explain, he decided to look in on Maddie.

"We were sleeping in different bedrooms," he explained. "When I work late . . . Anyway, it was just luck. Or maybe God. But if I hadn't looked in, the doc says she would have been gone."

He had found her crumpled on the floor in her shortie pajamas. Lying in a pool of vomit. He thought at first she had drunk too much and had passed out. But then, when he couldn't rouse her, he became frightened.

"I panicked," he said. "I admit it. I thought she was gone. I couldn't see her breathing. I mean, her chest wasn't going up and down or anything."

So he had called 911, and while he was waiting, he attempted to give mouth-to-mouth resuscitation. But he didn't know how to do it and was afraid he might be harming her.

"I just sort of blew in her mouth," he said, "but the guy in the ambulance said I didn't hurt her. He was the one who found the empty pill bottle in the bathroom. Phenobarbital. And there was an empty Scotch bottle that had rolled under the bed. The doc said if she hadn't vomited, she'd have been gone. It was that close."

Harry had ridden in the ambulance to Soames-Phillips, watching the attendant administer oxygen and inject stimulants.

"I kept repeating, 'Don't do this to me, Maddie,' " he said. "That's all I remember saying: 'Please don't do this to me.' Wasn't that a stupid, selfish thing to say? Listen, Zoe, I guess you know Maddie and I are separating. Maybe this was her way of, uh, you know, getting back at me. But I swear I never thought she'd pull anything like this. I mean, it was all friendly; we didn't fight or anything like that. No screaming. I never thought she'd . . ."

His voice trailed away.

"Maybe now you'll get back together again," Zoe said hopefully.

But he didn't answer, and after a while she left him and went in search of Maddie.

She found a young doctor scribbling on a clipboard outside the Intensive Care Unit. She asked him if she could see Mrs. Kurnitz.

"I'm Zoe Kohler," she said. "I'm her best friend. You can ask her husband. He's right down the hall."

He looked at her blankly.

"Why not?" he said finally, and again she thought of her gold bracelet. "She's not so bad. Puked up most of the stuff. She'll be dancing the fandango tomorrow night. But make it short."

Maddie was in a bed surrounded by white screens. She looked drained, waxen. Her eyes were closed. Zoe bent over her, took up a cool, limp hand. Maddie's eyes opened slowly. She stared at Zoe.

"Shit," she said in a wispy voice. "I fucked it up, didn't I? I can't do anything right."

"Oh, Maddie," Zoe Kohler said sorrowfully.

"I got the fucking pills down and then I figured I'd make sure by finishing the booze. But they tell me I upchucked."

"But you're alive," Zoe said.

"Hip, hip, hooray," Maddie said, turning her head to one side. "Is Harry still around?"

"He's right outside. Do you want to see him, Maddie?"

"What the hell for?"

"He's taking it hard. He's all broken up."

Maddie's mouth stretched in a grimace that wasn't mirth.

"He thinks it was because of him," she said, a statement, not a question. "The male ego. I couldn't care less."

"Then why . . . ?"

Maddie turned her head back to glare at Zoe.

"Because I just didn't want to wake up," she said. "Another day. Another stupid, empty, fucking day. Harry's got nothing to do with it. It's me."

"Maddie, I . . . Maddie, I don't understand."

"What's the point?" she demanded. "Just what is the big, fucking point? Will you tell me that?"

Zoe was silent.

"Ah, shit," Maddie said. "What a downer it all is. Just being alive. Who needs it?"

"Maddie, you don't really feel like—"

"Don't tell me what I feel like, kiddo. You haven't a clue, not a clue. Oh, Christ, I'm sorry," she added immediately, her hand tightening on Zoe's. "You got your problems too, I know."

"But I thought you were—"

"All fun and games?" Maddie said, her mouth twisted. "A million laughs? You've got to be young for that, luv. When the tits begin to sag, it's time to take stock. I just figured I had the best of it and I didn't have the guts for what comes next. I'm a sprinter, sweetie, not a long distance runner."

"Do you really think you and Harry . . . ?"

"No way. It's finished. Kaput. He had a toss in the hay with his tootsie tonight, and then came home and found me gasping my last. Big tragedy. Instant guilt. So he's all busted up. By tomorrow night he'll be sore at me for spoiling his sleep. Oh hell, I'm not blaming him. But it's all over. He knows it and I know it."

"What will you do now, Maddie?"

"Do?" she said with a bright smile. "I'll tell you what I'll do. The worst. Go on living."

Out in the corridor, Zoe Kohler leaned a moment against the wall, her eyes closed.

If Maddie, if a woman like Maddie, couldn't win, no one could win. She didn't want to believe that, but there it was.

Dr. Oscar Stark called her at the office.

"Just checking on my favorite patient," he said cheerfully. "How are we feeling these days, Zoe?"

"I feel fine, doctor."

"Uh-huh. Taking your medication regularly?"

"Oh yes."

"No craving for salt?"

"No."

"What about tiredness? Feel weary at times? All washed out?"

"Oh no," she lied glibly, "nothing like that."

"Sleeping all right? Without pills?"

"I sleep well."

He sighed. "Not under any stress, are you, Zoe? Not necessarily physical stress, but any, uh, personal or emotional strains?"

"No."

"You're wearing that bracelet, aren't you? The medical identification bracelet? And carrying the kit?"

"Oh yes. Every day."

He was silent a moment, then said heartily, "Good! Well, I'll see you on—let me look it up—on the first of July, a Tuesday. Right?"

"Yes, doctor. That's correct."

"If any change occurs—any weakness, nausea, unusual weight loss, abdominal pains—you'll phone me, won't you?"

"Of course, doctor. Thank you for calling."

She thought it out carefully . . .

Newspapers had described the Hotel Ripper as being "flashily dressed." So she would have to forget her skin-tight skirts and revealing necklines. Also, it was now too warm to wear a coat of any kind to cover such a costume.

So, to avoid notice by the doorman of her apartment house and by police officers stationed in hotel cocktail lounges, she would dress conservatively. She would wear no wig. She would use only her usual minimal makeup.

That meant there was no reason for that pre-adventure trip up to the Filmore on West 72nd Street to effect a transformation. She could sally forth boldly, dressed conventionally, and take a cab to anywhere she wished.

She could not wear the WHY NOT? bracelet, of course, and her entire approach would have to be revised. She could not come on as "sexually available." Her clothes, manner, speech, appearance—all would have to be totally different from the published description of the Hotel Ripper.

Innocence! That was the answer! She knew how some men were excited by virginity. (Hadn't Kenneth been?) She would try to act as virginal as a woman of her age could. Why, some men even had a letch for cheerleaders and nubile girls in middies. She knew all that, and it would be fun to play the part.

There was a store on 40th Street, just east of Lexington Avenue, that sold women's clothing imported from Latin America. Blouses from Ecuador, skirts from Guatemala, bikinis from Brazil, huaraches, mantillas, lacy camisoles—and Mexican wedding gowns.

These last were white or cream-colored dresses of batiste or crinkled cotton, light as gossamer. They had full skirts that fell to the ankle, with modest necklines of embroidery or eyelet. The bell sleeves came below the elbow, and the entire loose dress swung, drifted, ballooned—fragile and chaste.

"A marvelous summer party dress," the salesclerk said. "Comfortable, airy—and so different."

"I'll take it," Zoe Kohler said.

She read the weekly hotel trade magazine avidly. There was a motor inn on 49th Street, west of Tenth Avenue: the Tribunal. It would be hosting a convention of college and university comptrollers during June 29th to July 2nd.

When Zoe Kohler looked up the Tribunal in the hotel directory, she found it was a relatively modest hostelry, only 180 rooms and suites, with coffee shop, dining room, a bar. And an outdoor cocktail lounge that overlooked a small swimming pool on the roof, six floors up.

The Tribunal seemed far enough removed from midtown Manhattan to have escaped the close surveillance of the police. And, being small, it was quite likely to be crowded with tourists and convention-goers. Zoe Kohler thought she would try the Tribunal. An outdoor cocktail lounge that overlooked a swimming pool. It sounded romantic.

Her menstrual cramps began on Sunday, June 29th. Not slowly, gradually, increasing in intensity as they usually did, but suddenly, with the force of a blow. She doubled over, sitting with her arms folded and clamped across her abdomen.

The pain came in throbs, leaving her shuddering. She imagined the soles of her feet ached and the roots of her hair burned. Deep within her was this wrenching twist, her entrails gripped and turned over. She wanted to scream.

She swallowed everything: Anacin, Midol, Demerol. She called Ernie and postponed their planned trip to Jones Beach. Then she got into a hot tub, light-headed and nauseated. She tried a glass of white wine, but hadn't finished it before she had to get out of the tub to throw up in the toilet.

Her weakness was so bad that she feared to move without gripping sink or doorjamb. She was uncoordinated, stumbled frequently, saw her own watery limbs floating away like feelers. She was troubled by double vision and, clasping a limp breast, felt her heart pound in a wild, disordered rhythm.

"What's happening to me?" she asked aloud, more distraught than panicky.

She spent all day in bed or lying in a hot bath. She ate nothing, since she felt always on the verge of nausea. Once, when she tried to lift a glass of water and the glass slipped from her strengthless fingers to crash on the kitchen floor, she wept.

She took two Tuinal and had a fitful sleep thronged with evil dreams. She awoke, not remembering the details, but filled with dread. Her nightgown was sodden with sweat, and she showered and changed before trying to sleep again.

She awoke late Monday morning, and told herself she felt better. She had inserted a tampon, but her period had not started. The knifing pain had subsided, but she was left with a leaden pressure that seemed to force her guts downward. She had a horrific image of voiding all her insides.

She dared not step on the scale, but could not ignore the skin discolorations in the crooks of her elbows, on her knees, between her fingers. Remembering Dr. Stark's test, she plucked at her pubis; several hairs came away, dry and wiry.

She called the Hotel Granger and spoke to Everett Pinckney. He was very understanding, and told her they'd manage without her for the day, and to take Tuesday off as well, if necessary.

She lay on the bed, blanket and sheet thrown aside. She looked down with shock and loathing at her own naked body.

She hadn't fully realized how thin she had become. Her hipbones jutted, poking up white, glassy skin. Her breasts lay flaccid, nipples withdrawn. Below, she could see a small tuft of dulled hair, bony knees, toes ridiculously long and prehensile: an animal's claws.

When she smelled her arm, she caught a whiff of ash. Her flesh was pudding; she could not make a fist. She was a shrunken sack, and when she explored herself, the sphincter was slack. She was emptied out and hollow.

She spent the afternoon dosing herself with all the drugs in her pharmacopeia. She got down a cup of soup and held it, then had a ham sandwich and a glass of wine. She soaked again in a tub, washed her hair, took a cold shower.

She worked frantically to revive her flagging body, ignoring the internal pain, her staggering gait. She forced herself to move slowly, carefully, precisely. She punished herself, breathing deeply, and willed herself to dress.

For it seemed to her that an adventure that night—all her adventures—were therapy, necessary to her well-being. She did not pursue the thought further than that realization: she would not be well, could not be well, unless she followed the dictates of her secret, secret heart.

It became a dream. No, not a dream, but a play in which she was at once actress and spectator. She was inside and outside. She observed herself with wonder, moving about resolutely, disciplining her flesh. She wanted to applaud this fierce, determined woman.

The Mexican wedding gown was a disaster; she knew it would never do. It hung on her wizened frame in folds. The neckline gaped. The hem seemed to sweep the floor. She was lost in it: a little girl dressed up in her mother's finery, lacking only the high-heeled pumps, wide-brimmed hat, smeared lipstick.

She put the gown aside and dressed simply in lisle turtleneck sweater, denim jumper, low-heeled pumps. When she inspected herself in the mirror, she saw a wan, tremulous, vulnerable woman. With a sharpened knife in her purse.

The rooftop cocktail lounge was bordered with tubs of natural greenery. The swimming pool, lighted from beneath, shone with a phosphorescent blue. An awning stretched over the tables was flowered with golden daisies.

A few late-evening swimmers chased and splashed with muted cries. From a hi-fi behind the bar came seductive, nostalgic tunes, fragile as tinsel. Life seemed slowed, made wry and gripping.

A somnolent waiter moved slowly, splay-footed. Clink of ice in tall glasses. Quiet murmurs, and then a sudden fountain of laughter. White faces in the gloom. Bared arms. Everyone lolled and dreamed.

The night itself was luminous, stars blotted by city glow. A soft breeze stroked. The darkness opened up and engulfed, making loneliness bittersweet and silence a blessing.

Zoe Kohler sat quietly in the shadows and thought herself invisible. She was hardly aware of the gleaming swimmers in the pool, the couples lounging at the outdoor tables. She thought vaguely that soon, soon, she would go downstairs to the crowded bar.

But she felt so calm, so indolent, she could not stir. It was the bemused repose of convalescence: all pain dulled, turmoil vanished, worry spent. Her body flowed; it just flowed, suffused with a liquid warmth.

There were two solitary men on the terrace. One, older, drank rapidly with desperate intentness, bent over his glass. The other, with hair to his shoulders and a wispy beard, seemed scarcely old enough to be served. He was drinking bottled beer, making each one last.

The bearded boy rose suddenly, his metal chair screeching on the tile. Everyone looked up. He stood a moment, embarrassed by the attention, and fussed with beer bottle and glass until he was ignored.

He came directly to Zoe's table.

"Pardon me, ma'am," he said in a low voice. "I was wondering if I might buy you a drink. Please?"

Zoe inspected him, tilting her head, trying to make him out in the twilight. He was very tall, very thin. Dressed in a tweed jacket too bulky for his frame, clean chinos, sueded bush boots.

Thin wrists stuck from the cuffs of his heavy jacket, and his big head seemed balanced on a stalk neck. His smile was hopeful. The long hair and scraggly beard were blond, sun-streaked. He seemed harmless.

"Sit down," she said softly. "We'll each buy our own drinks."

"Thank you," he said gratefully.

His name was Chet (for Chester) LaBranche, and he was from Waterville, Maine. But he lived and worked in Vermont, where he was assistant to the president of Barre Academy, which was called an academy but was actually a fully accredited coeducational liberal arts college with an enrollment of 437.

"I really shouldn't be here," he said, laughing happily. "But our comptroller came down with the flu or something, and we had already paid for the convention reservation and tickets and all, so Mrs. Bixby—she's the president—asked me if I wanted to come, and I jumped at the chance. It's my first time in the big city, so I'm pretty excited about it all."

"Having a good time?" Zoe asked, smiling.

"Well, I just got in this morning, and we had meetings most of the day, so I haven't had much time to look around, but it's sure big and noisy and dirty, isn't it?"

"It sure is."

"But tomorrow and Wednesday we'll have more time to ourselves, and I mean to look around some. What should I see?"

"Everything," she told him.

"Yes," he said, nodding vigorously, "everything. I mean to. Even if I stay up all night. I don't know when I'll get a chance like this again. I want to see the fountain where Zelda Fitzgerald went dunking and all the bars in Greenwich Village where Jack Kerouac hung out. I got a list of places I made out in my room and I aim to visit them all."

"You're staying here in the hotel?" she asked casually.

"Oh yes, ma'am. That was included in the convention tickets. I got me a nice room on the fifth floor, one flight down. Nice, big, shiny room."

"How old are you, Chet?"

"Going on twenty-five," he said, ducking his head. "I never have asked your name, ma'am, but you don't have to tell me unless you want to."

"Irene," she said.

He was enthusiastic about everything. It wasn't the beer he gulped down; it was him. He chattered along brightly, making her laugh with his descriptions of what life was like at the Barre Academy when they got snowed in, and the troubles he already had with New York cabdrivers.

She really enjoyed his youth, vitality, optimism. He hadn't yet been tainted. He trusted. It all lay ahead of him: a glittering world. He was going to become a professor of English Lit. He was going to travel to far-off places. He was going to own a home, raise a family. Everything.

He almost spluttered in his desire to get it all out, to explain this tremendous energy in him. His long hands made grand gestures. He squirmed, laughing at his own mad dreams, but believing them.

Zoe had three more glasses of white wine, and Chet had two more bottles of beer. She listened to him, smiling and nodding. Then, suddenly, the swimmers were gone, the pool was dimmed. Tables had emptied; they were the last. The sleepy waiter appeared with their bill.

"Chet, I'd like to see that list you made out," Zoe said. "The places you want to visit. Maybe I can suggest some others."

"Sure," he said promptly. "Great idea. We don't have to wait for the elevator. We can walk; it's only one flight down."

"Fine," she said.

She carried her glass of wine, and he carried his bottle and glass of beer. As he had said, his room was nice, big, and shiny. He showed it off proudly: the stack of fluffy towels, the neatly wrapped little bars of soap, the clean glasses and plastic ice bucket.

"And two beds!" he chortled, bouncing up and down on one of them. "Never thought I'd get to stay in a room with *two* beds! I may just sleep in both of them, taking turns. Just for the sheer luxury of it! Now . . . where's that list?"

They sat side by side on the edge of the bed, discussing his planned itinerary.

Never once did he touch her, say anything even mildly suggestive, or give her any reason to suspect he was other than he appeared to be: an innocent.

She turned suddenly, kissed his cheek.

"I like you," she said. "You're nice."

He stared at her, startled, eyes widening. Then he leaped to his feet, a convulsive jump.

"Yes, well . . ." he said, stammering. "I thank you. I guess maybe I've been boring you. Haven't I? I mean, talking about myself all night. Good Lord, I haven't given you a chance to open your mouth. We could go downstairs and have a nightcap. In the bar downstairs. Would you like that? Or maybe you want to split? I understand. That's all right. I mean if you want to go . . ."

She smiled, took his hand, drew him back down onto the bed.

"I don't want another drink, Chet," she said. "And I don't want to go. Not yet. Can't we talk for a few minutes?"

"Well . . . yeah . . . sure. I'd like that."

"Are you married, Chet?"

"Oh no. No, no."

"Girlfriend?"

"Uh, yes . . . sort of. Sure, she's a girlfriend. A junior at the Academy, which is against the rules because we're not supposed to date the students. You know? But this has been going on for, oh, maybe six or seven months now. And she's been sneaking out to meet me, but vacation started last week and we've got plans to see each other this summer."

"That's wonderful. Is she nice?"

"Oh yes. I think so. Very nice. Good fun—you know? I mean fun to be with. Alice. That's her name—Alice."

"I like that name."

"Yes, well, we usually meet out of town. I mean, the place isn't so big that people wouldn't notice, so we have to be careful. I have wheels, an old, beat-up crate, and sometimes we go to a roadhouse out of town. Sometimes, on a nice night, we'll just take a walk and talk."

"Is she pretty?"

"Oh yes. I think so. Not beautiful. I mean, she's not glamorous or anything like that. She wears glasses. She's very nearsighted. But I think she's pretty."

"Do you love her, Chet?"

He considered that a long moment.

"I don't know," he finally confessed. "I really don't know. I've given it a lot of thought. I mean, if I want to spend the rest of my life with her. I really don't know. But it's not something we have to decide right now. I mean, it's only been six or seven months. She's coming back for her senior year, so we'll have a chance to get to know each other better. Maybe it'll just, like, fade away, or maybe it'll become something. You know?"

She put her lips close to his ear, whispering . . .

"Have you had sex together?"

He blushed. "Well, ah, not exactly. I mean, we've done . . . things. But not, you know, all the way. I respect her."

"Does she have a good body?"

"Oh God—oh gosh, yes! She's really stacked. I mean, she's a swimmer and all. Doesn't smoke. Has a beer now and then. Keeps herself in very good shape. Very good. She's almost as tall as I am. Very slender with these big . . . you know . . ."

"Why haven't you had sex with her?"

"Well, uh . . . you know . . ."

She wouldn't let him off the hook. It was suddenly important to her to learn what Chet and Alice had done together.

"She wants to, doesn't she, Chet?"

"Oh yes. I think so. Sometimes we get started and it's very difficult to stop. Then we cool it. That's what we say to each other: 'Cool it!' Then we laugh, and get, uh, control again."

"You'd like to, wouldn't you?"

"Oh yes. I mean, at the moment, when we get all excited, I'd like to. I forget all my good intentions. I know that someday—some night rather—neither of us will say, 'Cool it!' And then . . ."

"Is she on the Pill?"

"Oh no! I asked her that and she said, 'What for?' I mean, she doesn't play around. She's right. Why should she take those dangerous drugs?"

"But what if you both get excited and don't say, 'Cool it,' and it happens, like you said? What if she gets pregnant?"

"No, no. I mean, I'd, uh, like take precautions. I'm not a virgin, Irene. I know about those things. I wouldn't do that to Alice."

She leaned forward, whispered in his ear again.

"Well, ah, yes," he said. "Yes, she could do that. If she wanted to. And I could, too, of course. I know about that."

"But you've never done it?"

"Well, uh, no. No, I've never done it."

"Why don't you take your clothes off?" Zoe Kohler said in a low voice. "I'd like to do it to you."

"You're kidding!"

"No, really, I want to. Don't you? Wouldn't you like the experience?"

She had said the right word. He wanted to experience everything.

"All right," he said. "But you must tell me what to do."

"You don't have to do anything," she assured him. "Just lie back and enjoy it. I have to go into the bathroom for a minute. You undress; I'll be right back."

His innocence was a rebuke to her. She was confused as to why this should be so. She didn't want to corrupt him; that would come soon enough. What she wanted to do, she decided, was to save him from corruption.

She thought this through as she undressed in the bathroom. It made a kind of hard sense. Because, despite how blameless he was now, she saw what would eventually happen to him, what he would become.

Years and the guilt of living would take their toll. He would lie and betray and cheat. His boy's body would swell at the same time his conscience would atrophy. He would become a swaggering man, bullying his way through life, scorning the human wreckage he left in his wake.

What was the worst, the absolute worst, was that he would never mourn his lost purity, but might recall it with an embarrassed laugh. He would be shamed by the memory, she knew. He would never regret his ruined goodness.

So she went back into the bedroom and slit his throat.

10

Thursday, June 5th . . .

"All right," Sergeant Abner Boone said, flipping through his notebook, "here's what we've got."

Standing and sitting around the splintered table in Midtown Precinct North. All of them smoking: cigarettes, cigars, and Lieutenant Crane chewing on a pipe. Emptied cardboard coffee cups on the table. The detritus of gulped sandwiches, containers of chop suey, a pizza box, wrappers and bags of junk food.

Air murky with smoke, barely stirred by the air conditioner. Sweat and disinfectant. No one commented or even noticed. They had all smelled worse odors. And battered rooms like this were home, familiar and comfortable.

"Nicholas Telemachus Pappatizos," Boone started. "Aka Nick Pappy, aka Poppa Nick, aka the Magician. Forty-two. Home address: Las Vegas. A fast man with the cards and dice. A small-time bentnose. Two convictions: eight months and thirteen months, here and there, for fraud and bunko. He got off twice on attempted rape and felonious assault."

"Good riddance," Detective Bentley said.

"The blood on the bathroom floor was definitely not his. Caucasian female. So it's confirmed; it's a female perp we're looking for."

"How do you figure the fight?" Detective Johnson asked.

"The PM shows sexual intercourse just before death," Boone went on, his voice toneless. "It could have been rape; he wasn't a nice guy. So after it's over, she gets her knife into him and starts cutting him up."

"That's another thing," Sergeant Broderick said. "She's obviously got a new knife. My guys are wasting their time trying to track the one that got broke."

"Right," Boone said. "Drop it; we were too late. We can use your guys on people who knew the convention schedule. We've got nearly two thousand names so far."

"Beautiful," Broderick said, but he wasn't really dismayed. No one was dismayed by the enormity of the search.

"Johnson," Boone said, "anything on the Mace?"

"Getting there," the detective said. "The stuff was sold to a lot of security outfits, armored car fleets, and so forth. Anyone who could prove a legitimate need. We're tracking them down. Every can of it."

"Keep on it. Bentley, what about that waitress from the Hotel Coolidge? The Ashley kill. His scarred hands."

"We check with her mother every day, sarge. She still hasn't called in from the Coast. Now we're tracking down her friends in case anyone knows where she is."

"As long as you're following up . . . Lieutenant? Anything new?"

"Nothing so far on the possibles. Some have moved, some are out of town, some are dead. I wouldn't say it looks promising."

"How did the decoys miss her at the Adler?" Edward X. Delaney demanded.

"Who the hell knows?" Bentley said angrily. "We had both bars in the place covered. Maybe she brought him in off the street."

"No," Delaney said stonily. "That's not her way. She's no street quiff. She knew there were conventions there. The lobby maybe, or the dining room. But it wasn't on the street."

They were all silent for a moment, trying to figure ways to stop her before she hit again.

"It should be about June twenty-ninth," Boone said, "to July second. In that time period. It's not too early to plan what more we can do. Intelligent suggestions gratefully received."

There were hard barks of laughter and the meeting broke up. Sergeant Boone drew Delaney aside.

"Chief," he said, "got a little time?"

"Sure. As much as you want. What's up?"

"There's a guy waiting in my office. A doctor. Dr. Patrick Ho. How's that for a name—Ho? He's some kind of an Oriental. Japanese, Chinese, Korean, or maybe from Vietnam or Cambodia. Whatever. With a first name like Patrick, there had to be an Irishman in there somewhere—right? Anyway, he's with the Lab Services Section. He's the guy who ran the analysis on the blood from the bathroom floor and said it was Caucasian female."

"And?" Delaney said.

Boone shrugged helplessly. "Beats the hell out of me. He tracked me down to tell me there's something screwy about the blood. But I can't get it straight what he wants. Will you talk to him a minute, Chief? Maybe you can figure it out."

Dr. Patrick Ho was short, plump, bronzed. He looked like a young Buddha with a flattop of reddish hair. When Boone introduced Delaney, he bowed and giggled. His hand was soft. The Chief noted the manicured nails.

"Ah," he said, in a high, flutey voice. "So nice. An honor. Everyone has heard of you, sir."

"Thank you," Delaney said. "Now, what's this about—"

"Your exploits," Dr. Ho went on enthusiastically, his dark eyes shining. "Your deductive ability. I, myself, would like to be a detective. But unfortunately I am only a lowly scientist, condemned to—"

"Let's sit down," Delaney said. "For a minute," he added hopefully.

They pulled chairs up to Boone's littered desk. The sergeant passed around cigarettes. The little doctor leaped to his feet with a gold Dunhill lighter at the ready. He closed the lighter after holding it for Boone and Delaney, then flicked it again for his own cigarette.

"Ah," he giggled, "never three on a light. Am I correct?"

He sat down again and looked at them, back and forth, beaming.

He was a jolly sight. A face like a peach with ruby-red lips. Tiny ears hugged his skull. Those dark eyes bulged slightly, and he had the smallest teeth Delaney had ever seen. A child's teeth: perfect miniatures.

His gestures were a ballet, graceful and flowing. His expression was never in repose, but he smiled, frowned, grimaced, pursed those full lips, pouted, made little moues. He was, Delaney decided, a very scrutable Oriental.

"Dr. Ho," the Chief said, "about the blood . . . There's no doubt it's from a Caucasian female?"

"No doubt!" the doctor cried. "No doubt whatsoever!"

"Then what . . . ?"

Dr. Ho leaned forward, looking at them in a conspiratorial manner. He held one pudgy forefinger aloft.

"That blood," he said in almost a whisper, "has a very high potassium count."

Delaney and Boone looked at each other.

"Uh, doctor," the sergeant said, "what does that mean? I mean, what's the significance?"

Dr. Ho leaned back, crossed his little legs daintily. He stared at the ceiling.

"Ah, at the moment," he said dreamily, "it has no significance. It means only what I said: a high potassium count. But I must tell you I feel, I *know,* it has a significance, if only we knew what it was. Normal blood does not have such a high potassium level."

Edward X. Delaney was getting interested. He hitched his chair closer to Dr. Patrick Ho, got a whiff of the man's flowery cologne, and leaned hastily back.

"You're saying the potassium content of that blood is abnormal?"

"Ah, yes!" the doctor said, grinning, nodding madly. "Precisely. Abnormal."

"And what could cause the abnormality?"

"Oh, many things. Many, many things."

Again, Delaney and Boone glanced at each other. The sergeant's shoulders rose slightly in a small shrug.

"Well, doctor," Boone said, sighing, "I don't see how that's going to help our investigation."

Dr. Patrick Ho frowned, then showed his little teeth, then pouted. Then he leaned forward, began to speak rapidly.

"Ah, I have said I wish to be a detective. I am but a lowly scientist—let me speak the truth: I am but a lowly technician; nothing more—but in a way, I *am* a detective. I detect what can be learned from a drop of blood, a chip of paint, a piece of glass, a hair. And about this high-potassium blood, I have a suspicion. No, I have a—a—what is the word?"

"A hunch?" Delaney offered.

The doctor laughed with delight. "What a word! A hunch! Exactly. Something is wrong with this blood. The high potassium should not be there. So I would like to make a much more thorough analysis of this puzzling blood."

"So?" Sergeant Boone said. "Why don't you?"

Dr. Ho sighed deeply. His face collapsed into such a woebegone expression that he seemed close to tears. This time he held up two fingers. He gripped one by the tip. He talked around his shortened cigarette, tilting his head to keep the smoke out of his eyes.

"One," he said, "we are, of course, very busy. A certain amount of time must be allotted to each task. I have, at this moment, many things assigned to me. All must be accomplished. I would like to be relieved—temporarily, of course," he added hastily, "of everything but the detection of this strange blood. Second," he said, folding down one finger, switching his grip to the other, "second, I must tell you in all honesty that we do not have the equipment in our laboratory necessary for the subtle blood analysis I wish to make."

"And where is this equipment available?" Delaney asked.

"The Medical Examiner has it," Dr. Ho said sorrowfully.

"So?" Boone said again. "Ask them to do the analysis."

That expressive face twisted. "Ah," the doctor said in an anguished voice, "but then it is out of my hands. You understand?"

Delaney looked at him intently. This little man was trying to score points, to further his career. Nothing wrong with that. In fact, in the right circumstances, it might be admirable. But he also might be wasting everyone's time.

"Let me get this straight," the Chief said. "What you'd like is to be temporarily relieved of all your other duties and assigned only to the analysis of the blood found on the bathroom floor at the Hotel Adler. And then you'd like to use the machines or whatever in the Medical Examiner's office to make that analysis. Have I got it right?"

Dr. Ho slapped his plump thigh. His eyes glowed with happiness . . . briefly.

"Exactly," he said. "Precisely." Then his face fell; the glee disappeared. "But you must understand that between my section and the Medical Examiner's office there is, ah, I would not say bad feeling, oh no, but there is, ah . . . what shall I say? Competition! Yes, there is competition. Professional jealousy perhaps. A certain amount of secrecy involved. You understand?" he pleaded.

Indeed, Edward X. Delaney did understand. It was nothing new and nothing unusual. Since when was there perfect, wholehearted cooperation between the branches of any large organization, even if their aims were identical?

The FBI vs. local cops. The army vs. the air force. The navy vs. the Marines. The Senate vs. the House of Representatives. The federal government vs. the states. Infighting was a way of life, and it wasn't all bad. Competing jealousies were a good counter for smug indolence.

"All right," the Chief said, "you want us to get you assigned full time to this analysis and you want us to get the ME's office to cooperate. Correct?"

Dr. Patrick Ho bent forward from the waist, put a soft hand on Delaney's arm. "You are a very sympathetic man," he said gratefully.

The Chief, who hated to be touched by strangers, or even by friends, jerked his arm away. He rose swiftly to his feet.

"We'll let you know, doctor. As soon as possible."

There was a round of half-bows and handshaking. They watched Dr. Ho dance from the room.

"A whacko," Sergeant Boone said.

"Mmm," Delaney said.

They slumped back in their chairs. They stared at each other.

"What do you think, Chief?"

"A long shot."

"I think it's a lot of bullshit," Boone said angrily. "Thorsen is the only man who could give Ho what he wants, and he'd have to pull a lot of strings and crack a lot of skulls to do it. I just don't have the juice."

"I understand that."

"But if I go to Thorsen with that cockamamie story of potassium in the blood, he'll think I'm some kind of a nut."

"That's true," Delaney said sympathetically. "On the other hand, if you turn him down cold, that crazy doctor is liable to go over your head. Then, if he gets action and it turns out to be something, your name is mud."

"Yeah," the sergeant said miserably, "I know."

"It may be nothing, but I think you should move on it."

"That's easy—" Boone started to say, then shut his mouth so abruptly that his teeth clicked.

The Chief looked at him steadily.

"I know what you're thinking, sergeant—that I've got nothing to lose, but you have. I understand all that. But I don't think you can afford to do nothing. Look, suppose we do this . . . I'll call Thorsen and tell him the doctor came to see me, but you sat in on the meet. I'll recommend he gets Dr. Ho what he wants and I'll tell him you'll go along. That way the blame is on me if it turns sour. I couldn't care less. If it turns out to be something, you'll be on record as having been on it from the start."

Abner Boone thought it over.

"Yeah," he said finally. "Let's do it that way. Thanks, Chief."

Delaney tried to call Thorsen from Boone's office, but the Deputy Commissioner was in a meeting. The Chief said he'd try him later from home.

He waved so-long to the sergeant and walked home slowly through Central Park. It was a hot, steamy day, but he didn't take off his hat or doff his jacket. He rarely complained about the weather. He was constantly amazed at people who never seemed to learn that in the summer it was hot and in the winter it was cold.

As usual, Monica was out somewhere. He went upstairs to take off jacket, vest, and tie. Then he peeled off his sodden shirt and undershirt and wiped his torso cool with a soaked washcloth. He pulled on a knitted polo shirt of Sea Island cotton.

He inspected the contents of the refrigerator. On the previous night, they had had veal cutlets dredged in seasoned flour (with paprika) and then sauteed in butter with onion flakes and garlic chips. There was enough cold veal left over to make a decent sandwich.

He used white bread spread thinly with Russian dressing. He added slices of red onion and a light dusting of freshly ground pepper. He carried the sandwich and a cold can of Ballantine Ale into the study.

While he ate and drank, he searched through his home medical encyclopedia and found the section on potassium. All it said was that potassium was a chemical element present in the human body, usually in combination with sodium salts.

The section on blood was longer and more detailed. Among other things, it said that the red fluid was a very complex substance, and plasma (the liquid part of the blood) carried organic and inorganic elements that had to be transported from one part of the body to another.

The blood also carried gases and secretions from the endocrine glands (hormones) as well as enzymes, proteins, etc. Serious imbalance in blood chemistry, the encyclopedia said, was usually indicative of physiological malfunction.

He put the book aside and finished his sandwich and beer. He called Thorsen again, and this time he got through. He told the Deputy Commissioner about the visit of Dr. Patrick Ho, from the Lab Services Section.

He made it sound like the doctor had come to see him, and that Sergeant

Boone was present at the meeting. He explained what it was Dr. Ho wanted and urged that they cooperate. He said Sergeant Boone agreed.

Ivar Thorsen was dubious.

"Pretty thin stuff, Edward," he said. "As I understand it, he hasn't got a clue as to why there's so much potassium in the blood or what it means."

"That's correct. That's what he wants to find out."

"Well, suppose he does find out, and the killer is popping potassium pills for some medical reason—how does that help us? My God, Edward, maybe the Hotel Ripper is a banana freak. She wolfs down bananas like mad. That would account for the potassium. So what? Are we going to arrest every woman in New York who eats bananas?"

"Ivar, I think we ought to give this guy a chance. It may turn up zilch. Granted. But we haven't got so goddamned much that we can afford to ignore anything."

"You really think it might amount to something?"

"We'll never know until we try, will we?"

Thorsen groaned. "Well . . . all right. The Lab Services Unit will be no problem. I can get this Ho assigned to us on temporary duty. The Medical Examiner's office is something else again. I don't swing much clout there, but I'll see what I can do."

"Thank you, Ivar."

"Edward," Thorsen said, almost pleading, "are we going to get her?"

Delaney was astounded.

"Of course," he said.

Newspapermen and television commentators reported no progress was being made in the investigation. SEARCH FOR RIPPER STALLED, one headline announced. The public seemed to take a ghoulish pleasure in reading how many summer conventions, hotel reservations, and tours had been canceled.

The Mayor's office took the flak from the business community and passed it along to the Police Commissioner. The PC, in turn, leaned on Deputy Commissioner Thorsen. And he, being a decent man, refused to scream at the men in his command, knowing they were doing everything that could be done, and working their asses off.

"But give me something," he begged. *"Anything!* A bone we can throw to the media."

Actually, progress was being made, but it was slow, tedious, foot-flattening labor, and didn't yield the kind of results that make headlines. The list of women who had access to the convention schedule was growing, and Detective Aaron Johnson's men were checking out every can of Chemical Mace and other tear gas delivered to the New York area.

Dr. Patrick Ho had been given what he wanted, and three days later he reported back to Sergeant Boone and Delaney. He was flushed and breathless.

"Ah, it is looking good," he said in his musical voice. "Very, very good."

"What?" Boone demanded. "What did you find out?"

"Listen to this," Ho said triumphantly. "In addition to the high potassium content, the sodium, chloride, and bicarbonate levels are very low. Isn't that wonderful!"

Boone made a sound of disgust.

"What does that mean, doctor?" Delaney asked.

"Ah, it is much too early to say," Dr. Ho said judiciously. "But definite abnormalities exist. Also, we have isolated two substances we cannot identify. Is that not exciting?"

"Maybe it would be," the sergeant said, "if you knew what they were."

"Where do you go from here?" the Chief asked.

"There are, in this marvelous city, two excellent hospitals with splendid hematology departments. They have beautiful hardware. I shall take our slides and samples to these hospitals, and they will tell me what these unidentified substances are."

"Listen," Sergeant Boone said hoarsely, "are we going to have to pay for this?"

"Oh no," Dr. Patrick Ho said, shocked. "It is their civic duty. I shall convince them."

Delaney looked at the little man with admiration.

"You know, doctor," he said, "I think you will."

Later, Boone said, "We're getting scammed. The guy's a loser."

On June 16th, Detective Daniel Bentley arrived late for the morning meeting at Midtown Precinct North. He came striding into the room, glowing.

"Bingo!" he shouted. "We got something."

"Oh Lord," Ivar Thorsen intoned, "let it be something good."

"Twice a day," Bentley said, "we been checking with the mother of that cocktail waitress who worked the New Orleans Room at the Hotel Coolidge the night Jerome Ashley got washed. The girl went out to the Coast and she hasn't called her mother yet. So we started checking out her pals. We found a boyfriend who's on probation after doing eighteen months for B-and-E. So we could lean on him—right? He gets a call last night from this chick . . ." Here Bentley consulted his notebook. "Her name is Anne Rogovich. Anyway, she calls her old boyfriend, they talk, and she gives him her number out there. Then he calls us like he's been told. I called the girl an hour ago. It's early in the morning on the Coast and I woke her up—but what the hell."

"Get to it," Boone said.

"Yeah, she worked the New Orleans Room the night Ashley was offed. Yeah, she remembers serving a guy with badly scarred hands. She says he was sitting with a woman. Not much of a physical description: tall, slender, darkish, heavy on the makeup. Strawberry blond wig. But she remembers the clothes better. Very flashy. A green silk dress, skimpy as a slip. Skinny shoulder straps. This Anne Rogovich remembers because she really dug that dress and wondered what it cost. Also, the woman with Ashley was wearing a bracelet. Gold links. With big gold letters that spelled out WHY NOT?"

"WHY NOT?" Boone said. "Beautiful. The dress she can change, but that bracelet might be something. Broderick, how about your guys checking it out? Who makes it and who sells it. Trace it to the stores. Maybe it was bought on a charge; you never can tell."

"Yeah," Broderick said, "we'll get on it."

"Did she remember anything else?" the sergeant asked.

"That's all I could get out of her," Bentley reported. "But she was half-asleep. I'll try her again later today."

"Good, good, good," the Deputy Commissioner said, rubbing his palms together. "Can this Anne Rogovich make the woman with Ashley if she sees her again?"

"She says no," Bentley said. "The clothes, yes; the woman, no."

"Still," Thorsen said happily, "it's something. The media will have a field day with that bracelet. WHY NOT? That should keep them off our backs for a while."

"Deputy," Edward X. Delaney said, "could I see you outside for a minute? Alone?"

"Sure, Edward," Thorsen said genially. "We're all finished in here, aren't we?"

Delaney closed the door of Sergeant Boone's office. Thorsen took the swivel chair behind the desk. Delaney remained standing. Slowly, methodically, he bit the tip off a cigar, threw it into the wastebasket. Then he twirled the cigar in his lips, lighted it carefully, puffed.

He stood braced, feet spread. His hands were clasped behind him, cigar clenched in his teeth. He looked at Thorsen critically through the smoke.

"Ivar," he said coldly, "you're a goddamned idiot."

Thorsen rose from his chair slowly, his face white. Chilled eyes stared directly at Delaney. He leaned forward until his knuckles were pressing the desktop. The Admiral's body was hunched, rigid.

"You're going to release it all, aren't you?" Delaney went on. "The physical description, the clothes, the bracelet . . . You're going to go public."

"That's right," the Deputy Commissioner said tightly.

"Then I'll tell you exactly what's going to happen. As soon as this woman reads it in the papers, the next time she goes out to kill she's going to change the color of her wig or leave it off completely. She's going to dress like a schoolmarm or a librarian. And she's going to drop that bracelet down the nearest sewer."

"We'll have to take that chance," Thorsen said tonelessly.

"Goddamnit!" Delaney exploded. "You release that stuff, and we're back to square one. Who the hell are the decoys going to look for? Without the wig and flashy clothes and bracelet, she'll look like a million other women. You're making the same stupid mistake Slavin did—talking too much."

"My responsibility is to alert possible victims," Thorsen said. "To circulate as complete a description as possible so people know who to look for. My first job is to protect the public."

"Bull*shit!*" Delaney said disgustedly. "Your first job is to protect the NYPD. The money men and the media are dumping all over you, so you figure to toss them a bone to prove the Department is on the job and making progress. So for the sake of your fucking public relations, you're going to jeopardize the whole goddamned investigation."

They glared at each other, eyes locked, both pressing forward aggressively. Their friendship would survive this, they knew. Their friendship wasn't at issue. It was their wills that were in conflict—and not for the first time.

Ivar Thorsen sat down again, as slowly as he had stood up. He sat on the edge of the chair. His thin fingers drummed silently on the desk. He never took his eyes from Delaney's.

"All right," he said, "there's some truth in what you say. *Some* truth. But you're getting your ass in an uproar because you can't or won't see the value of good public relations. I happen to believe the public's perception of the Department—the image, if that's what you want to call it—is just as important as the Department's performance. We could be the greatest hotshot cops in the world, and what the hell good would that do if we were perceived as a bunch of nincompoops, Keystone Kops jumping in the air and chasing dogs? I'm not saying the image is primary; it's not. Performance comes first, and is the foundation of the image. You want more cops on the street, don't you? You want better pay, better training, better equipment? How the hell do you expect us to ask for those things if the politicians and the public see us as a disorganized mob of hopeless bunglers?"

"I'm just saying that for the sake of keeping the press off your neck for a few days, you're making it a lot tougher to break this thing."

"Maybe," Thorsen said. "And what do you think would happen if we tried to keep this Anne Rogovich under wraps and the papers got onto it somehow? How would I explain why the public wasn't alerted to what the killer looks like and what she wears? They'd crucify us!"

"Look," Delaney said, "we can go around and around on this. We have different priorities, that's all."

"The hell we do," the Admiral said. "I want to put her down as much as you do. More. But it's an ego thing with you. Isn't that right—isn't it an ego thing?"

Delaney was silent.

"You've got tunnel vision on this case, Edward. All you can see is stopping a killer. Fine. You're a cop; that's all you're supposed to be thinking about. But there are other, uh, considerations that I've got to be aware of. And the Department's reputation is one of them. You're involved in the present. I am, too. But I've also got to think about the future."

"I still say you're fucking up the investigation," Delaney said stubbornly.

Ivar Thorsen sighed. "I don't think so. Possibly making it more difficult, but I think the benefits outweigh the risks. I may be wrong, I admit, but that's my best judgment. And that's the way it's going to be."

They were silent, still staring at each other. Finally Thorsen spoke softly . . .

"By the way, I happen to know we'd never have gotten onto this Anne Rogovich if you hadn't sent Bentley's men back to question if anyone remembered a man with scarred hands. That was good work."

The Chief grunted.

"Edward," the Deputy said, "you want off?"

"No," Delaney said, "I don't want off."

"What *is* it?" Monica said. "You've been a pain in the ass all night."

"Have I?" he said morosely. "I guess I have."

They were in their beds, both sitting up, both trying to read. The overhead light was on, and the bedside lamp. The window air conditioner was humming, and would until they agreed it was time to sleep. Then it would be turned off and the other window opened wide.

Now Monica had pushed her glasses atop her head. She had closed her book, a forefinger inserted to mark her place. She had turned toward her husband. Her words might have been challenging, but her tone was troubled and solicitous.

He told her about his run-in with Ivar Thorsen, repeating the conversation as accurately as he could. She listened in silence. When he finished, and asked, "What do you think?" she was quiet a moment longer. Then:

"You really think that's what she'll do? I mean, leave off the wig and bracelet and dress plainly?"

"Monica," he said, "this is not a stupid woman. She's no bimbo peddling her ass or a spaced-out wacko with a nose full of shit. Everything so far points to careful planning, smart reactions to unforeseen happenings, and very, very cool determination. She's going to read that description in the papers—or hear it on TV—and she's going to realize we're on to her disguise. Then she'll go in the opposite direction."

"How can you be sure it *is* a disguise? Maybe she dresses that way ordinarily."

"No, no. She was trying to change her appearance; I'm sure of it. First of all, a woman of her intelligence wouldn't ordinarily dress that way. Also, she knew the chances were good that someone would see her with one of the victims and remember her. So she'd want to look as different as possible from the way she does in everyday life."

"What you're saying is that in everyday life she looks like a schoolmarm or librarian—like you told Ivar?"

"Well . . . I'd guess she's a very ordinary looking lady. Dresses conventionally. Acts in a very conservative manner. Maybe even a dull woman. That's the way I see her. Mousy. Until she breaks out and kills."

"You make her sound schizophrenic."

"Oh no. I don't think she's that. No, she knows who she is. She can function in society and not make waves. But she's a psychopath. A walking, functioning psychopath."

"Thank you, doctor. And why does she kill?"

"Who the hell knows?" he said crossly. "She has her reasons. Maybe they wouldn't make sense to anyone else, but they make sense to her. It's a completely different kind of logic. Oh yes, crazies have a logic all their own. And it *does* make sense—if you accept their original premises. For instance, if you really and truly believe that the earth is flat, then it makes sense not to travel too far or you might fall off the edge. The premise is nutty, but the reasoning that follows from it is logical."

"I'd really like to know her," Monica said slowly. "I mean, talk to her. I'd like to know what's going through her mind."

"Her mind?" Delaney said. "I don't think you'd like it in there. Listen, when I was having that go-around with Ivar, he said something that bothers me. That's why I've been so grouchy all night. He said, 'It's an ego thing with you.' "

"What did he mean by that?"

"I think he was saying that this case has become a personal thing with me. That I'm out to prove that I'm smarter than the Hotel Ripper. That I can plan better, react faster, outthink her. That I'm *superior* to her."

"You mean you don't want a woman to get the better of you?"

"Come on! Don't get your feminist balls in an uproar. No, Ivar just meant that I see this thing as a personal challenge."

"And is he right?"

"Oh shit," he said roughly. "Who the hell has a coherent philosophy or a beautifully organized chart of beliefs that doesn't get daily scratching-outs and additions? Maybe the ego thing is *part* of it, but it's not *all* of it. There are other things."

"Like what?"

"Like the simple, basic belief that killing is wrong. Like the belief that the law, with all its stupidities and fuckups, is still the best we've been able to devise after all these thousands of years, and any assault on the law should be punished. And also, homicide isn't only an assault on the law, it's an attack against humanity."

"That I don't follow."

"All right, then murder is a crime against life. Does that make more sense?"

"You mean all life? Cows? And the birds and the bees and the flowers?"

"You should have been a Jesuit," he said, smiling. "But you know what I mean. I'm just saying that human life should not be taken lightly. Maybe there are more important things, but life itself is important enough so that anyone who destroys it for selfish motives should be punished."

"And you think this woman, this Hotel Ripper, has selfish motives?"

"*All* killers have selfish motives. Even those who say they were just obeying the command of God. When you get right down to it, they're just doing it because it makes them feel good."

She was incredulous. "You think this woman is killing because it makes her feel good?"

"Sure," he said cheerfully. "No doubt about it."

"That's awful."

"Is it? We all act from self-interest, don't we?"

"Edward, you don't really believe that, do you?"

"Of course I do. And what's so awful about it? The only problem is that most people spend their lives trying to figure out where their best interest lies, and nine times out of ten they're wrong."

"But I suppose you know where your best interest lies?"

"That's easy. In your bed."

"Pig."

About an hour later he turned off the air conditioner.

Delaney had no sooner settled down in the study to read his morning *Times* when the phone rang. The caller was Sergeant Abner Boone.

"Good morning, Chief."

"Morning, sergeant."

"Sorry to bother you so early, sir, but I was wondering if you were planning to drop by the precinct today."

"I wasn't, no. Should I?"

"Well, ah, I'm going to ask a favor."

"Sure. What gives?"

"I got a call from that Dr. Patrick Ho. He's got the hospital reports on the blood analysis and wants to come over to talk to me. He told me a little about it on the phone, and, Chief, I can't make any sense out of it at all. I'm up to my ass in paperwork and I was wondering if you'd be willing to talk to Dr. Ho at your place. Keep him out of my hair."

Delaney reflected that Boone was beginning to show the pressure. He was becoming increasingly dour and snappish. He should be pushing Dr. Ho for results, not trying to weasel out of talking to the man.

"You don't like him much, do you, sergeant?" he said.

"No, sir, I don't," Boone said. "He smells like a fruitcake and he treats this whole thing like some kind of scientific riddle. I still think he's just trying to make points and wasting our time in the process."

"Could be," Delaney said, thinking that maybe Boone simply wanted to disassociate himself from a loser.

"Will you deal with him, sir?"

"Sure," the Chief said genially. "Give him my address. I'll be in all morning."

Dr. Patrick Ho arrived about an hour later and made an immediate hit with Monica. She was in the kitchen, preparing a salad, and the doctor insisted on showing her how to make radish rosettes and how to slice a celery stalk so it resembled an exotic bloom.

Delaney finally got him into the study and provided him with a cup of tea. He then sat in his swivel chair, benignly watching Dr. Ho flip through a stack of papers he pulled from a battered briefcase.

"So?" the Chief said. "How did you make out with the hospitals?"

"Ah, splendid," the beaming little man said. "They were very cooperative when I explained why their aid was absolutely vital. And it was something to tell their families and friends—no? That they worked on the Hotel Ripper case."

"And were you able to identify the two unknown substances in the killer's blood?"

"Ah, yes. Where is it? Ah, here it is. Yes, yes. High potassium, low sodium, chloride, and bicarbonate, as we already knew. The two previously unidentified substances were high levels of ACTH and MSH."

He looked up at Delaney, delighted but modest, as if expecting a round of applause.

"ACTH and MSH?" the Chief asked.

"Exactly. Abnormally high levels."

"Doctor," Delaney said with great patience, "what are ACTH and MSH?"

"Pituitary hormones," Dr. Ho said happily. "They would not be present at such levels in normal blood. And something I find very, *very* interesting is that MSH is a melanocyte-stimulating hormone. I would be willing to venture the opinion that the woman whose blood this is has noticeable skin discolorations. A darkening, like a very heavy suntan, but perhaps grayish or dirty-looking."

"All over her body?"

"Oh no. I doubt that. But in exposed portions of the skin. Face, neck, hands, and so forth. Possibly on the elbows and nipples. Points of friction or pressure."

"Interesting," Delaney said, "what you can deduce from a blood analysis. Tell me, doctor, is it possible to identify an individual from an analysis of the blood? Like fingerprints?"

"Oh no," Dr. Ho said. "No, no, no. Perhaps, someday, the genetic code, but not the blood. You see, this liquid is affected by what we eat, what we drink, drugs that may be ingested, and so forth. The chemical composition of the blood is constantly changing, weekly, daily, almost minute to minute. So as a means of positive identification, I fear it would be without value. However, a complete blood profile can be a marvelous clue to the physical condition of the donor. And that is what we now have: a complete blood profile."

"Those hormones you mentioned—what were they?"

"ACTH and MSH."

"Yes. You said they were present in abnormally high levels in the killer's blood?"

"That is correct."

"Well, why is that? I mean, what would cause those high levels?"

"Illness," the doctor said with delight. "I would say that almost certainly the woman who owned this blood is suffering from some disease. Or at least some serious physiological malfunction. Chief Delaney, this is very odd blood. Very peculiar indeed."

"Would you care to make a guess as to what the illness might be?"

"Ah, no," Dr. Patrick Ho confessed, frowning sorrowfully. "That is beyond my experience and training. Also, the hematologists I consulted were unable to hazard a guess as to the illness, disease, or perhaps genetic fault that might be producing this curious blood."

"Well . . ." Delaney said, rocking back in his chair, lacing fingers across his stomach, "then I guess we're stymied, aren't we? End of the road."

Dr. Ho was horrified. His dark eyes widened, rosy lips pouted, plump hands fluttered in the air.

"Ah, no!" he protested. "No, no, no! I have obtained the names of the three best diagnosticians in New York. I will take our blood profile to these doctors and they will tell me what the illness is."

Delaney laughed. "You never give up, do you?"

Dr. Patrick Ho sobered. He looked at the Chief with eyes suddenly shrewd and piercing.

"No," he said, "I never give up. Do you?"

"No," Delaney said and stood to shake hands.

On the way out, Dr. Ho stopped at the kitchen and showed Monica how to slice raw carrots into attractive curls.

On June 25th, at the morning meeting of the Hotel Ripper task force in Midtown Precinct North, certain personnel changes were decided on.

Lieutenant Wilson T. Crane's squad was reduced to a minimum and most of his men assigned to the task of compiling and organizing the list of women who might have had access to the convention schedule. Lieutenant Crane was put in command of this group.

Detective Daniel Bentley's squad was also reduced, the men being switched to Detective Aaron Johnson's small army who were attempting to track down purchases of Chemical Mace and other tear gases in the New York area.

Detective Bentley was assigned to work with a police artist on sketches prepared from the scant description furnished by cocktail waitress Anne Rogovich.

Sergeant Thomas K. Broderick was given additional men to expedite the questioning of clerks in department stores and jewelry shops where the WHY NOT? bracelet was sold.

Everyone recognized that all these personnel shifts were merely paper changes and represented no significant breakthroughs. Still, progress was being made, and it was estimated that within a week, questioning of individual women on the convention schedule access list could begin.

And Detective Johnson reported that at the same time his men could start personal visits to the purchasers of tear gas. Every container, gun, and generator would be physically examined by Johnson's crew—or an explanation demanded for its absence.

It was decided that everyone in the task force—deskmen and street cops alike—would be on duty during the nights of June 29th through July 2nd. Midtown Manhattan would be flooded with uniformed and plainclothes officers from 8:00 P.M., to 2:00 A.M.

In addition, squad cars and unmarked vehicles would continually tour the streets of this section, and some would be parked in front of the larger hotels that were hosting conventions. The Crime Scene Unit was alerted and a command post established once again in Midtown Precinct South.

A larger number of policewomen in mufti were added to the stakeout crews in hotel bars and cocktail lounges. The reasoning here was that the women might be better able to spot suspicious behavior in another female.

It was debated whether or not an appeal should be issued asking the public to avoid the midtown area on the nights in question. It was decided the warning would be counterproductive.

"We'd have wackos flocking in from Boston to Philly," was the consensus.

When the meeting broke up, Delaney and Sergeant Boone walked out into the corridor to find a beaming Dr. Patrick Ho awaiting them. The sergeant gave the Chief a look of anguished entreaty.

"Please," he begged in a low voice, "you take him. Use my office." He hurried away.

After an exchange of polite pleasantries, during which the doctor inquired after the health of the Chief's wife, the two men went into Boone's office. Delaney closed the door to muffle the loud talk, laughter, and shouts in the hallway.

He took the swivel chair. Dr. Ho sat in a battered wooden armchair and crossed his short legs delicately, smoothing his trouser crease to avoid wrinkles.

"Well . . ." Delaney said, "I hope you have some good news to report."

"Ah, regrettably no," Dr. Ho said sadly, making his face into a theatrical mask of sorrow.

Then Delaney wondered if Boone might be right. Perhaps this busy little man was jerking them around and wanted nothing but a vacation from his regular job.

"You saw the diagnosticians?" he asked, more sharply than he had intended.

"I did indeed," the doctor said, nodding vigorously. "These are very big, important men, and they were exceedingly kind to lend their assistance."

"But no soap, eh?"

"I beg your pardon?"

"They couldn't say what the illness was?"

"Ah, no, they could not. All three agreed it is a most unusual blood profile, completely unique in their experience. Two of them refused to venture any opinion, or even a guess. They said that in the absence of an actual physical examination, they would require much more documentation: X rays, tissue samples, urinalysis, electrocardiograms, scans, sputum and feces tests, and so forth. The third man also would not offer an opinion solely on the basis of the blood profile. However, he suggested a hyperactive pituitary might be involved, but beyond that he would not go."

"Uh-huh," Delaney said. "Well, I can't really blame them. We didn't give them a whole hell of a lot to go on. So that's it? We've taken it as far as we can go?"

"Oh no!" Dr. Patrick Ho said. "No, no, no! I have more, ah, arrows in my quiver."

"I thought you might," the Chief said. "What now?"

Dr. Ho leaned forward, serious and intent.

"There are, in this marvelous country, several diagnostic computers. A fine one at the University of Pittsburgh, another at Stanford Medical, one at the National Library of Medicine, and so forth. Now these computers have stored in their memory banks many thousand symptoms and manifestations of disease. When a series of such manifestations is given to the machine, it is able, sometimes, to make a diagnosis, name the disease, and prescribe treatment."

Delaney sat upright.

"My God," he said, "I had no idea such computers existed. That's wonderful!"

"Ah, yes," the doctor said, gratified by the Chief's reaction, "I think so, too. If insufficient input is fed to the computers, they cannot always make a firm diagnosis, of course. But in such cases they can sometimes furnish several possibilities."

"And you want to send your blood profile to the computers?"

"Precisely," Dr. Ho said, blinking happily. "I would also include the sex of the subject and what physical description we have. I have prepared long telegrams telling the authorities the nature of the emergency and requesting computer time for a diagnosis."

"I don't see why not," Delaney said slowly. "Having started this, we might as well see it through."

"Ah, there is one small problem," the doctor said, almost shyly. "These telegrams will be costly. I would like official authorization."

"Sure," Delaney said, shrugging. "In for a penny, in for a pound. Send them from this phone right here. If you get any flak, say they were authorized by Deputy Commissioner Ivar Thorsen. I'll square it with him."

"Ah, thank you very much, sir. You are most understanding, and I am in your debt."

Dr. Ho rummaged through his scruffy briefcase and brought out several sheets of paper. Delaney let him have the swivel chair and the doctor prepared to phone.

"Tell me, Dr. Ho," the Chief said, "just as a matter of curiosity . . . If the computers don't come up with a diagnosis, what will you do then?"

"Oh," the little man said cheerfully, "I'll think of something."

Delaney stared at him.

"I'll bet you will," he said.

On July 1st, a Tuesday, at 10:14 A.M., a call was received at 911 reporting a violent death at the Tribunal Motor Inn on 49th Street west of Tenth Avenue. The caller identified himself as the Tribunal's chief of security.

The alert was forwarded to Midtown North. The precinct duty sergeant dispatched a foot patrolman in the vicinity via radio, two uniformed officers in a squad car, and two plainclothesmen in an unmarked car.

He also informed commanders of the Hotel Ripper task force who were, at the time, holding their morning meeting upstairs in the precinct house. Sergeant Abner Boone sent Detectives Bentley and Johnson to check it out.

While they were waiting for the Yes or No call, the others sat in silence, smoking, sipping stale coffee from soggy cardboard containers. Edward X. Delaney rose to locate the Tribunal on a precinct map Scotch-taped to the wall. Deputy Commissioner Thorsen joined him.

"What do you think, Edward?" he asked in a low voice.

"Not exactly midtown," the Chief replied, "but close enough."

They sat down again and waited. No one spoke. They could hear the noises of a busy precinct coming from the lower floors. They could even hear the bubbling sound as Lieutenant Crane blew through his pipe stem to clear it.

When the phone rang, all the men in the room jerked convulsively. They watched Boone pick it up in a hard grip, his knuckles white.

"Sergeant Boone," he said throatily.

He listened a moment. He hung up the phone. He turned a tight face to the others.

"Let's go," he said.

They went with a rush, chairs clattering over, men pouring from offices, feet pounding down the stairs.

"What's the goddamn hurry?" Sergeant Broderick said in a surly voice. "She's long gone."

Then engines starting up, blare of horns, the wail of sirens. Delaney rode in Deputy Thorsen's car, the uniformed driver swinging wildly onto Eighth Avenue, west on 55th Street to Ninth Avenue, south to 49th Street.

"She fucked us again," the Admiral said wrathfully, and the Chief mused idly on how rarely Thorsen used language like that.

By the time they pulled up with a squeal of brakes in front of the Tribunal, the street was already choked with police vehicles, vans, an ambulance. A crowd was growing, pushed back by precinct cops until barricades could be erected.

The hotel was already cordoned: no one in or out without showing identification. Motor inn staff, residents, and visitors were being lined up in the lobby for questioning. A uniformed officer guarding the elevator bank sent them up to the fifth floor.

There was a mob in the corridor, most of them clustered about Room 508. Sergeant Boone stood in the doorway, his face stony.

"It was her all right," he said, his voice empty. "Throat slashed, stab wounds in the nuts. The clunk was Chester LaBranche, twenty-four, from Barre, Vermont. He was here for some kind of a college convention."

"A convention again," Thorsen said bitterly. "And twenty-four. A kid!"

"Did we have any decoys in the place?" Delaney asked.

"No," Boone said shortly. "The place is small and this neighborhood isn't exactly Times Square, so we didn't cover it."

The Deputy Commissioner started to say something, then shut his mouth.

Tommy Callahan came to the doorway.

"Naked," he reported. "Half on and half off the bed. No signs of a struggle. Looks like the early kills when she came up behind them. All the blood appears to be his. We'll scrape the bathroom drains, but it doesn't look good."

Lou Gorki shouldered him out of the way. The Crime Scene Unit man was holding a wineglass by two fingers spread wide inside. There was a half-inch of amber liquid at the bottom. The outside of the glass was whitened with powder.

"It's wine all right," Gorki said. "I dipped a finger. Chablis. Vintage of yesterday. But the kicker is that there's also a half-empty bottle of beer and a glass. No guy is going to drink beer and wine at the same time. Good prints on both. I figure this wineglass was hers."

"Check it out," Boone said.

"Sure," Gorki said. "We'll take everything downtown for the transfers. At least now we got a make if we ever pull someone in on this thing."

"Sarge," Detective Johnson said from behind them, "I think maybe we lucked onto something. I got a waiter upstairs who says he might have seen her."

They trooped after him to a staircase at the end of the corridor, closed off with a red Exit sign above the door.

"This guy's name is Tony Pizzi," Johnson said as they climbed the concrete stairs. "He's on the day shift today, but yesterday he worked from six until two. He hustles drinks in the outdoor lounge by the pool. Then, when the pool and bar closed at midnight, he went downstairs to help out in the main bar. He thinks he served LaBranche and a woman up here. Bottled beer and white wine."

Anthony Pizzi was a sleepy-eyed man, short, chunky rather than fat. He was wearing a white apron cinched up under his armpits. The apron bulged with the bulk of his belly.

He had a fleshy, saturnine face cut in half with a narrow black mustache, straight across, cheek to cheek. His teeth were almonds, and he had a raspy New York voice. Delaney figured the accent for Brooklyn, probably Bushwick.

They got him seated at a corner table and hunched around him on metal chairs. A bartender, polishing one glass, watched them intently, but a man cleaning the pool with a long-handled screen paid no attention.

"Tony," Detective Johnson said, "will you go through it again, please, for these men? When you came on duty, what you did, what you saw. The whole schmeer."

"I come on duty at six o'clock," Pizzi started, "and—"

"This was yesterday?" Boone interrupted sharply.

"Yeah. Yesterday. Monday. So I come on duty at six o'clock, and there's a few people in the pool, not many, but at that time we're busy at the bar. The cocktail crowd, y'unnerstan. Martinis and Manhattans. We got one waiter here, me, and one bartender. In the afternoon, you can buy a sandwich, like, but not after six. So's people will go down to the dining room, y'unnerstan. So the crowd thins out like till nine-ten, around there, and then we begin to fill up again, and people come up for a swim."

Sergeant Boone was the interrogator.

"What time do you close?"

"Twelve. On the dot. Then anyone he wants to keep on drinking, he's got to go down to the lobby bar. Unless he wants to drink in his room, y'unnerstan. Anyways, last night about ten-eleven, like that, a couple of people in the pool, all the tables taken . . . Not that I'm all that rushed, y'unnerstan, with the tables filled. This is a small place; look around. Mostly couples and parties of four. Two guys by theirselves and one dame. The guys are double bourbons on the rocks and bottled Millers. The dame is white wine. The bourbon guy is like maybe fifty, around there, lushing like there's no tomorrow, and the beer guy is nursing his bottles. The wine dame is sipping away, not fast, not slow."

"You allow unescorted women up here?"

"Why not? If they conduct theirselves in a ladylike manner, y'unnerstan, they can drink up a storm—who cares?"

"Describe the young guy, Tony. The one drinking beer by himself."

"He's like—oh, about twenty-five, I'd guess. Tall, real tall, and thin. He's got long blond hair, like down to his shoulders and all over his ears, and a beard. But not a hippie, y'unnerstan. He's clean and dressed nice."

"What was he wearing—do you remember?"

"Khaki pants and a sports jacket."

They looked at Boone. The sergeant nodded grimly.

"Those were the clothes he took off," he said. "That was him. What about the woman, Tony. Can you describe her?"

"I din get a good look. She's sitting over there at that small table. See? Next to the palms. At night, most of the light comes from around the pool, so she's in shadow, y'unnerstan. About forty, I'd guess, give or take."

"Tall?"

"Yeah, I'd say so. Maybe five-six or -seven."

"Wearing a hat?"

"No hat. Brown hair. Medium. Cut short."

"How was she dressed?"

"Very plain. Nothing flashy. White turtleneck sweater. One of those denim things with shoulder straps."

"Was she pretty?"

"Nah. You'd never look at her once. Flat-chested. Flat heels. No makeup. A nothing."

"All right, now we got the woman by herself drinking white wine and the young blond guy by himself drinking beer. How did they get together?"

"The kid stands up, takes his bottle and glass, and goes over to her table. I'm watching him, y'unnerstan, because if she screams bloody murder, then I'll have to go over and tell him to cool it. But he talks and she talks, and I see them smiling, and after a while he sits down with her, and they keep talking and smiling, so I couldn't care less."

"Did you hear what they were talking about?"

"Nah. Who wants to listen to that bullshit? When they signal me, I bring another round of drinks: That's all I'm getting paid for. Not to listen to bullshit."

"When they left, did they leave together?"

"Sure. They were the last to go. That's how come I remember them so good. The place emptied out and I had to go over and tell them we was closing. So they paid their bill and left."

"Who paid the bill?"

"They each paid their own tabs. That was okay by me; they both left a tip so I did all right."

"Did you see where they went? To the elevators?"

"I din see. I went to the bar with the money and checks. When I come back, they was gone. My tips was on the table. Also, they took their glasses with them."

"Wasn't that unusual?"

"Nah. People staying here at the hotel, they don't finish a drink, they take it down to their rooms with them. The maids find the glasses and return them up here. No one loses."

"So they left around midnight?"

"Right to the minute."

Sergeant Boone looked at Delaney. "Chief?" he asked.

"Tony," Delaney said, "this woman—can you tell us more about her?"

"Like what?"

"Can you guess what she weighed?"

"Skinny. Couldn't have been more than one-twenty. Probably less."

"What about her voice?"

"Nothing special. Low. Polite."

"Her posture?"

"I din notice. Sorry."

"You're doing fine. You didn't happen to notice if she was wearing a gold bracelet, did you?"

"I don't remember seeing no gold bracelet."

"You said she was plain looking?"

"Yeah. A kind of a long face."

"If you had to guess what kind of work she does, what would you guess?"

"A secretary maybe. Like that."

"Did she touch the young guy?"

"Touch him?"

"His cheek. Stroke his hair. Put her hand on his arm. Anything like that?"

"You mean was she coming on? Nah, nothing like that."

"Did you ever see either of them before?"

"Never."

"Together or separately? Never been here before?"

"I never saw them."

"Did they act like they knew each other? Like old friends meeting by accident?"

"Nah. It was a pickup, pure and simple."

"When they left at midnight, would you say they were drunk?"

"No way. I could look up the bill, but I'd say he had three-four beers and she had three-four wines. But they wasn't drunk."

"Feeling no pain?"

"Not even that. Just relaxed and friendly. No trouble. When I told them we was closing, they din make no fuss."

"Do you remember the color of the woman's eyes?"

"I din see."

"Guess."

"Brown."

"Did you think they were guests here at the hotel?"

"Who knows? They come and go. Also, we get a lot of outsiders stop by for a drink. Off the street, y'unnerstan."

"Was the woman wearing perfume?"

"Don't remember any if she was."

"Anything at all you recall about her? Anything we haven't asked?"

"No, not really. She was nothing special, y'unnerstan. Just another woman."

"Uh-huh. Thank you, Tony. That's all I've got. Sergeant?"

"Thanks for your help, Tony," Boone said. "Detective Johnson will take you over to the station house and get a signed statement. Don't worry about getting docked; we'll make it right with your boss."

"Sure, I don't mind. You think this woman put him under?"

"Could be."

"She the Hotel Ripper?"

"Johnson," Boone said, gesturing, and the detective led Anthony Pizzi away.

"Good witness," Delaney said. "Those hooded eyes fooled me. He doesn't miss much. Hit him again in a day or so, sergeant. He'll be thinking about it, and maybe he'll remember more things."

"I suppose you blame me, Edward," Ivar Thorsen said.

"Blame you? For what?"

"She did what you said she'd do—left off the wig and bracelet, dressed plainly. After she read the newspaper stories."

Delaney shrugged. "Under the bridge and over the dam. Even if she had dressed up like a tart, I think she would have murdered LaBranche and walked away. Maybe it worked out for the best; now we got a firmer description of what she really looks like. Sergeant, don't forget to have Bentley take Anthony Pizzi to the police artist. Maybe they can refine that sketch."

"Do it today," Boone promised. "Anything else, Chief?"

"Nooo, not really."

"Something bothering you, Edward?"

"Up to now she's been so goddamned clever. Made sure she picked up her victims in a big, crowded place so no one would remember her. Made sure she wiped her prints clean. Now, all of a sudden, she meets the guy in a small place. Lets him pick her up in a way that people will recall. Stays late until they're the only two left. The waiter was sure to remember. Then carries her wineglass down to his room and leaves it there with prints all over it. Stupid, stupid, stupid! I can't understand it. It's just not like her."

"Maybe," Ivar Thorsen said slowly, "maybe she wants to be caught."

Delaney looked at him. "You think so? It's possible, but that's a fancy-schmancy explanation. Maybe the reason is simpler than that. Maybe she's just tired."

"Tired?"

"Weary. Fatigued. Can you imagine what the stress must be like? Picking up these strangers, any one of whom could be a sadistic killer himself. Then going up against them with a pocket knife. Killing them and destroying any evidence that would point to her. My God, the strain of doing all that, month after month."

"You think she's falling apart?" Boone asked.

"It makes sense, doesn't it? Especially when she reads the papers and realizes that little by little we're getting closer. I think the tension is beginning to get to her. She's not thinking straight anymore. She's forgetting things. The pressure is building up. Yes, sergeant, I think she's cracking."

"Is there anything more we could be doing?" Thorsen asked anxiously.

"Finish that sketch," Delaney said, "and get it out to all the newspapers and TV stations. Better put extra men on to handle the calls. Start immediately on individual interviews with every woman between the ages of, say, twenty-five and fifty, on the convention schedule access list. Get Johnson's men started on the physical examination of every tear gas container sold in New York."

"Right," Sergeant Boone said. "We'll put on the heat."

"You better," Delaney said drily. "We've only got another twenty-six days."

"I'm not sure I'll be around then," Deputy Commissioner Thorsen said.

They looked at him and realized he wasn't joking.

Delaney left the motor inn, pushed through the crowd on the street, and caught a cab going uptown on Tenth Avenue. He sat crossways on the back seat, stretching out his legs.

He thought of Thorsen's last comment. He reckoned the Admiral might weather this latest unsolved killing, but if there was another late in July, Thorsen would be tossed to the wolves and a new commander brought in.

It would be a hard, cruel thing to do, and would put an effective end to the Deputy's career in the NYPD. But Ivar knew the risk when he accepted the job of stopping the Hotel Ripper. Delaney could imagine the man's fury with this "plain looking, nothing special" woman whose fate was linked with his.

Monica met him in the hallway and put a hand on his arm. She had evidently heard the news on the radio, for she looked at him with shocked eyes.

"Another one?" she said.

He nodded.

"Edward," she said, almost angrily, "when is this going to stop?"

"Soon," he said. "I hope. We're getting there, but it's slow work. Ivar won't—"

"Edward," she interrupted, "Dr. Ho is waiting for you in the living room. I told him I didn't know when you'd be back, but he said he had to see you."

"All right," Delaney said, sighing. "I'll see what he wants now."

He hung his skimmer away in the hall closet, then opened the door to the living room.

The moment he appeared, Dr. Patrick Ho bounced to his feet. His eyes were burning with triumph. He waved a sheaf of yellow telegrams wildly.

"Addison's disease!" he shouted. "Addison's disease!"

11

July 1, Tuesday . . .

There had been a brief, hard summer squall just before Zoe Kohler left work. When she came out onto Madison Avenue, the pavement was steaming, gutters running with filth. The clogged air bit and stank of wet char.

She walked down to the office of Dr. Oscar Stark. She passed a liquor store, saw in the window a display of wines. She thought of the wineglass she had left in the hotel room of Chester LaBranche.

It was not a serious oversight—her fingerprints were not on file, anywhere—but the slipup bothered her. In many ways—in the Hotel Granger office, in the clean order of her home—she was a perfectionist. She knew it and found pride in it.

So this minor error annoyed her. It was the first mistake she could not blame on chance or accident. It depressed her because it tainted her adventure, made it bumbling happenstance instead of a clear statement of her will.

"Did you hear about the new murder?" the receptionist asked excitedly. "The Hotel Ripper again."

"I heard," Zoe Kohler said. "It's awful."

"Just awful," the woman agreed.

When Dr. Stark came into the examination room, preceded by a plume of cigar smoke, the first thing he said was, "Where's your bracelet?"

Her heart surged, then settled when she realized he was not referring to the gold links with the WHY NOT? legend, but to her medical identification strap stating she was a victim of Addison's disease.

"Uh, I took a shower this morning," she said, "and forgot to put it back on."

"Oh sure," he said. "But the kit's in your purse, isn't it?" Then, when she didn't answer, he said, "Zoe, Zoe, what am I going to do with you?"

He scanned the clipboard Gladys handed him. Then he commanded Zoe to stand and drop the sheet. He hitched the wheeled stool closer until his face was only inches from her sunken abdomen.

"Look at you," he said wrathfully. "Skin and bones! And look at this . . . and this . . . and this . . ."

He showed her the bronzy discolorations on her knees, elbows, knuckles, nipples. Then he plucked at her pubic hair, displayed what came away.

"See?" he demanded. "See? You're taking your medication?"

"Yes, I am. Every day."

He grunted. The remainder of the examination was conducted in silence. Because she was having her period, the pelvic probing and Pap smear were omitted.

It seemed to Zoe that he was not as gentle as usual. He was rough, almost savage, in his handling of her body. He ignored her gasps and groans.

"I'll see you in my office," he said grimly, picking up his cigar and stomping out.

He seemed a little calmer when she sat down facing him across his littered desk. He was, she saw, writing rapidly in her file.

Finally he tossed the pen aside. He relit his cold cigar. He pushed his glasses atop the halo of billowing white hair. He talked to the ceiling . . .

"Weight down," he said tonelessly. "Blood pressure up. Pulse rapid. Hyperpigmentation pronounced."

He brought his gaze down to stare into her eyes.

"Have you injured yourself?"

"No. Just that little cut on my leg. I told—"

"Have you been fasting? Have you stopped eating completely?"

"Of course not."

"Then you must be under some severe emotional or psychological stress that is affecting your body chemistry."

She was silent.

"Zoe," he said again in a kindlier tone, "what am I going to do with you? You come to me for advice and help. To assist you when you're ill or, better yet, to keep you healthy. Am I correct? For this, you pay me a fee, and I do my best. A nice relationship. But how can I do my job when you lie to me?"

"I don't lie to you," she said hotly.

He held up a palm. "All right, you don't lie. A poor choice of words. I apologize. But you withhold information from me, information I need to do my job. How can I help you if you refuse to tell me what I need to know?"

"I answer all your questions," she said.

"You don't," he said furiously. "You never tell me what I need to know. All right now, let's calm down, let's not get excited. We'll try again, very quietly, very logically. You are still taking the prescribed amount of cortisol?"

"Yes."

"And the salt tablets?"

"Yes."

"Do you have a craving for additional salt?"

"No."

"Your diet is well-balanced? You aren't on some faddish diet to lose weight fast?"

"No. I eat well."

"Any vomiting?"

"No."

"Nausea? Upset stomach?"

"No."

"Weakness?"

"Only during my period."

"Diarrhea or constipation?"

"No."

"When I probed your abdomen, you groaned."

"You hurt," she said.

"No," he said, "*you* hurt. The abdomen is tender?"

"I'm having my period," she protested.

"Uh-huh. And you're not wearing your bracelet or carrying your emergency kit?"

She didn't answer.

"Zoe," he said gently, "I want to put you in the hospital."

"No," she said immediately.

"Only for tests," he urged. "To find out what's going on here. I don't want to wait for your blood and urine tests; I want you in the hospital now. The last thing in the world we want is an Addisonian crisis. Believe me, it's no fun. We can prevent that if you go into the hospital now, and we can make tests I can't do here."

"I don't want to go into a hospital," she said. "I don't like hospitals."

"Who does? But sometimes they're necessary."

"No."

He sighed. "I can't knock you on the head and drag you there. Zoe, I think you should consult another physician. I think you may be happier with another doctor."

"I won't be happier. I don't want another doctor."

"All right, then *I'll* be happier. You won't tell me the truth. You won't follow my advice. I've done all I can for you. I really do think another physician will be better for both of us."

"No," she said firmly. "You can refuse to treat me if you want, but if you do, I won't go to anyone else. I just won't go to *any* other doctor."

They stared at each other. Something like a fearful wariness came into his eyes.

"Zoe," he said in a low voice, "I think there is a problem there. I mean a special problem that is not physical, that has nothing to do with Addison's, but is fueling the disease. You won't tell me about it, that's plain. I know a good man, a psychiatrist—will you talk to him?"

"What for? I don't have a special problem. Maybe I just need more medicine. Or a different medicine."

He drummed fingers on the desktop, looking at her reflectively. She sat quietly, legs crossed at the ankles, hands placidly clasped in her lap. She was expressionless, composed. Spine straight, head held high.

"I'll tell you exactly what I'm going to do," he said quietly. "I am going to wait until I have the results of your blood tests and urinalysis. If they show what I expect, I am going to call you and ask you once again to go into the hospital for further tests and treatment. If, at that time, you again refuse, I am going to call or wire your parents in Minnesota. I have their names and address in your file. I will explain the situation to them."

"You wouldn't," she said, gasping.

"Oh yes," he said, "I would, and will. At that time, the decision will be yours, and theirs. I'll have done everything I can possibly do. After that, it's out of my hands."

"And you'll just forget all about me," she said, beginning to weep.

"No," he said sadly, "I won't do that."

She stumbled home in the waning light of a summer night. The sky as bronzed as the tainted patches on her flesh. She saw, with dread, how ugly people were. Snout of pig and fang of snake.

It was a city of gargoyles, their lesions plain as hers. She could almost hear the howls and moans. The city writhed. "Special problems" everywhere. She was locked in a colony of the damned, the disease in or out, but festering.

Those answers she had given to Dr. Stark's questions—they were not lies, exactly.

She was aware of everything: her weakness, nausea, vertigo, salt craving, diarrhea. But she sloughed over these things, telling herself they were temporary, of no consequence. To admit them to Dr. Stark would give them an importance, a significance she knew was unwarranted.

And when he asked about emotional and psychological stress—well, that was simply prying into matters of no concern to him. She knew what he was doing, and was determined to block him. Her adventures were hers alone, private and secret.

Still, she was saddened by his threat to turn her away. Rejection again. Just as Kenneth had rejected her. And her father. He had rejected by ignoring her, but it was all the same.

She was still musing about rejection and how men did it with a sneer or a laugh, spurning something tender and yearning they could not appreciate and did not deserve, when Ernest Mittle called her soon after she returned home.

Ernie hadn't rejected her. He phoned almost every night, and they saw each other at least once a week and sometimes twice. She thought of him as a link, her only anchor to a gentle world that promised. No gargoyles or cries of pain in that good land.

He knew she had gone to the doctor for her monthly checkup, and asked how she made out.

She said everything was fine, she had passed with flying colors, but the doctor wanted her to eat more and put on a little weight.

He said that was marvelous because he wanted her to come down to his place on Saturday night for dinner. He was going to roast a small turkey.

She said that sounded like fun, and she would bring some of those strawberry tarts he liked. Then she asked him if he had heard anything about Maddie and Harry Kurnitz.

He said he had learned nothing new, but Mr. Kurnitz was still seeing the blonde, and was very irritable lately, and had Zoe heard about the latest Hotel Ripper killing, and wasn't it horrible?

She said yes, she had heard about it, and it was horrible, and had Ernie definitely scheduled his summer vacation?

He said he'd know by next week, and he hoped Zoe could get the same vacation time, and who was she going to vote for?

So it went: a phone conversation that lasted a half-hour. Just chatter, laughs, gossip. Nothing important in the content. But the voices were there. Even in talking about the weather, the voices were there. The soft tones.

"Good night, darling," he said finally. "I'll call you tomorrow."

"Good night, dear," she said. "Sleep well."

"You, too. I love you, Zoe."

"I love you, Ernie. Take care of yourself."

"You, too. I'll see you on Saturday, but I'll speak to you before that."

"Tomorrow night?"

"Oh yes, I'll call."

"Good. I love you, Ernie."

"I love you, sweetheart."

"Thank you for calling."

"Oh Zoe," he said, "be happy."

"I am," she said, "when I talk to you. When I'm with you. When I think of you."

"Think of me frequently," he said, laughing. "Promise?"

"I promise," she said, "if you'll dream of me. Will you?"

"I promise. Love you, darling."

"Love you."

She hung up, smiling. He had not rejected her, would not. Never once, not ever, had he criticized the way she looked, what she did, how she lived. He loved her for what she was and had no desire to change her.

"Mrs. Ernest Mittle." She spoke the title aloud. Then tried, "Mrs. Zoe Mittle."

He was not an exciting man, nor was he a challenge. There was no mystery to him. But he was caring and tender. She knew she was stronger than he, and loved him more for his weakness.

She would not have him different. Oh no. Never. She had her fill of male bluster and swagger. Maddie might call him "Mister Meek," but Maddie was incapable of seeing the sweet innocence of meekness, the scented fragility, as an infant is fragrant and vulnerable, shocked by hurt.

Zoe Kohler showered before she went to bed, not looking at her knobbed, discolored body. In bed, she dreamed that with Ernie at her side, always, as husband and helpmate, she might no longer have need for adventures.

Then the void would be filled, the ache dissolved. She would regain her health. She would blossom. Just blossom! They would create a world of two, and there would be no place for the cruel, the ugly, or the brutish.

July 2, Wednesday . . .

"Goddamn it!" Abner Boone shouted, and slapped a palm on the desktop. "Then you're not certain it definitely is this Addison's disease?"

Dr. Patrick Ho blinked at the sergeant's violence.

"Ah, no," he said regretfully. "Not certain. Not definite. But Addison's was first on the lists of possibilities from all computers queried. When a definite diagnosis cannot be computed because of lack of sufficient input, a list of possibilities is given with probability ratings. Addison's had the highest rating on all the lists."

"What probability?" Boone demanded. "What percentage?"

"Ah, a little above thirty percent."

"Jesus Christ!" the sergeant said disgustedly.

They were jammed into Boone's cramped office: the sergeant, Dr. Ho, Delaney, and Deputy Commissioner Thorsen.

"Let me get this straight," Thorsen said. "There's a thirty percent possibility that our killer is suffering from Addison's disease. Is that correct?"

"Ah, yes."

The Admiral looked at Delaney. "Edward?"

"Dr. Ho," the Chief said, "what is the possibility rating of the second highest ranked diagnosis?"

"Less than ten."

"So Addison's disease has three times the probability of the second diagnosis?"

"Yes."

"But still only about one chance in three of being accurate?"

"That is so."

"Mighty small odds to move on," Boone said glumly.

"Even if it was only one percent," Delaney said, "we'd have to move on it. We've got no choice. Doctor, I think you better tell us a little more about Addison's disease. I don't believe any of us knows exactly what it is."

"Ah, yes," Dr. Patrick Ho said, beaming. "Very understandable. It is quite rare. A physician might practice for fifty years and never treat a case."

"Just how rare?" Delaney said sharply. "Give us some numbers."

"Ah, I have been studying the available literature on the disease. One authority states the incidence is one case per hundred thousand population. Other estimates are slightly higher. There is, you understand, no registry of victims. I would guess, in the New York metropolitan area, possibly two hundred cases, but closer to one hundred. I am sorry I cannot be more precise, but there is simply no way of knowing."

"All right," Delaney said, "let's split the difference and say there are a hundred and fifty cases, with maybe thirty or forty in Manhattan. That's rare enough. Now, what exactly is this Addison's disease?"

Dr. Ho stood immediately and unbuttoned the jacket and vest of his natty tan poplin suit. A soft belly bulged over his knitted belt. Enthusiastically, he dug the fingers of both hands into an area below the rib cage.

"Ah, here," he said. "Approximately. Near the kidneys. Two glands called the adrenals. I will try to keep this as nontechnical as possible. These adrenal glands have a center portion called the medulla, and a covering or rind called the cortex. All right so far?"

He looked around the room. There were no questions from the other three men, so the doctor rebuttoned his vest and sat down again. He crossed his little legs slowly, adjusting the trouser crease with care.

"Now," he went on, "the adrenals secrete several important hormones. The medulla secretes adrenaline, for instance. You have heard of adrenaline? The cortex secretes cortisol, which you probably know as cortisone. The adrenals also secrete sex hormones. Of sex, of course, you have probably also heard."

The doctor giggled.

"Get on with it," Sergeant Boone growled.

"Ah, yes. Sometimes the cortex, the covering of the adrenal glands, is damaged, or even destroyed. This can be the result of tuberculosis, a fungal infection, a tumor, and other causes. When the cortex of the adrenals is damaged or destroyed, it cannot produce cortisol. The results can be catastrophic. Weakness, weight loss, nausea and vomiting, low blood pressure, abdominal pains, and so forth. If untreated, the course of the disease is invariably fatal."

"And if it's treated?" Delaney asked.

"Ah, there is the problem. Because it is such a rare disorder, and because so few doctors are familiar with the symptoms, the disease is sometimes not diagnosed correctly. The early manifestations, such as weakness, nausea, constipation, and so forth, could simply indicate a viral infection or the flu. But as the disease progresses, one symptom appears that is almost a certain clue: portions of the body—the elbows, knees, knuckles, the lips and creases of the palms—become discolored. These can be tan, brown, or bronze patches, like suntan. Sometimes they are bluish-black, sometimes gray. The reason for this discoloration is very interesting."

He paused and looked about brightly. He had their attention; there was no doubt of that.

"There is a small gland in the brain called the pituitary, sometimes known as the 'master gland.' It produces secretions that affect almost all functions of the body. The pituitary and the adrenals have a kind of feedback relationship. The pituitary produces two hormones, ACTH and MSH, which stimulate the adrenal cortex to produce cortisol which, in turn, helps keep the ACTH and MSH at normal levels. But when the adrenal cortex is damaged or destroyed, the levels of ACTH and MSH build up in the blood. That is what has happened to our killer. Now, MSH is a melanocyte-stimulating hormone. That is, it controls the melanin in the skin. Melanin is the dark brown or black pigmentation. So when there is an abnormally high level of MSH, there is an accumulation of melanin, which causes discoloration of the skin and is an indication to diagnosticians that the patient is suffering from adrenal cortical insufficiency, or Addison's disease."

Dr. Patrick Ho ended on a triumphant note, as if he had just proved out a particularly difficult mathematical theorem. QED.

"All right," Delaney said, "I've followed you so far. I think. And the high potassium level and the other stuff?"

"Also classic indications of Addison's disease. Especially the low sodium level."

"Tell me, doctor," Thorsen said, "if someone has Addison's disease, can you tell by looking at them? Those skin discolorations, for instance?"

"Ah, no," Dr. Ho said. "No, no, no. With proper medication and diet, an Addisonian victim would look as normal as any of us. They are somewhat like diabetics in that they must take synthetic cortisol for the remainder of their lives and watch their salt intake carefully. But otherwise they can live active lives, exercise, work, have sex, raise families, and so forth. There is no evidence that Addison's disease, adequately treated, shortens life expectancy."

"Wait a minute," Delaney said, frowning. "Something here doesn't jibe. Assuming our killer has Addison's disease and is being treated for it, her blood wouldn't show all those characteristics, would it?"

"Ah-ha!" Dr. Ho cried, slapping his palms together gleefully. "You are absolutely correct. One possibility is that the killer is in the primary stages of Addison's and has not yet sought treatment. Another possibility is that she has sought treatment, but her disease has not been correctly diagnosed. Another possibility is that her disorder has been properly diagnosed and prescribed for, but she is not taking the proper medication, for whatever reason."

"That's a helluva lot of possibilities," Boone grumbled.

"Ah, yes," the doctor said, not at all daunted. "But there is yet another possibility. Addisonian crisis may be brought on by acute stress such as vomiting, an injury, an infection, a surgical procedure, even a tooth extraction. And, I venture to say, by a prolonged period of severe mental, emotional, or psychic stress."

They stared at him, slowly grasping what he was telling them.

"What you're saying," Delaney said, "is that you believe the Hotel Ripper is suffering from Addison's disease. That she is being treated for it. But the treatment isn't having the effect it should have because of the stress of ripping open the throats of six strangers in hotel rooms. Is that it?"

"Ah, yes," Dr. Ho said placidly. "I believe that is a definite possibility."

"That's crazy!" Sergeant Boone burst out.

"Is it?" the doctor said. "What's so crazy? Surely you will not deny the influence of mental and emotional attitudes on physical health? The close relationship has been firmly established. You can will yourself to live and will yourself to die. All I am saying is that the physical health of this woman could be adversely affected by the strains and fear connected with her horrible activities. There may be a psychological factor at work here as well. If she acknowledges the evil of what she is doing, sees herself as a worthless individual not fit for society, that too might affect her health."

"Look," Deputy Thorsen said, "let's not go off into left field trying to figure out the emotional and psychological quirks of this woman. We'll leave that to the psychiatrists after we've caught her. But let's just stick to what we've got. You think she's suffering from Addison's disease, and either it's not being adequately treated or she's ignoring the treatment, and the stress of these murders is killing her. That sounds silly, but it's what you're saying, isn't it?"

"Approximately," Dr. Ho said in a low voice.

"So?" the Admiral said. "Where do we go from here? How do we begin finding everyone in New York City suffering from Addison's disease?"

They stared at each other a moment.

"Go to all the doctors?" Sergeant Boone questioned. "Ask them if they're treating anyone with the disease?"

Edward X. Delaney wagged his big head, side to side.

"Won't work, sergeant," he said. "You know the laws of confidentiality regarding privileged information between doctor and patient. The doctors will tell us to go screw and the courts will back them up."

"Edward," Thorsen said, "suppose we go to all the doctors in the city and instead of demanding the names of any patients they're treating for Addison's disease, we just ask a general question, like, 'Are you treating anyone for Addison's'?"

Delaney thought a moment before he answered:

"If a physician wants to cooperate with the cops, I think he could answer a general question like that without violating the law or his code of ethics. But what the hell good would it do? If a doctor answered, 'Yes,' then our next question would have to be, 'What is the patient's name and address?' Then he'd tell us to get lost and we'd be right back where we started."

They sat in silence, staring at their hands, the walls, the ceiling, trying to come up with *something*.

"Dr. Ho," the Chief said, "in answer to one of the Deputy's questions, you said an Addisonian victim would not have those skin discolorations if she was receiving the proper treatment. Right?"

"That is correct."

"But our killer obviously isn't getting the proper treatment or, for whatever reason, it isn't working the way it should. Her blood is all fucked up. Does that mean she would have the skin discolorations?"

"Ah, I would say possibly. Even probably, judging by the high MSH level."

"Could the discolorations be seen? On the street, I mean, if she was dressed in everyday clothes? Would a witness notice the blotches?"

"Ah, I would say no. Not on the elbows, knees, palms of the hands, etcetera. If it spread heavily to hands and face, then of course it would be noticeable. But by that time the victim would probably be hospitalized."

"How do the laws of privileged information apply to hospitals?" Boone asked.

"Same as to physicians," Delaney said. "In hospitals, patients are under a doctor's care. All information is privileged."

"Shit," Boone said.

"Perhaps," Dr. Ho said tentatively, "the Mayor would be willing to make a personal appeal to all the doctors of the city, asking for their cooperation in this civic emergency."

The Deputy Commissioner looked at him pityingly.

"I don't believe the Mayor would care to put himself in the position of urging physicians publicly to break the law. He had enough trouble just getting that offer of a fifty-thousand-dollar reward past the Council. No, doctor, don't expect any help from the politicos. They have their own problems."

They all went back to staring into the middle distance.

"The problem here is identification," the Chief said. "How do we identify all the victims of Addison's disease in New York?"

"Wait," Dr. Patrick Ho said, holding up a plump palm.

They looked at him.

"A problem of identification," the doctor mused. "All the papers I read on

Addison's were written for physicians, and gave the history of the disease, symptoms, treatment, and so forth. Without fail, every author recommended the Addisonian victim be instructed to wear a medical identification bracelet stating that he suffered from the disease. Also, the bracelet carries his name and address, and the name, address, and phone number of his doctor. This is in case of emergency, you understand. An automobile accident, sudden injury, or fainting."

"Go on," Delaney said, hunching forward on his chair. "This is beginning to sound good."

"Also, the patient should carry a small kit at all times. In the kit is a sterile syringe containing a hydrocortisone solution ready for injection in an emergency, with instructions for use."

"Better and better," Delaney said. "And where do you get a bracelet and kit like that?"

"Ah, I do not know," Dr. Ho confessed. "But I would guess the sources are limited. That is, you could not walk into just any drugstore in the city and expect to buy such specialized equipment. It would have to be a medical supply house, I would think, or a pharmacy that handles rare and difficult prescriptions."

"There can't be many places like that in the city," Sergeant Boone said slowly.

"Edward," Thorsen said, "do the laws of privileged information apply to prescriptions in drugstores?"

"I'd say not," the Chief said. "I think you take a prescription in and then it's between you and the pharmacist. It's out of the doctor's hands, and the pharmacist can reveal the names of the patient and the doctor who wrote the prescription."

"I better get a legal ruling on it," the Deputy said.

"Good idea," Delaney said. "Meanwhile, sergeant, I think you better organize a crew to track down the places that sell those medical identification bracelets and kits to people with Addison's disease."

"Long shot," Boone said doubtfully.

"Sure it is," Delaney said. "And that convention schedule access list is a long shot. And the list of tear gas customers is a long shot. But every list makes the odds shorter. We get enough lists, and crosscheck them, we're going to come up with some good possibles."

"Oh, I love this work!" Dr. Patrick Ho cried, his dark eyes gleaming.

They looked at him.

July 7 and 8, Monday and Tuesday . . .

Zoe Kohler sat primly at her desk in the security section of the Hotel Granger. She had finished four letters for Everett Pinckney, placed the neatly typed pages and envelopes on his desk. She had completed a tentative summer vacation schedule, requesting August 11–22 for herself since those were the weeks Ernest Mittle would be off.

She leafed idly through the pages of the current issue of the hotel trade magazine. The lead article reported that the New York association had raised its reward for capture of the Hotel Ripper. That brought the total of rewards offered to more than $100,000.

Mr. Pinckney came in with the signed letters and handed them to her for mailing.

"Perfect job, Zoe," he said. "As usual." He noticed the magazine on her desk and snapped his fingers. "I've been meaning to tell you," he said, "and it keeps slipping my mind. Last week a detective came by the manager's office and got a list of everyone in the hotel who sees that magazine."

"A detective, Mr. Pinckney? From the police department?"

"That's what his ID said. He wouldn't tell us what it was all about, just wanted the names of everyone who saw the magazine. Said they were checking the entire mailing list of the publisher."

"That's odd," Zoe said, her voice toneless.

"Isn't it?" Pinckney said. "I guessed it might have something to do with the Hotel Ripper case, but he wouldn't say. Can you imagine how big a job that will be? Why, we get six copies ourselves, and I suppose thousands are distributed. The list of people who read it must be endless."

"It's certainly a strange thing to do," Zoe said.

"Well," Pinckney said, shrugging, "I suppose they have their reasons. Whatever it is, I haven't heard any more about it."

He went back into his office and a moment later she heard the sound of his desk drawer being opened and the clink of bottle and glass.

She sat there staring down at the journal. She wondered if Mr. Pinckney's guess was correct, that the detective's request had something to do with the Hotel Ripper case. She could not conceive what the connection might be. As he said, thousands of people had access to the magazine.

Still, the incident was unsettling; it left her feeling uneasy and somehow threatened. She had a sense of the initiative slipping from her hands. Once again in her life she was being moved and manipulated by forces outside herself.

She had the same feeling of being pushed in directions she did not wish to go when, late in the afternoon, Dr. Oscar Stark phoned.

"Zoe," he said without preamble, "I want you in the hospital as soon as possible. Your tests are back and the results are even more disturbing than I thought they'd be. I talked over your case with a friend of mine, a very capable endocrinologist, and he agrees with me that you belong in a hospital before we have an Addisonian crisis."

"I won't go," she said flatly. "I don't need a hospital. I'm perfectly all right."

"Now you listen to me, young lady," he said sharply. "You are not perfectly all right. You are suffering from a pernicious disease that requires constant treatment and monitoring. All your vital signs point to a serious deterioration of your condition. We've got to find out why. I'm not talking about an operation; I'm talking about tests and observation. If you refuse, I can't be responsible for the consequences."

"No," she said, "I won't go to a hospital."

He was silent a moment.

"Very well," he said. "The only thing left for me to do is contact your parents. Then, unless you change your mind, I must ask you to consult another physician. I'm sorry, Zoe," he said softly before he hung up.

She could not have said exactly why she was being so obdurate. She did not doubt Dr. Stark's expertise. She supposed he was correct; she was seriously ill and her health was degenerating rapidly.

She told herself she could not endure the indignity of a hospital, of being naked before unfeeling strangers, to be poked and prodded, her body wastes examined critically, her flesh treated as a particularly vile and worthless cut of meat.

And there was also a secret fear that, somehow, in a hospital, she might be restored to perfect health, but in the process be deprived of those private pains and pleasures that were so precious to her.

She did not fully comprehend how this might happen, but the alarm was there, that hospital treatment would mollify those surges of insensate strength and will she felt during her adventures. They would reduce her to a dull, enduring beast and quench the one spark that set her above the animal people who thronged the city's streets.

She was special in this way only. She had excited the dread of millions, had caused fury and confusion in the minds of the police, had influenced the course of events of which, heretofore, she had been merely another victim.

A hospital might end all that. It might rob her of her last remaining uniqueness. It might, in fact, destroy the uncommon soul of Zoe Kohler.

That evening, on the way home, she stopped for a light dinner at the Madison Avenue luncheonette she frequented. She had a salad of cottage cheese and fresh fruit slices. She sat at the counter, drank an iced tea, and dabbed her lips delicately with a paper napkin.

By the time she reached her apartment, she had put the whole idea of hospitals from her mind, just as she was able to ignore the now obvious manifestations of her body's growing decrepitude. She took her pills and nostrums automatically, with the vague hope that she might wake the following morning cured and whole.

But a new shock awaited her on Tuesday. She was seated at her desk, sipping coffee and leafing through *The New York Times*. There, on the first page of the second section, was a headline: POLICE RELEASE NEW "RIPPER" SKETCH.

Beneath the legend was a two-column-wide drawing in line and wash. The moment Zoe Kohler saw it, she looked about wildly, then slapped another section of the paper over the sketch.

Finally, when her heart stopped thudding and she was able to breathe normally, she uncovered the drawing again and stared at it long and hard.

She thought it was so *like*. The hair was incorrectly drawn, her face was too long and thin, but the artist had caught the shape of her eyebrows, straight lips, the pointed chin.

The more she stared, the more the drawing seemed to resemble her. She could not understand why hotel employees did not rush into her office, crowd around her desk, point at her with accusing fingers.

Surely Mr. Pinckney, Barney McMillan, or Joe Levine would note the resemblance; they were trained investigators. And if not them, then Ernest Mittle, Maddie Kurnitz, or Dr. Stark would see her in that revealing sketch and begin to wonder, to question.

Or, if none of her friends or acquaintances, it might be a passerby, a stranger on the street. She had an awfull fantasy of a sudden shout, hue and cry, a frantic chase, capture. And possibly a beating by the maddened mob. A lynching.

It was not fear that moved her so much as embarrassment. She could never endure the ignominy of a public confrontation like that: the crazed eyes, wet mouths, the obscenities. Rather die immediately than face that humiliation.

She read the newspaper article printed beneath the drawing, and noted the detailed description of the clothing she had worn to the Tribunal Motor Inn. She supposed that she had been seen having a drink with that boy, and witnesses had told the police.

There was even mention that she drank white wine, though nothing was said about fingerprints. But the police suggested the woman they sought spoke in a low, polite voice, wore her hair quite short, dressed plainly, and might be employed as a secretary.

It was fascinating, in a strange way, to read this description of herself. It was like seeing one's image in a mirror that was a reflection of an image in another mirror. Reality was twice removed; the original was slightly distorted and wavery.

There was no doubt it was Zoe Kohler, but it was a remote woman, divorced from herself. It was a likeness, a very good likeness, with her hair, face, body, clothes. But it was not her. It was a replica.

Carefully she scissored the drawing from the newspaper, folded it, put it deep in her purse. Then, thinking that someone might notice the clipped page, she carried the whole newspaper to the trash room and dug it into a garbage can.

She hurried home from work that evening, keeping her head lowered, resisting an urge to hold her purse up in front of her face. No one took any notice of her. As usual, she was the invisible woman.

Safe in her apartment, she sat with a glass of iced vodka and inspected that damning sketch again. It seemed incredible that no one had recognized her.

As she stared at the drawing, she felt once again the sensation of disorientation. Like the printed description, the portrait was her and yet it was not her. It was a blurred likeness. She wondered if her body's rot had spread to her face, and this was a representation of dissolution.

She was still inspecting the drawing, eagerly, hungrily, trying to find meaning in it, when her parents called from Minnesota.

"Baby," her father said, "this is Dad, and Mother is on the extension."

"Hello, Dad, Mother. How are you?"

"Oh, Zoe!" her mother wailed, and began weeping noisily.

"Now, Mother," her father said, "you promised you wouldn't. Baby, we got a call from a doctor there in New York. Man named Stark. He your doctor?"

"Yes, Dad."

"Well, he says you're sick, baby. He says you should be in a hospital."

"Oh, Dad, that's silly. I was feeling down for a few days, but I'm all right now. You know how doctors are."

"Are you telling the truth, Zoe?" her mother asked tearfully.

"Mother, I'm perfectly all right. I'm taking my medicine and eating well. There's absolutely nothing wrong with me."

"Well, you certainly sound all right, baby. Are you sure you don't want me or Mother to come to New York?"

"Not on my account, Dad. There's just no need for it."

"Well, uh, as Mother wrote you, we were planning a trip to Hawaii this summer, but we can . . ."

"Oh, Dad, don't change your plans. I'm really in very good health."

"What do you weigh, Zoe?"

"About the same, Mother. Maybe a pound or two less, but I'll get that back."

"Well, why the hell did that New York doctor call us, baby? He got me and your mother all upset."

"Dad, you know how doctors are; the least little thing and they want to put you in the hospital."

"Have you missed work, Zoe?"

"Not a single day, Mother. That proves I'm all right, doesn't it?"

"Listen, baby, we're not going to Hawaii until late in July. Do you think you'll be able to get out here on your vacation?"

"I don't know when my vacation is, Dad. When I find out, I'll write you, and maybe we can work something out, even if it's only for a few days."

"Have you met anyone, Zoe?" her mother asked. "You know—a nice boy?"

"Well, there's one fellow I've been seeing. He's very nice."

"What does he do, baby?"

"I'm not sure, Dad. I know he's taking courses in computers."

"Computers? Hey, sounds like a smart fellow."

"He is, Dad. I think you'd like him."

"Well, that's fine, baby. I'm glad you're getting out and, uh, socializing. And it's good to hear you're feeling okay. That damned doctor scared us."

"I'm feeling fine, Dad, really I am."

"Now listen to me, Zoe," her mother said. "I want you to call us at least once a week. You can reverse the charges. All right, Dad?"

"Of course, Mother. Baby, you do that. Call at least once a week and reverse the charges."

"All right, Dad."

"You take care of yourself now, y'hear?"

"I will. Thank you for calling. Goodbye, Mother. Goodbye, Dad."

"Goodbye, Zoe."

"Goodbye, baby."

She hung up, and when she looked at her hands, they were trembling. Her parents always had that effect: made her nervous, defensive. Made her feel guilty. Not once during the call had she said, "I love you." But then, neither had they.

She ate a sandwich of something she couldn't taste. She drank another vodka, and swallowed vitamins, minerals, two Anacin, and a Valium. Then she took a shower, pulled on her threadbare robe.

She sat on the living room couch, drained by the conversation with her parents. It had taken energy, even bravado, to speak brightly, optimistically, to calm their fears and forestall their coming to New York and seeing her in her present state.

She supposed that when they thought of her, they remembered a little girl in a spotless pinafore. White gloves, knee-length cotton socks, and shiny black shoes with straps. A cute hat with flowers. A red plastic purse on a brass chain.

Zoe Kohler opened her robe, looked down, and saw what had become of that little girl. Tears came to her eyes, and she wondered how it had happened, and why it had happened.

As a child, when balked, scolded, or ignored, she had wished her tormentor dead. If her mother died, or her father, or a certain teacher, then Zoe's troubles would end, and she would be happy.

She had wished Kenneth dead. Not *wished* it exactly, but dreamed often of how her burdens would be lightened if he were gone. Once she had even fantasized that Maddie Kurnitz might die, and Zoe would comfort the widower, and he would look at her with new eyes.

All her life she had seen the death of others as the solution to her problems. Now, looking at her spoiled flesh, she realized that only her own death would put a stop to . . .

She was sick, and she was tired, and that thin, sour man she saw as "police" was stalking closer and closer. She wished *him* dead, but knew it could not be. He would persevere and . . .

That drawing was so accurate that it was only a matter of time until . . .

She might return to her parents' home and pretend . . .

Thoughts, unfinished, whirled by so rapidly that she felt faint with the flickering speed, the brief intensity. She closed her eyes, made tight fists. She hung on until her mind slowed, cleared, and she was able to concentrate on what she wanted to do, and find the resolve to do it.

She phoned Ernest Mittle.

"Ernie," she said, "do you *really* love me?"

July 11 and 12, Friday and Saturday . . .

Detective Sergeant Thomas K. Broderick and his squad had been assigned the task of tracing the WHY NOT? bracelet worn by the Hotel Ripper, but it was proving to be another dead end. Too many stores carried the bracelet, too many had been sold for cash; it was impossible to track every one.

So Broderick and his crew were pulled off the bracelet search and given the task of finding victims of Addison's disease who had purchased a medical identification bracelet and emergency kit in New York.

Broderick decided to start with the island of Manhattan, and the Yellow Pages were the first place he looked for names and addresses of medical supply houses.

Then he talked to police surgeons and to a small number of physicians who were police buffs or "groupies" and who were happy to cooperate with the NYPD as long as they weren't asked to violate the law or their professional ethics.

From these sources, Broderick compiled a list of places that might conceivably sell the things he was trying to trace. Then he divided his list into neighborhoods. Then he sent his men out to pound the pavements.

Most of the pharmacists they visited were willing to help. Those who weren't received a follow-up visit from Broderick or Sergeant Abner Boone. Both men were armed with opinions from the Legal Division of the NYPD, stating that the courts had held that communications to druggists and prescriptions given to them by customers were not confidential and not protected from disclosure.

"Of course," Boone would say, "if you want to fight this, and hire yourself a high-priced lawyer, and spend weeks sitting around in court, then I'll have to get a subpoena."

Cooperation was 100 percent.

As the names and addresses of Addisonian victims began to come in, Broderick's deskmen put aside the obviously masculine names and compiled a list only of the women. This list, in turn, was broken down into separate files for each borough of New York, and one for out-of-town addresses.

"It's all so mechanical!" Monica Delaney exclaimed.

"Mechanical?" the Chief said. "What the hell's mechanical about it? How do you think detectives work?"

"Well, maybe not mechanical," she said. "But you're all acting like bookkeepers. Like accountants."

"That's what we are," he said. "Accountants."

"Wise-ass," she said.

They were having dinner at P. J. Moriarty on Third Avenue. It was a fine, comfortable Irish bar and restaurant with Tiffany lampshades and smoke-mellowed wood paneling. For some unaccountable reason, a toy electric train ran around the bar on a track suspended from the ceiling.

They had started with dry Beefeater martinis. Then slabs of herring in cream sauce. Then pot roast with potato pancakes. With Canadian ale. Then black coffee and Armagnac. They were both blessed with good digestions.

"The greatest of God's gifts," Delaney was fond of remarking.

During dinner, he had told her about Dr. Ho's report on Addison's disease, and exactly how Sergeant Broderick's men were going about the search for Addisonian victims in New York.

"He says his list should be completed by late today," he concluded. "Tomorrow morning I'm going down to the precinct. We'll crosscheck the lists and see if we have anything."

"And if you don't?"

He shrugged. "We'll keep plugging. Every murder in the series has revealed more. Eventually we'll get her."

"Edward, if you find out who it is—what then?"

"Depends. Do we have enough evidence for an arrest? For an indictment?"

"You won't, uh . . ."

He looked at her, smiling slightly.

"Go in with guns blazing and cut her down? No, dear, we won't do that. I don't believe this woman will be armed. With a gun, that is. I think she'll come along quietly. Almost with relief."

"Then what? I mean, if you have enough evidence for an arrest and an indictment? What will happen to her then?"

He filled their coffee cups from the pewter pot.

"Depends," he said again. "If she gets a smart lawyer, he'll probably try to plead insanity. Seems to me that slitting the throats of six strangers is pretty good prima facie evidence of insanity. But even if she's adjudged capable of standing trial and is convicted, she'll get off with the minimum."

"Edward! Why? After what she's done?"

"Because she's a woman."

"You're joking?"

"I'm not joking. Want me to quote the numbers to you? I don't need Thomas Handry's research. The judicial system in this country is about fifty years behind the times as far as equality between men and women goes. Almost invariably females will receive lighter sentences than males for identical or comparable crimes. And when it comes to homicide, juries and judges seem to have a built-in bias that works in favor of women. They can literally get away with murder."

"But surely not the Hotel Ripper?"

"Don't be too sure of that. A good defense attorney will put her on the stand dressed in something conservative and black with a white Peter Pan collar. She'll speak in a low, trembling voice and dab at her eyes with a balled-up Kleenex. Remember when we were first arguing about whether the Hotel Ripper could be a woman, and you asked people at one of your meetings? All the men said a woman couldn't commit crimes like that and all the women said she could. Well, an experienced defense lawyer knows that, even if he doesn't know why. If he's got a female client accused of homicide, he'll try to get an all-male jury. Most of the men in this country still have a completely false concept of women's sensibilities. They think women are inherently incapable of killing. So they vote not guilty. That's why I think there should be an ECA."

"An ECA?"

"Sure," he said innocently. "To go along with the ERA, the Equal Rights Amendment. ECA, the Equal Conviction Amendment."

"Bastard," she said, kicking him under the table.

They walked home slowly through the warm, sticky summer night.

"Edward," Monica said, "back there in the restaurant you said you thought the killer would surrender quietly, with relief. Why relief?"

"I think she's getting tired," Delaney said, and explained to his wife why he believed that. "Also, Dr. Ho thinks that emotional stress could be triggering an Addisonian crisis. It all ties in: a sick woman coming to the end of her rope."

"Then you believe she *is* sick?"

"Physically, not mentally. She knows the difference between right and wrong. But the laws regarding insanity and culpability are so screwed-up that it's impossible to predict how a judge or jury might decide. They could say she's usually sane but killed in moments of overwhelming madness. Temporary insanity. It's really not important. Well, it is important, but it's not the concern of cops. Our only job is to stop her."

"Good luck tomorrow morning," Monica said faintly. "Will you call me?"

He took her arm.

"If you want me to," he said.

Edward X. Delaney slept well that night. In the morning he was amused to find himself dressing with special care for the meeting at Midtown Precinct North.

"Like I was going to a wedding," he mentioned to Monica. "Or a funeral."

He wore a three-piece suit of navy blue tropical worsted, a white shirt with starched collar, a wide cravat of maroon rep. His wife tucked a foulard square into the breast pocket of his jacket, one flowered edge showing. Delaney poked the silk down the moment he was out of the house.

As many men as possible crowded into the conference room upstairs at Midtown Precinct North. Lieutenant Crane, Sergeant Broderick, Boone, Bentley, Delaney, and Thorsen got the chairs. The others stood against the walls. Men milled about in the corridor outside, waiting for news. Good or bad.

"Okay, Tom," Sergeant Boone said to Broderick, "it's all yours."

"What I got here first," the detective sergeant said, "is an alphabetical list of female victims of Addison's living in Manhattan. Sixteen names."

"Right," Lieutenant Wilson T. Crane said, shuffling through the stack of typed lists in front of him. "What I have is a list of females who work or reside in Manhattan and who, one way or another, have access to a schedule of hotel conventions. Let's go . . ."

"First name," Broderick said, "is Alzanas. A-l-z-a-n-a-s. Marie. That's Marie Alzanas."

Lieutenant Crane pored over his list, flipped a page.

"No," he said, "haven't got her. Next?"

"Carson, Elizabeth J. That's C-a-r-s-o-n."

"Carson, Carson, Carson . . . I've got a Muriel Carson."

"No good. This one is Elizabeth J. Next name is Domani, Doris. That's D-o-m-a-n-i."

"No, no Domani."

"Edwards, Marilyn B. E-d-w-a-r-d-s."

"No Marilyn B. Edwards."

The roll call of names continued slowly. The other men in the room were silent. The men in the hallway had quieted. They could hear noises from downstairs, the occasional sound of a siren starting up. But their part of the building seemed hushed, waiting . . .

"Jackson," Sergeant Broderick intoned. "Grace T. Jackson. J-a-c-k-s-o-n."

"No Grace T. Jackson," Lieutenant Crane said. "Next?"

"Kohler. K-o-h-l-e-r. First name Zoe. Z-o-e. That's Zoe Kohler."

Crane's finger ran down the page. Stopped. He looked up.

"Got her," he said. "Zoe Kohler."

A sigh like a wind in the room. Men slumped, expressionless. They lighted cigarettes.

"All right," Sergeant Boone said, "finish the list. There may be more than one."

They waited quietly, patiently, while Sergeant Broderick completed his list of names. Zoe Kohler was the only name duplicated on Crane's convention schedule access list.

"Zoe Kohler," Delaney said. "Where did you find her, Broderick?"

"She bought a medical ID bracelet for Addison's disease and an emergency kit at a pharmacy on Twenty-third Street."

"Crane?" the Chief asked.

"We've got her listed at the Hotel Granger on Madison and Forty-sixth Street. Access to the hotel trade magazine that publishes the convention schedule every week."

They stared at each other, looks going around the room, no one wanting to speak.

"Sergeant," Delaney said to Abner Boone, "is Johnson down at Midtown South?"

"If he's not there, one of his guys will be. The phone is manned."

"Give him a call. Ask if the Hotel Granger, Madison and Forty-sixth, is on the list of tear gas customers."

They all listened as Boone made the call. He asked the man at the other end to check the list for the Hotel Granger. He heard the reply, grunted his thanks, hung up. He looked around at the waiting men.

"Bingo," he said softly. "The security chief at the Granger bought the stuff. Four pocket-size spray dispensers and three grenades."

Sergeant Broderick pushed his chair back with a clatter.

"Let's pick her up," he said loudly.

Delaney whirled on him furiously.

"What are you going to do?" he demanded. "Beat a confession out of her with a rubber hose? What kind of a garbage arrest would that be? She's got Addison's disease, she reads a hotel trade magazine, and the place where she works bought some tear gas. Take that to the DA and he'll throw your ass out the window."

"What do you suggest, Edward?" Thorsen asked.

"Button her up. At least two men on her around the clock. Better include a policewoman on the tail, in case she goes into a john. Put an undercover man where she works. Broderick, where does she live?"

The sergeant consulted his file.

"Thirty-ninth Street, east. The address sounds like it would be near Lex."

"Probably an apartment house. If it is, get an undercover man in there as a porter or something. Find a friendly judge and get a phone tap authorization. Around the clock. I mean, know exactly where she is every minute of the day and night. Where she goes. Who her friends are. It'll give us time to do more digging."

"Like what, Chief?" Boone said.

"A lot of things. How did she get hold of the tear gas, for instance. Get a photo of her with a long-distance lens and show it to that waiter at the Tribunal and to the cocktail waitress out on the Coast."

"I've got her doctor's name and address," Sergeant Broderick offered.

"It's a possibility," Delaney said. "He probably won't talk, but it's worth a try. The important thing is to keep this woman covered until she proves out, one way or the other. Meanwhile, Broderick, I suggest you check the rest of your lists against Lieutenant Crane's. There may be more duplications."

Deputy Thorsen, Delaney, and Boone left the conference room and went into the sergeant's office. The men in the corridor had heard the news and were talking excitedly.

"Sergeant," the Chief said, "you're going to have your hands full keeping a lid on this. If Zoe Kohler's name gets to reporters, and they print it, we're finished. She'll go back into the woodwork."

"Wait a minute, Edward," Thorsen said. "What are you figuring—that she'll try another kill, and we catch her at it?"

"It may come to that," Delaney said grimly. "I hope not, but it may turn out to be the only way we can make a case. She's due again late this month."

"Jesus," Sergeant Boone breathed, "that's a dangerous way to make a case. If we fuck it up, we'll have another stiff on our hands and we'll all be out on the street."

"It may be the only way," Delaney insisted stubbornly. "I don't like it any more than you do, but we may have to let her try. Meanwhile, make sure your men keep their mouths shut."

"Yeah," Boone said, "I better give them the word right now."

"And while you're at it," the Chief said, "call Johnson again. Tell him not to send a man to check out that tear gas at the Hotel Granger until we figure out how to handle it and give him the word."

"Right," Boone said. "I'll take care of it."

He left the office.

"Edward," Thorsen said nervously, "are you serious about letting that woman try another killing?"

"Ivar," Delaney said patiently, "it may turn out to be the only way we can step on her. You better be prepared for it. Right now, at this moment, we haven't got enough for a clean arrest, let alone an indictment. Believe me, nothing makes a stronger case than 'caught in the act.' "

"If we catch her in time," the Deputy said mournfully.

Delaney shrugged. "Sometimes you have to take the risk. But it may not come to that. We've got two weeks before she hits again. If she follows the pattern, that is. We can do a lot in two weeks. With the round-the-clock tail and the phone tap, we may be able to make a case before she tries again."

"We've *got* to," Thorsen said desperately.

"Sure," Delaney said.

July 13, Sunday . . .

She was weary of gnarled thoughts and knotted dreams. There came a time when only surrender seemed feasible. Peace at any price.

She could endure no more. Those attractive, smartly dressed, *happy* women she saw on the streets . . . The men who whispered dreadful things or just glanced at her derisively . . . It was a city of enemies, a foreign place. Sickened by her own substance, she wanted to be gone.

"You look so solemn," Ernest Mittle said. "I feel so good, and you look so sad."

"Do I?" she said, squeezing his hand. "I'm sorry. Just thinking."

"When you called me the other night, you sounded so *down.* Is something wrong, darling?"

"Not a thing," she said brightly. "I'm just fine. Where are we going?"

"It's a secret," he said. "Do you like secrets?"

"I love secrets," she said.

He had met her in the lobby of her apartment house. She saw at once that he was jangling with nervous excitement, almost dancing with eagerness. And he was dressed in his best summer suit, a light blue, pin-striped seersucker. He wore a dark blue polka-dotted bowtie and, in his buttonhole, a small cornflower.

He insisted on taking a taxi, showing the driver an address scrawled on a slip of paper. In the back seat of the cab, he held her hand and chattered about the weather, his job, thc plans he was making for their vacation together.

The cab headed downtown and then across Manhattan Bridge. Laughing delightedly, Ernie confessed that they were going for Sunday brunch at a restaurant built on a barge moored on the Brooklyn waterfront.

"The food is supposed to be good," he said, "and the view of the Manhattan skyline is fantastic. Okay?"

"Of course," she said. "I just hope it isn't too expensive."

"Oh well," he said, bowing his head, "it's sort of, uh, you know, an occasion."

They weren't able to get a window table in the restaurant, but from where they sat they had a good view of the East River, the sweep of the Brooklyn Bridge and, in the background, the swords of Manhattan slashing the pellucid sky.

They had Bloody Marys to start, and then scrambled eggs with ham steaks, toasted English muffins with guava marmalade, and a small green salad. Black coffee and raspberry sherbet for dessert.

The food was good, and the service efficient but too swift; they were finished and handed their check in less than an hour. On their way out, they passed a growing crowd of customers waiting hopefully behind a chain.

"A popular place," Ernie said when they were outside. "Well, the food is all right, and the prices are reasonable. First time I've ever eaten on a boat."

"It's different," Zoe said, "and I enjoyed it. Thank you, dear."

The restaurant had set up a number of park benches facing the Manhattan shore. Zoe and Ernie sat on the bench closest to the water. They watched a red tugboat push a string of barges upriver against the current.

The sun was bright and hot, but a salt-tanged breeze washed the air. A few small clouds, scoops of vanilla ice cream, drifted lazily. Smoke-colored gulls perched atop wharf pilings, preening their feathers.

And there in the distance, shimmering, were the golden spires of Manhattan. They gave back the sun in a million gleams. The city burned, prancing, a painted backdrop for a giant theater, a cosmic play.

"Oh, Zoe," Ernest Mittle breathed, "isn't it lovely?"

"Yes," she said, but she lowered her eyes. She didn't want to admit that the city could have beauty and grace.

He turned on the bench so he could face her. He took both her hands between his. She raised her eyes to look at him. His vivacity had vanished. Now he seemed solemn, almost grave.

"Uh," he said in a low voice, "there's something I want to talk to you about."

"What is it, dear?" she said anxiously. "Is something the matter? Is it something I did?"

"Oh no, no," he protested. "No, nothing's the matter. Uh, darling, I've been thinking about you a lot. Every minute. I mean, at work and walking down the street and when I'm home alone and before I go to sleep. I think about you all the time. And, uh, well, I've decided I want to be with you all the time. Forever." He finished with a rush: "Because I love you so much, and I want to marry you, Zoe. Darling . . . Please?"

She looked into his eyes and blinked to keep from weeping.

"Oh, Ernie—" she started.

"Listen a minute," he said hoarsely. He released her hands, swung back to face the river, hunched over on the bench. "I know I'm not so much. I mean, I have a good job and all, and I'm not afraid of hard work, and I think I'll do better. But I'm not much to look at, I know—not exactly every woman's dream. But I do love you, Zoe. More than I've ever loved anyone or anything, and I want to spend the rest of my life with you. I've thought this over very carefully, and I'm sure this is what I want to do. You're in my mind all the time, and I love you so much that sometimes it almost hurts, and I feel like crying. I know that's silly, but that's the way I feel."

"Oh, Ernie," she said again. She took him by the shoulders, turned him to her. She hugged him close, his face pressed into her neck. She held him tightly, stroking his fine, flaxen hair. She moved him away, saw tears in his eyes.

She kissed his soft lips tenderly and put her palm to his cheek.

"Thank you, darling," she said. "Thank you, thank you, thank you. You don't know how much that means to me, knowing how much you care. It's the nicest, sweetest thing that's ever happened to me, and I'm so proud."

"We could make a go of it, Zoe," he pleaded. "Really we could. We'd have to work at it, of course, but I know we could do it. When I finish my computer course, I'll get a better job. And I have some money in the bank. Not a lot, but *some.* So we wouldn't starve or anything like that. And you could move into my place. For the time being, I mean, until we can find a bigger place. And I have—"

"Shh, shh," she whispered, putting a finger on his lips. "Let me catch my breath for a minute. It isn't every day a girl . . ."

They sat immobile. She held his face between her palms and stared into his brimming eyes.

"You love me that much, darling?" she said in a low voice.

"I do, I do!" he declared. "I'd do anything for you, Zoe, I swear it. Except leave you. Don't ask me to do that."

"No," she said, smiling sadly. "I won't ask you to do that."

"There's no one else, is there?" he asked anxiously.

"Oh no. There's no one else."

"Zoe, I can understand that you might feel . . . Well, you know, having been married once and it didn't work out, you might feel, uh, very careful before you marry again. But I'd try very hard, darling, really I would. As hard as I can to be a good husband and make you happy."

"I know you would, Ernie. You're a dear, sweet man, and I love you."

"Then . . . ?"

"Oh, darling, I can't answer right now, this minute. I'm in a whirl. You'll have to give me time to think about—"

"Of course," he said hastily, "I understand. I didn't expect to sweep you off your feet or anything like that. But you will think about it, won't you?"

"Oh sweetheart, of course I will."

"Well . . ." he said, giggling nervously, "just to keep reminding you, I bought you this . . ."

He fumbled in the side pocket of his jacket, brought out a little velvet-covered ring box. He opened it.

"World's smallest diamond," he said, laughing. "But it's pretty, isn't it, Zoe? Isn't it pretty?"

"It's beautiful," she said, looking down at the twinkling stone set in a silver band. "Just beautiful."

"Try it on," he urged. "I didn't know your size, so it may be too tight or too large. But the man said it can be adjusted or even exchanged for a different size."

She slipped the ring onto her bony finger. It hung loosely.

"Too large," she said regretfully. She took off the ring and placed it carefully back into the box.

"It can be fixed," he assured her. "Zoe, your fingers are so thin. And what's this brown stain here?"

"I burned myself," she said swiftly. "On a hot pan. It'll clear up."

"Better see about it. Does it hurt?"

"Oh no. It's nothing. It'll go away."

She tried to return the ring box to him, but he wouldn't take it.

"You keep it, dear," he said. "Put it someplace where you'll see it every day and think about what I asked you. Will you do that, Zoe?"

"I don't need the ring to remind me," she said, smiling. "Oh, Ernie, it was so kind of you. And the ring is lovely. It truly is."

"You like it? Really?"

"It's the most beautiful ring in the world, and you're the most beautiful man."

"Say Yes, darling. Think it over, remember how much I love you, and say Yes."

That night, alone in her apartment, Zoe Kohler put the ring on her finger again, making a fist so it wouldn't slip off. Staring down at that shining circlet, she became aware of happiness as a conscious choice, hers for the taking.

She would call Dr. Stark and agree to enter a hospital. She would do whatever was necessary, endure any mortification to regain her health. She would throw out all her unnecessary pills and capsules. She would stop drinking, eat only good, nutritious food.

She would fill out, and her skin would become smooth and pure. She would make her body beautiful, slender and willowy. Her breath would be sweet and her monthly cramps would vanish as she grew content.

She would end her adventures because there would no longer be a need for them. The police would grow tired of the search, and the Hotel Ripper would fade from the headlines. In a few weeks or months the whole thing would be forgotten.

She would marry Ernest Mittle. Yes, and send an announcement to her ex-husband! Ernie would move in with her because her apartment was larger. She would keep her job at the Hotel Granger until Ernie was launched on a successful career in computers.

They would take turns cooking, and hurry home each night just to be together and talk to each other. They would go on wonderful vacations together, walk deserted beaches and swim in an endless sea.

They would make love gently, tenderly, and find bliss. Then they would sleep in each other's arms and wake to make love again, with smiles. They would find joy in each other's body, in their shared passion. They would not do anything ugly.

Their closeness would keep the brutal city at bay, would defend against the world's cruelty. *They* would be the world, a world of two, and nothing would daunt or defeat them.

Then they would have a child. Perhaps two. They would create a family of their own. With their clean, bright children, they would defy the darkness.

She replaced the ring in its box and hid it far back in the bureau drawer, next to the WHY NOT? bracelet. She went to sleep smiling, still living her dream.

It all seemed possible.

* * *

July 15–18, Tuesday to Friday . . .

Detective Daniel ("Dapper Dan") Bentley was given responsibility for the physical surveillance of Zoe Kohler. He used three crews, each on duty for eight hours. Each team consisted of two male and one female police officers.

Most of their time was spent in an unmarked police vehicle parked outside the subject's apartment house on East 39th Street or the Hotel Granger on Madison Avenue. The car was changed every day in an effort to prevent easy recognition by the suspect.

When Zoe Kohler walked to work, went to lunch, or just went shopping or on an innocent errand, one of the surveillance team tailed her on foot, keeping in touch with the stakeout car by walkie-talkie.

In addition to this close physical watch, a court order for a wiretap was obtained. With the cooperation of the owner of Zoe's apartment house, a tap and tape recorder were installed in the basement, hooked up to her telephone terminal. Two-man crews were on duty around the clock.

Gradually, a description of the subject and a time-habit pattern were assembled in the command post at Midtown Precinct North. The existence of Ernest Mittle and Madeline Kurnitz was established by phone call traces, and investigation begun of their relationship with the suspect.

Also, by means of a collect call made by the subject, the names and address of her parents were obtained. Following Zoe when she visited her bank resulted in an examination of her bank account and credit rating.

Slowly, the profile of the subject was filled in, with a complete physical description, personal history, her present job, employment record, friends, habits, etc. None of this, of course, added to or subtracted from her validity as a suspect, but it did give substance to the woman. In Midtown North, they began to speak familiarly of her as "Zoe." A friend of the family.

Photographs were taken from the surveillance car by a police photographer using a telephoto lens. Blowups of the best pictures were flown to the Coast by a New York detective and shown to Anne Rogovich, the former cocktail waitress. The result was negative; she could not identify the suspect as the woman she had seen with the late Jerome Ashley.

The same disappointment resulted when the photos were shown to Anthony Pizzi, the waiter at the Tribunal Motor Inn. So Mr. Pizzi was installed in the surveillance car and given an actual look at the subject. He still could not provide positive identification.

But not all inquiries were fruitless . . .

A long, involved discussion was held on how best to determine the disposition of tear gas purchased by Everett Pinckney, security chief of the Hotel Granger.

"The problem here," Delaney said, "is that if he gave her a can of the stuff, or she pinched it, then questions about it are sure to spook her. If she still has the can—maybe it's half-full—she's sure to dump it. And if she's already gotten rid of it, the questions will give her a chance to frame a story."

"Maybe we can tell this Pinckney to keep his trap shut," Sergeant Boone said.

"You can tell him," the Chief said, "but don't take it to the bank." He thought a moment, then: "Look, let's handle this in a conventional way. Just go in, verify the purchase with Pinckney, and say we'll be back in a week or so for a physical count of the containers he bought. Treat it very casually. If he mentions it to her, it may scare her into doing something foolish. Johnson, can you handle it?"

"I'll do it personally," the detective said. "No sweat. I want to get a look at the lady anyway."

So Detective Aaron Johnson visited Security Chief Everett Pinckney at the Hotel Granger. His cover story was that he was investigating a wholesale burglary of Chemical Mace and was tracing the serial numbers of every can sold in the New York area.

"The good news," he reported later, "is that this Pinckney admits the purchase, and says he handed out the spray dispensers to his assistants, including Zoe. He's got the grenades right there in his office and says he'll collect the spray cans from the others for examination. The bad news is that I didn't get to see her; she was out to lunch or some such."

That, at least, proved Zoe's access to a can of tear gas. It was a plus but, as Sergeant Boone said, "a little bitty plus."

More important was the result of a search of Zoe Kohler's apartment, a completely illegal enterprise. It was planned at a meeting attended only by Delaney, Boone, and Detective Bentley. Deputy Commissioner Ivar Thorsen was deliberately not informed of the plan; the Chief wanted to shield him from guilty knowledge.

"We can get a man in there easy," Abner Boone explained to Bentley. "The owner will go along. Our guy will be a maintenance man, porter, repairman, or whatever—in case any of the tenants spot him and ask questions. He'll go in when she's at work; we'll verify that with the tails."

"The problem," Delaney said, "is that he'll have to pick the lock. We don't want to ask the owner for a passkey. The fewer people who know about this, the better. Also, we need a fast guy, someone who'll get in, toss the place, and be out in, say, an hour or less."

"Got just the guy," Bentley said promptly. "Ramon Gonzales, a PR. Naturally, we call him 'Speedy.' He's a fast man on locks and he'll be in and out of there so quick and so slick no one will notice a thing. What does he look for?"

"A spray dispenser of tear gas," Boone said. "A pocket knife, or jackknife, switchblade—anything like that. Also, a gold link bracelet with the words WHY NOT? on it. And clothes, flashy clothes. A dark green dress with skinny straps. High-heeled shoes. She wore those to the Ashley kill. And a white turtleneck sweater and a denim thing with shoulder straps. The stuff she was wearing when she wasted the LaBranche boy. Anything else, Chief?"

"Yes," Delaney said. "Tell him to look for nylon wigs. Black and strawberry blond. Tell this Speedy Gonzales to wear gloves and to touch as little as possible, move things as little as possible. And don't, for God's sake, bring anything out with him. Leave everything exactly where it is."

"She'll never know she had a visitor," Bentley assured them.

Two days later, he was back with a report. He consulted a notebook, flipping the pages as he talked . . .

"No problems," he said. "Speedy didn't see anyone except the guy on the lobby desk who talked a minute or two but didn't ask any questions. The owner had told him to expect a guy who was going to make an estimate on cleaning the hallway rugs. Speedy got into Zoe's apartment with no trouble. He says the locks were a joke. He was inside less than an hour, gave the place a complete toss. He found that WHY NOT? bracelet and the dark green dress with thin shoulder straps. Her clothes are mostly plain and dull, but the fancy stuff is hidden in the back of a closet. A lot of hooker's dresses there, Speedy says. He didn't find any knife or can of tear gas."

"The wigs?" Delaney asked.

"Oh yeah. Black and blond. Both nylon. In the same closet with the whore's duds. High-heeled shoes in there, too. And in a dresser drawer, way in the back, black lace underwear and fancy shit like that."

"Did he say anything about what the apartment was like?" the Chief said.

"Very neat," Bentley reported. "Very clean. Spotless."

"That figures," Delaney said.

Late on Friday afternoon, July 18th, the Chief met with Deputy Commissioner Thorsen at a back table in a seedy tavern on Eighth Avenue. There were only a few solitary drinkers at the bar. The waitress, wearing a leotard and black net hose, brought their Scotch-and-waters and left them alone.

"How's it going, Edward?" Thorsen asked.

Delaney flipped a palm back and forth. "Some good, some bad," he said.

"But is it *her?*" the Deputy said.

"No doubt about that. It's her, all right."

"But you still don't want to pick her up?"

"Not yet."

"We've got about a week, Edward. Then she's due to hit again."

"I'm aware of that, Ivar."

The Admiral sat back, sighing. He lifted his glass around on the Formica tabletop, making damp interlocking circles.

"You're a hard man, Edward."

"Not so hard," Delaney said. "I'm just trying to make a case for you."

"Since when has any case been airtight?"

"I didn't say an airtight case. Just a strong case that has a chance in the courts."

Thorsen stared at him reflectively.

"Sometimes I think you and I are—well, maybe not on opposing sides, but we see this thing from different viewpoints. All I want to do is stop these killings. And you—"

"That's all I want," Delaney said stolidly.

"No, that's not all you want. You want to squash the woman."

"And what do you want—to let her walk away whistling? That's exactly what will happen if we pull her in now."

"Look," Thorsen said, "let's get our priorities straight. You're convinced she's the killer?"

"Yes."

"All right, now suppose we pull her in, even charge her, and eventually she walks. But she's not going to kill again, is she? She's going to behave, knowing we'll keep an eye on her. So the killings will end, won't they? Even if she walks?"

"And what about George Puller, Frederick Wolheim, Jerome Ashley, and all the rest? Just tough titty for them—right?"

"Edward, our main job is crime prevention. And if pulling her in now can prevent a crime, then I say let's do it."

"Prevention is only part of the job. Another part is crime detection and punishment."

"Let's have another drink," Ivar Thorsen said, signaling the waitress and pointing at their empty glasses.

They were silent while they were being served. Then Thorsen tried again . . .

"On the basis of what we know now," he said, "we can probably get search warrants for her apartment and office. Agreed?"

"Probably. But unless you find the weapon used, with her prints on it and stains of blood from her last kill, what have you got?"

"Maybe we'll find that WHY NOT? bracelet."

"Hundreds of them were sold. Probably thousands. It would mean nothing."

"The tear gas container?"

"Even if we find it, there's no proof it was the one used on Bergdorfer. Ditto the clothes she wore. And the wigs. Ivar, that's all the sleaziest kind of circumstantial evidence. A good defense attorney would make mincemeat of a prosecution based on that."

"She's got Addison's disease."

"So have fifteen other women living in Manhattan. I know you think we've got a lot on her. We have. Enough to convince me that she's the Hotel Ripper. But it's been a long time since you've testified in court. You've forgotten that there's a fucking big gap between knowing and proving. We have enough to know we have the right perp, but we have shit-all when it comes to proving. I tell you frankly that I don't think the DA will go for an indictment on the basis of what we've got. He's looking for good arrests and convictions. Like everyone else, he's not particularly enamored of lost causes."

"I still say we have enough to bring her in for questioning. Even if we don't find anything new in her apartment or office, we can throw the fear of God into her. She won't slit any more throats."

"You're sure of that? Positive? That she won't leave the city, move somewhere else, change her name, and take up her hobby again?"

"That's some other city's problem."

Delaney grunted. "Ivar, you're all heart."

"You know what I mean. I volunteered for this job because I figured if anyone could find the Hotel Ripper, you could. All right, you've done it, and I want you to know how much I appreciate what you've done. But the whole point of the thing was to bring this series of homicides to an end. It seems to me that we can do that now by picking her up and telling her what we know. Trial and conviction are secondary to stopping her."

"Then it's bye-bye, birdie," Delaney said. "That's not right."

Ivar Thorsen slapped his palms on the table.

"No wonder they called you 'Iron Balls,' " he said. "You've got to be the most stubborn, opinionated man I've ever met. You just won't give."

"I know what's right," Delaney said woodenly.

The Admiral took a deep breath.

"I'll give you another week," he said. "That's, uh, Friday the twenty-fifth. If we have nothing more on her by then, I'm bringing her in anyhow. I just can't take the risk of letting her try another slashing."

"Shit," Delaney said.

He strode home through the sultry twilight. He went through Central Park, trying to walk off his anger. Intellectually, he could understand the reasoning behind Ivar Thorsen's decision. But that didn't make it any better. It was all political.

"Political." What a shifty word! Political was everything weak, sly, expedient, and unctuous. Political was doing the right things for the wrong reasons, and the wrong things for the right reasons.

Ivar had his career and the Department's reputation to think about. In that connotation, he was doing the "right" thing, the political thing. But he was also letting a murderess stroll away from her crimes; that was what it amounted to.

Delaney planned how they could smash her. It would be an audacious scheme, but with foresight and a bit of luck, they could pull it off.

Not letting her out on the prowl to pick up some innocent slob, going with him to his hotel room, and then ripping his throat. With the cops tailing her and breaking in at the last minute to catch her with the knife in her hand and the victim-to-be still alive. That would never work.

It would have to be a carefully plotted scam, using a police decoy. The guy selected would have to be a real cowboy, with quick reflexes and the balls to see it through. He'd have charm, be physically presentable, and have enough acting ability to play the role of an out-of-town salesman or convention-goer.

He would have a room in a midtown hotel, and they would wire it like a computer, with mikes, a two-way mirror, and maybe a TV tape camera filming the whole thing. A squad of hard guys in the adjoining room, of course, ready to come on like Gangbusters.

She'd be tailed to the hotel she selected and the cowboy would be alerted. He'd make the pickup or let her pick him up. Then he'd take her back to his hotel room. The pickup would be the dicey part. Once the cowboy made the meet, the rest should go like silk.

It would be important that even the appearance of entrapment be avoided, but that could be worked out. With luck they'd be able to grab her in the act, with her trusty little jackknife open and ready. Let her try to walk away from that!

Delaney admitted it was a chancy gamble, but Goddamnit, it *could* work. And it would cut through all the legal bullshit, all the court arguments about the admissibility of circumstantial evidence. It would be irrefutable proof that Zoe Kohler was a bloody killer.

But the politicians said No, don't take the risk, all we want to do is stop her, and start booking conventions again, and if she walks, that's too bad, but we stopped her, didn't we?

Edward X. Delaney made a grimace of disgust. The law was the law, and murder was wrong, and every time you weaseled, you weakened the whole body of the law, the good book it had taken so many centuries to write.

By God, if he was on active duty and in command, he would smash her! If the cowboy didn't succeed, then Delaney would try something else. She might kill again, and again, but in the end he'd hang her by the heels, and the best defense attorney in the world couldn't prevent those words: "Guilty as charged."

By the time he arrived home, he was sodden with sweat, his face reddened, and he was puffing with exhaustion.

"What happened to you?" Monica asked curiously. "You look like you've been wrestling with the devil."

"Something like that," he said.

July 22, Tuesday . . .

She did not wake pure and whole—and knew she never would. The abdominal pains were constant now, almost as severe as menstrual cramps. Weakness buckled her knees; she frequently felt giddy and feared she might faint on the street.

She continued to lose weight; her flesh deflated over her joints; she seemed all knobs and edges. The discolored blotches grew; she watched with dulled horror as whole patches of skin took on a grayish-brown hue.

Everything was wrong. She felt nausea, and vomited. She suddenly had a craving for salt and began taking three, four, then five tablets a day. She tried to eat only bland foods, but was afflicted first with constipation, then with diarrhea.

Her dream of happiness, on the night following Ernest Mittle's proposal of marriage, had vanished. Now she said aloud: "I am sick and tired of being sick and tired."

When Madeline Kurnitz called to ask her to lunch, Zoe tried to beg off, not certain she had the strength and fearful of what Maddie might say about her appearance.

But the other woman insisted, even agreeing to lunch in the dining room of the Hotel Granger.

"I want you to meet someone," Maddie said, giggling.

"Who?"

"You'll see!"

Zoe reserved a table for three and was already seated when Maddie arrived. With her was a tall, stalwart youth who couldn't have been more than twenty-two or twenty-three. Maddie was hanging on to his arm possessively, looking up at his face, and whispering something that made him laugh.

She hardly glanced at Zoe. Just said, "Christ, you're skinny," and then introduced her escort.

"Kiddo, this stud is Jack. Keep your hands off; I saw him first. Jack, this is Zoe, my best friend. My only friend. Say, 'Hello, Zoe, how are you?' You can manage that, can't you?"

"Hello, Zoe," Jack said with a flash of white teeth, "how are you?"

"See?" Maddie said. "He can handle a simple sentence. Jack isn't so great in the brains department, luv, but with what he's got, who needs brains? Hey, hey, how's about a little drink? My first today."

"Your first in the last fifteen minutes," Jack said.

"Isn't he cute?" Maddie said, stroking the boy's cheek. "I'm teaching him to sit up and beg."

It was the other way around; Zoe was shocked by *her* appearance. Maddie had put on more loose weight, and it bulged, unbraed and ungirdled, in a straining dress of red silk crepe, with a side seam gaping and stains down the front.

Her freckled cleavage was on prominent display, and she wore no hose. Her feet, in the skimpiest of strap sandals, were soiled with street dirt. Her legs had been carelessly shaved; a swath of black fuzz ran down one calf.

It was her face that showed most clearly her loss: clown makeup wildly applied, powder caked in smut lines on her neck, a false eyelash hanging loose, lipstick streaked and crooked.

There she sat, a blob of a woman, all appetite. It seemed to Zoe that her voice had become louder and screakier. She shouted for drinks, yelled for menus, laughing in high-pitched whinnies.

Zoe hung her head as other diners turned to stare. But Maddie was impervious to their disapproval. She held hands with Jack, popped shrimp into his mouth, pinched his cheek. One of her hands was busy beneath the tablecloth.

". . . so Harry moved out," Maddie chattered on, "and Jack moved in. A beautiful exchange. Now the lawyers are fighting it out. Jack, baby, you have a steak; you've got to keep up your strength, you stallion, you!"

He sat there with a vacant grin, enjoying her ministrations, accepting them as his due. His golden hair was coiffed in artful waves. His complexion was a bronzed tan, lips sculpted, nose straight and patrician. A profile that belonged on a coin.

"Isn't he precious?" Maddie said fondly, staring at him with hungry eyes. "I found him parking cars at some roadhouse on Long Island. I got him cleaned up, properly barbered and dressed, and look at him now. A treasure! Maddie's own sweet treasure."

She was, Zoe realized, quite drunk, for in addition to her usual ebullience, there was something else: almost an hysteria. Plus a note of nasty cruelty when she spoke of the young man as if he were a curious object.

Either he did not comprehend her malicious gibes or chose to ignore them. He said little, grinned continuously, and ate steadily. He poked food into an already full mouth and masticated slowly with heavy movements of his powerful jaw.

"We're off for Bermuda," Maddie said, "or is it the Bahamas? I'm always getting the two of them fucked up. Anyway, we're going to do the tropical paradise bit for a month, drink rum out of coconut shells, and skinny-dip in the moonlight. How does that scenario grab you, kiddo? What does a thirsty gal have to do to get another drink in this dump?"

She ate very little, Zoe noted, but she drank at a frantic rate, gulping, wiping her mouth with the back of her hand when liquid trickled down her chin. But never once did she let go of Jack. She hung on to his arm, shoulder, thigh.

Zoe, remembering the brash bravado of a younger Maddie, was terrified by the woman's dissolution. Frightened not only for Maddie but at what it presaged for her own future.

For this woman, as a girl, had been the best of them. She was courageous and independent. She swaggered through life, dauntless and unafraid. She *lived,* and never feared tomorrow. She dared and she challenged, and never asked the price or counted the cost.

Now here she was, drunk, wild, feverish, her flesh puddled, holding on desperately to a handsome boy young enough to be her son. Behind the bright glitter of her mascaraed eyes grew a dark terror.

If this woman could be defeated, this brave, free, indefatigable woman, what hope in life was there for Zoe Kohler? She was so much weaker than Madeline Kurnitz. She was timid and fearful. She was *smaller*. When giants were toppled, what chance was there for midgets?

They finished their hectic meal and Maddie threw bills to the waiter.

"The son of a bitch cut off my credit cards," she muttered.

She rose unsteadily to her feet and Jack slid an arm about her thick waist. She tottered, staring glassily at Zoe.

"You changing jobs, kiddo?" she asked.

"No, Maddie. I haven't even been looking. Why do you ask?"

"Dunno. Some guy called me a few days ago, said you had applied for a job and gave me as a reference. Wanted to know how long I had known you, what I knew about your private life, and all that bullshit."

"I don't understand. I haven't applied for any job."

"Ah, the hell with it. Probably some weirdo. I'll call you when I get back from paradise."

"Take care of yourself, Maddie."

"Fuck that. Jack's going to take care of me. Aren't you, lover boy?"

She watched them stagger out, Jack half-supporting the porcine woman. Zoe walked slowly back to her office, dread seeping in as she realized the implications of what Maddie had said.

Someone was making inquiries about her, about her personal history and private life. She knew who it was—that stretched, dour man labeled "police," who would not give up the search and would not be content until Zoe Kohler was dead and gone.

She slumped at her desk, skeleton hands folded. She stared at those shrunken claws. They looked as if they had been soaked in brine. She thought of her approaching menstrual period and wondered dully if blood could flow from such a desiccated corpus.

"Hello there!" Everett Pinckney said brightly, weaving before her desk. "Have a good lunch?"

"Very nice," Zoe said, trying to smile. "Is there something I can do for you, Mr. Pinckney?"

He beamed at her, making an obvious effort to focus his eyes and concentrate on what he wanted to say. He leaned forward, knuckles propped on her desk. She could smell his whiskey-tainted breath.

"Yes," he said. "Well, uh . . . Zoe, remember that tear gas I gave you? The spray can? The little one for your purse?"

"I remember."

"Well, have you got it with you? In your purse? In your desk?"

She stared at him.

"Silly thing," he went on. "A detective was around. He's investigating a burglary and has to check the serial numbers of all the cans sold in New York. I asked McMillan and Joe Levine to bring theirs in. You still have yours, don't you? Didn't squirt anyone with it, did you?" He giggled.

"I don't have it with me, Mr. Pinckney," she said slowly.

"Oh. It's home, is it?"

"Yes," she said, thinking sluggishly. "I have it at home."

"Well, bring it in, will you, please? By Friday? The detective is coming back. Once he checks the number, you can have the can again. No problem."

He smiled glassily and tottered into his own office.

Stronger now, it returned: the sense of being moved and manipulated. Events had escaped her power. They were pressing her back into her natural role of victim. She had lost all initiative; she was being controlled.

She thought wildly of what she might do. Claim an attack by a would-be rapist whom she had repulsed with tear gas? Defended herself against a vicious dog? But she had already told Mr. Pinckney she had the dispenser at home.

Finally, she decided miserably, she could do nothing but tell him she had lost or misplaced the container.

Not for a moment did she believe the detective's claim of investigating a burglary. He was investigating *her,* and what would happen when he was told Zoe Kohler had "lost or misplaced" her dispenser, she didn't wish to imagine. It was all so depressing she could not even wonder how they had traced the tear gas to her.

That evening, when she returned to her apartment, she did something completely irrational. She searched her apartment for the tear gas container, knowing she had disposed of it. The worst thing was that she *knew* she was acting irrationally but could not stop herself.

Of course she did not find the dispenser. But she found something else. Or rather, several things . . .

When she had placed Ernest Mittle's engagement ring far in the back of the dresser drawer, she had paused a moment to open the box and take a final look at the pretty stone. Then she had shoved the box away, but remembered very well that it opened to the front.

When she found it, the box was turned around in its hiding place. Now the hinge was to the front, the box opened from the rear.

When she had put way her nylon wigs, wrapped in tissue, the blond wig was on top, the black beneath. Now they were reversed.

The stacks of her pantyhose and lingerie had been disturbed. She always left them with their front edges neatly aligned. Now the piles showed they had been handled. They were not messy; they were neat. But not the way she had left them.

Perhaps someone less precise and finicky than Zoe Kohler would never have noticed. But she noticed, and was immediately convinced that someone had been in her apartment and had searched through her possessions.

She went at once to her front window. Drawing the drape cautiously aside, she peeked out. She did not see the white-shirted watcher in the shadows of the apartment across the street. She did not see him, but was certain he was there.

She made no connection between the voyeur and the search of her personal belongings. She knew only that her privacy was once again being cruelly violated; people wanted to know her secrets. They would keep trying, and there was no way she could stop them.

When Ernest Mittle called, she made a determined effort to sound cheerful and loving. They chatted for a long time, and she kept asking questions about his job, his computer classes, his vacation plans—anything to keep him talking and hold the darkness back.

"Zoe," he said finally, "I don't, uh, want to pressure you or anything, but have you been thinking about it?"

It took her a moment to realize what he meant.

"Of course, I've been thinking about it, darling," she said. "Every minute."

"Well, I meant every word I said to you. And now I'm surer than ever in my own mind. This is what I want to do. I just don't want to live without you, Zoe."

"Ernie, you're the sweetest and most considerate man I've ever met. You're *so* considerate."

"Yes . . . well . . . uh . . . when do you think you'll decide? Soon?"

"Oh yes. Soon. Very soon."

"Listen," he said eagerly, "I have classes Friday night. I get out about eight-thirty or so. How's about my picking up a bottle of white wine and dropping by? I mean, it'll be Friday night and all, and we can talk and get squared away on our vacation. Okay?"

She didn't have the strength to object. Everyone was pushing her—even Ernie.

"Of course," she said dully. "Friday night?"

"About nine," he said happily. "See you then. Take care of yourself, dear."

"Yes," she said. "You, too."

He hung up and she sat there staring at the phone in her hand. Without questioning why, she called Dr. Oscar Stark. She got his answering service, of course. The operator asked if she'd care to leave a message.

"No," Zoe Kohler said, "no message."

She wandered into the kitchen. She opened the cabinet door. She stared at the rows and rows of pills, capsules, ampules, powders, medicines. They all seemed so foolish. Toys.

She closed the door without taking anything. Not even her cortisol. Not even a salt tablet. Nothing would make her a new woman. She was condemned to be her.

She thought vaguely that she should eat something, but just the idea of food roiled her stomach. She poured a glass of chilled vodka and took it into the living room.

She slouched on the couch, staring into the darkness. She tried to concentrate and feel the workings of her body. She felt only deep pain, a malaise that sapped her spirit and dulled her senses.

Was this the onset of death—this total surrender to the agony of living? Peace, peace. Something warm and comfortable. Something familiar and close. It seemed precious to her, this going over. The hurt ended . . .

She was conscious that she was weeping, surprised that her dried flesh could squeeze out that moisture. The warm, thin tears slid down her cheeks, and she did not wipe them away. She found a glory in this evidence of her miserableness.

"Poor Zoe Kohler," she said aloud, and the spoken words affected her so strongly that she gasped and sobbed.

What she could not understand, would never understand, was what she had done to deserve this wretchedness.

She had always dressed neatly and kept herself clean. She had never used dirty words. She had been polite and kind to everyone. Whom had she hurt? She had tried, always, to conduct herself like a lady.

There may have been a few times, very few, when she had forgotten herself, denied her nature, and acted in a crude and vulgar manner. But most of her life had been above reproach, spotless, obeying all the rules her mother had taught her.

She had moved through her days refined and gentle, low-voiced, and thoughtful of the feelings of others. She had worked hard to succeed as dutiful daughter and loving wife.

And it had all, *all,* come to this: sitting in the darkness and weeping. Smelling her body's rot. Hounded by unfeeling men who would not stop prying into things of no concern of theirs.

Poor Zoe Kohler. All hope gone, all passion spent. Only pain remained.

July 23 and 24, Wednesday and Thursday . . .

Delaney had to *see* her; he could not help himself.

"You can learn a lot about people by observing them," he explained to Monica. "How they walk, how they gesture. Do they rub their eyes or pick their nose? How they light a cigarette. Do they wait for a traffic light or run through traffic? Any nervous habits? How they dress. The colors and style. Do they constantly blink? Lick their lips? And so forth."

His wife listened to this recital in silence, head bowed, eyes on the mending in her lap.

"Well?" he demanded.

"Well what?"

"I just thought you might have a comment."

"No, I have no comment."

"Maybe it'll help me understand her better. Why she did what she did. Clues to her personality."

"Whatever you say, dear," she said.

He looked at her suspiciously. He didn't trust her complaisant moods.

He told Abner Boone what he wanted to do, and the sergeant had no objections.

"Better let Bentley know, Chief," he suggested. "He can tell his spooks you'll be tailing her too. In case they spot you and call out the troops."

"They won't spot me," Delaney said, offended.

But he spotted *them:* the unmarked cars parked near the Hotel Granger and Zoe Kohler's apartment house, the plainclothes policewomen who followed the suspect on foot. Some of the shadows were good, some clumsy. But Zoe seemed oblivious to them all.

He picked her up on 39th Street and Lexington Avenue at 8:43 on Wednesday morning and followed her to the Granger. He hung around for a while, then wandered into the hotel and inspected the lobby, dining room, cocktail bar.

He was back at noon, and when she came out for lunch, he tailed her to a fast-food joint on Third Avenue, then back to the Granger. At five o'clock he returned to follow her home. He never took his eyes off her.

"What's she like?" Monica asked that night.

"So ordinary," he said, "she's outstanding. Miss Nothing."

"Pretty?"

"No, but not ugly. Plain. Just plain. She could do a lot more with herself than she does. She wears no makeup that I could see. Hair a kind of mousy color. Her clothes are browns and tans and grays. Earth colors. She moves very slowly, cautiously. Almost like an invalid, or at least like a woman twice her age. Once I saw her stop and hang on to a lamppost as if she suddenly felt weak or faint. Sensible shoes. Sensible clothes. Nothing bright or cheerful about her. She carries a shoulder bag but hangs on to it with both hands. I'd guess the knife is in the bag. When she confronts anyone on the sidewalk, she's always the first to step aside. She never crosses against the lights, even when there's no traffic. Very careful. Very conservative. Very law-abiding. When she went out to lunch, I thought I saw her talking to herself, but I'm not sure."

"Edward, how long are you going to keep this up—following her?"

"You think it's morbid curiosity, don't you?"

"Don't be silly."

"Sure you do," he said. "But it's not. The woman fascinates me; I admit it."

"That I believe," Monica said. "Does she look sad?"

"Sad?" He considered that a moment. "Not so much sad as defeated. Her posture is bad; she slumps; the sins of the world on her shoulders. And her complexion is awful. Muddy pale. I think I was right and Dr. Ho was right; she's cracking."

"I wish you wouldn't do it, Edward—follow her, I mean."

"Why not?"

"I don't know . . . It just seems indecent."

"You are a dear, sweet woman," he told her, "and you don't know what the hell you're talking about."

He went through the same routine on Thursday. He maneuvered so he walked toward her as she headed up Madison Avenue on her way to work. He passed quite close and got a good look at her features.

They seemed drawn and shrunken to him, nose sharpened, cheeks caved. Her lips were dry and slightly parted. The eyes seemed focused on worlds away. There was a somnolence about that face. She could have been a sleepwalker.

No breasts that he could see. She appeared flat as a board.

He was there a few minutes after 5:00 P.M., when she exited from the Hotel Granger and turned downtown on Madison. Delaney was behind her. Bentley's policewoman was across the avenue.

The suspect walked south on Madison, then went into a luncheonette. Delaney strolled to the corner, turned, came back. He stood in front of the restaurant, ostensibly inspecting the menu Scotch-taped inside the plate glass window.

Zoe Kohler was seated at the counter, waiting to be served. Everyone in the place was busy eating or talking. No one paid any attention to the activity on the street, to a big, lumpy man peering through the front window.

Delaney walked on, looked in a few shop windows, came back to the luncheonette. Now Zoe had a plate before her and was drinking a glass of something that looked like iced tea.

If he had been a man given to theatrical gestures, he would have slapped his forehead in disgust and dismay. He had forgotten. They all had forgotten. How could they have been so fucking *stupid?*

He loitered about the front of the luncheonette. He looked at his watch occasionally to give the impression of a man waiting for a late date. He saw Zoe Kohler pat her lips with a paper napkin, gather up purse and check, begin to rise.

He was inside immediately, almost rushing. As she moved toward the cashier's desk, he brushed by her.

"I beg your pardon," he said, raising his hat and stepping aside.

She gave him a shy, timorous smile: a flicker.

He let her go and slid onto the counter stool she had just left. In front of him was most of a tunafish salad plate and dregs of iced tea in a tall glass. He linked his hands around the glass without touching it.

A porky, middle-aged waitress with a mustache and bad feet stopped in front of him. She took out her pad.

"Waddle it be?" she asked, patting her orange hair. "The meatloaf is good."

"I'd like to see the manager, please."

She peered at him. "What's wrong?"

"Nothing's wrong," he said, smiling at her. "I'd just like to see the manager."

She turned toward the back of the luncheonette.

"Hey, you, Stan," she yelled.

A man back there talking to two seated customers looked up. The waitress jerked her head toward Delaney. The manager came forward slowly. He stood at the Chief's shoulder.

"What seems to be the trouble?" he asked.

"No trouble," Delaney said. "This iced-tea glass here—I've got a dozen at home just like it. But my kid broke one. I'd like to fill out the set. Would you sell me this glass for a buck?"

"You want to buy that glass for a dollar?" Stan said.

"That's right. To fill out my set of a dozen. How about it?"

"A pleasure," the manager said. "I've got six dozen more you can have at the same price."

"No," Delaney said, laughing, "just one will do."

"Let me get you a clean one," the porky waitress said, reaching for Zoe Kohler's glass.

"No, no," Delaney said hastily, protecting the glass with his linked hands. "This one will be fine."

Waitress and manager looked at each other and shrugged. Delaney handed over a dollar bill. Touching the glass gingerly with two fingers spread inside, he wrapped it loosely in paper napkins, taking care not to wipe or smudge the outside.

He had to walk two blocks before he found a sidewalk phone that worked. He set the wrapped glass carefully atop the phone and called Sergeant Abner Boone at Midtown Precinct North. He explained what he had.

"God *damn* it!" Boone exploded. "We're *idiots!* We could have had prints from her office or apartment a week ago."

"I know," Delaney said consolingly. "It's my fault as much as anyone's. Listen, sergeant, if you get a match with that wineglass from the Tribunal, it's not proof positive that she wasted the LaBranche kid. It's just evidence that she was at the scene."

"That's good enough for me," Boone said grimly. "Where are you, Chief? I'll get a car, pick up the glass myself, and take it to the lab."

Delaney gave him the location. "After they check it out, will you call me at home and let me know?"

"Of course."

"Better call Thorsen and tell him, too. Yes or no."

"I'll do that," Abner Boone said. "Thank you, sir," he added gratefully.

Delaney was grumpy all evening. He hunched over his plate, eating pork roast and applesauce in silence. Not even complimenting Monica on the bowl of sliced strawberries with a sprinkle of Cointreau to give it a tang.

It wasn't until they had taken their coffee into the air-conditioned living room that she said: "Okay, buster, what's bothering you?"

"Politics," he said disgustedly, and told her about his argument with Ivar Thorsen.

"He was right and I was right. Considering his priorities and responsibilities, picking the woman up and getting her out of circulation makes sense. But I still think going for prosecution and conviction makes more sense."

Then he told Monica what he had just done: obtaining Zoe Kohler's fingerprints for a match with the prints found on the wineglass at the Tribunal Motor Inn.

"So I handed Ivar more inconclusive evidence," he said wryly. "If the prints match, he's sure to pick her up. But he'll never get a conviction on the basis of what we've got."

"If you feel that strongly about it," Monica said, "you could have forgotten all about the prints."

"You're joking, of course."

"Of course."

"The habits of thirty years die hard," he said, sighing. "I had to get her prints. But no one will believe me when I tell them that even a perfect match won't put her behind bars. Her attorney will say, 'Sure, she had a drink with the guy in his hotel room—and so what? He was still alive when she left.' Those prints won't prove she slashed his throat. Just that she was there. And another thing is—"

The phone rang then.

"That'll be Boone," Delaney said, rising. "I'll take it in the study."

But it wasn't the sergeant; it was Deputy Commissioner Ivar Thorsen, and he couldn't keep the excitement out of his voice.

"Thank you, Edward," he said. "Thank you, thank you. We got a perfect match on the prints. I had a long talk with the DA's man and he thinks we've got enough now to go for an indictment. So we're bringing her in. It'll take all day tomorrow to get the paperwork set and plan the arrest. We'll probably take her Saturday morning at her apartment. Want to come along?"

Delaney paused. "All right, Ivar," he said finally. "If that's what you want to do. I'd like a favor: will you ask Dr. Patrick Ho if he wants to be in on it? That man contributed a lot; he should be in at the end."

"Yes, Edward, I'll contact him."

"One more thing . . . I'd like Thomas Handry to be there."

"Who's Thomas Handry?"

"He's on the *Times.*"

"You want a *reporter* to be there?"

"I owe him."

Thorsen sighed. "All right, Edward, if you say so. And thank you again; you did a splendid job."

"Yeah," Delaney said dispiritedly, but Thorsen had already hung up.

He went back into the living room and repeated the phone conversation to Monica.

"So that's that," he concluded. "If she keeps her nerve and doesn't say a goddamn word until she gets a smart lawyer, I think she'll beat it."

"But the murders will end?"

"Yes. Probably."

She looked at him narrowly.

"But that's not enough for you, is it? You want her punished."

"Don't you?"

"Of course—if it can be done legally. But most of all I want the killings to stop. Edward, don't you think you're being vindictive?"

He rose suddenly. "Think I'll pour myself a brandy. Get you one?"

"All right. A small one."

He brought their cognacs from the study, then settled back again into his worn armchair.

"Why do you think I'm being vindictive?"

"Your whole attitude. You want to catch this woman in the act, even if it means risking a man's life. You want, above all, to see her punished for what she's done. You want her to suffer. It's really become an obsession with you. I don't think you'd feel that strongly if the Hotel Ripper was a man. Then you'd be satisfied just to get him off the streets."

"Come on, Monica, what kind of bullshit is that? The next thing you'll be saying is that I hate women."

"No, I'd never say that because I know it's not true. Just the opposite. I think you have some very old-fashioned, romantic ideas about women. And because this particular woman has flouted those beliefs, those cherished ideals, you feel very vengeful toward her."

He took a swig of brandy. "Nonsense. I've dealt with female criminals before. Some of them killers."

"But none like Zoe Kohler—right? All the female murderers in your experience killed from passion or greed or because they were drunk or something like that. Am I correct?"

"Well . . ." he said grudgingly, "maybe."

"You told me so yourself. But now you find a female killer who's intelligent, plans well, kills coldly with no apparent motive, and it shatters all your preconceptions about women. And not only does it destroy your romantic fancies, but I think it scares you—in a way."

He was silent.

"Because if a woman can act in this way, then you don't know anything at all about women. Isn't that what scares you? Now you've discovered that women are as capable as men. Capable of evil, in this case. But if that's true, then they must also be as capable of good, of creativity, of invention and art. It's upsetting all the prejudices you have and maybe even weren't aware of. Suddenly you have to revise your thinking about women, all your old, ingrained opinions, and that can be a painful process. I think that's why you want more than the killings ended. You want revenge against this woman who has caused such an upheaval in all your notions of what women are and how they should act."

"Thank you, doctor, for the fifty-cent analysis," he said. "I'm not saying you're completely wrong, but you *are* mistaken if you think I would have felt any differently if the Hotel Ripper was a man. You have to pay for your sins in this world, regardless of your sex."

"Edward, how long has it been since you've been to church."

"You mean for mass or confession? About thirty-five years."

"Well, you haven't lost your faith."

"The good sisters beat it into me. But my faith, as you call it, has nothing to do with the church."

"No?"

"No. I'm for civilization and against the swamp. It's as simple as that."

"And that is simple. You believe in God, don't you?"

"I believe in a Supreme Being, whatever you want to call him, her, or it."

"You probably call it the Top Cop."

He laughed. "You're not too far wrong. Well, the Top Cop has given us the word in a body of works called the law. Don't tell me how rickety, inefficient, and leaky the law is; I know better than you. But it's the best we've been able to come up with so far. Let's hope it'll be improved as the human race stumbles along. But even in the way it exists today, it's the only thing that stands between civilization and the swamp. It's a wall, a dike. And anyone who knocks a hole in the wall should be punished."

"And what about understanding? Compassion? Justice?"

"The law and justice are not always identical, my dear. Any street cop can tell you that. In this case, I think both the law and justice would be best served if Zoe Kohler was put away for the rest of her life."

"And if New York still had the death penalty, you'd want her electrocuted, or hanged, or gassed, or shot?"

"Yes."

July 25, Friday . . .

Her pubic hair had almost totally disappeared; only a few weak wisps survived. And the hair on her legs and in her armpits had apparently ceased to grow. She had the feeling of being *peeled,* to end up as a skinless grape, a quivering jelly. Clothing rasped her tender skin.

She took a cab to work that morning, not certain she had the strength to walk or push her way aboard a crowded bus. In the office, she was afraid she might drop the tray of coffee and pastries. Every movement was an effort, every breath a pain.

"Did you bring it in, Zoe?" Everett Pinckney asked.

She looked at him blankly. "What?"

"The tear gas dispenser," he said.

She felt a sudden anguish in her groin. A needle. She knew her period was due in a day, but this was something different: a steel sliver. But she did not wince. She endured, expressionless.

"I lost it," she said in a low voice. "Or misplaced it. I can't find it."

He was bewildered.

"Zoe," he said, "a thing like that—how could you lose it or misplace it?"

She didn't answer.

"What am I going to do?" he asked helplessly. "The cop will come back. He'll want to know. He'll want to talk to you."

"All right," she said, "I'll talk to him. I just don't have it."

He was not a man to bluster. He just stood, wavering . . .

"Well . . ." he said, "all right," and left her alone.

The rest of the day vanished. She didn't know where it went. She swam in agony, her body pulsing. She wanted to weep, cry out, claw her aching flesh from the bones. The world about her whirled dizzily. It would not stop.

She walked home slowly, her steps faltering. Passersby were a streaming blur. The earth sank beneath her feet. She heard a roaring above the traffic din, smelled scorch, and in her mouth was a taste of old copper.

She turned into the luncheonette, too weak to continue her journey.

"Hullo, dearie," the porky waitress said. "The usual?"

Zoe nodded.

"Wanna hear somepin nutty?" the waitress asked, setting a place for her. "Right after you was in here last night, a guy comes in and buys the iced tea glass you drank out of. Said he had glasses just like it at home, but his kid broke one, and he wanted to fill the set. Paid a dollar for it."

"The glass I used?"

"Crazy, huh? Din even want a clean one. Just wrapped up the dirty glass in paper napkins and rushed out with it. Well, it takes all kinds . . ."

"Was he tall and thin?" Zoe Kohler asked. "With a sour expression?"

"Nah. He was tall all right, but a heavyset guy. Middle sixties maybe. Why? You know him?"

"No," Zoe said listlessly, "I don't know him."

She was still thinking clearly enough to realize what had happened. Now *they* had her fingerprints. *They* would compare them with the prints on the wineglass she left at the Tribunal. *They* would be sure now. *They* would come for her and kill her.

She left her food uneaten. She headed home with stumbling steps. The pains in her abdomen were almost shrill in their intensity.

She wondered if her period had started. She had not inserted a tampon and feared to look behind her; perhaps she was leaving a spotted trail on the sidewalk. And following the spoor came the thin, dour man, nose down and sniffing. A true bloodhound.

At home, she locked and bolted her door, put on the chain. She looked wearily about her trig apartment. She had always been neat. Her mother never had to tell her to tidy her room.

"A place for everything and everything in its place," her mother was fond of remarking.

She slipped shoes from her shrunken feet. She sat upright in a straight chair in the living room, hands folded primly on her lap. She watched dusk, twilight, darkness seep into the silent room.

Perhaps she fainted, dozed, dreamed; it was impossible to know. She saw a deserted landscape. Nothing there but gray smoke curling.

Then, as it thinned to fog, vapor, she saw a cracked and bloodless land. A jigsaw of caked mud. Craters and crusted holes venting steam. A barren world. No life stirring.

How long she sat there, her mind intent on this naked vision, she could not have said. Yet when her telephone rang, she rose, quite sane, turned on the light, picked up the phone. The lobby attendant: could Mr. Mittle come up?

She greeted Ernie with a smile, almost as happy as his. They kissed, and he told her she was getting dreadfully thin, and he would have to fatten her up. She touched his cheek lovingly, so moved was she by his concern.

The white wine he carried was already chilled. She brought a corkscrew and glasses from the kitchen. They sat close together on the couch. They clinked glasses and looked into each other's eyes.

"How do you feel, darling?" he asked anxiously.

"Better now," she said. "You're here."

He groaned with pleasure, kissed her poor, shriveled fingers.

He prattled on about his computer class, his job, their vacation plans. She smiled and nodded, nodded and smiled, searching his face. And all the time . . .

"Well," he said briskly, slapping one knee as if they had come to the moment of decision in an important business haggle, "have you thought about it, Zoe? Will you marry me?"

"Ernie, are you sure . . . ?"

He rose and began to stalk about the dimly lighted room, carrying his wineglass.

"I certainly am sure," he said stoutly. "Zoe, I know this is the most important decision of my life, and I've considered it very carefully. Yes, I'm sure. I want to spend the rest of my life with you. No two ways about *that!* I know I don't have a great deal to offer you, but still . . . Love—you know? And a promise to work hard at making you happy."

"I have nothing to offer," she said faintly. "Less than nothing."

"Don't say that," he cried.

He sat down again at her side. He put his glass on the cocktail table. He held her bony shoulders.

"Don't say that, darling," he said tenderly. "You have all I want. You *are* all I want. I just don't want to live without you. Say Yes."

She stared at him, and through his clear, hopeful features saw again that sere, damned landscape, the gray smoke curling.

"All right," she said in a low voice. "Yes."

"Oh, Zoe!" he said, clasped her to him, kissed her closed eyes, her dry lips. She put her arms softly about him, felt his warmth, his aliveness.

He moved her away.

"When?" he demanded. "When?"

She smiled. "Whenever you say, dear."

"As soon as possible. The sooner the better. Listen, I've been thinking about it, planning it, and I'll tell you what I think would be best. If you don't agree, you tell me—all right? I mean, this is just my idea, and you might have some totally different idea on how we should do it, and if you do, I want you to tell me. Zoe? All right?"

"Of course, Ernie."

"Well, I thought a small, quiet wedding. Just a few close friends. Unless you want your parents here?"

"Oh no."

"And I don't want my family. Mostly because they can't afford to make the trip. Unless you want to go to Minnesota for the wedding?"

"No, let's have it here. A few close friends."

"Right," he said enthusiastically. "And the money we save, we can spend on the, uh, you know, honeymoon. Just a small ceremony. If you like, we could have a reception afterward at my place or here at your place. Or we could rent a room at a hotel or restaurant. What do you think?"

"Let's keep it small and quiet," she said. "Not make a big, expensive fuss. We could have it right here."

"Maybe we could have it catered," he said brightly. "It wouldn't cost so much. You know, just a light buffet, sandwiches maybe, and champagne. Like that."

"I think that would be plenty," she said firmly. "Keep it short and simple."

"Exactly," he said, laughing gleefully. "Short and simple. See? We're agreeing already! Oh Zoe, we're going to be so happy."

He embraced her again. She gently disengaged herself to fill their wineglasses. They tinked rims in a solemn toast.

"We've got so much to do," he said nervously. "We've got to sit down together and make out lists. You know—schedules and who to invite and the church and all. And when we should—"

"Ernie," she said, putting a palm to his hot cheek, "do you really love me?"

"I do!" he groaned, turning his face to kiss her palm. "I really do. More than anything or anyone in my life."

"And I love you," Zoe Kohler said. "You're the kindest man I've ever known. The sweetest and nicest. I want to be with you always."

"Always," he vowed. "Always together."

She brought her face close, looked deep into his eyes.

"Darling," she said softly, "do you remember when we talked about—uh—you know—going to bed together? Sex?"

"Yes. I remember."

"We agreed there had to be love and tenderness and understanding."

"Oh yes."

"Or it was just nothing. Like animals. We said that, Ernie—remember?"

"Of course. That's the way I feel."

"I know you do, dear. And I do, too. Well, if we love each other and we're going to get married, couldn't we . . . ?"

"Oh Zoe," he said. "Oh my darling. You mean now? Tonight?"

"Why not?" she said. "Couldn't we? It's all right, isn't it?"

"Of course it's all right. It's wonderful, marvelous, just great. Because we do love each other and we're going to spend the rest of our lives together."

"You're sure?" she said. "You won't be, uh, offended?"

"How can you think that? It'll be sweet. So sweet. It'll be right."

"Oh yes," she breathed. "It will be right. I feel it. Don't you feel it, darling?"

He nodded dumbly.

"Let's go into the bedroom," she whispered. "Bring the wine. You get undressed and get into bed. I have to go into the bathroom for a few minutes, but I'll be right out."

"Is the front door locked?" he said, his voice choked.

"Darling," she said, kissing his lips. "My sweetheart. My lover."

She took her purse into the bathroom. She closed and locked the door. She undressed slowly. When she was naked, she inspected herself. She had not yet begun to bleed.

She waited a few moments, seated on the closed toilet seat. Finally she rose, opened the knife, held it in her right hand. She draped a towel across her forearm. She did not look at herself in the medicine cabinet mirror.

She unlocked the door. She peeked out. The bedside lamp was on. Ernest Mittle was lying on his back, hands clasped behind his head. The sheet was drawn up to his waist. His torso was white, hairless, shiny.

He turned his head to look toward her.

"Darling," she called with a trilly laugh, "look away. I'm embarrassed."

He smiled and rolled onto his side, away from her. She crossed the carpeted floor quickly, suddenly strong, suddenly resolute. She bent over him. The towel dropped away.

"Oh lover," she breathed.

The blade went into soft cheese. His body leaped frantically, but with her left hand and knee she pressed him down. The knife caught on something in his neck, but she sawed determinedly until it sliced through.

Out it went, the blood, in a spray, a fountain, a gush. She held him down until his threshings weakened and ceased. Then he just flowed, and she tipped the torn head over the edge of the bed to let him drain onto the rug.

She rolled him back. She pulled the sodden sheet down. She raised the knife high to complete her ritual. But her hand faltered, halted, came slowly down. She could not do it. Still, she murmured, "There, there, there," as she headed for the bathroom.

She tossed the bloodied knife aside. She inspected herself curiously. Only her hands, right arm, and left knee were stained and glittering.

She showered in hot water, lathering thickly with her imported soap. She rinsed, lathered again, rinsed again. She stepped from the tub and made no effort to wash away the pink tinge on the porcelain.

She dried thoroughly, then used her floral-scented cologne and a deodorant spray. She combed her hair quickly. She powdered neck, shoulders, armpits, the insides of her shrunken thighs.

It took her a few moments to find the Mexican wedding dress she had bought long ago and had never worn. She pulled it over her head. The crinkled cotton slid down over her naked flesh with a whisper.

The gown came to her blotched ankles, hung as loosely as a tent. But it was a creamy white, unblemished, as pure and virginal as the pinafores she had worn when she was Daddy's little girl and all her parents' friends had said she was "a real little lady."

Ernest Mittle's engagement ring twisted on her skinny finger. Working carefully, so as not to cut herself, she snipped a thin strip of Band-Aid. This she wound around and around the back part of the ring.

Then, when she worked it on, the fattened ring hung and stuck to her finger. It would never come loose.

She went into the kitchen, opened the cabinet door. In her pharmacopeia she found a full container of sleeping pills and a few left in another. She took both jars and a bottle of vodka into the bedroom. She set them carefully on the floor alongside the bed.

She checked the front door to make certain it was locked, bolted, and chained. Then she turned out all the lights in the apartment. Moving cautiously, she found her way back to the bedroom.

She sat on the edge of the bed. She took four of the pills, washed them down with a swallow of vodka. She didn't want to drink too much, remembering what had happened to Maddie Kurnitz.

Then she stripped the soaked sheet from the bed and let it fall at the foot. She got into bed alongside Ernest Mittle, wearing her oversized wedding gown and taped ring. She moved pills and vodka onto the bedside table. She took four more pills, a larger swallow of vodka.

She waited . . .

She thought it might come suddenly, blackness descending. But it did not; it took time. She gulped pills and swallowed vodka, and once she patted Ernie's cooling hip and repeated, "There, there . . ."

The scene she had been seeing all night, the blasted landscape, came back, but hazed and softened. The pitted ground slowly vanished, and only the curling smoke was left, the fog, the vapor.

But soon enough that was gone. She thought she said something aloud, but did not know what it meant. All she was conscious of was that pain had ceased.

And for that she was thankful.

July 26, Saturday . . .

"Surveillance reported ten minutes ago," Sergeant Abner Boone said, consulting his notes.

"Is she still there?" Thorsen said sharply.

"Yes, sir. Got home about six-forty last night. Hasn't been out since."

"Any phone calls?" Delaney asked.

"One," Boone said. "About nine o'clock last night. The deskman in the lobby, asking if Ernest Mittle could come up."

"Mittle?" Detective Bentley said. "He's the boyfriend."

"He didn't leave," Boone said. "He's still up there."

"Shacking up?" Sergeant Broderick said.

"He never did that before," Detective Johnson said.

"Well, apparently both of them are still up there."

"Maybe he's closer to this than we figured," Broderick said. "Maybe he's been in on it all along."

"We'll soon find out," Boone said.

"How do we do this?" Ivar Thorsen asked.

"Maybe I've overplanned it," Boone said, "but rather be safe than sorry. Two cars at Lex and Third to block off her street. Precinct men for crowd control. The two guys on the wiretap will cover the basement. One man posted at each end of her hallway. Then we'll go in."

"What if she doesn't open up?" Thomas Handry said.

"We'll get the lobby man to use his passkeys," Boone said. "He's got them; I checked. Deputy, you, the Chief and I go in first. Uh, and Dr. Ho and Handry. Bentley, Johnson, and Broderick to follow. We got a floor plan of her apartment from the owner, and those guys will spread out fast to make sure she doesn't have a chance to dump anything. Sound okay?"

They all looked at Delaney.

"I don't think she'll try to run," he said, "but it won't do any harm to have a man on the roof."

"Right," Boone said, "we'll do it." He looked at his watch. "Coming up to ten o'clock. Let's get this show on the road."

Delaney, Dr. Patrick Ho, Sergeant Boone, and Thorsen rode in the Deputy's car.

"Ah, will there be any shooting?" Dr. Ho asked nervously.

"God forbid," Boone said.

"I want this to go down quickly and quietly," the Admiral said.

"Get her and the boyfriend out of there as soon as possible," Delaney advised. "Then you can tear the place apart."

"You have the warrants, sergeant?" Thorsen asked.

Boone tapped his breast pocket. "Right here, sir. She's signed, sealed, and delivered."

Thorsen remarked on the beauty of the morning; a bare sun rising in a strong sky. He said the papers had predicted rain, but at the moment it looked like a perfect July day.

It went with a minimum of confusion. The screening cars sealed off the block. Two uniformed officers were posted at the outer door of the apartment house. Precinct men began to set up barricades.

The others piled into the lobby. Uniformed men went first, hands on their holstered revolvers. The lobby attendant looked up, saw them coming. He turned white. Sergeant Boone showed the warrants. The man couldn't stop nodding.

They waited a few moments for the roof and corridor men to get in position. Then they crowded into the elevators, taking the lobby attendant along with them.

They gathered outside her door. Boone waved the others aside, then knocked on the door with his knuckles.

No response.

He banged on the door with his fist, then put his ear to the panel.

"Nothing," he reported. "No sounds at all." He gestured to the lobby attendant. "Open it up."

The man's hands were shaking so hard he couldn't insert the passkeys. Boone took them from him, turned both locks. The door opened a few inches, then caught on the chain.

"I've got a bolt-cutter in my car," Sergeant Broderick said.

"Wait a minute," Delaney said. He turned to the attendant. "Gas or electric ranges?" he asked.

"Gas."

The Chief stepped close, put his face near the narrow opening, sniffed deeply. "Nothing," he reported and stepped aside.

Sergeant Boone took his place.

"Police officers," he yelled. "We've got a warrant. Open up."

No answer.

"They've got to be in there," Thorsen said nervously.

"Should I get the bolt-cutter?" Broderick asked.

Boone looked to Delaney.

"Kick it in," the Chief said curtly.

The sergeant stood directly in front of the door. He drew up his leg until his knee almost touched his chin. He drove his foot forward at the spot where the chain showed. Wood splintered, the chain swung free, the door slammed open.

They rushed in, jostling each other. The searchers spread out. Thorsen, Delaney, Dr. Ho, Handry, and Boone stood in the living room, looking around.

"Clean and neat," the Chief said, nodding.

"Sarge!" Johnson yelled from the bedroom. "In here!"

They went in, clustered around the bed. They stared down. The drained man with his raw throat gaping wide. The puttied woman wrapped in cloth as thin as a shroud.

"Shit," Sergeant Boone said bitterly.

Delaney motioned to Dr. Ho. The little man stepped close, put two fingers to the side of Zoe Kohler's neck.

"Ah, yes," he said gently. "She is quite, quite deceased."

He peered closely at the empty pill bottles but did not touch them. The vodka bottle was on its side on the rug, a little clear liquid left.

"Barbiturates?" Handry asked Dr. Ho.

"Ah, I would say so. And the liquor. Usually a lethal combination."

Ivar Thorsen took a deep breath, hands on his hips. Then he turned away.

"You'll have to clean up this mess, sergeant," he said. "Do what you have to do."

Thorsen and Delaney took the elevator down together.

"She killed him?" the Deputy said. "Then did the Dutch?"

"Looks like it."

"How do you figure it?"

"I don't," Delaney said.

Outside, on the sidewalk, a crowd was beginning to gather. They pushed their way through. They walked slowly to the Deputy's car.

"I'll have to call a press conference," Thorsen said, "but I could use a drink first. How about you, Edward?"

"I'll pass."

"I'll buy," the Deputy offered.

"Thanks, Ivar," Edward X. Delaney said, smiling briefly. "Some other time. I think I'll go home. Monica is waiting for me."